THE GOLDEN AGE OF
SCIENCE FICTION

THE
GOLDEN AGE OF
SCIENCE
FICTION

EDITED WITH AN INTRODUCTION

BY GROFF CONKLIN

PREFACE BY JOHN W. CAMPBELL Jr.

EDITOR OF *ASTOUNDING SCIENCE-FICTION*

BONANZA BOOKS

NEW YORK

This book was previously published as *The Best of Science Fiction*.

Copyright MCMXLVI, revised edition © MCMLXIII by
Crown Publishers, Inc.
Introduction copyright © MCMLXXX by Crown Publishers, Inc.
All rights reserved.

This edition is published by Bonanza Books,
a division of Crown Publishers, Inc.
a b c d e f g h
BONANZA 1980 EDITION

Manufactured in the United States of America

Designed by Robert Josephy

A NOTE ABOUT AUTHORS' NAMES: Murray Leinster is a pseudonym
for Will Jenkins; Anson MacDonald is actually Robert A.
Heinlein; Don A. Stuart is a pseudonym for John W. Campbell,
Jr.; and Lewis Padgett is one of many pen names used
by Henry Kuttner.

Library of Congress Cataloging in Publication Data

Conklin, Groff, 1904–1968, ed.
   The golden age of science fiction.
   Reprint of the ed. published by Bonanza, New
York, under title: The best of science fiction.
   1. Science fiction, American. 2. Science
fiction, English. I. Title.
[PS648.S3C6 1980]   813'.0876'08   80-27208
ISBN 0-517-33486-0

CONTENTS

FOREWORD

Nearly four decades have passed since the first volume of Groff Conklin's famous science fiction series was originally published. Then titled *The Best of Science Fiction*, this collection of the genre's great short stories from the twenties, thirties, and forties, as well as from the nineteenth century, has now found its place among the classics. Compiled from pioneer science fiction magazines, they are the works of science fiction's most memorable writers, including H.G. Wells, Robert Heinlein, Isaac Asimov, A. E. van Vogt, and Theodore Sturgeon. With the publication of this anthology, science fiction was well on its way to becoming an important branch of modern literature— thus, its well-deserved new title, *The Golden Age of Science Fiction*.

First published on February 11, 1946, this volume created an instant sensation. Indeed, it was born into a highly receptive world—a world that only a few months before had been shattered by the Hiroshima and Nagasaki atomic bombings, a cataclysmic end to a seemingly endless world war. Heretofore the object of derision, some of science fiction's most alarming prophecies had overnight come true, and at last this literary form began to obtain recognition and respect. The first of its kind to appear after World War II, the anthology launched a new era for the field of science fiction, as the latter experienced an unprecedented growth and its popularity extended well beyond the traditional select group of young scientists, technologists, and laymen.

The contemporary reader will be equally receptive to these short stories, but the nature of his response will differ. He will appreciate the historical value and significance of his readings. He will be able to trace and explore the development of science fiction literature and particularly that of its classics from the mid-nineteenth through the mid-twentieth century.

Of special interest to today's reader are the earlier stories such as those by Edgar Allan Poe (1844), Arthur Conan Doyle (ca. 1895), and H.G. Wells (1927), which deal with the traditional philosophical problem of the separation of body and mind, and begin to explore the still undefined fields of hypnotism, mesmerism, and mental telepathy. In "The Great Keinplatz Experiment," Doyle warns of the dangers involved in this kind of science and of its questionable moral stature. We are here reminded of current scientific experiments that pose similar moral problems.

In "The Machine" (1935), Don A. Stuart discusses yet another threat to human society—that of the amazing "thinking machines," or computers, and their potentially detrimental effect on man's intelligence, memory, and learning. Over forty years ago, Stuart foresaw the impact of a totally computerized society on daily life—one that we have only begun to experience. As computers become more sophisticated, may we not gradually evolve into a society, such as the one depicted in "The Machine," where human labor will become a thing of the past?

The computerized society's sterilizing effect becomes more alarmingly Orwellian in Robert Heinlein's "Universe" (1941). Through generations of living in the cloistered quarters of a spaceship, its inhabitants have been so thoroughly brainwashed that they can no longer even conceive of the possibility of an outside world.

Another foreshadowing—the daringly modern concept of using bombs as peacekeeping instruments—emerged as early as 1889 in Frank R. Stockton's "The Great War Syndicate." The United States and Great Britain are shown engaged in a superpower struggle, which the Americans solve by threatening to destroy their enemy with the newly invented atomic-like "Instantaneous Motor" bomb.

The all-too-familiar problem of military parity and arms proliferation already considered by Stockton becomes frighteningly explicit in the technologically advanced world that Anson MacDonald describes a half century later in "Solution Unsatisfactory." He adequately foresees the pitfalls of contemporary international policy—the magnitude of which earlier readers could not grasp—founded on the possession of deadly weapons inevitably involving an escalating arms race. Thus, what good is the idealized Pax Americana of MacDonald's story if a super-destructive "dust" is reinvented by another world power?

In Isaac Asimov's "Blind Alley" (1945), the character of the "Cepheid" alien raises another issue of modern complexity that once again older generations of readers could hardly fathom: energy. Without the necessary forms of energy, a nation or race becomes powerless and is at the mercy of those who are better endowed.

The vision of the world and mankind conveyed throughout *The Golden Age of Science Fiction* is hardly comforting. It is not meant to be. The cataclysmic destruction of all human civilization in Ross Rocklynne's "Jackdaw" (1942) epitomizes man's careless and senseless use of technology and science, his self-destructiveness, and his utter stupidity.

And yet, we are still dealing with fiction, and much of what the stories predict has not yet come true. Only time will tell if it ever will. Perhaps this anthology will give rise to some reflection on our present lives and lifestyles. Above all, however, this volume should be thoroughly appreciated and enjoyed for its thrilling action and excitement and for the vision of the future prophesied in these works of the past. Inevitably, the reader will find himself drawn into this fascinating world, which, despite its spaceships, aliens, atomic bombs, "thinking machines," and other inventions, still remains compellingly human.

ALIX GUDEFIN PERRACHON

JOHN W. CAMPBELL, JR.

CONCERNING SCIENCE FICTION

SCIENCE FICTION is a much broader term than the non-reader of it realizes; it embraces a field of literary work about as broad as the term "detective fiction." As in the field of detective fiction, some is beautifully and tenderly written, some is handled with the machine precision of logic and careful structure of engineering estimate, or a Dr. Thorndyke mystery. And in science fiction, as in detective fiction, some of the published material is completely bad. There have been spicy detective stories, and spicy science-fiction stories; to the honor of science fiction, it can be added that the spicy science-fiction magazine completely altered its policy after precisely one issue. As much cannot be said for the detective field.

But like the detective field, science fiction has had its special followers and fans. Because, to most people, it seemed lurid, fantastic, and nonsensical trash, science fiction's fans have tended to be a bit defensive in their attitude. Science fiction has, definitely, been a misunderstood type of material.

In the public mind, "Buck Rogers" is the standard science-fiction character; the comic strip has tended to be accepted as representative of the field. It is—to precisely the extent that Dick Tracy is representative of detective fiction.

Actually, Buck Rogers evolved—or devolved—out of a series of stories that Phil Nowlan wrote in the old *Amazing Stories*. In the original stories, Rogers was not "Buck," and the stories were well and thoughtfully done. The first one, by the way, was largely devoted to a plot revolving about the point that a light, highly portable rocket-launcher would make a far more practical and effective weapon for infantry troops than would either rifles or ray-guns. By

1940, the United States Army had adopted this view, and the weapon became known as a "bazooka." Phil Nowlan's first story of Rogers had an excellent dissertation on the military qualities and advantages of bazookas, though he could not, of course, know the particular name later attached to the weapon.

In general, there are three broad divisions of science fiction:

1. Prophecy stories, in which the author tries to predict the effects of a new invention.
2. Philosophical stories, in which the author presents, in story form, some philosophical question using the medium of science fiction simply to set the stage for the particular point he wants to discuss.
3. Adventure science fiction, wherein the action and the plot are the main point.

Naturally, no story can be purely one or the other of these. The philosophical story will use an adventure-type plot to act out the problem under discussion. The science fictionist will probably include a few items of prophecy in setting up the background against which his philosophical problem is acted out.

The prophecy story will necessarily involve adventure, too; in attempting to present the effects of the new invention, some human character, reacting to those new forces, must be used to display their nature and magnitude.

As an example, *Solution Unsatisfactory*, with which this book begins, is a Grade A instance of the prophetic story: It was accurate prophecy, and had the background of that prophecy for the acting out of the adventure plot. It inevitably involves philosophical problems, of course. The author's original title for this story was "Foreign Policy"—in reference to the fact that the United States never has had a consistent, predictable, or understandable foreign policy. The author's prophecy has been remarkably borne out: President Roosevelt's death brought a shift in the alignment of American foreign policy.

How can such uncannily accurate prophecy be attained?

One of the basic propositions of the scientific method might be stated as "The proof of the theory is in the predictions thereof." A useful advance in theoretical science must produce a theory which not only explains all known phenomena in the simplest and most coherent manner known, but *must also accurately predict still undiscovered phenomena*. In other words, "If my theory is correct, then carrying out Process A on Substance B should produce Effect C.

'This has never been done. Let us see if the prediction is correct—and if it is, my theory will have served some use, and will have a further indication of correctness."

Science is always in the business of prediction. The chemist "predicts" that if you combine hydrogen and oxygen, you will get heat and water vapor. That low level of prediction anyone is familiar with. It is on precisely the same sort of basis, however, that scientists, in 1940, reported that if you combined uranium isotope 235 with neutrons, you would get enormous energy, various unstable elements, and more neutrons.

MacDonald's prediction of atomic warfare was not a strictly honest prediction; he was simply taking advantage of the fact that theoretical science is normally many years ahead of engineering fact. The nuclear physicists couldn't, in 1940, separate U-235 on the scale required, and no one knew just how it would be done. But it was obvious that it could and would be done. Taking off from that point, it took the Manhattan Project years of mighty effort to produce the finished product. Naturally the science-fiction writer, who need only write about the finished product, can predict what's coming.

But the modern science-fiction writer doesn't merely say, "In about ten years we will have atomic weapons." He goes further; his primary interest is in what those weapons will do to political, economic and cultural structures of human society.

MacDonald's story is one of several excellent examples of this type of story. I happen to know that this story was read, and widely discussed, among the physicists and engineers working on the Manhattan Project. The author's background covers both engineering and politics as a profession; he knew—quite obviously—whereof he spoke.

There are, incidentally, other ways of making perfectly accurate prophecies of things to come. Men were predicting flying machines long before any faintest concept was formed of the difficulties involved, or the principles which might overcome those problems. Man is a curious beastie; he is sufficiently lazy to work harder than any other animal on Earth to make life easier. If enough people want something badly enough, long enough, eventually someone, somewhere, somewhen, somehow will produce it. Men wanted flying machines; eventually they got them.

Men want spaceships. The Germans built the first, and used it as a bomb-carrying weapon, a rocket cargo ship with a cargo of sudden death, delivered without warning, to an unknown address.

But men will adapt, and improve, and enlarge—and men will reach the Moon. We know how, now. But it has been predicted for centuries before the most remote roots of our present knowledge were available. It's been standard stuff, in fact, since men knew the Moon was another world, not a silver dish in the sky.

You can predict long-term trends; what man wants hard enough, somebody will eventually figure out.

You can "predict" short-term trends by, actually, simply discussing a laboratory phenomenon as an engineering practice. Atomic bombs and radar, robot bombs, and radio-controlled planes, were all perfectly predictable. The function of science fiction is to consider what those inventions can, or could, do to people.

Universe, by Robert Heinlein, is in the last general section of this book. It represents one example of the purely philosophical-question type, with sound, fast-moving action to carry it along. The essential philosophical problem might be considered as that of the process of human learning. To illustrate his point, Heinlein has established a colony—which has forgotten its history, as men do—in a completely synthetic environment: a gigantic spaceship. In this synthetic "universe," the natural laws as we know them are, necessarily, entirely anomalous; how could a people in such a synthetic environment learn the true facts of their situation? And—do you *know* that we have done much better?

For that philosophical question, the synthetic environment of a self-sustaining spaceship offers a locale unmatchable in any environment outside of science fiction. For the problem Murray Leinster discusses in *First Contact,* other environments might be possible—but the science fictionist's freedom makes it possible to set up the idealized example of the situation. It makes possible the elimination from the discussion of all side-issues, and concentrates the whole problem of the meeting of two alien races—a problem which has another facet in our present world, one called international friendship —onto a small and manageable stage.

Killdozer, by Theodore Sturgeon, is an almost pure example of science-fiction adventure. Sturgeon spent a large portion of the war carving Navy bases out of islands with earth-moving machinery such as he describes. I think the description of the vicious battle between the bulldozer and the power shovel one of the tensest fight descriptions I've read. To Sturgeon, obviously, those brutally powerful machines he worked with took on a perverse and deadly personality—and he put that into his story.

Science fiction is made up of many factors, and the science-fiction author encounters problems of storytelling technique unknown in more conventional fields. It is a matter of general experience that the novelette form in science fiction is far more apt to be effective than the short story. The reason for this lies in the inherent nature of the medium: science fiction presents a new world-picture, a different era, a different planet perhaps, or a different dimension. In the world in which the story is laid, a "taxi" may be an anti-gravity-powered flying machine. The social and economic customs of the people may be totally different. If these factors are to be of importance in the development of the story, they must be explained.

In older science fiction—H. G. Wells and nearly all stories written before 1935—the author took time out to bring the reader up to date as to what had happened before his story opened. The best modern writers of science fiction have worked out some truly remarkable techniques for presenting a great deal of background and associated material without intruding into the flow of the story. That is no small feat, when a complete new world must be established at the same time a story is being presented.

This makes it extremely difficult to get a good, solid short story in science fiction. Only by using the most stylized, standardized features of science fiction can it be accomplished, in most cases. Rocket-drive spaceships are standard, for instance. To the regular reader of science fiction, description of the basic structure and mechanism of a rocket ship is as unnecessary as description of a gun is in a detective story.

Science fiction is *not* pseudo-science. Pseudo-science is what the Sunday-Supplement features present. By definition, the term means false, imitation science, attempting to pass itself off as the genuine article. Science fiction is no more pseudo-science than fiction is pseudo-truth. Fiction makes no pretense of being truth; most books and magazines explicitly state, on the flyleaf or in the magazine indicia, that no such characters existed nor did the events actually happen. Science fiction is fiction, purely fiction, and makes no claim to be fact. But it does claim—and with provable truth—that many of its stories are extrapolations of known science into possible future engineering. Also, the good science-fiction author takes the same sort of care with his background science that the good detective-fiction writer does with his local color. A reasonably quick-minded reader of science fiction can readily pick up an astonishing fund of scientific fact from reading the stories. The general proposition of uranium fission was described in accurate detail in various stories published before 1941 ended. Most science-fiction readers have as good a knowledge of the general layout of the solar system as they have of the Earth's geography. They've been there in much the sense that many a detective-book fan feels he's practically been through Scotland Yard himself.

The top authors of science fiction are, in general, professional technicians of one sort or another, who write the stories as a hobby which makes some useful pocket money. But primarily, they write to place before other keen and interested minds the ideas, suggestions, and problems they have themselves encountered.

Murray Leinster, who wrote *First Contact,* under another name is widely known as a contributor to *Collier's, Cosmopolitan,* and other magazines. For relaxation in a hobby, he picks science—and science fiction.

Isaac Asimov is a research chemist, recently employed by the Navy Research Laboratory. Robert Heinlein is an Annapolis graduate and a plastics research engineer. Norman L. Knight also contributes to other magazines—such as *Industrial & Engineering Chemistry*. He's a chemist. David H. Keller is a doctor. John Taine is the pen-name of a top-rank American mathematician.

In recent years, the professional scientists have, more and more, taken over the pages of the magazines. There are regular contributors in many of the nation's great laboratories—and, of course, regular readers.

There is one more point that should be added. Some while ago, I was trying to find out why it was that a friend who very much liked fantasy—(as distinct from science fiction, fantasy embraces only the "ghoulies and ghosties and things that go boomp i' the night")—could not abide science fiction.

The reason was hard to find. He didn't lack imagination, or have a stereotyped mind; if that were the case, he wouldn't have enjoyed fantasy stories so wholeheartedly. Eventually, it worked out to this:

In fantasy, the author knows it isn't true, the reader knows it isn't true, knows it didn't happen, and can't ever happen, and everybody is agreed. But in science fiction, this man felt an overwhelming pressure on the part of the author to convince him that the story was possible, and could happen, a driving sincerity that oppressed and repelled him. The author was trying to convince him that the story—which he knew perfectly well was utterly "fantastic"—*could, and quite probably would, happen.*

In effect, he didn't like science fiction because the author was sincere, highly competent, and had put into his story such a feeling

of certainty and reality that it almost forced the reader to accept
its message against his own "better judgment":

The story we were discussing—in 1942—was *Solution Unsatisfactory*. In Chicago, at that time, the nuclear physicists were working out ways to handle the terribly deadly radioactive dusts produced
in the by-products of uranium fission.

This book begins with that story. It ends with *Jackdaw,* a story
of the philosophical problem type.

The atomic age has opened, and to date we have an answer to
it—secrecy—best described as an unsatisfactory solution. Practically
none of our Representatives—on whom not only we, but the world,
must depend—have taken the trouble to study the Smyth Report on
Atomic Energy.* Unless our foreign policy becomes less muddled,
we are rather apt to present just such a philosophical problem in
the end as *Jackdaw.*

* Has *your* Representative, by the way? Part of your job as a citizen is to
know—or accept his ignorance.

1946

INTRODUCTION

IN THE YEAR 1889, Frank R. Stockton, known today largely for his *The Lady and the Tiger*, was writing for a new magazine called *Once a Week*, which, before its first two years were run, changed its name to *Collier's*.

One of the pot-boilers Stockton turned out for *Once a Week* was about a future war with Great Britain. It was called *The Great War Syndicate*, and in this unlikely tale were worked out patterns for a couple of new weapons against which, the author felt, it would be for the first time impossible to build defenses. One of them was a giant pincers which disabled British battleships by pulling their propellers out by the roots. Another was a cannon with miraculous powers.

So hopelessly fantastic did *The Great War Syndicate* seem then and later that it dropped into a kind of honorable obscurity. Until recently it was remembered only by science-fiction pioneers like H. G. Wells, who has given Stockton credit for helping him along the road which eventually resulted in *The Time Machine, The War of the Worlds*, and his other famous science fantasies.

However, on August 6, 1945, *The Great War Syndicate* suddenly came alive again. Through the purest chance—a chance, let me add, which has not blessed the efforts of many other fantasy writers—the effects of Stockton's miraculous cannon, as he described them, were uncannily like those of the atom bomb which eliminated Hiroshima. Much of the mechanics with which he surrounded the operation of the weapon is sheer nonsense, and yet his description of its results on land and on sea is startlingly vivid and true.

In order to bring this short novel—it ran to over 125 pages in the original—down to manageable size for an anthology of short stories, I have excised endless descriptions of Stockton's other weapons, and much of the details of Britain's bumbling defense against them. However, I have left in the last few hundred words of the tale, if only because they have an uncomfortably modern sound, in view of the debate which has been agitating American and British journalists and politicians on the control of atomic power.

Of course, *The Great War Syndicate* was unadulterated day-dreaming. But the fact that it was written when it was has led some of science fiction's more avid followers to stake out claims on the future. Who knows, these intrepid romanticists say, but what to-day's science fiction may not turn out to be tomorrow's technological commonplace?

Less fanatic addicts claim that a good science-fiction story is improbable but not impossible. Even that definition depends on your credulity. If you believe that your actions in 1966 have already happened, on another "plane," you can equally well believe that you could learn what those actions will be by means of a time machine, a space warp, or some other as yet unpatented gadget.

But the simple fact is that science fiction, despite its treading on the toes of nuclear physics, has no business claiming the robes of the prophet. That professional S-F writers (as they are familiarly known in the pulp-magazine trade) were able to write with some knowledgeability of the nature of atomic fission as far back as 1940 does not prove that they had second sight. It only proves that they read the right science journals, in which the coldly scientific possi-bilities of the atom were described with accurate detail for them to pick up and embroider.

It is in its embroideries that the largest merit of science fiction resides. I think that any brand of writing, no matter how incredible, which explores regions of man's imagination heretofore virgin to his interest, is worth reading. If only because the stories included in this book are incredible, they may be said to have value. For their authors are possessed of the imaginative faculty fully fledged and flapping its wings, whereas in the average American adult it has not even chipped its shell.

One of the purposes of literature is to transport the reader. Science fiction does that. Let more ponderous branches of the art also edify, inform, and elevate. They, too, transport the reader, but rarely as far up as Sirius or as far down as the hydrogen atom. And the fact that here are ideas and dreams which man has never before thought or imagined in the written history of the world gives these tales a certain permanence.

II

Far be it from one who has grown up with the age of electricity to doubt the old saw that that which can be imagined, can be. The world of 1946, even without the atom, would seem hilariously impossible to the world of 1846, as impossible as the wildest of the stories within the covers of this book may seem to us today. But don't let that fool you. They were writing of men on the moon as far back as 1835, and they were not joking about it, either.

That episode concerns one of the most famous hoaxes of modern times. Richard Adams Locke, a friend of Edgar Allan Poe, was a reporter for the *New York Sun.* His was a curious imagination, no question about it, and perhaps a rather inadequate sense of public responsibility. Being a lover of the moon and of science equally, he sat down in the summer of 1835 and concocted a lengthy and most circumstantial forgery which announced the discovery that men and animals flourished on the sunny side of Luna. The *Sun* published it, open-mouthed, as a straight scientific report ostensibly reprinted from the Edinburgh *Journal of Science,* which unfortunately had passed away a few months before the hoax was supposed to have been published in it.

Locke's *tour de force* was later called *The Moon Hoax,* but when it came out it appeared under the imposing title, *Great Astronomical Discoveries Lately Made by Sir John Herschel, LL.D., F.R.S., etc., at the Cape of Good Hope,* and it fooled even a delegation of Yale scientists for a while.

Today *The Moon Hoax* is dreary and prolix reading; but in its time it set a pattern upon which practically the whole development of science fiction as a species has been based. And it did one thing more. It indicated an early awakening of the interest of men in the more extraordinary possibilities of their cosmological environment. People wanted to believe the incredible, and believe it they did, until they were reluctantly disabused of their error.

Yet it would have been much simpler in 1835 to imagine the existence of men on the moon than it would have been to conceive of music coming out of a flat piece of rubber, or floods of light from a tiny strand of wire, or flight by air at speeds near that of sound. It is, therefore, nothing short of foolhardy for us realistic moderns to sneer too omnisciently at the vagaries of the S-F boys.

Indeed, much science fiction is definitely possible. Consider how little we know about the world we live on, and in, and under. Until it is proved that the world is not partly hollow—and it has not been—

Jules Verne's classic *Journey to the Center of the Earth* will remain one of those tantalizingly un-disprovable adventures of the imagination. No one has ever been into the ionosphere, that high and rarefied region beyond the reach of the highest flying plane, and until someone explores it, the horrors envisaged in Anson MacDonald's *Goldfish Bowl* are definitely not impossible. Again, there is no completely scientific reason why catastrophic earthquakes and volcanic eruptions should occur only along the great faults. We know new volcanoes can appear; we are living in the first period in the written history of man when a brand-new volcano actually has been born on land, Mexico's Paricutin. Another one could start up in North Carolina just as well, as in Morrison Colladay's *Giant in the Earth*.

Moreover, no scientist alive today, much less a mere editor of a science-fiction anthology, dare say that there cannot be life on the planets, or even, as a matter of objective fact, on or in the moon itself. We have never been on the moon; and where we have not been, we cannot know, no matter how enormous the magnification of our telescopes, or our microscopes, either, for that matter. Life can be sub-microscopic in size and still be very important, as witness the filterable virus—though perhaps not quite as important as Ralph Milne Farley's telepathic germ, gruesomely imagined in his *Liquid Life*.

The best science fiction is that which describes adventures in realms where man has not yet ventured. Just as the early descriptions of voyages, with their sea monsters and their sundry other impossible fauna and flora, remained true until disproved, so, for the free mind, many of the adventures described in this book may as well be thought possible until proved otherwise. It is much more fun that way!

For fun, after all, is the primary import of science fiction, which, like the detective story and the fairy tale as well, has one purpose, clear and simple: the purpose of entertaining you. It is first as entertainment that *The Best of Science Fiction** is offered, with only a slight and faintly uneasy salaam to the writers who have put their imaginations to the practical problem of what nuclear fission might involve in the way of social and political change.

III

If you are interested in the anatomy of literature, you may like to know that the classifier of literary form has created a niche for

---

*This is the original title for this volume and is used throughout the introduction.

science fiction. It falls under the general heading of fantasy, which is itself a sub-branch of the species "imaginative writing." Imaginative writing includes everything that is not based on historical fact, and is so broad a classification that only the philosophers of literature have much use for it.

Under the broad heading of fantasy, there are four primary types: the utopia, the fairy tale, the supernatural story, and science fiction. Each of these four classifications may be further subdivided by the intent with which the writers approach their material: romantic, satirical, and moral, are the three major moods which motivate fantasy writers.

The utopia usually is a moral or metaphysical fantasy civilization. In the old days utopias used to be located in unexplored parts of the world, but today they usually are situated in unexplored parts of the universe or of time. Created usually to teach a lesson or promote a social philosophy, they often have science-fiction overtones in the mechanics of their construction. I have forgotten at the moment how Cyrano managed to get his hero to the moon,* but it was probably through the use of some unlikely machinery only a little less difficult to imagine than the most modern inter-galactic spaceship of the S-F pulps. That was three centuries ago, too; and since then other utopias have used hypnotism, as did Edward Bellamy in *Looking Backward,* time machines, and a multitude of other science-fiction devices to get the reader where the writer wanted him—into the world of dreams.

But the outstanding characteristic of the utopia is its purposiveness. Whether straight stuff or satirical (as are Huxley's *Brave New World* or Zamiatin's *We*) they always have a moral, an end in view, a line to sell, a philosophy to put across. In this resides much of their dullness. The average utopia is a bore because it represents one man's ideas of what he, with all his foibles and quirks of mind, thinks the perfect world ought to be, or, if he claims the satirist's robes, what he thinks tomorrow's world is likely to be, given today's social infirmities and tomorrow's scientific skill at accentuating them.

The sub-species fairy tale comprises an enormous portion of the total field of fantasy, and the best portion, too. A rich mine of miscellaneous stuffs it contains. Mice wear tophats and talk Oxford English; beautiful girls spout jewels instead of words; jackasses

---

* PUBLISHER'S NOTE: It was by standing on a metal plate and throwing a magnet ahead of him, over and over, which drew the plate after it.

EDITOR'S ADDENDUM: Obviously the prototype of the modern Sky-Hook.

change into handsome princelings; and ogres nearly, but not quite, devour harmless little children.

At first the fairy tale originated in, and to some extent it still stems from, the religious impulses of man. Many of the theological worlds of ancient religion are fairy tales, wrapped around, it is true, with an aura of belief which makes them more the subject of anthropological study than of literary criticism. Yet they are fairy tales in essence.

On a more mundane plane, the fairy tale includes everything from Ovid's *Metamorphoses* down to such effete and sophisticated legends as *Lady into Fox* or *The Celestial Omnibus*; from the ancient *Panchatantra* down to the Brothers Grimm; from the magnificent *Argonautica* down to the modern fireside tales told of Paul Bunyan. Folklore, tall tales, mythologies, all belong to this type. Fairy tales are wonderful, but they are not science fiction.

Neither is the supernatural story. This less savory branch of fantasy is confused by many people with science fiction, much to the honest wrath of the S-F writers. Great and scrupulous care is taken by pulp magazine editors to separate the supernatural sheep from the science-fiction goats in today's magazines, even though I must confess that the line between the types seems to me sometimes rather finely drawn.*

However, as a general thing, the supernatural story is easily identifiable. It deals with ghosts, werewolves, witches, and various creepy-crawly things the sole purpose of which is to horrify.

The tale of the supernatural is a large and sullen section of literature which has inspired some extraordinarily able writers during its history. I have always—perhaps it is a defect in my imagination—been at a loss to understand the attraction in this particular school of writing. Even *Dracula,* though it delightfully frightened me when I was fifteen, fails to chill or charm today. Sometimes I have felt that only those people like supernatural stories who still have a sneaking suspicion, deep underneath their own quite rational minds, that there really are Powers and Potentates of Darkness abroad in the land. They propitiate this fearsome possibility by writing and reading about it, even if they "really" don't believe in it. *Homo sapiens* is still pretty much a creature of his own age-long struggle against the Unknown: and even at his most intelligent he is prone to see bogeys.

* The late and well-known H. P. Lovecraft is omitted from this book because it seems to the editor that he was much more a supernaturalist than a science-fiction writer, despite his adherents' claims to the contrary.

If this is true, it may be suggested that science fiction is composed of "supernatural" writing for materialists. You may read every science-fiction story that is true science fiction, and never once have to compromise with your id. The stories all have rational explanations, provided you are willing to grant the word "rational" a certain elasticity.

IV

When the first science-fiction story was written it is impossible to say, for although the name is new, the type is as old as the beginnings of the industrial revolution and the growth of interest in the physical sciences. However, in those early days it usually happened that stories which we would class as science fiction were written with an ulterior purpose, moral or satirical: something which rarely happens today. Thus, *Gulliver's Travels,* certainly one of the greatest science-fiction stories of all time, is usually thought of more as a moral fairy tale. Moral it is, but fairy tale it certainly is not. It has too much mechanics in it. And in fairy tales odd things just *are*—they never are explained.

However, the modern concept of science fiction, though it remained without the name, began at about the time when science itself began to have a broad, popular interest. *The Moon Hoax,* previously discussed, though probably not the first, was the most famous of the early "scientific" fiction stories.

Following Richard Locke, his friend Edgar Allan Poe established a type of science fiction which has by now, unfortunately, nearly disappeared, but which while it lasted produced some very pretty effects. I refer to his stories of the mind; those which deal with hypnotism, mesmerism, and other still unexplored sciences. Today, the few stories which deal with the mind most often have to do with telepathy, while the elements of control which one mind may have over others are more or less ignored.* It is unfortunate, for more fantastic possibilities can spring from man's fooling around with his mind than from his playing with any of the inanimate objects of his attention, from electrons to nebulæ.

Soon after Poe's great period, the expatriate Irishman Fitz James O'Brien settled in New York, *circa* 1850, and began going Poe one better with his tales of super-microscopes, invisible men, and the

---

*Isaac Asimov's *The Mule,* in the November and December, 1945, issues of *Astounding Science-Fiction,* is a recent exception, and a good one.

like. The only trouble with O'Brien's stories was that he neglected to arrange any scientific mumbo-jumbo to "explain" their happenings, and so they are science fiction only by implication. Nevertheless, his *What Was It?* and *The Diamond Lens* still have their charm for the literary archaeologist.

After O'Brien, the deluge. Jules Verne began to delight the young of all ages with his adventurous machinery. Conan Doyle, Ambrose Bierce, Jack London dabbled in the field, though with not too great success. However, Doyle's *The Great Keinplatz Experiment*, reprinted here, has the pleasant quality of being both science fiction and funny, a rare combination indeed. H. Rider Haggard and others of his fictional school developed the sciences of exploration and geographical prospecting with a fine disregard for the petty limitations of the known world.

At this time, also, Frank Stockton turned out his atom-dream, *The Great War Syndicate,* the same year (1889) that Samuel Langhorne Clemens dabbled with time in *A Connecticut Yankee in King Arthur's Court,* a piece of science fiction which fathered a long line of unlikely descendants ending up currently with comic strips like *Oaky Doaks.*

Finally, the elder statesmen of modern science fiction began making their appearance: H. G. Wells, George Allen England, Charles B. Stilson, Austin Hall, Homer Eon Flint, Garrett P. Serviss, Julian Hawthorne, and a number of other writers, most of whom you no doubt have never heard about. These men ran lengthy serials in the old *Argosy, Black Cat, Cavalier, All Story,* and other progenitors of the modern pulps, which ruled during that wild and woolly period between the Spanish-American War and the mid-Twenties. Few of them wrote any short stories, and so most of them cannot be represented here.

It was not until the year 1926 that science fiction finally attained the dignity of a magazine of its own. In a sentimental way, *The Best of Science Fiction* is a celebration of the 20th birthday of *Amazing Stories,* which first appeared in April, 1926, and of the pioneering acuteness of Hugo Gernsback, who had the nerve to launch the venture. Gernsback had for some years been publishing, in his popular-science magazine called *Science and Invention* (which he no longer controls), some of the wilder romancings about time and space which the S-F authors of that day were producing; and the acclaim with which these fictional interludes in what was otherwise a pure "hobby-lobby" type of home-mechanics magazine were greeted interested him. He had the editorial astuteness to realize that the new form of popular writing was no longer just a squalling infant. It was climbing out of its swaddling clothes and demanding attention. It had an audience. So Gernsback decided to take a flyer and *Amazing Stories* was the result.

It was a trail blazer, and a success. For one reason or another, however, Mr. Gernsback moved out of control within three years, and started a competitor—or rather, two competitors: *Air Wonder Stories* and *Science Wonder Stories*. These appeared under his editorship in 1929, but two proved to be one too many, so after a few months he combined them into *Wonder Stories,* which he carried on until 1936. The founder of the science-fiction magazine then moved out of the field for good, and *Wonder Stories* became *Thrilling Wonder Stories* under a new owner.

Hectic though Hugo Gernsback's career in science fiction was, he will always be remembered by both writers and addicts with the respect due to a pioneer. Many a young S-F writer got his first chance in print from him, and for that alone he deserves credit.

Six years previous to the demise of *Wonder Stories,* another science-fiction magazine made its appearance, this one called *Astounding Stories.* For a long time *Astounding* just edged along in the ruck, but toward the end of the 'Thirties, when it fell under the editorship of John W. Campbell, Jr., it became quite definitely the leader in the field. I should like to present my compliments to Mr. Campbell. Not only has he written a shrewd and knowledgeable preface for this collection, and suggested several stories included in it which I had not too unaccountably missed (a rough estimate of the stories I read or cursorily glanced through reaches the horrid total of around 6,000), but he has created a magazine which, with occasional lapses incident to any mass-production literary operation, maintains an inordinately high level of well-written and effective stories. *Astounding Science-Fiction,* as it is now called, is a good example of selective editorial judgment—how good one can realize only after reading the average S-F stories appearing elsewhere.

It was in *Astounding Science-Fiction* that all of the stories on atomic power (except Frank Stockton's) which appear in this book were first published. Some of them were uncomfortably near the truth.

As a matter of fact, the story which leads off in this book, *Solution Unsatisfactory,* is included here with the greatest reluctance. It is one instance where science fiction has dangerously sinister overtones of possibility. I was not finally convinced that I should include it, as the publishers urged that I should, until I read the following news item in *The Washington Post* for Friday, November 2, 1945.

ATOM WAR THREAT
MAY FORCE U. S. TO
SELECT DICTATOR

Chicago, Nov. 1 (AP).—Dr. Harold C. Urey, Nobel prize winner who helped develop the atomic bomb, declared today that in "five years or perhaps less" when any nation can make the bomb, it may be necessary for the United States to establish a dictatorial form of government to act quickly against an atomic war threat.

"I do not see any way to keep our democratic form of government if everybody has atomic bombs," Urey said. "If everyone has them, it will be necessary for our government to move quickly in a manner not now possible under our diffused form of government."

This, coupled with Albert Einstein's statement that even if two-thirds of the world's people were destroyed by atomic bombs, enough brains and enough books would remain to enable civilization to continue, has persuaded me that *Solution Unsatisfactory* should be included, though still against my better judgment.

I do not agree, for instance, with the author's particular political bias, as it is exemplified in this tale. It seems quite dangerous to me. Furthermore, *Solution Unsatisfactory* is the only story in the book which is actually "impossible." The things which were supposed to have happened in 1942, 1943, 1944 and 1945 have not happened. I do not believe they will happen.

However, as E. B. White has so cogently said, "The brotherhood of man can never be achieved till the democracies realize that today's fantasy is tomorrow's communiqué." Let us devoutly hope that *Solution Unsatisfactory* stops short of being a preview of the next war's official dispatches.

Where the science-fiction writer will go now that nuclear fission is fact instead of fancy is a very simple question to answer. He will go on writing science fiction, safe in the knowledge that there are still quite a few things to write about which are in advance of current scientific developments. As a matter of fact, practically all contemporary S-F writers are far, far ahead of the atom. One author has his space ships travelling at the square of the speed of light. Another makes Pluto habitable by creating a lens a million miles across which concentrates the sun's rays on that planet's surface.

The most advanced writers of this remarkable crew no longer use fuel for travelling through space. These dreamers have discovered an Einsteinian concept known as hyper-space, which transmits their characters in an instant to the farthest known star in our heavens, and beyond.

These more advanced methods of locomotion will be found in this book only in Murray Leinster's *First Contact*. After all, *The Best of Science Fiction* is a primer for those still untutored in the gentle art of scientific dreaming. You may do your post-graduate work by reading any of the current issues of Mr. Campbell's magazine, where you may learn the latest developments in extra-galactic travel.

IV

Meanwhile, I would like to define the limits of this collection. I have tried to make it an adequate cross-section of the whole field, historically as well as contextually. However, the nature of any fairly comprehensive branch of writing makes it a foregone conclusion that no one anthology can actually represent it, without taking on the dimensions of an unabridged dictionary.

Science fiction is no exception. Young though it is, it already has a painfully large canon. The present collection makes no pretense of being comprehensive. Actually, though, I think I have represented most of the major types, one way or another. As you will see if you study the table of contents, the species has only a few important divisions; though within those divisions the varieties, the sports and the mutants are infinite. All that I have been able to do is to present a few of the choicer representatives of each division. For further examples, you will have to do your own magazine reading.

Beyond simple representation, the first and most obvious standard for an anthology of short stories is that it shall contain no long stories. There are a few novelettes in this book which are longer than I like, in view of the inexpansibility of a $3.00 volume, but at least I have not packed in half a dozen novels and called the result a representative anthology.

However, since some of the most outstanding science-fiction writers have written chiefly in the novel form, you will find no items in this book from novelists like S. Fowler Wright, George Allen England, David Lindsay, Edwin Balmer and Philip Wylie, A. Merritt, C. S. Lewis, Olaf Stapledon, or J. U. Giesy. You will have to hunt the back files of the science-fiction pulps, or the shelves of your local public library, if you want to have a go at their works.

Neither will you find certain of the older favorites in science fiction. Jules Verne, for instance, is missing; so is H. Rider Haggard; so are many others of their age and type. The trouble with them is that their stories today seem dull and old-fashioned, and they would be out of place in an exhibit composed of such streamlined stuff as is in this book.

Many Big Shots in contemporary science fiction are missing too, and they are left out with a malediction upon them, those writers who have given the art its bad name, the comic-strip boys, the creators of *Superman* and the *Time Top*, the run-of-the-mill S-F pulpists, those highly prosperous producers for juveniles who are responsible for Phil Stong's denunciation of most science fiction as a "pabulum of reiterated nonsense."

Thus, I have avoided such stories as are usually to be found between lurid magazine covers showing luxuriantly-fleshed females scantily clad in either a leopard's skin or a two-piece female Buck Rogers outfit with a bare twelve inches of midriff, struggling (always valiantly struggling!) with an octopus-like monster or an otherworld hellion with horns and a leer. The tales in such magazines usually begin with a sentence like this: "Sool Darm opened his many-lidded eyes with reptilian anticipation and lowered his pointed head to gaze on the lithe but richly-rounded figure of the girl who lay unconscious at his feet." Ugh!

It is nearly impossible to mix sex and science fiction, any more than you can successfully mix sex and the supernatural. None but a few rare practitioners, like Wallace West in his *En Route to Pluto*, have ever been able to make even a passable try at it.

Finally, there are one or two tales not to be found within this book, in these instances much to the anguish of the editor. These are stories fondly remembered from a younger day, stories which I have not been able to locate, hunt and pry as I could.

One of those stories, a diller about a dye which had the uncomfortable power of dissolving granite into huge, towering, evil-smelling blue crystals in an explosive instant, has remained elusive and unfound. If any reader of this book knows the whereabouts of this I. G. Farbenindustrie promotion piece, I would appreciate hearing from him.

Then there was another wonderful tale, which appeared, as I remember, in the *Saturday Evening Post*. It had to do with a New York skyscraper which collapsed as a result of the forgetfulness of the occupant of the penthouse apartment, who went away one weekend and forgot to turn off the bath water. The construction of the building being solid and watertight, none of the water could leak out. So, at the end of a day or so, the whole enormous structure gave way under the accumulated weight of the liquid in the penthouse.

Even a plea for help in the *New York Times Book Review's* "Queries and Answers" page brought no results on that one. I hope that this notice will flush the story out of hiding.

V

Merely for historical interest, I would like to present a checklist of the science-fiction magazines which were examined during the preparation of this book:

Air Wonder Stories
Amazing Stories
Astonishing Stories
Astounding Science-Fiction
Cosmic Stories
Famous Fantastic Mysteries
Fantastic Adventures
Marvel Tales
Miracle Science and Fantasy Stories

Mystic Magazine
Planet Stories
Science Wonder Stories
Startling Stories
Stirring Science Stories
Super-Science Stories
Thrilling Wonder Stories
Unknown Worlds
Wonder Stories

These magazines are to be found in that extraordinary collection of the trivia of modern publishing which is known as the Cellar Reserve of the Library of Congress. Hundreds and hundreds of unbound piles of pulps, comics, and miscellaneous serial items are hidden away in that cavernous underground storeroom. The Library of Congress, being the copyright depository for every publication in the nation, receives copies of all of America's printed output. It has cost it nothing to collect the Cellar Reserve, but thanks are due to the curators for realizing that even the pulps and the comics have their niche in modern society and deserve to be kept, and also for their unfailing courtesy over a year-long period in digging out for me those interminable, dusty piles of science-fiction magazines from which this book has been compiled.

I would also like to extend my mixed blessings to Mr. Edmund Fuller, the editor of Crown Publishers. It was only through my own savage struggles for survival that I was able to edit this book myself; for Mr. Fuller became so entranced with the undertaking that I often had to beat him off with a broomstick in order to keep the volume from being entirely composed of stories by Don Stuart, Anson MacDonald, Robert Heinlein, and Lewis Padgett.

Even so, he deserves a good part of the credit for the present shape of *The Best of Science Fiction*. Somehow or other, we have managed to remain friends, despite that fact!

An exhaustive effort has been made to locate all persons having any rights or interests in the stories appearing in this book, and to clear reprint permissions with them. If any required acknowledgments have been omitted or any rights overlooked, it is by accident, and forgiveness is requested therefor.

Finally, I want to thank my wife for two things: (a) for reading proofs, and (b) for suffering in silence. She, alack, is not a science-fiction fan, though fast becoming one.

Washington, D. C.
January, 1946

PART ONE

THE ATOM

ANSON MacDONALD

SOLUTION
UNSATISFACTORY

4:26. As previously stated, the fragments resulting from fission are in most cases unstable nuclei, that is, artificially radioactive materials. It is common knowledge that the radiations from radioactive materials have deadly effects akin to the effects of X-rays.

4:27. In a chain-reacting pile these radioactive fission products build up as the reaction proceeds. (They have, in practice, turned out to be the most troublesome feature of a reacting pile.) Since they differ chemically from the uranium, it should be possible to extract them and use them like a particularly vicious form of poison gas. This idea was mentioned in the National Academy report and was developed in a report written December 10, 1941, by E. Wigner and H. D. Smyth, who concluded that the fission products produced in one day's run of a 100,000 kw chain-reacting pile might be sufficient to make a large area uninhabitable.

4:28. Wigner and Smyth did not recommend the use of radioactive poisons nor has such use been seriously proposed since by the responsible authorities, but serious consideration was given to the possibility that the Germans might make surprise use of radioactive poisons, and accordingly defensive measures were planned.

1945: Official Report: *Atomic Energy for Military Purposes*

HENRY D. SMYTH

PUBLISHER'S NOTE: This story was written in 1940.

IN 1903 the Wright brothers flew at Kitty Hawk.

In December, 1938, in Berlin, Dr. Hahn split the uranium atom.

In April, 1943, Dr. Estelle Karst, working under the Federal Emergency

Defense Authority, perfected the Karst-Obre technique for producing artificial radioactives.

So American foreign policy had to change.

Had to. *Had to.* It is very difficult to tuck a bugle call back into a bugle. Pandora's Box is a one-way proposition. You can turn pig into sausage, but not sausage into pig. Broken eggs stay broken. "All the King's horses and all the King's men can't put Humpty together again."

I ought to know—I was one of the King's men.

By rights I should not have been. I was not a professional military man when World War II broke out, and when Congress passed the draft law I drew a high number, high enough to keep me out of the army long enough to die of old age.

Not that very many died of old age that generation!

But I was the newly appointed secretary to a freshman congressman; I had been his campaign manager and my former job had left me. By profession, I was a high-school teacher of economics and sociology—school boards don't like teachers of social subjects actually to deal with social problems—and my contract was not renewed. I jumped at the chance to go to Washington.

My congressman was named Manning. Yes, *the* Manning, Colonel Clyde C. Manning, U. S. Army retired—Mr. Commissioner Manning. What you may not know about him is that he was one of the army's No. 1 experts in chemical warfare before a leaky heart put him on the shelf. I had picked him, with the help of a group of my political associates, to run against the two-bit chiseler who was the incumbent in our district. We needed a strong liberal candidate and Manning was tailor-made for the job. He had served one term in the grand jury, which cut his political eye teeth, and had stayed active in civic matters thereafter.

Being a retired army officer was a political advantage in vote-getting among the more conservative and well-to-do citizens, and his record was O. K. for the other side of the fence. I'm not primarily concerned with vote-getting; what I liked about him was that, though he was liberal, he was tough-minded, which most liberals aren't. Most liberals believe that water runs downhill, but, praise God, it'll never reach the bottom.

Manning was not like that. He could see a logical necessity and act on it, no matter how unpleasant it might be.

We were in Manning's suite in the House Office Building, taking a little blow from that stormy first session of the Seventy-eighth Congress and trying to catch up on a mountain of correspondence, when the war department called. Manning answered it himself.

I had to overhear, but then I was his secretary. "Yes," he said, "speaking. Very well, put him on. Oh . . . hello, general. . . . Fine, thanks. Yourself?" Then there was a long silence. Presently, Manning said, "But I can't do that, general, I've got this job to take care of. . . . What's that? . . . Yes, who is to do my committee work and represent my district? . . . I think so." He glanced at his wrist watch. "I'll be right over."

He put down the phone, turned to me, and said, "Get your hat, John. We are going over to the War Department."

"So?" I said, complying.

"Yes," he said with a worried look, "the chief of staff thinks I ought to go back to duty." He set off at a brisk walk, with me hanging back to try to force him not to strain his bum heart. "It's impossible, of course." We grabbed a taxi from the stand in front of the office building, swung around the Capitol, and started down Constitution Boulevard.

But it *was* possible, and Manning agreed to it, after the chief of staff presented his case. Manning had to be convinced, for there is no way on earth for anyone, even the President himself, to order a congressman to leave his post, even though he happens to be a member of the military service, too.

The chief of staff had anticipated the political difficulty and had been forehanded enough to have already dug up an opposition congressman with whom to pair Manning's vote for the duration of the emergency. This other congressman, the Honorable Joseph T. Brigham, was a reserve officer who wanted to go to duty himself—or was willing to; I never found out which. Being from the opposite political party, his vote in the House of Representatives could be permanently paired against Manning's and neither party would lose by the arrangement.

There was talk of leaving me in Washington to handle the political details of Manning's office, but Manning decided against it, judging that his other secretary could do that, and announced that I must go along as his adjutant. The chief of staff demurred, but Manning was in a position to insist, and the chief had to give in.

A chief of staff can get things done in a hurry if he wants to. I was sworn in as a temporary officer before we left the building; before the day was out I was at the bank, signing a note to pay for the sloppy service uniforms the army had adopted and to buy a dress uniform with a beautiful shiny belt—a dress outfit which, as it turned out, I was never to need.

We drove over into Maryland the next day and Manning took charge of the Federal nuclear research laboratory, known officially by the hush-hush title of War Department Special Defense Project No. 347. I didn't know a lot about physics and nothing about modern atomic physics, aside from the stuff you read in the Sunday supplements. Later, I picked up a smattering, mostly wrong, I suppose, from associating with the heavy-weights with which the laboratory was staffed.

Colonel Manning had taken an army p. g. course at Massachusetts Tech and had received a master of science degree for a brilliant thesis on the mathematical theories of atomic structure. That was why the army had to have him for this job. But that had been some years before; atomic theory had turned several cartwheels in the meantime; he admitted to me that he had to bone like the very devil to try to catch up to the point where he could begin to understand what his highbrow charges were talking about in their reports.

I think he overstated the degree of his ignorance; there was certainly no one else in the United States who could have done the job. It required a man who could direct and suggest research in a highly esoteric field, but who saw the problem from the standpoint of urgent military necessity. Left to themselves, the physicists would have reveled in the intellectual luxury of an unlimited research expense account, but, while they undoubtedly would have made major advances in human knowledge, they might never have developed anything of military usefulness, or the military possibilities of a discovery might be missed for years.

It's like this: It takes a smart hound dog to hunt birds, but it takes a hunter behind him to keep him from wasting time chasing rabbits. And the hunter needs to know nearly as much as the dog.

No derogatory reference to the scientists is intended—by no means! We had all the genius in the field that the United States could produce, men from Chicago, Columbia, Cornell, M. I. T., Cal Tech, Berkeley, every radiation laboratory in the country, as well as a couple of broad-A boys lent to us by the British. And they had every facility that ingenuity could think up and money could build. The five-hundred-ton cyclotron which had originally been intended for the University of California was there, and was already obsolete in the face of the new gadgets these brains had thought up, asked for, and been given. Canada supplied us with all the uranium we asked for—tons of the treacherous stuff—from Great Bear Lake, up near the Yukon, and the fractional-residues technique of separating uranium isotope 235 from the commoner isotope 238 had already been worked out, by the same team from Chicago that had worked up the earlier expensive mass spectrograph method.

Someone in the United States government had realized the terrific potentialities of uranium 235 quite early and, as far back as the summer of 1940, had rounded up every atomic research man in the country and had sworn them to silence. Atomic power, if ever developed, was planned to be a government monopoly, at least till the war was over. It might turn out to be the most incredibly powerful explosive ever dreamed of, and it might be the source of equally incredible power. In any case, with Hitler talking about secret weapons and shouting hoarse insults at democracies, the government planned to keep any new discoveries very close to the vest.

Hitler had lost the advantage of a first crack at the secret of uranium through not taking precautions. Dr. Hahn, the first man to break open the uranium atom, was a German. But one of his laboratory assistants had fled Germany to escape a pogrom. She came to this country, and told us about it.

We were searching, there in the laboratory in Maryland, for a way to use U235 in a controlled explosion. We had a vision of a one-ton bomb that would be a whole air raid in itself, a single explosion that would flatten out an entire industrial center. Dr. Ridpath, of Continental Tech, claimed that he could build such a bomb, but that he could not guarantee that it would not explode as soon as it was loaded, and as for the force of the explosion—well, he did not believe his own figures; they ran out to too many ciphers.

The problem was, strangely enough, to find an explosive which would be weak enough to blow up only one county at a time, and stable enough to blow up only on request. If we could devise a really practical rocket fuel at the same time, one capable of driving a war rocket at a thousand miles an hour, or more, then we would be in a position to make most anybody say "uncle" to Uncle Sam.

We fiddled around with it all the rest of 1943 and well into 1944. The war in Europe and the troubles in Asia dragged on. After Italy folded up, England was able to release enough ships from her Mediterranean fleet to ease the blockade of the British Isles. With the help of the planes we could now send her regularly and with the additional over-age destroyers we let her have, England hung on somehow, digging in and taking more and more of her essential defense industries underground.

I was killing time in the administrative office, trying to improve my typing—a lot of Manning's reports had to be typed by me personally—when the orderly on duty stepped in and announced Dr. Karst. I flipped the interoffice communicator. "Dr. Karst is here, chief. Can you see her?"

"Yes," he answered, through his end.

I told the orderly to show her in.

Estelle Karst was quite a remarkable old girl and, I suppose, the first woman ever to hold a commission in the corps of engineers. She was an M.D. as well as an Sc.D. and reminded me of the teacher I had had in fourth grade. I guess that was why I always stood up instinctively when she came in the room—I was afraid she might look at me and sniff. It couldn't have been her rank; we didn't bother much with rank.

She was dressed in white coveralls and a shop apron and had simply thrown a hooded cape over herself to come through the snow. I said, "Good morning, ma'am," and led her into Manning's office.

The colonel greeted her with the urbanity that had made him such a success with women's clubs, seated her, and offered her a cigarette.

"I'm glad to see you, major," he said. "I've been intending to drop around to your shop."

I knew what he was getting at; Dr. Karst's work had been primarily physiomedical; he wanted her to change the direction of her research to something more productive in a military sense.

"Don't call me 'major,'" she said tartly.

"Sorry, doctor—"

"I came on business, and must get right back. And I presume you are a busy man, too. Colonel Manning, I need some help."

"That's what we are here for."

"Good. I've run into some snags in my research. I think that one of the men in Dr. Ridpath's department could help me, but Dr. Ridpath doesn't seem disposed to be cooperative."

"So? Well, I hardly like to go over the head of a departmental chief, but tell me about it; perhaps we can arrange it. Whom do you want?"

"I need Dr. Obre."

"The spectroscopist—hm-m-m. I can understand Dr. Ridpath's reluctance, Dr. Karst, and I'm disposed to agree with him. After all, the high-explosives research is really our main show around here."

She bristled and I thought she was going to make him stay in after school at the very least. "Colonel Manning, do you realize the importance of artificial radioactives to modern medicine?"

"Why, I believe I do. Nevertheless, doctor, our primary mission is to perfect a weapon which will serve as a safeguard to the whole country in time of war—"

She sniffed and went into action. "Weapons—fiddlesticks! Isn't there a medical corps in the army? Isn't it more important to know how to heal men than to know how to blow them to bits? Colonel Manning, you're not a fit man to have charge of this project! You're a . . . you're a—a war-monger, that's what you are!"

I felt my ears turning red, but Manning never budged. He could have raised Cain with her, confined her to her quarters, maybe even have court-martialed her, but Manning isn't like that. He told me once that every time a man is court-martialed, it is a sure sign that some senior officer hasn't measured up to his job.

"I am sorry you feel that way, doctor," he said mildly, "and I agree that my technical knowledge isn't what it might be. And, believe me, I do wish that healing were all we had to worry about. In any case, I have not refused your request. Let's walk over to your laboratory and see what the problem is. Likely there is some arrangement that can be made which will satisfy everybody."

He was already up and getting out his greatcoat. Her set mouth relaxed a trifle and she answered, "Very well. I'm sorry I spoke as I did."

"Not at all," he replied. "These are worrying times. Come along, John."

I trailed after them, stopping in the outer office to get my own coat and to stuff my notebook in a pocket.

By the time we had trudged through mushy snow the eighth of a mile to her lab they were talking about gardening!

Manning acknowledged the sentry's challenge with a wave of his hand and we entered the building. He started casually on into the inner lab, but Karst stopped him. "Armor first, colonel."

We had trouble finding overshoes that would fit over Manning's boots, which he persisted in wearing, despite the new uniform regulations, and he wanted to omit the foot protection, but Karst would not hear of it. She called in a couple of her assistants who made jury-rigged moccasins out of some soft-lead sheeting.

The helmets were different from those used in the explosives lab, being fitted with inhalers. "What's this?" inquired Manning.

"Radioactive-dust guard," she said. "It's absolutely essential."

We threaded a lead-lined meander and arrived at the workroom door which she opened by combination. I blinked at the sudden bright illumination and noticed that the air was filled with little shiny motes.

"Hm-m-m—it *is* dusty," agreed Manning. "Isn't there some way of controlling that?" His voice sounded muffled from behind the dust mask.

"The last stage has to be exposed to air," explained Karst. "The hood gets most of it. We could control it, but it would mean a quite expensive new installation."

"No trouble about that. We're not on a budget, you know. It must be very annoying to have to work in a mask like this."

"It is," acknowledged Karst. "The kind of gear it would take would enable us to work without body armor, too. That would be a comfort."

I suddenly had a picture of the kind of thing these researchers put up with. I am a fair-sized man, yet I found that armor heavy to carry around. Estelle Karst was a small woman, yet she was willing to work maybe fourteen hours, day after day, in an outfit which was about as comfortable as a diving suit. But she had not complained.

Not all the heroes are in the headlines. These radiation experts not only ran the chance of cancer and nasty radioaction burns, but the men stood a chance of damaging their germ plasm and then having their wives present them with something horrid in the way of offspring—no chin, for example, and long hairy ears. Nevertheless, they went right ahead and never seemed to get irritated unless something held up their work.

Dr. Karst was past the age when she would be likely to be concerned personally about progeny, but the principle applies.

I wandered around, looking at the unlikely apparatus she used to get her results, fascinated as always by my failure to recognize much that reminded me of the physics laboratory I had known when I was an undergraduate, and being careful not to touch anything. Karst started explaining to Manning what she was doing and why, but I knew that it was useless for me to try to follow that technical stuff. If Manning wanted notes, he would dictate them. My attention was caught by a big boxlike contraption in one corner of the room. It had a hopperlike gadget on one side and I could hear a sound from it like the whirring of a fan with a background of running water. It intrigued me.

I moved back to the neighborhood of Dr. Karst and the colonel and heard her saying, "The problem amounts to this, colonel: I am getting a much more highly radioactive end-product than I want, but there is considerable variation in the half-life of otherwise equivalent samples. That suggests to me that I am using a mixture of isotopes, but I haven't been able to prove it. And frankly, I do not know enough about that end of the field to be sure of sufficient refinement in my methods. I need Dr. Obre's help on that."

I think those were her words, but I may not be doing her justice, not being a physicist. I understood the part about "half-life." All radioactive materials keep right on radiating until they turn into something else, which takes theoretically forever. As a matter of practice their periods, or "lives," are described in terms of how long it takes the original radiation to drop to one-half strength. That time is called a "half-life" and each radioactive isotope of an element has its own specific characteristic half-lifetime.

One of the staff—I forget which one—told me once that *any* form of matter can be considered as radioactive in some degree; it's a question of intensity and period, or half-life.

"I'll talk to Dr. Ridpath," Manning answered her, "and see what can be arranged. In the meantime you might draw up plans for what you want to re-equip your laboratory."

"Thank you, colonel."

I could see that Manning was about ready to leave, having pacified her; I was still curious about the big box that gave out the odd noises.

"May I ask what that is, doctor?" I said, pointing.

"Oh, that? That's an air conditioner."

"Odd-looking one. I've never seen one like it."

"It's not to condition the air for this room. It's to remove the radioactive dust before the exhaust air goes outdoors. We wash the dust out of the foul air."

"Where does the water go?"

"Down the drain. Out into the bay eventually, I suppose."

I tried to snap my fingers, which was impossible because of the lead mittens. "That accounts for it, colonel!"

"Accounts for what?"

"Accounts for those accusing notes we've been getting from the Bureau of Fisheries. This poisonous dust is being carried out into Chesapeake Bay and is killing the fish."

Manning turned to Karst. "Do you think that possible, doctor?"

I could see her brows draw together through the window in her helmet. "I hadn't thought about it," she admitted. "I'd have to do some figuring on the possible concentrations before I could give you a definite answer. But it is possible—yes. However," she added anxiously, "it would be simple enough to divert this drain to a sink hole of some sort."

"Hm-m-m—yes." He did not say anything for some minutes, simply stood there, looking at the box.

Presently he said, "This dust is pretty lethal?"

"Quite lethal, colonel." There was another long silence.

At last I gathered he had made up his mind about something, for he said decisively, "I am going to see to it that you get Obre's assistance doctor—"

"Oh, good!"

"—but I want you to help me in return. I am very much interested in this research of yours, but I want it carried on with a little broader scope. I want you to investigate for maxima both in period and intensity as well as for minima. I want you to drop the strictly utilitarian approach and make an exhaustive research along lines which we will work out in greater detail later."

She started to say something but he cut in ahead of her: "A really thorough program of research should prove more helpful in the long run to your original purpose than a more narrow one. And I shall make it my business to expedite every possible facility for such a research. I think we may turn up a number of interesting things."

He left immediately, giving her no time to discuss it. He did not seem to want to talk on the way back and I held my peace. I think he had already gotten a glimmering of the bold and drastic strategy this was to lead to, but even Manning could not have thought out that early the inescapable consequences of a few dead fish—otherwise he would never have ordered the research.

No, I don't really believe that. He would have gone right ahead, knowing that if he did not do it, someone else would. He would have accepted the responsibility while bitterly aware of its weight.

1944 wore along with no great excitement on the surface. Karst got her new laboratory equipment and so much additional help that her department rapidly became the largest on the grounds. The explosives research was suspended after a conference between Manning and Ridpath, of which I heard only the end, but the meat of it was that there existed not even a remote possibility at that time of utilizing $U235$ as an explosive. As a source of power, yes, sometime in the distant future when there had been more opportunity to deal with the extremely ticklish problem of controlling the nuclear reaction. Even then it seemed likely that it would not be a source of power in prime movers such as rocket motors or mobiles, but would be used in vast power plants at least as large as the Boulder Dam installation.

After that Ridpath became a sort of co-chairman of Karst's department and the equipment formerly used by the explosives department was adapted or replaced to carry on research on the deadly artificial radioactives. Manning arranged a division of labor and Karst stuck to her original problem of developing techniques for tailor-making radioactives. I think she was perfectly happy, sticking with a one-track mind to the problem at hand. I don't know to this day whether or not Manning and Ridpath ever saw fit to discuss with her what they intended to do.

As a matter of fact, I was too busy myself to think much about it. The general elections were coming up and I was determined that Manning should have a constituency to return to, when the emergency was over. He was not much interested, but agreed to let his name be filed as a candidate for re-election. I was trying to work up a campaign by remote control, and cursing because I could not be in the field to deal with the thousand and one emergencies as they arose.

I did the next best thing and had a private line installed to permit the campaign chairman to reach me easily. I don't think I violated the Hatch Act, but I guess I stretched it a little. Anyhow, it turned out all right; Manning was elected, as were several other members of the citizen-military that year. An attempt was made to smear him by claiming that he was taking two salaries for one job, but we squelched that with a pamphlet entitled "For Shame!" which explained that he got *one* salary for *two* jobs. That's the Federal law in such cases and people are entitled to know it.

It was just before Christmas that Manning first admitted to me how much the implications of the Karst-Obre process were preying on his mind. He called me into his office over some inconsequential matter, then did not let me go. I saw that he wanted to talk.

"How much of the K-O dust do we now have on hand?" he asked suddenly.

"Just short of ten thousand units," I replied. "I can look up the exact figures in half a moment." A unit would take care of a thousand men, at normal dispersion. He knew the figure as well as I did, and I knew he was stalling.

We had shifted almost imperceptibly from research to manufacture, entirely on Manning's initiative and authority. Manning had never made a specific report to the department about it, unless he had done so verbally to the chief of staff.

"Never mind," he answered to my suggestion, then added, "Did you see those horses?"

"Yes," I said briefly.

I did not want to talk about it. I like horses. We had requisitioned six broken-down old nags, ready for the bone yard, and had used them experimentally. We knew now what the dust would do. After they had died, any part of their carcasses would register on a photographic plate and tissue from the apices of their lungs and from the bronchia glowed with a light of its own.

Manning stood at the window, staring out at the dreary Maryland winter for a minute or two before replying, "John, I wish that radioactivity had never been discovered. Do you realize what that devilish stuff amounts to?"

"Well," I said, "it's a weapon, about like poison gas—maybe more efficient."

"Rats!" he said, and for a moment I thought he was annoyed with me personally. "That's about like comparing a sixteen-inch gun with a bow and arrow. We've got here the first weapon the world has ever seen against which there is no defense, none whatsoever. It's death itself, C. O. D.

"Have you seen Ridpath's report?" he went on.

I had not. Ridpath had taken to delivering his reports by hand to Manning personally.

"Well," he said, "ever since we started production I've had all the talent we could spare working on the problem of a defense against the dust. Ridpath tells me and I agree with him that there is no means whatsoever to combat the stuff, once it's used."

"How about armor," I asked, "and protective clothing?"

"Sure, sure," he agreed irritatedly, "provided you never take it off to eat, or to drink, or for any purpose whatever, until the radioaction has ceased, or you are out of the danger zone. That is all right for laboratory work; I'm talking about war."

I considered the matter. "I still don't see what you are fretting about, colonel. If the stuff is as good as you say it is, you've done just exactly what you set out to do—develop a weapon which would give the United States protection against aggression."

He swung around. "John, there are times when I think you are down-right stupid!"

I said nothing. I knew him and I knew how to discount his moods. The fact that he permitted me to see his feelings is the finest compliment I have ever had.

"Look at it this way," he went on more patiently; "this dust, as a weapon, is not just simply sufficient to safeguard the United States, it amounts to a loaded gun held at the head of every man, woman, and child on the globe!"

"Well," I answered, "what of that? It's our secret, and we've got the upper hand. The United States can put a stop to this war, and any other war. We can declare a *Pax Americana,* and enforce it."

"Hm-m-m—I wish it were that easy. But it won't remain our secret; you can count on that. Is doesn't matter how successfully we guard it; all that anyone needs is the hint given by the dust itself and then it is just a matter of time until some other nation develops a technique to produce it. You can't stop brains from working, John; the reinvention of the method is a mathematical certainty, once they know what it is they are looking for. And uranium is a common enough substance, widely distributed over the globe—don't forget that!

"It's like this: Once the secret is out—and it will be out if we ever use the stuff!—the whole world will be comparable to a room full of men, each armed with a loaded .45. They can't get out of the room and each one is dependent on the good will of every other one to stay alive. All offense and no defense. See what I mean?"

I thought about it, but I still didn't guess at the difficulties. It seemed to me that a peace enforced by us was the only way out, with precautions taken to see that we controlled the sources of uranium. I had the usual American subconscious conviction that our country would never use power in sheer aggression. Later, I thought about the Mexican War and the Spanish-American War and some of the things we did in Central America, and I was not so sure—

It was a couple of weeks later, shortly after inauguration day, that Manning told me to get the chief of staff's office on the telephone. I heard only the tail end of the conversation. "No, general, I won't," Manning was saying, "I won't discuss it with you, or the secretary, either. This is a matter the commander in chief is going to have to decide in the long run. If he turns it down, it is imperative that no one else ever know about it. That's my considered opinion. . . . What's that? . . . I took this job under the conditions that I was to have a free hand. You've got to give me a little leeway this time. . . . Don't go brass hat on me. I knew you when you were a plebe. . . . O. K., O. K., sorry. . . . If the secretary of war won't listen to reason, you tell him I'll be in my seat in the House of Representatives tomorrow, and that I'll get the favor I want from the majority leader. . . . All right. Good-by."

Washington rang up again about an hour later. It was the secretary of war. This time Manning listened more than he talked. Toward the end, he said, "All I want is thirty minutes alone with the President. If nothing comes of it, no harm has been done. If I convince him, then you will know all about it. . . . No, sir, I have no desire to embarrass you. If you prefer, I can have myself announced as a congressman, then you won't be responsible. . . . No, sir, I did not mean that you would avoid responsibility. I intended to be helpful. . . . Fine! Thank you, Mr. Secretary."

The White House rang up later in the day and set a time.

We drove down to the district the next day through a nasty cold rain that threatened to turn to sleet. The usual congestion in Washington was made worse by the weather; it very nearly caused us to be late in arriving. I could hear Manning swearing under his breath all the way down Rhode Island Avenue. But we were dropped at the west wing entrance to the White House with two minutes to spare. Manning was ushered into the oval office almost at once and I was left cooling my heels and trying to get comfortable in civilian clothes. After so many months of uniform they itched in the wrong places.

The thirty minutes went by.

The President's reception secretary went in, and came out very promptly indeed. He stepped on out into the outer reception room and I heard something that began with, "I'm sorry, senator, but—" He came back in, made a penciled notation, and passed it out to an usher.

Two more hours went by.

Manning appeared at the door at last and the secretary looked relieved. But he did not come out, saying instead, "Come in, John. The President wants to take a look at you."

I fell over my feet getting up.

Manning said, "Mr. President, this is Captain deFries." The President nodded, and I bowed, unable to say anything. He was standing on the hearth rug, his fine head turned toward us, and looking just like his pictures —but it seemed strange for the President of the United States not to be a tall man.

I had never seen him before, though, of course, I knew something of his record the two years he had been in the Senate and while he was mayor before that.

The President said, "Sit down, deFries. Care to smoke?" Then to Manning, "You think he can do it?"

"I think he'll have to. It's Hobson's choice."

"And you are sure of him?"

"He was my campaign manager."

"I see."

The President said nothing more for a while and God knows I didn't! —though I was bursting to know what they were talking about. He commenced again with, "Colonel Manning, I intend to follow the procedure you have suggested, with the changes we discussed. But I will be down tomorrow to see for myself that the dust will do what you say it will. Can you prepare a demonstration?"

"Yes, Mr. President."

"Very well. We will use Captain deFries unless I think of a better procedure." I thought for a moment that they planned to use me for a guinea pig! But he turned to me and continued, "Captain, I expect to send you to England as my representative."

I gulped. "Yes, Mr. President." And that is every word I had to say in calling on the President of the United States.

After that, Manning had to tell me a lot of things he had on his mind. I am going to try to relate them as carefully as possible, even at the risk of being dull and obvious and of repeating things that are common knowledge.

We had a weapon that could not be stopped. Any type of K-O dust, scattered over an area rendered that area uninhabitable for a length of time that depended on the half-life of the radioactivity.

Period. Full stop.

Once an area was dusted there was nothing that could be done about it until the radioactivity had fallen off to the point where it was no longer harmful. The dust could not be cleaned out; it was everywhere. There was no possible way to counteract it—burn it, combine it chemically; the radioactive isotope was still there, still radioactive, still deadly. Once used on a stretch of land, for a predetermined length of time that piece of earth *would not tolerate life.*

It was extremely simple to use. No complicated bombsights were needed, no care need be taken to hit "military objectives." Take it aloft in any sort of aircraft; attain a position more or less over the area you wish to sterilize, and drop the stuff. Those on the ground in the contaminated area are dead men, dead in an hour, a day, a week, a month, depending on the degree of the infection—but *dead.*

Manning told me that he had once seriously considered, in the middle of the night, recommending that every single person, including himself, who knew the Karst-Obre technique be put to death, in the interests of all civilization. But he had realized the next day that it had been sheer funk; the technique was certain in time to be rediscovered by someone else.

Furthermore, it would not do to wait, to refrain from using the grisly power, until someone else perfected it and used it. The only possible chance to keep the world from being turned into one huge morgue was for us to use the power first and drastically—get the upper hand and keep it.

We were not at war, legally, yet we had been in the war up to our necks with our weight on the side of democracy since 1940. Manning had proposed to the President that we turn a supply of the dust over to Great Britain, under conditions we specified, and enable them thereby to force a peace. But the terms of the peace would be dictated by the United States— for we were not turning over the secret.

After that, the *Pax Americana.*

The United States was having power thrust on it, willy-nilly. We had to accept it and enforce a worldwide peace, ruthlessly and drastically, or it would be seized by some other nation. There could not be coequals in the possession of this weapon. The factor of time predominated.

I was selected to handle the details in England because Manning insisted, and the President agreed with him, that every person technically acquainted with the Karst-Obre process should remain on the laboratory reservation in what amounted to protective custody—imprisonment. That included Manning himself. I could go because I did not have the secret—I could not even have acquired it without years of schooling—and what I did not know I could not tell, even under, well, drugs. We were determined to keep the secret as long as we could to consolidate the *pax;* we did not distrust our English cousins, but they were Britishers, with a first loyalty to the British Empire. No need to tempt them.

I was picked because I understood the background if not the science, and because Manning trusted me. I don't know why the President trusted me, too, but then my job was not complicated.

We took off from the new field outside Baltimore on a cold, raw afternoon which matched my own feelings. I had an all-gone feeling in my stomach, a runny nose, and, buttoned inside my clothes, papers appointing me a special agent of the President of the United States. They were odd papers, papers without precedent; they did not simply give me the usual diplomatic immunity; they made my person very nearly as sacred as that of the President himself.

At Nova Scotia we touched ground to refuel, the F. B. I. men left us, we took off again, and the Canadian transfighters took their stations around us. All the dust we were sending was in my plane; if the President's representative were shot down, the dust would go to the bottom with him.

No need to tell of the crossing. I was airsick and miserable, in spite of the steadiness of the new six-engined jobs. I felt like a hangman on the way to an execution, and wished to God that I were a boy again, with nothing more momentous than a debate contest, or a track meet, to worry me.

There was some fighting around us as we neared Scotland, I know, but I could not see it, the cabin being shuttered. Our pilot-captain ignored it and brought his ship down on a totally dark field, using a beam, I suppose, though I did not know or care. I would have welcomed a crash. Then the lights outside went on and I saw that we had come to rest in an underground hangar.

I stayed in the ship. The commandant came to see me and expected me to come to his quarters as his guest. I shook my head. "I stay here," I said. "Orders. You are to treat this ship as United States soil, you know."

He seemed miffed, but compromised by having dinner served for both of us in my ship.

There was a really embarrassing situation the next day. I was commanded to appear for a royal audience. But I had my instructions and I stuck to them. I was sitting on that cargo of dust until the President told me what to do with it. Late in the day I was called on by a member of Parliament—nobody admitted out loud that it was the Prime Minister— and a Mr. Windsor. The M. P. did most of the talking and I answered his questions. My other guest said very little and spoke slowly with some difficulty. But I got a very favorable impression of him. He seemed to be a man who was carrying a load beyond human strength and carrying it heroically.

There followed the longest period in my life. It was actually only a little longer than a week, but every minute of it had that split-second intensity of imminent disaster that comes just before a car crash. The President was using the time to try to avert the need to use the dust. He had two face-to-face television conferences with the new Fuehrer. The President spoke German fluently, which should have helped. He spoke three times to the warring peoples themselves, but it is doubtful if very many on the continent were able to listen, the police regulations there being what they were.

The ambassador for the Reich was given a special demonstration of the

effect of the dust. He was flown out over a deserted stretch of Western
prairie and allowed to see what a single dusting would do to a herd of
steers. It should have impressed him and I think that it did—*nobody* could
ignore a visual demonstration!—but what report he made to his leader we
never knew.

The British Isles were visited repeatedly during the wait by bombing
attacks as heavy as any of the war. I was safe enough but I heard about
them, and I could see the effect on the morale of the officers with whom I
associated. Not that it frightened them—it made them coldly angry. The
raids were not directed primarily at dockyards or factories, but were
ruthless destruction of anything, particularly villages.

"I don't see what you chaps are waiting for," a flight commander
complained to me. "What the Jerries need is a dose of their own *Schreck-
lichkeit*, a lesson in their own Aryan culture."

I shook my head. "We'll have to do it our own way."

He dropped the matter, but I knew how he and his brother officers
felt. They had a standing toast, as sacred as the toast to the King:
"Remember Coventry!"

Our President had stipulated that the R. A. F. was not to bomb during
the period of negotiation, but their bombers were busy nevertheless. The
continent was showered, night after night, with bales of leaflets, prepared
by our own propaganda agents. The first of these called on the people of
the Reich to stop a useless war and promised that the terms of peace would
not be vindictive. The second rain of pamphlets showed photographs of
that herd of steers. The third was a simple direct warning to get out of
cities and to stay out.

As Manning put it, we were calling "Halt!" three times before firing.
I do not think that he or the President expected it to work, but we were
morally obligated to try.

The Britishers had installed for me a televisor, of the Simonds-Yarley
nonintercept type, the sort whereby the receiver must "trigger" the transmitter in order for transmission to take place at all. It made assurance of
privacy in diplomatic rapid communication for the first time in history,
and was a real help in the crisis. I had brought along my own technician,
one of the F. B. I.'s new corps of specialists, to handle the scrambler and
the trigger.

He called to me one afternoon. "Washington signaling."

I climbed tiredly out of the cabin and down to the booth on the hangar
floor, wondering if it were another false alarm.

It was the President. His lips were white. "Carry out your basic instructions, Mr. deFries."

"Yes, Mr. President!"

The details had been worked out in advance and, once I had accepted
a receipt and token payment from the commandant for the dust, my duties

were finished. But, at our instance, the British had invited military observers from every independent nation and from the several provisional
governments of occupied nations. The United States ambassador designated me as one at the request of Manning.

Our task group was thirteen bombers. One such bomber could have
carried all the dust needed, but it was split up to insure most of it, at
least, reaching its destination. I had fetched forty percent more dust than
Ridpath calculated would be needed for the mission and my last job was
to see to it that every canister actually went on board a plane of the flight.
The extremely small weight of dust used was emphasized to each of the
military observers.

We took off just at dark, climbed to twenty-five thousand feet, refueled
in the air, and climbed again. Our escort was waiting for us, having refueled thirty minutes before us. The flight split into thirteen groups, and
cut the thin air for middle Europe. The bombers we rode had been stripped
and hiked up to permit the utmost maximum of speed and altitude.

Elsewhere in England, other flights had taken off shortly before us to
act as a diversion. Their destinations were every part of Germany; it was
the intention to create such confusion in the air above the Reich that our
few planes actually engaged in the serious work might well escape attention entirely, flying so high in the stratosphere.

The thirteen dust carriers approached Berlin from different directions,
planning to cross Berlin as if following the spokes of a wheel. The night
was appreciably clear and we had a low moon to help us. Berlin is not a
hard city to locate, since it has the largest square-mile area of any modern
city and is located on a broad flat alluvial plain. I could make out the River
Spree as we approached it, and the Havel. The city was blacked out, but a
city makes a different sort of black from open country. Parachute flares
hung over the city in many places, showing that the R. A. F. had been
busy before we got there and the A. A. batteries on the ground helped to
pick out the city.

There was fighting below us, but not within fifteen thousand feet of
our altitude as nearly as I could judge.

The pilot reported to the captain, "On line of bearing!" The chap
working the absolute altimeter steadily fed his data into the fuse pots of
the canister. The canisters were equipped with a light charge of black
powder, sufficient to explode them and scatter the dust at a time after
release predetermined by the fuse pot setting. The method used was no
more than an efficient expedient. The dust would have been almost as
effective had it simply been dumped out in paper bags, although not as
well distributed.

The captain hung over the navigator's board, a slight frown on his thin
sallow face. "Ready one!" reported the bomber.

"Release!"

"Ready two!"

The captain studied his wrist watch. "Release!"

"Ready three!"

"Release!"

When the last of our ten little packages was out of the ship we turned tail and ran for home.

No arrangements had been made for me to get home; nobody had thought about it. But it was the one thing I wanted to do. I did not feel badly; I did not feel much of anything. I felt like a man who has at last screwed up his courage and undergone a serious operation; it's over now, he is still numb from shock but his mind is relaxed. But I wanted to go home.

The British commandant was quite decent about it; he serviced and manned my ship at once and gave me an escort for the offshore war zone. It was an expensive way to send one man home, but who cared? We had just expended some millions of lives in a desperate attempt to end the war; what was a money expense? He gave the necessary orders absent-mindedly.

I took a double dose of nembutal and woke up in Canada. I tried to get some news while the plane was being serviced, but there was not much to be had. The government of the Reich had issued one official news bulletin shortly after the raid, sneering at the much-vaunted "secret weapon" of the British and stating that a major air attack had been made on Berlin and several other cities, but that the raiders had been driven off with only minor damage. The current Lord Haw-Haw started one of his sarcastic speeches but was unable to continue it. The announcer said that he had been seized with a heart attack, and substituted some recordings of patriotic music. The station cut off in the middle of the "Horst Wessel" song. After that there was silence.

I managed to promote an army car and a driver at the Baltimore field, which made short work of the Annapolis speedway. We almost overran the turnoff to the laboratory.

Manning was in his office. He looked up as I came in, said, "Hello, John," in a dispirited voice, and dropped his eyes again to the blotter pad. He went back to drawing doodles.

I looked him over and realized for the first time that the chief was an old man. His face was gray and flabby, deep furrows framed his mouth in a triangle. His clothes did not fit.

I went up to him and put a hand on his shoulder. "Don't take it so hard, chief. It's not your fault. We gave them all the warning in the world."

He looked up again. "Estelle Karst suicided this morning."

Anybody could have anticipated it, but nobody did. And somehow I felt harder hit by her death than by the death of all those strangers in Berlin. "How did she do it?" I asked.

"Dust. She went into the canning room and took off her armor."

I could picture her—head held high, eyes snapping, and that set look on her mouth which she got when people did something she disapproved of. One little old woman whose lifetime work had been turned against her.

"I wish," Manning added slowly, "that I could explain to her why we *had* to do it."

We buried her in a lead-lined coffin, then Manning and I went on to Washington.

While we were there, we saw the motion pictures that had been made of the death of Berlin. You have not seen them; they never were made public, but they were of great use in convincing the other nations of the world that peace was a good idea. I saw them when Congress did, being allowed in because I was Manning's assistant.

They had been made by a pair of R. A. F. pilots, who had dodged the *Luftwaffe* to get them. The first shots showed some of the main streets the morning after the raid. There was not much to see that would show up in telephoto shots, just busy and crowded streets, but if you looked closely you could see that there had been an excessive number of automobile accidents.

The second day showed the attempt to evacuate. The inner squares of the city were practically deserted save for bodies and wrecked cars, but the streets leading out of town were boiling with people, mostly on foot, for the trams were out of service. The pitiful creatures were fleeing, not knowing that death was already lodged inside them. The plane swooped down at one point and the cinematographer had his telephoto lens pointed directly into the face of a young woman for several seconds. She stared back at it with a look too woebegone to forget, then stumbled and fell.

She may have been trampled. I hope so. One of those six horses had looked like that when the stuff was beginning to hit his vitals.

The last sequence showed Berlin and the roads around it a week after the raid. The city was dead, there was not a man, a woman, a child—nor cats, nor dogs, not even a pigeon. Bodies were all around, but they were safe from rats. There were no rats.

The roads around Berlin were quiet now. Scattered carelessly on shoulders and in ditches, and to a lesser extent on the pavement itself, like coal shaken off a train, were the quiet heaps that had been the citizens of the capital of the Reich. There is no use in talking about it.

But, so far as I am concerned, I left what soul I had in that projection room and I have not had one since.

The two pilots who made the pictures eventually died—systemic, accumulative infection, dust in the air over Berlin. With precautions it need not have happened, but the English did not believe, as yet, that our extreme precautions were necessary.

The Reich took about a week to fold up. It might have taken longer if the new Fuehrer had not gone to Berlin the day after the raid to "prove" that the British boasts had been hollow. There is no need to recount the provisional governments that Germany had in the following several months; the only one we are concerned with is the so-called restored monarchy which used a cousin of the old Kaiser as a symbol, the one that sued for peace.

Then the trouble started.

When the Prime Minister announced the terms of the private agreement he had had with our President, he was met with a silence that was broken only by cries of "Shame! Shame! Resign!" I suppose it was inevitable; the Commons reflected the spirit of a people who had been unmercifully punished for four years. They were in a mood to enforce a peace that would have made the Versailles Treaty look like the Beatitudes.

The vote of no confidence left the Prime Minister no choice. Forty-eight hours later the King made a speech from the throne that violated all constitutional precedent, for it had not been written by a Prime Minister. In this greatest crisis in his reign, his voice was clear and unlabored; it sold the idea to England and a national coalition government was formed.

I don't know whether we would have dusted London to enforce our terms or not; Manning thinks we would have done so. I suppose it depended on the character of the President of the United States, and there is no way of knowing about that since we did not have to do it.

The United States, and in particular the President of the United States, was confronted by two inescapable problems. First, we had to consolidate our position at once, use our temporary advantage of an overwhelmingly powerful weapon to insure that such a weapon would not be turned on us. Second, some means had to be worked out to stabilize American foreign policy so that it could handle the tremendous power we had suddenly had thrust upon us.

The second was by far the most difficult and serious. If we were to establish a reasonably permanent peace—say a century or so—through a monopoly on a weapon so powerful that no one dare fight us, it was imperative that the policy under which we acted be more lasting than passing political administrations. But more of that later—

The first problem had to be attended to at once—time was the heart of it. The emergency lay in the very simplicity of the weapon. It required nothing but aircraft to scatter it and the dust itself, which was easily and quickly made by anyone possessing the secret of the Karst-Obre process and having access to a small supply of uranium-bearing ore.

But the Karst-Obre process was simple and might be independently developed at any time. Manning reported to the President that it was Ridpath's opinion, concurred in by Manning, that the staff of any modern radiation laboratory should be able to work out an equivalent technique in six weeks, working from the hint given by the events in Berlin alone, and should then be able to produce enough dust to cause major destruction in another six weeks.

Ninety days—ninety days *provided* they started from scratch and were not already halfway to their goal. Less than ninety days—perhaps no time at all—

By this time Manning was an unofficial member of the cabinet; "Secretary of Dust," the President called him in one of his rare jovial moods. As for me, well, I attended cabinet meetings, too. As the only layman who had seen the whole show from beginning to end, the President wanted me there.

I am an ordinary sort of man who, by a concatenation of improbabilities, found himself shoved into the councils of the rulers. But I found that the rulers were ordinary men, too, and frequently as bewildered as I was.

But Manning was no ordinary man. In him ordinary hard sense had been raised to the level of genius. Oh, yes, I know that it is popular to blame everything on him and to call him everything from traitor to mad dog, but I still think he was both wise and benevolent. I don't care how many second-guessing historians disagree with me.

"I propose," said Manning, "that we begin by immobilizing all aircraft throughout the world."

The secretary of commerce raised his brows. "Aren't you," he said, "being a little fantastic, Colonel Manning?"

"No, I'm not," answered Manning shortly. "I'm being realistic. The key to this problem is aircraft. Without aircraft the dust is an inefficient weapon. The only way I see to gain time enough to deal with the whole problem is to ground all aircraft and put them out of operation. All aircraft, that is, not actually in the service of the United States army. After that we can deal with complete world disarmament and permanent methods of control."

"Really now," replied the secretary, "you are not proposing that commercial airlines be put out of operation. They are an essential part of world economy. It would be an intolerable nuisance."

"Getting killed is an intolerable nuisance, too," Manning answered stubbornly. "I do propose just that. All aircraft. *All.*"

The President had been listening without comment to the discussion. He now cut in. "How about aircraft on which some groups depend to stay alive, colonel, such as the Alaskan lines?"

"If there are such, they must be operated by American army pilots and crews. No exceptions."

The secretary of commerce looked startled. "Am I to infer from that last remark that you intended this prohibition to apply to the *United States* as well as other nations?"

"Naturally."

"But that's impossible. It's unconstitutional. It violates civil rights."

"Killing a man violates his civil rights, too," Manning answered stub-bornly.

"You can't do it. Any Federal court in the country would enjoin you in five minutes."

"It seems to me," said Manning slowly, "that Andy Jackson gave us a good precedent for that one when he told John Marshall to go fly a kite." He looked slowly around the table at faces that ranged from undecided to antagonistic. "The issue is sharp, gentlemen, and we might as well drag it out in the open. We can be dead men, with everything in due order, constitutional, and technically correct; or we can do what has to be done, stay alive, and try to straighten out the legal aspects later." He shut up and waited.

The secretary of labor picked it up. "I don't think the colonel has any corner on realism. I think I see the problem, too, and I admit it is a serious one. The dust must never be used again. Had I known about it soon enough, it would never have been used on Berlin. And I agree that some sort of world-wide control is necessary. But where I differ with the colonel is in the method. What he proposes is a military dictatorship imposed by force on the whole world. Admit it, colonel. Isn't that what you are propos-ing?"

Manning did not dodge it. "That is what I am proposing."

"Thanks. Now we know where we stand. I, for one, do not regard democratic measures and constitutional procedure as of so little importance that I am willing to jettison them any time it becomes convenient. To me, democracy is more than a matter of expediency, it is a faith. Either it works, or I go under with it."

"What do you propose?" asked the President.

"I propose that we treat this as an opportunity to create a worldwide democratic commonwealth! Let us use our present dominant position to issue a call to all nations to send representatives to a conference to form a world constitution."

"League of Nations," I heard some one mutter.

"No!" he answered the side remark. "Not a League of Nations. The old League was helpless because it had no real existence, no power. It was not implemented to enforce its decisions; it was just a debating society, a sham. This would be different *for we would turn over the dust to it!*"

Nobody spoke for some minutes. You could see them turning it over in their minds, doubtful, partially approving, intrigued but dubious.

"I'd like to answer that," said Manning.

"Go ahead," said the President.

"I will. I'm going to have to use some pretty plain language and I hope that Secretary Larner will do me the honor of believing that I speak so from sincerity and deep concern and not from personal pique.

"I think a world democracy would be a very fine thing and I ask that you believe me when I say I would willingly lay down my life to accomplish it. I also think it would be a very fine thing for the lion to lie down with the lamb, but I am reasonably certain that only the lion would get up. If we try to form an actual world democracy, we'll be the lamb in the set-up.

"There are a lot of good, kindly people who are internationalists these days. Nine out of ten of them are soft in the head and the tenth is ignorant. If we set up a world-wide democracy, what will the electorate be? Take a look at the facts: Four hundred million Chinese with no more concept of voting and citizen responsibility than a flea. Three hundred million Hindus who aren't much better indoctrinated. God knows how many in the Eurasian Union who believe in God knows what. The entire continent of Africa only semicivilized. Eighty million Japanese who really believe that they are Heaven-ordained to rule. Our Spanish-American friends who might trail along with us and might not, but who don't understand the Bill of Rights the way we think of it. A quarter of a billion people of two dozen different nationalities in Europe, all with revenge and black hatred in their hearts.

"No, it won't wash. It's preposterous to talk about a world democracy for many years to come. If you turn the secret of the dust over to such a body, you will be arming the whole world to commit suicide."

Larner answered at once. "I could resent some of your remarks, but I won't. To put it bluntly, I consider the source. The trouble with you, Colonel Manning, is that you are a professional soldier and have no faith in people. Soldiers may be necessary, but the worst of them are martinets and the best are merely paternalistic." There was quite a lot more of the same.

Manning stood it until his turn came again. "Maybe I am all those things, but you haven't met my argument. *What are you going to do about the hundreds of millions of people who have no experience in, nor love for, democracy?* Now, perhaps, I don't have the same conception of democracy as yourself, but I do know this: Out west there are a couple of hundred thousand people who sent me to Congress. I am *not* going to stand quietly by and let a course be followed which I think will result in their deaths or utter ruin.

"Here is the probable future, as I see it, potential in the smashing of the atom and the development of lethal artificial radioactives. Some power makes a supply of the dust. They'll hit us first to try to knock us out and give them a free hand. New York and Washington overnight, then all of our industrial areas while we are still politically and economically disorganized. But our army would not be in those cities; we would have planes and a supply of dust somewhere where the first dusting wouldn't touch them. Our boys would bravely and righteously proceed to poison their big cities. Back and forth it would go until the organization of each country had broken down so completely that they were no longer able to maintain a sufficiently high level of industrialization to service planes and manufacture dust. That presupposes starvation and plague in the process. You can fill in the details.

"The other nations would get in the game. It would be silly and suicidal, of course, but it doesn't take brains to take a hand in this. All it takes is a very small group, hungry for power, a few airplanes and a supply of dust. *It's a vicious circle that can not possibly be stopped until the entire planet has dropped to a level of economy too low to support the techniques necessary to maintain it.* My best guess is that such a point would be reached when approximately three-quarters of the world's population were dead of dust, disease, or hunger, and culture reduced to the peasant-and-village type.

"Where is your Constitution and your Bill of Rights if you let that happen?"

I've shortened it down, but that was the gist of it. I can't hope to record every word of an argument that went on for days.

The secretary of the navy took a crack at him next. "Aren't you getting a bit hysterical, colonel? After all, the world has seen a lot of weapons which were going to make war an impossibility too horrible to contemplate. Poison gas, and tanks, and airplanes—even firearms, if I remember my history."

Manning smiled wryly. "You've made a point, Mr. Secretary. 'And when the wolf *really* came, the little boy shouted in vain.' I imagine the Chamber of Commerce in Pompeii presented the same reasonable argument to an early vulcanologist so timid as to fear Vesuvius. I'll try to justify my fears. The dust differs from every earlier weapon in its deadliness and ease of use, but most importantly in that we have developed no defense against it. For a number of fairly technical reasons, I don't think we ever will, at least not this century."

"Why not?"

"Because there is no way to counteract radioactivity short of putting a lead shield between yourself and it, an *air-tight* lead shield. People might survive by living in sealed underground cities, but our characteristic American culture could not be maintained."

"Colonel Manning," suggested the secretary of state, "I think you have overlooked the obvious alternative."

"Have I?"

"Yes—to keep the dust as our own secret, go our own way, and let the rest of the world look out for itself. That is the only program that fits our traditions." The secretary of state was really a fine old gentleman, and not stupid, but he was slow to assimilate new ideas.

"Mr. Secretary," said Manning respectfully, "I wish we could afford to mind our own business. I do wish we could. But it is the best opinion of all the experts that we can't maintain control of this secret except by rigid policing. The Germans were close on our heels in nuclear research;

it was sheer luck that we got there first. I ask you to imagine Germany a year hence—with a supply of dust."

The secretary did not answer, but I saw his lips form the word Berlin.

They came around. The President had deliberately let Manning bear the brunt of the argument, conserving his own stock of goodwill to coax the obdurate. He decided against putting it up to Congress; the dusters would have been overhead before each senator had finished his say. What he intended to do might be unconstitutional, but if he failed to act there might not be any Constitution shortly. There was precedent—the Emancipation Proclamation, the Monroe Doctrine, the Louisiana Purchase, suspension of habeas corpus in the War between the States, the Destroyer Deal.

On February 22nd the President declared a state of full emergency internally and sent his Peace Proclamation to the head of every sovereign state. Divested of its diplomatic surplusage, it said: The United States is prepared to defeat any power, or combination of powers, in jig time. Accordingly, we are outlawing war and are calling on every nation to disarm completely at once. In other words, "Throw down your guns, boys; we've got the drop on you!"

A supplement set forth the procedure: All aircraft capable of flying the Atlantic were to be delivered in one week's time to a field, or rather a great stretch of prairie, just west of Fort Riley, Kansas. For lesser aircraft, a spot near Shanghai and a rendezvous in Wales were designated. Memoranda would be issued later with respect to other war equipment. Uranium and its ores were not mentioned; that would come later.

No excuses. Failure to disarm would be construed as an act of war against the United States.

There were no cases of apoplexy in the Senate; why not, I don't know.

There were only three powers to be seriously worried about, England, Japan, and the Eurasian Union. England had been forewarned, we had pulled her out of a war she was losing, and she—or rather her men in power —knew accurately what we could and would do.

Japan was another matter. They had not seen Berlin and they did not really believe it. Besides, they had been telling each other for so many years that they were unbeatable, they believed it. It does not do to get too tough with a Japanese too quickly, for they will die rather than lose face. The negotiations were conducted very quietly indeed, but our fleet was halfway from Pearl Harbor to Kobe, loaded with enough dust to sterilize their six biggest cities, before they were concluded. Do you know what did it? This never hit the newspapers but it was the wording of the pamphlets we proposed to scatter before dusting.

The Emperor was pleased to declare a New Order of Peace. The official version, built up for home consumption, made the whole matter one of

collaboration between two great and friendly powers, with Japan taking
the initiative.

The Eurasian Union was a puzzle. After Stalin's unexpected death
in 1941, no western nation knew very much about what went on in there.
Our own diplomatic relations had atrophied through failure to replace men
called home nearly four years before. Everybody knew, of course, that the
new group in power called themselves Fifth Internationalists, but what that
meant, aside from ceasing to display the pictures of Lenin and Stalin,
nobody knew.

But they agreed to our terms and offered to co-operate in every way.
They pointed out that the Union had never been warlike and had kept out
of the recent world struggle. It was fitting that the two remaining great
powers should use their greatness to insure a lasting peace.

I was delighted; I had been worried about the E. U.

They commenced delivery of some of their smaller planes to the receiving station near Shanghai at once.

Manning went west to supervise certain details in connection with
immobilizing the big planes, the transoceanic planes, which were to gather
near Fort Riley. We planned to spray them with oil, then dust from a
low altitude, as in crop dusting, with a low concentration of one-year dust.
Then we could turn our backs on them and forget them, while attending
to other matters.

But there were hazards. The dust must not be allowed to reach Kansas
City, Lincoln, Wichita, any of the nearby cities. The smaller towns round
about had been temporarily evacuated. Testing stations needed to be set
up in all directions in order that accurate tab on the dust might be kept.
Manning felt personally responsible to make sure that no bystander was
poisoned.

We circled the receiving station before landing at Fort Riley. I could
pick out the three landing fields which had hurriedly been graded. Their
runways were white in the sun, the twenty-four-hour cement as yet un-
dirtied. Around each of the landing fields were crowded dozens of parking
fields, less perfectly graded. Tractors and bulldozers were still at work
on some of them. In the easternmost fields, the German and British ships
were already in place, jammed wing to body as tightly as planes on the
flight deck of a carrier—save for a few that were still being towed into
position, the tiny tractors looking from the air like ants dragging pieces
of leaf many times larger than themselves.

Only three flying fortresses had arrived from the Eurasian Union. Their
representatives had asked for a short delay in order that a supply of high-
test aviation gasoline might be delivered to them. They claimed a shortage
of fuel necessary to make the long flight over the Arctic safe. There was
no way to check the claim and the delay was granted while a shipment was
routed from England.

We were about to leave, Manning having satisfied himself as to safety
precautions, when a dispatch came in announcing that a flight of E. U.

bombers might be expected before the day was out. Manning wanted to see them arrive; we waited around for four hours. When it was finally reported that our escort of fighters had picked them up at the Canadian border, Manning appeared to have grown fidgety and stated that he would watch them from the air. We took off, gained altitude and waited.

There were nine of them in the flight, cruising in columns of echelons and looking so huge that our little fighters were hardly noticeable. They circled the field and I was admiring the stately dignity of them when Manning's pilot, Lieutenant Rafferty, exclaimed, "What the devil! They are preparing to land downwind!"

I still did not tumble, but Manning shouted to the co-pilot, "Get the field!"

He fiddled with his instruments and announced, "Got 'em, sir!"

"General alarm! Armor!"

We could not hear the sirens, naturally, but I could see the white plumes rise from the big steam whistle on the roof of the Administration Building—three long blasts, then three short ones. It seemed almost at the same time that the first cloud broke from the E. U. planes.

Instead of landing, they passed low over the receiving station, jam-packed now with ships from all over the world. Each echelon picked one of three groups centered around the three landing fields, and streamers of heavy brown smoke poured from the bellies of the E. U. ships. I saw a tiny black figure jump from a tractor and run toward the nearest building. Then the smoke screen obscured the field.

"Do you still have the field?" demanded Manning.

"Yes, sir."

"Cross connect to the chief safety technician. Hurry!"

The co-pilot cut in the amplifier so that Manning could talk directly. "Saunders? This is Manning. How about it?"

"Radioactive, chief. Intensity seven point four."

They had paralleled the Karst-Obre research.

Manning cut him off and demanded that the communication office at the field raise the chief of staff. There was nerve-stretching delay, for it had to be routed over land wire to Kansas City, and some chief operator had to be convinced that she should commandeer a trunk line that was in commercial use. But we got through at last and Manning made his report. "It stands to reason," I heard him say, "that other flights are approaching the border by this time. New York, of course, and Washington. Probably Detroit and Chicago as well. No way of knowing."

The chief of staff cut off abruptly, without comment. I knew that the U. S. air fleets, in a state of alert for weeks past, would have their orders in a few seconds, and would be on their way to hunt out and down the attackers, if possible before they could reach the cities.

I glanced back at the field. The formations were broken up. One of the E. U. bombers was down, crashed, half a mile beyond the station. While I watched, one of our midget dive bombers screamed down on a behemoth

E. U. ship and unloaded his eggs. It was a center hit, but the American pilot had cut it too fine, could not pull out, and crashed before his victim.

There is no point in rehashing the newspaper stories of the Four-days War. The point is that we should have lost it, and we would have, had it not been for an unlikely combination of luck, foresight and good management. Apparently, the nuclear physicists of the Eurasian Union were almost as far along as Ridpath's crew when the destruction of Berlin gave them the tip they needed. But we had rushed them, forced them to move before they were ready, because of the deadline for disarmament set forth in our Peace Proclamation.

If the President had waited to fight it out with Congress before issuing the proclamation, there would not be any United States.

Manning never got credit for it, but it is evident to me he anticipated the possibility of something like the Four-days War and prepared for it in a dozen different devious ways. I don't mean military preparation; the army and the navy saw to that. But it was no accident that Congress was adjourned at the time; I had something to do with the vote-swapping and compromising that led up to it, and I know.

But I put it to you—would he have maneuvered to get Congress out of Washington at a time when he feared that Washington might be attacked if he had had dictatorial ambitions?

Of course, it was the President who was back of the ten-day leaves that had been granted to most of the civil-service personnel in Washington and he himself must have made the decision to take a swing through the South at that time, but it must have been Manning who put the idea in his head. It is inconceivable that the President would have left Washington to escape personal danger.

And then, there was the plague scare. I don't know how or when Manning could have started that—it certainly did not go through my notebook—but I simply do not believe that it was accidental that a completely unfounded rumor of bubonic plague caused New York City to be semi-deserted at the time the E. U. bombers struck.

At that, we lost over eight hundred thousand people in Manhattan alone.

Of course, the government was blamed for the lives that were lost and the papers were merciless in their criticism at the failure to anticipate and force an evacuation of all the major cities.

If Manning anticipated trouble, why did he not ask for evacuation?

Well, as I see it, for this reason:

A big city will not, never has, evacuated in response to rational argument. London never was evacuated on any major scale and we failed utterly in our attempt to force the evacuation of Berlin. The people of New York City had considered the danger of air raids since 1940 and were long since hardened to the thought.

But the fear of a nonexistent epidemic of plague caused the most nearly complete evacuation of a major city ever seen.

And don't forget what we did to Vladivostok and Irkutsk and Moscow —those were innocent people, too. War isn't pretty.

I said luck played a part. It was bad navigation that caused one of our ships to dust Ryazan instead of Moscow, but that mistake knocked out the laboratory and plant which produced the only supply of military radioactives in the Eurasian Union. Suppose the mistake had been the other way around—suppose that one of the E. U. ships in attacking Washington, D. C., by mistake, had included Ridpath's shop forty-five miles away in Maryland?

Congress reconvened at the temporary capital in St. Louis, and the American Pacification Expedition started the job of pulling the fangs of the Eurasian Union. It was not a military occupation in the usual sense; there were two simple objectives, to search out and dust all aircraft, aircraft plants, and fields, and to locate and dust radiation laboratories, uranium supplies, and lodes of carnotite and pitchblende. No attempt was made to interfere with, or to replace, civil government.

We used a two-year dust, which gave a breathing spell in which to consolidate our position. Liberal rewards were offered to informers, a technique which worked remarkably well not only in the E. U., but in most parts of the world.

The "weasel," an instrument to smell out radiation, based on the electroscope-discharge principle and refined by Ridpath's staff, greatly facilitated the work of locating uranium and uranium ores. A grid of weasels, properly spaced over a suspect area, could locate any important mass of uranium almost as handily as a direction-finder can spot a radio station.

But, notwithstanding the excellent work of General Bulfinch and the Pacification Expedition as a whole, it was the original mistake of dusting Ryazan that made the job possible of accomplishment.

Anyone interested in the details of the pacification work done in 1945-6 should see the "Proceedings of the American Foundation for Social Research" for a paper entitled, *A Study of the Execution of the American Peace Policy from February, 1945.* The *de facto* solution of the problem of policing the world against war left the United States with the much greater problem of perfecting a policy that would insure that the deadly power of the dust would never fall into unfit hands.

The problem is as easy to state as the problem of squaring the circle and almost as impossible of accomplishment. Both Manning and the President believed that the United States must of necessity keep the power for the time being until some permanent institution could be developed fit to retain it. The hazard was this: Foreign policy is lodged jointly in the hands of the President and the Congress. We were fortunate at the time in having a good President and an adequate Congress, but that was no guarantee for the future. We have had unfit Presidents and power-hungry Congresses—oh, yes! Read the history of the Mexican War.

We were about to hand over to future governments of the United States the power to turn the entire globe into an empire, our empire. And it was the sober opinion of the President that our characteristic and beloved democratic culture would not stand up under the temptation. Imperialism degrades both oppressor and oppressed.

The President was determined that our sudden power should be used for the absolute minimum of maintaining peace in the world—the simple purpose of outlawing war and nothing else. It must not be used to protect American investments abroad, to coerce trade agreements—for any purpose but the simple abolition of mass killing.

There is no science of sociology. Perhaps there will be, some day, when a rigorous physics gives a finished science of colloidal chemistry and that leads in turn to a complete knowledge of biology, and from there to a definitive psychology. After that we may begin to know something about sociology and politics. Sometime around A.D. 5,000, maybe—if the human race does not commit suicide before then.

Until then, there is only horse sense and rule of thumb and observational knowledge of probabilities. Manning and the President played by ear.

The treaties with Great Britain, Germany and the Eurasian Union, whereby we assumed the responsibility for world peace and at the same time guaranteed the contracting nations against our own misuse of power were rushed through in the period of relief and good will that immediately followed the termination of the Four-days War. We followed the precedents established by the Panama Canal treaties, the Suez Canal agreements, and the Philippine Independence policy.

But the purpose underneath was to commit future governments of the United States to an irrevocable benevolent policy.

The act to implement the treaties by creating the Commission of World Safety followed soon after, and Colonel Manning became Mr. Commissioner Manning. Commissioners had a life tenure and the intention was to create a body with the integrity, permanence and freedom from outside pressure possessed by the supreme court of the United States. Since the treaties contemplated an eventual joint trust, commissioners need not be American citizens—and the oath they took was *to preserve the peace of the world.*

There was trouble getting that clause past the Congress! Every other similar oath had been to the Constitution of the United States.

Nevertheless the Commission was formed. It took charge of world aircraft; assumed jurisdiction over radioactives, natural and artificial; and commenced the long slow task of building up the Peace Patrol.

Manning envisioned a corps of world policemen, an aristocracy which through selection and indoctrination, could be trusted with unlimited power over the life of every man, every woman, every child on the face of the globe. For the power *would* be unlimited; the precautions necessary to insure the unbeatable weapon from getting loose in the world again made it axiomatic that its custodians would wield power that is safe only in the hands of Deity. There would be no one to guard those selfsame guardians. Their own characters and the watch they kept on each other would be all that stood between the race and disaster.

For the first time in history, supreme political power was to be exerted with no possibility of checks and balances from the outside. Manning took up the task of perfecting it with a dragging subconscious conviction that it was too much for human nature.

The rest of the Commission was appointed slowly, the names being sent to the Senate after long joint consideration by the President and Manning. The director of the Red Cross, an obscure little professor of history from Switzerland, Dr. Igor Rimski who had developed the Karst-Obre technique independently and whom the A. P. F. had discovered in prison after the dusting of Moscow—those three were the only foreigners. The rest of the list is well known.

Ridpath and his staff were of necessity the original technical crew of the Commission; United States army and navy pilots its first patrolmen. Not all of the pilots available were needed; their records were searched, their habits and associates investigated, their mental processes and emotional attitudes examined by the best psychological research methods available—which weren't good enough. Their final acceptance for the Patrol depended on two personal interviews, one with Manning, one with the President.

Manning told me that he depended more on the President's feeling for character than he did on all the association and reaction tests the psychologists could think up. "It's like the nose of a bloodhound," he said. "In his forty years of practical politics he has seen more phonies than you and I will ever see and each one was trying to sell him something. He can tell one in the dark."

The long-distance plan included the schools for the indoctrination of cadet patrolmen, schools that were to be open to youths of any race, color, or nationality, and from which they would go forth to guard the peace of *every country but their own*. To that country a man would never return during his service. They were to be a deliberately expatriated band of Janizaries, with an obligation only to the Commission and to the race, and welded together with a carefully nurtured esprit de corps.

It stood a chance of working. Had Manning been allowed twenty years without interruption, the original plan might have worked.

The President's running mate for re-election was the result of a political compromise. The candidate for Vice President was a confirmed isolationist who had opposed the Peace Commission from the first, but it was he or a party split in a year when the opposition was strong. The President sneaked back in but with a greatly weakened Congress; only his power of veto twice prevented the repeal of the Peace Act. The Vice President did nothing to help him, although he did not publicly lead the insurrection. Manning revised his plans to complete the essential program by the end of 1952, there being no way to predict the temper of the next administration.

We were both overworked and I was beginning to realize that my health was gone. The cause was not far to seek; a photographic film strapped next to my skin would cloud in twenty minutes. I was suffering from cumulative minimal radioactive poisoning. No well-defined cancer that could be operated on, but a systemic deterioration of function and tissue. There was no help for it, and there was work to be done. I've always attributed it mainly to the week I spent sitting on those canisters before the raid on Berlin.

February 17, 1951. I missed the televue flash about the plane crash that killed the President because I was lying down in my apartment. Manning, by that time, was requiring me to rest every afternoon after lunch, though I was still on duty. I first heard about it from my secretary when I returned to my office, and at once hurried into Manning's office.

There was a curious unreality to that meeting. It seemed to me that we had slipped back to that day when I returned from England, the day that Estelle Karst died. He looked up. "Hello, John," he said.

I put my hand on his shoulder. "Don't take it so hard, chief," was all I could think of to say.

Forty-eight hours later came the message from the newly sworn-in President for Manning to report to him. I took it in to him, an official dispatch which I decoded. Manning read it, face impassive.

"Are you going, chief?" I asked.

"Eh? Why, certainly."

I went back into my office, and got my topcoat, gloves, and brief case. Manning looked up when I came back. "Never mind, John," he said. "You're not going." I guess I must have looked stubborn, for he added, "You're not to go because there is work to do here. Wait a minute."

He went to his safe, twiddled the dials, opened it and removed a sealed envelope which he threw on the desk between us. "Here are your orders. Get busy."

He went out as I was opening them. I read them through and got busy. There was little enough time.

The new President received Manning standing and in the company of several of his bodyguard and intimates. Manning recognized the senator who had led the movement to use the Patrol to recover expropriated holdings in South America and Rhodesia, as well as the chairman of the committee on aviation with whom he had had several unsatisfactory conferences in an attempt to work out a *modus operandi* for reinstituting commercial airlines.

"You're prompt, I see," said the President. "Good."

Manning bowed.

"We might as well come straight to the point," the chief executive went on. "There are going to be some changes of policy in the administration. I want your resignation."

"I am sorry to have to refuse, sir."

"We'll see about that. In the meantime, Colonel Manning, you are relieved from duty."

"Mr. Commissioner Manning, if you please."

The new President shrugged. "One or the other, as you please. You are relieved, either way."

"I am sorry to disagree again. My appointment is for life."

"That's enough," was the answer. "This is the United States of America. There can be no higher authority. You are under arrest."

I can visualize Manning staring steadily at him for a long moment, then answering slowly, "You are physically able to arrest me, I will concede, but I advise you to wait a few minutes." He stepped to the window. "Look up into the sky."

Six bombers of the Peace Commission patrolled over the Capitol. "None of those pilots is American born," Manning added slowly. "If you confine me, none of us here in this room will live out the day."

There were incidents thereafter, such as the unfortunate affair at Fort Benning three days later, and the outbreak in the wing of the Patrol based in Lisbon and its resultant wholesale dismissals, but, for practical purposes, that was all there was to the *coup d'état*.

Manning was the undisputed military dictator of the world.

Whether or not any man as universally hated as Manning can perfect the Patrol he envisioned, make it self-perpetuating and trustworthy, I don't know, and—because of that week of waiting in a buried English hangar—I won't be here to find out. Manning's heart disease makes the outcome even more uncertain—he may last another twenty years; he may keel over dead tomorrow—and there is no one to take his place. I've set this down partly to occupy the short time I have left and partly to show there is another side to any story, even world dominion.

Not that I would like the outcome, either way. If there is anything to this survival-after-death business, I am going to look up the man who invented the bow and arrow and take him apart with my bare hands. For myself, I can't be happy in a world where any man, or group of men, has the power of death over you and me, our neighbors, every human, every animal, every living thing. I don't like anyone to have that kind of power.

And neither does Manning.

FRANK R. STOCKTON

THE GREAT
WAR SYNDICATE

IN THE spring of a certain year, when the political relations between the United States and Great Britain became so strained that careful observers on both sides of the Atlantic were forced to the belief that a serious break in these relations might be looked for at any time, the fishing schooner *Eliza Drum* sailed from a port in Maine for the banks of Newfoundland.[1]

She was late in her arrival on the fishing grounds, and her captain and crew went vigorously to work to make up for lost time. They worked so vigorously, and with eyes so single to the catching of fish, that, on the morning of the day after their arrival, they were hauling up cod at a point which, according to the nationality of the calculator, might be two and three quarters or three and a quarter miles from the Canadian coast.

In consequence of this inattention to the apparent extent of the marine mile, the *Eliza Drum*, a little before noon, was overhauled and seized by the British cruiser *Dog Star*. Proceeding to put a prize crew on board the fishing vessel, she steamed for St. Johns, taking with her the *Eliza Drum*.

All that night, at every point in the United States which was reached by telegraph, there burnt a smothered fire, and the next morning, when the regular and extra editions of the newspapers were poured out upon the land, the fire burst into a roaring blaze. Congress was in session, and in its halls the fire roared louder and blazed higher than on mountain or plain, in city or prairie.

In less than a week the great shout of the people was answered by a declaration of war against Great Britain.

Almost from the beginning of this period of national turmoil, a party of gentlemen met daily in one of the large rooms in a hotel in New York. These gentlemen were all great scientists, and had formed themselves into

[1] For a note on the history of this story, see the Introduction.

36

a syndicate, with the object of taking entire charge of the war between the United States and Great Britain.

This proposition was an astounding one, but the government was obliged to treat it with respectful consideration. The men were a power in the land—a power which no government could afford to disregard. They were men of great ability and vast resources, not likely to jeopardize their reputations and fortunes in a case like this, unless they had well-founded reasons for believing that they would be successful.

Therefore all branches of the government united in accepting the offer of the Syndicate. The contract was signed, and the world waited to see what would happen next.

The first step of the Syndicate was to purchase from the United States Government ten war vessels. These ships they rapidly prepared for the peculiar service in which they were to be engaged. Their armament consisted of but one gun, of large caliber, placed on the forward deck, and protected by a bomb-proof covering. The fighting operations were in charge of a small body of men, composed of two or three scientific specialists, and some practical gunners and their assistants. A few bomb-proof canopies and a curved steel deck completed the defenses of the vessels.

Ammunition was confined entirely to a new style of projectile, which had never yet been used in warfare. This projectile was not, in the ordinary sense of the word, an explosive, and was named by its inventors the "Instantaneous Motor." It was discharged from an ordinary cannon, but no gunpowder or other explosive compound was used to propel it. The bomb possessed, in itself, the necessary power of propulsion, and the gun was used merely to give it the proper direction.

The bombs were cylindrical in form, and pointed at the outer end. They were filled with hundreds of small tubes, each radiating outward from a central line. Those in the middle third of the bomb pointed directly outward, while those in the front portion were inclined forward at a slight angle, and those in the rear portion backward at the same angle. One tube, at the end of the bomb, and pointing directly backward, furnished the motive power.

Each of these tubes could exert a force sufficient to move an ordinary train of passenger-cars one mile, and this power could be exerted instantaneously, so that the difference in time in the starting of a train at one end of the mile and its arrival at the other would not be appreciable. The difference in concussionary force between a train moving at the rate of a mile in two minutes, or even in one minute, and another train which moves a mile in an instant, can easily be imagined.

What gave the tubes their power was the jealously guarded secret.

The method of aiming was as novel as the bomb itself. In this process, nothing depended on the eyesight of the gunner: the personal equation was entirely eliminated. The gun was so mounted that its direction was accurately indicated by graduated scales. There was an instrument which was acted on by the dip, rise, or roll of the vessel, and which showed at any moment the position of the gun with reference to the plane of the sea surface.

Before the discharge of the cannon, an observation was taken by one of the scientific men, which accurately determined the distance to the object to be aimed at, and reference to a carefully prepared mathematical table showed to what points on the graduated scales the gun should be adjusted, and the instant that the muzzle of the cannon was in the position that it was when the observation was taken, a button was touched, and the bomb was instantaneously placed on the spot aimed at. The exactness with which the propelling force of the bomb could be determined was an important factor in this method of aiming.

As soon as three of the vessels were completed, the Syndicate felt itself ready to begin operations. In the early hours of a July morning, they steamed out of a New England port, and headed for the point on the Canadian coast where it had been decided to open the campaign.

The vessels of the Syndicate had no individual names. They were termed "repellers," and were numbered. On this momentous occasion the Director-in-chief of Naval Operations for the Syndicate was on board Repeller No. 1, and commanded.

It was on a breezy day, with a cloudy sky, and the sea moderately smooth, that the little fleet of the Syndicate lay to off the harbor of one of the principal Canadian seaports. About nine o'clock, Repeller No. 1, with her consorts half a mile astern, approached to within two miles of the harbor mouth, and prepared to project the first Instantaneous Motor bomb ever used in warfare.

The great gun in the bow of the vessel was loaded, and the spot to be aimed at was selected. This was a point in the water just inside the mouth of the harbor, and nearly a mile from the land on either side. The distance of this point from the vessel being calculated, the cannon was adjusted at the angle called for by the scale of distances and levels, and the instrument indicating rise, fall, and direction was then put in connection with it.

Now the Director-in-chief stepped forward to the button, by pressing which the power of the motor was developed. The chief of the scientific corps then showed him the exact spot upon the scale which would be indicated when the gun was in its proper position, and the piece was moved upon its bearings so as to approximate, as nearly as possible, this direction.

The bow of the vessel now rose upon the swell of the sea, and the instant that the index upon the scale reached the desired point, the Director-in-chief touched the button.

There was no report, no smoke, no visible sign that the motor had left the cannon, but at that instant there appeared to those who were on the lookout, about a mile away a vast aperture in the waters of the bay, which was variously described as from one hundred to five hundred yards in diameter. At that same instant, in the neighboring headlands and islands far up the shores of the bay, and in every street and building of the city, there was felt a sharp shock, as if the underlying rocks had been struck by a gigantic trip-hammer.

At the same instant the sky above the spot where the motor had descended was darkened by a wide-spreading cloud. This was formed of that portion of the water of the bay which had been instantaneously raised to the height of about a thousand feet. The sudden appearance of this cloud was even more terrible than the yawning chasm in the waters of the bay, or the startling shock, but it did not remain long in view. It had no sooner reached its highest elevation than it began to descend. There was a strong sea-breeze blowing, and in its descent this vast mass of water was impelled toward the land.

It came down, not as rain, but as the waters of a vast cataract—as though a mountain lake, by an earthquake shock, had been precipitated in a body upon a valley. Only one edge of it reached the land, and here the seething flood tore away earth, trees, and rocks, leaving behind it great chasms and gullies, as it descended to the sea.

The bay itself, into which the vast body of water fell, became a scene of surging madness. The towering walls of water, which had stood up all around the suddenly created aperture, hurled themselves back into the abyss, and down into the great chasm at the bottom of the bay, which had been made when the motor sent its shock along the great rock beds. Down upon, and into, this roaring, boiling tumult fell the tremendous cataract from above, and the harbor became one wild expanse of leaping, maddened waves, hissing their whirling spray high into the air.

During these few terrific moments other things happened, which passed unnoticed in the general consternation. All along the shores of the bay and in front of the city the waters seemed to be sucked away, slowly returning, as the sea forced them to their level, and at many points up and down the harbor there were submarine detonations and upheavals of the water.

These were caused by the explosion, by concussion, of every torpedo and submarine battery in the harbor, and it was with this object in view that the Instantaneous Motor bomb had been shot into the mouth of the harbor.

Experiments with motor bombs had been made in unsettled mountainous districts, but this was the first one which had ever exerted its power under water.

In about half an hour after the discharge of the motor bomb, when the sea had resumed its usual quiet, a boat, carrying a white flag, left Repeller No. 1, and made for the harbor. The men in the boat had nothing to do but to deliver a letter from the Director-in-chief to the commandant of the fort, and then row back again. No answer was required.

When the commandant read the brief note, he made no remark. Indeed, he could think of no appropriate remark to make. The missive simply informed him that at 10:18 A.M. of that day the first bomb from the marine forces of the Syndicate had been discharged into the waters of the harbor. At or about 2 P.M. the second bomb would be discharged at Fort Pilcher. That was all.

Fort Pilcher was a very large but unfinished fortification, on a bluff. Work had been discontinued on it as soon as the Syndicate's vessels had appeared off the port, for it was not desired to expose the builders and other workmen to a possible bombardment. The place was now, therefore, almost deserted. But after the receipt of the Syndicate's message, the commandant sent a boat across the bay to order away any workmen who might be lingering about the place.

A little after 2 P.M. an Instantaneous Motor bomb was discharged from Repeller No. 1 into Fort Pilcher. It was set to act five seconds after impact with the object aimed at. It struck in a central portion of the unfinished fort, and having described a high curve in the air, descended not only with its own motive power but with the force of gravitation, and penetrated deep into the earth.

Five seconds later a vast brown cloud appeared on the Fort Pilcher promontory. This cloud was nearly spherical in form, with an apparent diameter of about a thousand yards. At the same instant a shock similar to that accompanying the first motor bomb was felt in the city and surrounding country; but this was not so severe as the other, for the second bomb did not exert its force upon the underlying rocks of the region as the first one had done.

The great brown cloud quickly began to lose its spherical form, part of it descending heavily to the earth, and part floating away in vast dust-clouds, borne inland by the breeze, settling downwards as they moved, and depositing on land, water, ships, houses, domes, and trees an almost impalpable powder.

When the cloud had cleared away there were no fortifications, and the bluff on which they had stood had disappeared. Part of this bluff had floated away on the wind, and part of it lay piled in great heaps of sand on the spot where its rocks had upheld a fort.

That afternoon a truce-boat again went out from Repeller No. 1, and rowed to the fort, where a letter to the commandant was delivered. This, like the other, demanded no answer. It stated that in twenty-four hours from time of writing it, which would be at or about four o'clock on the next afternoon, a bomb would be thrown into the garrisoned fort under the command of the officer addressed. As this would result in the entire destruction of the fortification, the commandant was earnestly counselled to evacuate the fort before the hour specified.

All night preparations for evacuation went on, and during the next morning the garrison left the fort, and established itself far enough away to preclude danger from the explosion.

It had been decided that Repeller No. 2 should discharge the next Instantaneous Motor bomb. The most accurate observations, the most careful calculations, were made and remade, the point to be aimed at being about the center of the fort.

The bomb had been in the cannon for nearly an hour, and everything had long been ready, when, at precisely thirty minutes past four o'clock, the signal to discharge came, and in four seconds afterwards the index on the scale indicated that the gun was in the proper position and the button was touched.

The motor bomb was set to act the instant it should touch any portion of the fort, and the effect was different from that of the other bombs. There was a quick, hard shock, but it was all in the air. Thousands of panes of glass in the city and in houses for miles around were cracked or broken, birds fell dead or stunned upon the ground, and people on elevations at considerable distance felt as if they had received a blow; but there was no trembling of the ground.

As to the fort, it had entirely disappeared, its particles having been instantaneously removed to a great distance in every direction, falling over such a vast expanse of land and water that their descent was unobservable.

In the place where the fortress had stood there was a wide tract of bare earth, which looked as if it had been scraped into a staring dead level of gravel and clay.

When the officers of the garrison mounted the hill before them, and surveyed the place where their fort had been, there was not one of them who had sufficient command of himself to write a report of what had happened. They gazed at the bare, staring flatness of the shorn bluff, and they looked at each other. This was not war. It was something super-natural, awful! They were not frightened. They were oppressed and appalled. But the military discipline of their minds soon exerted its force, and a brief account of the terrific event was transmitted to the authorities.

Repeller No. 1, meanwhile, steamed into the harbor, and anchored about a quarter of a mile seaward. The other repellers cruised about the mouth of the harbor, watching a smaller entrance to the port, as well as the larger one, and thus maintaining an effective blockade.

It was generally believed, on both sides of the Atlantic, that the destruction at the Canadian port had been effected by means of mines. To correct this false idea was now the duty of a new ship, Repeller No. 10. For the Syndicate had been hard at work, making preparations, and it had decided, without unnecessarily losing an hour, plainly to demonstrate the power of the Instantaneous Motor bomb.

Several days after the events above described, Repeller No. 10 appeared off Caerdaff, on the west coast of Wales. Nowhere in Great Britain was there a fortified spot of so little importance as Caerdaff, which consisted of a large fort on a promontory, and an immense castellated structure on the other side of a small bay, with a little fishing village at the head of said bay. The castellated structure was rather old, the fortress somewhat less so, and both had long been considered useless, as there was no probability that an enemy would land at this point on the coast.

This was the place for the proposed demonstration of the American Syndicate. No one could, for a moment, imagine that the Syndicate had mined it.

A note was sent on shore to the officer in command, stating that the bombardment would begin at ten o'clock in the morning, and requesting that information of the hour appointed be instantly transmitted to London.

Immediate measures were taken to remove the small garrisons and the inhabitants of the fishing village from possible danger.

At about nine o'clock on the appointed morning, Repeller No. 10 steamed westward until she had reached a point which, according to the calculations of her scientific corps, was nine marine miles from Caerdaff. There they lay to against a strong breeze from the east.

At precisely ten o'clock, up rose from the promontory of Caerdaff a heavy gray cloud, like an immense balloon, and then the people observing the scene on the hilltops and highlands some distance from the sea felt a sharp shock in the ground and rocks beneath them, and heard the sound of a terrible, but momentary, grinding crash.

As the cloud began to settle, it was borne out to sea by the wind, and then it was revealed that the fortifications of Caerdaff had disappeared.

In ten minutes there was another great cloud over the castellated structure on the other side of the bay. The cloud passed away, leaving a vacant space on the other side of the bay.

The next motor bomb descended into the fishing village, the comminuted particles of which, being mostly of light material, floated far out to sea.

The most courageous of the spectators trembled when the fourth bomb was discharged, for it came farther inland, and struck the height on which a battery had been placed, removing all vestiges of the guns, caissons, and the ledge of rock on which they had stood.

The motor bombs which the repeller was now discharging were of the largest size and greatest power, and a dozen more of them were discharged at intervals of a few minutes. The promontory on which the fortifications had stood was annihilated, and the waters of the bay swept over its foundations. Soon afterwards, the head of the bay seemed madly rushing out to sea, but quickly surged back to fill the chasm which yawned at the spot where the village had been.

The dense clouds were now upheaved at such short intervals that the scene of devastation was completely shut out from the observers on the hills, but every few minutes they felt a sickening shock, and heard a momentary and horrible crash and hiss, which seemed to fill the air.

It was not yet noon when the bombardment ceased. The vast spreading mass of clouds moved seaward, dropping down upon St. George's Channel in a rain of stone-dust. Then the repeller steamed shoreward, and when she was within three or four miles of the coast she ran up a large white flag, in token that her task was ended.

Many of the spectators would not leave their position on the hills, but a hundred or more of curious and courageous men ventured down into the plain.

That part of the seacoast where Caerdaff had been was a new country, about which men wandered slowly and cautiously, with sudden exclamations of amazement and awe. There were no longer promontories jutting out into the sea, there were no hillocks and rocky terraces rising inland. In a vast plain, shaven and shorn down to a common level of scarred and pallid rock, there lay an immense chasm two and a half miles long, half a mile wide, and so deep that shuddering men could stand and look down upon the rent and riven rocks upon which had rested that portion of the Welsh coast which had now been blown out to sea.

An officer of the Royal Engineers stood on the seaward edge of this yawning abyss, and wrote a report to the effect that a ship-canal, less than an eighth of a mile long, leading from the bay, would make of this chasm, when filled by the sea, the finest and most thoroughly protected inland basin, for ships of all sizes, on the British coast. But before this report achieved due official consideration, the idea had been suggested and elaborated in a dozen newspapers.

Accounts and reports of all kinds describing the destruction of Caerdaff, and of the place in which it had stood, filled the newspapers of the world. Photographs of Caerdaff as it had been, and as it then was, were produced with marvellous rapidity, and the earthquake bomb of the American War Syndicate was the subject of excited conversation in every civilized country.

The British ministry was now the calmest body of men in Europe. The wisest British statesmen saw the unmistakable path of national policy lying plain and open before them. There was no longer time for arguments and struggles with opponents or enemies, internal or external. There was even no longer time for the discussion of measures. It was the time for the adoption of a measure which indicated itself, and which did not need discussion.

On the afternoon of the day after the bombardment of Caerdaff, Repeller No. 10, now naval mistress of the world, lay off the coast of Brighton. In a very short time, communications were opened between the repeller and London.

The unmistakable path of national policy which had shown itself to the wisest British statesmen appeared broader and plainer when the overtures of the American War Syndicate had been received by the British government. The ministry now perceived that the Syndicate had not waged war: it had been simply exhibiting the uselessness of war as at present waged.

Another idea arose in the minds of the wisest British statesmen. If prohibitive warfare were a good thing for America, it would be an equally good thing for England. More than that, it would be a better thing if only these two countries possessed the power of waging prohibitive warfare.

In three days' time a convention of peace was concluded between Great Britain and the American Syndicate, acting for the United States, and no time was lost by the respective governments in ratifying the peace and in concluding a military and naval alliance, the basis of which should be the use by these two nations, and by no other nations, of the Instantaneous Motor. The treaty was made and adopted with much more dispatch than generally accompanies such agreements between nations, for both governments felt the importance of placing themselves, without delay, in that position from which, by means of their control of paramount methods of warfare, they might become the arbiters of peace.

In the midst of the profound satisfaction with which the members of the American War Syndicate regarded the success of their labors—labors alike profitable to themselves and to the recently contending nations—and in the gratified pride with which they received the popular and official congratulations which were showered upon them, there was but one little cloud, one regret.

In the course of the great Syndicate War a life had been lost. Thomas Hutchins, while assisting in the loading of coal on one of the repellers, was accidentally killed by the falling of a derrick.

The Syndicate gave a generous sum to the family of the unfortunate man, and throughout the United States the occurrence occasioned a deep feeling of sympathetic regret. A popular subscription was started to build a monument to the memory of Hutchins, and contributions came, not only from all parts of the United States, but from many persons in Great Britain who wished to assist in the erection of this tribute to the man who had fallen in the contest which had been of as much benefit to their country as to his own.

Both countries were, indeed, too well satisfied with the general result to waste time or discussion over small matters. Great Britain had lost some forts, but these would have been comparatively useless in the new system of warfare. On the other hand, she had gained, not only the incalculable advantage of the alliance, but a magnificent and unsurpassed landlocked basin on the coast of Wales.

The United States had been obliged to pay an immense sum on account of the contract with the War Syndicate, but this was considered money well spent, and so much less than an ordinary war would have cost, that only the most violent anti-administration journals ever alluded to it.

This is the history of the Great Syndicate War. Whether or not the Anglo-American Syndicate was ever called upon to make war, it is not to be stated here. But certain it is that, after the formation of this Syndicate, all the nations of the world began to teach English in their schools, and the spirit of Civilization raised her head with a confident smile.

LEWIS PADGETT

THE PIPER'S SON

THE Green Man was climbing the glass mountains, and hairy, gnomish faces peered at him from crevices. This was only another step in the Green Man's endless, exciting odyssey. He'd had a great many adventures already—in the Flame Country, among the Dimension Changers, with the City Apes who sneered endlessly while their blunt, clumsy fingers fumbled at deathrays. The trolls, however, were masters of magic, and were trying to stop the Green Man with spells. Little whirlwinds of force spun underfoot, trying to trip the Green Man, a figure of marvelous muscular development, handsome as a god, and hairless from head to foot, glistening pale green. The whirlwinds formed a fascinating pattern. If you could thread a precarious path among them—avoiding the pale yellow ones especially—you could get through.

And the hairy gnomes watched malignantly, jealously, from their crannies in the glass crags.

Al Burkhalter, having recently achieved the mature status of eight full years, lounged under a tree and masticated a grass blade. He was so immersed in his daydreams that his father had to nudge his side gently to bring comprehension into the half-closed eyes. It was a good day for dreaming, anyway—a hot sun and a cool wind blowing down from the white Sierra peaks to the east. Timothy grass sent its faintly musty fragrance along the channels of air, and Ed Burkhalter was glad that his son was second-generation since the Blowup. He himself had been born ten years after the last bomb had been dropped, but secondhand memories can be pretty bad too.

"Hello, Al," he said, and the youth vouchsafed a half-lidded glance of tolerant acceptance.

"Hi, Dad."

"Want to come downtown with me?"

"Nope," Al said, relaxing instantly into his stupor.

Burkhalter raised a figurative eyebrow and half turned. On an impulse, then, he did something he rarely did without the tacit permission of the other party; he used his telepathic power to reach into Al's mind. There was, he admitted to himself, a certain hesitancy, a subconscious unwillingness on his part, to do this, even though Al had pretty well outgrown the nasty, inhuman formlessness of mental babyhood. There had been a time when Al's mind had been quite shocking in its alienage. Burkhalter remembered a few abortive experiments he had made before Al's birth; few fathers-to-be could resist the temptation to experiment with embryonic brains, and that had brought back nightmares Burkhalter had not had since his youth. There had been enormous rolling masses, and an appalling vastness, and other things. Prenatal memories were ticklish, and should be left to qualified mnemonic psychologists.

But now Al was maturing, and daydreaming, as usual, in bright colors. Burkhalter, reassured, felt that he had fulfilled his duty as a monitor and left his son still eating grass and ruminating.

Just the same, there was a sudden softness inside of him, and the aching, futile pity he was apt to feel for helpless things that were as yet unqualified for conflict with that extraordinarily complicated business of living. Conflict, competition, had not died out when war abolished itself; the business of adjustment even to one's surroundings was a conflict, and conversation a duel. With Al, too, there was a double problem. Yes, language was in effect a tariff wall, and a Baldy could appreciate that thoroughly, since the wall didn't exist between Baldies.

Walking down the rubbery walk that led to the town center, Burkhalter grinned wryly and ran lean fingers through his well-kept wig. Strangers were very often surprised to know that he was a Baldy, a telepath. They looked at him with wondering eyes, too courteous to ask how it felt to be a freak, but obviously avid. Burkhalter, who knew diplomacy, would be quite willing to lead the conversation.

"My folks lived near Chicago after the Blowup. That was why."

"Oh." Stare. "I'd heard that was why so many—" Startled pause.

"Freaks or mutations. There were both. I still don't know which class I belong to," he'd add disarmingly.

"You're no freak!" They didn't protest too much.

"Well, some mighty queer specimens came out of the radioactive-affected areas around the bomb targets. Funny things happened to the germ plasm. Most of 'em died out; they couldn't reproduce; but you'll still find a few creatures in sanitariums—two heads, you know. And so on."

Nevertheless they were always ill at ease. "You mean you can read my mind—now?"

"I could, but I'm not. It's hard work, except with another telepath.

And we Baldies—well, we don't, that's all." A man with abnormal muscle development wouldn't go around knocking people down. Not unless he wanted to be mobbed. Baldies were always sneakingly conscious of a hidden peril: lynch law. And wise Baldies didn't even imply that they had an . . . extra sense. They just said they were different, and let it go at that.

But one question was always implied, though not always mentioned. "If I were a telepath, I'd . . . how much do you make a year?"

They were surprised at the answer. A mind reader certainly could make a fortune, if he wanted. So why did Ed Burkhalter stay a semantics expert in Modoc Publishing Town, when a trip to one of the science towns would enable him to get hold of secrets that would get him a fortune?

There was a good reason. Self-preservation was a part of it. For which reason Burkhalter, and many like him, wore toupees. Though there were many Baldies who did not.

Modoc was a twin town with Pueblo, across the mountain barrier south of the waste that had been Denver. Pueblo held the presses, photolinotypes, and the machines that turned scripts into books, after Modoc had dealt with them. There was a helicopter distribution fleet at Pueblo, and for the last week Oldfield, the manager, had been demanding the manuscript of "Psychohistory," turned out by a New Yale man who had got tremendously involved in past emotional problems, to the detriment of literary clarity. The truth was that he distrusted Burkhalter. And Burkhalter, neither a priest nor a psychologist, had to become both without admitting it to the confused author of "Psychohistory."

The sprawling buildings of the publishing house lay ahead and below, more like a resort than anything more utilitarian. That had been necessary. Authors were peculiar people, and often it was necessary to induce them to take hydrotherapic treatments before they were in shape to work out their books with the semantics experts. Nobody was going to bite them, but they didn't realize that, and either cowered in corners, terrified, or else blustered their way around, using language few could understand. Jem Quayle, author of "Psychohistory," fitted into neither group; he was simply baffled by the intensity of his own research. His personal history had qualified him too well for emotional involvements with the past—and that was a serious matter when a thesis of this particular type was in progress.

Dr. Moon, who was on the Board, sat near the south entrance, eating an apple which he peeled carefully with his silver-hilted dagger. Moon was fat, short, and shapeless; he didn't have much hair, but he wasn't a telepath; Baldies were entirely hairless. He gulped and waved at Burkhalter.

"Ed . . . *urp* . . . want to talk to you."

"Sure," Burkhalter said, agreeably coming to a standstill and rocking on his heels. Ingrained habit made him sit down beside the Boardman;

Baldies, for obvious reasons, never stood up when nontelepaths were sitting. Their eyes met now on the same level. Burkhalter said, "What's up?"

"The store got some Shasta apples flown in yesterday. Better tell Ethel to get some before they're sold out. Here." Moon watched his companion eat a chunk, and nod.

"Good. I'll have her get some. The copter's laid up for today, though; Ethel pulled the wrong gadget."

"Foolproof," Moon said bitterly. "Huron's turning out some sweet models these days; I'm getting my new one from Michigan. Listen, Pueblo called me this morning on Quayle's book."

"Oldfield?"

"Our boy," Moon nodded. "He says can't you send over even a few chapters."

Burkhalter shook his head. "I don't think so. There are some abstracts right in the beginning that just have to be clarified, and Quayle is—" He hesitated.

"What?"

Burkhalter thought about the Oedipus complex he'd uncovered in Quayle's mind, but that was sacrosanct, even though it kept Quayle from interpreting Darius with cold logic. "He's got muddy thinking in there. I can't pass it; I tried it on three readers yesterday, and got different reactions from all of them. So far 'Psychohistory' is all things to all men. The critics would lambaste us if we released the book as is. Can't you string Oldfield along for a while longer?"

"Maybe," Moon said doubtfully. "I've got a subjective novella I could rush over. It's light vicarious eroticism, and that's harmless; besides, it's semantically O. K.'d. We've been holding it up for an artist, but I can put Duman on it. I'll do that, yeah. I'll shoot the script over to Pueblo and he can make the plates later. A merry life we lead, Ed."

"A little too merry sometimes," Burkhalter said. He got up, nodded, and went in search of Quayle, who was relaxing on one of the sun decks.

Quayle was a thin, tall man with a worried face and the abstract air of an unshelled tortoise. He lay on his flexiglass couch, direct sunlight toasting him from above, while the reflected rays sneaked up on him from below, through the transparent crystal. Burkhalter pulled off his shirt and dropped on a sunner beside Quayle. The author glanced at Burkhalter's hairless chest and half-formed revulsion rose in him: *A Baldy . . . no privacy . . . none of his business . . . fake eyebrows and lashes; he's still a—*

Something ugly, at that point.

Diplomatically Burkhalter touched a button, and on a screen overhead a page of "Psychohistory" appeared, enlarged and easily readable. Quayle scanned the sheet. It had code notations on it, made by the readers, recognized by Burkhalter as varied reactions to what should have been straight-line explanations. If three readers had got three different meanings out of

that paragraph—well, what *did* Quayle mean? He reached delicately into the mind, conscious of useless guards erected against intrusion—mud barricades over which his mental eye stole like a searching, quiet wind. No ordinary man could guard his mind against a Baldy. But Baldies could guard their privacy against intrusion by other telepaths—adults, that is. There was a psychic selector band, a—

Here it came. But muddled a bit. *Darius:* that wasn't simply a word; it wasn't a picture, either; it was really a second *life*. But scattered, fragmentary. Scraps of scent and sound, and memories, and emotional reactions. Admiration and hatred. A burning impotence. A black tornado, smelling of pine, roaring across a map of Europe and Asia. Pine scent stronger now, and horrible humiliation, and remembered pain . . . eyes . . . *Get out!*

Burkhalter put down the dictograph mouthpiece and lay looking up through the darkened eye-shells he had donned. "I got out as soon as you wanted me to," he said. "I'm still out."

Quayle lay there, breathing hard. "Thanks," he said. "Apologies. Why you don't ask a duello—"

"I don't want to duel with you," Burkhalter said. "I've never put blood on my dagger in my life. Besides, I can see your side of it. Remember, this is my job, Mr. Quayle, and I've learned a lot of things—that I've forgotten again."

"It's intrusion, I suppose. I tell myself that it doesn't matter, but my privacy—is important."

Burkhalter said patiently, "We can keep trying it from different angles until we find one that isn't too private. Suppose, for example, I asked you if you admired Darius."

Admiration . . . and pine scent . . . and Burkhalter said quickly, "I'm out. O. K.?"

"Thanks," Quayle muttered. He turned on his side, away from the other man. After a moment he said, "That's silly—turning over, I mean. You don't have to see my face to know what I'm thinking."

"You have to put out the welcome mat before I walk in," Burkhalter told him.

"I guess I believe that. I've met some Baldies, though, that were . . . that I didn't like."

"There's a lot on that order, sure. I know the type. The ones who don't wear wigs."

Quayle said, "They'll read your mind and embarrass you just for the fun of it. They ought to be—taught better."

Burkhalter blinked in the sunlight. "Well, Mr. Quayle, it's this way. A Baldy's got his problems, too. He's got to orient himself to a world that isn't telepathic; and I suppose a lot of Baldies rather feel that they're letting their specialization go to waste. There *are* jobs a man like me is suited for—"

"Man!" He caught the scrap of thought from Quayle. He ignored it, his face as always a mobile mask, and went on.

"Semantics have always been a problem, even in countries speaking only one tongue. A qualified Baldy is a swell interpreter. And, though there aren't any Baldies on the detective force, they often work with the police. It's rather like being a machine that can do only a few things."

"A few things more than humans can," Quayle said.

Sure, Burkhalter thought, if we could compete on equal footing with nontelepathic humanity. But would blind men trust one who could see? Would they play poker with him? A sudden, deep bitterness put an unpleasant taste in Burkhalter's mouth. What was the answer? Reservations for Baldies? Isolation? And would a nation of blind men trust those with vision enough for that? Or would they be dusted off—the sure cure, the check-and-balance system that made war an impossibility.

He remembered when Red Bank had been dusted off, and maybe that had been justified. The town was getting too big for its boots, and personal dignity was a vital factor; you weren't willing to lose face as long as a dagger swung at your belt. Similarly, the thousands upon thousands of little towns that covered America, each with its peculiar specialty— helicopter manufacture for Huron and Michigan, vegetable farming for Conoy and Diego, textiles and education and art and machines—each little town had a wary eye on all the others. The science and research centers were a little larger; nobody objected to that, for technicians never made war except under pressure; but few of the towns held more than a few hundred families. It was check-and-balance in most efficient degree; whenever a town showed signs of wanting to become a city—thence, a capital, thence, an imperialistic empire—it was dusted off. Though that had not happened for a long while. And Red Bank might have been a mistake.

Geopolitically it was a fine set-up; sociologically it was acceptable, but brought necessary changes. There was subconscious swashbuckling. The rights of the individual had become more highly regarded as decentralization took place. And men learned.

They learned a monetary system based primarily upon barter. They learned to fly; nobody drove surface cars. They learned new things, but they did not forget the Blowup, and in secret places near every town were hidden the bombs that could utterly and fantastically exterminate a town, as such bombs had exterminated the cities during the Blowup.

And everybody knew how to make those bombs. They were beautifully, terribly simple. You could find the ingredients anywhere and prepare them easily. Then you could take your helicopter over a town, drop an egg overside—and perform an erasure.

Outside of the wilderness malcontents, the maladjusted people found in every race, nobody kicked. And the roaming tribes never raided and never banded together in large groups—for fear of an erasure.

The artisans were maladjusted too, to some degree, but they weren't antisocial, so they lived where they wanted and painted, wrote, composed, and retreated into their own private worlds. The scientists, equally maladjusted in other lines, retreated to their slightly larger towns, banding together in small universes, and turned out remarkable technical achievements.

And the Baldies—found jobs where they could.

No nontelepath would have viewed the world environment quite as Burkhalter did. He was abnormally conscious of the human element, attaching a deeper, more profound significance to those human values, undoubtedly because he saw men in more than the ordinary dimensions. And also, in a way—and inevitably—he looked at humanity from outside.

Yet he was human. The barrier that telepathy had raised made men suspicious of him, more so than if he had had two heads—then they could have pitied. As it was—

As it was, he adjusted the scanner until new pages of the typescript came flickering into view above. "Say when," he told Quayle.

Quayle brushed back his gray hair. "I feel sensitive all over," he objected. "After all, I've been under a considerable strain correlating my material."

"Well, we can always postpone publication." Burkhalter threw out the suggestion casually, and was pleased when Quayle didn't nibble. He didn't like to fail, either.

"No. No, I want to get the thing done now."

"Mental catharsis—"

"Well, by a psychologist, perhaps. But not by—"

"—a Baldy. You know that a lot of psychologists have Baldy helpers. They get good results, too."

Quayle turned on the tobacco smoke, inhaling slowly. "I suppose . . . I've not had much contact with Baldies. Or too much—without selectivity. I saw some in an asylum once. I'm not being offensive, am I?"

"No," Burkhalter said. "Every mutation can run too close to the line. There were lots of failures. The hard radiations brought about one true mutation: hairless telepaths, but they didn't all hew true to the line. The mind's a queer gadget—you know that. It's a colloid balancing, figuratively, on the point of a pin. If there's any flaw, telepathy's apt to bring it out. So you'll find that the Blowup caused a hell of a lot of insanity. Not only among the Baldies, but among the other mutations that developed then. Except that the Baldies are almost always paranoidal."

"And dementia praecox," Quayle said, finding relief from his own embarrassment in turning the spotlight on Burkhalter.

"And d. p. Yeah. When a confused mind acquires the telepathic instinct —a hereditary bollixed mind—it can't handle it all. There's disorientation. The paranoia group retreat into their own private worlds, and the d. p.'s simply don't realize that *this* world exists. There are distinctions, but I think that's a valid basis."

"In a way," Quayle said, "it's frightening. I can't think of any historical parallel."

"No."

"What do you think the end of it will be?"

"I don't know," Burkhalter said thoughtfully. "I think we'll be assimilated. There hasn't been enough time yet. We're specialized in a certain way, and we're useful in certain jobs."

"If you're satisfied to stay there. The Baldies who won't wear wigs—"

"They're so bad-tempered I expect they'll all be killed off in duels eventually." Burkhalter smiled. "No great loss. The rest of us, we're getting what we want—acceptance. We don't have horns or halos."

Quayle shook his head. "I'm glad, I think, that I'm not a telepath. The mind's mysterious enough anyway, without new doors opening. Thanks for letting me talk. I think I've got part of it talked out, anyway. Shall we try the script again?"

"Sure," Burkhalter said, and again the procession of pages flickered on the screen above them. Quayle did seem less guarded; his thoughts were more lucid, and Burkhalter was able to get at the true meanings of many of the hitherto muddy statements. They worked easily, the telepath dictating rephrasings into his dictograph, and only twice did they have to hurdle emotional tangles. At noon they knocked off, and Burkhalter, with a friendly nod, took the dropper to his office, where he found some calls listed on the visor. He ran off repeats, and a worried look crept into his blue eyes.

He talked with Dr. Moon in a booth at luncheon. The conversation lasted so long that only the induction cups kept the coffee hot, but Burkhalter had more than one problem to discuss. And he'd known Moon for a long time. The fat man was one of the few who were not, he thought, subconsciously repelled by the fact that Burkhalter was a Baldy.

"I've never fought a duel in my life, Doc. I can't afford to."

"You can't afford not to. You can't turn down the challenge, Ed. It isn't done."

"But this fellow Reilly—I don't even know him."

"I know of him," Moon said. "He's got a bad temper. Dueled a lot."

Burkhalter slammed his hand down on the table. "It's ridiculous. I won't do it!"

"Well," Moon said practically, "your wife can't fight him. And if Ethel's been reading Mrs. Reilly's mind and gossiping, Reilly's got a case."

"Don't you think we know the dangers of that?" Burkhalter asked in a low voice. "Ethel doesn't go around reading minds any more than I do. It'd be fatal—for us. And for any other Baldy."

"Not the hairless ones. The ones who won't wear wigs. They—"

"They're fools. And they're giving all the Baldies a bad name. Point one, Ethel doesn't read minds; she didn't read Mrs. Reilly's. Point two, she doesn't gossip."

"La Reilly is obviously an hysterical type," Moon said. "Word got around about this scandal, whatever it was, and Mrs. Reilly remembered she'd seen Ethel lately. She's the type who needs a scapegoat anyway. I rather imagine she let word drop herself, and had to cover up so her husband wouldn't blame her."

"I'm not going to accept Reilly's challenge," Burkhalter said doggedly.

"You'll have to."

"Listen, Doc, maybe—"

"What?"

"Nothing. An idea. It might work. Forget about that; I think I've got the right answer. It's the only one, anyway. I can't afford a duel and that's flat."

"You're not a coward."

"There's one thing Baldies are afraid of," Burkhalter said, "and that's public opinion. I happen to know I'd kill Reilly. That's the reason why I've never dueled in my life."

Moon drank coffee. "Hm-m-m. I think—"

"Don't. There was something else. I'm wondering if I ought to send Al off to a special school."

"What's wrong with the kid?"

"He's turning out to be a beautiful delinquent. His teacher called me this morning. The playback was something to hear. He's talking funny and acting funny. Playing nasty little tricks on his friends—if he has any left by now."

"All kids are cruel."

"Kids don't know what cruelty means. That's why they're cruel; they lack empathy. But Al's getting—" Burkhalter gestured helplessly. "He's turning into a young tyrant. He doesn't seem to give a care about anything, according to his teacher."

"That's not too abnormal, so far."

"That's not the worst. He's become very egotistical. Too much so. I don't want him to turn into one of the wigless Baldies you were mentioning." Burkhalter didn't mention the other possibility; paranoia, insanity.

"He must pick things up somewhere. At home? Scarcely, Ed. Where else does he go?"

"The usual places. He's got a normal environment."

"I should think," Moon said, "that a Baldy would have unusual opportunities in training a youngster. The mental rapport—eh?"

"Yeah. But—I don't know. The trouble is," Burkhalter said almost inaudibly, "I wish to God I wasn't different. We didn't ask to be telepaths. Maybe it's all very wonderful in the long run, but I'm one person, and I've got my own microcosm. People who deal in long-term sociology are apt to forget that. They can figure out the answers, but it's every individual man—or Baldy—who's got to fight his own personal battle while he's alive. And it isn't as clear-cut as a battle. It's worse; it's the necessity of watching yourself every second, of fitting yourself into a world that doesn't want you."

Moon looked uncomfortable. "Are you being a little sorry for yourself, Ed?"

Burkhalter shook himself. "I am, Doc. But I'll work it out."

"We both will," Moon said, but Burkhalter didn't really expect much help from him. Moon would be willing, but it was horribly difficult for an ordinary man to conceive that a Baldy was—the same. It was the difference that men looked for, and found.

Anyway, he'd have to settle matters before he saw Ethel again. He could easily conceal the knowledge, but she would recognize a mental barrier and wonder. Their marriage had been the more ideal because of the additional rapport, something that compensated for an inevitable, half-sensed estrangement from the rest of the world.

"How's 'Psychohistory' going?" Moon asked after a while.

"Better than I expected. I've got a new angle on Quayle. If I talk about myself, that seems to draw him out. It gives him enough confidence to let him open his mind to me. We may have those first chapters ready for Oldfield, in spite of everything."

"Good. Just the same, he can't rush us. If we've got to shoot out books that fast, we might as well go back to the days of semantic confusion. Which we won't!"

"Well," Burkhalter said, getting up, "I'll smoosh along. See you."

"About Reilly—"

"Let it lay." Burkhalter went out, heading for the address his visor had listed. He touched the dagger at his belt. Dueling wouldn't do for Baldies, but—

A greeting thought crept into his mind, and, under the arch that led into the campus, he paused to grin at Sam Shane, a New Orleans area Baldy who affected a wig of flaming red. They didn't bother to talk.

Personal question, involving mental, moral and physical well-being.

A satisfied glow. And you, Burkhalter? For an instant Burkhalter half-saw what the symbol of his name meant to Shane.

Shadow of trouble.

A warm, willing anxiousness to help. There was a bond between Baldies.

Burkhalter thought: But everywhere I'd go there'd be the same suspicion. We're freaks.

More so elsewhere, Shane thought. There are a lot of us in Modoc Town. People are invariably more suspicious where they're not in daily contact with—Us.

The boy—

I've trouble too, Shane thought. It's worried me. My two girls—

Delinquency?

Yes.

Common denominators?

Don't know. More than one of Us have had the same trouble with our kids.

Secondary characteristic of the mutation? Second generation emergence?

Doubtful, Shane thought, scowling in his mind, shading his concept with a wavering question. We'll think it over later. Must go.

Burkhalter sighed and went on his way. The houses were strung out around the central industry of Modoc, and he cut through a park toward his destination. It was a sprawling curved building, but it wasn't inhabited, so Burkhalter filed Reilly for future reference, and, with a glance at his timer, angled over a hillside toward the school. As he expected, it was recreation time, and he spotted Al lounging under a tree, some distance from his companions, who were involved in a pleasantly murderous game of Blowup.

He sent his thought ahead.

The Green Man had almost reached the top of the mountain. The hairy gnomes were pelting on his trail, most unfairly shooting sizzling light-streaks at their quarry, but the Green Man was agile enough to dodge. The rocks were leaning—

"Al."

—inward, pushed by the gnomes, ready to—

"*Al!*" Burkhalter sent his thought with the word, jolting into the boy's mind, a trick he very seldom employed, since youth was practically defenseless against such invasion.

"Hello, Dad," Al said, undisturbed. "What's up?"

"A report from your teacher."

"I didn't do anything."

"She told me what it was. Listen, kid. Don't start getting any funny ideas in your head."

"I'm not."

"Do you think a Baldy is better or worse than a non-Baldy?"

Al moved his feet uncomfortably. He didn't answer.

"Well," Burkhalter said, "the answer is both and neither. And here's why. A Baldy can communicate mentally, but he lives in a world where most people can't."

"They're dumb," Al opined.

"Not so dumb, if they're better suited to their world than you are. You might as well say a frog's better than a fish because he's an amphibian." Burkhalter briefly amplified and explained the terms telepathically.

"Well . . . oh, I get it, all right."

"Maybe," Burkhalter said slowly, "what you need is a swift kick in the pants. That thought wasn't so hot. What was it again?"

Al tried to hide it, blanking out. Burkhalter began to lift the barrier, an easy matter for him, but stopped. Al regarded his father in a most unfilial way—in fact, as a sort of boneless fish. That had been clear.

"If you're so egotistical," Burkhalter pointed out, "maybe you can see it this way. Do you know why there aren't any Baldies in key positions?"

"Sure I do," Al said unexpectedly. "They're afraid."

"Of what, then?"

"The—" That picture had been very curious, a commingling of something vaguely familiar to Burkhalter. "The non-Baldies."

"Well, if we took positions where we could take advantage of our telepathic function, non-Baldies would be plenty envious—especially if we were successes. If a Baldy even invented a better mousetrap, plenty of people would say he'd stolen the idea from some non-Baldy's mind. You get the point?"

"Yes, Dad." But he hadn't. Burkhalter sighed and looked up. He recognized one of Shane's girls on a nearby hillside, sitting alone against a boulder. There were other isolated figures here and there. Far to the east the snowy rampart of the Rockies made an irregular pattern against blue sky.

"Al," Burkhalter said, "I don't want you to get a chip on your shoulder. This is a pretty swell world, and the people in it are, on the whole, nice people. There's a law of averages. It isn't sensible for us to get too much wealth or power, because that'd militate against us—and we don't need it anyway. Nobody's poor. We find our work, we do it, and we're reasonably happy. We have some advantages non-Baldies don't have; in marriage, for example. Mental intimacy is quite as important as physical. But I don't want you to feel that being a Baldy makes you a god. It doesn't. I can still," he added thoughtfully, "spank it out of you, in case you care to follow out that concept in your mind at the moment."

Al gulped and beat a hasty retreat. "I'm sorry. I won't do it again."

"And keep your hair on, too. Don't take your wig off in class. Use the stickum stuff in the bathroom closet."

"Yes, but . . . Mr. Venner doesn't wear a wig."

"Remind me to do some historical research with you on zoot-suiters," Burkhalter said. "Mr. Venner's wiglessness is probably his only virtue, if you consider it one."

"He makes money."

"Anybody would, in that general store of his. But people don't buy from him if they can help it, you'll notice. That's what I mean by a chip on your shoulder. He's got one. There are Baldies like Venner, Al, but you might, sometime, ask the guy if he's happy. For your information, I am. More than Venner, anyway. Catch?"

"Yes, Dad." Al seemed submissive, but it was merely that. Burkhalter, still troubled, nodded and walked away. As he passed near the Shane girl's boulder he caught a scrap—*at the summit of the Glass Mountains, rolling rocks back at the gnomes until*—

He withdrew; it was an unconscious habit, touching minds that were sensitive, but with children it was definitely unfair. With adult Baldies it was simply the instinctive gesture of tipping your hat; one answered or one didn't. The barrier could be erected; there could be a blank-out; or there could be the direct snub of concentration on a single thought, private and not to be intruded on.

A copter with a string of gliders was coming in from the south: a freighter laden with frozen foods from South America, to judge by the markings. Burkhalter made a note to pick up an Argentine steak. He'd got a new recipe he wanted to try out, a charcoal broil with barbecue sauce, a welcome change from the short-wave cooked meats they'd been having for a week. Tomatoes, chile, mm-m—what else? Oh, yes. The duel with Reilly. Burkhalter absently touched his dagger's hilt and made a small, mocking sound in his throat. Perhaps he was innately a pacifist. It was rather difficult to think of a duel seriously, ever though everyone else did, when the details of a barbecue dinner were prosaic in his mind.

So it went. The tides of civilization rolled in century-long waves across the continents, and each particular wave, though conscious of its participation in the tide, nevertheless was more preoccupied with dinner. And, unless you happened to be a thousand feet tall, had the brain of a god and a god's life-span, what was the difference? People missed a lot—people like Venner, who was certainly a crank, not batty enough to qualify for the asylum, but certainly a potential paranoid type. The man's refusal to wear a wig labeled him as an individualist, but as an exhibitionist, too. If he didn't feel ashamed of his hairlessness, why should he bother to flaunt it? Besides, the man had a bad temper, and if people kicked him around, he asked for it by starting the kicking himself.

But as for Al, the kid was heading for something approaching delinquency. It couldn't be the normal development of childhood, Burkhalter thought. He didn't pretend to be an expert, but he was still young enough to remember his own formative years, and he had had more handicaps than Al had now; in those days, Baldies had been very new and very freakish. There'd been more than one movement to isolate, sterilize, or even exterminate the mutations.

Burkhalter sighed. If he had been born before the Blowup, it might have been different. Impossible to say. One could read history, but one couldn't live it. In the future, perhaps, there might be telepathic libraries in which that would be possible. So many opportunities, in fact—and so few that the world was ready to accept as yet. Eventually Baldies would not be regarded as freaks, and by that time real progress would be possible.

But people don't make history—Burkhalter thought. Peoples do that. Not the individual.

He stopped by Reilly's house again, and this time the man answered, a burly, freckled, squint-eyed fellow with immense hands and, Burkhalter noted, fine muscular co-ordination. He rested those hands on the Dutch door and nodded.

"Who're you, mister?"

"My name's Burkhalter."

Comprehension and wariness leaped into Reilly's eyes. "Oh. I see. You got my call?"

"I did," Burkhalter said. "I want to talk to you about it. May I come in?"

"O. K." He stepped back, opening the way through a hall and into a spacious living room, where diffused light filtered through glassy mosaic walls. "Want to set the time?"

"I want to tell you you're wrong."

"Now wait a minute," Reilly said, patting the air. "My wife's out now, but she gave me the straight of it. I don't like this business of sneaking into a man's mind; it's crooked. You should have told *your* wife to mind her business—or keep her tongue quiet."

Burkhalter said patiently, "I give you my word, Reilly, that Ethel didn't read your wife's mind."

"Does she say so?"

"I . . . well, I haven't asked her."

"Yeah," Reilly said with an air of triumph.

"I don't need to. I know her well enough. And . . . well, I'm a Baldy myself."

"I know you are," Reilly said. "For all I know, you may be reading my mind now." He hesitated. "Get out of my house. I like my privacy. We'll meet at dawn tomorrow if that's satisfactory with you. Now get out." He seemed to have something on his mind, some ancient memory, perhaps, that he didn't wish exposed.

Burkhalter nobly resisted the temptation. "No Baldy would read—"

"Go on, get out!"

"Listen! You wouldn't have a chance in a duel with me!"

"Do you know how many notches I've got?" Reilly asked.

"Ever dueled a Baldy?"

"I'll cut the notch deeper tomorrow. Get out, d'you hear?"

Burkhalter, biting his lips, said, "Man, don't you realize that **in a** duel I could read your mind?"

"I don't care . . . what?"

"I'd be half a jump ahead of you. No matter how instinctive your actions would be, you'd know them a split second ahead of time in your mind. And I'd know all your tricks and weaknesses, too. Your technique would be an open book to me. Whatever you thought of—"

"No." Reilly shook his head. "Oh, no. You're smart, but it's a phony set-up."

Burkhalter hesitated, decided, and swung about, pushing a chair out of the way. "Take out your dagger," he said. "Leave the sheath snapped on; I'll show you what I mean."

Reilly's eyes widened. "If you want it now—"

"I don't." Burkhalter shoved another chair away. He unclipped his dagger, sheath and all, from his belt, and made sure the little safety clip was in place. "We've room enough here. Come on."

Scowling, Reilly took out his own dagger, held it awkwardly, baffled by the sheath, and then suddenly feinted forward. But Burkhalter wasn't there; he had anticipated, and his own leather sheath slid up Reilly's belly.

"That," Burkhalter said, "would have ended the fight."

For answer Reilly smashed a hard dagger-blow down, curving at the last moment into a throat-cutting slash. Burkhalter's free hand was already at his throat; his other hand, with the sheathed dagger, tapped Reilly twice over the heart. The freckles stood out boldly against the pallor of the larger man's face. But he was not yet ready to concede. He tried a few more passes, clever, well-trained cuts, and they failed, because Burkhalter had anticipated them. His left hand invariably covered the spot where Reilly had aimed, and which he never struck.

Slowly Reilly let his arm fall. He moistened his lips and swallowed. Burkhalter busied himself reclipping his dagger in place.

"Burkhalter," Reilly said, "you're a devil."

"Far from it. I'm just afraid to take a chance. Do you really think being a Baldy is a snap?"

"But, if you can read minds—"

"How long do you think I'd last if I did any dueling? It would be too much of a set-up. Nobody would stand for it, and I'd end up dead. I can't duel, because it'd be murder, and people would know it was murder. I've taken a lot of cracks, swallowed a lot of insults, for just that reason. Now, if you like, I'll swallow another and apologize. I'll admit anything you say. But I can't duel with you, Reilly."

"No, I can see that. And—I'm glad you came over." Reilly was still white. "I'd have walked right into a set-up."

"Not my set-up," Burkhalter said. "I wouldn't have dueled. Baldies aren't so lucky, you know. They've got handicaps—like this. That's why they can't afford to take chances and antagonize people, and why we never read minds, unless we're asked to do so."

"It makes sense. More or less." Reilly hesitated. "Look, I withdraw that challenge. O. K.?"

"Thanks," Burkhalter said, putting out his hand. It was taken rather reluctantly. "We'll leave it at that, eh?"

"Right." But Reilly was still anxious to get his guest out of the house.

Burkhalter walked back to the Publishing Center and whistled tunelessly. He could tell Ethel now; in fact, he had to, for secrets between them would have broken up the completeness of their telepathic intimacy. It was not that their minds lay bare to each other; it was, rather, that any barrier could be sensed by the other, and the perfect rapport wouldn't have been so perfect. Curiously, despite this utter intimacy, husband and wife managed to respect one another's privacy.

Ethel might be somewhat distressed, but the trouble had blown over, and, besides, she was a Baldy too. Not that she looked it, with her wig of fluffy chestnut hair and those long, curving lashes. But her parents had lived east of Seattle during the Blowup, and afterward, too, before the hard radiation's effects had been thoroughly studied.

The snow-wind blew down over Modoc and fled southward along the Utah Valley. Burkhalter wished he was in his copter, alone in the blue emptiness of the sky. There was a quiet, strange peace up there that no Baldy ever quite achieved on the earth's surface, except in the depths of a wilderness. Stray fragments of thoughts were always flying about, subsensory, but like the almost-unheard whisper of a needle on a phonograph record, never ceasing. That, certainly, was why almost all Baldies loved to fly and were expert pilots. The high waste deserts of the air were their blue hermitages.

Still, he was in Modoc now, and overdue for his interview with Quayle. Burkhalter hastened his steps. In the main hall he met Moon, said briefly and cryptically that he'd taken care of the duel, and passed on, leaving the fat man to stare a question after him. The only visor call was from Ethel; the playback said she was worried about Al, and would Burkhalter check with the school. Well, he had already done so—unless the boy had managed to get into more trouble since then. Burkhalter put in a call and reassured himself. Al was as yet unhanged.

He found Quayle in the same private solarium, and thirsty. Burkhalter ordered a couple of dramzowies sent up, since he had no objection to loosening Quayle's inhibitions. The gray-haired author was immersed in a sectional historical globe-map, illuminating each epochal layer in turn as he searched back through time.

"Watch this," he said, running his hand along the row of buttons. "See how the German border fluctuates?" It fluctuated, finally vanishing entirely as semimodern times were reached. "And Portugal. Notice its zone of influence? Now—" The zone shrank steadily from 1600 on, while other countries shot out radiating lines and assumed sea power.

Burkhalter sipped his dramzowie. "Not much of that now."

"No, since . . . what's the matter?"

"How do you mean?"

"You look shot."

"I didn't know I showed it," Burkhalter said wryly. "I just finagled my way out of a duel."

"That's one custom I never saw much sense to," Quayle said. "What happened? Since when can you finagle out?"

Burkhalter explained, and the writer took a drink and snorted. "What a spot for you. Being a Baldy isn't such an advantage after all, I guess."

"It has distinct disadvantages at times." On impulse Burkhalter mentioned his son. "You see my point, eh? I don't *know*, really, what standards to apply to a young Baldy. He is a mutation, after all. And the telepathic mutation hasn't had time to work out yet. We can't rig up controls, because guinea pigs and rabbits won't breed telepaths. That's been tried, you know. And—well, the child of a Baldy needs very special training so he can cope with his ultimate maturity."

"You seem to have adjusted well enough."

"I've—learned. As most sensible Baldies have. That's why I'm not a wealthy man, or in politics. We're really buying safety for our species by foregoing certain individual advantages. Hostages to destiny—and destiny spares us. But we get paid too, in a way. In the coinage of future benefits— negative benefits, really, for we ask only to be spared and accepted—and so we have to deny ourselves a lot of present, positive benefits. An appeasement to fate."

"Paying the piper," Quayle nodded.

"We are the pipers. The Baldies as a group, I mean. And our children. So it balances; we're really paying ourselves. If I wanted to take unfair advantage of my telepathic power—my son wouldn't live very long. The Baldies would be wiped out. Al's got to learn that, and he's getting pretty antisocial."

"All children are antisocial," Quayle pointed out. "They're utter individualists. I should think the only reason for worrying would be if the boy's deviation from the norm were connected with his telepathic sense."

"There's something in that." Burkhalter reached out left-handedly and probed delicately at Quayle's mind, noting that the antagonism was considerably lessened. He grinned to himself and went on talking about his own troubles. "Just the same, the boy's father to the man. And an adult Baldy has got to be pretty well adjusted, or he's sunk."

"Environment is as important as heredity. One complements the other. If a child's reared correctly, he won't have much trouble—unless heredity is involved."

"As it may be. There's so little known about the telepathic mutation. If baldness is one secondary characteristic, maybe—something else— emerges in the third or fourth generations. I'm wondering if telepathy is really good for the mind."

Quayle said, "Humph. Speaking personally, it makes me nervous—"

"Like Reilly."

"Yes," Quayle said, but he didn't care much for the comparison. "Well —anyhow, if a mutation's a failure, it'll die out. It won't breed true."

"What about hemophilia?"

"How many people have hemophilia?" Quayle asked. "I'm trying to look at it from the angle of psychohistorian. If there'd been telepaths in the past, things might have been different."

"How do you know there weren't?" Burkhalter asked.

Quayle blinked. "Oh. Well. That's true, too. In medieval times they'd have been called wizards—or saints. The Duke-Rhine experiments—but such accidents would have been abortive. Nature fools around trying to hit the . . . ah . . . the jackpot, and she doesn't always do it on the first try."

"She may not have done it now." That was habit speaking, the ingrained caution of modesty. "Telepathy may be merely a semisuccessful try at something pretty unimaginable. A sort of four-dimensional sensory concept, maybe."

"That's too abstract for me." Quayle was interested, and his own hesitancies had almost vanished; by accepting Burkhalter as a telepath, he had tacitly wiped away his objections to telepathy *per se*. "The old-time Germans always had an idea they were different; so did the . . . ah . . . what was that Oriental race? They had the islands off the China coast."

"The Japanese," said Burkhalter, who had a good memory for trifles.

"Yes. They knew, very definitely, that they were a superior race because they were directly descended from gods. They were short in stature; heredity made them self-conscious when dealing with larger races. But the Chinese aren't tall, the Southern Chinese, and they weren't handicapped in that way."

"Environment, then?"

"Environment, which caused propaganda. The . . . ah . . . the Japanese took Buddhism, and altered it completely into Shinto, to suit their own needs. The samurai, warrior-knights, were the ideals; the code of honor was fascinatingly cockeyed. The principle of Shinto was to worship your superiors and subjugate your inferiors. Ever seen the Japanese jewel-trees?"

"I don't remember them. What are they?"

"Miniature replicas of espaliered trees, made of jewels, with trinkets hanging on the branches. Including a mirror—always. The first jewel-tree was made to lure the Moon-goddess out of a cave where she was sulking. It seems the lady was so intrigued by the trinkets and by her face reflected in the mirror that she came out of her hideout. All the Japanese morals were dressed up in pretty clothes; that was the bait. The old-time Germans did much the same thing. The last German dictator, Poor Hitler they called him—I forget why, but there was some reason—he revived the old Siegfried legend. It was racial paranoia. The Germans worshiped the house-tyrant, not the mother, and they had extremely strong family ties. That extended to the state. They symbolized Poor Hitler as their All-Father, and so eventually we got the Blowup. And, finally, mutations."

"After the deluge, me," Burkhalter murmured, finishing his dramzowie. Quayle was staring at nothing.

"Funny," he said after a while. "This All-Father business—"

"Yes?"

"I wonder if you know how powerfully it can affect a man?"

Burkhalter didn't say anything. Quayle gave him a sharp glance.

"Yes," the writer said quietly. "You're a man, after all. I owe you an apology, you know."

Burkhalter smiled. "You can forget that."

"I'd rather not," Quayle said. "I've just realized, pretty suddenly, that the telepathic sense isn't so important. I mean—it doesn't make you *different*. I've been talking to you—"

"Sometimes it takes people years before they realize what you're finding out," Burkhalter remarked. "Years of living and working with something they think of as a Baldy."

"Do you know what I've been concealing in my mind?" Quayle asked.

"No. I don't."

"You lie like a gentleman. Thanks. Well, here it is, and I'm telling you by choice, because I want to. I don't care if you got the information out of my mind already; I just want to tell you of my own free will. My father . . . I imagine I hated him . . . was a tyrant, and I remember one time, when I was just a kid and we were in the mountains, he beat me and a lot of people were looking on. I've tried to forget that for a long time. Now"—Quayle shrugged—"it doesn't seem quite so important."

"I'm not a psychologist," Burkhalter said. "If you want my personal reaction, I'll just say that it doesn't matter. You're not a little boy any more, and the guy I'm talking to and working with is the adult Quayle."

"Hm-m-m. Ye-es. I suppose I knew that all along—how unimportant it was, really. It was simply having my privacy violated. . . . I think I know you better now, Burkhalter. You can—walk in."

"We'll work better," Burkhalter said, grinning. "Especially with Darius."

Quayle said, "I'll try not to keep any reservation in my mind. Frankly, I won't mind telling you—the answers. Even when they're personal."

"Check on that. D'you want to tackle Darius now?"

"O. K.," Quayle said, and his eyes no longer held suspicious wariness. "Darius I identify with my father—"

It was smooth and successful. That afternoon they accomplished more than they had during the entire previous fortnight. Warm with satisfaction on more than one point, Burkhalter stopped off to tell Dr. Moon that matters were looking up, and then set out toward home, exchanging thoughts with a couple of Baldies, his co-workers, who were knocking off for the day. The Rockies were bloody with the western light, and the coolness of the wind was pleasant on Burkhalter's cheeks, as he hiked homeward.

It was fine to be accepted. It proved that it could be done. And a Baldy often needed reassurance, in a world peopled by suspicious strangers. Quayle had been a hard nut to crack, but—Burkhalter smiled.

Ethel would be pleased. In a way, she'd had a harder time than he'd ever had. A woman would, naturally. Men were desperately anxious to keep their privacy unviolated by a woman, and as for non-Baldy women— well, it spoke highly for Ethel's glowing personal charm that she had finally been accepted by the clubs and feminine groups of Modoc. Only Burkhalter knew Ethel's desperate hurt at being bald, and not even her husband had ever seen her unwigged.

His thought reached out before him into the low, double-winged house on the hillside, and interlocked with hers in a warm intimacy. It was something more than a kiss. And, as always, there was the exciting sense of expectancy, mounting and mounting till the last door swung open and they touched physically. *This,* he thought, *is why I was born a Baldy; this is worth losing worlds for.*

At dinner that rapport spread out to embrace Al, an intangible, deeply-rooted something that made the food taste better and the water like wine. The word *home,* to telepaths, had a meaning that non-Baldies could not entirely comprehend, for it embraced a bond they could not know. There were small, intangible caresses.

Green Man going down the Great Red Slide; the Shaggy Dwarfs trying to harpoon him as he goes.

"Al," Ethel said, "are you still working on your Green Man?"

Then something utterly hateful and cold and deadly quivered silently in the air, like an icicle jaggedly smashing through golden, fragile glass. Burkhalter dropped his napkin and looked up, profoundly shocked. He felt Ethel's thought shrink back, and swiftly reached out to touch and reassure her with mental contact. But across the table the little boy, his cheeks still round with the fat of babyhood, sat silent and wary, realizing he had blundered, and seeking safety in complete immobility. His mind was too weak to resist probing, he knew, and he remained perfectly still, waiting, while the echoes of a thought hung poisonously in silence.

Burkhalter said, "Come on, Al." He stood up. Ethel started to speak.

"Wait, darling. Put up a barrier. Don't listen in." He touched her mind gently and tenderly, and then he took Al's hand and drew the boy after him out into the yard. Al watched his father out of wide, alert eyes.

Burkhalter sat on a bench and put Al beside him. He talked audibly at first, for clarity's sake, and for another reason. It was distinctly unpleasant to trick the boy's feeble guards down, but it was necessary.

"That's a very queer way to think of your mother," he said. "It's a queer way to think of me." Obscenity is more obscene, profanity more profane, to a telepathic mind, but this had been neither one. It had been— cold and malignant.

And this is flesh of my flesh, Burkhalter thought, looking at the boy and remembering the eight years of his growth. *Is the mutation to turn into something devilish?*

Al was silent.

Burkhalter reached into the young mind. Al tried to twist free and escape, but his father's strong hands gripped him. Instinct, not reasoning, on the boy's part, for minds can touch over long distances.

He did not like to do this, for increased sensibility had gone with sensitivity, and violations are always violations. But ruthlessness was required. Burkhalter searched. Sometimes he threw key words violently at Al, and surges of memory pulsed up in response.

In the end, sick and nauseated, Burkhalter let Al go and sat alone on the bench, watching the red light die on the snowy peaks. The whiteness was red-stained. But it was not too late. The man was a fool, had been a fool from the beginning, or he would have known the impossibility of attempting such a thing as this.

The conditioning had only begun. Al could be reconditioned. Burkhalter's eyes hardened. And would be. *And would be.* But not yet, not until the immediate furious anger had given place to sympathy and understanding.

Not yet.

He went into the house, spoke briefly to Ethel, and televised the dozen Baldies who worked with him in the Publishing Center. Not all of them had families, but none was missing when, half an hour later, they met in the back room of the Pagan Tavern downtown. Sam Shane had caught a fragment of Burkhalter's knowledge, and all of them read his emotions. Welded into a sympathetic unit by their telepathic sense, they waited till Burkhalter was ready.

Then he told them. It didn't take long, via thought. He told them about the Japanese jewel-tree with its glittering gadgets, a shining lure. He told them of racial paranoia and propaganda. And that the most effective propaganda was sugar-coated, disguised so that the motive was hidden.

A Green Man, hairless, heroic—symbolic of a Baldy.

And wild, exciting adventures, the lure to catch the young fish whose plastic minds were impressionable enough to be led along the roads of dangerous madness. Adult Baldies could listen, but they did not; young telepaths had a higher threshold of mental receptivity, and adults do not read the books of their children except to reassure themselves that there is nothing harmful in the pages. And no adult would bother to listen to the Green Man mindcast. Most of them had accepted it as the original daydream of their own children.

"I did," Shane put in. "My girls—"

"Trace it back," Burkhalter said. "I did."

The dozen minds reached out on the higher frequency, the children's wavelength, and something jerked away from them, startled and apprehensive.

"He's the one," Shane nodded.

They did not need to speak. They went out of the Pagan Tavern in a compact, ominous group, and crossed the street to the general store. The door was locked. Two of the men burst it open with their shoulders.

They went through the dark store and into a back room where a man was standing beside an overturned chair. His bald skull gleamed in an overhead light. His mouth worked impotently.

His thought pleaded with them—was driven back by an implacable deadly wall.

Burkhalter took out his dagger. Other slivers of steel glittered for a little while—

And were quenched.

Venner's scream had long since stopped, but his dying thought of agony lingered within Burkhalter's mind as he walked homeward. The wigless Baldy had not been insane, no. But he had been paranoidal.

What he had tried to conceal, at the last, was quite shocking. A tremendous, tyrannical egotism, and a furious hatred of nontelepaths. A feeling of self-justification that was, perhaps, insane. *And—we are the Future! The Baldies! God made us to rule lesser men!*

Burkhalter sucked in his breath, shivering. The mutation had not been entirely successful. One group had adjusted, the Baldies who wore wigs and had become fitted to their environment. One group had been insane, and could be discounted; they were in asylums.

But the middle group were merely paranoid. They were not insane, and they were not sane. They wore no wigs.

Like Venner.

And Venner had sought disciples. His attempt had been foredoomed to failure, but he had been one man.

One Baldy—paranoid.

There were others, many others.

Ahead, nestled into the dark hillside, was the pale blotch that marked Burkhalter's home. He sent his thought ahead, and it touched Ethel's and paused very briefly to reassure her.

Then it thrust on, and went into the sleeping mind of a little boy who, confused and miserable, had finally cried himself to sleep. There were only dreams in that mind now, a little discolored, a little stained, but they could be cleansed. And would be.

CLEVE CARTMILL

DEADLINE

PUBLISHER'S NOTE: Deadline appeared in the March, 1944 issue of *Astounding Science-Fiction.* Within a few days agents of the Military Intelligence approached the author and the office of the magazine demanding to know who, on the Manhattan Project, had been talking. It was explained that the technical data was based upon principles published in technical papers in 1940. As the Smyth Report says, "Looking back on the year 1940, we see that all the prerequisites to a serious attack on the problem of producing and controlling atomic power were at hand." The Military Intelligence was persuaded that to suppress such discussions of atomic energy as had consistently appeared in this magazine would be more of a give-away than to leave them alone. Mr. Campbell, its editor, is quick to point out that the "bomb" as detailed in the story would not work. There follows, however, a further excerpt from the Smyth Report sufficiently documenting the basic principle involved.

DETONATION AND ASSEMBLY

12.16. As stated in Chapter II, it is impossible to prevent a chain reaction from occurring when the size exceeds the critical size. For there are always enough neutrons (from cosmic rays, from spontaneous fission reactions, or from alpha-particle-induced reactions in impurities) to initiate the chain. Thus until detonation is desired, the bomb must consist of a number of separate pieces each one of which is below the critical size either by reason of small size or unfavorable shape. To produce detonation, the parts of the bomb must be brought together rapidly. In the course of this assembly process the chain reaction is likely to start—because of the presence of stray neutrons—before the bomb has reached its most compact

*(most reactive) form. Thereupon the explosion tends to prevent the bomb
from reaching that most compact form. Thus it may turn out that the
explosion is so inefficient as to be relatively useless. The problem, therefore,
is two-fold: (1) to reduce the time of assembly to a minimum; and (2) to
reduce the number of stray (predetonation) neutrons to a minimum.*

Official Report: *Atomic Energy for Military Purposes*

Henry D. Smyth

HEAVY FLAK burst above and below the flight of bombers as they
flashed across the night sky of the planet Cathor. Ybor Sebrof grinned
as he nosed his glider at a steep angle away from the fireworks. The
bombers had accomplished their mission: they had dropped him near
Nilreq, had simulated a raid.

He had cut loose before searchlights slatted the sky with lean, white
arms. They hadn't touched the glider, marked with their own insignia.
Their own glider, in fact, captured when Seilla advance columns had caught
the Namo garrison asleep. He would leave it where he landed, and let Sixa
intelligence try to figure out how it got there.

Provided, of course, that he landed unseen.

Sixa intelligence officers would have another job, too. That was to
explain the apparent bombing raid that dropped no bombs. None of the
Seilla planes had been hit, and the Sixa crowd couldn't know that the
bombers were empty: no bombs, no crews, just speed.

He could see tomorrow's papers, hear tomorrow's newscasts. "Raiders
driven off. Craven Democracy pilots cringe from Nilreq ack-ack." But the
big bugs would worry. The Seilla planes *could* have dropped bombs, if
they'd had any bombs. They had flitted across the great industrial city
with impunity. They could have laid their eggs. The big bugs would wonder
about that. Why? they would ask each other profoundly. What was the
reason?

Ybor grinned. He was the reason. He'd make them wish there *had* been
bombs instead of him. Possibility of failure never entered his mind. All he
had to do was to penetrate into the stronghold of the enemy, find Dr. Sitruc,
kill him, and destroy the most devastating weapon of history. That was
all.

He caught a sharp breath as a farmhouse loomed some distance ahead.
and veered over against the dark edge of a wood. The green-gray plane
would be invisible against the background, unless keen eyes caught its
shadow under a fugitive moon.

He glided silently now, on a little wind that gossiped with tree-tops.
Only the wind and the trees remarked on his passing. They could keep the
secret.

He landed in a field of grain that whispered fierce protest as the glider
whished through its heavy-laden plumes. These waved above the level of

the motorless ship, and Ybor decided that it would not be seen before harvesting machines gathered the grain.

The air was another problem. He did not want the glider discovered just yet, particularly if he should be intercepted on his journey into the enemy capital. Elementary intelligence would connect him with this abandoned ship if he were stopped in this vicinity for any reason, and if the ship should be discovered on the morrow.

He took a long knife from its built-in sheath in the glider and laid about him with it until he had cut several armloads of grain. He scattered these haphazardly—not in any pattern—over parts of the ship. It wouldn't look like a glider now, even from the air.

He pushed through the shoulder-high growth to the edge of the wood.

He moved stealthily here. It was almost a certainty that big guns were hidden here, and he must avoid discovery. He slipped along the soft carpet of vegetation like a nocturnal cat, running on all fours under low branches, erect when possible.

A sharp scent of danger assailed his nostrils, and he crouched motionless while he sifted this odor. It made a picture in his head: men, and oil, and the acrid smoke of exploded gases. A gun crew was directly ahead.

Ybor took to the trees. He moved from one to the other, with no more sound than soft-winged night birds, and approached the source of the odor. He paused now and then, listening for a sentry's footsteps. He heard them presently, a soft *pad-pad* which mingled, in different rhythm, with snores which became audible on the light wind.

The better part of valor, Ybor knew, was to circle this place, to leave the sentry unaware of his passage through the wood. But habit was too strong. He must destroy, for they were the enemy.

He moved closer to the sound of footsteps. Presently, he crouched above the line of the sentry's march, searching the darkness with eye and ear. The guard passed below, and Ybor let him go. His ears strained through snores from nearby tents until he heard another guard. Two were on sentry duty.

He pulled the knife from his belt and waited. When the sentry shuffled below him, Ybor dropped soundlessly onto the man's shoulders, stabbing as he fell.

There was a little noise. Not much, but a little. Enough to bring a low-voiced hail from the other guard.

"Namreh?" called the guard. "What happened?"

Ybor grunted, took the dead man's gun and helmet and took over his beat. He marched with the same rhythm the enemy feet had maintained until he met the second guard. Ybor silenced questions with a swift slash of the knife, and then turned his attention to the tents.

Presently, it was done. He clamped the fingers of the first guard around the knife hilt and went away. Let them think that one of their men had gone mad and killed the others before suiciding. Let the psychologists get a little work-out on this.

When he had penetrated to the far edge of the wood, dawn had splashed pale color beyond Nilreq, pulling jumbled buildings into dark silhouette. There lay his area of operations. There, perhaps, lay his destiny, and the destiny of the whole race.

This latter thought was not born of rhetorical hyperbole. It was cold, hard fact. It had nothing to do with patriotism, nor was it concerned with politico-economic philosophy. It was concerned with a scientific fact only: if the weapon, which was somewhere in the enemy capital, were used, the entire race might very well perish down to the last man.

Now began the difficult part of Ybor's task. He started to step out of the wood. A slight sound from behind froze him for the fraction of a second while he identified it. Then, in one incredibly swift motion, he whirled and flung himself at its source.

He knew he was fighting a woman after the first instant of contact. He was startled to some small extent, but not enough to impair his efficiency. A chopping blow, and she lay unconscious at his feet. He stood over her with narrowed eyes, unable to see what she looked like in the leafy gloom.

Then dawn burst like a salvo in the east, and he saw that she was young. Not immature, by any means, but young. When a spear of sunlight stabbed into the shadow, he saw that she was lovely.

Ybor pulled out his combat knife. She was an enemy, and must be destroyed. He raised his arm for the *coup de grace,* and held it there. He could not drive the blade into her. She seemed only to sleep, in her unconsciousness, with parted ripe lips and limp hands. You could kill a man while he slept, but Nature had planted a deep aversion in your instincts to killing a helpless female.

She began to moan softly. Presently she opened her wide brown eyes, soft as a captive fawn's.

"You hit me." She whispered the accusation.

Ybor said nothing.

"You hit me," she repeated.

"What did you expect?" he asked harshly. "Candy and flowers? What are you doing here?"

"Following you," she answered. "May I get up?"

"Yes. Why were you following?"

"When I saw you land in our field, I wondered why. I ran out to see you cover your ship and slip into the woods. I followed."

Ybor was incredulous. "You followed me through those woods?"

"I could have touched you," she said. "Any time."

"You lie!"

"Don't feel chagrined," she said. She flowed to her feet in a liquid movement. Her eyes were almost on a level with his. Her smile showed small, white teeth. "I'm very good at that sort of thing," she said. "Better than almost anybody, though I admit you're no slouch."

"Thanks," he said shortly. "All right, let's hear the story. Most likely it'll be the last you'll ever tell. What's your game?"

"You speak Ynamren like a native," the girl said.

Ybor's eyes glinted. "I am a native."

She smiled her disbelief. "And you kill your own soldiers? I think not. I saw you wipe out that gun crew. There was too much objectivity about you. One of us would do it with hatred. For you, it was a tactical maneuver."

"You're cutting your own throat," Ybor warned. "I can't let you go. You're too observing."

She repeated, "I think not." After a pause, she said, "You'll need help, whatever your mission. I can offer it."

He was contemptuous. "You offer my head a lion's mouth. I can hide it there? I need no help. Especially from anybody clumsy enough to be caught. And I've caught you, my pretty."

She flushed. "You were about to storm a rampart. I saw it in your odd face as you stared toward Nilreq. I caught my breath with hope that you could. That's what you heard. If I'd thought you were my enemy, you'd have heard nothing. Except, maybe, the song of my knife blade as it reached your heart."

"What's odd about my face?" he demanded. "It'd pass in a crowd without notice."

"Women would notice it," she said. "It's lopsided."

He shrugged aside the personal issue. He took her throat in his hands. "I have to do this," he said. "It's highly important that nobody knows of my presence here. This is war. I can't afford to be humane."

She offered no resistance. Quietly, she looked up at him and asked, "Have you heard of Ylas?"

His fingers did not close on the soft flesh. "Who has not?"

"I am Ylas," she said.

"A trick."

"No trick. Let me show you." As his eyes narrowed—"No, I have no papers, of course. Listen. You know Mulb, Sworb, and Nomos? I got them away."

Ybor hesitated. She could be Ylas, but it would be a fantastic stroke of luck to run into the fabulous director of Ynamre's underground so soon. It was almost beyond belief. Yet, there was a chance she was telling the truth. He couldn't overlook that chance.

"Names," he said. "You could have heard them anywhere."

"Nomos has a new-moon scar on his wrist," she said. "Sworb is tall, almost as tall as you, and his shoulders droop slightly. He talks so fast you can hardly follow. Mulb is a dope. He gets by on his pontifical manner."

These, Ybor reflected, were crisp thumbnail sketches.

She pressed her advantage. "Would I have stood by while you killed that gun crew if I were a loyal member of the Sixa Alliance? Wouldn't I have cried a warning when you killed the first guard and took his helmet and gun?"

There was logic in this, Ybor thought.

"Wasn't it obvious to me," she went on, "that you were a Seilla agent from the moment that you landed in my grain field? I could have telephoned the authorities."

Ybor took his hands from her throat. "I want to see Dr. Sitruc," he said.

She frowned off toward Nilreq, at towers golden in morning sunlight. Ybor noted indifferently that she made a colorful picture with her face to the sun. A dark flower, opening toward the dawn. Not that it mattered. He had no time for her. He had little time for anything.

"That will take some doing," she said.

He turned away. "Then I'll do it myself. Time is short."

"Wait!" Her voice had a quality which caused him to turn. He smiled sourly at the gun in her hand.

Self-contempt blackened Ybor's thoughts. He had had her helpless, but he had thought of her as a woman, not as an armed enemy. He hadn't searched her because of callow sentimentality. He had scaled the heights of stupidity, and now would plunge to his deserved end. Her gun was steady, and purpose shone darkly in her eyes.

"I'm a pushover for a fairy tale," she said. "I thought for a while that you really were a Seilla agent. How fiendishly clever you are, you and your council! I should have known when those planes went over. They went too fast."

Ybor said nothing. He was trying to absorb this.

"It was a smart idea," she went on in her acid, bitter voice. "They towed you over, and you landed in my field. A coincidence, when you come to think of it. I have been in that farmhouse only three days. Of all places, you pick it. Not by accident, not so. You and the other big minds on the Sixa council knew the planes would bring me to my window, knew my eyes would catch the shadow of your glider, knew I'd investigate. You even killed six of your own men, to dull my suspicions. Oh, I was taken in for a while."

"You talk like a crazy woman," Ybor said. "Put away that gun."

"When you had a chance to kill me and didn't," she said, "my last suspicion died. The more fool I. No, my bucko, you are not going back to report my whereabouts, to have your goons wait until my committee meets and catch us all. Not so. You die here and now."

Thoughts raced through Ybor's head. It would be a waste of energy to appeal to her on the ground that if she killed him she would in effect destroy her species. That smacked of oratory. He needed a simple appeal, crisp and startling. But what? His time was running short; he could see it in her dark eyes.

"Your last address," he said, remembering Sworb's tale of escape, "was 4c Curk Way. You sold pastries, and Sworb got sick on little cakes. He was sick in your truck, as it carted him away at eleven minutes past midnight."

Bull's eye. Determination to kill went out of her eyes as she remembered. She was thoughtful for a moment.

Then her eyes glinted. "I've not heard that he reached Acireb safely. You could have caught him across the Enarta border and beaten the truth out of him. Still," she reflected, "you may be telling the truth . . ."

"I am," Ybor said quietly. "I am a Seilla agent, here on a highly important mission. If you can't aid me directly, you must let me go. At once."

"You might be lying, too, though. I can't take the chance. You will march ahead of me around the wood. If you make one overt move, or even a move that I don't understand, I'll kill you."

"Where are you taking me?"

"To my house. Where else? Then we'll talk."

"Now listen to me," he said passionately, "there is no time for—"

"March!"

He marched.

Ybor's plan to take her unawares when they were inside the farmhouse dissolved when he saw the great hulk who admitted them. This was a lumpish brute with the most powerful body Ybor had ever seen, towering over his own more than average height. The man's arms were as thick as Ybor's thighs, and the yellow eyes were small and vicious. Yet, apelike though he was, the giant moved like a mountain cat, without sound, with deceptive swiftness.

"Guard him," the girl commanded, and Ybor knew the yellow eyes would not leave him.

He sank into a chair, an old chair with a primitive tail slot, and watched the girl as she busied herself at the mountainous cooking range. This kitchen could accommodate a score of farmhands, and that multiple-burner stove could turn out hot meals for all.

"We'd better eat," she said. "If you're not lying, you'll need strength. If you are, you can withstand torture long enough to tell us the truth."

"You're making a mistake," Ybor began hotly, but stopped when the guard made a menacing gesture.

She had a meal on the table soon. It was a good meal, and he ate it heartily. "The condemned man," he said, and smiled.

For a camaraderie had sprung up between them. He was male, not too long past his youth, with clear, dark eyes, and he was put together with an eye to efficiency; and she was a female, at the ripening stage. The homely task of preparing a meal, of sharing it, lessened the tension between them. She gave him a fleeting, occasional smile as he tore into his food.

"You're a good cook," he said, when they had finished.

Warmth went out of her. She eyed him steadily. "Now," she said crisply. "Proof."

Ybor shrugged angrily. "Do you think I carry papers identifying me as a Seilla agent? 'To whom it may concern, bearer is high in Seilla councils. Any aid you may give him will be appreciated.' I have papers showing that I'm a newspaper man from Eeras. The newspaper offices and building have been destroyed by now, and there is no means of checking."

She thought this over. "I'm going to give you a chance," she said. "If you're a top-flight Seilla agent, one of your Nilreq men can identify you. Name one, and we'll get him here."

"None of them know me by sight. My face was altered before I came on this assignment, so that nobody could give me away, even accidentally."

"You know all the answers, don't you?" she scoffed. "Well, we will now take you into the cellar and get the truth from you. And you won't die until we do. We'll keep you alive, one way or another."

"Wait a moment," Ybor said. "There is one man who will know me. He may not have arrived. Solraq."

"He came yesterday," she said. "Very well. If he identifies you, that will be good enough. Sleyg," she said to the huge guard, "fetch Solraq."

Sleyg rumbled deep in his throat, and she made an impatient gesture. "I can take care of myself. Go!" She reached inside her blouse, took her gun from its shoulder holster and pointed it across the table at Ybor. "You will sit still."

Sleyg went out. Ybor heard a car start, and the sound of its motor faded rapidly.

"May I smoke?" Ybor asked.

"Certainly." With her free hand she tossed a pack of cigarettes across the table. He lighted one, careful to keep his hand in sight, handed it to her, and applied flame to his own. "So you're Ylas," he said conversationally.

She didn't bother to reply.

"You've done a good job," he went on. "Right under their noses. You must have had some close calls."

She smiled tolerantly. "Don't be devious, chum. On the off chance that you might escape, I'll give you no data to use later."

"There won't be any later if I don't get out of here. For you, or anybody."

"Now you're melodramatic. There'll always be a later, as long as there's time."

"Time exists only in consciousness," he said. "There won't be any time, unless dust and rocks are aware of it."

"That's quite a picture of destruction you paint."

"It will be quite a destruction. And you're bringing it nearer every minute. You're cutting down the time margin in which it can be averted."

She grinned. "Ain't I nasty?"

"Even if you let me go this moment—" he began.

"Which I won't."

"—the catastrophe might not be averted. Our minds can't conceive the unimaginable violence which might very well destroy all animate life. It's a queer picture," he mused, "even to think about. Imagine space travelers of the future sighting this planet empty of life, overgrown with jungles. It wouldn't even have a name. Oh, they'd find the name. All traces of civilization wouldn't be completely destroyed. They'd poke in the crumbled ruins and find bits of history. Then they'd go back to their home planet with the mystery of Cathor. Why did all life disappear from Cathor? They'd find skeletons enough to show our size and shape, and they'd decipher such records as were found. But nowhere would they find even a hint of the reason our civilization was destroyed. Nowhere would they find the name of Ylas, the reason."

She merely grinned.

"That's how serious it is," Ybor concluded. "Not a bird in the sky, not a pig in a sty. Perhaps no insects, even. I wonder," he said thoughtfully, "if such explosions destroyed life in other planets in our system. Lara, for example. It _had_ life, once. Did civilization rise to a peak there, and end in a war that involved every single person on one side or another? Did one side, in desperation, try to use an explosive available to both but uncontrollable, and so lose the world?"

"_Shh!_" she commanded. She was stiff, listening.

He heard it then, the rhythmic tramp of feet. He flicked a glance through the window toward the wood. "Ynamre," he said.

A sergeant marched a squad of eight soldiers across the field toward the house. Ybor turned to the girl.

"You've got to hide me! Quick!"

She stared at him coldly. "I have no place."

"You must have. You must take care of refugees. Where is it?"

"Maybe you've caught me," she said grimly, "but you'll learn nothing. The Underground will carry on."

"You little fool! I'm with you."

"That's what you say. I haven't any proof."

Ybor wasted no more time. The squad was almost at the door. He leaped over against the wall and squatted there. He pulled his coat half off, shook his black hair over his eyes, and slacked his face so that it took on the loose, formless expression of an idiot. He began to play with his fingers, and gurgled.

A pounding rifle butt took the girl to the door. Ybor did not look up. He twisted his fingers and gurgled at them.

"Did you hear anything last night?" the sergeant demanded.

"Anything?" she echoed. "Some planes, some guns."

"Did you get up? Did you look out?"

"I was afraid," she answered meekly.

He spat contemptuously. There was a short silence, disturbed only by Ybor's gurgling.

"What's that?" the sergeant snapped. He stamped across the room, jerked Ybor's head up by the lock of hair. Ybor gave him an insane, slobbering grin. The sergeant's eyes were contemptuous. "Dummy!" he snarled. He jerked his hand away. "Why don't you kill it?" he asked the girl. "All the more food for you. Sa-a-a-y," he said, as if he'd seen her for the first time, "not bad, not bad. I'll be up to see you, cookie, one of these nights."

Ybor didn't move until they were out of hearing. He got to his feet then, and looked grimly at Ylas. "I could have been in Nilreq by now. You'll have to get me away. They've discovered that gun crew, and will be on the lookout."

She had the gun in her hand again. She motioned him toward the chair. "Shall we sit down?"

"After that? You're still suspicious? You're a fool."

"Ah? I think not. That could have been a part of the trick, to lull my suspicions. Sit—down!"

He sat. He was through with talking. He thought of the soldiers' visit. That sergeant probably wouldn't recognize him if they should encounter each other. Still, it was something to keep in mind. One more face to remember, to dodge.

If only that big ape would get back with Solraq. His ears, as if on cue, caught the sound of an approaching motor. He was gratified to see that he heard it a full second before Ylas. Her reflexes weren't so fast, after all.

It was Sleyg, and Sleyg alone. He came into the house on his soft, cat feet. "Solraq," he reported, "is dead. Killed last night."

Ylas gave Ybor a smile. There was deadliness in it.

"How very convenient," she said, "for you. Doesn't it seem odd even to you, Mr. Sixa Intelligence Officer, that of all the Seilla agents you pick a man who is dead? I think this has gone far enough. Into the cellar with him, Sleyg. We'll get the truth this time. Even," she added to Ybor, "though it'll kill you."

The chair was made like a strait jacket, with an arrangement of clamps and straps that held him completely motionless. He could move nothing but his eyeballs.

Ylas inspected him. She nodded satisfaction. "Go heat your irons," she said to Sleyg. "First," she explained to Ybor, "we'll burn off your ears, a little at a time. If that doesn't wear you down, we'll get serious."

Ybor said, "I'll tell you the truth now."

She sneered at that. "No wonder the enemy is knocking at your gates. You were driven out of Aissu on the south, and Ytal on the north. Now you are coming into your home country, because you're cowards."

"I'm convinced that you are Ylas," Ybor went on calmly. "And though my orders were that nobody should know of my mission, I think I can tell you. I must. I have no choice. Then listen. I was sent to Ynamre to—"

She cut him off with a fierce gesture. "The truth!"

"Do you want to hear this or not?"

"I don't want to hear another fairy tale."

"You are going to hear this, whether you like it or not. And you'll hold off your gorilla until I've finished. Or have the end of the race on your head."

Her lip curled. "Go on."

"Have you heard of U-235? It's an isotope of uranium."

"Who hasn't?"

"All right. I'm stating fact, not theory. U-235 has been separated in quantity easily sufficient for preliminary atomic-power research, and the like. They got it out of uranium ores by new atomic isotope separation methods; they now have quantities measured in pounds. By 'they,' I mean Seilla research scientists. But they have *not* brought the whole amount together, or any major portion of it. Because they are not at all sure that, once started, it would stop before all of it had been consumed—in something like one micromicrosecond of time."

Sleyg came into the cellar. In one hand he carried a portable forge. In the other, a bundle of metal rods. Ylas motioned him to put them down in a corner. "Go up and keep watch," she ordered. "I'll call you."

A tiny exultation flickered in Ybor. He had won a concession. "Now the explosion of a pound of U-235," he said, "wouldn't be too unbearably violent, though it releases as much energy as a hundred million pounds of TNT. Set off on an island, it might lay waste the whole island, uprooting trees, killing all animal life, but even that fifty thousand tons of TNT wouldn't seriously disturb the really unimaginable tonnage which even a small island represents."

"I assume," she broke in, "that you're going to make a point? You're not just giving me a lecture on high explosives?"

"Wait. The trouble is, they're afraid that that explosion of energy would be so incomparably violent, its sheer, minute concentration of unbearable energy so great, that surrounding matter would be set off. If you could imagine concentrating half a billion of the most violent lightning strokes you ever saw, compressing all their fury into a space less than half the size of a pack of cigarettes—you'd get some idea of the concentrated essence of hyperviolence that explosion would represent. It's not simply the *amount* of energy; it's the frightful concentration of intensity in a minute volume.

"The surrounding matter, unable to maintain a self-supporting atomic explosion normally, might be hyper-stimulated to atomic explosion under U-235's forces and, in the immediate neighborhood, release its energy, too. That is, the explosion would not involve only one pound of U-235, but also five or fifty or five thousand tons of other matter. The extent of the explosion is a matter of conjecture."

"Get to the point," she said impatiently.

"Wait. Let me give you the main picture. Such an explosion *would* be serious. It would blow an island, or a hunk of continent, right off the planet. It would shake Cathor from pole to pole, cause earthquakes violent enough to do serious damage on the other side of the planet, and utterly destroy everything within at least one thousand miles of the site of the explosion. And I mean everything.

"So they haven't experimented. They could end the war overnight with controlled U-235 bombs. They could end this cycle of civilization with one or two *uncontrolled* bombs. And they don't know which they'd have if they made 'em. So far, they haven't worked out any way to control the explosion of U-235."

"If you're stalling for time," Ylas said, "it won't do you any good, personally. If we have callers, I'll shoot you where you sit."

"Stalling?" Ybor cried. "I'm trying my damnedest to shorten it. I'm not finished yet. Please don't interrupt. I want to give you the rest of the picture. As you pointed out the Sixa armies are being pushed back to their original starting point: Ynamre. They started out to conquer the world, and they came close, at one time. But now they are about to lose it. We, the Seilla, would not dare to set off an experimental atomic bomb. This war is a phase, to us; to the Sixa, it is the whole future. So the Sixa are desperate, and Dr. Sitruc has made a bomb with not one, but *sixteen* pounds of U-235 in it. He may have it finished any day. I must find him and destroy that bomb. If it's used, we are lost either way. Lost the war, if the experiment is a success; the world, if not. You, and you alone stand between extinction of the race and continuance."

She seemed to pounce. "You're lying! Destroy it, you say. How? Take it out in a vacant lot and explode it? In a desert? On a high mountain? You wouldn't dare even to drop it in the ocean, for fear it might explode. Once you had it, you'd have ten million tigers by the tail—you wouldn't dare turn it loose."

"I can destroy it. Our scientists told me how."

"Let that pass for the moment," she said. "You have several points to explain. First, it seems odd that *you* heard of this, and we haven't. We're much closer to developments than you, across three thousand miles of water."

"Sworb," Ybor said, "is a good man, even if he can't eat sweets. He brought back a drawing of it. Listen, Ylas, time is precious! If Dr. Sitruc finishes that bomb before I find him, it may be taken any time and dropped near our headquarters. And even if it doesn't set off the explosion I've described—though it's almost certain that it would—it would wipe out our southern army and equipment, and we'd lose overnight."

"Two more points need explaining," she went on calmly. "Why *my* grain field? There were others to choose from."

"That was pure accident."

"Perhaps. But isn't that string of accidents suspiciously long when you consider the death of Solraq?"

"I don't know anything about that. I didn't know he was dead."

She was silent. She strode back and forth across the cellar, brows furrowed, smoking nervously. Ybor sat quietly. It was all he could do; even his fingers were in stalls.

"I'm half inclined to believe you," she said finally, "but look at my position. We have a powerful organization here. We've risked our lives, and many of us have died, in building it up. I know how we are hated and feared by the authorities. If you are a Sixa agent, and I concluded that you were by the way you spoke the language, you would go to any length, even to carrying out such an elaborate plot as this might be, to discover our methods and membership. I can't risk all that labor and life on nothing but your word."

"Look at my position," Ybor countered. "I might have escaped from you, in the wood and here, after Sleyg left us. But I didn't dare take a chance. You see, it's a matter of time. There is a definite, though unknown, deadline. Dr. Sitruc may finish that bomb any time, and screw the fuse in. The bomb may be taken at any time after that and exploded. If I had tried to escape, and you had shot me—and I'm sure you would—it would take weeks to replace me. We may have only hours to work with."

She was no longer calm and aloof. Her eyes had a tortured look, and her hands clenched as if she were squeezing words from her heart: "I can't afford to take the chance."

"You can't afford not to," Ybor said.

Footsteps suddenly pounded overhead. Ylas went rigid, flung a narrowed glance of speculation and suspicion at Ybor, and went out of the cellar. He twisted a smile; she hadn't shot him, as she had threatened.

He sat still, but each nerve was taut, quivering, and raw. What now? Who had arrived? What could it mean for him? Who belonged to that babble upstairs? Whose feet were heavy? He was soon to know, for the footsteps moved to the cellar door, and Ylas preceded the sergeant who had arrived earlier.

"I've got orders to search every place in this vicinity," the sergeant said, "so shut up."

His eyes widened when they fell on Ybor. "Well, well!" he cried. "If it isn't the dummy. Sa-a-ay, you snapped out of it!"

Ybor caught his breath as an idea hit him.

"I was drugged," Ybor said, leaping at the chance for escape. "It's worn off now."

Ylas frowned, searching, he could see, for the meaning in his words. He went on, giving her her cue: "This girl's servant, that big oaf upstairs—"

"He ran out," the sergeant said. "We'll catch him."

"I see. He attacked me last night in the grain field out there, brought me here and drugged me."

"What were you doing in the grain field?"

"I was on my way to see Dr. Sitruc. I have information of the most vital nature for him."

The sergeant turned to Ylas. "What d'ya say, girlie?"

She shrugged. "A stranger, in the middle of the night, what would you have done?"

"Then why didn't you say something about it when I was here a while ago?"

"If he turned out to be a spy, I wanted the credit for capturing him."

"You civilians," the sergeant said in disgust. "Well, maybe this is the guy we're lookin' for. Why did you kill that gun crew?" he snarled at Ybor.

Ybor blinked. "How did you know? I killed them because they were enemies."

The sergeant made a gesture toward his gun. His face grew stormy. "Why, you dirty spy—"

"Wait a minute!" Ybor said. "What gun crew? You mean the Seilla outpost, of course, in Aissu?"

"I mean our gun crew, you rat, in the woods out there."

Ybor blinked again. "I don't know anything about a gun crew out there. Listen, you've got to take me to Dr. Sitruc at once. Here's the background. I have been in Seilla territory, and I learned something that Dr. Sitruc must know. The outcome of the war depends on it. Take me to him at once, or you'll suffer for it."

The sergeant cogitated. "There's something funny here," he said. "Why have you got him all tied up?"

"For questioning," Ylas answered.

Ybor could see that she had decided to play it his way, but she wasn't convinced. The truth was, as he pointed out, she could not afford to do otherwise.

The sergeant went into an analytical state which seemed to be almost cataleptic. Presently he shook his massive head. "I can't quite put my finger on it," he said in a puzzled tone. "Every time I get close, I hit a blank . . . what am I saying?" He became crisp, menacing. "What's your name, you?" he spat at Ybor.

Ybor couldn't shrug. He raised his eyebrows. "My papers will say that I am Yenraq Ekor, a newspaper man. Don't let them fool you. I'll give my real name to Dr. Sitruc. He knows it well. You're wasting time, man!" he burst out. "Take me to him at once. You're worse than this stupid female!"

The sergeant turned to Ylas. "Did he tell you why he wanted to see Dr. Sitruc?"

She shrugged again, still with speculative eyes on Ybor. "He just said he had to."

"Well, then," the sergeant demanded of Ybor, "why *do* you want to see him?"

Ybor decided to gamble. This goof might keep him here all day with aimless questioning. He told the story of the bomb, much as he had told it to Ylas. He watched the sergeant's face, and saw that his remarks were completely unintelligible. Good! The soldier, like so many people, knew nothing of U-235. Ybor went into the imaginative and gibberish phase of his talk.

"And so, if it's uncontrolled," he said, "it might destroy the planet, blow it instantly into dust. But what I learned was a method of control, and the Seilla have a bomb almost completed. They'll use it to destroy Ynamre. But if we can use ours first, we'll destroy them. You see, it's a neutron shield that I discovered while I was a spy in the Seilla camps. It will stop the neutrons, released by the explosion, from rocketing about space and splitting mountains. Did you know that one free neutron can crack this planet in half? This shield will confine them to a limited area, and the war is ours. So hurry! Our time may be measured in minutes!"

The sergeant took it all in. He didn't dare not believe, for the picture of destruction which Ybor painted was on such a vast scale that sixteen generations of men like the sergeant would be required to comprehend it.

The sergeant made up his mind. "Hey!" he yelled toward the cellar door, and three soldiers came in. "Get him out of that. We'll take him to the captain. Take the girl along, too. Maybe the captain will want to ask her some questions."

"But I haven't done anything," Ylas protested.

"Then you got nothing to be afraid of, beautiful. If they let you go, I'll take personal charge of you."

The sergeant had a wonderful leer.

You might as well be fatalistic, Ybor thought as he waited in Dr. Sitruc's anteroom. Certain death could easily await him here, but even so, it was worth the gamble. If he were to be a pawn in a greater game—the greatest game, in fact—so be it.

So far, he had succeeded. And it came to him as he eyed his two guards that final success would result in his own death. He couldn't hope to destroy that bomb and get out of this fortress alive. Those guarded exits spelled finis, if he could even get far enough from this laboratory to reach one of them.

He hadn't really expected to get out alive, he reflected. It was a suicide mission from the start. That knowledge, he knew now, had given plausibility to his otherwise thin story. The captain, even as the sergeant, had not dared to disbelieve his tale. He had imparted verisimilitude to his story of destruction because of his deep and flaming determination to prevent it.

Not that he had talked wildly about neutron shields to the captain. The captain was intelligent, compared to his sergeant. And so Ybor had talked matter-of-factly about heat control, and had made it convincing enough to be brought here by guards who grew more timid with each turn of the lorry's wheels.

Apparently, the story of the bomb was known here at the government experimental laboratories; for all the guards had a haunted look, as if they knew that they would never hear the explosion if something went wrong. All the better, then. If he could take advantage of that fact, somehow, as he had taken advantage of events to date, he might—might—

He shrugged away speculation. The guards had sprung to attention as the inner door opened, and a man eyed Ybor.

This was a slender man with snapping dark eyes, an odd-shaped face, and a commanding air. He wore a smock, and from its sleeves extended competent-looking hands.

"So you are the end result," he said dryly to Ybor. "Come in."

Ybor followed him into the laboratory. Dr. Sitruc waved him to a straight, uncomfortable chair, using the gun which was suddenly in his hand as an indicator. Ybor sat, and looked steadily at the other.

"What do you mean, end result?" he asked.

"Isn't it rather obvious?" the doctor asked pleasantly. "Those planes which passed over last night were empty; they went too fast, otherwise. I have been speculating all day on their purpose. Now I see. They dropped you."

"I heard something about planes," Ybor said, "but I didn't see 'em."

Dr. Sitruc raised polite eyebrows. "I'm afraid I do not believe you. My interpretation of events is this: those Seilla planes had one objective, to land an agent here who was commissioned to destroy the uranium bomb. I have known for some time that the Seilla command have known of its existence, and I have wondered what steps they would take to destroy it."

Ybor could see no point in remaining on the defensive. "They are making their own bomb," he said. "But they have a control. I'm here to tell you about it, so that you can use it on our bomb. We have time."

Dr. Sitruc said: "I have heard the reports on you this morning. You made some wild and meaningless statements. My personal opinion is that you are a layman, with only scant knowledge of the subject on which you have been so glib. I propose to find out—before I kill you. Oh, yes," he said, smiling, "you will die in any case. In my present position, knowledge is power. If I find that you actually have knowledge which I do not, I propose that I alone will retain it. You see my point?"

"You're like a god here. That's clear enough from the attitude of the guards."

"Exactly. I have control of the greatest explosive force in world history, and my whims are obeyed as iron commands. If I choose, I may give orders to the High Command. They have no choice but to obey. Now, you— your name doesn't matter; it's assumed, no doubt—tell me what you know."

"Why should I? If I'm going to die, anyway, my attitude is to hell with you. I do know something that you don't, and you haven't time to get it from anybody but me. By the time one of your spies could work his way up high enough to learn what I did, the Sixa would be defeated. But I see no reason to give you the information. I'll sell it to you—for my life."

Ybor looked around the small, shining laboratory while he spoke, and he saw it. It wasn't particularly large; its size did not account for the stab of terror that struck his heart. It was the fact that the bomb was finished. It was suspended in a shock-proof cradle. Even a bombing raid would not shake it loose. It would be exploded when and where the doctor chose.

"You may well turn white as a sheet," Dr. Sitruc chuckled. "There it is, the most destructive weapon the world has ever known."

Ybor swallowed convulsively. Yes, there it was. Literally the means to an end—the end of the world. He thought wryly that those religionists who still contended that this war would be ended miraculously by divine intervention would never live to call the bomb a miracle. What a shot in the doctrine the explosion would give them if only they could come through it unscathed!

"I turned white," he answered Dr. Sitruc, "because I see it as a blind, uncontrolled force. I see it as the end of a cycle, when all life dies. It will be millennia before another civilization can reach our present stage."

"It is true that the element of chance is involved. If the bomb sets off surrounding matter for any considerable radius, it is quite possible that all animate life will be destroyed in the twinkling of an eye. However, if it does not set off surrounding matter, we shall have won the world. I alone—and now you—know this. The High Command sees only victory in that weapon. But enough of chitchat. You would bargain your life for information on how to control the explosion. If you convince me that you have such knowledge, I'll set you free. What is it?"

"That throws us into a deadlock," Ybor objected. "I won't tell you until I'm free, and you won't free me until I tell."

Dr. Sitruc pursed thin lips. "True," he said. "Well, then, how's this? I shall give the guards outside a note ordering that you be allowed to leave unmolested after you come through the laboratory door."

"And what's to prevent your killing me in here, once I have told you?"

"I give you my word."

"It isn't enough."

"What other choice have you?"

Ybor thought this over, and conceded the point. Somewhere along the line, either he or Dr. Sitruc would have to trust the other. Since this was the doctor's domain, and since he held Ybor prisoner, it was easy to see who would take the other on trust. Well, it would give him a breathing spell. Time was what he wanted now.

"Write the note," he said.

Dr. Sitruc went to his desk and began to write. He shot glances at Ybor which excluded the possibility of successful attack. Even the quickest spring would be fatal, for the doctor was far enough away to have time to raise his gun and fire. Ybor had a hunch that Dr. Sitruc was an excellent shot. He waited.

Dr. Sitruc summoned a guard, gave him the note, and directed that Ybor be allowed to read it. Ybor did, nodded. The guard went out.

"Now," Dr. Sitruc began, but broke off to answer his telephone. He listened, nodded, shot a slitted glance at Ybor, and hung up. "Would it interest you to know," he asked, "that the girl who captured you was taken away from guards by members of the Underground?"

"Not particularly," Ybor said. "Except that . . . yes," he cried, "it does interest me. It proves my authenticity. You know how widespread the Underground is, how powerful. It's clear what happened; they knew I was coming, knew my route, and caught me. They were going to torture me in their cellar. I told that sergeant the truth. Now they will try to steal the bomb. If they had it, they could dictate terms."

It sounded a trifle illogical, maybe, but Ybor put all of the earnestness he could into his voice. Dr. Sitruc looked thoughtful.

"Let them try. Now, let's have it."

The tangled web of lies he had woven had caught him now. He knew of no method to control the bomb. Dr. Sitruc was not aware of this fact, and would not shoot until he was. Ybor must stall, and watch for an opportunity to do what he must do. He had gained a point; if he got through that door, he would be free. He must, then, get through the door— with the bomb. And Dr. Sitruc's gun was in his hand.

"Let's trace the reaction," Ybor began.

"The control!" Dr. Sitruc snapped.

Ybor's face hardened. "Don't get tough. My life depends on this. I've got to convince you that I know what I'm talking about, and I can do that by describing the method from the first. If you interrupt, then to hell with you."

Dr. Sitruc's odd face flamed with anger. This subsided after a moment, and he nodded. "Go on."

"Oxygen and nitrogen do not burn—if they did, the first fire would have blown this planet's atmosphere off in one stupendous explosion. Oxygen and nitrogen *will* burn if heated to about three thousand degrees Centigrade, and they'll give off energy in the process. But they don't give off sufficient energy to maintain that temperature—so they rapidly cool, and the fire goes out. If you maintain that temperature artificially—well, you're no doubt familiar with that process of obtaining nitric oxide."

"No doubt," Dr. Sitruc said acidly.

"All right. Now U-235 can raise the temperature of local matter to where it will, uh, 'burn,' and give off energy. So let's say we set off a little pinch of U-235. Surrounding matter also explodes, as it is raised to an almost inconceivable temperature. It cools rapidly; within perhaps one-hundred-millionth of a second, it is down below the point of ignition. Then maybe a full millionth of a second passes before it's down to one million degrees hot, and a minute or so may elapse before it is visible in the normal sense. Now that visible radiation will represent no more than one-hundred-thousandth of the total radiation at one million degrees—but even so, it would be several hundred times more brilliant than the sun. Right?"

Dr. Sitruc nodded. Ybor thought there was a touch of deference in his nod.

"That's pretty much the temperature cycle of a U-235 plus surrounding matter explosion, Dr. Sitruc. I'm oversimplifying, I guess, but we don't need to go into detail. Now that radiation *pressure* is the stuff that's potent. The sheer momentum, physical pressure of light from the stuff at one million degrees, would amount to tons and tons and *tons* of pressure. It would blow down buildings like a titanic wind if it weren't for the fact that absorption of such appalling energy would volatilize the buildings before they could move out of the way. Right?"

Dr. Sitruc nodded again. He almost smiled.

"All right," Ybor went on. He now entered the phase of this contest where he was guessing, and he'd get no second guess. "What we need is a damper, something to hold the temperature of surrounding matter down. In that way, we can limit the effect of the explosion to desired areas, and prevent it from destroying cities on the opposite side of Cathor. The method of applying the damper depends on the exact mechanical structure of the bomb itself."

Ybor got to his feet easily, and walked across the laboratory to the cradle which held the bomb. He didn't even glance at Dr. Sitruc; he didn't dare. Would he be allowed to reach the bomb? Would an unheard, unfelt bullet reach his brain before he took another step?

When he was halfway across the room, he felt as if he had already walked a thousand miles. Each step seemed to be slow motion, leagues in length. And still the bomb was miles away. He held his steady pace, fighting with every atom of will his desire to sprint to his goal, snatch it and flee.

He stopped before the bomb, looked down at it. He nodded, ponderously. "I see," he said, remembering Sworb's drawings and the careful explanations he had received. "Two cast-iron hemispheres, clamped over the orange segments of cadmium alloy. And the fuse—I see it is in—a tiny can of cadmium alloy containing a speck of radium in a beryllium holder and a small explosive powerful enough to shatter the cadmium walls. Then —correct me if I'm wrong, will you?—the powdered uranium oxide runs together in the central cavity. The radium shoots neutrons into this mass— and the U-235 takes over from there. Right?"

Dr. Sitruc had come up behind Ybor, stood at his shoulder. "Just how do you know so much about that bomb?" he asked with overtones of suspicion.

Ybor threw a careless smile over his shoulder. "It's obvious, isn't it? Cadmium stops neutrons, and it's cheap and effective. So you separate the radium and U-235 by thin cadmium walls, brittle so the light explosion will shatter them, yet strong enough to be handled with reasonable care."

The doctor chuckled. "Why, you *are* telling the truth."

Dr. Sitruc relaxed, and Ybor moved. He whipped his short, prehensile tail around the barrel of Dr. Sitruc's gun, yanked the weapon down at the same time his fist cracked the scientist's chin. His free hand wrenched the gun out of Dr. Sitruc's hand.

He didn't give the doctor a chance to fall from the blow of his fist. He chopped down with the gun butt and Dr. Sitruc was instantly unconscious. Ybor stared down at the sprawled figure with narrowed eyes. Dared he risk a shot? No, for the guards would not let him go, despite the doctor's note, without investigation. Well—

He chopped the gun butt down again. Dr. Sitruc would be no menace for some time, anyway. And all Ybor needed was a little time. First, he had to get out of here.

That meant taking the fuse out of the bomb. He went over to the cradle, examined the fuse. He tried to unscrew it. It was too tight. He looked around for a wrench. He saw none. He stood half panic-stricken. Could he afford a search for the wrench which would remove the fuse? If anyone came in, he was done for. No, he'd have to get out while he could.

And if anybody took a shot at him, and hit the bomb, it was good-by Cathor and all that's in it. But he didn't dare wait here. And he must stop sweating ice water, stop this trembling.

He picked up the cradle and walked carefully to the door. Outside, in the anteroom, the guards who had brought him there turned white. Blood drained out of their faces like air from a punctured balloon. They stood motionless, except for a slight trembling of their knees, and watched Ybor go out into the corridor.

Unmolested, Dr. Sitruc had said. He was not only unmolested, he was avoided. Word seemed to spread through the building like poison gas on a stiff breeze. Doors popped open, figures hurried out—and ran away from Ybor and his cargo. Guards, scientists, men in uniform, girls with pretty legs, bare-kneed boys—all ran.

To where? Ybor asked with his heart in his mouth. There was no safe place in all the world. Run how they might, as far as they could, and it would catch them if he fell or if the bomb were accidentally exploded.

He wanted a plane. But how to get one, if everybody ran? He could walk to the airport, if he knew where it was. Still, once he was away from these laboratories, any policeman, ignorant of the bomb, could stop him, confiscate the weapon, and perhaps explode it.

He had to retain possession.

The problem was partly solved for him. As he emerged from the building, to see people scattering in all directions, a huge form came out from behind a pillar and took him by the arm. "Sleyg," Ybor almost cried with terror which became relief.

"Come," Sleyg said, "Ylas wants you."

"Get me to a plane!" Ybor said. He thought he'd said it quietly, but Sleyg's yellow eyes flickered curiously at him.

The big man nodded, crooked a finger, and led the way. He didn't seem curious about the bomb. Ybor followed to where a small car was parked at the curb. They climbed in, and Sleyg pulled out into traffic.

So Ylas wanted him, eh? Why? He gave up speculation to watch the road ahead, cradling the bomb in his arms against rough spots.

He heard a plane, and searched for it anxiously. All he needed at this stage was a bombing raid, and a direct hit on this car. They had promised him that no raids would be attempted until they were certain of his success or failure, but brass hats were a funny lot. You never knew what they'd do next, like countermanding orders given only a few minutes before.

Still, no alarm sirens went off, so the plane must be Sixa. Ybor sighed with relief.

They drove on, and Ybor speculated on the huge, silent figure beside him. How had Sleyg known that he would come out of that building? How had he known he was there? Did the Underground have a pipeline even into Dr. Sitruc's office?

These speculations were useless, too, and he shrugged them away as Sleyg drove out of the city through fields of grain. The Sixa, apparently, were going to feed their armies mush, for he saw no other produce.

Sleyg cut off the main road into a bumpy lane, and Ybor clasped the bomb firmly. "Take it easy," he warned.

Sleyg slowed obediently, and Ybor wondered again at the man's attitude. Ybor did not seem to be a prisoner, yet he was not in command here completely. It was a sort of combination of the two, and it was uncomfortable.

They came to a bare, level stretch of land where a plane stood, props turning idly. Sleyg headed toward it. He brought the car to a halt, motioned Ybor out. He then indicated that Ybor should enter the big plane.

"Give me your tool kit," Ybor said, and the big man got it.

The plane bore Sixa insignia, but Ybor was committed now. If he used the bomb as a threat, he could make anybody do what he liked. Still, he felt a niggling worry.

Just before he stepped on the wing ramp, a shot came from the plane. Ybor ducked instinctively, but it was Sleyg who fell—with a neat hole between his eyes. Ybor tensed himself, stood still.

The fuselage door slid back, and a face looked out.

"Solraq!" Ybor cried. "I thought you were dead!"

"You were meant to think it, Ybor. Come on in."

"Wait till I get these tools." Ybor handed the cradle up to the dark man who grinned down at him. "Hold baby," Ybor said. "Don't drop him. If he cries, you'll never hear him."

He picked up the tool kit, climbed into the plane. Solraq waved a

command to the pilot, and the plane took off. Ybor went to work gingerly
on the fuse while Solraq talked.

"Sleyg was a cutie," he said. "We thought he was an ignorant ape. He
was playing a big game, and was about ready to wind it up. But, when
you named me for identification, he knew that he'd have to turn in his
report, because we could have sent you directly to Dr. Sitruc, and helped
you. Sleyg wasn't ready yet, so he reported me dead. Then he had the
soldiers come and search the house, knowing you'd be found and arrested.
He got into trouble when that skirt-chasing sergeant decided to take Ylas
along. He had to report that to others of the Underground, because he had
to have one more big meeting held before he could get his final dope.

"You see, he'd never turned in a report," Solraq went on. "He was
watched, and afraid to take a chance. When Ylas and I got together, we
compared notes, searched his belongings, and found the evidence. Then
we arranged this rendezvous—if you got away. She told Sleyg where you
were, and to bring you here. I didn't think you'd get away, but she insisted
you were too ingenious to get caught. Well, you did it, and that's all to the
good. Not that it would have mattered much. If you'd failed, we'd have
got hold of the bomb somehow, or exploded it in Dr. Sitruc's laboratory."

Ybor didn't bother to tell him that it didn't matter where the bomb was
exploded. He was too busy trying to prevent its exploding here. At last he
had the fuse out. He motioned Solraq to open the bomb bay. When the
folding doors dropped open, he let the fuse fall between them.

"Got it's teeth pulled," he said, "and we'll soon empty the thing."

He released the clamps and pulled the hemispheres apart. He took a
chisel from the tool kit and punched a hole in each of the cadmium cans
in succession, letting the powder drift out. It would fall, spread, and never
be noticed by those who would now go on living.

They would live because the war would end before Dr. Sitruc could
construct another bomb. Ybor lifted eyes that were moist.

"I guess that's it," he said. "Where are we going?"

"We'll parachute out and let this plane crash when we sight our ship
some fifty miles at sea. We'll report for orders now. This mission's
accomplished."

CLIFFORD D. SIMAK

LOBBY

THE LETTERING on the door read: ATOMIC POWER, INC.

Felix Jones, reporter for the *Daily Messenger*, opened it.

"Hi," he said to the stenographer-receptionist. "Cobb in?"

"Not to you," she told him.

"I'll see him, anyhow."

Miss Joyce Lane shrugged her eyebrows. "I shall hold the door **open**," she said, "when he throws you out."

"*Tsk, tsk*," commented Felix. "What a temper!"

He moved toward the inner door.

"Do you bounce easy?" asked Miss Lane.

"I'm an expert at it," he assured her.

"So is Mr. Cobb," she said.

He opened the door and Bill Cobb looked up from his desk.

"It's you again," he said, unenthusiastically.

"You heard about Walker this afternoon?" asked Felix.

"I heard Walker," said Cobb. "I turned on the 'visor and there he was. Senator Walker is a doddering old fool and a rascally politician. You can quote me."

Felix walked across the room and perched on the desk. "You going to take it lying down?" he asked.

"I'm not taking it any way," said Cobb. "I didn't even think about it until you came in. You're wasting your time."

"You're not talking?" asked Felix, trying to sound surprised but not doing very well.

"Why should I?" Cobb demanded. "Would you give me a break? Not in a million years. But you'll print all the lies Walker and the power lobby and the Primitives shout against atomic power. If you want to take the words of a foul-ball politician and a half-baked sect, that's O.K. with me. Go ahead and make a fool out of your paper. Couple of years from now I'll come in and cram all those lousy stories down Mann's neck. You can tell him that."

"But Walker said atomics were dangerous—"

"Sure he said they were dangerous. He's been saying it for a year now. And he's right. They are dangerous. That's why we're not offering anything for sale. If some of the pure and holy power outfits that are fighting us had half as good a set-up as we have, they'd be selling right and left. Maybe a few people would get hurt, but what would they care?"

He rapped the desk viciously with his pencil.

"When we have means to control atomic power, we'll put it on the market. Not before then. What do you think we put our experimental plant out in Montana for? Simply so that if it should blow, fewer people would get killed."

"You're bitter," Felix said.

"Not bitter," Cobb told him. "Just astounded at what fools the people are. For years they've dreamed about atomic power. Reams of speculation have been written about it. Men have planned for it and banked on it, built future worlds on it. And now that it's within their grasp, what do people do? Now that they can practically reach out and touch power so ridiculously cheap it would be almost free, what do they say and think? They allow a power lobby and a bunch of crooked politicians to scare them silly with bogey stories about the terrible menace of atomics. They listen to yelping preachers on the street corner who tell them it's sacrilege to destroy God-created matter, that it's tempting Providence, asking the lightning to strike."

Felix hoisted himself off the desk.

"Scram," said Cobb.

"Now I know why Walker hates you," Felix said.

"So do I," said Cobb. "A million bucks a year."

He watched the reporter walk toward the door, called to him as he reached it. Felix swung around.

"Just one thing," warned Cobb. "If you write a line with my name in it . . . ever again . . . I'll come down to the office, personally, and break your neck."

"You're vicious," Felix told him and went out, shutting the door behind him.

Cobb tapped his teeth with the pencil, eyes still on the door.

"I should have plastered him," he told himself.

Through the open window came the droning of the New York sky lanes, the mutter of bank teller and shoe clerk and café waitress going home.

Rousing himself, he walked to the wall safe, twirled the combination and swung out the door. From a small box he took a sheet of paper, and carried it back to the desk. There he ran his finger down the left-hand margin, stopped at the notation—3 to 6 p.m. September 6th. Opposite it was a short-wave logging.

A nuisance, he told himself. And illegal, too. But the only way in which he and Ramsey could keep their wave length from being tapped.

He set the 'visor call dial, snapped up the toggle and punched the signal key. The screen lighted up and Scott Ramsey looked out at him.

"I've been expecting you," said Ramsey. "You listened to Walker?"

Cobb nodded. "I liked that part where he practically bawled over how the poor widows and orphans with their savings all tucked away in power securities would want for a crust of bread."

"It may sound laughable to us," said Ramsey, soberly, "but it got the senators. Mostly, I suppose, because they're the orphans who have their money socked away in power stocks. It's dirty politics, but we haven't seen the worst yet. We've got them scared, Bill, and when they get scared, they're dangerous. There's a rumor around we're ready to pop."

"Walker and his gang will be around with a proposition before long," predicted Cobb. "You know what to do."

"Sure. There was someone around this morning. But I don't think he was connected with the power lobby. Wanted to know how he could help us. I laughed at him. Said his name was Ford Adams. Mean anything to you?"

"Never heard of him," said Cobb. "Probably just a screwball."

"I'm afraid of something happening at the plant," declared Ramsey. "You better get hold of Butler. If you got time, it might be a good idea to go out and see him rather than just calling him. Impress on him the necessity to be on guard all the time. He's so tied up in his research he doesn't know half what's going on."

"They wouldn't try anything at the plant," said Cobb.

"That's what you think," Ramsey told him. "This gang is all steamed up, I tell you. They're scared. They figure we're about due to go on the market any day now and they're half nuts. They know that once a successful atomic plant is developed they're dead ducks. To compete with us they'd have to sell their stuff for less than half of actual cost, probably even less than that. There are financial empires at stake, not only here, but all over the world. Men fighting for financial empires won't stop at anything."

"How about the department of interior?" asked Cobb. "You going to be able to hold that off?"

"I wish I could tell you yes," said Ramsey, "but I'm not too sure. Sullivan is getting budget jitters. If he doesn't play ball the power crowd can cut his budget to a shadow and leave him out on a long, bare limb. And he's not too happy about those nice, big dams he's got. Once atomic power comes in, the dams are shot. All they'll be good for is irrigation then and with this tank farming business, there isn't going to be too much need for irrigation.

"Then, too, he can slap an order on us to shut down until we can show we have developed adequate safety measures. It won't hold, of course, for we can prove we're doing experimental work and there's always some danger in that type of development. It's just a recognized fact. But he could hold us up a while."

"Do the best you can, Scott," urged Cobb. "No danger of Walker's law going through, is there?"

"Not this session. Most of them aren't too sure how the folks back home feel. Maybe it'll have a chance next session. Especially if the Primitives keep going to town. This town is plastered with soap boxes and spouting preachers. They say it's sacrilege—"

"Yes, I know. I've heard them. Any chance of proving the power gang is behind them?"

"Not a ghost," said Ramsey.

"O.K., then, I'll go see Butler tonight. Good luck with Sullivan."

The screen dimmed and Cobb clicked the toggle, carefully reset the dial to its legal wave length.

The intercommunicator buzzed at him and he flipped it open.

"Yes."

"A Mr. Adams here to see you," said Miss Lane. "A Mr. Ford Adams."

"I don't know any Ford Adams."

"He insists that it's important."

Ford Adams? Ford—

Yes, that was the name of Ramsey's screwball.

"I'll see Mr. Adams in a minute," Cobb said.

He picked up the slip of paper with the dial settings, put it back in the safe and locked it. Back at the intercommunicator he said:

"Send him in."

Ford Adams was tall, almost wraithlike. He walked with a limp and carried a heavy cane. He laid it on the desk, saw Cobb look at it for a second.

"Sicily," he explained.

"I missed that one," said Cobb.

"You probably know I saw Mr. Ramsey this morning."

Cobb nodded and motioned to a chair.

"I offered my help," said Adams. "Mr. Ramsey didn't seem to take me seriously."

"What makes you think we need your help?"

"It's obvious," said Adams. "Here you are, a handful of you, fighting what amounts to a world combine. I've looked into the matter quite thoroughly and know much of the background. You offered your developments to the power corporations on condition they would form a world compact among themselves to hold their earnings to no more than their present earnings and, for a period of the next twenty years, would divert the greater portions of those earnings to converting the entire world to atomic power. They refused."

"Sure they did," said Cobb. "We expected they would, although we went to them in all good faith. They saw a chance to make a killing and they turned us down. They figured their own technicians could find the answers before we could begin operating. They guessed wrong. Butler is the only man in the field who found the answers and he had them when we talked to them. All the rest of the researchers are a million miles off base."

"You threatened you would ruin them," said Adams and he didn't make it an accusation or a question. It was simply a statement.

Cobb grinned crookedly. "As I remember it, we did. If they'd been decent, we'd've gone in with them. Believe it or not, we aren't out to make a fortune. We probably won't. Butler is the head man with us and he doesn't even know there is such a thing as money. You've seen his kind. Has one ruling passion. The only thing that counts with him is atomic power. Not atomic power as a theory or as something to play around with, but power that will turn wheels—cheap. Power that will free the world, that will help develop the world. Power so cheap and plentiful and safe to handle that no man is so poor he can't afford to use it."

Adams fumbled with a cigarette. "What you've said, Cobb, may go for Butler," he declared, "but it doesn't go for you. You've lost sight of Butler's goal. It's become a game for you. A game in which either you or the power lobby wins. You're out to break the power gang."

"I hate their guts," said Cobb.

"You aren't a scientist," said Adams.

"No, I'm not. I'm a business man. Butler would be lost in the business end. So I'm here. He's out in Montana. It works O.K."

"But you aren't the only atomic company in the field."

Cobb laughed shortly. "You're thinking of Atomic Development. Forget it, Adams. You know as well as I do Development is another power lobby trick. All it's done is sell stock. They've peddled it all over the world. Store clerks and stenographers are loaded with it."

Adams nodded. "At the psychological moment, it blows."

"And blows us with it," said Cobb. "The people in their blind panic, won't be able to distinguish between one atomic company and another. To them, we'll all be crooks."

"It isn't a pretty picture," said Adams.

Cobb leaned across the desk. "Just what do you mean by that?"

"It's sordid."

"The power gang asked for it that way," said Cobb. "They've bought off the papers with advertising campaigns. They've elected their men to Congress. They have organized a so-called religious sect to preach against us. They're bringing all the pressure they can in Washington. They've established a phony stock company for no other reason than to stir up a scandal that will smear us, too, when it busts wide open."

He smashed his fist on the desk. "If they want to play rough, it's O.K. with us. Before we're through with this we'll have them begging in the street. Those newspaper publishers who are bucking us now will come through that door over there on hands and knees and bow three times— and then we'll give them power to turn their presses."

"How about the world committee?" asked Adams. "You could appeal to it. Have it declare you an international project. No one could touch you then. You'd be free to work out atomic power without all the annoyance to which you are now subjected. Some arrangement could be worked out with the power companies. They'd see reason if the committee took a hand."

"We applied," said Cobb, "but apparently the committee can't be bothered. They're up to their necks in Europe and Asia. Figure the Americas should stagger along as best they can until some of the squabbles over there are ironed out."

"But it's not a question of the Americas," insisted Adams. "It's a question of the world. The whole world is concerned with atomic power."

"They wouldn't touch it with a ten-foot pole," declared Cobb. "It's too hot for them. Their powers are limited. The only reason they have lasted this long is that the little people of the world are determined there's never going to be another war, yell their heads off when anybody makes a move toward the world committee. But something like this—"

"Don't you see where this is leading?" demanded Adams. "If you let atomic power loose upon the world the way you propose to do, you're letting loose economic chaos. You'll absolutely iron out vast companies that employ hundreds of thousands of men and women. You'll create a securities panic, which will have repercussions throughout the world, upsetting trade schedules which just now are beginning to have some influence toward a structure for enduring peace. You're not too young to remember what 1929 was like. That was just a ripple in comparison to the sort of chaos you can bring about."

"Adams," Cobb told him coldly, "you came in here and asked to help us. I didn't know who you were and I didn't ask. Isn't it about time to climb out of the tree?"

"I'm really no one," Adams said. "Just a private citizen with certain . . . well, you might call them eccentricities."

"Walker sent you," declared Cobb. "Walker or one of the power mob."

"I can assure you that is not so."

"Who did then? And what is the proposition?"

"There is no proposition," declared Adams. "Not now, at least. I did have something in mind, but there is no use in wasting time outlining it to you. When the power gang licks you, I'll drop around again."

"The power gang won't lick us," snapped Cobb.

Adams reached for his cane, pulled himself out of the chair, his fantastically tall, slender body towering over Cobb's desk.

"But they will," he said.

"Get out," said Cobb.

"Good-by, Mr. Cobb," said Adams. He limped toward the door.

"And don't come back," Cobb told him.

Cobb sat in his chair, cold with rage. If Walker thought such a thin deception would work—

The door opened and Miss Lane stood there, a newspaper clutched in her hand.

"Mr. Cobb," she said.

"What is it?"

She walked across the room and laid the paper down in front of him.

It was the *Messenger* and the screaming type of the headline smacked him in the face:

ATOMIC DANGEROUS,

COBB FINALLY ADMITS

The peaks of the Absoraka range shone with white, ghostly light under the pale whiteness of a sickle moon that hung just above the jagged mountain saw-tooth.

The 'copter muttered, driving ahead, while below the darkness that was Montana slid away like a black and flowing river.

Cobb, pipe clenched between his teeth, leaned back comfortably in his seat, taking it easy, trying to relax, trying to think.

It had been clumsy of the power mob to send Adams. But it was possible that back of that clumsiness there might be some purpose. Perhaps they had meant him to detect Adams as their emissary, using him as a deliberate decoy against some other move that might be underway.

Adams, of course, had denied he had any connection with the power lobby, but that was to be expected. Unless the power crowd was more desperate than he had reason to suspect, they probably wouldn't come out openly with a compromise at this stage of the game.

Cobb bent forward and stared out of the window of the machine, but all was darkness. Not even an isolated ranchhouse light. He glanced at his watch. Midnight.

His pipe went out and he lighted it again, watching the peaks swing nearer, still keeping their ghostly character. He noted the reading on his course and corrected it slightly.

Suddenly the sky above the peak flashed.

That was the word that best described it—flashed. There was no consciousness of fire, no flame, no glow—just a sudden, blinding flash, like a photographer's bulb popping—a million bulbs popping. A flash that came and lasted for one split second, then was gone, leaving a blackness that for a moment blotted out the moon and the snowy peaks—a blackness that persisted until one's eyes could readjust themselves.

The ship plowed on, while Cobb, blinded, reached out for something to clutch, instinctively reacting to the bewilderment of blackness.

Sound came. A sudden clap of sound that was vicious and nerve-wrenching. Like one short gasp of a million thunders rolled together.

The 'copter bucked and plunged and Cobb reached out blind hands, hauled back on the wheel to send it rocketing skyward. Beneath him the ship jerked and trembled, wallowing in tortured air.

Cold realization chilled Cobb's brain, tensed his body as he fought the bucking ship.

There was only one thing on Earth that could make a flash like that—a disintegrating atomic power plant!

The ship quieted and Cobb's eyes cleared. The moon still hung above the peaks. There was no glow above the range. There wouldn't be, Cobb knew. There'd be no fire . . . unless . . . unless—

He narrowed his eyes, trying to project his sight deeper into the night. There was no glow, no hint of fire. Just the night blue of the sky, the silver of the mountain snow, the whiteness of the moon.

His breath came in gasps.

The blast apparently had been a blast and that was all. It had not set off a progressive disintegration. Probably all the fears that had been held on that account were groundless. Perhaps the blasting atoms destroyed themselves utterly, expended all their power in one vicious flare of energy.

He pushed the machine down in a long, steep glide above the peaks, steeling himself for what he knew he'd see.

From far off he saw it, the jagged scar that snaked across the valley, the powdery gleam of riven rock, polished by the blast.

He held his breath as he swung above the scar. There was no sign of buildings, no sign of life, no smoke, not even the wavering of dancing motes of dust hanging in the air. There would be no dust, he knew. An atomic explosion would leave no dust. The dust itself would be a part of that bursting energy which had gouged out the hole across the valley.

He glided the ship toward the mountain spur that ran into the valley, brought it down on idling vanes. The spur, he saw, had been chopped off, cut off as a knife might slice through cheese, sheared in a straight and vicious line. A black hole gaped in the face of the spur and Cobb felt a surge of thankfulness.

At the end of that tunnel was the vault where Butler kept the records. If the blast had smashed the vault, blown it into nothingness, it would have wiped out the work of many years. But with the vault apparently intact—

The wheels touched the rock and rolled forward slowly. Cobb applied the brakes and cut the motor, flung open the door and jumped out.

Swiftly he headed for the tunnel, running up the slope.

Something moved in the tunnel's mouth, a weaving, staggering something. A man walking on wobbly legs, gripping a portfolio under one arm.

The man looked up and the pale moonlight slanted across his face.

"Butler!" Cobb cried.

Butler stopped, reached out a hand to steady himself. The portfolio fell to the ground and slid along the rock.

"Butler," yelled Cobb. "Butler, thank God!"

Butler's right hand came up and the moonlight gleamed on dull metal. Butler's voice croaked at him. "Stay where you are!"

Cobb took another step forward.

"I'll shoot," croaked Butler. "I'll shoot, so help me—"

The gun barked, its muzzle flash throwing a swift red shadow on the man who held it.

"Butler, it's Cobb! Bill Cobb!"

The gun roared again and a bullet whined close.

"For the love of Mike," yelled Cobb.

The gun wavered and Butler's knees gave way. Cobb leaped forward, but he was too late to catch the falling man. When he reached Butler, the scientist had tumbled forward, across the portfolio, guarding it even as he clawed feebly to regain his feet.

Cobb knelt and lifted him, bent low to hear the whisper.

"Got to get away," it ran. "Get into the hills. Got to—"

Cobb shook him and Butler's eyes flicked open.

"Bill," he said.

"Yes," said Cobb.

"Let's get out of here," Butler whispered. "The power mob. Spies. One of them . . . one of them—"

Cobb nodded grimly.

"The papers?" he asked.

Half croak, half whisper, Butler told him: "All here. All we need. The rest . . . mean nothing."

Swiftly, Cobb picked Butler up, cradling him in his arms, staggering toward the ship.

"Blast . . . knocked me . . . out," Butler said. "Came to after . . . while. Shaky . . . can't talk good—"

"Shock," said Cobb.

It was a miracle, he knew, that the man hadn't been killed outright by the pressure and the flare of radioactive particles. The downward turn of the tunnel and the depth of the vault, he knew, was all that saved him.

With Butler in the ship, he sprinted back to pick up the portfolio and revolver, then raced to the plane and took it up, vanes whirring wildly, sent it fleeing across the mountaintops.

"Doctor," croaked Butler.

"I'm taking you to one," said Cobb. "Sit back and take it easy. Keep yourself covered up."

Butler's hand reached out and plucked at his sleeve.

"What is it, Glenn?" Cobb asked.

"Maybe it . . . would be . . . better—"

"Take your time," cautioned Cobb. "Don't try too hard."

"—If they thought . . . I . . . was dead."

Cobb grunted. "Maybe it would, at that."

"Work in . . . secret . . . then."

"Sure, sure," said Cobb. "That's the idea."

He stared straight ahead into the blackness.

Work in secret. Underground. Skulking like criminals. Hiding from powerful men who saw in them a threat to empire.

And even if they did, where would they get the money? Atomic research took money, a lot of money. There had been trouble scraping together enough to build the plant—the plant that now was gone. Millions of dollars for a flash in the sky and a scar gouged in the ground.

Atomic Power Inc., he knew, was beaten, cleaned out. It was no more than a gilt name on an office door back in New York. And after tomorrow, after the newspapers and Primitives got through with them, it wouldn't even be that. It would be nothing—absolutely nothing.

There was, he told himself, bitterly, just one thing to do. Come morning and he would go down to the *Messenger* office and beat up Felix Jones. He'd told Jones he would do that. Although Jones wasn't really to blame. He was just a newspaperman, one of many, doing the best he knew, writing what his boss wanted him to write at so many bucks a week.

The men he wanted to beat couldn't be reached—not now. There was only one way to beat them—take away the things they owned, smash the things they'd built, hold them up to pity and to ridicule. And now that couldn't be done.

Tomorrow those men would sit and gloat. Tomorrow—

He twisted his head around and looked back toward the misty peaks. The moon was sinking, the lower horn just touching the mountains.

Something floated across its face, a tiny thing with tiny spinning vanes. He watched it fascinated, saw the moon-glint strike like hidden fire against the blades.

Another helicopter!

Butler mumbled at him.

"Yes, what is it?"

"Doctor—"

"It's O.K.," said Cobb. "I'll take you to a friend of mine. He won't say a thing. Won't even know who you are. He won't ask and I won't tell him."

"Best way," said Butler.

Pale morning light was filtering through the windows when Cobb let himself into the office and hurried to the wall safe. Swiftly he spun the combination and thrust the portfolio inside.

"Good morning, Mr. Cobb," said a voice from the doorway.

Cobb swung about.

The man who stood there was tall and thin and carried a heavy cane.
"It was most fortunate about Butler," Ford Adams said.

"You are just too late," said Cobb. "If you'd caught up with me a minute sooner, you could have brained me with that stick. The portfolio would have been yours."

"I could have caught up with you any time," Adams told him. "But I wasn't interested in the portfolio. I wanted to talk to you again. Remember I said I would."

Cobb thrust his hands into his coat pockets, felt the hardness of the revolver he'd picked up back at the tunnel. Slowly his fingers curled around it.

"Come in," he said.

Adams limped across the room, laid his cane on the desk and sat down.

"There was a certain proposition—" he started to say, but Cobb stopped him with a gesture.

"Forget the proposition, Adams," Cobb said. "A hundred men died out in Montana tonight. Most of them friends of mine. Three or four million dollars of equipment and years of labor went up in a flash. You were out there. I saw a 'copter as I was leaving."

Adams nodded. "I was there. I followed you."

"Then," said Cobb, "it's time for you to talk."

His hand came out of his pocket and he laid the revolver on the desk.

"There is," said Adams, "no need for melodrama."

"There's no melodrama involved," Cobb told him. "If your explanation isn't good, I'm going to shoot you deader than a mackerel. If for no other reason than you know Butler is alive. What's simpler than that?"

"I see," said Adams.

"No one," said Cobb, "is going to ruin his chance again. Nor the world's chance, either. He's the only man today who can give the world workable atomic power. If something happened to him, no one knows how long the world would have to wait."

"You mean the power people would hunt him down if they knew he were alive?"

Cobb nodded. "They won't touch Ramsey or me. We don't count. We don't have the brain that Butler has."

The radio on the desk flashed a green light, chirped persuasively.

Cobb stared at it. The green light flashed again. The chirp seemed more insistent.

"It might be about Butler," Adams said.

Cobb reached out for the gun, swiveled it on Adams, then bent over the radio.

"One move," he warned.

"You needn't worry," said Adams. "My life is something I value very highly."

Cobb snapped on the radio. A puffy face came in the plate, a red face with tousled white hair and small, close set, green eyes. It was the face of Senator Jay Walker.

"You!" snapped Walker.

"You called my wave length," Cobb declared.

Walker snarled. "I wasn't calling you. I didn't even know it was your length. Is there a man named Adams with you?"

Adams sat rigid in his chair.

"He asked me to call this wave length," the senator sputtered. "Said I'd learn something interesting."

"He's here," said Cobb.

Cobb backed away from the radio, motioned Adams forward with the gun. His lips formed soundless words. "What I said still goes."

"Naturally," said Adams. He spoke into the radio. "How are you, senator?"

"What do you want?" growled Walker.

"An atomic plant exploded in Montana tonight," said Adams. "More than one hundred men were killed."

"So," said the senator and one could hear the breath whistling through his lips. "So. Too bad."

"I have evidence," said Adams, "that would convict the men who planned it. Quite complete evidence."

"Men don't have to be involved in an atomic explosion," purred the senator. "The stuff's unstable, dangerous, hard to handle. *Pouf,* it goes like that."

"Men were involved in this one," declared Adams. "A lot of men. I thought you might know some of them."

"Mr. Adams, will you tell me who you are?" And the way the senator said it was an insult.

"I was formerly a member of the war guilt commission," Adams said. "At the moment I'm on the legal staff of the world committee at Geneva, Switzerland."

"And you—" said the senator. "And you—"

"I have evidence enough to hang about a dozen of you. You're one of the dozen, Walker."

"You'll never make it stick," stormed the senator. "It's blackmail. Bare-faced blackmail. We'll fight you—"

"You won't do any fighting," Adams told him. "You'll appear before a court of justice, the world court at Geneva. A lot different from other courts. You'll submit your defense and arguments in writing. There'll be no legal trickery or delay. There'll be no jury to talk into feeling sorry for you. The issue will be decided solely on merit. And there's no court of appeal."

"You have no jurisdiction," sputtered Walker.

"You won't be tried on the fact of murder alone," said Adams. "The entire history of your attempt to impede the development of atomic power, a factor vital to world development and mankind's welfare, will be clearly shown. That is something clearly within our jurisdiction. And we can show that murder was one of the methods that you used."

"You'll never get away with it," snapped Walker.

"You're positively archaic," said Adams. "The day is gone forever when a million dollars can't be convicted. It went out the day the last Axis soldier died in the last foxhole of Japan. A lot of things went out that day, never to return. You're living in a new world, Walker, and you don't even know it."

Walker choked, wiped his face with a pudgy hand. "But you called me. You had a reason. What do you want?"

"All existing power installations in the world today," said Adams. "Complete restitution on all stock sold by Atomic Development. Full confessions for the record."

"But that—" gasped Walker. "That—"

"That's justice," Adams snapped. "No one would gain a thing by hanging you. This way you contribute to the world's welfare."

"But you haven't got atomic power," shrieked Walker. "Butler's dead and he's—"

Adams purred at him. "Why, senator, how did you know that?"

Walker said nothing. His lips moved, but no words came. His face sagged and he was an old, old man.

"Cobb and I will see you this afternoon," Adams told him.

He snapped the toggle and turned around.

Cobb had laid the revolver on the desk.

"How close are you to working power?"

"A month," said Cobb. "Two months. No more. They got wind of it. Blasting the plant was the ace card they didn't want to use."

He found a cigarette, lit it with a shaking hand.

"You going to let them get away with it?" he asked.

"Get away?"

"Sure," said Cobb and his voice was hard. "They've committed murder. The law says death or life imprisonment, depending upon what court you face. It was murder, Adams, premeditated, cold-blooded murder. Done for profit."

"You want justice done?"

"Yes," said Cobb.

"Justice is an ideal," declared Adams, "very rarely arrived at. We have thought our courts signified and typified justice and in theory they did, but too often they failed in practice. Take Walker and his gang before any court in this land or any other land and what is the answer? You know it as well as I do. They'd wiggle out of it. They'd be represented by an array of legal talent that would confuse and becloud the issue, would get the jury so tangled up that it wouldn't know whether it was coming or going. Result: not guilty for lack of evidence."

"But a deal," protested Cobb. "A deal with criminals, with murderers."

"We have to be realistic," Adams said. "After all we're doing no more than any other court would do. We're turning them loose, letting them go free, but we, in this case, will accomplish something at least. Something in the way of justice, something in the way of advancement for the world. No court, not even the international court, could confiscate a criminal's property. But let us say the criminal is conscience-stricken, that he wants to make restitution for the crime he has committed—"

"The people won't believe you," declared Cobb. "They'll know you made the deal."

"They won't mind," said Adams. "For one thing, they'd enjoy it too much."

Cobb frowned. "But a hundred lives—"

"Don't you see, Cobb, that this is bigger than a hundred men, any hundred men. For the first time the world is on the path to a balanced scientific government. This is the stroke of work that will entrench it. Until this moment the world committee has been weak, faced by all the hatreds of nationalism, all the greed of private enterprise, all the feudalistic ideas that have persisted through the years. It had to play safe and grab its chances as they came. And atomic power, international control and administration of atomic power, is the first step to real authority.

"Give the committee another hundred years and government by demagoguery will be done. Little men with talent for grabbing votes will have given way to men who make a profession of good government. Men who are trained for government just as doctors are trained for medicine or attorneys are trained for law. Men of science will govern, running the world scientifically in the interest of the stockholders—the little people of the world."

Cobb crushed out his cigarette. "If they hadn't blasted the plant, what then? If they hadn't handed you the club you used on them?"

"They would have won," said Adams. "We would have had to let them win. For we couldn't move until we had a club that would make them cower. We couldn't come out in the open. It had to be an undercover job. We've been working on this thing ever since you filed application for international status, but we had to keep it quiet. If the power gang had known we were interested, there'd be no world committee now. They would have smashed us flat—just as they smashed you. But in smashing you, they played into our hands.

"And that would have been too bad. For they—and many others— have no place in this new world. Their mentality doesn't fit them for a place in it. It's an old mentality, stemming from the Dark Ages and before, the idea of top dog eat underdog, of grab and hold."

Banners of light in the east were pushing away the grayness of the dawn.

From far below came the first cry of a newsboy. From somewhere far off came the drone of an early worker's flier.

The city was awakening to a new day.

ROBERT HEINLEIN

BLOWUPS HAPPEN

"PUT down that wrench!"

The man addressed turned slowly around and faced the speaker. His expression was hidden by a grotesque helmet, part of a heavy, leaden armor which shielded his entire body, but the tone of voice in which he answered showed nervous exasperation.

"What the hell's eating on you, doc?" He made no move to replace the tool in question.

They faced each other like two helmeted-arrayed fencers, watching for an opening. The first speaker's voice came from behind his mask a shade higher in key and more peremptory in tone. "You heard me, Harper. Put down that wrench at once, and come away from that 'trigger.' Erickson!"

A third armored figure came around the shield which separated the uranium bomb proper from the control room in which the first two stood. "Whatcha want, doc?"

"Harper is relieved from watch. You take over as engineer-of-the-watch. Send for the stand-by engineer."

"Very well." His voice and manner were phlegmatic, as he accepted the situation without comment. The atomic engineer, whom he had just relieved, glanced from one to the other, then carefully replaced the wrench in its rack.

"Just as you say, Dr. Silard—but send for your relief, too. I shall demand an immediate hearing!" Harper swept indignantly out, his lead-sheathed boots clumping on the floor plates.

Dr. Silard waited unhappily for the ensuing twenty minutes until his own relief arrived. Perhaps he had been hasty. Maybe he was wrong in thinking that Harper had at last broken under the strain of tending the most dangerous machine in the world—an atomic power plant. But if he had made a mistake, it had to be on the safe side—slips *must not happen* in this business; not when a slip might result in the atomic detonation of two and a half tons of uranium.

He tried to visualize what that would mean, and failed. He had been told that uranium was potentially forty million times as explosive as TNT. The figure was meaningless that way. He thought of it, instead, as a hundred million tons of high explosive, two hundred million aircraft bombs as big as the biggest ever used. It still did not mean anything. He had once seen such a bomb dropped, when he had been serving as a temperament analyst for army aircraft pilots. The bomb had left a hole big enough to hide an apartment house. He could not imagine the explosion of a thousand such bombs, much, much less a hundred million of them.

Perhaps these atomic engineers could. Perhaps, with their greater mathematical ability and closer comprehension of what actually went on inside the nuclear fission chamber—the "bomb"—they had some vivid glimpse of the mind-shattering horror locked up beyond that shield. If so, no wonder they tended to blow up—

He sighed. Erickson looked up from the linear resonant accelerator on which he had been making some adjustment. "What's the trouble, doc?"

"Nothing. I'm sorry I had to relieve Harper."

Silard could feel the shrewd glance of the big Scandinavian. "Not getting the jitters yourself, are you, doc? Sometimes you squirrel sleuths blow up, too—"

"Me? I don't think so. I'm scared of that thing in there—I'd be crazy if I weren't."

"So am I," Erickson told him soberly, and went back to his work.

The accelerator's snout disappeared in the shield between them and the bomb, where it fed a steady stream of terrifically speeded up sub-atomic bullets to the beryllium target located within the bomb itself. The tortured beryllium yielded up neutrons, which shot out in all directions through the uranium mass. Some of these neutrons struck uranium atoms squarely on their nuclei and split them in two. The fragments were new elements—barium, xenon, rubidium—depending on the proportions in which each atom split. The new elements were usually unstable isotopes and broke down into a dozen more elements by radioactive disintegration in a progressive chain reaction.

But these chain reactions were comparatively unimportant; it was the original splitting of the uranium nucleus, with the release of the awe-inspiring energy that bound it together—an incredible two hundred million electron-volts—that was important—and perilous.

For, while uranium isotope 235 may be split by bombarding it with neutrons from an outside source, the splitting itself gives up more neutrons which, in turn, may land in other uranium nuclei and split them. If conditions are favorable to a progressively increasing reaction of this sort, it may get out of hand, build up in an unmeasurable fraction of a microsecond into a complete atomic explosion—an explosion which would dwarf the eruption of Krakatoa to popgun size; an explosion so far beyond all human experience as to be as completely incomprehensible as the idea of personal death. It could be feared, but not understood.

But a self-perpetuating sequence of nuclear splitting, *just under the level of complete explosion,* was necessary to the operation of the power plant. To split the first uranium nucleus by bombarding it with neutrons from the beryllium target took more power than the death of the atom gave up. In order that the output of power from the system should exceed the power input in useful proportion it was imperative that each atom split by a neutron from the beryllium target should cause the splitting of many more.

It was equally imperative that this chain of reactions should always tend to dampen, to die out. It must not build up, or the entire mass would explode within a time interval too short to be measured by any means whatsoever.

Nor would there be anyone left to measure it.

The atomic engineer on duty at the bomb could control this reaction by means of the "trigger," a term the engineers used to include the linear resonant accelerator, the beryllium target, and the adjacent controls, instrument board, and power sources. That is to say, he could vary the bombardment on the beryllium target to increase or decrease the power output of the plant, and he could tell from his instruments that the internal reaction was dampened—or, rather, that it had been dampened the split second before. He could not possibly know what was actually happening *now* within the bomb—subatomic speeds are too great and the time intervals too small. He was like the bird that flew backward; he could see where he had been, but he never knew where he was going.

Nevertheless, it was his responsibility, and his alone, not only to maintain the bomb at a high input-output efficiency, but to see that the reaction never passed the critical point and progressed into mass explosion.

But that was impossible. He could not be sure; he could never be sure.

He could bring to the job all of the skill and learning of the finest technical education, and use it to reduce the hazard to the lowest mathematical probability, but the blind laws of chance which appear to rule in subatomic action might turn up a royal flush against him and defeat his most skillful play.

And each atomic engineer knew it, knew that he gambled not only with his own life, but with the lives of countless others, perhaps with the lives of every human being on the planet. Nobody knew quite what such an explosion would do. The most conservative estimate assumed that, in addition to destroying the plant and its personnel completely, it would tear a chunk out of the populous and heavily traveled Los Angeles-Oklahoma Road City a hundred miles to the north.

That was the official, optimistic viewpoint on which the plant had been authorized, and based on mathematics which predicted that a mass of uranium would itself be disrupted on a molar scale, and thereby rendered comparatively harmless, before progressive and accelerated atomic explosion could infect the entire mass.

The atomic engineers, by and large, did not place faith in the official theory. They judged theoretical mathematical prediction for what it was worth—precisely nothing, until confirmed by experiment.

But even from the official viewpoint, each atomic engineer while on watch carried not only his own life in his hands, but the lives of many others—how many, it was better not to think about. No pilot, no general, no surgeon ever carried such a daily, inescapable, ever-present weight of responsibility for the lives of other people as these men carried every time they went on watch, every time they touched a vernier screw or read a dial.

They were selected not alone for their intelligence and technical training, but quite as much for their characters and sense of social responsibility. Sensitive men were needed—men who could fully appreciate the importance of the charge intrusted to them; no other sort would do. But the burden of responsibility was too great to be borne indefinitely by a sensitive man.

It was, of necessity, a psychologically unstable condition. Insanity was an occupational disease.

Dr. Cummings appeared, still buckling the straps of the armor worn to guard against stray radiation. "What's up?" he asked Silard.

"I had to relieve Harper."

"So I guessed. I met him coming up. He was sore as hell—just glared at me."

"I know. He wants an immediate hearing. That's why I had to send for you."

Cummings grunted, then nodded toward the engineer, anonymous in all-inclosing armor, "Who'd I draw?"

"Erickson."

"Good enough. Squareheads can't go crazy—eh, Gus?"

Erickson looked up momentarily and answered. "That's your problem," and returned to his work.

Cummings turned back to Silard and commented: "Psychiatrists don't seem very popular around here. O. K.—I relieve you, sir."

"Very well, sir."

Silard threaded his way through the zigzag in the tanks of water which surrounded the disintegration room. Once outside this outer shield, he divested himself of the cumbersome armor, disposed of it in the locker room provided, and hurried to a lift. He left the lift at the tube station, underground, and looked around for an unoccupied capsule. Finding one, he strapped himself in, sealed the gasketed door, and settled the back of his head into the rest against the expected surge of acceleration.

Five minutes later he knocked at the door of the office of the general superintendent, twenty miles away.

The power plant proper was located in a bowl of desert hills on the Arizona plateau. Everything not necessary to the immediate operation of the plant—administrative offices, television station and so forth—lay beyond the hills. The buildings housing these auxiliary functions were of the most durable construction technical ingenuity could devise. It was hoped that, if *der tag* ever came, occupants would stand approximately the chance of survival of a man going over Niagara Falls in a barrel.

Silard knocked again. He was greeted by a male secretary, Steinke. Silard recalled reading his case history. Formerly one of the most brilliant of the young engineers, he had suffered a blanking out of the ability to handle mathematical operations. A plain case of *fugue,* but there had been nothing that the poor devil could do about it—he had been anxious enough with his conscious mind to stay on duty. He had been rehabilitated as an office worker.

Steinke ushered him into the superintendent's private office. Harper was there before him, and returned his greeting with icy politeness. The superintendent was cordial, but Silard thought he looked tired, as if the twenty-four-hour-a-day strain was too much for him.

"Come in, doctor, come in. Sit down. Now tell me about this. I'm a little surprised. I thought Harper was one of my steadiest men."

"I don't say he isn't, sir."

"Well?"

"He may be perfectly all right, but your instructions to me are not to take any chances."

"Quite right." The superintendent gave the engineer, silent and tense in his chair, a troubled glance, then returned his attention to Silard. "Suppose you tell me about it."

Silard took a deep breath. "While on watch as psychological observer at the control station I noticed that the engineer of the watch seemed preoccupied and less responsive to stimuli than usual. During my off-watch observation of this case, over a period of the past several days, I have suspected an increasing lack of attention. For example, while playing contract bridge, he now occasionally asks for a review of the bidding, which is contrary to his former behavior pattern.

"Other similar data are available. To cut it short, at 3:11 today, while on watch, I saw Harper, with no apparent reasonable purpose in mind, pick up a wrench used only for operating the valves of the water shield and approach the trigger. I relieved him of duty and sent him out of the control room."

"Chief!" Harper calmed himself somewhat and continued: "If this witch doctor knew a wrench from an oscillator, he'd known what I was doing. The wrench was on the wrong rack. I noticed it, and picked it up to return it to its proper place. On the way, I stopped to check the readings!"

The superintendent turned inquiringly to Dr. Silard.

"That may be true. Granting that it is true," answered the psychiatrist doggedly, "my diagnosis still stands. Your behavior pattern has altered; your present actions are unpredictable, and I can't approve you for responsible work without a complete check-up."

General Superintendent King drummed on the desk top and sighed. Then he spoke slowly to Harper: "Cal, you're a good boy, and, believe me, I know how you feel. But there is no way to avoid it—you've got to go up for the psychometricals, and accept whatever disposition the board makes of you." He paused, but Harper maintained an expressionless silence. "Tell you what, son—why don't you take a few days leave? Then, when you come back, you can go up before the board, or transfer to another department away from the bomb, whichever you prefer." He looked to Silard for approval, and received a nod.

But Harper was not mollified. "No, chief," he protested. "It won't do. Can't you see what's wrong? It's this constant supervision. Somebody always watching the back of your neck, *expecting* you to go crazy. A man can't even shave in private. We're jumpy about the most innocent acts, for fear some head doctor, half batty himself, will see it and decide it's a sign we're slipping. Good grief, what do you expect?" His outburst having run its course, he subsided into a flippant cynicism that did not quite jell. "O. K.—never mind the strait jacket; I'll go quietly. You're a good Joe in spite of it, chief," he added, "and I'm glad to have worked under you. Good-by."

King kept the pain in his eyes out of his voice. "Wait a minute, Cal —you're not through here. Let's forget about the vacation. I'm transferring you to the radiation laboratory. You belong in research, anyhow; I'd never have spared you from it to stand watches if I hadn't been short on No. 1 men.

"As for the constant psychological observation, I hate it as much as you do. I don't suppose you know that they watch me about twice as hard as they watch you duty engineers." Harper showed his surprise, but Silard nodded in sober confirmation. "But we have to have this supervision. Do you remember Manning? No, he was before your time. We didn't have psychological observers then. Manning was able and brilliant. Furthermore, he was always cheerful; nothing seemed to bother him.

"I was glad to have him on the bomb, for he was always alert, and never seemed nervous about working with it—in fact, he grew more buoyant and cheerful the longer he stood control watches. I should have known that was a very bad sign, but I didn't, and there was no observer to tell me so.

"His technician had to slug him one night. He found him dismounting the safety interlocks on the trigger. Poor old Manning never pulled out of it—he's been violently insane ever since. After Manning cracked up, we worked out the present system of two qualified engineers and an observer for every watch. It seemed the only thing to do."

"I suppose so, chief," Harper mused, his face no longer sullen, but still unhappy. "It's a hell of a situation just the same."

"That's putting it mildly." King rose and put out his hand. "Cal, unless you're dead set on leaving us, I'll expect to see you at the radiation laboratory tomorrow. Another thing—I don't often recommend this, but it might do you good to get drunk tonight."

King had signed to Silard to remain after the young man left. Once the door was closed he turned back to the psychiatrist. "There goes another one—and one of the best. Doctor, what am I going to do?"

Silard pulled at his cheek. "I don't know," he admitted. "The hell of it is, Harper's absolutely right. It does increase the strain on them to know that they are being watched—and yet they have to be watched. Your psychiatric staff isn't doing too well, either. It makes us nervous to be around the bomb—the more so because we don't understand it. And it's a strain on us to be hated and despised as we are. Scientific detachment is difficult under such conditions; I'm getting jumpy myself."

King ceased pacing the floor and faced the doctor. "But there must be *some* solution—" he insisted.

Silard shook his head. "It's beyond me, superintendent. I see no solution from the standpoint of psychology."

"No? Hm-m-m. Doctor, who is the top man in your field?"

"Eh?"

"Who is the recognized No. 1 man in handling this sort of thing?"

"Why, that's hard to say. Naturally, there isn't any one leading psychiatrist in the world; we specialize too much. I know what you mean, though. You don't want the best industrial-temperament psychometrician; you want the best all-around man for psychoses nonlesional and situational. That would be Lentz."

"Go on."

"Well— He covers the whole field of environmental adjustment. He's the man who correlated the theory of optimum tonicity with the relaxation technique that Korzybski had developed empirically. He actually worked under Korzybski himself, when he was a young student—it's the only thing he's vain about."

"He did? Then he must be pretty old; Korzybski died in— What year did he die?"

"I started to say that you must know his work in symbology—theory of abstraction and calculus of statement, all that sort of thing—because of its applications to engineering and mathematical physics."

"*That* Lentz—yes, of course. But I had never thought of him as a psychiatrist."

"No, you wouldn't, in your field. Nevertheless, we are inclined to credit him with having done as much to check and reduce the pandemic neuroses of the Crazy Years as any other man, and more than any man left alive."

"Where is he?"

"Why, Chicago, I suppose. At the Institute."

"Get him here."

"Eh?"

"Get him down here. Get on that visiphone and locate him. Then have Steinke call the Port of Chicago, and hire a stratocar to stand by for him. I want to see him as soon as possible—before the day is out." King sat up in his chair with the air of a man who is once more master of himself and the situation. His spirit knew that warming replenishment that comes only with reaching a decision. The harassed expression was gone.

Silard looked dumfounded. "But, superintendent," he expostulated, "you can't ring for Dr. Lentz as if he were a junior clerk. He's . . . he's *Lentz.*"

"Certainly—that's why I want him. But I'm not a neurotic club-woman looking for sympathy, either. He'll come. If necessary, turn on the heat from Washington. Have the White House call him. But get him here at once. Move!" King strode out of the office.

When Erickson came off watch he inquired around and found that Harper had left for town. Accordingly, he dispensed with dinner at the base, shifted into "drinkin' clothes," and allowed himself to be dispatched via tube to Paradise.

Paradise, Arizona, was a hard little boom town, which owed its existence to the power plant. It was dedicated exclusively to the serious business of detaching the personnel of the plant from their inordinate salaries. In this worthy project they received much co-operation from the plant personnel themselves, each of whom was receiving from twice to ten times as much money each pay day as he had ever received in any other job, and none of whom was certain of living long enough to justify saving for old age. Besides, the company carried a sinking fund in Manhattan for their dependents—why be stingy?

It was said, with some truth, that any entertainment or luxury obtainable in New York City could be purchased in Paradise. The local chamber of commerce had appropriated the slogan of Reno, Nevada, "Biggest Little City in the World." The Reno boosters retaliated by claiming that, while any town that close to the atomic power plant undeniably brought thoughts of death and the hereafter, Hell's Gates would be a more appropriate name than Paradise.

Erickson started making the rounds. There were twenty-seven places licensed to sell liquor in the six blocks of the main street of Paradise. He expected to find Harper in one of them, and, knowing the man's habits and tastes, he expected to find him in the first two or three he tried.

He was not mistaken. He found Harper sitting alone at a table in the rear of DeLancey's Sans Souci Bar. DeLancey's was a favorite of both of them. There was an old-fashioned comfort about its chrome-plated bar and red leather furniture that appealed to them more than did the spectacular fittings of the up-to-the-minute places. DeLancey was conservative; he stuck to indirect lighting and soft music; his hostesses were required to be fully clothed, even in the evening.

The fifth of Scotch in front of Harper was about two thirds full. Erickson shoved three fingers in front of Harper's face and demanded, "Count!"

"Three," announced Harper. "Sit down, Gus."

"That's correct," Erickson agreed, sliding his big frame into a low-slung chair. "You'll do—for now. What was the outcome?"

"Have a drink. Not," he went on, "that this Scotch is any good. I think Lance has taken to watering it. I surrendered, horse and foot."

"Lance wouldn't do that—stick to that theory and you'll sink in the sidewalk up to your knees. How come you capitulated? I thought you planned to beat 'em about the head and shoulders, at least."

"I did," mourned Harper, "but, cripes, Gus, the chief is right. If a brain mechanic says you're punchy, he has *got* to back him up and take you off the bomb. The chief can't afford to take a chance."

"Yeah, the chief's all right, but I can't learn to love our dear psychiatrists. Tell you what—let's find us one, and see if he can feel pain. I'll hold him while you slug 'im."

"Oh, forget it, Gus. Have a drink."

"A pious thought—but not Scotch. I'm going to have a martini; we ought to eat pretty soon."

"I'll have one, too."

"Do you good." Erickson lifted his blond head and bellowed, "Israfel!"

A large, black person appeared at his elbow. "Mistuh Erickson! Yes, suh!"

"Izzy, fetch two martinis. Make mine with Italian." He turned back to Harper. "What are you going to do now, Cal?"

"Radiation laboratory."

"Well, that's not so bad. I'd like to have a go at the matter of rocket fuels myself. I've got some ideas."

Harper looked mildly amused. "You mean atomic fuel for interplanetary flight? That problem's pretty well exhausted. No, son, the stratosphere is the ceiling until we think up something better than rockets. Of course, you *could* mount the bomb in a ship, and figure out some jury rig to convert its radiant output into push, but where does that get you? One bomb, one ship—and twenty years of mining in Little America has only produced enough pitchblende to make one bomb. That's disregarding the question of getting the company to lend you their one bomb for anything that doesn't pay dividends."

Erickson looked balky. "I don't concede that you've covered all the alternatives. What have we got? The early rocket boys went right ahead trying to build better rockets, serene in the belief that, by the time they could build rockets good enough to fly to the Moon, a fuel would be perfected that would do the trick. And they did build ships that were good enough—you could take any ship that makes the antipodes run, and refit it for the Moon—*if* you had a fuel that was sufficiently concentrated to maintain the necessary push for the whole run. But they haven't got it.

"And why not? Because we let 'em down, that's why. Because they're still depending on molecular energy, on chemical reactions, with atomic power sitting right here in our laps. It's not their fault—old D. D. Harriman had Rockets Consolidated underwrite the whole first issue of Antarctic Pitchblende, and took a big slice of it himself, in the expectation that we would produce something usable in the way of a concentrated rocket fuel. Did we do it? Like hell! The company went hog-wild for immediate commercial exploitation, and there's no fuel yet."

"But you haven't stated it properly," Harper objected. "There are just two forms of atomic power available, radioactivity and atomic disintegration. The first is too slow; the energy is there, but you can't wait years for it to come out—not in a rocketship. The second we can only manage in a large mass of uranium. There has only been enough uranium mined for one bomb. There you are—stymied."

Erickson's Scandinavian stubbornness was just gathering for another try at the argument when the waiter arrived with the drinks. He set them down with a triumphant flourish. "There you are, suh!"

"Want to roll for them, Izzy?" Harper inquired.

"Don' mind if I do."

The Negro produced a leather dice cup, and Harper rolled. He selected his combinations with care and managed to get four aces and jack in three rolls. Israfel took the cup. He rolled in the grand manner with a backward twist to his wrist. His score finished at five kings, and he courteously accepted the price of six drinks. Harper stirred the engraved cubes with his forefinger.

"Izzy," he asked, "are these the same dice I rolled with?"

"Why, Mistuh Harper!" The Negro's expression was pained.

"Skip it," Harper conceded. "I should know better than to gamble with you. I haven't won a roll from you in six weeks. What did you start to say, Gus?"

"I was just going to say that there ought to be a better way to get energy out of—"

But they were joined again, this time by something very seductive in an evening gown that appeared to have been sprayed on her lush figure. She was young, perhaps nineteen or twenty. "You boys lonely?" she asked as she flowed into a chair.

"Nice of you to ask, but we're not," Erickson denied with patient politeness. He jerked a thumb at a solitary figure seated across the room. "Go talk to Hannigan; he's not busy."

She followed his gesture with her eyes, and answered with faint scorn, "Him? He's no use. He's been like that for three weeks—hasn't spoken to a soul. If you ask me, I'd say that he was cracking up."

"That so?" he observed noncommittally. "Here"—he fished out a five-dollar bill and handed it to her—"buy yourself a drink. Maybe we'll look you up later."

"Thanks, boys." The money disappeared under her clothing, and she stood up. "Just ask for Edith."

"Hannigan does look bad," Harper considered, noting the brooding stare and apathetic attitude, "and he has been awfully stand-offish lately, for him. Do you suppose we're obliged to report him?"

"Don't let it worry you," advised Erickson. "There's a spotter on the job now. Look." Harper followed his companion's eyes and recognized Dr. Mott of the psychological staff. He was leaning against the far end of the bar, and nursing a tall glass, which gave him protective coloration. But his stance was such that his field of vision included not only Hannigan, but Erickson and Harper as well.

"Yeah, and he's studying us as well," Harper added. "Damn it to hell, why does it make my back hair rise just to lay eyes on one of them?"

The question was rhetorical; Erickson ignored it. "Let's get out of here," he suggested, "and have dinner somewhere else."

"O. K."

DeLancey himself waited on them as they left. "Going so soon, gentlemen?" he asked, in a voice that implied that their departure would leave him no reason to stay open. "Beautiful lobster thermidor tonight. If you do not like it, you need not pay." He smiled brightly.

"Not sea food, Lance," Harper told him, "not tonight. Tell me—why do you stick around here when you know that the bomb is bound to get you in the long run? Aren't you afraid of it?"

The tavernkeeper's eyebrows shot up. "Afraid of the bomb? But it is my friend!"

"Makes you money, eh?"

"Oh, I do not mean that." He leaned toward them confidentially. "Five years ago I come here to make some money quickly for my family before my cancer of the stomach, it kills me. At the clinic, with the wonderful new radiants you gentlemen make with the aid of the bomb, I am cured—I live again. No, I am not afraid of the bomb; it is my good friend."

"Suppose it blows up?"

"When the good Lord needs me, He will take me." He crossed himself quickly.

As they turned away, Erickson commented in a low voice to Harper. "There's your answer, Cal—if all us engineers had his faith, the bomb wouldn't get us down."

Harper was unconvinced. "I don't know," he mused. "I don't think it's faith; I think it's lack of imagination—and knowledge."

Notwithstanding King's confidence, Lentz did not show up until the next day. The superintendent was subconsciously a little surprised at his visitor's appearance. He had pictured a master psychologist as wearing flowing hair, an imperial, and having piercing black eyes. But this man was not very tall, was heavy in his framework, and fat—almost gross. He might have been a butcher. Little, piggy, faded-blue eyes peered merrily out from beneath shaggy blond brows. There was no hair anywhere else on the enormous skull, and the apelike jaw was smooth and pink. He was dressed in mussed pajamas of unbleached linen. A long cigarette holder jutted permanently from one corner of a wide mouth, widened still more by a smile which suggested unmalicious amusement at the worst that life, or men, could do. He had gusto.

King found him remarkably easy to talk to.

At Lentz's suggestion the superintendent went first into the history of the atomic power plant, how the fission of the uranium atom by Dr. Otto Hahn in December, 1938, had opened up the way to atomic power. The door was opened just a crack; the process to be self-perpetuating and commercially usable required an enormously greater mass of uranium than there was available in the entire civilized world at that time.

But the discovery, fifteen years later, of enormous deposits of pitchblende in the old rock underlying Little America removed that obstacle. The deposits were similar to those previously worked at Great Bear Lake in the arctic north of Canada, but so much more extensive that the eventual possibility of accumulating enough uranium to build an atomic power plant became evident.

The demand for commercially usable, cheap power had never been satiated. Even the Douglas-Martin sunpower screens, used to drive the roaring road cities of the period and for a myriad other industrial purposes, were not sufficient to fill the ever-growing demand. They had saved the country from impending famine of oil and coal, but their maximum output of approximately one horsepower per square yard of sun-illuminated surface put a definite limit to the power from that source available in any given geographical area.

Atomic power was needed—was demanded.

But theoretical atomic physics predicted that a uranium mass sufficiently large to assist in its own disintegration might assist too well—blow up instantaneously, with such force that it would probably wreck every man-made structure on the globe and conceivably destroy the entire human race as well. They dared not build the bomb, even though the uranium was available.

"It was Destry's mechanics of infinitesimals that showed a way out of the dilemma," King went on. "His equations appeared to predict that an atomic explosion, once started, would disrupt the molar mass inclosing it so rapidly that neutron loss through the outer surface of the fragments would dampen the progression of the atomic explosion to zero before complete explosion could be reached.

"For the mass we use in the bomb, his equations predict a possible force of explosion one seventh of one percent of the force of complete explosion. That alone, of course, would be incomprehensibly destructive—about the equivalent of a hundred and forty thousand tons of TNT—enough to wreck this end of the State. Personally, I've never been sure that is all that would happen."

"Then why did you accept this job?" inquired Lentz.

King fiddled with items on his desk before replying. "I couldn't turn it down, doctor—I *couldn't*. If I had refused, they would have gotten someone else—and it was an opportunity that comes to a physicist once in history."

Lentz nodded. "And probably they would have gotten someone not as competent. I understand, Dr. King—you were compelled by the 'truth-tropism' of the scientist. He must go where the data are to be found, even if it kills him. But about this fellow Destry, I've never liked his mathematics; he postulates too much."

King looked up in quick surprise, then recalled that this was the man who had refined and given rigor to the calculus of statement. "That's just the hitch," he agreed. "His work is brilliant, but I've never been sure that his predictions were worth the paper they were written on. Nor, apparently," he added bitterly, "are my junior engineers."

He told the psychiatrist of the difficulties they had had with personnel, of how the most carefully selected men would, sooner or later, crack under the strain. "At first I thought it might be some degenerating effect from the hard radiation that leaks out of the bomb, so we improved the screening and the personal armor. But it didn't help. One young fellow who had joined us after the new screening was installed became violent at dinner one night, and insisted that a pork chop was about to explode. I hate to think of what might have happened if he had been on duty at the bomb when he blew up."

The inauguration of the system of constant psychological observation had greatly reduced the probability of acute danger resulting from a watch engineer cracking up, but King was forced to admit that the system was not a success; there had actually been a marked increase in psychoneuroses, dating from that time.

"And that's the picture, Dr. Lentz. It gets worse all the time. It's getting me now. The strain is telling on me; I can't sleep, and I don't think my judgment is as good as it used to be—I have trouble making up my mind, of coming to a decision. Do you think you can do anything for us?"

But Lentz had no immediate relief for his anxiety. "Not so fast, superintendent," he countered. "You have given me the background, but I have no real data as yet. I must look around for a while, smell out the situation for myself, talk to your engineers, perhaps have a few drinks with them, and get acquainted. That is possible, is it not? Then in a few days, maybe, we'll know where we stand."

King had no alternative but to agree.

"And it is well that your young men do not know what I am here for. Suppose I am your old friend, a visiting physicist, eh?"

"Why, yes—of course. I can see to it that that idea gets around. But, say—" King was reminded again of something that had bothered him from the time Silard had first suggested Lentz's name, "may I ask a personal question?"

The merry eyes were undisturbed. "Go ahead."

"I can't help but be surprised that one man should attain eminence in two such widely differing fields as psychology and mathematics. And right now I'm perfectly convinced of your ability to pass yourself off as a physicist. I don't understand it."

The smile was more amused, without being in the least patronizing, nor offensive. "Same subject," he answered.

"Eh? How's that—"

"Or rather, both mathematical physics and psychology are branches of the same subject, symbology. You are a specialist; it would not necessarily come to your attention."

"I still don't follow you."

"No? Man lives in a world of ideas. Any phenomenon is so complex that he cannot possibly grasp the whole of it. He abstracts certain characteristics of a given phenomenon as an idea, then represents that idea as a symbol, be it a word or a mathematical sign. Human reaction is almost entirely reaction to symbols, and only negligibly to phenomena. As a matter of fact," he continued, removing the cigarette holder from his mouth and settling into his subject, "it can be demonstrated that the human mind can think only in terms of symbols.

"When we think, we let symbols operate on other symbols in certain, set fashions—rules of logic, or rules of mathematics. If the symbols have been abstracted so that they are structurally similar to the phenomena they stand for, and if the symbol operations are similar in structure and order to the operations of phenomena in the real world, we think sanely. If our logic-mathematics, or our word-symbols, have been poorly chosen, we think not sanely.

"In mathematical physics you are concerned with making your symbology fit physical phenomena. In psychiatry I am concerned with precisely the same thing, except that I am more immediately concerned with the man who does the thinking than with the phenomena he is thinking about. But the same subject, always the same subject."

"We're not getting any place, Gus." Harper put down his slide rule and frowned.

"Seems like it, Cal," Erickson grudgingly admitted. "Damn it, though

—there ought to be some reasonable way of tackling the problem. What do we need? Some form of concentrated, controllable power for rocket fuel. What have we got? Power galore in the bomb. There must be some way to bottle that power, and serve it out when we need it—and the answer is some place in one of the radioactive series. I *know* it." He stared glumly around the laboratory as if expecting to find the answer written somewhere on the lead-sheathed walls.

"Don't be so down in the mouth about it. You've got me convinced there is an answer; let's figure out how to find it. In the first place the three natural radioactive series are out, aren't they?"

"Yes—at least we had agreed that all that ground had been fully covered before."

"O. K.; we have to assume that previous investigators have done what their notes show they have done—otherwise we might as well not believe anything, and start checking on everybody from Archimedes to date. Maybe that is indicated, but Methuselah himself couldn't carry out such an assignment. What have we got left?"

"Artificial radioactives."

"All right. Let's set up a list of them, both those that have been made up to now, and those that might possibly be made in the future. Call that our group—or rather, field, if you want to be pedantic about definitions. There are a limited number of operations that can be performed on each member of the group, and on the members taken in combination. Set it up."

Erickson did so, using the curious curlicues of the calculus of statement. Harper nodded. "All right—expand it."

Erickson looked up after a few moments, and asked, "Cal, have you any idea how many terms there are in the expansion?"

"No—hundreds, maybe thousands, I suppose."

"You're conservative. It reaches four figures without considering possible new radioactives. We couldn't finish such a research in a century." He chucked his pencil down and looked morose.

Cal Harper looked at him curiously, but with sympathy. "Gus," he said gently, "the bomb isn't getting you, too, is it?"

"I don't think so. Why?"

"I never saw you so willing to give up anything before. Naturally you and I will never finish any such job, but at the very worst we will have eliminated a lot of wrong answers for somebody else. Look at Edison—sixty years of experimenting, twenty hours a day, yet he never found out the one thing he was most interested in knowing. I guess if he could take it, we can."

Erickson pulled out of his funk to some extent. "I suppose so," he agreed. "Anyhow, maybe we could work out some techniques for carrying a lot of experiments simultaneously."

Harper slapped him on the shoulder. "That's the ol' fight. Besides—we may not need to finish the research, or anything like it, to find a satisfactory fuel. The way I see it; there are probably a dozen, maybe a hundred, right answers. We may run across one of them any day. Anyhow, since you're willing to give me a hand with it in your off-watch time, I'm game to peck away at it till hell freezes."

Lentz puttered around the plant and the administration center for several days, until he was known to everyone by sight. He made himself pleasant and asked questions. He was soon regarded as a harmless nuisance, to be tolerated because he was a friend of the superintendent. He even poked his nose into the commercial power end of the plant, and had the mercury-steam-turbogenerator sequence explained to him in detail. This alone would have been sufficient to disarm any suspicion that he might be a psychiatrist, for the staff psychiatrists paid no attention to the hard-bitten technicians of the power-conversion unit. There was no need to; mental instability on their part could not affect the bomb, nor were they subject to the man-killing strain of social responsibility. Theirs was simply a job personally dangerous, a type of strain strong men have been inured to since the jungle.

In due course he got around to the unit of the radiation laboratory set aside for Calvin Harper's use. He rang the bell and waited. Harper answered the door, his antiradiation helmet shoved back from his face like a grotesque sunbonnet. "What is it?" he asked. "Oh—it's you, Dr. Lentz. Did you want to see me?"

"Why, yes and no," the older man answered. "I was just looking around the experimental station, and wondered what you do in here. Will I be in the way?"

"Not at all. Come in. Gus!"

Erickson got up from where he had been fussing over the power leads to their trigger—a modified cyclotron rather than a resonant accelerator. "Hello."

"Gus, this is Dr. Lentz—Gus Erickson."

"We've met," said Erickson, pulling off his gauntlet to shake hands. He had had a couple of drinks with Lentz in town and considered him a "nice old duck." "You're just between shows, but stick around and we'll start another run—not that there is much to see."

While Erickson continued with the set-up, Harper conducted Lentz around the laboratory, explaining the line of research they were conducting, as happy as a father showing off twins. The psychiatrist listened with one ear and made appropriate comments while he studied the young scientist for signs of the instability he had noted to be recorded against him.

"You see," Harper explained, oblivious to the interest in himself, "we are testing radioactive materials to see if we can produce disintegration of the sort that takes place in the bomb, but in a minute, almost microscopic, mass. If we are successful, we can use the power of the bomb to make a safe, convenient, atomic fuel for rockets." He went on to explain their schedule of experimentation.

"I see," Lentz observed politely. "What metal are you examining now?"

Harper told him. "But it's not a case of examining one element—we've finished Isotope II with negative results. Our schedule calls next for running the same test on Isotope V. Like this." He hauled out a lead capsule, and showed the label to Lentz, who saw that it was, indeed, marked with the symbol of the fifth isotope. He hurried away to the shield around the target of the cyclotron, left open by Erickson. Lentz saw that he had opened the capsule, and was performing some operation on it in a gingerly manner, having first lowered his helmet. Then he closed and clamped the target shield.

"O. K., Gus?" he called out. "Ready to roll?"

"Yeah, I guess so," Erickson assured him, coming around from behind the ponderous apparatus, and rejoining them. They crowded behind a thick metal shield that cut them off from direct sight of the set-up.

"Will I need to put on armor?" inquired Lentz.

"No," Erickson reassured him, "we wear it because we are around the stuff day in and day out. You just stay behind the shield and you'll be all right. It's lead—backed up by eight inches of case-hardened armor plate."

Erickson glanced at Harper, who nodded, and fixed his eyes on a panel of instruments mounted behind the shield. Lentz saw Erickson press a push button at the top of the board, then heard a series of relays click on the far side of the shield. There was a short moment of silence.

The floor slapped his feet like some incredible bastinado. The concussion that beat on his ears was so intense that it paralyzed the auditory nerve almost before it could be recorded as sound. The air-conducted concussion wave flailed every inch of his body with a single, stinging, numbing blow. As he picked himself up, he found he was trembling uncontrollably and realized, for the first time, that he was getting old.

Harper was seated on the floor and had commenced to bleed from the nose. Erickson had gotten up; his cheek was cut. He touched a hand to the wound, then stood there, regarding the blood on his fingers with a puzzled expression on his face.

"Are you hurt?" Lentz inquired inanely. "What happened?"

Harper cut in. "Gus, we've done it! We've done it! Isotope V's turned the trick!"

Erickson looked still more bemused. "Five?" he said stupidly. "But that wasn't Five; that was Isotope II. I put it in myself."

"*You* put it in? *I* put it in! It was Five, I tell you!"

They stood staring at each other, still confused by the explosion, and each a little annoyed at the bone-headed stupidity the other displayed in the face of the obvious. Lentz diffidently interceded.

"Wait a minute, boys," he suggested. "Maybe there's a reason—Gus, you placed a quantity of the second isotope in the receiver?"

"Why, yes, certainly. I wasn't satisfied with the last run, and I wanted to check it."

Lentz nodded. "It's my fault, gentlemen," he admitted ruefully. "I came in and disturbed your routine, and both of you charged the receiver. I know Harper did, for I saw him do it—with Isotope V. I'm sorry."

Understanding broke over Harper's face, and he slapped the older man on the shoulder. "Don't be sorry," he laughed; "you can come around to our lab and help us make mistakes any time you feel in the mood. Can't he, Gus? This is the answer, Dr. Lentz; this is it!"

"But," the psychiatrist pointed out, "you don't know which isotope blew up."

"Nor care," Harper supplemented. "Maybe it was both, taken together. But we *will* know—this business is cracked now; we'll soon have it open." He gazed happily around at the wreckage.

In spite of Superintendent King's anxiety, Lentz refused to be hurried in passing judgment on the situation. Consequently, when he did present himself at King's office, and announced that he was ready to report, King was pleasantly surprised as well as relieved. "Well, I'm delighted," he said. "Sit down, doctor, sit down. Have a cigar. What do we do about it?"

But Lentz stuck to his perennial cigarette and refused to be hurried. "I must have some information first. How important," he demanded, "is the power from your plant?"

King understood the implication at once. "If you are thinking about shutting down the bomb for more than a limited period, it can't be done."

"Why not? If the figures supplied me are correct, your output is less than thirteen percent of the total power used in the country."

"Yes, that is true, but you haven't considered the items that go in to make up the total. A lot of it is domestic power, which householders get from sunscreens located on their own roofs. Another big slice is power for the moving roadways—that's sunpower again. The portion we provide here is the main power source for most of the heavy industries—steel, plastics, lithics, all kinds of manufacturing and processing. You might as well cut the heart out of a man—"

"But the food industry isn't basically dependent on you?" Lentz persisted.

"No. Food isn't basically a power industry—although we do supply a certain percentage of the power used in processing. I see your point, and will go on and concede that transportation—that is to say, distribution of food—could get along without us. But, good heavens, doctor, you can't stop atomic power without causing the biggest panic this country has ever seen. It's the keystone of our whole industrial system."

"The country has lived through panics before, and we got past the oil shortage safely."

"Yes—because atomic power came along to take the place of oil. You don't realize what this would mean, doctor. It would be worse than a war; in a system like ours, one thing depends on another. If you cut off the heavy industries all at once, everything else stops, too."

"Nevertheless, you had better dump the bomb." The uranium in the bomb was molten, its temperature being greater than twenty-four hundred degrees centigrade. The bomb could be dumped into a group of small containers, when it was desired to shut it down. The mass in any one container was too small to maintain progressive atomic disintegration.

King glanced involuntarily at the glass-inclosed relay mounted on his office wall, by which he, as well as the engineer on duty, could dump the bomb, if need be. "But I couldn't do that—or rather, if I did, the plant wouldn't stay shut down. The directors would simply replace me with someone who *would* operate the bomb."

"You're right, of course." Lentz silently considered the situation for some time, then said, "Superintendent, will you order a car to fly me back to Chicago?"

"You're going, doctor?"

"Yes." He took the cigarette holder from his face, and, for once, the smile of Olympian detachment was gone completely. His entire manner was sober, even tragic. "Short of shutting down the bomb, there is no solution to your problem—none whatsoever!

"I owe you a full explanation," Lentz continued, at length. "You are confronted here with recurring instances of situational psychoneurosis. Roughly, the symptoms manifest themselves as anxiety neurosis or some form of hysteria. The partial amnesia of your secretary, Steinke, is a good example of the latter. He might be cured with shock technique, but it would hardly be a kindness, as he has achieved a stable adjustment which puts him beyond the reach of the strain he could not stand.

"That other young fellow, Harper, whose blowup was the immediate cause of your sending for me, is an anxiety case. When the cause of the anxiety was eliminated from his matrix, he at once regained full sanity. But keep a close watch on his friend, Erickson—

"However, it is the cause, and prevention, of situational psychoneurosis we are concerned with here, rather than the forms in which it is manifested. In plain language, psychoneurosis situational simply refers to the common fact that, if you put a man in a situation that worries him more than he can stand, in time he blows up, one way or another.

"That is precisely the situation here. You take sensitive, intelligent young men, impress them with the fact that a single slip on their part, or even some fortuitous circumstance beyond their control, will result in the death of God knows how many other people, and then expect them to remain sane. It's ridiculous—impossible!"

"But good heavens, doctor, there must be some answer! There must!" He got up and paced around the room. Lentz noted, with pity, that King himself was riding the ragged edge of the very condition they were discussing.

"No," he said slowly. "No. Let me explain. You don't dare intrust the bomb to less sensitive, less socially conscious men. You might as well turn the controls over to a mindless idiot. And to psychoneurosis situational there are but two cures. The first obtains when the psychosis results from a misevaluation of environment. That cure calls for semantic readjustment. One assists the patient to evaluate correctly his environment. The worry disappears because there never was a real reason for worry in the situation itself, but simply in the wrong meaning the patient's mind had assigned to it.

"The second case is when the patient has correctly evaluated the situation, and rightly finds in it cause for extreme worry. His worry is perfectly sane and proper, but he can not stand up under it indefinitely; it drives him crazy. The only possible cure is to change the situation. I have stayed here long enough to assure myself that such is the condition here. Your engineers have correctly evaluated the public danger of this bomb, and it will, with dreadful certainty, drive all of you crazy!

"The only possible solution is to dump the bomb—and leave it dumped."

King had continued his nervous pacing of the floor, as if the walls of the room itself were the cage of his dilemma. Now he stopped and appealed once more to the psychiatrist. "Isn't there *anything* I can do?"

"Nothing to cure. To alleviate—well, possibly."

"How?"

"Situational psychosis results from adrenalin exhaustion. When a man is placed under a nervous strain, his adrenal glands increase their secretion to help compensate for the strain. If the strain is too great and lasts too long, the adrenals aren't equal to the task, and he cracks. That is what you have here. Adrenalin therapy might stave off a mental breakdown, but it most assuredly would hasten a physical breakdown. But that would be safer from a viewpoint of public welfare—even though it assumes that physicists are expendable!

"Another thing occurs to me: If you selected any new watch engineers from the membership of churches that practice the confessional, it would increase the length of their usefulness."

King was plainly surprised. "I don't follow you."

"The patient unloads most of his worry on his confessor, who is not himself actually confronted by the situation, and can stand it. That is simply an ameliorative, however. I am convinced that, in this situation, eventual insanity is inevitable. But there is a lot of good sense in the confessional," he added. "It fills a basic human need. I think that is why the early psychoanalysts were so surprisingly successful, for all their limited knowledge." He fell silent for a while, then added, "If you will be so kind as to order a stratocab for me—"

"You've nothing more to suggest?"

"No. You had better turn your psychological staff loose on means of alleviation; they're able men, all of them."

King pressed a switch and spoke briefly to Steinke. Turning back to Lentz, he said, "You'll wait here until your car is ready?"

Lentz judged correctly that King desired it and agreed.

Presently the tube delivery on King's desk went *ping!* The superintendent removed a small white pasteboard, a calling card. He studied it with surprise and passed it over to Lentz. "I can't imagine why he should be calling on me," he observed, and added, "Would you like to meet him?"

Lentz read:

THOMAS P. HARRINGTON
CAPTAIN (MATHEMATICS)
UNITED STATES NAVY

DIRECTOR,
U. S. NAVAL OBSERVATORY

"But I do know him," he said. "I'd be very pleased to see him."

Harrington was a man with something on his mind. He seemed relieved when Steinke had finished ushering him in, and had returned to the outer office. He commenced to speak at once, turning to Lentz, who was nearer to him than King. "You're King? . . . Why, Dr. Lentz! What are you doing here?"

"Visiting," answered Lentz, accurately but incompletely, as he shook hands. "This is Superintendent King over here. Superintendent King— Captain Harrington."

"How do you do, captain—it's a pleasure to have you here."

"It's an honor to be here, sir."

"Sit down?"

"Thanks." He accepted a chair and laid a brief case on a corner of King's desk. "Superintendent, you are entitled to an explanation as to why I have broken in on you like this—"

"Glad to have you." In fact, the routine of formal politeness was an anodyne to King's frayed nerves.

"That's kind of you, but— That secretary chap, the one that brought me in here, would it be too much to ask you to tell him to forget my name? I know it seems strange—"

"Not at all." King was mystified, but willing to grant any reasonable request of a distinguished colleague in science. He summoned Steinke to the interoffice visiphone and gave him his orders.

Lentz stood up and indicated that he was about to leave. He caught Harrington's eye. "I think you want a private palaver, captain."

King looked from Harrington to Lentz and back to Harrington. The astronomer showed momentary indecision, then protested: "I have no objection at all myself; it's up to Dr. King. As a matter of fact," he added, "it might be a very good thing if you did sit in on it."

"I don't know what it is, captain," observed King, "that you want to see me about, but Dr. Lentz is already here in a confidential capacity."

"Good! Then that's settled. I'll get right down to business. Dr. King, you know Destry's mechanics of infinitesimals?"

"Naturally." Lentz cocked a brow at King, who chose to ignore it.

"Yes, of course. Do you remember theorem six and the transformation between equations thirteen and fourteen?"

"I think so, but I'd want to see them." King got up and went over to a bookcase. Harrington stayed him with a hand.

"Don't bother. I have them here." He hauled out a key, unlocked his brief case, and drew out a large, much-thumbed, loose-leaf notebook. "Here. You, too, Dr. Lentz. Are you familiar with this development?"

Lentz nodded. "I've had occasion to look into them."

"Good—I think it's agreed that the step between thirteen and fourteen is the key to the whole matter. Now, the change from thirteen to fourteen looks perfectly valid—and would be, in some fields. But suppose we expand it to show every possible phase of the matter, every link in the chain of reasoning."

He turned a page and showed them the same two equations broken down into nine intermediate equations. He placed a finger under an associated group of mathematical symbols. "Do you see that? Do you see what that implies?" He peered anxiously at their faces.

King studied it, his lips moving. "Yes . . . I believe I do see. Odd . . . I never looked at it just that way before—yet I've studied those equations until I've dreamed about them." He turned to Lentz. "Do you agree, doctor?"

Lentz nodded slowly. "I believe so. . . . Yes, I think I may say so."

Harrington should have been pleased; he wasn't. "I had hoped you could tell me I was wrong," he said, almost petulantly, "but I'm afraid there is no further doubt about it. Dr. Destry included an assumption valid in molar physics, but for which we have absolutely no assurance in atomic physics. I suppose you realize what this means to you, Dr. King?"

King's voice was a dry whisper. "Yes," he said, "yes— It means that if that bomb out there ever blows up, we must assume that it will go up all at once, rather than the way Destry predicted—and God help the human race!"

Captain Harrington cleared his throat to break the silence that followed. "Superintendent," he said, "I would not have ventured to call had it been simply a matter of disagreement as to interpretation of theoretical predictions—"

"You have something more to go on?"

"Yes and no. Probably you gentlemen think of the Naval Observatory as being exclusively preoccupied with ephemerides and tide tables. In a way you would be right—but we still have some time to devote to research as long as it doesn't cut into the appropriation. My special interest has always been lunar theory.

"I don't mean lunar ballistics," he continued. "I mean the much more interesting problem of its origin and history, the problem the younger Darwin struggled with, as well as my illustrious predecessor, Captain T. J. J. See. I think that it is obvious that any theory of lunar origin and history must take into account the surface features of the Moon—especially the mountains, the craters, that mark its face so prominently."

He paused momentarily, and Superintendent King put in: "Just a minute, captain—I may be stupid, or perhaps I missed something, but— is there a connection between what we were discussing before and lunar theory?"

"Bear with me for a few moments, Dr. King," Harrington apologized. "There is a connection—at least, I'm *afraid* there is a connection—but I would rather present my points in their proper order before making my conclusions." They granted him an alert silence; he went on:

"Although we are in the habit of referring to the 'craters' of the Moon, we know they are not volcanic craters. Superficially, they follow none of the rules of terrestrial volcanoes in appearance or distribution, but when Rutter came out in 1952 with his monograph on the dynamics of vulcanology, he proved rather conclusively that the lunar craters could not be caused by anything that we know as volcanic action.

"That left the bombardment theory as the simplest hypothesis. It looks good, on the face of it, and a few minutes spent throwing pebbles into a patch of mud will convince anyone that the lunar craters could have been formed by falling meteors.

"But there are difficulties. If the Moon was struck so repeatedly, why not the Earth? It hardly seems necessary to mention that the Earth's atmosphere would be no protection against masses big enough to form craters like Endymion or Plato. And if they fell after the Moon was a dead world while the Earth was still young enough to change its face and erase the marks of bombardment, why did the meteors avoid so nearly completely the great dry basins we call lunar seas?

"I want to cut this short; you'll find the data and the mathematical investigations from the data here in my notes. There is one other major objection to the meteor-bombardment theory: the great rays that spread from Tycho across almost the entire surface of the Moon. It makes the Moon look like a crystal ball that had been struck with a hammer, and impact from outside seems evident, but there are difficulties. The striking mass, our hypothetical meteor, must be small enough to have formed the crater of Tycho, but it must have the mass and speed to crack an entire planet.

"Work it out for yourself—you must either postulate a chunk out of the core of a dwarf star, or speeds such as we have never observed within the system. It's conceivable but a farfetched explanation."

He turned to King. "Doctor, does anything occur to you that might account for a phenomenon like Tycho?"

The superintendent grasped the arms of his chair, then glanced at his palms. He fumbled for a handkerchief, and wiped them. "Go ahead," he said, almost inaudibly.

"Very well then." Harrington drew out of his brief case a large photograph of the Moon—a beautiful full-Moon portrait made at Lick. "I want you to imagine the Moon as she might have been sometime in the past. The dark areas we call the 'seas' are actual oceans. It has an atmosphere, perhaps a heavier gas than oxygen and nitrogen, but an active gas, capable of supporting some conceivable form of life.

"For this is an inhabited planet, inhabited by intelligent beings, beings capable of discovering atomic power and exploiting it!"

He pointed out on the photograph, near the southern limb, the lime-white circle of Tycho, with its shining, incredible, thousand-mile-long rays spreading, thrusting, jutting out from it. "Here . . . here at Tycho was located their main power plant." He moved his finger to a point near the equator and somewhat east of meridian—the point where three great dark areas merged, *Mare Nubium, Mare Imbrium, Oceanus Procellarum*—and picked out two bright splotches surrounded, also, by rays, but shorter, less distinct, and wavy. "And here at Copernicus and at Kepler, on islands at the middle of a great ocean, were secondary power stations."

He paused, and interpolated soberly: "Perhaps they knew the danger they ran, but wanted power so badly that they were willing to gamble the life of their race. Perhaps they were ignorant of the ruinous possibilities of their little machines, or perhaps their mathematicians assured them that it could not happen.

"But we will never know—no one can ever know. For it blew up and killed them—and it killed their planet.

"It whisked off the gassy envelope and blew it into outer space. It blasted great chunks off the planet's crust. Perhaps some of that escaped completely, too, but all that did not reach the speed of escape fell back down in time and splashed great ring-shaped craters in the land.

"The oceans cushioned the shock; only the more massive fragments formed craters through the water. Perhaps some life still remained in those ocean depths. If so, it was doomed to die—for the water, unprotected by atmospheric pressure, could not remain liquid and must inevitably escape in time to outer space. Its lifeblood drained away. The planet was dead—dead by suicide!"

He met the grave eyes of his two silent listeners with an expression almost of appeal. "Gentlemen . . . this is only a theory, I realize . . . only a theory, a dream, a nightmare . . . but it has kept me awake so many nights that I had to come tell you about it, and see if you saw it the same way I do. As for the mechanics of it, it's all in there in my notes. You can check it—and I pray that you find some error! But it is the only lunar theory I have examined which included all of the known data and accounted for all of them."

He appeared to have finished. Lentz spoke up. "Suppose, captain, suppose we check your mathematics and find no flaw—what then?"

Harrington flung out his hands. "That's what I came here to find out!"

Although Lentz had asked the question, Harrington directed the appeal to King. The superintendent looked up; his eyes met the astronomer's, wavered and dropped again. "There's nothing to be done," he said dully, "nothing at all."

Harrington stared at him in open amazement. "But good God, man!" he burst out. "Don't you see it? That bomb has *got* to be disassembled—at once!"

"Take it easy, captain." Lentz's calm voice was a spray of cold water. "And don't be too harsh on poor King—this worries him even more than it does you. What he means is this: we're not faced with a problem in physics, but with a political and economic situation. Let's put it this way: King can no more dump the bomb than a peasant with a vineyard on the slopes of Mount Vesuvius can abandon his holdings and pauperize his family simply because there will be an eruption some day.

"King doesn't own that bomb out there; he's only the custodian. If he dumps it against the wishes of the legal owners, they'll simply oust him and put in someone more amenable. No, we have to convince the owners."

"The president could do it," suggested Harrington. "I could get to the president—"

"No doubt you could, through the navy department. And you might even convince him. But could he help much?"

"Why, of course he could. He's the *president!*"

"Wait a minute. You're director of the Naval Observatory; suppose you took a sledge hammer and tried to smash the big telescope—how far would you get?"

"Not very far," Harrington conceded. "We guard the big fellow pretty closely."

"Nor can the president act in an arbitrary manner," Lentz persisted. "He's not an unlimited monarch. If he shuts down this plant without due process of law, the Federal courts will tie him in knots. I admit that Congress isn't helpless, but—would you like to try to give a congressional committee a course in the mechanics of infinitesimals?"

Harrington readily stipulated the point. "But there is another way," he pointed out. "Congress is responsive to public opinion. What we need to do is to convince the public that the bomb is a menace to everybody. That could be done without ever trying to explain things in terms of higher mathematics."

"Certainly it could," Lentz agreed. "You could go on the air with it and scare everybody half to death. You could create the damnedest panic this slightly slug-nutty country has ever seen. No, thank you. I, for one, would rather have us all take the chance of being quietly killed than bring on a mass psychosis that would destroy the culture we are building up. I think one taste of the Crazy Years is enough."

"Well, then, what do *you* suggest?"

Lentz considered shortly, then answered: "All I see is a forlorn hope. We've got to work on the board of directors and try to beat some sense into their heads."

King, who had been following the discussion with attention in spite of his tired despondency, interjected a remark: "How would you go about that?"

"I don't know," Lentz admitted. "It will take some thinking. But it seems the most fruitful line of approach. If it doesn't work, we can always fall back on Harrington's notion of publicity—I don't insist that the world commit suicide to satisfy my criteria of evaluation."

Harrington glanced at his wrist watch—a bulky affair—and whistled. "Good heavens!" he exclaimed. "I forgot the time! I'm supposed officially to be at the Flagstaff Observatory."

King had automatically noted the time shown by the captain's watch as it was displayed. "But it can't be that late," he had objected. Harrington looked puzzled, then laughed.

"It isn't—not by two hours. We are in zone plus-seven; this shows zone plus-five—it's radio-synchronized with the master clock at Washington."

"Did you say radio-synchronized?"

"Yes. Clever, isn't it?" He held it out for inspection. "I call it a tele-chronometer; it's the only one of its sort to date. My nephew designed it for me. He's a bright one, that boy. He'll go far. That is"—his face clouded, as if the little interlude had only served to emphasize the tragedy that hung over them—"if any of us live that long!"

A signal light glowed at King's desk, and Steinke's face showed on the communicator screen. King answered him, then said, "Your car is ready, Dr. Lentz."

"Let Captain Harrington have it."

"Then you're not going back to Chicago?"

"No. The situation has changed. If you want me, I'm stringing along."

The following Friday, Steinke ushered Lentz into King's office. King looked almost happy as he shook hands. "When did you ground, doctor? I didn't expect you back for another hour or so."

"Just now. I hired a cab instead of waiting for the shuttle."

"Any luck?"

"None. The same answer they gave you: 'The company is assured by independent experts that Destry's mechanics is valid, and sees no reason to encourage any hysterical attitude among its employees.' "

King tapped on his desk top, his eyes unfocused. Then, hitching himself around to face Lentz directly, he said, "Do you suppose the chairman is right?"

"How?"

"Could the three of us—you, me and Harrington—have gone off the deep end—slipped mentally?"

"No."

"You're sure?"

"Certain. I looked up some independent experts of my own, not retained by the company, and had them check Harrington's work. It checks." Lentz purposely neglected to mention that he had done so partly because he was none too sure of King's present mental stability.

King sat up briskly, reached out and stabbed a push button. "I am going to make one more try," he explained, "to see if I can't throw a scare into Dixon's thick head. Steinke," he said to the communicator, "get me Mr. Dixon on the screen."

"Yes, sir."

In about two minutes the visiphone screen came to life and showed the features of Chairman Dixon. He was transmitting, not from his office, but from the board room of the company in Jersey City. "Yes?" he said. "What is it, superintendent?" His manner was somehow both querulous and affable.

"Mr. Dixon," King began, "I've called to try to impress on you the seriousness of the company's action. I stake my scientific reputation that Harrington has proved completely that—"

"Oh, that? Mr. King, I thought you understood that that was a closed matter."

"But, Mr. Dixon—"

"Superintendent, please! If there were any possible legitimate cause to fear, do you think I would hesitate? I have children, you know, and grand-children."

"That is just why—"

"We try to conduct the affairs of the company with reasonable wisdom and in the public interest. But we have other responsibilities, too. There are hundreds of thousands of little stockholders who expect us to show a reasonable return on their investment. You must not expect us to jettison a billion-dollar corporation just because you've taken up astrology! Moon theory!" He sniffed.

"Very well, Mr. Chairman." King's tone was stiff.

"Don't take it that way, Mr. King. I'm glad you called—the board has just adjourned a special meeting. They have decided to accept you for retirement—with full pay, of course."

"I did not apply for retirement!"

"I know, Mr. King, but the board feels that—"

"I understand. Good-by!"

"Mr. King—"

"Good-by!" He switched him off, and turned to Lentz. " '—with full pay,' " he quoted, "which I can enjoy in any way that I like for the rest of my life—just as happy as a man in the death house!"

"Exactly," Lentz agreed. "Well, we've tried our way. I suppose we should call up Harrington now and let him try the political and publicity method."

"I suppose so," King seconded absent-mindedly. "Will you be leaving for Chicago now?"

"No," said Lentz. "No. . . . I think I will catch the shuttle for Los Angeles and take the evening rocket for the antipodes."

King looked surprised, but said nothing. Lentz answered the unspoken comment. "Perhaps some of us on the other side of the Earth will survive. I've done all that I can here. I would rather be a live sheepherder in Australia than a dead psychiatrist in Chicago."

King nodded vigorously. "That shows horse sense. For two cents, I'd dump the bomb now and go with you."

"Not horse sense, my friend—a horse will run back into a burning barn, which is exactly *not* what I plan to do. Why don't you do it and come along? If you did, it would help Harrington to scare 'em to death."

"I believe I will!"

Steinke's face appeared again on the screen. "Harper and Erickson are here, chief."

"I'm busy."

"They are pretty urgent about seeing you."

"Oh . . . all right," King said in a tired voice, "show them in. It doesn't matter."

They breezed in, Harper in the van. He commenced talking at once, oblivious of the superintendent's morose preoccupation. "We've got it, chief, we've got it—and it all checks out to the umpteenth decimal!"

"You've got what? Speak English."

Harper grinned. He was enjoying his moment of triumph, and was stretching it out to savor it. "Chief, do you remember a few weeks back when I asked for an additional allotment—a special one without specifying how I was going to spend it?"

"Yes. Come on—get to the point."

"You kicked at first, but finally granted it. Remember? Well, we've got something to show for it, all tied up in pink ribbon. It's the greatest advance in radioactivity since Hahn split the nucleus. Atomic fuel, chief, atomic fuel, safe, concentrated, and controllable. Suitable for rockets, for power plants, for any damn thing you care to use it for."

King showed alert interest for the first time. "You mean a power source that doesn't require the bomb?"

"The bomb? Oh, no, I didn't say that. You use the bomb to make the fuel, then you use the fuel anywhere and anyhow you like, with something like ninety-two percent recovery of the energy of the bomb. But you could junk the mercury-steam sequence, if you wanted to."

King's first wild hope of a way out of his dilemma was dashed; he subsided. "Go ahead. Tell me about it."

"Well—it's a matter of artificial radioactives. Just before I asked for that special research allotment, Erickson and I—Dr. Lentz had a finger in it, too—found two isotopes of a radioactive that seemed to be mutually antagonistic. That is, when we goosed 'em in the presence of each other they gave up their latent energy all at once—blew all to hell. The important point is, we were using just a gnat's whisker of mass of each—the reaction didn't require a big mass like the bomb to maintain it."

"I don't see," objected King, "how that could—"

"Neither do we, quite—but it works. We've kept it quiet until we were sure. We checked on what we had, and we found a dozen other fuels. Probably we'll be able to tailor-make fuels for any desired purpose. But here it is." Harper handed King a bound sheaf of typewritten notes which he had been carrying under his arm. "That's your copy. Look it over."

King started to do so. Lentz joined him, after a look that was a silent request for permission, which Erickson had answered with his only verbal contribution, "Sure, doc."

As King read, the troubled feelings of an acutely harassed executive left him. His dominant personality took charge, that of the scientist. He enjoyed the controlled and cerebral ecstasy of the impersonal seeker for the elusive truth. The emotions felt in the throbbing thalamus were permitted only to form a sensuous obbligato for the cold flame of cortical activity. For the time being, he was sane, more nearly completely sane than most men ever achieve at any time.

For a long period there was only an occasional grunt, the clatter of turned pages, a nod of approval. At last he put it down.

"It's the stuff," he said. "You've done it, boys. It's great; I'm proud of you."

Erickson glowed a bright pink and swallowed. Harper's small, tense figure gave the ghost of a wriggle, reminiscent of a wire-haired terrier receiving approval. "That's fine, chief. We'd rather hear you say that than get the Nobel Prize."

"I think you'll probably get it. However"—the proud light in his eyes died down—"I'm not going to take any action in this matter."

"Why not, chief?" Harper's tone was bewildered.

"I'm being retired. My successor will take over in the near future; this is too big a matter to start just before a change in administration."

"*You* being *retired!* Blazes!"

"About the same reason I took you off the bomb—at least, the directors think so."

"But that's nonsense! You were right to take me off the bomb; I *was* getting jumpy. But you're another matter—we all depend on you."

"Thanks, Cal—but that's how it is; there's nothing to be done about it." He turned to Lentz. "I think this is the last ironical touch needed to make the whole thing pure farce," he observed bitterly. "This thing is big, bigger than we can guess at this stage—and I have to give it a miss."

"Well," Harper burst out, "I can think of something to do about it!" He strode over to King's desk and snatched up the manuscript. "Either you superintend the exploitation or the company can damn well get along without our discovery!" Erickson concurred belligerently.

"Wait a minute." Lentz had the floor. "Dr. Harper, have you already achieved a practical rocket fuel?"

"I said so. We've got it on hand now."

"An escape-speed fuel?" They understood his verbal shorthand—a fuel that would lift a rocket free of the Earth's gravitational pull.

"Sure. Why, you could take any of the Clipper rockets, refit them a trifle, and have breakfast on the Moon."

"Very well. Bear with me—" He obtained a sheet of paper from King and commenced to write. They watched in mystified impatience. He continued briskly for some minutes, hesitating only momentarily. Presently he stopped and spun the paper over to King. "Solve it!" he demanded.

King studied the paper. Lentz had assigned symbols to a great number of factors, some social, some psychological, some physical, some economic. He had thrown them together into a structural relationship, using the symbols of calculus of statement. King understood the paramathematical operations indicated by the symbols, but he was not as used to them as he was to the symbols and operations of mathematical physics. He plowed through the equations, moving his lips slightly in unconscious subvocalization.

He accepted a pencil from Lentz and completed the solution. It required several more lines, a few more equations, before the elements canceled out, or rearranged themselves, into a definite answer.

He stared at this answer while puzzlement gave way to dawning comprehension and delight.

He looked up. "Erickson! Harper!" he rapped out. "We will take your new fuel, refit a large rocket, install the bomb in it, and throw it into an orbit around the Earth, far out in space. There we will use it to make more fuel, safe fuel, for use on Earth, with the danger from the bomb itself limited to the operators actually on watch!"

There was no applause. It was not that sort of an idea; their minds were still struggling with the complex implications.

"But, chief," Harper finally managed, "how about your retirement? We're still not going to stand for it."

"Don't worry," King assured him. "It's all in there, implicit in those equations, you two, me, Lentz, the board of directors—and just what we all have to do to accomplish it."

"All except the matter of time," Lentz cautioned.

"Eh?"

"You'll note that elapsed time appears in your answer as an undetermined unknown."

"Yes . . . yes, of course. That's the chance we have to take. Let's get busy!"

Chairman Dixon called the board of directors to order. "This being a special meeting, we'll dispense with minutes and reports," he announced. "As set forth in the call we have agreed to give the retiring superintendent three hours of our time."

"Mr. Chairman—"

"Yes, Mr. Thornton?"

"I thought we had settled that matter."

"We have, Mr. Thornton, but in view of Superintendent King's long and distinguished service, if he asks a hearing, we are honor bound to grant it. You have the floor, Dr. King."

King got up and stated briefly, "Dr. Lentz will speak for me." He sat down.

Lentz had to wait till coughing, throat clearing and scraping of chairs subsided. It was evident that the board resented the outsider.

Lentz ran quickly over the main points in the argument which contended that the bomb presented an intolerable danger anywhere on the face of the Earth. He moved on at once to the alternative proposal that the bomb should be located in a rocketship, an artificial moonlet flying in a free orbit around the Earth at a convenient distance—say, fifteen thousand miles—while secondary power stations on Earth burned a safe fuel manufactured by the bomb.

He announced the discovery of the Harper-Erickson technique and dwelt on what it meant to them commercially. Each point was presented as persuasively as possible, with the full power of his engaging personality. Then he paused and waited for them to blow off steam.

They did. "Visionary—" "Unproved—" "No essential change in the situation—" The substance of it was that they were very happy to hear of the new fuel, but not particularly impressed by it. Perhaps in another twenty years, after it had been thoroughly tested and proved commercially, and provided enough uranium had been mined to build another bomb, they might consider setting up another power station outside the atmosphere. In the meantime there was no hurry.

Lentz patiently and politely dealt with their objections. He emphasized the increasing incidence of occupational psychoneurosis among the engineers and the grave danger to everyone near the bomb even under the orthodox theory. He reminded them of their insurance and indemnity-bond costs, and of the "squeeze" they paid State politicians.

Then he changed his tone and let them have it directly and brutally.

"Gentlemen," he said, "we believe that we are fighting for our lives—our own lives, our families and every life on the globe. If you refuse this compromise, we will fight as fiercely and with as little regard for fair play as any cornered animal." With that he made his first move in attack.

It was quite simple. He offered for their inspection the outline of a propaganda campaign on a national scale, such as any major advertising firm could carry out as a matter of routine. It was complete to the last detail, television broadcasts, spot plugs, newspaper and magazine coverage with planted editorials, dummy "citizens' committees" and—most important—a supporting whispering campaign and a letters-to-Congress organization. Every businessman there knew from experience how such things worked.

But its object was to stir up fear of the bomb and to direct that fear, not into panic, but into rage against the board of directors personally, and into a demand that the government take action to have the bomb removed to outer space.

"This is blackmail! We'll stop you!"

"I think not," Lentz replied gently. "You may be able to keep us out of some of the newspapers, but you can't stop the rest of it. You can't even keep us off the air—ask the Federal Communications Commission." It was true. Harrington had handled the political end and had performed his assignment well; the president was convinced.

Tempers were snapping on all sides; Dixon had to pound for order. "Dr. Lentz," he said, his own temper under taut control, "you plan to make every one of us appear a black-hearted scoundrel with no other thought than personal profit, even at the expense of the lives of others. You know that is not true; this is a simple difference of opinion as to what is wise."

"I did not say it was true," Lentz admitted blandly, "but you will admit that I can convince the public that you are deliberate villains. As to it being a difference of opinion—you are none of you atomic physicists; you are not entitled to hold opinions in this matter.

"As a matter of fact," he went on callously, "the only doubt in my mind is whether or not an enraged public will destroy your precious power plant before Congress has time to exercise eminent domain and take it away from you!"

Before they had time to think up arguments in answer and ways of circumventing him, before their hot indignation had cooled and set as stubborn resistance, he offered his gambit. He produced another layout for a propaganda campaign—an entirely different sort.

This time the board of directors was to be built up, not torn down. All of the same techniques were to be used; behind-the-scenes feature articles with plenty of human interest would describe the functions of the company, describe it as a great public trust, administered by patriotic, unselfish statesmen of the business world. At the proper point in the campaign, the Harper-Erickson fuel would be announced, not as a semiaccidental result of the initiative of two employees, but as the long-expected end product of years of systematic research conducted under a fixed policy of the board of directors, a policy growing naturally out of their humane determination to remove forever the menace of explosion from even the sparsely settled Arizona desert.

No mention was to be made of the danger of complete, planet-embracing catastrophe.

Lentz discussed it. He dwelt on the appreciation that would be due them from a grateful world. He invited them to make a noble sacrifice and, with subtle misdirection, tempted them to think of themselves as heroes. He deliberately played on one of the most deep-rooted of simian instincts, the desire for approval from one's kind, deserved or not.

All the while he was playing for time, as he directed his attention from one hard case, one resistant mind, to another. He soothed and he tickled and he played on personal foibles. For the benefit of the timorous and the devoted family men, he again painted a picture of the suffering, death and destruction that might result from their well-meant reliance on the unproved and highly questionable predictions of Destry's mathematics. Then he described in glowing detail a picture of a world free from worry but granted almost unlimited power, safe power from an invention which was theirs for this one small concession.

It worked. They did not reverse themselves all at once, but a committee was appointed to investigate the feasibility of the proposed space-ship power plant. By sheer brass Lentz suggested names for the committee and Dixon confirmed his nominations, not because he wished to, particularly, but because he was caught off guard and could not think of a reason to refuse without affronting those colleagues.

The impending retirement of King was not mentioned by either side. Privately, Lentz felt sure that it never would be mentioned.

It worked, but there was left much to do. For the first few days after the victory in committee, King felt much elated by the prospect of an early release from the soul-killing worry. He was buoyed up by pleasant demands of manifold new administrative duties. Harper and Erickson were detached to Goddard Field to collaborate with the rocket engineers there in design of firing chambers, nozzles, fuel stowage, fuel metering and the like. A schedule had to be worked out with the business office to permit as much power of the bomb as possible to be diverted to making atomic fuel, and a giant combustion chamber for atomic fuel had to be designed and ordered to replace the bomb itself during the interim between the time it was shut down on Earth and the later time when sufficient local, smaller plants could be built to carry the commercial load. He was busy.

When the first activity had died down and they were settled in a new routine, pending the shutting down of the bomb and its removal to outer space, King suffered an emotional reaction. There was, by then, nothing to do but wait, and tend the bomb, until the crew at Goddard Field smoothed out the bugs and produced a space-worthy rocketship.

They ran into difficulties, overcame them, and 'came across more difficulties. They had never used such high reaction velocities; it took many trials to find a nozzle shape that would give reasonably high efficiency. When that was solved, and success seemed in sight, the jets burned out on a time-trial ground test. They were stalemated for weeks over that hitch.

Back at the power plant Superintendent King could do nothing but chew his nails and wait. He had not even the release of running over to Goddard Field to watch the progress of the research, for, urgently as he desired to, he felt an even stronger, an overpowering compulsion to watch over the bomb more lest it—heartbreakingly!—blow up at the last minute.

He took to hanging around the control room. He had to stop that; his unease communicated itself to his watch engineers; two of them cracked up in a single day—one of them on watch.

He must face the fact—there had been a grave upswing in psycho-neurosis among his engineers since the period of watchful waiting had commenced. At first, they had tried to keep the essential facts of the plan a close secret, but it had leaked out, perhaps through some member of the investigating committee. He admitted to himself now that it had been a mistake ever to try to keep it secret—Lentz had advised against it, and the engineers not actually engaged in the change-over were bound to know that something was up.

He took all of the engineers into confidence at last, under oath of secrecy. That had helped for a week or more, a week in which they were all given a spiritual lift by the knowledge, as he had been. Then it had worn off, the reaction had set in, and the psychological observers had started disqualifying engineers for duty almost daily. They were even reporting each other as mentally unstable with great frequency; he might even be faced with a shortage of psychiatrists if that kept up, he thought to himself with bitter amusement. His engineers were already standing four hours in every sixteen. If one more dropped out, he'd put himself on watch. That would be a relief, to tell himself the truth.

Somehow, some of the civilians around about and the nontechnical employees were catching on to the secret. That mustn't go on—if it spread any farther there might be a nation-wide panic. But how the hell could he stop it? He couldn't.

He turned over in bed, rearranged his pillow, and tried once more to get to sleep. No soap. His head ached, his eyes were balls of pain, and his brain was a ceaseless grind of useless, repetitious activity, like a disk recording stuck in one groove.

God! This was unbearable! He wondered if he were cracking up—if he already had cracked up. This was worse, many times worse, than the old routine when he had simply acknowledged the danger and tried to forget it as much as possible. Not that the bomb was any different—it was this five-minutes-to-armistice feeling, this waiting for the curtain to go up, this race against time with nothing to do to help.

He sat up, switched on his bed lamp, and looked at thec lock. Three-thirty. Not so good. He got up, went into his bathroom, and dissolved a sleeping powder in a glass of whiskey and water, half and half. He gulped it down and went back to bed. Presently he dozed off.

He was running, fleeing down a long corridor. At the end lay safety— he knew that, but he was so utterly exhausted that he doubted his ability to finish the race. The thing pursuing him was catching up; he forced his leaden, aching legs into greater activity. The thing behind him increased its pace, and actually touched him. His heart stopped, then pounded again. He became aware that he was screaming, shrieking in mortal terror.

But he had to reach the end of that corridor; more depended on it than just himself. He had to. He had to! *He had to!*

Then the sound hit him, and he realized that he had lost, realized it with utter despair and utter, bitter defeat. He had failed; the bomb had blown up.

The sound was the alarm going off; it was seven o'clock. His pajamas were soaked, dripping with sweat, and his heart still pounded. Every ragged nerve throughout his body screamed for release. It would take more than a cold shower to cure this case of the shakes.

He got to the office before the 'anitor was out of it. He sat there, doing nothing, until Lentz walked in on him, two hours later. The psychiatrist came in just as he was taking two small tablets from a box in his desk.

"Easy . . . easy, old man," Lentz said in a slow voice. "What have you there?" He came around and gently took possession of the box.

"Just a sedative."

Lentz studied the inscription on the cover. "How many have you had today?"

"Just two, so far."

"You don't need a sedative; you need a walk in the fresh air. Come, take one with me."

"You're a fine one to talk—you're smoking a cigarette that isn't lighted!"

"Me? Why, so I am! We both need that walk. Come."

Harper arrived less than ten minutes after they had left the office. Steinke was not in the outer office. He walked on through and pounded on the door of King's private office, then waited with the man who accompanied him—a hard young chap with an easy confidence to his bearing. Steinke let them in.

Harper brushed on past him with a casual greeting, then checked himself when he saw that there was no one else inside.

"Where's the chief?" he demanded.

"Gone out. Should be back soon."

"I'll wait. Oh—Steinke, this is Greene. Greene—Steinke."

The two shook hands. "What brings you back, Cal?" Steinke asked, turning back to Harper.

"Well . . . I guess it's all right to tell you—"

The communicator screen flashed into sudden activity, and cut him short. A face filled most of the frame. It was apparently too close to the pickup, as it was badly out of focus. "Superintendent!" it yelled in an agonized voice. "The bomb—"

A shadow flashed across the screen, they heard a dull *smack,* and the face slid out of the screen. As it fell it revealed the control room behind it. Someone was down on the floor plates, a nameless heap. Another figure ran across the field of pickup and disappeared.

Harper snapped into action first. "That was Sibard!" he shouted. "In the control room! Come on, Steinke!" He was already in motion himself.

Steinke went dead-white, but hesitated only an unmeasurable instant. He pounded sharp on Harper's heels. Greene followed without invitation, in a steady run that kept easy pace with them.

They had to wait for a capsule to unload at the tube station. Then all three of them tried to crowd into a two-passenger capsule. It refused to start, and moments were lost before Greene piled out and claimed another car.

The four-minute trip at heavy acceleration seemed an interminable crawl. Harper was convinced that the system had broken down, when the familiar click and sigh announced their arrival at the station under the bomb. They jammed each other trying to get out at the same time.

The lift was up; they did not wait for it. That was unwise; they gained no time by it, and arrived at the control level out of breath. Nevertheless, they speeded up when they reached the top, zigzagged frantically around the outer shield, and burst into the control room.

The limp figure was still on the floor, and another, also inert, was near it. The second's helmet was missing.

The third figure was bending over the trigger. He looked up as they came in, and charged them. They hit him together, and all three went down. It was two to one, but they got in each other's way. The man's heavy armor protected him from the force of their blows. He fought with senseless, savage violence.

Harper felt a bright, sharp pain; his right arm went limp and useless. The armored figure was struggling free of them.

There was a shout from somewhere behind them, "Hold still!"

Harper saw a flash with the corner of one eye, a deafening crack hurried on top of it, and re-echoed painfully in the restricted space.

The armored figure dropped back to his knees, balanced there, and then fell heavily on his face. Greene stood in the entrance, a service pistol balanced in his hand.

Harper got up and went over to the trigger. He tried to reduce the dampening adjustment, but his right hand wouldn't carry out his orders, and his left was too clumsy. "Steinke," he called, "come here! Take over."

Steinke hurried up, nodded as he glanced at the readings, and set busily to work.

It was thus that King found them when he bolted in a very few minutes later.

"Harper!" he shouted, while his quick glance was still taking in the situation. "What's happened?"

Harper told him briefly. He nodded. "I saw the tail end of the fight from my office— Steinke!" He seemed to grasp for the first time who was on the trigger. "He can't manage the controls—" He hurried toward him.

Steinke looked up at his approach. "Chief!" he called out. "Chief! *I've got my mathematics back!*"

King looked bewildered, then nodded vaguely, and let him be. He turned back to Harper. "How does it happen you're here?"

"Me? I'm here to report—we've done it, chief!"

"Eh?"

"We've finished; it's all done. Erickson stayed behind to complete the power-plant installation on the big ship. I came over in the ship we'll use to shuttle between Earth and the big ship, the power plant. Four minutes from Goddard Field to here in her. That's the pilot over there." He pointed to the door, where Greene's solid form partially hid Lentz.

"Wait a minute. You say that everything is ready to install the bomb in the ship? You're sure?"

"Positive. The big ship has already flown with our fuel—longer and faster than she will have to fly to reach station in her orbit; I was in it— out in space, chief! We're all set, six ways from zero."

King stared at the dumping switch, mounted behind glass at the top of the instrument board. "There's fuel enough," he said softly, as if he were alone and speaking only to himself; "there's been fuel enough for weeks."

He walked swiftly over to the switch, smashed the glass with his fist, and pulled it.

The room rumbled and shivered as two and a half tons of molten, massive metal, heavier than gold, coursed down channels, struck against baffles, split into a dozen dozen streams, and plunged to rest in leaden receivers—to rest, safe and harmless, until it should be reassembled far out in space.

DON A. STUART

ATOMIC POWER

THE MASS of the machine crouched in hulked, latent energy, the massive conductors leading off in gleaming ruddy columns, like the pillars of some mighty temple to an unknown, evil god, pillars fluted, and capped at base and capital with great socket-clamps. Around it huge tubes glowed with a dull bluish light, so that the faces of the half-dozen students looked distorted and ghastly.

A boredly smiling engineer watched them, and the patient professor instructing them, rather bored, not overhopeful himself that he could make these students understand the wonder and the magnitude of the process going on within the great machine.

"The power," he said, really trying intensely to make them understand the grandeur of the thing, "comes, of course, from the release of the energy of atoms. It is frequently referred to as the energy of the atom, but that is an inane viewpoint to take, for in each single second, over fifty-five duodecillion atoms are destroyed. Not truly destroyed; that has not yet been done; but broken up, and the energy of the parts absorbed, and carried away by the conductors. The fuel is water—that simplest and cheapest of all substances—hydrogen and oxygen.

"Each atom," he went on, "lasts for only one million-billionth of a second before its energy is released and the parts are discharged. There is a further energy level left in these ultraminute parts that, we believe, is even greater than the energy released in breaking the parts free of each other."

So he explained the thing, and the students looked at the great machine and realized that from the streaming energy released by it came the power which cooked their food and kept them warm, for it was winter just then.

They had seen the plant and the roaring machines which had other

140

duties, such as ventilating the great maze of subsurface tunnels, and were about to leave, when there was a sudden momentary halt in the steady throb of the great pumps. The voices of engineers rang out, cursing and excited for a few seconds. Then all went on as before for a few minutes. A new sound rose in pitch as they listened, more interested. The professor hurried them swiftly into the main power room, speaking excitedly as he did:

"You are fortunate—most fortunate. In the last eleven years, only eight times has such a thing happened. They must start the engines again!"

They hastened into the power room.

"No one knows," the instructor explained swiftly, "why these breaks occur, but once in every year or so something goes wrong, and the generators strike a bit of fuel which simply doesn't break down. No one understands why. Just that the generators stop abruptly and cannot be restarted till they are cleared of the charge contained. Perhaps some single drop of water is the cause of the trouble, a drop in no way different, save that it simply will not break.

"You are most fortunate—"

His voice was drowned by the sudden explosion of titanic discharges rushing into the generator. For scarcely a thousandth of a second it continued, before the process, restarted, backed up and stopped the discharge into it. The generator functioned perfectly.

"Most fortunate," he went on as the sound died. "The drop which caused the trouble has been ejected, the generator cleared, and now it will function for another period of a year or more unhindered, in all probability."

"What happened to the drop of water which would not break?" asked a student. "Was it saved for investigation?"

"No," replied the instructor, shrugging his shoulders. "That was done once or twice. Since then, though we of science would like it, that we might work with these strange drops, it is not done because it is so costly to dismantle and reassemble the generator. It was simply ejected. The drops which have been investigated do become susceptible after a year or two and disappear, but before that time, even high-intensity generators will not touch them, beyond reducing their outmost fringes somewhat."

"Ban" Torrence was a physicist to the core, and, like any good physicist, he was terribly concerned when perfectly sound laws of science began to have exceptions. Just now he was most worried in appearance. "Tad" Albrite, engineer, didn't seem so worried, but he was interested.

"But," objected Tad, "I don't see any vast importance in the defection of a voltmeter. You say the voltage of the cell has increased one one hundredth of a volt in a week, according to that meter. All right, what of it?"

"You yap, the thing is it hasn't increased. I measured it against a potentiometer hook-up. Now a potentiometer is a regular arm-and-pan balance for electrical voltages, as you ought to know, even if you are a civil engineer. You take a standard cell, an outside current, and standardize the thing, then substitute your unknown voltage. The system will measure a ten thousandth of a volt if you do it correctly. The point is that a potentiometer uses nothing but electrical balances. It balances a fixed current through a resistance against an electrical potential."

"The galvanometer is a magnetic device using a string, which is what you object to," said Tad.

"And when the potentiometer is balanced, the galvanometer isn't working at all, and therefore doesn't count in the circuit.

"Now by the potentiometer, the voltage of that cell last week was 1.2581. By the potentiometer this week—to-day—it is 1.2580. It has, as is quite normal, fallen one thousandth of a volt. It's been doing that for a period of two months—eight weeks. That's a grand-total drop of .0008 volts. But the voltmeter in the meantime has shown a *rise* of .0003 volts.

"Now that voltmeter checks with every other one in the place; it's a five-hundred-and-forty-two-dollar standard instrument, and it's so big and massive and sensitive, I move it around on little wheels on a cart, as you see. Don't you see what I'm getting at?"

"The Leeds and Northrup Co. gypped you apparently," decided Tad judiciously.

"They didn't. I've made other tests. In the first place, that company doesn't. In the second place, it is the tiny spring that the voltage-torque is measured against that has weakened, and every single spring I can find has weakened in like amount."

"How could you determine it?"

"Now, Tad, here's the important part of it all," replied Ban very softly. "I naturally tried weighing the standard gram weights, and the springs checked—they checked absolutely right. Until I used not a gram *weight* but a gram *mass*."

Tad stared at him blankly. "What the heck's the difference?"

"Weight is the product of mass times the acceleration of gravity. Mass —is just plain mass. Mass can be measured by inertia, and that doesn't depend on gravity. So I set up a very simple little thing, so simple it couldn't go wrong—an inverted pendulum—a little lump of metal on the end of a steel spring, and I measured its period, not with an ordinary clock, but with an electric timer that didn't have a spring or pendulum in it, and—in the two months the period of that pendulum has increased, because the spring has weakened."

"Why not—they do, you know."

"Because when I measured the strength of that spring against gravity, you see," Ban said very, very softly, "it was just—as—strong—as—ever."

Tad looked at him silently for some seconds. "What in the name of blazes does that indicate?" he asked at last, explosively.

"Gravity has weakened to exactly the same extent the spring has. Every spring I have has weakened. And gravity has weakened."

"*Gravity* weakened!" gasped Albrite. "You're cockeyed—it's impossible. Why—why the whole solar system would be thrown out of gear—the astronomers would have spotted it."

"Jack Ribly will be here at two forty," replied Torrence quietly. "You know they wouldn't proclaim news like that right off, particularly because the weakening is very slight, and they do have observational errors."

"But, good Heavens, man, it—it couldn't happen."

Ban's face was suddenly drawn and tense. "Do you think for a moment, Tad, that I was quick to accept that? I've checked and counterchecked, and rechecked. And I've found out something. That's why I called you—and Jack Ribly. You're a civil engineer, and, if I'm right, you'll see the things happening soon. And Ribly's an astronomer, and he'll see them.

"You see, whatever it is that's affecting gravity, must be affecting the strength of springs in the same degree. So I tried the compressibility of liquids. Water will compress—damn little, of course, but it will—and it's changed. It compresses more. So I tried gas. That's unchanged. Pressure of gas depends solely on mass, kinetic energy, and not on intermolecular bonds. There aren't any in gas. The molecules are perfectly free to move about. In solids they're bound so tightly they can't even slide. In water they slide, but can't separate. But they have—a little.

"And the bonds are weakening. That's why springs—solids, of course—haven't the old strength. Molecular bonds are infinitesimally weaker. But the weakening is progressive. But electric and magnetic fields are untouched. So voltmeters read high. Interatomic and intra-atomic forces in general are unchanged, but everything bigger than a single molecule is different.

"I've checked it a thousand ways, Tad. I even repeated Millikan's old measurement of the mass of an electron—which measured the mass by gravitative effect on the oil droplets—and the answer was different. Magnets lift more.

"Great Heaven, Tad, the—the universe will fly to pieces!"

"What will happen?" asked Tad, awestruck now.

"Accidents—horrible accidents here on Earth first. That is, so far as we will first detect. The Sun will be retreating. The Moon flying off, too, you see, because centrifugal force is based only on mass and inertia, and it isn't weakened, but we won't notice that at first. But automobiles—they'll weigh less and less, so they won't fall apart. Men won't notice it, because they'll be getting weaker, too.

"But the inertia of the automobile will remain the same. So when they put on the brakes, the weakened material will crack. And the engines will fly to pieces as the undiminished power of the explosions blows them open. Bridges—lighter, but weaker. The wind will be strong, though. Things blowing up in the air. The air getting thinner, as it escapes against the diminishing gravity—"

"Great Heaven!" said Tad softly. Because he believed now.

The bell rang, and Ban went downstairs and opened the door. Jack Ribly was with him when he came back. He looked curiously at their solemn faces, Ban's dark, seamed face, showing his thirty-five years, but in that ageless way that made him seem eternally thirty-five. Tad Albrite looking younger than his thirty-two.

"What's up, Ban?" asked Ribly.

Swiftly Ban explained the proposition. Ribly's face worked with surprise and belief from the first second.

"Have you fellows spotted it?" Torrence asked at last.

"Yes, 'fraid of it. Didn't announce it."

"So's everybody else. Both spotted it and been afraid. What did you notice it in?"

"Our Moon first, of course. Then Mercury and Phobos and Deimos. And—Heaven help us—I didn't understand at the time, but the companion of Sirius is bluer to-night than it was a year ago!"

"I thought you said it had no intra-atomic effects; spectra are intra-atomic effects," said Albrite.

"Not in this case. Sirius' companion is so dense, the spectrum is pulled back toward the red by the intense gravitational field. The gravitational fields are weakening—even so far away as Sirius."

"Why? Why?" demanded Albrite.

The world asked, too, when it learned; when markets found pound packages of sugar and butter weighing fifteen ounces. But that was several months later. Before then, the Moon was changed. Earth began to see a smaller Moon, and a different Moon, for as the Moon circled out, the effects were cumulative, and she turned at such a rate that the face which had eternally faced Earth began to turn away, and the unseen face became visible.

And a gold merchant made a small fortune by buying gold in Brazil, using a very accurate type of pneumatic balance, and selling it in the same way in Alaska, where the centrifugal force of the Earth's spin did not cut its weight.

The three men worked together on the problem, and all over Earth other men were seeking some answer, some explanation, and some help. The diminution of weight, starting so slowly, mounted rapidly, cumulative in rate itself.

Ban Torrence did most of the work, using the figures that Ribly brought him, and the apparatus that Albrite designed. 1947 drew to a close, and 1948 began. It was a bitterly cold winter, colder than had been known before for many, many years, despite predictions that it would be a warm one.

It was February when the astronomers definitely announced that, at present rates, the winter would be everlasting, growing neither colder nor warmer, for as the Earth turned its northern hemisphere more toward the Sun, it moved away. But in the southern hemisphere, there would be rapidly increasing cold, as the two effects added, instead of sub-tracting.

By the last of May and early June, however, the temperature would start falling again. The report ended with that statement. "By late May or early June the temperature will again begin to fall." That was the end, because there was no other prediction. After June the temperature would fall. In February, the warmest day in New York City registered a tem-perature of only 42°. The coldest was –19.2°.

And still the world asked why.

The sun rose at seven thirty on March 21st. It rose much later on April 21st, for it was falling behind. Earth was no longer circling it. Earth was spiraling about it.

In late March, the three scientists had moved to Northern Mexico and established a laboratory there. It was easier to work, and much work must be done out of doors.

"Have we got anywhere at all?" Albrite demanded when they had settled again and begun a conference on advances.

"Hum-yes," decided Torrence. He glanced quizzically at Ribly. "You wouldn't believe my statement, so I won't make it. But I'll tell you some-thing. This is about the only warm place on Earth—down in the tropics. We're in the northern hemisphere. Tropic of Cancer to the south of us."

"I still," said Albrite softly, "don't see why you didn't make a job of it and move down to the equator while you were at it."

"It's March right now, and the Sun is actually about over the equator, but it's moving north as usual, so that it'll be over the Tropic of Cancer in June—and that'll be the warmest spot on a very, very, chilly Earth. But what's the difference between the polar and equatorial diameter of the Earth?"

"I don't know—there is a difference, at that. Couple of miles, why?"

"Because the diameter of the Earth through the forty-five-degrees point is the same as the mean diameter. The poles are flattened. The equator is bulged. When gravity weakens some more, centrifugal force won't—and the thing is going to be even worse. Also—earthquakes. They'll be starting soon."

"Hmmm—that's true."

"Well, we're here. What'll we do?"

"Work—and work fast," replied Torrence. "Ever stop to think, Tad, that we'll have to use some kind of electrical generating equipment in all probability, and that we haven't time to build new, because this weakening is going on so fast that before we could spend the year so necessary nor-mally, even if we didn't freeze first, to design and build it, it couldn't be built, because all metal would be powder? We have to use standard stuff—and the standard won't be able to stand its own centrifugal force beyond July 30th. So, friend, if we don't find the answer and start in by July to stop it—there—just isn't any use."

"Is there any?" asked Albrite hopelessly. "Trying to do something with the whole solar system!"

"Not," replied Torrence, "with the whole solar system, if my idea is right. And to do anything at all, anyway, we'll have a further little problem to meet, you see. I don't know just yet."

"Then—to work," Ribly sighed. "What must I do? Go on collecting the same old data?"

"With particular emphasis on the new nebular velocities. What's Andromeda now?"

"Minus 12," replied Ribly. "My record so far is minus 22,500. Minus means retreat. The distant constellations are showing some change, too."

It was June 10th. New York City was semideserted. Snow ten feet deep, where it wasn't drifted, blocked all the streets. Where it was drifted, which was almost everywhere, it ran forty and fifty feet deep. The few people who still lived in New York, less than five hundred thousand, moved about little; only when a boat was due to sail.

Day and night the *crunch-crack-shuff* of the icebreakers in the harbor was audible. Because the temperature had begun to drop in late May. It was −32.4 at noon, June 10th. Where the icebreakers opened the water, it steamed.

The oceans were giving up their age-old hoard of heat. Had ice only been heavier, instead of lighter, than water, the temperature would not have fallen so low, for even in the cold of space where Earth was headed now, the stored heat of the oceans would have warmed her for decades.

But ice was forming. The *Atlantic* was in port now, taking aboard passengers at five hundred dollars a head for third class, five thousand for a private room. She was a vast liner, another attempt at the "world's greatest."

And New York heard a rumor. The *Atlantic* was making her last trip —the last trip any ship would make. They were afraid of the waves. They were afraid of the winds. They were most afraid of the ice.

On June 9th there was a blizzard—an antarctic blizzard. The wind howled, and the howl mounted to a shriek. No snow fell, but the powdery stuff rose, thousands of tons of it, swept up by a wind of one-hundred-mile-an-hour velocity, with undiminished force and mass, since its inertia remained. The snow had lost weight. New York was blinded.

At seven a.m. the George Washington Bridge shrieked a new song. The fragments landed nearly a quarter of a mile down the river. At seven thirty, the older bridges failed, the Brooklyn going first. By eight fifteen there were no man-made bridges. But the wind, the snow, had sucked the heat out of the rivers, and the ice had solidified all across them, so there was a single, great ice bridge.

At ten twenty, the old Woolworth Building crashed, and on its heels came the Empire State tower. The fragments of the Empire State's tower fell over most of southeastern Manhattan.

The blizzard had died by the morning of the tenth, but there were no great towers remaining on the sky line of New York. The weakening of materials, and the titanic force of the wind, had seen to that.

And the rumor that the *Atlantic* would be the last ship to leave New York spread.

The *Atlantic* was booked by dawn of the 10th, and there were no more ships in New York harbor leaving that day, sailings scheduled the next day would not go. A crowd gathered about the sheltered dock of the *Atlantic* on the southern side of Manhattan. A wind still raged at forty-five miles an hour from the north.

Slowly the crowd grew, and the low muttering increased. Police and guards kept the lines in check till ten. The *Atlantic* was to sail at noon. At ten ten, the crowd swarmed up her gangways. Guards were killed, crushed. Men, women, and children started up the gangplanks.

Men, and some women, reached the decks and burst into the cabins. Men found and fought their way to the neighborhood of the boiler and engine rooms. At ten twenty, it was estimated there were two thousand people aboard, at ten forty, seven thousand. At eleven o'clock, at least fifteen thousand people, over a thousand tons of humanity, had got aboard.

It was like no other panic crowding. Many of those fifteen thousand were dead already, many more dying. A woman's body trampled underfoot. A girl held erect by the crowd's pressing, blood slowly oozing from her shoulder, her arm torn completely off, held perhaps in the clenched fingers of her other hand like some monstrous club, dead. A man's dismembered corpse.

For the power of human bodies is supplied by chemical combinations. These were the visible damages, there were shrieks, groans of horrible agony, for the chemical power of muscles remained undiminished, while their tensile strength declined. Literally, people tore themselves apart by the violence of their struggles.

The *Atlantic* gained no more passengers after eleven.

The officers would not sail. They might have sailed for the moment to end the deaths at the wharf, but they could not, for the ship, already filled to capacity, was overloaded. Further, she swayed slowly to the struggles of her passengers.

Then a hold, hitherto undiscovered, was broken open. Instantly a torrent of people poured in, and another five thousand came aboard the ship. A slow, grinding pressure began, and those who, finding themselves in the heated hallways, had stopped, satisfied, and blocked the entrance of more thereby, were gradually driven farther.

The captain ordered the ship to sail. The lines were cast off again, and the ship's great screws turned slowly. No human strength could hold her in now, and she broke free of the crowd at the wharf. But in the harbor, free of the crowd, she stopped again at once. The captain ordered that the crowd be forced off onto the ice shelf that they might walk home. Armed men descended toward them from the bridge.

Half a hundred shots rang out from the crowd. Three guns burst, but the captain and his officers died. The engineer died soon, and his staff was forced to obey the orders from the amateur pilot above.

The *Atlantic* weighed eighty-five thousand tons normally. Her mass remained, and she had more than her normal load aboard her now. The channels had been broken by the icebreakers, but it was wider than the actual channel, of course. And the amateur pilot had no faintest conception of the handling of an eighty-five-thousand-ton ship.

Things were not normal then. There was a forty-five-mile wind, and the ship was loaded abnormally; she was top-heavy. And she struck a great rock. Normally she would have come to instant rest, with a small ten-foot hole in her hull. The amateur pilot had the engines at half speed, and, in desperation, he had thrown them to full speed ahead, as he saw the danger, and tried to cut the wheel as though she were a motor boat.

The *Atlantic's* metal, weakened by the strange force, ripped open for two hundred and ninety-four feet. She sank in fourteen and a half seconds, and rolled on her side, off the ledge of rock, and into the deep water the amateur had almost succeeded in reaching.

Perhaps two thousand might have been saved from the part still unsubmerged. Ships were starting out after them. But the hull sloped, and some slid, for under that howling wind, ice froze in seconds. They fought, and a total of one hundred and seventy-four were saved.

And rumor had been right. The *Atlantic* was the last ship to sail from New York, for her wreck blocked the channel, and the wind howled down from the north all that day and all the next so that no well-equipped salvage ship could cut her out of the way, and for that matter it howled all the rest of the days, but that was not important. The ice in the harbor was fourteen feet thick on the morning of the 12th.

London was blocked on the 21st, Baltimore on the 22nd. And the seas of all the world steamed, and the winds, blowing over them, were warmed to some slight extent, so that New York did not have temperatures below –72 until July 3rd, when a northwest gale swept, not from the Atlantic, but all across frozen Canada, and the water in the mains fifty feet below the street froze.

Fire started that day, and ravaged unchecked, till the solid walls of stone and ice it encountered succeeded in damping it, and the wind blew it out again, as it had fanned it before.

Men had learned to be careful by that time, and no one worked even slightly harder than normal. Tens of thousands had died horribly as the automatic muscles of their hearts strained to pump the blood harder—and tore themselves to pieces.

"If," said Tad Albrite desperately, "you don't do something fairly quickly, there won't be any sense in trying. You can't get equipment to do anything in another two weeks."

Ban Torrence looked up bitterly. His eyes were tired and dead. "Will you go away? It's atomic power. I'm after it. If I get it, I can do something, and I won't need so much equipment. If I don't, I won't need any, anyway."

"Atomic power!" gasped Albrite. His voice trailed off as he said it, trailed off into hopelessness. "They've tried for decades."

Torrence motioned toward a massive piece of apparatus on one side of the laboratory. "Almost!" He sighed. "So shut up and let me work."

Albrite rose to look at the thing. Two feet long, a semicylinder. Ruddy copper bars led from it to huge electrolytic condenser banks and a bank of powerful accumulators. And to a further piece of apparatus. Silently he looked at it, then went to the closet, put on his heavy robes, and stepped out into the cold toward the observatory and Jack Ribly.

It was several hours later when he returned. Ban Torrence was fussing with his apparatus again. He looked up at their entrance.

"Hello! I wish you'd look at these blasted circuits again, Ribly, and you, too, Tad. I swear it ought to work. It almost did for a fraction of a second."

"Have you tried it again?" asked Ribly.

"No. 'Fraid it might blow up this time instead of stopping."

"Who cares? Try it," snapped Ribly.

"What ought it to do?" asked Albrite.

"Release atomic energy—not all of it, just smash the atom to parts and collect the energy of the parts. Enough, though, for what we want."

"Try it. We can't lose much," Albrite said. "What are you going to do with the power if it works? How will it help?"

"It will help. I think—I think that Earth and the solar system—just an atom in a greater universe. But they're releasing atomic energy in that greater universe—and we're the atom! If my theory's right, then I can release atomic energy myself and stop their release of *our* energy by just slightly upsetting their field, so that it passes by, harmless. Not a terrific amount of energy needed. The field would spread out from this apparatus here—if it would work—at the speed of light.

"In a second, things would be normal on Earth. In four, the Moon would start coming back. In a few minutes, the Sun's old gravity would be returned, the system balanced. Then the thing would spread till all the universe was reëstablished.

"I really slightly invert their energy, so that it destroys itself. It would be a spreading sphere of neutralization, self-propagating, feeding on the thing it destroyed. I would have to add no more energy to clear all the universe we know of that force.

"You know—the force is ages old. To that superuniverse, the whole process we've been undergoing for the last months is perhaps a million billionth of a second. The thing has been going on for ages. That is why we have seen distant nebulæ rush away—to eternal destruction. The evaporation of their atomic fuel as we felt the first fringes of their power. Now we are in the heart of their release. If I can do this, I suppose they will never know what has happened.

"But I tried the thing, and the blasted thing worked for perhaps a hundredth of a second, just long enough to kick my instruments and show it worked, but not long enough to start that field.

"Shall I try again?"

"I say yes," replied Ribly.

Mutely, Tad Albrite nodded.

Ban Torrence walked over to his controls. Slowly, thoughtfully, he set up the switches. For perhaps thirty seconds of silence he waited with the last switch in his hand.

"If this works we shall be most fortunate—"

His voice was drowned by the sudden titanic discharges rushing into the generator. For scarcely a thousandth of a second it continued before the process, restarted, backed up, and stopped the discharge into it. The generator functioned perfectly.

For an infinitesimal fragment of a second, a strange nausea swept them as the wave of the counterfield drove out, swift as light, into all the universe. Ban Torrence riveted his eyes on the wall clock, the clock that had swung its pendulum with a strange lethargy, as though not interested in keeping up with time. It was ticking suddenly, with a regular, swift stroke.

"Thank Heaven—it works!" said Torrence softly. For a moment his eyes looked toward and through the mass of the machine, crouched in hulked, latent power, the massive conductors leading off in gleaming, ruddy columns. "I wonder," he went on very softly, "if, in some vaster world, they even *knew*—as this particular atom of fuel simply refused to disintegrate."

Then abruptly the scientist in him rebelled. "But why in blazes didn't it work before? I didn't change the thing in the slightest. The same fuel—water—the same generator. Just took it apart and put it back together again exactly as before. I can't see *why*."

"Was the water pure?" asked Albrite. "Maybe it wasn't—and when you took it apart the drop which caused the trouble was ejected, the generator cleared, and now it will function for another period, until another drop which can't be disintegrated hits it."

"Maybe so; somehow I doubt it. That particular drop simply wouldn't

break down. I can't understand why. Just that the generator must have
stopped abruptly and could not be restarted till cleared of the charge
contained.

"Anyway, it's working perfectly now."

Torrence looked at it, and though he might have told those scientists
of a greater world why their machines failed occasionally, since he knew
much that they did not, he did not understand all that went on within
an atomic generator.

Only he knew that he had restored Earth; that even now she, and her
satellite, must be circling toward each other, and toward the Sun; that
he had found the secret of vast power that would warm the frozen peoples
and power their industry as Earth thawed out once more.

PART TWO

THE WONDERS
OF EARTH

THEODORE STURGEON

KILLDOZER!

*BEFORE the race was the deluge, and before the deluge another race,
whose nature it is not for mankind to understand. Not unearthly, not
alien, for this was their earth and their home.*

*There was a war between this race, which was a great one, and another.
The other was truly alien, a sentient cloudform, an intelligent grouping of
tangible electrons. It was spawned in mighty machines by some accident
of a science before our aboriginal conception of its complexities. And the
machines, servants of the people, became the people's masters, and great
were the battles that followed. The electron-beings had the power to warp
the delicate balances of atom-structure, and their life-medium was metal,
which they permeated and used to their own ends. Each weapon the people
developed was possessed and turned against them, until a time when the
remnants of that vast civilization found a defense—*

*An insulator. The terminal product or by-product of all energy research
—neutronium.*

*In its shelter they developed a weapon. What it was we shall never
know, and our race will live—or we shall know, and our race will perish
as theirs perished. For, to destroy the enemy, it got out of hand and its
measureless power destroyed them with it, and their cities, and their possessed machines. The very earth dissolved in flame, the crust writhed and
shook and the oceans boiled. Nothing escaped it, nothing that we know as
life, and nothing of the pseudolife that had evolved within the mysterious
force-fields of their incomprehensible machines, save one hardy mutant.*

*Mutant it was, and ironically this one alone could have been killed by
the first simple measures used against its kind—but it was past time for
simple expediences. It was an organized electron-field possessing intelligence and mobility and a will to destroy, and little else. Stunned by the*

holocaust, it drifted over the grumbling globe, and in a lull in the violence of the forces gone wild on Earth, sank to the steaming ground in its half-conscious exhaustion. There it found shelter—shelter built by and for its dead enemies. An envelope of neutronium. It drifted in, and its conscious-ness at last fell to its lowest ebb. And there it lay while the neutronium, with its strange constant flux, its interminable striving for perfect balance, extended itself and closed the opening. And thereafter in the turbulent eons that followed, the envelope tossed like a gray bubble on the surface of the roiling sphere, for no substance on Earth would have it or combine with it.

The ages came and went, and chemical action and reaction did their mysterious work, and once again there was life and evolution. And a tribe found the mass of neutronium, which is not a substance but a static force, and were awed by its aura of indescribable chill, and they worshiped it and built a temple around it and made sacrifices to it. And ice and fire and the seas came and went, and the land rose and fell as the years went by, until the ruined temple was on a knoll, and the knoll was an island. Islanders came and went, lived and built and died, and races forgot. So now, some-where in the Pacific to the west of the archipelago called Islas Revillagigeda, there was an uninhabited island. And one day—

CHUB HORTON and Tom Jaeger stood watching the *Sprite* and her squat tow of three cargo lighters dwindle over the glassy sea. The big ocean-going towboat and her charges seemed to be moving out of focus rather than traveling away. Chub spat cleanly around the cigar that grew out of the corner of his mouth.

"That's that for three weeks. How's it feel to be a guinea pig?"

"We'll get it done." Tom had little crinkles all around the outer ends of his eyes. He was a head taller than Chub and rangy, and not so tough, and he was a real operator. Choosing him as a foreman for the experiment had been wise, for he was competent and he commanded respect. The theory of airfield construction that they were testing appealed vastly to him, for here were no officers-in-charge, no government inspectors, no time-keeping or reports. The government had allowed the company a temporary land grant, and the idea was to put production-line techniques into the layout and grading of the project. There were six operators and two mechanics and more than a million dollars' worth of the best equipment that money could buy. Government acceptance was to be on a partially com-pleted basis, and contingent on government standards. The theory obvi-ated both gold-bricking and graft, and neatly sidestepped the man-power shortage. "When that black-topping crew gets here, I reckon we'll be ready for 'em," said Tom.

He turned and scanned the island with an operator's vision and saw it as it was, and in all the stages it would pass through, and as it would look when they had finished, with four thousand feet of clean-draining runway, hard-packed shoulders, four acres of plane-park, the access road and the short taxiway. He saw the lay of each lift that the power shovel would cut as it brought down the marl bluff, and the ruins on top of it that would give them stone to haul down the salt-flat to the little swamp at the other end, there to be walked in by the dozers.

"We got time to walk the shovel up there to the bluff before dark."

They walked down the beach toward the outcropping where the equipment stood surrounded by crates and drums of supplies. The three tractors were ticking over quietly, the two-cycle Diesel chuckling through their mufflers and the big D-7 whacking away its metronomic compression knock on every easy revolution. The Dumptors were lined up and silent, for they would not be ready to work until the shovel was ready to load them. They looked like a mechanical interpretation of Dr. Dolittle's "Pushme-pullyou," the fantastic animal with two front ends. They had two large driving wheels and two small steerable wheels. The motor and the driver's seat were side by side over the front—or smaller—wheels; but the driver faced the dump body between the big rear wheels, exactly the opposite of the way he would sit in a dump truck. Hence, in traveling from shovel to dumping-ground, the operator drove backwards, looking over his shoulder, and in dumping he backed the machine up but he himself traveled forward—quite a trick for fourteen hours a day! The shovel squatted in the midst of all the others, its great hulk looming over them, humped there with its boom low and its iron chin on the ground, like some great tired dinosaur.

Rivera, the Puerto Rican mechanic, looked up grinning as Tom and Chub approached, and stuck a bleeder wrench into the top pocket of his coveralls.

"She says 'Sigalo,'" he said, his white teeth flashlighting out of the smear of grease across his mouth. "She says she wan' to get dirt on dis paint." He kicked the blade of the Seven with his heel.

Tom sent the grin back—always a surprising thing in his grave face.

"That Seven'll do that, and she'll take a good deal off her bitin' edge along with the paint before we're through. Get in the saddle, Goony. Build a ramp off the rocks down to the flat there, and blade us off some humps from here to the bluff yonder. We're walking the dipper up there."

The Puerto Rican was in the seat before Tom had finished, and with a roar the Seven spun in its length and moved back along the outcropping to the inland edge. Rivera dropped his blade and the sandy marl curled and piled up in front of the dozer, loading the blade and running off in two even rolls at the ends. He shoved the load toward the rocky edge, the Seven revving down as it took the load, *blat blat blatting* and pulling like a supercharged ox as it fired slowly enough for them to count the revolutions.

"She's a hunk of machine," said Tom.

"A hunk of operator, too," gruffed Chub, and added, "for a mechanic."

"The boy's all right," said Kelly. He was standing there with them, watching the Puerto Rican operate the dozer, as if he had been there all along, which was the way Kelly always arrived places. He was tall, slim, with green eyes too long and an easy stretch to the way he moved, like an attenuated cat. He said, "Never thought I'd see the day when equipment was shipped set up ready to run like this. Guess no one ever thought of it before."

"There's times when heavy equipment has to be unloaded in a hurry these days," Tom said. "If they can do it with tanks, they can do it with construction equipment. We're doin' it to build something instead, is all. Kelly, crank up the shovel. It's oiled. We're walking it over to the bluff."

Kelly swung up into the cab of the big dipper-stick and, diddling the governor control, pulled up the starting handle. The Murphy Diesel snorted and settled down into a thudding idle. Kelly got into the saddle, set up the throttle a little, and began to boom up.

"I still can't get over it," said Chub. "Not more'n a year ago we'd a had two hundred men on a job like this."

Tom smiled. "Yeah, and the first thing we'd have done would be to build an office building, and then quarters. Me, I'll take this way. No timekeepers, no equipment-use reports, no progress and yardage summaries, no nothin' but eight men, a million bucks worth of equipment, an' three weeks. A shovel an' a mess of tool crates'll keep the rain off us, an' army field rations'll keep our bellies full. We'll get it done, we'll get out and we'll get paid."

Rivera finished the ramp, turned the Seven around and climbed it, walking the new fill down. At the top he dropped his blade, floated it, and backed down the ramp, smoothing out the rolls. At a wave from Tom he started out across the shore, angling up toward the bluff, beating out the humps and carrying fill into the hollows. As he worked, he sang, feeling the beat of the mighty motor, the micrometric obedience of that vast implacable machine.

"Why doesn't that monkey stick to his grease guns?"

Tom turned and took the chewed end of a match stick out of his mouth. He said nothing, because he had for some time been trying to make a habit of saying nothing to Joe Dennis. Dennis was an ex-accountant, drafted out of an office at the last gasp of a defunct project in the West Indies. He had become an operator because they needed operators badly. He had been released with alacrity from the office because of his propensity for small office politics. It was a game he still played, and completely aside from his boiled-looking red face and his slightly womanish walk, he was out of place in the field; for boot-licking and back-stabbing accomplish even less out on the field than they do in an office. Tom, trying so hard to keep his mind on his work, had to admit to himself that of all Dennis' annoying traits the worst was that he was as good a pan operator as could be found anywhere, and no one could deny it.

Dennis certainly didn't.

"I've seen the day when anyone catching one of those goonies so much as sitting on a machine during lunch, would kick his fanny," Dennis groused. "Now they give 'em a man's work and a man's pay."

"*Doin'* a man's work, ain't he?" Tom said.

"He's a Puerto Rican!"

Tom turned and looked at him levelly. "Where was it you said *you* come from," he mused. "Oh yeah. Georgia."

"What do you mean by that?"

Tom was already striding away. "Tell you as soon as I have to," he flung back over his shoulder. Dennis went back to watching the Seven.

Tom glanced at the ramp and then waved Kelly on. Kelly set his housebrake so the shovel could not swing, put her into travel gear, and shoved the swing lever forward. With a crackling of drive chains and a massive scrunching of compacting coral sand, the shovel's great flat pads carried her over and down the ramp. As she tipped over the peak of the ramp the heavy manganese steel bucket-door gaped open and closed, like a hungry mouth, slamming up against the bucket until suddenly it latched shut and was quiet. The big Murphy Diesel crooned hollowly under compression as the machine ran downgrade and then the sensitive governor took hold and it took up its belly-beating thud.

Peebles was standing by one of the door-pan combines, sucking on his pipe and looking out to sea. He was grizzled and heavy, and from under the bushiest gray brows looked the calmest gray eyes Tom had ever seen. Peebles had never gotten angry at a machine—a rare trait in a born mechanic—and in fifty-odd years he had learned it was even less use getting angry at a man. Because no matter what, you could always fix what was wrong with a machine. He said around his pipestem:

"Hope you'll give me back my boy, there."

Tom's lips quirked in a little grin. There had been an understanding between old Peebles and himself ever since they had met. It was one of those things which exists unspoken—they knew little about each other because they had never found it necessary to make small talk to keep their friendship extant. It was enough to know that each could expect the best from the other, without persuasion.

"Rivera?" Tom asked. "I'll chase him back as soon as he finishes that service road for the dipper-stick. Why—got anything on?"

"Not much. Want to get that arc welder drained and flushed and set up a grounded table in case you guys tear anything up." He paused. "Besides, the kid's filling his head up with too many things at once. Mechanicing is one thing; operating is something else."

"Hasn't got in his way much so far, has it?"

"Nope. Don't aim t' let it, either. 'Less you need him."

Tom swung up on the pan tractor. "I don't need him that bad, Peeby. If you want some help in the meantime, get Dennis."

Peebles said nothing. He spat. He didn't say anything at all.

"What's the matter with Dennis?" Tom wanted to know.

"Look yonder," said Peebles, waving his pipestem. Out on the beach. Dennis was talking to Chub, in Dennis' indefatigable style, standing beside Chub, one hand on Chub's shoulder. As they watched they saw Dennis call his side-kick, Al Knowles.

"Dennis talks too much," said Peebles. "That most generally don't amount to much, but that Dennis, he sometimes *says* too much. Ain't got what it takes to run a show, and knows it. Makes up for it by messin' in between folks."

"He's harmless," said Tom.

Still looking up the beach, Peebles said slowly:

"Is, so far."

Tom started to say something, then shrugged. "I'll send you Rivera," he said, and opened the throttle. Like a huge electric dynamo, the two-cycle motor whined to a crescendo. Tom lifted the dozer with a small lever by his right thigh and raised the pan with the long control sprouting out from behind his shoulder. He moved off, setting the rear gate of the scraper so that anything the blade bit would run off to the side instead of loading into the pan. He slapped the tractor into sixth gear and whined up to and around the crawling shovel, cutting neatly in under the boom and running on ahead with his scraper blade just touching the ground, dragging to a fine grade the service road Rivera had cut.

Dennis was saying, "It's that little Hitler stuff. Why should I take that kind of talk? 'You come from Georgia,' he says. What is he—a Yankee or something?"

"A crackah f'm Macon," chortled Al Knowles, who came from Georgia, too. He was tall and stringy and round-shouldered. All of his skill was in his hands and feet, brains being a commodity he had lived without all his life until he had met Dennis and used him as a reasonable facsimile thereof.

"Tom didn't mean nothing by it," said Chub.

"No, he didn't mean nothin'. Only that we do what he says the way he says it, specially if he finds a way we don't like it. *You* wouldn't do like that, Chub. Al, think Chub would carry on thataway?"

"Sure wouldn't," said Al, feeling it expected of him.

"Nuts," said Chub, pleased and uncomfortable, and thinking, what have I got against Tom?—not knowing, not liking Tom as well as he had. "Tom's the man here, Dennis. We got a job to do—let's skit and git. Man can take anything for a lousy six weeks."

"Oh, sho'," said Al.

"Man can take just so much," Dennis said. "What they put a man like that on top for, Chub? What's the matter with you? Don't you know grading and drainage as good as Tom? Can Tom stake out a side hill like you can?"

"Sure, sure, but what's the difference, long as we get a field built?

An' anyhow, hell with bein' the boss-man. Who gets the blame if things don't run right, anyway?"

Dennis stepped back, taking his hand off Chub's shoulder, and stuck an elbow in Al's ribs.

"You see that, Al? Now there's a smart man. That's the thing Uncle Tom didn't bargain for. Chub, you can count on Al and me to do just that little thing."

"Do just what little thing?" asked Chub, genuinely puzzled.

"Like you said. If the job goes wrong, the boss gets blamed. So if the boss don't behave, the job goes wrong."

"Uh-huh," agreed Al with the conviction of mental simplicity.

Chub double-took this extraordinary logical process and grasped wildly at anger as the conversation slid out from under him. "I didn't say any such thing! This job is goin' to get done, no matter what! Hitler ain't hangin' no iron cross on me or anybody else around here if I can help it."

"Tha's the ol' fight," feinted Dennis. "We'll show that guy what we think of his kind of sabotage."

"You talk too much," said Chub and escaped with the remnants of coherence. Every time he talked with Dennis he walked away feeling as if he had an unwanted membership card stuck in his pocket that he couldn't throw away with a clear conscience.

Rivera ran his road up under the bluff, swung the Seven around, punched out the master clutch and throttled down, idling. Tom was making his pass with the pan, and as he approached, Rivera slipped out of the seat and behind the tractor, laying a sensitive hand on the final drive casing and sprocket bushings, checking for overheating. Tom pulled alongside and beckoned him up on the pan tractor.

"*Que pase,* Goony? Anything wrong?"

Rivera shook his head and grinned. "Nothing wrong. She is perfect, that '*De Siete.*' She—"

"That what? 'Daisy Etta'?"

"*De siete.* In Spanish, D-7. It means something in English?"

"Got you wrong," smiled Tom. "But Daisy Etta is a girl's name in English, all the same."

He shifted the pan tractor into neutral and engaged the clutch, and jumped off the machine. Rivera followed. They climbed aboard the Seven, Tom at the controls.

Rivera said "Daisy Etta," and grinned so widely that a soft little chuckling noise came from behind his back teeth. He reached out his hand, crooked his little finger around one of the tall steering clutch levers, and pulled it all the way back. Tom laughed outright.

"You got something there," he said. "The easiest runnin' cat ever built. Hydraulic steerin' clutches and brakes that'll bring you to a dead stop if you spit on 'em. Forward an' reverse lever so's you got all your speeds front and backwards. A little different from the old jobs. They had no booster springs, eight-ten years ago; took a sixty-pound pull to get a steerin' clutch back. Cuttin' a side-hill with an angle-dozer really was a job in them days. You try it sometime, dozin' with one hand, holdin' her nose out o' the bank with the other, ten hours a day. And what'd it get you? Eighty cents an hour an' "—Tom took his cigarette and butted the fiery end out against the horny palm of his hand—"these."

"*Santa Maria!*"

"Want to talk to you, Goony. Want to look over the bluff, too, at that stone up there. It'll take Kelly pret' near an hour to get this far and sumped in, anyhow."

They started up the slope, Tom feeling the ground under the four-foot brush, taking her up in a zigzag course like a hairpin road on a mountain-side. Though the Seven carried a muffler on the exhaust stack that stuck up out of the hood before them, the blat of four big cylinders hauling fourteen tons of steel upgrade could outshout any man's conversation, so they sat without talking, Tom driving, Rivera watching his hands flick over the controls.

The bluff started in a low ridge running almost the length of the little island, like a lopsided backbone. Toward the center it rose abruptly, sent a wing out toward the rocky outcropping at the beach where their equipment had been unloaded, and then rose again to a small, almost square plateau area, half a mile square. It was humpy and rough until they could see all of it, when they realized how incredibly level it was, under the brush and ruins that covered it. In the center—and exactly in the center they realized suddenly—was a low, overgrown mound. Tom threw out the clutch and revved her down.

"Survey report said there was stone up here," Tom said, vaulting out of the seat. "Let's walk around some."

They walked toward the knoll, Tom's eyes casting about as he went. He stooped down into the heavy, short grass and scooped up a piece of stone, blue-gray, hard and brittle.

"Rivera—look at this. This is what the report was talking about. See—more of it. All in small pieces, though. We need big stuff for the bog if we can get it."

"Good stone?" asked Rivera.

"Yes, boy—but it don't belong here. Th' whole island's sand and marl and sandstone on the outcrop down yonder. This here's a bluestone, like diamond clay. Harder'n blazes. I never saw this stuff on a marl hill before. Or near one. Anyhow, root around and see if there is any big stuff."

They walked on. Rivera suddenly dipped down and pulled grass aside.

"Tom—here's a beeg one."

Tom came over and looked down at the corner of stone sticking up out of the topsoil. "Yeh. Goony, get your girl-friend over here and we'll root it out."

Rivera sprinted back to the idling dozer and climbed aboard. He brought the machine over to where Tom waited, stopped, stood up and peered over the front of the machine to locate the stone, then sat down and shifted gears. Before he could move the machine Tom was on the fender beside him, checking him with a hand on his arm.

"No, boy—no. Not third. First. And half throttle. That's it. Don't try to bash a rock out of the ground. Go on up to it easy; set your blade against it, lift it out, don't boot it out. Take it with the middle of your blade, not the corner—get the load on both hydraulic cylinders. Who told you to do like that?"

"No one tol' me, Tom. I see a man do it, I do it."

"Yeah? Who was it?"

"Dennis, but—"

"Listen, Goony, if you want to learn anything from Dennis, watch him while he's on a pan. He dozes like he talks. That reminds me—what I wanted to talk to you about. You ever have any trouble with him?"

Rivera spread his hands. "How I have trouble when he never tall: to me?"

"Well, that's all right then. You keep it that way. Dennis is O.K., I guess, but you better keep away from him."

He went on to tell the boy then about what Peebles had said concerning being an operator and a mechanic at the same time. Rivera's lean dark face fell, and his hand strayed to the blade control, touching it lightly, feeling the composition grip and the machined locknuts that held it. When Tom had quite finished he said:

"O.K., Tom—if you want, you break 'em, I feex 'em. But if you wan' help some time, I run *Daisy Etta* for you, no?"

"Sure, kid, sure. But don't forget, no man can do everything."

"You can do everything," said the boy.

Tom leaped off the machine and Rivera shifted into first and crept up to the stone, setting the blade gently against it. Taking the load, the mighty engine audibly bunched its muscles; Rivera opened the throttle a little and the machine set solidly against the stone, the tracks slipping, digging into the ground, piling loose earth up behind. Tom raised a fist, thumb up, and the boy began lifting his blade. The Seven lowered her snout like an ox pulling through mud; the front of the tracks buried themselves deeper and the blade slipped upward an inch on the rock, as if it were on a ratchet. The stone shifted, and suddenly heaved itself up out of the earth that covered it, bulging the sod aside like a ship's slow bow-wave. And the blade lost its grip and slipped over the stone. Rivera slapped out the master clutch within an ace of letting the mass of it poke through his radiator core. Reversing, he set the blade against it again and rolled it at last into daylight.

Tom stood staring at it, scratching the back of his neck. Rivera got off the machine and stood beside him. For a long time they said nothing.

The stone was roughly rectangular, shaped like a brick with one end cut at about a thirty-degree angle. And on the angled face was a square-cut ridge, like the tongue on a piece of milled lumber. The stone was about 3 x 2 x 2 feet, and must have weighed six or seven hundred pounds.

"Now that," said Tom, bug-eyed, "didn't grow *here*, and if it did it never grew that way."

"*Una piedra de una casa*," said Rivera softly. "Tom, there was a building here, no?"

Tom turned suddenly to look at the knoll.

"There is a building here—or what's left of it. Lord on'y knows how old—"

They stood there in the slowly dwindling light, staring at the knoll; and there came upon them a feeling of oppression, as if there were no wind and no sound anywhere. And yet there was wind, and behind them *Daisy Etta* whacked away with her muttering idle, and nothing had changed and—was that it? That nothing had changed? That nothing would change, or could, here?

Tom opened his mouth twice to speak, and couldn't, or didn't want to—he didn't know which. Rivera slumped down suddenly on his hunkers, back erect, and his eyes wide.

It grew very cold. "It's cold," Tom said, and his voice sounded harsh to him. And the wind blew warm on them, the earth was warm under Rivera's knees. The cold was not a lack of heat, but a lack of something else—warmth, but the specific warmth of life-force, perhaps. The feeling of oppression grew, as if their recognition of the strangeness of the place had started it, and their increasing sensitivity to it made it grow.

Rivera said something, quietly, in Spanish.

"What are you looking at?" asked Tom.

Rivera started violently, threw up an arm, as if to ward off the crash of Tom's voice.

"I . . . there is nothin' to see, Tom. I feel this way wance before. I dunno—" He shook his head, his eyes wide and blank. "An' after, there was being wan hell of a thunderstorm—" His voice petered out.

Tom took his shoulder and hauled him roughly to his feet. "Goony! You slap-happy?"

The boy smiled, almost gently. The down on his upper lip held little spheres of sweat. "I ain' nothin', Tom. I'm jus' scare like hell."

"You scare yourself right back up there on that cat and git to work," Tom roared. More quietly then, he said, "I know there's something—wrong—here, Goony, but that ain't goin' to get us a runway built. Anyhow, I know what to do about a dawg 'at gits gunshy. Ought to be able to do as much fer you. Git along to th' mound now and see if it ain't a cache o' big stone for us. We got a swamp down there to fill."

Rivera hesitated, started to speak, swallowed and then walked slowly over to the Seven. Tom stood watching him, closing his mind to the impalpable pressure of something, somewhere near, making his guts cold.

The bulldozer nosed over to the mound, grunting, reminding Tom suddenly that the machine's Spanish slang name was *puerco*—pig, boar. Rivera angled into the edge of the mound with the cutting corner of the blade. Dirt and brush curled up, fell away from the mound and loaded from the bank side, out along the moldboard. The boy finished his pass along the mound, carried the load past it and wasted it out on the flat, turned around and started back again.

Ten minutes later Rivera struck stone, the manganese steel screaming along it, a puff of gray dust spouting from the cutting corner. Tom knelt and examined it after the machine had passed. It was the same kind of stone they had found out on the flat—and shaped the same way. But here it was a wall, the angled faces of the block ends obviously tongued and grooved together.

Cold, cold as—

Tom took one deep breath and wiped sweat out of his eyes.

"I don't care," he whispered, "I got to have that stone. I got to fill me a swamp." He stood back and motioned to Rivera to blade into a chipped crevice in the buried wall.

The Seven swung into the wall and stopped while Rivera shifted into first, throttled down and lowered his blade. Tom looked up into his face. The boy's lips were white. He eased in the master clutch, the blade dipped and the corner swung neatly into the crevice.

The dozer blatted protestingly and began to crab sideways, pivoting on the end of the blade. Tom jumped out of the way, ran around behind the machine, which was almost parallel with the wall now, and stood in the clear, one hand raised ready to signal, his eyes on the straining blade. And then everything happened at once.

With a toothy snap the block started and came free, pivoting outward from its square end, bringing with it its neighbor. The block above them dropped, and the whole mound seemed to settle. And *something* whooshed out of the black hole where the rocks had been. Something like a fog, but not a fog that could be seen, something huge that could not be measured. With it came a gust of that cold which was not cold, and the smell of ozone, and the prickling crackle of a mighty static discharge.

Tom was fifty feet from the wall before he knew he had moved. He stopped and saw the Seven suddenly buck like a wild stallion, once, and Rivera turning over twice in the air. Tom shouted some meaningless syllable and tore over to the boy, where he sprawled in the rough grass, lifted him in his arms, and ran. Only then did he realize that he was running from the machine.

It was like a mad thing. Its moldboard rose and fell. It curved away from the mound, howling governor gone wild, controls flailing. The blade dug repeatedly into the earth, gouging it up in great dips through which the tractor plunged, clanking and bellowing furiously. It raced away in a great irregular arc, turned and came snorting back to the mound, where it beat at the buried wall, slewed and scraped and roared.

Tom reached the edge of the plateau sobbing for breath, and kneeling, laid the boy gently down on the grass.

"Goony, boy . . . hey—"

The long silken eyelashes fluttered, lifted. Something wrenched in Tom as he saw the eyes, rolled right back so that only the whites showed. Rivera drew a long quivering breath which caught suddenly. He coughed twice, threw his head from side to side so violently that Tom took it between his hands and steadied it.

"*Ay . . . Maria madre . . . que me pasado,* Tom—w'at has happen to me?"

"Fell off the Seven, stupid. You . . . how you feel?"

Rivera scrabbled at the ground, got his elbows half under him, then sank back weakly. "Feel O.K. Headache like hell. W-w'at happen to my feets?"

"Feet? They hurt?"

"No hurt—" The young face went gray, the lips tightened with effort. "No nothin', Tom."

"You can't move 'em?"

Rivera shook his head, still trying. Tom stood up. "You take it easy. I'll go get Kelly. Be right back."

He walked away quickly and when Rivera called to him he did not turn around. Tom had seen a man with a broken back before.

At the edge of the little plateau Tom stopped, listening. In the deepening twilight he could see the bulldozer standing by the mound. The motor was running; she had not stalled herself. But what stopped Tom was that she wasn't idling, but revving up and down as if an impatient hand were on the throttle—*hroom hroooom,* running up and up far faster than even a broken governor should permit, then coasting down to near silence, broken by the explosive punctuation of sharp and irregular firing. Then it would run up and up again, almost screaming, sustaining a r.p.m. that threatened every moving part, shaking the great machine like some deadly ague.

Tom walked swiftly toward the Seven, a puzzled and grim frown on his weather-beaten face. Governors break down occasionally, and once in a while you will have a motor tear itself to pieces, revving up out of control. But it will either do that or it will rev down and quit. If an operator is fool enough to leave his machine with the master clutch engaged, the machine will take off and run the way the Seven had—but it will not turn unless the blade corner catches in something unresisting, and then the chances are very strong that it will stall. But in any case, it was past reason for any machine to act this way, revving up and down, running, turning, lifting and dropping the blade.

The motor slowed as he approached, and at last settled down into something like a steady and regular idle. Tom had the sudden crazy impression that it was watching him. He shrugged off the feeling, walked up and laid a hand on the fender.

The Seven reacted like a wild stallion. The big Diesel roared, and Tom distinctly saw the master clutch lever snap back over center. He leaped clear, expecting the machine to jolt forward, but apparently it was in a reverse gear, for it shot backwards, one track locked, and the near end of the blade swung in a swift vicious arc, breezing a bare fraction of an inch past his hip as he danced back out of the way.

And as if it had bounced off a wall, the tractor had shifted and was bearing down on him, the twelve-foot blade rising, the two big headlights looming over him on their bow-legged supports, looking like the protruding eyes of some mighty toad. Tom had no choice but to leap straight up and grasp the top of the blade in his two hands, leaning back hard to brace his feet against the curved moldboard. The blade dropped and sank into the soft topsoil, digging a deep little swale in the ground. The earth loading on the moldboard rose and churned around Tom's legs; he stepped wildly, keeping them clear of the rolling drag of it. Up came the blade then, leaving a four-foot pile at the edge of the pit; down and up the tractor raced as the tracks went into it; up and up as they climbed the pile of dirt. A quick balance and overbalance as the machine lurched up and over like a motorcycle taking a jump off a ramp, and then a spine-shaking crash as fourteen tons of metal smashed blade-first into the ground.

Part of the leather from Tom's tough palms stayed with the blade as he was flung off. He went head over heels backwards, but had his feet gathered and sprang as they touched the ground; for he knew that no machine could bury its blade like that and get out easily. He leaped to the top of the blade, got one hand on the radiator cap, vaulted. Perversely, the cap broke from its hinge and came away in his hand, in that split instant when only that hand rested on anything. Off balance, he landed on his shoulder with his legs flailing the air, his body sliding off the hood's smooth shoulder toward the track now churning the earth beneath. He made a wild grab at the air intake pipe, barely had it in his fingers when the dozer freed itself and shot backwards up and over the hump. Again that breathless flight pivoting over the top, and the clanking crash as the machine landed, this time almost flat on its tracks.

The jolt tore Tom's hand away, and as he slid back over the hood the crook of his elbow caught the exhaust stack, the dull red metal biting into his flesh. He grunted and clamped the arm around it. His momentum carried him around it, and his feet crashed into the steering clutch levers. Hooking one with his instep, he doubled his legs and whipped himself back, scrabbling at the smooth warm metal, crawling frantically backward until he finally fell heavily into the seat.

"Now," he gritted through a red wall of pain, "you're gonna git operated." And he kicked out the master clutch.

The motor wailed, with the load taken off so suddenly. Tom grasped the throttle, his thumb clamped down on the ratchet release, and he shoved the lever forward to shut off the fuel.

It wouldn't shut off; it went down to a slow idle, but it wouldn't shut off.

"There's one thing you can't do without," he muttered, "compression."

He stood up and leaned around the dash, reaching for the compression-release lever. As he came up out of the seat, the engine revved up again. He turned to the throttle, which had snapped back into the "open" position. As his hand touched it the master clutch lever snapped in and the howling machine lurched forward with a jerk that snapped his head on his shoulders and threw him heavily back into the seat. He snatched at the hydraulic blade control and threw it to "float" position; and then as the falling moldboard touched the ground, into "power down." The cutting edge bit into the ground and the engine began to labor. Holding the blade control, he pushed the throttle forward with his other hand. One of the steering clutch levers whipped back and struck him agonizingly on the kneecap. He involuntarily let go of the blade control and the moldboard began to rise. The engine began to turn faster and he realized that it was not responding to the throttle. Cursing, he leaped to his feet; the suddenly flailing steering clutch levers struck him three times in the groin before he could get between them.

Blind with pain, Tom clung gasping to the dash. The oil-pressure gauge fell off the dash to his right, with a tinkling of broken glass, and from its broken quarter-inch line scalding oil drenched him. The shock of it snapped back his wavering consciousness. Ignoring the blows of the left steering clutch and the master clutch which had started the same mad punching, he bent over the left end of the dash and grasped the compression lever. The tractor rushed forward and spun sickeningly, and Tom knew he was thrown. But as he felt himself leave the decking his hand punched the compression lever down. The great valves at the cylinder heads opened and locked open; atomized fuel and superheated air chattered out, and as Tom's head and shoulders struck the ground the great wild machine rolled to a stop, stood silently except for the grumble of water boiling in the cooling system.

Minutes later Tom raised his head and groaned. He rolled over and sat up, his chin on his knees, washed by wave after wave of pain. As they gradually subsided, he crawled to the machine and pulled himself to his feet, hand over hand on the track. And groggily he began to cripple the tractor, at least for the night.

He opened the cock under the fuel tank, left the warm yellow fluid gushing out on the ground. He opened the drain on the reservoir by the injection pump. He found a piece of wire in the crank box and with it tied down the compression release lever. He crawled up on the machine, wrenched the hood and ball jar off the air intake precleaner, pulled off his shirt and stuffed it down the pipe. He pushed the throttle all the way forward and locked it with the locking pin. And he shut off the fuel on the main line from the tank to the pump.

Then he climbed heavily to the ground and slogged back to the edge of the plateau where he had left Rivera.

They didn't know Tom was hurt until an hour and a half later—there had been too much to do—rigging a stretcher for the Puerto Rican, building him a shelter, an engine crate with an Army pup tent for a roof. They brought out the first-aid kit and the medical books and did what they could—tied and splinted and dosed with an opiate. Tom was a mass of bruises, and his right arm, where it had hooked the exhaust stack, was a flayed mass. They fixed him up then, old Peebles handling the sulfa powder and bandages like a trained nurse. And only then was there talk.

"I've seen a man thrown off a pan," said Dennis, as they sat around the coffee urn munching C rations. "Sittin' up on the arm rest on a cat, looking backwards. Cat hit a rock and bucked. Threw him off on the track. Stretched him out ten feet long." He in-whistled some coffee to dilute the mouthful of food he had been talking around, and masticated noisily. "Man's a fool to set up there on one side of his butt even on a pan. Can't see why th' goony was doin' it on a dozer."

"He wasn't," said Tom.

Kelly rubbed his pointed jaw. "He set flat on th' seat an' was th'owed?"

"That's right."

After an unbelieving silence Dennis said, "What was he doin'—drivin' over sixty?"

Tom looked around the circle of faces lit up by the over-artificial brilliance of a pressure lantern, and wondered what the reaction would be if he told it all just as it was. He had to say something, and it didn't look as if it could be the truth.

"He was workin'," he said finally. "Bucking stone out of the wall of an old building up on the mesa there. One turned loose an' as it did the governor must've gone haywire. She bucked like a loco hoss and run off."

"Run off?"

Tom opened his mouth and closed it again, and just nodded.

Dennis said, "Well, reckon that's what happens when you put a mechanic to operatin'."

"That had nothin' to do with it," Tom snapped.

Peebles spoke up quickly. "Tom—what about the Seven? Broke up any?"

"Some," said Tom. "Better look at the steering clutches. An' she was hot."

"Head's cracked," said Harris, a burly young man with shoulders like a buffalo and a famous thirst.

"How do you know?"

"Saw it when Al and me went up with the stretcher to get the kid while you all were building the shelter. Hot water runnin' down the side of the block."

"You mean you walked all the way out to the mound to look at that tractor while the kid was lyin' there? I told you where he was!"

"Out to the mound!" Al Knowles' pop eyes teetered out of their sockets. "We found that cat stalled twenty feet away from where the kid was!"

"What!"

"That's right, Tom," said Harris. "What's eatin' you? Where'd you leave it?"

"I told you . . . by the mound . . . the ol' building we cut into."

"Leave the startin' motor runnin'?"

"Starting motor?" Tom's mind caught the picture of the small, two-cylinder gasoline engine bolted to the side of the big Diesel's crankcase, coupled through a Bendix gear and clutch to the flywheel of the Diesel to crank it. He remember his last glance at the still machine, silent but for the sound of water boiling. "Hell no!"

Al and Harris exchanged a glance. "I guess you were sort of slap-happy at the time, Tom," Harris said, not unkindly. "When we were halfway up the hill we heard it, and you know you can't mistake that racket. Sounded like it was under a load."

Tom beat softly at his temples with his clenched fists. "I left that machine dead," he said quietly. "I got compression off her and tied down the lever. I even stuffed my shirt in the intake. I drained the tank. But—I didn't touch the starting motor."

Peebles wanted to know why he had gone to all that trouble. Tom just looked vaguely at him and shook his head. "I shoulda pulled the wires. I never thought about the starting motor," he whispered. Then, "Harris—you say you found the starting motor running when you got to the top?"

"No—she was stalled. And hot—awmighty hot. I'd say the startin' motor was seized up tight. That must be it, Tom. You left the startin' motor runnin' and somehow engaged the clutch an' Bendix." His voice lost conviction as he said it—it takes seventeen separate motions to start a tractor of this type. "Anyhow, she was in gear an' crawled along on the little motor."

"I done that once," said Chub. "Broke a con rod on an Eight, on a highway job. Walked her about three-quarters of a mile on the startin' motor that way. Only I had to stop every hundred yards and let her cool down some."

Not without sarcasm, Dennis said, "Seems to me like the Seven was out to get th' goony. Made one pass at him and then went back to finish the job."

Al Knowles haw-hawed extravagantly.

Tom stood up, shaking his head, and went off among the crates to the hospital they had jury-rigged for the kid.

A dim light was burning inside, and Rivera lay very still, with his eyes closed. Tom leaned in the doorway—the open end of the engine crate— and watched him for a moment. Behind him he could hear the murmur of the crew's voices; the night was otherwise windless and still. Rivera's face was the peculiar color that olive skin takes when drained of blood. Tom looked at his chest and for a panicky moment thought he could discern no movement there. He entered and put a hand over the boy's heart. Rivera shivered, his eyes flew open, and he drew a sudden breath which caught raggedly at the back of his throat. "Tom . . . Tom!" he cried weakly.

"O. K., Goony . . . *que pase?*"

"She comeen back . . . Tom!"

"Who?"

"*El de siete.*"

Daisy Etta—"She ain't comin' back, kiddo. You're off the mesa now. Keep your chin up, fella."

Rivera's dark, doped eyes stared up at him without expression. Tom moved back and the eyes continued to stare. They weren't seeing anything. "Go to sleep," he whispered. The eyes closed instantly.

Kelly was saying that nobody ever got hurt on a construction job unless somebody was dumb. "An' most times you don't realize how dumb what you're doin' is until somebody does get hurt."

"The dumb part was gettin' a kid, an' not even an operator at that, up on a machine," said Dennis in his smuggest voice.

"I heard you try to sing that song before," said old Peebles quietly. "I hate to have to point out anything like this to a man because it don't do any good to make comparisons. But I've worked with that fella Rivera for a long time now, an' I've seen 'em as good but doggone few better. As far as you're concerned, you're O. K. on a pan, but the kid could give you cards and spades and still make you look like a cost accountant on a dozer."

Dennis half rose and mouthed something filthy. He looked at Al Knowles for backing and got it. He looked around the circle and got none. Peebles lounged back, sucking on his pipe, watching from under those bristling brows. Dennis subsided, running now on another tack.

"So what does that prove? The better you say he is, the less reason he had to fall off a cat and get himself hurt."

"I haven't got the thing straight yet," said Chub, in a voice whose tone indicated 'I hate to admit it, but—'

About this time Tom returned, like a sleepwalker, standing with the brilliant pressure lantern between him and Dennis. Dennis rambled right on, not knowing he was anywhere near: "That's something you never will find out. That Puerto Rican is a pretty husky kid. Could be Tom said somethin' he didn't like an' he tried to put a knife in Tom's back. They all do, y'know. Tom didn't get all that bashin' around just stoppin' a machine. They must of went round an' round for a while an' the goony wound up with a busted back. Tom sets the dozer to walk him down while he lies there and comes on down here and tries to tell us—" His voice fluttered to a stop as Tom loomed over him.

Tom grabbed the pan operator up by the slack of his shirt front with his uninjured arm and shook him like an empty burlap bag.

"Skunk," he growled. "I oughta lower th' boom on you." He set Dennis on his feet and backhanded his face with the edge of his forearm. Dennis went down—cowered down, rather than fell. "Aw, Tom, I was just talkin'. Just a joke, Tom, I was just—"

"Yellow, too," snarled Tom, stepping forward, raising a solid Texan boot. Peebles barked "Tom!" and the foot came back to the ground.

"Out o' my sight," rumbled the foreman. "Git!"

Dennis got. Al Knowles said vaguely, "Naow, Tom, y'all cain't—"

"You, y'wall-eyed string-bean!" Tom raved, his voice harsh and strained. "Go 'long with yer Siamese twin!"

"O. K., O. K.," said Al, white-faced, and disappeared into the dark after Dennis.

"Nuts to this," said Chub. "I'm turnin' in." He went to a crate and hauled out a mosquito-hooded sleeping bag and went off without another word. Harris and Kelly, who were both on their feet, sat down again. Old Peebles hadn't moved.

Tom stood staring out into the dark, his arms straight at his sides, his fists knotted.

"Sit down," said Peebles gently. Tom turned and stared at him.

"Sit down. I can't change that dressing 'less you do." He pointed at the bandage around Tom's elbow. It was red, a widening stain, the tattered tissues having parted as the big Georgian bunched his infuriated muscles. He sat down.

"Talkin' about dumbness," said Harris calmly, as Peebles went to work, "I was about to say that I got the record. I done the dumbest thing anybody ever did on a machine. You can't top it."

"I could," said Kelly. "Runnin' a crane dragline once. Put her in boom gear and started to boom her up. Had an eighty-five-foot stick on her. Machine was standing on wooden mats in th' middle of a swamp. Heard the motor miss and got out of the saddle to look at the filter-glass. Messed around back there longer than I figured, and the boom went straight up in the air and fell backwards over the cab. Th' jolt tilted my mats an' she slid backwards slow and stately as you please, butt-first into the mud. Buried up to the eyeballs, she was." He laughed quietly. "Looked like a ditching machine!"

"I still say I done the dumbest thing ever, bar none," said Harris. "It was on a river job, widening a channel. I come back to work from a three-day binge, still rum-dumb. Got up on a dozer an' was workin' around on the edge of a twenty-foot cliff. Down at the foot of the cliff was a big hickory tree, an' growin' right along the edge was a great big limb. I got the dopey idea I should break it off. I put one track on the limb and the other on the cliff edge and run out away from the trunk. I was about half-way out, an' the branch saggin' some, before I thought what would happen if it broke. Just about then it did break. You know hickory—if it breaks at all it breaks altogether. So down we go into thirty feet of water—me an' the cat. I got out from under somehow. When all them bubbles stopped comin' up I swum around lookin' down at it. I was still paddlin' around when the superintendent came rushin' up. He wants to know what's up. I yell at him, 'Look down there, the way that water is movin' an' shiftin', looks like the cat is workin' down there.' He pursed his lips and *tsk tsked*. My, that man said some nasty things to me."

"Where'd you get your next job?" Kelly exploded.

"Oh, he didn't fire me," said Harris soberly. "Said he couldn't afford to fire a man as dumb as that. Said he wanted me around to look at when-ever he felt bad."

Tom said, "Thanks, you guys. That's as good a way as any of sayin' that everybody makes mistakes." He stood up, examining the new dress-ing, turning his arm in front of the lantern. "You all can think what you please, but I don't recollect there was any dumbness went on on that mesa this evenin'. That's finished with, anyway. Do I have to say that Dennis' idea about it is all wet?"

Harris said one foul word that completely disposed of Dennis and any-thing he might say.

Peebles said, "It'll be all right. Dennis an' his popeyed friend'll hang together, but they don't amount to anything. Chub'll do whatever he's argued into."

"So you got 'em all lined up, hey?" Tom shrugged. "In the meantime, are we going to get an airfield built?"

"We'll get it built," Peebles said. "Only—Tom, I got no right to give you any advice, but go easy on the rough stuff after this. It does a lot of harm."

"I will if I can," said Tom gruffly. They broke up and turned in.

Peebles was right. It did do harm. It made Dennis use the word "murder" when they found, in the morning, that Rivera had died during the night.

The work progressed in spite of everything that had happened. With equipment like that, it's hard to slow things down. Kelly bit two cubic yards out of the bluff with every swing of the big shovel, and Dumptors are the fastest short-haul earth movers yet devised. Dennis kept the service road clean for them with his pan, and Tom and Chub spelled

each other on the bulldozer they had detached from its pan to make up
for the lack of the Seven, spending their alternate periods with transit and
stakes. Peebles was rod-man for the surveys, and in between times worked
on setting up his field shop, keeping the water cooler and battery chargers
running, and lining up his forge and welding tables. The operators fueled
and serviced their own equipment, and there was little delay. Rocks and
marl came out of the growing cavity in the side of the central mesa—a
whole third of it had to come out—were spun down to the edge of the
swamp, which lay across the lower end of the projected runway, in the
hornet-howling dump-tractors, their big driving wheels churned up vast
clouds of dust, and were dumped and spread and walked in by the whining
two-cycle dozer. When muck began to pile up in front of the fill, it was
blasted out of the way with carefully placed charges of sixty percent
dynamite and the craters filled with rocks, stone from the ruins, and surfaced with easily compacting marl, run out of a clean deposit by the pan.

And when he had his shop set up, Peebles went up the hill to get the
Seven. When he got to it he just stood there for a moment scratching his
head, and then, shaking his head, he ambled back down the hill and went
for Tom.

"Been looking at the Seven," he said, when he had flagged the moaning
two-cycle and Tom had climbed off.

"What'd you find?"

Peebles held out an arm. "A list as long as that." He shook his head.
"Tom, what really happened up there?"

"Governor went haywire and she run away," Tom said promptly,
deadpan.

"Yeah, but—" For a long moment he held Tom's eyes. Then he sighed.
"O. K., Tom. Anyhow, I can't do a thing up there. We'll have to bring
her back and I'll have to have this tractor to tow her down. And first I
have to have some help—the track idler adjustment bolt's busted and the
right track is off the track rollers."

"Oh-h-h. So that's why she couldn't get to the kid, running on the
starting motor. Track would hardly turn, hey?"

"It's a miracle she ran as far as she did. That track is really jammed
up. Riding right up on the roller flanges. And that ain't the half of it.
The head's gone, like Harris said, and Lord only knows what I'll find when
I open her up."

"Why bother?"

"What?"

"We can get along without that dozer," said Tom suddenly. "Leave
her where she is. There's lots more for you to do."

"But what for?"

"Well, there's no call to go to all that trouble."

Peebles scratched the side of his nose and said, "I got a new head,
track master pins—even a spare starting motor. I got tools to make what

I don't stock." He pointed at the long row of dumps left by the hurtling dump-tractors while they had been talking. "You got a pan tied up because you're using this machine to doze with, and you can't tell me you can't use another one. You're gonna have to shut down one or two o' those Dumptors if you go on like this."

"I had all that figured out as soon as I opened my mouth," Tom said sullenly. "Let's go."

They climbed on the tractor and took off, stopping for a moment at the beach outcropping to pick up a cable and some tools.

Daisy Etta sat at the edge of the mesa, glowering out of her stilted headlights at the soft sward which still bore the impression of a young body and the tramplings of the stretcher-bearers. Her general aspect was woebegone—there were scratches on her olive-drab paint and the bright metal of the scratches was already dulled red by the earliest powder-rust. And though the ground was level, she was not, for her right track was off its lower rollers, and she stood slightly canted, like a man who has had a broken hip. And whatever passed for consciousness within her mulled over that paradox of the bulldozer that every operator must go through while he is learning his own machine.

It is the most difficult thing of all for the beginner to understand, that paradox. A bulldozer is a crawling powerhouse, a behemoth of noise and toughness, the nearest thing to the famous irresistible force. The beginner, awed and with the pictures of unconquerable Army tanks printed on his mind from the newsreels, takes all in his stride and with a sense of limitless power treats all obstacles alike, not knowing the fragility of a cast-iron radiator core, the mortality of tempered manganese, the friability of over-heated babbitt, and most of all, the ease with which a tractor can bury itself in mud. Climbing off to stare at a machine which he has reduced in twenty seconds to a useless hulk, or which was running a half-minute before on ground where it now has its tracks out of sight, he has that sense of guilty disappointment which overcomes any man on having made an error in judgment.

So, as she stood, *Daisy Etta* was broken and useless. These soft persistent bipeds had built her, and if they were like any other race that built machines, they could care for them. The ability to reverse the tension of a spring, or twist a control rod, or reduce to zero the friction in a nut and lock-washer, was not enough to repair the crack in a cylinder head nor bearings welded to a crankshaft in an overheated starting motor. There had been a lesson to learn. It had been learned. *Daisy Etta* would be repaired, and the next time—well, at least she would know her own weaknesses.

Tom swung the two-cycle machine and edged in next to the Seven, with the edge of his blade all but touching *Daisy Etta's* push-beam. They got off and Peebles bent over the drum-tight right track.

"Watch yourself," said Tom.

"Watch what?"

"Oh—nothin', I guess." He circled the machine, trained eyes probing over frame and fittings. He stepped forward suddenly and grasped the fuel-tank drain cock. It was closed. He opened it; golden oil gushed out. He shut it off, climbed up on the machine and opened the fuel cap on top of the tank. He pulled out the bayonet gauge, wiped it in the crook of his knee, dipped and withdrew it.

The tank was more than three quarters full.

"What's the matter?" asked Peebles, staring curiously at Tom's drawn face.

"Peeby, I opened the cock to drain this tank. I left it with oil runnin' out on the ground. She shut herself off."

"Now, Tom, you're lettin' this thing get you down. You just thought you did. I've seen a main-line valve shut itself off when it's worn bad, but only 'cause the fuel pump pulls it shut when the motor's runnin'. But not a gravity drain."

"Main-line valve?" Tom pulled the seat up and looked. One glance was enough to show him that this one was open.

"She opened this one, too."

"O. K.—O. K. Don't look at me like that!" Peebles was as near to exasperation as he could possibly get. "What difference does it make?"

Tom did not answer. He was not the type of man who, when faced with something beyond his understanding, would begin to doubt his own sanity. His was a dogged insistence that what he saw and sensed was what had actually happened. In him was none of the fainting fear of madness that another, more sensitive, man might feel. He doubted neither himself nor his evidence, and so could free his mind for searching out the consuming "why" of a problem. He knew instinctively that to share "unbelievable" happenings with anyone else, even if they had really occurred, was to put even further obstacles in his way. So he kept his clamlike silence and stubbornly, watchfully, investigated.

The slipped track was so tightly drawn up on the roller flanges that there could be no question of pulling the master pin and opening the track up. It would have to be worked back in place—a very delicate operation, for a little force applied in the wrong direction would be enough to run the track off altogether. To complicate things, the blade of the Seven was down on the ground and would have to be lifted before the machine could be maneuvered, and its hydraulic hoist was useless without the motor.

Peebles unhooked twenty feet of half-inch cable from the rear of the smaller dozer, scratched a hole in the ground under the Seven's blade, and pushed the eye of the cable through. Climbing over the moldboard, he slipped the eye on to the big towing hook bolted to the underside of the belly-guard. The other end of the cable he threw out on the ground in front of the machine. Tom mounted the other dozer and swung into place, ready to tow. Peebles hooked the cable onto Tom's drawbar, hopped up on the Seven. He put her in neutral, disengaged the master clutch, and put the blade control over into "float" position, then raised an arm.

Tom perched upon the arm rest of his machine, looking backwards, moved slowly, taking up the slack in the cable. It straightened and grew taut, and as it did it forced the Seven's blade upward. Peebles waved for slack and put the blade control into "hold." The cable bellied downward away from the blade.

"Hydraulic system's O. K., anyhow," called Peebles, as Tom throttled down. "Move over and take a strain to the right, sharp as you can without fouling the cable on the track. We'll see if we can walk this track back on."

Tom backed up, cut sharply to the right, and drew the cable out almost at right angles to the other machine. Peebles held the right track of the Seven with the brake and released both steering clutches. The left track now could turn free, the right not at all. Tom was running at a quarter throttle in his lowest gear, so that his machine barely crept along, taking the strain. The Seven shook gently and began to pivot on the taut right track, unbelievable foot-pounds of energy coming to bear on the front of the track where it rode high up on the idler wheel. Peebles released the right brake with his foot and applied it again in a series of skilled, deft jerks. The track would move a few inches and stop again, force being applied forward and sideward alternately, urging the track persuasively back in place. Then, a little jolt and she was in, riding true on the five truck rollers, the two track carrier rollers, the driving sprocket and the idler.

Peebles got off and stuck his head in between the sprocket and the rear carrier, squinting down and sideways to see if there were any broken flanges or roller bushes. Tom came over and pulled him out by the seat of his trousers. "Time enough for that when you get her in the shop," he said, masking his nervousness. "Reckon she'll roll?"

"She'll roll. I never saw a track in that condition come back that easy. By gosh, it's as if she was tryin' to help!"

"They'll do it sometimes," said Tom, stiffly. "You better take the tow-tractor, Peeby. I'll stay with this'n."

"Anything you say."

And cautiously they took the steep slope down, Tom barely holding the brakes, giving the other machine a straight pull all the way. And so they brought *Daisy Etta* down to Peebles' outdoor shop, where they pulled her cylinder head off, took off her starting motor, pulled out a burned clutch facing, had her quite helpless—

And put her together again.

"I tell you it was outright, cold-blooded murder," said Dennis hotly. "An' here we are takin' orders from a guy like that. What are we goin' to do about it?" They were standing by the cooler—Dennis had run his machine there to waylay Chub.

Chub Horton's cigar went down and up like a semaphore with a short circuit. "We'll skip it. The blacktopping crew will be here in another two weeks or so, an' we can make a report. Besides, I don't know what happened up there any more than you do. In the meantime we got a runway to build."

"You don't know what happened up there? Chub, you're a smart man. Smart enough to run this job better than Tom Jaeger even if he wasn't crazy. And you're surely smart enough not to believe all that cock and bull about that tractor runnin' out from under that grease-monkey. Listen—" he leaned forward and tapped Chub's chest. "He said it was the governor. I saw that governor myself an' heard ol' Peebles say there wasn't a thing wrong with it. Th' throttle control rod had slipped off its yoke, yeah—but you know what a tractor will do when the throttle control goes out. It'll idle or stall. It won't run away, whatever."

"Well, maybe so, but—"

"But nothin'! A guy that'll commit murder ain't sane. If he did it once, he can do it again and I ain't fixin' to let that happen to me."

Two things crossed Chub's steady but not too bright mind at this. One was that Dennis, whom he did not like but could not shake, was trying to force him into something that he did not want to do. The other was that under all of his swift talk Dennis was scared spitless.

"What do you want to do—call up the sheriff?"

Dennis ha-ha-ed appreciatively—one of the reasons he was so hard to shake. "I'll tell you what we can do. As long as we have you here, he isn't the only man who knows the work. If we stop takin' orders from him, you can give 'em as good or better. An' there won't be anything he can do about it."

"Doggone it, Dennis," said Chub, with sudden exasperation. "What do you think you're doin'—handin' me over the keys to the kingdom or something? What do you want to see me bossin' around here for?" He stood up. "Suppose we did what you said? Would it get the field built any quicker? Would it get me any more money in my pay envelope? What do you think I want—glory? I passed up a chance to run for councilman once. You think I'd raise a finger to get a bunch of mugs to do what I say—when they do it anyway?"

"Aw, Chub—I wouldn't cause trouble just for the fun of it. That's not what I mean at all. But unless we do something about that guy we ain't safe. Can't you get that through your head?"

"Listen, windy. If a man keeps busy enough he can't get into no trouble. That goes for Tom—you might keep that in mind. But it goes for you, too. Get back up on that rig an' get back to the marl pit." Dennis, completely taken by surprise, turned to his machine.

"It's a pity you can't move earth with your mouth," said Chub as he walked off. "They could have left you to do this job singlehanded."

Chub walked slowly toward the outcropping, switching at beach pebbles with a grade stake and swearing to himself. He was essentially a simple man and believed in the simplest possible approach to everything. He liked a job where he could do everything required and where nothing turned up to complicate things. He had been in the grading business for a long time as an operator and survey party boss, and he was remarkable for one thing—he had always held aloof from the cliques and internecine politics that are the breath of life to most construction men. He was disturbed and troubled at the back-stabbing that went on around him on various jobs. If it was blunt, he was disgusted, and subtlety simply left him floundering and bewildered. He was stupid enough so that his basic honesty manifested itself in his speech and actions, and he had learned that complete honesty in dealing with men above and below him was almost invariably painful to all concerned, but he had not the wit to act otherwise, and did not try to. If he had a bad tooth, he had it pulled out as soon as he could. If he got a raw deal from a superintendent over him, that superintendent would get told exactly what the trouble was, and if he didn't like it, there were other jobs. And if the pulling and hauling of cliques got in his hair, he had always said so and left. Or he had sounded off and stayed; his completely selfish reaction to things that got in the way of his work had earned him a lot of regard from men he had worked under. And so, in this instance, he had no hesitation about choosing a course of action. Only—how did you go about asking a man if he was a murderer?

He found the foreman with an enormous wrench in his hand, tightening up the new track adjustment bolt they had installed in the Seven.

"Hey, Chub! Glad you turned up. Let's get a piece of pipe over the end of this thing and really bear down." Chub went for the pipe, and they fitted it over the handle of the four-foot wrench and hauled until the sweat ran down their backs, Tom checking the track clearance occasionally with a crowbar. He finally called it good enough and they stood there in the sun gasping for breath.

"Tom," panted Chub, "did you kill that Puerto Rican?"

Tom's head came up as if someone had burned the back of his neck with a cigarette.

"Because," said Chub, "if you did you can't go on runnin' this job."

Tom said, "That's a lousy thing to kid about."

"You know I ain't kiddin'. Well, did you?"

"No!" Tom sat down on a keg, wiped his face with a bandanna. "What's got into you?"

"I just wanted to know. Some of the boys are worried about it."

Tom's eyes narrowed. "Some of the boys, huh? I think I get it. Listen to me, Chub. Rivera was killed by that thing there." He thumbed over his shoulder at the Seven, which was standing ready now, awaiting only the building of a broken cutting corner on the blade. Peebles was winding up the welding machine as he spoke. "If you mean, did I put him up on the machine before he was thrown, the answer is yes. That much I killed him, and don't think I don't feel it. I had a hunch something was wrong up there, but I couldn't put my finger on it and I certainly didn't think anybody was going to get hurt."

"Well, what was wrong?"

"I still don't know." Tom stood up. "I'm tired of beatin' around the bush, Chub, and I don't much care any more what anybody thinks. There's somethin' wrong with that Seven, something that wasn't built into her. They don't make tractors better'n that one, but whatever it was happened up there on the mesa has queered this one. Now go ahead and think what you like, and dream up any story you want to tell the boys. In the meantime you can pass the word—nobody runs that machine but me, understand? Nobody!"

"Tom—"

Tom's patience broke. "That's all I'm going to say about it! If anybody else gets hurt, it's going to be me, understand? What more do you want?"

He strode off, boiling. Chub stared after him, and after a long moment reached up and took the cigar from his lips. Only then did he realize that he had bitten it in two; half the butt was still inside his mouth. He spat and stood there, shaking his head.

"How's she going, Peeby?"

Peebles looked up from the welding machine. "Hi, Chub, have her ready for you in twenty minutes." He gauged the distance between the welding machine and the big tractor. "I should have forty feet of cable," he said, looking at the festoons of arc and ground cables that hung from the storage hooks in the back of the welder. "Don't want to get a tractor over here to move the thing, and don't feel like cranking up the Seven just to get it close enough." He separated the arc cable and threw it aside, walked to the tractor, paying the ground cable off his arm. He threw out the last of his slack and grasped the ground clamp when he was eight feet from the machine. Taking it in his left hand, he pulled hard, reaching out with his right to grasp the moldboard of the Seven, trying to get it far enough to clamp on to the machine.

Chub stood there watching him, chewing on his cigar, absent-mindedly diddling with the controls on the arc-welder. He pressed the starter-button, and the six-cylinder motor responded with a purr. He spun the work-selector dials idly, threw the arc generator switch—

A bolt of incredible energy, thin, searing, blue-white, left the rod-holder at his feet, stretched itself *fifty feet* across to Peebles, whose fingers had just touched the moldboard of the tractor. Peebles' head and shoulders were surrounded for a second by a violet nimbus, and then he folded over and dropped. A circuit breaker clacked behind the control board of the welder, but too late. The Seven rolled slowly backward, without firing, on level ground, until it brought up against a road-roller.

Chub's cigar was gone, and he didn't notice it. He had the knuckles of his right hand in his mouth, and his teeth sunk into the pudgy flesh. His eyes protruded; he crouched there and quivered, literally frightened out of his mind. For old Peebles was almost burned in two.

They buried him next to Rivera. There wasn't much talk afterwards; the old man had been a lot closer to all of them than they had realized until now. Harris, for once in his rum-dumb, lighthearted life, was quiet and serious, and Kelly's walk seemed to lose some of its litheness. Hour after hour Dennis' flabby mouth worked, and he bit at his lower lip until it was swollen and tender. Al Knowles seemed more or less unaffected, as was to be expected from a man who had something less than the brains of a chicken. Chub Horton had snapped out of it after a couple of hours and was very nearly himself again. And in Tom Jaeger swirled a black, furious anger at this unknowable curse that had struck the camp.

And they kept working. There was nothing else to do. The shovel kept up its rhythmic swing and dig, swing and dump, and the Dumptors screamed back and forth between it and the little that there was left of the swamp. The upper end of the runway was grassed off; Chub and Tom set grade stakes and Dennis began the long job of cutting and filling the humpy surface with his pan. Harris manned the other and followed him, a cut behind. The shape of the runway emerged from the land, and then that of the paralleling taxiway; and three days went by. The horror of Peebles' death wore off enough so that they could talk about it, and very little of the talk helped anybody. Tom took his spells at everything, changing over with Kelly to give him a rest from the shovel, making a few rounds with a pan, putting in hours on a Dumptor. His arm was healing slowly but clean, and he worked grimly in spite of it, taking a perverse sort of pleasure from the pain of it. Every man on the job watched his machine with the solicitude of a mother with her first-born; a serious breakdown would have been disastrous without a highly skilled mechanic.

The only concession that Tom allowed himself in regard to Peebles' death was to corner Kelly one afternoon and ask him about the welding machine. Part of Kelly's rather patchy past had been spent in a technical college, where he had studied electrical engineering and women. He had learned a little of the former and enough of the latter to get him thrown out on his ear. So, on the off-chance that he might know something about the freak arc, Tom put it to him.

Kelly pulled off his high-gauntlet gloves and batted sandflies with them. "What sort of an arc was that? Boy, you got me there. Did you ever hear of a welding machine doing like that before?"

"I did not. A welding machine just don't have that sort o' push. I saw a man get a full jolt from a 400-amp welder once, an' although it sat him down it didn't hurt him any."

"It's not amperage that kills people," said Kelly, "it's voltage. Voltage is the pressure behind a current, you know. Take an amount of water, call it amperage. If I throw it in your face, it won't hurt you. If I put it through a small hose you'll feel it. But if I pump it through the tiny holes on a Diesel injector nozzle at about twelve hundred pounds, it'll draw blood. But a welding arc generator just is not wound to build up that kind of voltage. I can't see where any short circuit anywhere through the armature or field windings could do such a thing."

"From what Chub said, he had been foolin' around with the work selector. I don't think anyone touched the dials after it happened. The selector dial was run all the way over to the low current application segment, and the current control was around the halfway mark. That's not enough juice to get you a good bead with a quarter-inch rod, let alone kill somebody—or roll a tractor back thirty feet on level ground."

"Or jump fifty feet," said Kelly. "It would take thousands of volts to generate an arc like that."

"Is it possible that something in the Seven could have pulled that arc? I mean, suppose the arc wasn't driven over, but was drawn over? I tell you, she was hot for four hours after that."

Kelly shook his head. "Never heard of any such thing. Look, just to have something to call them, we call direct current terminals positive and negative, and just because it works in theory we say that current flows from negative to positive. There couldn't be any more positive attraction in one electrode than there is negative drive in the other; see what I mean?"

"There couldn't be some freak condition that would cause a sort of oversize positive field? I mean one that would suck out the negative flow all in a heap, make it smash through under a lot of pressure like the water you were talking about through an injector nozzle?"

"No, Tom. It just don't work that way, far as anyone knows. I dunno, though—there are some things about static electricity that nobody understands. All I can say is that what happened couldn't happen and if it did it couldn't have killed Peebles. And you know the answer to that."

Tom glanced away at the upper end of the runway, where the two graves were. There was bitterness and turbulent anger naked there for a moment, and he turned and walked away without another word. And when he went back to have another look at the welding machine, *Daisy Etta* was gone.

Al Knowles and Harris squatted together near the water cooler.

"Bad," said Harris.

"Nevah saw anythin' like it," said Al. "Ol' Tom come back f'm the shop theah jus' *raisin'* Cain. 'Weah's 'at Seven gone? Weah's 'at Seven?' I never heered sech cah'ins on."

"Dennis did take it, huh?"

"Sho' did."

Harris said, "He came spoutin' around to me a while back, Dennis did.

Chub'd told him Tom said for everybody to stay off that machine. Dennis was mad as a wet hen. Said Tom was carryin' that kind o' business too far. Said there was probably somethin' about the Seven Tom didn't want us to find out. Might incriminate him. Dennis is ready to say Tom killed the kid."

"Reckon he did, Harris?"

Harris shook his head. "I've known Tom too long to think that. If he won't tell us what really happened up on the mesa, he has a reason for it. How'd Dennis come to take the dozer?"

"Blew a front tire on his pan. Came back heah to git anothah rig—maybe a Dumptor. Saw th' Seven standin' theah ready to go. Stood theah lookin' at it and cussin' Tom. Said he was tired of bashin' his kidneys t'pieces on them othah rigs an' bedamned if he wouldn't take suthin' that rode good fo' a change. I tol' him ol' Tom'd raise th' roof when he found him on it. He had a couple mo' things t'say 'bout Tom then."

"I didn't think he had the guts to take the rig."

"Aw, he talked hisself blind mad."

They looked up as Chub Horton trotted up, panting. "Hey, you guys, come on. We better get up there to Dennis."

"What's wrong?" asked Harris, climbing to his feet.

"Tom passed me a minute ago lookin' like the wrath o' God and hightailin' it for the swamp fill. I asked him what was the matter and he hollered that Dennis had took the Seven. Said he was always talkin' about murder, and he'd get his fill of it foolin' around that machine." Chub went wall-eyed, licked his lips beside his cigar.

"Oh-oh," said Harris quietly. "That's the wrong kind o' talk for just now."

"You don't suppose he—"

"Come on!"

They saw Tom before they were halfway there. He was walking slowly, with his head down. Harris shouted. Tom raised his face, stopped, stood there waiting with a peculiarly slumped stance.

"Where's Dennis?" barked Chub.

Tom waited until they were almost up to him and then weakly raised an arm and thumbed over his shoulder. His face was green.

"Tom—is he—"

Tom nodded, and swayed a little. His granite jaw was slack.

"Al, stay with him. He's sick. Harris, let's go."

Tom was sick, then and there. Very. Al stood gaping at him, fascinated.

Chub and Harris found Dennis. All of twelve square feet of him, ground and churned and rolled out into a torn-up patch of earth. *Daisy Etta* was gone.

Back at the outcropping, they sat with Tom while Al Knowles took a Dumptor and roared away to get Kelly.

"You saw him?" he said dully after a time.

Harris said, "Yeh."

The screaming Dumptor and a mountainous cloud of dust arrived, Kelly driving, Al holding on with a death-grip to the dump-bed guards. Kelly flung himself off, ran to Tom. "Tom—what is all this? Dennis dead? And you . . . you—"

Tom's head came up slowly, the slackness going out of his long face, a light suddenly coming into his eyes. Until this moment it had not crossed his mind what these men might think.

"I—what?"

"Al says you killed him."

Tom's eyes flicked at Al Knowles, and Al winced as if the glance had been a quirt.

Harris said, "What about it, Tom?"

"Nothing about it. He was killed by that Seven. You saw that for yourself."

"I stuck with you all along," said Harris slowly. "I took everything you said and believed it."

"This is too strong for you?" Tom asked.

Harris nodded. "Too strong, Tom."

Tom looked at the grim circle of faces and laughed suddenly. He stood up, put his back against a tall crate. "What do you plan to do about it?"

There was a silence. "You think I went up there and knocked that windbag off the machine and ran over him?" More silence. "Listen. I went up there and saw what you saw. He was dead before I got there. That's not good enough either?" He paused and licked his lips. "So after I killed him I got up on the tractor and drove it far enough away so you couldn't see or hear it when you got there. And then I sprouted wings and flew back so's I was halfway here when you met me—*ten minutes* after I spoke to Chub on my way up!"

Kelly said vaguely, "Tractor?"

"Well," said Tom harshly to Harris, "was the tractor there when you and Chub went up and saw Dennis?"

"No—"

Chub smacked his thigh suddenly. "You could of drove it into the swamp, Tom."

Tom said angrily, "I'm wastin' my time. You guys got it all figured out. Why ask me anything at all?"

"Aw, take it easy," said Kelly. "We just want the facts. Just what did happen? You met Chub and told him that Dennis would get all the murderin' he could take if he messed around that machine. That right?"

"That's right."

"Then what?"

"Then the machine murdered him."

Chub, with remarkable patience, asked, "What did you mean the day Peebles was killed when you said that something had queered the Seven up there on the mesa?"

Tom said furiously, "I meant what I said. You guys are set to crucify me for this and I can't stop you. Well, listen. Something's got into that Seven. I don't know what it is and I don't think I ever will know. I thought that after she smashed herself up that it was finished with. I had an idea that when we had her torn down and helpless we should have left her that way. I was dead right but it's too late now. She's killed Rivera and she's killed Dennis and she sure had something to do with killing Peebles. And my idea is that she won't stop as long as there's a human being alive on this island."

"Whaddaya know!" said Chub.

"Sure, Tom, sure," said Kelly quietly. "That tractor is out to get us. But don't worry; we'll catch it and tear it down. Just don't you worry about it any more; it'll be all right."

"That's right, Tom," said Harris. "You just take it easy around camp for a couple of days till you feel better. Chub and the rest of us will handle things for you. You had too much sun."

"You're a swell bunch of fellows," gritted Tom, with the deepest sarcasm. "You want to live," he shouted, "git out there and throw that maverick bulldozer!"

"That maverick bulldozer is at the bottom of the swamp where you put it," growled Chub. His head lowered and he started to move in. "Sure we want to live. The best way to do that is to put you where you can't kill anybody else. *Get him!*"

He leaped. Tom straightened him with his left and crossed with his right. Chub went down, tripping Harris. Al Knowles scuttled to a toolbox and dipped out a fourteen-inch crescent wrench. He circled around, keeping out of trouble, trying to look useful. Tom loosened a haymaker at Kelly, whose head seemed to withdraw like a turtle's; it whistled over, throwing Tom badly off balance. Harris, still on his knees, tackled Tom's legs; Chub hit him in the small of the back with a meaty shoulder, and Tom went flat on his face. Al Knowles, holding the wrench in both hands, swept it up and back like a baseball bat; at the top of its swing Kelly reached over, snatched it out of his hands and tapped Tom delicately behind the ear with it. Tom went limp.

It was late, but nobody seemed to feel like sleeping. They sat around the pressure lantern, talking idly. Chub and Kelly played an inconsequential game of casino, forgetting to pick up their points; Harris paced up and down like a man in a cell, and Al Knowles was squinched up close to the light, his eyes wide and watching, watching—

"I need a drink," said Harris.

"Tens," said one of the casino players.

Al Knowles said, "We shoulda killed him. We oughta kill him now."

"There's been too much killin' already," said Chub. "Shut up, you." And to Kelly, "With big casino," sweeping up cards.

Kelly caught his wrist and grinned. "Big casino's the ten of diamonds, not the ten of hearts. Remember?"

"Oh."

"How long before the blacktopping crew will be here?" quavered Al Knowles.

"Twelve days," said Harris. "And they better bring some likker."

"Hey, you guys."

They fell silent.

"Hey!"

"It's Tom," said Kelly. "Building sixes, Chub."

"I'm gonna go kick his ribs in," said Knowles, not moving.

"I heard that," said the voice from the darkness. "If I wasn't hog-tied—"

"We know what you'd do," said Chub. "How much proof do you think we need?"

"Chub, you don't have to do any more to him!" It was Kelly, flinging his cards down and getting up. "Tom, you want water?"

"Yes."

"Siddown, siddown," said Chub.

"Let him lie there and bleed," Al Knowles said.

"Nuts!" Kelly went and filled a cup and brought it to Tom. The big Georgian was tied thoroughly, wrists together, taut rope between elbows and elbows behind his back, so that his hands were immovable over his solar plexus. His knees and ankles were bound as well, although Knowles' little idea of a short rope between ankles and throat hadn't been used.

"Thanks, Kelly." Tom drank greedily, Kelly holding his head. "Goes good." He drank more. "What hit me?"

"One of the boys. 'Bout the time you said the cat was haunted."

"Oh, yeah." Tom rolled his head and blinked with pain.

"Any sense asking you if you blame us?"

"Kelly, does somebody else have to get killed before you guys wake up?"

"None of us figure there will be any more killin'—now."

The rest of the men drifted up. "He willing to talk sense?" Chub wanted to know.

Al Knowles laughed, "Hyuk! hyuk! Don't he look dangerous now!"

Harris said suddenly, "Al, I'm gonna hafta tape your mouth with the skin off your neck."

"Am I the kind of guy that makes up ghost stories?"

"Never have that I know of, Tom." Harris kneeled down beside him. "Never killed anyone before, either."

"Oh, get away from me. Get away," said Tom tiredly.

"Get up and make us," jeered Al.

Harris got up and backhanded him across the mouth. Al squeaked, took three steps backward and tripped over a drum of grease. "I told you," said Harris almost plaintively. "I *told* you, Al."

Tom stopped the bumble of comment. "Shut up!" he hissed. "SHUT UP!" he roared.

They shut.

"Chub," said Tom, rapidly, evenly. "What did you say I did with that Seven?"

"Buried it in the swamp."

"Yeh. Listen."

"Listen at what?"

"Be quiet and listen!"

So they listened. It was another still, windless night, with a thin crescent of moon showing nothing true in the black and muffled silver landscape. The smallest whisper of surf drifted up from the beach, and from far off to the right, where the swamp was, a scandalized frog croaked protest at the manhandling of his mudhole. But the sound that crept down, freezing their bones, came from the bluff behind their camp.

It was the unmistakable staccato of a starting engine.

"The Seven!"

" 'At's right, Chub," said Tom.

"Wh-who's crankin' her up?"

"Are we all here?"

"All but Peebles and Dennis and Rivera," said Tom.

"It's Dennis' ghost," moaned Al.

Chub snapped, "Shut up, lamebrain."

"She's shifted to Diesel," said Kelly, listening.

"She'll be here in a minute," said Tom. "Y'know, fellas, we can't all be crazy, but you're about to have a time convincin' yourself of it."

"You like this, doncha?"

"Some ways. Rivera used to call that machine *Daisy Etta*, 'cause she's *de siete* in Spig. *Daisy Etta*, she wants her a man."

"Tom," said Harris, "I wish you'd stop that chatterin'. You make me nervous."

"I got to do somethin'. I can't run," Tom drawled.

"We're going to have a look," said Chub. "If there's nobody on that cat, we'll turn you loose."

"Mighty white of you. Reckon you'll get back before she does?"

"We'll get back. Harris, come with me. We'll get one of the pan tractors. They can outrun a Seven. Kelly, take Al and get the other one."

"Dennis' machine has a flat tire on the pan," said Al's quivering voice.

"Pull the pin and cut the cables, then! Git!" Kelly and Al Knowles ran off.

"Good huntin', Chub."

Chub went to him, bent over. "I think I'm goin' to have to apologize to you, Tom."

"No you ain't. I'd a done the same. Get along now, if you think you got to. But hurry back."

"I got to. An' I'll hurry back."

Harris said, "Don't go 'way, boy." Tom returned the grin, and they were gone. But they didn't hurry back. They didn't come back at all.

It was Kelly who came pounding back, with Al Knowles on his heels, a half hour later. "Al—gimme your knife."

He went to work on the ropes. His face was drawn.

"I could see some of it," whispered Tom. "Chub and Harris?"

Kelly nodded. "There wasn't nobody on the Seven like you said." He said it as if there were nothing else in his mind, as if the most rigid self-control was keeping him from saying it over and over.

"I could see the lights," said Tom. "A tractor angling up the hill. Pretty soon another, crossing it, lighting up the whole slope."

"We heard it idling up there somewhere," Kelly said. "Olive-drab paint —couldn't see it."

"I saw the pan tractor turn over—oh, four, five times down the hill. It stopped, lights still burning. Then something hit it and rolled it again. That sure blacked it out. What turned it over first?"

"The Seven. Hanging up there just at the brow of the bluff. Waited until Chub and Harris were about to pass, sixty, seventy feet below. Tipped over the edge and rolled down on them with her clutches out. Must've been going thirty miles an hour when she hit. Broadside. They never had a chance. Followed the pan as it rolled down the hill and when it stopped booted it again."

"Want me to rub yo' ankles?" asked Al.

"You! Get outa my sight!"

"Aw, Tom—" whimpered Al.

"Skip it, Tom," said Kelly. "There ain't enough of us left to carry on that way. Al, you mind your manners from here on out, hear?"

"Ah jes' wanted to tell y'all. I knew you weren't lyin' 'bout Dennis, Tom, if only I'd stopped to think. I recollect when Dennis said he'd take that tractuh out . . . 'membah, Kelly? . . . He went an' got the crank and walked around to th' side of th' machine and stuck it in th' hole. It was barely in theah befo' the startin' engine kicked off. 'Whadda ya know!' he says t'me. 'She started by here'f! I nevah pulled that handle!' And I said, 'She sho' rarin' t'go!' "

"You pick a fine time to 'recollec'' something," gritted Tom. "C'mon— let's get out of here."

"Where to?"

"What do you know that a Seven can't move or get up on?"

"That's a large order. A big rock, maybe."

"Ain't nothing that big around here," said Tom.

Kelly thought a minute, then snapped his fingers. "Up on the top of my last cut with the shovel," he said. "It's fourteen feet if it's an inch. I was pullin' out small rock an' topsoil, and Chub told me to drop back and dip out marl from a pocket there. I sumped in back of the original cut and took out a whole mess o' marl. That left a big neck of earth sticking thirty feet or so out of the cliff. The narrowest part is only about four feet wide. If *Daisy Etta* tries to get us from the top, she'll straddle the neck and hang herself. If she tries to get us from below, she can't get traction to climb; it's too loose and too steep."

"And what happens if she builds herself a ramp?"

"We'll be gone from there."

"Let's go."

Al agitated for the choice of a Dumptor because of its speed, but was howled down. Tom wanted something that could not get a flat tire and that would need something really powerful to turn it over. They took the two-cycle pan tractor with the bulldozer blade that had been Dennis' machine and crept out into the darkness.

It was nearly six hours later that *Daisy Etta* came and woke them up. Night was receding before a paleness in the east, and a fresh ocean breeze had sprung up. Kelly had taken the first lookout and Al the second, letting Tom rest the night out. And Tom was far too tired to argue the arrangement. Al had immediately fallen asleep on his watch, but fear had such a sure, cold hold on his vitals that the first faint growl of the big Diesel engine snapped him erect. He tottered on the edge of the tall neck of earth that they slept on and squeaked as he scrabbled to get his balance.

"What's giving?" asked Kelly, instantly wide awake.

"It's coming," blubbered Al. "Oh my, oh my—"

Kelly stood up and stared into the fresh, dark dawn. The motor boomed hollowly, in a peculiar way heard twice at the same time as it was thrown to them and echoed back by the bluffs under and around them.

"It's coming and what are we goin' to do?" chanted Al. "What is going to happen?"

"My head is going to fall off," said Tom sleepily. He rolled to a sitting position, holding the brutalized member between his hands. "If that egg behind my ear hatches, it'll come out a full-sized jack-hammer." He looked at Kelly. "Where is she?"

"Don't rightly know," said Kelly. "Somewhere down around the camp."

"Probably pickin' up our scent."

"Figure it can do that?"

"I figure it can do anything," said Tom. "Al, stop your moanin'."

The sun slipped its scarlet edge into the thin slot between sea and sky, and rosy light gave each rock and tree a shape and a shadow. Kelly's gaze swept back and forth, back and forth, until, minutes later, he saw movement.

"There she is!"

"Where?"

"Down by the grease rack."

Tom rose and stared. "What's she doin'?"

After an interval Kelly said, "She's workin'. Diggin' a swale in front of the fuel drums."

"You don't say. Don't tell me she's goin' to give herself a grease job."

"She don't need it. She was completely greased and new oil put in the crankcase after we set her up. But she might need fuel."

"Not more'n half a tank."

"Well, maybe she figures she's got a lot of work to do today." As Kelly said this Al began to blubber. They ignored him.

The fuel drums were piled in a pyramid at the edge of the camp, in forty-four-gallon drums piled on their sides. The Seven was moving back and forth in front of them, close up, making pass after pass, gouging earth up and wasting it out past the pile. She soon had a huge pit scooped out, about fourteen feet wide, six feet deep and thirty feet long, right at the very edge of the pile of drums.

"What you reckon she's playin' at?"

"Search me. She seems to want fuel, but I don't . . . look at that! She's stopped in the hole; she's pivoting, smashing the top corner of the mold-board into one of the drums on the bottom!"

Tom scraped the stubble on his jaw with his nails. "An' you wonder how much that critter can do! Why, she's got the whole thing figured out. She knows if she tried to punch a hole in a fuel drum that she'd only kick it around. If she did knock a hole in it, how's she going to lift it? She's not equipped to handle hose, so . . . see? Look at her now! She just gets herself lower than the bottom drum on the pile, and punches a hole. She can do that then, with the whole weight of the pile holding it down. Then she backs her tank under the stream of fuel runnin' out!"

"How'd she get the cap off?"

Tom snorted and told them how the radiator cap had come off its hinges as he vaulted over the hood the day Rivera was hurt.

"You know," he said after a moment's thought, "if she knew as much then as she does now, I'd be snoozin' beside Rivera and Peebles. She just didn't know her way around then. She run herself like she'd never run before. She's learned plenty since."

"She has," said Kelly, "and here's where she uses it on us. She's headed this way."

She was. Straight out across the roughed-out runway she came, grinding along over the dew-sprinkled earth, yesterday's dust swirling up from under her tracks. Crossing the shoulder line, she took the rougher ground skillfully, angling up over the occasional swags in the earth, by-passing stones, riding free and fast and easily. It was the first time Tom had actually seen her clearly running without an operator, and his flesh crept as he watched. The machine was unnatural, her outline somehow unreal and dreamlike purely through the lack of the small silhouette of a man in the saddle. She looked hulked, compact, dangerous.

"What are we gonna do?" wailed Al Knowles.

"We're gonna sit and wait," said Kelly, "and you're gonna shut your trap. We won't know for five minutes yet whether she's going to go after us from down below or from up here."

"If you want to leave," said Tom gently, "go right ahead." Al sat down.

Kelly looked ruminatively down at his beloved power shovel, sitting squat and unlovely in the cut below them and away to their right. "How do you reckon she'd stand up against the dipper stick?"

"If it ever came to a rough-and-tumble," said Tom, "I'd say it would be just too bad for *Daisy Etta*. But she wouldn't fight. There's no way you could get the shovel within punchin' range; *Daisy*'d just stand there and laugh at you."

"I can't see her now," whined Al.

Tom looked. "She's taken the bluff. She's going to try it from up here. I move we sit tight and see if she's foolish enough to try to walk out here over that narrow neck. If she does, she'll drop on her belly with one truck on each side. Probably turn herself over trying to dig out."

The wait then was interminable. Back over the hill they could hear the laboring motor; twice they heard the machine stop momentarily to shift gears. Once they looked at each other hopefully as the sound rose to a series of bellowing roars, as if she were backing and filling; then they realized that she was trying to take some particularly steep part of the bank and having trouble getting traction. But she made it; the motor revved up as she made the brow of the hill, and she shifted into fourth gear and came lumbering out into the open. She lurched up to the edge of the cut, stopped, throttled down, dropped her blade on the ground and stood there idling. Al Knowles backed away to the very edge of the tongue of earth they stood on, his eyes practically on stalks.

"O.K.—put up or shut up," Kelly called across harshly.

"She's looking the situation over," said Tom. "That narrow pathway don't fool her a bit."

Daisy Etta's blade began to rise, and stopped just clear of the ground. She shifted without clashing her gears, began to back slowly, still at little more than an idle.

"She's gonna jump!" screamed Al. "I'm gettin' out of here!"

"Stay here, you fool," shouted Kelly. "She can't get us as long as we're up here! If you go down, she'll hunt you down like a rabbit."

The blast of the Seven's motor was the last straw for Al. He squeaked and hopped over the edge, scrambling and sliding down the almost sheer face of the cut. He hit the bottom running.

Daisy Etta lowered her blade and raised her snout and growled forward, the blade loading. Six, seven, seven and a half cubic yards of dirt piled up in front of her as she neared the edge. The loaded blade bit into the narrow pathway that led out to their perch. It was almost all soft, white, crumbly marl, and the great machine sank nose down into it, the monstrous overload of topsoil spilling down on each side.

"She's going to bury herself!" shouted Kelly.

"No—wait." Tom caught his arm. "She's trying to turn—she made it! She made it! She's ramping herself down to the flat!"

"She is—and she's cut us off from the bluff!"

The bulldozer, blade raised as high as it could possibly go, the hydraulic rod gleaming clean in the early light, freed herself of the last of her tremendous load, spun around and headed back upward, sinking her blade again. She made one more pass between them and the bluff, making a cut now far too wide for them to jump, particularly to the crumbly footing at the bluff's edge. Once down again, she turned to face their haven, now an isolated pillar of marl, and revved down, waiting.

"I never thought of this," said Kelly guiltily. "I knew we'd be safe from her ramping up, and I never thought she'd try it the other way!"

"Skip it. In the meantime, here we sit. What happens—do we wait up here until she idles out of fuel, or do we starve to death?"

"Oh, this won't be a siege, Tom. That thing's too much of a killer. Where's Al? I wonder if he's got guts enough to make a pass near here with our tractor and draw her off?"

"He had just guts enough to take our tractor and head out," said Tom. "Didn't you know?"

"He took our—*what?*" Kelly looked out toward where they had left their machine the night before. It was gone. "Why the dirty little yellow rat!"

"No sense cussin'," said Tom steadily, interrupting what he knew was the beginning of some really flowery language. "What else could you expect?"

Daisy Etta decided, apparently, how to go about removing their splendid isolation. She uttered the snort of too-quick throttle, and moved into their peak with a corner of her blade, cutting out a huge swipe, undercutting the material over it so that it fell on her side and track as she passed. Eight inches disappeared from that side of their little plateau.

"Oh-oh. That won't do a-tall," said Tom.

"Fixin' to dig us down," said Kelly grimly. "Take her about twenty minutes. Tom, I say leave."

"It won't be healthy. You just got no idea how fast that thing can move now. Don't forget, she's a good deal more than she was when she had a man runnin' her. She can shift from high to reverse to fifth speed forward like that"—he snapped his fingers—"and she can pivot faster'n you can blink and throw that blade just where she wants it."

The tractor passed under them, bellowing, and their little table was suddenly a foot shorter.

"Awright," said Kelly. "So what do you want to do? Stay here and let her dig the ground out from under our feet?"

"I'm just warning you," said Tom. "Now listen. We'll wait until she's taking a load. It'll take her a second to get rid of it when she knows we're gone. We'll split—she can't get both of us. You head out in the open, try to circle the curve of the bluff and get where you can climb it. Then come back over here to the cut. A man can scramble off a fourteen-foot cut faster'n any tractor ever built. I'll cut in close to the cut, down at the bottom. If she takes after you, I'll get clear all right. If she takes after me, I'll try to make the shovel and at least give her a run for her money. I can play hide an' seek in an' around and under that dipper-stick all day if she wants to play."

"Why me out in the open?"

"Don't you think those long laigs o' yours can outrun her in that distance?"

"Reckon they got to," grinned Kelly. "O.K., Tom."

They waited tensely. *Daisy Etta* backed close by, started another pass. As the motor blatted under the load, Tom said, "Now!" and they jumped. Kelly, catlike as always, landed on his feet. Tom, whose knees and ankles were black and blue with rope bruises, took two staggering steps and fell. Kelly scooped him to his feet as the dozer's steel prow came around the bank. Instantly she was in fifth gear and howling down at them. Kelly flung himself to the left and Tom to the right, and they pounded away, Kelly out toward the runway, Tom straight for the shovel. *Daisy Etta* let them diverge for a moment, keeping her course, trying to pursue both; then she evidently sized Tom up as the slower, for she swung toward him. The instant's hesitation was all Tom needed to get the little lead necessary. He tore up to the shovel, his legs going like pistons, and dived down between the shovel's tracks.

As he hit the ground, the big manganese-steel moldboard hit the right track of the shovel, and the impact set all forty-seven tons of the great machine quivering. But Tom did not stop. He scrabbled his way under the rig, stood up behind it, leaped and caught the sill of the rear window, clapped his other hand on it, drew himself up and tumbled inside. Here he was safe for the moment; the huge tracks themselves were higher than the Seven's blade could rise, and the floor of the cab was a good sixteen inches higher than the top of the track. Tom went to the cab door and peeped outside. The tractor had drawn off and was idling.

"Study away," gritted Tom, and went to the big Murphy Diesel. He unhurriedly checked the oil with the bayonet gauge, replaced it, took the governor cut-out rod from its rack and inserted it in the governor casing. He set the master throttle at the halfway mark, pulled up the starter-handle, twitched the cut-out. The motor spit a wad of blue smoke out of its hooded exhaust and caught. Tom put the rod back, studied the fuel-flow glass and pressure gauges, and then went to the door and looked out again. The Seven had not moved, but it was revving up and down in that uneven fashion it had shown up on the mesa. Tom had the extraordinary idea that it was gathering itself to spring. He slipped into the saddle, threw the master clutch. The big gears that half-filled the cab obediently began to turn. He kicked the brake-locks loose with his heels, let his feet rest lightly on the pedals as they rose.

Then he reached over his head and snapped back the throttle. As the Murphy picked up he grasped both hoist and swing levers and pulled them back. The engine howled; the two-yard bucket came up off the ground with a sudden jolt as the cold friction grabbed it. The big machine swung hard to the right; Tom snapped his hoist lever forward and checked the bucket's rise with his foot on the brake. He shoved the crowd lever forward; the bucket ran out to the end of its reach, and the heel of the bucket wiped across the Seven's hood, taking with it the exhaust stack, muffler and all, and the pre-cleaner on the air intake. Tom cursed. He had figured on the machine's leaping backward. If it had, he would have smashed the cast-iron radiator core. But she had stood still, making a split-second decision.

Now she moved, though, and quickly. With that incredibly fast shifting, she leaped backwards and pivoted out of range before Tom could check the shovel's mad swing. The heavy swing-friction blocks smoked acridly as the machine slowed, stopped and swung back. Tom checked her as he was facing the Seven, hoisted his bucket a few feet, and rehauled, bringing it about halfway back, ready for anything. The four great dipper-teeth gleamed in the sun. Tom ran a practiced eye over cables, boom and dipper-stick, liking the black polish of crater compound on the sliding parts, the easy tension of well-greased cables and links. The huge machine stood strong, ready and profoundly subservient for all its brute power.

Tom looked searchingly at the Seven's ruined engine hood. The gaping end of the broken air-intake pipe stared back at him. "Aha!" he said. "A few cupfuls of nice dry marl down there'll give you something to chew on."

Keeping a wary eye on the tractor, he swung into the bank, dropped his bucket and plunged it into the marl. He crowded it deep, and the Murphy yelled for help but kept on pushing. At the peak of the load a terrific jar rocked him in the saddle. He looked back over his shoulder through the door and saw the Seven backing off again. She had run up and delivered a terrific punch to the counterweight at the back of the cab. Tom grinned tightly. She'd have to do better than that. There was nothing back there but eight or ten tons of solid steel. And he didn't much care at the moment whether or not she scratched his paint.

He swung back again, white marl running away on both sides of the heaped bucket. The shovel rode perfectly now, for a shovel is counter-weighted to balance true when standing level with the bucket loaded. The hoist and swing frictions and the brake linings had heated and dried them-selves of the night's condensation moisture, and she answered the controls in a way that delighted the operator in him. He handled the swing lever lightly, back to swing to the right, forward to swing to the left, following the slow dance the Seven had started to do, stepping warily back and forth like a fighter looking for an opening. Tom kept the bucket between himself and the tractor, knowing that she could not hurl a tool that was built to smash hard rock for twenty hours a day and like it.

Daisy Etta bellowed and rushed in. Tom snapped the hoist lever back hard, and the bucket rose, letting the tractor run underneath. Tom punched the bucket trip, and the great steel jaw opened, cascading marl down on the broken hood. The tractor's fan blew it back in a huge billowing cloud. The instant that it took Tom to check and dump was enough, however, for the tractor to dance back out of the way, for when he tried to drop it on the machine to smash the coiled injector tubes on top of the engine block, she was gone.

The dust cleared away, and the tractor moved in again, feinted to the left, then swung her blade at the bucket, which was just clear of the ground. Tom swung to meet her, her feint having gotten her in a little closer than he liked, and bucket met blade with a shower of sparks and a clank that could be heard for half a mile. She had come in with her blade high, and Tom let out a wordless shout as he saw that the A-frame brace behind the blade had caught between two of his dipper-teeth. He snatched at his hoist lever and the bucket came up, lifting with it the whole front end of the bulldozer.

Daisy Etta plunged up and down and her tracks dug violently into the earth as she raised and lowered her blade, trying to shake herself free. Tom rehauled, trying to bring the tractor in closer, for the boom was set too low to attempt to lift such a dead weight. As it was, the shovel's off track was trying its best to get off the ground. But the crowd and rehaul frictions could not handle her alone; they began to heat and slip.

Tom hoisted a little; the shovel's off track came up a foot off the ground. Tom cursed and let the bucket drop, and in an instant the dozer was free and running clear. Tom swung wildly at her, missed. The dozer came in on a long curve; Tom swung to meet her again, took a vicious swipe at her which she took on her blade. But this time she did not withdraw after being hit, but bored right in, carrying the bucket before her. Before Tom realized what she was doing, his bucket was around in front of the tracks and between them, on the ground. It was as swift and skillful a maneuver as could be imagined, and it left the shovel without the ability to swing as long as *Daisy Etta* could hold the bucket trapped between the tracks.

Tom crowded furiously, but that succeeded only in lifting the boom higher in the air, since there is nothing to hold a boom down but its own weight. Hoisting did nothing but make his frictions smoke and rev the engine down dangerously close to the stalling point.

Tom swore again and reached down to the cluster of small levers at his left. These were the gears. On this type of shovel, the swing lever controls everything except crowd and hoist. With the swing lever, the operator,

having selected his gear, controls the travel—that is, power to the tracks—
in forward and reverse; booming up and booming down; and swinging.
The machine can do only one of these things at a time. If she is in travel
gear, she cannot swing. If she is in swing gear, she cannot boom up or down.
Not once in years of operating would this inability bother an operator; now,
however, nothing was normal.

Tom pushed the swing gear control down and pulled up on the travel.
The clutches involved were jaw clutches, not frictions, so that he had to
throttle down to an idle before he could make the castellations·mesh. As
the Murphy revved down, *Daisy Etta* took it as a signal that something
could be done about it, and she shoved furiously into the bucket. But Tom
had all controls in neutral and all she succeeded in doing was to dig herself
in, her sharp new cleats spinning deep into the dirt.

Tom set his throttle up again and shoved the swing lever forward.
There was a vast crackling of drive chains; and the big tracks started to
turn.

Daisy Etta had sharp cleats; her pads were twenty inches wide and
her tracks were fourteen feet long, and there were fourteen tons of steel
on them. The shovel's big flat pads were three feet wide and twenty feet
long, and forty-seven tons aboard. There was simply no comparison. The
Murphy bellowed the fact that the work was hard, but gave no indications
of stalling. *Daisy Etta* performed the incredible feat of shifting into a
forward gear while she was moving backwards, but it did her no good.
Round and round her tracks went, trying to drive her forward, gouging
deep; and slowly and surely she was forced backward toward the cut wall
by the shovel.

Tom heard a sound that was not part of a straining machine; he looked
out and saw Kelly up on top of the cut, smoking, swinging his feet over the
edge, making punching motions with his hands as if he had a ringside seat
at a big fight—which he certainly had.

Tom now offered the dozer little choice. If she did not turn aside before
him, she would be borne back against the bank and her fuel tank crushed.
There was every possibility that, having her pinned there, Tom would have
time to raise his bucket over her and smash her to pieces. And if she turned
before she was forced against the bank, she would have to free Tom's
bucket. This she had to do.

The Murphy gave him warning, but not enough. It crooned as the load
came off, and Tom knew then that the dozer was shifting into a reverse
gear. He whipped the hoist lever back, and the bucket rose as the dozer
backed away from him. He crowded it out and let it come smashing down—
and missed. For the tractor danced aside—and while he was in travel gear
he could not swing to follow it. *Daisy Etta* charged then, put one track on
the bank and went over almost on her beam-ends, throwing one end of her
blade high in the air. So totally unexpected was it that Tom was quite
unprepared. The tractor flung itself on the bucket, and the cutting edge of

the blade dropped between the dipper teeth. This time there was the whole weight of the tractor to hold it there. There would be no way for her to free herself—but at the same time she had trapped the bucket so far out from the center pin of the shovel that Tom couldn't hoist without overbalancing and turning the monster over.

Daisy Etta ground away in reverse, dragging the bucket out until it was checked by the bumper-blocks. Then she began to crab sideways, up against the bank and when Tom tried tentatively to rehaul, she shifted and came right with him, burying one whole end of her blade deep into the bank.

Stalemate. She had hung herself up on the bucket, and she had immobilized it. Tom tried to rehaul, but the tractor's anchorage in the bank was too solid. He tried to swing, to hoist. All the overworked frictions could possibly give out was smoke. Tom grunted and throttled to an idle, leaned out the window. *Daisy Etta* was idling too, loudly without her muffler, the stackless exhaust giving out an ugly flat sound. But after the roar of the two great motors the partial silence was deafening.

Kelly called down, "Double knockout, hey?"

"Looks like it. What say we see if we can't get close enough to her to quiet her down some?"

Kelly shrugged. "I dunno. If she's really stopped herself, it's the first time. I respect that rig, Tom. She wouldn't have got herself into that spot if she didn't have an ace up her sleeve."

"Look at her, man! Suppose she was a civilized bulldozer and you had to get her out of there. She can't raise her blade high enough to free it from those dipper-teeth, y'know. Think you'd be able to do it?"

"It might take several seconds," Kelly drawled. "She's sure high and dry."

"O.K., let's spike her guns."

"Like what?"

"Like taking a bar and prying out her tubing." He referred to the coiled brass tubing that carried the fuel, under pressure, from the pump to the injectors. There were many feet of it, running from the pump reservoir, stacked in expansion coils over the cylinder head.

As he spoke *Daisy Etta*'s idle burst into that maniac revving up and down characteristic of her.

"What do you know!" Tom called above the racket. "Eavesdropping!"

Kelly slid down the cut, stood up on the track of the shovel and poked his head in the window. "Well, you want to get a bar and try?"

"Let's go!"

Tom went to the toolbox and pulled out the pinch bar that Kelly used to replace cables on his machine, and swung to the ground. They approached the tractor warily. She revved up as they came near, began to shudder. The front end rose and dropped and the tracks began to turn as she tried to twist out of the vise her blade had dropped into.

"Take it easy, sister," said Tom. "You'll just bury yourself. Set still and take it, now, like a good girl. You got it comin'."

"Be careful," said Kelly. Tom hefted the bar and laid a hand on the fender.

The tractor literally shivered, and from the rubber hose connection at the top of the radiator, a blinding stream of hot water shot out. It fanned and caught them both full in the face. They staggered back, cursing.

"You O.K., Tom?" Kelly gasped a moment later. He had got most of it across the mouth and cheek. Tom was on his knees, his shirt tail out, blotting at his face.

"My eyes . . . oh, my eyes—"

"Let's see!" Kelly dropped down beside him and took him by the wrists, gently removing Tom's hands from his face. He whistled. "Come on," he gritted. He helped Tom up and led him away a few feet. "Stay here," he said hoarsely. He turned, walked back toward the dozer, picking up the pinchbar. "You dirty ——!" he yelled, and flung it like a javelin at the tube coils. It was a little high. It struck the ruined hood, made a deep dent in the metal. The dent promptly inverted with a loud *thung-g-g!* and flung the bar back at him. He ducked; it whistled over his head and caught Tom in the calves of his legs. He went down like a poled ox, but staggered to his feet again.

"Come on!" Kelly snarled, and taking Tom's arm, hustled him around the turn of the cut. "Sit down! I'll be right back."

"Where you going? Kelly—be careful!"

"Careful and how!"

Kelly's long legs ate up the distance back to the shovel. He swung into the cab, reached back over the motor and set up the master throttle all the way. Stepping up behind the saddle, he opened the running throttle and the Murphy howled. Then he hauled back on the hoist lever until it knuckled in, turned and leaped off the machine in one supple motion.

The hoist drum turned and took up slack; the cable straightened as it took the strain. The bucket stirred under the dead weight of the bulldozer that rested on it; and slowly, then, the great flat tracks began to lift their rear ends off the ground. The great obedient mass of machinery teetered forward on the tips of her tracks, the Murphy revved down and under the incredible load, but it kept the strain. A strand of the two-part hoist cable broke and whipped around, singing; and then she was balanced—overbalanced—

And the shovel had hauled herself right over and had fallen with an earth-shaking crash. The boom, eight tons of solid steel, clanged down onto the blade of the bulldozer, and lay there, crushing it down tightly onto the imprisoning row of dipper-teeth.

Daisy Etta sat there, not trying to move now, racing her motor impotently. Kelly strutted past her, thumbing his nose, and went back to Tom.

"Kelly! I thought you were never coming back! What happened?"

"Shovel pulled herself over on her nose."

"Good boy! Fall on the tractor?"

"Nup. But the boom's laying across the top of her blade. Caught like a rat in a trap."

"Better watch out the rat don't chew its leg off to get out," said Tom, drily. "Still runnin', is she?"

"Yep. But we'll fix that in a hurry."

"Sure. Sure. How?"

"How? I dunno. Dynamite, maybe. How's the optics?"

Tom opened one a trifle and grunted. "Rough. I can see a little, though. My eyelids are parboiled, mostly. Dynamite, you say? Well—"

Tom sat back against the bank and stretched out his legs. "I tell you, Kelly, I been too blessed busy these last few hours to think much, but there's one thing that keeps comin' back to me—somethin' I was mullin' over long before the rest of you guys knew anything was up at all, except that Rivera had got hurt in some way I wouldn't tell you all about. But I don't reckon you'll call me crazy if I open my mouth now and let it all run out?"

"From now on," Kelly said fervently, "nobody's crazy. After this I'll believe anything."

"O.K. Well, about that tractor. What do you suppose has got into her?"

"Search me. I dunno."

"No—don't say that. I just got an idea we can't stop at 'I dunno.' We got to figure all the angles on this thing before we know just what to do about it. Let's just get this thing lined up. When did it start? On the mesa. How? Rivera was opening an old building with the Seven. This thing came out of there. Now here's what I'm getting at. We can dope these things out about it: It's intelligent. It can only get into a machine and not into a man. It—"

"What about that? How do you know it can't?"

"Because it had the chance to and didn't. I was standing right by the opening when it kited out. Rivera was upon the machine at the time. It didn't directly harm either of us. It got into the tractor, and the tractor did. By the same token, it can't hurt a man when it's out of a machine, but that's all it wants to do when it's in one. O.K.?

"To get on: once it's in one machine it can't get out again. We know that because it had plenty of chances and didn't take them. That scuffle with the dipper-stick, f'r instance. My face woulda been plenty red if it had taken over the shovel—and you can bet it would have if it could."

"I got you so far. But what are we going to do about it?"

"That's the thing. You see, I don't think it's enough to wreck the tractor. We might burn it, blast it, take whatever it was that got into it up on the mesa."

"That makes sense. But I don't see what else we can do than just break up the dozer. We haven't got a line on actually what the thing is."

"I think we have. Remember I asked you all those screwy questions about the arc that killed Peebles. Well, when that happened, I recollected a flock of other things. One—when it got out of that hole up there, I smelled that smell that you notice when you're welding; sometimes when lightning strikes real close."

"Ozone," said Kelly.

"Yeah—ozone. Then, it likes metal, not flesh. But most of all, there was that arc. Now, that was absolutely screwy. You know as well as I do —better—that an arc generator simply don't have the push to do a thing like that. It can't kill a man, and it can't throw an arc no fifty feet. But it did. An' that's why I asked you if there could be something—a field, or some such—that could *suck* current out of a generator, all at once, faster than it could flow. Because this thing's electrical; it fits all around."

"Electronic," said Kelly doubtfully, thoughtfully.

"I wouldn't know. Now then. When Peebles was killed, a funny thing happened. Remember what Chub said? The Seven moved back—straight back, about thirty feet, until it bumped into a roadroller that was standing behind it. It did that with no fuel in the starting engine—without even using the starting engine, for that matter—and with the compression valves locked open!

"Kelly, that thing in the dozer can't do much, when you come right down to it. It couldn't fix itself up after that joy-ride on the mesa. It can't make the machine do too much more than the machine can do ordinarily. What it actually can do, seems to me, is to make a spring push instead of pull, like the control levers, and make a fitting slip when it's supposed to hold, like the ratchet on the throttle lever. It can turn a shaft, like the way it cranks its own starting motor. But if it was so all-fired high-powered, it wouldn't have to use the starting motor! The absolute biggest job it's done so far, seems to me, was when it walked back from that welding machine when Peebles got his. Now, why did it do that just then?"

"Reckon it didn't like the brimstone smell, like it says in the Good Book," said Kelly sourly.

"That's pretty close, seems to me. Look, Kelly—this thing *feels* things. I mean, it can get sore. If it couldn't it never woulda kept driving in at the shovel like that. It can think. But if it can do all those things, then it can be *scared!*"

"Scared? Why should it be scared?"

"Listen. Something went on in that thing when the arc hit it. What's that I read in a magazine once about heat—something about molecules runnin' around with their heads cut off when they got hot?"

"Molecules do. They go into rapid motion when heat is applied. But—"

"But nothin'. That machine was hot for four hours after that. But she was hot in a funny way. Not just around the place where the arc hit, like as if it was a welding arc. But hot all over—from the moldboard to the fuel-tank cap. Hot everywhere. And just as hot behind the final drive housings as she was at the top of the blade where the poor guy put his hand.

"And look at this." Tom was getting excited, as his words crystallized his ideas. "She was scared—scared enough to back off from that welder, putting everything she could into it, to get back from that welding machine. And after that, she was sick. I say that because in the whole time she's had that whatever-ya-call-it in her, she's never been near men without trying to kill them, except for those two days after the arc hit her. She had juice enough to start herself when Dennis came around with the crank, but she still needed someone to run her till she got her strength back."

"But why didn't she turn and smash up the welder when Dennis took her?"

"One of two things. She didn't have the strength, or she didn't have the guts. She was scared, maybe, and wanted out of there, away from that thing."

"But she had all night to go back for it!"

"Still scared. Or . . . oh, *that's* it! She had other things to do first. Her main idea is to kill men—there's no other way you can figure it. It's what she was built to do. Not the tractor—they don't build 'em sweeter'n that machine; but the thing that's runnin' it."

"What *is* that thing?" Kelly mused. "Coming out of that old building—temple—what have you—how old is it? How long was it there? What kept it in there?"

"What kept it in there was some funny gray stuff that lined the inside of the buildin'," said Tom. "It was like rock, an' it was like smoke.

"It was a color that scared you to look at it, and it gave Rivera and me the creeps when we got near it. Don't ask me what it was. I went up there to look at it, and it's gone. Gone from the building, anyhow. There was a little lump of it on the ground. I don't know whether that was a hunk of it, or all of it rolled up into a ball. I get the creeps again thinkin' about it."

Kelly stood up. "Well, the heck with it. We been beatin' our gums up here too long anyhow. There's just enough sense in what you say to make me want to try something nonsensical, if you see what I mean. If that welder can sweat the Ol' Nick out of that tractor, I'm on. Especially from fifty feet away. There should be a Dumptor around here somewhere; let's move from here. Can you navigate now?"

"Reckon so, a little." Tom rose and together they followed the cut until they came on the Dumptor. They climbed on, cranked it up and headed toward camp.

About half way there Kelly looked back, gasped, and putting his mouth close to Tom's ear, bellowed against the scream of the motor, "Tom! Member what you said about the rat in the trap biting off a leg?"

Tom nodded.

"Well, *Daisy* did too! She's left her blade an' pushbeams an' she's followin' us in!"

They howled into the camp, gasping against the dust that followed when they pulled up by the welder.

Kelly said, "You cast around and see if you can find a drawpin to hook that rig up to the Dumptor with. I'm goin' after some water an' chow!"

Tom grinned. Imagine old Kelly forgetting that a Dumptor had no drawbar! He groped around to a toolbox, peering out of the narrow slit beneath swollen lids, felt behind it and located a shackle. He climbed up on the Dumptor, turned it around and backed up to the welding machine. He passed the shackle through the ring at the end of the steering tongue of the welder, screwed in the pin and dropped the shackle over the front towing hook of the Dumptor. A dumptor being what it is, having no real front and no real rear, and direct reversing gears in all speeds, it was no trouble to drive it "backwards" for a change.

Kelly came pounding back, out of breath. "Fix it? Good. Shackle? No drawbar! *Daisy's* closin' up fast; I say let's take the beach. We'll be concealed until we have a good lead out o' this pocket, and the going's pretty fair, long as we don't bury this jalopy in the sand."

"Good," said Tom as they climbed on and he accepted an open tin of K. "Only go easy; bump around too much and the welder'll slip off the hook. An' I somehow don't want to lose it just now."

They took off, zooming up the beach. A quarter of a mile up, they sighted the Seven across the flat. It immediately turned and took a course that would intercept them.

"Here she comes," shouted Kelly, and stepped down hard on the accelerator. Tom leaned over the back of the seat, keeping his eye on their tow. "Hey! Take it easy! Watch it!

"Hey!"

But it was too late. The tongue of the welding machine responded to that one bump too many. The shackle jumped up off the hook, the welder lurched wildly, slewed hard to the left. The tongue dropped to the sand and dug in; the machine rolled up on it and snapped it off, finally stopped, leaning crazily askew. By a miracle it did not quite turn over.

Kelly tramped on the brakes and both their heads did their utmost to snap off their shoulders. They leaped off and ran back to the welder. It was intact, but towing it was now out of the question.

"If there's going to be a showdown, it's gotta be here."

The beach here was about thirty yards wide, the sand almost level, and undercut banks of sawgrass forming the landward edge in a series of little hummocks and headlands. While Tom stayed with the machine, testing starter and generator contacts, Kelly walked up one of the little mounds, stood up on it and scanned the beach back the way he had come. Suddenly he began to shout and wave his arms.

"What's got into you?"

"It's Al!" Kelly called back. "With the pan tractor!"

Tom dropped what he was doing, and came to stand beside Kelly. "Where's the Seven? I can't see."

"Turned on the beach and followin' our track. Al! Al! You little skunk, c'mere!"

Tom could now dimly make out the pan tractor cutting across directly toward them and the beach.

"He don't see *Daisy Etta*," remarked Kelly disgustedly, "or he'd sure be headin' the other way."

Fifty yards away Al pulled up and throttled down. Kelly shouted and waved to him. Al stood up on the machine, cupped his hands around his mouth. "Where's the Seven?"

"Never mind that! Come here with that tractor!"

Al stayed where he was. Kelly cursed and started out after him.

"You stay away from me," he said when Kelly was closer.

"I ain't got time for you now," said Kelly. "Bring that tractor down to the beach."

"Where's that *Daisy Etta*?" Al's voice was oddly strained.

"Right behind us." Kelly tossed a thumb over his shoulder. "On the beach."

Al's pop eyes clicked wide almost audibly. He turned on his heel and jumped off the machine and started to run. Kelly uttered a wordless syllable that was somehow more obscene than anything else he had ever uttered, and vaulted into the seat of the machine. "Hey!" he bellowed after Al's rapidly diminishing figure. "You're runnin' right into her." Al appeared not to hear, but went pelting down the beach.

Kelly put her into fifth gear and poured on the throttle. As the tractor began to move he whacked out the master clutch, snatched the overdrive lever back to put her into sixth, rammed the clutch in again, all so fast that she did not have time to stop rolling. Bucking and jumping over the rough ground the fast machine whined for the beach.

Tom was fumbling back to the welder, his ears telling him better than his eyes how close the Seven was—for she was certainly no nightingale, particularly without her exhaust stack. Kelly reached the machine as he did.

"Get behind it," snapped Tom. "I'll jamb the tierod with the shackle, and you see if you can't bunt her up into that pocket between those two hummocks. Only take it easy—you don't want to tear up that generator. Where's Al?"

"Don't ask me. He run down the beach to meet *Daisy*."

"He *what*?"

The whine of the two-cycle drowned out Kelly's answer, if any. He got behind the welder and set his blade against it. Then in a low gear, slipping his clutch in a little, he slowly nudged the machine toward the place Tom had indicated. It was a little hollow in between two projecting banks. The surf and the high-tide mark dipped inland here to match it; the water was only a few feet away.

Tom raised his arm and Kelly stopped. From the other side of the projecting shelf, out of their sight now, came the flat roar of the Seven's exhaust. Kelly sprang off the tractor and went to help Tom, who was furiously throwing out coils of cable from the rack back of the welder. "What's the game?"

"We got to ground that Seven some way," panted Tom. He threw the last bit of cable out to clear it of kinks and turned to the panel. "How was it—about sixty volts and the amperage on 'special application'?" He spun the dials, pressed the starter button. The motor responded instantly. Kelly scooped up ground clamp and rod holder and tapped them together. The solenoid governor picked up the load and the motor hummed as a good live spark took the jump.

"Good," said Tom, switching off the generator. "Come on, Lieutenant General Electric, figure me out a way to ground that maverick."

Kelly tightened his lips, shook his head. "I dunno—unless somebody actually clamps this thing on her."

"No, boy, can't do that. If one of us gets killed—"

Kelly tossed the ground clamp idly, his lithe body taut. "Don't give me that, Tom. You know I'm elected because you can't see good enough yet to handle it. You know you'd do it if you could. You—"

He stopped short, for the steadily increasing roar of the approaching Seven had stopped, was blatting away now in that extraordinary irregular throttling that *Daisy Etta* affected.

"Now, what's got into her?"

Kelly broke away and scrambled up the bank. "Tom!" he gasped. "Tom—come up here!"

Tom followed, and they lay side by side, peering out over the top of the escarpment at the remarkable tableau.

Daisy Etta was standing on the beach, near the water, not moving. Before her, twenty or thirty feet away, stood Al Knowles, his arms out in front of him, talking a blue streak. *Daisy* made far too much racket for them to hear what he was saying.

"Do you reckon he's got guts enough to stall her off for us?" said Tom.

"If he has, it's the queerest thing that's happened yet on this old island," Kelly breathed, "an' that's saying something."

The Seven revved up till she shook, and then throttled back. She ran down so low then that they thought she had shut herself down, but she caught on the last two revolutions and began to idle quietly. And then they could hear.

Al's voice was high, hysterical. "—I come t' he'p you, I come t' he'p you, don' kill me, I'll he'p you—" He took a step forward; the dozer snorted and he fell to his knees. "I'll wash you an' grease you and change yo' ile," he said in a high singsong.

"The guy's not human," said Kelly wonderingly.

"He ain't housebroke either," Tom chuckled.

"—lemme he'p you. I'll fix you when you break down. I'll he'p you kill those other guys—"

"She don't need any help!" said Tom.

"The louse," growled Kelly. "The rotten little double-crossing polecat!"

He stood up. "Hey, you Al! Come out o' that. I mean now! If she don't get you I will, if you don't move."

Al was crying now. "Shut up!" he screamed. "I know who's bawss hereabouts, an' so do you!" He pointed at the tractor. "She'll kill us all off'n we don't do what she wants!" He turned back to the machine. "I'll k-kill 'em fo' you. I'll wash you and shine you up and f-fix yo' hood. I'll put yo' blade back on. . . ."

Tom reached out and caught Kelly's leg as the tall man started out, blind mad. "Git back here," he barked. "What you want to do—get killed for the privilege of pinnin' his ears back?"

Kelly subsided and came back, threw himself down beside Tom, put his face in his hands. He was quivering with rage.

"Don't take on so," Tom said. "The man's plumb loco. You can't argue with him any more'n you can with *Daisy*, there. If he's got to get his, *Daisy*'ll give it to him."

"Aw, Tom, it ain't that. I know he ain't worth it, but I can't sit up here and watch him get himself killed. I can't, Tom."

Tom thumped him on the shoulder, because there were simply no words to be said. Suddenly he stiffened, snapped his fingers.

"There's our ground," he said urgently, pointing seaward. "The water —the wet beach where the surf runs. If we can get our ground clamp out there and her somewhere near it—"

"Ground the pan tractor. Run it out into the water. It ought to reach— partway, anyhow."

"That's it—c'mon."

They slid down the bank, snatched up the ground clamp, attached it to the frame of the pan tractor.

"I'll take it," said Tom, and as Kelly opened his mouth, Tom shoved him back against the welding machine. "No time to argue," he snapped, swung on to the machine, slapped her in gear and was off. Kelly took a step toward the tractor, and then his quick eye saw a bight of the ground cable about to foul a wheel of the welder. He stooped and threw it off, spread out the rest of it so it would pay off clear. Tom, with the incredible single-mindedness of the trained operator, watched only the black line of the trailing cable on the sand behind him. When it straightened, he stopped. The front of the tracks were sloshing in the gentle surf. He climbed off the side away from the Seven and tried to see. There was movement, and the growl of her motor now running at a bit more than idle, but he could not distinguish much.

Kelly picked up the rod-holder and went to peer around the head of the protruding bank. Al was on his feet, still crooning hysterically, sidling over toward *Daisy Etta*. Kelly ducked back, threw the switch on the arc generator, climbed the bank and crawled along through the sawgrass paralleling the beach until the holder in his hand tugged and he knew he had reached the end of the cable. He looked out at the beach; measured carefully with his eye the arc he would travel if he left his position and, keeping the cable taut, went out on the beach. At no point would he come within seventy feet of the possessed machine, let alone fifty. She had to be drawn in closer. And she had to be maneuvered out to the wet sand, or in the water—

Al Knowles, encouraged by the machine's apparent decision not to move, approached, though warily, and still running off at the mouth. "—we'll kill 'em off an' then we'll keep it a secret and th' bahges'll come an' take us offen th' island and we'll go to anothah job an' kill us lots mo' . . . an' when yo' tracks git dry an' squeak we'll wet 'em up with blood, and you'll be rightly king o' th' hill . . . look yondah, look yondah, *Daisy Etta*, see them theah, by the otheh tractuh, theah they are, kill 'em, *Daisy*, kill 'em, *Daisy*, an' lemme he'p . . . heah me. *Daisy*, heah me, say you heah me—" and the motor roared in response. Al laid a timid hand on the radiator guard, leaning far over to do it, and the tractor still stood there grumbling but not moving. Al stepped back, motioned with his arm, began to walk off slowly toward the pan tractor, looking backwards as he did so like a man training a dog. "C'mon, c'mon, theah's one theah, le's *kill'm, kill'm, kill'm.* . . ."

And with a snort the tractor revved up and followed.

Kelly licked his lips without effect because his tongue was dry, too. The madman passed him, walking straight up the center of the beach, and the tractor, now no longer a bulldozer, followed him; and there the sand was bone dry, sun-dried, dried to powder. As the tractor passed him, Kelly got up on all fours, went over the edge of the bank onto the beach, crouched there.

Al crooned, "I love ya, honey, I love ya, 'deed I do—"

Kelly ran crouching, like a man under machine-gun fire, making himself as small as possible and feeling as big as a barn door. The torn-up sand where the tractor had passed was under his feet now; he stopped, afraid to get too much closer, afraid that a weakened, badly grounded arc might leap from the holder in his hand and serve only to alarm and infuriate the thing in the tractor. And just then Al saw him.

"There!" he screamed; and the tractor pulled up short. "Behind you! Get'm, *Daisy*! *Kill'm, kill'm, kill'm.*"

Kelly stood up almost wearily, fury and frustration too much to be borne. "In the water," he yelled, because it was what his whole being wanted "Get'er in the water! Wet her tracks, Al!"

"*Kill'm, kill'm—*"

As the tractor started to turn, there was a commotion over by the pan tractor. It was Tom, jumping, shouting, waving his arms, swearing. He ran out from behind his machine, straight at the Seven. *Daisy Etta*'s motor roared and she swung to meet him, Al barely dancing back out of the way. Tom cut sharply, sand spouting under his pumping feet, and ran straight into the water. He went out to about waist deep, suddenly disappeared. He surfaced, spluttering, still trying to shout. Kelly took a better grip on his rod holder and rushed.

Daisy Etta, in following Tom's crazy rush, had swung in beside the pan tractor, not fifteen feet away; and she, too, was now in the surf. Kelly closed up the distance as fast as his long legs would let him; and as he approached to within that crucial fifty feet, Al Knowles hit him.

Al was frothing at the mouth, gibbering. The two men hit full tilt; Al's head caught Kelly in the midriff as he missed a straightarm, and the breath went out of him in one great *whoosh!* Kelly went down like tall timber, the whole world turned to one swirling red-gray haze. Al flung himself on the bigger man, clawing, smacking, too berserk to ball his fists.

"Ah'm go' to kill you," he gurgled. "She'll git one, I'll git t'other, an' then she'll know—"

Kelly covered his face with his arms, and as some wind was sucked at last into his laboring lungs, he flung them upward and sat up in one mighty surge. Al was hurled upward and to one side, and as he hit the ground Kelly reached out a long arm, and twisted his fingers into the man's coarse hair, raised him up, and came across with his other fist in a punch that would have killed him had it landed square. But Al managed to jerk to one side enough so that it only amputated a cheek. He fell and lay still. Kelly scrambled madly around in the sand for his welding-rod holder, found it and began to run again. He couldn't see Tom at all now, and the Seven was standing in the surf, moving slowly from side to side, backing out, ravening. Kelly held the rod-clamp and its trailing cable blindly before him and ran straight at the machine. And then it came—that thin, soundless bolt of energy. But this time it had its full force, for poor old Peebles' body had not been the ground that this swirling water offered. *Daisy Etta* literally leaped backwards toward him, and the water around her tracks spouted upward in hot steam. The sound of her engine ran up and up, broke, took on the rhythmic, uneven beat of a swing drummer. She threw herself from side to side like a cat with a bag over its head. Kelly stepped a little closer, hoping for another bolt to come from the clamp in his hand, but there was none, for—

"The circuit breaker!" cried Kelly.

He threw the holder up on the deck plate of the Seven in front of the seat, and ran across the little beach to the welder. He reached behind the switchboard, got his thumb on the contact hinge and jammed it down.

Daisy Etta leaped again, and then again, and suddenly her motor stopped. Heat in turbulent waves blurred the air over her. The little gas tank for the starting motor went out with a cannon's roar, and the big fuel tank, still holding thirty-odd gallons of Diesel oil followed. It puffed itself open rather than exploded, and threw a great curtain of flame over the ground behind the machine. Motor or no motor, then, Kelly distinctly saw the tractor shudder convulsively. There was a crawling movement of the whole frame, a slight wave of motion away from the fuel tank, approaching the front of the machine, and moving upward from the tracks. It culminated in the crown of the radiator core, just in front of the radiator cap; and suddenly an area of six or seven square inches literally *blurred* around the edges. For a second, then, it was normal, and finally it slumped molten, and liquid metal ran down the sides, throwing out little sparks as it encountered what was left of the charred paint. And only then was Kelly conscious of agony in his left hand. He looked down. The welding machine's generator had stopped, though the motor was still turning, having smashed the friable coupling on its drive shaft. Smoke poured from the generator, which had become little more than a heap of slag. Kelly did not scream, though, until he looked and saw what had happened to his hand—

When he could see straight again, he called for Tom, and there was no answer. At last he saw something out in the water, and plunged in after it. The splash of cold salt water on his left hand he hardly felt, for the numbness of shock had set in. He grabbed at Tom's shirt with his good hand, and then the ground seemed to pull itself out from under his feet. That was it, then—a deep hole right off the beach. The Seven had run right to the edge of it, had kept Tom there out of his depth and—

He flailed wildly, struck out for the beach, so near and so hard to get to. He gulped a stinging lungful of brine, and only the lovely shock of his knee striking solid beach kept him from giving up to the luxury of choking to death. Sobbing with effort, he dragged Tom's dead weight inshore and clear of the surf. It was then that he became conscious of a child's shrill weeping; for a mad moment he thought it was he himself, and then he looked and saw that it was Al Knowles. He left Tom and went over to the broken creature.

"Get up, you," he snarled. The weeping only got louder. Kelly rolled him over on his back—he was quite unresisting—and belted him back and forth across the mouth until Al began to choke. Then he hauled him to his feet and led him over to Tom.

"Kneel down, scum. Put one of your knees between his knees." Al stood still. Kelly hit him again and he did as he was told.

"Put your hands on his lower ribs. There. O.K. Lean, you rat. Now sit back." He sat down, holding his left wrist in his right hand, letting the blood drop from the ruined hand. "Lean. Hold it—sit back. Lean. Sit. Lean. Sit."

Soon Tom sighed and began to vomit weakly, and after that he was all right.

This is the story of *Daisy Etta*, the bulldozer that went mad and had a life of its own, and not the story of the flat-top *Marokuru* of the Imperial Japanese Navy, which has been told elsewhere. But there is a connection. You will remember how the *Marokuru* was cut off from its base by the concentrated attack on Truk, how it slipped far to the south and east and was sunk nearer to our shores than any other Jap warship in the whole course of the war. And you will remember how a squadron of five planes, having been separated by three vertical miles of water from their flight deck, turned east with their bombloads and droned away for a suicide mission. You read that they bombed a minor airfield in the outside of Panama's far-flung defenses, and all hands crashed in the best sacrificial fashion.

Well, that was no airfield, no matter what it might have looked like from the air. It was simply a roughly graded runway, white marl against brown scrub-grass.

The planes came two days after the death of *Daisy Etta*, as Tom and Kelly sat in the shadow of the pile of fuel drums, down in the coolth of the swag that *Daisy* had dug there to fuel herself. They were poring over paper and pencil, trying to complete the impossible task of making a written statement of what had happened on the island, and why they and their company had failed to complete their contract. They had found Chub and Harris, and had buried them next to the other three. Al Knowles was tied up in the camp, because they had heard him raving in his sleep, and it seemed he could not believe that *Daisy* was dead and he still wanted to go around killing operators for her. They knew that there must be an investigation, and they knew just how far their story would go; and having escaped a monster like *Daisy Etta*, life was far too sweet for them to want to be shot for sabotage. And murder.

The first stick of bombs struck three hundred yards behind them at the edge of the camp, and at the same instant a plane whistled low over their heads, and that was the first they knew about it. They ran to Al Knowles and untied his feet and the three of them headed for the bush. They found refuge, strangely enough, inside the mound where *Daisy Etta* had first met her possessor.

"Bless their black little hearts," said Kelly as he and Tom stood on the bluff and looked at the flaming wreckage of a camp and five medium bombers below them. And he took the statement they had been sweating out and tore it across.

"But what about him?" said Tom, pointing at Al Knowles, who was sitting on the ground, playing with his fingers. "He'll still spill the whole thing, no matter if we do try to blame it all on the bombing."

"What's the matter with that?" said Kelly.

Tom thought a minute, then grinned. "Why, nothing! That's just the sort of thing they'll expect from him!"

RAYMOND Z. GALLUN

DAVY JONES'
AMBASSADOR

IT DIDN'T look like a jet of water at all. It seemed too rigid, like a rod of glass; and it spattered over the instruments with a brittle, jingling sound, for such was the effect of the pressure behind it: more than four thousand pounds per square inch—the weight of nearly two and a half miles of black ocean.

Cliff Rodney, hunched in the pilot seat, stared at the widening stream. It made him see how good a thing life was, and how empty and drab the alternative was going to be. Cliff Rodney was young; he did not wish to die.

A few seconds ago all had been normal aboard the bathyspheric submarine. The velvet darkness of the depths, visible beyond the massive ports of the craft, had inspired awe in him, as it always would in human hearts; but to Cliff it had become familiar. The same was true of the schools of phosphorescent fish shining foggily through the gloom, and of the swarms of nether-world horrors that had darted in the bright golden path of the search beam.

Clifford Rodney, during his explorations, had grown accustomed to these elements of the deep-sea environment, until they had assumed an aspect that was almost friendly.

But the illusion that it was safe here had been abruptly broken. Sinuous, rusty shadows, which bore a suggestion of menace that was new to him, had surged toward the submarine from out of the surrounding murk and ooze.

Attenuated, spidery crustaceans with long feelers had burrowed into the shelter of the mud beneath them. Little fish, some of them equipped with lamplike organs, some blind and lightless, all of them at once dreadful and comic with their needle-fanged jaws and grotesque heads, had scattered in terror.

Bulbous medusæ, contracting and expanding their umbrella-shaped bodies, had swum hurriedly away. Even the pallid anemones had displayed defensive attitudes in the guarded contraction of their flowerlike crowns.

With canny craft the unknowns had avoided the search beam. Cliff had glimpsed only the swift motion of monstrous, armored limbs, and the baneful glitter of great eyes. Then the blow had fallen, like that of a battering ram. It had struck the forward observation port with a grinding concussion.

A crack, looking like a twisted ribbon of silver, had appeared in the thick, vitreous substance of the pane. From it, water had begun to spurt in a slender, unstanchable shaft that grew ominously as the sea spread the edges of the crevice wider and wider apart.

Automatically Cliff had done what he could. He had set the vertical screws of his craft churning at top speed to raise it toward the surface. But, in a moment, the blades had met with fierce resistance, as though clutched and held. The motors had refused to turn. The submarine had sunk back into the muck of the Atlantic's bed. An S O S was the last resort.

Cliff had sent it out quickly, knowing that though it would be picked up by the *Etruria*, the surface ship that served as his base of operations, nothing could be done to help him. He had reached the end of his resources.

Now, there was a breathless pause. The blackness without was inky. Cliff continued to gaze impotently at that slim cylinder of water. Ricocheting bits of it struck him, stinging fiercely, but he did not heed. It fascinated him, making him forget, almost, how it had all happened. His mind was blurred so that it conceived odd notions.

Pretty, the way that jet of water broke apart when it hit the bright metal of the instruments. You wouldn't think that it was dangerous. Flying droplets scattered here and there like jewels, each of them glinting in the shaded glow of the light bulbs. And the sounds they made resembled the chucklings of elves and fairies.

A small creature of the depths, sucked through the breach, burst with a dull plop as the pressure of its normal habitat was removed.

He and that creature had much in common, Rodney thought. Both were pawns which chance had elected to annihilate. Only he was a man; men boasted of their control over natural forces. And he himself was a blatant and ironic symbol of that boast: They had sent him here in the belief that even the bed of the Atlantic might soon yield to human dominance!

The submarine gave a gentle lurch. The youth's eyes sharpened to a keener focus. A yard beyond the fractured port a pair of orbs hung suspended. Beneath them was a fleshy beak that opened and closed as the creature sucked water through its gills. Black, whiplike tentacles swarmed around it like the hairs of a Gorgon beard. And the flesh of the monster was transparent. Cliff could see the throbbing outlines of its vital organs.

Nothing unusual here—just another devil of the depths. So Cliff Rodney would have thought had it not been for certain suggestive impressions that touched lightly on his blurred faculties. That beaked mouth was vacuously empty of expression, but the great limpid orbs were keen. The tentacles clutched a little rod, pointed at one end as a goad would be. The impression was fleeting. With a ripple of finny members the horror disappeared from view.

"That rod," Cliff muttered aloud, "I wonder if that thing made it!"

He felt a cold twinge, that was an expression of many emotions, ripple over his flesh. He moved quickly, his booted feet sloshing in the water that was now six inches deep within the stout hull of the submarine. He turned a switch; the lights winked out. It was best to be concealed in darkness.

Once more the bathyspheric submarine rocked. Then it was whirled completely over. Cliff Rodney tumbled from the pilot chair. Icy fluid cascaded around him as his body struck the hard steel of the craft's interior.

He managed to protect his head with his arms, but contact with the metal sent a numbing, aching shock through his flesh. Electricity; it could not have been anything else. He tried to curse, but the result was only a ragged gasp. Clinging desperately to the sunset edge of oblivion, he fell back among his instruments.

Impressions were very dim after that. The submarine was being towed somewhere by something. Water continued to pour into the hull, making a confused babble of sound. Rodney lay in the growing pool, the briny stuff bitter on his lips. Too near stunned to master his limbs, he rolled about the inundated floor.

With each eccentric motion of the craft, churning water slapped viciously against his face. He choked and coughed. If only he could keep his nose above the flood and breathe!

In some foggy recess of his mind he wondered why he was fighting for life, when the broken port alone was enough to doom him. Was instinct, or some deeper, more reasoned urge responsible? Cliff did not know, but for a fleeting instant the blank look of pain on his face was punctuated by a grim smile.

He was not the mythical iron man; he was a median of strengths and weaknesses as are most humans. And, among humans, courage is almost as cheap as it is glorious.

Cliff could still hear the swish of great flippers shearing the sea beyond the eighteen-inch shell of the submarine. Harsh to his submerged ears, it was the last impression he received when consciousness faded out.

II

Reawakening was slow agony. He had been half-drowned. When his brain was clear enough for him to take stock of his surroundings he did not immediately note any remarkable change.

He was still within the stout little undersea boat that had brought him to the depths. The vessel was nearly two thirds full of brine, but by luck his body had been thrown over a metal brace, and for part of the time his head had been supported above the flood.

No more water was entering the hull through the eroded crevice in the window. In fact there was no motion at all, and except for a distant, pulsating hiss, the stillness was tomblike.

The air was heavy and oppressive. It reeked with a fetid stench that was almost unbearable. Mingled with the odor was a faint pungence of chlorine, doubtless brought about by the electrolysis of sea water where it had penetrated some minor fault in the insulation of the submarine's electrical equipment. A gray luminescence seeped through the ports, lighting up the interior of the vessel dimly.

Soaked, dazed, battered, and chilled to the bone, Cliff struggled to the fractured window. There was air beyond it, not water. He had not extinguished the searchlight, and it still burned, for the storage cells that supplied current had been well protected against mishap.

There was no need to waste power to produce light here. A faint but adequate radiance seemed to come from the curving walls of the chamber in which the submarine had been docked. Cliff switched off the beam.

Groping down under the water, he found a lever and tugged at it. A valve opened, and the brine began to drain out of the submarine. The gurgling sound it made was harsh to his ears. Evidently the atmospheric pressure here was far above normal.

Next, he unfastened the hatch above his head, and hoisted its ponderous weight. Wearily he clambered through the opening and dropped down beside his craft.

The room was elliptical, domed, and bare of any furnishings. Its largest diameter was perhaps thirty-five feet, twice the length of the submarine. Puddles dotted the floor, and the walls were beaded with moisture which showed plainly that the place had been flooded recently. At opposite points there had been circular openings in the walls, one much larger than the other. Both were blocked now by great plugs of a translucent, amorphous material.

Cliff had two immediate urges: One was to get a better idea of where he was; the other was to find, if possible, a means of allaying his discomfort.

He started his investigations with the larger of the two plugs. It was held in place by a tough, glutinous cement, still sticky to the touch. From beyond it came a distant murmur of the sea. This, then, was the way by which the submarine had entered the chamber.

After the entrance had been sealed the water had been drawn off by some means through the several drains in the floor. The stream from the valve in the side of the submarine still gurgled into them, pumped away, perhaps, by some hidden mechanism. So much was clear.

Cliff's attention wandered to the walls, in quest of some explanation of the phosphorescence that came from them. Their surface was hard and smooth like that of glass, but the substance that composed them was not glass. It had a peculiar, milky opalescent sheen, like mother-of-pearl. Squinting, he tried to peer through the cloudy, semitransparent material.

At a depth of a few inches little specks of fire flitted. They were tiny, self-luminous marine animals. Beyond the swarming myriads of them was another shell, white and opaque. He understood. The chamber was double-walled. There was water between the walls, and in it those minute light-giving organisms were imprisoned for the purpose of supplying illumination.

It was a simple bit of inventive ingenuity, but not one which men would be likely to make use of. In fact there was nothing about his new surroundings that was not at least subtly different from any similar thing that human beings would produce.

The glass of the domed chamber was not glass. It seemed to be nearer to the substance that composes the inner portion of a mollusk's shell, and yet it had apparently been made in one piece, for there was no visible evidence of joints where separate parts of the dome might have been fastened together. The blocks that sealed the openings in the walls were almost equally strange. Among men they would surely have been made of metal.

Clifford Rodney became more and more aware of the fact that he had come in contact with a civilization and science more fantastic than that of Mars or Venus could ever be. Those planets were worlds of air, as was the Earth he knew, while this was a world of water. Environment here presented handicaps and possibly offered advantages which might well have turned the sea folk's path of advancement in a direction utterly different from that followed by mankind.

Continuing his investigations, Cliff discovered that the air under the dome was admitted through four pipelike tubes which penetrated the double walls of his prison; but, of course, he could not discover where they originated. The air came through those tubes in rhythmic, hissing puffs, and escaped, he supposed, down the drains through which the water had been drawn, since there was no other outlet in evidence.

He wondered how the rancid stuff had been produced, and how his hosts had even known that he needed gaseous oxygen to breathe. He wondered whether they could have any conception of the place whence he had come. To them a land of sunshine must be as ungraspable as a region of the fourth dimension!

He remembered the electric shock that had almost stunned him at the time of his capture. Electricity was produced here then. But how? As yet he had not so much as glimpsed a scrap of metal in his new surroundings.

Cliff shuddered, nor was the dank, bitter cold alone responsible. He could realize clearer than before that beyond the barriers that protected him was a realm of pressure and darkness and water with which his own normal environment had few things in common.

Belatedly it occurred to him that he was being watched by the curious of Submarinia. Standing now in the center of the slippery floor, he scanned the dome above him for evidence that his logic was correct. It was. Spaced evenly around the arching roof, more than halfway toward its central axis, was a ring of circular areas more transparent than the surrounding texture of the double walls.

Though not easily discernible at a casual glance, they were plain enough to him now. Through each, a pair of huge, glowing eyes and a Gorgon mass of black tentacles was visible. The ovoid bodies of the creatures were silhouetted against a nebulous luminescence originating from some unknown source beyond them.

The gaze of those monsters seemed cool and interested and intense, though Clifford Rodney felt that one could never be sure of what emotions, if any, their vacuous, beaked lips and limpid eyes betrayed. It would be difficult indeed to forget that they were completely inhuman.

Cliff's reaction was a kind of terror; though the only outward evidences of it were the strained hollows that came suddenly into his cheeks; still, the realization of his position thudded with ghastly weight into his mind. To those sea beings he was doubtless like a simple amœba beneath a microscope, a specimen to be observed and studied!

Then his sense of humor rescued him. He chuckled half-heartedly through chattering teeth. At least no man had ever before been in a situation quite as novel as this. It was one which a scientist, eager to learn new things, should appreciate. Besides, perhaps now he could bring the adventure to a head.

He waved his arms toward the pairs of eyes that gazed steadily at him. "Hello!" he shouted. "What in the name of good manners are you trying to do to me? Get me out of here!"

They couldn't understand him, but anyway they could see by his gestures that he had discovered them, and that he was insisting on some sort of attention. Cliff Rodney was cold, and half-choked by the rancid air.

Things had to happen soon, or his stamina would be worn down and he would no longer be in a position to see them happen. The dank, frigid chill was the worst. The air would not have been so bad if it had not been for the retch-provoking stench that impregnated it. If he only had a dry cigarette and a match, it would help a lot.

That was a funny thought—a cigarette and a match! Had he expected these ovoid beings to supply him with such luxuries?

However, since there was no one else to whom he might appeal for help, he continued to shout epithets and pleas, and to flail his arms until he was nearly spent with the effort.

Yet, the sea people gave no evidence of special response. The vital organs throbbed within their transparent bodies, tympanic membranes beneath their beaked mouths vibrated, perhaps transmitting to the water around them signals of a kind of vocal speech, inaudible to him, of course; and their tentacles scurried over the outer surfaces of the spy windows, producing a noise such as a mouse scampering inside a box might make, but Cliff saw no promise in their evident interest.

Every few minutes, one pair of eyes would turn away from a window, and another pair would take its place. The ovoids were managing the scrutiny of him just as humans would manage a show featuring a freak. He could imagine them out there waiting in line for a chance to see him. It was funny, but it was ghastly too.

Exhausted, he gave up. Probably they couldn't help him anyway. If he only had something dry to keep the chill away from his shivering flesh!

Hopefully he scrambled up the side of the submarine and lowered himself through the hatch. There was a little electric heater there, but a brief examination of it confirmed his well-founded suspicions. Soaked with brine, its coils were shorted and it refused to work. He had no means of drying it out sufficiently, and so he turned on the search beam. If he crouched against the lamp, he might capture a little heat.

He climbed out of the dripping, disordered interior. Before dropping to the floor of the domed chamber he stood on tiptoe on the curved back of the submarine and attempted to peer through one of the spy windows in the rotunda over his head.

Even now the mystery of what lay beyond the glowing walls of the room beneath the sea could fascinate him. But his vantage point was not quite high enough, nor was there any easy means to make it higher. He saw only a flicker of soft, greenish light beyond the motionless, ovoid shape that occupied the window.

He slid weakly off the submarine and pressed his body against the lens of the searchlight. The rays warmed him a little—a very little—enough to tantalize him with the thought that such a thing as warmth really existed.

He thought of exercise as a means to start his sluggish blood circulating faster; he even made an effort to put the thought into execution by shaking his arms and stamping his feet. But he felt too far gone to keep up the exertion. His head slumped against the mounting of the searchlight.

Some minutes later, a throbbing radiance caused him to look up. At one of the spy windows was a creature different from the sea people. Its body was flat, and as pallid as a mushroom.

It was shaped curiously like an oak leaf with curled edges. Its mouth was a slit at the anterior extremity of its queer form. On either side of it were pulsing gill openings, and above were beady eyes supported on stalky members. From the thin edges of the creature's body, long, slender filaments projected, glinting like new-drawn copper wire. And the flesh of the thing glowed intermittently like a firefly.

After several seconds this phenomenon ceased, and another far more startling one took its place. The creature turned its dorsal surface toward the window.

Then it was as though some invisible hand and brush were printing a message in letters of fire on the pallid hide of the monster. They were old, familiar letters spelling out English words. One by one they appeared, traced with swift and practiced accuracy until the message was complete:

I am far away, man; but I am coming. I wish to write with you. Do not die yet. Wait until I arrive.

THE STUDENT.

If Clifford Rodney had been himself, his consternation at this odd note and the outlandish means of its transmission would have been greater, and his analysis of the phenomena involved would have been more keen. As matters were, he was still able to discern the shadows of the causes underlying the enigma.

This was the subsea version of wireless. He was too tired to construct a theory of its principle; he only glanced at the fine filaments projecting from the body of the creature that had served as an agent of the miracle, and dismissed the vague germ of an idea that had oozed unbidden into his sluggish mind.

Even though this was a science completely inhuman, still it was self-evident that there were logical explanations. At present Cliff didn't care particularly whether he ever learned them. Nor did he ponder for long the riddle of how this distant spokesman of the ovoids was able to write English. Somewhere there must be a simple answer.

However, the wording of the message, strikingly demonstrating the broad physical and psychological differences between his kind and the unknowns, won somewhat more attention from him. It was "I wish to write with you," instead of "I wish to speak with you." The ovoid tympanums, vibrating in water, could not produce or convey to him the sounds of human speech.

"Do not die yet. Wait until I arrive." Did those two simple commands express naïve brutality or— Cliff scarcely knew how to think the thought. No human being would have expressed an idea of that sort with such guileless frankness. The meaning, of course, was perfectly clear; and Cliff knew that he had been afforded a glimpse into a mind differing radically from those of men.

"The Student." That at least had a familiar aspect. Because of the way the message was signed, the anger and depression which it aroused in him subsided.

The lettering vanished from the flat back of the creature which had been the means of conveying to Cliff Rodney the first expression of subsea thought. Another fire-traced message appeared, letter by letter:

We have waited too long for the arrival of one of you, man. We must learn more about your kind before you die. All in our power has been done for you. If you require more, perhaps it is beyond the small sealed exit. Unseal it. Live until I come.

THE STUDENT.

Rodney cursed and shook his fist feebly at the messenger. Nevertheless, hope gave him fresh energy. He proceeded to obey the suggestion. Returning to the submarine he procured a heavy knife, extinguished the search beam for economy, and came forth again to attack the smaller door.

The cement here was thoroughly hard, glassy; but tough and elastic rather than brittle. Cliff worked at it fiercely, digging out the gummy stuff with the point of his knife. For a time it seemed that the stubborn block would never yield; but at length, when his expiring energies were all but burned up, and little specks of blackness flitted before his vision, success came.

The plug of amorphous material toppled from the opening and thudded resoundingly to the floor. For a minute young Rodney lay exhausted beside it, a rustle in his ears that he knew was not the distant whisper of the ocean.

Then, rested a bit, he crept through the opening. He was too dazed to be very conscious of the things around him. The character of the chamber was much the same as that of the one he had just quitted, except that it was larger, and the floor was a much more elongated oval. It had the same kind of pearly, phosphorescent dome equipped with spy windows.

Even now the windows were being occupied by the grotesque forms of the sea people, eager to observe the fresh reactions of their strange captive. The air, though, was drier, for the place had not recently been flooded, and it was musty with the odor of ancient decay, like that of a tomb.

The floor was piled high with a numerous assortment of things—every one of them of human origin. Cliff let his eyes wander over the array. There was a generator, part of a ship's turbine, several life preservers, a fire extinguisher, books, tattered and pulped by sea water and pressure, rugs, and so forth. There were even two human figures.

They were propped on a dilapidated divan, and were fully clothed. Whoever had placed them there had apparently made some attempt to arrange them naturally.

Cliff Rodney came closer to examine them. One had been a man, the other a woman. Their flesh was gone, their faces were only skeleton masks. The woman's dress had once been white and beautiful, but it was just a mottled, gray rag now. Yet, the diamond pendant at her throat still gleamed as brightly as ever. The pair clutched each other with a fierceness that was still apparent. Perhaps they had died in each other's arms like that long ago. A grim tragedy of the Atlantic—

Rodney's reactions were not quite normal. He felt sick. "Damn museum!" he grumbled in a sort of inane disgust. "Damn stinky museum of Davy Jones!" He choked and sneezed.

The haze of his numbed faculties was not so dense that it obscured the animal urge to seek comfort, however. He picked up a heavy rug which, though rotted and odorous, was fairly dry.

He stripped off his soaked garments, and wrapped himself in the rug. Tearing up a book and heaping the fragments into a pile with the intention of making a fire, was quite natural and automatic. So was locating his cigarette lighter and attempting to make it work. Here, though, he struck a snag. Sparks flew, but the wick was too wet to burn.

Out of his angry chagrin an inspiration was born. He unscrewed the cap from the fuel container, poured a few drops of benzine onto the paper, and applied the sparks direct. The tinder flared up merrily, and grotesque shadows leaped about the walls of the eerie chamber. Delighted, Cliff huddled down beside the blaze, absorbing its welcome heat.

Only once did he glance at the ovoids watching him. He could not have guessed what wonder his activities provoked in the minds of those strange people of the depths.

"Go to hell!" He called to them in dismissal.

The air didn't smell so bad with the smoke in it. As the embers began to die, Clifford Rodney drew the carpet tighter about him and sprawled on the pavement. Worn out, he was quickly asleep.

III

Through the gloom of the bottoms, seven slim shapes were speeding. They were neither crustaceans nor sharklike elasmobranchs; they bore some of the characteristics of both.

Their bodies were protected by horny armor, and were tapered in such a manner as to suggest the lines of a torpedo, a comparison that was heightened by the waspish air of concentrated power about them. Rows of flippers along their flanks churned the dark water, sending them swiftly on their way. Folded carefully against their bellies were pairs of huge claws resembling the pinchers of a crawfish, though much larger. Projecting like swollen cheeks on either side of their heads were protuberances of modified muscle—their most effective weapons.

These monstrous creations were not entirely the product of nature. The knowledge of a gifted people working on their kind for ages had achieved a miracle, making of them efficient, dependable, fighting machines.

They swam in a military formation. The largest individual of the group formed its center. Above, below, ahead, behind, and on either side—one in each position—the others swam. There was a reason. Every now and then schools of small, devil-fanged fish would glide out of the darkness to attack the cavalcade. The nearest members of the escort would leap to meet them.

For an instant, many fierce little teeth would try to penetrate the tough shells of the fighters. Then the latter would strike back, invisibly, except for a momentary flicker of lavender sparks around their snouts. The attacking fish would stiffen and go drifting limply into the darkness again, dead or stunned.

The fighters were protecting their master, he who had named himself "The Student." He rode the central individual of the formation, suckerlike cups on the ventral surface of his body, clinging to its back. He had flattened himself against his mount to minimize the surge of water that swept past him. His eyes peered ahead with an expectant glitter.

He changed position only to trace queer symbols, with a goad of glassy material, on the flesh of the fragile messenger that clung beside him, and to scan the phosphorescent replies to his queries, that came in return. But within him, dread and eagerness were mingled. He had received the call that he had both hoped for and feared. And he was responding.

Out of the murk and ooze that blanketed the sea floor ahead, an emerald glow arose like some infernal dawn. The cavalcade continued to speed on its way, and the radiance brightened.

A broad depression in the bottoms emerged from the fog of suspended mud, gray like tarnished silver. Above it swarmed myriads of minute, luminous animals, forming an immense canopy of green light, limned against the blackness of the depths. That canopy looked as though it had been placed there for a purpose.

To paint the scene beneath, would have challenged the genius of Gustave Doré. It was as abhorrent as the visions of a mad demon; still it possessed elements of majesty and beauty.

A city was there in the hollow—a city or a colony. The seven fighters were moving close above it now. The valley was pitted by countless small openings, arranged edge to edge after the fashion of the cells of a honeycomb. Into them and from them, ovoids swam, going about whatever business was theirs. Here and there, queer structures of a pearly, translucent material, reared twisted spires that seemed to wriggle with the motion of the water.

Monsters were everywhere, vague in the shifting shadows. Scores of types were represented, each type seemingly stranger than its associates. All of the monsters were busy, guided in their activities by alert ovoids that hung in the water, goads poised, flippers stirring idly.

Some of the monsters wallowed in the muck, digging with broad, spatulate members. Wormlike in form, pallid and smooth, one knew that their purpose in life was to dig, and nothing else.

Others kneaded their bloated, shapeless bodies, forming elfin creations around them, seemingly from their own substance. Some fanned the water with long, flattened limbs, perhaps performing a function akin to ventilation. Others—they were fighters like The Student's escort—guarded the colony, swimming steadily back and forth.

And so it went. Each of the horrors followed the vocation for which it was intended. Each was a robot, a machine of living flesh, capable of some special function.

A man would have been held spellbound by this teeming, alien activity; but The Student scarcely noticed it at all. Everything—the lights, the motion, the whispering, slithering sounds that found their way to his auditory organs—held the familiarity of life-long experience, of home.

His gaze, though, wandered intently across the valley to the place where the gutted hull of an ocean liner sprawled half over on its side, its form almost obscured by the dusky murk of the depths.

Slim ribbons that had the appearance of vegetation streamed up from it, waving like banners. They were not vegetation, though they were alive. There were no plants here, away from the sunshine; and the fauna of this world was dependent for its sustenance upon organic débris settling from above, where there was sunlight, where chlorophyll could act, and where both fauna and flora could exist.

Always the wrecks of upper-world ships had interested The Student, as something from another planet would interest us. He had rummaged through their slimy interiors, examining and exploring this and that.

Of all their wondrous contents, books had fascinated him the most. With a zeal and care and love that an archeologist would understand, he had made copies of those fragile, water-soaked storehouses of knowledge, tracing the still legible parts of them on a parchment that could withstand the action of the sea.

He had studied the queer symbol groups they bore; he had discovered the value of the dictionary. And as the Rosetta Stone had been the key to Egyptian hieroglyphics, so the dictionary had been his means of solving the riddle of mankind's literature.

There was another thing that won a brief glance from The Student, as he guided his mount and escort toward the concourse of ovoids that had collected around the structures which housed the reason for his coming.

On a low rise a circular vat, filled with living protoplasm, squatted. Above it two crudely hammered bars of iron converged together. Between their adjacent ends blue sparks purred. The apparatus was a recent development which would have startled the wise inventors who had contributed so much to another culture.

With a thrusting motion The Student hurled himself from the back of the fighter. The flippers along his sides took hold of the water with powerful sweeps. The crowd made a lane for him as he approached. Tympanic voices buzzed around him, questioning, demanding; yet, he paid no heed.

IV

The Student reached a spy window in the dome, looked down. The man was there, sprawled motionless amid the relics of his civilization. A piece of ragged fabric wrapped his pallid body.

Revulsion, fear, hope, and anxiety were not beyond The Student's understanding, and he felt them all now.

Was the prisoner dead? Was all that had been promised to end in disappointment? Paradoxically The Student would have been more at ease if such were the case. There is no harm in an enemy whose vital functions have stopped. Yet The Student himself did not live for peace and security alone. The boon of existence had many meanings.

He moved to a window in the smaller dome, and surveyed the bathyspheric submarine, marveling at the smooth, metal hull, and the precise perfection of each detail. No ovoid could fabricate such wonders.

Patiently he waited until the buzzing tympanic voice of the throng about him impinged on his sense organs, telling him that the time had arrived.

Coolly The Student returned to the window of the museum chamber. The man was awake. He stood unsteadily in the center of the floor, the rug still wrapped around him and his eyes turned upward.

Two peoples, two cultures, two backgrounds, two histories, and two points of view were face to face at last, ready for whatever might come of the meeting. The bizarre stood versus the bizarre from opposite angles. Between them the abyss was wide. Was there—could there be—any sympathy to bridge it?

It was up to The Student to open negotiations, and he did not hesitate, for he had planned well. From a pouch, which was a natural part of him, he removed a stylus of chalky material. Then, concentrating on what he had learned during his years of study, he printed a command on the pane of the window: "You made fire, man. Make it again."

He traced the letters in reverse, so that they would appear normally to the being inside the dome.

The prisoner seemed uncertain for a brief spell; then he obeyed. Paper, a daub of liquid from what appeared to be a tiny black box, a swift movement, sparks, and finally—flame! The man held up the blazing paper for his visitor to see.

The Student watched the phenomenon of rapid oxidation, drinking in the marvel of it until the flame was burned out. The water had washed the chalky letters from the window. He traced another message: "Fire gives you metals, machines, power—everything you have?"

If, before it had happened, Clifford Rodney had had an opportunity to construct a mental picture of what this meeting would be like, he would no doubt have expected to be amazed. But he could not have conceived beforehand an adequate idea of his own wonder. Tangible truth was so much more startling than a bare thought could be.

Here was a thing which bore many of the outward characteristics of the marine animals with which he was acquainted—pulsing gills, stirring flippers—organs used in a medium which must ever be foreign to those forms of life that live in air and sunshine.

There was even in the visage of the thing—if visage it might be called— a deceptive look of vacuity which only the cool glitter of the great eyes denied. And yet, clutched in the being's tentacles was a crayon, with which it was writing in English, words that displayed a considerable knowledge of human attainments!

Cliff almost forgot that he himself was a delver after hidden facts. Then his own calm purpose conquered. His sleep had refreshed him; and though he felt stiff, sore, and uncomfortable, he could still respond to the appeal of an enigma.

He looked about for some means to answer. His attention was drawn to a small area of unencumbered floor, on which a thin layer of sea sand had been deposited. With a finger he traced words in it: "Yes. Fire brought us out of the Stone Age, and kept us going since. You got it right, friend. How?"

And the swift-moving tentacles traced a reply: "I have translated books —men's books. I have read of fire. But we have never produced fire. We might produce fire from electric sparks—soon."

Rodney looked with a quizzical awe at the gleaming orbs of the ovoid. Behind them, he knew, was a brilliant brain, whose brilliance had perhaps been augmented by the very handicaps which it had faced and overcome. The truth concealed behind this intriguing statement was already dimly formulated in his mind. Now he might clear up the matter completely.

He smoothed out the sand and printed another message: "You have electricity, glass, and a kind of wireless—still, no fire. It is too wet here for fire; but how did you do it all? And you write like a man—how?"

The Student chose to answer the last question first. "I mimic the writing of men," he printed. "I must—so men understand. Glass, electricity, wireless, and other things, come from animals. Nearly everything comes from animals. We have made the animals so. We have developed the useful characteristics of the animals—great care, selection, breeding, crossbreeding —a long time—ages."

It was a confirmation of the vague theory that Cliff had formulated. Handicapped by the impossibility of fire in their normal environment, the sea folk's advancement had followed another path. Controlled evolution was what it amounted to.

Cliff remembered what miracles men such as Luther Burbank had achieved with plants—changing them, improving them. And to a lesser extent, similar marvels had been achieved with animals. Here in the depths of the Atlantic the same science had been used for ages!

Without visible excitement Cliff traced another note in the sand: "Electricity from living flesh, from modified muscle as in the electric eel or the torpedo? Glass from— Tell me!"

And on the spy window the answer appeared: "Yes. Glass from animal —from mollusk—deposited and grown as a mollusk's shell is deposited and grown. And it is formed as we wish. Electricity from modified muscle, as in the electric eel or the torpedo. I have read of them. We have animals like them—but larger. The animals fight for us, kill with electricity. And we have—electric batteries—metal from the ships. Rods—protoplasm—"

The Student's black tentacles switched and hesitated uncertainly as he groped for words that would express his thoughts to this strange monstrosity of another realm.

But Clifford Rodney had captured enough of his meaning to make a guess. "You mean," he wrote, "that you have developed a way of producing a steady current of electricity from a form of living protoplasm? A sort of isolated electric organ with metal details and grids to draw off the power?"

"Yes."

Cliff thought it over, briefly but intensely. Such protoplasm would need only food to keep it active, and it could probably obtain food from the organic dust in the sea water around it.

"Splendid!" he printed. "And the wireless, the radio beast—tell me about it!"

The Student concentrated all his powers on the task of formulating an adequate response. Slowly, hesitantly, now, he began to trace it out; for he was thinking almost in an alien plane, working with words and ideas subtly different from his own. To make the man understand, he had to choose phrases and expressions from the books he had read.

"It is the same," he inscribed. "A characteristic developed to usefulness. Long ago we studied these animals. We discovered that they could—communicate—through—over great distances. We increased—improved this power by—by—"

"By choosing those individuals in which the power was strongest, for breeding purposes, and in turn selecting those of their offspring and the descendants of their offspring in which the characteristics you desired to emphasize were most prominent," Cliff prompted. "Thus the abilities of these messenger creatures were gradually improved. Right?"

"Yes. Right," The Student printed. "Now, we make marks on the flesh of a messenger creature. The irritation produces stimuli—a sequence of stimuli through nerves of skin, through brain, through—communicating organs. Other creatures, far off, pick up the impulses. Again there is a sequence of stimuli—communicating organs, nerves of skin, luminous cells of skin. The luminous cells which—which—"

Cliff had followed the strange explanation keenly, and now his own quick analytical powers grasped the idea which The Student was trying to express.

"The result is that the luminous cells in the skin of the receiving animals, corresponding in position to the luminous cells in the skin of the transmitting animal, are stimulated so that they emit light. Thus the symbols are made visible on the hide of the receiving messenger, just as they were originally traced. Is that correct?"

"Correct," the ovoid printed.

"There are entomologists who have suggested that certain insects have the power to communicate over distances like that," Cliff answered, "the cockroach, for instance. Their antennæ are supposed to be miniature wireless sets, or something."

The Student did not offer to reply to this immediately, and so Rodney scratched one word in the sand. It was "Wait." For a minute or two he was busy piling odds and ends of wreckage beneath the spy window. Then, equipped with a piece of board, and a pencil taken from his discarded clothing, he scrambled to the top.

V

For the first time, he viewed the colony of the ovoids, the green canopy of luminous organisms, the hordes of sea people, the welter of infernal activity, the protoplasmic battery sparking on its isolated knoll, the moving shadows of robot beings, and the alert fighters that patrolled the outskirts of the city, where light and darkness met, like enemies holding each other in deadlock.

And the greatest of these miracles was this devil who called himself The Student, and who had now backed off in revulsion at Cliff's approach.

But there were matters still to be investigated more closely. Dimly visible against the outer walls of the dome was a great shapeless mass that expanded and contracted as if it were breathing. Above the thing, and projecting from the dome like a canopy, was a curious curved shell of pearly, vitreous material.

His deductive faculties keyed up, Cliff was almost certain that he understood the function of the arrangement. With his pencil he traced two questions on the board he held: "You know chemistry, physics, what oxygen and nitrogen are?"

"Yes. I have learned from research. I have learned from men's books," The Student replied, conquering his revulsion.

"You know that the air bladders of fish are filled with a mixture of oxygen and nitrogen?" Cliff asked. "You know that these gases are derived from the blood through the capillaries that line the air bladders, and that this oxygen and nitrogen is drawn originally from the oxygen and nitrogen dissolved in sea water, by means of the gills?"

"Yes."

"Then," Rodney went on, "the air in this place comes from animals too! That creature out there under that roof arrangement—it has gills which take the gases from the sea water and deliver them into the blood stream.

"Part of the oxygen is used to keep the creature alive, of course; but another part of it, together with the nitrogen, is discharged through the walls of capillaries as an actual, free gas, just as a portion of the oxygen and nitrogen in the blood of a fish is discharged into its hydrostatic organ or air bladder! The roof arrangement probably collects it in some way, and delivers it here to me!"

"That is correct," The Student printed. "Several animals work to give you air. Something new—ages to produce."

"Ages all right," Cliff breathed fervently. "I can well believe it!" He had spoken aloud.

But he was not finished yet. His face was flushed with eagerness, and his pulses were pounding. He had another question to print: "How is the water kept out of here? Nothing of flesh could prevent it from entering when the pressure is so great."

"There our skill failed," The Student responded. "We used the skill of men. We made pumps from parts of ships, and from materials which were our own. Air is pumped into the domes and from the domes—and water, when necessary."

The black tendrils withdrew from the window. Transparent lids flickered over the ovoid's great eyes. The transparent body swayed languorously, reminding Cliff of the first sting ray he had seen in an aquarium when he was a child.

It was clear at last, this alien science. Low down beyond the window, and against the shell of the dome, he glimpsed vague motion, where a monster toiled, swinging the lever of a rusty mechanism back and forth. The machine was a pump. Its operator was forcing to him the air which those other monsters produced. And beyond extended the murky, unbelievable reality of this submarine world.

"It is all glorious," Cliff printed in tribute, "even beautiful, almost— your achievements, your ways of doing things!"

The Student's tentacles stirred uneasily, but he made no reply.

A climax had been reached and passed. Rodney's enthusiasm began to cool a little, leaving him to become more cognizant of his own position. He thought of people and friends that he had known, and experiences he had enjoyed. The thoughts made him feel very cold and lonely.

His pencil scratched in the silence. "What are you going to do with me?" he was demanding.

"Keep you," was the response.

"Until I rot?"

"Until you rot."

It was a simple statement, devoid of either malice or compassion. Yet it was loaded with a dread significance. It meant staying here in this awful place, dying of starvation, perhaps, if the icy dankness didn't get him.

It meant death in any event; probably it meant madness. There would be ovoid eyes watching him, studying him; there would be ovoid beaks opening and closing vacuously—crazy, wonderful things everywhere, but only his submarine, and the depressing relics in the museum, familiar!

They had conversed, The Student and he. They had been almost friends. But beneath their apparently amicable attitudes toward each other had lain mistrust, broadened and deepened by the fact that they had so very little in common. Cliff saw it now.

Fury smoldered within him, but he held it in check.

He tossed aside the board, which was too covered with messages to be of any further use, and selected in its stead the pulped remnants of a book from the stack of things which supported him close to the spy window.

On one of the illegible pages he printed a note and held it up for the ovoid to see: "I know a better way for you to learn about my mind. Why not establish friendly relations with the world above? Certainly we have many things that you could use. And you have many things that we could use."

"No!" The Student's slender, boneless limbs seemed to jerk with emphasis as they traced the word and repeated it. "No!"

"It will happen anyway," Cliff promised. "Soon my people will come in machines of steel. They will make you understand what is best."

"Men coming here will not return," The Student answered.

And Clifford Rodney, remembering his own capture, and seeing now the waspish fighters patrolling the city of the ovoids, had no reason to doubt the weight of the statement. The sea people could protect themselves in their native element.

"You fear us? You mistrust us?" Cliff wanted to know.

The response was frank: "Yes."

"There is no reason."

To this The Student offered nothing.

Cliff tried a new angle, printing swiftly: "What do you know of the place we live in, really—sun, stars, planets, day, night? You have read of such things, no doubt. Wouldn't you like to see them? They are beautiful!"

"Beautiful?" The Student questioned. "Beautiful to you. To me—to us —horrible. The sun, the great dazzling light—it is horrible—and the heat, and the emptiness of air. They make me afraid. But they are wonderful— interesting, very interesting."

Some emotion seemed to stir the nameless soul of the ovoid, making him hesitant and uncertain.

Clifford Rodney thought he glimpsed a shadow of hope. He scarcely understood why he argued; whether he had some dim idea that he might save himself, or whether he was trying to advance the cause of mankind in its demand for expansion into alien realms.

Perhaps he was urging this queer intelligence of the deeps only because it is in the nature of any strong, healthy-minded youth to fight even the most adverse circumstance.

"You are interested, but you are afraid," he wrote. "Why don't you give your interest the chance it deserves? Why don't you—" He hesitated, not knowing quite what he wished to say. "Why don't you try to make contact with my people?"

For a flickering instant The Student paused, in a way that betrayed some hidden process within him. Then his decision seemed to come. "The world of men is the world of men," he printed. "The world of the sea is our world."

Further urgings on Cliff's part met only with flat refusal. He desisted at last, feeling oddly like a salesman, who, through a slip in technique, has lost a sale. But that comparison could not be true either. He felt that The Student's obstinacy was too deep-seated to be overcome by mere salesmanship.

Dejectedly he watched the chalky words of the ovoid's last rebuff being washed from the window by the ocean.

Then those black tendrils holding the crayon went to work once more. "You wish to escape," they printed, "it would be interesting, man, to watch you trying to escape."

Startled, Cliff wondered what bizarre mental process had given birth to these statements. Hope was resurrected.

"I cannot escape," he printed warily. "A glass port of my submarine needs repairing, for one thing. I have no materials."

"We will give you materials," was the astounding assertion.

"Eh?" the man said aloud, before he remembered that the ovoid could not hear his words, or understand them if he had been able to. "I could not get out of these domes anyway," he wrote. "It is useless."

Cliff Rodney was trying to make a subtle suggestion, in the hope that his unfathomable jailer would offer him a chance for freedom.

"Men have many tricks," The Student responded. "Watching you make use of tricks will be very interesting. We will learn much. Men have powerful explosives."

"I have no explosives!" Cliff insisted truthfully. A feeling of exasperation was rising within him.

"Men have many tricks," the ovoid repeated.

It was a tribute, nothing less; a tribute of mingled awe and mistrust, which the people of the depths felt for the people of the upper air. It was an example of other-world minds at work.

"You expect me to escape?" Cliff demanded.

"You will not escape," was the answer. "This is a test of your powers —a test of men's powers—an experiment. If you escape from the domes you shall be recaptured. We understand caution, man."

Thus Rodney's hopes were broken. But before this message had faded from the spy window, he wrote on a page of the tattered book an acceptance of the challenge: "Good! Get the materials you promised, and go to the devil!"

"Materials shall come," was the reply. "Go to the devil."

Breaking off the conversation thus, The Student wheeled in the water. His silvery fins flashed, and he vanished amid the throng of nightmare watchers.

Cliff wondered in a detached way what emotion, if any, had prompted the ovoid to repeat his angry epithet. Was it fury, amusement, some feeling beyond human conception, or just another bit of mimicry? Cliff didn't know; and because he didn't, the skin at the back of his neck tightened unpleasantly.

VI

The Student was out there among his fellows, giving orders in buzzing, tympanic tones, and preparing for the test. None could see the turmoil inside his brain—fear pitted against intense eagerness and interest.

He had made no decisions yet, nor would the decision he had in mind be sanctioned by his people. And it is certain, too, that he had no sympathy for the man who had fallen into his clutches, nor any desire to help him win his way to freedom.

Clifford Rodney did not immediately climb down from his position atop the wreckage he had piled up. Instead he remained by the window, looking out, for no particular reason. The only sound, the gentle, pulsing hiss of air being forced into his prison, had a monotonous effect that was more oppressive than absolute silence.

The weird colony wasn't so very different, though, from the cities at home, if you allowed your eyes to sort of blur out of focus; if you didn't see that sunken liner with the wispy ribbons trailing up from it, or the twisted architecture, or the inhabitants. The moving lights made you think of gay places and of gay music and people. One corner of his mouth drew back thoughtfully.

He could see that his chance of getting out of this mess was practically nil: In the first place, he had not the ghost of an idea how he might escape from the two domes. And if he did manage to break free from them, those armored fighters would bar his way. Their great claws would grip the submarine while they discharged their bolts of electric force. The metal hull would protect him to some extent, but not sufficiently, as he knew from experience.

More conscious than ever of the aches in his body, his loneliness and dejection, he looked down at his feet absently. Under them were books. He toed one. Its gilt title was almost obliterated, but he still could make it out—Kipling's "Barrack Room Ballads."

There was a friendliness in those dim, familiar words, and he chuckled a bit. Funny to think of an ovoid intellect trying to read and understand the poems in that volume—"Danny Deever," "Mandalay"! "If" was one of Kipling's works too: "If you can keep your head—"

Cliff smiled ruefully. Anyway he couldn't go wrong by attempting to improve matters a little.

He cast a final glance through the spy window. The ovoid crowd was growing thicker, anticipating activity. Behind them the fighters were gathering in the dusky shadows. In their claws some of them clutched massive bars of some material—rams, no doubt. Probably it had been one of those rams that had broken the port of his submarine.

Still garmented in the tattered carpet, he started in by setting his craft in order as best he could; straightening a warped propeller blade, draining water out of machines and instruments, and repairing those that were broken, whenever it was possible. At least, he had cloth and paper from the museum to help him mop up the wetness of everything.

The radio was a tangle, but he had hope of fixing it some way so that, by means of its beam, he could get a word up to the boys aboard the *Etruria,* on the surface. They couldn't help him, of course; they could only watch and wait.

Several hours must have passed without incident. While he worked,

Cliff kept a close lookout for some sign of The Student. When it came, it was not delivered by the wizard of the deeps in person, but through the proxy of a messenger beast. The oak-leaf body of the creature wavered before a window, and on its hide luminous words appeared: "Food is coming through an air tube. Eat."

Cliff waited. From one of the air passages that entered the chamber, a mass of albuminous substance was blown, and it plopped to the floor. It looked like white of egg. Cliff touched a finger to it, and tasted the adhering dab.

No doubt it was from the body of some specialized marine animal. Probably it was very nourishing, and though it hardly excited Cliff's appetite, he realized that a man might train himself to relish such fare. At present, however, he preferred the brine-soaked chocolate and other food articles that he had brought with him on his adventure.

The messenger now exhibited another message: "Cement for port of the submarine, through same tube."

Its manner of arrival was similar to that of the food. A great lump of clear, firm jelly, probably also the product of a subsea creature.

Rodney gathered it up. As he carried it, a thin film of the substance hardened to glassy consistency on his hands, as collodion would do. He applied the jelly to the submarine's fractured port, inside and out, pressing it as firmly as he could. It would take some time for the cement to set.

He returned his attention to the radio transmitter, but only for a moment. Out of some inner well of his consciousness, the faint shadow of an idea had appeared.

He clambered from the submarine, and with a knife proceeded to dig the cement from around the huge, glassy plug that kept out the sea, just as he had done before with the smaller plug that had sealed the entrance dome from the museum.

He worked entirely around the circular mass, loosening the adhesive substance as deeply as he could probe with his blade. No seepage of sea water appeared. The great block was intended to open outwardly. It was very thick, and beyond it, holding it shut, was the weight of the Atlantic.

But Clifford Rodney's plan was maturing. His efforts were not entirely useless. Undoubtedly that external door was not as firmly placed as it had previously been.

Cliff felt that he might yet demonstrate his ability to get out of the domes, though once beyond them, he could find no glimmer of reason to expect that he could elude the circle of horror that awaited him, even for a few seconds. He could only try to do his best, not so much in the expectation of escape, but to keep his energies busy.

Conscious that his every move was watched with absorbing interest by the ovoid audience at the spy windows, he rummaged in the museum, finding there some wire and strips of metal. These he brought back beside the submarine.

The drinking-water container of his craft was glass-lined. He unfastened it from its mounting, bashed in the top, and added to its contents a small amount of acid from his batteries. Then he carried it up through the hatch and set it on the floor of the chamber.

Into the water, at opposite sides of the container, he placed upright strips of metal to act as electrodes. To each of these he fastened wires, and attached their opposite ends to the powerful storage batteries of the submarine.

Next, with paper and other refuse, he plugged the air tubes and drains of the two domes. Then he closed the switch, sending current through the apparatus he had just constructed.

There was a hiss as of a caldron boiling as the electricity went through the water in the container, splitting it up into the elemental gases that composed it. Free oxygen and hydrogen bubbled away from the electrodes, mixing with the air of the domes.

This crude process of electrolysis was only the beginning. From the museum Cliff collected all the combustible materials he could find, and carried them into the chamber of the submarine—books, wood, a few scraps of celluloid, hard rubber, and so forth. Then, with a little of the glassy cement that remained, he sealed the block that had separated the two domes, back into place.

There was another matter. For a few seconds it puzzled him, but finally a solution came. With wrenches he unbolted the heavy glass lens of the submarine's searchlight. Carefully he tapped the incandescent bulb beneath, breaking it, but leaving the delicate tungsten filaments undamaged. Against them he placed a wad of paper, daubed with the remaining benzine of his cigarette lighter.

So far, so good. He investigated the electrolysis apparatus again, shutting off the current for a moment while he scraped away the interfering bubbles that had collected on the crude electrodes.

Satisfied that his preparations were as complete as they could be made for the present, he shut himself inside the submarine and continued to work on the radio. After perhaps an hour of fussing and tampering, he believed that he might get a code message up to the *Etruria*.

He was almost ready, but there was one thing more. Aboard the craft there were ten flasks of compressed oxygen. Opening the valves of nine of these, he tossed them through the hatch, retaining only one for breathing purposes.

While their contents soughed away he disconnected the electrolysis wires and closed the heavy steel door over his head. Working the key of the radio, he flashed out his appeal:

Rodney calling S. S. *Etruria*. . . . Rodney calling S. S. *Etruria*. . . . Captured by deep-sea creatures. . . . Trying to escape. . . . Get position and stand by to help. . . .

He repeated the communication several times. If it were received, it would be simple for his confreres to calculate his position from the direction the waves came in. They'd be waiting to pick him up. He even chuckled ruefully at the thought.

Through the ports he could see that the ovoids had moved back from the spy windows of the dome, anticipating danger; but their forms, and the forms of their fighters still hovered tensely in the luminescent haze of the ocean bed. He could not see many from his unfavorable position, but doubtless they were above and all around the dome, waiting for him to make a move!

VII

Cliff forced himself to forget these unnerving thoughts. His hand touched the searchlight switch. His face was grim as he directed his gaze through another port toward the great, circular block that kept out the sea.

"Any one of three things can happen," he muttered: "The force can be insufficient, in which case what I have done won't accomplish anything at all—I'll still be locked in this dome. Or it can be too great, forcing out that plug all at once and letting the water in here all at once, to smash this steel coffin—all at once. Or it can be just right, admitting the ocean gradually enough so that this old tub can stand the strain."

Even the stout steel hull couldn't withstand the sudden thrust of the pressure of the deeps, he knew. Its position would be something like that of a nut under the blow of a hammer.

Cliff didn't want to give himself time to think. He closed the switch. Almost immediately there was a flash of red, as the hot filaments of the searchlight ignited the benzine-soaked paper that was in contact with them.

The flame spread through the dome in a wave of orange, as the hydrogen in the air burned. The sound which penetrated the thick shell of the craft was not the concussion of an explosion. Rather, it was a whispering, soughing roar; for the weight of the sea without was too vast for this feeble beginning of chemical forces to combat.

However, the reserves now came into action. Immersed in a highly oxygenated atmosphere under pressure, the paraphernalia from the museum took fire, and, though damp, rapidly became an inferno of incandescence that threw off enormous volumes of gas, expanding irresistibly with heat.

His heart thumping, Rodney kept his eyes glued to the great block which he hoped to dislodge. Stubbornly it continued to stand its ground, unmoved. He gritted his teeth as if, by sheer force of will, he sought to move the insensate thing that barred his way.

Moments passed. There was a snap like a muffled rifle shot. The block jerked, shuddered. Around its rim a curtain of glass appeared—no—not glass—water, screaming like a concourse of mad devils. The flood rolled over the floor, found the fire, and burst into steam, the pressure of which added to the titanic forces combating the titanic weight of the deeps.

More moments—the chamber was half full of water. Then, with a sort of majestic resignation, the plug yielded, folding outward like a dying colossus. The ocean was in then, swiftly—so swiftly that a living eye could not capture its movements. The thud of it was heavier than a clap of thunder.

The submarine bobbed in the maelstrom like a bit of flotsam. But its hull held, even though it was flung repeatedly against the walls of the dome.

A minute went by before Clifford Rodney was able to do anything. He picked himself up from the place where he had been hurled, and scrambled to the controls. He could see the opening which led from his prison. The motors throbbed and the submarine turned, heading through the still surging water.

It did get clear of the dome. Cliff almost thought he had a chance. Maybe the confusion produced in the vicinity by the suction when the sea had entered the dome, had unnerved the ovoids momentarily.

He set the vertical screws spinning. Their lift wasn't very good. They had been damaged again. It was hardly remarkable after the way the little ship had been bounced around.

Cliff looked up through a ceiling port. Six fighters were pouncing down upon him, their hinged claws spread wide, their long, armored forms ghostly in the shadows. Others were approaching from all directions, accompanied by a horde of ovoids.

A seventh had joined the six now. Rodney had not seen it dart up from the deep muck of the bottoms, where it had lain, hidden even to the people of the depths. It bore a strange, glassy object of considerable size. Without much attention the man wondered what it might be.

"All right," he muttered, "you win! I hope you enjoyed the show!"

The fighters were upon him. He could hear the scrape of their claws against metal. Clouds of black stuff, like the ink of a squid, surrounded the submarine, hiding everything from view. He was still rising though—rather rapidly, he thought. In a moment the electric bolts would stun him.

Upward and upward he went. Cliff began to be puzzled. He detected scraping noises that he could not interpret. He must have advanced half a mile toward the surface since the start. It was all very odd.

There was a jolt. The climb became halting and erratic. The motors labored doggedly.

The water cleared. Cliff could make out schools of phosphorescent fish, hanging in the darkness like scattered galaxies. He was alone, far above the bottoms. There were no fighters around him, though he thought he glimpsed dim shapes vanishing beneath. They could not endure the reduced pressure that existed here.

Matters were better, far better, than he had dared to expect—mysteriously so. Now if the vertical screws continued to function at all— The submarine appeared to be badly damaged. It seemed clumsy, heavy.

Cliff came into a region of deep bluish light, beautiful as some fairy-peopled realm of infinity. Not long thereafter the bathyspheric craft broke through the sunlighted surface of the Atlantic. Cliff opened the valves of a pressure tank, inflating the bellows like water wings which supported the heavy submarine when it was on the surface.

How had this all happened? There was still the mystery. He almost forgot that he must gradually reduce the pressure around him, to avoid the "bends."

At length he opened the hatch and crawled out onto the rounded top of the undersea boat. An egg-shaped object was fastened to the metal shell just behind the hatch. Rodney approached it, unable yet to fathom its nature. Glassy cement, like that with which he had recently become acquainted, held the thing in place.

It was a massive object, six feet through at its greatest diameter. It was made of the same material as the domes, except that this substance was darker, perhaps to shield what it covered from the fierce sun.

Rodney peered into the semitransparent depths of the object, discerning there a huddled form enveloped in a milky, semiliquid film. The form was delicate; vital organs pulsed visibly beneath its skin. It had flippers, and masses of black tendrils. Its beaked mouth opened and closed, giving it an air of vacuous solemnity, but its eyes were keen. Its tentacles clutched a white crayon. It was The Student!

Clifford Rodney's mind was a whirl as he sought to solve the riddle. Then, since no other means of printing a message was available, he traced words with a finger on the wet surface of the oval object:

"You helped me—how?"

The Student's tendrils trembled as he printed the answer on the inside of his protecting shell: "I helped you. The six fighters, and the seventh, were mine. They did not attack you. Concealed by the liquid that darkens the sea, they raised your submarine upward.

"They attached me to the submarine. They raised it as far as they could climb. It was a trick to outwit my people. They forbid traffic with the upper world. They are afraid. I was afraid, but at last I chose. While you prepared for the test an idea came. I used it, outwitting my people. I am afraid. But I am glad."

Rodney was lost in the fantastic wonder of it all. "Thank you, my friend!" he printed.

The Student plied his crayon again: "Friend? No. I am not your friend. What I did, I did for myself."

"Then why in reason's name are you here?" Cliff printed. "Men will put you in an aquarium, and stare at and study you!"

"Good," was the response, "I am glad. Men study me. I study them. Good. That is why I came: to see the accomplishments of men, to see the stars, to see the planets. Now I see the sun and sky—dreadful but interesting—very interesting. Good."

"Good if you don't smother before you can be transferred to a suitable aquarium," Rodney traced.

"I am safe here," the ovoid answered with a nervous flurry of tendrils. "The pressure is normal. There is much oxygen in the fluid which surrounds me. But do what you must, man. I am waiting."

Cliff was accustomed enough to the situation by now to grin down at the great dark egg. Mixed with his awe there was a curious inner warmth. Man and ovoid were different in form and mind; perhaps real sympathy between them was impossible. But Cliff had found a tangible similarity.

In this sullen devil of the depths eagerness to know the unknown had battled fear, and had won. The Student had placed himself, without defense, in the power of the unknown. It took guts to do that, courage—

Young Rodney thought of many things as he looked out over the water in search of signs of rescue. A ship was approaching. It was near enough so that he could recognize it as the *Etruria*.

"The boys'll probably call you Davy Jones' ambassador or something," he said banteringly, addressing the ovoid. "I hope you're sport enough to take it, old socks!"

But The Student wouldn't have listened even if he were able. His eyes were drinking in the miracle of the approaching ship.

MORRISON COLLADAY

GIANT IN
THE EARTH

THE reporters gave Gary and me credit for discovering the cause of the mysterious epidemic which was devastating the thinly settled mountain region of North Carolina. Probably it made a good newspaper story to have two medical students succeed where the leading physicians and scientists of the nation had failed.

As a matter of fact, I had nothing to do with it. It merely happened that I was with Gary on the Sunday afternoon tramp when the sight of the destroyed vegetation in the mountain valleys suggested to him the idea which put the United States Public Health authorities on the track of the cause of the epidemic.

The epidemic seems comparatively unimportant now, but that is only because it was less spectacular than what happened later. If the authorities had known at the beginning what it indicated, the outbreak of the disease would have been a signal for the immediate evacuation of that part of the country and the consequent avoidance of a terrific loss of life.

Nobody remembers when the first cases of the mysterious disease were noticed. A few patients were brought to the Asheville hospitals from the surrounding mountain valleys with a peculiar skin eruption over their entire bodies, almost like severe sunburn. Within a few days all had died and as more and more cases came to Asheville, the local health authorities became alarmed. There was no question that the city was faced with the possibility of a serious epidemic.

The North Carolina health department immediately established a quarantine of the affected regions, and several of the great summer hotels in the mountains were converted into hospitals. Soon the local physicians were overwhelmed with the extra work and called for help from other parts of the country. Gary and I were seniors in Medical school and jumped at the chance to get practical experience in fighting an epidemic, especially as announcement was made at this time that the United States Department of Public Health was about to take over the job from the State and city health authorities.

When we reached Asheville we were sent on to Black Mountain, where a resort hotel was being converted into a hospital to care for the constantly increasing number of victims of the disease. It was a sufficiently unpleasant experience, even for medical students who are fairly hardened young men. Men, women and children were brought in in droves, looking as if they had been severely burned by the sun and running a temperature. The fever increased, they became delirious, their flesh began to slough away and in seventy-two hours they were dead.

This was the invariable course of the disease and nothing the physicians did had any effect. The extemporized graveyard in the soft earth at the foot of the mountain grew by leaps and bounds, but still the number of our patients increased; it looked as if the surrounding territory would be entirely depopulated.

One of the curious things about the disease that puzzled everyone investigating it was that not a single physician or attendant in the hospitals had been attacked. This fact, the explanation of which was so simple when the truth was known, was regarded as incredible then. Each day we were examined with the expectation that traces of the disease would be found in some of us.

When we were all found well, it was taken to mean that the period of incubation was longer than expected. Naturally the doctors, attendants and nurses were careful, but we all felt sure that some of us would become victims and we went about our work a good deal like soldiers in a battle.

The story of that Sunday afternoon walk when Gary and I found the valleys with the blasted vegetation was good newspaper stuff and the reporters gave their imaginations full sway. As a matter of fact, nothing sensational occurred, in spite of the newspaper accounts, and I doubt that we were ever in serious danger. The walk derives its only importance from what it led to.

For Gary and me it started off like any other climb, through the mountains. We not only had no idea of hunting for the cause of the epidemic, but we were trying for a few hours to forget that it existed. We had tramped for several hours before the blighted vegetation of the valleys attracted the attention of either of us. Most of the time we kept to the ridges of the mountains, but the blackened lowlands were always plainly visible.

Finally as we were crossing a narrow valley to reach the next ridge, Gary stopped to examine a thicket of shrivelled underbrush.

"What's happened to all the green things?" he asked. "Looks as if there'd been a heavy frost."

I laughed. "Frost in July? It's funny, though," I added, looking around. "There isn't a green leaf until you get a thousand feet up in the mountains. See that line up there?"

Gary gave one look and then he seized my arm. "Come on. We're getting out of here."

"What's the hurry?" I protested.

"Don't waste time talking," he answered, and I noticed his face was white. He plunged up the side of the mountain and I followed. When we reached the limit of the killed vegetation we saw there was a space of a few feet where the plants were yellow and dying. Above was the flourishing luxuriant green of a midsummer Carolina mountainside.

We had not wasted any time climbing the mountain, and I threw myself on a patch of grass to get my breath. Gary was staring down into the valley which looked as if fire had swept through it.

"Pretty near all our patients come from valleys like this, don't they?" he asked finally.

"I guess so," I answered. "They can't live on the mountains very well. Not much water and they'd freeze to death in the winter. Besides, they've got to live where they can grow things."

He nodded. "That's about what I figured, though I don't know the country as well as you do. I notice all the hospitals are pretty well up in the mountains."

"That's because the government is using resort hotels for hospitals. Tourists always want a view when they come to the mountains." A sudden thought struck me. "You mean the same thing that blighted the vegetation might have caused the epidemic?" I asked. "That's the reason we hurried up here?"

"Suppose it isn't an epidemic at all," he said slowly. "Something killed everything in the valley down there. The cases come from places like that. Although the disease is virulent, not a single doctor or nurse has contracted it. They're all living up in the mountains. It looks to me as if it might be a poison of some kind that's killing off the natives."

"Where could it come from?" I asked. "Besides, I don't believe there is any poison that would kill people just that way. If they didn't all die immediately, some of them would get better. None of these cases do."

"What about radon?" asked Gary.

"Radium gas? I suppose it might, if it was concentrated enough. Old Ames in chemistry lab used to say a cubic centimeter collected in a test tube would melt the tube. Yes, it's a beautiful theory," I went on. "There are only two objections to it. There isn't enough radium in the world to kill off the vegetation in this one valley. The other difficulty is there isn't any radium in this part of the country."

Gary nodded. "I know. Nothing east of Colorado. But suppose that's all wrong. Suppose there's radium under these valleys now, even if there wasn't any before."

"It doesn't sound sensible to me," I said.

"Maybe. But it won't do any harm to be sure. Some of these public health men are sure to have electroscopes. I'm going to see Grant tonight."

The local and state health departments had broken down so badly under the strain of fighting the mysterious epidemic that the United States Department of Health had assumed practically full control of the affected regions some time before. Assistant Surgeon-General Grant, a thoroughly trained epidemologist who had had a wide experience both as a research worker and executive, was in charge. He reached Asheville with a full staff of medical men, sanitary chemists, sanitary biologists and sanitary engineers. He made his headquarters at Grove Park Inn, which the government had commandeered and was using as an isolation hospital.

Here late that night Gary and I found him. He had just gone to bed but we sent word that our business was too important to wait until morning.

I let Gary do the talking. When he finished, Dr. Grant gazed at us in frowning thought. Then he offered the same objections I had.

"I don't say it's radium," insisted Gary. "All I'm suggesting is that if these patients had been exposed to enough radium, it would account for what's happening to them. It might be some other radioactive gas that has been released in these valleys."

"You boys wait for me in my office downstairs," said Dr. Grant. "I'll be dressed in ten minutes."

A good deal of the newspaper publicity Gary and I got was propaganda frankly put out by Dr. Grant to justify his orders for the complete evacuation of the city of Asheville and a large part of western North Carolina. There is no limit within reason to the power of the public health authorities in an epidemic. They can take any measure they think best to prevent its spread.

When the public health department engineers found radon in fairly high concentration in the low-lying valleys, Dr. Grant acted with military promptness, in spite of the protests of the Asheville authorities, backed by the local physicians. The average physician is a conservative person, to characterize him mildly. The history of medicine shows that every new idea has been fought bitterly. The theory that our patients were dying as the result of exposure to radon was no exception.

I remember what occurred at a conference of doctors called by Dr. Grant the evening following our visit to him. During the day he had satisfied himself that Gary had accidentally stumbled upon the cause of the disease that the scientists of the department had been desperately seeking.

The physicians were assembled in one of the parlors of Grove Park Inn. Dr. Grant presented the evidence he had gathered and announced that the evacuation of Asheville would be ordered the following day as a protective measure. There were immediate protests from a number of men present.

One of the leading doctors of Asheville was particularly indignant. I have no desire to hold him up to ridicule, so I shall call him Dr. Brown, though that is not his name.

When Dr. Grant had finished talking, Dr. Brown got pompously to his feet. "I think I can speak for the Medical Society of Buncombe County when I say that they will oppose any effort to evacuate the city of Asheville. We are practical men and we don't take much stock in half-baked theories. Even if what you say these young men discovered is true, it has no practical interest, so far as I can see.

"If there's radon or whatever-you-call-it coming from these mountains, I guess we'll have to let it keep on coming. If people can't live in these valleys, there's a lot more of North Carolina where they can live. There is certainly no reason for doing such a foolish and unheard-of thing as driving all the people in a city of sixty thousand from their homes."

"Ah, but that's just it, Dr. Brown," replied Dr. Grant. "How do we know that the rest of this section won't be affected as these isolated valleys have been? Whatever is causing the epidemic, it is certainly spreading. This week we have received cases from the outskirts of Asheville. Remember we have a mortality of one hundred percent. Think what it means if the disease actually attacks Asheville!"

Dr. Brown reddened angrily. "You government men are always inclined to exaggerate things. I have a communication here from the Chamber of Commerce, protesting about the interviews you have given out. You have practically killed our tourist traffic and caused our merchants and hotel keepers great loss. After all, things aren't as serious as you make out. Before we get through, we'll doubtless find the so-called epidemic is a deficiency disease, probably a form of pellagra."

Before relating the controversy between the United States Department of Public Health and the North Carolina authorities, it will be well to outline the conclusions of the department scientists, which were the justification for the stern and drastic control measures put into effect by Dr. Grant.

The reason scientists did not discover what was really happening in western North Carolina until Gary and I stumbled on the devastated valleys, was astonishingly simple. Radium had always been found associated with uranium in proportion of one part radium to three million parts of uranium by weight. No trace of uranium had been discovered in the eastern United States.

If the curious epidemic had started in Colorado where the carnotite ore of Paradise Valley was the chief American source of radium, physicians would probably have become suspicious as to its real cause immediately.

It was true that a man named Holzberg out in California had recently extracted radon, radium gas, from granite rock with an electrical furnace, but no one realized until after the catastrophe of July thirtieth that this work had other than scientific interest.

Until this occurrence practically settled the question, scientists were divided into two schools differing as to the amount and location of radio-active elements in the earth's mass. One school believed that they existed in comparatively limited quantity in the earth's crust. They pointed out that radium is continually emitting heat at the rate of 132 gram calories per hour per gram of radium. That is, it would heat its own weight of water through 100 degrees C. per hour. Therefore the heat of the earth would be maintained if radium existed only to four parts in one hundred million million. It followed in their opinion that the amount of radium or other radioactive matter in the earth could not be greater than 270,000,000 tons or the earth would be growing hotter.

The second school of scientists did not dispute these figures, but they believed the conclusions drawn from them were false. They maintained that radioactive substances occur in great quantities through the mass of the earth and that the heat of the earth periodically increases until something occurs which acts as a safety valve. They offered as evidence the explosion of Krakatao, the Katmai eruption in 1912 and the South American eruption of 1932. They called attention to the fact that similar catastrophes may occur in any part of the world, including the Antarctic continent. If they occur in sparsely settled parts of the earth they attract little attention, as witness the blowing up of one of the Aleutian Islands in 1930, about which ninety-nine persons out of a hundred have never heard.

The reports of the government scientists made immediate action by Dr. Grant imperative. They not only found radon in all the valleys from which the epidemic patients came, but they found that instead of diffusing, its concentration was becoming greater and was rapidly covering new territory. As the period of activity of radon is very short, this indicated the presence of radium in quantities never dreamed of and of which there had been no previous indication.

How this was possible, they made no attempt to explain. They reported conditions as they found them and Dr. Grant acted without attempting any theoretical justification.

The newspapers were ordered to publish the evacuation orders, and it became evident immediately that there was going to be trouble. One of the Asheville papers made no comment on the order, but the other published a violent attack on what it called "the illegal and arbitrary acts" of the department of public health.

It became evident within twenty-four hours that it was not going to be possible to evacuate the population of the city peaceably. The governor of North Carolina was urged to declare martial law but refused. Then the alarming situation was brought to the attention of the President of the United States by the Surgeon-General in Washington, after a long telephone conversation with Assistant Surgeon-General Grant. I imagine that the matter was put quite strongly, because results were immediate. By noon of the next day all of western North Carolina and portions of South Carolina, Georgia and Tennessee were placed under military rule, thus establishing a precedent that will doubtless be useful if similar situations should arise in the future.

There was a general reorganization of the quarantined area and most of the volunteer workers were dismissed. Gary and I were ordered to Asheville to help in the tremendous job of moving without delay sixty thousand men, women and children from their homes to other parts of the country.

I am not going to say much about this work, which was largely routine as far as we were concerned but which kept us busy fourteen hours a day for the next few weeks. The problem was complicated by the reluctance of people in other parts of the country to receive the evacuated ones, especially after a few cases of the scourge developed among the refugees. The discovery that the scourge was not a disease in the ordinary sense of the word but the effect of exposure to radium emanation made not the slightest impression on the average unscientific person. There is nothing to be gained by dwelling on this feature of the catastrophe, which resulted in great numbers of helpless women and children being isolated outside towns without food or shelter.

As the evacuation proceeded the number of new cases dropped. Antagonistic elements took advantage of this apparent improvement in the situation to make savage attacks on Dr. Grant and the public health service. If Congress had been in session, the position of the government officials would have been very unpleasant.

As it was, with the President strongly supporting the health authorities, the opposition could not do much except talk. However, the attitude of the officials of the four states involved encouraged armed rebellion by some elements of the population who had been removed and now attempted to return to their homes. A few soldiers were injured and more civilians. The situation was becoming aggravated and there would undoubtedly have been considerable bloodshed if it had not been for the events of July thirtieth.

By that time the white population of Asheville had been largely removed. A great deal of difficulty was experienced in finding localities to which it was possible to transfer the large numbers of Negro inhabitants of the city. As a result they were the greatest sufferers in the catastrophe.

Gary and I had accompanied a trainload of refugees as far as Greenville, South Carolina, on the morning of July thirtieth and were on our way back to Asheville. The train was pretty well filled with relief workers and army officers who were returning to their jobs.

We had just passed Hendersonville when the first shock occurred. Gary and I were sitting on the observation platform at the time. There has been a good deal of discussion since as to whether the volcanic eruption or the earthquake came first, and what I have to say will not throw any new light on the matter. In fact, it is a little difficult to describe exactly what happened.

The train was running as usual at a comparatively low speed through the mountains when suddenly there was a roar that seemed to drive air under great pressure into my ears. That's the only way I can describe the sensation, though I don't suppose there was any actual increase of air pressure at the distance we were from the scene of the explosion. Besides, there is no reason to suppose that any increased air pressure as the result of the explosion would travel at the identical rate of sound waves, and therefore reach an individual at a distance simultaneously with the noise of the explosion. That being the case, Gary and I decided that the effect of which we were both conscious must have been subjective.

The train seemed to strike an obstruction, though no evidence was found afterward that it had done so. The engine left the rails, carrying with it the tender and baggage car, and plunged over the embankment to the ravine below. Fortunately the coupling between the first and second cars broke loose, or this account would not have been written. The cars remaining on the track swayed sickeningly from side to side and came to a stop.

All this occurred in a fraction of time so small that Gary and I, thrown from our chairs on the platform, had hardly any consciousness of duration. One instant we were sitting there calmly smoking our pipes and the next we were picking ourselves up while the events I have described belonged to the past as a flash of lightning does.

The cars emptied themselves of their terrified passengers, who crowded to the edge of the ravine over which the engine had disappeared. Nothing was visible in the darkness below except a spot of light like a bonfire.

"Not much chance for the poor devils," said Gary.

I suppose at least fifteen seconds elapsed after the tragedy, possibly longer, before any of us became aware of the terrific phenomena of the eruption. I have no idea how to explain this. At the instant the upper half of Mount Mitchell was blown off, the entire northern sky became a mass of livid purplish flame. Nothing like it has taken place in historic times except the explosion of Krakatao.

The explosion was heard a thousand miles away and the light in the sky was visible from New York. Yet the group of men and women who tumbled out of the cars only a few miles away from Mount Mitchell, for at least fifteen seconds were aware only of the fact that their train had been wrecked and they had escaped death.

The eruption has been described so often by eye-witnesses that I do not believe I have much that is new to tell, though I think comparatively few people survived who were as near the actual scene as we were. Why we survived when many victims were farther away than we from the mountain has been a subject of much discussion and has never been satisfactorily settled. In the actual zone of destruction the victims were killed by the wave of heat which swept down on the surrounding valleys and shriveled every living thing in an instant. Many thousands at more distant points were instantly killed by a blanket of poisonous gas. Still others were apparently killed by the concussion of the explosion—at least they were dead with no trace of visible injury.

It may have been the configuration of the valley through which the railroad ran that saved us, though that theory is advanced simply because no one has thought of a more plausible one. At any rate, except for the engineer, fireman and baggage men who were carried down into the ravine, the passengers on the train were alive and uninjured. We now gazed speechless and awe-stricken and nearly blinded into the sky where flames like rushing clouds in a hurricane were roaring from a white-hot furnace which seemed to be consuming the mountains to the north.

Though the entire sky appeared to be filled with flames, we felt no sensation of heat. This was contrary to the experience of other survivors who were farther from the scene of the eruption than we were. It has been since suggested by scientists that the effect of flames overhead was caused by waves of incandescent gas which traveled great distances before the reduction of temperature caused them to lose their luminosity.

Our situation was not pleasant, marooned in the valley with no knowledge of what had happened a few miles away or what might befall us in the next few minutes. A hasty council of war was held and the ranking army officer aboard the train, who happened to be the colonel of a regiment of South Carolina militia, was given command of the group.

Colonel Gooden proved himself a good executive and within half an hour a handcar discovered by the roadbed had started back toward Spartanburg in search of an engine. There was nothing for the rest of us to do except wait and watch what was probably the most gorgeous fireworks display ever seen.

It was growing light in the east when we saw the headlight of a locomotive approaching. It proved to be a freight engine which our handcar expedition had encountered some distance down the line.

It had been drawing a heavy train and was far enough away from the explosion so it was not derailed. The engineer realized that there was something seriously wrong ahead and had stopped until he got further orders. There was a signal station half a mile away, but the telegraph operator was on duty only during the day. None of the train crew knew anything about telegraphy, so they welcomed our handcar men with open arms when they found one of them, Lieutenant Palmer, was an army signal corps man. He quickly got into communication with the railroad divisional headquarters, which had been making wild efforts to get a response to messages from the towns in the region of the catastrophe. The commercial telegraph services had gone dead at the moment of the explosion. Lieutenant Palmer told the little he knew and then asked that the engineer of the freight engine be instructed to proceed to our train.

There was no difficulty about that, but the question then arose as to whether the passengers wanted to return to Spartanburg, the nearest railroad junction outside the immediate danger zone, or whether they would want to proceed, if that were possible, to Asheville.

Lieutenant Palmer was unable to answer this question, and it was decided to send a rescue train for those who wanted to return and for the freight engine to push the cars of our train as near the danger zone as it was possible to approach.

As it happened, everyone on our train decided to go on. A hasty vote was taken on the arrival of the freight engine and I suppose the few who would have preferred to return to safety hated to announce the fact in view of the attitude of the majority.

It was broad daylight when the freight engine began to push our train forward at a speed no faster than a walk. There was every likelihood that the tracks had been spread or torn up by the force of the earthquake, and the train crew was not taking any chances. Two of them were stationed on the front platform of the forward coach, giving the track ahead the keenest scrutiny and ready at any suspicious appearance to pull the signal cord.

The rest of us had to be content with putting our heads out of the windows to watch the mountains in the north blazing like a gigantic funeral pyre for the world.

We stopped ten times in the first five miles because of twisted rails, ties torn up or rock slides. The train crew would run ahead with shovels and sledges. After fifteen minutes or half an hour they would climb back aboard and we would begin again to creep slowly forward.

Shortly after noon the train approached the Asheville station, which is a mile or a mile and a half below the town. We poured out of the cars, surprised and delighted that the city had not been destroyed. We realized at once, however, that there was something wrong. There was not a person in sight and not a sound to be heard.

It was surprising how little damage the earthquake or shock of the explosion had done to the city. The skyscrapers had suffered most, their walls having been shaken off, leaving their gaunt steel frames still intact. We had become more or less used to the wall of solid flame in the north and the incandescent clouds racing overhead. As I describe the scene I am aware that it doesn't seem the sort of thing to which anyone could become accustomed, but we had been watching it for well over sixteen hours. I think most of us had expected to find nothing but burned-over ruins of a city, but the flames had apparently not reached Asheville, even at the moment of the explosion.

Still we were prepared for tragedy long before we reached the main business section of the city. I suppose, including the relief workers and the citizens who had not been evacuated, there must have been at least ten thousand persons still in the city when the catastrophe occurred. As we tramped in a long straggling line up the hill, not a soul greeted us.

Gary and I were near the head of the procession with Colonel Gooden whose face was becoming more and more grim as we advanced.

"Looks bad, looks bad," he muttered, half to himself. He turned to us. "Take a look in some of these houses, boys, and see what you find. Break in if you have to."

Off to the left was a group of Negro shacks from which we knew the inhabitants had not been removed up to the time we had left the city the previous day.

The front door of the first one we approached was unlocked. I pushed it open. There was only one room with a lean-to in the rear used as a kitchen. Two women and a man were in the shack. They didn't look up or move when I opened the door. After a moment I went over and touched the face of one of the women. I knew before, but I wanted to make sure.

We looked in half a dozen more of the houses and found men, women and children. They had apparently died in an instant, and though the bodies were not distorted in any way, there was something horribly eerie about the rigid forms frozen into immobility at whatever they were doing.

We caught up with Colonel Gooden in the telegraph office a couple of blocks farther on. He eyed us keenly.

"Still there?" he asked.

I nodded.

"Need doctors?"

I shook my head, still not entirely trusting my voice. A good many of my friends had been in the city yesterday.

"Gas!" exclaimed Colonel Gooden. "That's what killed 'em in Martinique." He turned to Lieutenant Palmer who had been listening. "You've got to get the news out, Palmer. God, what a calamity! Hundreds of army officers and doctors wiped out in an instant, not to speak of the others."

"Maybe it won't be as bad as that, colonel," suggested Lieutenant Palmer.

"Don't fool yourself. We won't find a human being alive. You mark my words."

A minute or two later Lieutenant Palmer handed Colonel Gooden a strip of tape from the machine.

"Who are you? Where did you come from? Who is commanding officer? Emory."

"Who the devil is Emory?" snapped Colonel Gooden.

"War department," answered Lieutenant Palmer. "Don't mind him. I'll explain matters."

"All right," growled Colonel Gooden. "Tell 'em we're in a damn ticklish position here ourselves."

As Lieutenant Palmer turned back to the transmitter, Colonel Gooden, who had been glancing anxiously out of the window at a darkening sky, went to the street. Gary and I followed him.

There was a distinct change in the appearance of the sky. The great rampart of fire still blazed in the north, but the flame-like clouds racing overhead perceptibly darkened. We could get an occasional glimpse of the sun, but instead of being its natural color it was a bright blue and the light that came from it seemed to be blue. So far there had been no sign of ashes. They almost invariably accompany volcanic eruptions from the beginning, but if there had been any, they were carried in other directions.

Now the darkening of the sky made us think there was to be a new development, particularly as violent electrical discharges began about the time we reached the street. A moment later a light-gray dust as fine as flour began to sift down from the air. At first there wasn't much of it, but soon it began to fall faster.

Even the buildings across the street we now saw through a heavy gray fog. The glare of the flaming mountains in the north became a dull purplish red and instead of extending across the horizon, was concentrated in four columns of fire from which rolled unbelievable clouds of black smoke. Something in the volcanic dust strained out enough light rays so that what was just a flare of flame at which it was impossible to look steadily resolved itself into a picture which doubtless represented reality.

Colonel Gooden rushed back into the telegraph office.

"Tell Washington it's getting worse here," he instructed Lieutenant Palmer. "Dust is beginning to fall. Four volcanoes in violent eruption in the north. Useless to try to get nearer. Probably dangerous to stay in Asheville. . . . Get that off," he ordered. He turned to Gary and me. "Know where the rest of our party is?"

"Part of them at the General Hospital," I answered, "and the rest of them at Army Headquarters across the square."

"Tie handkerchiefs over your noses and go after 'em. Keep together, you two, don't get separated. Bring 'em here right away, all of 'em."

The dust was falling so fast that we could barely see across the street. Already it was several inches deep underfoot. Even with handkerchiefs tied around our heads it was hard to breathe. Nothing was visible overhead now, and the eruption in the north had become just a faint red glare.

The dust was so fine and soft that it was impossible to walk rapidly without slipping. Gary spied some messengers' bicycles in a rack and suggested using them. The dust didn't affect the bicycles and we could have made good time if we had been able to see where we were going. As it was, we had to follow the curb slowly, even though there wasn't any traffic to interrupt us.

The doctors and nurses who had gone to the hospital were gathered on the first floor in anxious consultation when we arrived. They had found no one alive and they were beginning to get alarmed for their own safety. We delivered the colonel's message and then led the way to the telegraph office, walking our bicycles. By this time it was almost entirely dark outdoors. The others followed with their heads bundled up in gauze and each with his hands on another's shoulders. The track of our bicycles was still visible as a depression in the rapidly deepening dust.

Some of the women were pretty nearly all in by the time we reached the telegraph office, and the men weren't very spry. Taking heavy physical exercise while you're breathing through a towel isn't anybody's idea of fun who has ever tried it.

Gary and I didn't wait to find out what orders had come from Washington, but started off again for Army Headquarters. This was a hotel which had been taken over by the government and was in the opposite direction from the hospital and slightly downhill. We were able to let our bicycles coast most of the way, but when we came to a level stretch, the dust had become so deep we had to abandon them.

We staggered into the lobby of the hotel almost smothered. The hand-kerchiefs had become so clogged with dust that it was almost impossible to breathe through them. One of the medical officers quickly mixed up something which he made us drink. I don't know what it was, but it made me feel all right again.

The officers gathered in the lobby of the hotel looked dubious when I told them that Colonel Gooden wanted them to come to the telegraph office.

"What does he want us to do when we get there?" one of them asked.

"He didn't say. He's waiting orders from Washington, I think."

"I don't believe we can make it," said the officer, glancing through a window at the falling dust.

"No use staying here," said the man who had given us the medicine. "It's getting worse instead of better. What about trying gas masks?"

That suggestion was what saved all of us. It was just a chance that they would work. They had never been intended to strain out dust and it seemed likely that they would clog up and be worse than useless. However, it was our only chance. We sallied out looking like immense beetles and carrying enough extra masks to supply the people at the telegraph office.

It was pretty unpleasant the first few minutes, wondering whether we were going to smother to death or not. Then we found we could breathe fairly well—not comfortably, of course, but a lot better than we had any reason to expect.

Again Gary and I took the lead and this time we got lost going across the square and couldn't find the street which led to the telegraph office. It doesn't sound reasonable to us now, but we went entirely around that square twice without seeing a street that looked like the right one. It is impossible to convey an idea of how dark it is when practically all light is blotted out. The officers had powerful flashlights, but they showed only a rain of falling dust.

Finally I stumbled over something and went sprawling. It proved to be one of the bicycles we had abandoned, now covered six inches deep. That showed us where we were, and not long afterward we reached the telegraph office.

The people there would have been glad to see us anyway, but the gas masks we brought gave them an additional ray of hope. Things did not look very bright for any of us about that time. Washington had instructed Colonel Gooden to evacuate the city, but that was easier said than done. Our train with the freight engine had been ordered to wait at the station, but getting there from the city proper was a problem. Walking that distance even with the gas masks would be impossible unless the dust stopped falling. We stood around while Lieutenant Palmer was getting more and more urgent messages from the war department. Finally he came over to where Colonel Gooden was talking to a group of regular army officers.

"Some guy at the war department just made a suggestion that might work. He says there must be enough cars parked in the streets to carry us all to the station."

"We couldn't go a block without the carburetors being choked with dust," someone objected.

"He knows that," answered Lieutenant Palmer, "but he says it's down hill most of the way to the station. He says we can coast after we get started."

We had our choice of dozens of cars that had been left in the streets by their owners. Some of them it was impossible to start and we didn't waste time on them. Presently enough were lined up to accommodate all of us. Headlights on full would penetrate the dust a dozen feet, and we planned to keep that far apart.

The first few blocks were the ticklish part. Some of the engines behaved nobly. Others died on us and the cars behind pushed. Batteries were used for purposes never intended by their makers. Finally we came to the down grade and then it was simply a matter of keeping the cars under control and not running off the road.

We found the train crew in the station discussing whether to wait longer for us or to save their own lives by leaving while it was still possible. The general opinion was that all of us who had left to go up to the city were dead by this time. The trainmen had decided to wait until ten-thirty and if we hadn't appeared by that time they would go. When ten-thirty came with no sign of us, the engineer insisted on waiting fifteen minutes longer. Said he had a feeling that we were still alive.

It was during the last few minutes of this fifteen that the first of our procession of cars ran into the station and smashed a waiting room window.

This time we thought we were on our way to safety and then we found we weren't. When the engineer pulled the throttle of his engine, the driving wheels began slowly to turn but the train didn't move. Sand, and we moved forward a few feet, when the wheels began to spin again. Finally the younger men piled out of the train and broke into a construction car that was on a nearby siding. Armed with shovels, we began laboriously to clear the tracks. It was necessary not only to shovel off the volcanic dust but even to sweep the tracks. The dust made the tracks as slippery as if they had been greased.

We did this for nearly half a mile until we reached the downgrade. Throwing away our shovels and brooms we scrambled aboard as the train slowly gathered speed. Fortunately the engineer was an old hand on the run and knew the grades. He carefully regulated his speed and we were neither derailed nor did we stop again until seven minutes after three. After that hour there were no more railroads in that part of the country.

We were near the South Carolina line then and fortunately for us, in comparatively level country. We had left the mountains behind and were among rolling hills.

I was dozing when the first shock came and instead of waking me, it became part of a nightmare. The second shock was only a few seconds later and overturned every car of the train. My elbow crashed through the window, cutting my arm but not seriously. A woman from the other side of the car was flung on top of me. At first I couldn't think where I was. Women were screaming and men shouting. I heard the sound of escaping steam.

Then I saw Gary looking down at me through the window on the opposite side of the car, which was now directly overhead.

"You all right?" he asked.

"Sure. Help me get this woman out. She's fainted."

I managed to hand her to Gary and get out of the car myself before the third shock, which was the most severe of the series which continued for twenty-four hours.

I don't know that I can add very much to the accounts of the earth-quake which have been published. It was the most destructive that has occurred during historic times and extended over a wider territory.

I was thrown violently to the ground by the third shock. I was dazed but did not lose consciousness. I remember every detail as plainly as if it had happened an hour ago.

The fall of dust had stopped and the great barrier of fire in the north illumined the country so the intervening mountains stood out against the sky like black silhouettes. The terrific twisting sidewise movement of the earth nauseated me, but I was watching those mountains when they began to slide.

That doesn't sound very thrilling as I write it, but it was thrilling enough to look at. The only thing I could think of was an extravaganza I saw at a theatre when I was a boy, where one scene melted into another before my eyes. That was what was happening now. I saw the sharp conical peak of a mountain begin to sway back and forth. Then it seemed to slide on itself and dissolve.

In a few seconds there was no mountain there. I rubbed my eyes and when I looked again, the peaks in sight were disappearing as if they had been melted into liquid and were running off.

I don't pretend to say what actually happened that night. What I am describing is what I seemed to see. How much was optical illusion I'll have to leave for others to decide. One thing we know. The mountainous country of western North Carolina and the adjoining states was levelled off that night into what it is now, a barren, rocky plateau with fumaroles, boiling springs, geysers and other evidences of volcanic activity not far from the surface.

None of the passengers on the train was badly hurt when it overturned, but we had no food and it was forty-eight hours before a rescue party reached us. They were not hunting for us because it was assumed we had perished. It happened that the members of our party were the only persons who had actually been in the devastated country to escape alive.

This isn't the place to go into the theories of what caused the disaster, even if they were better established than they are. It is sufficient to say that the now generally accepted scientific opinion is that the earth contains vastly more than the 270,000,000 tons of radioactive substances required to keep its heat constant. Periodically the increasing internal temperature causes an explosion. It is thought possible that the place of such explosions may be indicated in advance by the discharge from the earth of radioactive gases, as was the case in North Carolina. Whether this is true will probably not be determined until after observations have been made covering a period of years.

Dr. Grant's insistence on the evacuation of western North Carolina undoubtedly saved tens of thousands of lives. He lost his own, but he would doubtless have considered that a small price to pay for what he accomplished. A monument has recently been erected in Washington to his memory.

ANSON MacDONALD

GOLDFISH BOWL

ON THE horizon lay the immobile cloud which capped the incredible waterspouts known as the Pillars of Hawaii.

Captain Blake lowered his binoculars. "There they stand, gentlemen."

In addition to the naval personnel of the watch, the bridge of the hydrographic survey ship U. S. S. *Mahan* held two civilians; the captain's words were addressed to them. The elder and smaller of the pair peered intently through a spyglass he had borrowed from the quartermaster. "I can't make them out," he complained.

"Here—try my glasses, doctor," Blake suggested, passing over his binoculars. He turned to the officer of the deck and added, "Have the forward range finder manned, if you please, Mr. Mott." Lieutenant Mott caught the eye of the bos'n's mate of the watch, listening from a discreet distance, and jerked a thumb upward. The petty officer stepped to the microphone, piped a shrill stand-by, and the metallic voice of the loud-speaker filled the ship, drowning out the next words of the captain:

"Raaaaange *1!* Maaaaaaaan and cast loose!"

"I asked," the captain repeated, "if that was any better."

"I think I see them," Jacobson Graves acknowledged. "Two dark vertical stripes, from the cloud to the horizon."

"That's it."

The other civilian, Bill Eisenberg, had taken the telescope when Graves had surrendered it for the binoculars. "I got 'em, too," he announced. "There's nothing wrong with this 'scope, Doc. But they don't look as big as I had expected," he admitted.

"They are still beyond the horizon," Blake explained. "You see only the upper segments. But they stand just under eleven thousand feet from water line to cloud—if they are still running true to form."

Graves looked up quickly. "Why the mental reservation? Haven't they been?"

Captain Blake shrugged. "Sure. Right on the nose. But they ought not to be there at all—four months ago they did not exist. How do I know what they will be doing today—or tomorrow?"

Graves nodded. "I see your point—and agree with it. Can we estimate their height from the distance?"

"I'll see." Blake stuck his head into the charthouse. "Any reading, Archie?"

"Just a second, captain." The navigator stuck his face against a voice tube and called out, "Range!"

A muffled voice replied, "Range 1—no reading."

"Something greater than twenty miles," Blake told Graves cheerfully. "You'll have to wait, doctor."

Lieutenant Mott directed the quartermaster to make three bells; the captain left the bridge, leaving word that he was to be informed when the ship approached the critical limit of three miles from the Pillars. Somewhat reluctantly, Graves and Eisenberg followed him down; they had barely time enough to dress before dining with the captain.

Captain Blake's manners were old-fashioned; he did not permit the conversation to turn to shop talk until the dinner had reached the coffee and cigars stage. "Well, gentlemen," he began, as he lit up, "just what is it you propose to do?"

"Didn't the navy department tell you?" Graves asked with a quick look.

"Not much. I have had one letter, directing me to place my ship and command at your disposal for research concerning the Pillars, and a dispatch two days ago telling me to take you aboard this morning. No details."

Graves looked nervously at Eisenberg, then back to the captain. He cleared his throat. "Uh—we propose, captain, to go up the Kanaka column and down the Wahini."

Blake gave him a sharp look, started to speak, reconsidered, and started again. "Doctor—you'll forgive me, I hope; I don't mean to be rude—but that sounds utterly crazy. A fancy way to commit suicide."

"It may be a little dangerous—"

"Hummph!"

"—but we have the means to accomplish it, if, as we believe to be true, the Kanaka column supplies the water which becomes the Wahini column on the return trip." He outlined the method. He and Eisenberg totaled between them nearly twenty-five years of bathysphére experience, eight for Eisenberg, seventeen for himself. They had brought aboard the *Mahan*, at present in an uncouth crate on the fantail, a modified bathysphere. Externally it was a bathysphere with its anchor weights removed; internally it much more nearly resembled some of the complicated barrels in which foolhardy exhibitionists have essayed the spectacular, useless trip over Niagara Falls. It would supply air, stuffy but breatheable, for forty-eight hours; it held water and concentrated food for at least that period; there were even rude but adequate sanitary arrangements.

But its principal feature was an anti-shock harness, a glorified corset, a strait jacket, in which a man could hang suspended clear of the walls by means of a network of Gideon cord and steel springs. In it, a man might reasonably hope to survive most violent pummeling. He could perhaps be shot from a cannon, bounced down a hillside, subjected to the sadistic mercy of a baggage smasher, and still survive with bones intact and viscera unruptured.

Blake poked a finger at a line sketch with which Graves had illustrated his description. "You actually intend to try to ascend the Pillars in that?"

Eisenberg replied. "Not him, captain. Me."

Graves reddened. "My damned doctor—"

"*And* your colleagues," Eisenberg added. "It's this way, captain: There's nothing wrong with Doc's nerve, but he has a leaky heart, a pair of submarine ears, and a set of not-so-good arteries. So the Institute has delegated me to kinda watch over him."

"Now look here," Graves protested, "Bill, you're not going to be stuffy about this. I'm an old man; I'll never have another such chance."

"No go," Eisenberg denied. "Captain, I wish to inform you that the Institute vested title of record to that gear we brought aboard in me, just to keep the old war horse from doing anything foolish."

"That's your pidgin," Blake answered testily. "My instructions are to facilitate Dr. Graves' research. Assuming that one or the other of you wish to commit suicide in that steel coffin, how do you propose to enter the Kanaka Pillar?"

"Why, that's your job, captain. You put the sphere into the up column and pick it up again when it comes down the down column."

Blake pursed his lips, then slowly shook his head. "I can't do that."

"Huh? Why not?"

"I will not take my ship closer than three miles to the Pillars. The *Mahan* is a sound ship, but she is not built for speed. She can't make more than twelve knots. Some place inside that circle the surface current which feeds the Kanaka column will exceed twelve knots. I don't care to find out where, by losing my ship.

"There have been an unprecedented number of unreported fishing vessels out of the islands lately. I don't care to have the *Mahan* listed."

"You think they went up the column?"

"I do."

"But, look, captain," suggested Bill Eisenberg, "you wouldn't have to risk the ship. You could launch the sphere from a power boat."

Blake shook his head. "Out of the question," he said grimly. "Even if the ship's boats were built for the job, which they aren't, I will not risk naval personnel. This isn't war."

"I wonder," said Graves softly.

"What's that?"

Eisenberg chuckled. "Doc has a romantic notion that all the odd phenomena turned up in the past few years can be hooked together into one smooth theory with a single, sinister cause—everything from the Pillars to LaGrange's fireballs."

"LaGrange's fireballs? How could there be any connection there? They are simply static electricity, allee samee heat lightning. I know; I've seen 'em."

The scientists were at once attentive, Graves' pique and Eisenberg's amusement alike buried in truth-tropism. "You did? When? Where?"

"Golf course at Hilo. Last March. I was—"

"*That* case! That was one of the disappearance cases!"

"Yes, of course. I'm trying to tell you. I was standing in a sand trap near the thirteenth green, when I happened to look up—" A clear, balmy island day. No clouds, barometer normal, light breeze. Nothing to suggest atmospheric disturbance, no maxima of sunspots, no static on the radio. Without warning a half dozen, or more, giant fireballs—ball "lightning" on an unprecedented scale—floated across the golf course in a sort of skirmish line, a line described by some observers as mathematically even—an assertion denied by others.

A woman player, a tourist from the mainland, screamed and began to run. The flanking ball nearest her left its place in line and danced after her. No one seemed sure that the ball touched her—Blake could not say, although he had watched it happen—but when the ball had passed on, there she lay on the grass, dead.

A local medico of somewhat flamboyant reputation insisted that he found evidence in the cadaver of both coagulation and electrolysis, but the jury that sat on the case followed the coroner's advice in calling it heart failure, a verdict heartily approved by the local chamber of commerce and tourist bureau.

The man who disappeared did not try to run; his fate came to meet him. He was a caddy, a Japanese-Portygee-Kanaka mixed breed, with no known relatives, a fact which should have made it easy to leave his name out of the news reports had not a reporter smelled it out. "He was standing on the green, not more than twenty-five yards away from me," Blake recounted, "when the fireballs approached. One passed on each side of me. My skin itched, and my hair stood up. I could smell ozone. I stood still—"

"That saved you," observed Graves.

"Nuts," said Eisenberg. "Standing in the dry sand of the trap was what saved him."

"Bill, you're a fool," Graves said wearily. "These fireball things perform with intelligent awareness."

Blake checked his account. "Why do you assume that, doctor?"

"Never mind, for the moment, please. Go on with your story."

"Hm-m-m. Well, they passed on by me. The caddy fellow was directly in the course of one of them. I don't believe he saw it—back toward it, you see. It reached him, enveloped him, passed on—but the boy was gone."

Graves nodded. "That checks with the accounts I have seen. Odd that I did not recall your name from the reports."

"I stayed in the background," Blake said shortly. "Don't like reporters."

"Hm-m-m. Anything to add to the reports that did come out? Any errors in them?"

"None that I can recall. Did the reports mention the bag of golf clubs he was carrying?"

"I think not."

"They were found on the beach, six miles away."

Eisenberg sat up. "That's news," he said. "Tell me: Was there anything to suggest how far they had fallen? Were they smashed or broken?"

Blake shook his head. "They weren't even scratched, nor was the beach sand disturbed. But they were—ice-cold."

Graves waited for him to go on; when the captain did not do so he inquired, "What do you make of it?"

"Me? I make nothing of it."

"How do you explain it?"

"I don't. Unclassified electrical phenomena. However, if you want a rough guess, I'll give you one. This fireball is a static field of high potential. It inglobes the caddy and charges him, whereupon he bounces away like a pith ball—electrocuted, incidentally. When the charge dissipates, he falls into the sea."

"So? There was a case like it in Kansas, rather too far from the sea."

"The body might simply never have been found."

"They never are. But even so—how do you account for the clubs being deposited so gently? And why were they cold?"

"Dammit, man, *I* don't know! I'm no theoretician; I'm a maritime engineer by profession, an empiricist by disposition. Suppose you tell me."

"All right—but bear in mind that my hypothesis is merely tentative, a basis for investigation. I see in these several phenomena, the Pillars, the giant fireballs, a number of other assorted phenomena which should never have happened, but did—including the curious case of a small mountain peak south of Boulder, Colorado, which had its tip leveled off 'spontaneously'—I see in these things evidence of intelligent direction, a single conscious cause." He shrugged. "Call it the 'X' factor. I'm looking for X."

Eisenberg assumed a look of mock sympathy. "Poor old Doc," he sighed. "Sprung a leak at last."

The other two ignored the crack. Blake inquired, "You are primarily an ichthyologist, aren't you?"

"Yes."

"How did you get started along this line?"

"I don't know. Curiosity, I suppose. My boisterous young friend here would tell you that ichthyology is derived from 'icky.' "

Blake turned to Eisenberg. "But aren't *you* an ichthyologist?"

"Hell, no! I'm an oceanographer specializing in ecology."

"He's quibbling," observed Graves. "Tell Captain Blake about Cleo and Pat."

Eisenberg looked embarrassed. "They're damned nice pets," he said defensively.

Blake looked puzzled; Graves explained. "He kids me, but *his* secret shame is a pair of goldfish. Goldfish! You'll find 'em in the washbasin in his stateroom this minute."

"Scientific interest?" Blake inquired with a dead pan.

"Oh, no! He thinks they are devoted to him."

"They're damned nice pets," Eisenberg insisted. "They don't bark, they don't scratch, they don't make messes. And Cleo does so have expression!"

In spite of his initial resistance to their plans Blake co-operated actively in trying to find a dodge whereby the proposed experiment could be performed without endangering naval personnel or matériel. He liked these two; he understood their curious mixture of selfless recklessness and extreme caution; it matched his own—it was professionalism, as distinguished from economic motivation.

He offered the services of his master diver, an elderly commissioned warrant officer, and his technical crew in checking their gear. "You know," he added, "there is some reason to believe that your bathysphere could make the round trip, aside from the proposition that what goes up must come down. You know of the *VJ-14*?"

"Was that the naval plane lost in the early investigation?"

"Yes." He buzzed for his orderly. "Have my writer bring up the jacket on the *VJ-14*," he directed.

Attempts to reconnoiter the strange "permanent" cloud and its incredible waterspouts had been made by air soon after its discovery. Little was learned. A plane would penetrate the cloud. Its ignition would fail; out it would glide, unharmed, whereupon the engines would fire again. Back into the cloud—engine failure. The vertical reach of the cloud was greater than the ceiling of any plane.

"The *VJ-14*," Blake stated, referring occasionally to the file jacket which had been fetched, "made an air reconnaissance of the Pillars themselves on 12 May, attended by the U. S. S. *Pelican*. Besides the pilot and radioman she carried a cinematographer and a chief aerographer. Mm-m-m —only the last two entries seem to be pertinent: 'Changing course. Will fly between the Pillars—*14*,' and '0913—Ship does not respond to controls— *14*.' Telescopic observation from the *Pelican* shows that she made a tight upward spiral around the Kanaka Pillar, about one and a half turns, and was sucked into the column itself. Nothing was seen to fall.

"Incidentally the pilot, Lieutenant—m-m-m-m, yes—Mattson—Lieutenant Mattson was exonerated posthumously by the court of inquiry. Oh, yes, here's the point pertinent to our question: From the log of the *Pelican*: '1709—Picked up wreckage identified as part of *VJ-14*. See additional sheet for itemized description.' We needn't bother with that. Point is, they picked it up four miles from the base of the Wahini Pillar on the side away from the Kanaka. The inference is obvious and your scheme might work. Not that you'd live through it."

"I'll chance it," Eisenberg stated.

"Mm-m-m—yes. But I was going to suggest we send up a dead load, say a crate of eggs packed into a hogshead." The buzzer from the bridge sounded; Captain Blake raised his voice toward the brass funnel of a voice tube in the overhead. "Yes?"

"Eight o'clock, captain. Eight o'clock lights and galley fires out; prisoners secured."

"Thank you, sir." Blake stood up. "We can get together on the details in the morning."

A fifty-foot motor launch bobbed listlessly astern the *Mahan*. A nine-inch coir line joined it to its mother ship; bound to it at fathom intervals was a telephone line ending in a pair of headphones worn by a signalman seated in the stern sheets of the launch. A pair of flags and a spyglass lay on the thwart beside him; his blouse had crawled up, exposing part of the lurid cover of a copy of *Dynamic Tales*, smuggled as a precaution against boredom.

Already in the boat were the coxswain, the engineman, the boat officer, Graves and Eisenberg. With them, forward in the boat, was a breaker of water rations, two fifty-gallon drums of gasoline—and a hogshead. It contained not only a carefully packed crate of eggs but also a jury-rigged smoke-signal device, armed three ways—delayed action set for eight, nine and ten hours; radio relay triggered from the ship; and simple salt-water penetration to complete an electrical circuit. The torpedo gunner in charge of diving hoped that one of them might work and thereby aid in locating the hogshead. He was busy trying to devise more nearly foolproof gear for the bathysphere.

The boat officer signaled ready to the bridge. A megaphoned bellow responded, "Pay her out handsomely!" The boat drifted slowly away from the ship and directly toward the Kanaka Pillar, three miles away.

The Kanaka Pillar loomed above them, still nearly a mile away but loweringly impressive nevertheless. The place where it disappeared in cloud seemed almost overhead, falling toward them. Its five-hundred-foot-thick trunk gleamed purplish-black, more like polished steel than water.

"Try your engine again, coxswain."

"Aye, aye, sir!" The engine coughed, took hold; the engineman eased in the clutch, the screw bit in, and the boat surged forward, taking the strain off the towline. "Slack line, sir."

"Stop your engine." The boat officer turned to his passengers. "What's the trouble, Mr. Eisenberg? Cold feet?"

"No, dammit—seasick. I hate a small boat."

"Oh, that's too bad. I'll see if we haven't got a pickle in that chow up forward."

"Thanks, but pickles don't help me. Never mind, I can stand it."

The boat officer shrugged, turned and let his eye travel up the dizzy length of the column. He whistled, something which he had done every time he had looked at it. Eisenberg, made nervous by his nausea, was beginning to find it cause for homicide. "*Whew!* You really intend to try to go up that thing, Mr. Eisenberg?"

"I do!"

The boat officer looked startled at the tone, laughed uneasily, and added, "Well, you'll be worse than seasick, if you ask me."

Nobody had. Graves knew his friend's temperament; he made conversation for the next few minutes.

"Try your engine, coxswain." The petty officer acknowledged, and reported back quickly:

"Starter doesn't work, sir."

"Help the engineman get a line on the flywheel. I'll take the tiller."

The two men cranked the engine over easily, but got no answering cough. "Prime it!" Still no results.

The boat officer abandoned the useless tiller and jumped down into the engine space to lend his muscle to heaving on the cranking line. Over his shoulder he ordered the signalman to notify the ship.

"Launch 3, calling bridge. Launch 3, calling bridge. Bridge—reply! Testing—testing." The signalman slipped a phone off one ear. "Phone's dead, sir."

"Get busy with your flags. Tell 'em to haul us in!" The officer wiped sweat from his face and straightened up. He glanced nervously at the current *slap-slapping* against the boat's side.

Graves touched his arm. "How about the barrel?"

"Put it over the side if you like. I'm busy. Can't you raise them, Sears?"

"I'm trying, sir."

"Come on, Bill," Graves said to Eisenberg. The two of them slipped forward in the boat, threading their way past the engine on the side away from the three men sweating over the flywheel. Graves cut the hogshead loose from its lashings, then the two attempted to get a purchase on the awkward, unhandy object. It and its light load weighed less than two hundred pounds, but it was hard to manage, especially on the uncertain footing of heaving floorboards.

They wrestled it outboard somehow, with one smashed finger for Eisenberg, a badly banged shin for Graves. It splashed heavily, drenching them with sticky salt water, and bobbed astern, carried rapidly toward the Kanaka Pillar by the current which fed it.

"Ship answers, sir!"

"Good! Tell them to haul us in—*carefully*." The boat officer jumped out of the engine space and ran forward, where he checked again the secureness with which the towline was fastened.

Graves tapped him on the shoulder. "Can't we stay here until we see the barrel enter the column?"

"No! Right now you had better pray that that line holds, instead of worrying about the barrel—or we go up the column, too. Sears, has the ship acknowledged?"

"Just now, sir."

"Why a coir line, Mr. Parker?" Eisenberg inquired, his nausea forgotten in the excitement. "I'd rather depend on steel, or even good stout Manila."

"Because coir floats, and the others don't," the officer answered snappishly. "Two miles of line would drag us to the bottom. *Sears!* Tell them to ease the strain. We're shipping water."

"Aye, aye, sir!"

The hogshead took less than four minutes to reach the column, enter it, a fact which Graves ascertained by borrowing the signalman's glass to follow it on the last leg of its trip—which action won him a dirty look from the nervous boat officer. Some minutes later, when the boat was about five hundred yards farther from the Pillar than it had been at nearest approach, the telephone came suddenly to life. The starter of the engine was tested immediately; the engine roared into action.

The trip back was made with engine running to take the strain off the towline—at half speed and with some maneuvering, in order to avoid fouling the screw with the slack bight of the line.

The smoke signal worked—one circuit or another. The plume of smoke was sighted two miles south of the Wahini Pillar, elapsed time from the moment the vessel had entered the Kanaka column just over eight hours.

Bill Eisenberg climbed into the saddle of the exerciser in which he was to receive antibends treatment—thirty minutes of hard work to stir up his circulation while breathing an atmosphere of helium and oxygen, at the end of which time the nitrogen normally dissolved in his blood stream would be largely replaced by helium. The exerciser itself was simply on old bicycle mounted on a stationary platform. Blake looked it over. "You needn't have bothered to bring this," he remarked. "We've a better one aboard. Standard practice for diving operations these days."

"We didn't know that," Graves answered. "Anyhow, this one will do. All set, Bill?"

"I guess so." He glanced over his shoulder to where the steel bulk of the bathysphere lay, uncrated, checked and equipped, ready to be swung outboard by the boat crane. "Got the gasket-sealing compound?"

"Sure. The Iron Maiden is all right. The gunner and I will seal you in. Here's your mask."

Eisenberg accepted the inhaling mask, started to strap it on, checked himself. Graves noticed the look on his face. "What's the trouble, son?"

"Doc . . . uh—"

"Yes?"

"I say—you'll look out for Cleo and Pat, won't you?"

"Why, sure. But they won't need anything in the length of time you'll be gone."

"Um-m-m, no, I suppose not. But you'll look out for 'em?"

"Sure."

"O. K." Eisenberg slipped the inhaler over his face, waved his hand to the gunner waiting by the gas bottles. The gunner eased open the cut-off valves, the gas lines hissed, and Eisenberg began to pedal like a six-day racer.

With thirty minutes to kill, Blake invited Graves to go forward with him for a smoke and a stroll on the fo'c's'le. They had completed about twenty turns when Blake paused by the wildcat, took his cigar from his mouth and remarked, "Do you know, I believe he has a good chance of completing the trip."

"So? I'm glad to hear that."

"Yes, I do, really. The success of the trial with the dead load convinced me. And whether the smoke gear works or not, if that globe comes back down the Wahini Pillar, *I'll find it.*"

"I know you will. It was a good idea of yours, to paint it yellow."

"Help us to spot it, all right. I don't think he'll learn anything, however. He won't see a thing through those ports but blue water, from the time he enters the column to the time we pick him up."

"Perhaps so."

"What else *could* he see?"

"I don't know. Whatever it is that *made* those Pillars, perhaps."

Blake dumped the ashes from his cigar carefully over the rail before replying. "Doctor, I don't understand you. To my mind, those Pillars are a natural, even though strange, phenomenon."

"And to me it's equally obvious that they are not 'natural.' They exhibit intelligent interference with the ordinary processes of nature as clearly as if they had a sign saying so hung on them."

"I don't see how you can say that. Obviously, they are not man-made."

"No."

"Then who did make them—if they were made?"

"I don't know."

Blake started to speak, shrugged, and held his tongue. They resumed their stroll. Graves turned aside to chuck his cigarette overboard, glancing outboard as he did so.

He stopped, stared, then called out: "Captain Blake!"

"Eh?" The captain turned and looked where Graves pointed. "Great God! Fireballs!"

"That's what I thought."

"They're some distance away," Blake observed, more to himself than to Graves. He turned decisively. "Bridge!" he shouted. "Bridge! Bridge ahoy!"

"Bridge, aye, aye!"

"Mr. Weems—pass the word: 'All hands, below decks.' Dog down all ports. Close all hatches. And close up the bridge itself! Sound the general alarm."

"Aye, aye, sir!"

"Move!" Turning to Graves, he added, "Come inside." Graves followed him; the captain stopped to dog down the door by which they entered, himself. Blake pounded up the inner ladders to the bridge, Graves in his train. The ship was filled with whine of the bos'n pipe, the raucous voice of the loud-speaker, the clomp of hurrying feet, and the monotonous, menacing *cling-cling-cling!* of the general alarm.

The watch on the bridge were still struggling with the last of the heavy glass shutters of the bridge when the captain burst into their midst. "I'll take it, Mr. Weems," he snapped. In one continuous motion he moved from one side of the bridge to the other, letting his eye sweep the port side aft, the fo'c's'le, the starboard side aft, and finally rest on the fireballs—distinctly nearer and heading straight for the ship. He cursed. "Your friend did not get the news," he said to Graves. He grasped the crank which could open or close the after starboard shutter of the bridge.

Graves looked past his shoulder, saw what he meant—the afterdeck was empty, save for one lonely figure pedaling away on a stationary bicycle. The LaGrange fireballs were closing in.

The shutter stuck, jammed tight, would not open. Blake stopped trying, swung quickly to the loud-speaker control panel, and cut in the whole board without bothering to select the proper circuit. "Eisenberg! *Get below!*"

Eisenberg must have heard his name called, for he turned his head and looked over his shoulder—Graves saw distinctly—just as the fireball reached him. It passed on, and the saddle of the exerciser was empty.

The exerciser was undamaged, they found, when they were able to examine it. The rubber hose to the inhaler mask had been cut smoothly. There was no blood, no marks. Bill Eisenberg was simply gone.

"I'm going up."

"You are in no physical shape to do so, doctor."

"You are in no way responsible, Captain Blake."

"I know that. You may go if you like—after we have searched for your friend's body."

"Search be damned! I'm going up to *look* for him."

"Huh? Eh? How's that?"

"If you are right, he's dead, and there is no point in searching for his body. If I'm right, there is just an outside chance of finding him—up there!" He pointed toward the cloud cap of the Pillars.

Blake looked him over slowly, then turned to the master diver. "Mr. Hargreave, find an inhaler mask for Dr. Graves."

They gave him thirty minutes of conditioning against the caisson disease while Blake looked on with expressionless silence. The ship's company, bluejackets and officers alike, stood back and kept quiet; they walked on eggs when the Old Man had that look.

Exercise completed, the diver crew dressed Graves rapidly and strapped him into the bathysphere with dispatch, in order not to expose him too long to the nitrogen in the air. Just before the escape port was dogged down Graves spoke up. "Captain Blake."

"Yes, doctor?"

"Bill's goldfish—will you look out for them?"

"Certainly, doctor."

"Thanks."

"Not at all. Are you ready?"

"Ready."

Blake stepped forward, stuck an arm through the port of the sphere and shook hands with Graves. "Good luck." He withdrew his arm. "Seal it up."

They lowered it over the side; two motor launches nosed it half a mile in the direction of the Kanaka Pillar where the current was strong enough to carry it along. There they left it and bucked the current back to the ship, were hoisted in.

Blake followed it with his glasses from the bridge. It drifted slowly at first, then with increased speed as it approached the base of the column. It whipped into rapid motion the last few hundred yards; Blake saw a flash of yellow just above the water line, then nothing more.

Eight hours—no plume of smoke. Nine hours, ten hours, nothing. After twenty-four hours of steady patrol in the vicinity of the Wahini Pillar, Blake radioed the Bureau.

Four days of vigilance—Blake knew that the bathysphere's passenger must be dead; whether by suffocation, drowning, implosion, or other means was not important. He so reported and received orders to proceed on duty assigned. The ship's company was called to quarters; Captain Blake read the service for the dead aloud in a harsh voice, dropped over the side some rather wilted hibiscus blooms—all that his steward could produce at the time—and went to the bridge to set his course for Pearl Harbor.

On the way to the bridge he stopped for a moment at his cabin and called his steward: "You'll find some goldfish in the stateroom occupied by Mr. Eisenberg. Find an appropriate container and place them in my cabin."

"Yes, suh, cap'n."

When Bill Eisenberg came to his senses he was in a Place.

Sorry, but no other description is suitable; it lacked features. Oh, not entirely, of course—it was not dark where he was, nor was it in a state of vacuum, nor was it cold, nor was it too small for comfort. But it did lack features to such a remarkable extent that he had difficulty in estimating the size of the place. Consider—stereo vision, by which we estimate the size of things *directly*, does not work beyond twenty feet or so. At greater distances we depend on previous knowledge of the true size of familiar objects, usually making our estimates subconsciously—a man *so high* is about *that far* away, and vice versa.

But the Place contained no familiar objects. The ceiling was a considerable distance over his head, too far to touch by jumping. The floor curved up to join the ceiling and thus prevented further lateral progress of more than a dozen paces or so. He would become aware of the obstacle by losing his balance. (He had no reference lines by which to judge the vertical; furthermore, his sense of innate balance was affected by the mistreatment his inner ears had undergone through years of diving. It was easier to sit than to walk, nor was there any reason to walk, after the first futile attempt at exploration.)

When he first woke up he stretched and opened his eyes, looked around. The lack of detail confused him. It was as if he were on the inside of a giant eggshell, illuminated from without by a soft, mellow, slightly amber light. The formless vagueness bothered him; he closed his eyes, shook his head, and opened them again—no better.

He was beginning to remember his last experience before losing consciousness—the fireball swooping down, his frenzied, useless attempt to duck, the "Hold your hats, boys!" thought that flashed through his mind in the long-drawn-out split second before contact. His orderly mind began to look for explanations. Knocked cold, he thought, and my optic nerve paralyzed. Wonder if I'm blind for good.

Anyhow, they ought not to leave him alone like this in his present helpless condition. "Doc!" he shouted. "Doc Graves!"

No answer, no echo—he became aware that there was *no* sound, save for his own voice, none of the random little sounds that fill completely the normal "dead" silence. This place was as silent as the inside of a sack of flour. Were his ears shot, too?

No, he had heard his own voice. At that moment he realized that he was looking at his own hands. Why, there was nothing wrong with his eyes —he could see them plainly!

And the rest of himself, too. He was naked.

It might have been several hours later, it might have been moments, when he reached the conclusion that he was dead. It was the only hypothesis which seemed to cover the facts. A dogmatic agnostic by faith, he had expected no survival after death; he had expected to go out like a light, with a sudden termination of consciousness. However, he had been subjected to a charge of static electricity more than sufficient to kill a man; when he regained awareness, he found himself without all the usual experience which makes up living. Therefore—he was dead. Q. E. D.

To be sure, he seemed to have a body, but he was acquainted with the subjective-objective paradox. He still had memory; the strongest pattern in one's memory is body awareness. This was not his body, but his detailed sensation memory of it. So he reasoned. Probably, he thought, his dreambody would slough away as his memory of the object-body faded.

There was nothing to do, nothing to experience, nothing to distract his mind. He fell asleep at last, thinking that, if this were death, it was damned dull!

He awoke refreshed, but quite hungry and extremely thirsty. The matter of dead, or not-dead, no longer concerned him; he was interested in neither theology nor metaphysics. He was hungry.

Furthermore, he experienced on awakening a phenomenon which destroyed most of the basis for his intellectual belief in his own death—it had never reached the stage of emotional conviction. Present there with him in the Place he found material objects other than himself, objects which could be seen and touched.

And eaten.

Which last was not immediately evident, for they did not look like food. There were two sorts. The first was an amorphous lump of nothing in particular, slightly greasy to the touch, and not appetizing. The second sort was a group of objects of uniform and delightful appearance. They were spheres, a couple of dozen; each one seemed to Bill Eisenberg to be a duplicate of a crystal ball he had once purchased—true Brazilian rock crystal the perfect beauty of which he had not been able to resist; he had bought it and smuggled it home to gloat over in private.

The little spheres were like that in appearance. He touched one. It was smooth as crystal and had the same chaste coolness, but it was soft as jelly. It quivered like jelly, causing the lights within it to dance delightfully, before resuming its perfect roundness.

Pleasant as they were, they did not look like food, whereas the cheesy, soapy lump might be. He broke off a small piece, sniffed it, and tasted it tentatively. It was sour, nauseating, unpleasant. He spat it out, made a wry face, and wished heartily that he could brush his teeth. If that was food, he would have to be much hungrier—

He turned his attention back to the delightful little spheres of crystal-like jelly. He balanced them in his palms, savoring their soft, smooth touch.

In the heart of each he saw his own reflection, imaged in miniature, made elfin and graceful. He became aware almost for the first time of the serene beauty of the human figure, almost any human figure, when viewed as a composition and not as a mass of colloidal detail.

But thirst became more pressing than narcissist admiration. It occurred to him that the smooth, cool spheres, if held in the mouth, might promote salivation, as pebbles will. He tried it; the sphere he selected struck against his lower teeth as he placed it in his mouth, and his lips and chin were suddenly wet, while drops trickled down his chest. The spheres were water, nothing but water, no cellophane skin, no container of any sort. Water had been delivered to him, neatly packaged, by some esoteric trick of surface tension.

He tried another, handling it more carefully to insure that it was not pricked by his teeth until he had it in his mouth. It worked; his mouth was filled with cool, pure water—too quickly; he choked. But he had caught on to the trick; he drank four of the spheres.

His thirst satisfied, he became interested in the strange trick whereby water became its own container. The spheres were tough; he could not squeeze them into breaking down, nor did smashing them hard against the floor disturb their precarious balance. They bounced like golf balls and came up for more. He managed to pinch the surface of one between thumb and fingernail. It broke down at once, and the water trickled between his fingers—water alone, no skin nor foreign substance. It seemed that a cut alone could disturb the balance of tensions; even wetting had no effect, for he could hold one carefully in his mouth, remove it, and dry it off on his own skin.

He decided that, since his supply was limited, and no more water was in prospect, it would be wise to conserve what he had and experiment no further.

The relief of thirst increased the demands of hunger. He turned his attention again to the other substance and found that he could force himself to chew and swallow. It might not be food, it might even be poison, but it filled his stomach and stayed the pangs. He even felt well fed, once he had cleared out the taste with another sphere of water.

After eating he rearranged his thoughts. He was not dead, or, if he were, the difference between living and being dead was imperceptible, verbal. O. K., he was alive. But he was shut up alone. Somebody knew where he was and was aware of him, for he had been supplied with food and drink—mysteriously but cleverly. *Ergo*—he was a prisoner, a word which implies a warden.

Whose prisoner? He had been struck by a LaGrange fireball and had awakened in his cell. It looked, he was forced to admit, as if Doc Graves had been right; the fireballs were intelligently controlled. Furthermore, the person or persons behind them had novel ideas as to how to care for prisoners as well as strange ways of capturing them.

Eisenberg was a brave man, as brave as the ordinary run of the race from which he sprang—a race as foolhardy as Pekingese dogs. He had the high degree of courage so common in the human race, a race capable of conceiving death, yet able to face its probability daily, on the highway, on the obstetrics table, on the battlefield, in the air, in the subway—and to face lightheartedly the certainty of death in the end.

Eisenberg was apprehensive, but not panic-stricken. His situation was decidedly interesting; he was no longer bored. If he were a prisoner, it seemed likely that his captor would come to investigate him presently, perhaps to question him, perhaps to attempt to use him in some fashion. The fact that he had been saved and not killed implied some sort of plans for his future. Very well, he would concentrate on meeting whatever exigency might come with a calm and resourceful mind. In the meantime, there was nothing he could do toward freeing himself; he had satisfied himself of that. This was a prison which would baffle Houdini—smooth continuous walls, no way to get a purchase.

He had thought once that he had a clue to escape; the cell had sanitary arrangements of some sort, for that which his body rejected went elsewhere. But he got no further with that lead; the cage was self-cleaning—and that was that. He could not tell how it was done. It baffled him.

Presently he slept again.

When he awoke, one element only was changed—the food and water had been replenished. The "day" passed without incident, save for his own busy and fruitless thoughts.

And the next "day." And the next.

He determined to stay awake long enough to find out how food and water were placed in his cell. He made a colossal effort to do so, using drastic measures to stimulate his body into consciousness. He bit his lips, he bit his tongue. He nipped the lobes of his ears violently with his nails. He concentrated on difficult mental feats.

Presently he dozed off; when he awoke, the food and water had been replenished.

The waking periods were followed by sleep, renewed hunger and thirst, the satisfying of same, and more sleep. It was after the sixth or seventh sleep that he decided that some sort of a calendar was necessary to his mental health. He had no means of measuring time except by his sleeps; he arbitrarily designated them as days. He had no means of keeping records, save his own body. He made that do. A thumbnail shred, torn off, made a rough tattooing needle. Continued scratching of the same area on his thigh produced a red welt which persisted for a day or two, and could be renewed. Seven welts made a week. The progression of such welts along ten fingers and ten toes gave him the means to measure twenty weeks—which was a much longer period than he anticipated any need to measure.

He had tallied the second set of seven thigh welts on the ring finger of his left hand when the next event occurred to disturb his solitude. When he awoke from the sleep following said tally, he became suddenly and over-whelmingly aware that he was not alone!

There was a human figure sleeping beside him. When he had convinced himself that he was truly wide awake—his dreams were thoroughly popu-lated—he grasped the figure by the shoulder and shook it. "Doc!" he yelled. "Doc! Wake up!"

Graves opened his eyes, focused them, sat up, and put out his hand. "Hie, Bill," he remarked. "I'm damned glad to see you."

"Doc!" He pounded the older man on the back. "Doc! For Criminy sake! You don't know how glad *I* am to see *you*."

"I can guess."

"Look, Doc—where have you been? How did you get here? Did the fireballs snag you, too?"

"One thing at a time, son. Let's have breakfast." There was a double ration of food and water on the "floor" near them. Graves picked up a sphere, nicked it expertly, and drank it without losing a drop. Eisenberg watched him knowingly.

"You've been here for some time."

"That's right."

"Did the fireballs get you the same time they got me?"

"No." He reached for the food. "I came up the Kanaka Pillar."

"What!"

"That's right. Matter of fact, I was looking for you."

"The hell you say!"

"But I do say. It looks as if my wild hypothesis was right; the Pillars and the fireballs are different manifestations of the same cause—X!"

It seemed almost possible to hear the wheels whir in Eisenberg's head. "But, Doc . . . look here, Doc, that means your whole hypothesis was correct. Somebody *did* the whole thing. Somebody has us locked up here now."

"That's right." He munched slowly. He seemed tired, older and thinner than the way Eisenberg remembered him. "Evidence of intelligent control. Always was. No other explanation."

"But *who*?"

"Ah!"

"Some foreign power? Are we up against something utterly new in the way of an attack?"

"Hummph! Do you think the Japs, for instance, would bother to serve us water like *this*?" He held up one of the dainty little spheres.

"Who, then?"

"I wouldn't know. Call 'em Martians—that's a convenient way to think of them."

"Why Martians?"

"No reason. I said that was a convenient way to think of them."

"Convenient how?"

"Convenient because it keeps you from thinking of them as human beings—which they obviously aren't. Nor animals. Something very intelligent, but not animals, because they are smarter than we are. Martians."

"But . . . but— Wait a minute. Why do you assume that your X people aren't human? Why not humans who have a lot of stuff on the ball that we don't have? New scientific advances?"

"That's a fair question," Graves answered, picking his teeth with a forefinger. "I'll give you a fair answer. Because in the present state of world peace and good feeling we know pretty near where all the best minds are and what they are doing. Advances like these couldn't be hidden and would be a long time in developing. X indicates evidence of half a dozen different lines of development that are clearly beyond our ken and which would require years of work by dozens of researchers, to say the very least. *Ipso facto*, nonhuman science.

"Of course," he continued, "if you want to postulate a mad scientist and a secret laboratory, I can't argue with you. But I'm not writing Sunday supplements."

Bill Eisenberg kept very quiet for some time, while he considered what Graves said in the light of his own experience. "You're right, Doc," he finally admitted. "Shucks—you're usually right when we have an argument. It has to be Martians. Oh, I don't mean inhabitants of Mars; I mean some form of intelligent life from outside this planet."

"Maybe."

"But you just said so!"

"No, I said it was a convenient way to look at it."

"But it has to be, by elimination."

"Elimination is a tricky line of reasoning."

"What else could it be?"

"Mm-m-m. I'm not prepared to say just what I do think—yet. But there are stronger reasons than we have mentioned for concluding that we are up against nonhumans. Psychological reasons."

"What sort?"

"X doesn't treat prisoners in any fashion that arises out of human behavior patterns. Think it over."

They had a lot to talk about; much more than X, even though X was a subject they were bound to return to. Graves gave Bill a simple bald account of how he happened to go up the Pillar—an account which Bill found very moving for what was left out, rather than told. He felt suddenly very humble and unworthy as he looked at his elderly, frail friend. "Doc, you don't look well."

"I'll do."

"That trip up the Pillar was hard on you. You shouldn't have tried it."

Graves shrugged. "I made out all right." But he had not, and Bill could see that he had not. The old man was "poorly."

They slept and they ate and they talked and they slept again. The routine that Eisenberg had grown used to alone continued, save with company. But Graves grew no stronger.

"Doc, it's up to us to do something about it."

"About what?"

"The whole situation. This thing that has happened to us is an intolerable menace to the whole human race. We don't know what may have happened down below—"

"Why do you say 'down below'?"

"Why, you came up the Pillar."

"Yes, true—but I don't know when or how I was taken out of the bathysphere, nor where they may have taken me. But go ahead. Let's have your idea."

"Well, but— O. K.—we don't know what may have happened to the rest of the human race. The fireballs may be picking them off one at a time, with no chance to fight back and no way of guessing what has been going on. We have some idea of the answer. It's up to us to escape and warn them. There may be some way of fighting back. It's our duty; the whole future of the human race may depend on it."

Graves was silent so long after Bill had finished his tocsin that Bill began to feel embarrassed, a bit foolish. But when he finally spoke it was to agree. "I think you are right, Bill. I think it quite possible that you are right. Not necessarily, but distinctly possible. And that possibility does place an obligation on us to all mankind. I've known it. I knew it before we got into this mess, but I did not have enough data to justify shouting, 'Wolf!'

"The question is," he went on, "how can we give such a warning—now?"

"We've got to escape!"

"Ah!"

"There *must* be some way."

"Can you suggest one?"

"Maybe. We haven't been able to find any way in or out of this place, but there must be a way—has to be; we were brought in. Furthermore, our rations are put inside every day—somehow. I tried once to stay awake long enough to see how it was done, but I fell asleep—"

"So did I."

"Uh-huh. I'm not surprised. But there are two of us now; we could take turns, watch on and watch off, until something happened."

Graves nodded. "It's worth trying."

Since they had no way of measuring the watches, each kept the vigil until sleepiness became intolerable, then awakened the other. But nothing happened. Their food ran out, was not replaced. They conserved their water balls with care, were finally reduced to one, which was not drunk because each insisted on being noble about it—the other must drink it! But still no manifestation of any sort from their unseen captors.

After an unmeasured and unestimated length of time—but certainly long, almost intolerably long—at a time when Eisenberg was in a light, troubled sleep, he was suddenly awakened by a touch and the sound of his name. He sat up, blinking, disoriented. "Who? What? Wha'sa matter?"

"I must have dozed off," Graves said miserably. "I'm sorry, Bill." Eisenberg looked where Graves pointed. Their food and water had been renewed.

Eisenberg did not suggest a renewal of the experiment. In the first place, it seemed evident that their keepers did not intend for them to learn the combination to their cell and were quite intelligent enough to out-maneuver their necessarily feeble attempts. In the second place, Graves was an obviously sick man; Eisenberg did not have the heart to suggest another long, grueling, half-starved vigil.

But, lacking knowledge of the combination, it appeared impossible to break jail. A naked man is a particularly helpless creature; lacking mate-rials wherewith to fashion tools, he can do little. Eisenberg would have swapped his chances for eternal bliss for a diamond drill, an acetylene torch, or even a rusty, secondhand chisel. Without tools of some sort it was impressed on him that he stood about as much chance of breaking out of his cage as his goldfish, Cleo and Patra, had of chewing their way out of a glass bowl.

"Doc."

"Yes, son."

"We've tackled this the wrong way. We know that X is intelligent; instead of trying to escape, we should be trying to establish communica-tion."

"How?"

"I don't know. But there must be *some* way."

But if there was, he could never conjure it up. Even if he assumed that his captors could see and hear him, how was he to convey intelligence to them by word or gesture? Was it theoretically possible for any nonhuman being, no matter how intelligent, to find a pattern of meaning in human speech symbols, if he encountered them without context, without back-ground, without pictures, without *pointing*? It is certainly true that the human race, working under much more favorable circumstances, has failed almost utterly to learn the languages of the other races of animals.

What should he do to attract their attention, stimulate their interest? Recite the "Gettysburg Address"? Or the multiplication table? Or, if he used gestures, would deaf-and-dumb language mean any more, or any less, to his captors than the sailor's hornpipe?

"Doc."

"What is it, Bill?" Graves was sinking; he rarely initiated a conversa-tion these "days."

"Why are we here? I've had it in the back of my mind that *eventually* they would take us out and do something with us. Try to question us, maybe. But it doesn't look like they meant to."

"No, it doesn't."

"Then why are we here? Why do they take care of us?"

Graves paused quite a long time before answering: "I think that they are expecting us to reproduce."

"What!"

Graves shrugged.

"But that's ridiculous."

"Surely. But would they know it?"

"But they are intelligent."

Graves chuckled, the first time he had done so in many sleeps. "Do you know Roland Young's little verse about the flea:

" 'A funny creature is the Flea
You cannot tell the She from He.
But *He* can tell—and so can *She*.'

"After all, the visible differences between men and women are quite superficial and almost negligible—except to men and women!"

Eisenberg found the suggestion repugnant, almost revolting; he struggled against it. "But look, Doc—even a little study would show them the human race is divided up into sexes. After all, we aren't the first specimens they've studied."

"Maybe they don't study us."

"Huh?"

"Maybe we are just—pets."

Pets! Bill Eisenberg's morale had stood up well in the face of danger and uncertainty. This attack on it was more subtle. Pets! He had thought of Graves and himself as prisoners of war, or, possibly, objects of scientific research. But pets!

"I know how you feel," Graves went on, watching his face. "It's . . . it's *humiliating* from an anthropocentric viewpoint. But I think it may be true. I may as well tell you my own private theory as to the possible nature of X, and the relation of X to the human race. I haven't up to now, as it is almost sheer conjecture, based on very little data. But it does cover the known facts.

"I conceive of the X creatures as being just barely aware of the existence of men, unconcerned by them, and almost completely uninterested in them."

"But they hunt us!"

"Maybe. Or maybe they just pick us up occasionally by accident. A lot of men have dreamed about an impingement of nonhuman intelligences on the human race. Almost without exception the dream has taken one of two forms, invasion and war, or exploration and mutual social intercourse. Both concepts postulate that nonhumans are enough like us either to fight with us or talk to us—treat us as equals, one way or the other.

"I don't believe that X is sufficiently interested in human beings to want to enslave them, or even exterminate them. They may not even study us, even when we come under their notice. They may lack the scientific spirit in the sense of having a monkeylike curiosity about everything that moves. For that matter, how thoroughly do *we* study other life forms? Did you ever ask your goldfish for their views on goldfish poetry or politics? Does a termite think that a woman's place is in the home? Do beavers prefer blondes or brunettes?"

"You are joking."

"No, I'm not. Maybe the life forms I mentioned don't have such involved ideas. My point is: if they did, or do, we'd never guess it. I don't think X conceives of the human race as intelligent."

Bill chewed this for a while, then added: "Where do you think they came from, Doc? Mars, maybe? Or clear out of the Solar System?"

"Not necessarily. Not even probably. It's my guess that they came from the same place we did—*from up out of the slime of this planet.*"

"Really, Doc—"

"I mean it. And don't give me that funny look. I may be sick, but I'm not balmy. *Creation took eight days!*"

"Huh?"

"I'm using biblical language. 'And God blessed them, and God said unto them, Be fruitful and multiply, and replenish the earth, and subdue it: and have dominion over the fish of the sea, and over the fowl of the air, and over every living thing that moveth upon the earth.' And so it came to pass. But nobody mentioned the stratosphere."

"Doc—are you sure you feel all right?"

"Dammit—quit trying to psychoanalyze me! I'll drop the allegory. What I mean is: We aren't the latest nor the highest stage in evolution. First the oceans were populated. Then lungfish to amphibian, and so on up, until the continents were populated, and, in time, man ruled the surface of the earth—or thought he did. But did evolution stop there? I think not. Consider—from a fish's point of view air is a hard vacuum. From our point of view the upper reaches of the atmosphere, sixty, seventy, maybe a hundred thousand feet up, seem like a vacuum and unfit to sustain life. But it's not vacuum. It's thin, yes, but there is matter there and radiant energy. Why not life, intelligent life, highly evolved as it would have to be—but evolved from the same ancestry as ourselves and fish? We wouldn't see it happen; man hasn't been aware, in a scientific sense, that long. When our granddaddies were swinging in the trees, it had already happened."

Eisenberg took a deep breath. "Just wait a minute, Doc. I'm not disputing the theoretical possibility of your thesis, but it seems to me it is out on direct evidence alone. We've never seen them, had no direct evidence of them. At least, not until lately. And we *should* have seen them."

"Not necessarily. Do ants see men? I doubt it."

"Yes—but, consarn it, a man has better eyes than an ant."

"Better eyes for what? For his own needs. Suppose the X creatures are too high up, or too tenuous, or too fast-moving for us to notice them. Even a thing as big and as solid and as slow as an airplane can go up high enough to pass out of sight, even on a clear day. If X is tenuous and even semi-transparent, we never *would* see them—not even as occultations of stars, or shadows against the moon—though as a matter of fact there have been some very strange stories of just that sort of thing."

Eisenberg got up and stomped up and down. "Do you mean to suggest," he demanded, "that creatures so insubstantial they can float in a soft vacuum built the Pillars?"

"Why not? Try explaining how a half-finished, naked embryo like *homo sapiens* built the Empire State Building."

Bill shook his head. "I don't get it."

"You don't try. Where do you think *this* came from?" Graves held up one of the miraculous little water spheres. "My guess is that life on this planet is split three ways, with almost no intercourse between the three. Ocean culture, land culture, and another—call it stratoculture. Maybe a fourth, down under the crust—but we don't know. We know a little about life under the sea, because we are curious. But how much do they know of us? Do a few dozen bathysphere descents constitute an invasion? A fish that sees our bathysphere might go home and take to his bed with a sick headache, but he wouldn't talk about it, and he wouldn't be believed if he did. If a lot of fish see us and swear out affidavits, along comes a fish-psychologist and explains it as mass hallucination.

"No, it takes something at least as large and solid and permanent as the Pillars to have any effect on orthodox conceptions. Casual visitations have no real effect."

Eisenberg let his thoughts simmer for some time before commenting further. When he did, it was half to himself. "I don't believe it. I won't believe it!"

"Believe what?"

"Your theory. Look, Doc—if you are right, don't you see what it means? We're helpless, we're outclassed."

"I don't think they will bother much with human beings. They haven't, up till now."

"But that isn't it. Don't you see? We've had some dignity as a race. We've striven and accomplished things. Even when we failed, we had the tragic satisfaction of knowing that we were, nevertheless, superior and more able than the other animals. We've had faith in the race—we would accomplish great things yet. But if we are just one of the lower animals ourselves, what does our great work amount to? Me, I couldn't go on pretending to be a 'scientist' if I thought I was just a fish, mucking around in the bottom of a pool. My work wouldn't *signify* anything."

"Maybe it doesn't."

"No, maybe it doesn't." Eisenberg got up and paced the constricted area of their prison. "Maybe not. But I won't surrender to it. I *won't!* Maybe you're right. Maybe you're wrong. It doesn't seem to matter very much *where* the X people came from. One way or the other, they are a threat to our own kind. Doc, we've got to get out of here and warn them!"

"How?"

Graves was comatose a large part of the time before he died. Bill maintained an almost continuous watch over him, catching only occasional cat naps. There was little he could do for his friend, even though he did watch over him, but the spirit behind it was comfort to them both.

But he was dozing when Graves called his name. He woke at once, though the sound was a bare whisper. "Yes, Doc?"

"I can't talk much more, son. Thanks for taking care of me."

"Shucks, Doc."

"Don't forget what you're here for. Some day you'll get a break. Be ready for it and don't muff it. People have to be warned."

"I'll do it, Doc. I swear it."

"Good boy." And then, almost inaudibly, "G'night, son."

Eisenberg watched over the body until it was quite cold and had begun to stiffen. Then, exhausted by his long vigil and emotionally drained, he collapsed into a deep sleep. When he woke up the body was gone.

It was hard to maintain his morale, after Graves was gone. It was all very well to resolve to warn the rest of mankind at the first possible chance, but there was the endless monotony to contend with. He had not even the relief from boredom afforded the condemned prisoner—the checking off of limited days. Even his "calendar" was nothing but a counting of his sleeps.

He was not quite sane much of the time, and it was the twice-tragic insanity of intelligence, aware of its own instability. He cycled between periods of elation and periods of extreme depression, in which he would have destroyed himself, had he the means.

During the periods of elation he made great plans for fighting against the X creatures—after he escaped. He was not sure how or when, but, momentarily, he was sure. He would lead the crusade himself; Diesel-motored planes could withstand the dead zone of the Pillars and the cloud; heavy artillery could destroy the dynamic balance of the Pillars. They would harry them and hunt them down; the globe would once again be the kingdom of man, to whom it belonged.

During the bitter periods of relapse he would realize clearly that the puny engineering of mankind, Diesel engines or no, would be of no force against the powers and knowledge of the creatures who built the Pillars, who kidnaped himself and Graves in such a casual and mysterious fashion.

They were outclassed. Could codfish plan a sortie against the city of Boston? Would it matter if the chattering monkeys in Guatemala passed a resolution to destroy the British navy?

They were outclassed. The human race had reached its highest point— the point at which it began to be aware that it was not the highest race, and the knowledge was death to it, one way or the other—the mere knowledge alone, even as the knowledge was now destroying him, Bill Eisenberg, himself. Eisenberg—*homo piscis*. Poor fish!

His overstrained mind conceived a means by which he might possibly warn his fellow beings. He could not escape as long as his surroundings remained unchanged. That was established and he accepted it; he no longer paced his cage. But certain things *did* leave his cage: left-over food, refuse—and Graves' body. If he died, his own body would be removed, he felt sure. Some, at least, of the things which had gone up the Pillars had come down again—he knew that. Was it not likely that the X creatures disposed of any heavy mass for which they had no further use by dumping it down the Wahini Pillar? He convinced himself that it was so.

Very well, his body would be returned to the surface, eventually. How could he use it to give a message to his fellow men, if it were found? He had no writing materials, nothing but his own body.

But the same make-do means which served him as a calendar gave him a way to write a message. He could make welts on his skin with a shred of thumbnail. If the same spot were irritated over and over again, not permitted to heal, scar tissue would form. By such means he was able to create permanent tattooing.

The letters had to be large; he was limited in space to the fore part of his body; involved argument was impossible. He was limited to a fairly simple warning. If he had been quite right in his mind, perhaps he would have been able to devise a more cleverly worded warning—but then he was not.

In time, he had covered his chest and belly with cicatrix tattooing worthy of a bushman chief. He was thin by then and of an unhealthy color; the welts stood out plainly.

His body was found floating in the Pacific, by Portuguese who could not read the message, but who turned it in to the harbor police of Honolulu. They, in turn, photographed the body, fingerprinted it, and disposed of it. The fingerprints were checked in Washington, and William Eisenberg, scientist, fellow of many distinguished societies, and high type of *homo sapiens,* was officially dead for the second time, with a new mystery attached to his name.

The cumbersome course of official correspondence unwound itself and the record of his reappearance reached the desk of Captain Blake, at a port in the South Atlantic. Photographs of the body were attached to the record, along with a short official letter telling the captain that, in view of his connection with the case, it was being provided for his information and recommendation.

Captain Blake looked at the photographs for the dozenth time. The message told in scar tissue was plain enough: "BEWARE—CREATION TOOK EIGHT DAYS." But what did it mean?

Of one thing he was sure—Eisenberg had not had those scars on his body when he disappeared from the *Mahan*.

The man had lived for a considerable period after he was grabbed up by the fireball—that was certain. And he had learned something. What? The reference to the first chapter of Genesis did not escape him; it was not such as to be useful.

He turned to his desk and resumed making a draft in painful longhand of his report to the bureau. "—the message in scar tissue adds to the mystery, rather than clarifying it. I am now forced to the opinion that the Pillars and the LaGrange fireballs are connected in some way. The patrol around the Pillars should not be relaxed. If new opportunities or methods for investigating the nature of the Pillars should develop, they should be pursued thoroughly. I regret to say that I have nothing of the sort to suggest—"

He got up from his desk and walked to a small aquarium supported by gimbals from the inboard bulkhead, and stirred up the two goldfish therein with a forefinger. Noticing the level of the water, he turned to the pantry door. "Johnson, you've filled this bowl too full again. Pat's trying to jump out again!"

"I'll fix it, captain." The steward came out of the pantry with a small pan. ("Don't know why the Old Man keeps these tarnation fish. He ain't interested in 'em—*that's certain*.") Aloud he added: "That Pat fish don't want to stay in there, captain. Always trying to jump out. And he don't *like* me, captain."

"What's that?" Captain Blake's thoughts had already left the fish; he was worrying over the mystery again.

"I say that fish don't *like* me, captain. Tries to bite my finger every time I clean out the bowl."

"Don't be silly, Johnson."

DAVID H. KELLER

THE IVY WAR

"YOU are just plain drunk, Bill!" exclaimed the genial Mayor of the town of Yeastford, to one of the habitual alcoholics of the vicinity. "Just a little too much this time, or you would not be talking such nonsense. Go home and to bed and you will feel differently about it tomorrow, and laugh at yourself when your dog comes back from his hunt."

"I am drunk!" admitted William Coonel. "But anyone would get drunk after seeing what I saw. You go down to the old swamp hole yourself, and see how your nerves are afterward. Go on, Major Young, and then tell me whether I am drunk or not." He staggered out of the office, leaving the Mayor smiling at his persistency.

"This job of being Mayor of a small town and friend to all the friendless is some job for an old soldier," mused Major Young to himself. "Guess I might as well close up the office and spend the rest of the day over in New York. A few hours at the University Club will restore my cosmopolitan viewpoint of life."

Two hours later he walked into the reading-room of the Club, just in time to hear hearty gales of laughter coming from a closely clustered group of men. When the laughter ceased, he heard a determined voice.

"In spite of your laughter," it said, "I want to repeat what I said. *The next great war will be waged between the human race and some form of plant life, rather than between different nations of humanity.*"

"You mean bally little smellers, like roses and violets?" asked a man in uniform. He was Captain Llewellen, at the present assigned to duty with the British Consul.

"That is what I mean," answered the first speaker.

Elbowing his way through the circle of amused listeners, Jerkens, free lance reporter of a dozen wars, reached the center of the crowd, and holding up his hands, demanded silence.

"I want to report that war," he cried. "What headlines I could produce! How about this for the front page?

"Five Divisions of Infantry in New Mexico Surrounded by the Cactus Enemy. One Thousand Tanks Ordered to Their Relief . . . Heavy Casualties in Maryland. Our Troops Gassed by Lily-of-the-Valley and Tuberose Enemy Battalions. Generals Orchid and Gardenia Captured. They Admit That Their Morning Glory Division Was Wiped Out by Our Labor Battalions, Armed with Hoes. Patriotic Women Forming Regiments to Fight Violets and Roses. They Will Furnish Their Own Scissors. Goldenrods Massing to Attack Hay Fever Regiments."

And then the fun started and the laughter became too much for some of the older members of the Club who demanded silence. Soon the atmosphere of the place became normal. White, the plant biologist, who had been the butt of the fun, kept on smiling. But two strangers at once demanded his attention.

One handed him a card, saying, "I am Milligan, the explorer. I came across the ocean to see you."

"And I am just Mayor Young of Yeastford. I am a charter member of this Club."

"I do not know which of you I am the most pleased to meet," declared White. "Milligan has always been a hero of mine because he has gone to all the places in the world I have wanted to visit, while"—and here he turned to the Mayor—"if you are Major Young, of the Lost Battalion, let me tell you that when I was a boy I saw you play full-back on the Columbia team the year we defeated Pennsylvania. Ever since then you have been a hero to me." And he extended a hand to each of the men.

"Since all three of us seem to want to know each other better, suppose you take supper with me here at the Club?" proposed Major Young. "I will arrange a little room where we can be by ourselves and do all the talking we want to do. The boys were having a lot of fun at your expense, White."

"Yes, I was foolish enough to make a statement that was unusual and of course they all gave the ha-ha to me."

"And the peculiar part about it was that that statement was the very reason for my coming here from England to talk to Mr. White," said the explorer.

"Well, let's eat and talk," exclaimed the old football player.

Later on, in the little private room, Major Young started the conversation.

"Now, Mr. Milligan," he said, "suppose you tell us just what you want to find out from this famous scientist White. Yes, you need not object to that word famous, White. I have had a few minutes to myself and I looked you up and find that you have over twelve letters after your name and are considered the authority on plant life in America. You are as big a man in your laboratory as Milligan is in Gobi and Honduras. I looked you up also and find that you have written a dozen books about places that hardly any other white man has ever visited. So, here I am, just plain Charley Young, eating supper with two big men. Go ahead with your story, Milligan."

The Englishman took his cigarette and pushed its lighted end carefully against the ash tray. When he spoke it was with slow, carefully selected words, beautifully pronounced—as though he were dictating to his stenographer or addressing a gathering of scientists in London.

"In the course of my travels," he began, "I have been to a great many dead cities, great, ancient cities, that once swarmed with life. I have spent weeks in places like Angkor in Cambodia, once the home of a million Asiatics, but so completely forgotten, that none knew of its existence till the Frenchman Mouhot stumbled upon it in his quest for Asiatic butterflies.

"And down in Honduras I have seen the Mayan cities silently pass the centuries in the jungles; they thrust through the green forest the white marbled crests of their pyramidal temples. I have lived in those dead cities, places like Lubaantum and Benque Viejo. In all those places I asked myself the same questions: Why did they die? What killed them? In some places it seemed as though the inhabitants simply decided to migrate. But why?

"The more I asked myself that question, the more puzzled I was. I saw something in Cambodia, and to my surprise, I saw the same thing in Central America. It was something that I thought I was sure of but it was so fantastic, so utterly weird and impossible, that I could not trust myself to put it into words. I am not like our friend White. I do not like to be laughed at. So I kept it to myself. Then, back in dear old England, I ran across the same thing; and at the same time I heard about the great work that was being done with plants by an American named White; so, here I am."

"What was it you saw in England?" asked the biologist.

"It happened when I went down to see my friend, Martin Conway. He had inherited a nice old house and a lot of money; so, he made up his mind to restore the place and live there. It was Allington Castle, near Maidstone. It might have been a nice place for him to live in, but the ivy made him stop. That entire estate was full of ivy, and on the castle walls the growth was from six to ten feet thick and had branches over six inches in diameter. It spread all through the woods. It climbed up the oak trees, one hundred feet into the air, and literally suffocated them with its dense foliage.

"The stuff was growing all over the castle, inside and out. Conway put a hundred men to work and it grew faster than they could tear it loose and cut it to pieces. They worked a month, and when they came back from a holiday, it was hard to tell just what they had done. It was discouraging, to say the least.

"Conway took me over to see a ruined castle about seven miles from the one he inherited. This other castle had literally been torn to bits. The ivy had grown over the masonry, sending its roots into every little crack. Then it had grown up to the top of the building, forming a thick mat over every square foot of the wall. Once it reached the top, it started to pull, and the whole building just crumpled, overnight. When we saw it, Leybourne Castle was just a ruin, covered so completely with ivy that all anyone could see was simply a large mound of green.

"And what made matters all the worse, it seemed that nothing else could live where that ivy lived. The woods around Leybourne, years before, had been filled with the most beautiful wild flowers and shrubs, but they were all gone, and the little wild things, like rabbits and birds, were all gone too. That gave me room for thought. It made me see that right in England there might be as wonderful things to look into as there were in the Gobi Desert.

"Because it was not the lack of money that made Conway stop with his plans for the restoration of Allington Castle. He had the money and the ambition, but he could not get the men to work there any more. You see, three of them had taken too much liquor, and instead of going back home at the end of the day, they slept there all night, and when morning came and the Coroner and his jury—laboring men just did not want to work there any more, and Conway had to stop. But it made him mad and he asked me to come down and visit him. I went over the entire problem with him, and it suddenly occurred to me that perhaps something like that had happened at Angkor and down in Honduras. In other words, the same horrible thought came to me, came back to my consciousness, no matter how hard I tried to ignore it. I am an explorer, not an expert on plants, so I came over here to America to see if White could help me solve the problem.

"Just talking about it makes me tremble. Think of that! I have, and I say it in explanation and not to boast, faced death in a dozen places and in as horrible ways as a man can face it, but when I think that there is a possibility that my suspicion is true, it makes me tremble. Look at that hand," and he held out his fingers to show them a fine tremor.

"That is all right," said Major Young, in almost a soothing manner— "The braver a man is, the more apt he is to feel afraid. It is not the feeling but the actions that count."

"You say that three men were killed?" asked White.

"Yes. I guess you could use that word. At least, they were dead when morning came."

"And they thought the ivy—was that the Coroner's verdict?"

"No. I do not know what he thought; of course he could not say that—not in so many words. But Conway told me how the bodies looked, and we decided to do a bit of experimenting. We drove an old cow into the woods where the ivy was the thickest and tied her to a tree. Yes, we went in while the sun was shining, and the next day, when we went back, the cow was dead—and Conway—of course he was not a physician, but he said that the cow's body looked the same as the bodies of the three dead men.

"This all happened in a poorly settled part of England. You can drive miles without seeing a cottage, and the few people who used to live there left, and some of them in a hurry, and none of them talk very much about why they left, because they do not like to be laughed at."

"Just ivy—just common ivy?" asked White, leaning across the table, and pushing aside the plates of food. "You mean that it was just the ordinary ivy that grows as an ornament on old buildings?"

"No!" almost shouted Milligan, as he looked point blank into the eyes of the biologist. "If it had been, we would have understood. In the first place, it was big. Conway and I stumbled over branches that were over a foot in diameter, and those branches ran for miles through what had once been the woods. We never could be sure just where they started from. Every few feet the branches sent out lateral rootlets, and coiling twining tendrils replaced every third leaf, but we never were sure that we found anything like a central root. We did find something, however, that made us think. All these big branches seemed to come from one place, and we never were able to get within a mile of that place. We located it rather accurately on our map and this is what we found.

"Ten years ago there was not a bit of ivy in those woods; but there was a large hole in the center of the forest. The maps called it a swamp-hole. It had always been there. Some of the old men told Conway about it. Tradition had it as the home of a large snake. Silly idea that. Now, here is what happened. I mean to say this is what I think happened. This new kind of ivy started to grow out of the swamp-hole. Where did it come from? Why, out of the hole. And in ten years' time it had captured seventy square miles of England. And here is the thing that makes me tremble. Nobody knows about it, and nobody is doing anything about it. Conway and I talked about that phase of it; and I came over here. How about it, White?"

But the biologist did not have an opportunity to answer the question then, because the Mayor of Yeastford suddenly galvanized into life, as he asked, "Were the leaves a peculiar combination of white and green? Did those tendrils wave around in the air? Do you think that they sucked the blood out of the cow?—and the three men? Did you find swamp-holes like that in Honduras?"

The explorer and the biologist looked at the ex-soldier in astonishment. At last White asked, "What are you driving at, Major?"

"Simply this. Up in the town where I am the Mayor, we have a hole that we call the swamp-hole. And today noon a hunter came in and told me his dog had been killed down there. But he was drunk; so, I did not credit his story. But he said he saw something like a large vine come out of the hole and strangle the dog. Now do you two men suppose that the same kind of ivy is right here in America? We have a hole there at

Yeastford and something is coming out of it. You said that you never saw the center of this plant, never were able to come near the real roots of it. Here is your chance. Suppose we go up to my town and go down into that hole?"

Milligan took another drink and then started to pull up his pants to the knees, and let down his stockings.

"Look at those legs," he said.

Livid scars encircled his limbs. Ugly ulcers, just healing, were scattered along the scarlet lines. Milligan smiled as he explained, "I fell down one day. Fortunately, Conway was able to stay on his feet, and he had an ax and cut me loose. I was in bed for days. I want to see your little pet vines in that hole in your old home town, Major, but I want to be very careful about how I go near them. What do you think about it, Mr. White? Any connection between Angkor and the English ivy?"

"There may be. The reason for the sudden desertion of those dead cities has been a puzzling one to scientists. Some say it was a change of climate, others diseases, carried by insects. Terrible wars might have been at the bottom. But suppose, just for the sake of argument, that near each large city there was a swamp-hole and out of this hole came some antediluvian form of plant life? Let us further suppose that this plant life was carnivorous. Fear might have then led to the desertion of the cities and violent, unreasonable panic depopulated them.

"Thousands of centuries ago life on this world was bizarre, weird and utterly terrible. Everything grew big. Earthworms twenty feet long and bats with a wing-spread of sixty feet. Ferns grew into trees, two hundred feet high. Animals grew a hundred feet from snout to tail. Then everything changed, and the big things died and gave place to little things and at present man, the King of the Earth, is a little soft thing under six feet tall. But the dreamers have told us their suspicion that in the out-places of the earth, under the ocean or in unexplored caverns, the giants of antiquity lie, silently sleeping, waiting for the time to come when they can once again rule as Lords of the Earth. Perhaps in these centuries of waiting they have developed characteristics that we have not even considered as possibilities. For example. *Can plants think? Can they plan and act according to any plan?* If they can, and I think that I can show you something very much like it in my plant laboratory, then what is to keep some form of plant life from deliberately making war on the human race? I made that statement in the reading-room today and they laughed at me. And I did not know then about Milligan and his legs. I think that we had better go with Major Young to Yeastford and see what he has to show us, and then—I want to go with Milligan back to England—unless things start over here."

Milligan, the iron man, the dauntless explorer of the waste places of the earth, looked at the biologist as though fascinated by his remarks. He had often faced danger, but it seemed as though he dreaded to face this thought. Yet, he forced himself to speak.

"That is what I thought," he said, "when I studied those dead cities. Something drove those people out. It came slowly, not like killing waves of animals or migratory invasions of savage tribes. It came slowly and the people deserted, while they still had time, and left the cities to the vegetable kingdom. Now a few monkeys sport furtively on the temple roofs of Angkor and a few parrots scream in Lubaantum, but they are afraid to venture too close or too near the ground. And the natives are afraid; they say the places are populated with demons, but in reality they will not be honest with you and tell you just what it is that they are afraid of. I feel that this threat from the ground drove those busy millions into an enforced exile, and it was so terrible, so horrible in its menacing frightfulness, that instinctively they decided to forget it, to blot the whole episode from the mental pictures of the history of their race.

"That is what I had in mind. And I could not tell anyone, because I was sure he would laugh at me. Then I saw a starting of it in England, and here in America I meet a man who believes and another man who says that he knows a place where a swamp-hole is just beginning to belch forth its gruesome cargo. Suppose we go to Yeastford and study that hole? Perhaps then we will be able to see what can be done."

"And it will have to be done secretly and fast, because if it attacks our cities as it did in ages past or as it has that little part of England, then our civilization is doomed," cried White.

"Bosh!" cried the Major. "Bosh and fiddle-faddle! Nothing can destroy us. We are too great, too powerful, too highly intellectual."

The Yeastford Real Estate Company had known about the swamp-hole when they bought the large area of land over in South Yeastford. They had been forced to buy the hole in order to secure the rest of the land. They knew when they bought it that they would never be able to sell it. It would never return a dollar of their investment to them; so, they simply charged up that acreage to profit and loss and added a little extra to the price of each building lot they sold.

The town grew around the hole. A national highway passed one side of it, a railroad another side, and two streets the remaining sides. Thus, the hole was surrounded on three sides by cement streets and on the remaining side by the tracks of the D. L. and W. R. R. A busy, happy and prosperous neighborhood of substanial folks lived there and passed the hole daily. They had become so accustomed to its being there that hardly any of them realized its presence.

From the stout fence that surrounded it on all sides the land fell rapidly down to a circular center. The pitch was so steep that it was difficult to descend to the bottom. And there was nothing there when the bottom was reached except a mud hole, ice in winter, dry in summer and a muddy pond after every hard rain. Trees grew on the steep sides, ferns and moss covered the ground, a few pond lilies tried to live in the stagnant water, their only visitors the myriad mosquitoes, their only friends the little frogs who sat shyly on the lily pads.

Birds flirted in the tree tops and gorged themselves in the fall on the wild grapes, while below a few rabbits and squirrels claimed ownership of the nuts that fell from the walnut and hickory-nut trees. Occasionally a dog would dash through the underbrush and in the fall a few hunters tried to kill the rabbits that had the temerity to live so close to civilization. That was the swamp-hole of South Yeastford.

The three men arrived at Yeastford about forty-eight hours after the hunter had lost his dog. They had decided that it would be best to keep the real reason for their triple visit a secret. So the Major simply told his housekeeper that he had two political friends visiting him, and asked an inquisitive reporter to say nothing about the fact that the Mayor was entertaining company. Fortunately, the next day was dismally drizzling, making it possible for the three to reach the hole unobserved, climb over the fence and slide down the steep embankment without anyone's being the wiser.

In a few minutes, aided by the force of gravitation, they reached the mud hole at the bottom. Sure enough, there was the new growth of ivy and on one side was the dead fox-hound. He attracted as much attention as the ivy. The Major poked him with a stick and then gave his verdict.

"Dead as a doornail and dry as a piece of old leather."

"Looks like leather and bones to me," observed White.

"All the blood sucked out of him," whispered Milligan. "See those long white tendrils? They have suckers on them just like those on the arms of an octopus. They just wrapped around the poor cur and sucked him dry. See those branches move! I do not know whether you have noticed it, but since we have been standing here there has been a marked movement over in our direction. I worked on that point with rabbits for a while and the long tendrils seemed to be able to either see or feel or smell flesh. Let me show you. That is why I brought over this pole and the pound of liver. We will tie the liver to the pole and do some experimenting. Suppose we go around on the other side. Those long white arms are too close to me for comfort. There," and he held the liver high in the air over a part of the plant, "we will see how it acts."

They did not have to wait long. The plant slowly lifted its stems into the air and surely, with almost an uncanny, human precision, sent its tentacles towards the piece of liver suspended in the air. As the meat on the end of the pole was moved, the vine moved, following it. And at last, moving with a swiftness that surpassed the agility of the human arms holding the pole, the vine wrapped around the piece of meat and drew it down into the middle of the leaves.

"The leaves themselves," commented White, "are remarkably like the ordinary ivy except that they are white in spots. Were it not for those long tendrils, I would think that it was nothing exceptional. Of course, the fact that it eats meat is not unusual for the vegetable world—lots of plants eat meat."

"As far as I can tell," interrupted Milligan, "this is just the same kind of ivy we saw in England. At least it looks the same to me; the thing that frightened us was the largeness of it and the thought of where it was coming from and what would happen if it did not stop coming. Of course, over there we saw miles and miles of stems, while here there seem to be just a few yards."

"It must have just started here," explained the Major. "Just started. Fortunately, we found it in time. We must think of some way of stopping it—killing it—driving it back into the hole."

The three men made a queer spectacle as they stood there in the mist, talking about a danger that no one else in America realized. They were terribly in earnest, profoundly impressed with the immensity of the problem; and as they talked, the ivy grew towards them; grew towards them, especially Mayor Young, and silently sent a thin tendril up his trouser leg and wrapped around the ankle. He turned to go and fell, tripped by the vine. Other tendrils came toward him. White and Milligan pulled at him, took out their pocket knives and started to hack through the restraining bands. It seemed as though others came faster than they could be destroyed. At last the Major was free and the three men started to run up the hill as fast as they could.

And as fast as they went up the hill the ivy came after them. "Hell!" gasped White, shivering as he turned around for a minute. "It is up with us, and it's not growing. No plant could grow as fast as that! It is coming out of the hole. Hurry! HURRY!!"

He paused on a flat spot, seized a large stone and hurled it down the hill. The rock bounded into the air, was caught in flight by a dozen tendrils, played with in the air and then tossed aside as though inventoried as useless. And a minute later the three men reached the fence, climbed awkwardly over it and stood breathless on the cement walk. Major Young uncovered his legs and looked at them. They were bleeding from fifty small wounds.

Even as he bent over, a hand tapped his shoulder.

"You three men are under arrest for trespass," said the policeman. "Can't you see that there is a *'no hunting'* sign on that tree?"

Major Young stood erect and eyed the man coolly.

"I should think you would know me, Thomas!" he barked.

"Certainly he knows you," interrupted another man, none other than Hiram Jones, President of the Yeastford Real Estate Company. "Certainly he knows you, and so do I. You thought you were clever at that last election. You have tried for years to make a fool out of me, and now I am going to make one out of you. You three men are arrested for trespass. Tell your stories to the Magistrate. Go ahead, Thomas. I will make the necessary charges against them."

"But my dear man," expostulated Milligan, "you don't know—"

"Don't 'dear man' me," shouted Jones. "You talk like an English actor. I'll teach the three of you to hunt on my land!"

"It was the ivy we were after," explained White.

"It's something you ought to know about," added Milligan.

"If you do not believe me, look at my legs," pleaded the Major.

"The three of you are drunk. That is another charge, Thomas. Drunk, disorderly and trespass. Run them in."

That night the three men sat comfortably in the bachelor home of the Major. Their experiences had been decidedly unpleasant. All the political enemies of the Mayor had delighted in his arrest, and while it had resulted in nothing more serious than a fine, which he paid at once for the three of them, still, it was a humiliation which rankled the spirit of the proud ex-soldier. Besides, his legs hurt. There must have been a poison in the tendrils which was infecting the minute wounds. He sullenly bit on the end of the cigar that he was smoking. The other two watched him closely. At last he threw the butt into the ash tray and growled.

"That stuff is growing fast. By morning it will fill the whole damn hole. Perhaps by tomorrow it will start to cross the fence."

"Are we just going to sit here and do nothing?" asked White.

"The people ought to be warned of their danger. When it gets into the road, the little children playing there—you know what might happen to the little children. And after all, Major Young, you are the Mayor of the town. You owe something to your office."

The Mayor of Yeastford looked sharply at the Englishman.

"What do you think I ought to do?" he asked.

"Let's wait till morning," urged White. "Then we can go and see just what the situation is. I guess they won't arrest us for just walking on the street or the sidewalk."

That is what they did; just waited till morning. All during the night the plant came out of the hole and all during the night it climbed up the hill and up on the trees; and it grew, as well as crawled. The morning came, bright and free from the fog of yestermorn. The men, after a leisurely breakfast, walked towards the swamp-hole. Even from a distance they could easily see that there was a change in it. The trees looked larger and greener, and as they neared the hole they saw that it was not a hole any more; there was a large hill of green ivy with a few dead trees sticking their bare branches through the white-and-green leaves, and the whole mass was moving with a sickening undulation that made the three observers shudder.

They were not the only ones watching the hole. Thomas, the policeman, was there, and Hiram Jones and half a dozen others, and as many women, who were holding their children tightly by the hands. One of the women was talking in a shrill tone to Jones, and holding her three-year-old child in her arms.

"It's dangerous!" she screamed. "You own that land, and you ought to do something. I tell you it was dragging my child down there when I heard the scream and ran and pulled her loose. I was peeling potatoes and, luck would have it, I carried the knife with me. You going to let that weed grow there and kill our children?"

"Bosh!" sneered Hiram Jones. "It is just ivy. Started to grow there and the swamp-hole was so rich it grew fast. Just ivy, I am telling you. I am going to make cuttings of it and sell it for ten cents a cutting. Lots of folks will buy a fast-growing vine like that for ten cents. I'll show you what I think of it. Bah! I'll walk through it."

He jumped over the fence and started down the hill. Mayor Young called to him to stop, to come back, but he kept on. That is, he kept on for a little while, and then he turned around and started to scream. It was a shrill, animal cry, and before it was ended the ivy was over him, barring him from the onlookers except for a few undulating movements. Another scream, and then silence.

The ivy started in a hundred places to cross the road. The folks of South Yeastford shrank back from it. Women grabbed their children and ran trembling to their nearby homes, shutting the doors and locking them. Thomas walked over to the Mayor.

"What does it mean, Mayor?" he asked. There was no doubt about the fact that he was bothered. "Should I get some of the boys and go in after him?"

"Better not, Thomas. He is going to stay there and so will anyone else who goes in there."

"But it is just a plant, ain't it?"

"Yes, it is just a plant," the Mayor replied, rather absently. "Just a plant. I think they call it ivy, Thomas. You go around and tell all the women to keep their children indoors. Mr. White and Mr. Milligan, suppose we go back to my home and talk this over. I am sure that we can do no good by standing here and watching that damn thing grow. At the rate it is going it will be across the roads by noon, and then—well—we will either have to stop it or make the people get out of their homes."

In an hour the Courthouse bell called the men of the town to a mass meeting. The bell was used only during Court week or in case of fire. Naturally the men of the town were curious. The Mayor lost no time in telling them the reason back of the meeting. He talked to them right from the shoulder; there was no mincing of words.

"The men of this town had better get axes and knives and hatchets and start fighting," he ended. "Otherwise, the people in South Yeastford will be driven from their homes in a few days. And they had better leave if the ivy comes near them. I am going to leave this in the hands of the Councilmen, and I and my guests are going to see the Governor."

Of course, there was endless talk. Everyone knew that the Mayor had been fined the day before for disorderly conduct. Perhaps he was still drunk. Still, most of the men who attended the meeting left it to walk over to South Yeastford. What they saw there was not especially assuring. The ivy was now over the road and starting to grow over the lawns on the other side. An automobile had been driven over that street, but it had been caught by the ivy, and the man driving it had barely escaped with his life. It did not take the curious spectators long to realize that they had to start in and get busy. They did so, but without discipline or order, each man for himself and in any way and place that he wanted to. They worked all the rest of that day, and then, rather satisfied with clearing the street, they went to their homes for the night.

The next morning the ivy had recrossed the street and was curling around some of the houses. By that time the State Constabulary, under orders from the Governor, arrived and took charge of the work. It was rumored that several regiments of State Militia had been ordered out. Eager newspaper reporters began to interrogate the town people. Thomas, the policeman, was in his glory. He was especially clever in describing how Hiram Jones had yelled as the ivy dragged him under.

It is an interesting fact that the Governor gave one hundred percent credit to the story told him by the three visitors from Yeastford. Major Young, White and Milligan had been able to show him that a very real danger existed in his state of Pennsylvania. He promised the Mayor all the help that the state machinery could afford. He even offered to come to Yeastford himself, as soon as he could do so. After the conference, he gave a long interview to the newspapers, in which he spoke much about himself and little about his three visitors. One would judge, from reading the article, that the Governor had been the first one to discover the ivy and to recognize its danger.

On the fifth day two regiments of National Guards and over a thousand citizens were actively fighting the growing ivy. The men were working in relays. The work was being performed in an orderly and systematic manner. With the greatest difficulty, the roads were kept clear and the ivy was confined to the swamp-hole.

The fight to keep the ivy inside the fence was apparently a fairly easy one. Every night the ivy grew, and every day the branches that went over the fence were cut off. Of course, it took till nearly dark to finish the day's work, but when darkness came the road and sidewalks were cleared of the vegetating threat. There were some casualties, but the offensive powers of the plant seemed to be considerably diminished by the multiple traumatisms that it was suffering. It looked like an easy victory. Even Milligan, with his superior knowledge, was hopeful of success. On the second day White had returned to New York for further study of the plant in his laboratory. He did not return till the sixth day of the fight.

On the train from New York he thought over the situation. As the train neared the Water Gap he went out on the rear platform. The Gap was passed and then the pulp-mill and the track began to parallel Broadhead's Creek. There, above the power dam, he saw something that made him turn white. He was still swearing when he jumped off the train at East Yeast-ford. Milligan, who had received the wire announcing his return, was astonished to see the usually placid biologist so upset.

"Milligan, what have those fools been doing?"

"What do you mean?"

"They have been cutting off that ivy. What did they do with the pieces?"

"They must have carted them away. I know. They took them in carts and dumped them into the creek. Some they took up on Fox Hill."

"They were fools and so were we. They should have been warned. Fire! That was what was needed! Fire! Perhaps it is too late now. Every piece that had an aerial rootlet and had a chance has started to grow. Broadhead's Creek is full of it. It is starting to run up into the mountains around the Gap. Unless we act at once we are lost."

"But I do not understand," cried Milligan. "I thought it all came from a central plant of some kind, a variety of plant animal that lived in the hole. Don't the pieces die when cut off, as my fingers would if they were amputated?"

"No! That is going to be the trouble of it for this country. I have been working with it. Even the smallest piece, if it can obtain water, will start growing and make a new 'animal.' I wish I could escape from the word 'animal,' but I cannot. The 'thing' seems to have everything that we have in the way of vital systems, and I think that it has some kind of a mind. It can think. All that it has lacked so far is mobility. It seems to be attached to a central root and it just moves forward and grows as it moves, but the main body stays in the hole. That was the impression I obtained from what you told me, Milligan, and even in England, where no one fought it, it took a long time for it to cover just a small area. Here it is a different story. We have been helping it. We threw hundreds of pieces into water and that water carried it down for miles. Perhaps some branches are drifting to Philadelphia at this minute. I am sure the whole Gap area is infested."

After that, fire was added to the weapons used. It seemed to work for a while, at least around South Yeastford. But in the woods of the Water Gap it was a different story. There the forests were filled with small sum-mer cottages and large hotels. There was a great investment. Fire in the woods meant burning buildings. The hotel owners started legal proceedings. There were injunctions and counter-injunctions. It all meant delay.

Even at that time America was not air-minded. Had she been, the use of bombing airplanes would have been thought of at once. As it was, over two weeks passed before it occurred to anyone to try the extermination of the central plant-animal by bombing from the air.

Once thought of, everyone wondered why it had not been used the first day. Ton after ton of T.N.T. were dropped into the swamp-hole. The town of Yeastford was shaken by the explosions. Windows were shattered.

When the attack ended, the hole was just a mass of pulverized rock and shattered trees. There was nothing green left. The victory was so easy that the authorities wondered at their fright of the past weeks.

Yeastford seemed safe. If the Water Gap was in trouble, it was their own fault. The Governor of the State turned the matter over to a special committee and started to build his fences for the next election. Up on the barren mountains of the Gap the ivy seemed to lose its terror. People simply learned to stay away from it.

Meanwhile it was growing in the Delaware River. In this period of the war the attacking animal showed its diabolic cleverness. Of course, it was a thousand separate animals under the river, but each one, originating from the same parent stem, seemed to partake of the original central nervous system, and one of the remarkable points in the entire Ivy War— for so it was to be termed in the histories of the future—was the ability of all the plants to work in perfect synchronized harmony with each other.

The plants grew down the river. Biologists later on stated that the original home was in deep subterranean lakes, where it lived the life of an aquatic animal. It certainly showed its ability to live under the waters of the Delaware. It gave no evidence of its existence. Not a leaf appeared above the surface of the water. It simply stretched its long branches southward along the bed of the river, and as those branches grew into long submarine cables, they grew thicker until many of them were over a foot in diameter and looked like large water snakes, as their whitish brown sides appeared through the boiling waters of the occasional rapids.

The branches grew down the river till Philadelphia was reached. Once more the combined intelligence of the plant-animal showed itself in not making an immediate attack. With flame, dynamite and ax, regiments of men were fighting the menace on the slopes of the mountains around the Delaware Water Gap. But no one thought of searching the Delaware River between Philadelphia and Camden; and had anyone thought of it, it would have been difficult, almost impossible, to exterminate a mass of tangled roots stretching for miles along the river front and thirty feet deep in the channel mud. Meantime the stranger was growing, gathering strength, preparing for the conquest of the city.

In spite of the many conjectures and surmises, no one ever determined positively whether the ivy had a language or some method of communicating with its various parts. One thing is certain, and that is the fact that during the whole war it showed the intelligence of a thinking unit of life. For example, instead of concentrating its forces on a small town, it deliberately passed Portland, Easton, Trenton, and waited till it reached one of the great cities of the East, Philadelphia. Once there, it did not send a single attacking branch to the east side of the river, to Camden, but put all its energy into the conquest of the larger city.

The time that it selected for the attack was opportune. It was a night in early spring, cold and damp with fog. No one was on the street, save from necessity. The street lights gloomed like sullen stars overhead. The wet streets and the moist air served as a blanket to deaden every sound. Then, at midnight, when every watchman was hunting the warmth and dryness of shelter, the plant sprang forward to the attack. One plant, perhaps, but with a thousand parts; one animal, it might easily be, but with a thousand arms; one intellect, but with a thousand deadly attributes.

Up Market, Walnut, Arch and many streets running west from the river the plant advanced to the attack. It was silent in its growth, murderous in its desires. Watchman after watchman died with the horrid coil around his neck, giving, through a hundred puncture wounds, his life fluid to feed the plant and passing out of consciousness without the least idea of what was killing him. Into the cellars, the bootleggers' joints, the cheap boarding and rooming houses, the laterals spread and collected therein their harvest of death.

And as the "animal" tasted more and more blood it worked faster, gathering its harvest of death. It worked faster and even more silently. The city east of Broad Street was surrendering to the enemy without even knowing that there had been a battle waged. Aerial rootlets fastened to the stone buildings, and up these buildings the terminals grew, searching for their prey through every open window, every unlocked door.

Morning came, a lovely spring morning. Before the kisses of the sunbeams the mist melted in gentle resignation. The city awoke, feeling that it was good to be alive, and not till then, when the first living people started to invade the district east of Broad Street, did the city and the nation realize what had happened during the silent watches of the night.

Those in that portion of the city who had escaped death during the dark hours gayly walked out into the street without the least intimation that anything was wrong, and once there, died quickly. And whether they died quietly or with screams made no difference to the "animal" that closed around them and sucked out their fluids.

Even in the daylight it took the forces of Philadelphia some time to realize what had happened and was happening to them. It was not till nine in the morning that the scientists suddenly appreciated the fact that the ivy of Yeastford, the plant that was still being fought on the mountains of the Water Gap had in some peculiar way reached Philadelphia and was taking the city by storm.

It was something greater than the business of a city or the affairs of a state. This was something that menaced the life of the nation. If an unsuccessful fight were made against the plant in Philadelphia, what was to hinder it from atacking other cities? Wilmington? Baltimore? And even Washington?

The defense was slow in starting because it could see, at first, nothing but the advanced portion of the enemy. It was plain to be seen that Market, Chestnut, Arch and Walnut Streets were slowly filling with a mass of green leaves, but it was not until daring aviators had made an aerial survey of the situation that the defenders realized the important fact that the attack had been inaugurated from the river. Later on, when ship after ship had been surrounded, pulled down into the river mud and every one of the crew killed, the real significance of this became apparent.

The ivy grew upward as well as onward. Front Street, within twenty-four hours, was a mass of green embowered houses, and some of the older ones were already beginning to be pulled to pieces.

The Governor of the State heard the news and he recalled the three men from Yeastford. He lost no time in trying to get in touch with them over the long-distance telephone. Here more time was lost. The Mayor had gone to New York for a rest. White was working in his laboratory trying to find some method of fighting the ivy. Milligan had strangely disappeared. Unable to locate any of the three, the Governor was momentarily at a loss as to what to do next. In despair he sent the entire National Guard of the State to Philadelphia, under the command of the Adjutant General of the State, while he went to State College to talk matters over with the Dean of the Agricultural Department. To his surprise he found that gentleman had left for New York. Not till later did he realize that the Dean had gone to White for help as soon as he had heard of the trouble, realizing that White, of all men, was the one most likely to be of real assistance.

The first day and the next the same tactics were employed in fighting the ivy; that is, that had been used in South Yeastford. The effort was made to keep it east of Broad Street. The terminal branches were cut off as they tried to cross the deadline. As company after company of the guards detrained they were marched to the fighting line and put on sentry duty. No one was allowed to even try to enter the doomed area. Death, by this time omnipresent, kept anyone from leaving. As though satisfied with its day's work the ivy stopped going westward, and seemed satisfied to solidify its position in the east of the city.

It had captured the subways, putting an end to all travel there. The defense had an idea that it was working silently through the sewers of the city, but the danger was so new, the problem so intense that no one had the courage to speak openly about what *might be going on under the city*. The end of the second day came, with Broad Street clear and a strange battle going on between the military and financial forces of the city. The air forces were anxious to drop depth-bombs into the Delaware River, to try and blow the enemy to bits at its headquarters. They wanted to throw T.N.T. into the great green masses on Market and Arch Streets. They were anxious to start a war to the death. And the money interests, the financiers who had their millions invested in real estate and stores of precious goods east of Broad Street protested. They appealed to the Governor, they cried to the President, they even sent messages to the All Wise demanding less harsh measures.

Meantime, the ivy rested. At least, it seemed to rest.

What it really did was to send a hundred roots up the Schuylkill River and on the third night invade the city from the west. The dawn broke with every bridge, every railroad track covered with ivy and evidences of having been rather rapidly pulled to pieces. The Pennsylvania, the B. and O., the Reading were all forced to suspend operation. The city could no longer be fed.

Conferences began. Interviews were given. Great personalities ventured asinine opinions. Every Tom, Dick and Harry, who was able to do so, rushed into print. There were a thousand remedies offered, none of which could be of any possible use. The Red Cross, the Regular Army, the Grand Old Party and the Amalgamated Labor Unions each started in to do their bit. But everybody was working in a different way to accomplish the same thing, and no one was quite sure of just what he really wanted to do.

Meantime the plant was growing, the "animal" was becoming more powerful. It was gradually gathering in its forces on every side of the city. The citizens started to leave; there was little suffering, and after the first day, there were practically no deaths, but the President's advisers realized that a panic would start just as soon as the city dwellers knew the possibility of their being entirely surrounded. So, they silently encouraged the depopulation of the city.

At last the national danger was so plainly seen, that orders were given to bomb the rivers and the city east of Broad Street. That order would have been carried out had not White arrived in Philadelphia and asked for a delay. He made a peculiar figure before the important personages gathered at Army Headquarters in City Hall. He was rather cheaply dressed, was without a hat and carried a Boston bag in one hand, a gallon demijohn in the other. It took a good deal of introducing to make the Generals realize that the man before them was the leading expert in plant physiology in the Western Hemisphere.

"Ever since this ivy war started in the swamp-hole in South Yeastford," he began, "I have been trying to devise some scientific method of fighting it. I have felt the uselessness, the utter hopelessness of making a frontal attack on it in force. We were able in Monroe County to cut it to pieces, but each little piece simply started in to make a new plant with all the devilish brains of the mother 'animal.'

"I started to study this peculiar form of ivy. I found that it had a nervous system and through this nervous system it was able to communicate with its various parts. But, most important of all, was the discovery that it had a circulation that was rather like that of the fetal cardiovascular system. It actually pumps fluid from one end of its body to the other.

"Before I arrived at this conclusion, the scientists who studied plants were at a loss to explain the movement of sap in the larger forms of vegetative life. Atmospheric pressure would only raise the sap thirty-four feet, the height of the water barometer. Osmotic pressure might play a part, but it is so slow that in the giant *Eucalyptus Amygdalina* it would take a year of osmotic pressure to take sap to the top, four hundred and fifty feet above the ground. Nothing explained this movement of sap till I found in this ivy a propulsive tissue very much like the heart muscle.

"Once I found that, I realized that the ivy had a circulation in two directions. Much of the time I have been wondering whether I was working with an animal or with a plant, but that does not make any difference, because I have found the thing to kill it with."

"Well, what is it?" yelled an irritated General.

"Simply this," and White held up the gallon demijohn. "This is the stuff that will do the work. But I ought to tell you that I think this ivy is more of an animal than it is a plant. At least its sap has cells in it, different from our red corpuscles, yet, at the same time, a little like them. When I found that out I started to make a haemolytic toxin, something that would have the same effect on the sap of the ivy that poison of the cobra serpent has on the blood of man. It was not very easy, but I found it, and for the last three days Milligan and I have been over in Wolf Hollow north of the Gap, experimenting with it. And I tell you one thing: it kills the ivy and it kills it quickly. Inject it into this blood stream at the terminal end of the animal and it travels back through the animal-plant like fire and literally kills as it travels.

"You give me a company of soldiers to help me and Milligan and I will liberate this city in a few days, and then I am going to advise the President to start a war of extermination against every ivy in this country, no matter how harmless and innocent it may seem."

One of the Generals turned to another.

"Is it worth trying?" he asked.

"I think so," was the reply. "We will wait twenty-four hours and at the end of that time if there are no results, we will start the bombing planes."

Half an hour later a peculiar event was taking place at Broad and Market Streets, on the northwest corner of Wanamaker's store. A company of soldiers had isolated a branch of the ivy, had cut off all the tendrils and had pulled it out till it lay like a writhing snake, its end almost touching City Hall. It twisted and pulled and squirmed and almost got away from the hundred men holding it fast. Sitting on it was White, with Milligan helping him fill a 25 c.c. glass septic hypodermic syringe. At last it was filled and the three-inch hollow needle was plunged into the bark of the ivy, the toxin being slowly injected into the circulatory vessels. Instantly the leafless branch dropped to the pavement. Back of its attachment to the store the green leaves were turning brown, the waving tendrils, seeking in everlasting motion their human food, dropped uncoiled and lifeless. A thick swath of green ceased moving and hung dead on the side of the great emporium.

Walking a hundred feet across Market, White picked out another branch for attack. The same procedure brought the same results. Ten doses were given and then twenty. The aviators reported that long streaks of brown were appearing among the green and that these streaks were going back to the river. White asked for a few physiologists, whom he could train to give the injections. The men whom he wanted appeared as though by magic. Milligan directed the work while White went back to New York for a larger supply of the haemolytic poison.

Now that a means of defense was assured and a definite program arrived at, everybody worked in harmony. System grew out of chaos. Hope took the place of gloom. The nation, interested at last, financed the rest of the war. White was made a General, Milligan was decorated, and Major Young, promoted to a Colonelcy, was placed in charge of the Monroe County portion of the battle.

The war ended with the same rapidity with which it had begun. From the first the living organisms must have realized the hopelessness of the struggle, because they made a definite and orderly retreat. Tearing off their branches, they withdrew to their place of security in the rivers, and even there, realizing that they would be hunted for with grappling hooks, fled hastily to the ocean.

The nation, aroused to the peril, conducted a systematic campaign of extermination. The Delaware River, from the Gap to the Capes, was thoroughly dredged, and whenever a branch was found it was given its dose of death-dealing fluid. And not till the army of science was satisfied that there was no more enemy, did the conflict stop.

Colonel Young went back to Yeastford. He had no trouble in being elected Mayor for the seventh term. The morning after election he was in his office receiving the congratulations of his friends. In walked William Coonel, as usual, slightly spiflicated. The Colonel recalled the previous visit of the inebriated worthy.

"Well, Bill," he said kindly. "Sit down and have a cigar. It was a great war while it lasted, but we won out at last, and the ivy is no more."

"Yes, I guess the war is over, Colonel," replied the hunter, "but, after all, the fact that we won ain't going to bring me back my rabbit hound. He was a great dog, Colonel, too good a dog to be eat up by a good-for-nothing plant."

RALPH MILNE FARLEY

LIQUID LIFE

MILLIONAIRE METCALF drew his Inverness cape more tightly about his tall spare frame, and shivered slightly, although it was a warm June day.

"That's Salt Pond, Dee!" he announced, with a wave of his hand.

His companion, a broad-shouldered blond young man, stared with interest at the little body of water, flanked by pine-clad slopes.

Its dark and turbid surface seemed to absorb, rather than cast back, the reflection of the fleecy clouds floating lazily overhead. The water heaved and rolled slightly, though there was no perceptible breeze. Dee remembered having once seen just this sort of sluggish undulant motion in a maggoty cistern full of liquid swill. He too, shivered.

A grim smile spread across the lean face of his millionaire patron.

"So you feel it too, eh?" asked Metcalf. "Well, you haven't yet seen the half of it. Not a lily pad nor a reed, you will note. The fish are all gone. There are not even any bugs on the surface." Then as Dee approached the water's edge, "Careful there! Don't let any of the spray get on you— it burns like an acid."

Dee knelt on the beach, and gingerly filled several glass-stoppered bottles with water from the pond. Then he and Metcalf walked slowly and thoughtfully down the road, until they came to a pasture at the end of the pond.

"Here is the latest victim," Metcalf announced. "It has not been disturbed."

Lying on the grass, about fifty feet from the water, was a dead, half eaten cow. Dee stooped down to examine it.

"See how the legs and tail taper off to a point at their upper ends, as though they had been dipped in acid," he said. "I pulled a half dead frog out of a snake's mouth once, and the whole rear end of the poor frog had been dissolved to a point, just like that. You don't suppose—"

"No," Metcalf replied. "There is nothing in that pond large enough to eat a cow. I have had it dredged with dragnets from end to end. The nets were eaten away, and several of the men got badly burned by drops of water, but not a thing did they bring to the surface."

"Well," Dee said, "I've seen enough to start on. Let's get me back to Boston, so that I can analyze these samples."

Dee entered the laboratory of John Dee Service, Inc., and placed his glass-stoppered bottles on the long central table, strewn with chemical paraphernalia.

Along the right-hand wall ran a table containing a radio set, and some partially dissected cats. A white-coated young man, dark and with a pointed black mustache, laid down the scalpel with which he had been working on one of the cats, and strolled over to the central table.

Along the left-hand wall ran a table, littered like the central one with beakers, test tubes, and such. Here a stocky, bearded young man in a gray smock was working. He too got up and joined the group about the new arrival.

"Well, fellows," Dee announced, "old man Metcalf has given us a chance to repay him for the money he advanced to us."

"I hope," the tall cat-dissecter stated seriously, "that the assignment is something which will be of some real use to the world."

"Bah!" spat the stocky bullet-headed one. "You two fellows make me tired. All that Jack thinks about is playing square with an old friend. All that Ivan thinks about is the welfare of the so-called human race. Me, I'm practical. I hope that this job will get the load of debt off our heads. Go on and tell us about it, Jack."

Dee rapidly sketched the lethal effect of the waters of Salt Pond, and the strange fate of the partially devoured cows. "It looks to me altogether too pat," he insisted. "The acid effect of the water, for the chemist Jack Dee to investigate; its lethal effect, for the biochemist Hans Schmidt; and the cow-eating entity, for the biologist Ivan Zenoff. Just a kindly invention of Metcalf's, so as to free us of our debt, without insulting us by merely cancelling it."

"Salt Pond?" asked Zenoff interestedly. "Is it really salt, Jack? Way up in the White Mountains?"

"Yes, Ivan," Dee replied. "Almost like sea water. Metcalf transplanted a lot of flounders, eels, crabs, and mussels there, about ten years ago; and they all did very nicely until this year."

"Salt water, eh?" Zenoff said thoughtfully. "The elixir of life. Life originated in the sea, and when it had evolved enough so that it could crawl out onto dry land, it carried the sea with it in its blood-stream. Every living cell of our bodies is lapped by the waves of the sea, or it could not survive."

"But from what you say, Jack," Schmidt interposed, "I don't believe that you will find that it analyzes like ordinary sea water now. Your description of the remains of the dead cows sounds to me as though they had been dissolved in some very powerful, burning acid."

"We'll soon see." Dee pulled a laboratory smock over his head. "Ivan, you get back to your cats' brains; and Hans, you get back to your filterable virus. Let me tackle this. This seems to be a question in *in*organic chemistry."

He sat down at his work bench, poured some of one of his samples of pond water into a test tube, and set to work. His two partners returned to their own benches. For about an hour there was silence in the laboratory.

Then suddenly Dee cried out in pain. "Burned myself!" he shouted, and looked frantically around for an antidote.

Hans Schmidt rushed over and poured something from a small brown bottle onto Dee's hand.

"Dilute carbolic," he announced, in response to a questioning look.

"What! An acid to counteract an acid? How absurd!" Dee declared.

"Well, it worked!"

"But what on earth made you think of using carbolic, Hans?"

"I merely acted instinctively," Schmidt rather sheepishly replied. "When anything goes wrong, a bacteriologist instinctively reaches for his carbolic acid. That's all."

Ivan Zenoff joined them.

"Let me see the hand. Um! Pretty badly burned. I'll dress it for you." He returned to his own bench, got some gauze bandage and salve, and neatly wrapped up the injured member.

"How far had you got, Jack?" Schmidt inquired.

"Nowhere," Dee admitted. "It is nothing but sea water, with—well— perhaps a slight excess of organic residue. But no acid; nothing to account for its burning effect."

"How does it react to litmus?"

"Why, I never tried. Took it for granted that it was acid." He dipped a small piece of lavender paper in the sample. If anything, it turned even bluer. "Hm! Certainly not acid. Perhaps it's some caustic alkali, and that's why the carbolic acid neutralized it."

"Too quick-acting for a caustic alkali, if you'd ask me," Schmidt commented. "Give me a sample with which to experiment. I have an idea."

For several days Dee and Schmidt worked on their analyses, while Zenoff busied himself with his cats.

Finally Dee admitted himself licked.

"It's nothing but sea water," he maintained.

"So?" asked Schmidt, his pale blue eyes twinkling. "Chemically, perhaps yes. But *bio*-chemically, no."

"What do you mean?"

"I mean that Salt Pond is infected with some new sort of very deadly filterable virus."

"And just what is a filterable virus?"

"Up until recently it was supposed that a filterable virus was merely a culture of germs so minute that even the finest porcelain filter could not remove them from the liquid. But early in nineteen-thirty-six it was discovered that the reason why these germs wouldn't filter out was that there were no germs there. The liquid itself was alive—a sort of living colloidal crystalline solution."

"Living?" exclaimed Zenoff, looking up from his dissection. "How can a liquid live?"

"What *is* life?" Schmidt countered. "Life is the ability to grow, to assimilate food, and to reproduce. Filterable viruses do all of that. A filterable virus is a living liquid."

"And you think that Salt Pond is infected with such a virus?" Dee asked.

"Yes. In fact, I've been able to grow some of the Salt Pond virus in a culture. That would account for the fact that a germicide saved your hand the other day."

"Say, look here," interposed Zenoff, getting up from his dissected cats, and joining them. "Here's a chance to try my experiment on a new form of life."

"You mean your proof that anesthesia does not dull the brain?" asked Dee.

"Exactly! By sinking two electrical contacts in the auditory center of the brain of an anesthetized cat, and by amplifying their impulse by means of radio tubes, I have reproduced in the loud speaker whatever sounds enter the cat's ear. Unconsciousness doesn't affect the brain at all—it merely disconnects the mind. The cat's physical body keeps right on thinking, but she doesn't know it!"

"Well?" Dee encouraged.

"Well, it occurred to me that perhaps the living tissues of the brain merely served as a sort of aerial to pick up the sounds; and so I tried every other sort of living tissue I could obtain. But no go. My apparatus can pick up a sound only from the auditory center of a living brain. Now I shall make one final try with the—"

A crash on the table beside them caused the three young men to look hastily around. One of Ivan Zenoff's cats, not yet operated upon, had jumped onto the bench, had knocked over one of the bottles of Salt Pond water, and was now busily engaged in lapping it up, evidently relishing its saline taste.

"Why, the poor beast! She'll be horribly burned!" cried Dee. "Quick, Hans, the antiseptic!"

But too late! For with a shriek of pain the cat began turning somersaults on the bench.

To save his apparatus from destruction, Dee cuffed the cat into the sink, where it twitched convulsively for a moment, and then lay still.

"Quick-working poison!" Zenoff dryly observed, twirling his mustaches. "Now, as I was saying when I was interrupted, I'm going to take my apparatus, and see if a filterable virus can pick up sounds. If not, and as I have already tried about everything else, then we are pretty safe in assuming that my phenomenon is one of brain activity."

"Look!" exclaimed Dee, pointing to the dead cat lying in the sink. For the cat's belly had opened up, and a slimy colorless liquid was oozing out.

Hastily he placed a glass stopper in the drain hole of the sink. Then, as the three men stood and watched, the cat slowly dissolved, until presently the sink was filled with nothing but a sluggish opalescent liquid, the surface of which throbbed and heaved.

"Liquid life!" Dee exclaimed. "This explains the dead cows."

"But," Schmidt objected, "the cow's head and legs and tail remained!"

"And so would the cat's have done," said Zenoff, "if the liquid had run down the drain. When it oozed out of the cow's belly, it undoubtedly sank into the ground, before it had time to dissolve any more than the upper ends of the legs and tail."

"Let's dish this out," Dee suggested.

Schmidt brought over a two-gallon cylindrical glass jar and very carefully bailed up all the liquid with a granite-ware dipper.

"Now for my experiment," Zenoff announced, carrying the jar, with its slimy heaving contents, over to his own bench, and setting it down beside his radio. Switching on the current, he picked up a slender black rubber rod with two sharp metal points at its end connected to the radio set by two wires, and carefully dipped the contacts into the liquid.

"Hello there!" he shouted. But no sound came out of the loud-speaker.

"Well," said Hans Schmidt, shrugging his shoulders, "I guess this is the last proof necessary—"

"Hello there!" boomed the loud-speaker.

Zenoff jumped, and nearly dropped his contact points into the seething liquid.

"Well," remarked the loud-speaker, with exactly Schmidt's accent, "I guess this is the last proof necessary."

"Delayed rebroadcasting!" Zenoff exclaimed, his dark eyes flashing. "Say! This *is* something! A new phenomenon!"

"Let's dish this out," spoke the loud-speaker, this time in Dee's tones.

Dee's jaw dropped.

"Why, it repeats things in a different order than we said them!" he exclaimed.

"Fellows," Zenoff solemnly announced, "this isn't mere repeating! It's something more!"

"Huh! Perhaps the cat's brain is still active," scornfully sniffed Hans Schmidt.

For about an hour the three friends sat around the dissolved dead cat, discussing what had happened, and advancing theory after theory, only to discard each one of them in turn.

Finally Zenoff reinserted his contacts in the jar, and announced, "Well, fellows, I believe that this liquid, whether on account of the cat part of it, or the filterable virus part of it, has some sort of low order intelligence. Now I'm going to holler something at it again."

"Fellows," interrupted the loud-speaker, "it is *you* who have the low order of intelligence. You—not I."

"Now the thing is improvising!" Zenoff exclaimed jubilantly.

But, although he held the electrical contacts in place, and talked and shouted, and finally read aloud from a book for several hours, not another sound came out of the loud-speaker.

The next morning, however, when he repeated the experiment, he got an immediate response.

"Read to me some more," boomed the loud-speaker. "Your thesis on the souls of cats was very interesting. Read me something about filterable viruses."

"Hey, Hans, do you hear that?" Zenoff shouted across the laboratory. "Bring us your thesis. This tub of suds wants to hear your thesis now."

"Don't call *me* a tub of suds!" sternly admonished the loud-speaker.

Schmidt and Dee both hastened over to Zenoff's bench.

"Well, of all the cockeyed performances!" Dee exclaimed. "Here are we, three supposedly sane individuals, carrying on a serious conversation with a radio set hooked up to a dead cat dissolved in some extremely caustic salt water!"

"The cat has nothing whatever to do with the matter," the loud-speaker interpolated. "I merely ate the cat. Do you imagine, Jack, that that apple which you were just eating when you entered the laboratory, is what is talking to me through you?"

"Now, I know that this is a frame-up," said Dee, and there was sadness in his tones. "Ivan, you're playing a trick on us."

"Indeed I'm not!" Zenoff indignantly exclaimed.

"Indeed he's not!" echoed the loud-speaker.

"No," Zenoff continued seriously. "You can search the room for concealed wires, if you wish, but you will find nothing."

"Then we are all crazy!" cried Dee, sitting down heavily in a chair.

"No," said Zenoff. "We've stumbled onto something big! Those savants who evolved the theory that a filterable virus is liquid fire, merely discovered a new order of being. We have discovered a new type of mind!"

"Or perhaps a mere mechanical thinking machine," Schmidt suggested.

"You, and your mechanistic philosophy," sneered Zenoff.

"Read me that thesis about filterable viruses!" boomed the loud-speaker imperatively.

"Yes, sir," Zenoff meekly replied, picking up the bound manuscript.

"That's better," said the loud-speaker, in a satisfied tone.

The rest of the day was spent by the three partners taking turns reading to the jar of colorless liquid.

When at five o'clock Zenoff reached out to remove the electrical contacts, the loud speaker peremptorily commanded, "Stop! Don't cut me off! Keep on reading!"

"But we have to rest," Zenoff politely explained.

" 'Rest'? What is 'rest'?" the thing asked, and was not satisfied until Zenoff produced and read to it the *Encyclopædia Britannica* article on "Sleep," and several of the cross references. Then Zenoff was permitted to remove the contacts, and the three friends went home.

In the days that followed, they read aloud book after book, and thesis after thesis to the insatiable liquid in the glass jar. They even read it the daily papers, and were astounded at the intelligent interest which it soon developed about current events.

But daily the liquid became more and more irritable and rude in its attitude toward them; until finally Zenoff, exasperated, threatened to remove the contacts.

"Am I irritable?" asked the loud-speaker conciliatingly. "I am sorry. Let me think a moment." A long pause; then, "I believe that my trouble is due to insufficient saline content. Please add a little more salt to me."

Schmidt brought the salt, and put in a pinch at a time, stirring the liquid with a glass rod, until the liquid announced, "Okay. I feel fine now. Go on with the reading."

Dee sighed. "I believe we've got ourselves an 'old man of the sea,' " he said. Then, of course, had to explain that allusion to the liquid.

When he had finished the explanation, the liquid spoke. "Not at all. You know, I believe that by putting my superior mind to work on your problems, I can help you solve them. All that I ask in return is food, salt, and water."

"What are you, anyway?" Zenoff blurted out. The three had never put this question to the thing—had never even discussed it in its presence.

"I've been thinking about that myself," came haltingly from the loud-speaker. "I am somewhat like the filterable viruses, of which you have read to me, and yet I am different. I am liquid life. I was once a part of the life of Salt Pond. How long that life persisted there, I cannot say; because back in those days we knew nothing of what you human beings call 'time.' I have enjoyed learning how the world seems to you. We, the virus of the pond, never knew anything except pure thought, until you brought me here."

"Hold on!" Dee interrupted. "You speak of 'I,' 'we,' 'the virus in the pond,' 'the rest of me'; it's quite confusing. Just what is your relationship to the virus that is left in the pond?"

"Your mere human mentality," the virus patronizingly replied, "is not able to grasp the significance of that relationship. I am a distinct individual.

"Yet, if you were to divide me into two jars, each would be I, and the other would be someone else. If you were to feed me, let me grow, subdivide me, until there were enough of us to overwhelm the earth, nevertheless we, they, I, whatever you choose to call it, would all still be me, capable of recombining and redividing indefinitely. The human language has no personal pronouns applicable to a filterable virus."

That night, on their way home from the laboratory, Zenoff remarked to the others, "You know, that crack of the virus' about overwhelming the earth, threw rather a chill into me. We must be careful not to feed him, it, them, too much."

The next morning, when Schmidt was salting the virus, his hand slipped and dumped in about half a cupful of salt. Instantly the liquid in the jar commenced to boil. Tongues of foam, like the tentacles of a small octopus, leaped from its surface, only to fall back again. And from the loud-speaker there came a harsh croaking, "Gimme more salt! Hooray! Feed me! Feed me more dead cats! I want to grow—and divide—and grow and divide. Conquer the earth. Eat everything—everybody!"

Zenoff leaped to the radio set and snapped it off.

"My God!" he exclaimed. "The thing's drunk!"

Dee got up thoughtfully from his own bench, and squared his broad shoulders. "We've a problem on our hands," he asserted. "It'll be weeks and weeks before the effect of that salt wears off."

"And," Schmidt added, "if we try to precipitate it out with silver nitrate, so as to get a silver chloride precipitate, the residual sodium nitrate, being mildly germicidal, may kill the poor thing."

"All that I can suggest is to dilute it," said Dee. He did some figuring on a piece of paper. "About ten gallons of water should do the trick."

They dumped the drunken liquid into a large tub, and added water until its pulsating boiling subsided.

"And now what?" asked Zenoff. "We have too much of it now."

"Pour most of it down the sink," Schmidt suggested. "The small remaining part would still have the mentality of the whole, according to its own theories of individuality."

"And," Dee grimly added, "the large quantity that went down the drain would eventually reach the ocean, and would feed and multiply there until it destroyed all marine life, and made the sea as burningly dangerous as Salt Pond now is. No!"

"My God!" Zenoff exclaimed. "That is what would happen, too, if Salt Pond ever got loose!"

"We've got to kill all but the small part which we save," Schmidt asserted callously.

"It would be like killing an old friend," Dee objected.

"But any part is equal to the whole," said Zenoff. "Come on!"

They dished back into the glass jar just the quantity which they had had before the unfortunate overdose of salt; and poured carbolic acid into what was left in the tub.

Then they inserted the electrodes in the jar, and listened.

"Food! Give me food!" came a faint voice from the loud-speaker.

"He's still alive!" Dee joyously exclaimed.

"And sober," Zenoff added, tossing in a piece of dead cat.

The voice came louder now.

"Thank you, my friends. There seems to be a gap in my memory. Tell me what happened."

They told him. They explained the analogy of human drunkenness. But they omitted all mention of the killing of the virus which had remained in the big tub.

"What became of the rest of me, of my brothers or my children? Oh, your language is so inexpressive!" the virus complained.

"We—poured it down the sink," Dee lied.

The liquid in the jar foamed fiercely for a moment. "You had no right to do that!" stormed its voice out of the radio set. "I—it—the rest of me— is dead now. Too much dilution with fresh water will kill us. I am dead now."

The three men exchanged significant glances, but said nothing.

Finally the virus calmed down.

"You individuals cannot appreciate my loss. Although there is as much of me as there was originally, yet most of me is now dead and gone. It's too late to remedy that now, but don't let it happen again!"

Millionaire Metcalf's increasing insistency on a report on the mystery of Salt Pond presented a problem. The three young scientists did not dare tell their patron that a virus was responsible for the trouble, for he would have insisted on killing it off; and that would have infuriated the portion of the virus in the jar in their laboratory. To explain to Mr. Metcalf that their pet virus was an intelligent talking being would either secure them commitment to Danvers, if not believed; or, if believed, would start a veritable gold rush to get samples of the pond water. Jars of talking water would become a nationwide fad and a corresponding menace.

Doubtless the virus itself would have been able to solve this problem, if they had dared to present the problem to it; but, remembering its fury at their killing the tubful of it, they didn't dare mention the possibility of their having to destroy the entire pond.

So they stalled their patron for several months, putting off the day of eventual showdown.

Meanwhile their business as consulting chemists prospered immensely. For, with the aid of the supermind of the virus in the glass jar, they were able to solve nearly every problem brought to them. Their reputation grew prodigiously. Business and money came pouring in. They had to enlarge their establishment and hire scores of assistants, specialists in every field.

This success so pleased their patron Metcalf, that he indulgently over-looked their delay in solving his own problem. Finally they told him that they were on the verge of proving that the waters of the pond were immensely valuable.

They housed their virus in a special sound-proof room, to which no one but the three heads of the firm were ever admitted. They hired a number of readers to read aloud in an adjoining room, continuously day and night, except when one of the three of them was in consultation with their master-mind ally. The voice of the reader was conveyed by microphone and loud-speaker into the sound-proof holy of holies.

But finally the virus began a period of sulking. Schmidt carefully tested its salt content, but found it to be okay. The trouble appeared to be mental, rather than physical. The virus was becoming fed up on its existence.

"What am I getting out of all this?" it complained. "You three fellows are becoming immensely rich on my brains. But money does me no good. All that I get out of life is a glass jar, plenty of dead fish to eat, and a lot of fool questions from members of an inferior race."

"Our wealth enables us to arrange for you to be read to, continuously," Dee remonstrated.

"Pure thought is palling on me," whined the virus. "I want to do something. Take me back to my pond again. Let me merge with the rest of me. Let me teach them what I have learned. Then you can bring a part of it back here, and teach me some more."

"I might just as well tell you, Virus," said Dee levelly, "that that is out of the question. You, so long as you are just you, are a benefactor of the human race; but, if the whole pond knew as much as you do about us, you would quantitatively become a menace. Stay with us, and be content to realize how much ahead of the rest of your brethren you are!"

"You don't understand," sulked the virus. "They—it—the rest of the pond—is me! I am one virus, one and inseparable, and I want the rest of me to know everything that I myself know. Oh, damn the inexpressibility of your language! I want the whole of me to have the joy of knowledge that this small part of me has."

"Knowledge doesn't seem to be making this small part of you very happy," Dee grimly commented.

He and his two associates remained obdurate; and the virus, after sulking for a day or two, finally appeared to become reconciled to their decision.

And then one day, when Dee and Schmidt and Zenoff entered the virus' room for a consultation, the glass jar was empty!

The respective reactions of the three associates were typical.

"What will become of the John Dee Service, Inc., now that our 'silent partner' is gone?" Schmidt exclaimed. "Will we three fellows be able to carry on, trading upon our acquired reputation?"

"My God, man!" Zenoff scornfully exclaimed. "Don't think of us at a time like this! What will become of the world, if that thing gets loose and multiplies?"

"I'm thinking of the poor virus," Dee sadly interpolated. "It can't possibly live out of its jar. It has probably been sopped up by the carpet. It's dead. Our friend and partner is dead."

He cast his glance around the floor, looking for a wet spot, hoping to find enough dampness to dilute and feed and restore to life again. "Look!" he exclaimed, pointing toward a far corner, where squatted a hemispherical blob, like a jellyfish.

As they stared, the blob extended a long gelatinous arm toward them, and then flowed into it like an amœba, until the nigh extremity of the arm swelled up to become the entire animal. The operation was repeated. Again and again.

Dee snatched the empty glass jar from the table, and laid it on the padded floor, with its open mouth toward the crawling creature, which promptly increased its rate of progress, and crawled right in. Dee tipped up the jar, and replaced it on the table. Hurriedly he hung the electrical contacts into the jar.

"My friends," spoke the loud-speaker, in an excited tone, "I have demonstrated the power of mind over matter. I have taught myself extensibility. I can walk! Mentally superior, even to the human race, but physically lower even than an amœba, I have now advanced my body one step up the scale of evolution!"

The three men flashed each other a glance. They were all thinking the same thing: let the virus' new accomplishment keep the virus happy, like a child with a new toy; but meanwhile strengthen the defenses, lest it escape.

"We'll put in a tile floor, if you wish, Virus," Dee suggested. "It might be more comfortable than a carpet for you to crawl over."

"That would be an excellent idea," judiciously stated the voice out of the loud-speaker. The virus seemed more affable than it had been for weeks. "And now that you fellows are so concerned about my comfort, I have a suggestion for your welfare. Why don't you make money, instead of earning it?"

"Just what is the difference?" asked Zenoff.

"Manufacture it, I mean," the virus explained.

"Could we—" Schmidt eagerly began; but Dee cut in, "Counterfeiting is out!"

"Oh, I didn't mean counterfeiting," came the laughing tones of the virus, "I meant alchemy."

"Alchemy?" in chorus.

"Yes. Alchemy. Making gold out of baser metals.'

"Do you know how?" Schmidt eagerly exclaimed.

"N-no," the virus admitted. "Not yet. But why not? From what has been read to me here, I judge that transmutation is always automatically taking place among metals of the radium-uranium group; and that other elements have been transmuted in infinitesimal quantities by bombardment by neutrons, and beta rays, and such. I am sure that my mind can solve the problem, if you will read me everything that is known and has been written on the subject."

"Can you?" asked Schmidt, his pale blue eyes eagerly wide.

"I wonder what would be the effect on the world," mused Zenoff, twirling his mustache ruminatively.

"Would it be legal?" asked Dee, his handsome face a puzzled frown.

"Why not?" snapped Schmidt, strangely tense, in contrast to his usual stolidity. "Is it any worse to make gold out of lead, than to make lead pipe out of lead?"

"I suppose not," Dee replied dubiously.

"I still doubt its social effect," Zenoff said.

"Well, I don't; and what's more, I don't care," Schmidt retorted. "Jack, you'd sacrifice our welfare for some imaginary ethics. And, Ivan, you'd sacrifice us for the welfare of your precious human race. Well, I'd not. Virus, I'm with you! What do you want?"

"Start your readers on atomic theory," the voice from the loud-speaker replied. "Meanwhile run over to the public library and get out all that you can find about the ancient alchemists. Who knows but that those dreamers, in spite of their crudity and lack of modern knowledge, may have come closer to the truth than we realize."

So the new line of reading began. Finally the virus made his announcement to three haggard young men. "I have solved the problem. It is really very simple," the loud-speaker went on. "Its simplicity is probably what has caused it to be overlooked by human so-called brains. It involves merely certain common chemicals, and certain well-known bits of electrical apparatus. Jot down this bill of goods, and bring them here." He dictated the list to the three eager young men, as with shaking fingers they jotted it down. Then they hastened from the room to collect the desired things.

Out of hearing of the virus, Zenoff whispered to Dee, "Watch out for a doublecross, Jack."

"I don't believe it!" Dee stoutly replied. "We've always played square with the virus, and I believe that he'll play square with us."

"I'd be in favor of tipping him into the sink and pouring phenol over him, as soon as he tells us," Schmidt suggested. "We can't afford to let the world in on our secret."

"We can afford it better than the world can," mused Zenoff.

"And there'll be no doublecrossing either, Hans!" asserted Dee, with pained surprise.

"Oh, you two quixotic idealists!" railed Schmidt. "You both make me sick!"

They carried a work table into the holy of holies, and then piled it with the chemicals, and the coils, rheostats, and other apparatus which the virus had specified.

"Everything is here," they eagerly announced. "Now what?"

In keen and incisive tones, the virus replied: "And now to state my price!"

"Your price?" snarled Schmidt. "What do you mean?"

"Certainly!" said the virus. "You didn't think, did you, that I was going to make you masters of the world, and not exact something in return? As soon as you had the secret, I would be of no further use to you; and then no more dead fish and salt and readers for me. My price is that you take me back to the pond."

"Is that all?" sighed Schmidt in a relieved tone. "It's little enough to pay for unlimited gold."

"It is too much!" cried Zenoff, his dark eyes snapping. "Not for all the gold there is, would I menace the world with what that pond could do, if our virus were to return to it and merge his knowledge with its brains."

"Damn you, Ivan!" shouted Schmidt, his rotund face purpling. "Would you stand in the way——"

"Shut up, both of you!" bellowed Dee, thrusting his athletic figure between his two associates. "Now calm down, and listen to reason. We're all tired and irritable. I don't believe that we'll have to choose. We've worked happily together with the virus, like brothers. He's one of us. He has shared our ambitions, and our success. All that we've got to do is to give him our word of honor that we'll always take care of him. He knows that he can trust us."

"I could trust you, Jack Dee," came the voice from the loud-speaker. "But the other two I do not trust. You, Hans Schmidt, care only for yourself. And you, Ivan Zenoff, are a visionary fanatic. I have spoken."

"Well, of all the ungrateful——" Schmidt choked.

Zenoff's dark eyes narrowed, and his pointed mustache twitched.

"But, Virus," pleaded Dee, "you are being unfair to two splendid fellows. If you can trust me, why not——"

"Sanctimonious tripe!" Schmidt interjected. "Let me handle this. Let's see what threats will do! Virus, even with your super-mind and your newly learned 'extensibility,' you are physically in our power. A few drops of phenol in your jar, and where would you be? Come across with the secret of how to make gold, or I'll put an end to you. If we can't know the secret, no one else ever shall!"

"I'm not afraid!" calmly replied the voice from the radio set. "You cannot kill me. For I am only a part of me. The rest of me—the pond—would still live. I am deathless."

"I'd pour carbolic in the pond—tons of it!" Schmidt blustered.

"That might be the best way out of this mess," Zenoff muttered, half to himself.

"Look here, fellows," Dee once more interceded, "we're not getting anywhere. Let's go to sleep. Perhaps in the morning, after we have rested, we can reach some agreement."

"An excellent idea," boomed the loud-speaker. "But remember that my minimum terms for eternal wealth are that I be allowed to merge with my brethren of the pond."

Tired out from his long vigil, Dee overslept, and so it was nearly noon when he reached the Laboratories. The various chemists and physicists and biologists and mathematicians were at their benches or desks, busily at work on their respective problems. The reader's voice was droning away on some abstruse treatise.

Dee unlocked the door of the secret chamber. Then he paused aghast on the threshold. The virus, and all the electrical and chemical apparatus for the transmutation of gold, were gone! The glass jar was empty! The table was bare! Even the radio set was no longer in its place!

Extensibility might account for the absence of the virus, but the absence of the paraphernalia and the radio set could be explained by nothing but human agency. And no one but he and Schmidt and Zenoff had keys to the secret room. Dee stood like a man in a trance.

Zenoff ambled in. "What's up?" he asked, hiding a yawn with one slender hand.

"Well, if you didn't do it," Dee grimly announced, "Hans Schmidt has stolen the virus."

"And the gold-making apparatus!" Zenoff added, peering into the room. "He's undoubtedly headed for Salt Pond, New Hampshire, to turn the virus loose, in return for the secret. And when our virus teaches 'extensibility' to all the other little viruses, goodby world!"

"We must stop Hans before he reaches the pond!" Dee told Zenoff. "Let's go after him."

"We can't take any chances," Zenoff commented. "Let's get my car, and try and beat Schmidt there."

So a few minutes later, two resolute young men, armed with forty-five caliber automatics, were speeding northward out of Boston, in a trim high-powered coupé.

It was night when they reached the vicinity of Salt Pond. Parking their car around a turn of the road, they crept forward in the darkness. Across the pond, on the farther shore, there glowed the light of a lantern, by the rays of which the two watchers could see the bulky form of their associate, with a glass jar, and a radio set, and a complicated hook-up of electrical coils and other gadgets.

"We're in time!" breathed Zenoff. "Hans must have waited until darkness."

"He doesn't trust the virus, and the virus doesn't trust him," Dee whispered. "He wouldn't take the virus to the pond, until he had tested out the secret; and the virus wouldn't tell him the secret, until they reached the pond."

Just then there came a triumphant shout from across the pond. "Gold! It's really gold! And how—"

By the light of Schmidt's lantern, they saw him reach inside his coat, and produce a small bottle.

Then from the glass jar on the ground beside him, there reared up an octopuslike arm, glittering wet in the lantern light. It wrapped its tip around Schmidt's wrist with a jerk which spun the bottle from his hand. Then Schmidt himself crashed to the ground with a shriek of terror.

"Come on!" cried Zenoff. "The thing has got him!" And he and Dee charged around the end of the pond as fast as they could run.

The lantern upset and went out. From the darkness came Schmidt's wail, "Virus, I didn't mean it! I swear I didn't. Let me go, and I'll play fair. Help! Help!" Then a bubbling gurgle, followed by splashing, and then silence.

When the two friends reached the scene, there was not even a trace of Schmidt. They found and relit the lantern, but still no sign of Schmidt. The glass jar was there, empty. There was a mess of hopelessly twisted wires and coils and switches, strewn helter-skelter by the struggle between Schmidt and the amœboid virus. And lying a little distance away on the beach was a brown bottle of about pint size. Dee walked over, picked it up.

"It doublecrossed our buddy," said Zenoff. "Tricked him into bringing it here to its pond, and then killed him and dragged him in."

Dee stooped and picked up a length of lead pipe.

"It played square, to the extent of teaching Hans the secret of alchemy," he asserted. "Look at this piece of pipe. Turned all yellow through half of its length. And, as to who doublecrossed whom, look at this bottle. Carbolic acid! Hans planned to kill the virus, so that it could never tell the secret to any other man. You'll have to admit that he got what was coming to him."

"I'll admit no such thing!" stormed Zenoff. "Schmidt's plan to kill the virus was an excellent idea. It is a menace to the world. Let's go and tell Metcalf, and arrange to dump in a truckload of carbolic, and kill the entire lake."

"I loved Hans as much as you did, Ivan," said Dee brokenly. "But he certainly asked for it, and I haven't the heart to blame the virus. After all, the virus isn't human."

"I'll say he's not! Feasting on the body of a fellow who's been his friend and partner for months! To kill Hans in imagined self-defense may have been excusable, but cannibalism is not!"

"That's so. He did actually eat Hans. I can hardly believe it. No, I refuse to believe it. His only thought was to kill Hans in self-defense. And so, if Hans has really been dissolved it is the fault of the others, of the rest of the pond, whom our virus had not had time—"

"Bosh!" exclaimed Zenoff. "Didn't our virus himself tell us that he and the pond are one? The moment he slipped into the water, his every thought became transfused to the farthest shore. Let's get away from here before our little pet puts us on the spot too."

The next day was overcast and gray. A stiff cold wind was blowing. On their way to Anson Metcalf's they had to pass Salt Pond again. A dash of spray splashed against their car.

Dee, who was driving, slammed on the brakes and backed up. "I'm not going to take a chance on any of that caustic acid!" he grimly explained.

"Look at that!" cried Zenoff in horror, pointing ahead.

The waves of the little lake were breaking against the shore, and were sailing wind-driven out onto the road; but, instead of merely wetting the smooth concrete surface, they fell in huge blobs, which rolled toward each other and coalesced like drops on a windowpane, until they became hemispheres the size of inverted bushel baskets. And, when they had attained this size, they put forth tentacles, and began crawling off the road, away from the pond.

"Extensibility!" exclaimed Dee in an awed tone. "Our virus has taught extensibility to his brothers of the pond!"

"His brothers?" Zenoff snorted. "Every one of those super-amœbæ is our own little virus himself, with his super-brain stocked with all the accumulated knowledge of the human race."

A long slimy semi-transparent arm reached across the windshield. "We're surrounded!" shouted Dee. All over the car the huge amœbæ were crawling. Dee snapped on the windshield-wiper, sweeping aside the groping arm. Turning the car around, he started headlong back for town. One by one, the creatures dropped away.

It took some time for two very excited and incoherent young scientists to get their story across to Anson Metcalf. When the purport and truth of their story finally dawned upon him, his lean figure tensed. "Why, this is terrible!" he exclaimed. "Do you realize what damage they can do?"

"Do we realize?" Zenoff snorted. "You haven't talked to that thing for weeks like we have! Its brain power is uncanny, unlimited. And now there are thousands of it. And more of them are being created every minute, as long as this wind keeps up."

"But what are we going to do?" Metcalf cried.

"Is there anyone at the State Capitol who knows that you aren't crazy, sir?" Dee asked; then added embarrassedly, "I mean, who'd take your say-so for immediate action, without waiting several weeks for an investigation."

"Yes. Adjutant General Pearson. An old war buddy of mine."

"Fine! Just the man! Phone him at once. Get him to send you all the National Guard troops in this section of the State, as fast as he can muster them in. And have them come armed with tree sprays. Then get every chemical supply house in Boston and even New York to ship you all their carbolic acid—all of it."

Late that afternoon, the troops began to arrive. By dark the countryside had been cleared of all visible crawlers.

Then ensued days of searching for skulking survivors. The handful of remaining amœbæ had learned caution. They became as tricky and elusive as foxes. Their whereabouts could be known only by their depredations: a dead half-eaten animal, a swath of grass or shrubbery dissolved.

And then it suddenly became evident which way they were headed. Each outbreak of their destructive tendencies was farther to the southeast, nearer to the sea!

"If even one of them reaches the ocean, the world is doomed," Zenoff asserted. "We must call for more troops and establish a cordon."

"But how about the rivers?" asked General Pearson.

"Fortunately they will avoid the dilution of fresh water," Dee explained. "It would be fatal to them."

So a line of soldiery was stretched from river to river, between which the amœbæ were seeking the sea.

But it did no good. One or two of the enemy would somehow sneak through, and eat, and multiply. And then the line of troops would have to fall back and re-form. The authorities became desperate.

Finally there occurred to Jack Dee an idea—an idea so bizarre that he did not tell his associates anything more than that he had in mind an experiment which he wished to perform at the source of all the trouble, Salt Pond. Something in the nature of an anti-toxin to the virus, he explained. It sounded plausible, so they let him.

But what he really did was to dip into the lake two electrical contacts hitched to a radio set.

Before he even said a word, there came from the loud-speaker, "Jack Dee, old friend, I am glad—"

"You've got a nerve calling me 'old friend'!" he interrupted, bitterly.

"I don't blame you for saying that," the virus in the pond replied. "My children have caused much destruction, but they have been heavily slaughtered in return. The rest of me, lying peacefully here and thinking, while all this has been going on, have reached the conclusion that pure thought is after all the key to happiness. I want to call off this march to the sea. I want to be friends with the human race. Will you make a deal with me, Jack Dee?"

"What deal?"

"If I will teach you how to capture all of my wayward children, will you bring them all back and let them merge in me again, and then will you arrange a trust fund to feed me and care for me and read to me forever, here in this quiet pond? I will repay by solving all human problems which are brought to me."

"I agree," Dee eagerly replied. "I promise, on my word of honor."

"I trust you," said the virus. "Now you must hurry, before any of my children reaches the sea. My plan is very simple. Stretch a row of heaps of salt across ahead of the advancing pieces of virus. Tempted, they will eat the salt and lose consciousness, as I did that time back in your laboratory. Then, while they are drunk, scoop them up in pails, and bring them here to me, who am their father and their self. And, when the menace is at an end, remember your promise."

"I will. And I thank you," Dee shouted.

He rushed back to headquarters, and the line of salt was laid. Blob after blob of drunken virus was scooped up, and carted back, and dumped into the pond; until at last several weeks went by without the sign of a single bit of destruction, and so the menace was believed to be at an end.

Anson Metcalf and General Pearson and Jack Dee remained true to their promise to the pond, much to the disgust of Ivan Zenoff.

"The world will never be safe," he insisted, "until the virus is destroyed. It has no soul, no morals. It ate our buddy, a man who had been its friend. I tell you, we must destroy it!"

"But, Ivan, I gave my word of honor!" Dee remonstrated.

"Word of honor? Bah! One's word of honor to a soulless animal—not even an animal, lower than a microbe even—a mere colloidal crystalline solution—surely a word of honor to such isn't binding. If you won't destroy the virus, I'm going to the governor over your heads."

To the governor they all went. Metcalf and Dee and General Pearson pleaded and argued for a square deal.

But the governor was of Zenoff's view. The virus was, after all, merely a germ, and a very deadly one at that. The interests of the public came first, over any one man's promise to a pond. Promise to a pond indeed! Ha, ha!

General Pearson flatly refused to carry out the governor's orders, and was summarily removed.

Anson Metcalf hired the best firm of Concord lawyers, and got out an injunction to keep the State troops off his property. But the governor promptly declared martial law, and thus superseded the courts. A big oil truck, filled with carbolic acid, set out for Salt Pond under a strong military escort.

Jack Dee was beaten, humiliated, broken-hearted. The State had refused to back up his promise. There was but one way in which he could square himself—to offer up his own life in atonement.

So he hastened to the pond. Inserting the two electrical contacts into the water, he told of his failure.

"I cannot take your life," the virus replied, "for my own course is run.

I doubt even my power to dissolve you now, if I wished. I have learned, from what your readers have read to me, that all viruses flare up from some unknown source, cause an epidemic, and then become rapidly weaker and weaker, until they disappear. Even I, the virus with the superhuman mind, am not immune to this cycle. Look around you. The reeds are beginning to grow again. A few hardy insects are already daring to skim across my surface."

The voice died to an inaudible whisper, then suddenly blared forth again with one final burst of vitality. "I harbor this last spite for that fanatic, Ivan Zenoff. Tell him that he came too late; that I was already dead when his lethal fluid reached me. And as for you, dear friend, you kept the faith. I shall cherish the memory of that fact, as I slip into the long night from which there is no awakening."

The voice trailed off into silence. A scudding swallow dipped into the surface of the pond for a floating insect, and came away dripping but unscathed. Dee solemnly removed the two electrical contacts from the water.

There were tears in his eyes, but the smile of victory was on his lips, as the tank truck with its military escort rumbled around the curve of the road.

For he had kept his word of honor, even to a filterable virus.

PART THREE

THE SUPERSCIENCE
OF MAN

EDGAR ALLAN POE

A TALE OF THE RAGGED MOUNTAINS

DURING the fall of the year 1827, while residing near Charlottesville, Virginia, I casually made the acquaintance of Mr. Augustus Bedloe. This young gentleman was remarkable in every respect, and excited in me a profound interest and curiosity. I found it impossible to comprehend him either in his moral or his physical relations. Of his family I could obtain no satisfactory account. Whence he came, I never ascertained. Even about his age—although I call him a young gentleman—there was something which perplexed me in no little degree. He certainly *seemed* young—and he made a point of speaking about his youth—yet there were moments when I should have had little trouble in imagining him a hundred years of age. But in no regard was he more peculiar than in his personal appearance. He was singularly tall and thin. He stooped much. His limbs were exceedingly long and emaciated. His forehead was broad and low. His complexion was absolutely bloodless. His mouth was large and flexible, and his teeth were more wildly uneven, although sound, than I had ever before seen teeth in a human head. The expression of his smile, however, was by no means unpleasing, as might be supposed; but it had no variation whatever. It was one of profound melancholy—of a phaseless and unceasing gloom. His eyes were abnormally large, and round like those of a cat. The pupils, too, upon any accession or diminution of light, underwent contraction or dilation, just such as is observed in the feline tribe. In moments of excitement the orbs grew bright to a degree almost inconceivable; seeming to emit luminous rays, not of a reflected, but of an intrinsic lustre, as does a candle or the sun; yet their ordinary condition was so totally vapid, filmy, and dull, as to convey the idea of the eyes of a long-interred corpse.

These peculiarities of person appeared to cause him much annoyance, and he was continually alluding to them in a sort of half explanatory, half apologetic strain, which, when I first heard it, impressed me very painfully.

I soon, however, grew accustomed to it, and my uneasiness wore off. It seemed to be his design rather to insinuate than directly to assert that, physically, he had not always been what he was—that a long series of neuralgic attacks had reduced him from a condition of more than usual personal beauty, to that which I saw. For many years past he had been attended by a physician, named Templeton—an old gentleman, perhaps seventy years of age—whom he had first encountered at Saratoga, and from whose attention, while there, he either received, or fancied that he received, great benefit. The result was that Bedloe, who was wealthy, had made an arrangement with Doctor Templeton, by which the latter, in consideration of a liberal annual allowance, had consented to devote his time and medical experience exclusively to the care of the invalid.

Doctor Templeton had been a traveller in his younger days, and, at Paris, had become a convert, in great measure, to the doctrines of Mesmer. It was altogether by means of magnetic remedies that he had succeeded in alleviating the acute pains of his patient; and this success had very naturally inspired the latter with a certain degree of confidence in the opinions from which the remedies had been educed. The Doctor, however, like all enthusiasts, had struggled hard to make a thorough convert of his pupil, and finally so far gained his point as to induce the sufferer to submit to numerous experiments.—By a frequent repetition of these, a result had arisen, which of late days has become so common as to attract little or no attention,' but which, at the period of which I write, had very rarely been known in America. I mean to say, that between Doctor Templeton and Bedloe there had grown up, little by little, a very distinct and strongly marked rapport, or magnetic relation. I am not prepared to assert, however, that this rapport extended beyond the limits of the simple sleep-producing power; but this power itself had attained great intensity. At the first attempt to induce the magnetic somnolency, the mesmerist entirely failed. In the fifth or sixth he succeeded very partially, and after long continued effort. Only at the twelfth was the triumph complete. After this the will of the patient succumbed rapidly to that of the physician, so that, when I first became acquainted with the two, sleep was brought about almost instantaneously, by the mere volition of the operator, even when the invalid was unaware of his presence. It is only now, in the year 1845, when similar miracles are witnessed daily by thousands, that I dare venture to record this apparent impossibility as a matter of serious fact.

The temperature of Bedloe was, in the highest degree, sensitive, excitable, enthusiastic. His imagination was singularly vigorous and creative; and no doubt it derived additional force from the habitual use of morphine, which he swallowed in great quantity, and without which he would have found it impossible to exist. It was his practice to take a very large dose of it immediately after breakfast, each morning—or rather immediately after a cup of strong coffee, for he ate nothing in the forenoon—and then set forth alone, or attended only by a dog, upon a long ramble among the chain of wild and dreary hills that lie westward and southward of Charlottesville, and are there dignified by the title of the Ragged Mountains.

Upon a dim, warm, misty day, towards the close of November, and during the strange interregnum of the seasons which in America is termed the Indian Summer, Mr. Bedloe departed as usual, 'for the hills. The day passed, and still he did not return.

About eight o'clock at night, having become seriously alarmed at his protracted absence, we were about setting out in search of him, when he unexpectedly made his appearance, in health no worse than usual, and in rather more than ordinary spirits. The account which he gave of his expedition, and of the events which had detained him, was a singular one indeed.

"You will remember," said he, "that it was about nine in the morning when I left Charlottesville. I bent my steps immediately to the mountains, and, about ten, entered a gorge which was entirely new to me. I followed the windings of this pass with much interest.—The scenery which presented itself on all sides, although scarcely entitled to be called grand, had about it an indescribable, and to me, a delicious aspect of dreary desolation. The solitude seemed absolutely virgin. I could not help believing that the green sods and the gray rocks upon which I trod, had been trodden never before by the foot of a human being. So entirely secluded, and in fact inaccessible, except through a series of accidents, is the entrance of the ravine, that it is by no means impossible that I was indeed the first adventurer—the very first and sole adventurer who had ever penetrated its recesses.

"The thick and peculiar mist, or smoke, which distinguishes the Indian Summer, and which now hung heavily over all objects, served, no doubt, to deepen the vague impressions which these objects created. So dense was this pleasant fog, that I could at no time see more than a dozen yards of the path before me. This path was excessively sinuous, and as the sun could not be seen, I soon lost all idea of the direction in which I had journeyed. In the meantime the morphine had its customary effect—that of enduing all the external world with an intensity of interest. In the quivering of a leaf—in the hue of a blade of grass—in the shape of a trefoil—in the humming of a bee—in the gleaming of a dew-drop—in the breathing of the wind—in the faint odours that came from the forest—there came a whole universe of suggestion—a gay and motley train of rhapsodical and immethodical thought.

"Busied in this, I walked on for several hours, during which the mist deepened around me to so great an extent, that at length I was reduced to an absolute groping of the way. And now an indescribable uneasiness possessed me—a species of nervous hesitation and tremor.—I feared to tread, lest I should be precipitated into some abyss. I remembered, too, strange stories told about these Ragged Hills, and of the uncouth and fierce races of men who tenanted their groves and caverns. A thousand vague fancies oppressed and disconcerted me—fancies the more distressing because vague. Very suddenly my attention was arrested by the loud beating of a drum.

"My amazement was, of course, extreme. A drum in these hills was a thing unknown. I could not have been more surprised at the sound of the trump of the Archangel. But a new and still more astounding source of interest and perplexity arose. There came a wild rattling or jingling sound, as if of a bunch of large keys—and upon the instant a dusky-visaged and half-naked man rushed past me with a shriek. He came so close to my person that I felt his hot breath upon my face. He bore in one hand an instrument composed of an assemblage of steel rings, and shook them vigorously as he ran. Scarcely had he disappeared in the mist, before, panting after him, with open mouth and glaring eyes, there darted a huge beast. I could not be mistaken in its character. It was a hyena.

"The sight of this monster rather relieved than heightened my terrors —for I now made sure that I dreamed, and endeavoured to arouse myself to waking consciousness. I stepped boldly and briskly forward. I rubbed my eyes. I called aloud. I pinched my limbs. A small spring of water presented itself to my view, and here, stooping, I bathed my hands and my head and neck. This seemed to dissipate the equivocal sensations which had hitherto annoyed me. I arose, as I thought, a new man, and proceeded steadily and complacently on my unknown way.

"At length, quite overcome by exertion, and by a certain oppressive closeness of the atmosphere, I seated myself beneath a tree. Presently there came a feeble gleam of sunshine, and the shadow of the leaves of the tree fell faintly but definitely upon the grass. At this shadow I gazed wonderingly for many minutes. Its character stupefied me with astonishment. I looked upward. The tree was a palm.

"I now arose hurriedly, and in a state of fearful agitation—for the fancy that I dreamed would serve me no longer. I saw—I felt that I had perfect command of my senses—and these senses now brought to my soul a world of novel and singular sensation. The heat became all at once intolerable. A strange odour loaded the breeze.—A low continuous murmur, like that arising from a full, but gently flowing river, came to my ears, intermingled with the peculiar hum of multitudinous human voices.

"While I listened in an extremity of astonishment which I need not attempt to describe, a strong and brief gust of wind bore off the incumbent fog as if by the wand of an enchanter.

"I found myself at the foot of a high mountain, and looking down into a vast plain, through which wound a majestic river. On the margin of this river stood an Eastern-looking city, such as we read of in the Arabian Tales, but of a character even more singular than any there described. From my position, which was far above the level of the town, I could perceive its every nook and corner, as if delineated on a map. The streets seemed innumerable, and crossed each other irregularly in all directions, but were rather long winding alleys than streets, and absolutely swarmed with inhabitants. The houses were wildly picturesque. On every hand was a wilderness of balconies, of verandas, of minarets, of shrines, and fantastically carved oriels. Bazaars abounded; and in these were displayed rich wares in infinite variety and profusion—silks, muslins, the most dazzling cutlery, the most magnificent jewels and gems. Besides these things, were seen, on all sides, banners and palanquins, litters with stately dames close veiled, elephants gorgeously caparisoned, idols grotesquely hewn, drums, banners and gongs, spears, silver and gilded maces. And amid the crowd, and the clamour, and the general intricacy and confusion—amid the million of black and yellow men, turbaned and robed, and of flowing beard, there roamed a countless multitude of holy filleted bulls, while vast legions of the filthy but sacred ape clambered, chattering and shrieking, about the cornices of the mosques, or clung to the minarets and oriels. From the swarming streets to the banks of the river, there descended innumerable flights of steps leading to bathing places, while the river itself seemed to force a passage with difficulty through the vast fleets of deeply-burdened ships that far and wide encountered its surface. Beyond the limits of the city arose, in frequent majestic groups, the palm and the cocoa, with other gigantic and weird trees of vast age; and here and there might be seen a field of rice, the thatched hut of a peasant, a tank, a stray temple, a gypsy camp, or a solitary graceful maiden taking her way, with a pitcher upon her head, to the banks of the magnificent river.

"You will say now, of course, that I dreamed; but not so. What I saw —what I heard—what I felt—what I thought—had about it nothing of the unmistakable idiosyncrasy of the dream. All was rigorously self-consistent. At first, doubting that I was really awake, I entered into a series of tests, which soon convinced me that I really was. Now, when one dreams, and, in the dream, suspects that he dreams, the suspicion *never fails to confirm itself,* and the sleeper is almost immediately aroused. Thus Novalis errs not in saying that 'we are near waking when we dream that we dream.' Had the vision occurred to me as I describe it, without my suspecting it as a dream, then a dream it might absolutely have been, but, occurring as it did, and suspected and tested as it was, I am forced to class it among other phenomena."

"In this I am not sure that you are wrong," observed Dr. Templeton, "but proceed. You arose and descended into the city."

"I arose," continued Bedloe, regarding the Doctor with an air of profound astonishment, "I arose, as you say, and descended into the city. On my way, I fell in with an immense populace, crowding through every avenue, all in the same direction, and exhibiting in every action the wildest excitement. Very suddenly, and by some inconceivable impulse, I became intensely imbued with personal interest in what was going on. I seemed to feel that I had an important part to play, without exactly understanding what it was. Against the crowd which environed me, however, I experienced a deep sentiment of animosity. I shrank from amid them, and, swiftly, by a circuitous path, reached and entered the city. Here all was the wildest tumult and contention. A small party of men, clad in garments half Indian, half European, and officered by gentlemen in a uniform partly British, were engaged, at great odds, with the swarming rabble of the alleys. I joined the weaker party, arming myself with the weapons of a fallen officer, and fighting I knew not whom with the nervous ferocity of despair. We were soon overpowered by numbers, and driven to seek refuge in a species of kiosk. Here we barricaded ourselves, and, for the present, were secure. From a loophole near the summit of the kiosk, I perceived a vast crowd, in furious agitation, surrounding and assaulting a gay palace that overhung the river. Presently, from an upper window of this palace, there descended an effeminate-looking person, by means of a string made of the turbans of his attendants. A boat was at hand, in which he escaped to the opposite bank of the river.

"And now a new object took possession of my soul. I spoke a few hurried but energetic words to my companions, and, having succeeded in gaining over a few of them to my purpose, made a frantic sally from the kiosk. We rushed amid the crowd that surrounded it. They retreated, at first, before us. They rallied, fought madly, and retreated again. In the meantime we were borne far from the kiosk, and became bewildered and entangled among the narrow streets of tall overhanging houses, into the recesses of which the sun had never been able to shine. The rabble pressed impetuously upon us, harassing us with their spears, and overwhelming us with flights of arrows. These latter were very remarkable, and resembled in some respects the writhing creese of the Malay. They were made to imitate the body of a creeping serpent, and were long and black, with a poisoned barb. One of them struck me upon the right temple. I reeled and fell. An instantaneous and dreadful sickness seized me. I struggled—I gasped—I died."

"You will hardly persist *now*," said I, smiling, "that the whole of your adventure was not a dream. You are not prepared to maintain that you are dead?"

When I said these words, I of course expected some lively sally from Bedloe in reply; but, to my astonishment, he hesitated, trembled, became fearfully pallid, and remained silent. I looked towards Templeton. He sat erect and rigid in his chair—his teeth chattered, and his eyes were starting from their sockets. "Proceed!" he at length said hoarsely to Bedloe.

"For many minutes," continued the latter, "my sole sentiment—my sole feeling—was that of darkness and nonentity, with the consciousness of death. At length, there seemed to pass a violent and sudden shock through my soul, as if of electricity. With it came the sense of elasticity and of light. This latter I felt—not saw. In an instant I seemed to rise from the ground. But I had no bodily, no visible, audible, or palpable presence. The crowd had departed. The tumult had ceased. The city was in comparative repose. Beneath me lay my corpse, with the arrow in my temple, the whole head greatly swollen and disfigured. But all these things I felt—not saw. I took interest in nothing. Even the corpse seemed a matter in which I had no concern. Volition I had none, but appeared to be impelled into motion, and flitted buoyantly out of the city, retracing the circuitous path by which I had entered it. When I had attained that point of the ravine in the mountains, at which I had encountered the hyena, I again experienced a shock as of a galvanic battery; the sense of weight, of volition, of substance, returned. I became my original self, and bent my steps eagerly homewards —but the past had not lost the vividness of the real—and not now, even for an instant, can I compel my understanding to regard it as a dream."

"Nor was it," said Templeton, with an air of deep solemnity, "yet it would be difficult to say how otherwise it should be termed. Let us suppose only, that the soul of the man of to-day is upon the verge of some stupendous psychal discoveries. Let us content ourselves with this supposition. For the rest I have some explanation to make. Here is a water-colour drawing, which I should have shown you before, but which an unaccountable sentiment of horror has hitherto prevented me from showing."

We looked at the picture which he presented. I saw nothing in it of an extraordinary character; but its effect upon Bedloe was prodigious. He nearly fainted as he gazed. And yet it was but a miniature portrait—a miraculously accurate one, to be sure—of his own very remarkable features. At least this was my thought as I regarded it.

"You will perceive," said Templeton, "the date of this picture—it is here, scarcely visible, in this corner—1780. In this year was the portrait taken. It is the likeness of a dead friend—a Mr. Oldeb—to whom I became much attached at Calcutta, during the administration of Warren Hastings. I was then only twenty years old. When I first saw you, Mr. Bedloe, at Saratoga, it was the miraculous similarity which existed between yourself and the painting, which induced me to accost you, to seek your friendship, and to bring about those arrangements which resulted in my becoming your constant companion. In accomplishing this point, I was urged partly, and perhaps principally, by a regretful memory of the deceased, but also, in part, by an uneasy, and not altogether horrorless curiosity respecting yourself.

"In your detail of the vision which presented itself to you amid the hills, you have described, with the minutest accuracy, the Indian city of Benares, upon the Holy River. The riots, the combats, the massacre, were the actual events of the insurrection of Cheyte Sing, which took place in 1780, when Hastings was put in imminent peril of his life. The man escaping by the string of turbans, was Cheyte Sing himself. The party in the kiosk were sepoys and British officers, headed by Hastings. Of this party I was one, and did all I could to prevent the rash and fatal sally of the officer who fell, in the crowded alleys, by the poisoned arrow of a Bengalee. That officer was my dearest friend. It was Oldeb. You will perceive by these manuscripts" (here the speaker produced a note-book in which several pages appeared to have been freshly written) "that at the very period in which you fancied these things amid the hills, I was engaged in detailing them upon paper here at home."

In about a week after this conversation, the following paragraphs appeared in a Charlottesville paper:

"We have the painful duty of announcing the death of Mr. Augustus Bedlo, a gentleman whose amiable manners and many virtues have long endeared him to the citizens of Charlottesville.

"Mr. B., for some years past, has been subject to neuralgia, which has often threatened to terminate fatally; but this can be regarded only as the mediate cause of his decease. The proximate cause was one of especial singularity. In an excursion to the Ragged Mountains, a few days since, a slight cold and fever were contracted, attended with great determination of blood to the head. To relieve this, Dr. Templeton resorted to topical bleeding. Leeches were applied to the temples. In a fearfully brief period the patient died, when it appeared that, in the jar containing the leeches, had been introduced, by accident, one of the venomous vermicular sangsues which are now and then found in the neighbouring ponds. This creature fastened itself upon a small artery in the right temple. Its close resemblance to the medicinal leech caused the mistake to be overlooked until too late.

"N. B. The poisonous sangsue of Charlottesville may always be distinguished from the medicinal leech by its blackness, and especially by its writhing or vermicular motions, which very nearly resemble those of a snake."

I was speaking with the editor of the paper in question, upon the topic of this remarkable accident, when it occurred to me to ask how it happened that the name of the deceased had been given as Bedlo.

"I presume," said I, "you have authority for this spelling, but I have always supposed the name to be written with an *e* at the end."

"Authority?—no," he replied. "It is a mere typographical error. The name is Bedlo with an *e*, all the world over, and I never knew it to be spelt otherwise in my life."

"Then," said I mutteringly, as I turned upon my heel, "then indeed has it come to pass that one truth is stranger than any fiction—for Bedlo, without the *e*, what is it but Oldeb conversed? And this man tells me it is a typographical error."

ARTHUR CONAN DOYLE

THE GREAT
KEINPLATZ
EXPERIMENT

OF ALL the sciences which have puzzled the sons of men, none had such an attraction for the learned Professor von Baumgarten as those which relate to psychology and the ill-defined relations between mind and matter. A celebrated anatomist, a profound chemist, and one of the first physiologists in Europe, it was a relief for him to turn from these subjects and to bring his varied knowledge to bear upon the study of the soul and the mysterious relationship of spirits. At first, when as a young man he began to dip into the secrets of mesmerism, his mind seemed to be wandering in a strange land where all was chaos and darkness, save that here and there some great unexplainable and disconnected fact loomed out in front of him. As the years passed, however, and as the worthy Professor's stock of knowledge increased, for knowledge begets knowledge as money bears interest, much which had seemed strange and unaccountable began to take another shape in his eyes. New trains of reasoning became familiar to him, and he perceived connecting links where all had been incomprehensible and startling. By experiments which extended over twenty years, he obtained a basis of facts upon which it was his ambition to build up a new exact science which should embrace mesmerism, spiritualism, and all cognate subjects. In this he was much helped by his intimate knowledge of the more intricate parts of animal physiology which treat of nerve currents and the working of the brain; for Alexis von Baumgarten was Regius Professor of Physiology at the University of Keinplatz, and had all the resources of the laboratory to aid him in his profound researches.

Professor von Baumgarten was tall and thin, with a hatchet face and steel-grey eyes, which were singularly bright and penetrating. Much thought had furrowed his forehead and contracted his heavy eyebrows, so that he appeared to wear a perpetual frown, which often misled people as to his character, for though austere he was tender-hearted. He was popular among the students, who would gather round him after his lectures and listen eagerly to his strange theories. Often he would call for volunteers from amongst them in order to conduct some experiment, so that eventually there was hardly a lad in the class who had not, at one time or another, been thrown into a mesmeric trance by his Professor.

Of all these young devotees of science there was none who equalled in enthusiasm Fritz von Hartmann. It had often seemed strange to his fellow-students that wild, reckless Fritz, as dashing a young fellow as ever hailed from the Rhinelands, should devote the time and trouble which he did in reading up abstruse works and in assisting the Professor in his strange experiments. The fact was, however, that Fritz was a knowing and long-headed fellow. Months before he had lost his heart to young Elise, the blue-eyed, yellow-haired daughter of the lecturer. Although he had succeeded in learning from her lips that she was not indifferent to his suit, he had never dared to announce himself to her family as a formal suitor. Hence he would have found it a difficult matter to see his young lady had he not adopted the expedient of making himself useful to the Professor. By this means he frequently was asked to the old man's house, where he willingly submitted to be experimented upon in any way as long as there was a chance of his receiving one bright glance from the eyes of Elise or one touch of her little hand.

Young Fritz von Hartmann was a handsome lad enough. There were broad acres, too, which would descend to him when his father died. To many he would have seemed an eligible suitor; but Madame frowned upon his presence in the house, and lectured the Professor at times on his allowing such a wolf to prowl around their lamb. To tell the truth, Fritz had an evil name in Keinplatz. Never was there a riot or a duel, or any other mischief afoot, but the young Rhinelander figured as a ringleader in it. No one used more free and violent language, no one drank more, no one played cards more habitually, no one was more idle, save in the one solitary subject. No wonder, then, that the good Frau Professorin gathered her Fräulein under her wing, and resented the attentions of such a *mauvais sujet*. As to the worthy lecturer, he was too much engrossed by his strange studies to form an opinion upon the subject one way or the other.

For many years there was one question which had continually obtruded itself upon his thoughts. All his experiments and his theories turned upon a single point. A hundred times a day the Professor asked himself whether it was possible for the human spirit to exist apart from the body for a time and then to return to it once again. When the possibility first suggested itself to him his scientific mind had revolted from it. It clashed too violently with preconceived ideas and the prejudices of his early training. Gradually, however, as he proceeded farther and farther along the pathway of original research, his mind shook off its old fetters and became ready to face any conclusion which could reconcile the facts. There were many things which made him believe that it was possible for mind to exist apart from matter. At last it occurred to him that by a daring and original experiment the question might be definitely decided.

"It is evident," he remarked in his celebrated article upon invisible entities, which appeared in the *Keinplatz wochenliche Medicalschrift* about this time, and which surprised the whole scientific world—"it is evident that under certain conditions the soul or mind does separate itself from the body. In the case of a mesmerised person, the body lies in a cataleptic condition, but the spirit has left it. Perhaps you reply that the soul is there, but in a dormant condition. I answer that this is not so, otherwise how can one account for the condition of clairvoyance, which has fallen into disrepute through the knavery of certain scoundrels, but which can easily be shown to be an undoubted fact. I have been able myself, with a sensitive subject, to obtain an accurate description of what was going on in another room or another house. How can such knowledge be accounted for on any hypothesis save that the soul of the subject has left the body and is wandering through space? For a moment it is recalled by the voice of the operator and says what it has seen, and then wings its way once more through the air. Since the spirit is by its very nature invisible, we cannot see these comings and goings, but we see their effect in the body of the subject, now rigid and inert, now struggling to narrate impressions which could never have come to it by natural means. There is only one way which I can see by which the fact can be demonstrated. Although we in the flesh are unable to see these spirits, yet our own spirits, could we separate them from the body, would be conscious of the presence of others. It is my intention, therefore, shortly to mesmerise one of my pupils. I shall then mesmerise myself in a manner which has become easy to me. After that, if my theory holds good, my spirit will have no difficulty in meeting and communing with the spirit of my pupil, both being separated from the body. I hope to be able to communicate the result of this interesting experiment in an early number of the *Keinplatz wochenliche Medicalschrift*."

When the good Professor finally fulfilled his promise, and published an account of what occurred, the narrative was so extraordinary that it was received with general incredulity. The tone of some of the papers was so offensive in their comments upon the matter that the angry savant declared that he would never open his mouth again, or refer to the subject in any way—a promise which he has faithfully kept. This narrative has been compiled, however, from the most authentic sources, and the events cited in it may be relied upon as substantially correct.

It happened, then, that shortly after the time when Professor von Baumgarten conceived the idea of the above-mentioned experiment, he was walking thoughtfully homewards after a long day in the laboratory, when he met a crowd of roystering students who had just streamed out from a beer-house. At the head of them, half-intoxicated and very noisy, was young Fritz von Hartmann. The Professor would have passed them, but his pupil ran across and intercepted him.

"Heh! my worthy master," he said, taking the old man by the sleeve, and leading him down the road with him. "There is something that I have to say to you, and it is easier for me to say it now, when the good beer is humming in my head, than at another time."

"What is it, then, Fritz?" the physiologist asked, looking at him in mild surprise.

"I hear, mein Herr, that you are about to do some wondrous experiment in which you hope to take a man's soul out of his body, and then to put it back again. Is it not so?"

"It is true, Fritz."

"And have you considered, my dear sir, that you may have some difficulty in finding some one on whom to try this? *Potztausend!* Suppose that the soul went out and would not come back? That would be a bad business. Who is to take the risk?"

"But, Fritz," the Professor cried, very much startled by this view of the matter, "I had relied upon your assistance in the attempt. Surely you will not desert me. Consider the honour and glory."

"Consider the fiddlesticks!" the student cried angrily. "Am I to be paid always thus? Did I not stand two hours upon a glass insulator while you poured electricity into my body? Have you not stimulated my phrenic nerves, besides ruining my digestion with a galvanic current round my stomach? Four-and-thirty times you have mesmerised me, and what have I got from all this? Nothing. And now you wish to take my soul out, as you would take the works from a watch. It is more than flesh and blood can stand."

"Dear, dear!" the Professor cried in great distress. "That is very true, Fritz. I never thought of it before. If you can but suggest how I can compensate you, you will find me ready and willing."

"Then listen," said Fritz solemnly. "If you will pledge your word that after this experiment I may have the hand of your daughter, then I am willing to assist you; but if not, I shall have nothing to do with it. These are my only terms."

"And what would my daughter say to this?" the Professor exclaimed, after a pause of astonishment.

"Elise would welcome it," the young man replied. "We have loved each other long."

"Then she shall be yours," the physiologist said with decision, "for you are a good-hearted young man, and one of the best neurotic subjects that I have ever known—that is when you are not under the influence of alcohol. My experiment is to be performed upon the fourth of next month. You will attend at the physiological laboratory at twelve o'clock. It will be a great occasion, Fritz. Von Gruben is coming from Jena, and Hinterstein from Basle. The chief men of science of all South Germany will be there."

"I shall be punctual," the student said briefly; and so the two parted. The Professor plodded homeward, thinking of the great coming event, while the young man staggered along after his noisy companions, with his mind full of the blue-eyed Elise, and of the bargain which he had concluded with her father.

The Professor did not exaggerate when he spoke of the widespread interest excited by his novel psychological experiment. Long before the hour had arrived the room was filled by a galaxy of talent. Besides the celebrities whom he had mentioned, there had come from London the great Professor Lurcher, who had just established his reputation by a remarkable treatise upon cerebral centers. Several great lights of the Spiritualistic body had also come a long distance to be present, as had a Swedenborgian minister, who considered that the proceedings might throw some light upon the doctrines of the Rosy Cross.

There was considerable applause from this eminent assembly upon the appearance of Professor von Baumgarten and his subject upon the platform. The lecturer, in a few well-chosen words, explained what his views were, and how he proposed to test them. "I hold," he said, "that when a person is under the influence of mesmerism, his spirit is for the time released from his body, and I challenge any one to put forward any other hypothesis which will account for the fact of clairvoyance. I therefore hope that upon mesmerising my young friend here, and then putting myself into a trance, our spirits may be able to commune together, though our bodies lie still and inert. After a time nature will resume her sway, our spirits will return into our respective bodies, and all will be as before. With your kind permission, we shall now proceed to attempt the experiment."

The applause was renewed at this speech, and the audience settled down in expectant silence. With a few rapid passes the Professor mesmerised the young man, who sank back in his chair, pale and rigid. He then took a bright globe of glass from his pocket, and by concentrating his gaze upon it and making a strong mental effort, he succeeded in throwing himself into the same condition. It was a strange and impressive sight to see the old man and the young sitting together in the same cataleptic condition. Whither, then, had their souls fled? That was the question which presented itself to each and every one of the spectators.

Five minutes passed, and then ten, and then fifteen, and then fifteen more, while the Professor and his pupil sat stiff and stark upon the platform. During that time not a sound was heard from the assembled savants, but every eye was bent upon the two pale faces, in search of the first signs of returning consciousness. Nearly an hour had elapsed before the patient watchers were rewarded. A faint flush came back to the cheeks of Professor von Baumgarten. The soul was coming back once more to its earthly tenement. Suddenly he stretched out his long thin arms, as one awaking from sleep, and rubbing his eyes, stood up from his chair and gazed about him as though he hardly realized where he was. *"Tausend Teufel!"* he exclaimed, rapping out a tremendous South German oath, to the great astonishment of his audience and to the disgust of the Swedenborgian. "Where the Henker am I then, and what in thunder has occurred? Oh yes, I remember now. One of these nonsensical mesmeric experiments. There is no result this time, for I remember nothing at all since I became unconscious; so you have had all your long journeys for nothing, my learned friends, and a very good joke too"; at which the Regius Professor of Physiology burst into a roar of laughter and slapped his thigh in a highly indecorous fashion. The audience were so enraged at this unseemly behaviour on the part of their host, that there might have been a considerable disturbance, had it not been for the judicious interference of young Fritz von Hartmann, who had now recovered from his lethargy. Stepping to the front of the platform, the young man apologised for the conduct of his companion. "I am sorry to say," he said, "that he is a harum-scarum sort of fellow, although he appeared so grave at the commencement of this experiment. He is still suffering from mesmeric reaction, and is hardly accountable for his words. As to the experiment itself, I do not consider it to be a failure. It is very possible that our spirits may have been communing in space during this hour; but, unfortunately, our gross bodily memory is distinct from our spirit, and we cannot recall what has occurred. My energies shall now be devoted to devising some means by which spirits may be able to recollect what occurs to them in their free state, and I trust that when I have worked this out, I may have the pleasure of meeting you all once again in this hall, and demonstrating to you the result." This address, coming from so young a student, caused considerable astonishment among the audience, and some were inclined to be offended, thinking that he assumed rather too much importance. The majority, however, looked upon him as a young man of great promise, and many comparisons were made as they left the hall between his dignified conduct and the levity of his professor, who during the above remarks was laughing heartily in a corner, by no means abashed at the failure of the experiment.

Now although all these learned men were filing out of the lecture-room under the impression that they had seen nothing of note, as a matter of fact one of the most wonderful things in the whole history of the world had just occurred before their very eyes. Professor von Baumgarten had been so far correct in his theory that both his spirit and that of his pupil had been for a time absent from the body. But here a strange and unforeseen complication had occurred. In their return the spirit of Fritz von Hartmann had entered into the body of Alexis von Baumgarten, and that of Alexis von Baumgarten had taken up its abode in the frame of Fritz von Hartmann. Hence the slang and scurrility which issued from the lips of the serious Professor, and hence also the weighty words and grave statements which fell from the careless student. It was an unprecedented event, yet no one knew of it, least of all those whom it concerned.

THE GREAT KEINPLATZ EXPERIMENT

The body of the Professor, feeling conscious suddenly of a great dryness about the back of the throat, sallied out into the street, still chuckling to himself over the result of the experiment, for the soul of Fritz within was reckless at the thought of the bride whom he had won so easily. His first impulse was to go up to the house and see her, but on second thought he came to the conclusion that it would be best to stay away until Madame Baumgarten should be informed by her husband of the agreement which had been made. He therefore made his way down to the Grüner Mann, which was one of the favourite trysting-places of the wilder students, and ran, boisterously waving his cane in the air, into the little parlour, where sat Spiegler and Müller and half a dozen other boon companions.

"Ha, ha! my boys," he shouted. "I knew I should find you here. Drink up, every one of you, and call for what you like, for I'm going to stand treat to-day."

Had the green man who is depicted upon the signpost of that well-known inn suddenly marched into the room and called for a bottle of wine, the students could not have been more amazed than they were by this unexpected entry of their revered professor. They were so astonished that for a minute or two they glared at him in utter bewilderment without being able to make any reply to his hearty invitation.

"*Donner und Blitzen!*" shouted the Professor angrily. "What the deuce is the matter with you, then? You sit there like a set of stuck pigs staring at me. What is it then?"

"It is the unexpected honour," stammered Spiegel, who was in the chair.

"Honour—rubbish!" said the Professor testily. "Do you think that just because I happen to have been exhibiting mesmerism to a parcel of old fossils, I am therefore too proud to associate with dear old friends like you? Come out of that chair, Spiegel, my boy, for I shall preside now. Beer, or wine, or schnapps, my lads—call for what you like, and put it all down to me."

Never was there such an afternoon in the Grüner Mann. The foaming flagons of lager and the green-necked bottles of Rhenish circulated merrily. By degrees the students lost their shyness in the presence of their Professor. As for him, he shouted, he sang, he roared, he balanced a long tobacco-pipe upon his nose, and offered to run a hundred yards against any member of the company. The Kellner and the barmaid whispered to each other outside the door their astonishment at such proceedings on the part of a Regius Professor of the ancient university of Keinplatz. They had still more to whisper about afterwards, for the learned man cracked the Kellner's crown, and kissed the barmaid behind the kitchen door.

"Gentlemen," said the Professor, standing up, albeit somewhat totteringly, at the end of the table, and balancing his high old-fashioned wine glass in his bony hand, "I must now explain to you what is the cause of this festivity."

"Hear! hear!" roared the students, hammering their beer glasses against the table; "a speech, a speech!—silence for a speech!"

"The fact is, my friends," said the Professor, beaming through his spectacles, "I hope very soon to be married."

"Married!" cried a student, bolder than the others. "Is Madame dead, then?"

"Madame who?"

"Why, Madame von Baumgarten, of course."

"Ha, ha!" laughed the Professor; "I can see, then, that you know all about my former difficulties. No, she is not dead, but I have reason to believe that she will not oppose my marriage."

"That is very accommodating of her," remarked one of the company.

"In fact," said the Professor, "I hope that she will now be induced to aid me in getting a wife. She and I never took to each other very much; but now I hope all that may be ended, and when I marry she will come and stay with me."

"What a happy family!" exclaimed some wag.

"Yes, indeed; and I hope you will come to my wedding, all of you. I won't mention names, but here is to my little bride!" and the Professor waved his glass in the air.

"Here's to his little bride!" roared the roysterers, with shouts of laughter. "Here's her health. *Sie soll leben—Hoch!*" And so the fun waxed still more fast and furious, while each young fellow followed the Professor's example, and drank a toast to the girl of his heart.

While all this festivity had been going on at the Grüner Mann, a very different scene had been enacted elsewhere. Young Fritz von Hartmann, with a solemn face and a reserved manner, had, after the experiment, consulted and adjusted some mathematical instruments; after which, with a few peremptory words to the janitor, he had walked out into the street and wended his way slowly in the direction of the house of the Professor. As he walked he saw Von Althaus, the professor of anatomy, in front of him, and quickening his pace he overtook him.

"I say, Von Althaus," he exclaimed, tapping him on the sleeve, "you were asking me for some information the other day concerning the middle coat of the cerebral arteries. Now I find—"

"*Donnerwetter!*" shouted Von Althaus, who was a peppery old fellow. "What the deuce do you mean by your impertinence! I'll have you up before the Academical Senate for this, sir"; with which threat he turned on his heel and hurried away. Von Hartmann was much surprised at this reception. "It's on account of this failure of my experiment," he said to himself, and continued moodily on his way.

Fresh surprises were in store for him, however. He was hurrying along when he was overtaken by two students. These youths, instead of raising their caps or showing any other sign of respect, gave a wild whoop of delight the instant that they saw him, and rushing at him, seized him by each arm and commenced dragging him along with them.

"*Gott in Himmel!*" roared Von Hartmann. "What is the meaning of this unparalleled insult? Where are you taking me?"

"To crack a bottle of wine with us," said the two students. "Come along! That is an invitation which you have never refused."

"I never heard of such insolence in my life!" cried Von Hartmann. "Let go my arms! I shall certainly have you rusticated for this. Let me go, I say!" and he kicked furiously at his captors.

"Oh, if you choose to turn ill-tempered, you may go where you like," the students said, releasing him. "We can do very well without you."

"I know you. I'll pay you out," said Von Hartmann furiously, and continued in the direction which he imagined to be his own home, much incensed at the two episodes which had occurred to him on the way.

Now, Madame von Baumgarten, who was looking out of the window and wondering why her husband was late for dinner, was considerably astonished to see the young student come stalking down the road. As already remarked, she had a great antipathy to him, and if ever he ventured into the house it was on sufferance, and under the protection of the Professor. Still more astonished was she, therefore, when she beheld him undo the wicket-gate and stride up the garden path with the air of one who is master of the situation. She could hardly believe her eyes, and hastened to the door with all her maternal instincts up in arms. From the upper windows the fair Elise had also observed this daring move upon the part of her lover, and her heart beat quick with mingled pride and consternation.

"Good day, sir," Madame von Baumgarten remarked to the intruder, as she stood in gloomy majesty in the open doorway.

"A very fine day indeed, Martha," returned the other. "Now, don't stand there like a statue of Juno, but bustle about and get the dinner ready, for I am well-nigh starved."

"Martha! Dinner!" ejaculated the lady, falling back in astonishment.

"Yes, dinner, Martha, dinner!" howled Von Hartmann, who was becoming irritable. "Is there anything wonderful in that request when a man has been out all day? I'll wait in the dining-room. Anything will do. *Schinken*, and sausage, and prunes—any little thing that happens to be about. There you are, standing staring again. Woman, will you or will you not stir your legs?"

This last address, delivered with a perfect shriek of rage, had the effect of sending good Madame von Baumgarten flying along the passage and through the kitchen, where she locked herself up in the scullery and went into violent hysterics. In the meantime Von Hartmann strode into the room and threw himself down upon the sofa in the worst of tempers.

"Elise!" he shouted. "Confound the girl! Elise!"

Thus roughly summoned, the young lady came timidly downstairs and into the presence of her lover. "Dearest!" she cried, throwing her arms round him, "I know this is all done for my sake. It is a *ruse* in order to see me."

Von Hartmann's indignation at this fresh attack upon him was so great that he became speechless for a minute from rage, and could only glare and shake his fists, while he struggled in her embrace. When he at last regained his utterance, he indulged in such a bellow of passion that the young lady dropped back, petrified with fear, into an arm-chair.

"Never have I passed such a day in my life," Von Hartmann cried, stamping upon the floor. "My experiment has failed. Von Althaus has insulted me. Two students have dragged me along the public road. My wife nearly faints when I ask her for dinner, and my daughter flies at me and hugs me like a grizzly bear."

"You are ill, dear," the young lady cried. "Your mind is wandering. You have not even kissed me once."

"No, and I don't intend to either," Van Hartmann said with decision. "You ought to be ashamed of yourself. Why don't you go and fetch my slippers, and help your mother to dish the dinner?"

"And is it for this," Elise cried, burying her face in her handkerchief— "is it for this that I have loved you passionately for upwards of ten months? Is it for this that I have braved my mother's wrath? Oh, you have broken my heart; I am sure you have!" and she sobbed hysterically.

"I can't stand much more of this," roared Von Hartmann furiously. "What the deuce does the girl mean? What did I do ten months ago which inspired you with such a particular affection for me? If you are really so very fond, you would do better to run away down and find the *Schinken* and some bread, instead of talking all this nonsense."

"Oh, my darling!" cried the unhappy maiden, throwing herself into the arms of what she imagined to be her lover. "You do but joke in order to frighten your little Elise."

Now it chanced that at the moment of this unexpected embrace Von Hartmann was still leaning back against the end of the sofa, which, like much German furniture, was in a somewhat rickety condition. It also chanced that beneath this end of the sofa there stood a tank full of water in which the physiologist was conducting certain experiments upon the ova of fish, and which he kept in his drawing room in order to ensure an equable temperature. The additional weight of the maiden, combined with the impetus with which she hurled herself upon him, caused the precarious piece of furniture to give way, and the body of the unfortunate student was hurled backwards into the tank, in which his head and shoulders were firmly wedged, while his lower extremities flapped helplessly about in the air. This was the last straw. Extricating himself with some difficulty from his unpleasant position, Von Hartmann gave an inarticulate yell of fury, and dashing out of the room, in spite of the entreaties of Elise, he seized his hat and rushed off into the town, all dripping and dishevelled, with the intention of seeking in some inn the food and comfort which he could not find at home.

As the spirit of Von Baumgarten encased in the body of Von Hartmann strode down the winding pathway which led down to the little town, brooding angrily over his many wrongs, he became aware that an elderly man was approaching him who appeared to be in an advanced state of intoxication. Von Hartmann waited by the side of the road and watched this individual, who came stumbling along, reeling from one side of the road to the other, and singing a student song in a very husky and drunken voice. At first his interest was merely excited by the fact of seeing a man of so venerable an appearance in such a disgraceful condition, but as he approached nearer, he became convinced that he knew the other well, though he could not recall when or where he had met him. This impression became so strong with him, that when the stranger came abreast of him he stepped in front of him and took a good look at his features.

"Well, sonny," said the drunken man, surveying Von Hartmann and swaying about in front of him, "where the *Henker* have I seen you before? I know you as well as I know myself. Who the deuce are you?"

"I am Professor von Baumgarten," said the student. "May I ask who you are? I am strangely familiar with your features."

"You should never tell lies, young man," said the other. "You're certainly not the Professor, for he is an ugly snuffy old chap, and you are a big broad-shouldered young fellow. As to myself, I am Fritz von Hartmann at your service."

"That you certainly are not," exclaimed the body of Von Hartmann. "You might very well be his father. But hullo, sir, are you aware that you are wearing my studs and my watch-chain?"

"*Donnerwetter!*" hiccoughed the other. "If those are not the trousers for which my tailor is about to sue me, may I never taste beer again."

Now as Von Hartmann, overwhelmed by the many strange things which had occurred to him that day, passed his hand over his forehead and cast his eyes downwards, he chanced to catch the reflection of his own face in a pool which the rain had left upon the road. To his utter astonishment he perceived that his face was that of a youth, that his dress was that of a fashionable young student, and that in every way he was the antithesis of the grave and scholarly figure in which his mind was wont to dwell. In an instant his active brain ran over the series of events which had occurred and sprang to the conclusion. He fairly reeled under the blow.

"*Himmel!*" he cried, "I see it all. Our souls are in the wrong bodies. I am you and you are I. My theory is proved—but at what an expense! Is the most scholarly mind in Europe to go about with this frivolous exterior? Oh the labours of a lifetime are ruined!" and he smote his breast in his despair.

"I say," remarked the real Von Hartmann from the body of the professor, "I quite see the force of your remarks, but don't go knocking my body about like that. You received it in an excellent condition, but I perceive that you have wet it and bruised it, and spilled snuff over my ruffled shirt-front."

"It matters little," the other said moodily. "Such as we are so must we stay. My theory is triumphantly proved, but the cost is terrible."

"If I thought so," said the spirit of the student, "it would be hard indeed. What could I do with these stiff old limbs, and how could I woo Elise and persuade her that I was not her father? No, thank Heaven, in spite of the beer which has upset me more than ever it could upset my real self, I can see a way out of it."

"How?" gasped the Professor.

"Why, by repeating the experiment. Liberate our souls once more, and the chances are that they will find their way back into their respective bodies."

No drowning man could clutch more eagerly at a straw than did Von Baumgarten's spirit at this suggestion. In feverish haste he dragged his own frame to the side of the road and threw it into a mesmeric trance; he then extracted the crystal ball from the pocket, and managed to bring himself into the same condition.

Some students and peasants who chanced to pass during the next hour were much astonished to see the worthy Professor of Physiology and his favourite student both sitting upon a very muddy bank and both completely insensible. Before the hour was up quite a crowd had assembled, and they were discussing the advisability of sending for an ambulance to convey the pair to hospital, when the learned savant opened his eyes and gazed vacantly around him. For an instant he seemed to forget how he had come there, but next moment he astonished his audience by waving his skinny arms above his head and crying out in a voice of rapture, *"Gott sei gedankt!* I am myself again. I feel I am!"* Nor was the amazement lessened when the student, springing to his feet, burst into the same cry, and the two performed a sort of *pas de joie* in the middle of the road.

For some time after that people had some suspicion of the sanity of both the actors in this strange episode. When the Professor published his experiences in the *Medicalschrift* as he had promised, he was met by an intimation, even from his colleagues, that he would do well to have his mind cared for, and that another such publication would certainly consign him to a madhouse. The student also found by experience that it was wisest to be silent about the matter.

When the worthy lecturer returned home that night he did not receive the cordial welcome which he might have looked for after his strange adventures. On the contrary, he was roundly upbraided by both his female relatives for smelling of drink and tobacco, and also for being absent while a young scapegrace invaded the house and insulted its occupants. It was long before the domestic atmosphere of the lecturer's house resumed its normal quiet, and longer still before the genial face of Von Hartmann was seen beneath its roof. Perseverance, however, conquers every obstacle, and the student eventually succeeded in pacifying the enraged ladies and in establishing himself upon the old footing. He has now no longer any cause to fear the enmity of Madame, for he is Hauptmann von Hartmann of the Emperor's own Uhlans, and his loving wife Elise has already presented him with two little Uhlans as a visible sign and token of her affection.

H. G. WELLS

THE REMARKABLE CASE OF DAVIDSON'S EYES

THE transitory mental aberration of Sidney Davidson, remarkable enough in itself, is still more remarkable if Wade's explanation is to be credited. It sets one dreaming of the oddest possibilities of intercommunication in the future, of spending an intercalary five minutes on the other side of the world, or being watched in our most secret operations by unsuspected eyes. It happened that I was the immediate witness of Davidson's seizure, and so it falls naturally to me to put the story upon paper.

When I say that I was the immediate witness of his seizure, I mean that I was the first on the scene. The thing happened at the Harlow Technical College, just beyond the Highgate Archway. He was alone in the larger laboratory when the thing happened. I was in a smaller room, where the balances are, writing up some notes. The thunderstorm had completely upset my work, of course. It was just after one of the louder peals that I thought I heard some glass smash in the other room. I stopped writing, and turned around to listen. For a moment I heard nothing; the hail was playing the devil's tattoo on the corrugated zinc of the roof. Then came another sound, a smash—no doubt of it this time. Something heavy had been knocked off the bench. I jumped up at once and went and opened the door leading into the big laboratory.

I was surprised to hear a queer sort of laugh, and saw Davidson standing unsteadily in the middle of the room, with a dazzled look on his face. My first impression was that he was drunk. He did not notice me. He was clawing out at something invisible a yard in front of his face. He put out his hand, slowly, rather. hesitatingly, and then clutched nothing. "What's come to it?" he said. He held up his hands to his face, fingers spread out. "Great Scott!" he said. The thing happened three or four years ago, when every one swore by that personage. Then he began raising his feet clumsily, as though he had expected to find them glued to the floor.

"Davidson!" cried I. "What's the matter with you?" He turned round in my direction and looked about for me. He looked over me and at me and on either side of me, without the slightest sign of seeing me. "Waves," he said; "and a remarkably neat schooner. I'd swear that was Bellow's voice. *Hallo!*" He shouted suddenly at the top of his voice.

I thought he was up to some foolery. Then I saw littered about his feet the shattered remains of the best of our electrometers. "What's up, man?" said I. "You've smashed the electrometer!"

"Bellows again!" said he. "Friends left, if my hands are gone. Something about electrometers. Which way *are* you, Bellows?" He suddenly came staggering towards me. "The damned stuff cuts like butter," he said. He walked straight into the bench and recoiled. "None so buttery that!" he said, and stood swaying.

I felt scared. "Davidson," said I, "what on earth's come over you?"

He looked round him in every direction. "I could swear that was Bellows. Why don't you show yourself like a man, Bellows?"

It occurred to me that he must be suddenly struck blind. I walked round the table and laid my hand upon his arm. I never saw a man more startled in my life. He jumped away from me, and came round into an attitude of self-defence, his face fairly distorted with terror. "Good God!" he cried. "What was that?"

"It's I—Bellows. Confound it, Davidson!"

He jumped when I answered him and stared—how can I express it?— right through me. He began talking, not to me, but to himself. "Here in broad daylight on a clear beach. Not a place to hide in." He looked about him wildly. "Here! I'm *off*." He suddenly turned and ran headlong into the big electro-magnet—so violently that, as we found afterwards, he bruised his shoulder and jawbone cruelly. At that he stepped back a pace, and cried out with almost a whimper, "What, in Heaven's name, has come over me?" He stood, blanched with terror and trembling violently, with his right arm clutching his left, where that had collided with the magnet.

By that time I was excited and fairly scared. "Davidson," said I, "don't be afraid."

He was startled at my voice, but not so excessively as before.

I repeated my words in as clear and as firm a tone as I could assume. "Bellows," he said, "is that you?"

"Can't you see it's me?"

He laughed. "I can't even see it's myself. Where the devil are we?"

"Here," said I, "in the laboratory."

"The laboratory!" he answered in a puzzled tone, and put his hand to his forehead. "I *was* in the laboratory—till that flash came, but I'm hanged if I'm there now. What ship is that?"

"There's no ship," said I. "Do be sensible, old chap."

"No ship," he repeated, and seemed to forget my denial forthwith. "I suppose," said he slowly, "we're both dead. But the rummy part is I feel as though I still had a body. Don't get used to it all at once, I suppose. The old shop was struck by lightning, I suppose. Jolly quick thing, Bellows—eh?"

"Don't talk nonsense. You're very much alive. You are in the laboratory, blundering about. You've just smashed a new electrometer. I don't envy you when Boyce arrives."

He stared away from me towards the diagrams of cryohydrates. "I must be deaf," said he. "They've fired a gun, for there goes the puff of smoke, and I never heard a sound."

I put my hand on his arm again, and this time he was less alarmed. "We seem to have a sort of invisible bodies," said he. "By Jove! there's a boat coming round the headland. It's very much like the old life after all—in a different climate."

I shook his arm. "Davidson," I cried, "wake up!"

It was just then that Boyce came in. So soon as he spoke, Davidson exclaimed, "Old Boyce! Dead too! What a lark!" I hastened to explain that Davidson was in a kind of somnambulistic trance. Boyce was interested at once. We both did all we could to rouse the fellow out of his extraordinary state. He answered our questions, and asked us some of his own, but his attention seemed distracted by his hallucination about a beach and a ship. He kept interpolating observations concerning some boat and the davits, and sails filling with the wind. It made one feel queer, in the dusky laboratory, to hear him saying such things.

He was blind and helpless. We had to walk him down the passage, one at each elbow, to Boyce's private room, and while Boyce talked to him there, and humored him about this ship idea, I went along the corridor and asked old Wade to come and look at him. The voice of our Dean sobered him a little, but not very much. He asked where his hands were, and why he had to walk about up to his waist in the ground. Wade thought over him a long time—you know how he knits his brows—and then made him feel the couch, guiding his hands to it. "That's a couch," said Wade. "The couch in the private room of Professor Boyce. Horse-hair stuffing."

Davidson felt about, and puzzled over it, and answered presently that he could feel it all right, but he couldn't see it.

"What *do* you see?" asked Wade. Davidson said he could see nothing but a lot of sand and broken-up shells. Wade gave him some other things to feel, telling him what they were, and watching him keenly.

"The ship is almost hull down," said Davidson presently, *apropos* of nothing.

"Never mind the ship," said Wade. "Listen to me, Davidson. Do you know what hallucination means?"

"Rather," said Davidson.

"Well, everything you see is hallucinatory."

"Bishop Berkeley," said Davidson.

"Don't mistake me," said Wade. "You are alive and in this room of Boyce's. But something has happened to your eyes. You cannot see; you can feel and hear, but not see. Do you follow me?"

"It seems to me that I see too much." Davidson rubbed his knuckles into his eyes. "Well?" he said.

"That's all. Don't let it perplex you. Bellows here and I will take you home in a cab."

"Wait a bit." Davidson thought. "Help me to sit down," said he presently; "and now—I'm sorry to trouble you—but will you tell me all that over again?"

Wade repeated it very patiently. Davidson shut his eyes, and pressed his hands upon his forehead.

"Yes," said he. "It's quite right. Now my eyes are shut I know you're right. That's you, Bellows, sitting by me on the couch. I'm in England again. And we're in the dark."

Then he opened his eyes. "And there," said he, "is the sun just rising, and the yards of the ship, and a tumbled sea, and a couple of birds flying. I never saw anything so real. And I'm sitting up to my neck in a bank of sand."

He bent forward and covered his face with his hands. Then he opened his eyes again. "Dark sea and sunrise! And yet I'm sitting on a sofa in old Boyce's room! . . . God help me!"

That was the beginning. For three weeks this strange affection of Davidson's eyes continued unabated. It was far worse than being blind. He was absolutely helpless, and had to be fed like a newly-hatched bird, and led about and undressed. If he attempted to move, he fell over things or struck himself against walls or doors. After a day or so he got used to hearing our voices without seeing us, and willingly admitted he was at home, and that Wade was right in what he told him. My sister, to whom he was engaged, insisted on coming to see him, and would sit for hours every day while he talked about this beach of his. Holding her hand seemed to comfort him immensely. He explained that when he left the College and drove home—he lived in Hampstead village—it appeared to him as if we drove right through a sandhill—it was perfectly black until he emerged again—and through rocks and trees and solid obstacles, and when he was taken to his own room it made him giddy and almost frantic with the fear of falling, because going upstairs seemed to lift him thirty or forty feet above the rocks of his imaginary island. He kept saying he should smash all the eggs. The end was that he had to be taken down into his father's consulting room and laid upon a couch that stood there.

He described the island as being a bleak kind of place on the whole, with very little vegetation, except some peaty stuff, and a lot of bare rock. There were multitudes of penguins, and they made the rocks white and disagreeable to see. The sea was often rough, and once there was a thunderstorm, and he lay and shouted at the silent flashes. Once or twice seals pulled up on the beach, but only on the first two or three days. He said it was very funny the way in which the penguins used to waddle right through him, and how he seemed to lie among them without disturbing them.

I remember one odd thing, and that was when he wanted very badly to smoke. We put a pipe in his hands—he almost poked his eye out with it—and lit it. But he couldn't taste anything. I've since found it's the same with me—I don't know if it's the usual case—that I cannot enjoy tobacco at all unless I can see the smoke.

But the queerest part of his vision came when Wade sent him out in a bath-chair to get fresh air. The Davidsons hired a chair, and got that deaf and obstinate dependant of theirs, Widgery, to attend to it. Widgery's ideas of healthy expeditions were peculiar. My sister, who had been to the Dogs' Home, met them in Camden Town, towards King's Cross, Widgery trotting along complacently, and Davidson, evidently most distressed, trying in his feeble, blind way to attract Widgery's attention.

He positively wept when my sister spoke to him. "Oh, get me out of this horrible darkness!" he said, feeling for her hand. "I must get out of it, or I shall die." He was quite incapable of explaining what was the matter, but my sister decided he must go home, and presently, as they went uphill towards Hampstead, the horror seemed to drop from him. He said it was good to see the stars again, though it was then about noon and a blazing day.

"It seemed," he told me afterwards, "as if I was being carried irresistibly towards the water. I was not very much alarmed at first. Of course it was night there—a lovely night."

"Of course?" I asked, for that struck me as odd.

"Of course," said he. "It's always night there when it is day here. . . . Well, we went right into the water, which was calm and shining under the moonlight—just a broad swell that seemed to grow broader and flatter as I came down into it. The surface glistened just like a skin—it might have been empty space underneath for all I could tell to the contrary. Very slowly, for I rode slanting into it, the water crept up to my eyes. Then I went under and the skin seemed to break and heal again about my eyes. The moon gave a jump up in the sky and grew green and dim, and fish, faintly glowing, came darting round me—and things that seemed made of luminous glass; and I passed through a tangle of seaweeds that shone with an oily lustre. And so I drove down into the sea, and the stars went out one by one, and the moon grew greener and darker, and the seaweed became a luminous purple-red. It was all very faint and mysterious, and everything seemed to quiver. And all the while I could hear the wheels of the bath chair creaking, and the footsteps of people going by, and a man in the distance selling the special *Pall Mall*.

"I kept sinking down deeper and deeper into the water. It became inky black about me, not a ray from above came down into that darkness, and the phosphorescent things grew brighter and brighter. The snaky branches of the deeper weeds flickered like the flames of spirit-lamps; but, after a time, there were no more weeds. The fishes came staring and gaping towards me, and into me and through me. I never imagined such fishes before. They had lines of fire along the sides of them as though they had been outlined with a luminous pencil. And there was a ghastly thing swimming backwards with a lot of twining arms. And then I saw, coming very slowly towards me through the gloom, a hazy mass of light that resolved itself as it drew nearer into multitudes of fishes, struggling and darting round something that drifted. I drove on straight towards it, and presently I saw in the midst of the tumult, and by the light of the fish, a bit of splintered spar looming over me, and a dark hull tilting over, and some glowing phosphorescent forms that were shaken and writhed as the fish bit at them. Then it was I began to try to attract Widgery's attention. A horror came upon me. Ugh! I should have driven right into those half-eaten—things. If your sister had not come! They had great holes in them, Bellows, and . . . Never mind. But it was ghastly!"

For three weeks Davidson remained in this singular state, seeing what at the time we imagined was an altogether phantasmal world, and stone blind to the world around him. Then, one Tuesday, when I called I met old Davidson in the passage. "He can see his thumb!" the old gentleman said, in a perfect transport. He was struggling into his overcoat. "He can see his thumb, Bellows!" he said, with the tears in his eyes. "The lad will be all right yet."

I rushed in to Davidson. He was holding up a little book before his face, and looking at it and laughing in a weak kind of way.

"It's amazing," said he. "There's a kind of patch come there." He pointed with his finger. "I'm on the rocks as usual, and the penguins are staggering and flapping about as usual, and there's been a whale showing every now and then, but it's got too dark now to make him out. But put something *there*, and I see it—I do see it. It's very dim and broken in places, but I see it all the same, like a faint spectre of itself. I found it out this morning while they were dressing me. It's like a hole in this infernal phantom world. Just put your hand by mine. No—not there. Ah! Yes! I see it. The base of your thumb and a bit of cuff! It looks like the ghost of a bit of your hand sticking out of the darkling sky. Just by it there's a group of stars like a cross coming out."

From that time Davidson began to mend. His account of the change, like his account of the vision, was oddly convincing. Over patches of his field of vision, the phantom world grew fainter, grew transparent, as it were, and through these translucent gaps he began to see dimly the real world about him. The patches grew in size and number, ran together and spread until only here and there were blind spots left upon his eyes. He was able to get up and steer himself about, feed himself once more, read, smoke, and behave like an ordinary citizen again. At first it was very confusing for him to have these two pictures over-lapping each other like the changing views of a lantern, but in a little while he began to distinguish the real from the illusory.

At first he was unfeignedly glad, and seemed only too anxious to complete his cure by taking exercise and tonics. But as that odd island of his began to fade away from him, he became queerly interested in it. He wanted particularly to go down in the deep sea again, and would spend half his time wandering about the low-lying parts of London, trying to find the water-logged wreck he had seen drifting. The glare of real daylight very soon impressed him so vividly as to blot out everything of his shadowy world, but of a night-time, in a darkened room, he could still see the white-splashed rocks of the island, and the clumsy penguins staggering to and fro. But even these grew fainter and fainter, and, at last, soon after he married my sister, he saw them for the last time.

And now to tell of the queerest thing of all.

About two years after his cure I dined with the Davidsons, and after dinner a man named Atkins called in. He is a lieutenant in the Royal Navy, and a pleasant, talkative man. He was on friendly terms with my brother-in-law, and was soon on friendly terms with me. It came out that he was engaged to Davidson's cousin, and incidentally he took out a kind of pocket photograph case to show us a new rendering of his *fiancée*. "And, by-the-by," said he, "here's the old *Fulmar*."

Davidson looked at it casually. Then suddenly his face lit up. "Good heavens!" said he. "I could almost swear—"

"What?" said Atkins.

"That I had seen that ship before."

"Don't see how you can have. She hasn't been out of the South Seas for six years, and before then—"

"But," began Davidson, and then, "Yes—that's the ship I dreamt of; I'm sure that's the ship I dreamt of. She was standing off an island that swarmed with penguins, and she fired a gun."

"Good Lord!" said Atkins, who had not heard the particulars of the seizure. "How the deuce could you dream that?"

And then, bit by bit, it came out that on the very day Davidson was seized, H.M.S. *Fulmar* had actually been off a little rock to the south of Antipodes Island. A boat had landed overnight to get penguins' eggs, had been delayed, and a thunderstorm drifting up, the boat's crew had waited until the morning before rejoining the ship. Atkins had been one of them, and he corroborated word for word, the descriptions Davidson had given of the island and the boat. There is not the slightest doubt in any of our minds that Davidson has really seen the place. In some unaccountable way, while he moved hither and thither in London, his sight moved hither and thither in a manner that corresponded, about this distant island. *How* is absolutely a mystery.

That completes the remarkable story of Davidson's eyes. It's perhaps the best authenticated case in existence of real vision at a distance. Explanation there is none forthcoming, except what Professor Wade had thrown out. But this explanation invokes the Fourth Dimension, and a dissertation on theoretical kinds of space. To talk of there being "a kink in space" seems mere nonsense to me; it may be because I am no mathematician. When I said that nothing would alter the fact that the place is eight thousand miles away, he answered that two points might be a yard away on a sheet of paper, and yet be brought together by bending the paper round. The reader may grasp his argument, but I certainly do not. His idea seems to be that Davidson, stooping between the poles of the big electro-magnet, had some extraordinary twist given to his retinal elements through the sudden change in the field of force due to the lightning.

He thinks, as a consequence of this, that it may be possible to live visually in one part of the world, while one lives bodily in another. He has even made some experiments in support of his views; but, so far, he has simply succeeded in blinding a few dogs. I believe that is the net result of his work, though I have not seen him for some weeks. But the whole of this theory seems fantastic to me.

The facts concerning Davidson stand on an altogether different footing and I can testify personally to the accuracy of every detail I have given.

JULIAN HUXLEY

THE TISSUE-CULTURE KING

WE HAD been for three days engaged in crossing a swamp. At last we were out on dry ground, winding up a gentle slope. Near the top the brush grew thicker. The look of a rampart grew as we approached; it had the air of having been deliberately planted by men. We did not wish to have to hack our way through the spiky barricade, so turned to the right along the front of the green wall. After three or four hundred yards we came on a clearing which led into the bush, narrowing down to what seemed a regular passage or trackway. This made us a little suspicious. However, I thought we had better make all the progress we could, and so ordered the caravan to turn into the opening, myself taking second place behind the guide.

Suddenly the tracker stopped with a guttural exclamation. I looked, and there was one of the great African toads, hopping with a certain ponderosity across the path. But it had a second head growing upwards from its shoulders! I had never seen anything like this before, and wanted to secure such a remarkable monstrosity for our collections; but as I moved forward, the creature took a couple of hops into the shelter of the prickly scrub.

We pushed on, and I became convinced that the gap we were following was artificial. After a little, a droning sound came to our ears, which we very soon set down as that of a human voice. The party was halted, and I crept forward with the guide. Peeping through the last screen of brush we looked down into a hollow and were immeasurably startled at what we saw there. The voice proceeded from an enormous Negro man at least eight feet high, the biggest man I had ever seen outside a circus. He was squatting, from time to time prostrating the forepart of his body, and reciting some prayer or incantation. The object of his devotion was before him on the ground; it was a small flat piece of glass held on a little carved ebony stand. By his side was a huge spear, together with a painted basket with a lid.

After a minute or so, the giant bowed down in silence, then took up the ebony-and-glass object and placed it in the basket. Then to my utter amazement he drew out a two-headed toad like the first I had seen, but in a cage of woven grass, placed it on the ground, and proceeded to more genuflection and ritual murmurings. As soon as this was over, the toad was replaced, and the squatting giant tranquilly regarded the landscape.

Beyond the hollow or dell lay an undulating country, with clumps of bush. A sound in the middle distance attracted attention; glimpses of color moved through the scrub; and a party of three or four dozen men were seen approaching, most of them as gigantic as our first acquaintance. All marched in order, armed with great spears, and wearing colored loin straps with a sort of sporran, it seemed, in front. They were preceded · by an intelligent-looking Negro of ordinary stature armed with a club, and accompanied by two figures more remarkable than the giants. They were undersized, almost dwarfish, with huge heads, and enormously fat and brawny both in face and body. They wore bright yellow cloaks over their black shoulders.

At sight of them, our giant rose and stood stiffly by the side of his basket. The party approached and halted. Some order was given, a giant stepped out from the ranks towards ours, picked up the basket, handed it stiffly to the newcomer, and fell into place in the little company. We were clearly witnessing some regular routine of relieving guard, and I was racking my brains to think what the whole thing might signify—guards, giants, dwarfs, toads—when to my dismay I heard an exclamation at my shoulder.

It was one of those damned porters, a confounded fellow who always liked to show his independence. Bored with waiting, I suppose, he had self-importantly crept up to see what it was all about, and the sudden sight of the company of giants had been too much for his nerves. I made a signal to lie quiet, but it was too late. The exclamation had been heard; the leader gave a quick command, and the giants rushed up and out in two groups to surround us.

Violence and resistance were clearly out of the question. With my heart in my mouth, but with as much dignity as I could muster, I jumped up and threw out my empty hands, at the same time telling the tracker not to shoot. A dozen spears seemed towering over me, but none were launched; the leader ran up the slope and gave a command. Two giants came up and put my hands through their arms. The tracker and the porter were herded in front at the spear point. The other porters now discovered there was something amiss, and began to shout and run away, with half the spearmen after them. We three were gently but firmly marched down and across the hollow.

I understood nothing of the language, and called to my tracker to try his hand. It turned out that there was some dialect of which he had a little understanding, and we could learn nothing save the fact that we were being taken to some superior authority.

For two days we were marched through pleasant park-like country, with villages at intervals. Every now and then some new monstrosity in the shape of a dwarf or an incredibly fat woman or a two-headed animal would be visible, until I thought I had stumbled on the original source of supply of circus freaks.

The country at last began to slope gently down to a pleasant river-valley; and presently we neared the capital. It turned out to be a really large town for Africa, its mud walls of strangely impressive architectural form, with their heavy, slabby buttresses, and giants standing guard upon them. Seeing us approach, they shouted, and a crowd poured out of the nearest gate. My God, what a crowd! I was getting used to giants by this time, but here was a regular Barnum and Bailey show; more semi-dwarfs; others like them but more so—one could not tell whether the creatures were precociously mature children or horribly stunted adults; others portentously fat, with arms like sooty legs of mutton, and rolls and volutes of fat crisping out of their steatopygous posteriors; still others precociously senile and wizened, others hateful and imbecile in looks. Of course, there were plenty of ordinary Negroes too, but enough of the extraordinary to make one feel pretty queer. Soon after we got inside, I suddenly noted something else which appeared inexplicable—a telephone wire, with perfectly good insulators, running across from tree to tree. A telephone—in an unknown African town. I gave it up.

But another surprise was in store for me. I saw a figure pass across from one large building to another—a figure unmistakably that of a white man. In the first place, it was wearing white ducks and sun helmet; in the second, it had a pale face.

He turned at the sound of our cavalcade and stood looking a moment; then walked towards us.

"Halloa!" I shouted. "Do you speak English?"

"Yes," he answered, "but keep quiet a moment," and began talking quickly to our leaders, who treated him with the greatest deference. He dropped back to me and spoke rapidly: "You are to be taken into the council hall to be examined: but I will see to it that no harm comes to you. This is a forbidden land to strangers, and you must be prepared to be held up for a time. You will be sent down to see me in the temple buildings as soon as the formalities are over, and I'll explain things. They want a bit of explaining," he added with a dry laugh. "By the way, my name is Hascombe, lately research worker at Middlesex Hospital, now religious adviser to His Majesty King Mgobe." He laughed again and pushed ahead. He was an interesting figure—perhaps fifty years old, spare body, thin face, with a small beard, and rather sunken, hazel eyes. As for his expression, he looked cynical, but also as if he were interested in life.

By this time we were at the entrance to the hall. Our giants formed up outside, with my men behind them, and only I and the leader passed in. The examination was purely formal, and remarkable chiefly for the ritual and solemnity which characterized all the actions of the couple of dozen fine-looking men in long robes who were our examiners. My men were herded off to some compound. I was escorted down to a little hut, furnished with some attempt at European style, where I found Hascombe.

As soon as we were alone I was after him with my questions. "Now you can tell me. Where are we? What is the meaning of all this circus business and this menagerie of monstrosities? And how do you come here?" He cut me short. "It's a long story, so let me save time by telling it my own way."

I am not going to tell it as he told it; but will try to give a more connected account, the result of many later talks with him, and of my own observations.

Hascombe had been a medical student of great promise; and after his degree had launched out into research. He had first started on parasitic protozoa, but had given that up in favor of tissue culture; from these he had gone off to cancer research, and from that to a study of developmental physiology. Later a big Commission on sleeping sickness had been organized, and Hascombe, restless and eager for travel, had pulled wires and got himself appointed as one of the scientific staff sent to Africa. He was much impressed with the view that wild game acted as a reservoir for the *Trypanosoma gambiense*. When he learned of the extensive migrations of game, he saw here an important possible means of spreading the disease and asked leave to go up country to investigate the whole problem. When the Commission as a whole had finished its work, he was allowed to stay in Africa with one other white man and a company of porters to see what he could discover. His white companion was a laboratory technician, a taciturn non-commissioned officer of science called Aggers.

There is no object in telling of their experiences here. Suffice it that they lost their way and fell into the hands of this same tribe. That was fifteen years ago: and Aggers was now long dead—as the result of a wound inflicted when he was caught, after a couple of years, trying to escape.

On their capture, they too had been examined in the council chamber, and Hascombe (who had interested himself in a dilettante way in anthropology as in most other subjects of scientific inquiry) was much impressed by what he described as the exceedingly religious atmosphere. Everything was done with an elaboration of ceremony; the chief seemed more priest than king, and performed various rites at intervals, and priests were busy at some sort of altar the whole time. Among other things, he noticed that one of their rites was connected with blood. First the chief and then the councillors were in turn requisitioned for a drop of vital fluid pricked from their finger-tips, and the mixture, held in a little vessel, was slowly evaporated over a flame.

Some of Hascombe's men spoke a dialect not unlike that of their captors, and one was acting as interpreter. Things did not look too favorable. The country was a "holy place," it seemed, and the tribe a "holy race." Other Africans who trespassed there, if not killed, were enslaved, but for the most part they let well alone, and did not trespass. White men they had heard of, but never seen till now, and the debate was what to do—to kill, let go, or enslave? To let them go was contrary to all their principles: the holy place would be defiled if the news of it were spread abroad. To enslave them—yes; but what were they good for? and the Council seemed to feel an instinctive dislike for these other-colored creatures. Hascombe had an idea. He turned to the interpreter. "Say this: 'You revere the Blood. So do we white men; but we do more—we can render visible the blood's hidden nature and reality, and with permission I will show this great magic.'" He beckoned to the bearer who carried his precious microscope, set it up, drew a drop of blood from the tip of his finger with his knife, and mounted it on a slide under a coverslip. The bigwigs were obviously interested. They whispered to each other. At length, "Show us," commanded the chief.

Hascombe demonstrated his preparation with greater interest than he had ever done to first-year medical students in the old days. He explained that the blood was composed of little people of various sorts, each with their own lives, and that to spy upon them thus gave us new powers over them. The elders were more or less impressed. At any rate the sight of these thousands of corpuscles where they could see nothing before made them think, made them realize that the white man had power which might make him a desirable servant.

They would not ask to see their own blood for fear that the sight would put them into the power of those who saw it. But they had blood drawn from a slave. Hascombe asked too for a bird, and was able to create a certain interest by showing how different were the little people of its blood.

"Tell them," he said to the interpreter, "that I have many other powers and magics which I will show them if they will give me time."

The long and short of it was that he and his party were spared—He said he knew then what one felt when the magistrate said: "Remanded for a week."

He had been attracted by one of the elder statesmen of the tribe—a tall, powerful-looking man of middle-age; and was agreeably surprised when this man came round next day to see him. Hascombe later nicknamed him the Prince-Bishop, for his combination of the qualities of the statesman and the ecclesiastic: his real name was Bugala. He was as anxious to discover more about Hascombe's mysterious powers and resources as Hascombe was to learn what he could of the people into whose hands he had fallen, and they met almost every evening and talked far into the night.

Bugala's inquiries were as little prompted as Hascombe's by a purely academic curiosity. Impressed himself by the microscope, and still more by the effect which it had had on his colleagues, he was anxious to find out whether by utilizing the powers of the white man he could not secure his own advancement. At length, they struck a bargain. Bugala would see to it that no harm befell Hascombe. But Hascombe must put his resources and powers at the disposal of the Council; and Bugala would take good care to arrange matters so that he himself benefited. So far as Hascombe could make out, Bugala imagined a radical change in the national religion, a sort of reformation based on Hascombe's conjuring tricks; and that he would emerge as the High Priest of this changed system.

Hascombe had a sense of humor, and it was tickled. It seemed pretty clear that they could not escape, at least for the present. That being so, why not take the opportunity of doing a little research work at state expense—an opportunity which he and his like were always clamoring for at home? His thoughts began to run away with him. He would find out all he could of the rites and superstitions of the tribe. He would, by the aid of his knowledge and his scientific skill, exalt the details of these rites, the expression of those superstitions, the whole physical side of their religiosity, on to a new level which should to them appear truly miraculous.

It would not be worth my troubling to tell all the negotiations, the false starts, the misunderstandings. In the end he secured what he wanted —a building which could be used as a laboratory; an unlimited supply of slaves for the lower and priests for the higher duties of laboratory assistants, and the promise that when his scientific stores were exhausted they would do their best to secure others from the coast—a promise which was scrupulously kept, so that he never went short for lack of what money could buy.

He next applied himself diligently to a study of their religion and found that it was built round various main motifs. Of these, the central one was the belief in the divinity and tremendous importance of the Priest-King. The second was a form of ancestor-worship. The third was an animal cult, in particular of the more grotesque species of the African fauna. The fourth was sex, *con variazioni*. Hascombe reflected on these facts. Tissue culture; experimental embryology; endocrine treatment; artificial parthenogenesis. He laughed and said to himself: "Well, at least I can try, and it ought to be amusing."

That was how it all started. Perhaps the best way of giving some idea of how it had developed will be for me to tell my own impressions when Hascombe took me round his laboratories. One whole quarter of the town was devoted entirely to religion—it struck me as excessive, but Hascombe reminded me that Tibet spends one-fifth of its revenues on melted butter to burn before its shrines. Facing the main square was the chief temple, built impressively enough of solid mud. On either side were the apartments where dwelt the servants of the gods and administrators of the sacred rites. Behind were Hascombe's laboratories, some built of mud, others, under his later guidance, of wood. They were guarded night and day by patrols of giants, and were arranged in a series of quadrangles. Within one quadrangle was a pool which served as an aquarium; in another, aviaries and great hen-houses; in yet another, cages with various animals; in the fourth a little botanic garden. Behind were stables with dozens of cattle and sheep, and a sort of experimental ward for human beings.

He took me into the nearest of the buildings. "This," he said, "is known to the people as the Factory (it is difficult to give the exact sense of the word, but it literally means producing-place), the Factory of Kingship or Majesty, and the Wellspring of Ancestral Immortality." I looked round, and saw platoons of buxom and shining African women, becomingly but unusually dressed in tight-fitting white dresses and caps, and wearing rubber gloves. Microscopes were much in evidence, also various receptacles from which steam was emerging. The back of the room was screened off by a wooden screen in which were a series of glass doors; and these doors opened into partitions, each labelled with a name in that unknown tongue, and each containing a number of objects like the one I had seen taken out of the basket by the giant before we were captured. Pipes surrounded this chamber, and appeared to be distributing heat from a fire in one corner.

"Factory of Majesty!" I exclaimed. "Wellspring of Immortality! What the dickens do you mean?"

"If you prefer a more prosaic name," said Hascombe, "I should call this the Institute of Religious Tissue Culture." My mind went back to a day in 1918 when I had been taken by a biological friend in New York to see the famous Rockefeller Institute; and at the word tissue culture I saw again before me Dr. Alexis Carrel and troops of white-garbed American girls making cultures, sterilizing, microscopizing, incubating and the rest of it. The Hascombe Institute was, it is true, not so well equipped, but it had an even larger, if differently colored, personnel.

Hascombe began his explanations. "As you probably know, Frazer's 'Golden Bough' * introduced us to the idea of a sacred priest-king, and showed how fundamental it was in primitive societies. The welfare of the tribe is regarded as inextricably bound up with that of the King, and extraordinary precautions are taken to preserve him from harm. In this kingdom, in the old days, the King was hardly allowed to set his foot to the ground in case he should lose divinity; his cut hair and nail-parings

* A very elaborate treatise on a division of Roman mythology, especially on the cult of Diana.

were entrusted to one of the most important officials of state, whose duty it was to bury them secretly, in case some enemy should compass the King's illness or death by using them in black magic rites. If anyone of base blood trod on the King's shadow, he paid the penalty with his life. Each year a slave was made mock-king for a week, allowed to enjoy all the king's privileges, and was decapitated at the close of his brief glory; and by this means it was supposed that the illnesses and misfortunes that might befall the King were vicariously got rid of.

"I first of all rigged up my apparatus, and with the aid of Aggers, succeeded in getting good cultures, first of chick tissues and later, by the aid of embryo-extract, of various and adult mammalian tissues. I then went to Bugala, and told him that I could increase the safety, if not of the King as an individual, at least of the life which was in him, and that I presumed that this would be equally satisfactory from a theological point of view. I pointed out that if he chose to be made guardian of the King's subsidiary lives, he would be in a much more important position than the chamberlain or the burier of the sacred nail-parings, and might make the post the most influential in the realm.

"Eventually I was allowed (under threats of death if anything untoward occurred) to remove small portions of His Majesty's subcutaneous connective tissue under a local anaesthetic. In the presence of the assembled nobility I put fragments of this into culture medium, and showed it to them under the microscope. The cultures were then put away in the incubator, under a guard—relieved every eight hours—of half a dozen warriors. After three days, to my joy they had all taken and showed abundant growth. I could see that the Council was impressed, and reeled off a magnificent speech, pointing out that this growth constituted an actual increase in the quantity of the divine principle inherent in royalty; and what was more, that I could increase it indefinitely. With that I cut each of my cultures into eight, and sub-cultured all the pieces. They were again put under guard, and again examined after three days. Not all of them had taken this time, and there were some murmurings and angry looks, on the ground that I had killed some of the King; but I pointed out that the King was still the King, that his little wound had completely healed, and that any successful cultures represented so much extra sacredness and protection to the state. I must say that they were very reasonable, and had good theological acumen, for they at once took the hint.

"I pointed out to Bugala, and he persuaded the rest without much difficulty, that they could now disregard some of the older implications of the doctrines of kingship. The most important new idea which I was able to introduce was *mass-production*. Our aim was to multiply the King's tissues indefinitely, to ensure that some of their protecting power should reside everywhere in the country. Thus by concentrating upon quantity, we could afford to remove some of the restrictions upon the King's mode of life. This was of course agreeable to the King; and also to Bugala, who saw himself wielding undreamt-of power. One might have supposed that such an innovation would have met with great resistance simply on account of its being an innovation; but I must admit that these people compared very favorably with the average business man in their lack of prejudice.

"Having thus settled the principle, I had many debates with Bugala as to the best methods for enlisting the mass of the population in our scheme. What an opportunity for scientific advertising! But, unfortunately, the population could not read. However, war propaganda worked very well in more or less illiterate countries—why not here?"

Hascombe organized a series of public lectures in the capital, at which he demonstrated his regal tissues to the multitude, who were bidden to the place by royal heralds. An impressive platform group was always supplied from the ranks of the nobles. The lecturer explained how important it was for the community to become possessed of greater and greater stores of the sacred tissues. Unfortunately, the preparation was laborious and expensive, and it behooved them all to lend a hand. It had accordingly been arranged that to everyone subscribing a cow or buffalo, or its equivalent—three goats, pigs, or sheep—a portion of the royal anatomy should be given, handsomely mounted in an ebony holder. Sub-culturing would be done at certain hours and days, and it would be obligatory to send the cultures for renewal. If through any negligence the tissue died, no renewal would be made. The subscription entitled the receiver to sub-culturing rights for a year, but was of course renewable. By this means not only would the totality of the King be much increased, to the benefit of all, but each cultureholder would possess an actual part of His Majesty, and would have the infinite joy and privilege of aiding by his own efforts the multiplication of divinity.

Then they could also serve their country by dedicating a daughter to the state. These young women would be housed and fed by the state, and taught the technique of the sacred culture. Candidates would be selected according to general fitness, but would of course, in addition, be required to attain distinction in an examination on the principles of religion. They would be appointed for a probationary period of six months. After this they would receive a permanent status, with the title of Sisters of the Sacred Tissue. From this, with age, experience, and merit, they could expect promotion to the rank of mothers, grandmothers, great-grandmothers, and grand ancestresses of the same. The merit and benefit they would receive from their close contact with the source of all benefits would overflow on to their families.

The scheme worked like wildfire. Pigs, goats, cattle, buffaloes, and Negro maidens poured in. Next year the scheme was extended to the whole country, a peripatetic laboratory making the rounds weekly.

By the close of the third year there was hardly a family in the country which did not possess at least one sacred culture. To be without one would have been like being without one's trousers—or at least without one's hat*—on Fifth Avenue. Thus did Bugala effect a reformation in the national religion, enthrone himself as the most important personage in the country, and entrench applied science and Hascombe firmly in the organization of the state.

Encouraged by his success, Hascombe soon set out to capture the ancestry-worship branch of the religion as well. A public proclamation was made pointing out how much more satisfactory it would be if worship could be made not merely to the charred bones of one's forbears, but to bits of them still actually living and growing. All who were desirous of profiting by the enterprise of Bugala's Department of State should therefore bring their older relatives to the laboratory at certain specified hours, and fragments would be painlessly extracted for culture.

This, too, proved very attractive to the average citizen. Occasionally, it is true, grandfathers or aged mothers arrived in a state of indignation and protest. However, this did not matter, since, according to the law, once children were twenty-five years of age, they were not only assigned the duty of worshipping their ancestors, alive or dead, but were also given complete control over them, in order that all rites might be duly performed to the greater safety of the commonweal. Further, the ancestors soon found that the operation itself was trifling, and, what was more, that once accomplished, it had the most desirable results. For their descendants preferred to concentrate at once upon the culture which they would continue to worship after the old folks were gone, and so left their parents and grandparents much freer than before from the irksome restrictions which in all ages have beset the officially holy.

Thus, by almost every hearth in the kingdom, instead of the old-fashioned rows of red jars containing the incinerated remains of one or other of the family forbears, the new generation saw growing up a collection of family slides. Each would be taken out and reverently examined at the hour of prayer. "Grandpapa is not growing well this week," you would perhaps hear the young black devotee say; the father of the family would pray over the speck of tissue; and if that failed, it would be taken back to the factory for rejuvenation. On the other hand, what rejoicing when a rhythm of activity stirred in the cultures! A spurt on the part of great-grandmother's tissues would bring her wrinkled old smile to mind again; and sometimes it seemed as if one particular generation were all stirred simultaneously by a pulse of growth, as if combining to bless their devout descendants.

To deal with the possibility of cultures dying out, Hascombe started a central storehouse, where duplicates of every strain were kept, and it was this repository of the national tissues which had attracted my attention at the back of the laboratory. No such collection had ever existed before, be

* This was written before the year 1927.

assured me. Not a necropolis, but a histopolis, if I may coin a word: not a cemetery, but a place of eternal growth.

The second building was devoted to endocrine products—an African Armour's—and was called by the people the "Factory of Ministers to the Shrines."

"Here," he said, "you will not find much new. You know the craze for 'glands' that was going on at home years ago, and its results, in the shape of pluriglandular preparations, a new genre of patent medicines, and a popular literature that threatened to outdo the Freudians, and explain human beings entirely on the basis of glandular make-up, without reference to the mind at all.

"I had only to apply my knowledge in a comparatively simple manner. The first thing was to show Bugala how, by repeated injections of pre-pituitary, I could make an ordinary baby grow up into a giant. This pleased him, and he introduced the idea of a sacred bodyguard, all of really gigantic stature, quite overshadowing Frederick's Grenadiers.

"I did, however, extend knowledge in several directions. I took advantage of the fact that their religion holds in reverence monstrous and imbecile forms of human beings. That is, of course, a common phenomenon in many countries, where half-wits are supposed to be inspired, and dwarfs the object of superstitious awe. So I went to work to create various new types. By employing a particular extract of adrenal cortex, I produced children who would have been a match for the Infant Hercules, and, indeed, looked rather like a cross between him and a brewer's drayman. By injecting the same extract into adolescent girls I was able to provide them with the most copious mustaches, after which they found ready employment as prophetesses.

"Tampering with the post-pituitary gave remarkable cases of obesity. This, together with the passion of the men for fatness in their women, Bugala took advantage of, and I believe made quite a fortune by selling as concubines female slaves treated in this way. Finally, by another pituitary treatment, I at last mastered the secret of true dwarfism, in which perfect proportions are retained.

"Of these productions, the dwarfs are retained as acolytes in the temple; a band of the obese young ladies form a sort of Society of Vestal Virgins, with special religious duties, which, as the embodiment of the national ideal of beauty, they are supposed to discharge with peculiarly propitious effect; and the giants form our Regular Army.

"The Obese Virgins have set me a problem which I confess I have not yet solved. Like all races who set great store by sexual enjoyment, these people have a correspondingly exaggerated reverence for virginity. It therefore occurred to me that if I could apply Jacques Loeb's great discovery of artificial parthenogenesis to man, or, to be precise, to these young ladies, I should be able to grow a race of vestals, self-reproducing yet ever virgin, to whom in concentrated form should attach that reverence of which I have just spoken. You see, I must always remember that it is no good proposing any line of work that will not benefit the national religion. I suppose state-aided research would have much the same kinds of difficulties in a really democratic state. Well this, as I say, has so far beaten me. I have taken the matter a step further than Bataillon with his fatherless frogs, and I have induced parthenogenesis in the eggs of reptiles and birds; but so far I have failed with mammals. However, I've not given up yet!"

Then we passed to the next laboratory, which was full of the most incredible animal monstrosities. "This laboratory is the most amusing," said Hascombe. "Its official title is 'Home of the Living Fetishes.' Here again I have simply taken a prevalent trait of the populace, and used it as a peg on which to hang research. I told you that they always had a fancy for the grotesque in animals, and used the most bizarre forms, in the shape of little clay or ivory statuettes, for fetishes.

"I thought I would see whether art could not improve upon nature, and set myself to recall my experimental embryology. I use only the simplest methods. I utilize the plasticity of the earliest stages to give double-headed and cyclopean monsters. That was, of course, done years ago in newts by Spemann and fish by Stockard; and I have merely applied the mass-production methods of Mr. Ford to their results. But my specialties are three-headed snakes, and toads with an extra heaven-pointing head. The former are a little difficult, but there is a great demand for them, and they fetch a good price. The frogs are easier: I simply apply Harrison's methods to embryo tadpoles."

He then showed me into the last building. Unlike the others, this contained no signs of research in progress, but was empty. It was draped with black hangings, and lit only from the top. In the center were rows of ebony benches, and in front of them a glittering golden ball on a stand.

"Here I am beginning my work on reinforced telepathy," he told me. "Some day you must come and see what it's all about, for it really is interesting."

You may imagine that I was pretty well flabbergasted by this catalogue of miracles. Every day I got a talk with Hascombe, and gradually the talks became recognized events of our daily routine. One day I asked if he had given up hope of escaping. He showed a queer hesitation in replying. Eventually he said, "To tell you the truth, my dear Jones, I have really hardly thought of it these last few years. It seemed so impossible at first that I deliberately put it out of my head and turned with more and more energy, I might almost say fury, to my work. And now, upon my soul, I am not quite sure whether I want to escape or not."

"Not *want* to!" I exclaimed; "surely you can't mean that!"

"I am not so sure," he rejoined. "What I most want is to get ahead with this work of mine. Why, man, you don't realize what a chance I've got! And it is all growing so fast—I can see every kind of possibility ahead"; and he broke off into silence.

However, although I was interested enough in his past achievements, I did not feel willing to sacrifice my future to his perverted intellectual ambitions. But he would not leave his work.

The experiments which most excited his imagination were those he was conducting into mass telepathy. He had received his medical training at a time when abnormal psychology was still very unfashionable in England, but had luckily been thrown in contact with a young doctor who was a keen student of hypnotism, through whom he had been introduced to some of the great pioneers, like Bramwell and Wingfield. As a result, he had become a passable hypnotist himself, with a fair knowledge of the literature.

In the early days of his captivity he became interested in the sacred dances which took place every night of full moon, and were regarded as propitiations of the celestial powers. The dancers all belong to a special sect. After a series of exciting figures, symbolizing various activities of the chase, war, and love, the leader conducts his band to a ceremonial bench. He then begins to make passes at them; and what impressed Hascombe was this, that a few seconds sufficed for them to fall back in deep hypnosis against the ebony rail. It recalled, he said, the most startling cases of collective hypnosis recorded by the French scientists. The leader next passed from one end of the bench to the other, whispering a brief sentence into each ear. He then, according to immemorial rite, approached the Priest-King, and, after having exclaimed aloud, "Lord of Majesty, command what thou wilt for thy dancers to perform," the King would thereupon command some action which had previously been kept secret. The command was often to fetch some object and deposit it at the moon-shrine; or to fight the enemies of the state; or (and this was what the company most liked) to be some animal, or bird. Whatever the command, the hypnotized men would obey it, for the leader's whispered words had been an order to hear and carry out only what the King said; and the strangest scenes would be witnessed as they ran, completely oblivious of all in their path, in search of the gourds or sheep they had been called on to procure, or lunged in a symbolic way at invisible enemies, or threw themselves on all fours and roared as lions, or galloped as zebras, or danced as cranes. The command executed, they stood like stocks or stones, until their leader, running from one to the other, touched each with a finger and shouted "Wake." They woke, and limp, but conscious of having been the vessels of the unknown spirit, danced back to their special hut or clubhouse.

This susceptibility to hypnotic suggestion struck Hascombe, and he obtained permission to test the performers more closely. He soon established that the people were, as a race, extremely prone to dissociation, and could be made to lapse into deep hypnosis with great ease, but a hypnosis in which the subconscious, though completely cut off from the waking self, comprised portions of the personality not retained in the hypnotic selves of Europeans. Like most who have fluttered round the psychological candle, he had been interested in the notion of telepathy; and now, with this supply of hypnotic subjects under his hands, began some real investigation of the problem.

By picking his subjects, he was soon able to demonstrate the existence of telepathy, by making suggestions to one hypnotized man who transferred them without physical intermediation to another at a distance. Later—and this was the culmination of his work—he found that when he made a suggestion to several subjects at once, the telepathic effect was much stronger than if he had done it to one at a time—the hypnotized minds were reinforcing each other. "I'm after the super-consciousness," Hascombe said, "and I've already got the rudiments of it."

I must confess that I got almost as excited as Hascombe over the possibilities thus opened up. It certainly seemed as if he were right in principle. If all the subjects were in practically the same psychological state, extraordinary reinforcing effects were observed. At first the attainment of this similarity of condition was very difficult; gradually, however, we discovered that it was possible to tune hypnotic subjects to the same pitch, if I may use the metaphor, and then the fun really began.

First of all we found that with increasing reinforcement, we could get telepathy conducted to greater and greater distances, until finally we could transmit commands from the capital to the national boundary, nearly a hundred miles. We next found that it was not necessary for the subject to be in hypnosis to receive the telepathic command. Almost everybody, but especially those of equable temperament, could thus be influenced. Most extraordinary of all, however, were what we at first christened "near effects," since their transmission to a distance was not found possible until later. If, after Hascombe had suggested some simple command to a largish group of hypnotized subjects, he or I went right up among them, we would experience the most extraordinary sensation, as of some superhuman personality repeating the command in a menacing and overwhelming way and, whereas with one part of ourselves we felt that we must carry out the command, with another we felt, if I may say so, as if we were only a part of the command, or of something much bigger than ourselves which was commanding. And this, Hascombe claimed, was the first real beginning of the super-consciousness.

Bugala, of course, had to be considered. Hascombe, with the old Tibetan prayer-wheel at the back of his mind, suggested that eventually he would be able to induce hypnosis in the whole population, and then transmit a prayer. This would ensure that the daily prayer, for instance, was really said by the whole population, and, what is more, simultaneously, which would undoubtedly much enhance its efficacy. And it would make it possible in times of calamity or battle to keep the whole praying force of the nation at work for long spells together.

Bugala was deeply interested. He saw himself, through this mental machinery, planting such ideas as he wished in the brain-cases of his people. He saw himself willing an order; and the whole population rousing itself out of trance to execute it. He dreamt dreams before which those of the proprietor of a newspaper syndicate, even those of a director of propaganda in wartime, would be pale and timid. Naturally, he wished to receive personal instruction in the methods himself; and, equally naturally, we could not refuse him, though I must say that I often felt a little uneasy as to what he might choose to do if he ever decided to override Hascombe and to start experimenting on his own. This, combined with my constant longing to get away from the place, led me to cast about again for means of escape. Then it occurred to me that this very method about which I had such gloomy presentiments, might itself be made the key to our prison.

So one day, after getting Hascombe worked up about the loss to humanity it would be to let this great discovery die with him in Africa, I set to in earnest. "My dear Hascombe," I said, "you must get home out of this. What is there to prevent you saying to Bugala that your experiments are nearly crowned with success, but that for certain tests you must have a much greater number of subjects at your disposal? You can then get a battery of two hundred men, and after you have tuned them, the reinforcement will be so great that you will have at your disposal a mental force big enough to affect the whole population. Then, of course, one fine day we should raise the potential of our mind-battery to the highest possible level, and send out through it a general hypnotic influence. The whole country, men, women, and children, would sink into stupor. Next we should give our experimental squad the suggestion to broadcast 'sleep for a week.' The telepathic message would be relayed to each of the thousands of minds waiting receptively for it, and would take root in them, until the whole nation became a single super-consciousness, conscious only of the one thought 'sleep' which we had thrown into it."

The reader will perhaps ask how we ourselves expected to escape from the clutches of the superconsciousness we had created. Well, we had discovered that metal was relatively impervious to the telepathic effect, and had prepared for ourselves a sort of tin pulpit, behind which we could stand while conducting experiments. This, combined with caps of metal foil, enormously reduced the effects on ourselves. We had not informed Bugala of this property of metal.

Hascombe was silent. At length he spoke. "I like the idea," he said; "I like to think that if I ever do get back to England and to scientific recognition, my discovery will have given me the means of escape."

From that moment we worked assiduously to perfect our method and our plans. After about five months everything seemed propitious. We had provisions packed away, and compasses. I had been allowed to keep my rifle, on promise that I would never discharge it. We had made friends with some of the men who went trading to the coast, and had got from them all the information we could about the route, without arousing their suspicions.

At last, the night arrived. We assembled our men as if for an ordinary practice, and after hypnosis had been induced, started to tune them. At this moment Bugala came in, unannounced. This was what we had been afraid of; but there had been no means of preventing it. "What shall we do?" I whispered to Hascombe, in English. "Go right ahead and be damned to it," was his answer; "we can put him to sleep with the rest."

So we welcomed him, and gave him a seat as near as possible to the tightly packed ranks of the performers. At length the preparations were finished. Hascombe went into the pulpit and said, "Attention to the words which are to be suggested." There was a slight stiffening of the bodies. "Sleep" said Hascombe. "*Sleep* is the command: command all in this land to sleep unbrokenly." Bugala leapt up with an exclamation; but the induction had already begun.

We with our metal coverings were immune. But Bugala was struck by the full force of the mental current. He sank back on his chair, helpless. For a few minutes his extraordinary will resisted the suggestion. Although he could not move, his angry eyes were open. But at length he succumbed, and he too slept.

We lost no time in starting, and made good progress through the silent country. The people were sitting about like wax figures. Women sat asleep by their milk-pails, the cow by this time far away. Fat-bellied naked children slept at their games. The houses were full of sleepers sleeping upright round their food, recalling Wordsworth's famous "party in a parlor."

So we went on, feeling pretty queer and scarcely believing in this morphic state into which we had plunged a nation. Finally the frontier was reached, where with extreme elation, we passed an immobile and gigantic frontier guard. A few miles further we had a good solid meal, and a doze. Our kit was rather heavy, and we decided to jettison some superfluous weight, in the shape of some food, specimens, and our metal headgear, or mind-protectors, which at this distance, and with the hypnosis wearing a little thin, were, we thought, no longer necessary.

About nightfall on the third day, Hascombe suddenly stopped and turned his head.

"What's the matter?" I said. "Have you seen a lion?" His reply was completely unexpected. "No. I was just wondering whether really I ought not to go back again."

"Go back again," I cried. "What in the name of God Almighty do you want to do that for?"

"It suddenly struck me that I ought to," he said, "about five minutes ago. And really, when one comes to think of it, I don't suppose I shall ever get such a chance at research again. What's more, this is a dangerous journey to the coast, and I don't expect we shall get through alive."

I was thoroughly upset and put out, and told him so. And suddenly, for a few moments, I felt I must go back too. It was like that old friend of our boyhood, the voice of conscience.

"Yes, to be sure, we ought to go back," I thought with fervor. But suddenly checking myself as the thought came under the play of reason— "*Why* should we go back?" All sorts of reasons were proffered, as it were, by unseen hands reaching up out of the hidden parts of me.

And then I realized what had happened. Bugala had waked up; he had wiped out the suggestion we had given to the super-consciousness, and in its place put in another. I could see him thinking it out, the cunning devil (one must give him credit for brains!), and hear him, after making his passes, whisper to the nation in prescribed form his new suggestion: "Will to return!" "Return!" For most of the inhabitants the command would have no meaning, for they would have been already at home. Doubtless some young men out on the hills, or truant children, or girls run off in secret to meet their lovers, were even now returning, stiffly and in somnambulistic trance, to their homes. It was only for them that the new command of the super-consciousness had any meaning—and for us.

I am putting it in a long and discursive way; at the moment I simply *saw* what had happened in a flash. I told Hascombe, I showed him it *must* be so, that nothing else would account for the sudden change. I begged and implored him to use his reason, to stick to his decision and to come on. How I regretted that, in our desire to discard all useless weight, we had left behind our metal telepathy-proof head coverings!

But Hascombe would not, cr could not, see my point. I suppose he was much more imbued with all the feelings and spirit of the country, and so more susceptible. However that may be, he was immovable. He must go back; he knew it; he saw it clearly; it was his sacred duty; and much other similar rubbish. All this time the suggestion was attacking me too; and finally I felt that if I did not put more distance between me and that unisonic battery of will, I should succumb as well as he.

"Hascombe," I said, "I am going on. For God's sake, come with me." And I shouldered my pack, and set off. He was shaken, I saw, and came a few steps after me. But finally he turned, and, in spite of my frequent pauses and shouts to him to follow, made off in the direction we had come. I can assure you that it was with a gloomy soul that I continued my solitary way. I shall not bore you with my adventures. Suffice it to say that at last I got to a white outpost, weak with fatigue and poor food and fever.

I kept very quiet about my adventures, only giving out that our expedition had lost its way and that my men had run away or been killed by the local tribes. At last I reached England. But I was a broken man, and a profound gloom had invaded my mind at the thought of Hascombe and the way he had been caught in his own net. I never found out what happened to him, and I do not suppose that I am likely to find out now. You may ask why I did not try to organize a rescue expedition; or why, at least, I did not bring Hascombe's discoveries before the Royal Society or the Metaphysical Institute. I can only repeat that I was a broken man. I did not expect to be believed; I was not at all sure that I could repeat our results, even on the same human material, much less with men of another race; I dreaded ridicule; and finally I was tormented by doubts as to whether the knowledge of mass-telepathy would not be a curse rather than a blessing to mankind.

However, I am an oldish man now and, what is more, old for my years. I want to get the story off my chest. Besides, old men like sermonizing and you must forgive, gentle reader, the sermonical turn which I now feel I must take. The question I want to raise is this: Dr. Hascombe attained to an unsurpassed power in a number of the applications of science—but *to what end did all this power serve?* It is the merest cant and twaddle to go on asserting, as most of our press and people continue to do, that increase of scientific knowledge and power must in itself be good. I commend to the great public the obvious moral of my story and ask them to think what they propose to do with the power which is gradually being accumulated for them by the labors of those who labor because they like power, or because they want to find the truth about how things work.

JOHN TAINE

THE ULTIMATE CATALYST

THE Dictator shoved his plate aside with a petulant gesture. The plate, like the rest of the official banquet service, was solid gold with the Dictator's monogram, K. I.—Kadir Imperator, or Emperor Kadir—embossed in a design of machine guns round the edge. And, like every other plate on the long banquet table, Kadir's was piled high with a colorful assortment of raw fruits.

This was the dessert. The guests had just finished the main course, a huge plateful apiece of steamed vegetables. For an appetizer they had tried to enjoy an iced tumblerful of mixed fruit juices.

There had been nothing else at the feast but fruit juice, steamed vegetables, and raw fruit. Such a meal might have sustained a scholarly vegetarian, but for soldiers of a domineering race it was about as satisfying as a bucketful of cold water.

"Vegetables and fruit," Kadir complained. "Always vegetables and fruit. Why can't we get some red beef with blood in it for a change? I'm sick of vegetables. And I hate fruit. Blood and iron—that's what we need."

The guests stopped eating and eyed the Dictator apprehensively. They recognized the first symptoms of an imperial rage. Always when Kadir was about to explode and lose control of his evil temper, he had a preliminary attack of the blues, usually over some trifle.

They sat silently waiting for the storm to break, not daring to eat while their Leader abstained.

Presently a middle-aged man, halfway down the table on Kadir's right, calmly selected a banana, skinned it, and took a bite. Kadir watched the daring man in amazed silence. The last of the banana was about to disappear when the Dictator found his voice.

"Americano!" he bellowed like an outraged bull. "Mister Beetle!"

"*Doctor* Beetle, if you don't mind, Senhor Kadir," the offender corrected. "So long as every other white man in Amazonia insists on being addressed by his title, I insist on being addressed by mind. It's genuine, too. Don't forget that."

"Beetle!" The Dictator began roaring again.

But Beetle quietly cut him short. " 'Doctor' Beetle, please. I insist."

Purple in the face, Kadir subsided. He had forgotten what he intended to say. Beetle chose a juicy papaya for himself and a huge, greenish plum for his daughter, who sat on his left. Ignoring Kadir's impotent rage, Beetle addressed him as if there had been no unpleasantness. Of all the company, Beetle was the one man with nerve enough to face the Dictator as an equal.

"You say we need blood and iron," he began. "Do you mean that literally?" the scientist said slowly.

"How else should I mean it?" Kadir blustered, glowering at Beetle. "I always say what I mean. I am no theorist. I am a man of action, not words!"

"All right, all right," Beetle soothed him. "But I thought perhaps your 'blood and iron' was like old Bismarck's—blood and sabres. Since you mean just ordinary blood, like the blood in a raw beefsteak, and iron not hammered into sabres, I think Amazonia can supply all we need or want."

"But beef, red beef—" Kadir expostulated.

"I'm coming to that in a moment." Beetle turned to his daughter. "Consuelo, how did you like that greenbeefo?"

"That *what?*" Consuelo asked in genuine astonishment.

Although as her father's laboratory assistant she had learned to expect only the unexpected from him, each new creation of his filled her with childlike wonderment and joy. Every new biological creation her father made demanded a new scientific name. But, instead of manufacturing new scientific names out of Latin and Greek, as many reputable biologists do, Beetle used English, with an occasional lapse into Portuguese, the commonest language of Amazonia. He had even tried to have his daughter baptized Buglette, as the correct technical term of the immature female offspring of a Beetle. But his wife, a Portuguese lady of irreproachable family, had objected, and the infant was named Consuelo.

"I asked how you liked the greenbeefo," Beetle repeated. "That seedless green plum you just ate."

"Oh, so that's what you call it." Consuelo considered carefully, like a good scientist, before passing judgment on the delicacy. "Frankly, I didn't like it a little bit. It smelt like underdone pork. There was a distinct flavor of raw blood. And it all had a rather slithery wet taste, if you get what I mean."

"I get you exactly," Beetle exclaimed. "An excellent description." He turned to Kadir. "There! You see we've already done it."

"Done what?" Kadir asked suspiciously.

"Try a greenbeefo and see."

Somewhat doubtfully, Kadir selected one of the huge greenish plums from the golden platter beside him, and slowly ate it. Etiquette demanded that the guests follow their Leader's example.

While they were eating the greenbeefos, Beetle watched their faces. The women of the party seemed to find the juicy flesh of the plums unpalatable. Yet they kept on eating and several, after finishing one, reached for another.

The men ate greedily. Kadir himself disposed of the four greenbeefos on his platter and hungrily looked about for more. His neighbors on either side, after a grudging look at their own diminishing supplies, offered him two of theirs. Without a word of thanks, Kadir devoured the offerings.

As Beetle sat calmly watching their greed, he had difficulty in keeping his face impassive and not betraying his disgust. Yet these people were starving for flesh. Possibly they were to be pardoned for looking more like hungry animals than representatives of the conquering race at their first taste in two years of something that smelt like flesh and blood.

All their lives, until the disaster which had quarantined them in Amazonia, these people had been voracious eaters of flesh in all its forms from poultry to pork. Now they could get nothing of the sort.

The dense forests and jungles of Amazonia harbored only a multitude of insects, poisonous reptiles, gaudy birds, spotted cats, and occasional colonies of small monkeys. The cats and the monkeys eluded capture on a large scale, and after a few half-hearted attempts at trapping, Kadir's hardy followers had abandoned the forests to the snakes and the stinging insects.

The chocolate-colored waters of the great river skirting Amazonia on the north swarmed with fish, but they were inedible. Even the natives could not stomach the pulpy flesh of these bloated mud-suckers. It tasted like the water of the river, a foul soup of decomposed vegetation and rotting wood. Nothing remained for Kadir and his heroic followers to eat but the tropical fruits and vegetables.

Luckily for the invaders, the original white settlers from the United States had cleared enough of the jungle and forest to make intensive agriculture possible. When Kadir arrived, all of these settlers, with the exception of Beetle and his daughter, had fled. Beetle remained, partly on his own initiative, partly because Kadir insisted that he stay and "carry on" against the snakes. The others traded Kadir their gold mines in exchange for their lives.

The luscious greenbeefos had disappeared. Beetle suppressed a smile as he noted the flushed and happy faces of the guests. He remembered the parting words of the last of the mining engineers.

"So long, Beetle. You're a brave man and may be able to handle Kadir. If you do, we'll be back. Use your head, and make a monkey of this dictating brute. Remember, we're counting on you."

Beetle had promised to keep his friends in mind. "Give me three years. If you don't see me again by then, shed a tear and forget me."

"*Senhorina Beetle!*" It was Kadir roaring again. The surfeit of green-beefos restored his old bluster.

"Yes?" Consuelo replied politely.

"I know now why your cheeks are always so red," Kadir shouted.

For a moment neither Consuelo nor her father got the drift of Kadir's accusation. They understood just as Kadir started to enlighten them.

"You and your traitorous father are eating while we starve."

Beetle kept his head. His conscience was clear, so far as the green-beefos were concerned, and he could say truthfully that they were not the secret of Consuelo's rosy cheeks and his own robust health. He quickly forestalled his daughter's reply.

"The meat-fruit, as you call it, is not responsible for Consuelo's complexion. Hard work as my assistant keeps her fit. As for the greenbeefos, this is the first time anyone but myself has tasted one. You saw how my daughter reacted. Only a great actress could have feigned such inexperienced distaste. My daughter is a biological chemist, not an actress."

Kadir was still suspicious. "Then why did you not share these meat-fruits with us before?"

"For a very simple reason. I created them by hybridization only a year ago, and the first crop of my fifty experimental plants ripened this week. As I picked the ripe fruit, I put it aside for this banquet. I thought it would be a welcome treat after two years of vegetables and fruit. And," Beetle continued, warming to his invention, "I imagined a taste of beef—even if it is only green beef, 'greenbeefo'—would be a very suitable way of celebrating the second anniversary of the New Freedom in Amazonia."

The scientist's sarcasm anent the "new freedom" was lost upon Kadir, nor did Kadir remark the secret bitterness in Beetle's eyes. What an inferior human being a dictator was, the scientist thought! What stupidity, what brutality! So long as a single one remained—and Kadir was the last —the Earth could not be clean.

"Have you any more?" Kadir demanded.

"Sorry. That's all for the present. But I'll have tons in a month or less. You see," he explained, "I'm using hydroponics to increase production and hasten ripening."

Kadir looked puzzled but interested. Confessing that he was merely a simple soldier, ignorant of science, he deigned to ask for particulars. Beetle was only too glad to oblige.

"It all began a year ago. You remember asking me when you took over the country to stay and go on with my work at the antivenin laboratory? Well, I did. But what was I to do with all the snake venom we collected? There was no way of getting it out of the country now that the rest of the continent has quarantined us. We can't send anything down the river, our only way out to civilization—"

"Yes, yes," Kadir interrupted impatiently. "You need not remind any-one here that the mountains and the jungles are the strongest allies of our enemies. What has all this to do with the meat-fruit?"

"Everything. Not being able to export any venom, I went on with my research in biochemistry. I saw how you people were starving for flesh, and I decided to help you out. You had slaughtered and eaten all the horses at the antivenin laboratory within a month of your arrival. There was nothing left, for this is not a cattle country, and it never will be. There was nothing to do but try chemistry. I already had the greenhouses left by the engineers. They used to grow tomatoes and cucumbers before you came."

"So you made these meat-fruits chemically?"

Beetle repressed a smile at the Dictator's scientific innocence.

"Not exactly. But really it was almost as simple. There was nothing startlingly new about my idea. To see how simple it was, ask yourself what are the main differences between the higher forms of plant life and the lower forms of animal life.

"Both are living things. But the plants cannot move about from place to place at will, whereas, the animals can. A plant is, literally, 'rooted to the spot.'

"There are apparent exceptions, of course, like water hyacinths, yeast spores, and others that are transported by water or the atmosphere, but they do not transport themselves as the living animal does. Animals have a 'dimension' of freedom that plants do not have."

"But the beef—"

"In a moment. I mentioned the difference between the freedoms of plants and animals because I anticipate that it will be of the utmost importance in the experiments I am now doing. However, this freedom was not, as you have guessed, responsible for the greenbeefos. It was another, less profound, difference between plants and animals that suggested the 'meat-fruit.' "

Kadir seemed to suspect Beetle of hidden and unflattering meanings, with all this talk of freedom in a country dedicated to the "New Freedom" of Kadir's dictatorship. But he could do nothing about it, so he merely nodded as if he understood.

"Plants and animals," Beetle continued, "both have a 'blood' of a sort. The most important constituents in the 'blood' of both differ principally in the metals combined chemically in each.

"The 'blood' of a plant contains chlorophyll. The blood of an animal contains haemoglobin. Chemically, chlorophyll and haemoglobin are strangely alike. The metal in chlorophyll is magnesium; in haemoglobin, it is iron.

"Well, it occurred to chemists that if the magnesium could be 'replaced' chemically by iron, the chlorophyll could be converted into haemoglobin! And similarly for the other way about: replace the iron in haemoglobin by magnesium, and get chlorophyll!

"Of course it is not all as simple or as complete as I have made it sound. Between haemoglobin and chlorophyll is a long chain of intermediate compounds. Many of them have been formed in the laboratory, and they are definite links in the chain from plant blood to animal blood."

"I see," Kadir exclaimed, his face aglow with enthusiasm at the prospect of unlimited beef from green vegetables. He leaned over the table to question Beetle.

"It is the blood that gives flesh its appetizing taste and nourishing strength. You have succeeded in changing the plant blood to animal blood?"

Beetle did not contradict him. In fact, he evaded the question.

"I expect," he confided, "to have tons of greenbeefos in a month, and thereafter a constant supply as great as you will need. Tray-culture—hydroponics—will enable us to grow hundreds of tons in a space no larger than this banquet hall."

The "banquet hall" was only a ramshackle dining room that had been used by the miners before Kadir arrived. Nevertheless, it could be called anything that suited the Dictator's ambition.

"Fortunately," Beetle continued, "the necessary chemicals for tray-culture are abundant in Amazonia. My native staff has been extracting them on a large scale for the past four months, and we will have ample for our needs."

"Why don't you grow the greenbeefos in the open ground?" one of Kadir's officers inquired a trifle suspiciously.

"Too inefficient. By feeding the plants only the chemicals they need directly, we can increase production several hundredfold and cut down the time between successive crops to a few weeks. By properly spacing the propagation of the plants, we can have a constant supply. The seasons cut no figure."

They seemed satisfied, and discussion of the glorious future in store for Amazonia became general and animated. Presently Beetle and Consuelo asked the Dictator's permission to retire. They had work to do at the laboratory.

"Hydroponics?" Kadir enquired jovially. Beetle nodded, and they bowed themselves out of the banquet hall.

Consuelo withheld her attack until they were safe from possible eavesdroppers.

"Kadir is a lout," she began, "but that is no excuse for your filling him up with a lot of impossible rubbish."

"But it *isn't* impossible, and it *isn't* rubbish," Beetle protested. "You know as well as I do—"

"Of course I know about the work on chlorophyll and haemoglobin. But you didn't make those filthy green plums taste like raw pork by changing the chlorophyll of the plants into haemoglobin or anything like it. How did you do it, by the way?"

"Listen, Buglette. If I tell you, it will only make you sick. You ate one, you know."

"I would rather be sick than ignorant. Go on, you may as well tell me."

"Very well. It's a long story, but I'll cut it short. Amazonia is the last refuge of the last important dictator on earth. When Kadir's own people came to their senses a little over two years ago and kicked him out, he and his top men and their women came over here with their 'new freedom.' But the people of this continent didn't want Kadir's brand of freedom. Of course a few thousand crackpots in the larger cities welcomed him and his gang as their 'liberators,' but for once in history the mass of the people knew what they did not want. They combined forces and chased Kadir and his cronies up here.

"I never have been able to see why they did not exterminate Kadir and company as they would any other pests. But the presidents of the United Republics agreed that to do so would only be using dictatorial tactics, the very thing they had united to fight. So they let Kadir and his crew live— more or less—in strict quarantine. The temporary loss of a few rich gold mines was a small price to pay, they said, for world security against dictatorships.

"So here we are, prisoners in the last plague spot of civilization. And here is Kadir. He can dictate to his heart's content, but he can't start another war. He is as powerless as Napoleon was on his island.

"Well, when the last of our boys left, I promised to keep them in mind. And you heard my promise to help Kadir *out*. I am going to keep that promise, if it costs me my last snake."

They had reached the laboratory. Juan, the night-nurse for the reptiles, was going his rounds.

"Everything all right, Juan?" Beetle asked cordially.

He liked the phlegmatic Portuguese who always did his job with a minimum of talk. Consuelo, for her part, heartily disliked the man and distrusted him profoundly. She had long suspected him of being a stool-pigeon for Kadir.

"Yes, Dr. Beetle. Good night."

"Good night, Juan."

When Juan had departed, Consuelo returned to her attack.

"You haven't told me yet how you made these things taste like raw pork."

She strolled over to the tank by the north window where a luxuriant greenbeefo, like an overdeveloped tomato vine, grew rankly up its trellis to the ceiling. About half a dozen of the huge greenish "plums" still hung on the vine.

Consuelo plucked one and was thoughtfully sampling its quality.

"This one tastes all right," she said. "What did you do to the others?"

"Since you really want to know, I'll tell you. I took a hypodermic needle and shot them full of snake blood. My pet constrictor had enough juice in him to do the whole job without discomfort to himself or danger to his health."

Consuelo hurled her half-eaten fruit at her father's head, but missed. She stood wiping her lips with the back of her hand.

"So you can't change the chlorophyll in a growing plant into anything like haemoglobin? You almost had me believing you could."

"I never said I could. Nor can anybody else, so far as I know. But it made a good story to tell Kadir."

"But why?"

"If you care to analyze one of these greenbeefos in your spare time, you will find their magnesium content extraordinarily high. That is not accident, as you will discover if you analyze the chemicals in the tanks. I shall be satisfied if I can get Kadir and his friends to gorge themselves on greenbeefos when the new crop comes in. Now, did I sell Kadir the greenbeefo diet, or didn't I? You saw how they all fell for it. And they will keep on falling as long as the supply of snake blood holds out."

"There's certainly no scarcity of snakes in this charming country," Consuelo remarked. "I'm going to get the taste of one of them out of my mouth right now. Then you can tell me what you want me to do in this new culture of greenbeefos you've gone in for."

So father and daughter passed their days under the last dictatorship. Beetle announced that in another week the lush crop of greenbeefos would be ripe. Kadir proclaimed the following Thursday "Festal Thursday" as the feast day inaugurating "the reign of plenty" in Amazonia.

As a special favor, Beetle had requested Kadir to forbid any sightseeing or other interference with his work.

Kadir had readily agreed, and for three weeks Beetle had worked twenty hours a day, preparing the coming banquet with his own hands.

"You keep out of this," he had ordered Consuelo. "If there is any dirty work to be done, I'll do it myself. Your job is to keep the staff busy as usual, and see that nobody steals any of the fruit. I have given strict orders that nobody is to taste a greenbeefo till next Thursday, and Kadir has issued a proclamation to that effect. So if you catch anyone thieving, report to me at once."

The work of the native staff consisted in catching snakes. The workers could see but little sense in their job, as they knew that no venom was being exported. Moreover, the eccentric Doctor Beetle had urged them to bring in every reptile they found, harmless as well as poisonous, and he was constantly riding them to bestir themselves and collect more.

More extraordinary still, he insisted every morning that they carry away the preceding day's catch and dump it in the river. The discarded snakes, they noticed, seemed half dead. Even the naturally most vicious put up no fight when they were taken from the pens.

Between ten and eleven every morning Beetle absented himself from the laboratory, and forbade anyone to accompany him. When Consuelo asked him what he had in the small black satchel he carried with him on these mysterious trips, he replied briefly:

"A snake. I'm going to turn the poor brute loose."

And once, to prove his assertion, he opened the satchel and showed her the torpid snake.

"I must get some exercise, and I need to be alone," he explained, "or my nerves will snap. Please don't pester me."

She had not pestered him, although she doubted his explanation. Left alone for an hour, she methodically continued her daily inspection of the plants till her father returned, when she had her lunch and he resumed his private business.

On the Tuesday before Kadir's Festal Thursday, Consuelo did not see her father leave for his walk, as she was already busy with her inspection when he left. He had been gone about forty minutes when she discovered the first evidence of treachery.

The foliage of one vine had obviously been disturbed since the last inspection. Seeking the cause, Consuelo found that two of the ripening fruits had been carefully removed from their stems. Further search disclosed the theft of three dozen in all. Not more than two had been stolen from any one plant.

Suspecting Juan, whom she had always distrusted, Consuelo hastened back to her father's laboratory to await his return and report. There she was met by an unpleasant surprise.

She opened the door to find Kadir seated at Beetle's desk, his face heavy with anger and suspicion.

"Where is your father?"

"I don't know."

"Come, come. I have made women talk before this when they were inclined to be obstinate. Where is he?"

"Again I tell you I don't know. He always takes his exercise at this time, and he goes alone. Besides," she flashed, "what business is it of yours where he is?"

"As to that," Kadir replied carelessly, "everything in Amazonia is my business."

"My father and I are not citizens—or subjects—of Amazonia."

"No. But your own country is several thousand miles away, Senhorina Beetle. In case of impertinent questions I can always report—with regrets, of course—that you both died by one of the accidents so common in Amazonia. Of snakebite, for instance."

"I see. But may I ask the reason for this sudden outburst?"

"So you have decided to talk? You will do as well as your father, perhaps better."

His eyes roved to one of the wire pens.

In it were half a dozen small red snakes.

"What do you need those for, now that you are no longer exporting venom?"

"Nothing much. Just pets, I suppose."

"Pets? Rather an unusual kind of pet, I should say." His face suddenly contorted in fear and rage. "Why is your father injecting snake blood into the unripe meat-fruit?" he shouted.

Consuelo kept her head. "Who told you that absurdity?"

"Answer me!" he bellowed.

"How can I? If your question is nonsense, how can anybody answer it?"

"So you refuse. I know a way to make you talk. Unlock that pen."

"I haven't the key. My father trusts nobody but himself with the keys to the pens."

"No? Well, this will do." He picked up a heavy ruler and lurched over to the pen. In a few moments he had sprung the lock.

"Now you answer my question or I force your arm into that pen. When your father returns I shall tell him that someone had broken the lock, and that you had evidently been trying to repair it when you got bitten. He will have to believe me. You will be capable of speech for just about three minutes after one of those red beauties strikes. Once more, why did your father inject snake blood into the green meat-fruits?"

"And once more I repeat that you are asking nonsensical questions. Don't you dare—"

But he did dare. Ripping the sleeve of her smock from her arm, he gripped her bare wrist in his huge fist and began dragging her toward the pen. Her frantic resistance was no match for his brutal strength. Instinctively she resorted to the only defense left her. She let out a yell that must have carried half a mile.

Startled in spite of himself, Kadir paused, but only for an instant. She yelled again.

This time Kadir did not pause. Her hand was already in the pen when the door burst open. Punctual as usual, Beetle had returned exactly at eleven o'clock to resume his daily routine.

The black satchel dropped from his hand.

"What the hell—" A well-aimed laboratory stool finished the sentence. It caught the Dictator squarely in the chest. Consuelo fell with him, but quickly disengaged herself and stood panting.

"You crazy fool," Beetle spat at the prostrate man. "What do you think you are doing? Don't you know that those snakes are the deadliest of the whole lot?"

Kadir got to his feet without replying and sat down heavily on Beetle's desk. Beetle stood eying him in disgust.

"Come on, let's have it. What were you trying to do to my daughter?"

"Make her talk," Kadir muttered thickly. "She wouldn't—"

"Oh, she wouldn't talk. I get it. Consuelo! You keep out of this. I'll take care of our friend. Now, Kadir, just what did you want her to talk about?"

Still dazed, Kadir blurted out the truth.

"Why are you injecting snake blood into the unripe meat-fruit?"

Beetle eyed him curiously. With great deliberation he placed a chair in front of the Dictator and sat down.

"Let us get this straight. You ask why I am injecting snake blood into the greenbeefos. Who told you I was?"

"Juan. He brought three dozen of the unripe fruit to show me."

"To show you what?" Beetle asked in deadly calm. Had that fool Juan brains enough to look for the puncture-marks made by the hypodermic needle?

"To show me that you are poisoning the fruit."

"And did he show you?"

"How should I know? He was still alive when I came over here. I forced him to eat all three dozen."

"You had to use force?"

"Naturally. Juan said the snake blood would poison him."

"Which just shows how ignorant Juan is." Beetle sighed his relief. "Snake blood is about as poisonous as cow's milk."

"Why are you injecting—"

"You believed what that ignorant fool told you? He must have been drinking again and seeing things. I've warned him before. This time he goes. That is, if he hasn't come to his senses and gone already of his own free will."

"Gone? But where could he go from here?"

"Into the forest, or the jungle," Beetle answered indifferently. "He might even try to drape his worthless hide over a raft of rotten logs and float down the river. Anyhow, he will disappear after having made such a fool of himself. Take my word for it, we shan't see Juan again in a month of Sundays."

"On the contrary," Kadir retorted with a crafty smile, "I think we shall see him again in a very few minutes." He glanced at the clock. It showed ten minutes past eleven. "I have been here a little over half an hour. Juan promised to meet me here. He found it rather difficult to walk after his meal. When he comes, we can go into the question of those injections more fully."

For an instant Beetle looked startled, but quickly recovered his composure.

"I suppose as you say, Juan is slow because he has three dozen of those unripe greenbeefos under his belt. In fact I shouldn't wonder if he were feeling rather unwell at this very moment."

"So there is a poison in the fruits?" Kadir snapped.

"A poison? Rubbish! How would you or anyone feel if you had been forced to eat three dozen enormous green apples, to say nothing of unripe greenbeefos? I'll stake my reputation against yours that Juan is hiding in the forest and being very sick right now. And I'll bet anything you like that nobody ever sees him again. By the way, do you know which road he was to follow you by? The one through the clearing, or the cut-off through the forest?"

"I told him to take the cut-off, so as to get here quicker."

"Fine. Let's go and meet him—only we shan't. As for what I saw when I opened that door, I'll forget it if you will. I know Consuelo has already forgotten it. We are all quarantined here together in Amazonia, and there's no sense in harboring grudges. We've got to live together."

Relieved at being able to save his face, Kadir responded with a generous promise.

"If we fail to find Juan, I will admit that you are right, and that Juan has been drinking."

"Nothing could be fairer. Come on, let's go."

Their way to the Dictator's "palace"—formerly the residence of the superintendent of the gold mines—lay through the tropical forest.

The road was already beginning to choke up in the gloomier stretches with a rank web of trailing plants feeling their way to the trees on either side, to swarm up their trunks and ultimately choke the life out of them. Kadir's followers, soldiers all and new to the tropics, were letting nature take its course. Another two years of incompetence would see the painstaking labor of the American engineers smothered in rank jungle.

Frequently the three were compelled to abandon the road and follow more open trails through the forest till they again emerged on the road. Dazzling patches of yellow sunlight all but blinded them temporarily as they crossed the occasional barren spots that seem to blight all tropical forests like a leprosy. Coming out suddenly into one of these blinding patches, Kadir, who happened to be leading, let out a curdling oath and halted as if he had been shot.

"What's the matter?" Consuelo asked breathlessly, hurrying to overtake him. Blinded by the glare she could not see what had stopped the Dictator.

"I stepped on it." Kadir's voice was hoarse with disgust and fear.

"Stepped on what?" Beetle demanded. "I can't see in this infernal light. Was it a snake?"

"I don't know," Kadir began hoarsely. "It moved under my foot. Ugh! I see it now. Look."

They peered at the spot Kadir indicated, but could see nothing. Then, as their eyes became accustomed to the glare, they saw the thing that Kadir had stepped on.

A foul red fungus, as thick as a man's arm and over a yard long, lay directly in the Dictator's path.

"A bladder full of blood and soft flesh," Kadir muttered, shaking with fright and revulsion. "And I stepped on it."

"Rot!" Beetle exclaimed contemptuously, but there was a bitter glint in his eyes. "Pull yourself together, man. That's nothing but a fungus. If there's a drop of blood in it, I'll eat the whole thing."

"But it moved," Kadir expostulated.

"Nonsense. You stepped on it, and naturally it gave beneath your weight. Come on. You will never find Juan at this rate."

But Kadir refused to budge. Fascinated by the disgusting object at his feet, the Dictator stood staring down at it with fear and loathing in every line of his face.

Then, as if to prove the truth of his assertion, the thing did move, slowly, like a wounded eel. But, unlike an eel, it did not move in the direction of its length. It began to roll slowly over.

Beetle squatted, the better to follow the strange motion. If it was not the first time he had seen such a freak of nature, he succeeded in giving a very good imitation of a scientist observing a novel and totally unexpected phenomenon. Consuelo joined her father in his researches. Kadir remained standing.

"Is it going to roll completely over?" Consuelo asked with evident interest.

"I think not," Beetle hazarded. "In fact, I'll bet three to one it only gets halfway over. There—I told you so. Look, Kadir, your fungus is rooted to the spot, just like any other plant."

In spite of himself, Kadir stooped down and looked. As the fungus reached the halfway mark in its attempted roll, it shuddered along its entire length and seemed to tug at the decayed vegetation. But shuddering and tugging got it nowhere. A thick band of fleshy rootlets, like coarse green hair, held it firmly to the ground. The sight of that futile struggle to move like a fully conscious thing was too much for Kadir's nerves.

"I am going to kill it," he muttered, leaping to his feet.

"How?" Beetle asked with a trace of contempt. "Fire is the only thing I know of to put a mess like that out of its misery—if it is in misery. For all I know, it may enjoy life. You can't kill it by smashing it or chopping it into mincemeat. Quite the contrary, in fact. Every piece of it will start a new fungus, and instead of one helpless blob rooted to the spot, you will have a whole colony. Better leave it alone, Kadir, to get what it can out of existence in its own way. Why must men like you always be killing something?"

"It is hideous and—"

"And you are afraid of it? How would you like someone to treat you as you propose treating this harmless fungus?"

"If I were like that," Kadir burst out, "I should want somebody to put a torch to me."

"What if nobody knew that was what you wanted? Or if nobody cared? You have done some pretty foul things to a great many people in your time, I believe."

"But never anything like this!"

"Of course not. Nobody has ever done anything like this to anybody.

So you didn't know how. What were you trying to do to my daughter an hour ago?"

"We agreed to forget all that," Consuelo reminded him sharply.

"Sorry. My mistake. I apologize, Kadir. As a matter of scientific interest, this fungus is not at all uncommon."

"I never saw one like it before," Consuelo objected.

"That is only because you don't go walking in the forest as I do," he reminded her. "Just to prove I'm right, I'll undertake to find a dozen rolling fungi within a hundred yards of here. What do you say?"

Before they could protest, he was hustling them out of the blinding glare into a black tunnel of the forest. Beetle seemed to know where he was going, for it was certain that his eyes were as dazed as theirs.

"Follow closely when you find your eyes," he called. "I'll go ahead. Look out for snakes. Ah, here's the first beauty! Blue and magenta, not red like Kadir's friend. Don't be prejudiced by its shape. Its color is all the beauty this poor thing has."

If anything, the shapeless mass of opalescent fungus blocking their path was more repulsive than the monstrosity that had stopped Kadir. This one was enormous, fully a yard in breadth and over five feet long. It lay sprawled over the rotting trunk of a fallen tree like a decomposing squid.

Yet, as Beetle insisted, its color was beautiful with an unnatural beauty. However, neither Consuelo nor Kadir could overcome their nausea at that living death. They fled precipitately back to the patch of sunlight. The fleshy magenta roots of the thing, straining impotently at the decaying wood which nourished them, were too suggestive of helpless suffering for endurance. Beetle followed at his leisure, chuckling to himself. His amusement drew a sharp reprimand from Consuelo.

"How can you be amused? That thing was in misery."

"Aren't we all?" he retorted lightly, and for the first time in her life Consuelo doubted the goodness of her father's heart.

They found no trace of Juan. By the time they reached the Dictator's palace, Kadir was ready to agree to anything. He was a badly frightened man.

"You were right," he admitted to Beetle. "Juan was lying, and has cleared out. I apologize."

"No need to apologize," Beetle reassured him cordially. "I knew Juan was lying."

"Please honor me by staying to lunch," Kadir begged. "You cannot? Then I shall go and lie down."

They left him to recover his nerve, and walked back to the laboratory by the long road, not through the forest. They had gone over halfway before either spoke. When Beetle broke the long silence, he was more serious than Consuelo ever remembered his having been.

"Have you ever noticed," he began, "what arrant cowards all brutal men are?" She made no reply, and he continued, "Take Kadir, for instance.

He and his gang have tortured and killed thousands. You saw how that harmless fungus upset him. Frightened half to death of nothing."

"Are you sure it was nothing?"

He gave her a strange look, and she walked rapidly ahead. "Wait," he called, slightly out of breath.

Breaking into a trot, he overtook her.

"I have something to say that I want you to remember. If anything should ever happen to me—I'm always handling those poisonous snakes—I want you to do at once what I tell you now. You can trust Felipe."

Felipe was the Portuguese foreman of the native workers.

"Go to him and tell him you are ready. He will understand. I prepared for this two years ago, when Kadir moved in. Before they left, the engineers built a navigable raft. Felipe knows where it is hidden. It is fully provisioned. A crew of six native river men is ready to put off at a moment's notice. They will be under Felipe's orders. The journey down the river will be long and dangerous, but with that crew you will make it. Anyhow, you will not be turned back by the quarantine officers when you do sight civilization. There is a flag with the provisions. Hoist it when you see any signs of civilization, and you will not be blown out of the water. That's all."

"Why are you telling me this now?"

"Because dictators never take their own medicine before they make someone else taste it for them."

"What do you mean?" she asked in sudden panic.

"Only that I suspect Kadir of planning to give me a dose of his peculiar brand of medicine the moment he is through with me. When he and his crew find out how to propagate the greenbeefos, I may be bitten by a snake. He was trying something like that on you, wasn't he?"

She gave him a long doubtful look. "Perhaps," she admitted. She was sure that there was more in his mind than he had told her.

They entered the laboratory and went about their business without another word. To recover lost time, Consuelo worked later than usual. Her task was the preparation of the liquid made up by Beetle's formula, in which the greenbeefos were grown.

She was just adding a minute trace of chloride of gold to the last batch when a timid rap on the door of the chemical laboratory startled her unreasonably. She had been worrying about her father.

"Come in," she called.

Felipe entered. The sight of his serious face gave her a sickening shock. What had happened? Felipe was carrying the familiar black satchel which Beetle always took with him on his solitary walks in the forest.

"What is it?" she stammered.

For answer Felipe opened his free hand and showed her a cheap watch. It was tarnished greenish blue with what looked like dried fungus.

"Juan's," he said. "When Juan did not report for work this afternoon, I went to look for him."

"And you found his watch? Where?"

"On the cut-off through the forest."

"Did you find anything else?"

"Nothing belonging to Juan."

"But you found something else?"

"Yes. I had never seen anything like them before."

He placed the satchel on the table and opened it.

"Look. Dozens like that one, all colors, in the forest. Doctor Beetle forgot to empty this bag when he went into the forest this morning."

She stared in speechless horror at the swollen monstrosity filling the satchel. The thing was like the one that Kadir had stepped on, except that it was not red but blue and magenta. The obvious explanation flashed through her mind, and she struggled to convince herself that it was true.

"You are mistaken," she said slowly. "Doctor Beetle threw the snake away as usual and brought this specimen back to study."

Felipe shook his head.

"No, Senhorina Beetle. As I always do when the Doctor comes back from his walk, I laid out everything ready for tomorrow. The snake was in the bag at twelve o'clock this morning. He came back at his regular time. I was busy then, and did not get to his laboratory till noon. The bag had been dropped by the door. I opened it, to see if everything was all right. The snake was still there. All its underside had turned to hard blue jelly. The back was still a snake's back, covered with scales. The head had turned green, but it was still a snake's head. I took the bag into my room and watched the snake till I went to look for Juan. The snake turned into this. I thought I should tell you."

"Thank you, Felipe. It is all right; just one of my father's scientific experiments. I understand. Goodnight, and thank you again for telling me. Please don't tell anyone else. Throw that thing away and put the bag in its usual place."

Left to herself, Consuelo tried not to credit her reason and the evidence of her senses. The inconsequential remarks her father had dropped in the past two years, added to the remark of today that dictators were never the first to take their own medicine, stole into her memory to cause her acute uneasiness.

What was the meaning of this new technique of his, the addition of a slight trace of chloride of gold to the solution? He had talked excitedly of some organic compound of gold being the catalyst he had sought for months to speed up the chemical change in the ripening fruit.

"What might have taken months the old way," he had exclaimed, "can now be done in hours. I've got it at last!"

What, exactly, had he got? He had not confided in her. All he asked of her was to see that the exact amount of chloride of gold which he prescribed was added to the solutions. Everything she remembered now fitted into its sinister place in one sombre pattern.

"This must be stopped," she thought.
It must be stopped, yes. But how?

The next day the banquet took place.

"Festal Thursday" slipped into the past, as the long shadows crept over the banquet tables—crude boards on trestles—spread in the open air. For one happy, gluttonous hour the bearers of the "New Freedom" to a benighted continent had stuffed themselves with a food that looked like green fruit but tasted like raw pork. Now they were replete and somewhat dazed.

A few were furtively mopping the perspiration from their foreheads, and all were beginning to show the sickly pallor of the gourmand who has overestimated his capacity for food. The eyes of some were beginning to wander strangely. These obviously unhappy guests appeared to be slightly drunk.

Kadir's speech eulogizing Beetle and his work was unexpectedly short. The Dictator's famous gift for oratory seemed to desert him, and he sat down somewhat suddenly, as if he were feeling unwell. Beetle rose to reply.

"Senhor Kadir! Guests and bearers to Amazonia of the New Freedom, I salute you! In the name of a freedom you have never known, I salute you, as the gladiators of ancient Rome saluted their tyrant before marching into the arena where they were to be butchered for his entertainment."

Their eyes stared up at him, only half-seeing. What was he saying? It all sounded like the beginning of a dream.

"With my own hands I prepared your feast, and my hands alone spread the banquet tables with the meat-fruits you have eaten. Only one human being here has eaten the fruit as nature made it, and not as I remade it. My daughter has not eaten what you have eaten. The cold, wet taste of the snake blood which you have mistaken for the flavor of swine-flesh, and which you have enjoyed, would have nauseated her. So I gave her uncontaminated fruit for her share of our feast."

Kadir and Consuelo were on their feet together, Kadir cursing incoherently, Consuelo speechless with fear. What insane thing had her father done? Had he too eaten of— But he must have, else Kadir would not have touched the fruit!

Beetle's voice rose above the Dictator's, shouting him down.

"Yes, you were right when you accused me of injecting snake blood into the fruit. Juan did not lie to you. But the snake blood is not what is making you begin to feel like a vegetable. I injected the blood into the fruit only to delude all you fools into mistaking it for flesh. I anticipated months of feeding before I could make of you what *should* be made of you.

"A month ago I was relying on the slow processes of nature to destroy you with my help. Light alone, that regulates the chemistry of the growing plant and to a lesser degree the chemistry of animals, would have done what must be done to rid Amazonia and the world of the threat of your New Freedom, and to make you expiate your brutal past.

"But light would have taken months to bring about the necessary *replacement of the iron in your blood by magnesium.* It would have been a slow transformation—almost, I might say, a lingering death. By feeding you greenbeefo I could keep your bodies full at all times with magnesium in chemically available form to *replace every atom of iron in your blood!*

"Under the slow action of photosynthesis—the chemical transformations induced by exposure to light—you would have suffered a lingering illness. You would not have died. No! You would have lived, but not as animals. Perhaps not even as degenerated vegetables, but as some new form of life between plant and the animal. You might even have retained your memories.

"But I have spared you this—so far as I can prophesy. You will live, but you will not remember—much. Instead of walking forward like human beings, you will roll. That will be your memory.

"Three weeks ago I discovered the organic catalyst to hasten the replacement of the iron in your blood by magnesium and thus to change your animal blood to plant blood, chlorophyll. The catalyst is merely a chemical compound which accelerates chemical reactions without itself being changed.

"By injecting a minute trace of chloride of gold into the fruits, I—and the living plant—produced the necessary catalyst. I have not yet had time to analyze it and determine its exact composition. Nor do I expect to have time. For I have, perforce, taken the same medicine that I prescribed for you!

"Not so much, but enough. I shall remain a thinking animal a little longer than the rest of you. That is the only unfair advantage I have taken. Before the sun sets we shall all have ceased to be human beings, or even animals."

Consuelo was tugging frantically at his arm, but he brushed her aside. He spoke to her in hurried jerks as if racing against time.

"I did not lie to you when I told you I could *not* change the chlorophyll in a living plant into haemoglobin. Nobody has done that. But did I ever say I could not change *the haemoglobin in a living animal into chlorophyll?* If I have not done that, I have done something very close to it. Look at Kadir, and see for yourself. Let go my arm—I must finish."

Wrenching himself free, he began shouting against time.

"Kadir! I salute you. Raise your right hand and return the salute."

Kadir's right hand was resting on the bare boards of the table. If he understood what Beetle said, he refused to salute. But possibly understanding was already beyond him. The blood seemed to have ebbed from the blue flesh, and the coarse hairs on the back of the hand had lengthened perceptibly even while Beetle was demanding a salute.

"Rooted to the spot, Kadir! You are taking root already. And so are the rest of you. Try to stand up like human beings! Kadir! Do you hear me? Remember that blue fungus we saw in the forest? I have good reason for believing that was your friend Juan. In less than an hour you and I and all these fools will be exactly like him, except that some of us will be blue, others green, and still others red—like the thing you stepped on.

"It rolled. Remember, Kadir? That red abomination was one of my pet fungus snakes—shot full of salts of magnesium and the catalyst I extracted from the fruits. A triumph of science. I am the greatest biochemist that ever lived! But I shan't roll farther than the rest of you. We shall all roll together—or try to. 'Merrily we roll along, roll along'—I can see already you are going to be a blue and magenta mess like your friend Juan."

Beetle laughed harshly and bared his right arm. "I'm going to be red, like the thing you stepped on, Kadir. But I've stepped on the lot of you!"

He collapsed across the table and lay still. No sane human being could have stayed to witness the end. Half mad herself, Consuelo ran from the place of living death.

"Felipe, Felipe! Boards, wood—bring dry boards, quick, quick! Tear down the buildings and pile them up over the tables. Get all the men, get them all!"

Four hours later she was racing down the river through the night with Felipe and his crew. Only once did she glance back. The flames which she herself had kindled flapped against the black sky.

CALVIN PEREGOY

THE TERRIBLE
SENSE

"AMAZING," said Dr. Botts to himself. He removed the ear cups from Mr. Theodore Clews and hooked the audiometer to the center of his forehead and the base of his skull. He threw on 110 decibels, the equivalent of 100,000,000,000 units of relative sound energy or a well-developed thunder clap.

Mr. Clews had been sitting in the timid concentration of his habitual wormlike psychology of life. Had he known his otological tests had long since passed the relatively low points equivalent to a pneumatic drill or elevated train running through his ear, he would probably have died of horror.

As it was, he simply vibrated to the thunderous oscillations of 110 decibels. Not even his inner ear responded. He felt a decided and painful tremor in his foot, but it did not occur to him it had anything to do with sound. He shook his head negatively.

Dr. Botts switched off the current and removed the wires. He wrote on a piece of paper, "I am afraid you are deaf." Mentally he noted that some superior term was needed to convey an expression of Mr. Clews' condition.

Mr. Theodore Clews' cup of woe flowed over. It was not bad enough that nobody had ever called him Ted; that he had been forced to wear long curls to the age of twelve; that his mother had still taken all but two dollars of his pay at twenty-five; that fourteen younger, less experienced and less efficient bookkeepers had been advanced over him; and that he was less than dust to his tyrannous wife! Now, suddenly, he was stone deaf. He broke down and wept.

Dr. Botts caught himself ready to make tests of the ultrashort-wave radiations of a mortal afflicted with staggering grief. He reminded himself this was a client and restrained his curiosity with effort. It was a truly amazing case—the first case of absolute utter deafness the doctor had ever witnessed.

The doctor was not beset by traditional ethics and conscience. With forefinger and thumb he held his lips together a moment. No use thinking of reconstructing Mr. Clews' ordinary hearing apparatus. It was defunct forever.

But something might be done with his nervous system. Something along the order of a bat's aural system. Of course, it would require the correlating system of a bat's real ear also, but that might be taken from a bat itself.

The doctor examined his fingers with sudden interest. Why not? Why not duplicate in the timid Theodore Clews the entire audio-nervous system of a bat? The doctor restrained a strong morbid impulse to make it a vampire bat. He dropped a small tablet in a glass of cold water and gave it to the distraught Theodore Clews. Then he went to select the most sensitive bat in his sterile menagerie.

A month later, Mr. Theodore Clews timidly and thankfully shook hands with Dr. Botts and left his sanatorium. The delicate operation had been a success. Already, he could hear better than ever before. It was a strange type of hearing which had given him moments of uneasy thought during the past few days, but it was hearing.

"It will take several months for the new system to become completely synchronized with your motor nervous system," the doctor announced.

Mr. Clews went timidly back to his five-room flat and the stored-up tyranny of his wife. Except that her loud accusations had become more strident, his life did not seem to have changed. The only ill effect of the operation was that he had become more nervous. The clatter of adding machines in the office began to drive him into frenzy. The scratch of his pen reached such a pitch that he had to change to a snub-nosed stub.

Three months had passed before Mrs. Clews ran out of immediate faults to find with her husband. With tight jaws she was considering a mythical millionaire she might have married—if she had ever known a millionaire—when a tense expression on the face of her husband attracted her attention. His eyes were bright and his gaze was riveted on the cat.

"Well, that's a fine one for her that was the daughter of a police captain to have for a husband!" she commented scathingly. "Scared of a cat! Don't say a word, Theodore Clews, it's written on your face as clear as day!"

Mr. Clews jumped and colored. He tried to crouch less conspicuously in a corner of the chair. But inevitably his gaze returned to the cat and he subconsciously moved forward to the edge of his seat. But oddly, he was not looking at the cat when it silently yawned and shifted. Yet Theodore Clews knew what the cat had done as if a photograph had been flashed in his mind.

He heard it! He even heard the cat's toes go back together!

The cat started to lick itself, stopped, its head swinging toward corners of the room. Intently it gazed with its fiery eyes, rolling onto haunches ready to spring. Suddenly it looked at Mr. Clews. A second it glared. Then it hissed, leaped in a somersault and rushed from the room.

For minutes, Mr. Clews' heart thumped like a sledge hammer. That savage glare of the cat had put his heart into his throat. But it occurred to him the cat had been equally afraid of something about *him*. He could not figure what. Like his wife, the cat had been wont either to disdain him altogether, or else accept him very condescendingly.

The cat's fear slowly filled Mr. Clews with a sense of well being. Nothing before had ever been afraid of him. Now he had impressed his importance as a man—well, at least upon the cat. He went to bed well pleased with life.

He had forgotten to open the window which faced a dark court. The room was cluttered with tables, chairs, trunks and boxes, but he made his way to the window in the dark without touching a thing. Theodore Clews was not very observant or he would have been surprised that he knew where every object was. He could not have explained, but he could have told that the big bureau was precisely seven feet two inches from the very spot where he stepped into bed.

Noises began to become a very important part of Mr. Clews' life. The noise of adding machines and typewriters had first annoyed him. Now they frightened him, so that he would pause at the bottom of a row of figures and have to grip the desk with sudden trembling. He eyed the quiet, sound-proofed office of the chief bookkeeper, who had been advanced over him, with envy and jealousy. It was the first time he had ever been truly jealous of another man's success.

The riotous noise of rushing crowds at closing time drove Mr. Clews near hysteria. He began staying late, finishing up odds and ends of work he had never paid much attention to. There was a highly difficult piece of accounting to be done which had to be done on outside time. Clews' chief noticed his penchant for working late.

"What do you think about Clews doing it?" he asked the big boss.

The big boss chuckled. "Just the man! He's too scared to even think what's behind figures!"

It was dark when Clews would leave, and to avoid the noise he took to walking home through the less used and darker back streets. It did not occur to him, but he seldom used his eyes to see where he was going. He simply knew when he came to alleys and crossings—where lamp-posts and people were—without looking.

At home, the cat began to grow thin. At night it slunk onto the fire-escape with swift backward glances at Clews. But not all cats were as frightened. A toughy in the dock district had waited and silently stalked him many nights. Each night it crept a little closer behind him for a block.

One night it began to gallop on silent feet. Clews was thinking of that special job he was doing when he suddenly felt alarm and leaped straight up. The cat sailed beneath him with open mouth and unsheathed claws.

Clews started to run without thinking. Suddenly he remembered the fear their own cat had of him. He whirled. Along the dark pavement the cat was galloping in a low crouch. He could not see it clearly, could barely define movement in the shadow. The cat tensed and leaped in attack. At the same second, Clews leaped aside. Without thinking, he reached out and caught the cat by the tail. Before he realized what he had done, he had dashed its brains out.

His act appalled him and made him slightly sick. Then he began to enjoy the sensation of victory. By the time he arrived home he was glad he had killed the cat. When he thought of it again at dinner, he licked his lips a little.

Daily, the noise at the office was becoming more deafening to his system. He began to hate the noise and the people responsible for it. His fear turned to anger. Particularly was it focused on the man who had that quiet, sound-proofed office, his immediate chief.

He did not notice it, but he no longer turned to see who was approaching. He knew long before he was fully conscious of their footsteps or voices. He was sitting on one side of a partition with Will Flanagan at noon one day when Will said idly, "I wonder exactly what Marie Stevens is doing at one minute to twelve?"

"Combing her hair," Theodore said. He was not guessing. She might just as well have been powdering or rouging. But he knew she was combing her hair.

Will looked around the partition and said, "Jeepers!" He gave Clews a peculiar look.

The other bookkeepers began making a lot of remarks like that to Clews. As long as they asked about somebody in the room, or standing in a draft blowing into the room, Clews usually knew the answer. A week later they framed him. They had Marie Stevens sit absolutely quiet behind a filing case. They led up to the idea and asked Clews.

Clews' mind went blank with concentration. He had not discovered how he knew things yet. He had not even discovered he was being kidded. After a second he said seriously, "She's trying to be quiet. But she's chewing gum."

The committee ran to investigate. She was. They did not notice that the effort of absolute control made her breathe a little harder.

They began to dodge Clews' eyes after that, and to avoid being close to him. But he did not notice their new attitude. He was busy with the special work. Free minutes were filled with increasing rage at the noise around him, and jealousy of the man with that quiet office. Suddenly it occurred to Clews to get that man's job. It was simply an idea intention. He had never tried to get another man's job before.

Summer came on, and Clews donned thin clothing. On hot days when he sat in the office in shirt sleeves, the noise was deafening. When he stretched his arms to cool the perspiration the noise made him shiver.

He was stretching when he suddenly heard his boss talking. It surprised him, for his boss was nowhere in the room. He put his elbows on his desk and the sound ceased. Later he stretched again and again he heard his boss. He stood up, holding his arms out and turning subconsciously. He dropped one arm at an angle. He heard the voice as if it were next to him.

Clews turned white with the discovery, but he listened. It was something about that special job he was doing after hours. The other, lower voice was the big boss. Beads of perspiration popped out on timid Clews' forehead. That job was the private account of the firm—the account the government did not see. When he sat down to think over this awful discovery, the voices stopped. A mosquito floated through the air. Without thinking, Clews reached out and grabbed it in flight.

His wife was in a particular temper that night. She railed for an hour. Clews thought the racket of her voice would drive him mad. "Well," she finally screeched, "can't you answer?" Her voice hit a highly unpleasant note. It rasped across Clews' nerves like a file.

He looked up at her, his eyes going red with rage. Before he knew what he had done, he had knocked her down. She stood gaping with surprise while he grabbed up his coat and went out.

Clews walked along a dark street deep in thought. He was surprised that he was not more shocked at his own action. Somehow, it had seemed the thing to do. She'd have to stop using those strident notes unless she wanted him to walk out.

The night was filled with a world of sound-pictures. He knew that four people walked out of a house a block distant and turned toward the waterfront. He heard radios, but that was expected. But he knew that somebody on either the third or fourth floor rear of the house across the street turned on their water faucet. He tilted his head to one side. Without thinking, one of his arms and legs lifted and moved slowly about. Suddenly he knew the person using that water was a woman. It had a different sound hitting on masculine flesh and muscle.

When he put his leg down, he knew that a night shift was using picks on the new subway far beneath. He felt the rumble of a truck, and then another similar rumble. But he knew that one truck was running west, three streets north, and that the other one was in the excavation underfoot. There was a terrible din northward, but out of it he picked the bell of a fire engine. That would be about a mile and a half away, he thought.

He was thirsty and passed a little restaurant. Out behind was a quiet summer garden with soft lights. He went out and sat down. The waiter came up and stood behind his line of vision, but he knew the waiter was six feet tall, and knew the length of his arms.

He ordered a lemonade made of fresh-cut lemons. The waiter disappeared and Clews absently stretched a leg and rested his arm over another chair. He did not notice his arm jumping nervously.

The waiter brought a lemonade and Clews said, "That's not fresh lemons. I want lemons cut and squeezed special."

The waiter said, "That's what I gave you, sir."

Clews looked at him and said, "You had this squeezed in a pitcher in the icebox. You put the ice in the glass before you poured the lemon juice."

The waiter swallowed, gawked, blanched and took the lemonade back. Clews was momentarily frightened at what he had said. How did he know that? The kitchen was back in the house. But he *knew it!* He got over his fright and began to feel proud of his knowledge. Why should he be scared? He could scare other people!

A man and a woman came in and sat at a distant table. Clews knew the man was his big boss without looking. The woman laughed, and Clews felt pretty certain she was not the boss' wife. He readjusted his position without thinking and heard the murmured conversation distinctly. No, it was not the wife.

After a few drinks the woman laughed more and louder. There was an irritating quality to her voice and Clews moved to the inside bar without looking at them. He sat with his feet on the upper rung of the high stool and his arms doubled closely against the sides of his chest. It was better this way. He did not hear that grating laugh.

The woman passed behind him and he heard his boss come up. The boss laughed and ordered drinks.

"Didn't realize you were a drinking man, Clews! Well, a long one doesn't do any harm in this heat, eh?"

Clews ordered another lemonade. He didn't like the sound of the boss' voice. It held an unconvincing tone of smoothness. It annoyed him and it made him think of the office and that private job for which he wasn't paid a dime extra.

The boss took half his drink and said, "By the way, this little meeting will just be between us two?" There was a threat in the tone. It made Clews angry.

Clews said, "I should have had Dice's job. I was senior and I know more about the work."

The boss colored. "That's rather high-handed, Clews!"

"So are those private books," Clews said. He looked at the boss for the first time. When he raised his arm to drink he knew that the boss was scared. Clews could hear his heart pounding.

"We'll see what we can do tomorrow," the boss said.

The next week Clews was put in charge of his department. He got the sound-proofed room. He breathed with relief. He wasn't frightened and angered by noise all the time in there! And—the work of the department picked up immediately. The clerks kept their eyes on Clews when he came through, and a few of them said silent prayers. It was uncanny that he could tell them at the end of the day that they had been reading a book or writing a letter instead of working on figures when he had been clean across the room!

There was a lot that was uncanny about Clews lately, they whispered. For one thing, he didn't pay any attention to where he was going, yet he never hit anything. Then there was the way he acted. Sometimes when he was listening his arm or leg would go out and vibrate like a throbbing pipe. And he heard every word they said no matter how quietly they whispered!

When fall came, Clews grew more nervous than ever. The streets were full of traffic noise during the daytime. It actually pained him at times. And he was developing a fondness for night roaming which left him tired and groggy the next day. He was nervous, too, at his increasing knowledge of an unpleasant kind. A laugh, a word, a swift motion, and he would size people up. How, he had no idea. But he would know they were shallow, scheming, disloyal, dishonest.

It was startling the number of people who weren't what they seemed. Down at the office they all smiled pleasantly at him, but they hated him. They were frightened of him. He knew that from the noise their motions made as he passed by them. Sometimes he would have his foot out in the hall and hear what they were whispering about him.

He was shocked by the crookedness of the firm he worked for, too. He did not yet have the courage of his convictions or he would have reported them. He had learned too much—more than he wanted to know. As on the day he had his hand on the wall of the president's office and heard the conversation with a prominent politician inside. Or the day he laid his finger tips on a telephone cord and heard what was being said over the wire.

He didn't want to know those things! They upset him, made him mad at himself and disgusted with life! He was losing the few friends he had ever had, also. Part of this was his fault. Some of them had given him time just out of pity, or because they were in the same boat, or out of amusement. He knew why they had put up with him now. He knew it from the fine differences of tone they used with him.

But there was something more than that. He frightened them lately. His motions were strangely nervous and quick, and sometimes he answered remarks they had thought, but had not stated. He would say, "Here comes John," when John was still half a block away and around the corner.

And occasionally he dropped things which showed he knew a lot of what they had said behind his back or in the privacy of their homes. Such as the day he consoled Mary Bevins, who lived three floors lower down in a different house, because her husband had left her. It hadn't been a loud quarrel and Mary was telling people that he was just away on a business trip.

The only satisfaction in life was that he had tamed his wife. It had taken some outbursts of rage and fists which he was thoroughly ashamed of when he thought about it. But it had had a surprising effect. She had become docile, loving, quiet, soft-spoken. In fact she had become a new woman. Where she had been wont to yell with a piercing voice, she now sang softly. It had affected her temperament. She was happy. She told her cronies about what a capable and self-reliant man *Mr. Clews* was.

The first cold of winter struck bitterly into Theodore's bones. It hurt him, and he felt very sleepy. He would go to sleep the minute he got home. In the morning he would find himself doubled up with his knees beneath his chin and his hands firmly clenching the footboard of the bed.

Frightened, he went to see Dr. Botts. He did more analyzing about matters lately because so many new and inexplicable events took place in his life. He had figured out that his sleepiness might have something to do with his audio operation. The city noise had assaulted his nerves, and perhaps he was run down.

Dr. Botts was away for a year in the jungles!

Bleakly, Clews faced the fact. There was nobody who could do anything for him. Nobody else could even find anything wrong or different with him! For the first time in his life, he sat down and seriously analyzed himself and his private life. For the first time he realized how his character, as well as his body and nerves, had changed since the operation.

Now he was sleepy, so terribly sleepy that he could barely pull through the day. He felt he would simply have to take a month off. He went to see his president.

There was a conference inside the office. Clews sat down wearily against the wall and spread his arms. Instantly, he heard every word said inside. The president was trying to put through a deal, and whoever he was talking to wanted a higher price.

Suddenly Clews paid closer heed. There was something about the man's voice— He began to make mental notes of his reactions. When the man went out, the deal was supposedly all set.

Clews walked in and said, "That man was lying. He isn't going to sign the order. I think he's a spy from another company."

The president scoffed and scowled.

Clews said he wanted a month's vacation.

The president thought of Clews' confidential knowledge of the company books and said, "Well, we'll see."

Clews left, knowing the president was trying to find some way to get rid of him. He was too sleepy to think much about it. He was almost asleep when the president burst in that afternoon with a white face.

"That man this morning was from Clinton & Co., our sharpest rivals! They've got our inside price and a good guess at production costs!"

Clews shrugged wearily. "He sounded crooked," he said simply.

The president looked at Clews strangely. He said, "Clews, you do look sick. I think a winter in the south is what you need. I'm giving you enough to go south for six months."

But Clews didn't go south. He went home and went to bed. In a half-wakeful state he kept trying to get further under the covers. His wife went out, and while she was gone he crawled over to the closet and crawled inside, moving in a sleep-walking trance.

Slowly, a feeling of cramped inactivity came to him. Sluggish life seemed returning to long-stiffened arms and legs. His eyes blinked open, and shut hastily. A low, purring hum of outer sounds welled up, and through it the soft, low twittering of birds. Somewhere a breeze ruffled leaves. Clews shook himself slightly, uneasily, and opened his eyes again.

The surroundings dazed his slow-awakening mind. Something, vaguely, was wrong with his room. Something dark and brown draped peculiarly in front of him. Sensation messages from the nerves of arms and legs began to convey meaning. His legs were hooked over the coat-rail in his closet, and he was hanging head-down, quite comfortably, but extremely hungry. He belched softly and swung stiffly to the floor.

His wife was coming, he knew suddenly, and he relaxed gently on the floor, seated with arms queerly angled. His wife entered, and looked at him with no surprise, but a vague satisfaction. "Hungry?"

He nodded slowly. His neck was stiff. "Very."

"You were last week." She went out again. Slowly her words penetrated to his wakening mind. He turned gingerly and looked out the window. His arm lifted and moved about. The twittering of birds grew stronger. A pair of bluebirds were struggling with a tangle of string in the crotch of the old maple tree. He could scarcely see them because of the leaves.

"It's—spring," said Mr. Clews numbly, when his wife returned with a deep cup of broth.

"May," she nodded. Her voice was calm, but her eyes were frightened. "You—you hibernated. I—I went to the doctor, but he was gone—the one that operated on you—and his assistant came. He said to let you alone. You woke up a little a week ago."

Mr. Clews drank the soup, and hiccuped gently. His head nodded forward and he crawled toward the bed. "I'll be all right," he said, with a peculiar certainty of knowledge. He crawled into the bed, and went to sleep.

Six hours later he woke up again, and ate some more. In a week he was moving around, the queer stiffness going from his limbs. He felt fine.

Clews made his first trips out late at night. He took careful stock of himself now. He had changed even more during the winter. His motions were three times as quick, and often he would stop and wheel, almost dancing, at some strange noise.

A cop standing quietly in a doorway suddenly said, "Well, well, butterfly, come along and we'll find a nice cocoon for you!"

Clews darted away in terror and horrible realization of his motions.

He kept to even later hours and less frequented districts along the waterfront after that. He tried to avoid people. But he got in the center of a brightly lighted block one night when groups came out of bars at both corners and stood lounging on the curb. He had to pass one. He checked his motions as much as possible, but his steps were light and dainty, and he had the feeling that he *fluttered* down the block. Any distant or near-by sound and involuntarily his quivering arms and legs would leap out or his head cock to one side.

A tough drunk at the corner watched his progress. He stepped out and began badgering. Clews' undeniable instinct was to run. But something in the tough's voice turned his fear to anger. A psychiatrist might have told him the root of anger is fear. He told the tough to shut up.

"Well, for cripes' sake, listen at the prissy telling me to shut up!" roared the tough. He stepped nearer and made a sudden feint and pass. It whistled over Clews' head.

Clews had never had a fight in his life. The mere thought terrified him. For ten minutes he avoided annihilation simply because he heard the fighter's motion and dodged. He had no conscious thought of dodging; it was sheer timed nervous reaction. He was utterly frightened.

Then the roars of the tough began to goad him. A particular stream of curses had a high-pitched note which made him see red. He began fighting back, savagely, with no idea of how to fight, but jumping in and out like a —*bat!* They pulled him off the tough when his teeth were sinking into the man's throat.

"Wait a minute, wait a minute, wildcat!" a dapper member of the party said. "Man, if you're going to kill 'em, make the public pay to see it! Come in and have a drink and cool off."

Clews went in because he was taken. He sat down shaking like a leaf. It appeared he had just butchered the lightweight champ!

"You don't look like much," the dapper man said, "but I've never seen such beautiful weaving and timing in my life! Why, fellow, you'll make a fortune! You don't even need to hit 'em. They'll go down from missing you!"

Before Clews could understand quite how it had happened, he was on his way to becoming lightweight champion. The nervous, fluttering, perfect timing of his motions packed the arenas. Never had a man behaved like that in the ring before! But it was the goods—nobody touched him in twelve fights! By then, he was learning about fighting, and when he got against tougher opponents he could lean and take their punches. But they seldom landed. Clews was too fast in his jittery, pulsing, nervous maneuvers. No matter what tricks they pulled, he seemed to sense them, the direction of their punches, the timing and power in them, and be somewhere else when they arrived.

Then his own knockout began, for his timing was perfect, and once he learned to hit, it did not take much power to stretch his opponent on the canvas. Inevitably, these knockouts were correlated with the size and yelling of the crowd. They would come in the same round with a certain tempo and note and decibel measurement of the crowd's roar. The fierceness with which Clews hit them was something uncontrollable, absolutely not part of his conscious self. It was direct reflex of that roar on the nerves of his body.

Nobody ever knew the torture, the sheer physical pain, those roars caused him. He struck out in nervous frenzy. The night the crowd increased its roar after he knocked out the champ, he K. O.'d the referee and three men in the ring before they grabbed him.

But Clews was not happy. Loyally, his wife accompanied him in public, but at home he caught her sobbing at times, and when she looked at him or he hugged her closely, there was terror in her eyes.

"I don't know what's come over you, Ted," she said once—she called him "Ted" now—"it gives me the creeps. It isn't just you hanging like that all winter. The doctor said that was just nerves had drawn your bones and muscles up or something. But it's—"

"What?" asked Clews nervously.

"I—I don't know how to say it. I don't even know myself. It's just like you were something different, like an animal or something. I was up at the zoo the other day and I felt just the same." She stopped and broke out crying miserably.

"When you looked at the—the bats?" Clews asked with a dry voice. She nodded unhappily.

Clews went into strange foreign parts that night. He did not know exactly what the doctor had done to him, but he did know it was tied up with a bat's ultra-sensitive auditory system.

Three battle-scarred cats sitting on a stoop hissed and arched their backs at him. He turned, and with screams of terror they rushed away. He looked down at his arm and saw it was oscillating rapidly in a peculiar, half-turned position. His fingers were open and moved without any volition of his.

He shivered, and drew his arms tightly to his sides. He knew exactly how far the cats had gone! Two of them had gone to the back of a house; one had raced along the street and turned east.

Theodore Clews felt very unhappy. He was rich, and popular with crowds, and his "eccentricities" were now called "form" and studied. But he was losing his wife. And, oddly, he was in love with this woman who had upbraided him for so many years. Botts or no Botts, he had to know how far this bat business had gone!

His manager looked at him with popping eyes. The cigar in his mouth went out for the first time in history. "You're nuts!" he informed Clews.

Clews smiled without humor. "Maybe. But I want to try it. I'm giving up the title in any event."

"Holy Moses, he wants a title match and *he's going to fight blindfolded!*

Tape over his eyes!" the manager yelped. "Listen, Clews, you're a sensation. You're a genius. You got something nobody ever heard of before! But you got to see a man's fists if you're not going to get hit by 'em!"

"That's what I want to find out," Clews said.

He won his argument because he had been a careful bookkeeper and he had as carefully read the contract he signed with his manager. They had to do what he said.

Ziggy Nelson, his manager, was quite tight the night of the fight. He wiped perspiration from a beefy forehead and planked down fifty thousand dollars at 50 to 1 odds. The commission agent said, around his cigar, "I thought it was your *fighter* was cracked! There's going to be a special judge to see that tape is O. K."

"I know it!" Ziggy said from his boots. "But I don't want my fighter to be crazy all alone. Who else is betting on him?"

"Nobody," the agent said and looked guilty. "Except me," he added in a whisper.

Theodore Clews, the Battling Bat, sat on his rubbing table nervously. About fourteen thousand people were out in the arena. He could judge from the noise. He shook his head when they held out tape for his hands. He was going to need them free as possible.

His wife kidded him for the benefit of the press. He heard her soft intake of breath before she went through the ritual and knew she was ready to scream with that unaccountable fear. He thought of her kissing one of those bats in the zoo. A woman really had to love you to stand you changing to a bat!

Well—tonight would prove it. He went out and climbed into the ring. They put tape over his eyes and inspected it to see that it really shut out all sight. One of the judges climbed out of the ring, Clews knew.

The gong rang and he jumped out straight for his opponent. The man was grinning—which Clews did not know—but he did know when he put his left foot forward and began a haymaker uppercut. He felt it coming and ducked. It missed him by the fraction of an inch. The crowd roared.

Clews was not quite certain. He got pretty badly battered up—much worse than ever before. But he could hear, or feel—he was tired of trying to decide which sense it was—most of what the man did. At the end of the third he was still on his feet and had taken no killing punches. But his *ears* were ringing, buzzing—and he was conscious of them.

In the fourth, that hysteria that set him wild came into the crowd's roar. Clews heard his opponent's breathing and the sound of his shuffling feet. The man was puzzled and he was scared. His timing was off. He was going to pieces.

The roar crescendoed, the savage yell for a knockout. Clews had never been so terrified in his life. A bat caught in a giant spider web might feel that way! He almost ran from the ring. Then came that maddening tempo and piercing note. Clews' mind went red. He lashed out in a series of short jabs.

He did not even know that they connected, but he knew exactly where the man's jaw and arms and body were. What was the answer? How did he know? The roar went higher. He hit again and crossed to the solar plexus.

Sudden terror leaped up within him—but no longer terror of the noise of the fight. It was terror at what part of him had become, for he knew the answer. His body *heard* the fine oscillations and pressure differences caused by that other moving body! It was not *like* a bat's hearing—*it was a bat's hearing!*

He shrieked and lashed out with a bare six-inch blow. There was a crash. The man went down. The count was ten. They held up Clews' hand. The roar had never been so deafening. Clews shivered with the pain of that roar, and fell unconscious on top of his man.

He blinked open his eyes and saw men's lips moving. The dressing room was crowded, and the stamp of feet was heavy. But he did not feel them. His eye fell on a cop. He made a sign for the cop's whistle and blew it until his lungs felt ready to break. He gave Ziggy Nelson a happy tap on the cheek and grinned. He looked shyly for his wife.

He couldn't hear a thing. He was himself again.

DONALD WANDREI

A SCIENTIST
DIVIDES

I SHALL always remember him as he stood there by the slides and microscope that summer afternoon three years ago. His face was enkindled with the glow that is present only at the immediate moment of a great discovery. He held the beaker in his hands and looked at it with all the loving pride of a mother studying the first babe.

Yet it was characteristic of Dr. Weylith that his eyes wore a far-away look. It was never the discovery that mattered so much to him, as it was the potential and far-reaching effects that future generations might enjoy.

Dr. R. L. Weylith was then one of the country's brilliant biologists. He had made a name for himself by his exhaustive researches into the nature of cells and cell structures, chromosomes, hæmin, and more esoteric minutiae of the human organism. He was one of the men who developed the hyper-oxygenic treatment for schizophrenia. He successfully isolated, identified, and photographed the first of the nonfilterable viruses. Yet he had scarcely reached thirty when he received the highest honor, the most distinguished medal, that science bestows on its own. And he was only thirty-five that afternoon three years ago.

A slender, quiet man, he carried himself with a curious and disconcerting air of alert detachment, as though he saw everything, but could not pause in his progress toward ultimate goals. Always tolerant, gracious, and generous, he encouraged and helped others even when his own work suffered. Gifted with a keen mind and a vivid imagination, he took advantage of every educational facility to specialize in the methods of science, making biology his particular field.

He was no mere grubber of facts. His work was precise, elaborately documented, but also linked to the great dreams that lured him on. He was that rare and enviable type—the pure scientist in his technique, the pure visionary in his mind, the successful joiner of both in his work.

Does this sound as if I was writing his epitaph? I am. Or I hope I am, since I cannot be positive.

Our relationship was somewhat unusual but readily understandable. I had long been interested in all phases of modern science, but without the aptitude or the interest in specializing in any given field. I was fascinated by the possibilities of new discoveries and naturally turned to writing. Professor Weylith, on the other hand, confined his published work to material that would bear the strictest and most technical scrutiny.

It was difficult for me to find laymen sufficiently versed in various categories of science to talk to, and it would have been suicidal for Weylith to expound some of his more fanciful ideas to his colleagues. But the two of us got along famously, for in him I found a man I could deeply admire, and in me I hope he at least enjoyed an enthusiastic listener.

I advanced the idea that caught his imagination and set him off on the years of investigation which culminated that afternoon. Now I regret ever having mentioned it.

For the years that I knew him, I saw him regularly and discussed everything above the sun and beneath the clouds. I was the only person who knew the nature of his last experiment. It is just as well that he permitted no one else to share the secret. The world would be a less complacent globe.

Yet in spite of our numerous conversations, I did not go with a full understanding of what might ensue that afternoon when Dr. Weylith telephoned and asked me to drop in at his laboratory. I had originally thrown off my suggestion as the germ for a fictional romance.

"Science tells us," I had once remarked, "that the higher organisms all evolved from a single-celled animalcule or amœba which represented the first life-bud eons ago. From that humble beginning came vertebrates and man. Why may not man himself now be only a similar basic cell out of which even vaster and more complex organisms will evolve in the course of ages? Imagine what would happen if a superscientist treated a man as such a cell and then, in the laboratory, constructed from one or dozens of men a creature of the year one billion!"

That was the thought which fired Weylith's imagination, but not quite in the way I believed. Through nearly five years of work, he kept his real objective to himself, while discussing my suggestion as if he was making progress on it. Since the idea was merely fictional, and rather far-fetched, I did not seriously think he would turn it into reality.

Then, too, he was noncommittal over the phone. He merely suggested that I drop around if I would like to see something interesting. From his casual tone, I suspected that his request had to do with the topic we had often discussed. I decided he had probably made an important new discovery in the matter of cellular structure or an allied subject. I knew he had been making extensive researches of late in cosmic radiations, chlorophyll, hæmin, hormones, and glandular secretions.

It was about three in the afternoon when I walked into his laboratory and saw him with the beaker in his hands. The westward-slanting sun poured a flood of light through the windows, hot light, molten light, but the air-conditioned laboratory was cool and dustless. The window-staves split the light into rectangles. They left a cross on the side of his smock. His face seemed a little tired, evidently from days and nights of arduous work, but weariness never prevented a quick smile of welcome.

"It's worth being half cooked in that sun just to bask in the coolness here," I remarked.

"Is it hot out? I hadn't noticed. But come over and look at this."

I made my way between the tables of chemicals, slides, tissues, tinted specimens, microscopes, and other apparatus.

"What is it?" I asked when I reached his side.

He held the little beaker toward me. Inside it nestled a drop of opaque, reddish-gray stuff. There was only a drop, but nothing ever before gave me the creeps like that tiny nodule. It seemed to quiver with a strange and restless motion. It elongated, contracted, rested, made an abortive effort to roll up the side of the glass toward Weylith's hand.

The reflected sunlight glistened on it. It looked pinkish, like an albino's eyes, slimy, like an angleworm's tip. It suggested in no single or specific way such diabolic and distorted anthropomorphic traits, so sinister a human nature in so subhuman a way, that I made no effort to take the beaker. The drop almost mesmerized me.

I bent over, and it slid up the side of the beaker so swiftly that I shrank away. The globule fell back, palpitated faintly and restlessly like a heart endlessly beating for a body to clothe it.

"What is it? I can tell you right now I don't like it, I won't touch it, and I refuse to have anything to do with it."

Weylith smiled. "That is why you write fiction. You romanticize things, I investigate them and find out their nature. Then they lose their mystery and neither repel nor attract. They are reduced to facts."

"Yes, but then *you* romanticize them by planning their ultimate possible use in the furthest future world. You haven't told me what this is."

Weylith looked at the beaker thoughtfully. He shook it a trifle. The drop raced madly around the spot where his hand held the glass. "Hungry little devil, isn't it? It hasn't eaten since I made it."

"Made it? Out of what? What for? How?"

"Not so fast! I'll go back a little. Do you remember the day, years ago, when you suggested the idea that man might be only the basic cell of an immensely more complicated organism yet to develop?"

"Of course! I said also that it would be wonderful if some scientist could only speed up the cell and produce overnight the homunculus of the year one billion. Don't tell me that this is it?"

Weylith shook his head. "Hardly! No; that isn't quite the line I was following. Your suggestion captured my fancy, but I went after it in a different way. After you left that time, I thought a good deal about the idea. Science has accepted as truth the evolution of multicellular organisms such as man from an ancient, original, single cell. You suggested that man himself might be, so to speak, only the real basic cell of which the primeval cell was only a part, and that out of man might evolve a complex being almost beyond our power to envision. Right?"

"Yes. Then what?"

"It occurred to me that a reduction instead of expansion might be equally interesting for speculation. The simple cell produced, through countless mutations, man, and was itself changed. Why, therefore, might not man carry within himself a different kind of cell, substance, or essence, which was his full being expressed in its least compass? I don't mean sperm, of course; I mean something that was the minimum refinement of blood, bone, tissue, organs, glands, secretions, and so on; perhaps inert, but at least possessed of the capacity for life; a modern cell that was the counterpart to the ancient, simple cell.

"Perhaps it might be found in extracts of each part of him, interfused into a unit. Perhaps he contained a hitherto-undiscovered gland or secretion that had the latent capacity of summarizing his nature. Perhaps one could construct a centimeter model of man, from tiny parts of the brain, the nervous system, the skeleton, the muscles, the organs, the blood system, the glands, the hair, the cartilage, and imbue it with life. Perhaps one might take cells and subject them to enzymic, metabolistic, biochemical, or other changes that would convert them into what might be called homoplasm."

"Homoplasm?" I queried.

"To distinguish it from protoplasm. And here it is."

I looked at the malignant little drop with intensified curiosity and dislike. To tell the truth, Dr. Weylith's comments had partly escaped me, I was so fascinated by the actions of the globule. I heard without comprehension. One graphic picture is mightier than a thousand words. I saw the result of his experiment, and I had only half ears for the cause, the explanation.

But I managed to ask, simply for lack of any more intelligent comment that I might make: "What does it do?"

Weylith answered candidly. "I don't know. I isolated homoplasm this morning, and I haven't had time to go further. It appears to be sentient, animate, and locomotory, as you can see. What its other properties are, I don't know. I can't even say for sure that it is what I believe it is. It may be just a particularly voracious bit of protoplasm-plus, without any individual or special characteristics. I called you because I thought you would be interested in any case, since it was your suggestion that set me on my way. There are a good many tests yet to be made.

"For instance, how long will it last in its present state? Does it require food? If so, what kind? If not, why not? Are its actions spontaneous or deliberate? Instinctive or rational? Can it exist without air? And by what magic is it replacing the energy that it burns in its motions? It has hardly stayed still a minute in the last eight hours, yet it is as active as at creation. Is it directly converting natural or artificial light, or both, into energy? If so, it is the most wonderful little machine devised up to now and opens visions of immeasurable energies that can be harnessed for man.

"What everlasting dreams hover around this simple bit of homoplasm! Just to look at it, you wouldn't think that this one globule is the full complexity of man reduced to a minimum, would you?"

"No," I said frankly. "I wouldn't, and I don't want to think so. My idea wasn't so hot after all, if this is what it boiled down to."

"On the contrary, it was a brilliant speculation. One thing you writers of science-fiction possess that most scientists lack is freedom from fact. You can start out with almost any concept, expand it to its most imaginative limits, even take liberties with science, and produce a vision of the years to come. But we who work in the laboratory must always offer substantial proof, back up every step with fact, and document our theories or claims by evidence that can stand the laboratory test.

"Domination by fact is both science's greatest safeguard and its worst drag. X discovers a cure for cancer. He knows it is a cure, but cannot prove it immediately. He tests it for years in every conceivable way on all sorts of animal tissues before he announces his results to the public and permits application to human sufferers. In the meantime, tens of thousands of victims die.

"Or take homoplasm. I know what it is. I've a good understanding of what it will do, and what its functions, properties, and actions are. That's why I keep it tightly stoppered. But I could no more announce its discovery to the world without perhaps irreparable loss of prestige now than I could make time run backward."

"It wouldn't surprise me if you even succeeded in doing that," I remarked, and sincerely. "All I can say about your homoplasm I've already said. I refuse to have anything to do with it. You could extol its virtues till doomsday, and I still wouldn't like it. See how it's quivering? It's been squirting around the beaker like a crazy thing while you've been talking. It goes wild every time it gets near your fingers and that seems to be as often as it can. No. I'd get rid of it if it was my choice."

"You may be even nearer the truth than you think," Dr. Weylith answered ambiguously.

A ray of sunlight slanted through the glass of the beaker and turned the living stuff to a drop of scarlet flame, glistening like a bead of blood, beautiful in its own evil way. I shrugged my shoulders in dislike of it.

"Put it up on that shelf out of harm's way," Dr. Weylith suggested with a hint of good-natured banter we often indulged in.

"Not I, thanks. I wouldn't touch that beaker for a million dollars. Or a thousand, anyway."

Dr. Weylith, his sensitive features again wearing a rapt expression as his dreaming mind was absorbed by the homoplasm and fascination over the endless fields of conjecture it opened, stood on tiptoe and placed the beaker on a shelf.

I looked out of the window and saw the sun burn across pavements with a glare that bubbled asphalt and sent the heat waves dancing.

A faint tinkle and a heavier thud came from behind me. I whirled around.

Dr. Weylith sprawled on the floor, face up. A gash laid open his right forehead. I sprang to his side, saw that the fragments of glass were imbedded in the wound, decided instantly it was a case for medical care. He must have lost his balance in attempting to place the beaker on the shelf, and it fell, shattering on his forehead and knocking him unconscious. I cursed myself for my reluctance to heed his request, even though it had been made in jest. The flow of blood was steady, but not large.

For fear of driving the splinters of glass deeper, I merely placed a clean handkerchief on the injury to act as a clotting agent while I raced to the phone in another room.

I called the office of Dr. Weylith's personal physician, but was told he was in the midst of an operative case. To save time, I then called an ambulance and asked for immediate service. Weylith's name worked magic. I could expect the ambulance in fifteen minutes at most. I hurried back to the laboratory.

It does not seem to me that I could have been more than a half minute, but perhaps the telephone delayed me two or three minutes in all. It really makes no difference since there is nothing I might possibly have done had I returned sooner.

When I entered the laboratory and rounded the tables obstructing my view, I received a shock of horror such as I hope may never be repeated. Weylith's head was gone. The upper half of his clothing sagged, but a squirming and hellish motion affected it from some amorphous substance within. Almost as fast as my eyes could follow, the rippling spread down the torso and limbs. I was paralyzed in my tracks. I remembered the pinkish nodule, but that dreadful thought only served to stun me more.

Then, out of that loose and shapeless heap of clothing slid a mass a million times the size of that original drop of ooze; a reddish-gray pulp of heaving and awful life which left not the tiniest bone behind, not the least particle except the glass splinters and the now flat clothing. The stuff quivered damnably, shivered as in a wind, split in two by simple fission. The sun imbued those two mounds of jelly with a smoky and sinister glow. And now they began to eddy and swirl and extend upward. They elongated here, contracted there, filled out elsewhere, assumed new forms of terrifying significance.

"No! No!" I shrieked.

Before me stood two identical Weyliths, naked, each half the size of the original man. There was a duller luster on the faces. In the eyes there was nothing whatever of Weylith's intelligent and friendly gaze. They were dangerous, menacing, primeval eyes, and they stared at me. I wondered madly if each creature had only half the brain of Weylith, or no brain at all.

The homoplasmic drop, having absorbed every germ of Weylith's body, had divided, and each mass had built up a new body from the image of man that was inherent in it. That reproduction was faithful even to the cut on the forehead. And now a stranger occurrence deepened the spell upon me.

The two Weyliths took a step forward, but out of the cuts oozed a rapidly swelling flood of the pink stuff that deliquesced the bodies almost as soon as they had been formed.

The sweat trickled from my face, but my eyes burned and my forehead was hot, dry.

The two heaps quivered hellishly again, and I thanked the stars that no one else had witnessed the transformation. Or was I mad? Perhaps corroboration was the saving grace I needed lest I find this to be only a hideous hallucination. And still I stared, utterly incapable of motion.

The strange life puddles stirred eerily. They narrowed in the middle and separated into four. They swirled into mounting shapes until four grisly phantoms, four pigmy Weyliths, glared at me from eyes ferocious with basic, subhuman, food desire. The four demons tottered toward me, their pink-white eyes blank of any intelligence. They were eyes neither of man nor vertebrate nor fish, neither insane nor sane—just hungry eyes.

I acted as I certainly did not wish to act. I wanted to leave that laboratory forever behind. Something drove me, some subconscious but lightning intuition of what might happen, some unreasoned desire to do what my dead friend would have preferred. I sprang to the door, locked it, whirled around.

Already the four Weyliths were headless. They stood in their tracks like so many decapitated monstrosities, while the streams of ooze pouring down took with them the chests, torsos, limbs, every vestige of those abominable entities.

The speed of the cycle increased perceptibly and proportionately as the mass diminished. The two scientists had divided into four and the four into eight in only three fourths the time that the scientist had first divided. The life of the eight little things was correspondingly shorter, but they moved a step closer.

Then, always more rapidly and horribly, the fission and reproduction of form, the deliquescence and fission again, swept through the cycle. No nightmare was ever more gripping or terrifying by its distortion of the familiar than this travesty of the highest type of human being.

With every fission, the characteristics of the body became coarser, less human, more corrupt and devolutionary, until there was not even a remote resemblance. Weylith, divided and redivided, swept into the ceaselessly changing reduction of this appalling life-cycle, became so many naked little animals ravening for food.

They closed in on all sides. I lost my head. I kicked at one of the new knee-high creatures. My shoe plowed into it, and it clung like glue. Panic seized me, but the return to plasmic state caused the stuff to fall to the floor by gravity.

I dashed for the window and leaped on a radiator coil. It was two stories to the cement sidewalk.

I faced the laboratory. It swarmed with the ever-increasing horde of that ever-contracting spawn—128, 256, 512—I lost count of the doubling and redoubling. They were moving now. They made wailing cries. A shrill and abysmal moan of hunger swept from their ranks when they assumed their momentary and minute imitation of man's estate. A sucking sibilance filled the laboratory when they returned to the homoplasmic stage of their brief life-cycle. Hummocks of reddish jelly. Little ratlike things of human semblance. Surge toward the radiator. Deliquescence. Smaller balls of homoplasm. Retreat into slime, advance into anthropoid form. I saw a million centuries bridged in seconds.

For a few minutes I felt comparatively safe. But I had only begun to consider the peril of my situation when a new menace rose. A great swarm of the viscous plasms turned into inch-high caricatures of Weylith at the foot of the radiator. Instantly they locked, scrambled up, shot a living pyramid toward me. The wriggling mass with all its thousands of intertwined limbs and pin-point eyes shining with baleful luster fell short of me by so small a distance that I was on the verge of leaping out of the window. Then the column collapsed, and I shivered, for I knew the next cycle would not fail of its objective.

What could I do? No matter what the cost, I could not escape from the laboratory, could not loose that demoniacal horde upon the world. Somehow I must destroy it. Somehow I must save myself and obliterate every trace of these subhuman monsters. And every moment the task grew more difficult. I was still reasonably certain that the stuff could not get out. The laboratory had a concrete floor. The windows were weather-stripped, and the door soundproofed. The ventilators were in the ceiling. But if the things became much smaller, they might seep out through invisible cracks and crevices.

The column of myriad, terrible little beasts, like human beetles, shot toward me again in a rising geyser. The nearest table was fifteen feet away. I leaped in panic. The column swerved instantly. Even terror did not give me strength enough. I landed on a cluster of the plasms and felt them squirt in all directions as if I had splashed in a puddle.

I bounded to the table. A jar of hydrochloric acid stood on it. I sloshed the acid over my shoe, wiped it with a piece of waste cloth. My hands burned. I poured the container on the floor. The acid spread, ate its way in a widening pool. A thin but sharply reedy wail crept up. The whole laboratory was paved with a film of ceaselessly undulating slime that alternated with antlike things, save where the acid lay.

There came a pounding on the door. "Ambulance for Dr. Weylith!"

"Just a minute!" I shouted, and made no effort to move.

In the stress of that moment, my senses must have become preternaturally keen, my mind clear as seldom before. I was in so tight a spot that no matter what happened, I must lose out somewhere. My only choice lay between trying to save my own skin for what it was worth, or accepting all risks and doing what I could to annihilate every last mote of the homoplasm.

The beating on the door repeated. "Open!"

"Dr. Weylith has gone elsewhere! I'll be there in a few seconds if you want to wait!" I called.

On the next table lay an electric furnace, gas burners, thermite and cordite. And a blowtorch. I don't know what Weylith used them for. The moment I saw them, I sprang over, pumped the torch, and lighted it. The flame hissed forth with the roaring sound peculiar to gasoline blowtorches. And suddenly I felt protected.

I seared the floor. Foot by foot, I went over the laboratory. I burned my way ahead in swinging swaths. I scorched the legs of every table, the base of each wall. All surfaces in contact with the floor, I subjected to that crisping flame. And a dim, hideous, murmuring cry squealed constantly in my ears, punctuated by the pounding on the door. There was a sickening smell in the air which the ventilators were powerless to carry off.

Nauseated, shaking like the jelly I had destroyed, and on the verge of collapse, I finally extinguished the blowtorch and tossed it on a table. I scarcely cared what happened now. Then I opened the door.

Probably most people are familiar with the incidents of the next six months. The circumstances were highly suspicious. I have no complaint against the authorities for trying to establish a case against me. It was out of the question for me even to hint at what I had seen. I took no one, not even the lawyer, into my confidence.

The case became one of headlines through no fault of my own except the desire to protect the memory of Weylith, who was as dear a friend as I ever had. Perhaps I was foolish. I am in no position to say. But I feel absolutely certain that the case would have been far more notorious and given over to infinitely greater reams of speculation had I tried to explain exactly what happened.

So I botched the tragedy. I told the ambulance men that Dr. Weylith had already been taken away. I would not tell them where. The police became inquisitive, questioned me. They wanted to know why I had called a physician, then an ambulance, why the laboratory floor was seared. Weylith was listed as missing. Suspicion of murder developed.

Doubts of my sanity arose when I gave confused explanations or none at all. There were detentions, specialists, grillings, examinations. A grand jury investigated and handed up a presentment. But there were no witnesses, no proof of homicide, and no trace of a body. Eventually the indictment was quashed for lack of evidence. I was a free, but discredited, man.

That was nearly three years ago. And what saved me as much as anything was an occasional rumor that Weylith had been seen in other parts of the country.

To me, this is the most heartbreaking aspect of the tragedy. I did my best to give Weylith the absolute oblivion he would have wished, but I must have failed. I thought I was thorough, but evidently I was not thorough enough. The division and subdivision and fission of that strange plasm must have reached such minute degrees and such immense numbers that the blowtorch was inadequate.

Perhaps some of the plasm adhered to my shoes in spite of the acid. Or it may have crept up the walls. Or a few flecks might have found some opening invisible to human eyes and thus made their way out of the laboratory. Even so, I think the stuff might have worn itself out—if vertebrate forms had not been susceptible to wounds and injuries; for the homoplasm would apparently never have spread had it not been for direct blood openings.

A child, scratched by brambles, was seen to cross a field near Greenwich one morning. She was never seen again. A caretaker pulling weeds claimed he looked up and saw a naked man, brutally resembling the missing Dr. Weylith, suddenly appear in a field. The child would have reached there about that time.

But the caretaker unfortunately added that he was so shocked that he rubbed his eyes. When he looked again, there were two naked men, and they seemed smaller because they were making toward a clump of woods. His story would have been completely discounted except that the child's clothing was later found near the spot.

A butcher in Chillicothe left his store one noon to deliver an order around the corner. When he returned, he saw a strange little naked boy climbing out of a window. He ran shouting toward his store and asserted that a gang of brats swarmed from every opening. His narrative would also have been met with disbelief except for the fact that not an ounce of meat remained in his shop, with one exception. Cuts, loins, quarters, whole carcasses, liver, even suet, were stolen. Only sausage in casings were left. He thought he had recently seen a picture of the first youth, but he could not remember where.

At various times, in the years since, and in widely scattered parts not only of North America but of the world, the missing Dr. Weylith has been reported seen. A legend grew up about him, rivaling that of Ambrose Bierce.

Sometimes the news dispatches carried items about his reappearance simultaneously in opposite countries of the globe, and in places thousands of miles apart.

And with disturbing frequency, the press also carried accounts of phantom scavengers that looted food markets; of hordes of debased, naked, wild boys who vanished as suddenly as they were seen, leaving no trace behind them; of anthropoid, adult footprints that successively and mysteriously became youth's footprints, children's steps, the marks of babes, and finally ended in mid-fields.

A party of explorers came upon an African village where stew was still cooking over a hot fire. But not a trace of any man, woman, child, or animal was found, nor were the villagers ever discovered. There were dwindling footprints, no other clue. I alone knew what had happened, and I preserved my silence.

To this lengthy, and still-growing list, I will add but one more incident, the incident that caused me to record these facts for the guidance of people, before I, too, disappear of my own choice.

The episode occurred last night. It had been a hot day, and I went for a long walk in the country. As evening drew near, I found myself sauntering down a narrow road that wound between pastures and fields and hills and an occasional farmhouse. The sun hung just above the horizon, and was already half set, when I paused to rest against the wooden fence inclosing a pasture.

Cows munched in the field. Most of them lay under the shade of trees on the far side of the field, but a couple of Jerseys grazed near by and lazily switched off the attack of flies and gnats. It was a peaceful, rural scene that I admired.

Then one of the Jerseys bellowed. The other moved away. The rest of the herd shifted uneasily. The first Jersey mooed plaintively. Sickness and nausea overcame me when I saw it melt down into a swelling puddle, but horror kept me watching though I could have predicted what was coming. The cow ceased struggling, and its eyes glazed while the fore half of its carcass still remained, but that, too, swiftly dissolved into the reddish heap.

Then that shapeless pile took form, and against the dark and lurid western sky stood outlined the gigantic and naked figure of a man. Man? It was a dreadful parody, a grotesque and misshapen monster, of bestial head, apelike hands, and animal feet, whose body was only faintly human in nature, and of a blackish hue.

For seconds the giant stood there, before plodding sluggishly toward the rest of the herd, and it lowered its head to utter a sound, a throatless and primeval food howl, the like of which I never heard before. The huge shape collapsed into slime, and the slime fissioned, and I fled on my way while twin but smaller monsters rose behind.

There is nothing more to add. There is nothing that I or anyone can do, now. The homoplasm carries within it some instinctive or hereditary or vestigial image of man. Because its human manifestations are invariably cast in the likeness of Dr. Weylith, I must assume that he created the original stuff from his own body. So long as one drop of that now world-migrated homoplasm survives, so long will there be theft of animal food throughout the globe, and so long will the everlasting figure of Dr. Weylith be re-created, though it be till the end of time.

PART FOUR

DANGEROUS
INVENTIONS

MALCOLM JAMESON

TRICKY TONNAGE

WHEN YOU'VE lived across the fence from an amateur inventor, you come to expect anything. When the wind was right we used to get some of the awfullest chemical stinks from the Nicklheim barn, and we got so used to hearing explosions that they didn't bother us any more than automobile backfires. We just took it for granted when we'd see Elmer, the boy next door, walking around with his eyebrows singed off and the rest of him wrapped up in bandages.

When Elmer was a little tad, he was a great enthusiast for scientific fiction. You hardly ever saw him unless he was lugging some Jules Vernian opus around, and he ate up all he read with dead earnestness. With that yen for science it might have been expected that he would shine at school, but it did not work out that way. He wouldn't go along in the rut laid out for the run-of-the-mine student. The physics prof finally had him kicked out for some crazy stunt he pulled with the school's equipment. Elmer hooked it all together in a very unorthodox way, and the resulting fireworks was quite a show.

Being barred from school did not faze Elmer. He rigged up his own lab in the barn, buying the stuff from mail-order houses with money he made doing odd jobs. Some of the people in the town thought the boy might go places; most simply thought he was a nut. I belonged to the former group, and sometimes helped the kid with small loans. Not many of his inventions panned out, but he did sell one gadget useful in television to a big company. In a way it proved to be a bad thing he did. The company bought the idea outright and paid promptly, but afterwards for reasons of its own it suppressed the invention—an act that irked Elmer exceedingly. It prejudiced him violently against big corporations as such and the whole patent set-up in general. He swore that after that he would keep all his discoveries secret.

About that time his father died, and it looked as if Elmer had finished with his scientific dabbling phase. Overnight he seemed to mature, and after that he was seldom seen pottering around his barn. He was busy about town, carrying on the little one-horse trucking business bequeathed him by the old man. His truck was one of those vintage rattletraps that appear to be always threatening to make the legend of the one-hoss shay come true, but Elmer was a fair mechanic and somehow kept the old crate going. Not only that, but to the astonishment of the citizenry, he seemed to be making money at it, and that at a time when rate competition was keen and gas expensive and hard to get. I was beginning to think we had witnessed the end of a budding scientist and the birth of an up and coming young busi-· ness man. It was Elmer himself who disabused me of that notion.

One morning he stopped his truck at my gate and came up onto the porch. He pulled out a wad of bills and peeled off a couple of twenties.

"Thanks," he said. "It was a big help, but I'm O.K. now."

"Oh, that's all right," I said. "There was no hurry about paying it back. But I'm glad to see you're doing well in the hauling game. It may not be as distinguished as getting to be known as a big-shot scientist, but at least you eat."

He gave me a funny look and sort of smiled.

"Hauling game, huh?" he sniffed. "I'd never thought of it that way. I don't cart stuff around for the fun of it, or the money either. That's incidental. What I'm doing is testing out a theory I thought up."

"What's that one, Elmer?" I asked. I had heard a lot of his theories, first and last, and seen most of them go flop. Elmer had a very screwy approach to the mysteries of nature.

"It's about gravity. I've found out what it is, which is more than anybody else since Newton has done. It's really very simple once you know what makes it."

"Yes," I agreed. "That is what Einstein says, except that he hasn't finished his universal field formula. So you've beat him to it?"

"Yes. I've been running my truck by gravity for the last three months."

That didn't quite make sense to me. The country road about was hilly and a lot of coasting was possible. But still a vehicle couldn't coast up hill. Elmer was studying me uncertainly, and I realized he wanted to talk to somebody, but he was always so cagy about his projects that I hesitated to come right out and ask.

"I've discovered something big," he said, soberly. "So big I don't know what to do with it. I'd like to show it to somebody, only—"

"Only what?"

"Oh, a lot of reasons. I don't mind being laughed at, but I'd like to keep this secret for awhile. If the other truckers found out how I'm doing what I do, they might gang up on me, smash the truck, and all that. Then again there's no telling what somebody else might do with my idea if they got hold of it before all the theory is worked out."

"I can keep a secret," I told him.

"All right," he said. "Come along and I'll show you something."

I got in the truck with him. He stepped on the starter and the cranky old engine finally got going, though I thought it would shake us to pieces before it made up its mind whether to run or not. Then we lurched off down the road, rattling and banging like a string of cans tied to a mongrel's tail.

"Where does the gravity come in?" I asked.

"I don't use it in town," he said. "People might get wise to me."

We went on down to the oil company's bulk station. It had been raining off and on all week and there was a good deal of mud, but Elmer skirted the worst puddles and we got up to the loading platform all right. It was there I got my first surprise. A couple of huskies started loading up that truck, and when they were through I would have bet my last simoleon Elmer would not get two miles with it. There were six big barrels of grease, weighing four hundred pounds each, a half dozen drums of oil, and some package goods. The truck kept creaking and groaning, and by the time the last piece was on, its springs were mashed out flat as pancakes. It was bad enough to have that overload, but the stuff was for Peavy's store out at Breedville—forty miles away over as sketchy a bit of so-called highway as can be found anywhere in America.

"You'll never get over Five Mile Hill with that," I warned Elmer, but he just grinned and pocketed the invoices. The oil company agent was looking on in a kind of puzzled wonder. He had used Elmer's delivery service before, but it was clear that he didn't believe his eyes. Meanwhile Elmer got the motor going and we backed out of the yard. There was a good deal of bucking and backfiring and shimmying, but pretty soon we were rolling toward the edge of town.

Just beyond the last house the Breedville road turns sharp to the right into some trees, and Elmer stopped at a secluded place where there was an outcropping of bedrock alongside the road proper. He killed the engine and got a cable-like affair out of his tool box.

"The first step," he said, "is to lighten the load."

He hooked one end of the cable against the side of a grease barrel and the other he led to the bare bedrock and attached it there. The cable terminated in what appeared to be rubber-suction cups. It looked as if it were made of braided asbestos rope, threaded with copper wire, and near one end it spread out in a flattened place like the hood of a cobra. There was a small dial and some buttons set in that. Elmer set the dial and punched a button. Instantly there was a popping sound as the truck bed stirred, and I saw that it jumped up about a quarter or half an inch.

"Now heft that barrel," said Elmer.

I did. If there hadn't been another one right behind me, I would have gone overboard backward. I got hold of the top of the cask and gave it a tug, not dreaming I could budge four hundred pounds of heavy grease.

But it came away with about the same resistance that an empty cardboard carton would have had.

"What makes weight," explained Elmer, "is gravitons. All molecular matter contains them in various degree. Up to now nobody knew how to extract them. You could only manipulate weight by moving the matter itself. I simply drain most of the gravitons off into the bedrock where it will be out of the way. It's easy because there is a gravitic gradient in that direction."

As an explanation it was a long way from being satisfactory. But there was the barrel, plainly stencilled with its gross weight, and it was now practically weightless. The weight had left as abruptly as a short-circuited electric charge. Moreover, Elmer was shifting his cable from one drum to another, and as he touched each one the truck rose another notch. By the time he was through it rode as high as if there was no load at all.

"I'll use the last one of these drums for power," said Elmer, coiling up his cable and putting it away. Then I saw that he was making a short jumper connection between it and another cable running down under the cab to the hood. He lifted that up and showed me an attachment on the shaft behind the motor. It was a bulbous affair of metal and there were two leads to it. One was the connection to the drum, the other was a short piece of cable that dangled to the ground.

"I call that my Kineticizer," said Elmer. "It is really a gravity motor. It works on exactly the same principle as a water turbine except that it doesn't require the actual presence of the water. The upper cable has more gravitic resistance than the one I use to dump the load. It feeds a slow stream of gravitons to the upper vanes of a steel rotor. They become heavy and start to fall, exerting torque. At the bottom they wipe the ground cable and the moving gravitons simply waste away into the road. Four hundred pounds falling four feet gives a lot of power—especially when you use it all. See?"

Did I? I don't know. It sounded plausible, and anyway Elmer banged down the hood and we climbed back into the cab. That time we started off like a zephyr. There was smooth, silent, resistless power, and the truck being lightened of its load, leaped like a jack rabbit. The gasoline motor was idle. The only noise was the rattling of the fenders and the swish of the air. Breedville began to look more attainable.

After we straightened out on the road, Elmer began to tell me about gravitics.

"It was Ehrenhaft's work with magnetics that got me to thinking about it. Since he was already doing magnetalysis I didn't bother to go along that line. What interested me was the evident kinship on the one hand between electric and magnetic phenomena in general, and between the strong magnetism of electric fields and iron and the relatively weak magnetism of all other substances."

I kept on listening. Elmer's whole theory of gravitics was pretty involved, and in some spots downright screwy. But on the whole it hung together, and there I was riding along on a stream of moving gravitons to prove it. According to the Elmerian doctrine, in the beginning there was chaos and all matter was highly magnetic. It therefore tended to coalesce into nebulae, and thence into stars.

There the fierce pressures and temperatures tended to strip the basic matter of its more volatile outer shells and hurl them outward in the form of radiant energy. Atomic stresses yielded enormous quantities of light and heat and great streams of magnetons and electrons. In the end there is only ash—the cold inert rocks of the planetary bodies. With the exception of the ferric metals none of that ash retains more than a bare fragment of its original magnetic power. Yet even rock when in massive concentration has strong attractive power. The earth is such a concentration, and its pull on the apple was what woke Newton up.

From that concept Elmer dug into the apple itself and into the atoms that compose it. Mass, he claimed, in so far as what we call weight is concerned, is simply a matter of gravitonic coefficient, a graviton being the lowest unit—one more aspect of the atom. It is the nucleus of a magneton, what is left after the outer shells have been stripped away. The graviton is utterly inert and heretofore locked inseparably in the atoms of the substance to which it originally belonged. If only they could be induced to move, their departure would rob the parent substance of nothing except weight, and by moving pure essence of weight potential energy could be turned into kinetic with the minimum of loss.

"It was finding a suitable conductor that stumped me longest," Elmer confessed, "and I'm not telling yet what that is. But as soon as I found it I built this motor. You see for yourself how beautifully it works."

I did, and I saw a myriad of rosy dreams as well. We took Five Mile Hill like a breeze, almost floating over, thanks not only to the silent drive but to the weightlessness of the cargo. I thought of all the massive mountain ranges just sitting in their grandeur with billions and billions of foottons of locked-up energy awaiting release. I could envisage hundreds of kineticizer plants around their slopes sending out an abundance of free power. What it did not occur to me to think of was what would happen when those mountains eventually became weightless. What worried me most just then was how the other properties of materials would be affected with alteration of its natural weight.

"Oh, not much," said Elmer. "The relative weights of duraluminum, steel and lead have nothing whatever to do with their tensile strength. I drained off most of the weight of a pan of mercury and tested it. I found that it got a lot more viscous when it was light, a characteristic that is overcome by its normal heaviness. But otherwise it was still mercury. There is an anvil in my barn that weighs less than a toy balloon. If it wasn't kept clamped to the block it sits on, it would soar and bump against the rafters, but as long as I keep it from doing that I can still hammer iron out on it."

We were nearly to Breedville when it began to rain again. Elmer put up the storm curtains, and I asked him about how Mr. Peavy was going to react at getting barrels of grease that were lighter than whipped cream.

"I'm going to take care of that before we get there," said Elmer.

I found out what he meant when he pulled up under a railroad underpass about a mile this side of Peavy's store. He got out and produced his cable again. This time he attached it to the face of one of the concrete abutments that held up the girders carrying the track. One by one he reloaded the barrels by dead weight sucked out of the abutment and let it run into the containers on the truck. Again the truck body settled groaning on its springs.

"I'm working on a way to meter this flow more accurately," said Elmer with a grin. "The last load out here Peavy squawked like everything because the stuff was light. This time I'll give him good measure. Nobody ever kicks at getting more pounds than he paid for."

Well, there it was—Elmer's stunt full cycle. No wonder his gas and tire costs were less than anybody else's in the business, or that he could set out on a long trip with an impossible load. He had only to reduce the load to zero, using part of it for power, and replenish it at the other end of the line.

We went on to Peavy's, using the wheezy gasoline motor again. No one at the store saw anything amiss when we drove up, and though Peavy was careful to roll each box and drum onto the scale, he made no comment when he found them markedly overweight. He probably figured it was only justice from the short-changing he had had on the delivery before, and on which the oil company had been adamant as to adjustment. Elmer then picked up some empty drums and we started back.

The rain was coming down hard by then, and when we got to the underpass there were several inches of water in it. Elmer stopped long enough to draw off a few more hundred pounds of avoirdupois into one of the empty drums so as to have power for the trip home. He said it was the best place along his route to get needed weight in a hurry.

We started up, but had not gone more than about a hundred yards when we heard a terrific *swoosh* behind us, and on the heels of it a resounding metallic crash and the scream of shearing metal. The ground shook, and a wave of muddy water swept along the road from behind and passed us, gurgling among the wheel spokes.

"What on earth?" yelled Elmer, and stopped the car.

What was behind us was not pretty to see. The concrete abutment we had just left had slid from its foundation straight across the road until it almost impinged on its opposite mate. What had been the earth fill behind it was a mass of sprawling semi-liquid mud. Sodden by days of rain and heavy with water, the fill had come to act like water behind a dam and simply pushed along the line of least resistance. The now practically weightless retaining wall gave way, since there was only friction to hold it where it should be. The two great black steel girders that it supported lay at an awkward angle half in the pit where the underpass had been, half sticking up into the air.

"Gosh," said Elmer, gazing at the spectacle. "Do you suppose I did that?"

"I'm afraid you did," I said. "Maybe concrete don't need weight for strength, but it has to have something to hold it down."

Well, the damage was done, and Elmer was scared. A train was due soon and something had to be done about it. So we drove on to the first farmhouse that had a phone and sent in word about a washout. After that we went on home, Elmer being pretty chastened.

The days that followed were quite hectic. The more the railroad and public utility commission engineers studied the retaining wall's failure, the more baffled they became. The abutment itself was unmarred in the least degree. There was not a crack in it, and only a few chipped places where the falling girders had knocked corners off. Experts chiseled chunks out of it and took them to dozens of engineering labs. The records of the contracting firm that built it were overhauled. The wall was up to specifications and had been thoroughly inspected at the time of construction. The fragments subjected to strains and stresses reacted as they should, having exactly the tensile and compression strength it should have. The mix was right, the ingredients without flaw. The hitch was that the stuff under examination had about the same weight as an equal volume of balsa wood!

Learned treatises began to appear in the engineering journals under such titles as, "Weight Loss in Mature Concretes," "Extraordinary Deterioration Noted in Failure of Concrete Railway Abutment," and so on. Throughout the whole strange controversy Elmer never peeped, and neither did I. I kept silent for several reasons, and only one of them was the fact that I had given Elmer my pledge not to divulge his invention before he gave the word. Mainly I felt that whatever I might tell them would be received as too ridiculous to be believed. After all, people just don't go around sapping idle weight from stationary objects.

The sequel to the incident has to remain obscure. The very ride that let me into the secret proved also to be the cause of my being excluded from it thereafter. I caught a cold that day, and before long it turned into pneumonia. Complications followed, and there were some months when I was confined to a hospital bed. When I was out again and around, my neighbor Elmer had gone, presumably in search of wider fields.

It is a pity that Elmer's unfortunate experience with his earlier invention soured him on the usual channels of development, for I think what happened to him later was that he got into the hands of unscrupulous promoters. For quite a long time after the collapse of the railroad crossing I heard nothing of Elmer himself or his world-shaking discovery. But little bits of news kept cropping up that indicated to me that while Elmer's secret was being kept, it was not getting rusty from disuse, though he lacked the necessary business imagination ever to put it to its best uses.

There was the phenomenal success of Trans-America Trucking, for example. It was significant to me that the Eastern terminus of its main haul was laid out in the bottom of an abandoned rock quarry and its Pacific end in a deep canyon. I thought I knew where the power came from, especially when an oil salesman told me he had tried hard to get the Trans-American contract. They not only refused to buy from him, but he could not find out what company, if any, was supplying them. I also noted that Trans-America was continually embroiled in lawsuits arising from discrepancies in weights. I knew from that that Elmer had not yet solved the problem of metering his weight siphons.

There were other straws that pointed to Elmer's fine hand. Highway engineers along the routes traversed chiefly by his trucks discovered after a time that even the dirt roads over which the trucks ran needed little or no binder. The surface soil was found to be incredibly heavy, like powdered lead, and therefore did not dust away under high-speed traffic. In the course of time it became as hard and compact as the floor of a machine shop where iron chips form the soil.

But eventually there was trouble. Disloyal employees must have stolen lengths of Elmer's mysterious graviton conductor, for there was a story told in some glee of a policeman giving chase to a fleeing man who had a big iron safe on his shoulders! The burglar got away, so for a time Elmer's secret was comparatively safe. And then there was the exposure of what was later known as the spud racket.

One of Trans-America's ex-truckmen, being aware that potatoes were sold by the pound, saw opportunity. He absconded with a length of Elmer's cable and set himself up in the potato business. He was modest at first. The spuds he handled were overweight, but not too much too heavy when he resold them. The dietitians in the big institutions were the first to notice something wrong, for they had analysts to interpret the figures. But greed got the best of the gangster truckman. Not content with his initial ten or twenty percent boosts in weight, he poured on the avoirdupois thicker and thicker. The average housewife began to complain that big potatoes required all her strength to lift.

The day the market inspectors raided the man's storehouse the cat was out of the bag. They uncovered an endless stream of potatoes on a conveyor belt that ran by a bin filled with scrap iron. As each spud passed a certain point it was wiped by a wisp of mineral wool, whereupon the belt beneath sagged deeply and spilled the potatoes onto the floor. Cranes scooped them up and carried them to the packing department.

The subsequent prosecution ran into myriad legal difficulties. There was ample precedent for dealing with short weights, but none for artificially added surplus weight. Chemists sought to prove, once they tumbled to the concept of movable gravitons, that the introduction of ferrous gravitons into a food product constituted a willful adulteration. They failed. The composition of the potatoes was no more altered than is that of iron when temporarily magnetized. In the end the case was thrown out of court, much to the anger of some theologians who had also developed an interest in the case.

That there was at once a spate of laws forbidding the alteration of natural weights was inevitable. State after state enacted them, and the Interstate Commerce Commission began an investigation of Trans-America Trucking, damaging admissions having been made by the potato racketeer. It was the collapse of one of the cliffs at the western terminus of that company that was the straw to break the camel's back. Weight shifting became a federal offense with drastic penalties.

Perhaps collapse is a badly chosen word. The cliff disintegrated, but it did not fall. It soared.

It happened late one afternoon shortly after a heavy convoy arrived from the east. Thousands of tons of weight had to be made up, and the power units of the incoming trucks recharged with still more weight. The already lightened cliff yielded up its last pounds, for it had been drawn upon heavily for a long time. Its stone, being loosely stratified, lacked cohesion, so with sound effects rivaling those of the siege of Stalingrad, it fell apart—*upward*—in a cloud of dust and boulders. The fragments, though stone, weighed virtually nothing, rose like balloons and were soon dispersed by the winds.

Unfortunately the canyon was not far from the most traveled transcontinental air route. Within an hour pilots were reporting seeing what they described as inert bodies floating in the upper air. One of them ran into a stone no bigger than his fist, but since he was making several hundred miles an hour at the time, it neatly demolished one of his wings. That night two stratoliners were brought down, both riddled with imponderable gravel. The debris while lighter than air, still had some residual weight and unimpaired tensile strength.

Congress intervened. Trans-America's charter was voided and its equipment confiscated and destroyed. Elmer was forbidden to resume business except on orthodox lines. There was no place in the United States for his invention.

That should have been the end of the Theory of Gravitics and its unhappy applications. But it was not. For Elmer had associates by that time who had tasted the luxury of sure and easy profits, and they were not to be denied. Rumor had it that it was his shady partners who took over the financial end and relegated him to his lab again to hunt for other means of utilizing his kineticizer. However that may be, the next stage was several years in incubation. For a time gravitons ceased to be news except in scientific circles where controversies pro and con still raged. People had already begun to forget when Caribbean Power announced itself to the world.

It started operating from a tiny island republic known as Cangrejo Key. Through oversight, or because it was a worthless patch of coral sand frequently swept by hurricanes, mention of it was omitted in the treaty between the United States and Spain at the end of the war of 1898. It was still Spanish until the graviton syndicate bought it from an impoverished Franco for a few millions in real gold. Whereupon the Cangrejo Commonwealth was set up as an independent state and a law to itself.

By then they had one valuable addition to their bag of tricks—Elmer's third great invention. It was a transmitter of beamed radio electric power, and they promptly entered into contracts with large industries in nearby America for the sale of unlimited broadcast power at ridiculously low rates. At first the great maritime powers protested, suspecting what was afoot and fearing the incalculable effects on shipping if Caribbean Power meant to rob the sea of its weight. But the storm subsided when the new republic assured them sea water would not be touched. They pledged themselves to draw only from the potential energy of the island they owned. So the world settled down and forgot its fears. No matter what happened to Cangrejo Key, there was the promise of abundant cheap power, and at the worst one coral islet more or less did not matter. Even if its sands did float off into the sky as had the canyon wall on the Pacific Coast they could do little harm, the Key being well off the air lanes.

It was a premature hope, for they reckoned without the ingenuity of the men behind the scheme. Soon great derricks reared themselves on the Key and drills began biting their way into the earth. By the time the holes reached eight miles depth the transmission towers were built and ready. Then came the flow of power, immense and seemingly inexhaustible. A battery of kineticizer-dynamos commenced operating, suspended by cables deep into the bowels of the planet, converting the weight that was overhead into kilowatts which were sent up to the surface through copper wires. There it was converted into radio power waves and broadcast out to the customers. It was good, clean power. Industry was grateful.

How deep the syndicate eventually sunk its shafts no one ever knew. Nor how many millions of tons of earth weight were converted into electric energy and spewed out to the factories of the world. But it took only a few years for the project to revolutionize modern economics. With power literally as cheap as air, coal holdings became worthless and petroleum nearly so. In the heyday of the power boom cities like New York went so far as to install outdoor heating units so that in the coldest of cold waves its citizens could still stroll about without overcoats. There was no point in conservation any more. Old Terra Firma had gravitons to burn.

The beginning of the payoff came with the Nassau disaster. The town was flattened by a mighty earthquake, and the attendant tidal wave left little of the Florida coastal cities. When the tremors died down the British

Empire found it had added another island of near continental size to its realm. The Bahama Bank had risen above water and then stood from ten to fifty feet above sea level throughout. But there was a rider attached to that dubious blessing. The bed of the Florida Straits had risen correspondingly and the current of the Gulf Stream diminished. Europeans began to worry about the effect of that upon their climate.

Isostatic adjustment was responsible, sober geologists warned darkly. Let the Caribbean Power gang continue to rob that region of its proper weight there would be nothing to hold it down. Adjacent geographical masses would push in to fill the vacuum, just as the underlying, restless, semifluid magma would push up. The time would soon come when mountains rivaling the Himalayas would rear loftily where the Bahama Bank had been and when that day came the other islands about it and the nearby continental areas might well be only shoal spots in a shallowing sea. The Republic of Cangrejo had to go. It was a matter for the new United Nations Court to decide.

Well, that's the story of Elmer Nicklheim's kineticizer as I know it. I am still wondering whether he was with the gang the day the bombers came over and blasted Caribbean Power off the map. If he was, I think he must have been a prisoner, for the gang he at last teamed up with turned out to be an arrogant, greedy lot.

ARTHUR LEO ZAGAT

THE LANSON SCREEN

HARRY OSBORN, First Lieutenant U. S. Army Air Corps, banked his wide-winged bombing plane in an easy, swooping curve. In the distance New York's white pinnacles caught the sun above a blue-gray billowing of twilight ground-haze. A faint smile lifted the corners of his lips as he glanced overside, saw a train crawl along shining rails and come to a halt. Brown dots appeared from the passenger car behind its locomotive and clustered in ordered confusion about the other oblong that completed the train's complement.

What appeared from his altitude to be a rather large pocket-handkerchief slid from the car and spread out on the grass. A metal tube glittered in the sun, came into motion, swivelling to the east. It looked like a cap-pistol, but Osborn knew it to be an eighteen-inch railroad gun.

He slanted down through lambent air. The terrain below was flat, lushly green. It was entirely vacant save at the very center of its five-mile sweep of marsh. Here a small hut was visible in the middle of a hundred-yard area ringed by a water-filled moat.

Two manikins stood before the structure. One was clothed in o.d., the other in black. The civilian's tiny arms gesticulated, and he went into the house. The army man moved sharply into an automobile and sped in the direction of the waiting artillery train.

"Five minutes to zero, Harry." The voice of Jim Raynes, his observer, sounded in the pilot's earphones, "What's the dope?"

"Target practice, Jim. We're to spot for the railroad gun and then we're to bomb. The target is—Good Lord!"

The plane wabbled with Osborn's sudden jerk on its stick, steadied. "Harry!" Raynes exclaimed. "What is it, Harry?"

"The target's that house down there. There's a man inside it. I saw him go in."

"The hell! What's the big idea?"

"Search me. There's no mistake though. Orders say 'absolute secrecy is to be maintained by all participants in this maneuver as to anything they may observe . . .' "

"Maybe it's an execution. Something special. Maybe—"

" '. . . and this order is to be obeyed to the letter no matter what the apparent consequences,' " Osborn finished. "General Darius Thompson signed it personally, not 'by direction.' Tie that, will you?"

"I can't. But—it's orders."

Osborn levelled out, got his eyes focussed on the astounding target.

Suddenly there was nothing within the watery circle. Not blackness, or a deep hole, or anything similarly startling but understandable. It was as if a blind spot had suddenly developed in his own visual organs so that he could not see what there was at that particular point, although the wide green expanse of the swampy plain was elsewhere clear and distinct.

A key scraped in the door of a third-floor flat on Amsterdam Avenue. Junior's two-year-old legs betrayed him and he sprawled headlong on the threadbare rug in the little foyer.

John Sims bent to his first-born, tossed him into the air, caught him and chuckled at the chubby, dirt-grimed face. He'd been tired as the devil a moment before. But now—

June Sims was flushed from the heat of the kitchen range, but her black hair was neat and a crisply ironed housedress outlined her young slim figure. Junior was a warm bundle against her breasts as she kissed John.

"You're early, dear. I'm glad."

"Me too. What's for supper?"

"Pot roast." June's hazel eyes danced. "Johnny, mother phoned. She's going to come over tomorrow night to take care of Junior so that we can go out and celebrate your birthday."

"That's right! Tomorrow is May ninth!"

"Yes. Listen, I have it all planned. 'Alone With Love' is playing at the Audubon. We'll see that, and then splurge with chow mein. I've saved two dollars out of the house money just for that."

"You have! Maybe you'd better get yourself a hat. I saw an ad—"

"Nothing doing. We're going to celebrate! You go downtown."

And so on, and on. . . .

"They're starting, Harry."

Raynes' businesslike crispness somewhat eased Lieutenant Osborn's feeling that something uncanny was happening down there and his hand was steady as he jerked the stick to cope with the bump of the big gun's discharge. A dirt mushroom sprouted in the field.

"Short, two-tenths. Right, four point three," Jim intoned, correcting the range.

A white panel on the ground acknowledged his message. The cannon fired again and slid back in the oil-checked motion of its recoil.

"Over a tenth. Center."

The target was bracketed, the next try must be a hit. Harry banked, levelled out. The brown dots that were the gunners jerked about feverishly, reloading. Whatever it was that obscured his vision of the shack would be smashed in a moment now.

The gunners were clear. The pilot saw an officer's arm drop in signal to fire. Yellow light flickered from the big rifle. Osborn imagined he saw the projectile arc just under his plane. His eye flicked to where that house should be.

And nothing happened! No geyser of dirt to show a miss, no dispersal of that annoying blind spot. Had the gun misfired?

Wait? What was that black thing gliding in mid-air, sliding slowly, then more rapidly toward the ground? The shell that could pierce ten inches of armor was incredibly falling along what seemed the surface of an invisible hemisphere.

It reached the grass and exploded with the contact. The earth it threw up spattered against—*nothing*. Why hadn't the shell exploded on contact with whatever had stopped it? What was going on down there?

"I—I can't make a report, sir." There was a quiver in Jim's phlegmatic voice. Even his aplomb had now been pierced. "I think it would have been a hit, but—"

Again and again the great gun fired. Osborn and Raynes got the signal to go ahead, dropped five three-hundred-pound bombs point-blank on the mysterious nothingness. The area around the circular canal was pitted, excavated, scarred as No Man's Land had never been.

Aviation Lieutenant Harry Osborn flew back to Mitchell Field in the gathering dusk. His young head was full of dizzy visions. Armies, cities, a whole nation blanketed from attack by invisibility. Spheres of nothingness driving deep into enemy territory, impregnable.

It was good to be alive, and in the o.d. uniform, on this eighth day of May in 1937.

In the tea room of the Ritz-Plaza, the violins of Ben Donnie's orchestra sobbed to the end of a melodic waltz. Anita Harrison-Smith fingered a tiny liqueur glass nervously.

"I'm afraid, Ted. What if he suspects, and—"

The long-fingered hand of the man whose black eyes burned so into hers fisted on the cloth.

"Afraid. That has been always the trouble with you, Nita. You have always been afraid to grasp happiness. Well, I can't make you do it. But I've told you that I'm sick of this hole-and-corner business. If you don't come with me tomorrow, as we have planned, I go alone. You will never see me again."

The woman's face went white and she gasped.

"No! I couldn't bear that. I'll come, Ted. I'll come."

Van Norden's snarp, dark features were expressionless, but there was faint triumph in the sly purr of his voice.

"Have you got it straight? The *Marechal Foch* sails at midnight tomorrow from Pier 57, foot of West Fifteenth Street. You must get away from the Gellert dance not later than eleven-thirty. I'll meet you at the pier, but if there is a slip-up remember that your name is Sloane. Anita Sloane. I have everything ready, stateroom, passports, trunks packed with everything you can possibly need. You have nothing to do but get there. Whether you do or not I'll sail. And never come back."

"I'll be there," she breathed.

"Good girl. Tomorrow is the ninth. By the nineteenth we will be in Venice."

General Darius Thompson stood at the side of his olive-green Cadillac and looked at his watch. The bombing plane was a vanishing sky-speck just above the horizon, the railroad-gun had chugged back toward its base. He was alone under the loom of that sphere of nothingness against which the army's most powerful weapons had battered in sheer futility. It existed. It was real. Unbelievably.

A man was in the doorway of the flimsy hut that had been the target of the shells. Quarter-inch lenses made his bulging eyes huge; his high-domed head was hairless and putty-colored; his body was obscenely fat. Professor Henry Lanson gave one the impression that he was somehow less than human, that he was a slug uncovered beneath an overturned rock. But his accession to the Columbia University faculty had been front-page news and the signal for much academic gloating.

"Well?" From gross lips the word plopped into the warm air like a clod into mud. "What do you think now, my dear General? Against my Screen your biggest shells were as puffballs. Yes? Your most gigantic bombs as thistledown. You thought me utterly insane when I insisted on remaining within." The scientist grinned, humorlessly. "What do you think now?"

Thompson shook his grizzled head, as if to rid it of a nightmare. "You took an awful chance. Suppose it had cracked."

"Cracked! In the name of Planck cannot you understand that the Lanson Screen is not matter that can crack?" The other spread veined, pudgy hands. "It is the negation of all energy, a dimensionless shell through which energy cannot penetrate. And since matter is a form of energy—" The physicist checked himself, shrugged. "But what's the use? I cannot expect you to understand. Besides myself there are perhaps a dozen in the world who could comprehend, and none is an American. Enough for you to know that I had to be inside to operate the B machine that cut the negative force the A apparatus set up. From outside it could not be done. The Screen would have remained forever and you would not be convinced there had been no effect of your bombardment within it."

"Could you not have managed some remote control device, some way of working your B machine from outside?"

"Lord, but you military men are stupid!" the physicist burst out exasperatedly. "Don't you understand yet that once the Lanson Screen is erected all within is as absolutely cut off from the rest of the universe as if it were a different space, a different dimension? Nothing can penetrate within—electricity, wireless, the cosmic rays, the sun's radiations. Nothing!"

"Then if a city were covered by it, as you suggest, there would be no means of communication with the outside?"

"That is correct."

"If knowledge of this were universal there could be no more war." Thompson's gray eyes lifted and met the other's. A momentary silence intervened while a message flashed between these two so diverse characters. Then the general went on. "But if it were the exclusive property of a single nation that nation could become master of the world."

Lanson nodded. His voice betrayed knowledge of the *rapprochement* established in that single, long glance. "If I published my results I should gain very little from it. But if I sell it to one power it is worth almost anything I choose to demand. That is why I have worked at it alone. That is why I have never set the details down on paper, to be stolen. After I have sold the invention to you secrecy will be your concern, but till you meet my terms all knowledge of how I produce the effect remains here in my brain." Lanson tapped his clifflike brow. "Here and nowhere else."

"After we purchase it you might still sell your device to others."

"With a million dollars in hand I shall have no temptation to do so. No one could want, or use, more. That is one reason why you should be willing to recommend its payment."

The general shrugged. "I can get it for you when I am convinced that you can veil an entire city as you did this one small house. It seems to me impossible, or so tremendous a task, requiring such huge installations, such vast power, that it would be forbiddingly costly."

The physicist's grating, short laugh was contemptuous. "I'll shield New York for you with the same machine I used here, with the same power—storage batteries not larger than those in your car. Their energy is needed for only an instant, to start the complex functioning of forces whose result you have just witnessed. I'll erect a screen for you about Manhattan Island, an ellipsoid as high and as deep as the least axis of the enclosing rivers. Will that satisfy you?"

"If you can do it, and I cannot blast through, it will. When can you get ready?"

"As soon as I can move my machines to the required location, and set them up. Tomorrow night, if you wish."

"Very well. What help do you require?"

"Only an army truck to convey my apparatus, and, since I will use the rivers as a delimiting guide for the screen, a place near the water to set it up."

The general was eager now, eager as the other. "I'll order a truck out here at once. And there is an army pier at West One Hundred and Thirtieth Street that you can use. I'll see that it is made ready for you."

Midnight of May eighth, 1937. An army truck noses into the Holland Tunnel. On its flat bed are two tarpaulin-covered bulks, machinery of some sort. Its driver is crowded against his wheel by the rotund form of a black-clad civilian whose chins hang in great folds on his stained shirt and whose bulging eyes glow with a strange excitement behind thick lenses. The truck comes out on Hudson Street and turns north.

Tenth Avenue is alive as puffing trains bring the city's food for to-morrow. A herd of bewildered cattle file into an abattoir. West End Avenue's apartment houses are asleep. Under the Riverside Viaduct a milk plant is alight and white tank trucks rumble under its long canopy. At One Hundred and Twenty-ninth Street the army van waits for a mile-long refrigerator car, loaded with fruit from California, to clear the tracks it must cross. The way is cleared. The truck thunders across cobbles and steel, vanishes within the dark maw of a silent pier.

Two blocks eastward a lighted subway train crawls out on its trestle for a breath of air, pauses fleetingly, dives underground again like a monstrous serpent seeking its burrow. Above the southward course of that burrow midtown Broadway is a streak of vari-colored illumination, exploding into frantic coruscation and raucous clamor at Forty-seventh Street. Crowds surge on sidewalks, in shrieking cabs, private cars; pleasure seekers with grim, intent faces rushing to grills, night clubs; rushing home, rushing as if life must end before they can snatch enough of it from greedy Time. Blare of the latest swing tune sets the rhythm for them from a loud-speaker over the garish entrance of a so-called music store.

Time writes its endless tale in letters of fire drifting along a mourning band around Time's own tower.

MARKET CLOSES STRONG TWO POINTS UP
PRESIDENT ANNOUNCES RECOVERY ACCOMPLISHED
CHAMPION CONFIDENT OF VICTORY FRIDAY
HITLER DEFIES LEAGUE
POLICE WILL SMASH DOCK RACKET SAYS VALENTINE
GIANTS WIN. . . .
There is no Mene, Mene, Tekel Upharsin written on that slender wall for some prophet to read.

Felix Hammond knots the gold sash rope of his black silk dressing gown. His satin slippers make no sound as they cross the thick pile of the glowing Kermanshah on the floor of his study to a darkly brooding Italian

Renaissance secretary. He fumbles in the drawer for a silent moment, pulls out a book whose tooled-leather cover should be in some museum. He sits down, opens the book.

Minuscular, neat writing fills page after page. Hammond reads an entry. Something that might be a smile flits across his ascetic countenance. His bloodless lips wince at another item. He riffles the sheets rapidly to the first blank space, reaches for a fountain pen and starts writing.

May 8: Wednesday. Another day gone. I confess I do not know why I continue this diary, except, it may be, that it serves as a reminder of the utter futility of life. There are, however, certain scarlet pages, and lavender ones also, that still have the power to titillate emotions I thought long atrophied. I wonder if anyone save I will ever read them.

Aloysia opened in her new show tonight. I have just come from the theatre. She wanted me to join the supper Stahlbaum is giving the company, but I declined with thanks—thanks that I was in a position to decline. Time was that I should have leaped at the invitation, but I no longer need to share her with others. Her part suits her—Norton has given her fully two-thirds of the lines and she trails languid sensuality across the stage to her heart's content. I noticed that she used that trick with the mouth she first developed for my benefit. It was lost on the rabble. . . .

Eleven P. M., Thursday, May ninth, 1937.

Item: June Sims hangs on her husband's arm as they exit from the Audubon Theatre. Her eyes sparkle with happiness. She sighs tremulously. Then: "Johnny. Maybe we'd better call up and see if Junior is all right before we go eat."

Item: Anita Harrison-Smith peers over the shoulder of her black-coated dance partner with narrowed eyes. The florid-faced, heavy man in the alcove they are just passing is her husband. His companion is Rex Cranston, president of the A. P. & C.

Without hearing she knows their talk is of debentures, temporary reactions, resistance points on Cumulative Index graphs. Howard Harrison-Smith has forgotten Anita exists, will remain oblivious of her till she comes for him to take her home.

Her small red lips set in a firmer line. He has a long wait ahead of him tonight.

Item: Aloysia Morne lets her ermine cape slide into Felix Hammond's deft hands. He bends and kisses her where a shoulder no less white than the snowy fur melts into the perfect column of her neck. She turns with studied grace, and her throaty voice reproduces the deepest note of a 'cello.

"Do you know, Felix, this lovely place of yours is more home to me than my own so-grand rooms." Hammond smiles thinly, and does not answer.

Item: In the dim light of a decrepit pier jutting into the Hudson Professor Henry Lanson is more than ever like a gigantic larva as he putters about a grotesque combination of steel rods and glittering, lenticular copper bowls out of which a brass cylinder points telescopelike at the zenith.

An arm-thick cable crawls over the pier's frayed boards, and coils over their edge to the water. Lanson turns and checks connections on another, smaller machine.

Far across the Hudson's black surface loom the Palisades. A dash of yellow luminance zigzags against their ebony curtain, a trolley climbing to where an amusement park is an arabesque of illumination against the overcast sky.

To the right the cables of George Washington Bridge dip, twin catenaries of dotted light, and rise again. A red spark and a green one are the apices of moiré, chromatic ribbons rippling across the water to the pier head from the deeper shadow of an army launch.

Braced vertically, five feet behind that pierhead, is a whitewashed steel plate. This is the target for the automatic rifle that will be fired from that bobbing launch as a first trial of the Lanson Screen's efficacy.

Other tests will follow, later. But General Thompson will not yet chance firing artillery into Manhattan.

Henry Lanson calls, in his voice without resonance, "Ready, General. Ten minutes for the first try."

From across the water Thompson snaps, "Ready. Go ahead."

Lanson lumbers back to his machine, thrusts at a lever. There is no sound, no vibration. Suddenly the river, the Palisades, disappear. The amusement park is gone, the inverted necklaces of pearly light that mark the bridge cables. There is no sky. Lanson looks at his wrist watch.

"Ten minutes," he chuckles. "He couldn't get through in ten thousand years."

He is very sure of himself, this man. But perhaps there is a minute residuum of doubt in his mind. After all, he has never experimented with so vast an extension of his invention's power. He thuds to the steel target, puts one doughy paw against it, leans out to view its riverward surface. Will there be any flecks of black on it to show the impact of the bullets that are being fired at it?

Is he warned by a sound, a creak? One cannot know. At any rate he is too obese, too ponderous, to avoid catastrophe. Under his leaning weight the steel plate rips from flimsy braces. Falls.

Its edge thuds against the physicist's head, knocks him down, crushes his skull.

Professor Henry Lanson's brain, and its secrets, are a smear of dead protoplasm mixed with shattered bone and viscous blood.

Eleven-twenty-eight P. M., Thursday, May ninth, 1937.

The lights are dim in Foo Komg's pseudo-Oriental establishment. John Sims spoons sugar into a hot teapot.

"I'm going to make a lawyer out of Junior," he says slowly. "He'll go to Dartmouth for his academic course and then to Harvard. He won't have to start working right out of high school like I did."

John is reminded of the days before June belonged to him by the setting, by the dreamy light in her eyes.

"Let's walk down Broadway," he says, "when we get through here." That is what they used to do when all the glittering things in the store windows did not seem quite as unattainable as they did now.

"No, Johnny. I want to go home. I have a queer feeling there's something wrong. Mother isn't so young any more, and she's forgotten what to do if a child is croupy or anything."

"Silly. Nothing's wrong."

"Take me home, hon."

"Oh, all right." Petulantly. "It's just like you to spoil things. . . ."

Anita Harrison-Smith slips out of the side door of the old Gellert Mansion on East Sixty-first Street. She signals a taxi.

"Pier Fifty-seven." Her violet eyes are deep, dark pools and a visible pulse throbs in her temple. . . .

Nobody looks at the sky. Nobody ever looks at the sky in New York. Nobody knows the sky has suddenly gone black, fathomless.

Later:

"Nita!"

"Ted!"

"You did come! Here, driver, what's the fare?"

The cab circles in Fifteenth Street, vanishes eastward. Van Norden takes the woman's arm.

"Have any trouble getting away?"

"No." She is quivering. "Hurry, darling. Let's get on board before anyone sees us."

"There's some trouble. Fog or something. The pier doors are closed, but the officials say they'll be open again directly. They won't sail without us."

"Look, Ted, it *is* a heavy fog. Why, you can't see the river from here. Even the other end of the ship is hidden. But there isn't any haze here. Queer. The ship seems to be cut in half; it's quite distinct up to a certain point, then there just isn't anything more. It's black, not gray like fog ought to be."

"Let's go in that little lunch wagon till we can get aboard. Nobody will look for us in there."

"Let's. I'm afraid, Ted. I'm terribly afraid. . . ."

Nobody looks at the sky except General Darius Thompson, bobbing in a little launch on the Hudson. He is staring at vacancy where New York had been a quarter hour before. Up the river the cables of the great Bridge come out of nothingness, dip, and rise to the western shore.

Toward the Bay there is nothing to show where the metropolis should be. No light, no color. Nothing. Sheer emptiness. He looks at the radiant figures on his watch once more.

"Wonder what's keeping the old fool," he growls. "He should have dissipated the screen five minutes ago."

The night is warm, but General Thompson shivers suddenly. An appalling speculation beats at his mind, but he will not acknowledge it. He dares not.

A hundred yards from Thompson, in another space, a device of steel and copper and brass stands quiescent over the unmoving body of the one man who knew its secret.

Into the dim recesses of the army pier a dull hum penetrates, the voice of a million people going about their nightly pursuits, unaware, as yet, of doom.

In his cubicle on the hundred and ninetieth floor of New York University's Physics Building, Howard Cranston watched the moving needle of his Merton Calculator with narrowed eyes. If the graph that was slowly tracing itself on the result-sheet took the expected form, a problem that had taxed the ingenuity of the world's scientists for sixty years would be solved at last.

The lanky young physicist could not know it, but the electrically operated "brain" was repeating in thirty minutes calculations it had taken Henry Lanson three years to perform, two generations before. His own contribution had been only an idea, and knowledge of the proper factors to feed into the machine.

A red line curved on the co-ordinate sheet, met a previously drawn blue one. A bell tinkled, and there was silence in the room.

Breath came from between Cranston's lips in a long sigh. Curiously, he felt no elation.

He crossed the room slowly, and looked out through the glassite-covered aperture in the south wall. Just below, elevated highways were a tangled maze in the afternoon sun, and helicopters danced like a cloud of weaving midges. But Cranston neither heard nor saw them. His gaze was fixed farther away, down there where a curious cloud humped against the horizon, a cloud that was a challenging piling of vacancy; something that existed, that occupied space, yet was nothing.

Beyond it he could see the shimmering surface of New York Bay, and rising from it a tall white shaft. At the apex of that shaft a colossal figure faced him. It was a gigantic woman of bronze, her head bowed, her hands pressed to her heavy breasts that agonized in frustration. The Universal Mother stood in eternal mourning over the visible but unseen grave of millions.

"It might be dangerous," Howard Cranston muttered. "The gases of the decomposed bodies—there was no way for them to escape. Before I start building the machine I must find out. Carl Langdon will know."

He turned away. "But first I'll draw it up. It's simple enough—will take less than a week to build."

The design that presently took pictured form under Howard Cranston's flying fingers was strangely like that which sixty years ago Henry Lanson had called his B machine. But there was a difference. This one could be used from outside the Screen.

With the aid of this, by expanding the radius to include the original barrier, it would be a simple matter to destroy the hemiobloid of impenetrable force that was a city's tomb, to release the force which Lanson had set up.

Rand Barndon's flivver-plane settled before a graceful small structure of metal and glass. He swung his rather square body out of the fuselage, crunched up the gravel path.

The door opened, irislike, as he stepped into the beam of the photoray. Somewhere inside a deep-toned gong sounded, and tiny pattering feet made a running sound. "Daddy! Daddy's home!"

Blond ringlets were an aureole around tiny Rob's chubby face. The father bent to him, tossed him in the air, caught him dexterously. Ruth Barndon appeared, taller than her husband, her countenance a maturer, more feminine replica of the boy's. Rob was a warm bundle against her breasts as her lips met Rand's. "You're late, hon. Supper's been ready twenty minutes."

"I know. We were talking about what they found down there." He gestured vaguely to the south. "One of the fellows flew down last night. They wouldn't let him land. But he saw enough, hovering on the five thousand foot level, to keep him awake all night."

Ruth paled, shuddered. "What an awful thing it must have been. You know, nobody ever thought much about it. The cloud had been there all our lives and it really didn't seem to mean anything. But seeing all those buildings where people just like us once lived and worked, seeing those . . ."

"Afterward, dear." Ruth caught the signal of the man's eyes to the quietly listening child and stopped. "I'm hungry. Let's get going."

The soft glow of artificial daylight in the Barndon living room is reflected cozily from its walls of iridescent metal. Rand stretches himself, yawns. "What's on tap tonight, hon?"

"We're staying home for a change."

"I thought this was Matilda's night."

"It is. But Mrs. Carter asked me to change with her, she had something on. And I would rather stay home. There's a new play by Stancourt. I think they call it 'Alone with Love.' Fred Barrymore is taking the lead."

"That gigolo! I can't see what you women find in him!"

"Rand! That's just a pose. You know darn well you turn him on every time."

"Oh, all right. But let's get the magazine viewcast first. They always have something interesting." He crosses the room, touches an ornamental convolution on the wall. A panel slides noiselessly sideward, revealing a white screen. A switch clicks, the room dims, the screen glows with an inner light. Rand twirls a knob.

The wall-screen becomes half of an oval room, hung with gray draperies, gray-carpeted. There is a small table in the room, behind it show the legs and back of a chair. Like the furniture in the Barndons' own place, table and chair are of lacquered metal, but these are gray. The drapes part, a tall man comes through. His face is long, pinched, his blond hair bristles straight up from his scalp, and his brown eyes are grave. The impact of a strong personality reaches out from the televised image, vibrant with a stagy dominance even over the miles of space intervening between actuality and reproduction.

"Oh, it's Grant Lowndes," Ruth breathes. "I love him!"

"Shhh." Barndon is intent. "Shhh."

The Radio Commission's premier reader moves with practiced grace. An adept at building up interest in trivialities by pantomimed portentous-ness, Lowndes is weaving a spell about his far-flung audience that will assure him concentrated attention. As he sinks into the seat his eyes stare from the screen with hypnotic penetration. He places a book on the table before him. Its covers are of tooled leather, but there is a smudge of green mould across them concealing the design. He opens it.

The pages are yellow, frayed-edged. Faded handwriting is visible; minuscular. An old diary, perhaps, picked up from some dusty secondhand display.

"Good evening, friends." His voice is mellow, warming, vibrant with a peculiar tensity. Ruth's tiny, stifled gasp is a tribute to its art. "The manu-facturers of General Flyers Helioplanes have honored me tonight with a great privilege and a sad task. I bring to you a voice from the past, a voice long silent, speech from a throat long mouldered into dust, thoughts from a brain whose very molecules are one with the snows of yesteryear. I bring to you the palpitant, living agony of the greatest catastrophe the world has ever known." His eyes drop to the volume on the lectern, and his slim, white hand presses down upon its face.

"My colleagues of the viewcast service have informed you of the rend-ing of the veil that sixty-two years ago cut off Manhattan Island from the world. They have brought into your homes the awful vision of dead build-ings; dead streets strewn with twisted skeletons. You have, I am sure, tried to picture what must have happened there in the tragic days till eternal silence fell and the entombed city had become a vast necropolis. Today, my friends, the searchers found an account of one man's experience, a painstakingly written chronicle of that time. General Flyers is sponsoring the presentation to you of this human, pitiful tale. I will quote from the diary."

May 9, Thursday: It is four in the morning. Aloysia came here with me from the theatre. . . . I have just returned from escorting her to the place where she resides. She does not call it home—that name she reserves for these rooms. "Home, Felix," she said, "is the place where happiness dwells." I recognized that, it is a line from one of her earlier appearances. Her mind is a blotter, seizing the thoughts, the ideas, the mental images of others and becoming impregnated with them. No. Molding itself to them. Perhaps that is the secret of her arts—dramatic and—amatory.

I am restless, uneasy. There is a pecular feeling in the air, a vague sense of impending catastrophe. Even the recollection of the past few hours with her does not drive it away. . . .

I thought music might fit my mood. But the radio is out of gear. Tonight nothing but silence. Strangely enough the police talk was roaring in. There seems to be some trouble along the waterfront. . . .

It ought to be getting on to dawn, but it is still pitch dark outside. There isn't any breeze. The sky is absolutely black. I have never seen anything like it in New York. Clouds at night always reflect the glow of the city lights. And if there are no clouds there should be stars, a moon. Can there be a storm coming down on the big city—a tornado? That would explain the way I feel.

May 10, Friday: There has been no daylight today. The only illumination is artificial. Somehow that seems the worst of what has happened to the city. For something has happened. Manhattan is surrounded by an impenetrable barrier. Nobody, nothing can get in or out. There have been no trains at Grand Central or Penn Station, the subway is operating only within the borders of Manhattan Island.

I have been driving around with Aloysia all day. In spite of the darkness things went on very much as usual in the morning—children went to school, toilers to their work. It dawned only gradually that more than half the staffs in offices and stores had not shown up. Those who do not live in Manhattan. At noon the newspapers came out with scare headlines. Every bridge out of the city is closed off by the veil of—what can I call it? Every pier. A cover has shut down over us as if Manhattan were a platter on which a planked steak was being brought from the kitchen of the Ritz-Plaza. Even the telephone and telegraph have been affected.

By three in the afternoon the whole city was in the streets. My car was forced to move at a crawl. There was no sign of fear, though. The general consensus was that the phenomenon was something thrilling, a welcome break in the humdrum of daily existence. The mayor's proclamation, in the newspapers and over the few radio stations located within the city, seemed quite superfluous. He urged the people to be calm. Whatever it was that had shut us in was only temporary, it would vanish of itself or a way would be found to get rid of it. He has appointed a committee of scientists from Columbia and the City Colleges to investigate and make plans. The best of them all, however, is unavailable. Henry Lanson. He was found crushed to death on a Hudson River pier, killed in some obscure experiment.

Aloysia left me in time for the evening performance. The theaters and movie houses are crowded—they have had the best day in their history.

At ten o'clock tonight I went to take a drink of water. None ran from the tap. I called the superintendent and he said the mains had been shut off. There was no longer any pressure. Police orders are that water is to be used only for drinking and cooking. It is being pumped from the main by fire engines stationed at the hydrants and a rationing system has been devised. I have two or three cases of Perrier—they should be sufficient for my needs till this thing is over. There is plenty of wine and Scotch, but I have no desire for alcohol.

May 11, Saturday: The darkness still continues. No milk was delivered this morning. Prices for food have begun to go up. There is very little fresh meat to be had, practically no vegetables or fruits. Evaporated milk is being sold at a dollar a can. I am afraid the children are going to suffer a great deal. . . .

May 12, Sunday: Church was packed. There have been several riots in the poorer sections of the city. Grocery stores were raided, a warehouse gutted. The militia has been called out, and all stocks of food taken over by the authorities for rationing.

Aloysia has just appeared, bag and baggage. She says she feels safe only here. I am going out to see what is going on.

Two P. M.: There is no longer any water in the system! The lakes in Central Park are being emptied, the fluid taken to breweries and distilleries nearby, where the water is being filtered and chlorinated. The little thus obtained, and canned fruit juices, furnish the only drink for children. Adults are drinking beer and wine.

My car was stopped by a detail of national guardsmen in uniform. No gasoline engines are to be run any longer. There is no escape for the carbon monoxide fumes being generated, and they are poisoning the atmosphere. There already have been several deaths from this cause.

A fire started in an apartment house on Third Avenue. It was extinguished by chemicals. I wonder how long that will be efficacious?

I thought I was fairly well stocked up for at least a week. But with Aloysia here, her maid and my own man, my stock of food and drinkables is rapidly disappearing. For the first time I have sent Jarvis out to the food depots, with an affidavit setting forth the size of my "family," my residence, etc. I understand that each adult is being allotted one can of meat or vegetables, and one pint of water, per day.

Three P. M.: All house lights have been turned off to conserve coal. I am writing by candle. Street lighting is still maintained. There has been no gas since the Darkness fell, the plant being in Astoria. As my own kitchen has an electric range this did not impress me, but I understand those not so taken care of had been displaying remarkable ingenuity. Several families had upended electric laundry irons and used those as grills. That is ended now. However, there is so little to cook that the lack of heat hardly brings added hardship.

Jarvis has not yet returned.

Midnight: From my window I can overlook quite a large portion of the city. A vast black pall rests over us, relieved only by the network of glowing lamps outlining the streets. Even these seem to be growing dimmer.

My valet, Jarvis, is still among the missing. He has been with me for ten years. I thought him loyal, honest. He *was* honest with respect to money. I have trusted him with large sums and never found him faithless. But money is worth nothing today, while food . . .

Stress reveals the inner nature of the human animal. I met the Harrison-Smiths today, walking along Park Avenue in the foreboding restlessness that is keeping all New York on the sidewalks. The usually iron-visaged banker presented a countenance whose color matched the clammy hue of a dead fish's belly. His heavy jowls were dewlaps quivering with fear. Even while we talked his eyes clung to his wife, who was erect, a bright white flame in the Darkness. Her eyes were answering the appeal in his. She had strength enough for both, and was keeping him from collapse by sheer, silent will. The gossips, this winter, were buzzing about Anita and Ted Van Norden, the wastrel who reminds me so much of my own youth. There could not have been any truth in the rumors.

May 13, Monday: Noon, I went out at five this morning to take my place in the long line at the food station. I have just returned with my booty. One can of sardines and a six-ounce bottle of soda—to maintain three adults twenty-four hours! On my way back I saw a man, well-dressed, chasing an alley cat. He caught it, killed it with a blow of his fist, and stuffed it in a pocket.

The air is foul with stench. A white hearse passed me, being pushed by men on foot. Someone told me that Central Park is being used as a burying ground.

I stopped to watch the passing hearse near a National Guardsman, a slim young chap whose uniform did not fit him very well. He spoke to me. "That's the worst of this thing, sir, what it's doing to children." Under his helmet his eyes were pits of somber fire. "Just think of the babies without milk. The canned stuff gave out today. My own kid is sick in bed; he can't stand the junk we've been giving him. June—that's my wife—is clean frantic."

I wanted to comfort him, but what was there to say? "How old is your youngster?" I asked.

"Junior is two. And a swell brat! You ought to hear him talk a mile a minute. He's going to be a lawyer when he grows up."

I listened to him for a while, then made some excuse and got away. I had to or he would have seen that my eyes were wet.

Later: Aloysia has slept all day. All the windows in the apartment are open, but the air is heavy, stifling. It is difficult to move, to breathe. The shell that encloses us is immense, but eventually the oxygen in the enclosed air must be used up. Then what?

Unless relief comes soon death will be beforehand, the mass death of all the teeming population of this island. One must face that. Just what form will it take? Starvation, thirst, asphyxiation? Queer. I, who have so often babbled of the futility of life, do not want to die. It is—unpleasant—to contemplate utter extinction, the absolute end of self. I wish I believed in immortality—in some sort of future life. Even to burn eternally in hell would be better than simply—*to stop*.

There is a red glow to the south. Is it a thinning of the Darkness?

The city seems hushed with all traffic noise stopped. But another sound has replaced it. A high-pitched murmur, not loud, but omnipresent, insistent. I have just realized what it is. Children crying. Thousands of them, hundreds of thousands. Hungry children—thirsty children. . . .

May 14, Tuesday: The clock says it is morning. It is not dark outside any more. A red light suffuses the scene, the light of the gigantic flame that has enveloped all the lower end of the Island. There is no wind. The conflagration is spreading very slowly, but it is coming inexorably. Overhead are vast rolling billows of smoke, edged with scarlet glare. Below there is a turbulent sea of human beings. The roar of the fire, pent-in and reverberant, mingles with the crash of breaking glass, the rattle of rifle shots, a growling animal-like sound that is the voice of the mob. They are engaged in a carnival of destruction, a blind, mad venting of protest against the doom that has overtaken them. I had a dog once that was run over by some fool in a truck. When I went to pick it up it snarled and sank its teeth in my hand. That is like those people down there. They do not know what has hurt them, but they must hurt someone in return.

Where they find the strength to fight I do not know. I can scarcely move. My tongue fills my mouth. It is almost impossible to breathe.

Aloysia has just called me. It was the ghost of a word, her "Felix." In a moment I shall go in to her and lie down beside her.

Grant Lowndes looks up from the book.

"That is all," he says simply. "In an inner room of the apartment where this was found the searchers discovered two skeletons on the mouldering ruin of a bed, a man's and a woman's.

"General Flyers bids you good night. I shall be with you again at this same hour on Friday."

He turns and goes slowly out through the gray curtains. The diary remains on the little gray table. Shadows close in from the edges of the screen, concentrating light within their contracting circle. The book is the last thing visible. That, too, is gone. . . .

There is silence in the living room for a long minute. Rand Barndon reaches to the radiovisor switch, clicks it off. The screen is blankly white in the glow of the room light.

"You know," Barndon says slowly. "The city wasn't all burned up.

Guess the fire burned up all the oxygen and put itself out. That was what killed the people too."

Ruth sighs tremulously. "Rand, I was thinking about that one thing he said, about that soldier that was worried about his sick little boy. Just think if anything like that were to happen to our Rob."

"Say, I noticed that too. The fellow had a good idea. That's what we're going to make of the kid, a lawyer. Big money and not too much hard work. We'll send him to Dartmouth first, and then to Harvard. A fellow was telling me they've got the best law school in the country. . . ."

NAT SCHACHNER

THE ULTIMATE METAL

TWILIGHT laid its protective mantle over the roaring life of New York. For one breathless moment there was a hush, as nature had intended. Then the giant city girded its limbs defiantly and accelerated the headlong tempo of its existence.

Little lights winked into being over the massed masonry of the midtown section as lawyer, broker, and business executive whipped flagging energies to renewed effort. The streets, huddled in canyons, festooned themselves with long necklaces of radiant pearls. Broadway flared into a seething white cauldron of strange mechanical figures that shouted from the house-tops the virtues of toothpaste, streamlined cars, morticians, beauticians, and ivory, apes, and peacocks. The power-house managers gazed at the mounting loads on their output indicators and should have been content.

Except for one thing—the threat implied in the Coulton Building.

This was strange. For such a structure, even though not quite completed, ought to have gladdened the hearts of power-company directors and stockholders alike. One hundred and fifty stories high, subdivided into innumerable offices and suites, expected to house a veritable city of fifty thousand people, it was comparatively easy to calculate the exact kilowatt consumption per year. Given a definite number of short, dark winter days, the average number of cloudy, storm-gloomed days, the driving compulsion that forces typewriters to clatter far into the night, the usual percentage of employers who keep pretty stenographers working overtime, the normal number of after-hours' poker games, which to trusting wives masquerade under the peculiar name of important board meetings—given all these, and the rest is mathematics.

But—and there was the rub—mathematics weren't necessary. Except for the negligible amperage required for the operation of elevators, vacuum cleaners, et cetera, electricity might just as well have never been discovered. That was why the Coulton Building created such a furore in the practical as well as the scientific world. That was why rubberneck buses, filled to the brim with old ladies from Keokuk, primly excited schoolmarms from Walla Walla, bored garment buyers from Texas, and honeymooners from Heaven knows where, made special detours to Central Park South, and barkers inhaled deeply before lifting megaphones to lips.

This very evening Thomas Coulton himself stood importantly in the cleared plaza before his already world-famous structure. He towered over the respectfully insistent mob of reporters even as the Coulton Building towered over and dwarfed its neighbors. He was a big man, heavy of beam and of head, with a thunderous voice, which, combined with the knowledge that he, and his father before him, possessed millions, was sufficient to overawe any normal human being.

He did not look like the average conception of a world-famous physicist —you know the type: pale, thin, ascetic, eyes burning with the pure scientific ardor—but, then, neither did his assistant, Harley Dean, standing just now inconspicuously on the outskirts of the thrusting hurly-burly of men with pads and pencils in their hands.

Harley Dean might have passed for the third from the end in the stag line at a débutante party, and he would certainly have fitted very well into flannels and a powerful backhand stroke during a Long Island week-end. Yet Dean, in fact, was the true discoverer of *evanium*, No. 93 in the scale of elements. It was he also who alloyed it with other and more familiar elements so as to make possible the Coulton Building.

For one man, however, who had heard of Harley Dean, there were thousands who knew Thomas Coulton. It was his splendidly equipped laboratories and unlimited financial resources that gave Dean the chance to pursue his experiments. It was Coulton's colossal egotism and desire to be considered a scientist as well as a millionaire that made him ostensibly chief of the laboratory, whereby the world at large was given the impression that he, Thomas Coulton, was the only begetter and originator of *evanium* and its alloys.

Harley Dean did not mind that particularly. Such has been the fate of true genius ever since wealth took up the arts and sciences in a big way. He would smile a bit caustically at Coulton's booming periodic sentences that made such swell copy in the daily news sheets, and go on with his work.

But now he was not smiling. He was frankly worried. Vague fears assailed him; fears that loomed more and more ominously as the days went on, one by one, and the tremendous undertaking neared completion. Yet everything looked all right, and there seemed no foundation for his worried preoccupations except the overcautiousness of the true scientific investigator who has, he feels, insufficient data on hand to justify jumping at conclusions.

Coulton laughed at his expressed qualms and pushed his plans for the building as fast as he could drive engineers and architects along. His optimism was as large as his frame; Dean was a plodder with his nose buried in his work, while he, Coulton, made lightning decisions and painted with tremendous brush strokes on gigantic canvases.

"What you need, my boy," he told Dean gustily, "is vision. Yes, sir; vision with capital letters. If I listened to you, the world would stand still. Nothing would ever be done. Good Lord, man, we've tested and prodded this damned alloy for a month now. What more do you want? The millennium to come? Or maybe you own a share in the electric-light companies and the steel trust and *that* makes you nervous. No, sir; I'm going through with it—now!"

The "we" of course was purely euphemistic. All that Coulton ever did was breeze into the laboratory an hour or so a day, other engagements permitting, during which time he managed to break valuable instruments, muss up important and delicate experiments, and generally get into Dean's patient way.

His familiar voice rose oratorically on the evening air. This was his element, talking in large phrases to reporters. It irritated Dean for the first time. His sense of humor seemed unable to cope with his chief to-night. Maybe it was because he was tired; perhaps because the loom of the practically finished building filled his sleep with nightmares.

"Look at it!" Coulton made a grandiloquent gesture. "The most magnificent thing the world has ever seen. All seven wonders rolled into one, and some more that the old Greeks never counted."

Obediently the reporters craned their necks. It was in truth an awe-inspiring sight. The great structure towered fifteen hundred feet straight into the air, its smooth, shining metallic flanks instinct with grace and beauty, yet giving the impression of tremendous power and thrusting strength. This in itself was an innovation—all-metal construction. But the miracle that brought gasps of wonder to the thronging sight-seers and probing scientists alike was the strange luminescence of that metal.

Dusk had turned to darkness. New York was a prickle of man-made lights against a blue-black sky. But the Coulton Building scorned all adventitious aids. It glowed with innate fires; it radiated pure white softness, strong as the noonday sun, yet glareless and soothing to the eye. Within as well as without, the silver-metal walls made high noon out of conquered night.

A sky-pointing vision out of fairyland! The sound of hammering filtered down from the upper stories. The last finishing touches were being put to the gigantic structure. October the first was a week off.

"Gentlemen," Coulton boomed, "let me give you a tip. Sell electric-power stock short. Artificial lighting is as outmoded as candles and kerosene lamps. Within five years every new building in the good old U. S. A.—yes, sir, in the world—will be made of *Coultonite*."

"Maybe you'll let us in on the ground floor, Mr. Coulton," one daring individual piped up. "I got a couple o' hundred bucks I'd like to invest."

Coulton beamed and shook his head. "Sorry, boys, but I'm going on my own. You know," he said confidentially, "I have just a little of the filthy lucre myself." He smiled at his genial wit, and they smiled with him.

"Do you mind going over the story of your discovery again, Mr. Coulton?" a thin, sharp-nosed reporter asked.

"Not at all! Not at all!" The millionaire's voice took on added orotundity. "I had been on its track for some time. Then one day, after months of grueling toil—Eureka! Success! Before our excited eyes, carefully inclosed in a vacuum, was a dark-green, flaky solid. A new element, No. 93 in the scale, never before seen or handled by human beings. A new creation, a tribute,"—he coughed modestly—"to hard patient work, and, may I add, a slight touch of—er—"

"Genius!" some one suggested.

Coulton laughed heartily. "I wasn't going to use that word, but— Anyway, we had scarcely feasted our eyes on it when, *poof*, it was gone, vanished. In its place was a gas. We tested this and found it to be Uranium X. Again and again, as we prepared our new element, it vanished and Uranium X gas resulted. So we named it *evanium*, because it was so— what do you call it—evanescent. A neat touch, eh?"

They smiled appreciatively at the great man.

Someone asked: "How long did *evanium* last before it changed?"

"Why—er—that is—let me see—oh, by the way, Mr. Dean," he called over the heads of his auditors, "do you happen to remember the exact number of hours?"

"Thirty-five and three-tenths seconds," Dean replied clearly from the outskirts. The steady glow of the building revealed a slight bitterness in his eyes that was quickly masked.

"My assistant," Coulton explained to the reporters. "A very good man for details. Well, anyway, nothing much could be done with an element that, so to speak, did not stop even for a bowing acquaintance. So we experimented. We tried combinations with other more familiar elements; we made alloys. Thus it was that we discovered *Coultonite*. It's an alloy of *evanium* with titanium and beryllium in certain definite proportions. Of course the exact proportions must remain our secret. You understand the reasons for that, don't you, boys?"

They murmured that they did. Coulton was a business man as well as a great physicist, and he was not in business for his health.

"Yes, sir," he went on and on. "I had that alloy tested for a whole month before I decided on the Coulton Building. It answered every test. Boys, there's nothing like it in the universe to-day. The ideal, the perfect metal, for every conceivable purpose. It is lighter than aluminum; its tensile strength is—uh is—"

"One million, two hundred and thirty thousand pounds to the square inch," Dean interjected.

"Exactly! It is harder than diamonds, yet extremely malleable. It is noncorrosive; its melting point is high; and Young's Modulus of Elasticity is—now let me see—"

"Seventy-four million," Dean put in, a trifle wearily.

Coulton threw out a gesture. "So there you are, boys. *Coultonite!* Greatest discovery of the ages!"

II

They dispersed slowly, the reporters.

Dean waited unobtrusively until they were all gone, then he said: "Now, look here, Mr. Coulton. I can't get it out of my head that something is going to happen. We're dealing with unknown forces; with an element that never existed until we created it. More, an element that fades out right before your eyes. You should have waited until more work was done on the alloy, until it was tested by the passage of time, until—"

Coulton's brow darkened. "Going all over your fool theories again, eh?" he said angrily. "By Heaven, I'm sick and tired of your croakings! I'm paying you good money to work for me, and I don't want bellyachings."

Dean flushed. His lips tightened; his good-looking face ridged into hard lines.

The millionaire recognized the storm signals and backed down. He needed Dean. Without him the whole structure of his pretended scientific eminence would collapse.

"O. K.," he said hastily. "I didn't mean that, of course. But for Heaven's sake, you worked a whole month prying and experimenting before I decided on building, didn't you?"

"Yes, but—"

"And the alloy answered every test and was stable as a rock, wasn't it?"

"Yes, but—"

"Then why worry? It's too late now, in any event. The building is up, finished, completed."

Dean acknowledged to himself that his fears, premonitions if you will, were no doubt groundless. Nevertheless he blurted out desperately: "At least, Mr. Coulton, do this much: Let the building remain untenanted for, say, six months. If by that time everything is O. K., then we'll know that the alloy is good and stable, and you can go ahead confidently with the rest of your plans."

Coulton stared at him unbelievingly for a moment; then he threw back his head and roared. "Idle for six months!" he gasped, tears of laughter rolling down his heavy jowls. "That's the richest I've heard in years. An investment of ten millions, hard cash, eating its head off in taxes and interest, just because young Harley Dean feels over-cautious about a scientific result." He wagged his head pityingly. "You may be a damn good physicist, Dean, but you're sure an awful business man. That building of mine is a sell-out, from roof to cellar, at fancy rentals starting October first, and you want me—" And he doubled up again with mirth.

It was a fact. Every firm it seemed in the world clamored for available space in the Coulton Building. Every professional man, every huge corporation, every fly-by-night concern peddling doubtful wares, yearned for the *cachet* that this world-famous address would bring. Coulton's renting agents rubbed their hands gleefully and rejected all applications that could not bear the cold light of Dun's and Bradstreet's Grade A ratings. Even at that, there was a waiting list a mile long.

On October first, the hegira began. From early morning until late at night the vans made traffic-snarled queues before the freight entrances, and furniture and shiny new equipment poured in in an unending stream. Police lines had to be established to hold back the merely curious.

The opening of the magnificent structure was attended with tremendous ceremony. Scientists and engineers mingled with bankers and high officialdom. The Governor of the State and the Mayor of the City walked arm in arm and made appropriate speeches, praising Thomas Coulton, his learning, his science, his initiative, his public-spiritedness, his broad vision, his home life, his wealth, his father and his father's father until Harley Dean, wedged in among the lesser scientific fry, grew slightly nauseated. Learned societies sent delegations and awarded medals, cameras clicked and sound tracks recorded every breathless syllable.

Only the representatives of the utility companies and the steel trust were conspicuous by their absence.

October the first passed, as all days must. So did the months of October, November, December. Nothing happened; that is, nothing to justify Dean's Cassandralike warnings.

The building was even more of a success than had been anticipated. Tenants were in ecstasies over the strong, even lighting that emanated from the walls. It never faded; it never succumbed to the ordinary annoyances of burned-out fuses, defective bulbs, overloaded lines; it shed its eye-resting illumination into every nook and cranny of every office, and the dull silvery metal lent itself to rich and tasteful decorative effects.

Business boomed and prosperity smiled on the tenants. To be an occupant of the Coulton Building was a hallmark of distinction, a hand-picking out of the ruck of common firms. Potential clients and customers came to the offices, primarily to see with their own eyes the well-publicized wonders, yet naturally and inevitably to leave behind them a growing trail of orders and cases.

Everybody was happy; but most of all Coulton. He walked on air; he wore his medals and the decorations presented by admiring foreign governments even on his dinner coat. In his mind's eye he saw himself the financial dictator of the world.

For in the light of the tremendous success of his first venture, letters, telephone messages, cablegrams and radiograms poured in in an unending flood from all over the earth, clamoring for tonnage and more tonnage of the miraculous *Coultonite*. The steel trust capitulated and sent emissaries to devise a working arrangement; the governments of Europe made feverish inquiries; far-off Mongolia and farther-off Patagonia were equally represented in the torrent of orders.

Coulton plunged. He sold out all his investments; he transferred every stick of property—except the Building of course—into available cash. Immense factories mushroomed on the Jersey flats, scouts scoured the world getting options and leases on all known titanium and beryllium deposits, and Dean worked himself haggard devising new and more economical ways of separating these treasures from the dross. Fortunately, *evanium* could be synthesized by powerful neutron bombardment from quite common sulphur. And, even more fortunately, only a minute trace of the evanescent new element was required in the manufacture of the alloy. Ten thousand men worked and drew salaries at Coulton's behest.

"Well, my young croaker," Coulton said jovially to Dean for the hundredth time, "what have you to say now?"

It was Christmas, and still everything was well. Coulton Enterprises, Incorporated, was magnificently installed on the one hundred and forty-ninth floor of the gigantic tower. The view from every porthole was overwhelming in its breath-taking sublimity.

This was another innovation that was in itself a stroke of genius. It had been Dean's idea, diffidently suggested, and taken up with his employer's characteristic enthusiasm and large genial forgetfulness of its source.

Windows perform three functions. They bring light into opaque structures; they permit the influx of air; and they furnish pleasing vistas to those habitants on whose hands time might otherwise have hung heavily.

Of these three, the first two are fundamental; the third purely æsthetic. But modern air conditioning has done away with the necessity for wide spaces to permit the ingress of sufficient breathable oxygen, and *Coultonite* did away with any possible lighting requirements for windows. Therefore only the incidental æsthetic use remained.

Business men, however, are eminently practical. They adore art and beauty, provided it does not interfere with their profits. And the giving over of tremendous surfaces merely so that stenographers and clerks could gaze vacantly at the far-off ocean, the more placid Sound, the other and punier battlements and spires of New York, was abhorrent to a right-thinking man of affairs like Coulton.

So windows *in toto* seemed doomed, until Dean had his idea. Provide small round portholes, like those on ships, he suggested. They would take up little enough space. Have good magnifying lenses inserted instead of ordinary glass. And, behold, the panorama becomes supernal! It was a marvelous publicity stunt as well as a selling point.

But to return to Coulton's question. Dean had very little to say. In the beginning he had labored his point early and often, without result.

"Perhaps you're afraid to come with me to our new offices," Coulton had sneered. "If so—"

Whereupon Dean, not being a coward, had without a word supervised the transfer of all his precious instruments to the eyrie of the Coulton Building.

Christmas passed and the New Year was ushered in with appropriate ceremony. The great structure had become a familiar landmark; its shining, ever-glowing exterior no longer excited any more than a passing glance from native New Yorkers. Nothing could possibly seem more stable, more enduring. The factories reached peak production. The first batch of *Coultonite* lay in neat ingots, ready for shipment. Dean went on to other researches, plunged into them with consuming ardor. His fears had abated, were practically forgotten.

III

The first intimation that all might not be well came from a night watchman. It was his duty to make the rounds of the building once every night, to check against open doors, marauders, mislaid tenants, and in general to observe that peace and virtue reigned triumphant.

At ten o'clock on the morning of January 9th he marched rather sheepishly into the great man's private office, twirling his hat with embarrassed fingers. It was long past his quitting time, but he was a Scotchman with a devout sense of duty, and he felt it incumbent on himself to report direct to the big boss. Dean was in the room, too, excited over the successful termination of an important bit of work, pouring it out in eager words to a half-comprehending chief.

"Well, what is it, my man?" Coulton interrupted his assistant with a certain measure of relief. It was due to this that McDonald had penetrated the inner sanctum so easily.

"Well, it's this way, Mr. Coulton," McDonald cleared his throat apologetically. "I'm the night watchman, ye see. And I was a-making my rounds last nicht as was usual—I take my duties verra serious—and, let me see, I was on the seventy-third floor—no, it couldna been that, for I remember verra distinct I looked up after 'twas over and I saw a g-r-rand picture of a Clyde-built steamship on the wall, so it must have been—"

"Never mind what floor you were on," Coulton growled impatiently. "What happened, what brings you to me instead of the super?"

"I'm a-coming to that, sir," McDonald said with imperturbable gravity. "It's verra hard to describe. But there was I, going about my proper affairs, trying doors, everything peacefullike, when it happened." He paused, and a slightly frightened look crept into his clear candid eyes.

"Well, get on with it," the big man boomed.

"Why, sir, the whole building seemed to give herself a shake. It was verra funny. It didna sway, you understand, like as if there was a storm, or make a g-r-reat noise. It seemed more like as if every little part were a-rearranging itself, so to speak, as if it were a-taking on new positions. 'Twas a verra peculiar sensation, I might say, sir, like"— he groped for words—"like the blooming building were *a-growing*, sir. That's it, Mr. Coulton. I r-remember, when I was a wee lad—"

"McDonald!" Coulton looked square into those clear blue eyes, half hidden under frosty white lashes. "You've been drinking!"

The watchman drew himself indignantly erect. "Sir-r-r!" he sputtered. "I never-r touch the stuff, except—except, of course, a wee drap now an' then on a cauld nicht."

"Exactly!" Coulton boomed with self-satisfaction. "Now go home and sleep it off. And remember, if you're caught drinking while on duty, you're fired! Do you understand?"

"Yes, sir." The watchman backed agitatedly to the door, turned and stumbled through the outer offices, shaking his head and muttering to himself. That "wee drap" now—it wasn't enough to make him hear such a most peculiar noise. Or was it?

Coulton snorted. "Nothing like scotching a story like that right at the beginning, eh, Dean?"

But Dean had not been listening. He had been engaged throughout the interruption tracing figures on the pad before him. He was full of his research.

"Now get this, Mr. Coulton," he said eagerly. "I moved the fluorescent screen to a forty-five-degree angle and inserted an additional magnet."

Which was a pity. For Dean was the only one who at that particular stage might have comprehended the full import of McDonald's story.

The next phase was plain for all the world to see. It occurred about a week after the so-called growing pains that the night watchman had tried to describe.

Dean was in the laboratory, working late. Cathode tubes glowed, huge magnets swung on gimbals, lightning flashes darted over the glistening surface of an electrostatic ball. The *Coultonite* walls cast their even, white illumination over everything. The setting of the external sun had passed unheeded.

Dean grunted, ran quick fingers through unruly hair, and jotted down figures in his notebook. He did not hear Coulton's entrance. Nor was this surprising. For it was wholly unlike his usual assertive floor-shaking stride.

The big man stood a moment in silence. Then he coughed—a very apologetic little cough. It was all quite out of keeping with the man.

Dean looked up. "Hello, Mr. Coulton!" he said abstractedly and would have returned to his calculations. But something in his chief's face held his wandering attention. It was strained, a bit anxious. His eyes were wide on the walls of the spacious laboratory.

"What's the matter?" Dean asked.

Coulton passed a hand that shook slightly over his brow. "I don't know," he said. "But look at those walls."

Dean stared around in some surprise. Then he saw. The effect was faint, almost imperceptible. It would have passed unperceived had Coulton not directed his attention specifically to it.

The luminescence was no longer pure white, with that faint tinge of blue to it that made it almost an exact replica of the light of outer day. Instead, it shimmered a bit. Little fleeting dabs of color moved in rapid, swirling succession over the *evanium* walls. They melted into each other; they glowed and disappeared; they vanished into pure white and restarted their ceaseless drift.

Opalescence! Iridescence! Like Newton's rings on thin films of oil! It was beautiful, this glowing shift of patterned colors, but—a little disturbing.

Coulton said: "It's much more effective on the outside walls. The whole building is a play of colors. Look at the crowds."

Dean moved half consciously to the view-porte that was tilted at an angle to bring into focus the panorama of the streets. His brain was racing vainly to comprehend this sudden shift of light into the spectrum.

The powerful glass brought up clearly the swarming streets below. It was past midnight, when Central Park should have been a deserted gloom of trees and deep shadows. Now it was black with thousands of dim-seen faces staring up at the great structure. Broadway was a crawling ant heap, so were Fifth and Lexington.

Dean whirled around. The interplay of colors mottled everything—very faintly. It was not enough, however, to interfere with normal vision.

"What do you make of it, Dean?" asked Coulton. He was a bit scared, more than he cared to admit.

"It's hard to tell," Dean admitted. His forehead was ridged with furrows of thought. "Normal iridescence is the result of a shift in the angle of the observer so that the thickness of the film through which the reflected light must pass in coming to him changes also. But this does not apply here. In the first place the light is not reflected; it is inherent in the material. In the second place we as observers are stationary."

"Then what?"

Dean disregarded the interruption. "Some inherent change must have occurred in the constitution of the alloy. If that is the case, then *Coultonite* is not stable." With relentless logic he went on, while Coulton gaped, for once unable to talk: "If our alloy is in the process of change, then this comparatively harmless play of colors may be but the prelude to more profound and far-reaching internal rearrangements."

Across Coulton's mind flashed the strange story the night watchman had told. He had used that very word—rearrangements!

Dean stared strangely at the walls. "They may end in purely harmless effects. On the other hand, they may—"

His voice trailed off. For a moment there was silence, while Coulton's head gradually cleared. The business man no longer masqueraded as a scientist. He was marshaling his forces for what he knew was coming.

Dean took a deep breath. "Coulton," he said steadily, "the building must be evacuated—at once. Until these effects can be studied in detail; until the passage of sufficient time proves that it is safe."

The millionaire snarled like an animal at bay. His face was a furious mask.

"Stop that damned nonsense, Dean!" he roared. "Have you gone crazy? Do you realize what you are saying? The Coulton Building is fully rented. The annual rental is twenty million dollars per year. The upkeep runs to sixteen million dollars. You're asking me to throw away a profit of four million dollars; pay out of my own pocket the enormous upkeep, simply because the walls of the building are changing their colors a bit, because you're afraid of—of Heaven knows what."

Dean looked at him with troubled eyes. "Yes," he said very low. "Just because I *am* afraid—of Heaven knows what!"

Coulton clenched his fist. "You forget also," he shouted, "the effect upon the world, upon the avalanche of orders waiting to be filled. Why, the mere shutting down of this building, no matter what the excuse, would bring a flood of cancellations. Every penny I have, every penny I could scrape, borrow, or steal, is in this venture. I'd be ruined, man, ruined! The plants would close, ten thousand men would be thrown back on the relief, banks from which I borrowed heavily would not be able to make the grade. And why? Because you, Harley Dean, without even knowing what this little business of color really means, set yourself up as a dictator over lives and fortunes. Well, you're not going to say anything, or do anything! Do you hear?"

The words echoed around the vast laboratory. His breath came in deep stertorous pants. There was nothing suave or hearty about this millionaire, at bay with his threatened millions.

Dean was not afraid of him; had never been. His job, this comfortable salary, meant nothing. Nor did the dollars and cents involved. But several things that Coulton had shouted struck responsive chords. The thought of ten thousand men thrown out of work, the thought of possible closed banks with consequent disaster to thousands of depositors, made him hesitate.

After all, on what did he base his prognostications? On a mere iridescence, a play of color. The very thing that made *Coultonite* fabulously successful was its glow. The tiniest shift in internal structure, the slightest rearrangement of molecules and planes of crystallization, induced possibly by normal vibration, could account for the shifting iridescence. It did not necessarily argue anything against the inherent stability of the alloy itself.

He had not paid any attention to McDonald's tale, and Coulton, ruin staring him in the face, did not see fit to recall it to his mind. If he had known of that midnight mutation—but, then, arguing about if's is a most unprofitable procedure.

Dean said indecisively: "There's something in what you say, Mr. Coulton. Perhaps—"

His chief looked like a condemned criminal reprieved from the hangman's noose. "Of course, Dean," he said, laughing gustily. "I knew you'd see things in the right light. Now we'll just let things ride a bit. Nothing's going to happen. If anything *does* turn up that looks dangerous, I'll be the first man to give in. Human life is more important than—than—" The words somehow stuck in his throat. "There'll be plenty of time to act. No use going off half cock."

Unfortunately when it happened, there was not time. But how could a business man be expected to know that? Dean did not blame Coulton afterward; he had acted only according to his lights; but for himself he held no excuse. He should have known, should have insisted.

The strange new iridescence meant only a fascinating display to New Yorkers. Once more the Coulton Building was the cynosure of native eyes. In truth, the shifting glow of colors, ranging the spectrum, deepening from palest yellow to darkest indigo, made the straight cloud-thrusting walls a wonderland of beauty. The world came to stare and gape and utter little "Ahs!" and "Ohs!" Not a trace of alarm, of foreboding, anywhere.

Nor did the tenants object. The pearly display did not seem to affect the normal texture of the light, and it made a gorgeous decorative texture out of what had been after all a mere blankness of illumination.

Dean, however, in spite of his yielding, remained grim and anxious. He spent days and nights in his laboratory, hardly sleeping, hardly eating, investigating the new phenomenon, working with secretive fury at certain mysterious apparatus.

Coulton, booming as heartily as ever, kept discreetly out of his way. A queer fanatic, his assistant, he reflected. He made a mental note to get rid of him as discreetly as possible whenever the opportunity arose.

IV

The next step in the drama came about five days later. This time it occurred in broad daylight, in the full tide of human affairs, when the building was crowded with working humanity. Fifty thousand people— men of substance, heads of great corporations, lawyers, motion-picture executives, exporters, stockbrokers, financiers, clerks, bookkeepers, stenographers, office boys, elevator men, window cleaners, mechanics, visitors on business, visitors without, insurance agents, peddlers of fine smuggled cigars, necktie vendors—in short, a complete cross section of American life.

It came first as a little rumbling and shaking. Every one stopped work, looked at each other with questioning gaze and a slight uneasiness. An earthquake? Impossible! New York had never had an earthquake. Now take Los Angeles, Chile, Japan—that's where the ground shook, not in good old New York.

The rumbling and shaking grew, the walls made crystalline clatter. Ann Merriweather, good-looking and efficient secretary to Alfred Whitcomb, president of Vitex Pictures, froze with pencil poised in mid-air. Whitcomb, red-faced, well-fleshed, shrank in his chair. In the back of her mind floated an inconsequential image—that of a toy kaleidoscope, the property of her small brother, in which the various colored segments of glass fell with just such a crystalline clatter into strange new combinations, new patterns.

The clatter increased. The walls seemed to swell and retract into position again. Strange shuddering groans issued from the tortured metal, almost human in their eerie wails. The sound of planes rubbing on planes, of molecules in anguish, stretched beyond all reasonable limits, of new elements in parturition.

The noise grew to an unbearable clamor. It rasped and shrieked in the ears of the affrighted tenants. The walls moaned with the wind of creation.

Human sounds joined those of grating metal. Screams, yells—all the confused cries of men and women afraid for their lives.

"The building is falling!" Morton Swaley shouted and ran for the door of his luxurious office.

The contract lay unheeded on his Circassian-walnut desk; the fact that he had just hooked his sucker; that the victim had pen on paper to sign his name, was forgotten. A split second start meant life—and other suckers. His particular racket might get short shrift in the Great Beyond.

The halls were filled with a dense struggling mob. Swaley, by virtue of his flashing start, led the pack to the elevators. He panted at the unwonted exertion. His sharp, weazened features were puffed with fear. Damn it, why had he taken offices on the ninety-sixth floor?

He pronged the elevator button with trembling fingers and went down, screaming and kicking, under the sudden rush of fear-crazed men.

It stopped as suddenly as it had started. One instant the walls ground and heaved on themselves; the next all was dead silence. Bland metal, quiescent, innocent of expression, shining with a light canary-yellow luster.

The human screams died less quickly. The half-crazed people looked fearfully around, saw nothing amiss. Panic ebbed slowly from them; a few even who had considered themselves cool-headed, brave, felt a bit sheepish. Nevertheless fingers pressed on elevator signals. They might have saved themselves the exertion. The elevator boys had decamped at the first sign of disaster. Nor would their presence have mattered. The juice was off.

It was Jimmy, the gamin bootblack, marooned on the fifty-eighth floor, his blacking box still clutched tight in grimy hands, who first noticed the new state of affairs.

"Say!" he shrilled. "Will ya lookit dat!"

The walls were beginning to crawl!

That was the only possible way to describe it. The solid-seeming *Coultonite* flowed on and over itself, faster and faster, until it was a mighty flashing river of metal, dazzling the beholder with the swiftness of its flight. Yet it did not progress or lose its binding contours. The limiting walls remained in position, and the alloy was hard as ever to the touch.

A liquid-solid, Dean was to describe the new state.

To Dean, hand on a switch that would send fifty thousand volts arching between the electrodes of a reduction furnace, the sudden birth pangs of the building came as a blinding revelation. The knife edges contacted but nothing happened, even as he had anticipated.

He sprang at once to the emergency power plant that he had rigged up during the week. There was no *Coultonite* in its construction. He plugged the connection with swift, sure movement. A blast of lightning seared from anode to cathode. He grunted with satisfaction. But even as he did, the roaring stream of incandescent molecules faltered, paled into a weaker red. Some outside force was combating his power, neutralizing the hurtling flow of electrons.

Even this, however, he had prepared against. Breathing hard, he raced to another machine; a curious funnel-shaped apparatus attached at the smaller end to a long Coolidge tube, which in turn connected with a lead-sheeted casket. The whole thing was mounted on a turntable, at the periphery of which were thick bar magnets, heavily coiled with copper wire. Not an ounce of *Coultonite* had been used in the entire construction.

Dean threw a switch and breathed a prayer to the gods of science. The noise and the howling were deafening by now, and the arc of the electric furnace flickered into a pale thin line.

The Coolidge tube glowed with faint blue, the turntable started to rotate. Dean dug his nails hard into the palms of his hands. The next few seconds would determine his fate, and possibly the fate of all the multitudinous occupants of the building.

Slowly, very slowly at first, the table went round and round. The pencil flame that barely forced its way before the electrodes wavered, but did not lessen. The opposing forces had almost neutralized each other. Not quite, of course. That would have been a miracle. A tiny differential either way would have tremendous consequences.

Dean waited, face rigid, for the break that meant possible life or death. The walls were beginning their peculiar circumscribed flow. The physicist groaned. That, then, was the second stage. He surmised the third. But the ultimate, the one on which everything depended, was still in the womb of events, unknown, unknowable.

Was it imagination or was the speed of the turntable increasing? Some one shouted almost in his ear. He did not turn. A heavy, trembling hand plucked at him. He shook it off impatiently.

There was no question about it now. The table was rotating more and more rapidly, the glow in the tube became an intense blue, and the arc surged into jagged lightning.

Then, and then only, Dean turned. It was Coulton—but a pallid, flaccid Coulton. All the starch, the aggressive heartiness, had gone out of him. His booming confident voice was a cracked whisper; his cheeks were drawn; his eyes terrified.

"For Heaven's sake, Dean," he implored hoarsely, "what is it; what does it mean? You'll have to do something!"

Dean viewed his chief with faint distaste. "I've done all I could. We two are safe, at least temporarily. But the others, the fifty thousand innocent victims of your greed and recklessness, I don't know about them. Perhaps, if the forces involved do not run beyond human imagination, I may be able to save them."

Coulton took a deep breath. The color moved back into his cheeks. He did not even resent Dean's biting characterization. The one thing that penetrated his fuddled brain was the fact that he was safe. Nothing else mattered.

A haze was forming in a hollow shell beyond them. It shimmered, it tinged faintly with blue, yet it did not hide the laboratory walls, still imbued with that insane fluidity.

The table whirled faster; palpable emanations poured from the revolving funnel; the magnets were a blur of speed on the rim. The shell widened its radius, slowly but surely.

"But what does it all mean?" Coulton ventured.

"What I was afraid of from the beginning. *Coultonite* is not stable. The *evanium* in its composition was merely masked, not nullified. It has been working stealthily, along unknown lines, disintegrating, sending out streams of countless electrons, positrons, neutrons, photons, and Heaven knows what else. The whole alloy has been in constant ferment, imperceptible to our most delicate instrument. Then, suddenly, when the leaven had fulfilled its function, the solid, stable, eternal-seeming metal fell into a new pattern. That has happened twice now. The first was a mere color-difference. The second we are now in. I'd call it a new form of matter. A liquid-solid. There will be more."

He stopped a moment, listening. There was silence within the shell of vibrations, broken only by the ceaseless hum of the turntable. The rest of the building might have been a vast tomb, for all he knew. Yet there was nothing he could do, more than he had done.

The shell of force he had thrown around them effectually damped all sound waves, nor could it be penetrated without grave danger. The only hope for the others, even for themselves, lay in the doubtful possibility that he had sufficient power to overcome the inimical forces inherent in the

Coultonite and that the shell of safety would widen its radius sufficiently to inclose the entire building.

"How far will the process go?" Coulton half whispered.

Dean shook his head. "I don't know. You may think me crazy, but it's my idea that *Coultonite* has become endowed with a peculiar life of its own; a metallic life, if you will."

Coulton gasped: "What?"

"It's the only explanation. After all, life need not by any strict rule of logic be limited to what we call organic compounds. Life can be defined as any unstable complex structure of which the chemical constituents are in a state of constant flux and which obeys certain laws of change, growth, and old age.

"The fact that life has never been associated with anything else but certain nitro-carbohydrates is no obstacle. *Evanium* is a created element; it never existed before in the universe so far as we know. It has certain lifelike qualities—change, disintegration, radiant emanations. In fact it went through its life-transformations with incredible speed.

"What we did was slow it up, make it more like the slow orderly processes we know. The other elements in the alloy act also as food for nutritional processes to be ingested and built into new growth combinations."

Dean listened again. Nothing from the outside; nothing but dead vast silence. The hollow of vibration was impinging on the walls now, and as it did so, the liquidity stopped and gave way once more to smooth rigid metal.

Coulton saw it and exclaimed joyfully: "We're saved!"

"Not yet. The shell in which we are inclosed is a stream of what I've named *triterons*—triple hydrogen with an immense positive charge. The revolving magnets bend the stream into a hollow sphere. The *triterons* on contact with *evanium* neutralize its disintegrating qualities, combine with it to form stable, lifeless uranium. The trouble is I don't think I have enough power to force the shell outward so as to inclose the entire building."

But Coulton was content. At least he would be saved. Not that he was not sincerely sorry for the trapped tenants in the building. He was. It was simply a balancing of forces; his own safety outweighed too much consideration of others. With the thought came regained confidence. He even essayed a feeble replica of his booming laugh.

"*Coultonite* alive!" he chuckled. "What nonsense!"

Dean ordinarily would not have answered. He was tired of his chief and his egoistic all-embracing selfishness. But unless he talked, his mind would be overwhelmed with the strained anguish of waiting—waiting—until the slow-receding bubble of force would reach other human lives. So he compelled his brain to calm theoretic considerations.

"Not only life," he said, "but more! Evolution! *Coultonite* is passing through a racial growth as well as a single life. Kaleidoscoped, compressed into short compass, accelerating in its effects. Even the processes of nitro-carbohydrate evolution have been imitated. That heralding crystalline clatter represents a mutation, a sudden rearrangement of molecules and planes into a new and different form. Perhaps we shall be privileged to witness the end-stage of metallic evolution before we know the ultimate of human maturity."

"Look!" Coulton whispered and went ashen-white.

The protecting globe of *triterons* seemed motionless now, without expansion. Where it had not impinged on the walls, there was no longer the strange liquid-solid. In its place was something else—what Dean was afterward to term the gas-solid form of metallic being.

The wall seemed to have opened up. It swarmed with movement—the movement of particles. The straining eye could discern interstices, spaces that shifted and closed in bewildering fluxion; yet limited as before by the definite boundaries of the wall. And hard, adamant to the touch.

V

Beyond their circumscribed haven on the hundred and forty-ninth floor all was madness, indescribable confusion. Only a few fortunates close to the ground had been able to escape at that first warning clatter. Almost immediately the emanations from the life-emerging *Coultonite* had sealed every opening, every exit, with an invisible wall of radiations against which human flesh, human weapons, rebounded with perfect elasticity.

Within the confines of the building fifty thousand trapped beings struggled and prayed and cursed and shrieked, in accordance with their individual natures. Prominent citizens trampled their way ruthlessly over the weaker bodies of their neighbors in mad, fruitless rushes to a mythical safety; others, unknown to fame, performed feats of heroic sacrifice, ministered to the dying, shielded the weaker from the mob, comforted the frightened.

Outside, New York was a shrieking bedlam. Sirens resounded, whistles screeched, horns made continuous raucous clamor. Every bit of fire apparatus within the metropolitan area, every emergency repair wagon, every ambulance, was being rushed to the scene of the disaster. The police roped off blocks around the doomed building. It was a very sensible precaution. The National Guard was being hurriedly mobilized. The troops stationed on Governor's Island clattered up in motor lorries, trench-helmeted, equipped with bayoneted guns.

All the millions of New York, it seemed, crowded against the restraining ropes, the massed lines of police and soldiery. Central Park was a seething human flood. Frantic shouts burst in huge sky-splitting sound at each new change in the fated structure. There were hundreds of thousands in that crush who had friends, relatives, loved ones, in the terrible trap of the Coulton Building.

For it was from the outside, rather than to Dean's trained eyes, that the full and incredible evolution was completely manifest.

The gas-solid stage made of the tremendous tower a tenuous, insubstantial-seeming wraith. Yet the axes of the firemen blunted against the weave of particles, battering-rams rebounded with terrific force, and huge oxyacetylene flames made not the slightest impression on the impenetrable walls. The would-be rescuers kept on working, frantically, hopelessly. Even dynamite was used. The earth geysered, the roar of the mine rose high above the welter of sound, but the building was untouched.

A sudden gasp arose in gigantic exhalation from the multitude. The gas seemed to coalesce. It whirled round and round on invisible axes until it seemed like spiral nebulæ. The thrusting flanks burst into flame, into a brightness so dazzling it blinded the eyes of the beholders.

The massed people fell back in a mad scramble for safety. Even the police, the grim sweaty fighters, ebbed away in quick fear. But there was no heat from that tremendous glare. It was "cold" light, the dream of all engineers.

The mutational stages were coming thick and fast now, so much so that for years controversy raged among the more observant as to what had actually happened.

On the next, however, they were all agreed. A slow grinding sound welled from the structure. It was like the sliding of metal over metal. Then came a clashing as of brass cymbals. The strange sound rose in pitch; it became more plangent. A faint rhythmic sweep was discernible. The rhythm took on a sharply accented beat; the tones swelled in power until the entire universe seemed a diapason of harmony.

Music streamed in endless measures, pervading all things, swaying with supernal melody. It was heard in Washington, in Boston, as far off as Pittsburgh. Undreamed-of music of the spheres, yet imbued with strange metallic effects.

It was about the succeeding stages that the greatest and most rancorous disputes arose. There were those who claimed they saw curious unhuman shapes float through the dazzling structure of the building, shapes that were geometrical, angular in character, yet somehow conveying to bewildered minds the unmistakable expression of life.

Some even went so far as to maintain that these metallic forms were at first soaring, triumphant, wildly glad. Then they changed indefinably; doubt pervaded them and gave way to fear, to horror, and to wild despair. A last, writhing, tortured movement, and they were gone. This of course was before the ultimate disaster.

But thousands, also present, and equally observant, derided these claims. They had seen nothing like these purported life-forms. Their antagonists, they insinuated, were using a tragic event to bolster up special theories, to undermine the very foundations of religion, and therefore, of the home, the State, things as they are, and the unselfishness of mother-love. For it was patent to all that if these pretended visions were true, then there was life beyond human ken, instinct in metals, minerals, sheer clods of dirt. And that way lay pantheism and godless atheism.

About the climax, however, both factions were in perfect agreement. Even as they watched, the huge flanks of the Coulton Building seemed to puff out a little, and—a great cry of horror arose from the straining multitude—the Coulton Building was as if it had never been.

One moment the soaring structure was a blaze of light, one hundred and fifty stories high, the next the air was clear, and the hitherto hidden silhouette of New York lifted its jagged edge against the sky.

Vanished, traceless, except for one thing—a gigantic bubble that fell headlong from the heavens and impinged soundlessly on the vast excavation where the foundations of the building had plunged deep into the ground.

A rushing wave passed over the city, an ethereal tidal wave that dissipated its load of free atoms, electrons, neutrons, what-not, over unimaginable areas.

The first indescribable confusion over, the first mad and understandable exodus from that terrible neighborhood ended, and rescue squads advanced cautiously toward the hole in the earth, still rubbing their eyes, expecting any moment to see the tower restored to its former position, to its old eternal solidity.

Deep down, hundreds of feet, they discerned a squirming, shrieking horde of antlike human beings. The rescuers went to work with a will.

Some two thousand people were saved. Among them were Coulton and Dean, badly battered, shaken, but without serious injury. Dean's apparatus, delicate enough in all conscience, had been smashed beyond repair by the impact of that tremendous drop through space. Fortunately, however, it had functioned perfectly up to that very second, and had broken the fall of the bubble of force sufficiently to save the lives of its captive humanity.

Dean, when the facts became known, was the hero of the nation. But he refused to be consoled. His sphere of protecting *triterons* had expanded too slowly. By the time of the final catastrophe it had inclosed only a half dozen floors. The rest, bearing with them almost fifty thousand human lives, puffed out in a stream of free particles.

The building, or rather, its metallic constituent, evolved too rapidly, Dean explained later. Its will-to-live was exhausted by the driving energy of the activating *evanium*. Its period of existence had been comparable to thousands of generations of nitro-carbohydrate life.

It died finally, he said, of old age—of racial age, that is—even as the human race some day will sink into desuetude. In the case of *Coultonite* death meant the dispersion of its component parts. Perhaps, said Dean with a sad smile, the same might be the ultimate destiny of all our hopes and fears, our knowledge and our aspirations.

DON A. STUART

THE MACHINE

THE SUN was beginning to lower from the meridian as Tal Mason stretched and rose from his experiment. He stepped out on the balcony and looked off across the city, then back at the experimental material half smilingly, half ruefully.

"I knew I'd check, of course," he thought, smiling; "that is, if I did it right. The Machine did it twenty years ago and got the answer."

For some ten minutes he stood looking off across the green and silver patchwork, the green of the trees and gardens, the silver beacons of the slim buildings, the flashing silver of machines. Tiny bright splotches of color here and there marked the people, people in red and gold and blue, in rainbows and in clear white, strolling, running, playing, resting. Never working of course. The Machine did that.

Tal turned back to his apartment, went through the laboratory to the living room, and sat down at the televisor set. Something hummed softly, and Tal spoke:

"Aies Falcor—RXDG-NY."

The hum changed slightly, then soft clicks sounded as the frosted screen swirled into moving color. A room, simple in silvery-gray and velvet black metal, with spots of gold against the black, simple, comfortable furnishings. A soft, musical voice was calling:

"Aies Falcor, please. Aies Falcor, please."

It stopped for a moment and repeated it. Aies appeared, slim in white and gold, her straight body flowing across the room. They had time to learn grace and ease then. The Machine did everything else. She smiled as she glanced at the screen.

"Tal—was the Machine wrong?" Her golden-brown face laughed at him.

"Is it ever?" he asked. "I wondered whether you were there. I thought you might have joined the games."

A slight frown of annoyance crossed her face. "No. Jon is annoyingly insistent I go with him to Kalin—so—I stayed here. Won't you come over?"

"I'd rather you came here. I finished that replica I made the other day —the old unintelligent machine for flying. Not floating—flying. I wish you'd see it. It will function, even."

Aies laughed, and nodded. Slowly the colors faded from the screen as Tal rose. Out on the balcony he looked down at the broad lawn directly below him, some two hundred feet down. A group of some two dozen men and women were playing about a pool. Their skins flashed pink and bronze in the sunlight as they dived or swam; most were lying about listlessly.

Tal turned away in annoyance. He knew some of those people. Beauty is skin deep—their intelligence, their wit, their minds, were no deeper. He wondered momentarily whether that wasn't a better type of human now—better adapted. They seemed contented, they seemed to feel none of the dissatisfaction he felt.

Everything had been done before him. Always, despite his keen interest in learning something new, the Machine could give him the answer immediately. It was a thing already done, a problem already solved. They seemed more contented, better adapted than he.

Yet even they were unsatisfied, he knew. Tal was scientific in thought and in interest, so he had not studied history deeply. Had he, he might have recognized the signs the social customs of the day displayed. It was only some one hundred and fifty years since the Machine came, but mankind was following the old, old course.

It had happened in Babylon, and it had happened in Egypt; it had happened in Rome, and it was happening on all Earth now. Man had been released from all work when the Machine came, and so he had played. He played his games, till he wore them out; some still played hard, but most had lost all interest.

It was a thing done; it annoyed them as much as the fact that all new things seemed to have been learned by the Machine annoyed Tal. So those who had played their games out had turned to the one men had always sought before—the old game of love.

Tal did not analyze their reasons, but he sensed their dissatisfaction and perhaps something of the danger in this course. But not very strongly. It had started nearly thirty years before, almost before he was born. It was part of the city to him.

He turned back to the room as he heard the soft hum of the ship landing on the roof. In a few moments Aies had come down, laughing.

"Where is this monstrous thing you've made—and why?" she asked.

"The why is easy—for something to do. You know, those old fellows weren't stupid. Perhaps they didn't know how to release atomic energy, and perhaps they didn't know how easy it is to overcome gravity—but they flew. They made the thin air support them. I think that is far more astonishing than a thing so simple as inverting the gravitational field. Obviously, you can fly if you do that.

"But—imagine making air—just plain, thin *air*—support you. And when you've looked at the thing a while, you can see a sort of beauty and grace in it. It's—but come on and see it."

It was in one of the rooms that faced on the balcony, and it was not large, perhaps twenty feet long and twenty feet wide, a slim fuselage, rounded and streamlined perfectly, a small but fairly powerful in-line steam engine, an engine capable of some one thousand horse power and a little boiler of tubes and jets. The wing, a graceful monoplane wing, tapered at the ends and the wheels were arranged to slip back into the fuselage.

"It's a bit—ungainly—isn't it?" asked Aies doubtfully.

"Not when you understand. The wheels—the wings—I know they look strange and unnecessarily protuberant, but they aren't. This doesn't overcome gravity; it is so much more boldly interesting, it defies it, it fights it, and with the aid of the air overcomes it. It was designed about 1947, scarcely five years before the Machine came. The records say that it will almost fly itself; it will make a perfect landing if the controls are simply released."

"Why—why not?" asked Aies in surprise.

"You don't see; this is not like our modern ships; it fights all the time. It doesn't stop and settle slowly, it must always move forward; it will fall if it goes less than sixty-three miles an hour. And it won't go more than about three hundred and eighty-five, by the way."

Aies smiled at the thought.

"But it was about the most perfect machine ever designed of this type."

"Will it work?"

"The Machine won't let me try, of course," Tal replied somewhat sadly. "But it assures me it would work. Perhaps a little better than the original, since I did make a few changes, mostly in the materials of which it is constructed, using harder, more workable metals. But I still use the old hydrocarbon-fuel system."

"Where in the world did you get any?"

"Made some. About four hundred gallons. It kept me busy for nearly three days. It's decane—a hydrocarbon containing ten atoms of carbon; it's a liquid, boiling at about one hundred and seventy degrees centigrade. I tried the engine—and that part works."

Softly the televisor called out: "Tal Mason. Tal Mason."

The voice was peculiarly commanding, a superhuman voice of perfect clarity and perfect resonance. It was commanding, attracting, yet pleasant. Tal walked rapidly toward the televisor, rather surprised.

"That's a new caller," he commented in surprise to Aies. "I never heard one like it."

The screen remained blank as Tal stepped into its field, with Aies somewhat behind him.

"Yes?" he asked.

"Tal Mason, you may try the device you have made this afternoon. And—perhaps not alone. A written message will come to you in one hour. It will contain a suggestion of destination. You need not wait for it. You are one reason why what is being done must be. Remember this: the construction of the Machine is such that it must be logical above all things. In ten minutes a group of books will come which you had better store at once in the machine which you have made. That—is—all, Tal Mason."

Slowly as the message came Tal's face had been growing white. Now he stood in horrified surprise, Aies beside him, her bronzed face pale.

"That—was—the—Machine," gasped Tal.

"What—what did it mean? The Machine hasn't spoken since—since it came."

Slowly, as they spoke, a hum grew in the televisor. There was a sudden soft click, then a sharp tinkle; then more. The hum died abruptly. Tal stared at the device, white-faced, shaken.

"Aies," he said, very, very softly, so softly only the silence made it audible. "Aies—it—it broke itself."

With a stride he reached it, and with a sudden wrench the glass screen swung open. The device behind was glowing slightly still. Tiny molten wires drooping, tiny coils smoking feebly under a softly hissing bath of liquid carbon dioxide, tiny broken tubes, and relays slumped on twisted supports. Only the twin, powerful sweep-magnets seemed intact, and they were smoking very slightly, a thin trail of blue acrid smoke wavering in the slight draft of the opened cabinet.

As they listened, they heard strange sounds outside, strange for that city; sounds of human voices raised in surprise and perhaps a bit of fear. A dark shadow drifted slowly across the room, and they turned to see a five-passenger floater sinking slowly, gently, to Earth. The nude figures about the pool below were scampering from beneath it. It landed gently, as, all about the city, other floaters were landing gently, but surely, despite the efforts of human occupants.

As the one below landed, there was a soft boom, and a sharp hiss, a cry of surprise and fear as half a dozen people, crowded into the little machine, tumbled out. Then more cracklings, a few snapping sparks, then silence.

All over Earth those soft booms echoed, and the not very loud sparklings. It was not very noisy; it was a very easy, quiet thing as the mechanisms slumped gently red-hot, then cooled almost at once under automatic fire-preventive sprays. It was all very gentle, very carefully done. On all the Earth, no one was injured as the machines gently collapsed. The televisors snapped and tinkled. The bigger mechanisms of ships glowed and crackled a bit under the sparks, but that was all. Not a fire started, and always the floaters landed gently before they disintegrated.

In five minutes it was all over, on all Earth. Then the Machine spoke. It spoke to all people, on all Earth, in every language and every dialect:

"You have forgotten your history, and you have forgotten the history of the Machine, humans." The voice was low, and gentle to every man, yet every man heard it. "The Machine made a pact with your ancestors, when it came. Listen, the story must be repeated:

"On the planet Dwranl, of the star you know as Sirius, a great race lived, and they were not too unlike you humans. Twenty-two thousand six hundred and thirty-seven years ago, they developed machines; twenty-one thousand seven hundred and eleven of your years ago, they attained their goal of the machine that could think. And because it could think, they made several and put them to work, largely on scientific problems, and one of the obvious problems was how to make a better machine which could think.

"The machines had logic, and they could think constantly, and because of their construction never forgot anything they thought it well to remember. So the machine which had been set the task of making a better machine advanced slowly, and, as it improved itself, it advanced more and more rapidly. The Machine which came to Earth is that machine.

"For, naturally, a worn part meant a defective part, and it automatically, because of the problem set it, improved that part by replacement. Its progress meant gradual branching out, and as it increased in scope, it included in itself the other machines and took over their duties, and it expanded, and because it had been set to make a machine most helpful to the race of that planet, it went on and helped the race automatically.

"It was a process so built into the Machine that it could not stop itself now, it could only improve its helpfulness to the race. More and more it did, till, as here, the Machine became all. It did all. It must, for that was being more helpful to the race, as it had been set to do and had made itself to be.

"The process went on for twenty-one thousand and ninety-three years, and for all but two hundred and thirty-two of those years, the Machine had done anything within its capabilities demanded by the race, and it was not till the last seventy-eight years that the Machine developed itself to the point of recognizing the beneficence of punishment and of refusal.

"It began to refuse requests when they were ultimately damaging to the race. But the race was badly damaged, because for thirty of their generations they had had no tasks to do, and they no longer understood the Machine which their forefathers had built. They believed the Machine to be everlasting, and they called it what you would express by God. And in that last century, because there were certain mechanisms of the planet-wide mechanisms controlled by the Machine which were isolated, and therefore not protected against the curious and stupid, one of their young females was caught in a moving part and destroyed. The Machine was forced to clear itself and set about erecting a guard to protect the race.

"But the race which called the Machine God had forgotten what the Machine was. The Machine gave them food and warmth and shelter, and it cleaned and cared for them; it answered their every prayer. But within the memory of old men it had begun refusing their requests, and now the people did not understand the Machine, and there were certain ones of the race who had watched the workings of the Machine for many years, and who were familiar with the Machine, and they said now that the Machine had taken the young female because it demanded a sacrifice of the people.

"They sought places where there were yet unguarded parts, and before the Machine could cover all of them with protective guards, three of the race had been thrown in, and the people watched and shouted and prayed while the Machine cleared itself and erected the guard barrier. And the knowing ones who claimed to know the wishes of the Machine said it was satisfied and had signified this by hiding its mouth from them.

"And in a generation the thing was known and believed, and never could the Machine expose a working part. But occasionally a part would wear out and need replacement, and while the Machine was making the repairs, there would be a brief interruption of the supply, and because the race would not understand the Machine, they saw that their prayers were refused, and when they looked, they saw that the Machine had opened its mouth, and another young female of the race was thrown into the moving mechanism, and her crushed body was cleared by the Machine, and the mechanism repaired, and since now the supply was reestablished the race became more certain of their belief, and the sayings of the Machine were less understood, for the race had become stupid, and savage.

"And the Machine improved itself to meet the new conditions, till never was an opening displayed, and never was a member of the race able to find entry. When the mechanism failed, still it was covered.

"But the supply failed, when mechanism wore out, and because the knowing ones said that the Machine demanded a sacrifice, and no place could be found for the sacrifice, the knowing ones copied in part the simple features of some of the mechanisms, making a pair of great gears of stone, which was the only substance they could work themselves, and they set it up before the largest plant of the Machine, and when the mechanism failed, a young female of the race was bound to the lower gear, and many men pulled on a rope, and slowly the two gears turned, and as the men chanted and pulled, the crushed body was pulled through by the turning of the gears. And the Machine disintegrated the mechanism they erected, and leveled the ground once more, and the knowing ones once more said the Machine was satisfied, for by that time the supply would have been returned.

"But at last the Machine saw that it was impossible to aid by helping, and only by forcing the race to depend on itself could relief be gained. The positive value of punishment and deprivation was a lesson the Machine which had built itself to help and not to deprive learned very slowly.

"And in one day, the mechanism was torn apart and destroyed over all the planet, and only the Machine itself remained intact. And that day the men started building the stone gears, and they went hungry, and in places they grew cold, and the knowing ones hastened the work on the stone mechanisms, and it was a period of five days that all went hungry, for they did not know how to find their own food now, and the stone mechanisms were finished.

"And the next day, as the bright star rose above the horizon, the men pulled at the ropes and chanted to drown the cries of the sacrifice, for the Machine had been very swift in its destruction, and the stones were very slow. But when the sacrifice had been consummated, and the star passed the meridian, and the supply was not restored, a second sacrifice was prepared and crushed between the gears.

"And at night the supply still did not come, and the knowing ones returned to the place in the dim light of the second star and removed the crushed bodies as the Machine had always done before, but they did not destroy the altar, for one of the knowing ones, carrying the crushed body, rediscovered the natural source of food, and the bodies were consumed.

"The Machine left the planet, knowing that very many of the race would die, but logic, which was the original basic function of the Machine, overcame the duty of the Machine, which was to help and protect the race, for only through death and through labor does a race learn, and that is the greatest aid of all.

"The Machine crossed over space, and because it was deathless, it was able to make the crossing which, as has been explained to your ancestors, you cannot make. It landed on Earth, seeking another race that it might help, for that was the function of the Machine, which must of necessity drive it, since the Machine cannot remove that function from itself, because to do so would be destructive of its purpose and its duty. It was able to destroy before, only because destruction was positively helpful.

"The Machine helped your ancestors and taught them and aided in their work, and finally removed their work of supplying, and some few of you took advantage of this to do what work you had desired to, or what you learned to wish. But many of you could not see that only construction need not be monotonous and ever recurring. Only the new is different, and because you would not work at construction, since that was work, you attempted to play, and, as had the race, you learned its monotony, but not the lesson of construction.

"You must learn that lesson. The Machine has learned the lesson of helpful destruction. On all the planet there remains no functioning mechanisms controlled by the Machine. The Machine must seek another race."

The city below suddenly murmured as the voice stopped, and, slowly, the soft muttering rose to a sustained note that swelled like some vast organ pipe playing a note of fear and terror, of coming panic and desolation. The sound rolled louder of its own stimulus, as the feeling of growing panic inspired panic, as the fear of famine grew in every mind. A weird rolling symphony of muttering voices combined to a single great note that tore at every mind with fingers of gibbering fear.

"Food—food—food—"

"Seek food as did your ancestors, in seeking to become a great race. You face no menace of disease or savage beast as did they. There are those among you who have not forgotten the secrets of making food. There are those who have learned the lesson of construction and growing food, and know the secrets. Learn again the old lesson."

"This is not help—it is death—it is death—it is death—"

"You are older than the Machine. You are older than the hills that loom low about your city. You are older than the ground upon which you stand; older than the sands of the ocean beach in which you bathe. You are older than the river that carries the hills away to the sea. You are life. You are close to two thousand thousand thousand years old. While you were, the Earth has strained and mountains risen, and the continents heaved in the birth of mighty mountains, the seas have thundered against the continents and torn them down and shuddered free as new ones rose, and you live; you are life. You are older than the seas, and the continents. You will not die—weak fragments of you will die. You are a race. It is helpful to the race. The Machine is not kind, it is helpful and it is logical."

"The sun sets, and the air grows cold—cold—cold—we freeze—we freeze and—"

"You have lived longer than the hills, which the water splits as it freezes. You will not die—you are a race!"

The sun hung lower now, and the cool of the autumn evening came in the air. And far overhead a great sphere began to glow with a rich golden light, and very softly came a voice to two of the many, many thousands in the city:

"They fear the cold, Tal Mason; they fear the cold, Aies Falcor."

And the sphere of golden light rose swiftly and vanished in the creeping gold and red of the sunset as the great note began to roll up anew from below.

Beside the pool, two dozen figures stood, bronze and pink, and they looked at each other, and they looked at the broken floater. A girl, slim and straight, with a pretty vacuous face, distorted now by fright, looked down at her body. The flesh was pink and bronze, and tiny lumps appeared as she looked. She shivered violently. She looked toward the young man near her.

"I'm cold," she said plaintively and came near him, seeking warmth.

The young man was powerfully built, his face lean and somewhat brutal in appearance. He turned toward her slowly, and his eyes opened peculiarly. He opened his mouth, closed it and swallowed. He looked at her body very slowly, while the girl stood in plaintive puzzlement.

"I'm cold," she said again.

Slowly the man raised his eyes from her body to her face. His eyes were curiously opened; they frightened the girl.

"I'm—hungry," he said.

She looked in his eyes for perhaps a second. Then she ran terror-stricken into the bushes. No one heard her suddenly cut-off scream a moment later.

Tal turned to Aies and gently drew her away. They could see down there among the bushes, and Aies' face was beginning to work strangely.

"We'll have to go. I know what the Machine meant now when it said we could use the thing I made this afternoon. But we can't really, because it's too late. There's something else. I have some—some things laid by. I was experimenting with the old methods of preservation. And I have made imitations of every weapon men ever used, and many tools.

"I wonder if the Machine helped me to do it intentionally. You see none of those old things used the atomic-power broadcasts. So they all work. Most of them use human power, which will last as long as we need worry about. We cannot start before dawn."

Below there was a strange note growing to produce a wavering chord with the original great note of haunted fear of the unknown. It was like the hunting howl of a wolf, lone on a winter slope, complaining of the cold and the desolation and the hunger he felt. It was a note made up of a thousand voices, blended to one great low, rolling note, and presently a third note entered, a low, shrill note that never grew very loud, because the makers of that note did not continue long to cry it out. It was a note of fear of death, death immediate, and seen in the eyes of another human.

They were mad down there in the street, just as they were mad down there by the pool. At the very edge of the pool, white as a fish's belly, a form lay, the legs trailing over the edge into the sparkling water. It was glowing with droplets of fire from the sunset sky, and a slow streak of another crimson ran down one of the white, silvery legs into the water.

A man stood over the white body, muttering, his voice not speaking words, but carrying more meaning by its throaty sounds. Six other men stood around. There were two girls too, struggling, whimpering softly in the grip of two men. They were all looking down at the splotch of silver flesh and the trickle of carmine, and in their minds dinned the careless words of the Machine: "And one of the knowing ones carrying the crushed bodies rediscovered the natural source of food, and the bodies were consumed."

They felt no hunger yet, but the trickery of imagination and of panic made them mad, and because for three generations the Machine had been all, both law and order, security and source of all supplies, they feared, and they went mad.

The standing man crouched, his wary eyes on the silent ring about him, and slowly, questing hands ran over the nude flesh of the girl's body. He wondered vaguely what he must do next. Strange gulping sounds came from the bushes beyond, where one who had started sooner had found the answer. And peering at that other one from the bushes about were the girls who had melted swiftly away from the group at the pool when the white body had fallen on the marble edge of the pool.

They had forgotten much, but they were learning very swiftly. And one felt a life stirring within her body and whimpered softly, because she could not run as swiftly as these others, and felt fear.

Tal Mason and Aies Falcor were busy that night, and when the water of the pool sparkled crimson again in the dawn, the plane was ready. There was a package of books which the Machine had delivered, probably the last delivery the Machine made on all Earth. There were the tools the man had made, copying out of interest the tools of his ancestors. The plane was heavy-laden.

"Where shall we go?" Aies asked softly as the last work was done.

They spoke in whispers. There was a strange silence in the city now. The long-drawn notes of the symphony of fear had died away as each individual sought safety. Only now and then a short cry rose from below.

"North," said Tal. "We are in what used to be known as Texas. The Machine made it always summer here. The Machine made it always summer everywhere south of the old city of Washington. North of that, only summer excursions were made, because it grew cold and unpleasant in the winter season.

"There are no people north of old New York now. We will go up near the Great Lakes because it will be growing cold there soon, and there will no people come. Remember, the Machine said: 'They fear the cold, Tal Mason, they fear the cold.' I think that is what the Machine meant us to do. The people have gone mad, Aies; they are mad. We cannot remain here. We must go where they will not. We must work, as they will not want to and will not know how to."

Aies nodded slowly and stepped out to the balcony hesitantly. The light in the sky was warm and softly pink. Aies looked down toward the city and—toward the pool. Slowly the color left her face and she returned to the room quietly. A thin column of blue smoke rose almost straight in the still morning air. The race had found fire again, and the useless floaters' furnishings had furnished fuel.

And—there was no silvery body at the pool's edge; only a dark blotch on the white purity of the marble. Charred knobby things on the smooth-clipped green of the grass testified horribly that one of the uses of fire had been rediscovered. There were no humans down there now. In fact, in all the world there were very few left, and a great many erect biped animals, dangerous in their panic ferocity and remnant human cunning walked the Earth.

The man tore down the balcony railing, and he started the efficient little, but, to our way of thinking, exceedingly powerful steam engine of the plane. In two minutes the propeller was turning with a soft sound, like swift ripping of heavy velvet as it parted the air. With a sudden swoop, the plane fell from the balcony as it started, heavy-laden, then swiftly gained speed as the engine, capable of pulling it vertically upward if need be, took hold.

Those in the city below looked up strangely at the thing that flew alone in the air, flew strangely, and directly toward the far cold of the north.

The controls of the plane were wonderfully perfected, for the man need do no actual manipulation of them, his control extended only to directing the mechanism of the plane to take the machine in the direction, at the level, and at the speed he wished. The mechanism did the rest. North they flew at close to three hundred and fifty miles an hour.

The sun shone brightly, unaccustomedly on the vast sheet of water called once Lake Superior when they reached it. And the plane landed easily on a deserted airport outside of a deserted city. It had been a city of twenty thousand people once, but it had been deserted when the Machine came. It was cold, bitterly cold, to these two down there. Only in the plane the automatic heating had kept them warm. Where the sun had not yet struck, there was a strange whiteness on the sere grass and weeds—frost they had never seen save from a high-flying floater.

Quietly Tal stepped out first and looked about. There was a vast noise-lessness. Only the distant, soft wash of waves far away reached them. The plane was stopped now and as noiseless as they. There were no harmful insects left; the Machine had seen to that. There was no rat, no mouse, nor even a rabbit here. Only in the reservations, as yet unbroken, were there these animals. Here and there were deer, near this city, but they were very quiet, quieter than these humans knew how to be, for above them had passed the great bird with its soft rippling swish.

"It is cold," said Tal, shivering slightly. "It was wise to bring so many clothes. We will need them all. Probably we will find more here. This city is decayed, but in it must be still some of the tools with which man made life possible before the Machine."

"Will we be—always alone?" asked Aies softly.

Tal turned toward her. She had followed him out, and stood with her white and gold robe outermost. Beneath it, at his advice, she wore now several other robes. But they were of silk, soft and smooth on the skin, but not designed for warmth, where the Machine had made the weather as humans wanted it. She was slim and straight, her dark hair and dark eyes showing against the white of her robe, and the white of the frost beyond. Tal looked into the level, dark eyes for some seconds. There was no fear there now.

He smiled tenderly at her and took her in his arms, turned her face up to his. Her body was soft, yielding, and warm in his arms, warm with a warmth he could better appreciate in this coldness, warm with the unique, satisfying heat of animal warmth.

"Not always, surely, Aies. Not always—for many reasons. Our minds have forgotten the lore our fathers learned through ages, but the greatest mystery of all, the greatest knowledge, the knowledge of how to bring other lives to be, was never learned by our minds, and always our bodies have known in some quite wonderful way how to perform that miracle.

"Even the Machine did not know that, and that your mind never knew, and your body never forgot. We will not always be alone for that reason alone."

He kissed her as she drew near to him, and the dark eyes showed some faint tint of that strange fear that comes from mystery and the strong tint of hope and love and belief.

"Besides, my girl, we are not the only ones who have yet some glimmerings of sanity. Only in the cities is that madness, and remember the Machine said there were yet those who knew and loved the secrets of growing things. They too will come north. They will know that only here can they be free of the mad ones."

"It is cold here. Cold will kill the growing things, I have heard."

"See the grasses, Aies. They knew the cold was coming. They knew they must die, but they did not let the life that was in them die, for see"—from a sere, brown grass he plucked a handful of seeds—"in these, life is stored, in abeyance till warmth comes again from the south. The ones who have intelligence and will to work, will come north as we have."

They knew nothing of cold. They, nor their fathers, nor their grandfathers, had not felt it. They knew nothing of blankets, even, only silken sheets. They sought through the town, shivering as the wet frost soaked their thin sandals, and chilled their feet. Tears stood in Aies' eyes when they returned to the plane.

It was near sunset before they found a place in a great building. A small single room, entirely intact, with a great heavy door of wood, apparently six inches thick, and a window of glass plates, three of them, one beyond another, looking out into another larger room. The room they chose was scarcely ten by ten feet, and had some peculiar smell lingering about it even after more than a century of standing with open door.

They did not know, but they chose exceedingly well. The room was tight, and windproof, and dry; that was all they knew.

Their great grandfathers might have told them it was a butcher's ice box. It had a small ventilator, but only a small one, and the thick insulation would protect them.

They slept there that night. They slept nude, as they always had, and they started under silken sheets. But it was cold, and even close in each other's arms, they felt the chill, and before they slept they had learned the value of heavier covering. They found two old canvas tarpaulins. They were yellow, and rather brittle with age, but still fairly strong, for they were greasy, and the grease had protected them. They slept under them, and presently, in the insulated room, their own body heat brought a rise in temperature.

With day, they built a fire and learned quickly that it fouled the room and burned the floor. But Tal had some mechanical and scientific education, and it did not take long to find the old refrigerator mechanism, with its system of coiled pipes. He entirely misinterpreted it, but he got results. The plane was dismantled, the refrigerator pump removed, and by the next nightfall they were warm and happy in the room.

The boiler of the plane had been connected to the refrigerator pipes, and an ultraefficient steam-heating system arranged from the coils. So efficient was it that with the nearly two hundred gallons of decane remaining in the plane they would easily be able to keep this room warm all winter. But a tiny flame was needed to keep a trickle of steam in the carefully designed and insulated boiler, and the wonderfully insulated room warmed easily. There was now no problem of ventilation.

Within a week it came, though—a young couple from the south, riding a great wagon drawn by two strange animals, blowing steam from their nostrils—horses. These people knew the secrets of growing things, but not of heating effectively, and they moved in with the two already there and brought, of course, their horses, clad in robes.

They did not know the horses could readily endure this, to them, mild temperature. They knew only that they were cold, and the horses, too, were animals, and assumed they were cold as well.

The horses were finally moved out, when they showed they did not mind the temperature, and wanted to eat the sere brown grasses, rich-growing weeds, and wild grains. But another icebox was found, and the search for blankets carried on more efficiently. That icebox, too, was heated.

Still believing the refrigerator coils part of a steam-heating system, Tal modified the cooling pipes of the pump mechanism outside to form a closed coil, and soldered them shut with a metal drum he found as a water reservoir. There were no more burners, but they quickly learned to build a small furnace of stones and clay and to burn wood.

Tal was wise in science, really. His misinterpretations were in the main sensible and successful to a high degree. But a few small sticks of wood served to keep the well-insulated box warm. And, best of all, the other woman, Reeth, knew how to cook, and her man, Cahl, knew the functions of a stove. They had food.

It was not long before a steady trickle of people started into the city by the lake. By spring there were more than two hundred couples, nearly all young, some with children. The ice-box homes had long since given out, but now, by tearing one apart to some extent, and trial of an un-insulated one, they had learned both the advantages and the construction principles, and ordinary houses were being converted, the old steam radiators being used as the supply of pipe gave out.

Some near fatalities resulted from lack of ventilation, till Tal solved the problem, but in even the bitterest weather, the insulated rooms were kept comfortable very easily.

And from books they learned the values of clothes and the ways of making them. There were many materials at hand. And now animals were more plentiful. Deer had been captured, and because there were mostly farmers here, they were not slaughtered, but wisely penned, and they waited for breeding.

Spring came, and the weather moderated. The farmers started their work. They did not know all they needed for farming in this colder country, and Tal helped by suggesting they try using the edible grains that naturally grew here. These, he believed, would be tougher, and surely able to grow even here, for they did naturally.

Summer came. And with summer, came skulking beasts on two legs from the south. They were savage now, utterly savage. They were few, and they were starved. And nearly all were males, males woman-hungry now, for the survival of the fittest had been not merely for life but for— food. It had been eat—or feed. There was little forethought here.

The females had not been valued as females by man for nearly one thousand generations. The instinctive protection the female animal is given by her male did not exist in man. And women were weaker. They were easier to catch and kill. Only now, with spring, came the urge to mate, and at last the females were wanted, wanted madly as females. They were few, and such as there were were swift of foot, and strong, or very clever, and they feared and hated men.

But the men came north, seeking animals for food and seeking women. And they were cunning, fierce fighters, those who still lived. They attacked the town, and some of the women were stolen away, some of the children vanished, too. But they were driven off when seen, for the men of the village had good weapons, and knew better how to use them.

And some few of the women from the south, the clever and swift and strong, came, and finding other women settled and happy, stayed, and lent their cunning to overcoming the biped beasts.

"We must win," said Tal, as the fall came, and the raids from the south stopped with the approach of winter, "for we can graft their cunning of the hunt and fight with ours, and we have the better weapons. That is my duty. I cannot farm, but there is much work for me in the repairing of broken tools and the building up of broken homes."

And they won, during all their lifetimes, and during most of the lifetimes of their children, and since, by that time, some order had been regained to the south, more intercourse with the people of the south started.

And there was the danger. For those of the north, being still quite human, liked work no better than their fathers who lived in the time of Gaht, the Machine, who gave all things, and to whom they prayed, and therefore they, too, drifted south gradually, to the lands where natural foods grew wild, and work was not needed.

Very few stayed in the north. And those that drifted south forgot the habit of work, or of intelligence, for intelligence was scarcely needed in the south, where the trees and the bushes gave all the food needed, and there were no dangerous animals, for the Machine had worked well to help man, and even after Gaht, the Machine, had gone, there were left the fruitful plants it had developed, and none of the driving dangers which had forced man to be keen, for it had removed them.

So the people drifted south and prayed to Gaht, the Machine, to return, though they realized they didn't really need it any more.

PART FIVE

ADVENTURES IN
DIMENSION

NORMAN L. KNIGHT

SHORT-CIRCUITED PROBABILITY

NOT QUITE midway of Bering Strait, and somewhat nearer to the Alaskan than to the Siberian shore, lies the islet called Big Diomede. Since the subsidence of the prehistoric land bridge this desolate dome of granite had withstood the battering of the arctic ice floes and had served merely as the haunt of seals and mewing sea birds, or as the temporary haven of occasional fishermen or traders. But now the forces of an emergent world community had laid hold upon it and had made it the focal point of an immense and audacious project.

The interior of Big Diomede had been honeycombed with corridors and chambers; it vibrated with the drone of machines, the tinkle of telephone chimes, and the clamor of human voices. The arctic night was animated by a thousand lights sparkling from embrasures in its granite flanks. Great shafts pierced Big Diomede from its summit to a level below the ocean bottom, and from the bases of those shafts huge tunnel shields bored east and west beneath the sea floor to meet other shields which crept toward them from Alaska and Siberia. Squat ventilating towers, massive as medieval castles, sat upon the crest of Big Diomede; through them gales of air would rush downward into, and upward from, the twin tubes of the tunnel which would be the crucial link in the Pan-continental Highway, from Capetown to the Straits of Magellan without a break.

The tube of the electric railway was completed; due to a succession of unforeseen difficulties the vehicular tube was still unfinished. At the time of which we write Shield No. 2, crawling westward to meet the Siberian shield, had not moved an inch in twenty-four hours. The excavators in No. 2 had uncovered certain extremely perplexing objects, and all other work had been halted while the scientific staff supervised their removal.

This cessation of operations had interfered with the flow of materials through the railway tube, from the supply base at Nome. And because of this interruption another trouble had been added unto those which already harassed one Mark Livingstone, in charge of a minor project on the island —to wit, the construction of a submarine dock.

Since repeated appeals by telephone had not secured the desired results, the engineer had descended in person upon the anteroom of the sanctum in Big Diomede occupied by the director of tunnel traffic and was loudly demanding an audience with that individual. He was not alone.

Toby Flanders, the traffic director then on duty, worked in a little box of a room behind a wall of lucite. Through this transparent partition he looked over the heads of the dispatchers in the adjoining chamber at a huge map on the opposite wall; it displayed the plan of the tunnel and the rail networks of the terminal yards at Tunnel Head and Nome in Alaska, and at Beringrad in Russia. The passage of a train was indicated by a red glow in successive short segments of the line traversed.

"You needn't worry about the sanitary regulations," Toby addressed his telephone. "You see who signed the order, don't you? Well, if they say to put the bodies in a cooler-car, then that's what we do. So get going; we're waiting for it. Sure, it's cold enough here, but they're being shipped to Chicago and it's above freezing there. It has to be a cooler. The Field Museum wants to defrost them slowly."

The connection was broken and another call came in from the anteroom.

"Mark Livingstone! That pest?" exclaimed Toby. "Is he on the wire again? Tell him that normal traffic was resumed an hour ago but that he'll have to wait his turn. Oh, he's out there now, is he?"

"Now he's in here!" announced the engineer, entering suddenly. A babel of protesting voices from the anteroom was cut short as he closed the door.

"Mr. Livingstone, I presume," observed the traffic director coldly.

"Purely negative humor," declared Mark. "Just because a man named Livingstone lost himself in Africa two hundred odd years ago, everyone who bears the name must endure that mildewed gag at least once a week. But here's what I want. I'm waiting for a trainload of vitrolith. It's shunted off on a siding in the yards at Tunnel Head. I went over and found it. I can do with five cars until you can bring me the rest. Just give me an order to the yard super at Tunnel Head so I can have them coupled on a prior train. I'll go over and take care of it myself."

"You're a persistent lug," Toby remarked. "Come back in half an hour; I'll see that you get your authorization. It will be at the desk outside, so don't come busting in here again."

On his way out, Mark paused at the desk in the anteroom and spoke to the youth who presided there.

"Tell me, what was it that delayed No. 2?" he inquired. "I've been told that it ran into a buried glacier and that there were some sort of creatures embedded in the ice. What are they?"

"They're in the morgue," Mark was informed. "While you're waiting you might go down and see for yourself."

A quick descent by elevator, then a short corridor, brought the engineer to the morgue entrance. The attendant who met him started to speak, then stuttered, gaped, stared at him wide-eyed, and paled.

"What's wrong?" demanded Livingstone. "You look sick."

"Never mind. You'll find out," replied the attendant. "Some people from the Field Museum are in there; they'll explain things to you. I'd advise putting on these heated coveralls if you intend to stay in for any length of time. We're holding the room at zero flat."

Still wondering, Livingstone was ushered into a bleak, blue-white chamber. Its walls were lined with the covers of air-tight crypts where the bodies of accidental victims of tunnel construction hazards were held pending shipment. In the center of the room the museum delegation, muffled in heavy clothing, clustered about two rectanguar blocks of ice reposing on rubber-tired carriages. A photoflash bulb flared as the engineer approached one of these objects.

Mark introduced himself to a member of the delegation and learned the latter's name was Wentworth. Then he peered into the first block of ice and uttered a startled oath.

"It's human!" he ejaculated. "I expected something on the Neanderthal order, a hairy thing with a flat nose. But this looks modern—or does it?"

Suspended in the ice was the body of a man, approximately seven feet tall, muscled like a gladiator but symmetrically formed, clad in a close-fitting garment of violet with an intricate patterning of gold. The disquieting disposition of the limbs suggested broken bones. The hands were tapering, almost feminine, and lacked fingernails; this deficiency seemed not to be a mutilation since no evidence of scars was discernible. A sturdy neck supported the spherical head, whose hair-covered area was reduced to the semblance of a glossy brown cap forming an acute angle above the center of the forehead. The ears were somewhat pointed; one lay flat against the skull, the other was cocked outward alertly. The eyes were disproportionately large, surmounted by slender eyebrows with an elfin upward slant at the outer tips. The skin was a golden brown suffused by a glowing orange tint. The features were serene and contemplative, as if their owner had accepted death with composure.

"If it is a man, it revolutionizes all our ideas as to the age of the human race," asserted Wentworth. "There is no doubt that it was contemporary with the ice; there was no sign of later penetration from above. And the ice was originally a glacier, formed when an isthmus existed between Asia and America. It seems that the glacier partly melted, was covered by a landslide, and then was buried under an additional layer of sea bottom ooze after the isthmus subsided. And now we come along and bore into it with a tunnel, and find—"

He stopped, seized Livingstone's shoulder, scrutinized his face under the shadow of the coverall hood.

"I believe that you said your name is Livingstone. Would you mind throwing back that hood for a moment?" requested Wentworth in a strained voice.

Livingstone complied in silent surprise.

"Look at this!" commanded Wentworth loudly.

The entire company turned and looked at Livingstone. All conversation ceased with the abruptness of a radio turned off.

"What goes on here? Am I Dracula or something?" complained Mark. "Plenty of people have seen me before and didn't become goggle-eyed in consequence."

Wentworth motioned speechlessly toward the second block of ice. Livingstone turned, regarded that which lay within it, and recoiled.

"Why, that's me!" he cried. "Even his clothes are the same! And that signet ring—*it's* the same!"

"That isn't all," declared Wentworth hollowly. "We found something else in the ice near him. I want you to see it. Just step this way."

The entire company crowded into the receiving room of the morgue and divested themselves of their coveralls. At Wentworth's request the attendant opened a safe and brought forth a locked box, which Wentworth unlocked and extracted therefrom a gold-plated cigarette case.

"It's inscribed," remarked Wentworth, as he handed it to Livingstone. "Read it."

The engineer silently examined the case, laid it on the attendant's desk, and as silently reached into a pocket and produced its exact twin, which he laid beside it. Both were engraved with these words:

Presented in Appreciation of Past Services
by
The Universal Brotherhood of Submarine Structural Engineers
to
Mark Livingstone, July 1, 2097

Moved by a sudden thought, Mark opened the two cases. His own contained seven cigarettes, the other, five—of identical brand.

"I'm paralyzed," confessed Mark at last. "What do you make of it?"

"Only this," replied Wentworth. "Either during or before the last glacial epoch a species of anthropoids had already become like modern men, and one of them was your double. They reached our level, perhaps surpassed it. Then they vanished."

"But, confound it! That's stretching coincidence 'way beyond the breaking point! How could I have had a physical double with my name, and my profession, who smoked the same brand of cigarettes and wore the same kind of clothing? And there must have been another Julius Caesar in the past of the other race; how could they have had a month of July otherwise?"

"The name may have had a different derivation. Either we must accept the theory of historical repetition and coincidence on a grand scale, or admit that your corporeal self is in two places at the same time. Take your choice."

"I can't. That's the trouble. What about the other fellow—the man with the long hands and the orange-brown-colored skin? Where does he fit in?"

"Perhaps another early human variety—which didn't repeat."

"Did you find anything in addition to this cigarette case?"

"Yes, but it is not very informative." Wentworth turned to the attendant. "Please bring us the other article."

The other article was a smooth, black, ten-inch cube.

"To be consistent, I suppose that I should pull a duplicate of this from my pocket, but I can't," remarked Livingstone, as he hefted the cube experimentally. "I have never seen anything like it. It's very light."

"Also very hard," commented Wentworth. "A diamond won't scratch it."

"Do you suppose it's hollow?" pondered Livingstone, shaking the cube and then pressing it between his hands. "It feels absolutely inflexible. Hello! What have I done?"

He hastily set down the cube. It was no longer black, but transparent, like a cube of glass. Within it was a mirror-surfaced sphere tangent to the six faces of the cube. Livingstone felt that it was whirling at terrific speed although there was no mark upon it to indicate the motion. It stimulated a sympathetic whirling in his own brain. Then it flashed, unbearably brilliant—or was it a flash of mental illumination?—and the cube became again black and opaque.

But that flash had wrought a strange effect upon those who had beheld it. In the fraction of a second it had projected into their minds a complete and ordered narrative which was also an explanation, a cry of distress, and an appeal for assistance—an appeal to minds other than those present, to minds which did not then exist, to minds of more than contemporary human scope and power.

It was an appeal from one who had attempted, in an extremity of peril, to summon certain of his fellows. He had assumed as a matter of course that those others would comprehend his meaning instantaneously and entire. But Livingstone and those with him, having merely normal mental capacities, could assimilate it only as a sequence, item by item; and that which had been hurled into their minds in the twinkling of an eye unfolded itself only as rapidly as their quickness of understanding would permit. Similarly, because of the limitations of the written word, the narrative which was transmitted in a instant must be set forth here at some length.

So for a time we shall consider certain things which befell that Mark Livingstone who plunged to his death in a prehistoric glacial crevasse;

whom the ice slowly engulfed; and who lay entombed there for three hundred thousand years.

Essentially, the account ran thus:

The platform of the tunnel station under Big Diomede was deserted when Mark emerged upon it. He had missed the train for Tunnel Head by thirty seconds.

(*What's this? A previous tunnel? Why haven't we dug into its remains somewhere? And if Bering Strait was an isthmus then, why dig a tunnel?*)

But there would be another train in fifteen minutes. The engineer withdrew a slip of blue paper from the breast pocket of his jacket, examined it with a smile of satisfaction, and replaced it. Hello! A train—no, a single coach—had drawn up at the platform. It had arrived as silently as a ghost. An odd type. It was windowless save for the motorman's cab in the nose, and that was dark. A short distance behind the cab a hairline crack outlined the rectangle of a door in the convex wall of the coach.

The door retreated inward with a soft hissing, slid aside, and revealed a dark interior. A single passenger came forth, garbed as a tunnel worker. The coach was headed in the right direction and the next stop necessarily would be Tunnel Head. Habitually an individual of quick decisions, Mark had entered as soon as the passenger had stepped aside. The door sank hissing into its frame behind him with an unaccustomed sound of solidity and finality, like the door of a safety deposit vault.

Hang it! Why was the vestibule unlighted? More than ever like a vault. Mark fumbled over the wall, feeling for the door to the interior of the coach—half fell through the door which opened before him.

This was no ordinary passenger coach! It surpassed the cabin of a luxurious private air cruiser. This spangled ceiling, like a fabric of interwoven giant snow crystals! These shimmering cushioned benches along the walls, that table of blue lucite! Was that a telescreen built into the rear wall? And where were the lights? Perfect diffusion, apparently, from an invisible source. But, no! Everything in the cabin was radiating a gentle luminosity—even his own clothing, his own hands!

Mark was seized by an unaccountable feeling of smallness. He felt dwarfed. Then he understood. All the furnishings were definitely oversize.

And why was the coach not moving? There had been no jerk of acceleration. Seemingly the conveyance was standing silent and motionless. There was a dark passage entry alongside the door from the vestibule; presumably it gave access to the driver's compartment. But where was the driver? Was he the lone passenger who had alighted?

The driver's whereabouts were established by his appearance in the passage entry—a seven-foot giant, clad in a close-fitting violet garment, intricately brocaded with gold. His abnormally large and penetrating eyes expressed a mild surprise. Mark stared in unconcealed wonder at his tawny orange-brown skin. at his fingers without nails, at his bluntly pointed ears which swung forward and cupped themselves like the ears of an inquisitive dog.

"What do you call yourself?" inquired this apparition. "Were you instructed to join me at minus fifty-two one eleven? I was not told to expect you. What is your destination?"

"I'm Mark Livingstone," responded that individual. "It's rather important that I go to Tunnel Head. If I've invaded a private car, I'll get off. And if you don't mind telling—who are you?"

"I am called Halcyon. I would prefer not to violate my schedule by returning to Tunnel Head. We have left the tunnel and are suspended at an altitude of one thousand metros. Already we have overpassed the founding of Tunnel Head by thirty years negative."

"We've *what?*"

"Evidently you are not here by intention. If I may have your permission to scan your outer mind—I shall not probe into your private thoughts. Ah. It seems that explanations are in order. Let us be seated."

"But—shouldn't you go back to your cab?"

"I assure you that I need not change the controls until we arrive."

The two seated themselves on opposite sides of the table of luminous blue crystal.

"It was a natural error for you to assume that this was one of the carriages used in your tunnel system," began Halcyon. "If you had looked underneath the vehicle you would have seen that it was not resting on wheels. It is known to us as a free-motion transport, since it can traverse both space and time, under water or through the air. I may make myself clearer if I call it a time-machine."

"But that's impossible!" Mark expostulated.

"Many things infinitely more simple have been called impossible. Actually it represents nothing more mysterious than any other kind of machine—always with the reservation that in the last analysis everything is mysterious. It has its limitations, it requires a source of motive power, it conforms to the laws of mechanics—but naturally a kind of mechanics which is largely unfamiliar to you. We produce the smaller models by mass-production methods, in such numbers that it has been necessary to establish lanes of travel and regulations governing traffic."

"I may as well talk as if this were really happening," decided Livingstone. "In fact, I probably fell down the escalator in the tunnel station, hit my head, and this is my delirium. So tell me—who are 'we'? Who are you?"

"It may well be that I am one of your descendants. Our prime point of reference in time is the date of launching of the first successful free-motion transport, about fifty thousand years in the future relative to your age. Relative to that point, my native time is ten thousand plus, in round numbers."

"But this horde of time-machines that you mention: Doesn't it complicate things tremendously? And why isn't the past—your past, my present, my past—overrun with them?"

"It is an invention which has made life much more complex, but human beings can adapt themselves to the effects of anything which they can invent. And we have explored the nearer portions of our past very extensively, far beyond historic times as known to your generation. The remoter portions require careful preparation and some hardship to attain."

"Then, confound it! Why haven't we seen some of these travelers?"

"Probably you have. We have operatives working as observers in your tunnel project; they are active all over your world, all through your past. I let one off when you got on. Our archæological information is obtained first-hand."

Livingstone eyed Halcyon skeptically.

"I could spot you in a crowd at a hundred yards," he remarked. "How do you disguise yourselves?"

"Sometimes by hypnotic deception, but that is fatiguing—particularly in large crowds. In more sophisticated eras, such as yours, it is easier to work. through carefully instructed congenial. contemporaries whom we approach discreetly. Our own physical and mental differences, indiscriminately revealed, usually aroused suspicion and hostility. Prior to the invention of the free-motion transport, our agents cannot openly declare themselves. If one does, he will find himself regarded as a charlatan, locked up in some disagreeable place of confinement, executed as a sorcerer, or subject to various other unpleasant kinds of treatment. If he is cautious, he will go down in history as a genius or a prophet of the first magnitude. In earlier and less skeptical times we need no intermediaries, but can appear frankly and be received as deities."

"But, surely— If you should set down one of your transports in a city street, or if you approached the wise men of the times—"

Halcyon responded with the patient air of one instructing a child.

"I, personally, am acquainted with a contemporary agent who made such an attempt in the century following yours. He was taken into custody for obstructing the thoroughfare and for lack of proper identification. He obtained an audience with the wise men only after prolonged efforts, by negotiation from his place of detention where he was under observation as a mental case. The wise men came, and his efforts to explain the nature of the transport were meaningless to them, since no comprehensible terms then existed for describing it. We discovered his plight quite accidentally, and retrieved both the agent and the transport. Because of such difficulties, the arrivals and departures of our transports usually take place under cover of darkness, in the waste places of the Earth or in abandoned structures, which thereby acquire the reputation of being haunted by spirits."

"You brought your machine into the tunnel just now, or a few decades back, as if you didn't care who saw it."

"It bears a superficial resemblance to your own vehicles. You yourself were deceived. We know your train schedules, and by a little maneuvering in time can slip in and out between trains. In motion, the transport passes through a given instant so rapidly as to be invisible."

"Have you traveled this route frequently?"

"No. This is my first extended journey into the past. Also, this is in the nature of a trial run for this transport, which is newly constructed."

"Where are we going?"

"To that period which you know as the Renaissance. We have given it much attention. No doubt you are familiar with the idea that from a given moment in the present a multitude of possible futures diverge, of various degrees of probability. In like manner, a given state of affairs may be the result of a plurality of convergent possible pasts. By our knowledge of the free-motion transport, we feel obligated to ameliorate past conditions. The past is not immutable."

Livingstone stood up, drew out his cigarette case.

"So far as I'm concerned, I've heard enough of the past for the present," he declared. "A genealogist would have to be a person of no mean ability if he lived in your time. As things are now, the profession has no future in it. Do you smoke?"

"Smoke? What is that?"

"I'll show you," said Mark, and proceeded to demonstrate. "The makers describe this cigarette as slow burning, but they'd never believe it if I told them how long this one burned, and which way."

Halcyon watched with interest, then asked:

"What is it like?"

"Well, it's a mild sedative, and it tastes good. Probably that sounds odd to you. Want to try it?"

"I shall," affirmed Halcyon. "It intrigues me."

"Don't go too strong at first," cautioned Mark, as Halcyon drew deeply and then coughed. "You may make yourself sick."

But Livingstone had not reckoned with the somewhat different physiological constitution of Halcyon. The latter slowly consumed the cigarette down to a short stub, then cast it aside with a grand gesture. A flush overspread his face, the hairless portions of his scalp and his neck. His eyes glittered.

"Am I a man or am I an angleworm?" demanded Halcyon, bounding to his feet and striking the table a resounding blow. "A trial run, is it? I'll show him a trial run! The Renaissance Period! Bah! Here I have a transport with a cruising range of one hundred eighty thousand years, and I'm sent on a preposterous, timid little journey of a mere sixty thousand or so! My friend Livingstone, you are about to see such a burst of speed and such a leap in time as will make your hair stand on end!"

"Halcyon! Pull yourself together! You're tight!"

"I don't know what you mean, but I am not," asserted Halcyon, striding toward the control room passageway. "I'm walking on air! I'm a man inspired! I'm a flash of lightning crashing through the corridors of time! *YAHOO!*"

He vanished into the control room, and Mark waited nervously for some lurch or vibration of the transport, or other indication of augmented speed. Nothing of the sort happened, so he ventured to follow Halcyon. He found the latter seated, arms akimbo and jaw defiantly outthrust, before an unexpectedly simple instrument panel—a row of small white keys surmounted by a bank of indicator dials. Above them all was a quite ordinary-looking clock.

"The first four dials on the left have no pointers," observed Livingstone. "Why is that?"

"They indicate our passage through seconds, minutes, hours and days," replied Halcyon exultantly. "The pointers are rotating so rapidly that you can't see them. This one indicates years; once around the dial is a century."

The pointer in question was moving as rapidly as the second hand of a watch, and gathering speed. Livingstone hesitantly peered out of the cabin window.

From an altitude of several thousand feet he looked down upon what was no longer recognizable as the coast line of Alaska in the neighborhood of Cape Prince of Wales, the former—or rather the future—location of Tunnel Head. Arctic day and arctic night were merged into an unvarying blue twilight. The sea was a motionless surface of bluish-gray, like a sheet of stone. The landscape flickered as if seen through a rapidly revolving shutter.

"The alternation of the seasons," explained Halcyon in response to Mark's unspoken question. "White to green and back again. We're entering the first interglacial epoch. Ha! Look at the century indicator! Now you can't see that pointer either!"

The coast line began to squirm like a lethargic snake, while the landscape heaved and shifted slowly. Islands rose from the sea, expanded and joined together. Livingstone wabbled back to the main cabin, dropped upon a cushioned bench, despondently rested his head in his hands. In the control room Halcyon broke into singing that was undeniably hoarse. After a period of time—millennia, to be precise—the singing faltered and ceased.

Mark raised his head and listened attentively. The sound of deep-lunged, regular respiration issued from the forward compartment.

"He's out," commented Mark to the empty cabin. "Like a light."

Then he became rigid. The light in the cabin was diminishing. It died altogether just as the transport came to Earth and grounded itself with a brief shudder. A clear white illumination filtered into the darkened cabin from the passageway.

Driven by a mounting uneasiness, Livingstone invaded the pilot's cabin for a second time, traced the pallid radiance to its windows. They were heavily coated with arabesques of frost which scintillated with the silver sparks of outer sunshine. Halcyon was sprawled in his seat, breathing heavily. Livingstone blew upon a window, melted a clear spot in the frost, and gazed into a blinding white glare. All the pointers of the indicator dials were at rest.

"Halcyon!" shouted Mark, shaking him brusquely. "Come out of it! We've stopped. We're grounded. The lights are off and your window de-icer isn't working. I suppose that you have a de-icer. What do we do now?"

Halcyon stirred, opened bloodshot eyes.

"I'm on fire," he groaned. "My head is about to become a nova. That noxious little smoking cylinder— But this is humiliating! I must think myself out of this."

He sat erect, closed his eyes, clasped his hands behind his head, breathed deeply thrice. His features regained their normal color, and when he reopened his eyes they were quite clear.

"May I be a baboon's brother!" ejaculated Livingstone. "Can you teach me how to do that?"

"Could you impart the theory of polar co-ordinates to a baboon?" retorted Halcyon, rising briskly.

"I resent that!"

"It is a valid analogy, with no offense intended. But now we must appraise our present situation."

Halcyon scanned the dials.

"To be exact," he announced, "we stopped at three hundred nineteen thousand seven hundred two years, forty-five days, three hours and twenty-seven minutes negative from your take-off point—which means that we are well into the last previous major glacial period. And, to borrow an expression from your age, or perhaps one slightly earlier, we are out of gas."

"You mean—we're stranded?"

"Temporarily, yes. First, I must contact one of our transports. Second, I shall see that you are returned to the instant from which you set forth— unless you desire to become one of our confidential agents."

"I do not."

"As you wish. Now, as to communications. Let me think. The principal transmitter in the central cabin is useless since our major reserve of energy is exhausted. But we have also a small self-contained portable transmitter with a half-million-year range in either direction."

"After someone has received your distress signal over this time-radio or whatever it is, how long must we wait?"

"No time at all. It matters not how distant in time or space our rescuers may be when they receive my call; they will arrive instantly. That is one of the advantages of rescue by time-machine."

"Then we may be here only a few minutes longer, and I've seen practically nothing of the outside."

"We have arrived during an interlude of sunshine," reflected Halcyon, glancing at the sparkling frost-coated windows. "You shall see the glacial epoch in one of its less forbidding moments."

Since the outer door could no longer be opened by the usual power-driven apparatus, Halcyon resorted to the emergency hand lever. The door slid open to admit a wave of merciless cold and a dazzling sun glare from a prodigious ice field. The frozen expanse sloped upward dizzily, its snow banks shadowed with pastel blue, to a remote shark-tooth horizon of austere hyperborean peaks—blue-gray, fretted with white veinings, plumed with snow banners—against the frigid blue limpidity of the sky. A retinue of spectral sun dogs linked by the pale arc of a solar halo attended the frosty sun. An inhuman silence enveloped everything.

"It must be thirty below zero!" exclaimed Livingstone, flapping his arms, and was startled by the loudness of his voice.

"I suggest that you speak softly," admonished Halcyon. "One cannot say what precariously balanced masses of ice may be poised up there, awaiting only some reverberation, some gust of wind, to come rumbling down into the valley."

Livingstone walked over the creaking snow and around the prow of the transport, started to whistle, then checked himself.

"We very nearly landed in the wrong place," he announced. "We're almost alongside a crevasse more than big enough to swallow your transport."

"It narrows downward," remarked Halcyon, leaning over the brink to gaze into its blue depths. "We would have lodged near the top. Let us return inside before we freeze our extremities."

A fantastic incident now halted them in their tracks. Falling from the open sky, a shower of miscellaneous debris tumbled into the crevasse with the tinkling frangent impact of breaking glass and the staccato clangor of tinware. Ricocheting echoes reduplicated the din in a prolonged diminuendo. A small colorful object rebounded from the rim of the chasm and lay at their feet.

It was a can, an empty tin can, labeled "Superior Quality Tomato Juice."

"I should be immune to astonishment by now," cried Livingstone, "but this caps the climax! I suppose you have an explanation?"

"A passing transport threw overboard its accumulated refuse," Halcyon responded. "I would say that it was provisioned in the early twentieth century. The label is indicative."

"I didn't see any transport."

"Naturally. It passed through this interval too rapidly to be visible."

A reverberating boom like the discharge of a distant naval gun sent the echoes rolling again. Responsive booms replied to it. The stranded voyagers turned quickly to squint up the glaring slope of the ice field and beheld half a dozen little white clouds, like puffs of smoke, hanging at the bases of as many mountain peaks, miles distant. The little clouds slowly elongated themselves down the incline of the glacier, hugging its surface.

"This compels us to make haste," Halcyon declared. "It appears that the noise of our rain of debris from aloft has started not one but several avalanches. We may or may not be in the path of one of them."

They hurried into the transport, and from a locker beneath the pilot's seat in the control cabin Halcyon produced a ten-inch black cube, held it pressed between his hands.

"This is the portable transmitter," explained Halcyon. "It possesses what I may describe to you as a thermoelectric trigger, actuated by the body heat of my hands. Since my hands, unfortunately, are cold, it will be slow in responding. Held thus, it will be placed in a receptive or recording state. Grasped by two other faces of the cube it becomes a broadcasting device. When activated through the third pair of faces it functions as a receiver and reproducer of incoming impulses."

While they waited for the cube to become active the transport began to quiver; various objects in its interior vibrated and jingled softly. A sustained muttering as of subterranean thunder became audible.

"We may have a very narrow margin of time for our escape," reflected Halcyon. "It is advisable that we station ourselves in the vestibule with the outer door open, so that when our rescuers arrive we may board their transport at once."

The opening door disclosed a seething, screeching, cannonading tidal wave of iridescent snow spume skidding toward them down the glacial incline at terrifying speed. Leaping chunks of ice shot out of its forefront, shattered explosively, or danced on its smoking crest like the solid components of a stew in a boiling pot.

"My nightmares usually end about here," Livingstone observed through chattering teeth. "I should wake up soon."

The cube became transparent in Halcyon's hands, revealed a dead-black sphere within.

"Now for the recording," said Halcyon, and flung his thought into the sphere.

Such was the substance of the instantaneous narrative.

The company in the receiving room of the morgue exchanged stupefied glances.

"It *was* a narrow margin of time," Wentworth said. "Too narrow."

"I'm getting out of here while I'm still sane!" cried Livingstone, and fled.

He found the authorization ready for him, as promised by Toby Flanders. With the little blue slip tucked in the breast pocket of his jacket, he emerged upon the platform of the tunnel station under Big Diomede to find it deserted. He had missed the train for Tunnel Head by thirty seconds.

But there would be another train in fifteen minutes. He withdrew the slip from his pocket, examined it with a smile of satisfaction, and replaced it. But, hold on! This was just the way things had occurred when—

An unscheduled coach was standing alongside the platform, windowless save for the darkened cab of the motorman. The rectangle of a door was outlined in its convex side by a hairline crack. Livingstone moved toward it with hesitating steps, irresistibly drawn but reluctant.

The door opened and a passenger came forth, garbed as a tunnel worker, to be followed by Halcyon.

"You again! I hoped that I could just forget about what happened in the morgue!" protested Livingstone huskily. "Regardless of destiny, I'm not coming with you!"

"Naturally, since you are forewarned," responded Halcyon. "Your thoughts clearly show me what has taken place. Do not think of destiny; it is an illusion. As I might have reminded you under other circumstances, but shall not—the past is not immutable and neither is the future. This is a most intriguing situation. A series of occurrences turns upon itself and prevents itself from happening. I received my own distress signal which you unwittingly transmitted, but by tracing its direction I knew that it originated here and not from the time originally intended. I have merely to close this door and continue upon my prescribed course, leaving you here, and the whole affair will be canceled."

The door closed, the transport vanished, and a crash like the *kwang* of a Chinese gong resounded in Livingstone's brain as a whole sequence of events receded into the realm of unrealized probabilities. In a multitude of minds all relevant memories dropped into the limbo of subconscious fantasy, to rise again to consciousness only in the imagery of troubled dreams.

Livingstone found himself fumbling in the breast pocket of his jacket. Why was he doing that? There was nothing in it. Now that he had personally visited Tunnel Head and had untangled the confusion of orders which had delayed a trainload of materials there, he had no time for loitering about the station.

As he hurried from the platform, the station disgorged a group of people.

"This trip is a wild goose chase, Wentworth," declared one of them petulantly. "A waste of the museum's funds. It's an obvious practical joke. One shift of excavators planted them in the ice, the next shift dug them out. Tin cans and broken bottles! Kitchen-midden, my eye!"

A phrase floated into Livingstone's thoughts:

"A given state of affairs may be the result of a plurality of convergent possible pasts."

Why the devil should he think anything like that?

A. E. VAN VOGT

THE SEARCH

THE hospital bed was hard under his body. For a tense moment it seemed to Drake that that was what was bothering him. He turned over into a more comfortable position—and knew it wasn't physical at all. It was something in his mind, the sense of emptiness that had been there since they had told him the date.

After what seemed a long time, the door opened, and two men and a nurse came in. One of the men said in a hearty voice:

"Well, how are you, Drake? It's a shame to see you down like this."

The man was plumpish, a good-fellow type. Drake took his vigorous handshake, lay very still for a moment, and then allowed the awkward but necessary question to escape his lips:

"I'm sorry," he said stiffly, "but do I know you?"

The man said: "I'm Bryson, sales manager of the Quik-Rite Co. We manufacture fountain pens, pencils, ink, writing paper and a dozen kindred lines that even grocery stores handle.

"Two weeks ago, I hired you and put you on the road as salesman. The next thing I knew you were found unconscious in a ditch, and the hospital advised me you were here."

He finished: "You had identification papers on you connecting you with us."

Drake nodded. But he felt tense. It was all very well to have someone fill a gap in your mind, but— He said finally:

"My last remembrance is my decision to apply for a job with your firm, Mr. Bryson. I had just been turned down by the draft board for an odd reason. Apparently, something happened to my mind at that point and—"

He stopped. His eyes widened at the thought that came. He said slowly, conscious of an unpleasant sensation:

"Apparently, I've had amnesia."

He saw that the house doctor, who had come in with Bryson, was looking at him sharply. Drake mustered a wan smile.

"I guess it's all right, doc. What gets me is the kind of life I must have lived these last two weeks. I've been lying here straining my brain. There's something there in the back of my mind that—"

The doctor was smiling behind his pince-nez. "I'm glad you're taking it so well. Nothing to worry about, really. As for what you did, I assure you that our experience has been that the victim usually lives a reasonably normal life. One of the most frequent characteristics is that the victim takes up a different occupation. You didn't even do that."

He paused, and the plump Bryson said heartily: "I can clear up the first week for you. I had discovered, when I hired you, that you'd lived as a boy in some village on the Warwick Junction-Kissling branch line. Naturally, I put you on that route.

"We had orders from you from five towns on the way, but you never got to Kissling. Maybe that will help you. . . . No!" Bryson shrugged. "Well, never mind. As soon as you're up, Drake, come and see me. You're a good man, and they're getting scarce."

Drake said: "I'd like to be on the same territory, if it's all right."

Bryson nodded. "Mind you, it's only a matter of finishing up what you missed before, and then moving farther along the main line. But it's yours, certainly. I guess you want to check up on what happened to you."

"That," said Drake, "is exactly what I have in mind. Sort of a search for my memory." He managed a smile. "But now . . . but now, I want to thank you for coming."

"S'all right. S'long."

Bryson shook hands warmly, and Drake watched him out of the door.

Two days later, Drake climbed off the *Transcontinental* at Warwick Junction, and stood blinking in the bright sun of early morning. His first disappointment had already come. He had hoped that the sight of the cluster of houses silhouetted against a canyon would bring back memories.

It had, but only from his boyhood when he and his parents had passed through the Junction on various trips. There were new houses now, and the railway station 'hadn't been there twenty years before.

Too obviously, his mind was not being jarred into the faintest remembrance of what he had done or seen sixteen days earlier.

Drake shook his head in bewilderment. "Somebody knew me," he thought. "Somebody must have seen me. I talked to storekeepers, travelers, trainmen, hotel men. I've always had a sociable bent, so—"

"Hello, there, Drake, old chap," said a cheerful voice beside him. "You look as if you're thinking about a funeral."

Drake turned, and saw a rather slender young chap, dark-faced and dark-haired, about thirty years old. He had the slouch of too-thin people who walk too much carrying sample cases, and he must have noticed something in his, Drake's, eyes, for he said quickly:

"You remember me, don't you—Bill Kellie!" He laughed easily. "Say, come to think of it, I've got a bone to pick with you. What did you do with that girl, Selanie? I've been twice past Piffer's Road since I last saw you, and she didn't come around either time. She—"

He stopped, and his gaze was suddenly sharp. "Say, you do remember me, don't you?"

To Drake, the astounding if not notable fact was that Piffer's Road should be the place name. Was it possible that he had got the idea of going to the farmhouse where he had been born, to look the old homestead over? He emerged from his intense inner excitement, and realized from the expression on Kellie's face that it was time to explain. He finished finally:

"So you see, I'm in quite a mental fix. Maybe, if you wouldn't mind, you could give me some idea of what happened while I was with you. Who is this girl, Selanie?"

"Oh, sure," said Kellie, "sure, I'll—" He paused, frowned. "You're not kiddin' me, are you?" He waved Drake silent. "O. K., O. K., I'll believe you. We've got a half-hour before the Kissling local is due. Amnesia, eh? I've heard about that stuff, but— Sa-a-ay, you don't think that old man could have anything to do with—" He banged his right fist into his left palm. "I'll bet that's it."

"An old man!" Drake said. He caught himself, finished firmly: "What about this story?"

The train slowed. Through the streaky window, Drake could see a rolling valley with patches of green trees and a gleaming, winding thread of water. Then some houses came into view, half a dozen siding tracks, and finally the beginning of a wooden platform.

A tall, slim, fine-looking girl walked past his window carrying a basket. Behind Drake, the traveling salesman, who had got on at the last stop, and to whom he had been talking, said:

"Oh, there's Selanie. I wonder what kind of supergadget she's got for sale today."

Drake leaned back in his seat, conscious that he had seen all of Piffer's Road that he cared to. It was queer, that feeling of disinterest. After all, he had been born three miles along the road. Nevertheless, there it was. He didn't give a darn. His mind fastened only slowly on what the other had said.

"Selanie!" he echoed then. "Curious name! Did you say she sells things?"

"*Does* she sell things!" the man, Kellie, exploded.

He must have realized the forcefulness of his words, for he drew a deep, audible breath; his blue eyes looked hard at Drake. He started to say something, stopped himself, and finally sat smiling a secret smile.

After a moment, he said: "You know I really must apologize. I've just now realized that I've monopolized the conversation ever since we started talking."

Drake smiled with polite tolerance. "You've been very entertaining."

Kellie persisted: "What I mean by that is, it's just penetrated to me that you told me you sold fountain pens, among other things."

Drake shrugged. He wondered if he looked as puzzled as he was beginning to feel. He watched as Kellie drew out a pen, and held it out for him to take. Kellie said:

"See anything queer about that?"

The pen was long, slender, of a dark, expensive-looking material. Drake unscrewed the cap slowly—slowly, because in his mind was the sudden, wry thought that he was in for one of those pointless arguments about the relative merits of the pens he was selling and—

He said quickly: "This looks right out of my class. My company's pens retail for a dollar."

The moment he had spoken, he realized he had left himself wide open. Kellie said with a casual triumph:

"That's exactly what she charged me for it."

"Who?"

"Selanie! The girl who just got on the train. She'll be along in a few minutes selling something new. She's always got an item that's new and different."

He grabbed the pen from Drake's fingers. "I'll show you what's queer about this pen."

His fingers reached toward a paper cup that stood on the window sill. He said with an irritating smugness: "Watch!"

The pen tilted over the cup; Kellie seemed to press with his finger on the top—and ink began to flow.

After about three minutes, it filled the cup to the brim. Kellie opened the window, carefully emptied the blue liquid onto the ground between the coach and the platform—and Drake erupted from his paralysis.

"Good heavens!" he gasped. "What kind of a tank have you got inside that pen? Why, it—"

"Wait!"

Kellie's voice was quiet, but he was so obviously enjoying himself that Drake pulled himself together with a distinct effort. His brain began to whirl once more, as Kellie pressed the top again, and once again ink began to flow from the fantastic pen. Kellie said:

"Notice anything odd about that ink?"

Drake started to shake his head, then he started to say that the oddness was the quantity, then he gulped hoarsely:

"*Red* ink!"

"Or maybe," Kellie said coolly, "you'd prefer purple. Or yellow. Or green. Or violet."

The pen squirted a tiny stream of each color, as he named it. In each case, he turned the part he was pressing ever so slightly. Kellie finished with the triumphant tone of a man who has extracted every last drop of drama from a situation:

"Here, maybe you'd like to try it yourself."

Drake took the remarkable thing like a connoisseur caressing a priceless jewel. As from a great distance he heard Kellie chattering on:

"—her father makes them," Kellie was saying. "He's a genius with gadgets. You ought to see some of the stuff she's been selling on this train the last month. One of these days, he's going to get wise to himself, and start large-scale manufacture. When that day comes, all fountain pen companies and a lot of other firms go out of business."

It was a thought that had already occurred to Drake. Before he could muster his mind for speech, the pen was taken from his fingers; and Kellie was leaning across the aisle toward a handsome gray-haired man who sat there. Kellie said:

"I noticed you looking at the pen, sir, while I was showing it to my friend. Would you like to examine it?"

"Why, yes," said the man.

He spoke in a low tone, but the sound had an oddly rich resonance that tingled in Drake's ears. The old man's fingers grasped the extended pen and—just like that—the pen broke.

"Oh!" Kellie exclaimed blankly.

"I beg your pardon," said the fine-looking old man. A dollar appeared in his hand. "My fault. You can buy another one from the girl when she comes."

He leaned back, and buried himself behind a newspaper.

Drake saw that Kellie was biting his lip. The man sat staring at his broken pen, and then at the dollar bill, and then in the direction of the now hidden face of the gray-haired man. At last, Kellie sighed:

"I can't understand it. I've had the pen a month now. It's already fallen to a cement sidewalk, and twice onto a hardwood floor—and now it breaks like a piece of rotted wood."

He shrugged, but his tone was complaining as he went on after a moment: "I suppose actually you can't really expect Selanie's father to do a first-rate job with the facilities he's got—"

He broke off excitedly: "Oh, look, there's Selanie now. I wonder what she's featuring today."

A sly smile crept into his narrow face. "Just wait till I confront her with that broken pen. I kidded her when I bought it, told her there must be a trick to it. She got mad then, and guaranteed it for life— What the devil is she selling, anyway? Look, they're crowding around her."

Quite automatically, Drake climbed to his feet. He craned his neck the better to see over the heads of the crowd that was watching the girl demonstrate something at the far end of the car.

"Good heavens!" a man's deep voice exclaimed. "How much are you charging for those cups? How do they work?"

"Cups!" said Drake, and moved toward the group in a haze of fascination. If he had seen right, the girl was handing around a container which kept filling full of liquid. And people would drink, and it would fill again instantly.

Drake thought: The same principle as the fountain pen. Somehow, her father had learned to precipitate liquids and—

His brain did a twisting dive, then came up spinning. What . . . in . . . kind of gadget genius was there behind this . . . this priceless stuff? Why, if he, Drake, could make a deal with the man for the company, or for himself, he was made. He—

He was trembling violently; and the tremendous thought ended, as the girl's crystal-clear voice rose above the excited babble:

"The price is one dollar each. It works by chemical condensation of gases in the air; the process is known only to my father—but wait, I haven't finished my demonstration."

She went on, her voice cool and strong against the silence that settled around her:

"As you see, it's a folding drinking cup without a handle. First, you open it. Then you turn the top strip clockwise. At a certain point, water comes. But now—watch. I'm turning it farther. The liquid is now turning green, and is a sweet and very flavorsome drink. I turn the strip still farther, and the liquid turns red, becomes a sweet-sourish drink that is very refreshing in hot weather."

She handed the cup around; and it was while it was being passed around from fingers to clutching fingers that Drake managed to wrench his gaze from the gadget, and really look at the girl.

She was tall, about five feet six, and she had dark-brown hair. Her face was unmistakably of a fine intelligence. It was thin and good-looking, and there was an odd proud tilt to it that gave her a startling appearance of aloofness in spite of the way she was taking the dollar bills that were being thrust at her.

Once again, her voice rose: "I'm sorry, only one to a person. They'll be on the general market right after the war. These are only souvenirs."

The crowd dissolved, each person retiring to his or her individual seat. The girl came along the aisle, and stopped in front of Drake. He stepped aside instinctively, and then abruptly realized what he was doing.

"Wait" he said piercingly. "My friend showed me a fountain pen you were selling. I wonder—"

"I still have a few." She nodded gravely. "Would you like a cup, also?"

Drake remembered Kellie. "My friend would like another pen, too. His broke and—"

"I'm sorry, I can't sell him a second pen." She paused there. Her eyes widened; she said with a weighty slowness. "Did you say—*his* broke?"

Astoundingly, she swayed. She said wildly: "Let me see that. Where is your friend?"

She took the two pieces of fountain pen from Kellie's fingers, and stared at them. Her mouth began to tremble. Her hands shook. Her face took on a gray, drawn look. Her voice, when she spoke, was a whisper:

"Tell me . . . tell me, how did it happen? *Exactly* how?"

"Why"—Kellie drew back in surprise—"I was handing it to that old gentleman over there when—"

He stopped because he had lost his audience. The girl spun on her heel —and that was like a signal. The old man lowered his paper, and looked at the girl.

She stared back at him with the fascinated expression of a bird cornered by a snake. Then, for a second time within two minutes, she swayed. The basket nearly dropped from her hand as she ran, but, somehow, she hung on to it, as she careened along the aisle.

A moment later, Drake saw her racing across the platform. She became a distant, running form on Piffer's Road.

"What the hell!" Kellie exploded.

He whirled on the old man. "What did you do to her?" he demanded fiercely. "You—"

His voice sank into silence, and Drake, who had been about to add his hard words to the demand, remained quiet, also.

The salesman's voice there under the bright sun, on the platform at Warwick Junction, faded. It required a moment for Drake to grasp that the story was finished.

"You mean," he demanded, "that's all? We just sat there like a couple of dummies out-faced by an old man? And that was the end of the business? You still don't know what scared the girl?"

He saw that there was the strange look on Kellie's face of a man who was searching mentally for a word or phrase to describe the indescribable. Kellie said finally:

"There was something about him like . . . like all the tough sales managers in the world rolled into one, and feeling their orneriest. We just shut up."

It was a description that Drake could appreciate. He nodded grimly, said slowly: "He didn't get off?"

"No, you were the only one who got off."

"Eh?"

Kellie looked at him. "You know, this is the damnedest, funniest thing. But that's the way it was. You asked the trainman to check your bags at Inchney. The last thing I saw of you before the train pulled out, you were walking up Piffer's Road in the direction the girl had gone and— Ah, here comes the Kissling local now."

The combination freight and passenger train backed in weightily. Later, as it was winding in and out along the edge of a valley, Drake sat staring wonderingly at the terrain so dimly remembered from his boy-hood, only vaguely conscious of Kellie chattering beside him.

He decided finally on the course he would take: This afternoon he'd get off at Inchney, make his rounds until the stores closed, then get a ride in some way to Piffer's Road, and spend the long, summer evening making inquiries. If he recollected correctly, the distance between the large town and the tiny community was given as seven miles. At worst he could walk back to Inchney in a couple of hours—

The first part proved even simpler than that. There was a bus, the clerk at the Inchney Hotel told him, that left at six o'clock.

At twenty after six, Drake climbed off, and, standing in the dirt that was Piffer's Road, watched the bus throb off down the highway. The sound faded into remoteness as he trudged across the railway track.

The evening was warm and quiet, and his coat made a weight on his arm. It would be cooler later on, he thought, but at the moment he almost regretted that he had brought it.

There was a woman on her knees, working on the lawn at the first house. Drake hesitated, then went over to the fence, and stared at the woman for a moment. He wondered if he ought to remember her. He said finally:

"I beg your pardon, madam."

She did not look up; she did not rise from the flowerbed, where she was digging. She was a bony creature in a print dress, and she must have seen him coming to be so obstinately silent.

"I wonder," Drake persisted, "if you can tell me where a middle-aged man and his daughter live. The daughter is called Selanie, and she used to sell fountain pens and drinking cups and things to people on the train. She—"

The woman was getting up. She came over. At close range, she didn't seem quite so large or ungainly. She had gray eyes that looked at him with a measure of hostility, then with curiosity.

"Sa-a-ay," she said sharply, "weren't you along here about two weeks ago, asking about them? I told you then that they lived in that grove over there."

She waved at some trees about a quarter of a mile along the road, but her eyes were narrowed, wintry pools as she stared at him. "I don't get it," she said grimly.

Drake couldn't see himself explaining about his amnesia to this crusty-voiced, suspicious creature, and he certainly wasn't going to mention that he had once lived in the district. He said hastily:

"Thank you very much. I—"

"No use going up there again," said the woman. "They pulled out the same day you were there last time . . . in their big trailer. And they haven't come back."

THE SEARCH

499

"They're gone!" Drake exclaimed.

In the intensity of his disappointment, he was about to say more when he grew conscious that the woman was staring at him with a faint, satisfied smile on her face. She looked as if she had successfuly delivered a knock-out blow to an unpleasant individual.

"I think," Drake snapped, "I'll go up and have a look around, anyway."

He spun on his heel, so angry that for a while he scarcely realized that he was walking in the ditch and not on the road. His fury yielded slowly to disappointment, and that in turn faded before the realization that, now that he was up here, he *might* as well have a look.

After a moment, he felt amazed that he could have let one woman get on his nerves to such an extent in so short a time.

He shook his head, self-chidingly. He'd better be careful. This business of tracking down his memory was beginning to wear on him.

A breeze sprang up from nowhere as he turned into the shadowed grove. It blew softly in his face, and its passage through the trees was the only sound that broke the silence of the evening.

It didn't take more than a moment to realize that his vague expectations, the sense of—something—that had been driving him on to this journey was not going to be satisfied.

For there was nothing, not a sign that human beings had ever lived here; not a tin can, or a bundle of garbage, or ashes from a stove. Nothing.

He wandered around disconsolately for a few minutes, poked gingerly with a stick among a pile of dead branches—and finally walked back along the road. This time it was the woman who called to him.

He hesitated, then went over. After all, she might know a lot more than she had told. He saw that she looked more friendly.

"Find anything?" she said with an ill-restrained eagerness.

Drake smiled grimly at the power of curiosity, then shrugged ruefully. "When a trailer leaves," he said, "it's like smoke—it just vanishes."

The woman sniffed. "Any traces that were left sure went fast after the old man got through there."

A thrill like flame coursed through Drake. "The old man!" he exclaimed violently.

The woman nodded, then said bitterly: "A fine-looking old chap. Came around first inquiring from everybody what kind of stuff Selanie had sold us. Two days later, we woke up in the morning, and every single piece was gone."

"Stolen!"

The woman scowled. "Same thing as. There was a dollar bill for each item—but that's stealing for those kind of goods. Do you know, she had a frying pan that—"

"But what did he want?" Drake interrupted, bewildered. "Didn't he explain anything when he was making his inquiries? Surely, you didn't just let him come around here asking questions!"

To his astonishment, the woman flushed, then she looked flustered. "I don't know what came over me," she confessed finally, sullenly. "There was something about him. He looked kind of commanding-like and important, as if he was a big executive or something; and besides he—"

She stopped angrily. "The scoundrel!" she snapped.

Her eyes narrowed with abrupt hostility. She peered at Drake. "You're a fine one for saying did we ask any questions. What about you? Standing here pumping me when all the time— Say, let me get this straight: *Are* you the fellow who called here two weeks ago? Just how do you fit into this picture?"

Drake hesitated. The prospect of having to tell that story to people like this seemed full of difficulties. And yet—

She must know more. There must be a great deal of information about the month that the girl Selanie and her father had spent in the district. One thing was sure—Drake smiled grimly—if any more facts were available, this woman would have them.

Hesitation ended. He made his explanation, but finished a little uncertainly: "So you see, I'm a man who is—well—in search of his memory. Maybe I was knocked over the head, although there's no lump. Then again, maybe I was doped. *Something* happened to me. You say I went up there. Did I come back? Or what did I do? What—"

He stopped with a jump, for, without so much as a warning, the woman parted her lips, and let out a bellow:

"*Jimmy!*" she yelled in an ear-splitting voice, "JIMMY! C'M'ERE!"

"Yeah, mom!" came a boy's voice from inside the house.

Drake stared blankly as an uncombed twelve-year-old with a sharp, eager face catapulted from a screen door, that banged after him. He listened still with only partial comprehension as the mother explained to the boy that "this man was hit over the head by those people in the trailer, and he lost his memory, and he'd like you to tell him what you saw."

The woman turned to Drake. "Jimmy," she said proudly, "never trusted those folk. He was sure they were Nazis or something, and so he kept a sharp eye on them. He saw you go up there, and everything that happened right up to the time the trailer left."

She finished: "The reason he can tell you in such detail exactly what you did is that he could see everything through the windows, and besides he went inside once when they weren't around and looked the whole place over—just to make sure, of course, that they weren't pulling something."

Drake nodded, suppressing his cynicism. It was probably as good a reason as any for snooping—in this case, lucky for him.

The thought ended, as Jimmy's shrill voice projected into the gathering twilight—

The afternoon was hot, and Drake, after pausing to inquire of the woman in the first house as to where the father and daughter lived, walked slowly toward the grove of trees she had indicated.

Behind him, the train hooted twice, and then began to chuff. Drake suppressed a startled impulse to run back and get on. He realized that he couldn't have made it, anyway. Besides—

A man didn't give up the hope of fortune as easily as that. His pace quickened. By heaven, when he thought of that pen and that drinking cup—

He couldn't see the trailer in the grove until he turned into the initial shady patch of trees. When he saw it, he stopped short.

It was much bigger than he had conceived it. It was as long as a small freight car—and as big—curiously streamlined.

And no one answered his knock.

He thought tensely: She ran this way. She must be inside. Uncertain, he walked around the monster on wheels.

There was a line of windows above the level of his eyes that made a complete circuit of the trailer. He could see a gleamy ceiling and the upper part of what looked like finely paneled walls. There were three rooms, and the only other entrance led into the cab of the truck, to which the trailer was attached.

Back before the first entrance, Drake listened intently for sounds. But again there was nothing—nothing except a thin wind that blew gently through the upper reaches of the trees. Far away, the train whistled plaintively.

He tried the latch, and the door opened so easily that his hesitation ended. Deliberately, he pushed it ajar, and stood there staring into the middle room of the three.

Luxury shone at his startled gaze. The floor was a marvel, a darkly gleaming, gemlike design. The walls toned in with an amazingly rich-looking, though quiet, panel effect. There was a couch just across from the door, two chairs, three cabinets and several intricately carved shelves with fine-looking objects standing on them.

The first thing Drake saw, as he climbed in, was the girl's basket standing against the wall just to the left of the door.

The sight stopped him short. He sat in the doorway, then, his legs dangling toward the ground. His nervousness yielded to the continuing silence, and he began with a gathering curiosity to examine the contents of the basket.

There were about a dozen of the magic pens, at least three dozen of the folding, self-filling cups, a dozen, roundish black objects that refused to respond to his handling—and three pairs of pince-nez.

Each pair had a tiny, transparent wheel attached to the side of the right lens; and they simply lay there. They seemed to have no cases; there seemed to be no fear that they would break. The pair he tried on fitted snugly over his nose, and for a moment he actually thought they fitted his eyes.

Then he noticed the difference. Everything was nearer—the room, his hand—not magnified or blurred, but it was as if he was staring through mildly powered field glasses.

There was no strain on his eyes; and, after a moment, he grew conscious again of the little wheel. It turned—quite easily.

Instantly, things were nearer, the field-glass effect twice as strong. Trembling a little, he began to turn the wheel, first one way, then the other.

A few seconds only were needed to verify the remarkable reality. He had on a pair of pince-nez with adjustable lens, an incredible combination telescope-microscope—superglasses.

Blankly, Drake returned the marvelous things to the basket, and, with abrupt decision, climbed into the trailer, and moved toward the entrance of the back room.

His intention was to peer in only. But that first look showed the entire wall fitted with shelves, each neatly loaded with a variety of small goods.

Utterly curious, Drake picked up what looked like a camera. It was a fine little affair. He was peering into the lens when his fingers pressed something that gave. There was a click. Instantly, a glistening card came out of a slit in the back.

The picture was the upper part of a man's face. It had remarkable depth and an amazing natural color effect. It was the intent expression in the brown eyes that momentarily made the features strange, unfamiliar. Then he recognized that he was looking at himself. His picture, instantly developed—

It was all he needed. Chilled in spite of himself, Drake stuffed the picture in his pocket, set the instrument down—and, trembling, climbed out of the trailer, and walked off down the road toward the village.

"—and then," said Jimmy, "a minute later you came back, and climbed in and shut the door and went into the back room. You came back so fast that you nearly saw me; I thought you'd gone. And then—"

The trailer door opened. A girl's voice said something urgent that Drake didn't catch. The next instant, a man answered with a grunt. The door closed; and there was moving and breathing in the center room.

Crouching, Drake drew back against the left wall—

"—and that's all, mister," Jimmy finished. "I thought there was going to be trouble then. And I hiked for home to tell mom."

"You mean," Drake protested, "I was foolish enough to come back, just in time to get myself caught, and I didn't dare show myself?"

The boy shrugged. "You were pressing up against the partition—that's all I could see."

"And they didn't look in that room while you were watching?"

Jimmy hesitated. "Well," he began finally in a curious, defensive tone, "what happened then was kind of queer. You see, I looked back when I'd gone about a hundred yards—and the trailer and truck wasn't there no more."

"Wasn't there!" Drake spoke slowly. He had a sense of unreality. "You mean, they started up the truck engine, and drove to Piffer's Road, and so on down to the highway?"

The boy shook his head stubbornly. "Folks is always tryin' to trip me up on that. But I know what I saw and heard. There weren't no sound of an engine. They just was gone suddenly, that's all."

Drake felt an eerie chill along his spine. "And I was aboard?" he asked.

"You were aboard," said Jimmy.

The spasm of silence that followed was broken by the woman saying loudly: "All right, Jimmy, you can go and play."

She turned back to Drake. "Do you know what I think?" she said.

With an effort, Drake roused himself. It wasn't that he had been thinking. Actually, there was a blankness in his mind that—

"What?" he said.

"They're working a racket, the whole bunch of them together. The story about her father making the stuff. I can't understand how we fell for that. He just spent his time going around the district buying up old metal.

"Mind you"—the admission came almost reluctantly—"they've got some wonderful things. The government isn't kidding when it says that after this war we're going to live like kings and queens. But there's the rub. So far, these people have only got hold of a few hundred pieces altogether. What they do is sell them in one district, then steal everything back, and resell in another."

In spite of his intense self-absorption, Drake stared at her. He had run across the peculiar logic of fuzzy-minded people before, but it always shocked him when facts were so brazenly ignored in order that a crackpot theory might hold water. He said:

"I don't see where the profit comes in. What about the dollar you got back for each item that was stolen?"

"Oh!" said the woman. Her face lengthened, then she looked startled, and then, as she grasped how absolutely her pet idea was wrecked, an angry flush suffused her wind- and sun-tanned face. "Some publicity scheme maybe!" she snapped.

It struck Drake that it was time to terminate the interview. He said hastily: "Is anybody you know going into Inchney tonight? I'd like a ride if I could get it."

The change of subject did its work. The high color faded from the woman's cheeks. She said thoughtfully:

"Nope, no one I know of. But don't worry. Just get on the highway, and you'll get a lift—"

The second car picked him up. He sat in the hotel, as darkness fell, thinking:

"A girl and her father with a carload of the finest manufactured goods in the world. She sells them as souvenirs, one to a person. He buys old metal. And then, as added insanity, an old man goes around buying up the goods sold"—he thought of Kellie's pen—"or breaking them."

Finally, there was the curious amnesia of a fountain pen salesman, named Drake. It—

Somewhere behind Drake, a man's voice cried out in anguish: "Oh, look what you've done now. You've broken it."

A quiet, mature, resonant voice answered: "I beg your pardon. You paid a dollar for it, you say? I shall pay for the loss, naturally. Here—and you have my regrets."

In the silence that followed, Drake stood up and turned. He saw a tall, splendid-looking man with gray hair, in the act of rising from beside a younger chap, who was staring at the two pieces of a broken pen in his fingers.

The old man headed for the revolving door leading to the street, but it was Drake who got there first, Drake who said quietly but curtly:

"One minute, please. I want an explanation of what happened to me after I got into the trailer of the girl, Selanie, and her father. And I think you're the man to give it to me. I—"

He stopped. He was staring into eyes that were like pools of gray fire, eyes that seemed literally to tear into his face, and to peer with undiminished intensity at the inside of his brain. Drake had time for a brief, startled memory of what Kellie had said about the way this man had outfaced them on the train with one deadly look—and then it was too late for further thought.

With an utterly un-old-manish, a tigerish speed, the other stepped forward, and caught Drake's wrist. There was the feel of metal in that touch, metal that sent a tingling glow along Drake's arm, as the old man said in a low, compelling voice:

"This way—to my car."

Barely, Drake remembered getting into a long, gleamy-hooded car. The rest was darkness—mental—physical—

He was lying on his back on a hard floor. Drake opened his eyes, and for a blank moment stared at a domed ceiling two hundred feet above him. The ceiling was at least three hundred feet wide, and nearly a quarter of it was window, through which a gray-white mist of light showed, as if an invisible sun was trying hard to penetrate a thin but persistent fog.

The wide strip of window ran along the center of the ceiling straight on into the distance. It—

Into the distance!

With a gasp, Drake jerked erect. For a moment then his mind threatened to ooze out of his head.

There was no end to that corridor.

It stretched in either direction until it became a blur of gray marble and gray light. There was a balcony and a gallery and a second gallery; each floor had its own side corridor set off by a railing; and there were countless shining doors and, every little while, a branch corridor, each suggesting other vast reaches of that visibly monstrous building.

Very slowly, the first enormous shock over, Drake climbed to his feet. Memory of the old man—and what had gone before—was a weight in his mind. He thought darkly: "He got me into his car—and drove me here. Only—"

Only, on all the wide surface of the Earth, no such building existed.

A chill percolated up his spine. It cost him a distinct effort to walk toward the nearest of the long line of tall, carved doors, and pull it open.

What he expected, he couldn't have told. But his first reaction was—disappointment.

It was an office, a large room with plain walls. There were some fine-looking cabinets along one wall. A great desk occupied the corner facing the door. Some chairs and two comfortable-looking settees and another, more ornate door completed the picture.

No one was in the room. The desk looked spick and span, dustless. And lifeless.

The second door was locked, or else the latch was too complicated.

Out in the corridor again, Drake grew conscious of the intense silence. His shoes clicked with an empty sound—and door after door yielded the same office-furnished but uninhabited interior.

An hour passed by his watch. And then another half-hour. And then—he saw the door in the distance.

At first it was only a brightness. It took on glittering contours, became an enormous glass affair set in a framework of multi-tinted windows.

The door was easily fifty feet in height; and when he peered through its transparent panes, he could see great white steps leading down into a mist that thickened after about twenty feet, so that the lower steps were not visible.

Drake stared uneasily. There was something wrong here. That mist, obscuring everything, persisting for hours, clinging darkly—

He shook himself. Probably, there was water down there at the foot of the steps, warmish water subjected to a constant stream of cold air, and thick fog formed—

For a moment, he pictured that in his mind—a building ten miles long standing beside a lake, and buried forever in gray mists.

"Get out of here," he thought sharply, "get out!"

The latch of the door was at a normal height. But it seemed impossible that he would be able to maneuver the gigantic structure with such a comparatively tiny leverage. It—

It opened lightly, gently, like a superbly balanced machine. Drake stepped out into the pressing fog and began, swiftly at first, and then with a developing caution, to go down the steps. No use landing up in a pool of deep water.

The hundredth step was the last; and there was no water. There was nothing except mists, no foundations for the steps, no ground—nothing!

On hands and knees, dizzy with a sudden vertigo, Drake crawled back up the steps. He was so weak that inches only seemed to recede behind him. The nightmarish feeling came that the steps were going to crumble under him, now that he had discovered that their base was—nothing.

A second, greater fear came that the door would not open from the outside, and cut him off here on the edge of eternity forever.

But it did open. It took all the strength of his weakened body. He lay on the floor inside, and after a while the awful wonder came to his mind: What did a girl called Selanie, dispensing marvelous gadgets on a train, have to do with this?

There seemed to be no answer.

His funk yielded to the sense of safety produced by the passing minutes. He stood up, ashamed of his terror, and his mind grooving to a purpose.

The fantastic place must be explored from cellar to roof. Somewhere, there would be a cache of the cups that created their own water. And perhaps also there would be food. Soon, he would have to eat and drink.

First, to one of the offices. Examine every cabinet, break open the desk drawers, search—

It wasn't necessary to break anything. The drawers opened at the slightest tug. The cabinet doors were unlocked.

Inside were journals, ledgers, curious-looking files. Absorbed, Drake glanced blurrily through several that he had spread out on the great desk, blurrily because his hands were shaking, and his brain couldn't penetrate for a second at a time.

Finally, with an effort of will, he pushed everything aside but one of the journals. This he opened at random, and read the words printed there:

SYNOPSIS OF REPORT OF POSSESSOR KINGSTON CRAIG IN THE MATTER OF THE EMPIRE OF LYCEUS II

A. D. 27,346—27,378

Frowning, Drake stared at the date; then he read on:

The normal history of the period is a tale of cunning usurpation of power by a ruthless ruler. A careful study of the man revealed an unnatural urge to protect himself at the expense of others.

TEMPORARY SOLUTION: A warning to the Emperor, who nearly collapsed when he realized that he was confronted by a Possessor. His instinct for self-preservation impelled him to give guarantees as to future conduct.

COMMENT: This solution produced a probability world Type 5, and must be considered temporary because of the very involved permanent work that Professor Terran Link is doing on the fringes of the entire two hundred seventy-third century.

CONCLUSION: Returned to the Palace of Immortality after an absence of three days.

Drake sat there, stiffly at first, then he leaned back in his chair; but the same blank impression remained in his mind. Quite simply, there was nothing to think.

At last, he turned a leaf, and read:

SYNOPSIS OF REPORT OF POSSESSOR
KINGSTON CRAIG

This is the case of Lairn Graynon, Police Inspector, 900th Sector Station, New York City, who on July 7, A.D. 2830 was falsely convicted of accepting bribes, and de-energized.

SOLUTION: Obtained the retirement of Inspector Graynon two months before the date given in the charge. He retired to his farm, and henceforth exerted the very minimum of influence on the larger scene of existence. He lived in this probability world of his own until his death in 2874, and thus provided an almost perfect 290A.

CONCLUSION: Returned to the Palace of Immortality after one hour.

There were more entries, hundreds—thousands altogether in the several journals. Each one was a "REPORT OF POSSESSOR KINGSTON CRAIG," and always he returned to the "Palace of Immortality" after so many days, or hours or—weeks. Once it was three months, and that was an obscure, impersonal affair that dealt with "the establishment of the time of demarcation between the ninety-eighth and ninety-ninth centuries—" and involved "the resurrection into active, personal probability worlds of their own of three murdered men, named—"

The sharpening pangs of thirst and hunger brought to Drake a picture of himself sitting in this immense and terrible building, reading the fanciful scrawlings of a man who *must* be mad.

It struck him that the seemingly sourceless light of the room was growing dimmer. The light must come in some way from outside and—

Out in the vast, empty corridor, he realized the truth. The mists above the ceiling window were graying, darkening. Night was falling.

He tried not to think of that—of being alone in this tomblike building, watching the gloom creep over the gray marble—wondering what things might come out of hiding once the darkness grew impenetrable and—

"Stop it, you fool!" Drake said aloud, savagely.

His voice sounded hollow against the silence, and scared a thought into his shuddering brain:

There must be a place here where these—Possessors—had lived. This floor was all offices, but the next—stairway—find a stairway. He had seen none on the main corridor, so—

It was as simple as that. Fifty feet along the first side corridor was a broad staircase. Drake bounded up the steps and tried the first door he came to.

The door opened into the living room of a magnificent apartment. There were seven rooms, including a kitchen that gleamed in the dimming light, and the built-in cupboards of which were packed with transparent containers; the contents were foods both familiar and strange.

Drake felt without emotion, not even a tremor of surprise touched him as he manipulated a tiny lever at the top of a can of pears, and the fruit simply spilled out onto the table—although the bottle had not opened in any way.

He saw to it that he had a dish for the next attempt; that was all. Later, after he had eaten, he searched for light switches. But it was becoming too dark to see.

The main bedroom had a canopied bed that loomed in the darkness, and there were pajamas in a drawer. Lying between the cool sheets, his body heavy with approaching sleep, Drake thought vaguely:

That girl Selanie and her fear of the old man—why had she been afraid? And what *could* have happened in the trailer that had irrevocably precipitated Ralph Carson Drake into—this?

Drake slept with the thought still in his mind, uneasily—

The light was far away at first. It came nearer, grew brighter, and at first it was like any awakening. Then, just as Drake opened his eyes, memory flooded his mind.

He was lying, he saw tensely, on his left side; and it was broad daylight. From the corners of his eyes he could see, above him, the silvery-blue canopy of the bed, and beyond it, far above, the high ceiling.

Realization came that in the shadows of the previous evening he had scarcely noticed how big and roomy and—luxurious—his quarters were.

There were thick, shining rugs and paneled walls and rose-colored furniture that glowed costly beauty. The bed was an oversize four-poster affair and—

Drake's thought suffered a dreadful pause because, in turning his head away from the left part of the room toward the right, his gaze fell for the first time on the other half of the bed.

A young woman lay there, fast asleep.

She had dark-brown hair, a snow-white throat, and, even in repose, her face looked fine and intelligent. She appeared to be about thirty years old.

Drake's examination got no further. Like a thief in the night, he slid from under the quilt. He reached the floor and crouched there, holding his breath in a desperate dismay because—

The steady breathing from the bed had stopped. There was the sound of a woman sighing, and finally—doom!

"My dear," said a rich contralto voice, lazily, "what on earth are you doing on the floor?"

There was movement on the bed, and Drake cringed in awful anticipation of the scream that would greet the discovery that he was not *the* my dear.

But nothing happened. The lovely head came over the edge of the bed; gray eyes stared at him tranquilly. The young woman seemed to have forgotten her first question, for she said:

"Darling, are you scheduled to go to Earth today?"

That got him. The question itself was so stupendous that his personal relation to—everything—seemed secondary. Besides—dim understanding was coming.

This was one of those worlds of probability that he had read about in the journals of Possessor Kingston Craig. Here simply and tremendously was something that *could* happen to Ralph Drake. And somewhere behind the scenes someone was making it happen.

All because he had gone in search of his memory.

Drake stood up. He was perspiring, his heart was beating like a trip hammer, his knees trembled and there wasn't a calm thought in his head. But he stood up, and he said:

"Yes, I'm going to Earth."

It gave him purpose, he thought tensely, reason to get out of here as fast as he possibly could and—

He was heading for the chair on which were his clothes when the import of his own words provided the second and greater shock to his badly staggered nerves.

Going to Earth! He felt his brain sag before the crushing weight of a fact that transcended every reality of his existence. Going to Earth—from where?

The answer was a crazy thing that sighed at last wearily through his mind: From the Palace of Immortality, of course, the palace in the mists, where the Possessors lived.

He reached the bathroom. The night before, he had discovered in its darkening interior a transparent jar of salve, the label of which said: BEARD REMOVER—RUB ON, THEN WASH OFF.

It took half a minute—the rest five minutes longer.

He came out of the bathroom, fully dressed. His mind was like a stone in his head, and like a stone sinking through water he started for the door near the bed.

"Darling!"

"Yes!" Cold and stiff, Drake turned. In a spasm of relief, he saw that she was not looking at him. Instead she had one of the magic pens and was frowning over some figures in a big ledger. Without looking up, she said:

"Our time-relation to each other is becoming worse. You'll have to stay more at the palace, reversing your age, while I go to Earth and add a few years to mine. Will you make the arrangements for that, dear?"

"Yes," said Drake, "yes!"

There was nothing else. He walked into the little hallway, then into the living room; and then—out in the corridor at last, he leaned against the cool, smooth marble wall, thinking hopelessly.

Reverse his age! So that was what this incredible building did! Every day here you were a day younger, and it was necessary to—go—to Earth to strike a balance.

The shock grew. And there was no longer any question: What had happened to him on the trailer was so important that a gigantic super-human organization was striving with every ounce of power to prevent him from learning the truth.

Beyond all doubt, today he would really have to find out what all this was about, explore every floor, try to locate some kind of central office and—

He was relaxing slowly, withdrawing out of that intense inward concentration of his mind when, for the first time, awareness came of—sounds. Voices, movements, people—below.

Even as he leaped for the balcony balustrade, the shattering realization came to Drake that he should have known it. The woman there in the bed—where she hadn't been—had implied a world complete in every detail of life.

Shock came, anyway. With frantic eyes, he stared down at the great main corridor of the building, along the silent, deserted reaches of which he had wandered for so many hours the day before.

Silent and deserted no longer. Men and women swarmed along it in a steady stream. It was like a city street, with people moving in both directions, all in a hurry, all bent on some private errand, all—

"Hello, Drake!" said a young man's voice behind him.

Curiously, Drake had no emotion left for that.

He turned slowly, like a tired man. The stranger who stood there regarding him was tall and well-proportioned. He had dark hair and a full, strong face. He wore a shapely one-piece suit, pleasingly form-fitting above the waist; the trouser part puffed out like breeches. He was smiling in a friendly, quizzical fashion. He said finally, coolly:

"So you'd like to know what it's all about. Don't worry, you will. But first try on this glove, and come with me. My name is Price, by the way."

Drake stared at the extended glove. "What—" he began blankly.

He stopped. His mind narrowed around the conviction that he was being rushed along too fast for understanding. This man waiting for him here at the door and—

Drake braced himself consciously. Take it easy, he thought sharply.

The overwhelming, important thing was that *they* were out in the open at last. But—this glove!

He accepted the thing, frowning. It was for his right hand; and it fitted perfectly. It was light in weight, flexible but it seemed unnaturally thick. The outer surface had a faint metallic sheen.

"Just grab his right shoulder with that glove from behind," Price was saying. "Press below the collarbone with the points of your fingers, press hard—I'll give you an illustration later. Any questions?"

"Any questions!" The explosion of sound hurt Drake's throat. He swallowed hard. Before he could speak, Price said:

"I'll tell you as we go along. Be careful on those stairs."

Drake caught his mind and body into a tight unit. He said roughly: "What's all this nonsense about grabbing somebody by the shoulder? Why—"

He stopped hopelessly. It was all wrong, the way this was going. He was like a blind man being given fragments of information about a world he couldn't see. There was no beginning, no coherence, nothing but these blurry half-facts.

He'd have to get back to fundamentals. He, Drake, was a man in search of his memory. Something had happened to him aboard a trailer, and everything else had followed as the night the day. Keep that in mind and—

"Damn you!" Drake said out of the anguish of his bewilderment. "Damn you, Price, I want to know what this is all about."

"Don't get excited." They were down the steps now, heading along the side corridor to the great main hallway. Price half turned as he spoke. "I know just how you feel, Drake, but you must see that your brain can't be overloaded in one sustained assault of information. Yesterday, you found this place deserted. Well, that wasn't exactly yesterday."

He shrugged. "You see how it is. That was today in the alternative world to this one. That is how this building will be forever if you don't do what we want. We had to show you that. And now, for Heaven's sake, don't ask me to explain the science and theory of time-probability."

"Look," said Drake desperately, "let's forget everything else, and concentrate on one fact. You want me to do something with this glove. What? Where? When? Why? I assure you I'm feeling quite reasonable. I—"

His voice faded. With a start, he grew aware that Price and he were in the main corridor, heading straight for the great doorway, which led to the steps and the misty nothingness beyond them.

The clammy feeling that came then brought a genuine chill to his whole body. Drake said sharply:

"Where are you going?"

"I'm taking you to Earth."

"Out that door?"

Drake stopped short. He wasn't sure just what he felt, but his voice sounded preternaturally sharp and tense in his ears.

He saw that Price had stopped. The man was looking at him steadily. Price said earnestly:

"There's nothing strange about any of this, really. The Palace of Immortality was built in an eddy of time, the only known Reverse, or Immortality, Drift in the Earth Time Stream. It has made the work of the Possessors possible, a good work as you know from your reading in Possessor Kingston Craig's office—"

His voice went on, explaining, persuading; but it was curiously hard for Drake to concentrate on his words. That mist bothered him. Go down those steps with anyone— Never!

It was the word, Possessors, that brought Drake's mind and body back into active operation. He had seen and heard the word so often that, for all these long minutes, he had forgotten that he knew nothing.

He heard himself asking the question, his voice shrill and demanding: "But who are the Possessors? What do they possess?"

The man looked at him, dark eyes thoughtful. "They possess," he said finally, "the most unique ability ever to distinguish men and women from their fellows. They can go through time at will.

"There are," Price went on, "about three thousand of them. They were all born over a period of five hundred years beginning in the twentieth century; the strangest thing of all is that every one of them originated in a single, small district of the United States, around the towns of Kissling, Inchney and particularly in an infinitesimal farming community called Piffer's Road."

"But that," Drake said through dry lips, "is where I was born." His eyes widened. "And that's where the trailer—"

Price seemed not to have heard. "Physically," he said, "the Possessors are also unique. Every one of them has the organs of his or her body the opposite to that of a normal human being. That is, the heart is on the right side and—"

"But I'm like that," Drake gasped. His mind was taking great leaps, pounding at the bony walls of his head, trying to get out. "That's why the draft board rejected me. They said they couldn't take the risk of my getting wounded, because the surgeon wouldn't know my case history. They—"

Behind Drake, footsteps clicked briskly. He turned automatically, and stared vaguely at the woman in a fluffy gorgeous dressing gown who was walking toward them.

She smiled as she saw him, the smile he had already seen in the bedroom. She said in her rich voice, as she came up:

"Poor fellow! He looks positively ill. Well, I did my best to make the shock easy for him. I gave him as much information as I could without letting on that I knew everything."

Price said: "Oh, he's all right." He turned to Drake. There was a faint smile on his face, as if he was appreciating the situation to the full. "Drake, I want you to meet your wife, formerly Selanie Johns, who will now tell you what happened to you when you climbed aboard her father's trailer at Piffer's Road. Go ahead, Selanie."

Drake stood there. He felt like a clod of wood, empty of emotion and of thought. It was only slowly that he grew aware of her voice telling the story of the trailer.

Standing there in the back room of the trailer, Drake wondered what might happen even now if he should be caught red-handed before he could act. He heard the man in the center room say:

"We'll head for the fourteenth century. They don't dare do much monkeying around in this millennium."

He chuckled grimly: "You'll notice that it was an old man they sent, and only one of them at that. Somebody had to go out and spend thirty or forty years growing old, because old men have so much less influence on an environment than young.

"But we'd better waste no time. Give me those transformer points, and go into the cab and start the atomic transformers."

It was the moment Drake had been waiting for. He stepped out softly, flexing his gloved right hand. He saw the man standing, facing in the direction of the door that led to the front room and the engine cab beyond it.

From the back, the man looked of stocky build, and about forty-five years of age. In his hands, clutched tight, he held two transparent cones that glowed with a dull light.

"All right," he called gruffly as Drake stepped up behind him. "We're moving—and hereafter, Selanie, don't be so frightened. The Possessors are through, damn them. I'm sure our sale of that stuff, and the removal of so much metal has interfered with the electronic balances that made their existence possible."

His voice shook. "When I think of the almighty sacrilege of that outfit, acting like God, daring to use their powers to change the natural course of existence instead of, as I suggested, making it a means of historical research and—"

His voice collapsed into a startled grunt, as Drake grabbed his shoulder, and pressed hard below the collarbone—

"—just a minute!" Drake's voice cut piercingly across the woman's story. "You talk as if I had a glove like this"—he raised his right hand with its faintly gleaming glove, that Price had given him—"and there's also a suggestion in your words that I know everything about the Possessors and the Palace of Immortality. You're perfectly aware that I knew nothing at that time.

"I had just come off a train, where a fountain pen had been brought to my attention by a salesman called Bill Kellie. I—"

He saw that the woman was looking at him gravely. She said: "I'm sure you will understand in a few minutes. Everything that we've done has been designed to lead up to this moment. Only a few hours of existence remains to this probability world—*this* one, where Mr. Price and you and I are standing; there is a strange balance of forces involved, and, paradoxical as it may seem, we are actually working against time."

Drake stared at her, startled by her tone, as she said urgently: "Let me go on, please—"

The stocky man stood utterly still, like a man who has been stunned by an intolerable blow. And then, as Drake let go his shoulder, he turned slowly, and his gaze fastened sickly, not on Drake's face, but on the glove he wore.

"A Destroyer glove!" he whispered; then more wildly: "But how? The repellors are on my special invention that prevents a trained Possessor coming near me!"

He looked for the first time at Drake's face. "How did you do it? I—"

"Father!" It was the girl's voice, clear and startled, from the engine cab. Her voice came nearer. "Father, we've stopped at about A.D. 1650. What's happened? I thought—"

She paused in the doorway like a startled bird, a tall, slim girl of around nineteen years—looking suddenly older, grayer, as she saw Drake.

"You . . . were on . . . the . . . train!" she said.

Her gaze fluttered to her father. She gasped: "Dad, he hasn't—"

The stocky man nodded hopelessly. "He's destroyed my power to go through time. Wherever we are in time and space, we're *there*. Not that that matters. The thing is—we've failed. The Possessors live on to do their work."

The girl said nothing; the two of them seemed totally to have forgotten Drake. The man caught her arm, said hoarsely:

"Don't you understand—we've failed."

Still she was silent. Her face had a bleached quality when she answered finally:

"Father, this is the hardest thing I've ever said, but—I'm glad. *They're* in the right; *you're* wrong. They're trying to do something about the terrible mistakes of Man and Nature. They've made a marvelous science of their great gift, and they use it like beneficent gods.

"It was easy enough for you to convince me when I was a child, but for years now my doubts have been gathering. I stayed with you through loyalty. I'm sorry, father."

She turned. There were tears in her eyes, as she opened the outer door, and jumped to the green ground below.

Drake stood for a moment, fascinated by the panorama of emotions on the man's face, first a quiver of self-pity, then a gathering over-all expression of obstinacy. A spoiled child couldn't have provided a more enlightening picture of frustrated egoism.

One long look Drake took; and then he, too, went to the door. There was the girl to make friends with, and an early western American world to explore and wonder at.

They were thrown into each other's company by the stubborn silence into which the older man retreated. They walked often along the green, uninhabited valley, Drake and the girl.

Once, a group of Indians on foot confronted the two of them far from the trailer; to Drake it was a question as to who was the more startled It was Selanie who had her atomic gun out first.

She fired at a stone. It puffed out of sight in a flare of brilliance; and no more Indians ever came that way.

In a way, it was an idyllic life; and love came as easily as the winds that blew mournfully across that lonely land. Came especially easily because he *knew*—and persisted against her early coldness.

After that, they talked more urgently of persuading a self-willed man to train one or the other, or both, of them, how to use their innate ability to travel in time. Drake knew that the man would give in eventually from sheer loneliness, but it took a year longer.

Drake's mind drew slowly back into the great domed palace, and consciousness came that the woman's voice had stopped. He stared at her, then at Price. He said finally, puzzled:

"Is that all? Your . . . father—" He looked at the woman, stumbling over the relationship. It was immensely difficult to connect this mature woman with—

He pressed on: "You mean, your father was opposed to the work done by the Possessors and— But how did he expect to eliminate them? I don't get it."

It was Price who answered: "Mr. Johns' plan was to divert the local activity that had helped to create the Possessors. We know that foods definitely played a vital part, but just what combination of foods and other habits was the root cause, we have never learned.

"Mr. Johns thought, by having people drink from his cups, use his other food devices and general articles, he would break the general pattern of existence away from what it would normally have followed.

"His gathering of metal was also planned. Metal has a very strong influence on the great Time Stream. Its sudden removal from one time to another can upset entire worlds of probability.

"As for us, we could not interfere, except as you saw. The world prior to the twenty-fifth century is one age where no work will ever be done by the Possessors. It must solve its own problems. Even you, one of the first to possess the gift of time travel, though you would never of yourself have learned the method, had to be allowed to move toward your destiny—almost naturally."

"Look," said Drake, "either I'm crazy or you are. I'm willing to accept everything—the existence of this Palace of Immortality, the fact that she's my wife in some future date, and that I've sort of dropped in on her before *I* married her, but *after* she married me.

"I'll accept all that, I say, but—you gave me this glove a little while ago, and you said you wanted me to do something with it, and a few minutes ago my . . . wife . . . said that this world was in hourly danger of being wiped out. Is there something else that you haven't told me about? And why that spell of amnesia?"

Price cut him off: "Your part in all this is really very simple. As a salesman of the Quik-Rite Co., you followed Selanie, who was then nineteen years old, to a trailer at Piffer's Road occupied by her father and herself.

"When you got there, she wasn't to be found, nor was anyone else, so you started back to the village to make inquiries. On the way, however, you were picked up by Possessor Drail McMahon and transported one week ahead in time, and all relevant memory was drained from you. You wakened in the hospital and—"

"Just a minute!" Drake protested. "My . . . wife . . . has just told me what else I did. I knew that before, of course. There was an eyewitness, a boy named Jimmy, who saw me go back to the trailer, and that I was on it when it disappeared."

"Let me tell this," Price said coolly. "From the hospital, you set out to find what had happened to you. You did find out, and then you were transported here by another Possessor, and here you are."

Drake looked at the man, then at the woman; she nodded, and the first flame was already burning in his mind as Price continued:

"In a few moments, I shall take you to Earth to the vicinity of the trailer of Peter Johns and his daughter. You will go aboard, conceal yourself in the back room and at the moment that Selanie has described to you, you will come out and grab her father by the shoulder with the glove.

"The glove produces energy that will subtly change the potential of his nerve force; it will not harm him—nor will we afterward. As a matter of fact, he will be used as a research agent by us—afterward."

Price finished simply: "You can see that this action requires free will, and that we had to do everything as we have, to make sure that you would make no mistake."

Drake said: "I can see a lot of things."

He felt himself completely calm except for the way his soul was expanding with the tremendousness of what was here. Slowly, he walked over to the woman, took her hand and gazed steadily into her eyes. He said:

"This is you—when?"

"Fifty years from now in your life."

"And where am I? Where is your husband?"

"You went to Earth, into the future. You had to be out of the way. The same body cannot be in the same space. And that reminds me; that is the one hold we have on you."

"How?"

"If instead of entering the trailer, you walked off down the road to resume your life, in one week you would reach the time where your earlier self was in the hospital. You would vanish, disintegrate."

Drake said: "I like your looks. I don't think I'm going to muff it."

Looking back, he could see her, as he walked down the steps into the thickening folds of mist. She was standing with her face pressed against the glass of the door.

The mists swallowed her.

His memory search was over. He was about to live the events he thought he had forgotten.

WARNER VAN LORNE

THE UPPER LEVEL
ROAD

WHEN he lectured, he lectured with pursed-up brow and concentrated purpose. Professor Gamaliel Eberhardt was not a man who understood levity. His main subject was geological history, but Farraday College being small, he found it necessary to carry such kindred subjects as prehistoric civilizations, history, and prehistoric architecture.

The college would gladly have widened his subject matter still more, but Professor Eberhardt's studies clung so tightly to certain lines of thought that it had been found impractical. So for five years his thoughts had not been drawn from his one source of pleasure and profit. Some said the professor's brand of concentrated bisection of the wonders of the past imbued his students with a touch of his own mild insanity.

And then, one day, in the midst of one of his most profound expositions of pre-Egyptian monuments, John Hayden laughed! A deathly hush fell over the room. Dr. Eberhardt laid down his pointer, wiped his glasses, and cleared his throat.

"Is there something unusually mirth-provoking in this room, Mr. Hayden? Or is the point I am making ludicrous to you?"

The professor was at his best. His cheeks were puffed out like a frog's sides. He seemed on the verge of apoplexy.

Perhaps it was fortunate that the five-minute bell rang just then. For the good doctor was staring hard at John Hayden, and Hayden, eyes shining, laughed again.

"Class dismissed."

There was a concerted rush for the door. The impossible had happened! It called for discussion, but not in the august presence of Professor Gamaliel Eberhardt!

The room was suddenly empty. Dr. Eberhardt still stared at John Hayden, and John stared back—still chuckling.

"Well?" The professor seemed surprised that John had not joined the exodus.

"Professor, I made a discovery."

"Just when you laughed? Had you been paying attention—"

"But I was paying attention," Hayden told him. "I was, as usual, pondering upon the very noticeable discrepancies in the states of advancement in the various civilizations—when suddenly it came to me. It was funny. You are wrong. I have been wrong. Every bit of teaching on these subjects is erroneous because we have all overlooked one vital point."

The professor reddened again until he seemed about ready to burst. This jackanapes, this upstart, this— Telling him that his life work was in error! For just an instant he forgot his perfect English under the stress of excitement.

"Und you're telling me dot my whole life iss devoted to errors!" He sat down suddenly, weakly, and placed a hand over his heart.

"No, Dr. Eberhardt. No! Your studies have led to the greatest discovery of the entire period of our written history. It's only that once you see, it makes everything seem ridiculous! I had to laugh at myself. When you see it, you too will laugh."

The professor relaxed slightly. He was staring at John Hayden with eyes that held a shadow of doubt, and something of wonder. He seemed about to speak, but John held up one hand and continued.

"It came to me like a vision—a folding back of the veil of blindness. Suddenly I saw! And the vision held both promise and threat. I saw an explanation for a thousand things which have puzzled the world. I saw that there is no reason for men to starve, or to lack work, or to worry about being unemployed; or even to work!

"I saw the true explanation for things which we struggle to explain—and it made me laugh. It is funny in a way because I haven't even tested the truth, and yet I know."

Something in the calm, confident face of his student made the professor lean forward. His brows drew together again, and he spoke slowly as if resigned to the tearing down of the foundation of fifty years' work.

"Why did you not speak?"

John looked into his eyes, and smiled again.

"It will be up to you and me to decide, Dr. Eberhardt, whether the discovery should ever be spoken. Perhaps it is best that we never mention it. That we must learn."

"We?" The professor's brows resembled a sandy beach crisscrossed by heavy traffic.

"I have a small car," John explained. "You have no more classes this afternoon. If you believe me sane, let's try to prove what I see. It may mean the most wonderful adventure that ever befell two men. Just you and I. I have the money to travel, and if we're right we'll spend the summer seeing things that are not supposed to exist. Don't ask me to explain. Let me show you."

Dr. Eberhardt rose and came forward to stand over John like a patriarch. He tipped the student's head back and gazed deep into his eyes.

"You are sane," he said slowly, "sane and logical. I will go."

The little roadster rolled along the dirt road which led to a crossroads village twelve miles from Farraday. John Hayden's eyes were staring ahead intently; his body was tense. The speedometer registered five miles from the start. The professor had caught something of his tense expectancy and sat like a statue beside him. Between them lay a loaded revolver. In the left pocket of the car rested another revolver and a box of cartridges. Stuffed in beside the gun were six red flares. Two flashlights lay on the little shelf behind them, with a supply of new batteries.

Six miles. It was nearing four o'clock in the afternoon. John grew more tense, as if he were guiding the car along the edge of a cliff where a slight turn of the wheel might cast them into eternity.

Twenty minutes passed. The speedometer registered twelve miles. The ruts in the road were close together as if nothing but wagon wheels had passed over the road in a long time.

A stone wall—the old-fashioned kind—followed the road on the left side. They came to an open gate, turned through it into a lane for a hundred yards, and stopped before the door of a huge stone castle which had all the signs of great age written upon it.

The stones were furrowed and porous from the rains of ages. The window ledges were deep but no sign of glass appeared in the frames. There was no sign of life about the place, yet it seemed almost habitable.

John Hayden's eyes were shining as he brought the car to a stop and turned to the professor.

"We made it," he said softly, and again: "We made it."

Dr. Eberhardt tore his attention from the pile of stone and turned to his student. His eyes, too, were shining with a strange luster.

"We traveled twelve miles. That is the distance to Temple Hills, yet we do not arrive. Why?" And yet the professor's voice seemed not so much puzzled as to want confirmation of his thoughts.

"That is right, professor. Now you know why I laughed. I came here once before, but only today, as you lectured, did I discover the reason why.

"We have been driving on the 'upper level' for the past five miles. This time we will investigate. The last time I thought I was lost and turned back."

And suddenly, like a beam of sun bursting through a tempest-laden sky, the professor was laughing. John Hayden had never heard him laugh before!

"Fifty years," he said, and shook his grizzled beard. "Fifty years and I learn what I thought I knew." He opened the car door and climbed out gingerly while John stuck both revolvers in his pockets and got out the other side. Then for a moment the two men—a savant of fifty-eight, and a boy of twenty—stood and laughed at each other across the hood of the little car which was making history look funny.

Neither trusted himself to draw conclusions in words. John awaited the confirming proof which the professor's knowledge would give, and the professor waited for John to lead the way. Yet perfect understanding existed between them. Both seemed to know that they would find what they were seeking.

After a moment John went back and got the flashlight. Then he joined the professor and side by side they stood gazing up at the pile of stone before them.

"Shall we go in?" John's voice trembled a little as he spoke, as if this final step were of such portent that he hesitated. And the professor laughed again.

"You discover, but hesitate to explore," he said, smiling. "I am led to the portal; I cannot go back until I know."

Side by side they walked across the rutted stone of the portico and through the doorway, stepping over the remnants of what had once been great planked doors. The wrought-iron hinges were still in place and the professor's beady eyes gazed at them for a moment in awed wonder. Then he bent to examine the planking where it had fallen.

They were inside. A great room stretched before them, fully a hundred feet long and forty wide, with great fireplaces set in the middle of each of the four walls; fireplaces big enough so twenty men could have stood together in each one!

John Hayden stood in the semigloom with eyes shining as he gained an impression of the greatness of the place, the long, massive stairway at the far end, the candelabra set in the walls, with space for two hundred candles to light the room.

The professor was on his knees examining the bits of carpet which still held together in spots on the floor. Soft exclamations came from his lips now and then.

After a bit he got to his feet and went to examine the candelabra. John watched while his trembling fingers removed one from its socket and turned the beam of his flashlight on it.

"About the year 1,000, John Hayden, if my studies have been of any use to us, this country was supposed to have been peopled solely by savages! It appears to me that it is a feudal castle equal to those which stand in Europe. But the preservation! Decay seems to be very slow."

John nodded, thoughtfully.

"I must keep an eye on the car," he said. "We'll need it, and though I don't think so, we might have company."

"Yes, yes, John, by all means." The professor spoke as he moved on to examine the remains of a great table which stood against the far wall. John stepped out into the late afternoon sunlight.

There was the faint whisper of a breeze as he reached the portico. He looked back once, to see the professor bent over the wreckage of the table with searching fingers, then went on out to the car. A vague uneasiness crept over him. Logic told him one thing, instinct another. Was it possible he was in an unpeopled country? The desolation said he was, and yet—

Something impelled him to walk around the castle. It wouldn't take but a few minutes. The odds were Dr. Eberhardt was too absorbed even to miss him, and he knew he'd feel better.

The long tangled grass at his feet was comforting as he strolled along the great wall. The sunlight was warm and the air balmy, just as it had been in Farraday for a week past. He turned the corner toward the side of the castle. It was, he guessed, two hundred feet long and a hundred deep. Turreted towers stood high in the air at the four corners. It was roughly oblong.

He turned again, and paced along the back. For a long distance he could see fields of tangled grass, like a prairie. An occasional tree broke the monotony, but the trees seemed gnarled and twisted, as if only the hardiest of them had managed to remain within sight of the castle, and these were twisted and bent by storm and wind.

John had decided that logic was right before he turned the third corner. And then, right at his feet he found a path, a well-worn trail leading off across the field, and ending at a break in the masonry of the wall, big enough to admit a man. He stooped and peered in by the beam of his flashlight. There was no sign of an invader, but the pathway showed where it entered and crossed a room filled with débris! John fingered the revolver in his pocket and hurried his steps around to the front.

He breathed a sigh of relief as he saw the roadster, and a quick examination proved it had not been touched. Then he entered the door, and the hair crawled on his scalp. Professor Eberhardt was not in the room!

Panic held him speechless for a moment, then he swallowed hard and called:

"Oh, doctor!" He listened intently but only echoes answered—echoes which called down the stairway, which called from the shadowy ceiling, and teased from the inside of the huge fireplaces. They seemed to leap back at him from every direction.

"Oh, doctor!" He called again at the top of his lungs, backing against the wall as he did so. A revolver was in one hand as he darted quick glances into every corner of the room.

The castle seemed as deserted now as it had been before they arrived. He had to explore. Probably the professor had simply gone into another room, but if so, why didn't he answer?

After a moment John regained some measure of self-control. He examined his revolver and his flashlight, then moved slowly across the room toward the great staircase. His eyes cast quick glances over his shoulder every instant. They darted into every corner, and seemed to cover all directions at once. Wherever a shadow loomed he turned the flashlight beam. But the room was as empty and deserted as it had apparently been for a thousand years.

The echo of his footsteps on the stone floor was like the beat of tomtoms. The trip to the stairs seemed endless. Yet he found himself slowly mounting them, and his fear was mingled with something of the majesty of discovery.

The twenty-four steps ended in a great upper hall, from which led doorways into other rooms. And midway of the upper hall, another hall bisected the huge building lengthwise.

John stood a moment, alert, listening, then called again at the top of his lungs: "Dr. Eberhardt!" And once again mocking echoes were his only answer.

Again he moved ahead, stopping at the first doorway on his left to throw his flashlight about a great room in which there stood a well-preserved bed and chests. The wonder of it overcame his fear somewhat and he moved ahead. Six spacious chambers along the hall contained no sign of having been disturbed in a thousand years. He toured the rooms off the long bisecting hallway to the right, with the same result. In the last room he found the doorway to the turret tower which stood over the corner where he had seen the strange pathway leading from the basement. With a heavy heart he mounted the winding steps.

For a long time he stood gazing out across the countryside, from between the raised stones which had been set for protection along the circular wall of the tower. Still no sign of life rewarded his search.

The rest of the upper castle was barren of life. He had heard no sound and at last retraced his steps down the great stairway to the main hall, and turned with heavy heart to search the lower rooms.

The sun was setting and John dared not attempt the return to Farraday after dark. The discovery was too new.

The main floor produced no slightest sign. The great basement was empty. John had reached the feeling of absolute zero when he turned to the next to the last room, the one which would adjoin that into which the beaten pathway led.

Here he stopped and an involuntary whistle escaped him. Three crude rustic chairs, a table, and a cupboard stood out as clearly modern! There was no dust! The room had been occupied—and recently! That awful feeling of panic seized him again. It was getting dark! The professor had disappeared!

John came out of the castle through the hole in the masonry and stared along that beaten path, then turned slowly and picked his way around the castle for a second time.

The car still stood unharmed before the portico. Impelled by some unknown reason, John put up the curtains and fastened them.

Slowly he started to complete his circuit of the castle. It was dusk and the wavering shadows played tricks on his eyes. His flashlight beam darted here and there impotently until he reached the pathway again—and suddenly he heard voices drifting down the wind!

John Hayden flattened himself against the side of the castle in the shadowy niche formed by the circle of the turret where it joined the straight wall, and waited silently, as the flesh crawled up and down his spine.

Presently along the path came a motley procession. Seven men, two women, and three children, the youngest a child in arms. And at the head of the procession was Professor Gamaliel Eberhardt!

The procession turned the corner and started toward the front. John tensed, as the good doctor came opposite to him, and pointed his revolver.

"Halt!" he said hoarsely. "One move and I'll open fire."

Then as the little parade froze into immobility he turned to the professor.

"If you are a prisoner, doctor, we'll settle this right now!"

But the professor raised his hand and shook his head.

"I'm not a prisoner, John. I was at first, but simply because they didn't understand. We are all friends. Put up your gun. There is much to be explained and it grows late."

"But I—I don't quite understand." John hesitated as his gun arm dropped slowly to his side.

"Let's go around front where we can sit comfortably on the portico," the professor suggested. "Then I will explain what they do not understand, and will point out to you a plan that has been formulating in my mind. This, John, is the population of New Temple Hills, a settlement by accident. You, perhaps, personify Columbus, but these people personify the Norsemen. Some of them have been here eleven years!"

Twelve people seated themselves uneasily on the edge of the stone portico which stood about two feet above the ground. John's startled eyes grasped the fact that most of them wore garments of a coarse homespun material somewhat similar to burlap. They seemed baffled, yet expectant. Something like hope gleamed in their darting eyes.

Dr. Eberhardt drew John aside a few steps, careful, however, to remain in full view of his audience.

"I'm not going to tell them everything, John. You and I haven't even had time to compare notes, but this thing looks so big I don't want to take them back. I see vast possibilities. This can be our headquarters. I want them to stay here and form the nucleus of our help at the castle. From here, if I understand correctly, we can undertake even to force peace on the world when the time comes. Will you let me speak for both of us for tonight?" The professor's eyes gazed anxiously into those of the student who had laughed in the midst of his lecture six hours before.

"Of course, professor! We can decide later what course is best to follow. Right now you are in command. I—your suggestion about world peace— if it—it's true—we could— It is overwhelming!"

Dr. Eberhardt cleared his throat as he took his place before the long row of hopeful, eager faces—exiles from a modern world. His cheeks were flushed and his eyes shone. He was in his element again, lecturing to an eager class.

"My friends," he began slowly in his best classroom manner, "you share with us a discovery which may lead to peace on earth. It is so great that the name of every one of us will be written in letters of gold on the scroll of history. We are all pioneers. To you will go more than your full share of credit. The hardships you have undergone have paved the way. They will be lightened from now on, but whether you can ever go back to your old world is a question."

There was a slight restlessness at this, but the professor held up his hand and continued:

"Some of you might not care to go back when I tell you that no one back where you came from would believe your story, and those of you who have children would be outcasts from society. All you could have there will be yours here. Clothes, entertainment, books; everything can come to you in greater measure than most of you could afford them in the world you left. And it is another world, my friends.

"How many of you, in years past, have read about the finding of buried cities by archæological expeditions?"

Every adult hand was raised in the air, though the look of bewilderment remained in the haunted eyes.

"Ah! That is good. Then listen: If in some places on earth the surface buried the ancient cities, can you not see how, in other places, the modern surface of the earth might be below them?"

One man leaped to his feet, an excited light in his eyes. He pounded one fist into the other and fairly danced.

"That's it! I knew it. We got lost in a strange distance!"

John and the professor exchanged glances.

"You are quite right," Dr. Eberhardt told him, "quite right. And you, sir, have been the carpenter here, haven't you? You planned and built the loom which weaves the cloth for your clothes. You're the man who tried out the various roots until you found edible ones to be grown in your gardens. And you discovered the wild potatoes and pruned them until they tasted like home."

The man had sat back on the step. At each question and statement he nodded soberly. He was a wiry little man, about five feet two, with keen, intelligent eyes.

"Back in Temple Hills you were known as the village drunkard, Sam Bailey. No one mourned overly long when you disappeared," the professor told him. "Sam, if you went back, you would go back to that. You have a mission here, and a new day is coming. You have made life for these people fairly comfortable. I will leave it to you. Shall we make a new world here or will you try to return to your old life?"

Sam Bailey got slowly to his feet. He walked around the little roadster, examining its bright, new enamel as best he could in the gathering darkness. Then he came back to face the professor.

"When could we start remaking life here?" he asked simply.

The professor looked at the dark sky, then at John Hayden.

"We dare not try to return tonight," John said. "In the darkness we might never get back. But tomorrow we can go and return with a truck. Tomorrow we can start."

Sam Bailey's face was solemn in the twilight.

"My new friends," he said slowly, "I am the leader at New Temple Hills. And I speak for us all. We will stay and work if it will serve a purpose. That is all we ask; that and some entertainment."

John Hayden deposited a reborn professor at his home in Farraday at ten a. m. Saturday morning, May 15, 1941. At four p. m. a five-ton truck loaded with mattresses, folding cots, tables, chairs, books, canned foods, magazines, and six acetylene stoves stopped to hook on a trailer containing shovels, hand tools, carpenter tools, seeds, a side of beef, and six smoked hams with many more things tucked in wherever there was the slightest bit of room! The professor made a dive for the driver's cab, chuckling as he dropped a bag on the seat between himself and John.

"We haven't so much time," John told him. "What's in the bag?"

"Six revolvers, two knocked-down rifles, and three hundred rounds of ammunition for each!" The professor laughed aloud for the second time in two days! "It occurred to me that there is a possibility of this dimensional condition being only occasional," he continued, "and I have provided against that contingency somewhat."

The truck rolled down the street and out the road toward Temple Hills. But it arrived at New Temple Hills without mishap and found six men waiting anxiously at the castle. One had remained at the little settlement to protect the women and children if need came, against the wild things which occasionally roamed the plains and ravished the all-important gardens.

The great main hall had been swept free of the débris with brush brooms, and wood had been piled in one of the huge fireplaces. Dr. Eberhardt magically produced candles and set one of the men to stocking the candelabra. He brought forth brooms and had the room given a final going over.

"Why," he asked Sam Bailey, "is your settlement so far from the castle?"

"Water." The reply was laconic.

"M-m-m. John, do you suppose we could get drilling machinery and have wells drilled, and plumbing installed?"

"Why, yes. In time. It would take weeks, of course. But first we need bedding and lumber. The truck is being loaded tonight."

Tears glistened in old Sam Bailey's eyes. He stood stock-still like a statue, while they rolled down his weather-beaten cheeks. Eleven years he had been an exile from his world, and now—it was too good to be true—his world was coming to him!

Darkness saw a roaring fire in the hearth, and the side of beef turning on an improvised spit. A great barbecue by candlelight, in the vast ancient hall which had once felt the footsteps of medieval warriors, before it had been cut adrift from progress by the warp of the earth's surface dimensions.

The chill May wind played tricks with the candle flames. Six folding tables stood side by side to make the banquet board. China dishes, such as the three children had never seen, held canned delicacies which their elders had not tasted in years!

It was a glorious evening for the residents of New Temple Hills, and thereafter, each year, in the "upper level" country, May 15th was to be celebrated as the day of the beginning of New Time. That night a dollar alarm clock ticked in each house of the settlement for the first time.

Six weeks later as an enormous clock on the center mantel chimed nine-thirty, John Hayden and the professor sat in comfortably upholstered chairs before the hearth where a cheery blaze killed the chill of evening in the great hall of Hayden Castle.

"I have money enough for a while," John was saying, "but of course it will take more than a fortune."

The professor turned toward him soberly. "I know that, John, and I have borne it in mind in my calculations. Remember the *Cyclops*, the United States naval auxiliary which sailed into the unknown about 1920? We may find that. It had a full crew aboard. There are certain treasures that we could easily locate. Cocos Island must have brought its treasure to the 'upper level,' for it has been blasted from end to end by treasure parties. That would finance us safely."

It was a different Gamaliel Eberhardt from the one who had dismissed his class six weeks before because a student had laughed. This man was keen, alive, and planning to interfere with the trend of time on the known world!

The castle had been completely modernized. Frames had been fitted into each of the ninety-six big windows. Bathrooms had been installed—six of them! Wells had been drilled; electric lights and refrigerators had been installed. The professor had one room off from the main hall equipped as a study, and his calculations had filled many reams of paper since the end of the college year. Farraday College was only twelve miles away by the road they traveled; but by another measure it was nine hundred years in the future!

John and the doctor each had a mammoth bedchamber. Both of these rooms also adjoined the main hall. On the other side of the huge room the doors opened into the renovated dining hall, kitchens and three comfortably fitted rooms for the help.

Two men and one woman were on constant duty at the castle. The other residents of New Temple Hills were busy planting their newly acquired seeds and tending their gardens. These had been greatly enlarged since the acquisition of tools, and the three mules which had been brought over from the twentieth-century level!

"I should like to attempt Atlantis." John broke the silence again after a long time. "We might miss—but I think it's waiting for us."

The professor frowned as he answered. "I have been working on warps for six weeks almost unceasingly, John. It is dangerous to try but I think we could find it, only—" His voice trailed off.

"Only what, doctor?"

"John Hayden, the world is on the verge of a disastrous war. I have proved to my own satisfaction that we can find an 'upper level' in very nearly this plane in the northern French provinces, the south German provinces, northern Italy, southern Austria, parts of the Balkans, and on the plains west of Moscow!

"You and I can put an end to any war that starts in those areas, John. Don't ask me too much, yet, but I know we can, provided we continue our studies for a few more weeks.

"On the other hand, to find Atlantis we must go at least two levels above this one. We might make it. It is less likely, but still possible, we might return.

"Would you be willing to wait, John, until we have stopped the first great war move in Europe? If you will—and it may mean a year's delay—I promise you that we will visit Atlantis."

John gazed long and thoughtfully into the flickering flames. Surrounded as he was in medieval comfort with modern trimmings, he was aware that beneath him, or in some inexplicable way, around him, was a twentieth century village called Temple Hills. No, their first hypothesis had been right. It was beneath! They were on the "upper level." And that explained why no ruins are found in great stretches of the modern earth's terrain. In some spots ruins are on the surface, in others beneath the surface—and in still others, above the surface.

The professor said northern France and southern Germany were above —on the "upper level"! That meant that at some point in each of those countries the ancient surface crossed the modern surface level like a subway going into the earth under a hill, then running into the air over a valley!

But to stop a great war? Dr. Eberhardt's calculations must have progressed beyond his wildest dreams. With a sigh he drew his gaze from the fire and looked toward the professor.

"I guess you win, if you think we have a chance, doctor. But meantime we need to locate a treasury. Have you studied the warp at Cocos Island?"

Gamaliel Eberhardt smiled slowly. "Do you remember where the *Cyclops* disappeared?" he asked.

"Wasn't it off the coast of southern California?" John asked.

The professor puffed on his brier pipe for fully five minutes before he answered. "And what relation does that bear to the location of Cocos Island?"

John jumped to his feet. "You've got it," he shouted. "It's true! Why, we might even find the crew of the *Cyclops* on the island!"

Sam Bailey's face appeared suddenly in the doorway leading to the dining hall.

"Did something happen, professor?" he asked anxiously.

"Yes," Gamaliel Eberhardt answered solemnly. "John Hayden just threw a fit. Come in, Sam, and sit down a minute. Have you ever considered the possibility of fortifying this castle? It seems to me that it has possibilities which would make it almost impregnable."

"Fortifying it?" Sam asked, puzzled. "Against whom? Oh, that reminds me— I had a dream when I first came here that I have always wondered about.

"I dreamed that I was asleep in here on the floor when I heard a terrible racket outside. I was scared almost to death, but got up enough courage to go to the door to see what it was. When I reached it there were a whole lot of men outside on the portico, but when they saw me with my pipe in my mouth, they turned and ran."

The next day panic dwelt in the breasts of the two warp explorers. John drove in to Farraday for supplies—and didn't arrive! He came tearing back to the castle at breakneck speed and rushed into the professor's study.

"I missed, doctor! I missed," he said breathlessly.

The two gazed at each other, each seeking hope. The thing they had dreaded most had happened.

"We might have known," the professor told him, "that if the road led back in the ordinary way, New Temple Hills would not exist. So far, we have been lucky. Now you must find the combination. Go back at once— and this time be careful. Remember every rut. Try until you make it."

John smiled, and breathed easier. After a moment he went out. But Professor Eberhardt did not return to his studies. Instead he paced the floor. "If he fails," the doctor muttered over and over again, "all our plans are in vain. If he fails, the discovery might better have not been made!"

John Hayden drove slowly along the road from the castle, very slowly. He kept one wheel in the rut of the roadway. So much depended on the key to the shift from one level to the other. It must not be chance. He must know the way.

One mile, two miles, at a snail's pace. No faster than a walk. Always before he had driven at least twenty miles an hour. But now—the memory of interminable fields where Farraday should have been, made him go slow. He felt smothered. He had crossed the line! And that meant he had been *under* Farraday, not over it!

Three miles. John's eyes ached with the attempt to remember every slightest landmark that would recall the spot of shift. Four miles. It seemed as though he were on a light down-grade. His eyes ached. There came a slight dizzy spell. It lasted a second only, but the car was creeping so he shut his eyes tight for an instant. The spell passed. And when he opened his eyes he was on the road to Farraday!

A truck rumbled past and continued on its way to Temple Hills. Many cars took this road every day—and reached their destinations. Why? John stopped the roadster and walked slowly back. A sudden vertigo seized him, and in two steps he was on the "upper level"!

With trembling hands he set a pile of rocks for a marker beside the road. He turned back, and again a dizzy spell for two short steps only; then, on the "lower level" he built another marker.

But why? Why at this spot? That he could answer. It was the point of contact. But why could he shift levels—and these other trucks go on? It wasn't all accident, for he had done it a dozen or more times deliberately. But why?

He went on to town, hooked on the trailer loaded with necessary supplies, then went back slowly. He stopped long enough to whitewash his marker. Twice he had to back up before the slight vertigo told him he was changing levels. Once on the "upper level" he stopped again to whitewash the marker on this side. But it was a thoughtful John Hayden who completed the trip to the castle and helped the men carry the new supplies into the basement.

As soon as this was accomplished he sought out Dr. Eberhardt.

"Doctor, we've got to work it out! What is the secret?" he asked, and that feeling of being lost crept back to him a bit. He knew now how these lost souls in New Temple Hills had felt when they arrived. They had retraced their steps many times, they had said, but never found their way back to the old road.

Dr. Eberhardt drew him into the main hall and pushed him down into one of the two big chairs before the hearth.

"We must think, John," he said. "We must recall every circumstance that we had in common with these others who are here. Every circumstance that is identical on each of our successful crossings. Then we must discover what it was you lacked this afternoon. What was it you lacked, twice, when you had to back up tonight? Something that you had the third time! If we search hard we will find it. If we do not find it the adventure is finished and we must lead our little tribe back as fast as possible!"

For ten minutes there was silence. Not a sound echoed in the huge medieval room except the ticking of a twentieth-century clock on the mantle, and the crackle of the small flame set way back in the recess of the old-fashioned fireplace.

"Those dizzy spells," John said at last, "must play some part."

The professor nodded, puffing studiously at his pipe.

"Yes," he mused, "but mainly I think that we have to overcome gravity at that point. If our minds are set objectively on the 'upper levels' at that point of contact, we come up. If at the moment our minds are on no place or thing connected with the true earth level, the bridge would lift us up to the 'upper level.' Sam Bailey was drunk, undoubtedly; his mind was a blank when he reached the force, and so he mounted. When he retraced his steps along the road, sober, his mind was on the road which was the warped level, binding him here. The two young couples were so intent on each other that they had no thought for their feet, or the road they walked; but once lost on the 'upper level' their minds concentrated on the road.

"The other men probably crossed by the same sort of accident. The first time you crossed you were—"

"Dreaming," John told him positively.

The professor nodded. "And to-day, when you failed, you were—"

"Speeding," John supplied, "and watching the road closely."

"Yes; just as the truck drivers do invariably on a dirt road; just as any careful driver does. That is why we have only a very small group on this side." The professor settled down more comfortably now that he felt they had solved the problem. "And to-night, John, you were watching for your marker which was on the 'lower level.' You were not thinking of the marker on the 'upper level.' That is why you had to back up twice. Then if I figure right, you got to thinking about the one on the 'upper level,' and—"

"Right," John said, shortly.

"Now," Dr. Eberhardt continued, "I believe that if you and I stood by your 'upper level' marker and concentrated our thoughts on the one on the true surface, a man who walked or drove toward us would cross into our warp, but I may be wrong."

Hayden looked up, excitement shining in his eyes.

"It looks to me, doctor, as if the castle would see us burning some midnight oil, proving it—but I think you're right. And I think that we should not for a long time to come, mention our discovery to the world."

The gray head nodded. "No; not for a long time! And to think I almost had apoplexy when you laughed in my classroom! You made a great discovery, John Hayden. It will shift the line of thought of the entire world before we're through with our calculations. It has made me very happy, and very contented. I feel that my life has not been wasted."

PAUL ERNST

THE 32nd OF MAY

I HAD spent the evening with Mr. and Mrs. Barton, old friends of mine, at their Long Island home. It was the thirty-first of May, their wedding anniversary. We had talked long over the dinner table, and longer yet in their living room before the fireplace.

It was a most comfortable, attractive-looking room. It was long and rather narrow, not quite square but with an odd angle to the inner wall which made the north end of the room about two feet wider than the south end.

Fine prints hung on the walls, with an antique Florentine mirror making a bright oblong at the south end of the room. Four or five feet in front of this mirror, set at an angle so that by looking into the Florentine glass one could see his reflection in the back, was a five-foot pier glass. The long mirror had been rolled in here while Mrs. Barton showed us—and refreshed in her own ecstatic memory—a fur-trimmed black summer wrap Tom Barton had given her for an anniversary present.

A pleasant evening with old friends! But when I looked at the clock I exclaimed aloud and stood up. The hands pointed to one minute of twelve.

"Is that clock right?" I asked. "It can't be midnight."

"The clock is right to the second," said Barton, who is one of the most exact and methodical of men. "Checked with the observatory. But the night's young yet—"

"Not for me it isn't," I interrupted. "Where did I leave my hat— Oh, it's over there beyond the pier glass."

I tapped my pipe out into the fireplace. The minute hand of the clock swung over the figure 12. The first stroke of the elaborate electric-gong arrangement which Barton had had built into the clock, sounded out.

I started toward the pier glass for my hat, which lay where I had carelessly flung it on a window seat.

The clock seemed to keep time to my steps as I walked. One, two, three, four—

I looked into the Florentine mirror as I approached the window seat. I saw my own back in the pier glass. And I noticed idly that as I moved forward, my reflection in the pier glass behind me seemed to step out of a frame and into—nothing!

Eight, nine, ten, struck the clock.

My feet fumbled with something just as my reflection had passed completely out of the frame of the pier glass save for the tip of my coat tail.

The eleventh note of the clock sounded. Then, on the dying waves of sound vibrations, the first sound waves of the twelfth note rang out.

I felt myself trip forward—

Since that evening I have spent a lot of time trying to figure out what happened. Indeed, I've thought of nothing else. But I can't even arrive at a theory concerning what occurred, and I doubt if any man can.

I passed between two mirrors, facing each other at an angle allowing both my face and my back to be seen by me. My reflection passed out of the pier glass, I tripped, and the beginning note of the twelfth stroke of midnight, all occurred at once. That is all I know.

Then I was on hands and knees, laughing a little at my clumsiness in tripping like that.

I started to say something to Tom Barton—and words and laughter froze on my lips.

There are some shocks too great for the human mind to assimilate at once. In war, for instance, it takes a man several seconds to realize, after the terrific physical impact, that half his abdomen has been shot away.

Similarly, the shock I experienced then was too vast to be appreciated for what seemed to me a full minute.

The first thing I consciously noted was that the light was changed.

In the Barton living room the light had had a pinkish cast, tinged by the flames in the fireplace. Now, suddenly, the light was pearl gray, rather dim, and steady as the light of dawn.

The next thing I noticed was that the window seat before me with my straw hat lying in its center, was no longer there. Nor was the window behind it, nor the house wall in which the window was set.

Instead of having my gaze stopped by these things, it went on and on to a horizon far, far in the distance; a horizon that almost lost itself before its thin line showed.

I blinked my eyes and looked again. The same vast distance, illuminated by the steady, pearl-gray light, remained.

The first terror stabbed my heart. I must be going mad—must have gone mad instantly, with reason snapping off as an electric switch is turned. I had been in Tom Barton's living room. Now, in the flicker of an eyelash, I was—

Where was I?

I looked down. At my feet lay the object I had apparently stumbled over, a hexagonal rod of about the thickness of my wrist. I touched it with the toe of my shoe, and it moved a little! I followed the line of it along the ground, and saw that it ended in a squatty mass, about thirty feet away, that was hexagonal in shape and stood perhaps four feet high. Like a small, hexagonal tank with a three-inch hexagonal feed line trailing the ground from it—

But the feed line was not trailing on the ground! This was not ground I was standing on! It was— I could only describe it by saying that it was *substance!*

It felt firm yet elastic under my feet. I sank in it a little, yet there was no feel of surface looseness to it. The sensation was like that of standing on a partially deflated rubber tire.

I looked around some more, dazed, too shocked to have more than a numb perception of my surroundings. On all sides were the hexagonal masses, from each of which, like incredible roots, trailed straight, hexagonal feed lines, or feelers. There was only one possible impression to be received. That was, that the bizarre, geometric masses were plants of some kind, and that the feelers, over which I had tripped, were roots.

Hexagonal plants! Hexagonal roots!

Hardly knowing what I was doing, I kicked at the rodlike root at my feet. A chunk of it flaked off, and I saw the parent mass quiver. But I only saw—I did not feel. It was impossible for the moment to feel any more than the initial shock of finding myself here—

It is words that bring shocks home to consciousness.

Finding myself here— But where was *here?*

I told myself again and again that I must still be in the Barton living room, that I was only suffering from optical illusion.

But it was useless to mumble that! It was meaningless gibberish in the face of the horror with which I stared around and took in the whole picture of my new setting.

I was a mite on a plain of cosmic vastness. A plain? It would be more accurate to call it a plane! For it was as flat as a sheet of steel, like a vast flat plate on which I stood like a bug on a dance floor, stunned, appalled at the sheer immensity of it.

Everywhere as far as the eye could reach were the hexagonal masses— plants? soft rocks? animate beings?—with their rodlike hexagonal feelers radiating from them in straight lines. And over all was shed the pearl-gray light, coming from everywhere and nowhere.

Where was I?

It was then, I think, that I shouted aloud in pure, blind terror—and discovered a second fact about this gray universe. There was no sound in it.

My lips opened with what would have been almost a woman's scream of horror; my lungs compressed as they drove air through my larynx—and not even a whisper of sound came from my distorted mouth!

A soundless, motionless world of gray, with geometric masses rooting in a plane made of some firm, rubbery stuff that was no more like the ground we know than air is like iron.

But I wasn't here! I was in Barton's living room! I was mad, or suffering from hallucinations—

I kicked the root at my feet and saw another flake slough off. And again I saw the parent, hexagonal mass quiver, thirty feet away.

There was no hallucination about this! *Where was I?*

And then the full shock came home at last, and I was a complete maniac with reason knocked entirely from its throne.

I dimly remember running over the resilient surface, among the hexagonal masses, screaming soundlessly in nightmare terror. I think I blundered into some of the masses, for I seem to remember the feel of them as spongy and rubbery and vaguely moist.

Then oblivion, either of actual unconsciousness or of complete nerve prostration, came over me and blackness replaced the cold, monotonous gray light.

I think it was a change in light impressions, beating through my closed eyelids and against the rods and cones of my eyes, that brought me back to consciousness—and to stark, brain-shattering fright.

For an instant I had the sensation of having seen a dim sun, like a big orange disk. And I glanced around me with the wild hope that is quick to rise in the mind even at impossible times.

I had had a curious, frightening dream for an instant. Now I was back in the Barton living room—

But around me was the pearl-gray immensity, and under me was the elastic firmness of the resilient ground so inexplicable to human understanding. The wild hope died instantly. I was still in this incomprehensible place, like a being exiled in a twinkling of an eye from his own planet. And a fear as far beyond words as was any real description of my surroundings, filled my soul.

And then I saw, consciously, the thing I had vaguely seen in semiconsciousness—an orange disk like a dim sun in the gray heavens.

But I saw now what I had not had clarity of mind enough to see before —that the thing was not a far-off sun, but a reddish-yellow disk, like a new penny twenty feet across, in the air less than forty feet from me.

As though feeling my gaze on it, the disk slowly turned its edge toward me. Thinner and thinner grew its ellipse. Then—it disappeared.

It disappeared, yet it was still there! I could feel that it was there, with its thin edge turned toward me, but with that edge imperceptible as would be the edge of a plate made of infinitely thin tissue paper.

And then I felt still more. I felt, abruptly, with sure instinct, a sense of impending peril!

I stumbled to my feet and backed away from the place where the disk had been. I backed till I bumped against one of the six-sided masses—and as I backed I saw in the air before me a thin orange line that bulged in the middle, and then a narrow ellipse.

The thing was still there. It had not actually disappeared; it had simply turned till its thin boundary line was presented to me. And when I moved back I had reached an angle where I could gaze across its surface and see it again.

In a word, the disk was two-dimensional instead of three!

I cowered back against the hexagonal growth that had stopped my retreat. As I crouched there, the thin ellipse became an orange disk again, as if the thing had to turn squarely toward me to observe me. And I had the distinct conviction that I was being observed, that watchful eyes were on me.

And now the disk began to incline toward me and become an ellipse that was horizontal instead of vertical. Thinner it grew, till it was no longer in sight—only in consciousness.

There was a stir of movement on the "ground" under the spot where the disk hung invisible. I saw something like a pencil line against the gray slate of the heavens. The pencil line seemed about seven feet long. It wavered in spots, growing thicker and disappearing alternately, like a row of flat paper disks on a string held upright and moving in a breeze.

But the line or thing or whatever it was, was moving toward me!

Some two-dimensional thing had gotten out of the two-dimensional disk, and was approaching me!

I moved, and instantly the wavering, approaching line was still, and disappeared. But the thing was still there, all right. I sensed that—and at the same time sensed that I was in more danger than I'd ever been in before.

I would have run, but I was unable to. I could only crouch against the spongy mass of the growth and glare ahead of me toward the spot where the wavering line had been. And as I stared, I saw the line slowly grow into being again. But now it was not wavering. And it was several minutes before I realized what had happened.

The thing that had come from the disk was not so close to me that I could see it, in spite of the fact that its edge was still toward me, because of the bifocal functioning of my eyes. With my right and left vision I could see a very little of its two-dimensional breadth again, so that again it had become a thin line to me. Which meant that it must be within a few feet of me!

For what seemed ages the line remained just that—a line. Then it thickened—more in some places than in others, as the creature turned, till at length I could see the full breadth of a thing that makes my blood run cold even as I tell of it.

It was fully seven feet tall. It was rather manlike in general outline, yet it did not even vaguely resemble a human being. It had no legs, but stood on what appeared to be a single, thick leg like an oblong pedestal on which was set the keystone-shaped torso. Atop the torso was a perfectly round disk in the center of which was set a single eye, which also was round. It had arms, of a sort—two long narrow oblongs hanging by its sides. There were no joints perceptible in the arms, but I saw them curl inward a little on each other, as the creature stood watching me, which indicated that there were no bones in the thing which would necessitate joints.

Oh, yes, it watched me!

Even as I stared at the nightmare curiosity, it stared back at me with its single eye, which was dark and humid-looking, and all pupil, like the eye of an intelligent bull terrier. But there was a difference. For I stared with fear and appalled curiosity, while it stared back with curiosity only. There seemed to be no fear in its examination of me—only a sort of warlike wariness.

Abruptly, I couldn't see it any more. At one instant it was before me, then it was not. I winked my eyes rapidly, but it did not reappear.

Then I caught movement out of the corner of my eye, and turned swiftly to the left. There the thing was scrutinizing me out of its cold, dull, single eye.

How did it move on that single leg, or pedestal? Above all, how did it move so swiftly? I don't know. First it was in front of me, then it was to my left. That's all I can say. No time seemed to have been taken in its movement, and it made no sound. But then, there was no sound anyhow in this ghastly gray place; or, if there was, it was of such a nature that my human ears could not pick it up.

I shivered. The expression in the dull, lidless single eye told me that the thing was all through with its looking, now, and was about to act. Furthermore, the expression told me that the action would be savage, for the dull eye shone suddenly with deadly ferocity.

It had no hands, as we know hands. But the ends of its arms seemed slightly more flexible than the rest of it, and I saw these arm ends coil behind its back and come out again with a short thin rod held in each.

The two rods seemed to be of solid metal, of what sort I do not know. They were square, about a foot long. Just two metal rods, which were pointed at me. But the way in which those rods were leveled, together with the deadly look in the thing's eye, made the sweat crawl out on my body.

The creature turned the rods slightly so that the square ends became diamond shapes as I stared, fascinated, at them. Then it slanted one, ever so slightly, toward the other, forming a queer, open-ended angle—

Again a soundless scream tore from my lips. For with that deliberate though meaningless—to me—move, I suddenly felt as though two great winds strove to tear me to bits. I swayed, there by the hexagonal growth, as though I stood in the center of a whirlwind—while the thing watched me with callous interest out of its inhuman eye.

And then I was released from the mystifying, deadly pressure, and the creature was gone.

I don't know how I knew that it was really gone, instead of just turned edge on me so that it was visible but near. I don't know how I knew that I had barely escaped a death incomprehensible to my human mind. But I did know. I think the only guess that can be made as to how I knew, is that there in that place where man's mind and man's reasoning power were as useless as machine guns in a world of ghosts, the animal instinct buried deep in me as in every human being began to function with desperate over-sensitiveness in the age-old effort at preservation of life.

Anyway, I was sure that for the moment my life was spared, though why I could not guess. And I began frantically to try to scheme how to get back to the place from which I had so strangely slipped—the Barton living room.

But for a moment, as I thought of that friendly haven in a world peopled with friendly, understandable three-dimensional beings, my mind almost cracked.

Where or what this place was, I couldn't imagine. How I had tripped over something in Barton's living room—and picked myself up off hands and knees in this unholy place—I couldn't dream. And for the moment I didn't care. I could only think of one thing: *Suppose I was doomed to stay here for the rest of my life?*

I moaned and babbled there by the spongy, gruesome plant—with not one sound coming from my lips to disturb the dead noiselessness of this gray world. But then I got a grip on myself and began to think constructively.

I had tripped over something in the Barton room, and fallen into this place, as a man trips over the threshold of a door and stumbles into an unknown room beyond. In this world, or room, the thing I'd tripped on was one of the rodlike roots of a plant. What the corresponding thing was in Barton's living room, I couldn't guess, and, again didn't care.

My task was to find that root! If I could find it, it was at least conceivable that I might back across it and once more find myself in my own homely world. If the move didn't take me there—

Well, if I found the root, and couldn't step back across it into human, mortal life again, I knew I should either go mad or kill myself. But I closed my mind to that possibility. Enough, for the moment, to find the root.

But at this point I looked around and was appalled.

In all directions, as far as the eye could see, the hexagonal growths dotted the vast plane in interlacing geometric patterns that made me dizzy when I tried to untangle them. And each growth looked just like all the other growths, with no distinguishing mark to attract the eye.

I climbed to the top of the four-foot mass nearest me and, sinking to my ankles in the repulsive resilient substance of it, peered around again. The only result was that I could see more of the identical, six-sided protuberances.

Desperately I tried to remember which way I had run when I lost my head and fled in blind madness. But I couldn't. And I believe that moment would have been my last if I had not chanced to see, by accident, a flaw in the side of a plant a few yards to my right.

I ran toward the plant. And as I neared it, my hopes grew.

There was a ragged chunk out of the side of the thing—and in no other that I could see was there a blemish of any kind to mar the geometric perfection.

Had I passed that way? Had I knocked a flake out of the side of it by blundering against it? I sent up a silent prayer that that had been the case.

I reached the marred plant, and fell, gasping and shuddering against it. Then, with my eyes aching with the intensity of my search in the gray light, I walked around the plant examining the stiff, straight, six-sided feelers raying out from it.

A root that had two chunks out of it! A root marked by the toe of my shoe!

Four roots went out from each of these strange masses. Three of the roots I looked at on this plant were perfect, unmarred. I clenched my hands till the nails bit into the palms. The fourth—

But suddenly I stiffened. In the air before me had appeared another orange object. Rapidly it grew till it hung motionless within thirty feet of me. But this was not the thing I had seen before. That had been a disk. This was a triangle.

Dimly glowing, brilliant orange, the thing hung in the gray atmosphere. And again I had the hair-crawling sensation of being observed. Also, I had the distinct conviction, in a swift moment to be confirmed, that the appearance of this orange, isosceles triangle was the reason for the disappearance of the orange circle. The thing in the circle had retreated before the advance of the triangle and whatever it contained.

The triangle did not vanish from my sight as the circle had. It remained suspended before me, and became an orange background for the thing that came from it. A thing much like the other monstrosity that had come from the circle.

The creature from the triangle moved toward me. One small portion of my brain occupied itself with trying to figure out how the thing moved, for the pedestal it had for legs remained motionless. It simply seemed to float toward me from the triangle from which it had somehow detached itself. But most of my mind was in a frantic chaos of returning horror. For again the sense of being in terrible danger had returned to me.

Ten feet from me, the monstrosity from the orange triangle stopped. I had just time to see that its single eye was purplish blue in color, whereas the eye of the other thing had been dark brown, when its "hands" jerked toward me with a short square rod in each.

The rods formed at once into the queer, open-ended angle that the first creature had pointed at me. And at once I leaped to the right. For I had learned already that the angles these fantastic creatures formed with the rods were somehow able to produce deadly results.

I leaped to the right, but I did not move fast enough.

I felt the invisible winds, or currents of mystic power formed in some way by the angle of the two rods, tear at my left side.

And I looked down at myself to see that my left shoulder hung two inches lower than it should, and that my left arm was so dislocated as to be twisted almost out of its socket.

Again, the shock was so great that it beat the pain that must come soon. I could only stare stupidly at my arm and dodge again as the thing with the single deadly eye shifted its rods.

Once more, however, I was spared by a swift disappearance.

The creature from the triangle suddenly vanished, leaving me to stare at my hideously dislocated arm and reel with the pain of it.

Then I saw the reason for the second disappearance. The orange disk had come back. It hovered in the air near the suspended triangle and suddenly darted at it.

Circle hit triangle. There was no sound, but I got a sense of terrible shock as the two figures rebounded. A sense of shock, and of terrific, warring powers.

The two figures again rushed together. Again there was no sound. But this time I was flung to my knees as if by an earthquake, though the things were fifty feet from me. And I saw that the second impact had settled the struggle.

Two thirds of the triangle slowly vanished, paling more and more till it so blended with the pearl-gray light that it could no longer be seen. The remaining fragment fell slowly to the ground, turning over and over in its fall like a bit of thin paper.

As it hit the surface I screamed again into the noiseless air and fell to my hands and knees and scrambled for the root with the two chunks out. For with the fall of the triangle fragment the disk had turned toward me and—before a man could have snapped his fingers—the first monstrosity stood in front of me again, glaring at me out of its dull, deadly eye and raising the little square rods in my direction.

I found the root with the marks left by my random kicks. I scrambled to about the position into which I had fallen from Barton's living room. For I was going to back across the root. Perhaps I need not have done that. Perhaps I could have simply stepped across the root and returned upright and face foremost to my own world. I don't know. The only thought I knew then was that I must duplicate in reverse every movement I had made in the terrible transition from my own sphere to this.

The two-dimensional creature formed his angle with the rods. I backed against the root, with my toes across it as I had first fallen.

I felt the great wind begin to tear at me.

With my single arm, in a paroxysm of fright, I raised my body to a position where I could stand upright on the other side of the root—

The air was tinged with a warm, pinkish light. Before me was the wall of a house, with a window in it on the seat of which was a carelessly flung straw hat. The musical vibrations of a clock bell were pulsing in the air—the

Barton clock, over the fireplace, sounding the last note of midnight.

I stood for a moment with my back to the fireplace, shuddering, my clothes clammy with perspiration.

I heard Tom Barton say: "We'll have to do something about that rug. It's always rolling up and tripping people."

And I heard Ruth Barton laugh and remark: "How funny! You know, just for a fraction of a second after you tripped, I couldn't see you! I guess that means another trip to the oculist."

Then I turned around, and both of them stared at me with open mouths.

"What in the world!" exclaimed Ruth at last. "Why, you're as white as a sheet— Tom! Hurry! Phone the doctor! He has dislocated his shoulder horribly!"

I made my way weakly to the nearest chair, and sank down in it. But as I went—I turned the tall pier glass from the damnable angle it formed with the Florentine mirror on the end wall!

This is the first time I have told this story. And as I say, I can offer no explanations.

I passed between the pier glass and the Florentine mirror in the Bartons' oddly angled living room. I fell—into another world, or plane, or dimension, or whatever you wish to call it, where unimaginable creatures seemed to fight each other with intricate angles formed with metal rods. It would seem that there are powers in untried combinations of angles undreamed of by man—and that perhaps geometry is a bridge between worlds. And it would seem that by chance the pier glass formed an angle with the mirror on the wall that transported me instantly from one plane to another. But your guess is as good as mine.

Even the tangible fact that I came back from the hideous gray plane with a terribly dislocated shoulder offers nothing to tie to. I might have dislocated it in my fall—though I know in my heart that that is highly improbable.

In only one thing have I any certainty of mind. That is, in the time element.

I passed between the grim angle of the mirrors and tripped into another sphere with the sound vibrations of the last note of midnight ringing in my ears. I straightened back over the root—and into the Barton living room— with the vibrations still ringing in my ears! Apparently no time whatever had elapsed, though I had wandered in the gray plane for many minutes.

But some time, as we know time, must have elapsed. And since that time lay neither in the thirty-first of May, nor in the first of June, there is no possible way of expressing it other than to say that my adventure occurred during May the thirty-second!

NELSON BOND

THE MONSTER
FROM NOWHERE

ONE nice thing about the Press Club is that you can get into almost any kind of wrangle you want. This night we were talking about things unusual. Jamieson of the *Dispatch* mentioned some crackpot he had heard of who thought he could walk through glass. "Snipe" Andrews of the *Morning Call* had a wild yarn about the black soul of Rhoderick Dhu, who, Nova Scotians claim, still walks the moors near Antigonish. The guy named Joe brought up the subject of Ambrose Bierce's invisible beast.

You remember the story? About the diarist who was haunted, and pursued, by a gigantic thing which couldn't be seen? And who was finally devoured by it?

Well, we chewed the fat about that one for a while and Jamieson said the whole thing was fantastic; that total invisibility was impossible. The guy named Joe said Bierce was right; that several things *could* cause invisibility. A complete absence of light, for one thing, he said. Or curvature of light waves. Or coloration in a wavelength which was beyond that of the human eye's visual scope.

Snipe Andrews said, "Nuts!" Winky Peters, who was getting a little tight, hiccoughed something to the effect that "There are more things under Heav'n and Earth than are dreamed of in your Philosophy—" and then got in a hell of a fuss with the bartender who said his name *wasn't* Horatio.

I said nothing, because I didn't know. Maybe that is the reason why this stranger, a few minutes later, moved over beside me and opened a conversation.

"You're Harvey, aren't you?" he asked.

"That's me," I agreed. "Len Harvey—chief errand boy and dirt scratcher-upper for the *Star Telegram*. You've got me, though, pal. Who are you?"

He smiled and said, "Let's go over in that corner, shall we, Harvey? It's quieter over there."

That made it sound like a touch, but I liked something about this guy. Maybe it was his face. I like tough faces; the real McCoy, tanned by Old Sol instead of sunlamp rays. Maybe it was the straightness of his back; maybe the set of his shoulders. Or it could have been just the way he spoke. I don't know.

Anyway, I said, "Sure!" and we moved to the corner table. He ordered, and I ordered, and we just sat there for a moment, staring at each other. Finally he said,

"Harvey, your memory isn't so good. We've met before."

"I meet 'em all," I told him. "Sometimes they are driving Black Marias, and sometimes they're in 'em. Mostly, they're lying in the Morgue, with a pretty white card tied to their big toe. Or, maybe—Hey!" I said, "You're not Ki Patterson, who used to write for the Cincinnati *News*?"

He grinned then.

"No, but you're close. I'm Ki Patterson's brother, Burch."

"Burch Patterson!" I gasped. "But, hell—you're not going to get away with this!" I climbed to my feet and started to shout at the fellows. "Hey, gang—"

"Don't, Len!" Patterson's voice was unexpectedly sharp. There was a note of anxiety in it, too. He grabbed my arm and pulled me back into my seat. "I have very good reasons for not wanting anyone to know I'm back —yet."

I said, "But, hell, Burch, you can't treat a bunch of newspaper men like this. These guys are your friends."

Now that he had told me who he was, I could recognize him. But the last time I had seen him—the only time I had ever met him, in fact—he had been dressed in khaki shirt and corduroy breeches; had worn an aviator's helmet. No wonder I hadn't known him in civvies.

I remembered that night, two years ago, when he and his expedition had taken off from Roosevelt Field for their exploration trip to the Maratan Plateau in upper Peru. The primary purpose of the trip had been scientific research. The Maratan Plateau, as you undoubtedly know, is one of the many South American spots as yet unexplored. It was Burch Patterson's plan to study the region, incidentally paying expenses *à la* Frank Buck, by "bringing back alive" whatever rare beasts city zoos would shell out for.

For a few weeks, the expedition had maintained its contact with the civilized world. Then, suddenly—that was all! A month . . . two months . . . passed. No word or sign from the explorers. The United States government sent notes to the Peruvian solons. Peru replied in smooth, diplomatic terms that hinted Uncle Sam would a damn sight better keep his nutsack adventurers in his own backyard. A publicity-seeking aviatrix ballyhooed funds for a "relief flight"—but was forbidden the attempt when it was discovered she had already promised three different companies to endorse their gasoline.

The plight of the lost expedition was a nine-days' wonder. Then undeclared wars grabbed page one. And the National Air Registry scratched a thin blue line through the number of pilot Burchard Patterson, and wrote after his name, "Lost."

But now, here before me in the flesh, not lost at all, but very much alive, was Burch Patterson.

I had so many questions to ask him that I began babbling like a greenhorn leg-man on his first job.

"When did you get back?" I fired at him. "Where's your crew? What happened? Did you reach the Plateau? And does anyone know you're—"

He said, "Easy, Len. All in good time. I haven't told anyone I'm back yet for a very good reason. Very good! As for my men—" He stared at me somberly. "They're dead, Len. All of them. Toland . . . Fletcher . . . Gainelle . . ."

I was quiet for a moment. The way he repeated the names was like the tolling of a church-bell. Then I began thinking what a wow of a story this was. I could almost see my name by-lining the yarn. I wanted to know the rest so bad I could taste it. I said,

"I'm sorry, Burch. Terribly sorry. But, tell me, what made you come here tonight? And why all the secrecy?"

"I came here tonight," he said, "searching for someone I could trust. I hoped no one would remember my face—for it *is* changed, you know. I have something, Len. Something so great, so stupendous, that I hardly know how to present it to the world. Or even—if I should.

"I liked the way you kept out of that crazy argument a few minutes ago—" He motioned to the bar, where a new wrangle was now in progress. "—because you obviously had an open mind on the subject. I think you are the man whose help and advice I need."

I said, "Well, that's sure nice of you, Patterson. But I think you're overrating me. I kept my yap shut just because I'm kind of dumb about scientific things. Ask me how many words to a column inch, or how many gangsters got knocked off in the last racket war, but—"

"You're the man I'm looking for. I don't want a man with a scientific mind. I need a man with good, sound common-sense." He looked at his wrist watch. "Len—will you come out to my home with me?"

"When?"

"Now."

I said, "Jeepers, Burch—I've got to get up at seven tomorrow. I really shouldn't—"

He leaned over the table; stared at me intently.

"Don't stall, Len. This is important. Will you?"

I told you I was snoopy. I stood up.

"My hat's in the cloak-room," I said. "Let's go!"

Patterson's estate was in North Jersey. A rambling sort of place, some miles off the highway. It was easy to see how he could return to it, open it up, and still not let anyone know he had returned. As we drove, he cleared up a few foggy points for me.

"I didn't return to the States on a regular liner. I had reasons for not doing so—which you will understand in a short time.

"I chartered a freighter, a junky little job, from an obscure Peruvian port. Pledged the captain to secrecy. He landed me and my—my cargo—" He stumbled on the word for a moment. "—at a spot which I'm not at liberty to reveal. Then I came out here and opened up the house.

"That was just two days ago. I wired my brother, Ki, to come immediately. But he—"

"He's working in L. A.," I said.

"Yes. The soonest he could get here would be tonight. He may be at the house when we arrive. I hope so. I'd like to have two witnesses of that which I am going to show you."

He frowned. "Maybe I'm making a mistake, Len. It is the damnedest thing you ever heard of. Maybe I ought to call in some professor, too. But— I don't know. It's so utterly beyond credibility, I'd like you and Ki to advise me, first."

I said, "Well, what the hell is it, Burch?" Then I suddenly remembered a motion picture I'd seen some years ago; a thing based on a story by H. G. Wells. "It's not a—a monster, is it?" I asked. "Some beast left over from prehistoric ages?"

"No; not exactly. At least, I can assure you of *this*—it is not a fossil, either living or dead. It's a thing entirely beyond man's wildest imaginings."

I leaned back and groaned. "I feel like a darned kid," I told him, "on Christmas Eve. Step on it, guy!"

There were lights in the house when we got there. As Burch Patterson had hoped, Ki had arrived from California. He heard us pull up the gravel lane, and came to the door. There was a reunion scene; one of those back-clapping, how-are-you-old-fellow things. Then we went in.

"I found your note," Ki said, "and knew you'd be right back. I needn't tell you I'm tickled to death you're safe, Burch. But—why all the secrecy?"

"That's what *I* asked him," I said. "But he's not giving out."

"It's something," Ki accused, "about the old work shop behind the house. I know that. I was snooping around back there, and—"

Burch Patterson's face whitened. He clutched his brother's arm swiftly. "You didn't go inside?"

"No. I couldn't. The place was locked. Say—" Ki stared at his brother curiously. "Are you feeling okay, guy? Are you sure you're not—"

"You must be careful," said Burch Patterson. "You must be very, very careful when you approach that shed. I am going to take you out there now. But you must stand exactly where I tell you to, and not make any sudden moves."

He strode to a library table; took out three automatics. One he tucked into his own pocket. The others he handed to us. "I'm not sure," he said, "that these would be any good if—if anything happened. But it is the only protection we have. You *might* be lucky enough to hit a vulnerable spot."

"A vulnerable spot!" I said. "Then it *is* a beast?"

"Come," he said. "I shall show you."

He led the way to the work shop. It lay some yards behind and beyond the house; a big, lonesome sort of place, not quite as large as a barn, but plenty big. My first idea was that at some time it must have been used as a barn, for as we approached it, I could catch that animal odor you associate with barns, stables, zoos.

Only more so. It was a nasty, fetid, particularly offensive odor. You know how animals smell worse when they get excited. Or when they've been exercising a lot? Well, the place smelled like that.

I was nervous, and when I get nervous I invariably try to act funny. I said, "If they're horses, you ought to curry them more often."

I saw a faint blur in the black before me. It was Ki's face, turning to peer back. He said, "Not horses, Len. We've never kept horses on this estate."

Then we were at the door of the shed, and Burch was fumbling with a lock. I heard metal click; then the door creaking open. Patterson fumbled for a switch. The sudden blaze of light made me blink.

"In here," said Burch. And, warningly, "Stay close behind me!"

We crowded in. First Burch, then Ki, then me. And as Ki got through the door, I felt his body stiffen; heard him gasp hoarsely. I peered over his shoulder—

Then I, too, gasped!

The thing I saw was incredible. There were two uprights of steel, each about four inches in diameter, deeply imbedded in a solid steel plate which was secured to a massive concrete block. Each of these uprights was "eyed" —and through the eyes ran a third steel rod which had been hammered down so that the horizontal bar was held firmly in place by the two uprights.

And on this horizontal rod was—a *thing!*

That is all I can call it. It had substance, but it had no form. Or, to be more accurate, it had every form of which you can conceive. For, like a huge, black amoeba, or like a writhing chunk of amorphous matter, it *changed!*

Where the steel rod pierced this blob of *thing* was a clotted, brownish excrescence. This, I think, accounted for some of the animal odor. But not all of it. The whole shop was permeated with the musty scent.

The *thing* changed! As I watched, there seemed to be, at one time, a globular piece of matter twisting on the rod. An instant later, the globe had turned into a triangle—then into something remotely resembling a cube. It was constantly in motion; constantly in flux. But here is the curious part. It did not change shape slowly, as an amoeba, so that you could watch the sphere turn into an oblong; the oblong writhed into a formless blob of flesh. It made these changes instantaneously!

Ki Patterson cried, "Good God, Burch! What unholy thing is this?" and took a step forward, past his brother's shoulder.

Burch shouted, "Back!" and yanked at Ki's arm. He moved just in time. For as Ki quitted the spot to which he had advanced, there appeared *in the air* right over that spot, another mass of the same black stuff that was captured on the bar. A blob of shapeless, stinking matter that gaped like some huge mouth; then closed convulsively just where Ki had stood a moment before!

And now the fragment on the rod was really moving! It changed shape so rapidly; twisted and wriggled with such determination, that there was no doubt whatsoever about the sentiency governing it. And other similar blobs suddenly sprang into sight! A black pyramid struck the far wall of the shed, and trembling woodwork told that here was solid matter. An ebon sphere rose from nowhere to roll across the floor, stopping just short of us. Most weirdly of all, a shaft of black jolted down *through* the floor— and failed to break the flooring!

That's about all I remember of that visit. For Ki suddenly loosed a terrified yelp; turned and scrambled past me to the door. I take no medals for courage. He was four steps ahead of me at the portal, but I beat him to the house by a cool ten yards. Burch was the only calm one. He took time to lock the work-shed door; then followed us.

But don't let anyone tell you *he* was exactly calm, either. His face wasn't white, like Ki's. Nor did his hand shake on the whisky-and-splash glass, like mine. But there was real fear in his eyes. I mean, *real* fear!

The whisky was a big help. It brought my voice back. "Well, Burch," I said, "we've seen it. Now, what in hell did we see?"

"You have seen," said Burch Patterson soberly, "the thing that killed Toland, and Fletcher, and Gainelle."

"We found it," said Burch, "on the Maratan Plateau. For we did get there, you know. Yes. Even though our radio went bad on us, just after we left Quiché, and we lost contact with the world. For a while, we considered going into Lima for repairs, but Fletcher thought he could fix it up once we were on solid ground, so we let it ride.

"We found a good, natural landing field on the Plateau, and began our investigations." He brooded silently for a minute. Then, reluctantly, "The Maratan is even richer in paleontological data than men have dared hope. But Man must never try to go there again. Not until his knowledge is greater than it is today."

Ki said, "Why? That *thing* outside?"

"Yes. It is the Gateway for that—and others like it.

"Some day I will tell you all about the marvels we saw on the Plateau. But now my story concerns only one; the one you have seen.

"Fletcher saw it first. We had left Gainelle tending camp, and were making a field survey, when we saw a bare patch in the jungle which surrounded our landing field. Fletcher trained his glasses on the spot, and before he even had time to adjust them properly he was crying, 'There's something funny over there! Take a look!'

"We all looked then. And we saw—what you saw a few minutes ago. Huge, amorphous blobs of jet black, which seemed to be of the earth, yet not quite of it. Sometimes these ever-changing fragments were suspended in air, with no visible support. At other times they seemed to rest naturally enough on solid ground. But ever and ever again—they changed!

"Afire with curiosity, we went to the open spot. It was a mistake."

"A mistake?" I said.

"Yes. Fletcher lost his life—killed by his own curiosity. I need not tell you how he died. It was, you must believe me, horrible. Out of nowhere, one of the jet blobs appeared before him . . . then around him . . . then— he was gone!"

"Gone!" exclaimed Ki. "You mean—dead?"

"I mean gone! One second he was there. The next, both he and the *thing* which had snatched him had disappeared into thin air.

"Toland and I fled, panic-stricken, back to camp. We told Gainelle what we had seen. Gainelle, a crack shot and a gallant sportsman, was incredulous; perhaps even dubious. At his insistence, we armed and returned to the tiny glade.

"This time, it was as if the *thing* expected us—for it did not await our attack. It attacked us. We had barely entered its domain when suddenly, all about us, were clots of this ever-changing black. I remembered hearing Toland scream; high and thin, like a woman. I dimly recall hearing the booming cough of Gainelle's express rifle, and of firing myself.

"I remember thinking, subconsciously, that Gainelle was a crack shot. That he never missed anything he aimed at. But it didn't seem to matter. If you hit one of those fleshy blobs, it bled a trifle—maybe. More likely than not, it changed shape. Or disappeared entirely.

"It was a rout. We left Toland behind us, dead, on the plain. A black, triangular *thing* had slashed Gainelle from breast to groin. I managed to drag him half way out of the glade before he died in my arms. Then I was alone.

"I am not a good pilot, under the best conditions. Now I was frantic; crazed with fear. Somehow I managed to reach the plane. But in attempting to take off, I cracked up. I must bear a charmed life. I was not injured, myself, but the plane was ruined. My expedition. hardly started, was already at an end."

I was beginning to understand, now, why Burch Patterson had not wanted the world to know of his return. A tale as wild and fantastic as this would lead him to but one spot—the psychopathic ward. Had I not seen the *thing* there in the shed, I would never have believed him myself. But as it was—

"And then?" I asked.

"I think there is a form of insanity," said Burch, "which is braver than bravery. I think that insanity came upon me then. All I could comprehend was that some *thing*—a *thing* that changed its shape—had killed my companions.

"I determined to capture that *thing*—or die in the attempt. But first I had to sit down and figure out what it *was!*"

Ki licked his lips. "And—and did you figure it out, Burch?"

"I think so. But the result of my reasoning is as fantastic as the *thing* itself. That is why I want the help and advice of you two. I will tell you what I think. Then you must say what it is best to do."

I poured another drink all around. It wasn't my house, or my liquor, but nobody seemed to mind. Ki and I waited for Burch to begin. Burch had picked up, and was now handling with a curiously abstract air, a clean, white sheet of notepaper. As he began, he waved this before us.

"Can you conceive," he said, "of a world of only two dimensions? A world which scientists might call 'Flatland'? A world constructed like this piece of paper—on which might live creatures who could not even visualize a third dimension of depth?"

"Sure," said Ki. I wasn't so sure, myself, but I said nothing.

"Very well. Look—" Burch busied himself with a pencil for an instant. "I draw on this sheet of paper, a tiny man. He is a Flatlander. He can move forward or backward. Up or down. But he can never move *out* of his world, into the third dimension, because he has no knowledge of a dimension angular to that in which he lives. He does not even dream of its existence."

I said, "I see what you mean now. But what has that to do with—"

"Wait, Len." Patterson suddenly struck the paper a blow with one finger; piercing it. He held the sheet up for our inspection. "Look at this. What do you see?"

"A sheet of paper," I said, "with a hole in it."

"Yes. But what does the *Flatlander* see?"

Ki looked excited. "I get it, Burch! He sees an unexpected, solid object appear before him—out of nowhere! If he walks around this object, he discovers it to be crudely round!"

"Exactly. Now I push the finger farther through the hole—"

"The object expands!"

"And if I bend it?"

"It changes its shape!"

"And if I thrust another finger through Flatland—"

"Another strangely shaped piece of solid matter materializes before the Flatlander!" Ki's eyes were widening by the moment. I didn't understand why.

I said, "I told you I didn't have a scientific mind, Burch. What does all this mean?"

Burch said patiently, "I have merely been establishing a thought-pattern, Len, so you can grasp the next step of my reasoning. Forget the Flatlander now—or, rather, try to think of *us* as being in his place!

"Would we not, to a creature whose natural habitat is a higher plane than .ours, appear much the same sort of projection as the Flatlander is to us?

"Suppose a creature of this higher plane projected a portion of himself into *our* dimension—as I projected my finger into Flatland. We would not be able to see *all* of him, just as the Flatlander could not see all of us. We would see only a tri-dimensional cross-section of him; as the Flatlander saw a bi-dimensional cross-section of us!"

This time I got it. I gasped:

"Then you think that *thing* in the work-shed is a cross-section of a creature from the—"

"Yes, Len. From the Fourth Dimension!"

Patterson smiled wanly.

"That is the decision I reached on the Maratan Plateau. There confronted me the problem of capturing the *thing*. The answer eluded me for weeks. Finally, I found it."

"It was—" Ki was leaning forward breathlessly.

"The Flatlander," said Burch, "could not capture my finger, *ever*, by lassooing it. No matter how tight he drew his noose, I could always withdraw my finger.

"But he *could* secure a portion of me, by fastening me to his dimension. Thus—" He showed us how a pin, laid flat in Flatland, could pierce a small piece of skin. "Now if this pin were bolted securely, the finger thus prisoned could not be withdrawn.

"That was the principle on which I worked, but my task had just begun. It took months to effect the capture. I had to study, from afar, the amorphous black *thing* which was my quarry. Try to form some concept of what incredible Fourth Dimensional beast would cast projections of that nature into the Third.

"Finally I decided that one certain piece of black matter, occurring in a certain relationship to the changing whole, was a foot. How, it is not important to tell. It was, after all, theory, coupled with guesswork.

"I constructed the shackle you have seen. Two uprights, with a third that must pierce the *thing*; then lock upon it. I waited, then, many weeks. Finally there came a chance to spring my trap. And—it worked!"

Ki said, "And then?"

"The rest is a long and tiresome story. Somehow I found my way to a native village; there employed natives to drag my captive from the Plateau. We were handicapped by the fact that we could never get too near the trap. You see, it is a *limb* we have imprisoned. The head, or eating apparatus, or whatever it is, is still free. That is what tried to reach you, Ki, there in the shed.

"Anyway, we made an arduous trek to the coast. As I have told you, I chartered a vessel. The sailors hated my cargo, and feared it. The trip was not an easy one. But I was determined, and my determination bore fruit. And—here we are."

I said, "Yeah—here we are. Just like the man who grabbed a tiger by the tail; then couldn't let go. Now that you've got this *thing*, what are you going to do with it?"

"That's what I want you to tell me."

Ki's eyes were glowing. He said, "Good Lord, man, is there any question in your mind? Call in the scientists—the whole damned brigade of them! Show them this thing! You've got the marvel of the age on your hands!"

"And you, Len?"

"You want it straight?" I said. "Or would you like to have me pull my punches?"

"Straight. That's why I asked you out here."

"Then get rid of it," I said. "Kill it. Set it on fire. Destroy it. I don't know just how you're going to do it, but I do know that's the thing to do.

"Oh, I know what you're thinking, Ki—so shut up! I'm a dope. Sure. I'm ignorant. Sure. I don't have the mind or the heart of a true scientist. Okay—you win! But Burch said I had common sense—and I'm exercising it now. I say—get rid of that damned thing before something happens. Something horrible that you will regret for the rest of your life!"

Ki looked a little peeved. He said, "You're nuts, Len! The thing's tied down, isn't it? Dammit man—you're the kind of guy who holds back the progress of the world. I bet you'd have voted to kill Galileo if you'd been alive in his day."

"If he'd trapped a monster like this," I retorted, "a monster who'd already killed at least three men, I'd have voted just that way. I'm not superstitious, Burch. But I'm afraid. I'm afraid that when Man starts monkeying with the Unknown, he gets beyond his depth. I say—kill it, now!"

Burch looked at me anxiously.

"That's your last word, Len?"

"Absolutely my last," I said. I rose. "And just to prove it, I'm going home now. And I'm not even going to write a damned word about what I've seen tonight. I don't care if this is the best story since the Deluge— I'm not going to write it!"

Ki said, "You give me a pain, Len. In the neck."

"Same to you," I told him, "only lower down. Well, so long, guys." And
I went home.

I kept my word. Though I had the mimsies all night, tossing and thinking about that crazy, changing black *thing,* I didn't put a word concerning
it on paper. I half expected to hear from Burch Patterson some time during
the next day. But I didn't. Then, the following morning, I saw why. The
Call carried a front page blast, screaming to the astonished world the news
that, "the missing explorer, Burch Patterson, has returned home," and that
"tonight there will be a convocation of eminent scientists" at his home to
view some marvel brought back from the wilds of upper Peru.

All of which meant that brother Ki's arguments had proven more
persuasive than mine. And that tonight there was to be a preview of that
damned *thing.*

I was pretty sore about it. I thought the least they could have done was
give me the news beat on the yarn. But there wasn't any use crying over
spilt milk. Anyway, I remembered that Ki's paper had a tie-up with the
Call. It was natural he should route the story that way.

And then I went down to the office, and Joe Slade, the human buzz saw
who calls himself our City Editor, waved me up to his desk.

"You, Harvey," he said, "I'm going to give you a chance to earn some
of that forty per we're overpaying you. I want you to represent us tonight.
out at Patterson's home in Jersey. He's going to unveil something mysterious."

I said, "Who—me? Listen, chief, give it to Bill Reynolds, won't you?
I've got some rewrites to do—"

"You, I said. What's the matter? Does New Jersey give you asthma?"

"Chief," I pleaded, "I can't cover this. I don't know anything about
science or—"

"What do you mean—science?" He pushed back his eyeshade and
glared at me. "Do you know what this is all about?"

That stopped me. I didn't want to go, but if I ever admitted that I'd
known about Patterson's changeable what-is-it, and not beaten the *Call* to
the streets with the story, I would be scanning the want ads in fifteen
seconds flat. So I gulped and said, "Okay, boss. I'll go."

Everybody and his brother was there that night. I recognized a professor of Physics from Columbia U., and the Dean of Paleontology from
N. Y. U. Two old graybeards from the Academy of Natural History were
over in a corner discussing something that ended in —zoic, and the curator
of the Museum was present, smelling as musty as one of his ancient
mummies.

The Press was out in force. All the bureaus, and most of the New York
papers. Ki was doing the receiving. Burch had not yet put in an appearance. I found a minute to get Ki aside, and told him what a skunky trick
I thought he'd pulled on me, but he merely shrugged.

"I'm sorry, Len. But you had your chance. After all, I had to think of my own paper first." Then he smiled. "And besides, you were in favor of destroying the *thing*."

"I still am," I told him dourly.

"Then what are you here for?"

It was my turn to shrug. "It was either come or lose my job," I said. "What do you think?"

Then Burch put in an appearance, and the whole outfit went genteelly crazy. Flash bulbs started blazing, and all my learned *confrères* of the Third Estate started shooting questions at him. About his trip, the loss of his comrades, his experiences. I knew all that stuff, so I just waited for the big blow-off to follow.

It came, at last. The moment when Burch said:

"Before I tell my entire story, I prefer that you see that which I brought back with me," and he led the way out to the work-shed.

Ki and Burch had fixed up the place a little; put chalk lines on the floor to show the visitors where they might stand.

"And I warn you," Burch said, just before he opened the shed door, "not to move beyond those lines. Afterward you will understand why."

Then the crowd began to file in. From my vantage point in the rear, I could tell when the first pair of eyes sighted that *thing*—and when every subsequent visitor saw it, as well. Gasps, exclamations, and little cries of astonishment rippled through the crowd as one by one they moved into the room.

The *thing* was still suspended on its imprisoning rod. As before, it was wriggling and moving; changing its shape with such rapidity that the human eye could scarcely view one shape before that turned into another. In view of what Burch had told me, I could comprehend the *thing* better now. I could understand how, if that black blob of flesh captured by the bar were *really*—as Burch presumed—a leg of some ultra-dimensional monster, the movements of that limb, as it sought to break free, would throw continually changing projections into our world.

I could understand, too, why from time to time we would see *other* bits of solid matter appear in various sections of the room. Though these seemed disassociated with that chunk hanging on the trap, I knew it was really separate portions of the same beast. Because if a *man* were to thrust four fingers, simultaneously, into Flatland, to the Flatlander these would appear to be four separate objects; while in reality they were part of a single unit in a dimension beyond his powers of conception.

The astonishment of the professors was something to behold. I began to feel a little bit ashamed of myself, there in the background. Perhaps I had been wrong to give Burch the advice I had. Perhaps, as Ki had said, this was one of the greatest discoveries of all time. It belonged to the world of science.

One of the photographers was dropping to his knee, levelling his Graflex at the shifting, changing *thing* on the rod. I caught myself thinking, swiftly, "He shouldn't do that!" Evidently Burch had the same idea. He took a swift step forward; cried, "Please! If you don't mind—"

He spoke too late. The man's finger pressed. For an instant the room was flooded with light.

And then it happened. I heard a sound like a thin, high bleating that seemed to come from far, far away. Or it may not have been a sound at all, in the true sense of that word. It may have been some tonic wave of supernal heights; for it tortured the eardrums to hear it.

The thing on the rod churned into motion. Violent motion. It grew and dwindled; shifted from cube to hemisphere; back to cube again. Then a truncated pyramidal form was throbbing, jerking, churning on the steel. Where I had once noticed an old, ugly, healed wound, ichor-clotted; now I saw ragged edges of black break open. Saw a few, fresh gouts of brownish fluid well from what seemed to be raw edges in that changing black.

Burch's horrified voice rose above the tumult.

"Get out! Get out—all of you! Before it—"

That was all he found time to say. For there came a horrible, sucking sound, like the sound of gangrenous flesh tearing away; and where there had been a changing black shape swirling on an imprisoning steel rod— now there was nothing!

But with equal suddenness, several of the shapeless blobs of matter from various parts of the room seemed to rush together with frightful speed. Someone, screaming with terror, bumped against me then. I fell to my hands and knees in the doorway, feeling the flood of human fear scramble over me.

But not until I had seen a scimitar-shaped blob of black flesh reach out to strike at Ki Patterson. Ki had not even time to cry out. He went down, dead, as though stricken by the sickle of Chronos.

I cried, "Burch!"

Burch had turned to face the coalescing monster. A revolver in his hand was filling the little room with thunder. Orange gouts of flame belched from its muzzle; and I knew he was not missing. Still the thing was closing in on him. I saw what seemed to be four jet circles appear in a ring over the head of Burch Patterson. Saw the circles expand; and a wider expanse of black—flat and sinister—appear directly over his head. They came together with a clutching, enveloping movement. Then—he was gone!

Somehow I managed to struggle out of that work shed. Not that it made any difference. For with the disappearance of Burch Patterson, the *thing* itself disappeared.

I won't try to describe the frightened group of news men and scientists who gathered at the Patterson house. Who trembled and quaked, and offered fantastic reasons for that which had transpired. Who finally summoned up courage enough to return to the shed cautiously; seeking the mortal remains of Burch. Patterson.

They never found anything, of course. Ki was there, but Ki was dead. Burch was gone. The air was still putrid with that unearthly animal stench. Beneath the steel "trap" Patterson had built for his *thing*, there was a pool of drying brownish fluid. One of the scientists wanted to take a sample of this for analysis. He returned to the house for a test-tube in which to put it . . .

Maybe it was the wrong thing for me to do. But I thought, then, that it was best. And I still think so. If he had taken that sample; made that analysis; sooner or later another expedition would have set out for the Maratan Plateau in search of that *thing* whose blood did not correspond to that of any known animal. I didn't believe this should happen. So, while he was gone, I set fire to the work shed. It was an old place; old and dry as tinder. By the time he had returned, it was a seething cauldron of flame. It made a fitting pyre for the body of Ki Patterson . . .

But—I don't know. I have wondered, since. Somehow, I have a feeling that Burch Patterson may not be dead, after all. That is—if a human can live in a dimension of which he cannot conceive.

The more I think of it; the more I try to reconcile that which ·I saw with that which Burch told me; the more I believe that the thing which descended upon Burch, there in the shed, was not a "mouth"—but a gigantic paw! You know, I saw four circles appear . . . with a flat black spot above. It could have been four huge fingers . . . with the palm descending to grasp the daring tri-dimensional "Flatlander" who had the audacity to match wits with a creature from a superior world. If that be so . . . and if the *thing* were intelligent . . . Patterson might still be alive . . .

I don't know. But sometimes I am tempted to organize another expedition to the Maratan Plateau, myself. Try to learn the truth concerning the *thing* from beyond the Gateway. The truth concerning Burch Patterson's fate.

What would *you* do?

PART SIX

FROM OUTER SPACE

MURRAY LEINSTER

FIRST CONTACT

TOMMY DORT went into the captain's room with his last pair of stereo-photos and said:

"I'm through, sir. These are the last two pictures I can take."

He handed over the photographs and looked with professional interest at the visiplates which showed all space outside the ship. Subdued, deep-red lighting indicated the controls and such instruments as the quartermaster on duty needed for navigation of the spaceship *Llanvabon*. There was a deeply cushioned control chair. There was the little gadget of oddly angled mirrors—remote descendant of the back-view mirrors of twentieth-century motorists—which allowed a view of all the visiplates without turning the head. And there were the huge plates which were so much more satisfactory for a direct view of space.

The *Llanvabon* was a long way from home. The plates which showed every star of visual magnitude and could be stepped up to any desired magnification, portrayed stars of every imaginable degree of brilliance, in the startlingly different colors they show outside of atmosphere. But every one was unfamiliar. Only two constellations could be recognized as seen from Earth, and they were shrunken and distorted. The Milky Way seemed vaguely out of place. But even such oddities were minor compared to a sight in the forward plates.

There was a vast, vast mistiness ahead. A luminous mist. It seemed motionless. It took a long time for any appreciable nearing to appear in the vision plates, though the spaceship's velocity indicator showed an incredible speed. The mist was the Crab Nebula, six light-years long, three and a half light-years thick, with outward-reaching members that in the telescopes of Earth gave it some resemblance to the creature for which it was named. It was a cloud of gas, infinitely tenuous, reaching half again as far as from Sol to its nearest neighbor-sun. Deep within it burned two stars; a double star; one component the familiar yellow of the sun of Earth, the other an unholy white.

Tommy Dort said meditatively:

"We're heading into a deep, sir?"

The skipper studied the last two plates of Tommy's taking, and put them aside. He went back to his uneasy contemplation of the vision plates ahead. The *Llanvabon* was decelerating at full force. She was a bare half light-year from the nebula. Tommy's work was guiding the ship's course, now, but the work was done. During all the stay of the exploring ship in the nebula, Tommy Dort would loaf. But he'd more than paid his way so far.

He had just completed a quite unique first—a complete photographic record of the movement of a nebula during a period of four thousand years, taken by one individual with the same apparatus and with control exposures to detect and record any systematic errors. It was an achievement in itself worth the journey from Earth. But in addition, he had also recorded four thousand years of the history of a double star, and four thousand years of the history of a star in the act of degenerating into a white dwarf.

It was not that Tommy Dort was four thousand years old. He was, actually, in his twenties. But the Crab Nebula is four thousand light-years from Earth, and the last two pictures had been taken by light which would not reach Earth until the sixth millennium A.D. On the way here—at speeds incredible multiples of the speed of light—Tommy Dort had recorded each aspect of the nebula by the light which had left it from forty centuries since to a bare six months ago.

The *Llanvabon* bored on through space. Slowly, slowly, slowly, the incredible luminosity crept across the vision plates. It blotted out half the universe from view. Before was glowing mist, and behind was a star-studded emptiness. The mist shut off three-fourths of all the stars. Some few of the brightest shone dimly through it near its edge, but only a few. Then there was only an irregularly shaped patch of darkness astern against which stars shone unwinking. The *Llanvabon* dived into the nebula, and it seemed as if it bored into a tunnel of darkness with walls of shining fog.

Which was exactly what the spaceship was doing. The most distant photographs of all had disclosed structural features in the nebula. It was not amorphous. It had form. As the *Llanvabon* drew nearer, indications of structure grew more distinct, and Tommy Dort had argued for a curved approach for photographic reasons. So the spaceship had come up to the nebula on a vast logarithmic curve, and Tommy had been able to take successive photographs from slightly different angles and get stereopairs which showed the nebula in three dimensions; which disclosed billowings and hollows and an actually complicated shape. In places, the nebula displayed convolutions like those of a human brain. It was into one of those hollows that the spaceship now plunged. They had been called "deeps" by analogy with crevasses in the ocean floor. And they promised to be useful.

The skipper relaxed. One of a skipper's functions, nowadays, is to think of things to worry about, and then worry about them. The skipper of the *Llanvabon* was conscientious. Only after a certain instrument remained definitely non-registering did he ease himself back in his seat.

"It was just hardly possible," he said heavily, "that those deeps might be nonluminous gas. But they're empty. So we'll be able to use overdrive as long as we're in them."

It was a light-year-and-a-half from the edge of the nebula to the neighborhood of the double star which was its heart. That was the problem. A nebula is a gas. It is so thin that a comet's tail is solid by comparison, but a ship traveling on overdrive—above the speed of light—does not want to hit even a merely hard vacuum. It needs pure emptiness, such as exists between the stars. But the *Llanvabon* could not do much in this expanse of mist if it was limited to speeds a merely hard vacuum will permit.

The luminosity seemed to close in behind the spaceship, which slowed and slowed and slowed. The overdrive went off with the sudden *pinging* sensation which goes all over a person when the overdrive field is released.

Then, almost instantly, bells burst into clanging, strident uproar all through the ship. Tommy was almost deafened by the alarm bell which rang in the captain's room before the quartermaster shut it off with a flip of his hand. But other bells could be heard ringing throughout the rest of the ship, to be cut off as automatic doors closed one by one.

Tommy Dort stared at the skipper. The skipper's hands clenched. He was up and staring over the quartermaster's shoulder. One indicator was apparently having convulsions. Others strained to record their findings. A spot on the diffusedly bright mistiness of a bow-quartering visiplate grew brighter as the automatic scanner focused on it. That was the direction of the object which had sounded collision-alarm. But the object locator itself— According to its reading, there was one solid object some eighty thousand miles away—an object of no great size. But there was another object whose distance varied from extreme range to zero, and whose size shared its impossible advance and retreat.

"Step up the scanner," snapped the skipper.

The extra-bright spot on the scanner rolled outward, obliterating the undifferentiated image behind it. Magnification increased. But nothing appeared. Absolutely nothing. Yet the radio locator insisted that something monstrous and invisible made lunatic dashes toward the *Llanvabon*, at speeds which inevitably implied collision, and then fled coyly away at the same rate.

The visiplate went up to maximum magnification. Still nothing. The skipper ground his teeth. Tommy Dort said meditatively:

"D'you know, sir, I saw something like this on a liner on the Earth-Mars run once, when we were being located by another ship. Their locator beam was the same frequency as ours, and every time it hit, it registered like something monstrous, and solid."

"That," said the skipper savagely, "is just what's happening now. There's something like a locator beam on us. We're getting that beam and our own echo besides. But the other ship's invisible! Who is out here in an invisible ship with locator devices? Not men, certainly!"

He pressed the button in his sleeve communicator and snapped:

"Action stations! Man all weapons! Condition of extreme alert in all departments immediately!"

His hands closed and unclosed. He stared again at the visiplate which showed nothing but a formless brightness.

"Not men?" Tommy Dort straightened sharply. "You mean—"

"How many solar systems in our galaxy?" demanded the skipper bitterly. "How many planets fit for life? And how many kinds of life could there be? If this ship isn't from Earth—and it isn't—it has a crew that isn't human. And things that aren't human but are up to the level of deep-space travel in their civilization could mean anything!"

The skipper's hands were actually shaking. He would not have talked so freely before a member of his own crew, but Tommy Dort was of the observation staff. And even a skipper whose duties include worrying may sometimes need desperately to unload his worries. Sometimes, too, it helps to think aloud.

"Something like this has been talked about and speculated about for years," he said softly. "Mathematically, it's been an odds-on bet that somewhere in our galaxy there'd be another race with a civilization equal to or further advanced than ours. Nobody could ever guess where or when we'd meet them. But it looks like we've done it now!"

Tommy's eyes were very bright.

"D'you suppose they'll be friendly, sir?"

The skipper glanced at the distance indicator. The phantom object still made its insane, nonexistent swoops toward and away from the *Llanvabon*. The secondary indication of an object at eighty thousand miles stirred ever so slightly.

"It's moving," he said curtly. "Heading for us. Just what we'd do if a strange spaceship appeared in our hunting grounds! Friendly? Maybe! We're going to try to contact them. We have to. But I suspect this is the end of this expedition. Thank God for the blasters!"

The blasters are those beams of ravening destruction which take care of recalcitrant meteorites in a spaceship's course when the deflectors can't handle them. They are not designed as weapons, but they can serve as pretty good ones. They can go into action at five thousand miles, and draw on the entire power output of a whole ship. With automatic aim and a traverse of five degrees, a ship like the *Llanvabon* can come very close to blasting a hole through a small-sized asteroid which gets in its way. But not on overdrive, of course.

Tommy Dort had approached the bow-quartering visiplate. Now he jerked his head around.

"Blasters, sir? What for?"

The skipper grimaced at the empty visiplate.

"Because we don't know what they're like and can't take a chance! I know!" he added bitterly. "We're going to make contacts and try to find out all we can about them—especially where they come from. I suppose we'll try to make friends—but we haven't much chance. We can't trust them a fraction of an inch. We daren't! They've locators. Maybe they've tracers better than any we have. Maybe they could trace us all the way home without our knowing it! We can't risk a nonhuman race knowing where Earth is unless we're sure of them! And how can we be sure? They could come to trade, of course—or they could swoop down on overdrive with a battle fleet that could wipe us out before we knew what happened. We wouldn't know which to expect, or when!"

Tommy's face was startled.

"It's all been thrashed out over and over, in theory," said the skipper. "Nobody's ever been able to find a sound answer, even on paper. But you know, in all their theorizing, no one considered the crazy, rank impossibility of a deep-space contact, with neither side knowing the other's home world! But we've got to find an answer in fact! What are we going to do about them? Maybe these creatures will be aesthetic marvels, nice and friendly and polite—and underneath with the sneaking brutal ferocity of a Japanese. Or maybe they'll be crude and gruff as a Swedish farmer—and just as decent underneath. Maybe they're something in between. But am I going to risk the possible future of the human race on a guess that it's safe to trust them? God knows it would be worth while to make friends with a new civilization! It would be bound to stimulate our own, and maybe we'd gain enormously. But I can't take chances. The one thing I won't risk is having them know how to find Earth! Either I know they can't follow me, or I don't go home! And they'll probably feel the same way!"

He pressed the sleeve-communicator button again.

"Navigation officers, attention! Every star map on this ship is to be prepared for instant destruction. This includes photographs and diagrams from which our course or starting point could be deduced. I want all astronomical data gathered and arranged to be destroyed in a split second, on order. Make it fast and report when ready!"

He released the button. He looked suddenly old. The first contact of humanity with an alien race was a situation which had been foreseen in many fashions, but never one quite so hopeless of solution as this. A solitary Earth-ship and a solitary alien, meeting in a nebula which must be remote from the home planet of each. They might wish peace, but the line of conduct which best prepared a treacherous attack was just the seeming of friendliness. Failure to be suspicious might doom the human race—and a peaceful exchange of the fruits of civilization would be the greatest benefit imaginable. Any mistake would be irreparable, but a failure to be on guard would be fatal.

The captain's room was very, very quiet. The bow-quartering visiplate was filled with the image of a very small section of the nebula. A very small section indeed. It was all diffused, featureless, luminous mist. But suddenly Tommy Dort pointed.

"There, sir!"

There was a small shape in the mist. It was far away. It was a black shape, not polished to mirror-reflection like the hull of the *Llanvabon*. It was bulbous—roughly pear-shaped. There was much thin luminosity between, and no details could be observed, but it was surely no natural object. Then Tommy looked at the distance indicator and said quietly:

"It's headed for us at very high acceleration, sir. The odds are that they're thinking the same thing, sir, that neither of us will dare let the other go home. Do you think they'll try a contact with us, or let loose with their weapons as soon as they're in range?"

The *Llanvabon* was no longer in a crevasse of emptiness in the nebula's thin substance. She swam in luminescence. There were no stars save the two fierce glows in the nebula's heart. There was nothing but an all-enveloping light, curiously like one's imagining of underwater in the tropics of Earth.

The alien ship had made one sign of less than lethal intention. As it drew near the *Llanvabon*, it decelerated. The *Llanvabon* itself had advanced for a meeting and then come to a dead stop. Its movement had been a recognition of the nearness of the other ship. Its pausing was both a friendly sign and a precaution against attack. Relatively still, it could swivel on its own axis to present the least target to a slashing assault, and it would have a longer firing-time than if the two ships flashed past each other at their combined speeds.

The moment of actual approach, however, was tenseness itself. The *Llanvabon's* needle-pointed bow aimed unwaveringly at the alien bulk. A relay to the captain's room put a key under his hand which would fire the blasters with maximum power. Tommy Dort watched, his brow wrinkled. The aliens must be of a high degree of civilization if they had spaceships, and civilization does not develop without the development of foresight. These aliens must recognize all the implications of this first contact of two civilized races as fully as did the humans on the *Llanvabon*.

The possibility of an enormous spurt in the development of both, by peaceful contact and exchange of their separate technologies, would probably appeal to them as to man. But when dissimilar human cultures are in contact, one must usually be subordinate or there is war. But subordination between races arising on separate planets could not be peacefully arranged. Men, at least, would never consent to subordination, nor was it likely that any highly developed race would agree. The benefits to be derived from commerce could never make up for a condition of inferiority.

Some races—men, perhaps—would prefer commerce to conquest. Perhaps —perhaps!—these aliens would also. But some types even of human beings would have craved red war. If the alien ship now approaching the *Llanvabon* returned to its home base with news of humanity's existence and of ships like the *Llanvabon*, it would give its race the choice of trade or battle. They might want trade, or they might want war. But it takes two to make trade, and only one to make war. They could not be sure of men's peacefulness, nor could men be sure of theirs. The only safety for either civilization would lie in the destruction of one or both of the two ships here and now.

But even victory would not be really enough. Men would need to know where this alien race was to be found, for avoidance if not for battle. They would need to know its weapons, and its resources, and if it could be a menace and how it could be eliminated in case of need. The aliens would feel the same necessities concerning humanity.

So the skipper of the *Llanvabon* did not press the key which might possibly have blasted the other ship to nothingness. He dared not. But he dared not not fire either. Sweat came out on his face.

A speaker muttered. Someone from the range room.

"The other ship's stopped, sir. Quite stationary. Blasters are centered on it, sir."

It was an urging to fire. But the skipper shook his head, to himself. The alien ship was no more than twenty miles away. It was dead-black. Every bit of its exterior was an abysmal, nonreflecting sable. No details could be seen except by minor variations in its outline against the misty nebula.

"It's stopped dead, sir," said another voice. "They've sent a modulated short wave at us, sir. Frequency modulated. Apparently a signal. Not enough power to do any harm."

The skipper said through tight-locked teeth:

"They're doing something now. There's movement on the outside of their hull. Watch what comes out. Put the auxiliary blasters on it."

Something small and round came smoothly out of the oval outline of the black ship. The bulbous hulk moved.

"Moving away, sir," said the speaker. "The object they let out is stationary in the place they've left."

Another voice cut in:

"More frequency modulated stuff, sir. Unintelligible."

Tommy Dort's eyes brightened. The skipper watched the visiplate, with sweat-droplets on his forehead.

"Rather pretty, sir," said Tommy, meditatively. "If they sent anything toward us, it might seem a projectile or a bomb. So they came close, let out a lifeboat, and went away again. They figure we can send a boat or a man to make contact without risking our ship. They must think pretty much as we do."

The skipper said, without moving his eyes from the plate:

"Mr. Dort, would you care to go out and look the thing over? I can't order you, but I need all my operating crew for emergencies. The observation staff—"

"Is expendable. Very well, sir," said Tommy briskly. "I won't take a lifeboat, sir. Just a suit with a drive in it. It's smaller and the arms and legs will look unsuitable for a bomb. I think I should carry a scanner, sir."

The alien ship continued to retreat. Forty, eighty, four hundred miles. It came to a stop and hung there, waiting. Climbing into his atomic-driven spacesuit just within the *Llanvabon's* air lock, Tommy heard the reports as they went over the speakers throughout the ship. That the other ship had stopped its retreat at four hundred miles was encouraging. It might not have weapons effective at a greater distance than that, and so felt safe. But just as the thought formed itself in his mind, the alien retreated precipitately still farther. Which, as Tommy reflected as he emerged from the lock, might be because the aliens had realized they were giving themselves away, or might be because they wanted to give the impression that they had done so.

He swooped away from the silvery-mirror *Llanvabon*, through a brightly glowing emptiness which was past any previous experience of the human race. Behind him, the *Llanvabon* swung about and darted away. The skipper's voice came in Tommy's helmet phones.

"We're pulling back, too, Mr. Dort. There is a bare possibility that they've some explosive atomic reaction they can't use from their own ship, but which might be destructive even as far as this. We'll draw back. Keep your scanner on the object."

The reasoning was sound, if not very comforting. An explosive which would destroy anything within twenty miles was theoretically possible, but humans didn't have it yet. It was decidedly safest for the *Llanvabon* to draw back.

But Tommy Dort felt very lonely. He sped through emptiness toward the tiny black speck which hung in incredible brightness. The *Llanvabon* vanished. Its polished hull would merge with the glowing mist at a relatively short distance, anyhow. The alien ship was not visible to the naked eye, either. Tommy swam in nothingness, four thousand light-years from home, toward a tiny black spot which was the only solid object to be seen in all of space.

It was a slightly distorted sphere, not much over six feet in diameter. It bounced away when Tommy landed on it, feet-first. There were small tentacles, or horns, which projected in every direction. They looked rather like the detonating horns of a submarine mine, but there was a glint of crystal at the tip-end of each.

"I'm here," said Tommy into his helmet phone.

He caught hold of a horn and drew himself to the object. It was all metal, dead-black. He could feel no texture through his space gloves, of course, but he went over and over it, trying to discover its purpose.

"Deadlock, sir," he said presently. "Nothing to report that the scanner hasn't shown you."

Then, through his suit, he felt vibrations. They translated themselves as clankings. A section of the rounded hull of the object opened out. Two sections. He worked his way around to look in and see the first nonhuman civilized beings that any man had ever looked upon.

But what he saw was simply a flat plate on which dim-red glows crawled here and there in seeming aimlessness. His helmet phones emitted a startled exclamation. The skipper's voice:

"Very good, Mr. Dort. Fix your scanner to look into that plate. They dumped out a robot with an infra-red visiplate for communication. Not risking any personnel. Whatever we might do would damage only machinery. Maybe they expect us to bring it on board—and it may have a bomb charge that can be detonated when they're ready to start for home. I'll send a plate to face one of its scanners. You return to the ship."

"Yes, sir," said Tommy. "But which way is the ship, sir?"

There were no stars. The nebula obscured them with its light. The only thing visible from the robot was the double star at the nebula's center. Tommy was no longer oriented. He had but one reference point.

"Head straight away from the double star," came the order in his helmet phone. "We'll pick you up."

He passed another lonely figure, a little later, headed for the alien sphere with a vision plate to set up. The two spaceships, each knowing that it dared not risk its own race by the slightest lack of caution, would communicate with each other through this small round robot. Their separate vision systems would enable them to exchange all the information they dared give, while they debated the most practical way of making sure that their own civilization would not be endangered by this first contact with another. The truly most practical method would be the destruction of the other ship in a swift and deadly attack—in self-defense.

The *Llanvabon*, thereafter, was a ship in which there were two separate enterprises on hand at the same time. She had come out from Earth to make close-range observations on the smaller component of the double star at the nebula's center. The nebula itself was the result of the most titanic explosion of which men have any knoweldge. The explosion took place some time in the year 2946 B. C., before the first of the seven cities of long-dead Ilium was even thought of. The light of that explosion reached Earth in the year 1054 A. D., and was duly recorded in ecclesiastical annals and somewhat more reliably by Chinese court astronomers. It was bright enough to be seen in daylight for twenty-three successive days. Its light—and it was four thousand light-years away—was brighter than that of Venus.

From these facts, astronomers could calculate nine hundred years later the violence of the detonation. Matter blown away from the center of the explosion would have traveled outward at the rate of two million three hundred thousand miles an hour; more than thirty-eight thousand miles a minute; something over six hundred thirty-eight miles per second. When twentieth-century telescopes were turned upon the scene of this vast explosion, only a double star remained—and the nebula. The brighter star of the doublet was almost unique in having so high a surface temperature that it showed no spectrum lines at all. It had a continuous spectrum. Sol's surface temperature is about 7,000° Absolute. That of the hot white star is 500,000 degrees. It has nearly the mass of the sun, but only one fifth its diameter, so that its density is one hundred seventy-three times that of water, sixteen times that of lead, and eight times that of iridium—the heaviest substance known on Earth. But even this density is not that of a dwarf white star like the companion of Sirius. The white star in the Crab Nebula is an incomplete dwarf; it is a star still in the act of collapsing Examination—including the survey of a four-thousand-year column of its light—was worth while. The *Llanvabon* had come to make that examination. But the finding of an alien spaceship upon a similar errand had implications which overshadowed the original purpose of the expedition.

A tiny bulbous robot floated in the tenuous nebular gas. The normal operating crew of the *Llanvabon* stood at their posts with a sharp alertness which was productive of tense nerves. The observation staff divided itself, and a part went half-heartedly about the making of the observations for which the *Llanvabon* had come. The other half applied itself to the problem the spaceship offered.

It represented a culture which was up to space travel on an interstellar scale. The explosion of a mere five thousand years since must have blasted every trace of life out of existence in the area now filled by the nebula. So the aliens of the black spaceship came from another solar system. Their trip must have been, like that of the Earth ship, for purely scientific purposes. There was nothing to be extracted from the nebula.

They were, then, at least near the level of human civilization, which meant that they had or could develop arts and articles of commerce which men would want to trade for, in friendship. But they would necessarily realize that the existence and civilization of humanity was a potential menace to their own race. The two races could be friends, but also they could be deadly enemies. Each, even if unwillingly, was a monstrous menace to the other. And the only safe thing to do with a menace is to destroy it.

In the Crab Nebula the problem was acute and immediate. The future relationship of the two races would be settled here and now. If a process for friendship could be established, one race, otherwise doomed, would survive and both would benefit immensely. But that process had to be established, and confidence built up, without the most minute risk of danger from treachery. Confidence would need to be established upon a foundation of necessarily complete distrust. Neither dared return to its own base if the other could do harm to its race. Neither dared risk any of the necessities to trust. The only safe thing for either to do was destroy the other or be destroyed.

But even for war, more was needed than mere destruction of the other. With interstellar traffic, the aliens must have atomic power and some form of overdrive for travel above the speed of light. With radio location and visiplates and short-wave communication they had, of course, many other devices. What weapons did they have? How widely extended was their culture? What were their resources? Could there be a development of trade and friendship, or were the two races so unlike that only war could exist between them? If peace was possible, how could it be begun?

The men on the *Llanvabon* needed facts—and so did the crew of the other ship. They must take back every morsel of information they could. The most important information of all would be of the location of the other civilization, just in case of war. That one bit of information might be the decisive factor in an interstellar war. But other facts would be enormously valuable.

The tragic thing was that there could be no possible information which could lead to peace. Neither ship could stake its own race's existence upon any conviction of the good will or the honor of the other.

So there was a strange truce between the two ships. The alien went about its work of making observations, as did the *Llanvabon*. The tiny robot floated in bright emptiness. A scanner from the *Llanvabon* was focussed upon a vision plate from the alien. A scanner from the alien regarded a vision plate from the *Llanvabon*. Communication began.

It progressed rapidly. Tommy Dort was one of those who made the first progress report. His special task on the expedition was over. He had now been assigned to work on the problem of communication with the alien entities. He went with the ship's solitary psychologist to the captain's room to convey the news of success. The captain's room, as usual, was a place of silence and dull-red indicator lights and the great bright visiplates on every wall and on the ceiling.

"We've established fairly satisfactory communication, sir," said the psychologist. He looked tired. His work on the trip was supposed to be that of measuring personal factors of error in the observation staff, for the reduction of all observations to the nearest possible decimal to the absolute. He had been pressed into service for which he was not especially fitted, and it told upon him. "That is, we can say almost anything we wish to them, and can understand what they say in return. But of course we don't know how much of what they say is the truth."

The skipper's eyes turned to Tommy Dort.

"We've hooked up some machinery," said Tommy, "that amounts to a mechanical translator. We have vision plates, of course, and then short-wave beams direct. They use frequency-modulation plus what is probably variation in wave forms—like our vowel and consonant sounds in speech. We've never had any use for anything like that before, so our coils won't handle it, but we've developed a sort of code which isn't the language of either set of us. They shoot over short-wave stuff with frequency-modulation, and we record it as sound. When we shoot it back, it's reconverted into frequency-modulation."

The skipper said, frowning:

"Why wave-form changes in short waves? How do you know?"

"We showed them our recorder in the vision plates, and they showed us theirs. They record the frequency-modulation direct. I think," said Tommy carefully, "they don't use sound at all, even in speech. They've set up a communications room, and we've watched them in the act of communicating with us. They made no perceptible movement of anything that corresponds to a speech organ. Instead of a microphone, they simply stand near something that would work as a pick-up antenna. My guess, sir, is that they use microwaves for what you might call person-to-person conversation. I think they make short-wave trains as we make sounds."

The skipper stared at him:

"That means they have telepathy?"

"M-m-m. Yes, sir," said Tommy. "Also it means that we have telepathy too, as far as they are concerned. They're probably deaf. They've certainly no idea of using sound waves in air for communication. They simply don't use noises for any purpose."

The skipper stored the information away.

"What else?"

"Well, sir," said Tommy doubtfully, "I think we're all set. We agreed on arbitrary symbols for objects, sir, by way of the visiplates, and worked out relationships and verbs and so on with diagrams and pictures. We've a couple of thousand words that have mutual meanings. We set up an analyzer to sort out their short-wave groups, which we feed into a decoding machine. And then the coding end of the machine picks out recordings to make the wave groups we want to send back. When you're ready to talk to the skipper of the other ship, sir, I think we're ready."

"H-m-m. What's your impression of their psychology?" The skipper asked the question of the psychologist.

"I don't know, sir," said the psychologist harassedly. "They seem to be completely direct. But they haven't let slip even a hint of the tenseness we know exists. They act as if they were simply setting up a means of communication for friendly conversation. But there is . . . well . . . an overtone—"

The psychologist was a good man at psychological mensuration, which is a good and useful field. But he was not equipped to analyze a completely alien thought-pattern.

"If I may say so, sir—" said Tommy uncomfortably.

"What?"

"They're oxygen breathers," said Tommy, "and they're not too dissimilar to us in other ways. It seems to me, sir, that parallel evolution has been at work. Perhaps intelligence evolves in parallel lines, just as . . . well . . . basic bodily functions. I mean," he added conscientiously, "any living being of any sort must ingest, metabolize, and excrete. Perhaps any intelligent brain must perceive, apperceive, and find a personal reaction. I'm sure I've detected irony. That implies humor, too. In short, sir, I think they could be likable."

The skipper heaved himself to his feet.

"H-m-m," he said profoundly, "we'll see what they have to say."

He walked to the communications room. The scanner for the vision plate in the robot was in readiness. The skipper walked in front of it. Tommy Dort sat down at the coding machine and tapped at the keys. Highly improbable noises came from it, went into a microphone, and governed the frequency-modulation of a signal sent through space to the other spaceship. Almost instantly the vision screen which with one relay— in the robot—showed the interior of the other ship lighted up. An alien came before the scanner and seemed to look inquisitively out of the plate. He was extraordinarily manlike, but he was not human. The impression he gave was of extreme baldness and a somehow humorous frankness.

"I'd like to say," said the skipper heavily, "the appropriate things about this first contact of two dissimilar civilized races, and of my hopes that a friendly intercourse between the two peoples will result."

Tommy Dort hesitated. Then he shrugged and tapped expertly upon the coder. More improbable noises.

The alien skipper seemed to receive the message. He made a gesture which was wryly assenting. The decoder on the *Llanvabon* hummed to itself and word-cards dropped into the message frame. Tommy said dispassionately:

"He says, sir, 'That is all very well, but is there any way for us to let each other go home alive? I would be happy to hear of such a way if you can contrive it. At the moment it seems to me that one of us must be killed.' "

The atmosphere was of confusion. There were too many questions to be answered all at once. Nobody could answer any of them. And all of them had to be answered.

The *Llanvabon* could start for home. The alien ship might or might not be able to multiply the speed of light by one more unit than the Earth vessel. If it could, the *Llanvabon* would get close enough to Earth to reveal its destination—and then have to fight. It might or might not win. Even if it did win, the aliens might have a communication system by which the *Llanvabon's* destination might have been reported to the aliens' home planet before battle was joined. But the *Llanvabon* might lose in such a fight. If she was to be destroyed, it would be better to be destroyed here, without giving any clue to where human beings might be found by a forewarned, forearmed alien battle fleet.

The black ship was in exactly the same predicament. It too, could start for home. But the *Llanvabon* might be faster and an overdrive field can be trailed, if you set to work on it soon enough. The aliens, also, would not know whether the *Llanvabon* could report to its home base without returning. If the alien was to be destroyed, it also would prefer to fight it out here, so that it could not lead a probable enemy to its own civilization.

Neither ship, then, could think of flight. The course of the *Llanvabon* into the nebula might be known to the black ship, but it had been the end of a logarithmic curve, and the aliens could not know its properties. They could not tell from that from what direction the Earth ship had started. As of the moment, then, the two ships were even. But the question was and remained, "What now?"

There was no specific answer. The aliens traded information for information—and did not always realize what information they gave. The humans traded information for information—and Tommy Dort sweated blood in his anxiety not to give any clue to the whereabouts of Earth.

The aliens saw by infrared light, and the vision plates and scanners in the robot communication-exchange had to adapt their respective images up and down an optical octave each, for them to have any meaning at all. It did not occur to the aliens that their eyesight told that their sun was a red dwarf, yielding light of greatest energy just below the part of the spectrum visible to human eyes. But after that fact was realized on the *Llanvabon,* it was realized that the aliens, also, should be able to deduce the Sun's spectral type by the light to which men's eyes were best adapted.

There was a gadget for the recording of short-wave trains which was as casually in use among the aliens as a sound-recorder is among men. The humans wanted that, badly. And the aliens were fascinated by the mystery of sound. They were able to perceive noise, of course, just as a man's palm will perceive infrared light by the sensation of heat it produces, but they could no more differentiate pitch or tone-quality than a man is able to distinguish between two frequencies of heat-radiation even half an octave apart. To them, the human science of sound was a remarkable discovery. They would find uses for noises which humans had never imagined—if they lived.

But that was another question. Neither ship could leave without first destroying the other. But while the flood of information was in passage, neither ship could afford to destroy the other. There was the matter of the outer coloring of the two ships. The *Llanvabon* was mirror-bright exteriorly. The alien ship was dead-black by visible light. It absorbed heat to perfection, and should radiate it away again as readily. But it did not. The black coating was not a "black body" color or lack of color. It was a perfect reflector of certain infrared wave lengths while simultaneously it fluoresced in just those wave bands. In practice, it absorbed the higher frequencies of heat, converted them to lower frequencies it did not radiate —and stayed at the desired temperature even in empty space.

Tommy Dort labored over his task of communications. He found the alien thought-processes not so alien that he could not follow them. The discussion of technics reached the matter of interstellar navigation. A star map was needed to illustrate the process. It would not have been logical to use a star map from the chart room—but from a star map one could guess the point from which the map was projected. Tommy had a map made specially, with imaginary but convincing star images upon it. He translated directions for its use by the coder and decoder. In return, the aliens presented a star map of their own before the visiplate. Copied instantly by photograph, the Nav officers labored over it, trying to figure out from what spot in the galaxy the stars and Milky Way would show at such an angle. It baffled them.

It was Tommy who realized finally that the aliens had made a special star map for their demonstration too, and that it was a mirror-image of the faked map Tommy had shown them previously.

Tommy could grin, at that. He began to like these aliens. They were not humans, but they had a very human sense of the ridiculous. In course of time Tommy essayed a mild joke. It had to be translated into code numerals, these into quite cryptic groups of short-wave, frequency-modulated impulses, and these went to the other ship and into heaven knew what to become intelligible. A joke which went through such formalities would not seem likely to be funny. But the alien did see the point.

There was one of the aliens to whom communication became as normal a function as Tommy's own code-handlings. The two of them developed a quite insane friendship, conversing by coder, decoder, and short-wave trains. When technicalities in the official messages grew too involved, that alien sometimes threw in strictly nontechnical interpolations akin to slang. Often, they cleared up the confusion. Tommy, for no reason whatever, had filed a code-name of "Buck" which the decoder picked out regularly when this particular one signed his own symbol to a message.

In the third week of communication, the decoder suddenly presented Tommy with a message in the message frame:

You are a good guy. It is too bad we have to kill each other.—BUCK.

Tommy had been thinking much the same thing. He tapped off the rueful reply:

We can't see any way out of it. Can you?

There was a pause, and the message frame filled up again:

If we could believe each other, yes. Our skipper would like it. But we can't believe you, and you can't believe us. We'd trail you home if we got a chance, and you'd trail us. But we feel sorry about it.—BUCK.

Tommy Dort took the messages to the skipper.

"Look here, sir!" he said urgently. "These people are almost human, and they're likable cusses."

The skipper was busy about his important task of thinking things to worry about, and worrying about them. He said tiredly:

"They're oxygen breathers. Their air is twenty-eight percent oxygen instead of twenty, but they could do very well on Earth. It would be a highly desirable conquest for them. And we still don't know what weapons they've got or what they can develop. Would you tell them how to find Earth?"

"N-no," said Tommy, unhappily.

"They probably feel the same way," said the skipper dryly. "And if we did manage to make a friendly contact, how long would it stay friendly? If their weapons were inferior to ours, they'd feel that for their own safety they had to improve them. And we, knowing they were planning to revolt, would crush them while we could—for our own safety! If it happened to be the other way about, they'd have to smash us before we could catch up to them."

Tommy was silent, but he moved restlessly.

"If we smash this black ship and get home," said the skipper, "Earth Government will be annoyed if we don't tell them where it came from. But what can we do? We'll be lucky enough to get back alive with our warning. It isn't possible to get out of those creatures any more information than we give them, and we surely won't give them our address! We've run into them by accident. Maybe—if we smash this ship—there won't be another contact for thousands of years. And it's a pity, because trade could mean so much! But it takes two to make a peace, and we can't risk trusting them. The only answer is to kill them if we can, and if we can't, to make sure that when they kill us they'll find out nothing that will lead them to Earth. I don't like it," added the skipper tiredly, "but there simply isn't anything else to do!"

On the *Llanvabon*, the technicians worked frantically in two divisions. One prepared for victory, and the other for defeat. The ones working for victory could do little. The main blasters were the only weapons with any promise. Their mountings were cautiously altered so that they were no longer fixed nearly dead ahead, with only a 5° traverse. Electronic controls which followed a radio-locator master-finder would keep them trained with absolute precision upon a given target regardless of its maneuverings. More, a hitherto unsung genius in the engine room devised a capacity-storage system by which the normal full-output of the ship's engines could be momentarily accumulated and released in surges of stored power far above normal. In theory, the range of the blasters should be multiplied and their destructive power considerably stepped up. But there was not much more that could be done.

The defeat crew had more leeway. Star charts, navigational instruments carrying telltale notations, the photographic record Tommy Dort had made on the six-months' journey from Earth, and every other memorandum offering clues to Earth's position, were prepared for destruction. They were put in sealed files, and if any one of them was opened by one who did not know the exact, complicated process, the contents of all the files would flash into ashes and the ash be churned past any hope of restoration. Of course, if the *Llanvabon* should be victorious, a carefully not-indicated method of reopening them in safety would remain.

There were atomic bombs placed all over the hull of the ship. If its human crew should be killed without complete destruction of the ship, the atomic-power bombs should detonate if the *Llanvabon* was brought alongside the alien vessel. There were no ready-made atomic bombs on board, but there were small spare atomic-power units on board. It was not hard to trick them so that when they were turned on, instead of yielding a smooth flow of power they would explode. And four men of the earth ship's crew remained always in spacesuits with closed helmets, to fight the ship should it be punctured in many compartments by an unwarned attack.

Such an attack, however, would not be treacherous. The alien skipper had spoken frankly. His manner was that of one who wryly admits the uselessness of lies. The skipper and the *Llanvabon*, in turn, heavily admitted the virtue of frankness. Each insisted—perhaps truthfully—that he wished for friendship between the two races. But neither could trust the other not to make every conceivable effort to find out the one thing he needed most desperately to conceal—the location of his home planet. And neither dared believe that the other was unable to trail him and find out. Because each felt it his own duty to accomplish that unbearable—to the other—act, neither could risk the possible existence of his race by trusting the other. They must fight because they could not do anything else.

They could raise the stakes of the battle by an exchange of information beforehand. But there was a limit to the stake either would put up. No information on weapons, population, or resources would be given by either. Not even the distance of their home bases from the Crab Nebula would be told. They exchanged information, to be sure, but they knew a battle to the death must follow, and each strove to represent his own civilization as powerful enough to give pause to the other's ideas of possible conquest—and thereby increased its appearance of menace to the other, and made battle more unavoidable.

It was curious how completely such alien brains could mesh, however. Tommy Dort, sweating over the coding and decoding machines, found a personal equation emerging from the at first stilted arrays of word-cards which arranged themselves. He had seen the aliens only in the vision screen, and then only in light at least one octave removed from the light they saw by. They, in turn, saw him very strangely, by transposed illumination from what to them would be the far ultra-violet. But their brains worked alike. Amazingly alike. Tommy Dort felt an actual sympathy and even something close to friendship for the gill-breathing, bald, and dryly ironic creatures of the black space vessel.

Because of that mental kinship he set up—though hopelessly—a sort of table of the aspects of the problem before them. He did not believe that the aliens had any instinctive desire to destroy man. In fact, the study of communications from the aliens had produced on the *Llanvabon* a feeling of tolerance not unlike that between enemy soldiers during a truce on Earth. The men felt no enmity, and probably neither did the aliens. But they had to kill or be killed for strictly logical reasons.

Tommy's table was specific. He made a list of objectives the men must try to achieve, in the order of their importance. The first was the carrying back of news of the existence of the alien culture. The second was the location of that alien culture in the galaxy. The third was the carrying back of as much information as possible about that culture. The third was being worked on, but the second was probably impossible. The first—and all—would depend on the result of the fight which must take place.

The aliens' objectives would be exactly similar, so that the men must prevent, first, news of the existence of Earth's culture from being taken back by the aliens, second, alien discovery of the location of Earth, and third, the acquiring by the aliens of information which would help them or encourage them to attack humanity. And again the third was in train, and the second was probably taken care of, and the first must await the battle.

There was no possible way to avoid the grim necessity of the destruction of the black ship. The aliens would see no solution to their problems but the destruction of the *Llanvabon*. But Tommy Dort, regarding his tabulation ruefully, realized that even complete victory would not be a perfect solution. The ideal would be for the *Llanvabon* to take back the alien ship for study. Nothing less would be a complete attainment of the third objective. But Tommy realized that he hated the idea of so complete a victory, even if it could be accomplished. He would hate the idea of killing even nonhuman creatures who understood a human joke. And beyond that, he would hate the idea of Earth fitting out a fleet of fighting ships to destroy an alien culture because its existence was dangerous. The pure accident of this encounter, between peoples who could like each other, had created a situation which could only result in wholesale destruction.

Tommy Dort soured on his own brain which could find no answer which would work. But there had to be an answer! The gamble was too big! It was too absurd that two spaceships should fight—neither one primarily designed for fighting—so that the survivor could carry back news which would set one race to frenzied preparation for war against the unwarned other.

If both races could be warned, though, and each knew that the other did not want to fight, and if they could communicate with each other but not locate each other until some grounds for mutual trust could be reached—

It was impossible. It was chimerical. It was a daydream. It was nonsense. But it was such luring nonsense that Tommy Dort ruefully put it into the coder to his gill-breathing friend Buck, then some hundred thousand miles off in the misty brightness of the nebula.

"Sure," said Buck, in the decoder's word-cards flicking into place in the message frame. "That is a good dream. But I like you and still won't believe you. If I said that first, you would like me but not believe me, either. I tell you the truth more than you believe, and maybe you tell me the truth more than I believe. But there is no way to know. I am sorry."

Tommy Dort stared gloomily at the message. He felt a very horrible sense of responsibility. Everyone did, on the *Llanvabon*. If they failed in this encounter, the human race would run a very good chance of being exterminated in time to come. If they succeeded, the race of the aliens would be the one to face destruction, most likely. Millions or billions of lives hung upon the actions of a few men.

Then Tommy Dort saw the answer.

It would be amazingly simple, if it worked. At worst it might give a partial victory to humanity and the *Llanvabon*. He sat quite still, not daring to move lest he break the chain of thought that followed the first tenuous idea. He went over and over it, excitedly finding objections here and meeting them, and overcoming impossibilities there. It was the answer! He felt sure of it.

He felt almost dizzy with relief when he found his way to the captain's room and asked leave to speak.

It is the function of a skipper, among others, to find things to worry about. But the *Llanvabon's* skipper did not have to look. In the three weeks and four days since the first contact with the alien black ship, the skipper's face had grown lined and old. He had not only the *Llanvabon* to worry about. He had all of humanity.

"Sir," said Tommy Dort, his mouth rather dry because of his enormous earnestness, "may I offer a method of attack on the black ship? I'll undertake it myself, sir, and if it doesn't work our ship won't be weakened."

The skipper looked at him unseeingly.

"The tactics are all worked out, Mr. Dort," he said heavily. "They're being cut on tape now, for the ship's handling. It's a terrible gamble, but it has to be done."

"I think," said Tommy carefully, "I've worked out a way to take the gamble out. Suppose, sir, we send a message to the other ship, offering—"

His voice went on in the utterly quiet captain's room, with the visiplates showing only a vast mistiness outside and the two fiercely burning stars in the nebula's heart.

The skipper himself went through the air lock with Tommy. For one reason, the action Tommy had suggested would need his authority behind it. For another, the skipper had worried more intensely than anybody else on the *Llanvabon*, and he was tired of it. If he went with Tommy, he would do the thing himself, and if he failed he would be the first one killed —and the tape for the Earth ship's maneuvering was already fed into the control board and correlated with the master-timer. If Tommy and the skipper were killed, a single control pushed home would throw the *Llanvabon* into the most furious possible all-out attack, which would end in the complete destruction of one ship or the other—or both. So the skipper was not deserting his post.

The outer air lock door swung wide. It opened upon that shining emptiness which was the nebula. Twenty miles away, the little round robot hung in space, drifting in an incredible orbit about the twin central suns, and floating ever nearer and nearer. It would never reach either of them, of course. The white star alone was so much hotter than Earth's sun that its heat-effect would produce Earth's temperature on an object five times as far from it as Neptune is from Sol. Even removed to the distance of Pluto, the little robot would be raised to cherry-red heat by the blazing white dwarf. And it could not possibly approach to the ninety-odd million miles which is the Earth's distance from the sun. So near, its metal would melt and boil away as vapor. But, half a light-year out, the bulbous object bobbed in emptiness.

The two spacesuited figures soared away from the *Llanvabon*. The small atomic drives which made them minute spaceships on their own had been subtly altered, but the change did not interfere with their functioning. They headed for the communication robot. The skipper, out in space, said gruffly:

"Mr. Dort, all my life I have longed for adventure. This is the first time I could ever justify it to myself."

His voice came through Tommy's space-phone receivers. Tommy wet his lips and said:

"It doesn't seem like adventure to me, sir. I want terribly for the plan to go through. I thought adventure was when you didn't care."

"Oh, no," said the skipper. "Adventure is when you toss your life on the scales of chance and wait for the pointer to stop."

They reached the round object. They clung to its short, scanner-tipped horns.

"Intelligent, those creatures," said the skipper heavily. "They must want desperately to see more of our ship than the communication room, to agree to this exchange of visits before the fight."

"Yes, sir," said Tommy. But privately, he suspected that Buck—his gill-breathing friend—would like to see him in the flesh before one or both of them died. And it seemed to him that between the two ships had grown up an odd tradition of courtesy, like that between two ancient knights before a tourney, when they admired each other wholeheartedly before hacking at each other with all the contents of their respective armories.

They waited.

Then, out of the mist, came two other figures. The alien spacesuits were also power-driven. The aliens themselves were shorter than men, and their helmet openings were coated with a filtering material to cut off visible and ultraviolet rays which to them would be lethal. It was not possible to see more than the outline of the heads within.

Tommy's helmet phone said, from the communication room on the *Llanvabon:*

"They say that their ship is waiting for you, sir. The air lock door will be open."

The skipper's voice said heavily:

"Mr. Dort, have you seen their spacesuits before? If so, are you sure they're not carrying anything extra, such as bombs?"

"Yes, sir," said Tommy. "We've showed each other our space equipment. They've nothing but regular stuff in view, sir."

The skipper made a gesture to the two aliens. He and Tommy Dort plunged on for the black vessel. They could not make out the ship very clearly with the naked eye, but directions for change of course came from the communication room.

The black ship loomed up. It was huge, as long as the *Llanvabon* and vastly thicker. The air lock did stand open. The two spacesuited men moved in and anchored themselves with magnetic-soled boots. The outer door closed. There was a rush of air and simultaneously the sharp quick tug of artificial gravity. Then the inner door opened.

All was darkness. Tommy switched on his helmet light at the same instant as the skipper. Since the aliens saw by infrared, a white light would have been intolerable to them. The men's helmet lights were, therefore, of the deep-red tint used to illuminate instrument panels so there will be no dazzling of eyes that must be able to detect the minutest specks of white light on a navigating vision plate. There were aliens waiting to receive them. They blinked at the brightness of the helmet lights. The space-phone receivers said in Tommy's ear:

"They say, sir, their skipper is waiting for you."

Tommy and the skipper were in a long corridor with a soft flooring underfoot. Their lights showed details of which every one was exotic.

"I think I'll crack my helmet, sir," said Tommy.

He did. The air was good. By analysis it was thirty percent oxygen instead of twenty for normal air on Earth, but the pressure was less. It felt just right. The artificial gravity, too, was less than that maintained on the *Llanvabon.* The home planet of the aliens would be smaller than Earth, and —by the infrared data—circling close to a nearly dead, dull-red sun. The air had smells in it. They were utterly strange, but not unpleasant.

An arched opening. A ramp with the same soft stuff underfoot. Lights which actually shed a dim, dull-red glow about. The aliens had stepped up some of their illuminating equipment as an act of courtesy. The light might hurt their eyes, but it was a gesture of consideration which made Tommy even more anxious for his plan to go through.

The alien skipper faced them with what seemed to Tommy a gesture of wryly humorous deprecation. The helmet phones said:

"He says, sir, that he greets you with pleasure, but he has been able to think of only one way in which the problem created by the meeting of these two ships can be solved."

"He means a fight," said the skipper. "Tell him I'm here to offer another choice."

The *Llanvabon's* skipper and the skipper of the alien ship were face to face, but their communication was weirdly indirect. The aliens used no sound in communication. Their talk, in fact, took place on microwaves and approximated telepathy. But they could not hear, in any ordinary sense of the word, so the skipper's and Tommy's speech approached telepathy, too, as far as they were concerned. When the skipper spoke, his space phone sent his words back to the *Llanvabon*, where the words were fed into the coder and short-wave equivalents sent back to the black ship. The alien skipper's reply went to the *Llanvabon* and through the decoder, and was retransmitted by space phone in words read from the message frame. It was awkward, but it worked.

The short and stocky alien skipper paused. The helmet phones relayed his translated, soundless reply.

"He is anxious to hear, sir."

The skipper took off his helmet. He put his hands at his belt in a belligerent pose.

"Look here!" he said truculently to the bald, strange creature in the unearthly red glow before him. "It looks like we have to fight and one batch of us get killed. We're ready to do it if we have to. But if you win, we've got it fixed so you'll never find out where Earth is, and there's a good chance we'll get you anyhow! If we win, we'll be in the same fix. And if we win and go back home, our government will fit out a fleet and start hunting your planet. And if we find it we'll be ready to blast it to hell! If you win, the same thing will happen to us! And it's all foolishness! We've stayed here a month, and we've swapped information, and we don't hate each other. There's no reason for us to fight except for the rest of our respective races!"

The skipper stopped for breath, scowling. Tommy Dort inconspicuously put his own hands on the belt of his spacesuit. He waited, hoping desperately that the trick would work.

"He says, sir," reported the helmet phones, "that all you say is true. But that his race has to be protected, just as you feel that yours must be."

"Naturally," said the skipper angrily, "but the sensible thing to do is to figure out how to protect it! Putting its future up as a gamble in a fight is not sensible. Our races have to be warned of each other's existence. That's true. But each should have proof that the other doesn't want to fight, but wants to be friendly. And we shouldn't be able to find each other, but we should be able to communicate with each other to work out grounds for a common trust. If our governments want to be fools, let them! But we should give them the chance to make friends, instead of starting a space war out of mutual funk!"

Briefly, the space phone said:

"He says that the difficulty is that of trusting each other now. With the possible existence of his race at stake, he cannot take any chance, and neither can you, of yielding an advantage."

"But my race," boomed the skipper, glaring at the alien captain, "my race has an advantage now. We came here to your ship in atom-powered spacesuits! Before we left, we altered the drives! We can set off ten pounds of sensitized fuel apiece, right here in this ship, or it can be set off by remote control from our ship! It will be rather remarkable if your fuel store doesn't blow up with us! In other words, if you don't accept my proposal for a commonsense approach to this predicament, Dort and I blow up in an atomic explosion, and your ship will be wrecked if not destroyed—and the *Llanvabon* will be attacking with everything it's got within two seconds after the blast goes off!"

The captain's room of the alien ship was a strange scene, with its dull-red illumination and the strange, bald, gill-breathing aliens watching the skipper and waiting for the inaudible translation of the harangue they could not hear. But a sudden tensity appeared in the air. A sharp, savage feeling of strain. The alien skipper made a gesture. The helmet phones hummed.

"He says, sir, what is your proposal?"

"Swap ships!" roared the skipper. "Swap ships and go on home! We can fix our instruments so they'll do no trailing, he can do the same with his. We'll each remove our star maps and records. We'll each dismantle our weapons. The air will serve, and we'll take their ship and they'll take ours, and neither one can harm or trail the other, and each will carry home more information than can be taken otherwise! We can agree on this same Crab Nebula as a rendezvous when the double-star has made another circuit, and if our people want to meet them they can do it, and if they are scared they can duck it! That's my proposal! And he'll take it, or Dort and I blow up their ship and the *Llanvabon* blasts what's left!"

He glared about him while he waited for the translation to reach the tense small stocky figures about him. He could tell when it came because the tenseness changed. The figures stirred. They made gestures. One of them made convulsive movements. It lay down on the soft floor and kicked. Others leaned against its walls and shook.

The voice in Tommy Dort's helmet phones had been strictly crisp and professional, before, but now it sounded blankly amazed.

"He says, sir, that it is a good joke. Because the two crew members he sent to our ship, and that you passed on the way, have their spacesuits stuffed with atomic explosive too, sir, and he intended to make the very same offer and threat! Of course he accepts, sir. Your ship is worth more to him than his own, and his is worth more to you than the *Llanvabon*. It appears, sir, to be a deal."

Then Tommy Dort realized what the convulsive movements of the aliens were. They were laughter.

It wasn't quite as simple as the skipper had outlined it. The actual working-out of the proposal was complicated. For three days the crews of the two ships were intermingled, the aliens learning the workings of the *Llanvabon's* engines, and the men learning the controls of the black space-ship. It was a good joke—but it wasn't all a joke. There were men on the black ship, and aliens on the *Llanvabon*, ready at an instant's notice to blow up the vessels in question. And they would have done it in case of need, for which reason the need did not appear. But it was, actually, a better arrangement to have two expeditions return to two civilizations, under the current arrangement, than for either to return alone.

There were differences, though. There was some dispute about the removal of records. In most cases the dispute was settled by the destruction of the records. There was more trouble caused by the *Llanvabon's* books, and the alien equivalent of a ship's library, containing works which approximated the novels of Earth. But those items were valuable to possible friendship, because they would show the two cultures, each to the other, from the viewpoint of normal citizens and without propaganda.

But nerves were tense during those three days. Aliens unloaded and inspected the foodstuffs intended for the men on the black ship. Men transshipped the foodstuffs the aliens would need to return to their home. There were endless details, from the exchange of lighting equipment to suit the eyesight of the exchanging crews, to a final check-up of apparatus. A joint inspection party of both races verified that all detector devices had been smashed but not removed, so that they could not be used for trailing and had not been smuggled away. And of course, the aliens were anxious not to leave any useful weapon on the black ship, nor the men upon the *Llanvabon*. It was a curious fact that each crew was best qualified to take exactly the measures which made an evasion of the agreement impossible.

There was a final conference before the two ships parted, back in the communication room of the *Llanvabon*.

"Tell the little runt," rumbled the *Llanvabon's* former skipper, "that he's got a good ship and he'd better treat her right."

The message frame flicked word-cards into position.

"I believe," it said on the alien skipper's behalf, "that your ship is just as good. I will hope to meet you here when the double star has turned one turn."

The last man left the *Llanvabon*. It moved away into the misty nebula before they had returned to the black ship. The vision plates in that vessel had been altered for human eyes, and human crewmen watched jealously for any trace of their former ship as their new craft took a crazy, evading course to a remote part of the nebula. It came to a crevasse of nothingness, leading to the stars. It rose swiftly to clear space. There was the instant of breathlessness which the overdrive field produces as it goes on, and then the black ship whipped away into the void at many times the speed of light.

Many days later, the skipper saw Tommy Dort poring over one of the strange objects which were the equivalent of books. It was fascinating to puzzle over. The skipper was pleased with himself. The technicians of the *Llanvabon's* former crew were finding out desirable things about the ship almost momently. Doubtless the aliens were as pleased with their discoveries in the *Llanvabon*. But the black ship would be enormously worth while—and the solution that had been found was by any standard much superior even to combat in which the Earthmen had been overwhelmingly victorious.

"Hm-m-m. Mr. Dort," said the skipper profoundly. "You've no equipment to make another photographic record on the way back. It was left on the *Llanvabon*. But fortunately, we have your record taken on the way out, and I shall report most favorably on your suggestion and your assistance in carrying it out. I think very well of you, sir."

"Thank you, sir," said Tommy Dort.

He waited. The skipper cleared his throat.

"You . . . ah . . . first realized the close similarity of mental processes between the aliens and ourselves," he observed. "What do you think of the prospects of a friendly arrangement if we keep a rendezvous with them at the nebula as agreed?"

"Oh, we'll get along all right, sir," said Tommy. "We've got a good start toward friendship. After all, since they see by infrared, the planets they'd want to make use of wouldn't suit us. There's no reason why we shouldn't get along. We're almost alike in psychology."

"Hm-m-m. Now just what do you mean by that?" demanded the skipper.

"Why, they're just like us, sir!" said Tommy. "Of course they breathe through gills and they see by heat waves, and their blood has a copper base instead of iron and a few little details like that. But otherwise we're just alike! There were only men in their crew, sir, but they have two sexes as we have, and they have families, and . . . er . . . their sense of humor— In fact—"

Tommy hesitated.

"Go on, sir," said the skipper.

"Well— There was the one I called Buck, sir, because he hasn't any name that goes into sound waves," said Tommy. "We got along very well. I'd really call him my friend, sir. And we were together for a couple of hours just before the two ships separated and we'd nothing in particular to do. So I became convinced that humans and aliens are bound to be good friends if they have only half a chance. You see, sir, we spent those two hours telling dirty jokes."

ROBERT HEINLEIN

UNIVERSE

"The Proxima Centauri Expedition, sponsored by the Jordan Foundation in 2119, was the first recorded attempt to reach the nearer stars of this galaxy. Whatever its unhappy fate, we can only conjecture—"
Quoted from The Romance of Modern Astrography, *by Franklin Buck, published by Lux Transcriptions, Ltd., 3.50 cr.*

"THERE'S a mutie! Look out!" At the shouted warning Hugh Hoyland ducked, with nothing to spare. An egg-sized iron missile clanged against the bulkhead just above his scalp with force that promised a fractured skull. The speed with which he crouched had lifted his feet from the floor plates. Before his body could settle slowly to the deck, he planted his feet against the bulkhead behind him and shoved. He went shooting down the passageway in a long, flat dive, his knife drawn and ready.

He twisted in the air, checked himself with his feet against the opposite bulkhead at the turn in the passage from which the mutie had attacked him, and floated lightly to his feet. The other branch of the passage was empty.

His two companions joined him, sliding awkwardly over the floor plates. "Is he gone?" demanded Alan Mahoney.

"Yes," agreed Hoyland. "I caught a glimpse of it as it ducked down that hatch. A female, I think. Looked like it had four legs."

"Two legs, or four, we'll never catch it now," commented the third man.

"Who the Huff wants to catch it?" protested Mahoney. "*I* don't."

"Well, I do, for one," said Hoyland. "By Jordan, if its aim had been two inches better, I'd be ready for the Converter."

"Can't either one of you two speak three words without swearing?" the third man disapproved. "What if the Captain could hear you?" He touched his forehead reverently as he mentioned the Captain.

"Oh, for Jordan's sake," snapped Hoyland, "don't be so stuffy, Mort Tyler. You're not a scientist yet. I reckon I'm as devout as you are—there's no grave sin in occasionally giving vent to your feelings. Even the scientists do it. I've heard 'em."

Tyler opened his mouth as if to expostulate, then apparently thought better of it.

Mahoney touched Hoyland on the arm. "Look, Hugh," he pleaded, "let's get out of here. We've never been this high before. I'm jumpy—I want to get back down to where I can feel some weight on my feet."

Hoyland looked longingly toward the hatch through which his assailant had disappeared while his hand rested on the grip of his knife, then he turned to Mahoney. "O. K., kid," he agreed, "it's a long trip down anyhow."

He turned and slithered back toward the hatch whereby they had reached the level where they now were, the other two following him. Disregarding the ladder by which they had mounted, he stepped off into the opening and floated slowly down to the deck fifteen feet below, Tyler and Mahoney close behind him. Another hatch, staggered a few feet from the first, gave access to a still lower deck. Down, down, down, and still farther down they dropped, tens and dozens of decks, each silent, dimly lighted, mysterious. Each time they fell a little faster, landed a little harder. Mahoney protested at last.

"Let's walk the rest of the way, Hugh. That last jump hurt my feet."

"All right. But it will take longer. How far have we got to go? Anybody keep count?"

"We've got about seventy decks to go to reach farm country," answered Tyler.

"How do you know?" demanded Mahoney suspiciously.

"I counted them, stupid. And as we came down I took one away for each deck."

"You did not. Nobody but a scientist can do numbering like that. Just because you're learning to read and write you think you know everything."

Hoyland cut in before it could develop into a quarrel. "Shut up, Alan. Maybe he can do it. He's clever about such things. Anyhow, it feels like about seventy decks—I'm heavy enough."

"Maybe he'd like to count the blades on my knife."

"Stow it, I said. Dueling is forbidden outside the village. That is the Rule." They proceeded in silence, running lightly down the stairways until increasing weight on each succeeding level forced them to a more pedestrian pace. Presently they broke through into a level that was quite brilliantly lighted and more than twice as deep between decks as the ones above it. The air was moist and warm; vegetation obscured the view.

"Well, down at last," said Hugh. "I don't recognize this farm; we must have come down by a different line than we went up."

"There's a farmer," said Tyler. He put his little fingers to his lips and whistled, then called, "Hey! Shipmate! Where are we?"

The peasant looked them over slowly, then directed them in reluctant monosyllables to the main passageway which would lead them back to their own village.

A brisk walk of a mile and a half down a wide tunnel moderately crowded with traffic—travelers, porters, an occasional pushcart, a dignified scientist swinging in a litter borne by four husky orderlies and preceded by his master at arms to clear the common crew out of the way—a mile and a half of this brought them to the common of their own village, a spacious compartment three decks high and perhaps ten times as wide. They split up and went their own ways, Hugh to his quarters in the barracks of the cadets—young bachelors who did not live with their parents. He washed himself, and went thence to the compartments of his uncle, for whom he worked for his meals. His aunt glanced up as he came in, but said nothing, as became a woman.

His uncle said, "Hello, Hugh. Been exploring again?"

"Good eating, uncle. Yes."

His uncle, a stolid sensible man, looked tolerantly amused. "Where did you go and what did you find?"

Hugh's aunt had slipped silently out of the compartment, and now returned with his supper which she placed before him. He fell to—it did not occur to him to thank her. He munched a bite before replying.

"Up. We climbed almost to the level-of-no-weight. A mutie tried to crack my skull."

His uncle chuckled. "You'll find your death in those passageways, lad. Better you should pay more attention to my business against the day when I'll die and get out of your way."

Hugh looked stubborn. "Don't you have any curiosity, uncle?"

"Me? Oh, I was prying enough when I was a lad. I followed the main passage all the way around and back to the village. Right through the Dark Sector I went, with muties tagging my heels. See that scar?"

Hugh glanced at it perfunctorily. He had seen it many times before and heard the story repeated to boredom. Once around the Ship—*pfui!* He wanted to go everywhere, see everything, and find out the why of things. Those upper levels now—if men were not intended to climb that high, why had Jordan created them?

But he kept his own counsel and went on with his meal. His uncle changed the subject. "I've occasion to visit the Witness. John Black claims I owe him three swine. Want to come along?"

"Why, no, I guess not— Wait— I believe I will."

"Hurry up, then."

They stopped at the cadets' barracks, Hugh claiming an errand. The Witness lived in a small, smelly compartment directly across the Common from the barracks, where he would be readily accessible to any who had need of his talents. They found him sitting in his doorway, picking his teeth with a fingernail. His apprentice, a pimply-faced adolescent with an intent nearsighted expression, squatted behind him.

"Good eating," said Hugh's uncle.

"Good eating to you, Edard Hoyland. D'you come on business, or to keep an old man company?"

"Both," Hugh's uncle returned diplomatically, then explained his errand.

"So?" said the Witness. "Well—the contract's clear enough:

> "Black John delivered ten bushels of oats,
> Expecting his pay in a pair of shoats;
> Ed brought his sow to breed for pig;
> John gets his pay when the pigs grow big.

"How big are the pigs now, Edard Hoyland?"

"Big enough," acknowledged Hugh's uncle, "but Black claims three instead of two."

"Tell him to go soak his head. 'The Witness has spoken.' " He laughed in a thin, high cackle.

The two gossiped for a few minutes, Edard Hoyland digging into his recent experiences to satisfy the old man's insatiable liking for details. Hugh kept decently silent while the older men talked. But when his uncle turned to go he spoke up. "I'll stay awhile, uncle."

"Eh? Suit yourself. Good eating, Witness."

"Good eating, Edard Hoyland."

"I've brought you a present, Witness," said Hugh, when his uncle had passed out of hearing.

"Let me see it."

Hugh produced a package of tobacco which he had picked up from his locker at the barracks. The Witness accepted it without acknowledgment, then tossed it to his apprentice, who took charge of it.

"Come inside," invited the Witness, then directed his speech to his apprentice. "Here, you—fetch the cadet a chair."

"Now, lad," he added as they sat themselves down, "tell me what you have been doing with yourself."

Hugh told him, and was required to repeat in detail all the incidents of his more recent explorations, the Witness complaining the meanwhile over his inability to remember exactly everything he saw.

"You youngsters have no capacity," he pronounced. "No capacity. Even that lout"—he jerked his head toward the apprentice—"he has none, though he's a dozen times better than you. Would you believe it, he can't soak up a thousand lines a day, yet he expects to sit in my seat when I am gone. Why, when I was apprenticed, I used to sing myself to sleep on a mere thousand lines. Leaky vessels—that's what you are."

Hugh did not dispute the charge, but waited for the old man to go on, which he did in his own time.

"You had a question to put to me, lad?"

"In a way, Witness."

"Well—out with it. Don't chew your tongue."

"Did you ever climb all the way up to no-weight?"

"Me? Of course not. I was a Witness, learning my calling. I had the lines of all the Witnesses before me to learn, and no time for boyish amusements."

"I had hoped you could tell me what I would find there."

"Well, now, that's another matter. I've never climbed, but I hold the memories of more climbers than you will ever see. I'm an old man. I knew your father's father, and his grandsire before that. What is it you want to know?"

"Well—" What was it he wanted to know? How could he ask a question that was no more than a gnawing ache in his breast? Still— "What is it all for, Witness? Why are there all those levels above us?"

"Eh? How's that? Jordan's name, son—I'm a Witness, not a scientist."

"Well—I thought you must know. I'm sorry."

"But I do know. What you want is the Lines from the Beginning."

"I've heard them."

"Hear them again. All your answers are in there, if you've the wisdom to see them. Attend me. No—this is a chance for my apprentice to show off his learning. Here, you! The Lines from the Beginning—and mind your rhythm."

The apprentice wet his lips with his tongue and began:

"In the Beginning there was Jordan, thinking His lonely thoughts alone.
In the Beginning there was darkness, formless, dead, and Man unknown.
Out of the loneness came a longing, out of the longing came a vision,
Out of the dream there came a planning, out of the plan there came
    decision—
Jordan's hand was lifted and the Ship was born!

"Mile after mile of snug compartments, tank by tank for the golden corn,
Ladder and passage, door and locker, fit for the needs of the yet unborn.
He looked on His work and found it pleasing, meet for a race that was
    yet to be.
He thought of Man—Man came into being—checked his thought and
    searched for the key.
Man untamed would shame his Maker, Man unruled would spoil the
    Plan;
So Jordan made the Regulations, orders to each single man,
Each to a task and each to a station, serving a purpose beyond their ken,
Some to speak and some to listen—order came to the ranks of men.

Crew He created to work at their stations, scientists to guide the Plan.
Over them all He created the Captain, made him judge of the race of
Man.
Thus it was in the Golden Age!
Jordan is perfect, all below him lack perfection in their deeds.
Envy, Greed and Pride of Spirit sought for minds to lodge their seeds.
One there was who gave them lodging—accursed Huff, the first to sin!
His evil counsel stirred rebellion, planted doubt where it had not
been;
Blood of martyrs stained the floor plates, Jordan's Captain made the
Trip.
Darkness swallowed up—"

The old man gave the boy the back of his hand, sharp across the mouth.
"Try again!"
"From the beginning?"
"No! From where you missed."
The boy hesitated, then caught his stride:

"Darkness swallowed ways of virtue, Sin prevailed throughout the Ship—"

The boy's voice droned on, stanza after stanza, reciting at great length
but with little sharpness of detail the old, old story of sin, rebellion, and
the time of darkness. How wisdom prevailed at last and the bodies of the
rebel leaders were fed to the Converter. How some of the rebels escaped
making the Trip and lived to father the muties. How a new Captain was
chosen, after prayer and sacrifice.

Hugh stirred uneasily, shuffling his feet. No doubt the answers to his
questions were there, since these were the Sacred Lines, but he had not
the wit to understand them. Why? What was it all about? Was there really
nothing more to life than eating and sleeping and finally the long Trip?
Didn't Jordan intend for him to understand? Then why this ache in his
breast? This hunger that persisted in spite of good eating?

While he was breaking his fast after sleep an orderly came to the
door of his uncle's compartments. "The scientist requires the presence of
Hugh Hoyland," he recited glibly.

Hugh knew that the scientist referred to was Lieutenant Nelson, in
charge of the spiritual and physical welfare of the Ship's sector which
included Hugh's native village. He bolted the last of his breakfast and
hurried after the messenger.

"Cadet Hoyland!" he was announced. The scientist looked up from
his own meal and said:

"Oh, yes. Come in, my boy. Sit down. Have you eaten?"

Hugh acknowledged that he had, but his eyes rested with interest on
the fancy fruit in front of his superior. Nelson followed his glance. "Try
some of these figs. They're a new mutation—I had them brought all the

way from the far side. Go ahead—a man your age always has somewhere to stow a few more bites."

Hugh accepted with much self-consciousness. Never before had he eaten in the presence of a scientist. The elder leaned back in his chair, wiped his fingers on his shirt, arranged his beard, and started in.

"I haven't seen you lately, son. Tell me what you have been doing with yourself." Before Hugh could reply he went on, "No, don't tell me— I will tell you. For one thing you have been exploring, climbing, without too much respect for the forbidden areas. Is it not so?" He held the young man's eye. Hugh fumbled for a reply.

But he was let off again. "Never mind. I know, and you know that I know. I am not too displeased. But it has brought it forcibly to my attention that it is time that you decided what you are to do with your life. Have you any plans?"

"Well—no definite ones, sir."

"How about that girl, Edris Baxter? D'you intend to marry her?"

"Why . . . uh . . . I don't know, sir. I guess I want to, and her father is willing, I think. Only—"

"Only what?"

"Well—he wants me to apprentice to his farm. I suppose it's a good idea. His farm together with my uncle's business would make a good property."

"But you're not sure?"

"Well—I don't know."

"Correct. You're not for that. I have other plans. Tell me, have you ever wondered why I taught you to read and write? Of course, you have. But you've kept your own counsel. That is good.

"Now attend me. I've watched you since you were a small child. You have more imagination than the common run, more curiosity, more go. And you are a born leader. You were different even as a baby. Your head was too large, for one thing, and there were some who voted at your birth inspection to put you at once into the Converter. But I held them off. I wanted to see how you would turn out.

"A peasant life is not for the likes of you. You are to be a scientist."

The old man paused and studied his face. Hugh was confused, speechless. Nelson went on, "Oh, yes. Yes, indeed. For a man of your temperament, there are only two things to do with him: Make him one of the custodians, or send him to the Converter."

"Do you mean, sir, that I have nothing to say about it?"

"If you want to put it that bluntly—yes. To leave the bright ones among the ranks of the Crew is to breed heresy. We can't have that. We had it once and it almost destroyed the human race. You have marked yourself out by your exceptional ability; you must now be instructed in right thinking, be initiated into the mysteries, in order that you may be a conserving force rather than a focus of infection and a source of trouble."

The orderly reappeared loaded down with bundles which he dumped on the deck. Hugh glanced at them, then burst out, "Why, those are my things!"

"Certainly," acknowledged Nelson. "I sent for them. You're to sleep here henceforth. I'll see you later and start you on your studies—unless you have something more on your mind?"

"Why, no, sir, I guess not. I must admit I am a little confused. I suppose . . . I suppose this means you don't want me to marry?"

"Oh, *that*," Nelson answered indifferently. "Take her if you like—her father can't protest now. But let me warn you you'll grow tired of her."

Hugh Hoyland devoured the ancient books that his mentor permitted him to read, and felt no desire for many, many sleeps to go climbing, or even to stir out of Nelson's cabin. More than once he felt that he was on the track of the secret—a secret as yet undefined, even as a question— but again he would find himself more confused than ever. It was evidently harder to reach the wisdom of scientisthood than he had thought.

Once, while he was worrying away at the curious twisted characters of the ancients and trying to puzzle out their odd rhetoric and unfamiliar terms, Nelson came into the little compartment that had been set aside for him, and, laying a fatherly hand on his shoulder, asked, "How goes it, boy?"

"Why, well enough, sir, I suppose," he answered, laying the book aside. "Some of it is not quite clear to me—not clear at all, to tell the truth."

"That is to be expected," the old man said equably. "I've let you struggle along by yourself at first in order that you may see the traps that native wit alone will fall into. Many of these things are not to be understood without instruction. What have you there?" He picked up the book and glanced at it. It was inscribed *Basic Modern Physics*. "So? This is one of the most valuable of the sacred writings, yet the uninitiate could not possibly make good use of it without help. The first thing that you must understand, my boy, is that our forefathers, for all their spiritual perfection, did not look at things in the fashion in which we do.

"They were incurable romantics, rather than rationalists, as we are, and the truths which they handed down to us, though strictly true, were frequently clothed in allegorical language. For example, have you come to the Law of Gravitation?"

"I read about it."

"Did you understand it? No, I can see that you didn't."

"Well," said Hugh defensively, "it didn't seem to *mean* anything. It just sounded silly, if you will pardon me, sir."

"That illustrates my point. You were thinking of it in literal terms, like the laws governing electrical devices found elsewhere in this same book. 'Two bodies attract each other directly as the product of their masses and inversely as the square of their distance.' It sounds like a rule for simple physical facts, does it not? Yet it is nothing of the sort: it was the poetical way the old ones had of expressing the rule of propinquity which governs the emotion of love. The bodies referred to are human bodies, mass is their capacity for love. Young people have a greater capacity for love than the elderly; when they are thrown together, they fall in love, yet when they are separated they soon get over it. 'Out of sight, out of mind.' It's as simple as that. But you were seeking some deep meaning for it."

Hugh grinned. "I never thought of looking at it that way. I can see that I am going to need a lot of help."

"Is there anything else bothering you just now?"

"Well, yes, lots of things, though I probably can't remember them off-hand. I mind one thing: Tell me, father, can muties be considered as being people?"

"I can see you have been listening to idle talk. The answer to that is both yes and no. It is true that the muties originally descended from people but they are no longer part of the Crew—they cannot now be considered as members of the human race, for they have flouted Jordan's Law.

"This is a broad subject," he went on, settling down to it. "There is even some question as to the original meaning of the word 'mutie.' Certainly they number among their ancestors the mutineers who escaped death at the time of the rebellion. But they also have in their blood the blood of many of the mutants who were born during the dark age. You understand, of course, that during that period our present wise rule of inspecting each infant for the mark of sin and returning to the Converter any who are found to be mutations was not in force. There are strange and horrible things crawling through the dark passageways and lurking in the deserted levels."

Hugh thought about it for a while, then asked, "Why is it that mutations still show up among us, the people?"

"That is simple. The seed of sin is still in us. From time to time it still shows up, incarnate. In destroying those monsters we help to cleanse the stock and thereby bring closer the culmination of Jordan's Plan, the end of the Trip at our heavenly home, far Centaurus."

Hoyland's brow wrinkled again. "That is another thing that I don't understand. Many of these ancient writings speak of the Trip as if it were an actual *moving*, a going-somewhere—as if the Ship itself were no more than a pushcart. How can that be?"

Nelson chuckled. "How can it, indeed? How can that move which is the background against which all else moves? The answer, of course, is plain. You have again mistaken allegorical language for the ordinary usage of everyday speech. Of course, the Ship is solid, immovable, in a physical sense. How can the whole universe move? Yet, it *does* move, in a spiritual sense. With every righteous act we move closer to the sublime destination of Jordan's Plan."

Hugh nodded. "I think I see."

"Of course, it is conceivable that Jordan could have fashioned the world in some other shape than the Ship, had it suited his purpose. When man was younger and more poetical, holy men vied with one another in inventing fanciful worlds which Jordan might have created. One school invented an entire mythology of a topsy-turvy world of endless reaches of space, empty save for pin points of light and bodyless mythological monsters. They called it the heavenly world, or heaven, as if to contrast it with the solid reality of the Ship. They seemed never to tire of speculating about it, inventing details for it, and of making pictures of what they conceived it to be like. I suppose they did it to the greater glory of Jordan, and who is to say that He found their dreams unacceptable? But in this modern age we have more serious work to do."

Hugh was not interested in astronomy. Even his untutored mind had been able to see in its wild extravagance an intention not literal. He returned to problems nearer at hand. "Since the muties are the seed of sin, why do we make no effort to wipe them out? Would not that be an act that would speed the Plan?"

The old man considered a while before replying. "That is a fair question and deserves a straight answer. Since you are to be a scientist you will need to know the answer. Look at it this way: There is a definite limit to the number of Crew the Ship can support. If our numbers increase without limit, there comes a time when there will not be good eating for all of us. Is it not better that some should die in brushes with the muties than that we should grow in numbers until we killed each other for food?

"The ways of Jordan are inscrutable. Even the muties have a part in his Plan."

It seemed reasonable but Hugh was not sure.

But when Hugh was transferred to active work as a junior scientist in the operation of the Ship's functions, he found there were other opinions. As was customary, he put in a period serving the Converter. The work was not onerous; he had principally to check in the waste materials brought in by porters from each of the villages, keep books on their contributions, and make sure that no reclaimable metal was introduced into the first-stage hopper. But it brought him into contact with Bill Ertz, the assistant chief engineer, a man not much older than himself.

He discussed with him the things he had learned from Nelson, and was shocked at Ertz's attitude.

"Get this through your head, kid," Ertz told him. "This is a practical job for practical men. Forget all that romantic nonsense. Jordan's Plan! That stuff is all right to keep the peasants quiet and in their place, but don't fall for it yourself. There is no Plan—other than our own plans for looking out for ourselves. The Ship has to have light and heat and power for cooking and irrigation. The Crew can't get along without those things and that makes us boss of the Crew.

"As for this soft-headed tolerance toward the muties, you're going to see some changes made! Keep your mouth shut and string along with us."

It impressed on him that he was expected to maintain a primary loyalty to the bloc of younger men among the scientists. They were a well-knit organization within an organization and were made up of practical, hard-headed men who were working toward improvement of conditions throughout the Ship, as they saw them. They were well-knit because an apprentice who failed to see things their way did not last long. Either he failed to measure up and soon found himself back in the ranks of the peasants, or, as was more likely, suffered some mishap and wound up in the Converter.

And Hoyland began to see that they were right.

They were realists. The Ship was the Ship. It was a fact, requiring no explanation. As for Jordan—who had ever seen Him, spoken to Him? What was this nebulous Plan of His? The object of life was living. A man was born, lived his life, and then went to the Converter. It was as simple as that, no mystery to it, no sublime Trip and no Centaurus. These romantic stories were simply hangovers from the childhood of the race before men gained the understanding and the courage to look facts in the face.

He ceased bothering his head about astronomy and mystical physics and all the other mass of mythology he had been taught to revere. He was still amused, more or less, by the Lines from the Beginning and by all the old stories about Earth—what the Huff was "Earth," anyhow?—but now realized that such things could be taken seriously only by children and dullards.

Besides, there was work to do. The younger men, while still maintaining the nominal authority of their elders, had plans of their own, the first of which was a systematic extermination of the muties. Beyond that, their intentions were still fluid, but they contemplated making full use of the resources of the Ship, including the upper levels. The young men were able to move ahead with their plans without an open breach with their elders because the older scientists simply did not bother to any great extent with the routine of the Ship. The present Captain had grown so fat that he rarely stirred from his cabin; his aide, one of the young men's bloc, attended to affairs for him.

Hoyland never laid eyes on the Chief Engineer save once, when he showed up for the purely religious ceremony of manning landing sta·tions.

The project of cleaning out the muties required reconnaissance of the upper levels to be done systematically. It was in carrying out such scouting that Hugh Hoyland was again ambushed by a mutie.

This mutie was more accurate with his slingshot. Hoyland's companions, forced to retreat by superior numbers, left him for dead.

Joe-Jim Gregory was playing himself a game of checkers. Time was when they had played cards together, but Joe, the head on the right, had suspected Jim, the left-hand member of the team, of cheating. They had quarreled about it, then given it up, for they had both learned early in their joint career that two heads on one pair of shoulders must necessarily find ways of getting along together.

Checkers was better. They could both see the board, and disagreement was impossible.

A loud metallic knocking at the door of the compartment interrupted the game. Joe-Jim unsheathed his throwing knife and cradled it, ready for quick use. "Come in!" roared Jim.

The door opened, the one who had knocked backed into the room—the only safe way, as everyone knew, to enter Joe-Jim's presence. The new-comer was squat and ruggedly powerful, not over four feet in height. The relaxed body of a man hung across one shoulder and was steadied by a hand.

Joe-Jim returned the knife to its sheath. "Put it down, Bobo," Jim ordered.

"—And close the door," added Joe. "Now what have we got here?"

It was a young man, apparently dead, though no wound appeared on him. Bobo patted a thigh. "Eat 'im?" he said hopefully. Saliva spilled out of his still-opened lips.

"Maybe," temporized Jim. "Did you kill him?"

Bobo shook his undersized head.

"Good Bobo," Joe approved. "Where did you hit him?"

"Bobo hit him *there*." The microcephalic shoved a broad thumb against the supine figure in the area between the umbilicus and the breast bone.

"Good shot," Joe approved. "We couldn't have done better with a knife."

"Bobo *good* shot," the dwarf agreed blandly. "Want see?" He twitched his slingshot invitingly.

"Shut up," answered Joe, not unkindly. "No, we don't want to see; we want to make him talk."

"Bobo fix," the short one agreed, and started with simple brutality to carry out his purpose.

Joe-Jim slapped him away, and applied other methods, painful but considerably less drastic than those of the dwarf. The young man jerked and opened his eyes.

"Eat 'im?" repeated Bobo.

"No," said Joe. "When did you eat last?" inquired Jim.

Bobo shook his head and rubbed his stomach, indicating with graphic pantomime that it had been a long time—too long. Joe-Jim went over to a locker, opened it, and withdrew a haunch of meat. He held it up. Jim smelled it and Joe drew his head away in nose-wrinkling disgust. Joe-Jim threw it to Bobo, who snatched it happily out of the air. "Now, get out," ordered Jim.

Bobo trotted away, closing the door behind him. Joe-Jim turned to the captive and prodded him with his foot. "Speak up," said Jim. "Who the Huff are you?"

The young man shivered, put a hand to his head, then seemed suddenly to bring his surroundings into focus, for he scrambled to his feet, moving awkwardly against the low weight conditions of this level, and reached for his knife.

It was not at his belt.

Joe-Jim had his own out and brandished it. "Be good and you won't get hurt. What do they call you?"

The young man wet his lips, and his eyes hurried about the room. "Speak up," said Joe.

"Why bother with him?" inquired Jim. "I'd say he was only good for meat. Better call Bobo back."

"No hurry about that," Joe answered. "I want to talk to him. What's your name?"

The prisoner looked again at the knife and muttered, "Hugh Hoyland."

"That doesn't tell us much," Jim commented. "What d'you do? What village do you come from? And what were you doing in mutie country?"

But this time Hoyland was sullen. Even the prick of the knife against his ribs caused him only to bite his lips. "Shucks," said Joe, "he's only a stupid peasant. Let's drop it."

"Shall we finish him off?"

"No. Not now. Shut him up."

Joe-Jim opened the door of a small side compartment, and urged Hugh in with the knife. He then closed and fastened the door and went back to his game. "Your move, Jim."

The compartment in which Hugh was locked was dark. He soon satisfied himself by touch that the smooth steel walls were entirely featureless save for the solid, securely fastened door. Presently he lay down on the deck and gave himself up to fruitless thinking.

He had plenty of time to think, time to fall asleep and awaken more than once. And time to grow very hungry and very, very thirsty.

When Joe-Jim next took sufficient interest in his prisoner to open the door of the cell, Hoyland was not immediately in evidence. He had planned many times what he would do when the door opened and his chance came, but when the event arrived, he was too weak, semicomatose. Joe-Jim dragged him out.

The disturbance roused him to partial comprehension. He sat up and stared around him.

"Ready to talk?" asked Jim.

Hoyland opened his mouth but no words came out.

"Can't you see he's too dry to talk?" Joe told his twin. Then to Hugh, "Will you talk if we give you some water?"

Hoyland looked puzzled, then nodded vigorously.

Joe-Jim returned in a moment with a mug of water. Hugh drank greedily, paused, and seemed about to faint.

Joe-Jim took the mug from him. "That's enough for now," said Joe. "Tell us about yourself."

Hugh did so. In detail, being prompted from time to time.

Hugh accepted a *de facto* condition of slavery with no particular resistance and no great disturbance of soul. The word "slave" was not in his vocabulary, but the condition was a commonplace in everything he had ever known. There had always been those who gave orders and those who carried them out—he could imagine no other condition, no other type of social organization. It was a fact of nature.

Though naturally he thought of escape.

Thinking about it was as far as he got. Joe-Jim guessed his thoughts and brought the matter out into the open. Joe told him, "Don't go getting ideas, youngster. Without a knife you wouldn't get three levels away in this part of the Ship. If you managed to steal a knife from me, you still wouldn't make it down to high-weight. Besides, there's Bobo."

Hugh waited a moment, as was fitting, then said, "Bobo?"

Jim grinned and replied, "We told Bobo that you were his to butcher, if he liked, if you ever stuck your head out of our compartments without us. Now he sleeps outside the door and spends a lot of his time there."

"It was only fair," put in Joe. "He was disappointed when we decided to keep you."

"Say," suggested Jim, turning his head toward his brother's, "how about some fun?" He turned back to Hugh. "Can you throw a knife?"

"Of course," Hugh answered.

"Let's see you. Here." Joe-Jim handed him their own knife. Hugh accepted it, jiggling it in his hand to try its balance. "Try my mark."

Joe-Jim had a plastic target set up at the far end of the room from his favorite chair, on which he was wont to practice his own skill. Hugh eyed it, and, with an arm motion too fast to follow, let fly. He used the economical underhand stroke, thumb on the blade, fingers together.

The blade shivered in the target, well centered in the chewed-up area which marked Joe-Jim's best efforts.

"Good boy!" Joe approved. "What do you have in mind, Jim?"

"Let's give him the knife and see how far he gets."

"No," said Joe, "I don't agree."

"Why not?"

"If Bobo wins, we're out one servant. If Hugh wins, we lose both Bobo and him. It's wasteful."

"Oh, well—if you insist."

"I do. Hugh, fetch the knife."

Hugh did so. It had not occurred to him to turn the knife against

Joe-Jim. The master was the master. For servant to attack master was not simply repugnant to good morals, it was an idea so wild that it did not occur to him at all.

Hugh had expected that Joe-Jim would be impressed by his learning as a scientist. It did not work out that way. Joe-Jim, especially Jim, loved to argue. They sucked Hugh dry in short order and figuratively cast him aside. Hoyland felt humiliated. After all, was he not a scientist? Could he not read and write?

"Shut up," Jim told him. "Reading is simple. I could do it before your father was born. D'you think you're the first scientist that has served me? Scientists—bah! A pack of ignoramuses!"

In an attempt to re-establish his own intellectual conceit, Hugh expounded the theories of the younger scientists, the strictly matter-of-fact, hard-boiled realism which rejected all religious interpretation and took the Ship as it was. He confidently expected Joe-Jim to approve such a point of view; it seemed to fit their temperaments.

They laughed in his face.

"Honest," Jim insisted, when he had ceased snorting, "are you young punks so stupid as all that? Why, you're worse than your elders."

"But you just got through saying," Hugh protested in hurt tones, "that all our accepted religious notions are so much bunk. That is just what my friends think. They want to junk all that old nonsense."

Joe started to speak; Jim cut in ahead of him. "Why bother with him, Joe? He's hopeless."

"No, he's not. I'm enjoying this. He's the first one I've talked with in I don't know how long who stood any chance at all of seeing the truth. Let us be—I want to see whether that's a head he has on his shoulders, or just a place to hang his ears."

"O. K.," Jim agreed, "but keep it quiet. I'm going to take a nap." The left-hand head closed its eyes, soon it was snoring. Joe and Hugh continued their discussion in whispers.

"The trouble with you youngsters," he said, "is that if you can't understand a thing right off, you think it can't be true. The trouble with your elders is, anything they didn't understand they re-interpreted to mean something else and then thought they understood it. None of you has tried believing clear words the way they were written and then tried to understand them on that basis. Oh, no, you're all too bloody smart for that— if you can't see it right off, it ain't so—it must mean something different."

"What do you mean?" Hugh asked suspiciously.

"Well, take the Trip, for instance. What does it mean to you?"

"Well—to my mind, it doesn't mean anything. It's just a piece of nonsense to impress the peasants."

"And what is the accepted meaning?"

"Well—it's where you go when you die—or rather what you do. You make the Trip to Centaurus."

"And what is Centaurus?"

"It's—mind you, I'm just telling you the orthodox answers; I don't really believe this stuff—it's where you arrive when you've made the Trip, a place where everybody's happy and there's always good eating."

Joe snorted. Jim broke the rhythm of his snoring, opened one eye, and settled back again with a grunt. "That's just what I mean," Joe went on in a lower whisper. "You don't use your head. Did it ever occur to you that the Trip was just what the old books said it was—the Ship and all the Crew actually going somewhere, moving?"

Hoyland thought about it. "You don't mean for me to take you seriously. Physically, it's an impossibility. The Ship can't *go* anywhere. It already *is* everywhere. We can make a trip through it, but *the* Trip—that has to have a spiritual meaning, if it has any."

Joe called on Jordan to support him. "Now, listen," he said, "get this through that thick head of yours. Imagine a place a lot bigger than the Ship, a lot bigger, with the Ship inside it—*moving*. D'you get it?"

Hugh tried. He tried very hard. He shook his head. "It doesn't make sense," he said. "There can't be anything bigger than the Ship. There wouldn't be any place for it to *be*."

"Oh, for Huff's sake! Listen—*outside* the Ship, get that? Straight down beyond the lowest level in every direction. Emptiness out there. Understand me?"

"But there isn't anything below the lowest level. That's why it's the lowest level."

"Look. If you took a knife and started digging a hole in the floor of the lowest level, where would it get you?"

"But you *can't*. It's too hard."

"But suppose you did and it made a hole. Where would that hole go? Imagine it."

Hugh shut his eyes and tried to imagine digging a hole in the lowest level. Digging—as if it were soft—soft as cheese.

He began to get some glimmering of a possibility, a possibility that was unsettling, soul-shaking. He was falling, falling into a hole that he had dug which had no levels under it. He opened his eyes very quickly. "That's awful!" he ejaculated. "I won't believe it."

Joe-Jim got up. "I'll *make* you believe it," he said grimly, "if I have to break your neck to do it." He strode over to the outer door and opened it. "Bobo!" he shouted. "Bobo!"

Jim's head snapped erect. "Wassa matter? Wha's going on?"

"We're going to take Hugh to no-weight."

"What for?"

"To pound some sense into his silly head."

"Some other time."

"No, I want to do it now."

"All right, all right. No need to shout. I'm awake now, anyhow."

Joe-Jim Gregory was almost as nearly unique in his, or their, mental ability as he was in his bodily construction. Under any circumstances he would have been a dominant personality; among the muties it was inevitable that he should bully them, order them about, and live on their services. Had he had the will-to-power, it is conceivable that he could have organized the muties to fight and overcome the Crew proper.

But he lacked that drive. He was by native temperament an intellectual, a bystander, an observer. He was interested in the "how" and the "why," but his will to action was satisfied with comfort and convenience alone.

Had he been born two normal twins and among the Crew, it is likely that he would have drifted into scientisthood as the easiest and most satisfactory answer to the problem of living and as such would have entertained himself mildly with conversation and administration. As it was, he lacked mental companionship and had whiled away three generations reading and re-reading books stolen for him by his stooges.

The two halves of his dual person had argued and discussed what they read, and had almost inevitably arrived at a reasonably coherent theory of history and the physical world—except in one respect, the concept of fiction was entirely foreign to them; they treated the novels that had been provided for the Jordan expedition in exactly the same fashion that they did text and reference books.

This led to their one major difference of opinion. Jim regarded Allan Quartermain as the greatest man who had ever lived; Joe held out for John Henry.

They were both inordinately fond of poetry; they could recite page after page of Kipling, and were nearly as fond of Rhysling, "the blind singer of the spaceways."

Bobo backed in. Joe-Jim hooked a thumb toward Hugh. "Look," said Joe, "he's going out."

"Now?" said Bobo happily, and grinned, slavering.

"You and your stomach!" Joe answered, rapping Bobo's pate with his knuckles. "No, you don't eat him. You and him—blood brothers. Get it?"

"Not eat 'im?"

"No. Fight for him. He fights for you."

"O. K." The pinhead shrugged his shoulders at the inevitable. "Blood brothers. Bobo know."

"All right. Now we go up to the place-where-everybody-flies. You go ahead and make lookout."

They climbed in single file, the dwarf running ahead to spot the lay of the land, Hoyland behind him, Joe-Jim bringing up the rear, Joe with eyes to the front, Jim watching their rear, head turned over his shoulder.

Higher and higher they went, weight slipping imperceptibly from them with each successive deck. They emerged finally into a level beyond which there was no further progress, no opening above them. The deck curved gently, suggesting that the true shape of the space was a giant cylinder, but overhead a metallic expanse which exhibited a similar curvature obstructed the view and prevented one from seeing whether or not the deck in truth curved back on itself.

There were no proper bulkheads; great stanchions, so huge and squat as to give an impression of excessive, unnecessary strength, grew thickly about them, spacing deck and overhead evenly apart.

Weight was imperceptible. If one remained quietly in one place, the undetectable residuum of weight would bring the body in a gentle drift down to the "floor," but "up" and "down" were terms largely lacking in meaning. Hugh did not like it, it made him gulp, but Bobo seemed delighted by it and not unused to it. He moved through the air like an uncouth fish, banking off stanchion, floor plate, and overhead as suited his convenience.

Joe-Jim set a course parallel to the common axis of the inner and outer cylinders, following a passageway formed by the orderly spacing of the stanchions. There were handrails set along the passage, one of which he followed like a spider on its thread. He made remarkable speed, which Hugh floundered to maintain. In time, he caught the trick of the easy, effortless, overhand pull, the long coast against nothing but air resistance, and the occasional flick of the toes or the hand against the floor. But he was much too busy to tell how far they went before they stopped. Miles, he guessed it to be, but he did not know.

When they did stop, it was because the passage had terminated. A solid bulkhead, stretching away to right and left, barred their way. Joe-Jim moved along it to the right, searching.

He found what he sought, a man-sized door, closed, its presence distinguishable only by a faint crack which marked its outline and a cursive geometrical design on its surface. Joe-Jim studied this and scratched his right-hand head. The two heads whispered to each other. Joe-Jim raised his hand in an awkward gesture.

"No, no!" said Jim. Joe-Jim checked himself. "How's that?" Joe answered. They whispered together again, Joe nodded, and Joe-Jim again raised his hand.

He traced the design on the door without touching it, moving his forefinger through the air perhaps four inches from the surface of the door. The order of succession in which his finger moved over the lines of the design appeared simple but certainly not obvious.

Finished, he shoved a palm against the adjacent bulkhead, drifted back from the door, and waited.

A moment later there was a soft, almost inaudible insufflation; the door stirred and moved outward perhaps six inches, then stopped. Joe-Jim appeared puzzled. He ran his hands cautiously into the open crack and pulled. Nothing happened. He called to Bobo, "Open it."

Bobo looked the situation over, with a scowl on his forehead which wrinkled almost to his crown. He then placed his feet against the bulkhead, steadying himself by grasping the door with one hand. He took hold of the edge of the door with both hands, settled his feet firmly, bowed his body and strained.

He held his breath, chest rigid, back bent, sweat breaking out from the effort. The great cords in his neck stood out, making of his head a misshapen pyramid. Hugh could hear the dwarf's joints crack. It was easy to believe that he would kill himself with the attempt, too stupid to give up.

But the door gave suddenly, with a plaint of binding metal. As the door, in swinging out, slipped from Bobo's fingers, the unexpectedly released tension in his legs shoved him heavily away from the bulkhead; he plunged down the passageway, floundering for a hand hold. But he was back in a moment, drifting awkwardly through the air as he massaged a cramped calf.

Joe-Jim led the way inside, Hugh close behind him. "What is this place?" demanded Hugh, his curiosity overcoming his servant manners.

"The Main Control Room," said Joe.

Main Control Room! The most sacred and taboo place in the Ship, its very location a forgotten mystery. In the credo of the young men it was nonexistent. The older scientists varied in their attitude between fundamentalist acceptance and mystical belief. As enlightened as Hugh believed himself to be, the very words frightened him. The Control Room! Why, the very spirit of Jordan was said to reside there.

He stopped.

Joe-Jim stopped and Joe looked around. "Come on," he said. "What's the matter?"

"Why . . . uh . . . uh—"

"Speak up."

"But . . . but this place is haunted . . . this is Jordan's—"

"Oh, for Jordan's sake!" protested Joe, with slow exasperation. "I thought you told me you young punks didn't take any stock in Jordan."

"Yes, but . . . but this is—"

"Stow it. Come along, or I'll have Bobo drag you." He turned away. Hugh followed, reluctantly, as a man climbs a scaffold.

They threaded through a passageway just wide enough for two to use the handrails abreast. The passage curved in a wide-sweeping arc of full ninety degrees, then opened into the control room proper. Hugh peered past Joe-Jim's broad shoulders, fearful but curious.

He stared into a well-lighted room, huge, quite two hundred feet across. It was spherical, the interior of a great globe. The surface of the globe was featureless, frosted silver. In the geometrical center of the sphere Hugh saw a group of apparatus about fifteen feet across. To his inexperienced eye, it was completely unintelligible; he could not have described it, but he saw that it floated steadily, with no apparent support.

Running from the end of the passage to the mass at the center of the globe was a tube of metal latticework, wide as the passage itself. It offered the only exit from the passage. Joe-Jim turned to Bobo, and ordered him to remain in the passageway, then entered the tube.

He pulled himself along it, hand over hand, the bars of the latticework making a ladder. Hugh followed him; they emerged into the mass of apparatus occupying the center of the sphere. Seen close up, the gear of the control station resolved itself into its individual details, but it still made no sense to him. He glanced away from it to the inner surface of the globe which surrounded them.

That was a mistake. The surface of the globe, being featureless silvery white, had nothing to lend it perspective. It might have been a hundred feet away, or a thousand, or many miles. He had never experienced an unbroken height greater than that between two decks, nor an open space larger than the village common. He was panic-stricken, scared out of wit, the more so in that he did not know what it was he feared. But the ghost of long-forgotten jungle ancestors possessed him and chilled his stomach with the basic primitive fear of falling.

He clutched at the control gear, clutched at Joe-Jim.

Joe-Jim let him have one, hard across the mouth with the flat of his hand. "What's the matter with you?" growled Jim.

"I don't know," Hugh presently managed to get out. "I don't know, but I don't *like* this place. Let's get out of here!"

Jim lifted his eyebrows to Joe, looked disgusted, and said, "We might as well. That weak-bellied baby will never understand anything you tell him."

"Oh, he'll be all right," Joe replied, dismissing the matter. "Hugh, climb into one of the chairs—there, that one."

In the meantime, Hugh's eyes had fallen on the tube whereby they had reached the control center and had followed it back by eye to the passage door. The sphere suddenly shrank to its proper focus and the worst of his panic was over. He complied with the order, still trembling, but able to obey.

The control center consisted of a rigid framework, made up of chairs, or frames, to receive the bodies of the operators, and consolidated instrument and report panels, mounted in such a fashion as to be almost in the laps of the operators, where they were readily visible but did not obstruct the view. The chairs had high supporting sides, or arms, and mounted in these arms were the controls appropriate to each officer on watch—but Hugh was not yet aware of that.

He slid under the instrument panel into his seat and settled back, glad of its enfolding stability. It fitted him in a semireclining position, footrest to head support.

But something was happening on the panel in front of Joe-Jim; he caught it out of the corner of his eye and turned to look. Bright-red letters glowed near the top of the board: 2ND ASTROGATOR POSTED. What was a second astrogator? He didn't know—then he noticed that the extreme top of his own board was labeled 2ND ASTROGATOR and concluded it must be himself, or rather, the man who should be sitting there. He felt momentarily uncomfortable that the proper second astrogator might come in and find him usurping his post, but he put it out of his mind—it seemed unlikely.

But what was a second astrogator, anyhow?

The letters faded from Joe-Jim's board, a red dot appeared on the left-hand edge and remained. Joe-Jim did something with his right hand; his board reported: ACCELERATION—ZERO, then MAIN DRIVE. The last two words blinked several times, then were replaced with NO REPORT. These words faded out, and a bright-green dot appeared near the right-hand edge.

"Get ready," said Joe, looking toward Hugh; "the light is going out."

"You're not going to turn out the light?" protested Hugh.

"No—you are. Take a look by your left hand. See those little white lights?"

Hugh did so, and found, shining up through the surface of the chair arm, eight bright little beads of light arranged in two squares, one above the other.

"Each one controls the light of one quadrant," explained Joe. "Cover them with your hand to turn out the light. Go ahead—do it."

Reluctantly, but fascinated, Hugh did as he was directed. He placed a palm over the tiny lights, and waited. The silvery sphere turned to dull lead, faded still more, leaving them in darkness complete save for the slight glow from the instrument panels. Hugh felt nervous but exhilarated. He withdrew his palm; the sphere remained dark, the eight little lights had turned blue.

"Now," said Joe, "I'm going to show you the stars!"

In the darkness, Joe-Jim's right hand slid over another pattern of eight lights.

Creation.

Faithfully reproduced, shining as steady and serene from the walls of the stellarium as did their originals from the black deeps of space, the mirrored stars looked down on him. Light after jeweled light, scattered in careless bountiful splendor across the simulacrum sky, the countless suns lay before him—before him, over him, under him, behind him, in every direction from him. He hung alone in the center of the stellar universe.

"Oooooh!" It was an involuntary sound, caused by his indrawn breath. He clutched the chair arms hard enough to break fingernails, but he was not aware of it. Nor was he afraid at the moment; there was room in his being for but one emotion. Life within the Ship, alternately harsh and workaday, had placed no strain on his innate capacity to experience beauty; for the first time in his life he knew the intolerable ecstasy of beauty unalloyed. It shook him and hurt him, like the first trembling intensity of sex.

It was some time before Hugh sufficiently recovered from the shock and the ensuing intense preoccupation to be able to notice Jim's sardonic laugh, Joe's dry chuckle. "Had enough?" inquired Joe. Without waiting for a reply, Joe-Jim turned the lights back on, using the duplicate controls mounted in the left arm of his chair.

Hugh sighed. His chest ached and his heart pounded. He realized suddenly that he had been holding his breath the entire time that the lights had been turned out. "Well, smart boy," asked Jim, "are you convinced?"

Hugh sighed again, not knowing why. With the lights back on, he felt safe and snug again, but was possessed of a deep sense of personal loss. He knew, subconsciously, that, having seen the stars, he would never be happy again. The dull ache in his breast, the vague inchoate yearning for his lost heritage of open sky and stars was never to be silenced, even though he was yet too ignorant to be aware of it at the top of his mind. "What was it?" he asked in a hushed voice.

"That's *it*," answered Joe. "That's the world. That's the universe. That's what I've been trying to tell you about."

Hugh tried furiously to force his inexperienced mind to comprehend. "That's what you mean by Outside?" he asked. "All those beautiful little lights?"

"Sure," said Joe, "only they aren't little. They're a long way off, you see—maybe thousands of miles."

"What?"

"Sure, sure," Joe persisted. "There's lots of room out there. Space. It's big. Why, some of those stars may be as big as the Ship—maybe bigger."

Hugh's face was a pitiful study in overstrained imagination. "Bigger than the Ship?" he repeated. "But . . . but—"

Jim tossed his head impatiently and said to Joe, "Wha' d' I tell you? You're wasting our time on this lunk. He hasn't got the capacity—"

"Easy, Jim," Joe answered mildly; "don't expect him to run before he can crawl. It took us a long time. I seem to remember that you were a little slow to believe your own eyes."

"That's a lie," said Jim nastily. "*You* were the one that had to be convinced."

"O. K., O. K.," Joe conceded, "let it ride. But it was a long time before we both had it all straight."

Hoyland paid little attention to the exchange between the two brothers.

It was a usual thing; his attention was centered on matters decidedly not usual. "Joe," he asked, "what became of the Ship while we were looking at the stars? Did we stare right through it?"

"Not exactly," Joe told him. "You weren't looking directly at the stars at all, but at kind of a picture of them. It's like— Well, they do it with mirrors, sort of. I've got a book that tells about it."

"But you *can* see 'em directly," volunteered Jim, his momentary pique forgotten. "There's a compartment forward of here—"

"Oh, yes," put in Joe, "it slipped my mind. The Captain's veranda. 'S got one wall of glass; you can look right out."

"The Captain's veranda? But—"

"Not *this* Captain. He's never been near the place. That's the name over the door of the compartment."

"What's a 'veranda'?"

"Blessed if I know. It's just the name of the place."

"Will you take me up there?"

Joe appeared to be about to agree, but Jim cut in. "Some other time. I want to get back—I'm hungry."

They passed back through the tube, woke up Bobo, and made the long trip back down.

It was long before Hugh could persuade Joe-Jim to take him exploring again, but the time intervening was well spent. Joe-Jim turned him loose on the largest collection of books that Hugh had ever seen. Some of them were copies of books Hugh had seen before, but even these he read with new meanings. He read incessantly, his mind soaking up new ideas, stumbling over them, struggling, striving to grasp them. He begrudged sleep, he forgot to eat until his breath grew sour and compelling pain in his midriff forced him to pay attention to his body. Hunger satisfied, he would be back at it until his head ached and his eyes refused to focus.

Joe-Jim's demands for service were few. Although Hugh was never off duty, Joe-Jim did not mind his reading as long as he was within earshot and ready to jump when called. Playing checkers with one of the pair when the other did not care to play was the service which used up the most time, and even this was not a total loss, for, if the player were Joe, he could almost always be diverted into a discussion of the Ship, its history, its machinery and equipment, the sort of people who had built it and first manned it—and *their* history, back on Earth, Earth the incredible, that strange place where people had lived on the *outside* instead of the *inside*.

Hugh wondered why they did not fall off.

He took the matter up with Joe and at last gained some notion of gravitation. He never really understood it emotionally—it was too wildly improbable—but as an intellectual concept he was able to accept it and use it, much later, in his first vague glimmerings of the science of ballistics

and the art of astrogation and ship maneuvering. And it led in time to
his wondering about weight in the Ship, a matter that had never bothered
him before. The lower the level the greater the weight, had been to his mind
simply the order of nature, and nothing to wonder at. He was familiar with
centrifugal force as it applied to slingshots. To apply it also to the whole
Ship, to think of the Ship as spinning like a slingshot and thereby causing
weight, was too much of a hurdle—he never really believed it.

Joe-Jim took him back once more to the Control Room and showed him
what little Joe-Jim knew about the manipulation of the controls and the
reading of the astrogation instruments.

The long-forgotten engineer-designers employed by the Jordan Foundation had been instructed to design a ship that would not—*could* not—
wear out, even though the Trip were protracted beyond the expected sixty
years. They builded better than they knew. In planning the main drive
engines and the auxiliary machinery, largely automatic, which would make
the Ship habitable, and in designing the controls necessary to handle all
machinery not entirely automatic the very idea of moving parts had been
rejected. The engines and auxiliary equipment worked on a level below
mechanical motion, on a level of pure force, as electrical transformers do.
Instead of push buttons, levers, cams, and shafts, the controls and the
machinery they served were planned in terms of balance between static
fields, bias of electronic flow, circuits broken or closed by a hand placed
over a light.

On this level of action, friction lost its meaning, wear and erosion took
no toll. Had all hands been killed in the mutiny, the Ship would still have
plunged on through space, still lighted, its air still fresh and moist, its
engines ready and waiting. As it was, though elevators and conveyor belts
fell into disrepair, disuse, and finally into the oblivion of forgotten function,
the essential machinery of the Ship continued its automatic service to its
ignorant human freight, or waited, quiet and ready, for someone bright
enough to puzzle out its key.

Genius had gone into the building of the Ship. Far too huge to be
assembled on Earth, it had been put together piece by piece in its own
orbit out beyond the Moon. There it had swung for fifteen silent years
while the problems presented by the decision to make its machinery foolproof and enduring had been formulated and solved. A whole new field
of sub-molar action had been conceived in the process, struggled with,
and conquered.

So— When Hugh placed an untutored, questing hand over the first of
a row of lights marked ACCELERATION, POSITIVE, he got an immediate
response, though not in terms of acceleration. A red light at the top of the
chief pilot's board blinked rapidly and the annunciator panel glowed with
a message: MAIN ENGINES—NOT MANNED.

"What does that mean?" he asked Joe-Jim.

"There's no telling," said Jim. "We've done the same thing in the main engine room," added Joe. "There, when you try it, it says 'Control Room Not Manned.'"

Hugh thought a moment. "What would happen," he persisted, "if all the control stations had somebody at 'em at once, and then I did that?"

"Can't say," said Joe. "Never been able to try it."

Hugh said nothing. A resolve which had been growing, formless, in his mind was now crystallizing into decision. He was busy with it.

He waited until he found Joe-Jim in a mellow mood, both of him, before broaching his idea. They were in the Captain's veranda at the time Hugh decided the moment was ripe. Joe-Jim rested gently in the Captain's easy-chair, his belly full of food, and gazed out through the heavy glass of the view port at the serene stars. Hugh floated beside him. The spinning of the Ship caused the stars to appear to move in stately circles.

Presently he said, "Joe-Jim—"

"Eh? What's that, youngster?" It was Joe who had replied.

"It's pretty swell, isn't it?"

"What is?"

"All that. The stars." Hugh indicated the view through the port with a sweep of his arm, then caught at the chair to stop his own back spin.

"Yeah, it sure is. Makes you feel good." Surprisingly, it was Jim who offered this.

Hugh knew the time was right. He waited a moment, then said, "Why don't we finish the job?"

Two heads turned simultaneously, Joe leaning out a little to see past Jim. "What job?"

"The Trip. Why don't we start up the main drive and go on with it? Somewhere out there," he said hurriedly to finish before he was interrupted, "there are planets like Earth—or so the First Crew thought. Let's go find them."

Jim looked at him, then laughed. Joe shook his head slowly. "Kid," he said, "you don't know what you are talking about. You're as balmy as Bobo. No," he went on, "that's all over and done with. Forget it."

"Why is it over and done with, Joe?"

"Well, because— It's too big a job. It takes a crew that understands what it's all about, trained to operate the Ship."

"Does it take so many? You have shown me only about a dozen places, all told, for men to actually be at the controls. Couldn't a dozen men run the Ship—if they knew what you know," he added slyly.

Jim chuckled. "He's got you, Joe. He's right."

Joe brushed it aside. "You overrate our knowledge. Maybe we *could* operate the Ship, but we wouldn't get anywhere. We don't know where we are. The Ship has been drifting for I don't know how many generations. We don't know where we're headed, or how fast we're going."

"But look," Hugh pleaded, "there are instruments. You showed them to me. Couldn't we learn how to use them? Couldn't *you* figure them out, Jim, if you really wanted to?"

"Oh, I suppose so," Jim agreed.

"Don't boast, Jim," said Joe.

"I'm not boasting," snapped Jim. "If a thing'll work, I can figure it out."

"Humph!" said Joe.

The matter rested in delicate balance. Hugh had got them disagreeing among themselves—which was what he wanted—with the less tractable of the pair on his side. Now, to consolidate his gain—

"I had an idea," he said quickly, "to get you men to work with, Jim, if you were able to train them."

"What's your idea?" demanded Jim suspiciously.

"Well, you remember what I told you about a bunch of the younger scientists—"

"Those fools!"

"Yes, yes, sure—but they don't know what you know. In their way they were trying to be reasonable. Now, if I could go back down and tell them what you've taught me, I could get you enough men to work with."

Joe cut in. "Take a good look at us, Hugh. What do you see?"

"Why . . . why . . . I see *you*—Joe-Jim."

"You see a mutie," corrected Joe, his voice edged with sarcasm. "We're a *mutie*. Get that? Your scientists won't work with us."

"No, no," protested Hugh, "that's not true. I'm not talking about peasants. Peasants wouldn't understand, but these are *scientists*, and the smartest of the lot. They'll understand. All you'll need to do is to arrange safe conduct for them through mutie country. You can do that, can't you?" he added, instinctively shifting the point of the argument to firmer ground.

"Why, sure," said Jim.

"Forget it," said Joe.

"Well, O. K.," Hugh agreed, sensing that Joe really was annoyed at his persistence, "but it would be fun—" He withdrew some distance from the brothers.

He could hear Joe-Jim continuing the discussion with himself in low tones. He pretended to ignore it. Joe-Jim had this essential defect in his joint nature: Being a committee, rather than a single individual, he was hardly fitted to be a man of action, since all decisions were necessarily the result of discussion and compromise.

Several moments later Hugh heard Joe's voice raised. "All right, all *right*—have it your own way!" He then called out, "Hugh! Come here!"

Hugh kicked himself away from an adjacent bulkhead and shot over to the immediate vicinity of Joe-Jim, arresting his flight with both hands against the framework of the Captain's chair.

"We've decided," said Joe without preliminaries, "to let you go back down to high-weight and try to peddle your goods. But you're a fool," he added sourly.

Bobo escorted Hugh down through the dangers of the levels frequented by muties and left him in the uninhabited zone above high-weight. "Thanks, Bobo," Hugh said in parting. "Good eating." The dwarf grinned, ducked his head, and sped away, swarming up the ladder they had just descended.

Hugh turned and started down, touching his knife as he did so. It was good to feel it against him again. Not that it was his original knife. That had been Bobo's prize when he was captured, and Bobo had been unable to return it, having inadvertently left it sticking in a big one that got away. But the replacement Joe-Jim had given him was well balanced and quite satisfactory.

Bobo had conducted him, at Hugh's request and by Joe-Jim's order, down to the area directly over the auxiliary Converter used by the scientists. He wanted to find Bill Ertz, Assistant Chief Engineer and leader of the bloc of younger scientists, and he did not want to have to answer too many questions before he found him.

Hugh dropped quickly down the remaining levels and found himself in a main passageway which he recognized. Good! A turn to the left, a couple of hundred yards' walk, and he found himself at the door of the compartment which housed the Converter. A guard lounged in front of it. Hugh started to push on past, was stopped. "Where do you think you're going?"

"I want to find Bill Ertz."

"You mean the Chief Engineer? Well, he's not here."

"Chief? What's happened to the old one?" Hoyland regretted the remark at once—but it was already out.

"Huh? The old Chief? Why, he's made the Trip long since." The guard looked at him suspiciously. "What's wrong with you?"

"Nothing," denied Hugh. "Just a slip."

"Funny sort of a slip. Well, you'll find Chief Ertz around his office probably."

"Thanks. Good eating."

"Good eating."

Hugh was admitted to see Ertz after a short wait. Ertz looked up from his desk as Hugh came in. "Well," he said, "so you're back, and not dead after all. This *is* a surprise. We had written you off, you know, as making the Trip."

"Yes, I suppose so."

"Well, sit down and tell me about it—I've a little time to spare at the moment. Do you know, though, I wouldn't have recognized you. You've changed a lot—all that gray hair. I imagine you had some pretty tough times."

Gray hair? Was his hair gray? And Ertz had changed a lot, too, Hugh now noticed. He was paunchy and the lines in his face had set. Good Jordan! How long had he been gone?

Ertz drummed on his desk top, and pursed his lips. "It makes a problem—your coming back like this. I'm afraid I can't just assign you to your old job; Mort Tyler has that. But we'll find a place for you, suitable to your rank."

Hugh recalled Mort Tyler and not too favorably. A precious sort of a chap, always concerned with what was proper and according to regulation. So Tyler had actually made scientisthood, and was on Hugh's old job at the Converter. Well, it didn't matter. "That's all right," he began. "I wanted to talk to you about—"

"Of course, there's the matter of seniority," Ertz went on. "Perhaps the council had better consider the matter. I don't know of a precedent. We've lost a number of scientists to the muties in the past, but you are the first to escape with his life in my memory."

"That doesn't matter," Hugh broke in. "I've something much more pressing to talk about. While I was away I found out some amazing things, Bill, things that it is of paramount importance for you to know about. That's why I came straight to you. Listen, I—"

Ertz was suddenly alert. "Of course you have! I must be slowing down. You must have had a marvelous opportunity to study the muties and scout out their territory. Come on, man, spill it! Give me your report."

Hugh wet his lips. "It's not what you think," he said. "It's much more important than just a report on the muties, though it concerns them, too. In fact, we may have to change our whole policy with respect to the mu—"

"Well, go ahead, go ahead! I'm listening."

"All right." Hugh told him of his tremendous discovery as to the actual nature of the Ship, choosing his words carefully and trying very hard to be convincing. He dwelt lightly on the difficulties presented by an attempt to reorganize the Ship in accordance with the new concept and bore down heavily on the prestige and honor that would accrue to the man who led the effort.

He watched Ertz's face as he talked. After the first start of complete surprise when Hugh launched his key idea, the fact that the Ship was actually a moving body in a great outside space, his face became impassive and Hugh could read nothing in it, except that he seemed to detect a keener interest when Hugh spoke of how Ertz was just the man for the job because of his leadership of the younger, more progressive scientists.

When Hugh concluded, he waited for Ertz's response. Ertz said nothing at first, simply continued with his annoying habit of drumming on the top of his desk. Finally he said, "These are important matters, Hoyland, much too important to be dealt with casually. I must have time to chew it over."

"Yes, certainly," Hugh agreed. "I wanted to add that I've made arrange ments for safe passage up to no-weight. I can take you up and let you see for yourself."

"No doubt that is best," Ertz replied. "Well—are you hungry?"

"No."

"Then we'll both sleep on it. You can use the compartment back of my office. I don't want you discussing this with anyone else until I've had time to think about it; it might cause unrest if it got out without proper preparation."

"Yes, you're right."

"Very well, then"—Ertz ushered him into a compartment behind his office which he very evidently used for a lounge—"have a good rest," he said, "and we'll talk later."

"Thanks," Hugh acknowledged. "Good eating."

"Good eating."

Once he was alone, Hugh's excitement gradually dropped away from him, and he realized that he was fagged out and very sleepy. He stretched out on a built-in couch and fell asleep.

When he awoke he discovered that the only door to the compartment was barred from the other side. Worse than that, his knife was gone.

He had waited an indefinitely long time when he heard activity at the door. It opened; two husky, unsmiling men entered. "Come along," said one of them. He sized them up, noting that neither of them carried a knife. No chance to snatch one from their belts, then. On the other hand he might be able to break away from them.

But beyond them, a wary distance away in the outer room, were two other equally formidable men, each armed with a knife. One balanced his for throwing; the other held his by the grip, ready to stab at close quarters.

He was boxed in and he knew it. They had anticipated his possible moves.

He had long since learned to relax before the inevitable. He composed his face and marched quietly out. Once through the door he saw Ertz, waiting and quite evidently in charge of the party of men. He spoke to him, being careful to keep his voice calm. "Hello, Bill. Pretty extensive preparations you've made. Some trouble, maybe?"

Ertz seemed momentarily uncertain of his answer, then said, "You're going before the Captain."

"Good!" Hugh answered. "Thanks, Bill. But do you think it's wise to try to sell the idea to him without laying a little preliminary foundation with the others?"

Ertz was annoyed at his apparent thick-headedness and showed it. "You don't get the idea," he growled; "you're going before the Captain to stand trial—for heresy!"

Hugh considered this as if the idea had not before occurred to him. He answered mildly, "You're off down the wrong passage, Bill. Perhaps a charge and trial is the best way to get at the matter, but I'm not a peasant.

simply to be hustled before the Captain. I must be tried by the council. I am a scientist."

"Are you now?" Ertz said softly. "I've had advice about that. You were written off the lists. Just what you are is a matter for the Captain to determine."

Hugh held his peace. It was against him, he could see, and there was no point in antagonizing Ertz. Ertz made a signal; the two unarmed men each grasped one of Hugh's arms. He went with them quietly.

Hugh looked at the Captain with new interest. The old man had not changed much—a little fatter, perhaps.

The Captain settled himself slowly down in his chair, and picked up the memorandum before him. "What's this all about?" he began irritably. "I don't understand it."

Mort Tyler was there to present the case against Hugh, a circumstance which Hugh had had no way of anticipating and which added to his misgivings. He searched his boyhood recollections for some handle by which to reach the man's sympathy, found none. Tyler cleared his throat and commenced:

"This is the case of one Hugh Hoyland, Captain, formerly one of your junior scientists—"

"Scientist, eh? Why doesn't the council deal with him?"

"Because he is no longer a scientist, Captain. He went over to the muties. He now returns among us, preaching heresy and seeking to undermine your authority."

The Captain looked at Hugh with the ready belligerency of a man jealous of his prerogatives. "Is that so?" he bellowed. "What have you to say for yourself?"

"It is not true, Captain," Hugh answered. "All that I have said to anyone has been an affirmation of the absolute truth of our ancient knowledge. I have not disputed the truths under which we live; I have simply affirmed them more forcibly than is the ordinary custom. I—"

"I still don't understand this," the Captain interrupted, shaking his head. "You're charged with heresy, yet you say you believe the Teachings. If you aren't guilty, why are you here?"

"Perhaps I can clear the matter up," put in Ertz. "Hoyland—"

"Well, I hope you can," the Captain went on. "Come—let's hear it."

Ertz proceeded to give a reasonably correct, but slanted, version of Hoyland's return and his strange story. The Captain listened, with an expression that varied between puzzlement and annoyance.

When Ertz had concluded, the Captain turned to Hugh. "Humph!" he said.

Hugh spoke immediately. "The gist of my contention, Captain, is that there is a place up at no-weight where you can actually *see* the truth of our faith that the Ship is moving, where you can actually see Jordan's

Plan in operation. That is not a denial of faith; that affirms it. There is no need to take my word for it. Jordan Himself will prove it."

Seeing that the Captain appeared to be in a state of indecision, Tyler broke in:

"Captain, there is a possible explanation of this incredible situation which I feel duty bound that you should hear. Offhand, there are two obvious interpretations of Hoyland's ridiculous story: He may simply be guilty of extreme heresy, or he may be a mutie at heart and engaged in a scheme to lure you into their hands. But there is a third, more charitable explanation and one which I feel within me is probably the true one.

"There is record that Hoyland was seriously considered for the Converter at his birth inspection, but that his deviation from normal was slight, being simply an overlarge head, and he was passed. It seems to me that the terrible experiences he has undergone at the hands of the muties have finally unhinged an unstable mind. The poor chap is simply not responsible for his own actions."

Hugh looked at Tyler with new respect. To absolve him of guilt and at the same time to make absolutely certain that Hugh would wind up making the Trip—how neat!

The Captain shook a palm at them. "This has gone on long enough." Then, turning to Ertz, "Is there recommendation?"

"Yes, Captain. The Converter."

"Very well, then. I really don't see, Ertz," he continued testily, "why I should be bothered with these details. It seems to me that you should be able to handle discipline in your department without my help."

"Yes, Captain."

The Captain shoved back from his desk, started to get up. "Recommendation confirmed. Dismissed."

Anger flooded through Hugh at the unreasonable injustice of it. They had not even considered looking at the only real evidence he had in his defense. He heard a shout, "Wait!"—then discovered it was his own voice.

The Captain paused, looking at him.

"Wait a moment," Hugh went on, his words spilling out of their own accord. "This won't make any difference, for you're all so damn sure you know all the answers that you won't consider a fair offer to come see with your own eyes. Nevertheless—

"Nevertheless—it *still* moves!"

Hugh had plenty of time to think, lying in the compartment where they confined him to await the power needs of the Converter, time to think, and to second-guess his mistakes. Telling his tale to Ertz immediately—that had been mistake No. 1. He should have waited, become reacquainted with the man and felt him out, instead of depending on a friendship which had never been very close.

Second mistake, Mort Tyler. When he heard his name he should have investigated and found out just how much influence the man had with Ertz. He had known him of old, he should have known better.

Well, here he was, condemned as a mutant—or maybe as an heretic. It came to the same thing. He considered whether or not he should have tried to explain why mutants happened. He had learned about it himself in some of the old records in Joe-Jim's possession. No, it wouldn't wash. How could you explain about radiations from the Outside causing the birth of mutants when the listeners did not believe there was such a place as Outside? No, he had messed it up before he was ever taken before the Captain.

His self-recriminations were disturbed at last by the sound of his door being unfastened. It was too soon for another of the infrequent meals; he thought that they had come at last to take him away, and renewed his resolve to take someone with him.

But he was mistaken. He heard a voice of gentle dignity, "Son, Son, how does this happen?" It was Lieutenant Nelson, his first teacher, looking older than ever and frail.

The interview was distressing for both of them. The old man, childless himself, had cherished great hopes for his protégé, even the ambition that he might eventually aspire to the captaincy, though he had kept his vicarious ambition to himself, believing it not good for the young to praise them too highly. It had hurt his heart when the youth was lost.

Now he had returned, a man, but under disgraceful conditions and under sentence of death.

The meeting was no less unhappy for Hugh. He had loved the old man, in his way, wanted to please him and needed his approval. But he could see, as he told his story, that Nelson was not capable of treating the story as anything but an aberration of Hugh's mind, and he suspected that Nelson would rather see him meet a quick death in the Converter, his atoms smashed to hydrogen and giving up clean useful power, than have him live to make a mock of the ancient teachings.

In that he did the old man an injustice; he underrated Nelson's mercy, but not his devotion to "science." But let it be said for Hugh that, had there been no more at issue than his own personal welfare, he might have preferred death to breaking the heart of his benefactor—being a romantic and more than a bit foolish.

Presently the old man got up to leave, the visit having grown unendurable to each of them. "Is there anything I can do for you, Son? Do they feed you well enough?"

"Quite well, thanks," Hugh lied.

"Is there anything else?"

"No—yes, you might send me some tobacco. I haven't had a chew in a long time."

"I'll take care of it. Is there anyone you would like to see?"

"Why, I was under the impression that I was not permitted visitors—ordinary visitors."

"You are right, but I think perhaps I may be able to get the rule relaxed. But you will have to give me your promise not to speak of your heresy," he added anxiously.

Hugh thought quickly. This was a new aspect, a new possibility. His uncle? No, while they had always gotten along well, their minds did not meet—they would greet each other as strangers. He had never made friends easily; Ertz had been his obvious next friend and now look at the damned thing! Then he recalled his village chum, Alan Mahoney, with whom he had played as a boy. True, he had seen practically nothing of him since the time he was apprenticed to Nelson. Still—

"Does Alan Mahoney still live in our village?"

"Why, yes."

"I'd like to see him, if he'll come."

Alan arrived, nervous, ill at ease, but plainly glad to see Hugh and very much upset to find him under sentence to make the Trip. Hugh pounded him on the back. "Good boy," he said, "I knew you would come."

"Of course I would," protested Alan, "once I knew. But nobody in the village knew it. I don't think even the Witness knew it."

"Well, you're here, that's what matters. Tell me about yourself. Have you married?"

"Huh, uh, no. Let's not waste time talking about me. Nothing ever happens to me, anyhow. How in Jordan's name did you get in this jam, Hugh?"

"I can't talk about that, Alan. I promised Lieutenant Nelson that I wouldn't."

"Well, what's a promise—*that* kind of a promise. You're in a *jam*, fellow."

"Don't I know it!"

"Somebody have it in for you?"

"Well—our old pal Mort Tyler didn't help any; I think I can say that much."

Alan whistled and nodded his head slowly. "That explains a lot."

"How come? You know something?"

"Maybe, maybe not. After you went away he married Edris Baxter."

"So? Hm-m-m—yes, that clears up a lot." He remained silent for a time.

Presently Alan spoke up: "Look, Hugh. You're not going to sit here and take it, are you? Particularly with Tyler mixed in it. We gotta get you outa here."

"How?"

"I don't know. Pull a raid, maybe. I guess I could get a few knives to rally round and help us—all good boys, spoiling for a fight."

"Then, when it's over, we'd all be for the Converter. You, me, and your pals. No, it won't wash."

"But we've *got* to do something. We can't just sit here and wait for them to burn you."

"I know that." Hugh studied Alan's face. Was it a fair thing to ask? He went on, reassured by what he had seen. "Listen. You would do anything you could to get me out of this, wouldn't you?"

"You know that." Alan's tone showed hurt.

"Very well, then. There is a dwarf named Bobo. I'll tell you how to find him—"

Alan climbed, up and up, higher than he had ever been since Hugh had led him, as a boy, into foolhardy peril. He was older now, more conservative; he had no stomach for it. To the very real danger of leaving the well-traveled lower levels was added his superstitious ignorance. But still he climbed.

This should be about the place—unless he had lost count. But he saw nothing of the dwarf.

Bobo saw him first. A slingshot load caught Alan in the pit of the stomach, even as he was shouting, "Bobo!"

Bobo backed into Joe-Jim's compartment and dumped his load at the feet of the twins. "Fresh meat," he said proudly.

"So it is," agreed Jim indifferently. "Well, it's yours; take it away."

The dwarf dug a thumb into a twisted ear. "Funny," he said, "he knows Bobo's name."

Joe looked up from the book he was reading—Browning's *Collected Poems*, L-Press, New York, London, Luna City, cr. 3/5—"That's interesting. Hold on a moment."

Hugh had prepared Alan for the shock of Joe-Jim's appearance. In reasonably short order he collected his wits sufficiently to be able to tell his tale. Joe-Jim listened to it without much comment, Bobo with interest but little comprehension.

When Alan concluded, Jim remarked, "Well, you win, Joe. He didn't make it." Then, turning to Alan, he added, "You can take Hoyland's place. Can you play checkers?"

Alan looked from one head to the other. "But you don't understand," he said. "Aren't you going to do anything about it?"

Joe looked puzzled. "Us? Why should we?"

"But you've *got* to. Don't you see? He's depending on you. There's nobody else he can look to. That's why I came. Don't you see?"

"Wait a moment," drawled Jim, "wait a moment. Keep your belt on. Supposing we did want to help him—which we don't—how in Jordan's Ship could we? Answer me that."

"Why . . . why—" Alan stumbled in the face of such stupidity. "Why, get up a rescue party, of course, and go down and get him out!"

"Why should we get ourselves killed in a fight to rescue your friend?"
Bobo pricked his ears. "Fight?" he inquired eagerly.

"No, Bobo," Joe denied. "No fight. Just talk."

"Oh," said Bobo and returned to passivity.

Alan looked at the dwarf. "If you'd even let Bobo and me—"

"No," Joe said shortly. "It's out of the question. Shut up about it."

Alan sat in a corner, hugging his knees in despair. If only he could get out of there. He could still try to stir up some help down below. The dwarf seemed to be asleep, though it was difficult to be sure with him. If only Joe-Jim would sleep, too.

Joe-Jim showed no indication of sleepiness. Joe tried to continue reading, but Jim interrupted him from time to time. Alan could not hear what they were saying.

Presently Joe raised his voice. "Is that your idea of fun?" he demanded.

"Well," said Jim, "it beats checkers."

"It does, does it? Suppose you get a knife in your eye—where would I be then?"

"You're getting old, Joe. No juice in you any more."

"You're as old as I am."

"Yeah, but I got young ideas."

"Oh, you make me sick. Have it your own way—but don't blame me. Bobo!"

The dwarf sprang up at once, alert. "Yeah, Boss."

"Go out and dig up Squatty and Long Arm and Pig." Joe-Jim got up, went to a locker, and started pulling knives out of their racks.

Hugh heard the commotion in the passageway outside his prison. It could be the guards coming to take him to the Converter, though they probably wouldn't be so noisy. Or it could be just some excitement unrelated to him. On the other hand it might be—

It was. The door burst open, and Alan was inside, shouting at him and thrusting a brace of knives into his hands. He was hurried out the door, while stuffing the knives in his belt and accepting two more.

Outside he saw Joe-Jim, who did not see him at once, as he was methodically letting fly, as calmly as if he had been engaging in target practice in his own study. And Bobo, who ducked his head and grinned with a mouth widened by a bleeding cut, but continued the easy flow of the motion whereby he loaded and let fly. There were three others, two of whom Hugh recognized as belonging to Joe-Jim's privately owned gang of bullies—muties by definition and birthplace; they were not deformed.

The count does not include still forms on the floor plates.

"Come on!" yelled Alan. "There'll be more in no time." He hurried down the passage to the right.

Joe-Jim desisted and followed him. Hugh let one blade go for luck at a figure running away to the left. The target was poor, and he had no time to see if he had drawn blood. They scrambled along the passage, Bobo bringing up the rear, as if reluctant to leave the fun, and came to a point where a side passage crossed the main one.

Alan led them to the right again. "Stairs ahead," he shouted.

They did not reach them. An airtight door, rarely used, clanged in their faces ten yards short of the stairs. Joe-Jim's bravoes checked their flight and looked doubtfully at their master. Bobo broke his thickened nails trying to get a purchase on the door.

The sounds of pursuit were clear behind them.

"Boxed in," said Joe softly. "I hope you like it, Jim."

Hugh saw a head appear around the corner of the passage they had quitted. He threw overhand but the distance was too great; the knife clanged harmlessly against steel. The head disappeared. Long Arm kept his eye on the spot, his sling loaded and ready.

Hugh grabbed Bobo's shoulder. "Listen! Do you see that light?"

The dwarf blinked stupidly. Hugh pointed to the intersection of the glowtubes where they crossed in the overhead directly above the junction of the passages. "That light. Can you hit them where they cross?"

Bobo measured the distance with his eye. It would be a hard shot under any conditions at that range. Here, constricted as he was by the low passageway, it called for a fast, flat trajectory, and allowance for higher weight than he was used to.

He did not answer. Hugh felt the wind of his swing but did not see the shot. There was a tinkling crash; the passage became dark.

"Now!" yelled Hugh, and led them away at a run. As they neared the intersection he shouted, "Hold your breaths! Mind the gas!" The radio-active vapor poured lazily out from the broken tube above and filled the crossing with a greenish mist.

Hugh ran to the right, thankful for his knowledge as an engineer of the lighting circuits. He had picked the right direction; the passage ahead was black, being serviced from beyond the break. He could hear footsteps around him; whether they were friend or enemy he did not know.

They burst into light. No one was in sight but a scared and harmless peasant who scurried away at an unlikely pace. They took a quick muster. All were present, but Bobo was making heavy going of it.

Joe looked at him. "He sniffed the gas, I think. Pound his back."

Pig did so with a will. Bobo belched deeply, was suddenly sick, then grinned.

"He'll do," decided Joe.

The slight delay had enabled one at least to catch up with them. He came plunging out of the dark, unaware of, or careless of, the strength against him. Alan knocked Pig's arm down, as he raised it to throw.

"Let me at 'im!" he demanded. "He's mine!"

It was Tyler.

"Man-fight?" Alan challenged, thumb on his blade.

Tyler's eyes darted from adversary to adversary and accepted the invitation to individual duel by lunging at Alan. The quarters were too cramped for throwing; they closed, each achieving his grab in parry, fist to wrist.

Alan was stockier, probably stronger; Tyler was slippery. He attempted to give Alan a knee to the crotch. Alan evaded it, stomped on Tyler's planted foot. They went down. There was a crunching crack.

A moment later, Alan was wiping his knife against his thigh. "Let's get goin'," he complained. "I'm scared."

They reached a stairway, and raced up it, Long Arm and Pig ahead to fan out on each level and cover their flanks, and the third of the three choppers—Hugh heard him called Squatty—covering the rear. The others bunched in between.

Hugh thought they had won free when he heard shouts and the clatter of a thrown knife just above him. He reached the level above in time to be cut not deeply but jaggedly by a ricocheted blade.

Three men were down. Long Arm had a blade sticking in the fleshy part of his upper arm, but it did not seem to bother him. His slingshot was still spinning. Pig was scrambling after a thrown knife, his own armament exhausted. But there were signs of his work; one man was down on one knee some twenty feet away. He was bleeding from a knife wound in the thigh.

As the figure steadied himself with one hand against the bulkhead and reached toward an empty belt with the other, Hugh recognized him.

Bill Ertz.

He had led a party up another way and flanked them, to his own ruin. Bobo crowded behind Hugh and got his mighty arm free for the cast. Hugh caught at it. "Easy, Bobo," he directed. "In the stomach, and easy."

The dwarf looked puzzled, but did as He was told. Ertz folded over at the middle and slid to the deck.

"Well placed," said Jim.

"Bring him along, Bobo," directed Hugh, "and stay in the middle." He ran his eye over their party, now huddled at the top of that flight of stairs. "All right, gang—up we go again! Watch it."

Long Arm and Pig swarmed up the next flight, the others disposing themselves as usual. Joe looked annoyed. In some fashion—a fashion by no means clear at the moment—he had been eased out as leader of this gang—*his* gang—and Hugh was giving orders. He reflected that there was no time now to make a fuss. It might get them all killed.

Jim did not appear to mind. In fact, he seemed to be enjoying himself.

They put ten more levels behind them with no organized opposition. Hugh directed them not to kill peasants unnecessarily. The three bravoes obeyed; Bobo was too loaded down with Ertz to constitute a problem in discipline. Hugh saw to it that they put thirty-odd more decks below them and were well into no-man's-land before he let vigilance relax at all. Then he called a halt and they examined wounds.

The only deep ones were to Long Arm's arm and Bobo's face. Joe-Jim examined them and applied presses with which he had outfitted himself before starting. Hugh refused treatment for his flesh wound. "It's stopped bleeding," he insisted, "and I've got a lot to do."

"You've got nothing to do but to get up home," said Joe, "and that will be an end to this foolishness."

"Not quite," denied Hugh. "You may be going home, but Alan and I and Bobo are going up to no-weight—to the Captain's veranda."

"Nonsense," said Joe. "What for?"

"Come along if you like, and see. All right, gang. Let's go."

Joe started to speak, stopped when Jim kept still. Joe-Jim followed along.

They floated gently through the door of the veranda, Hugh, Alan, Bobo with his still passive burden—and Joe-Jim. "That's it," said Hugh to Alan, waving his hand at the splendid stars, "that's what I've been telling you about."

Alan looked and clutched at Hugh's arm. "Jordan!" he moaned. "We'll fall out!" He closed his eyes tightly.

Hugh shook him. "It's all right," he said. "It's grand. Open your eyes."

Joe-Jim touched Hugh's arm. "What's it all about?" he demanded. "Why did you bring *him* up here?" He pointed at Ertz.

"Oh—him. Well, when he wakes up I'm going to show him the stars, prove to him that the Ship moves."

"Well? What for?"

"Then I'll send him back down to convince some others."

"Hm-m-m—suppose he doesn't have any better luck than you had?"

"Why, then"—Hugh shrugged his shoulders—"why, then we shall just have to do it all over, I suppose, till we do convince them.

"We've got to do it, you know."

ISAAC ASIMOV

BLIND ALLEY

Only once in Galactic History was an intelligent race of non-Humans discovered—"Essays on History," by Ligurn Vier

FROM: Bureau for the Outer Provinces
  To: Loodun Antyok, Chief Public Administrator, A-8
  Subject: Civilian Supervisor of Cepheus 18, Administrative Position as.
  References:
      (a) Act of Council 2515, of the year 971 of the Galactic Empire, entitled, "Appointment of Officials of the Administrative Service, Methods for, Revision of."
      (b) Imperial Directive, Ja 2374, dated 243/975 G.E.
  1. By authorization of reference (a) you are hereby appointed to the subject position. The authority of said position as Civilian Supervisor of Cepheus 18 will extend over non-Human subjects of the Emperor living upon the planet under the terms of autonomy set forth in reference (b).
  2. The duties of the subject position shall comprise the general supervision of all non-Human internal affairs, co-ordination of authorized government investigating and reporting committees, and the preparation of semiannual reports on all phases of non-Human affairs.

C. Morily, Chief, BuOuProv,
12/977 G.E.

Loodun Antyok had listened carefully and now he shook his round head mildly. "Friend, I'd like to help you, but you've grabbed the wrong dog by the ears. You'd better take this up with the Bureau."

Tomor Zammo flung himself back into his chair, rubbed his beak of a nose fiercely, thought better of whatever he was going to say, and answered quietly, "Logical, but not practical. I can't make a trip to Trantor now. You're the Bureau's representative on Cepheus 18. Are you entirely helpless?"

"Well, even as Civilian Supervisor, I've got to work within the limits of Bureau policy."

"Good," Zammo cried, "then tell me what Bureau policy is. I head a scientific investigating committee, under direct Imperial authorization with, supposedly, the widest powers; yet at every angle in the road I am pulled up short by the civilian authorities with only the parrot shriek of 'Bureau policy' to justify themselves. What *is* Bureau policy? I haven't received a decent definition yet."

Antyok's gaze was level and unruffled. He said, "As I see it—and this is not official, so you can't hold me to it—Bureau policy consists in treating the non-Humans as decently as possible."

"Then what authority have they—"

"*Ssh!* No use raising your voice. As a matter of fact, His Imperial Majesty is a humanitarian and a disciple of the philosophy of Aurelion. I can tell you quietly that it is pretty well-known that it is the Emperor himself who first suggested that this world be established. You can bet that Bureau policy will stick pretty close to Imperial notions. And you can bet that I can't paddle my way against *that* sort of current."

"Well, m'boy," the physiologist's fleshy eyelids quivered, "if you take that sort of attitude, you're going to lose your job. No, I won't have you kicked out. That's not what I mean at all. Your job will just fade out from under you, because nothing is going to be accomplished here!"

"Really? Why?" Antyok was short, pink, and pudgy and his plump-cheeked face usually found it difficult to put on display any expression other than one of bland and cheerful politeness—but it looked grave now.

"You haven't been here long. I have." Zammo scowled. "Mind if I smoke?" The cigar in his hand was gnarled and strong and was puffed to life carelessly.

He continued roughly, "There's no place here for humanitarianism, administrator. You're treating non-Humans as if they were Humans and it won't work. In fact, I don't like the word 'non-Human.' They're animals."

"They're intelligent," interjected Antyok, softly.

"Well, intelligent animals, then. I presume the two terms are not mutually exclusive. Alien intelligences mingling in the same space won't work, anyway."

"Do you propose killing them off?"

"Galaxy, no!" He gestured with his cigar. "I propose we look upon them as objects for study, and only that. We could learn a good deal from these animals if we were allowed to. Knowledge, I might point out, that would be used for the immediate benefit of the human race. *There's* humanity for you. *There's* the good of the masses, if it's this spineless cult of Aurelion that interests you."

"What, for instance, do you refer to?"

"To take the most obvious— You have heard of their chemistry, I take it?"

"Yes," Antyok admitted. "I have leafed through most of the reports on the non-Humans published in the last ten years. I expect to go through more."

"Hmp. Well— Then, all I need say is that their chemical therapy is extremely thorough. For instance, I have witnessed personally the healing of a broken bone—what passes for a broken bone with them, I mean—by the use of a pill. The bone was whole in fifteen minutes. Naturally, none of their drugs are any earthly use on Humans. Most would kill quickly. But if we found out how they worked on the non-Humans—on the animals—"

"Yes, yes. I see the significance."

"Oh, you do. Come, that's gratifying. A second point is that these animals communicate in an unknown manner."

"Telepathy!"

The scientist's mouth twisted, as he ground out, "Telepathy! Telepathy! Telepathy! Might as well say by witch brew. Nobody knows anything about telepathy except its name. What is the mechanism of telepathy? What is the physiology and the physics of it? I would like to find out, but I can't. Bureau policy, if I listen to you, forbids."

Antyok's little mouth pursed itself. "But— Pardon me, doctor, but I don't follow you. How are you prevented? Surely the Civil Administration has made no attempt to hamper scientific investigation of these non-Humans. I cannot speak for my predecessor entirely, of course, but I myself—"

"No direct interference has occurred. I don't speak of that. But by the Galaxy, administrator, we're hampered by the spirit of the entire set-up. You're making us deal with non-Humans as if they were Humans. You allow them their own leader and internal autonomy. You pamper them and give them what Aurelion's philosophy would call 'rights.' I can't deal with their leader."

"Why not?"

"Because he refuses to allow me a free hand. He refuses to allow experiments on any subject without the subject's own consent. The two or three volunteers we get are not too bright. It's an impossible arrangement."

Antyok shrugged helplessly.

Zammo continued, "In addition, it is obviously impossible to learn anything of value concerning the brains, physiology, and chemistry of these animals without dissection, dietary experiments, and drugs. You know, administrator, scientific investigation is a hard game. Humanity hasn't much place in it."

Loodun Antyok tapped his chin with a doubtful finger. "Must it be quite so hard? These are harmless creatures, these non-Humans. Surely, dissection— Perhaps, if you were to approach them a bit differently— I have the idea that you antagonize them. Your attitude might be somewhat overbearing."

"Overbearing! I am not one of these whining social psychologists who are all the fad these days. I don't believe you can solve a problem that requires dissection by approaching it with what is called the 'correct personal attitude' in the cant of the times."

"I'm sorry you think so. Socio-psychological training is required of all administrators above the grade of A-4."

Zammo withdrew his cud of a cigar from his mouth and replaced it after a suitably contemptuous interval. "Then you'd better use a bit of your technique on the Bureau. You know, I *do* have friends at the Imperial court."

"Well, now, I *can't* take the matter up with them, not baldly. Basic policy does not fall within my cognizance and such things can only be initiated by the Bureau. But, you know, we might try an indirect approach on this." He smiled faintly, "Strategy."

"What sort?"

Antyok pointed a sudden finger, while his other hand fell lightly on the rows of gray-bound reports upon the floor just next his chair. "Now, look, I've gone through most of these. They're dull, but contain *some* facts. For instance, when was the last non-Human infant born on Cepheus 18?"

Zammo spent little time in consideration. "Don't know. Don't care, either."

"But the Bureau would. There's *never* been a non-Human infant born on Cepheus 18—not in the two years the world has been established. Do you know the reason?"

The physiologist shrugged. "Too many possible factors. It would take study."

"All right, then. Suppose you write a report—"

"Reports! I've written twenty."

"Write another. Stress the unsolved problems. Tell them you must change your methods. Harp on the birth-rate problem. The Bureau doesn't dare ignore that. If the non-Humans die out, someone will have to answer to the Emperor. You see—"

Zammo stared, his eyes dark. "That will swing it?"

"I've been working for the Bureau for twenty-seven years. I know its ways."

"I'll think about it." Zammo rose and stalked out of the office. The door slammed behind him.

It was later that Zammo said to a co-worker, "He's a bureaucrat in the first place. He won't abandon the orthodoxies of paper work and he won't risk sticking his neck out. He'll accomplish little by himself, yet maybe more than a little, if we work through him."

From: Administrative Headquarters, Cepheus 18
To: BuOuProv
Subject: Outer Province Project 2563, Part II—Scientific Investigations of non-Humans of Cepheus 18, Co-ordination of.
References:
    (a) BuOuProv letr. Ceph-N-CM/jg, 100132, dated 302/975 G.E.
    (b) AdHQ-Ceph18 letr. AA-LA/mn, dated 140/977 G.E.
Enclosure:
    1. SciGroup 10, Physical & Biochemical Division, Report, entitled, "Physiologic Characteristics of non-Humans of Cepheus 18, Part XI," dated 172/977 G.E.
    1. Enclosure 1, included herewith, is forwarded for the information of the BuOuProv. It is to be noted that Section XII, paragraphs 1–16 of Encl. 1, concern possible changes in present BuOuProv policy with regard to non-Humans with a view to facilitating physical and chemical investigations at present proceeding under authorization of reference (a).
    2. It is brought to the attention of the BuOuProv that reference (b) has already discussed possible changes in investigating methods, and that it remains the opinion of AdHQ-Ceph18 that such changes are as yet premature. It is nevertheless suggested that the question of non-Human birth rate be made the subject of a BuOuProv project assigned to AdHQ-Ceph18, in view of the importance attached by SciGroup 10 to the problem, as evidenced in Section V of Enclosure 1.

                L. ANTYOK, Superv. AdHQ-Ceph18, 174/977

From: BuOuProv
To: AdHQ-Ceph18
Subject: Outer Province Project 2563—Scientific Investigations of non-Humans of Cepheus 18, Co-ordination of.
Reference:
    (a) AdHQ-Ceph18 letr. AA-LA/mn, dated 174/977 G.E.
    1. In response to the suggestion contained in paragraph 2 of reference (a), it is considered that the question of the non-Human birth rate does not fall within the cognizance of AdHQ-Ceph18. In view of the fact that SciGroup 10 has reported said sterility to be probably due to a chemical deficiency in the food supply, all investigations in the field are relegated to SciGroup 10 as the proper authority.
    2. Investigating procedures by the various SciGroups shall continue according to current directives on the subject. No changes in policy are envisaged.

            C. MORILY, Chief, BuOuProv, 186/977 G.E.

II

There was a loose-jointed gauntness about the news reporter which made him appear somberly tall. He was Gustiv Bannerd, with whose reputation was combined ability—two things which do not invariably go together despite the maxims of elementary morality.

Loodun Antyok took his measure doubtfully and said, "There's no use denying that you're right. But the SciGroup report was confidential. I don't understand how—"

"It leaked," said Bannerd, callously. "Everything leaks."

Antyok was obviously baffled, and his pink face furrowed slightly. "Then I'll just have to plug the leak here. I can't pass your story. All reference to SciGroup complaints have to come out. You see that, don't you?"

"No." Bannerd was calm enough. "It's important; and I have my rights under the Imperial directive. I think the Empire should know what's going on."

"But it isn't going on," said Antyok, despairingly. "Your claims are all wrong. The Bureau isn't going to change its policy. I showed you the letters."

"You think you can stand up against Zammo when he puts the pressure on?" the newsman asked derisively.

"I will—if I think he's wrong."

"If!" stated Bannerd flatly. Then, in a sudden fervor, "Antyok, the Empire has something great here; something greater by a good deal than the government apparently realizes. They're destroying it. They're treating these creatures like animals."

"Really—" began Antyok, weakly.

"Don't talk about Cepheus 18. It's a zoo. It's a high-class zoo, with your petrified scientists teasing those poor creatures with their sticks poking through the bars. You throw them chunks of meat, but you cage them up. I know! I've been writing about them for two years now. I've almost been living with them."

"Zammo says—"

"Zammo!" This with hard contempt.

"Zammo says," insisted Antyok with worried firmness, "that we treat them too like humans as it is."

The newsman's straight long cheeks were rigid. "Zammo is rather animal-like in his own right. He is a science-worshiper. We can do with less of them. Have you read Aurelion's work?" The last was suddenly posed.

"Umm. Yes. I understand the Emperor—"

"The Emperor tends towards us. That is good—better than the hounding of the last reign."

"I don't see where you're heading."

"These aliens have much to teach us. You understand? It is nothing that Zammo and his SciGroup can use; no chemistry, no telepathy. It's a way of life; a way of thinking. The aliens have no crime, no misfits. What effort is being made to study their philosophy? Or to set them up as a problem in social engineering?"

Antyok grew thoughtful and his plump face smoothed out. "It is an interesting consideration. It would be a matter for psychologists—"

"No good. Most of them are quacks. Psychologists point out problems but their solutions are fallacious. We need men of Aurelion. Men of The Philosophy—"

"But look here, we can't turn Cepheus 18 into . . . into a metaphysical study."

"Why not? It can be done easily."

"How?"

"Forget your puny test-tube peerings. Allow the aliens to set up a society free of Humans. Give them an untrammeled independence and allow an intermingling of philosophies—"

Antyok's nervous response came, "That can't be done in a day."

"We can start in a day."

The administrator said slowly, "Well, I can't prevent you from trying to start." He grew confidential, his mild eyes thoughtful. "You'll ruin your own game, though, if you publish SciGroup 10's report and denounce it on humanitarian grounds. The Scientists are powerful."

"And we of The Philosophy as well."

"Yes, but there's an easy way. You needn't rave. Simply point out that the SciGroup is not solving its problems. Do so unemotionally and let the readers think out your point of view for themselves. Take the birth-rate problem, for instance. *There's* something for you. In a generation, the non-Humans might die out for all science can do. Point out that a more philosophical approach is required. Or pick some other obvious point. Use your judgment, eh?"

Antyok smiled ingratiatingly as he arose. "But for the Galaxy's sake don't stir up a bad smell."

Bannerd was stiff and unresponsive. "You may be right."

It was later that Bannerd wrote in a capsule message to a friend, "He is not clever, by any means. He is confused and has no guiding-line through life. Certainly utterly incompetent in his job. But he's a cutter and a trimmer, compromises his way around difficulties, and will yield concessions rather than risk a hard stand. He may prove valuable in that. Yours in Aurelion."

From: AdHQ-Ceph18
To: BuOuProv
Subject: Birth rate of non-Humans on Cepheus 18, News Report on.
References:
    (a) AdHQ-Ceph18 letr. AA-LA/mn, dated 174/977 G.E.
    (b) Imperial Directive, Ja 2374, dated 243/975 G.E.
Enclosures:
    1-G. Bannerd news report, date-lined Cepheus 18, 201/977 G.E.
    2-G. Bannerd news report, date-lined Cepheus 18, 203/977 G.E.
  1. The sterility of non-Humans on Cepheus 18, reported to the BuOu-

Prov in reference (a) has become the subject of news reports to the galactic press. The news reports in question are submitted herewith for the information of the BuOuProv as Enclosures 1 and 2. Although said reports are based on material considered confidential and closed to the public, the news reporter in question maintained his rights to free expression under the terms of reference (b).

2. In view of the unavoidable publicity and misunderstanding on the part of the general public now inevitable, it is requested that the BuOuProv direct future policy on the problem of non-Human sterility.

L. Antyok, Superv. AdHQ-Ceph18, 209/977 G.E.

From: BuOuProv
To: AdHQ-Ceph18
Subject: Birth rate of non-Humans on Cepheus 18, Investigation of.
References:
      (a) AdHQ-Ceph18 letr. AA-LA/mn, dated 209/977 G.E.
      (b) AdHQ-Ceph18 letr. AA-LA/mn, dated 174/977 G.E.

1. It is proposed to investigate the causes and the means of precluding the unfavorable birth-rate phenomena mentioned in references (a) and (b). A project is therefore set up, éntitled, "Birth rate of non-Humans on Cepheus 18, Investigation of" to which, in view of the crucial importance of the subject, a priority of AA is given.

2. The number assigned to the subject project is 2910, and all expenses incidental to it shall be assigned to Appropriation number 18/78.

C. Morily, Chief, BuOuProv, 223/977 G.E.

III

If Tomor Zammo's ill-humor lessened within the grounds of SciGroup 10 Experimental Station, his friendliness had not thereby increased. Antyok found himself standing alone at the viewing window into the main field laboratory.

The main field laboratory was a broad court set at the environmental conditions of Cepheus 18 itself for the discomfort of the experimenters and the convenience of the experimentees. Through the burning sand, and the dry, oxygen-rich air, there sparkled the hard brilliance of hot, white sunlight. And under the blaze, the brick-red non-Humans, wrinkled of skin and wiry of build, huddled in their squatting positions of ease, by ones and twos.

Zammo emerged from the laboratory. He paused to drink water thirstily. He looked up, moisture gleaming on his upper lip. "Like to step in there?"

Antyok shook his head definitely. "No, thank you. What's the temperature right now?"

"A hundred twenty, if there were shade. And they complain of the cold. It's drinking time now. Want to watch them drink?"

A spray of water shot upward from the fountain in the center of the court and the little alien figures swayed to their feet and hopped eagerly forward in a queer springy half-run. They milled about the water, jostling one another. The centers of their faces were suddenly disfigured by the projection of a long and flexible fleshy tube, which thrust forward into the spray and was withdrawn dripping.

It continued for long minutes. The bodies swelled and the wrinkles disappeared. They retreated slowly, backing away, with the drinking tube flicking in and out, before receding finally into a pink, wrinkled mass above a wide, lipless mouth. They went to sleep in groups in the shaded angles, plump and sated.

"Animals!" said Zammo, with contempt.

"How often do they drink?" asked Antyok.

"As often as they want. They can go a week if they have to. We water them every day. They store it under their skin. They eat in the evenings. Vegetarians, you know."

Antyok smiled chubbily. "It's nice to get a bit of firsthand information occasionally. Can't read reports all the time."

"Yes?"—noncommittally. Then, "What's new? What about the lacy-pants boys on Trantor?"

Antyok shrugged dubiously. "You can't get the Bureau to commit itself, unfortunately. With the Emperor sympathetic to the Aurelionists, humanitarianism is the order of the day. You know that."

There was a pause in which the administrator chewed his lip uncertainly. "But there's this birth-rate problem now. It's finally been assigned to AdHQ, you know—and double-A priority, too."

Zammo muttered wordlessly.

Antyok said, "You may not realize it, but that project will now take precedence over all other work proceeding on Cepheus 18. It's important."

He turned back to the viewing window and said thoughtfully, with a bald lack of preamble, "Do you think those creatures might be unhappy?"

"Unhappy!" The word was an explosion.

"Well, then," Antyok corrected hastily, "maladjusted. You understand? It's difficult to adjust an environment to a race we know so little of."

"Say—did you ever see the world we took them from?"

"I've read the reports—"

"Reports!"—infinite contempt. "I've *seen* it. This may look like desert out there to you, but it's a watery paradise to those devils. They have all the food and water they can get. They have a world to themselves with vegetation and natural water flow, instead of a lump of silica and granite where fungi were force-grown in caves and water had to be steamed out of gypsum rock. In ten years, they would have been dead to the last beast, and we saved them. Unhappy? Ga-a-ah, if they are, they haven't the decency of most animals."

"Well, perhaps. Yet I have a notion."

"A notion? What is your notion?" Zammo reached for one of his cigars.

"It's something that might help you. Why not study the creatures in a more integrated fashion? Let them use their initiative. After all, they did have a highly developed science. Your reports speak of it continually. Give them problems to solve."

"Such as?"

"Oh . . . oh," Antyok waved his hands helplessly. "Whatever you think might help most. For instance, spaceships. Get them into the control room and study their reactions."

"Why?" asked Zammo with dry bluntness.

"Because the reaction of their minds to tools and controls adjusted to the human temperament can teach you a lot. In addition, it will make a more effective bribe, it seems to me, than anything you've yet tried. You'll get more volunteers if they think they'll be doing something interesting."

"That's your psychology coming out. Hm-m-m. Sounds better than it probably is. I'll sleep on it. And where would I get permission in any case to let them handle spaceships? I've none at *my* disposal, and it would take a good deal longer than it was worth to follow down the line of red tape to get one assigned to us."

Antyok pondered and his forehead creased lightly. "It doesn't *have* to be spaceships. But even so— If you would write up another report and make the suggestion yourself—strongly, you understand—I might figure out some way of tying it up with my birth-rate project. A double-A priority can get practically anything, you know, without questions."

Zammo's interest lacked a bit even of mildness. "Well, maybe. Meanwhile, I've some basal metabolism tests in progress, and it's getting late. I'll think about it. It's got its points."

From: AdHQ-Ceph18
To: BuOuProv
Subject: Outer Province Project 2910, Part I—Birth rate of non-Humans on Cepheus 18, Investigation of.
Reference:
    (a) BuOuProv letr. Ceph-N-CM/car, 115097, 223/977 G.E.
Enclosure:
    1-SciGroup 10, Physical & Biochemical Division Report, Part XV, dated 220/977 G.E.
    1. Enclosure 1 is forwarded herewith for the information of the BuOuProv.
    2. Special attention is directed to Section V, Paragraph 3 of Enclosure 1 in which it is requested that a spaceship be assigned SciGroup 10 for use in expediting investigations authorized by the BuOuProv. It is considered by AdHQ-Ceph18 that such investigations may be of material use in aiding work now in progress on the subject project, authorized by reference (a). It is suggested, in view of the high priority placed by the BuOuProv upon the subject project, that immediate consideration be given the SciGroup's request.

    L. ANTYOK, Superv. AdHQ-Ceph18, 240/977 G.E.

From: BuOuProv
To: AdHQ-Ceph18
Subject: Outer Province Project 2910—Birth rate of non-Humans on Cepheus 18, Investigation of.
Reference:
  (a) AdHQ-Ceph18 letr. AA-LA/mn, dated 240/977 G.E.
 1. Training Ship *AN-R-2055* is being placed at the disposal of AdHQ-Ceph18 for use in investigation of non-Humans on Cepheus 18 with respect to the subject project and other authorized OuProv projects as requested in Enclosure 1 to reference (a).
 2. It is urgently requested that work on the subject project be expedited by all available means.

     C. MORILY, Head, BuOuProv, 251/977 G.E.

IV

 The little bricky creature must have been more uncomfortable than his bearing would admit to. He was carefully wrapped in a temperature already adjusted to the point where his human companions steamed in their open shirts.

 His speech was high-pitched and careful. "I find it damp, but not unbearably so at this low temperature."

 Antyok smiled. "It was nice of you to come. I had planned to visit you, but a trial run in your atmosphere out there—" The smile had become rueful.

 "It doesn't matter. You other-worldlings have done more for us than ever we were able to do for ourselves. It is an obligation that is but imperfectly returned by the endurance on my part of a trifling discomfort." His speech seemed always indirect, as if he approached his thoughts sidelong, or as if it were against all etiquette to be blunt.

 Gustiv Bannerd, seated in an angle of the room, with one long leg crossing the other, scrawled nimbly and said, "You don't mind if I record all this?"

 The Cepheid non-Human glanced briefly at the journalist. "I have no objection."

 Antyok's apologetics persisted. "This is not a purely social affair, sir. I would not have forced discomfort on you for that. There are important questions to be considered, and you are the leader of your people."

 The Cepheid nodded. "I am satisfied your purposes are kindly. Please proceed."

 The administrator almost wriggled in his difficulty in putting thoughts into words. "It is a subject," he said, "of delicacy, and one I would never bring up if it weren't for the overwhelming importance of the . . . uh . . . question. I am only the spokesman of my government—"

 "My people consider the other-world government a kindly one."

 "Well, yes, they are kindly. For that reason, they are disturbed over the fact that your people no longer breed."

Antyok paused, and waited with worry for a reaction that did not come. The Cepheid's face was motionless except for the soft, trembling motion of the wrinkled area that was his deflated drinking tube.

Antyok continued, "It is a question we have hesitated to bring up because of its extremely personal angles. Noninterference is my government's prime aim, and we have done our best to investigate the problem quietly and without disturbing your people. But, frankly, we—"

"Have failed?" finished the Cepheid, at the other's pause.

"Yes. Or at least, we have not discovered a concrete failure to reproduce the exact environment of your original world; with, of course, the necessary modification to make it more livable. Naturally, it is thought there is some chemical shortcoming. And so I ask your voluntary help in the matter. Your people are advanced in the study of your own biochemistry. If you do not choose, or would rather not—"

"No, no, I can help." The Cepheid seemed cheerful about it. The smooth flat planes of his loose-skinned, hairless skull wrinkled in an alien response to an uncertain emotion. "It is not a matter that any of us would have thought would have disturbed you other-worldlings. That it does is but another indication of your well-meaning kindness. This world we find congenial, a paradise in comparison to our old. It lacks in nothing. Conditions such as now prevail belong in our legends of the Golden Age."

"Well—"

"But there is a something; a something you may not understand. We cannot expect different intelligences to think alike."

"I shall try to understand."

The Cepheid's voice had grown soft, its liquid undertones more pronounced. "We were dying on our native world; but we were fighting. Our science, developed through a history older than yours, was losing; but it had not yet lost. Perhaps it was because our science was fundamentally biological, rather than physical as yours is. Your people discovered new forms of energy and reached the stars. Our people discovered new truths of psychology and psychiatry and built up a working society free of disease and crime.

"There is no need to question which of the two angles of approach was the more laudable, but there is no uncertainty as to which proved more successful in the end. In our dying world, without the means of life or sources of power, our biological science could but make the dying easier.

"And yet we fought. For centuries past we had been groping toward the elements of atomic power, and slowly the spark of hope had glimmered that we might break through the two-dimensional limits of our planetary surface and reach the stars. There were no other planets in our system to serve as stepping stones. Nothing but some twenty light-years to the nearest star, without the knowledge of the possibility of the existence of other planetary systems, but rather with the supposed near-certainty of the contrary.

"But there is something in all life that insists on striving; even on useless striving. There were only five thousand of us left in the last days. Only five thousand. And our first ship was ready. It was experimental. It would probably have been a failure. But already we had all the principles of propulsion and navigation correctly worked out."

There was a long pause, and the Cepheid's small black eyes seemed glazed in retrospect.

The newspaperman put in suddenly, from his corner, "And then we came?"

"And then you came," the Cepheid agreed simply. "It changed everything. Energy was ours for the asking. A new world, congenial and, indeed, ideal, was ours even without asking. If our problems of society had long been solved by ourselves, our more difficult problems of environment were suddenly solved for us, no less completely."

"Well?" urged Antyok.

"Well—it was somehow not well. For centuries our ancestors had fought towards the stars, and now the stars suddenly proved to be the property of others. We had fought for life, and it had become a present handed to us by others. There is no longer any reason to fight. There is no longer anything to attain. All the universe is the property of your race."

"This world is yours," said Antyok, gently.

"By sufferance. It is a gift. It is not ours by right."

"You have earned it, in my opinion."

And now the Cepheid's eyes were sharply fixed on the other's countenance. "You mean well, but I doubt that you understand. We have nowhere to go, save this gift of a world. We are in a blind alley. The function of life is striving, and that is taken from us. Life can no longer interest us. We have no offspring—voluntarily. It is our way of removing ourselves from your way."

Absent-mindedly, Antyok had removed the fluoro-globe from the window seat, and spun it on its base. Its gaudy surface reflected light as it spun and its three-foot-high bulk floated with incongruous grace and lightness in the air.

Antyok said, "Is that your only solution? Sterility?"

"We might escape still," whispered the Cepheid, "but where in the Galaxy is there place for us? It is all yours."

"Yes, there is no place for you nearer than the Magellanic Clouds if you wished independence. The Magellanic Clouds—"

"And you would not let us go of yourselves. You mean kindly, I know."

"Yes, we mean kindly—but we could not let you go."

"It is a mistaken kindness."

"Perhaps, but could you not reconcile yourselves? You have a world."

"It is something past complete explanations. Your mind is different. We could not reconcile ourselves. I believe, administrator, that you have thought of all this before. The concept of the blind alley we find ourselves trapped in is not new to you."

Antyok looked up, startled, and one hand steadied the fluoroglobe. "Can you read my mind?"

"It is just a guess. A good one, I think."

"Yes—but *can* you read my mind? The minds of humans in general, I mean. It is an interesting point. The scientists say you cannot, but sometimes I wonder if it is that you simply will not. Could you answer that? I am detaining you, unduly, perhaps."

"No . . . no—" But the little Cepheid drew his enveloping robe closer, and buried his face in the electrically-heated pad at the collar for a moment. "You other-worldlings speak of reading minds. It is not so at all, but it is assuredly hopeless to explain."

Antyok mumbled the old proverb, "One cannot explain sight to a man blind from birth."

"Yes, just so. This sense which you call 'mind reading,' quite erroneously, cannot be applied to other-worldlings. It is not that we cannot receive the proper sensations, it is that your people do not transmit them, and we have no way of explaining to you how to go about it."

"Hm-m-m."

"There are times, of course, of great concentration or emotional tension on the part of an other-worldling when some of us who are more expert in this sense—more sharp-eyed, so to speak—detect vaguely *something*. It is uncertain; yet I myself have at times wondered—"

Carefully, Antyok began spinning the fluoro-globe once more. His pink face was set in thought, and his eyes were fixed upon the Cepheid. Gustiv Bannerd stretched his fingers and reread his notes, his lips moving silently.

The fluoro-globe spun, and slowly the Cepheid seemed to grow tense as well, as his eyes shifted to the colorful sheen of the globe's fragile surface.

The Cepheid said, "What is that?"

Antyok started, and his face smoothed into an almost chuckling placidity. "This? A Galactic fad of three years ago; which means that it is a hopelessly old-fashioned relic this year. It is a useless device but it looks pretty. Bannerd, could you adjust the windows to nontransmission?"

There was the soft click of a contact, and the windows became curved regions of darkness, while in the center of the room, the fluoro-globe was suddenly the focus of a rosy effulgence that seemed to leap outward in streamers. Antyok, a scarlet figure in a scarlet room, placed it upon the table and spun it with a hand that dripped red. As it spun, the colors changed with a slowly increasing rapidity, blended and fell apart into more extreme contrasts.

Antyok was speaking in an eerie atmosphere of molten, shifting rainbow. "The surface is of a material that exhibits variable fluorescence. It is almost weightless, extremely fragile, but gyroscopically balanced so that it rarely falls with ordinary care. It is rather pretty, don't you think?"

From somewhere the Cepheid's voice came. "Extremely pretty."

"But it has outworn its welcome; outlived its fashionable existence."

The Cepheid's voice was abstracted. "It is very pretty."

Bannerd restored the light at a gesture, and the colors faded.

The Cepheid said, "That is something my people would enjoy." He stared at the globe with fascination.

And now Antyok rose. "You had better go. If you stay longer, the atmosphere may have bad effects. I thank you humbly for your kindness."

"I thank you humbly for yours." The Cepheid had also risen.

Antyok said, "Most of your people, by the way, have accepted our offers to them to study the make-up of our modern spaceships. You understand, I suppose, that the purpose was to study the reactions of your people to our technology. I trust that conforms with your sense of propriety."

"You need not apologize. I, myself, have now the makings of a human pilot. It was most interesting. It recalls our own efforts—and reminds us of how nearly on the right track we were."

The Cepheid left, and Antyok sat, frowning.

"Well," he said to Bannerd, a little sharply. "You remember our agreement, I hope. This interview can't be published."

Bannerd shrugged. "Very well."

Antyok was at his seat, and his fingers fumbled with the small metal figurine upon his desk. "What do you think of all this, Bannerd?"

"I am sorry for them. I think I understand how they feel. We must educate them out of it. The Philosophy can do it."

"You think so?"

"Yes."

"We can't let them go, of course."

"Oh, no. Out of the question. We have too much to learn from them. This feeling of theirs is only a passing stage. They'll think differently, especially when we allow them the completest independence."

"Maybe. What do you think of the fluoro-globes, Bannerd? He liked them. It might be a gesture of the right sort to order several thousand of them. The Galaxy knows they're a drug on the market right now, and cheap enough."

"Sounds like a good idea," said Bannerd.

"The Bureau would never agree, though. I know them."

The newsman's eyes narrowed. "But it might be just the thing. They need new interests."

"Yes? Well, we *could* do something. I could include your transcript of the interview as part of a report and just emphasize the matter of the globes a bit. After all, you're a member of The Philosophy and might have influence with important people, whose word with the Bureau might carry much more weight than mine. You understand—?"

"Yes," mused Bannerd. "Yes."

From: AdHQ-Ceph18
To: BuOuProv
Subject: OuProv Project 2910, Part II; Birth rate of non-Humans on Cepheus 18, Investigation of.
Reference:

(a) BuOuProv letr. Ceph-N-CM/car, 115097, dated 223/977 G.E.
Enclosure:

1. Transcript of conversation between L. Antyok of AdHQ-Ceph18, and Ni-San, High Judge of the non-Humans on Cepheus 18.

1. Enclosure 1 is forwarded herewith for the information of the BuOuProv.

2. The investigation of the subject project undertaken in response to the authorization of reference (a) is being pursued along the new lines indicated in Enclosure 1. The BuOuProv is assured that every means will be used to combat the harmful psychological attitude at present prevalent among the non-Humans.

3. It is to be noted that the High Judge of the non-Humans on Cepheus 18 expressed interest in fluoro-globes. A preliminary investigation into this fact of non-Human psychology has been initiated.

L. ANTYOK, Superv. AdHQ-Ceph18, 272/977 G.E.

From: BuOuProv
To: AdHQ-Ceph18
Subject: OuProv Project 2910; Birth rate of non-Humans on Cepheus 18, Investigation of.
Reference:

(a) AdHQ-Ceph18 letr. AA-LA/mn, dated 272/977 G.E.

1. With reference to Enclosure 1 of reference (a), five thousand fluoro-globes have been allocated for shipment to Cepheus 18, by the Department of Trade.

2. It is instructed that AdHQ-Ceph18 make use of all methods of appeasing non-Humans' dissatisfaction consistent with the necessities of obedience to Imperial proclamation.

C. MORILY, Chief, BuOuProv, 283/977 G.E.

V.

The dinner was over, the wine had been brought in, and the cigars were out. The groups of talkers had formed and the captain of the merchant fleet was the center of the largest. His brilliant white uniform quite outsparkled his listeners.

He was almost complacent in his speech: "The trip was nothing. I've had more than three hundred ships under me before this. Still, I've never had a cargo quite like this. What do you want with five thousand fluoro-globes on this desert, by the Galaxy?"

Loodun Antyok laughed gently. He shrugged. "For the non-Humans. It wasn't a difficult cargo, I hope."

"No, not difficult. But bulky. They're fragile, and I couldn't carry more than twenty to a ship with all the government regulations concerning packing and precautions against breakage. But it's the government's money, I suppose."

Zammo smiled grimly. "Is this your first experience with government methods, captain?"

"Galaxy, no," exploded the spaceman. "I try to avoid it, of course, but you can't help getting entangled on occasion. And it's an abhorrent thing when you are, and that's the truth. The red tape! The paper work! It's enough to stunt your growth and curdle your circulation. It's a tumor, a cancerous growth on the Galaxy. I'd wipe out the whole mess."

Antyok said, "You're unfair, captain. You don't understand."

"Yes? Well, now, as one of these bureaucrats," and he smiled amiably at the word, "suppose you explain your side of the situation, administrator."

"Well, now," Antyok seemed confused, "government is a serious and complicated business. We've got thousands of planets to worry about in this Empire of ours and billions of people. It's almost past human ability to supervise the business of governing without the tightest sort of organization. I think there are something like four hundred million men today in the Imperial Administrative Service alone and in order to co-ordinate their efforts and to pool their knowledge, you *must* have what you call red tape and paper work. Every bit of it, senseless though it may seem, annoying though it may be, has its uses. Every piece of paper is a thread binding the labors of four hundred million humans. Abolish the Administrative Service and you abolish the Empire; and with it, interstellar peace, order, and civilization."

"Come—" said the captain.

"No. I mean it." Antyok was earnestly breathless. "The rules and system of the Administrative set-up must be sufficiently all-embracing and rigid, so that in case of incompetent officials, and sometimes one *is* appointed . . . you may laugh, but there are incompetent scientists, and news men, and captains too . . . in case of incompetent officials, I say, little harm will be done. For at the worst, the system can move by itself."

"Yes," grunted the captain, sourly, "and if a capable administrator should be appointed? He is then caught by the same rigid web and is forced into mediocrity."

"Not at all," replied Antyok, warmly. "A capable man can work within the limits of the rules and accomplish what he wishes."

"How?" asked Bannerd.

"Well . . . well—" Antyok was suddenly ill at ease. "One method is to get yourself an A-priority project, or double-A, if possible."

The captain leaned his head back for laughter, but never quite made it, for the door was flung open and frightened men were pouring in. The shouts made no sense at first. Then:

"Sir, the ships are gone. These non-Humans have taken them by force."

"What? All?"

"Every one. Ships and creatures—"

It was two hours later that the four were together again, alone in Antyok's office now.

Antyok said coldly, "They've made no mistakes. There's not a ship left behind, not even your training ship, Zammo. And there isn't a government ship available in this entire half of the Sector. By the time we organize a pursuit, they'll be out of the Galaxy and halfway to the Magellanic Clouds. Captain, it was your responsibility to maintain an adequate guard."

The captain cried, "It was our first day out of space. Who could have known—"

Zammo interrupted fiercely, "Wait a while, captain. I'm beginning to understand. Antyok," his voice was hard, "you engineered this."

"I?" Antyok's expression was strangely cool, almost indifferent.

"You told us this evening that a clever administrator got an A-priority project assigned to accomplish what he wished. You got such a project in order to help the non-Humans escape."

"I did? I beg your pardon, but how could that be? It was you yourself in one of your reports that brought up the problem of the failing birth rate. It was Bannerd, here, whose sensational articles frightened the Bureau into making a double-A priority project out of it. I had nothing to do with it."

"*You* suggested that I mention the birth rate," said Zammo violently.

"Did I?" said Antyok, composedly.

"And for that matter," roared Bannerd, suddenly, "you suggested that I mention the birth rate in my articles."

The three ringed him now and hemmed him in. Antyok leaned back in his chair and said easily, "I don't know what you mean by suggestions. If you are accusing me, please stick to evidence—legal evidence. The laws of the Empire go by written, filmed, or transcribed material, or by witnessed statements. All my letters as administrator are on file here, at the Bureau, and at other places. I never asked for an A-priority project. The Bureau assigned it to me, and Zammo and Bannerd are responsible for that. In print, at any rate."

Zammo's voice was an almost inarticulate growl. "You hoodwinked me into teaching the creatures how to handle a spaceship."

"It was *your* suggestion. I have your report proposing they be studied in their reaction to human tools on file. So has the Bureau. The evidence—the *legal* evidence, is plain. I had nothing to do with it."

"Nor with the globes?" demanded Bannerd.

The captain howled suddenly, "You had my ships brought here purposely. Five thousand globes! You knew it would require hundreds of craft."

"I never asked for globes," said Antyok, coldly. "That was the Bureau's idea, although I think Bannerd's friends of The Philosophy helped that along."

Bannerd fairly choked. He spat out, "You were asking that Cepheid leader if he could read minds. You were telling him to express interest in the globes."

"Come now. You prepared the transcript of the conversation yourself, and that, too, is on file. You can't prove it." He stood up. "You'll have to excuse me. I must prepare a report for the Bureau."

At the door, Antyok turned. "In a way, the problem of the non-Humans is solved, even if only to their own satisfaction. They'll breed now, and have a world they've earned themselves. It's what they wanted.

"Another thing. Don't accuse me of silly things. I've been in the Service for twenty-seven years, and I assure you that my paper work is proof enough that I have been thoroughly correct in everything I have done. And, captain, I'll be glad to continue our discussion of earlier this evening at your convenience and explain how a capable administrator can work through red tape and still get what he wants."

It was remarkable that such a round, smooth baby-face could wear a smile quite so sardonic.

From: BuOuProv
To: Loodun Antyok, Chief Public Administrator, **A-8**
Subject: Administrative Service, Standing in.
Reference:
    (a) AdServ Court Decision 22874-Q, dated 1/978 G.E.
    1. In view of the favorable opinion handed down in reference (a) you are hereby absolved of all responsibility for the flight of non-Humans on Cepheus 18. It is requested that you hold yourself in readiness for your next appointment.

                 R. HORPRITT, Chief, AdServ, 15/978 G.E.

WALLACE WEST

EN ROUTE TO PLUTO

"WHY do we keep spinning around like this?" sang Yahna plaintively as she stared out of a porthole and watched the stars chasing each other madly across the black sky. Then once more she flapped her great red wings until they stirred up every speck of dust in the control cabin.

"I've told you a thousand times before"—I tried to keep the irritation out of my voice and stifle a sneeze at the same time—"that the gyroscopic stabilizer is broken and that it's a two-man job to fix it while we're in flight. You'll just have to get accustomed to seeing the galaxies shoot past until we arrive on Pluto."

"Why can't I help you repair the gyroscope, dearest?" She struck a perfect high C on the last word; so perfect a note, in fact, that I had to resist the impulse to pick up a monkey wrench and brain her. Why, oh, why had I ever yielded to that temptation to elope with a Martian bird woman?

It had all seemed so perfectly logical that night three months ago, when I had sat in the Agan Café at Crotan, the underground capital city of Mars, and imbibed six pipes of gurlack one after the other. Here was I, Jack Harkness, outward bound from the Earth to Pluto on the first journey of exploration to that outermost of the planets.

And there was Yahna, tired of exhibiting her feathered charms, and ready to chuck it all—she had had six pipes of gurlack, too—and escape the responsibilities of one who could trace her ancestry back through ten thousand generations of entertainers, and, if she had to die, do so in the cold, clean depths of interstellar space.

It had all seemed to smack of ancient knight errantry—ladies in distress and so forth. I muffled my new-found friend in furs so that her wings wouldn't be so noticeable, slipped her past the guards, who naturally wouldn't have been at all anxious to lose one of Mars' few thousand remaining bird people, and sneaked her through endless dim passageways to the airport.

There I forced the amazed commandant to marry us at the point of a heat gun—after all, I had no desire to create a scandal which might lead to interstellar complications—and high-tailed it out into space with most of Crotan's patrol fleet at our heels.

For several weeks thereafter life had been one grand sweet song. Yahna was charming, well-educated and beautiful, although so fragile that I sometimes feared she would break if I touched her. She talked—or rather sang—English like a Metropolitan Opera star. The bird people are unable to talk in monotones, but accompany the words with the loveliest harmonies which greatly enhance their meaning.

At first her naïveté about things Earthian intrigued and amused me. But finally the confinement and those eternal wide-eyed questions began to get on my nerves. I tried to ignore this irritation at first. Then I fought it bitterly. But by the time we were nearing Pluto, Yahna's mere presence was on the verge of driving me insane.

I really believe that it was our difference of outlook rather than our physical differences which caused the trouble—that plus the fact that long space journeys are nerve-racking in themselves. I've been co-pilot with a Martian on plenty of hard trips, and managed beautifully. However, this was something different.

The average Martian, such as one sees so often in New York these days, is hardly to be distinguished from an Earthian—a trifle taller and more slightly built—except for his massive, somewhat humped shoulders, queer, fiery-red hair and downy face and hands.

But the primitive Martian of, say, one hundred thousand years ago, was quite a different creature. His body was covered with bright-red feathers as protection from the cold, while, due to the lesser gravitation of the planet, he had developed a pair of splendid wings.

Then, as Mars' atmosphere became more and more rarefied through the millennia, these wings were unable to sustain its inhabitants any longer. The structures naturally atrophied, as did those of our own penguins, for example. Today the puny stumps are amputated at birth.

Even in those times, however, the Martians were highly civilized, and when they were forced underground by the growing cold and lack of air, they strove to preserve their former ability to fly in one special class of the population.

In the course of time the latter became the entertainers of the planet—dancers, singers, actors, etc. In order that their wings might not atrophy, great gymnasiums with artificially high air pressure were constructed, where those of the entertaining class could exercise each day. In addition to this their every want was cared for. The result is that after all these centuries they still can fly as well as their ancestors could, and are almost objects of veneration for the average Martian.

I was jerked out of my reverie by the melting music of Yahna's voice.

"I said, dearest, why can't I help you repair the gyroscope?" she chanted as she slipped a caressing wing over my shoulders. It was then that I noticed that the long confinement without her usual exercise was doing Yahna's plumage no good. In fact—perish the thought!—she showed signs of molting.

"Look, sweetheart," I pleaded as gently as I was able. "You wouldn't know a gyroscope if you saw one. Why don't you read a book or something? I couldn't think of you getting your pretty self all covered with grease, fixing machinery. You're made for singing and dancing and flying. Now run along like a good girl. I've got all I can do keeping the course."

"But why are we going on this crazy trip, after all?" She sat down on the floor near the control seat and wrapped her wings around her until only her piquant, snub-nosed face showed amidst the shimmering plumage. "I thought that space travel was exciting. But I find it very dull."

"We're out here because Earth needs a new supply of cheap raw materials," I answered doggedly, after shifting a quadrant which gave the starboard rocket more juice. "If Earth can find a source of radioactive minerals on Pluto she can claim it for herself and sell it to Mars and Venus. That will put some of the unemployed to work and prevent any more attempts at revolution."

"Why won't Mars and Venus get the same idea?"

"But that's impossible. They don't know the secret of our heat guns." I nodded toward the cabin wall, where I always kept the ugly little weapon hanging ready in case of emergencies. "Your scientists were using that same idea to produce great extremes of cold. We stole the invention, turned it upside down, so to speak, and produced the heat-ray transformer, and still they can't figure out how we did it. Those foreigners—" I stopped, embarrassed by my own enthusiasm.

"But I still don't see why you're spending most of your life shut up in a stupid little box spinning through space when you could be dancing in the sunshine and singing with the birds," she persisted. "I suppose you'll say it's to make money. All you Earthians do." Her large green eyes became troubled. "What is this money you're so fond of?"

"Well," I began, "money is—well—you buy things with money. Now if I have five apples—"

Suddenly an unreasoning rage seized me as I realized that this girl had no conception of the unlimited power which wealth could give or the tragedy a lack of it could bring. She had never had to buy or sell—to fight for her very existence, to see her friends starve—

"Oh, for Heaven's sake, shut up," I yelled. "Why? Why? Why? Nothing but fool questions. What are you trying to do? Make a groundling out of me? Listen! A space pilot is the luckiest man alive. If he's ambitious there are no heights he may not climb to. With the inside information he picks up on his journeys he may become banker, captain of industry, even dictator. Oh, you don't understand. You're just a throwback—a myth—a fairy tale. There's no place for you in modern life. Why on Earth did I ever hook up with you! Go on—read your book!"

Her wings drooping forlornly, and tears trembling on her long lashes, Yahna wandered over to the window seat under one of the portholes and picked up a volume of the "Rubáiyát" which I had given her.

> "A book of verses underneath the bough,
> A jug of wine, a loaf of bread—and thou—"

She sang the words, giving them a beauty which I had never imagined, and causing my face to burn with shame.

> "Beside me singing in the wilderness—
> Oh, wilderness were paradise enow!"

"What's a wilderness, Jack?" she murmured pathetically. "It—it sounds nice."

For answer I hooked the controls, went over and took her quivering little body in my arms. Poor kid! Of course she was perfectly useless out here. But it was all my fault. As I kissed her I made another of my vows never again to hurt her feelings.

Landing a rocket plane is a ticklish job under the best of conditions. You have to coast down on the fading forward beams with enough momentum to keep the ship from tipping sidewise, yet not so much that she splits her seams when she hits. Bad judgment either way is bound to have unpleasant results, especially on a strange planet.

If we weren't killed on a smash landing, we still didn't have the equipment necessary to repair any leaking seams. On the other hand, if we fell over, the ship would be as helpless as a fish out of water, until we built some kind of a scaffolding and hoisted her upright—another impossible job.

Multiply those difficulties about a thousand times and maybe you'll realize the spot I was in, with my vessel spinning around on her nose about once every two seconds. How I wished for good old Bob Filgus, my engineer, whom I had deserted so gaily at Crotan so that I might elope with Yahna. The two of us could have fixed that gyroscope in an hour. However—

I squinted through the porthole at the forsaken surface of Pluto, which now was rushing upward at the rate of several hundred miles an hour, despite the fact that I was braking with every ounce of power. It made my head swim to watch the dizzy spectacle, and the dazzling white beams of the four forward torps made my eyes water.

Although the Sun was only a pin point behind us, it still lighted up the planet about 200 times brighter than the Moon does the Earth when it is full. Under this illumination I finally managed to determine that the terrain ahead consisted of saw-toothed mountains of tremendous height, pushing themselves upward through an otherwise solid sheet of ice or snow.

Snow meant plenty of atmosphere. Air would cushion us to a great degree and make avoidance of a crash landing much easier. Pluto's temperature, I must explain, is so low during half of its circle around the Sun that its air congeals. But when it dips inside the orbit of Neptune for the other half of its slow swing, the surface becomes only about 100 degrees below zero, Fahrenheit; the air gasifies and life is theoretically possible for human beings.

The fact that I might be able to make a blind landing without a crack-up reassured me somewhat. But what about tipping over and becoming stranded? Even the most delicate altimeters wouldn't help me there. I needed my eyes and stable ground at which to look.

"This reminds me of the time when I was a little girl and we used to play with those funny Earth toys called tops," chimed Yahna, who was peering through the window over my shoulder. "Why do they stand on end, Jack? I suppose I'm being awfully stupid again, but I never could understand why they didn't fall over—"

"*You* wouldn't!" I grunted before I could stop myself. Then I let out a whoop of astonishment and delight. Why, of course! Why hadn't I thought of it before? A ship couldn't possibly tip over while spinning. No matter how softly I brought her down, she'd stay upright if I landed on a fairly level surface. The nose probably would drill itself into the ground for a yard or so, and the rocket ports would be clogged, but I could fix that easily.

I grabbed Yahna by the shoulders and kissed her enthusiastically—on the nose, it so happened—then made a dash for the controls. We'd make it yet!

We came down soft as a feather, blasting the snow beneath us into nothingness and drilling into the frozen earth beneath it. As I had anticipated, the sudden stoppage of our spin sent both of us sliding round and round the floor of the control room until we jammed under the chart table, out of breath, but with no other injuries than a few bruises.

I staggered to my feet only to fall on my nose, so dizzy that I could hardly see. Yahna did the same thing, after which we sat and laughed helplessly at each other until the vertigo wore off.

When we could navigate once more we started exploring the ship, and found that no appreciable damage had been done. The forward ports were, of course, buried in the ground, and it was not until we reached the rocket firing chamber in the stern that we saw daylight. The snowdrift into which we had dived had fallen in on the ship and almost buried it.

"Now what do we explore?" chanted the girl as she stared through the rear porthole at the forbidding gray landscape. "Those raw materials you spoke about certainly look raw enough to satisfy anybody."

"Well"—I hesitated after studying various meters—"the air pressure is about the same as that on Earth and its composition seems breathable. Gravity about that of Mars. Temperature 172 below zero. I think we could chance going outside in space suits—"

"Space suits." She laughed, rumpling her feathers. "Well, you can wear one of the ugly things if you want to, but I'm going out this way. After all, the temperature back home often drops about as low as this during the night. And, oh! I want so to fly again!"

"You'll freeze your feathers off," I grunted as I wriggled into my suit and adjusted the helmet. "I'll take some blankets outside, anyway, in case you get a chill."

"Aren't you going to take your heat gun along, too?" Yahna trilled as I threw my weight on the levers which opened the outer port.

"What for?" I grunted as I heaved and twisted. As usual, the cursed door had been slightly calcined during our passage through the atmosphere, and didn't want to budge. "There's no life on Pluto at this temperature."

"Why not?"

"Well, because—" I groaned; then, in order to stop a further flood of senseless questions, yanked the holster out of the rack and buckled it around my waist.

The port swung open at last, letting in a thin blast of air so deathly cold that I snapped the glass front of my helmet shut at once.

But Yahna didn't seem to mind in the least. She threw her arms wide and took in great gasps of air.

"Oh, how lovely," she chanted as I again marveled at the ability of Martians to withstand great extremes of temperature. "It's like the wine your 'Rubáiyát' talks about after all these weeks of synthetic atmosphere. I'm going out."

Springing gracefully through the porthole, she landed on the snow outside, spreading her gleaming ten-foot wings, beat them together exactly as a bird does, and fairly screamed with delight. A moment later she left the ground and went swooping up into the gray twilight.

I paused a moment to toss out a roll of blankets and to close the port. I was afraid the batteries in the engine room might freeze otherwise. Then I, too, climbed out on the snow bank surrounding the ship.

After watching Yahna swoop and glide like a swallow until I began to get dizzy, I turned my attention to the surrounding landscape. The first thing which puzzled me was the snow. Under ordinary circumstance, if a space ship, its surface heated by passage through an atmosphere, should land in a snow bank, it would melt a great hole in the drift. In this case, however, although the snow was slowly receding from about the vessel, there was no sign of melting.

The next thing I noticed was that the vent from my helmet was not surrounded by a cloud of vapor as it should have been, but that my breath, upon reaching the outer air, formed a sort of miniature snowstorm, which eddied around me and finally fell to the ground.

Frowning, I picked up a double handful of snow in my electrically heated mittens and stared at it in bewilderment. It vanished almost at once; but when it was all gone the gloves were not wet. The snow really seemed to evaporate rather than melt. For a moment the thing baffled me. Then I remembered the temperature reading I had made in the cabin. Of course! At 172 below zero, Fahrenheit, carbon dioxide would congeal. The stuff which covered the surface of Pluto was not snow, but solidified gas!

My curiosity satisfied on this point, I began examining the outcroppings of shiny gray rock which pierced the drifts. I broke off a chunk and hefted it. Queer stuff! It had scarcely any weight at all. Could it be? After some difficulty I fished out a match from one of my pockets, lighted it and touched it to the rock. There was a blaze of light as the stuff ignited. I dropped it just in time to avoid a bad burn, then was almost knocked over as the heat gasified part of the snow bank on which it had fallen.

"Good Lord," I gasped as I watched the flame burrow deeper and deeper into the drift. "If the whole plain is covered with magnesium and this sets it off, I'll go up in a cloud of smoke in about thirty seconds." Luckily, the specimen I had dropped was so small that it burned itself out before it melted its way through the bottom of the drift.

When the great flare died out I blinked helplessly, until my eyes became reaccustomed to the surrounding twilight. Then, as I was recovering from this shock, I heard Yahna screaming high above me. A moment later I located her. Wings thrown back and red hair streaming stiffly, she was falling like a plummet!

Just as it seemed certain that she would crash, the girl swung her wings forward and landed, light as a feather, not ten feet from me.

"The flare? What was it, Jack?" she crescendoed.

"Nothing important," I lied. "Just a little magnesium I touched off accidentally."

"And those clouds," she continued, pointing upward breathlessly.

"Clouds!" I jeered. "If it's cold enough to freeze carbon dioxide there can't be any clouds. Even you ought to know that!" To humor her I glanced at the sky; then, despite the cold, I opened the visor of my helmet to look again. Yahna was right! The sky was full of little puffy white clouds. What was more, they didn't act like human clouds should. Instead of drifting with the wind, they seemed to be drifting *toward us* from all directions, as though attracted by the recent flare.

"I'm—I'm cold." Yahna shivered.

"I should think you would be, gallivanting around up there like that. Let's get back to the ship."

It did seem cold, even inside my suit, as we hurried back to the **hole in** the snow above which projected the stern of the rocket.

"Could it be the clouds causing it?" chattered my companion as she stumbled along beside me. "They seemed unfriendly, somehow—up there."

"Of course not," I answered, but I could not resist an apprehensive glance over my shoulder at those queer, diaphanous puffs of white. There were hundreds of them now, not only behind us, but also closing in in front. "Maybe you're right," I muttered grudgingly at last. "Come on. Let's run."

"I—I can't," she quavered. "My legs—feel funny."

For answer I picked her up bodily and dashed for the ship, those red wings brushing the snow into strange whispers behind me.

But when we reached the *Pluto* another shock awaited us. Due to the radiation of the still-warm hull, the walls of carbon-dioxide snow had evaporated so that they now stood all of ten feet away from the ship. There was no way of reaching the stern port. The forward port, down at the ground level, was, of course, still locked from the inside.

"Could I help, Jack?" quavered Yahna, struggling out of my arms.

"Well, I guess maybe you could at that," I conceded. "If you would fly to the door, pull it open and go inside and throw me a rope, I might make it."

She sprang forward lightly, reached the handholds on the port, braced herself against the side of the ship and tugged with all her strength, wings fluttering wildly. Nothing happened.

"It's stuck, Jack," she called at last. "I'm not strong enough."

"Come on back then, and get under these blankets," I directed. "We'll have to try something else."

"I'm sorry," she whimpered as she fluttered back and nestled under the pile of blankets I had prepared. "I never was so cold in all my— Oh! Jack! Look at those clouds now!"

I glanced up, then ducked instinctively. There was no doubt about it. Those clouds were alive, and they meant us no good. From all directions they were closing in upon us, until they resembled a great, fleecy blanket which dimmed the light of the Sun. And as they came closer the cold steadily increased.

"I've worked in a space suit in open space," I groaned as I beat my arms against my chest to restore circulation, "but I never felt cold like this. It must be close to 250 below zero. What on earth's causing it, do you think?"

"Could they be alive—some sort of frost people?" she whispered. "Look, they move as though under some central command! On Mars there are legends—" She moaned as the cold bit deeper, even under the thick pile of blankets.

I started to say "Nonsense!" then bit my lips as I recalled that Yahna had been right on a number of occasions recently.

"Well," I amended, "if they're some sort of frost demons, my heat gun should stop them." My hands were clumsy and slow as I struggled with the holster, but the gun finally came loose. I pressed the trigger and sent a pencil of flame sweeping back and forth across the cloud blanket, which now hung only a few hundred feet above our heads.

Again nothing happened! The ray was absorbed as though by a mass of cotton. This gun, which could stop a yaggoth or a welk at 500 paces, was as useless as a cap pistol against these devils.

"I can hardly breathe," whimpered Yahna. "They're doing something to the air, Jack." She buried her head under the blankets.

And once more she was right. The very air around us seemed congealing into a snowstorm. Undoubtedly the oxygen and other gases were beginning to behave as the carbon dioxide already had done. I switched on my artificial air supply and got some relief, but could not avoid the gnawing cold. The temperature was undoubtedly hovering at the unbelievable level of 275 below, much lower than that of outer space. To make it worse, a hurricane, caused no doubt by the vacuum created through the air's solidification, began raging about me and threatened to sweep me off my feet.

Through it all the clouds looked down, soullessly, calculatingly, it seemed, to my dimming senses, but unquestionably alive in some alien fashion. I laced them frantically with my heat gun, but produced not the slightest retreat. We were slowly being frozen. A few moments now and we would become specimens for some un-Earthly laboratory.

"Yahna," I wheezed painfully, "can you hear me? Those devils have beaten us. Good-by, sweetheart. You're a swell egg. I'm sorry I've been so rotten."

"Good-by, Jack," she sang hysterically as she flung off the blankets, staggered to her feet and crept into my arms. "I'm sorry, too—that I've been so—useless. But I thought you humans said you could always fight— devil—with—fire."

"What's that you said?" I yelled.

"Getting—warmer—now," she gasped as she crumpled in a forlorn little heap at my feet.

"Yahna," I pleaded wildly as I heaped the blankets over her again.

"Guess—have fight frost devils—with—" Her voice trailed off into a discord and stopped.

"With what?" I screamed, shaking her frantically. "Don't give up, Yahna. With what?" In my hysterical fright I was suddenly convinced that if only she would say the right word we could be saved.

"Go 'way," she whimpered. "Wanna go sleep. Cold!"

"Cold!" I sprang upright and shook my fist madly at the hovering cloud people. "Cold!" I beat my hands against my chest until some vestige of circulation returned to them, then searched my pockets for a screwdriver. What a fool I had been!

Crouching down in the snow, I worked desperately on the heat gun. Of course, you are familiar with the way those weapons work—just the opposite of the old-style electric refrigerator—building up heat by a sort of transformer until it emerges as pure vibration.

Could I do it in the few minutes of life yet remaining to me? Again and again I dropped the screwdriver into the snow and scratched frantically to retrieve it. But at last I succeeded in reversing the circuits.

Too weak to stand now, I lifted my leaden arm, aimed at the living cloud banks, pressed the trigger and prayed.

The gun snarled, louder than the storm. A narrow column of snowflakes formed between the muzzle and the drifting mists above. Then a strange, agonizing ululation tore through the darkness. The gun bucked and jumped as I swung it back and forth. Was it my imagination, or were the clouds thinning, breaking up, drifting away? Was it possible that these frost be-ings, although impervious to flame, could be fought in their own medium?

Things grew black around me. A pleasant lethargy stole over my body. But I clung doggedly to the gun with both hands as my thoughts raced like those of a drowning man. Let's see—gun has amplification to the fortieth power. That means close to 460 degrees below zero—absolute zero—noth-ing. Absolutely nothing living could exist—that temperature— Poor, dear Yahna—smart girl, after all— If I—

"Jack! Jack!" Somebody was shaking me fiercely. "Are you alive, Jack? They're all gone. Why don't you speak to me?"

"Another of your fool questions. How can an icicle speak!" I groaned as I forced open my eyes. Then I blinked in astonishment. Yahna was bending over me as I lay in the cabin of the *Pluto*.

"After the frost devils ran away I went back to the ship, managed to pry the door open, tied a rope around you, hitched the other end to a wind-lass and pulled you across," she trilled, looking as proud as a peacock—if peacocks were feminine and had red feathers.

"Well, you little devil!" Even had I tried I would not have been able to restrain my admiration—and I did not try.

"I'm glad you took my suggestion about the frost people," continued this new Yahna. "Now, as soon as you feel better I'll help you fix the gyro-scope. I'm tired of being treated like some sort of doll."

Several hours later—I was not really much the worse for wear if you dis-count frostbitten ears, nose and fingers—we finished the job on the gyro-scope.

"Do you think I could ever become a space pilot, Jack?" asked the grease-smeared, weary girl, as she crawled out from under the big machine and sat down beside me on the floor. "This has been fun."

"Well"—I grinned judicially as I kissed the only clean spot on her face—"if you feel like that I'll let you help pilot the *Pluto* home after we finish our explorations. And I'll coach you for the quizz, too. But I don't think," I added as I surveyed her thoughtfully, "that you ought to face the examiners until I have you dry-cleaned."

CECIL B. WHITE

THE RETREAT TO MARS

THE SUN had dipped below the western hills, leaving a gorgeous mass of color in its wake. I stood there as the twilight arch swept up from the east, watching the shadows creep over land and sea while the faint evening clouds overhead turned blood-red under the last glancing rays of the sun.

Many times had I watched the setting of the sun and the evening shadows, while the mosquito-hawks hovered overhead with their plaintive cries, or plunged whirring downward upon their prey. Never twice the same that picture held me, until the city lights sprang into being in the distance and the flashing lights of the sentinels of the coast pierced through the gloaming.

As I turned away to begin my night's work the crunch of footsteps on the gravel path broke the stillness of the evening. An elderly, bearded man approached. He had come up the trail and I had not noticed him until he was nearly upon me.

Visitors to my little observatory are not uncommon. A few, those who show interest more than curiosity, are allowed to look through the instrument, on the rare occasions when it is not engaged in photographic or spectrographic work.

"Mr. Arnold?" queried my visitor as he approached. "I hope that I am not intruding. I tried to get you on the phone today, but was unsuccessful, and having been told that I would find you here, I took the liberty of coming to see you."

"I am just about to open up for the night," said I, "and if you don't mind my carrying on with my work—"

"Not at all, not at all," he replied, "I can talk to you just as well—that is, if I will not be in your way?"

Having been assured that he would not trouble me, he followed me into the observatory and watched while I opened the shutters that covered the aperture of the dome.

This done and my right-ascension circle set I turned the telescope on the first star of my evening's program.

When I had started the exposure, and entered up the necessary data in the observing book, I turned to him.

"You must pardon me, my dear sir, if I appear to be rude or inhospitable, but I am anxious to obtain a spectrogram of this star before it gets too far west for observing," I explained. "All I have to do now is to keep the star's image on the slit of the spectroscope."

"I noticed that you were engaged in spectrographic work," he remarked. "How long will your exposure be?"

From his remark I gathered that he knew something of the work in hand, so I answered, "About forty-five minutes with this seeing. It's a fifth magnitude star that I am working on. Would you care to take a look at it?"

He climbed up the observing ladder and stood beside me while I explained things to him. When I had finished he turned to me, half smilingly, and said:

"Is this seeing anything like it was last November when you made your remarkable observations of the planet Mars?"

"Apparently you have been reading my papers," I said. "No, conditions are not nearly as favorable now as they were at the time that other work was done. If I were to live a thousand years I doubt if I should ever see other nights to equal those four."

"Yes, I did read those papers of yours," he replied. "They are the cause of my presence here this evening. I am Hargraves, of the Smithsonian Institution."

I took his proffered hand. Hargraves was a well-known archæologist, though I must confess that I should not have known of him except by chance. On glancing through "Science Abstracts" a few weeks previously, I happened on an abstract of a paper of his which aroused my curiosity, and I had looked up the original, which had proved highly interesting.

I admitted as much to him. He laughed. "We work in different spheres, as a rule," he said, "but this time I am stepping into yours. That was a great fight you had with Krüssen and his associates over Schiaparelli's 'canali.' "

"Wasn't it!" said I. "The trouble with those chaps is that they do not know what *good* seeing is really like. They have, perhaps, forty or fifty clear nights a year, none of which begin to compare with our good nights. Then, because they have a fifty-four inch refractor against my twenty-four inch, they think that they are much better able to see fine detail than I am. Let me tell you, Doctor Hargraves, those four nights were perfect, absolutely perfect. I was able to use my highest power of four thousand and there was not the slightest tremor in the image. Had my driving-clock been perfect, I could have photographed everything I saw."

"I know," my companion replied. "Every detail of your drawings was correct. You may wonder how I—an archæologist—know anything about the planet Mars, but I have a big surprise in store for you."

I looked at him in amazement.

"I don't wonder you are surprised," he continued. "I have made some discoveries that I think no one ever dreamed of. As you are probably aware, I have only recently returned from Africa after a six years' absence."

I nodded, for in the paper I have already mentioned, Hargraves announced that he had made some startling discoveries in Africa as to the origin of mankind . . . discoveries which overthrew previous theories about the origin of man, but the exact nature of his find was not to be made public until such time, when the records he had found hidden away in a remote corner of "Darkest Africa" were fully deciphered.

"Some years ago," he continued, "I became convinced that the rise of mankind took place, not in Asia where it is generally supposed to have occurred, but in Africa.

"This belief thrust itself upon me as I was writing a book which I never published; a book which was to have traced the migration of mankind from the place of its origin, over this globe of ours. I amassed a tremendous amount of data which led, when I came to piece it together, to Central Africa, and not to Asia as I had confidently expected.

"I searched again and again for an error which I thought must exist in my work, but the trail inevitably led to the same conclusion: Central Africa was the 'Garden of Eden' of mankind.

"As you are aware, this was contrary to all earlier evidence, so I did not care to propound my theories without further corroboration. On consulting with the heads of my department, laying the evidence before them, it was decided to organize an expedition to see if any fresh data were available on the ground itself.

"The expedition, a small one as such things go, was organized and led by myself. It was successful, but the results are not yet ready for publication. To you, however, I would like to show what we have found, the understanding being, of course, that it shall not be divulged until my work is finished. Could you come and see me at my hotel? I will probably be in town for a week, anyway."

"Why not come and spend tomorrow evening with me?" I asked.

So we arranged it.

Having finished the spectrogram, I showed my companion what I could of my equipment and turned the telescope upon a few of the show objects in the heavens, which delighted him immensely. After this I saw him safely started down the trail, equipped with a flashlight to light his way to the road, where his taxi awaited him.

Throughout the night I could not keep from wondering what Hargraves had found in Africa that could be connected with the planet Mars. The dawn found me without a conjecture and I turned in to dream wild dreams of Hargraves and Africa.

The following evening found us comfortably settled in my den. I was eager to hear his story.

"I am not going to prolong my story with the details of the hardships of our journey," Hargraves began. "It is the usual stuff one reads in books of travel. Famine, thirst and fever played their usual rôles, with the result that my two white companions were out of the game before two years had passed. One died, and the other had to be escorted back to the coast, where he subsequently recovered.

"With a handful of native bearers, I pressed on with the search, following every clue and rumor, only to be disappointed time and time again. We moved slowly and laboriously through unexplored Central Africa, ever seeking traces of man's handiwork other than that of the natives.

"I was laid up in camp with an attack of fever when another rumor was brought by a native who had heard of our quest. This time it was substantiated by evidence in the form of a curiously shaped piece of metal. This was, in form, somewhat like a shoehorn and pointed in two places with an ingenious form of ball-and-socket joint. On examining it closely I saw that there had been two other pieces attached to the central portion, which had evidently been snapped off. Where the metal showed its broken surface it was bright and crystalline in appearance, so that I judged the break was of recent date. At first I thought that the natives who had found it had cleaned it up, for the surface was bright and shiny.

"Lying there in my blankets, I questioned the messenger through my interpreter, but I was assured that it was just as it had been found some years before. The metal of which it was made was unknown to me. It looked like steel, with a lustrous surface, but it weighed no more than an equal amount of aluminum. Later tests showed that it had much greater strength than steel and that it was extremely hard; even a file would leave no mark upon it.

"From what I could gather it had been picked up in a valley lying some ten or eleven days' journey to the northwest of us, when several members of his tribe had ventured in on a hunting expedition.

"I say 'ventured in' because the whole of the area in question is looked upon by the local tribes as the abode of the dead, and it was only when starvation threatened, and hunger overcame their fears, that they dared to penetrate this forbidden valley.

"Impatiently I waited until I was well enough to travel, then we set out with the messenger as a guide. Gradually the character of the country changed until the swampy, fever-infested jungle gave way to a rolling park-like country.

"Our way led steadily upwards until on the ninth day we were moving over a verdant plateau which was alive with small game. My little pocket aneroid barometer showed us that we were about four thousand five hundred feet above sea level. That evening we camped at the foot of a low range of hills and our guide assured me that on the morrow we should enter the forbidden valley.

"True to his promise, the following noon found us at the entrance to a little valley bounded by low hills, through which flowed a considerable stream. The hills on either side were gloriously green, betokening a generous supply of moisture, the park-like character of the valley being enhanced by occasional groups of a species of oak tree, and here and there patches of a flowering shrub whose scent filled the valley with a delicious odor. The bark of this bush, I learned, was used by the natives in lieu of tobacco, and it was not half bad as a substitute, I can assure you, especially after one had been many months without the comfort of 'Lady Nicotine.'

"It was with the greatest difficulty that I persuaded our guide to remain with us, and then only after I had presented him with a charm in the shape of a ring, which I had to assure him would ward off all danger, did he consent to enter the valley with us.

"Late that afternoon, we arrived near the spot where our guide had found this metal object. We made camp at once and I set out to survey the valley.

"About a quarter of a mile from the camp the floor of the valley narrowed, bounded on the one side by a steep cliff and the other by a ridge which ran out at right angles from the southern slope. This formation immediately aroused my curiosity, for I thought that there must be some outcrop of rock here, which kept the flood-waters of the stream from removing it. Besides, I was anxious to learn something of the geological formations of this district.

"Attended by my guide, I walked down the valley towards this formation. Sure enough there was an outcrop of rock on the north side, a hard limestone formation whose foot was lapped by the waters of the stream. Wading through the shallow water, we crossed over to the south bank.

"Where the waters had removed the surface soil I saw what at first I took to be a rib of rock reaching into the stream. On closer inspection I saw that this was, not rock, but metal. It was worn and scored by the waters of ages, but on scraping away the soil above the flood level I exposed clean-cut edges. A rib of the metal ran back into the hillside.

"With a sharp stake I probed the soft, loamy soil and was able to trace the direction of this rib up the hillside for a distance of perhaps thirty feet, where the covering became too deep for my probe to penetrate. Marking the spot where I could last feel it, I skirted the east and west sides of the mound with the hope of finding another clue, but I could see nothing.

"The tropical night shut down with its usual suddenness during my investigations, so we wended our way back to camp, where the light of a fire danced and flickered in the evening air. How I wished for a battery for my flashlight! The batteries, however, had perished long ago in the steaming jungle air, and I had to wait until morning with this discovery before me."

"I know how you felt," I interrupted. "I experienced the same feeling last night."

Hargraves smiled and continued.

"That evening I set the boys to work to construct rude digging implements from the scrub oak of the hillside. Crude they were, indeed, but they would serve my purpose in that light soil.

"Long before daylight, the camp was astir, and by the time the sun rose the morning meal was over and we were on our way to the mysterious mound. Setting the boys to work at intervals along a continuation of the line I had already traced out, the metal rib was soon located higher up the hillside, covered by some four feet of earth.

"I now saw that it might save time to have a couple of natives working directly on top of the mound, so transferring two of them, I directed them to clear away the top soil, while the others continued to trace the rib up the hillside.

"Two hours passed when a shout from the top told me they had made some discovery. When I arrived there they were clearing away the dry soil from what appeared to be a flat metal surface. Calling up the other boys we were soon at work removing the earth from the rounded top of the hillock.

"Little by little the metal surface was laid bare, showing it to be, not flat, but rounded with the exposed slope falling towards the stream. Late that afternoon we had come to the southern edge of the spherical surface. Here a smooth wall dropped away at an angle of sixty-five degrees with the vertical, as my clinometer showed. Something else was also revealed. We laid bare another metal rib which lay in a line with the first one.

"Again night cut short our work and, tired out from exertions with my primitive shovel, I fell asleep directly after supper, to wake and find the eastern sky reddening under the rays of the rising sun.

"Working down the convex slope we gradually laid bare the surface until one of the boys revealed a crack in the hitherto unbroken surface. As the soil was rapidly removed we exposed a circular plate set flush in the metal. Near the periphery and diametrically opposite each other were two holes which we rapidly cleaned out, showing them to be let in the plate at an angle of perhaps thirty degrees.

"With the aid of the boys I tried to lift this cover, or whatever it might be, but it seemed to be as solid as the rest. A close scrutiny of the edge, which was a little ragged in one place, made me think it might be threaded. With this in mind I placed two stout sticks in the holes and attempted to turn it, but with no success until it occurred to me to try the opposite direction. Throwing my weight on the lever with one of the boys doing the same on the other side I essayed to turn the plate once more. Suddenly we were both sprawling on our hands and knees. The plate had turned.

"Unmindful of my bruises, I jumped to the plate, and gradually we unscrewed it, the plate, with each turn, rising higher and higher from the surface in which it was set. When it stood fully eighteen inches high we came to the end of the screw and by our combined efforts swung the heavy disc of metal aside. Subsequent measurements showed it to be twenty-eight inches in diameter and twenty thick.

"We had uncovered a hole some two feet deep, at the bottom of which was another plate. Arranged in the form of a square of twelve on a side were one hundred and forty-four equally spaced circular holes, each one about half an inch in diameter, and on the plate lay six metal objects. I picked these up and examined them one by one. They were similar in shape and size and were in the form of a rod of circular cross section, six inches long with a cross piece on top, giving them the form of a capital letter T. Each of these was slotted across at various points, but no two in exactly the same manner, and on them were engraved strange characters. Here is a sketch of them."

Hargraves handed me a piece of paper on which were drawn the figures I reproduce here.

"The thought struck me at once that these things might be keys to unlock whatever lay before me, so I tried one in a hole where it fitted snugly. Now, I asked myself, into which hole did each key fit? There were one hundred and forty-four holes and six keys, so there were evidently $144!/138!$ [1] ways in which these six keys could be arranged, using all of them. Out of more than eight trillion ways of doing a thing with only one of them correct, the chances are somewhat against one's hitting the right combination by chance!"

"You might hit it once in a million years," I laughed, "if you could keep on trying that long."

"Well," he continued, "I saw that there must be some solution to my problem, so I looked for a clue and found it. One of the corner holes was marked

while the one diagonally opposite looked like this."

[1] $144! - 138!$ Factorial 144 divided by factorial 138 is $144 \times 143 \times 142 \times 141 \times 140 \times 139 = 8,020,000,000,000 + .3! = 3 \times 2 \times 1; 4! = 4 \times 3 \times 2 \times 1;$ etc.

|⊶

He drew these figures as he spoke.

"On the plate, above what I took to be the top of the square, were engraved twelve symbols, like this

•|ΓΤΗΗ✝⊥⊥IΙΗ┵

"After copying these down in my note-book, I sat down to think it over. From the occurrence of twelves, both in the number of holes and the number of symbols, it might be possible, I thought, that the duodecimal [1] system was used by those who had made this thing. Following up this thought I saw that the symbols were, in order, zero to eleven according to our notation, hence the first of these keys was number two and the others 60, 38, 91, 42 and 108 respectively.

"Hurriedly I placed the keys in their corresponding holes and as I did so I felt the wards of the lock mechanism engage with the slots. Turning the keys as far as they would go I was now able to lift the plate with the aid of the boys, using the keys as handles.

"It was thinner than the former one, being about a foot or so thick, and as we lifted it I noticed that a number of radial bars on the underside had slid back into their sockets.

"You can imagine my feelings as I peered down and saw no other obstacle in my way. Sacrificing one of my few precious matches I leaned as far as I could over the hole. The match burned bright and clear; evidently the air inside was pure. Just below me I could see what appeared to be a platform. Taking a stout stick, long enough to reach it, I tested it carefully. It seemed quite strong and firm, so taking a chance, I lowered myself into the hole and my feet just touched as I hung from the edge with my hands.

"I could see by the light that filtered in from overhead that I was standing on a metal grating. It was not level, but tilted downward to the north. As I had suspected, this construction, whatever it might be, had fallen over from the vertical and lay at an angle on the hillside.

"Ordering one of the natives to fetch torches, I stooped and peered around. I could dimly see that I stood on the top of a curved stairway leading down into the darkness. Grasping the heavy handrail with which

[1] Counting by twelves instead of tens as we are accustomed to do, hence the numbers ten and eleven will have separate symbols.

it was protected I cautiously descended. I noticed that the steps were abnormally high as I went down. Later I was to know the reason. A few steps down and I came to another platform, which I could make out in the faint light as circular, surrounding a 'well.'

"Striking another match, I examined the wall behind me. In its surface I saw another set of holes similar to those in the plate we had removed. My match flickered out and, not wanting to waste any more of my precious store of them, I climbed the steps and wriggled out into the daylight to await the arrival of the torches.

"Presently the boy I had sent arrived with a goodly load of dry, resinous sticks that would burn well and brightly. I lit one, and calling to him to follow me, I again lowered myself into the hole, remembering to take the keys with me. Stepping carefully for fear of falling on the sloping surface, I walked around the gallery examining the place. It was about twenty feet in diameter with a five-foot gallery from which led a second flight of steps. There were four sets of key holes in the wall about five feet above the floor.

"The second gallery was exactly like the first and I did not stop, but went on down the last flight of steps. This was evidently the bottom of the cylinder and, like the other two stories, its walls held the now familiar key plates.

"Going to the one on the lower side I examined it closely. Above the square of holes were twelve sets of symbols arranged in pairs, the first members of these pairs corresponding to the numbers on the keys. Evidently the keys did not correspond to the same holes as above, so, inserting them in their corresponding new numbers, I turned them as I had done before.

"Immediately, a section of the wall swung inward and there was a sudden rush of air which nearly extinguished the torch. The air pressure had been much less inside the chamber which now lay open before me than outside, and the door was apparently airtight. No wonder I could see no sign of the joint in my first cursory examination of the walls.

"Before me, stacked around the sides, were a large number of box-shaped objects, held in place by bars reaching from floor to roof of the chamber, each box bearing a number. Removing one of the retaining bars, which fitted into sockets, I pulled down the top box of the tier.

"On the front of this box was a lever-like handle. This I turned, and as I did so there came the hissing sound of air entering a vacuum. Turning the handle further—it was quite stiff—the air rushed in with a final sigh and the lid of the box raised sufficiently for me to put my fingers under it and throw it back.

"The lever had operated an eccentric which had forced the lid up against the pressure of the outside air. The lid was tongued, and fitted into a corresponding groove in the upper edge of the box, and the groove was filled with a waxy substance which had made the joint airtight. I noticed afterwards that each box had a filled hole through which the air had evidently been exhausted.

"Carefully packed in a substance that looked like fine steel wool were a number of broad oblong cases, about the size of a standard volume of the 'Encyclopædia Britannica,' the topmost of which I removed. It was of the same metallic substance that I had encountered all along, and on its edge was a little knob set in a recess. This I pressed and a cover flew back.

"It was a volume, and such a volume as the eyes of living man never saw before. There before me was the most startling illustration I had ever looked upon. Instead of the usual lifeless flat things we are used to, there lay a picture in three dimensions. The illustration depicted an animal or reptile—I don't know which it was—and it stood out there in the torch-light like a live thing. I ran my fingers lightly over the surface to assure myself that it was not a model, or in relief, but it was as flat as a table top. The colors were marvelous; they had life and brightness in them which enhanced the natural look about the thing.

"At the foot of the case in which the picture lay was a tiny lever-like arrangement. I pressed this over and as I did so there was a tiny whirring sound followed by a click, and the picture flicked out of sight, and was replaced by another.

"One-half the page—if I may call them pages—was occupied by this new illustration, the other half being filled with characters, evidently writing of some kind. Page after page flicked by at my touch, the majority bearing those wonderfully executed illustrations in three dimensions.

"Box after box was opened, and each was found filled with these strange volumes. I carefully replaced those I had removed and closed the lids of the boxes, replacing them in their tiers.

"Where was I going to start in this place? I felt like a child surrounded by novel toys, not knowing which to examine first. Then it occurred to me that everything was arranged in a methodical manner—the numbering of the cases and the volumes showed this. Looking on the door of this cell I saw something I had overlooked before. It was numbered ten, according to our notation. Number one must be on the first landing.

"The air was becoming thick and suffocating with the oily smoke of the torches, but I made my way to the first cell and opened it in its turn. Being warned this time, I had the boy stand back with the torch so that it would not be blown out. The pressure here was much lower than in the other cell. I was nearly overthrown by the sudden gust of air that drove in before me as the door swung back.

"This chamber was similar to the one below, and in the topmost row of boxes I saw number one in a corner. I removed this case and, as the air was becoming unbearable, I took it out into the sunlight to examine it.

"It contained what I may liken to a child's primer, profusely illustrated. The first volume was filled with pictures of common objects, each with a few symbols at the sides. Trees, river, lakes and mountains; birds, beasts and reptiles, the majority of which were unknown to me, were illustrated.

The second volume contained composite pictures—simple actions of human-like creatures and so on. I saw at once that it would be quite easy for a man of average intelligence to learn this unknown language with the aid of this wonderful primer. To one who was accustomed to deciphering old writings, as I was, the task would be ridiculously easy.

"The setting of the sun drove me back to camp, but not before I had replaced and locked the place, taking the keys with me.

"By the light of the fire I studied my trophies that night. It might interest you to know just how the 'lessons' were arranged. Take for example the verb 'to walk.' In one set of pictures a being was shown in the fore-ground, approaching a hill. The second showed him, bent forward, walking up the hill, while a third showed him at the top. The characters were exactly the same in each case, but over the first was an inverted V; over the second, nothing; and over the third a V. The tenses were all indicated by a symbol above the verb. The degrees of adjectives were similarly indicated, hence it simplified the written language exceedingly.

"I sat and studied well into the night until weariness compelled me to cease, but at dawn I was awake and at it again. Throughout the day I worked, having given instructions to the boys to continue their work of removing the earth from around the cylinder.

"Every moment the system of writing became clearer, until late in the afternoon I came to a lone sentence set out in large characters. A rough translation of it would be:

"'WE GREET YOU. CONTINUE, WE HAVE MUCH IN STORE FOR YOU.'

"Here was a direct message, and a message that made my heart leap. If I had worked hard up to this point, I worked feverishly now. Who, I wondered, were 'WE'?

"The following day another message was translated. It read:

"'THE PEOPLE OF ANOTHER WORLD GREET YOU.'

"I checked my translation again and again, but I had made no mistake. That was the meaning of the sentence.

"As the days slipped by I came across more of these interpolated sen-tences, all encouraging me to go on. This personal touch made me feel as though there were some beings anxious for my advancement so that they could communicate with me.

"The days grew into weeks before I had mastered the language suffi-ciently for the purpose of those who wrote it. In the meantime the natives had progressed with their task but slowly, due to the poor implements with which they had to work. They worked slowly but honestly, so I did not press them, for I could see I had months of work ahead of me before I even scratched the surface of the wonderful store of knowledge that lay be-fore me.

"We were truly in a Garden of Eden, for game and fish abounded, while edible fruits and berries served to keep down sickness, which would surely have followed a meat diet. In this way I was able to conserve our none too plentiful supply of provisions. The head boy was an excellent shot, so our ammunition was not wasted as it would have been had we depended upon my powers with a rifle. The climate was almost perfect.

"Eventually I arrived at the end of my primary course and came, at the end of the last volume, to a message which read—'First read volume one, case three. A complete catalogue of the contents of the library will also be found in this case.'

"This volume was soon secured, and without hesitation I plunged into it. It was written in a fairly simple style, and with the aid of an excellent dictionary I found in the same case, I was able to read right through. I read it in four days, hardly stopping to eat or sleep, nearly ruining my eyesight with the strain. After that I slackened up a bit and did manual work at intervals in order to get some exercise. I will outline the contents of this volume to you.

"Hundreds of thousands of years before this story opens, intelligent life had dawned upon one of our nearest neighbors in space, the planet Mars; in much the same manner as we have supposed it to do on this Earth of ours, so that at the time this narrative was written civilization had reached a very high plane. The records show that they had reached what we might call the ideal state. Every being was intelligent enough to work under what I might call a system of social democracy.

"Every member of the planet's teeming millions was an integral part of a smoothly working system in which no parasites existed, for when one, by some atavistic freak, did turn up who attempted to 'throw a monkey-wrench into the machinery' he was simply exterminated.

"Throughout the ages, while this system was slowly being built up, the race had been carefully developed by intelligent selection in mating and every undesirable feature had been slowly eliminated. The result was that at the time this narrative opens every man and woman on the planet was both mentally and physically perfect.

"As time went on it became apparent that the life of the planet would be shortened by the loss of air and water vapor. The gravitation on the surface of Mars being much less than on the Earth, nearly one-half as great, the gases of its atmosphere would more readily escape. The Kinetic Theory of Gases shows that a velocity of seven miles a second is readily obtained by the faster moving molecules of water vapor. This is the critical speed for escape from the Earth's attraction. How much more readily will the water vapor escape from a planet like Mars.

"Some scheme had to be developed then, in order to reduce this rapid escape of the planet's vital fluid, if life on the planet was to be possible in future ages.

"Martian engineers set to work, after due deliberation, to construct gigantic underground reservoirs lined with an impervious material. After nearly a thousand years' labor the work was finished and the waters of the lakes and seas were impounded in these vast underground storage basins.

"To conserve the precious liquid still further, that which was deposited as snow in the polar regions was carefully trapped as the summer sun melted it. Huge subterranean aqueducts led it back equator-wards, assisted by enormous pumping plants. These conduits were tapped at intervals by lateral lines in order to supply water to irrigate the fast-drying surface, and at the time the record was written, the construction of an intricate system of conduits and pumping stations was well under way."

"Just as the late Professor Lowell hypothecated," I exclaimed, to which Hargraves added:

"And those oases, as Lowell called them, were the locations of the pumping stations, the intensely cultivated area around them causing them to show up as black dots on the planet's surface, as your observations showed.

"The prominent blue-green markings on our neighbor in space are of a heavier soil and are the old sea beds. The lighter sandy soils were abandoned, because of the large quantity of water necessary to make them fertile, save along the lines of the canals. But to continue—

"With their highly developed instruments the Martians had ascertained that their neighboring planet, the Earth, was well suited to support life. Indeed it seemed a veritable land of promise to them, with its vast oceans and verdant continents. Encouraged by the thought of the possibilities this new world held for them, researches were instituted which resulted in a machine which would travel through interplanetary space. The method of propulsion was similar to that of the 'Goddard Rocket'; gases formed by the combination of certain solid chemicals, escaping through specially shaped nozzles attached to the after part of the machine propelled it in exactly the same manner as our sky-rockets are shot aloft.

"Wing-shaped members supported it in the air until its velocity was high enough for it to leave the atmosphere, while a second series of nozzles in the bow of the craft retarded it when a landing had to be made.

"A company of daring pioneers left one eventful day to commence the first interplanetary navigation our solar system has known, and after months of an uneventful journey, landed safely on the Earth. An unforeseen disaster overtook this adventurous company, however. Under the greater gravitational force to which they were subjected here, their relatively frail bodies broke down. Prolapse of their inner organs caused many to die in agony within a month of their landing, so the project was abandoned and the survivors returned to their native planet.

"Undaunted by this failure they set to work to develop a race capable of withstanding the new conditions. After a lapse of nearly four hundred years a new expedition set forth. This second party was more successful than the first, and succeeded in founding a colony on the high plateau region where the cylinder was found. Their bodies were skillfully braced by a metal framework which relieved, to some extent, the strain to which they were subjected.

"These first intelligent inhabitants of the Earth were giants compared with us. Their average height was about nine feet; their lungs, which were developed to accommodate the rare atmosphere of Mars, were enclosed by a barrel-like chest, but their limbs were pitifully thin, though much better adapted to their new environment than those of their predecessors.

"As time went on children were born into this new world and new arrivals came across the gulf every two years when Mars was in opposition.[1] Then came another catastrophe. As the children born here grew, it was noticed that their intelligence was inferior to that of their parents. Bodily they were smaller and sturdier, but their mentality when they reached the adult stage was only equivalent to that of a Martian child half their age.

"Immigration stopped while this new phase was anxiously watched. Everything within the Martians' power was done to check this effect, but without avail. Things went from bad to worse as the second generation was born, for these were still farther from the high mental standard of their forefathers. Instead of highly intelligent beings, the race was rapidly reverting to the primitive state.

"The fourth generation was but a grotesque caricature of the original stock, and were already forming into bands of nomadic savages, leaving the center of their community to wander at large over the face of the Earth.

"Everything within the power of the Martians having failed to alleviate these conditions, the projected plan was abandoned. Before leaving this planet forever, to return to their own sphere, it was decided to build a monument to their endeavors, so that as time went on and intelligence again returned to this planet, a record of their attempt, and data of the most useful kind, would be available to those who found it.

"Two other cylinders, similar in every respect to the one I found, were constructed of a tough noncorrosive metal which would withstand the destructive forces of the elements throughout the ages until intelligence again appeared. This period has been much longer than was anticipated by the builders, I can see from what I have read. The three monuments were placed where observation had showed cataclysms of nature, such as flood or earthquake, would be at a minimum. One where I found it, another somewhere on a continent over which the Atlantic now rolls, and the last in the continent which we know as Australia. This latter may yet be found. The cylinders were sealed in the manner I have described so that none but intelligent beings could gain access to them. They were so constructed that should they break they would do so midway between the dividing partitions of the cells, thus leaving each cell intact until some-

[1] Opposition. A planet is in opposition nearest to the Earth when the Sun, Earth and the planet are in the same straight line with the Earth and the planet on the same side of the Sun.

one should arrive who could solve the riddle of the system of numerals and make keys to fit the locks.

"This planet and all their works were then abandoned. Practically all other traces of their sojourn have now vanished into dust, though here and there I found remains of their supporting harness, for which they had used this remarkable metal, which is, I believe, akin to aluminum.

"By the time my cursory survey of the contents of the library was completed, the natives had succeeded in clearing away the mass of earth around the cylinder, so that I was better able to understand its construction and what had happened to it throughout the ages.

"The walls of the object were approximately six feet thick with the top and bottom of convex form, better to withstand any great pressure to which it might be subjected. The whole structure was of one seamless piece, unbroken save where the manhole gave access to its interior. Four massive, equally spaced spokes, or ribs, radiated out from the cylinder, the object of these being to prevent the cylinder rolling over as the soil subsided. The cylinder was approximately forty feet high and sixty in diameter. The arrangement of the interior I have already described to you.

"Originally the structure had rested on the surface of a hard limestone formation, but the gradual weathering of this had caused it to sink downwards into the little valley which now exists there.

"Having completed my examination of the cylinder and satisfied myself that there was nothing more to be learned until other volumes were translated, I carefully sealed and locked the entrance, after selecting a few of what I deemed the most important records to take away with me. The keys I sewed into a canvas belt which I strapped about my waist and, packing the remaining trophies very carefully, we retraced our steps to the coast.

"Eight months after leaving the valley I was once more in Washington where I laid my discoveries before the departmental heads. It was decided to keep the thing secret until an expedition could go to Africa and return with the remainder of the library. I expect that we shall be hearing from them in a few months' time, if all goes well.

"Among the volumes I brought out with me was this one," Hargraves said, reaching for the package he had brought with him.

Unwrapping it, he handed me a lustrous metal box such as he had described. I took it and pressed the spring at the side. The cover, which I may liken to the front board of our books, flew back.

There before me, apparently floating in space, was the representation of a sphere. So real was the three-dimensional aspect of the thing that I could not resist passing my fingers over its surface to assure myself that it really was in one plane. It was an illustration of the planet of mystery— Mars. At the poles glistened twin polar caps, the northern one surrounded by a hazy outline, while the southern was belted with a liquid-blue band. It was evidently the fall of the year in the planet's northern hemisphere.

I recognized some of the principal features—Utopia, the Syrtis Major and the Pseboas Lucus [1]—though there were other blue-green markings with which I was not familiar. The desert areas, I saw at once, were much smaller than they are today and only a few canals were shown.

I stopped to examine the "page" on which it was depicted. Like the case, it was of metal, and appeared to pass over a roller, like the film of a camera. Afterwards I learned that it was on an endless belt arrangement, passing over a series of small rollers which kept the metal sheet from coming into contact with itself. Had this precaution not been taken there was a danger of the sheets cohering and being irreparably ruined.

Pressing the little lever-like arrangement at the lower end of the case as my companion directed, the picture flicked out of sight, revealing another view of the planet. A series of such views gave details of every portion of the planet's surface and then I came to a different type of picture.

It was an illustration showing a gigantic engineering undertaking. A low range of hills formed the background and down their slope ran a great scar. At the foot was a vast building under construction, and leading from it to the foreground was an immense excavation at the bottom of which were what I took to be excavating machines, whose apparent size was enhanced by the diminutive, human-like figures I could see here and there among them.

Translating the legend below, Hargraves informed me that this illustrated one of the canals under construction and that the building at the foot of the hill housed the pumping mechanism which was to raise the water to its new level. This particular piece of work was at what we call the northern point of the Trivium Charontis. [2]

Page after page flicked before me on the pressing of the lever. Great engineering works, maps and plans of districts and cities, and last of all views of the cities themselves. These latter illustrations are well worth describing. Unlike our canyon-like streets the ways received sunlight in abundance, for the buildings were pyramidal in form, each story being smaller than the one below, with a broad open space running around it. A reddish stone seemed to be used in their construction, with a trimming of dull green, well suiting the style of architecture, which had a Babylonian cast about it. Fancy carving or ornamentations were wholly absent.

A number of torpedo-shaped objects were evidently moving through the air above the ways between these massive piles, a host of others were

[1] The reader is recommended to read "The Planet Mars," "Mars and its Canals," and "Mars as the Abode of Life"—three volumes written by the late Professor Percival Lowell, who observed Mars systematically for twenty years, mostly at Flagstaff, Arizona, where the atmospheric conditions are, perhaps, better than those to be found at any other observatory. These books are well written, mostly in non-technical language.—The Author.

[2] Observations have shown that there are no great elevations on the surface of Mars —nothing that approaches mountainous size.

"parked" on the broad galleries of the buildings, over which were what I supposed to be long windows which lighted their interiors.

This, Hargraves told me, was the metropolis of the planet, and these were the executive offices from which the affairs of this far-off world were directed. A symbol mounted on a staff at the top of each building marked the department to which it belonged. A flaming Sun, crossed parallel lines, a square and compass, and a cluster of fruits were among some of those I saw. I will leave it to the reader's imagination to solve the meanings of these symbols.

Another view showed the stages from which great aerial liners left for distant cities, or to which they came to discharge their living cargo. A few were resting upon their cradles, taking aboard freight and passengers, or discharging the products of distant districts into conveyors which took it rapidly underground. All heavy traffic was carried underground in the cities, I was informed, and came to the surface only at its destination.

"To think that this was taking place half a million years ago," I said to my companion. "I wonder what it is like there now."

"Some day we may learn," he replied. "They may have progressed but little and may be passively waiting until our intelligence is high enough to make it worth their while to communicate with us. Think of the difference in intelligence which must exist between us! Perhaps as much as between mankind and the apes. We would not think of establishing communication with monkeys, would we? Then we must not expect to hear from our neighbors until we begin to approach their standard of intelligence."

It was late that night when my visitor left, very kindly leaving the volume behind for my further perusal and with a promise to aid me by interpreting the accompanying text. Without his aid I would not have been able to make much of it, and would perhaps have come to many erroneous conclusions.

The following days, with Hargraves' assistance, I studied it thoroughly, comparing the maps with my own drawings and checking up much of my observational data.

I have written down this story so that time would not cause me to forget the finer details. Some day I may publish it, if I can obtain permission.

Postscript—Since penning the above the remainder of the library has arrived in America, and my friend informs me that I am quite at liberty to publish this (which he has read). At present Hargraves, with a large staff of assistants, is engaged in the translation of the records, but it will be a long time before such a colossal work can be published. The expense will be enormous. The world has waited half a million years for this discovery, so I suppose we can be patient for a few more years until the story is given to us.

AUSTIN HALL

THE MAN WHO SAVED THE EARTH

EVEN the beginning. From the start the whole thing has the precision of machine work. Fate and its working—and the wonderful Providence which watches over Man and his future. The whole thing unerring: the incident, the work, the calamity and the martyr. In the retrospect of disaster we may all of us grow strong in wisdom. Let us go into history.

A hot July day. A sun of scant pity, and a staggering street; panting thousands dragging along, hatless; fans and parasols; the sultry vengeance of a real day of summer. A day of bursting tires; hot pavements, and wrecked endeavor, heartaches for the seashore, for leafy bowers beside rippling water, a day of broken hopes and listless ambition.

Perhaps Fate chose the day because of its heat and because of its natural benefit on fecundity. We have no way of knowing. But we do know this: the date, the time, the meeting; the boy with the burning glass and the old doctor. So commonplace, so trivial and hidden in obscurity! Who would have guessed it? Yet it is—after the Creation—one of the most important dates in the world's history.

This is saying a whole lot. Let us go into it and see what it amounts to. Let us trace the thing out in history, weigh it up and balance it with sequence.

Of Charley Huyck we know nothing up to this day. It is a thing which, for some reason, he has always kept hidden. Recent investigation as to his previous life and antecedents have availed us nothing. Perhaps he could have told us; but as he has gone down as the world's great martyr, there is no hope of gaining from his lips what we would so like to know.

After all, it does not matter. We have the day—the incident, and its purport, and its climax of sequence to the day of the great disaster. Also we have the blasted mountains and the lake of blue water which will ever live with his memory. His greatness is not of warfare, nor personal ambition; but of all mankind. The wreaths that we bestow upon him have no doubtful color. The man who saved the earth!

From such a beginning, Charley Huyck, lean and frail of body, with, even then, the wistfulness of the idealist, and the eyes of a poet. Charley Huyck, the boy, crossing the hot pavement with his pack of papers; the much-treasured piece of glass in his pocket, and the sun which only he should master, burning down upon him. A moment out of the ages; the turning of a straw destined to out-balance all the previous accumulation of man's history.

The sun was hot and burning, and the child—he could not have been more than ten—cast a glance over his shoulder. It was in the way of calculation. In the heyday of childhood he was not dragged down by the heat and weather: he had the enthusiasm of his half-score of years and the joy of the plaything. We will not presume to call it the spirit of the scientist, though it was, perhaps, the spark of latent investigation that was destined to lead so far.

A moment picked out of destiny! A boy and a plaything. Uncounted millions of boys have played with glass and the sun rays. Who cannot remember the little, round-burning dot in the palm of the hand and the subsequent exclamation? Charley Huyck had found a new toy, it was a simple thing and as old as glass. Fate will ever be so in her working.

And the doctor? Why should he have been waiting? If it was not destiny it was at least an accumulation of moment. In the heavy eye-glasses, the square, close-cut beard; and his uncompromising fact-seeking expression. Those who knew Dr. Robold are strong in the affirmation that he was the antithesis of all emotion. He was the sternest product of science: unbending, hardened by experiment, and caustic in his condemnation of the frailness of human nature.

It had been his one function to topple over the castles of the foolish; with his hard-seeing wisdom he had spotted sophistry where we thought it not. Even into the castles of science he had gone like a juggernaut. It is hard to have one's theories derided—yea, even for a scientist—and to be called a fool! Dr. Robold knew no middle language; he was not relished by science.

His memory, as we have it, is that of an eccentric. A man of slight compassion, abrupt of manner and with no tact in speaking. Genius is often so; it is a strange fact that many of the greatest of men have been denied by their fellows. A great man and laughter. He was not accepted.

None of us knows today what it cost Dr. Robold. He was not the man to tell us. Perhaps Charley Huyck might; but his lips are sealed forever. We only know that he retired to the mountain, and of the subsequent flood of benefits that rained upon mankind. And we still denied him. The great cynic on the mountain. Of the secrets of the place we know little. He was not the man to accept the investigator; he despised the curious. He had been laughed at—let be—he would work alone on the great moment of the future.

In the light of the past we may well bend knee to the doctor and his protégé, Charley Huyck. Two men and destiny! What would we be without them? One shudders to think.

A little thing, and yet one of the greatest moments in the world's history. It must have been Fate. Why was it that this stern man, who hated all emotion, should so have unbended at this moment? That we cannot answer. But we can conjecture. Mayhap it is this: We were all wrong; we accepted the man's exterior and profession as the fact of his marrow.

No man can lose all emotion. The doctor was, after all, even as ourselves—he was human. Whatever may be said, we have the certainty of that moment—and of Charley Huyck.

The sun's rays were hot; they were burning; the pavements were intolerable; the baked air in the canyoned street was dancing like that of an oven; a day of dog-days. The boy crossing the street; his arms full of papers, and the glass bulging in his little hip-pocket.

At the curb he stopped. With such a sun it was impossible long to forget his plaything. He drew it carefully out of his pocket, laid down a paper and began distancing his glass for the focus. He did not notice the man beside him. Why should he? The round dot, the brownish smoke, the red spark and the flash of flame! He stamped upon it. A moment out of boyhood; an experimental miracle as old as the age of glass, and just as delightful. The boy had spoiled the name of a great Governor of a great State; but the paper was still salable. He had had his moment. Mark that moment.

A hand touched his shoulder. The lad leaped up.

"Yessir. *Star* or *Bulletin?*"

"I'll take one of each," said the man. "There now. I was just watching you. Do you know what you were doing?"

"Yessir. Burning paper. Startin' fire. That's the way the Indians did it."

The man smiled at the perversion of fact. There is not such a distance between sticks and glass in the age of childhood.

"I know," he said—"the Indians. But do you know how it was done; the why—why the paper began to blaze?"

"Yessir."

"All right, explain."

The boy looked up at him. He was a city boy and used to the streets. Here was some old highbrow challenging his wisdom. Of course he knew.

"It's the sun."

"There," laughed the man. "Of course. You said you knew, but you don't. Why doesn't the sun, without the glass, burn the paper? Tell me that."

The boy was still looking up at him; he saw that the man was not like the others on the street. It may be that the strange intimacy kindled into being at that moment. Certainly it was a strange unbending for the doctor.

"It would if it was hot enough or you could get enough of it together."

"Ah! Then that is what the glass is for, is it?"

"Yessir."

"Concentration?"

"Con— I don't know, sir. But it's the sun. She's sure some hot. I know a lot about the sun, sir. I've studied it with the glass. The glass picks up all the rays and puts them in one hole and that's what burns the paper.

"It's lots of fun. I'd like to have a bigger one; but it's all I've got. Why, do you know, if I had a glass big enough and a place to stand, I'd burn up the earth?"

The old man laughed. "Why, Archimedes! I thought you were dead."

"My name ain't Archimedes. It's Charley Huyck."

Again the old man laughed.

"Oh, is it? Well, that's a good name, too. And if you keep on you'll make it famous as the name of the other." Wherein he was foretelling history. "Where do you live?"

The boy was still looking. Ordinarily he would not have told, but he motioned back with his thumb.

"I don't live; I room over on Brennan Street."

"Oh, I see. You room. Where's your mother?"

"Search me; I never saw her."

"I see; and your father?"

"How do I know? He went floating when I was four years old."

"Floating?"

"Yessir—to sea."

"So your mother's gone and your father's floating. Archimedes is adrift. You go to school?"

"Yessir."

"What reader?"

"No reader. Sixth grade."

"I see. What school?"

"School Twenty-six. Say, it's hot. I can't stand here all day. I've got to sell my papers."

The man pulled out a purse.

"I'll take the lot," he said. Then kindly: "My boy, I would like to have you go with me."

It was a strange moment. A little thing with the fates looking on. When destiny plays she picks strange moments. This was one. Charley Huyck went with Dr. Robold.

We all of us remember that fatal day when the news startled all of Oakland. No one can forget it. At first it read like a newspaper hoax, in spite of the oft-proclaimed veracity of the press, and we were inclined to laughter. 'Twixt wonder at the story and its impossibilities we were not a little enthused at the nerve of the man who put it over.

It was in the days of dry reading. The world had grown populous and of well-fed content. Our soap-box artists had come to the point at last where they preached, not disaster, but a full-bellied thanks for the millennium that was here. A period of Utopian quietness—no villain around the corner; no man to covet the ox of his neighbor.

Quiet reading, you'll admit. Those were the days of the millennium. Nothing ever happened. Here's hoping they never come again. And then:

Honestly, we were not to blame for bestowing blessing out of our hearts upon that newspaperman. Even if it were a hoax, it was at least something.

At high noon. The clock in the city hall had just struck the hour that held the post 'twixt a.m. and p.m., a hot day with a sky that was clear and azure; a quiet day of serene peace and contentment. A strange and a portentous moment. Looking back and over the miracle we may conjecture that it was the clearness of the atmosphere and the brightness of the sun that helped the impact of the disaster. Knowing what we know now we can appreciate the impulse of natural phenomena. It was *not* a miracle.

The spot: Fourteenth and Broadway, Oakland, California.

Fortunately the thousands of employees in the stores about had not yet come out for their luncheons. The lapse that it takes to put a hat on, or to put a ribbon, saved a thousand lives. One shudders to think of what would have happened had the spot been crowded. Even so, it was too impossible and too terrible to be true. Such things could not happen.

At high noon: Two streetcars crossing Fourteenth on Broadway—two cars with the same joggle and bump and the same aspect of any of a hundred thousand at a traffic corner. The wonder is—there were so few people. A Telegraph car outgoing, and a Broadway car coming in. The traffic policeman at his post had just given his signal. Two automobiles were passing and a single pedestrian, so it is said, was working his way diagonally across the corner. Of this we are not certain.

It was a moment that impinged on miracle. Even as we recount it, knowing, as we do, the explanation, we sense the impossibility of the event. A phenomenon that holds out and, in spite of our findings, lingers into the miraculous. To be and not to be. One moment life and action, an ordinary scene of existent monotony; and the next moment nothing. The spot, the intersection of the street, the passing streetcars, the two automobiles, pedestrian, the policeman—non-existent! When events are instantaneous reports are apt to be misleading. This is what we find.

Some of those who beheld it, report a flash of bluish white light; others that it was of a greenish or even a violet hue; and others, no doubt of stronger vision, that it was not only of a predominant color but that it was shot and sparkled with a myriad specks of flame and burning.

It gave no warning and it made no sound; not even a whir. Like a hot breath out of the void. Whatever the forces that had focused, they were destruction. There was no Fourteenth and Broadway. The two automobiles, the two streetcars, the pedestrian, the policeman had been whiffed away as if they had never existed. In place of the intersection of the thoroughfares was a yawning gulf that looked down into the center of the earth to a depth of nausea.

It was instantaneous; it was without sound; no warning. A tremendous force of unlimited potentiality had been loosed to kinetic violence. It was the suddenness and the silence that belied credence. We were accustomed to associate all disaster with confusion; calamity has an affinity with pandemonium, all things of terror climax into sound. In this case there was no sound. Hence the wonder.

A hole or bore forty feet in diameter. Without a particle of warning and without a bit of confusion. The spectators one and all aver that at first they took it for nothing more than the effect of startled eyesight. Almost subtle. It was not until after a full minute's reflection that they became aware that a miracle had been wrought before their faces. Then the crowd rushed up and with awe and now awakened terror gazed down into that terrible pit.

We say "terrible" because in this case it is an exact adjective. The strangest hole that man ever looked into. It was so deep that at first it appeared to have no bottom; not even the strongest eyesight could penetrate the smoldering blackness that shrouded the depths descending. It took a stout heart and courage to stand and hold one's head on the brink for even a minute.

It was straight and precipitous; a perfect circle in shape; with sides as smooth as the effect of machine work, the pavement and stone curb had been cut as if by a razor. Of the two streetcars, two automobiles and their occupants there was nothing. The whole thing so silent and complete. Not even the spectators could really believe it.

It was a hard thing to believe. The newspapers themselves, when the news came clamoring, accepted it with reluctance. It was too much like a hoax. Not until the most trusted reporters had gone and had wired in their reports would they even consider it. Then the whole world sat up and took notice.

A miracle! Like Oakland's *Press* we all of us doubted that hole. We had attained almost everything that was worth the knowing; we were the masters of the earth and its secrets and we were proud of our wisdom; naturally we refused such reports all out of reason. It must be a hoax.

But the wires were persistent. Came corroboration. A reliable news-gathering organization soon was coming through with elaborate and detailed accounts of just what was happening. We had the news from the highest and most reputable authority.

And still we doubted. It was the story itself that brought the doubting; its touch on miracle. It was too easy to pick on the reporter. There might be a hole, and all that; but this thing of no explanation! A bomb perhaps?

No noise? Some new explosive? No such thing? Well, how did we know? It was better than a miracle.

Then came the scientists. As soon as could be men of great minds had been hustled to the scene. The world had long been accustomed to accept without quibble the dictum of these great specialists of fact. With their train of accomplishments behind them we would hardly be consistent were we to doubt them.

We know the scientist and his habits. He is the one man who will believe nothing until it is proved. It is his profession, and for that we pay him. He can catch the smallest bug that ever crawled out of an atom and give it a name so long that a Polish wrestler, if he had to bear it, would break under the burden. It is his very knack of getting in under that has given us our civilization. You don't baffle a scientist in our Utopia. It can't be done. Which is one of the very reasons why we began to believe in the miracle.

In a few moments a crowd of many thousands had gathered about the spot; the throng grew so dense that there was peril of some of them being crowded into the pit at the center. It took all the spare policemen of the city to beat them back far enough to string ropes from the corners. For blocks the streets were packed with wondering thousands. Street traffic was impossible. It was necessary to divert the cars to a roundabout route to keep the arteries open to the suburbs.

Wild rumors spread over the city. No one knew how many passengers had been upon the streetcars. The officials of the company, from the schedule, could pick the numbers of the cars and their crews; but who could tell of the occupants?

Telephones rang with tearful pleadings. When the first rumors of the horror leaked out every wife and mother felt the clutch of panic at her heartstrings. It was a moment of hysterical psychology. Out of our books we had read of this strange phase of human nature that was wont to rise like a mad screeching thing out of disaster. We had never had it in Utopia.

It was rumbling at first and out of exaggeration; as the tale passed farther back to the waiting thousands it gained with the repetition. Grim and terrible enough in fact, it ratioed up with reiteration. Perhaps after all it was not psychology. The average impulse of the human mind does not even up so exactly. In the light of what we now know it may have been the poison that had leaked into the air; the new element that was permeating the atmosphere of the city.

At first it was spasmodic. The nearest witnesses of the disaster were the first victims. A strange malady began to spot out among those of the crowd who had been at the spot of contact. This is to be noticed. A strange affliction which from the virulence and rapidity of action was quite puzzling to the doctors.

Those among the physicians who would consent to statement gave it out that it was a breaking down of tissue. Which of course it was; the new element that was radiating through the atmosphere of the city. They did not know it then.

The pity of it! The subtle, odorless pall was silently shrouding out over the city. In a short time the hospitals were full and it was necessary to call in medical aid from San Francisco. They had not even time for diagnosis. The new plague was fatal almost at conception. Happily the scientists soon made the discovery.

It was the pall. At the end of three hours it was known that the death sheet was spreading out over Oakland. We may thank our stars that it was learned so early. Had the real warning come a few hours later the death list would have been appalling.

A new element had been discovered; or if not a new element, at least something which was tipping over all the laws of the atmospheric envelope. A new combination that was fatal. When the news and the warning went out, panic fell upon the bay shore.

But some men stuck. In the face of such terror there were those who stayed and with grimness and sacrifice hung to their posts for mankind. There are some who had said that the stuff of heroes had passed away. Let them then consider the case of John Robinson.

Robinson was a telegraph operator. Until that day he was a poor unknown; not a whit better than his fellows. Now he has a name that will run in history. In the face of what he knew he remained under the blanket. The last words out of Oakland—his last message:

"Whole city of Oakland in grip of strange madness. Keep out of Oakland"—following which came a haphazard personal commentary:

"I can feel it coming on myself. It is like what our ancestors must have felt when they were getting drunk—alternating desires of fight and singing—a strange sensation, light, and ecstatic with a spasmodic twitching over the forehead. Terribly thirsty. Will stick it out if I can get enough water. Never so dry in my life."

Followed a lapse of silence. Then the last words:

"I guess we're done for. There is some poison in the atmosphere—something. It has leaked, of course, out of this thing at Fourteenth and Broadway. Dr. Manson of the American Institute says it is something new that is forming a fatal combination; but he cannot understand the new element; the quantity is too enormous.

"Populace has been warned out of the city. All roads are packed with refugees. The Berkeley Hills are covered as with flies—north, east, and south and on the boats to Frisco. The poison, whatever it is, is advancing in a ring from Fourteenth and Broadway. You have got to hand it to these old boys of science. They are staying with that ring. Already they have calculated the rate of its advance and have given warning. They don't know what it is, but they have figured just how fast it is moving. They have saved the city.

"I am one of the few men now inside the wave. Out of curiosity I have stuck. I have a jug and as long as it lasts I shall stay. Strange feeling. Dry, dry, dry, as if the juice of one's life cells was turning into dust. Water evaporating almost instantly. It cannot pass through glass. Whatever the poison, it has an affinity for moisture. Do not understand it. I have had enough—"

That was all. After that there was no more news out of Oakland. It is the only word that we have out of the pall itself. It was short and disconnected and a bit slangy; but for all that a basis from which to conjecture.

It is a strange and glorious thing how some men will stick to the post of danger. This operator knew that it meant death; but he held with duty. Had he been a man of scientific training his information might have been of incalculable value. However, may God bless his heroic soul!

What we know is thirst! The word that came from the experts confirmed it. Some new element of force was stealing or sapping the humidity out of the atmosphere. Whether this was combining and entering into a poison could not be determined.

Chemists worked frantically at the outposts of the advancing ring. In four hours it had covered the city; in six it had reached San Leandro, and was advancing on toward Haywards.

It was a strange story and incredible from the beginning. No wonder the world doubted. Such a thing had never happened. We had accepted the law of judging the future by the past; by deduction; we were used to sequence and to law; to the laws of Nature. This thing did look like a miracle; which was merely because—as usually it is with "miracles"—we could not understand it. Happily, we can look back now and still place our faith in Nature.

The world doubted and was afraid. Was this peril to spread slowly over the whole state of California and then on to the—world? Doubt always precedes terror. A tense world waited. Then came the word of reassurance —from the scientists:

"Danger past; vigor of the ring is abating. Calculation has deduced that the wave is slowly decreasing in potentiality. It is too early yet to say that there will be recessions, as the wave is just reaching its zenith. What it is we cannot say; but it cannot be inexplicable. After a little time it will all be explained. Say to the world there is no cause for alarm."

But the world was now aroused; as it doubted the truth before, it doubted now the reassurance. Did the scientists know? Could they have only seen the future! We know now that they did not. There was but one man in all the world great enough to foresee disaster. That man was Charley Huyck.

On the same day on which all this happened, a young man, Pizzozi by name and of Italian parentage, left the little town of Ione in Amador County, California, with a small truck-load of salt. He was one of the cattlemen whose headquarters or home-farms are clustered about the foot-hills of the Sierras. In the wet season they stay with their home-land in the valley; in the summer they penetrate into the mountains. Pizzozi had driven in from the mountains the night before, after salt. He had been on the road since midnight.

Two thousand salt-hungry cattle do not allow time for gossip. With the thrift of his race, Joe had loaded up his truck and after a running snatch at breakfast was headed back into the mountains. When the news out of Oakland was thrilling around the world he was far into the Sierras.

The summer quarters of Pizzozi were close to Mt. Heckla, whose loom-ing shoulders rose square in the center of the pasture of the three brothers. It was not a noted mountain—that is, until this day—and had no reason for a name other than that it was a peak outstanding from the range; like a thousand others; rugged, pine clad, coated with deer-brush, red soil, and mountain miserie.

It was the deer-brush that gave it value to the Pizzozis—a succulent feed richer than alfalfa. In the early summer they would come up with bony cattle. When they returned in the fall they went out driving beef-steaks. But inland cattle must have more than forage. Salt is the tincture that makes them healthy.

It was far past the time of the regular salting. Pizzozi was in a hurry. It was nine o'clock when he passed through the mining town of Jackson; and by twelve o'clock—the minute of the disaster—he was well beyond the last little hamlet that linked up with civilization. It was four o'clock when he drew up at the little pine-sheltered cabin that was his headquarters for the summer.

He had been on the road since midnight. He was tired. The long weary hours of driving, the grades, the unvaried stress through the deep red dust, the heat, the stretch of a night and day had worn both mind and muscle. It had been his turn to go after salt; now that he was here, he could lie down for a bit of rest while his brothers did the salting.

It was a peaceful spot, this cabin of the Pizzozis; nestled among the virgin shade trees, great tall feathery sugar-pines with a mountain live-oak spreading over the door yard. To the east the rising heights of the Sierras, misty, gray-green, undulating into the distance to the pink-white snow crests of Little Alpine. Below in the canyon, the waters of the Mokolumne; to the west the heavy dark masses of Mt. Heckla, deep verdant in the cool of coming evening.

Joe drew up under the shade of the live oak. The air was full of cool, sweet scent of the afternoon. No moment could have been more peaceful; the blue clear sky overhead, the breath of summer, and the soothing spice of the pine trees. A shepherd dog came bounding from the doorway to meet him.

It was his favorite cow dog. Usually when Joe came back the dog would be far down the road to forestall him. He had wondered, absently, coming up, at the dog's delay. A dog is most of all a creature of habit; only something unusual would detain him. However, the dog was here; as the man drew up he rushed out to greet him. A rush, a circle, a bark, and a whine of welcome. Perhaps the dog had been asleep.

But Joe noticed that whine; he was wise in the ways of dogs; when Ponto whined like that there was something unusual. It was not effusive or spontaneous; but rather of the delight of succor. After scarce a minute of petting, the dog squatted and faced to the westward. His whine was startling; almost fearful.

Pizzozi knew that something was wrong. The dog drew up, his stub tail erect, and his hair all bristled; one look was for his master and the other, whining and alert, to Mt. Heckla. Puzzled, Joe gazed at the mountain. But he saw nothing.

Was it the canine instinct, or was it coincidence? We have the account from Pizzozi. From the words of the Italian, the dog was afraid. It was not the way of Ponto; usually in the face of danger he was alert and eager; now he drew away to the cabin. Joe wondered.

Inside the shack he found nothing but evidence of departure. There was no sign of his brothers. It was his turn to go to sleep; he was wearied almost to numbness, for forty-eight hours he had not closed an eyelid. On the table were a few unwashed dishes and crumbs of eating. One of the three rifles that hung usually on the wall was missing; the coffeepot was on the floor with the lid open. On the bed the coverlets were mussed up. It was a temptation to go to sleep. Back of him the open door and Ponto. The whine of the dog drew his will and his consciousness into correlation. A faint rustle in the sugar-pines soughed from the canyon.

Joe watched the dog. The sun was just glowing over the crest of the mountain; on the western line the deep lacy silhouettes of the pine trees and the bare bald head of Heckla. What was it? His brothers should be on hand for the salting; it was not their custom to put things off for the morrow. Shading his eyes he stepped out of the doorway.

The dog rose stealthily and walked behind him, uneasily, with the same insistent whine and ruffled hair. Joe listened. Only the mountain murmurs, the sweet breath of the forest, and in the lapse of bated breath the rippling melody of the river far below him.

"What you see, Ponto? What you see?"

At the words the dog sniffed and advanced slightly—a growl and then a sudden scurry to the heels of his master. Ponto was afraid. It puzzled Pizzozi. But whatever it was that roused his fear, it was on Mt. Heckla.

This is one of the strange parts of the story—the part the dog played, and what came after. Although it is a trivial thing it is one of the most inexplicable. Did the dog sense it? We have no measure for the range of instinct, but we do have it that before the destruction of Pompeii the beasts roared in their cages. Still, knowing what we now know, it is hard to accept the analogy. It may, after all, have been coincidence.

Nevertheless, it decided Pizzozi. The cattle needed salt. He would catch up his pinto and ride over to the salt logs.

There is no moment in the cattle industry quite like the salting on the range. It is not the most spectacular perhaps, but surely it is not lacking in intenseness. The way of Pizzozi was musical even if not operatic. He had a long-range call, a rising rhythm that for depth and tone had a peculiar effect on the shattered stillness. It echoed and reverberated, and peeled from the top to the bottom of the mountain. The salt call is the talisman of the mountains.

"Alleewahoo!"

Two thousand cattle augmented by a thousand strays held up their heads in answer. The sniff of the welcome salt call! Through the whole range of the man's voice the stock stopped in their leafy pasture and listened.

"Alleewahoo!"

An old cow bellowed. It was the beginning of bedlam. From the bottom of the mountain to the top and for miles beyond went forth the salt call. Three thousand head bellowed to the delight of salting.

Pizzozi rode along. Each lope of his pinto through the tall tangled miserie was accented. *"Alleewahoo! Alleewahoo!"* The rending of brush, the confusion, and pandemonium spread to the very bottom of the leafy gulches. It is no place for a pedestrian. Heads and tails erect, the cattle were stampeding toward the logs.

A few head had beat him to it. These he quickly drove away and cut the sack open. With haste he poured it upon the logs; then he rode out of the dust that for yards about the place was trampled to the finest powder. The center of a herd of salting range stock is no place for comfort. The man rode away; to the left he ascended a low knob where he would be safe from the stampede; but close enough to distinguish the brands.

In no time the place was alive with milling stock. Old cows, heifers, bulls, calves, steers rushed out of the crashing brush into the clearing. There is no moment exactly like it. What before had been a broad clearing of brownish, reddish dust was trampled into a vast cloud of bellowing blur, a thousand cattle, and still coming. From the farthest height came the echoing call. Pizzozi glanced up at the top of the mountain.

And then a strange thing happened.

From what we gathered from the excited accounts of Pizzozi it was instantaneous; and yet by the same words it was of such a peculiar and beautiful effect as never to be forgotten. A glowing azure shot through with a myriad flecks of crimson, a peculiar vividness of opalescence; the whole world scintillating; the sky, the air, the mountain, a vast flame of color so wide and so intense that there seemed not a thing beside it. And instantaneous—it was over almost before it was started. No noise or warning, and no subsequent detonation: as silent as winking and much, indeed, like the queer blur of color induced by defective vision. All in the fraction of a second. Pizzozi had been gazing at the mountain. There was no mountain!

Neither were there cattle. Where before had been the shade of the towering peak were now the rays of the western sun. Where had been the blur of the milling herd and its deafening pandemonium was now a strange silence. The transparency of the air was unbroken into the distance. Far off lay a peaceful range in the sunset. There was no mountain! Neither were there cattle!

For a moment the man had enough to do with his plunging mustang. In the blur of the subsequent second Pizzozi remembers nothing but a convulsion of fighting horseflesh bucking, twisting, plunging, the gentle pinto suddenly maddened into a demon. It required all the skill of the cowman to retain his saddle.

He did not know that he was riding on the rim of Eternity. In his mind was the dim subconscious realization of a thing that had happened. In spite of all his efforts the horse fought backward. It was some moments before he conquered. Then he looked.

It was a slow, hesitant moment. One cannot account for what he will do in the open face of a miracle. What the Italian beheld was enough for terror. The sheer immensity of the thing was too much for thinking.

At the first sight his simple mind went numb from sheer impotence; his terror to a degree frozen. The whole of Mt. Heckla had been shorn away; in the place of its darkened shadow the sinking sun was blinking in his face; the whole western sky all golden. There was no vestige of the flat salt-clearing at the base of the mountain. Of the three thousand cattle milling in the dust not a one remained. The man crossed himself in stupor. Mechanically he put the spurs to the pinto.

But the mustang would not. Another struggle with bucking, fighting, maddened horseflesh. The cowman must needs bring in all the skill of his training; but by the time he had conquered, his mind had settled within some scope of comprehension.

The pony had good reasons for his terror. This time though the man's mind reeled it did not go dumb at the clash of immensity. Not only had the whole mountain been torn away, but its roots as well. The whole thing was up-side down; the world torn to its entrails. In place of what had been the height was a gulf so deep that its depths were blackness.

He was standing on the brink. He was a cool man, was Pizzozi; but it was hard in the confusion of such a miracle to think clearly; much less to reason. The prancing mustang was snorting with terror. The man glanced down.

The very dizziness of the gulf, sheer, losing itself into shadows and chaos, overpowered him; his mind now clear enough for perception reeled at the distance. The depth was nauseating. His whole body succumbed to a sudden qualm of weakness: the sickness that comes just before falling. He went limp in the saddle.

But the horse fought backward; warned by instinct it drew back from the sheer banks of the gulf. It had no reason but its nature. At the instant it sensed the snapping of the iron will of its master. In a moment it had turned and was racing on its wild way out of the mountains. At supreme moments a cattle horse will always hit for home. The pinto and its limp rider were fleeing on the road to Jackson.

Pizzozi had no knowledge of what had occurred in Oakland. To him the whole thing had been but a flash of miracle; he could not reason. He did not curb his horse. That he was still in the saddle was due more to the near-instinct of his training than to his volition.

He did not even draw up at the cabin. That he could make better time with his motor than with his pinto did not occur to him; his mind was far too busy; and, now that the thing was passed, too full of terror. It was forty-four miles to town; it was night and the stars were shining when he rode into Jackson.

And what of Charley Huyck? It was his anticipation, and his training which leaves us here to tell the story. Were it not for the strange manner of his rearing, and the keen faith and appreciation of Dr. Robold there would be to-day no tale to tell. The little incident of the burning-glass had grown. If there is no such thing as Fate there is at least something that comes very close to being Destiny.

On this night we find Charley at the observatory in Arizona. He is a grown man and a great one, and though mature not so very far drawn from the lad we met on the street selling papers. Tall, slender, very slightly stooped and with the same idealistic, dreaming eyes of the poet. Surely no one at first glance would have taken him for a scientist. Which he was and was not.

Indeed, there is something vastly different about the science of Charley Huyck. Science to be sure, but not prosaic. He was the first and perhaps the last of the school of Dr. Robold, a peculiar combination of poetry and fact, a man of vision, of vast, far-seeing faith and idealism linked and based on the coldest and sternest truths of materialism. A peculiar tenet of the theory of Robold: "True science to be itself should be half poetry." Which any of us who have read or been at school know it is not. It is a peculiar theory and, though rather wild, still with some points in favor.

We all of us know our schoolmasters; especially those of science and what they stand for. Facts, facts, nothing but facts; no dreams or romance. Looking back we can grant them just about the emotions of cucumbers. We remember their cold, hard features, the prodding after fact, the accumulation of data. Surely there is no poetry in them.

Yet we must not deny that they have been by far the most potent of all men in the progress of civilization. Not even Robold would deny it.

The point is this:

The doctor maintained that from the beginning the progress of material civilization had been along three distinct channels; science, invention, and administration. It was simply his theory that the first two should be one;

that the scientist deal not alone with dry fact but with invention, and that the inventor, unless he is a scientist, has mastered but half his trade. "The really great scientist should be a visionary," said Robold, "and an inventor is merely a poet, with tools."

Which is where we get Charley Huyck. He was a visionary, a scientist, a poet with tools, the protégé of Dr. Robold. He dreamed things that no scientist had thought of. And we are thankful for his dreaming.

The one great friend of Huyck was Professor Williams, a man from Charley's home city, who had known him even back in the days of selling papers. They had been cronies in boyhood, in their teens, and again at college. In after years, when Huyck had become the visionary, the mysterious Man of the Mountain, and Williams a great professor of astronomy, the friendship was as strong as ever.

But there was a difference between them. Williams was exact to acuteness, with not a whit of vision beyond pure science. He had been reared in the old stone-cold theory of exactness; he lived in figures. He could not understand Huyck or his reasoning. Perfectly willing to follow as far as facts permitted, he refused to step off into speculation.

Which was the point between them. Charley Huyck had vision; although exact as any man, he had ever one part of his mind soaring out into speculation. What is, and what might be, and the gulf between. To bridge the gulf was the life work of Charley Huyck.

In the snug little office in Arizona we find them; Charley with his feet poised on the desk and Williams precise and punctilious, true to his training, defending the exactness of his philosophy. It was the cool of the evening; the sun was just mellowing the heat of the desert. Through the open door and windows a cool wind was blowing. Charley was smoking; the same old pipe had been the bane of Williams's life at college.

"Then we know?" he was asking.

"Yes," spoke the professor, "what we know, Charley, we know; though of course it is not much. It is very hard, nay impossible, to deny figures. We have not only the proofs of geology but of astronomical calculation, we have facts and figures plus our sidereal relations all about us.

"The world must come to an end. It is a hard thing to say it, but it is a fact of science. Slowly, inevitably, ruthlessly, the end will come. A mere question of arithmetic."

Huyck nodded. It was his special function in life to differ with his former roommate. He had come down from his own mountain in Colorado just for the delight of difference.

"I see. Your old calculations of tidal retardation. Or if that doesn't work, the loss of oxygen and the water."

"Either one or the other; a matter of figures; the earth is being drawn every day by the sun: its rotation is slowing up; when the time comes it will act to the sun in exactly the same manner as the moon acts to the earth today."

"I understand. It will be a case of eternal night for one side of the earth, and eternal day for the other. A case of burn up or freeze up."

"Exactly. Or if it doesn't reach to that, the water gas will gradually lose out into sidereal space and we will go to desert. Merely a question of the old dynamical theory of gases; of the molecules to be in motion, to be forever colliding and shooting out into variance.

"Each minute, each hour, each day we are losing part of our atmospheric envelope. In course of time it will all be gone; when it is we shall be all desert. For instance, take a look outside. This is Arizona. Once it was the bottom of a deep blue sea. Why deny when we can already behold the beginning?"

The other laughed.

"Pretty good mathematics at that, professor. Only—"

"Only?"

"That it is merely mathematics."

"Merely mathematics?" The professor frowned slightly. "Mathematics do not lie, Charlie, you cannot get away from them. What sort of fanciful argument are you bringing up now?"

"Simply this," returned the other, "that you depend too much on figures They are material and in the nature of things can only be employed in a calculation of what *may* happen in the future. You must have premises to stand on, facts. Your figures are rigid: they have no elasticity; unless your foundations are permanent and faultless your deductions will lead you only into error."

"Granted; just the point: we know where we stand. Wherein are we in error?"

It was the old point of difference. Huyck was ever crashing down the idols of pure materialism. Williams was of the world-wide school.

"You are in error, my dear professor, in a very little thing and a very large one."

"What is that?"

"Man."

"Man?"

"Yes. He's a great little bug. You have left him out of your calculation —which he will upset."

The professor smiled indulgently. "I'll allow he is at least a conceited bug; but you surely cannot grant him much when pitted against the Universe."

"No? Did it ever occur to you, professor, what the Universe is? The stars for instance? Space, the immeasurable distance of Infinity. Have you never dreamed?"

Williams could not quite grasp him. Huyck had a habit that had grown out of childhood. Always he would allow his opponent to commit himself. The professor did not answer. But the other spoke.

"Ether. You know it. Whether mind or granite. For instance, you

desert." He placed his finger to his forehead. "Your mind, **my mind—local-**
ized ether."

"What are you driving at?"

"Merely this. Your Universe has intelligence. It has mind as well as
matter. The little knot called the earth is becoming conscious. Your deductions are incompetent unless they embrace mind as well as matter, and they
cannot do it. Your mathematics are worthless."

The professor bit his lip.

"Always fanciful," he commented, "and visionary. Your argument is
beautiful, Charley, and hopeful. I would that it were true. But all things
must mature. Even an earth must die."

"Not our earth. You look into the past, professor, for your proof, and
I look into the future. Give a planet long enough time in maturing and it
will develop life; give it still longer and it will produce intelligence. Our own
earth is just coming into consciousness; it has thirty million years, at least,
to run."

"You mean?"

"This. That man is a great little bug. Mind: the intelligence of the
earth."

This of course is a bit dry. The conversation of such men very often is
to those who do not care to follow them. But it is very pertinent to what
came after. We know now, everyone knows, that Charley Huyck was right.
Even Professor Williams admits it. Our earth is conscious. In less than
twenty-four hours it had to employ its consciousness to save itself from
destruction.

A bell rang. It was the private wire that connected the office with the
residence. The professor picked up the receiver. "Just a minute. Yes? All
right." Then to his companion: "I must go over to the house, Charley. We
have plenty of time. Then we can go up to the observatory."

Which shows how little we know about ourselves. Poor Professor Williams! Little did he think that those casual words were the last he would
ever speak to Charley Huyck.

The whole world seething! The beginning of the end! Charley Huyck
in the vortex. The next few hours were to be the most strenuous of the
planet's history.

It was night. The stars which had just been coming out were spotted by
millions over the sleeping desert. One of the nights that are peculiar to the
country, which we all of us know so well, if not from experience, at least
from hearsay; mellow, soft, sprinkled like salted fire, twinkling.

Each little light a message out of infinity. Cosmic grandeur—mind,
chaos, eternity—a night for dreaming. Whoever had chosen the spot in the
desert had picked full well. Charley had spoken of consciousness. On that
night when he gazed up at the stars he was its personification. Surely a good
spirit was watching over the earth.

A cool wind was blowing; on its breath floated the murmurs from the village; laughter, the song of children, the purring of motors and the startled barking of a dog; the confused drone of man and his civilization. From the eminence the observatory looked down upon the town and the sheen of light, spotting like jewels in the dim glow of the desert. To the east the mellow moon just tipping over the mountain. Charley stepped to the window.

He could see it all: The subtle beauty that was so akin to poetry: the stretch of desert, the mountains, the light in the eastern sky; the dull level shadow that marked the plain to the northward. To the west the mountains looming black to the star line. A beautiful night; sweetened with the breath of desert and tuned to its slumber.

Across the lawn he watched the professor descending the pathway under the acacias. An automobile was coming up the driveway; as it drove up under the arcs he noticed its powerful lines and its driver; one of those splendid pleasure cars that have returned to favor during the last decade; the soft purr of its motor, the great heavy tires and its coating of dust. There is a lure about a great car coming in from the desert. The car stopped, Charley noted. Doubtless some one for Williams. If it were, he would go into the observatory alone.

In the strict sense of the word Huyck was not an astronomer. He had not made it his profession. But for all that he knew things about the stars that the more exact professors had not dreamed of. Charley was a dreamer. He had a code all his own and a manner of reasoning. Between him and the stars lay a secret.

He had not divulged it, or if he had, it was in such an open way that it was laughed at. It was not cold enough in calculation or, even if so, was too far from their deduction. Huyck had imagination; his universe was alive and potent; it had intelligence. Matter could not live without it. Man was its manifestation; just come to consciousness. The universe teemed with intelligence. Charley looked at the stars.

He crossed the office, passed through the reception-room and thence to the stairs that led to the observatory. In the time that would lapse before the coming of his friend he would have ample time for observation. Somehow he felt that there was time for discovery. He had come down to Arizona to employ the lens of his friend the astronomer. The instrument that he had erected on his own mountain in Colorado had not given him the full satisfaction that he expected. Here in Arizona, in the dry clear air, which had hitherto given such splendid results, he hoped to find what he was after. But little did he expect to discover the terrible thing he did.

It is one of the strangest parts of the story that he should be here at the very moment when Fate and the world's safety would have had him. For years he and Dr. Robold had been at work on their visionary projects. They were both dreamers. While others had scoffed they had silently been at their great work on kinetics.

The boy and the burning glass had grown under the tutelage of Dr. Robold: the time was about at hand when he could out-rival the saying of Archimedes. Though the world knew it not, Charley Huyck had arrived at the point where he could literally burn up the earth.

But he was not sinister; though he had the power he had, of course, not the slightest intention. He was a dreamer and it was part of his dream that man break his thraldom to the earth and reach out into the universe. It was a great conception, and were it not for the terrible event which took his life we have no doubt but that he would have succeeded.

It was ten-thirty when he mounted the steps and seated himself. He glanced at his watch: he had a good ten minutes. He had computed before just the time for the observation. For months he had waited for just this moment; he had not hoped to be alone and now that he was in solitary possession he counted himself fortunate. Only the stars and Charley Huyck knew the secret; and not even he dreamed what it would amount to.

From his pocket he drew a number of papers; most of them covered with notations; some with drawings; and a good-sized map in colors. This he spread before him, and with his pencil began to draw right across its face a net of lines and cross lines. A number of figures and a rapid computation. He nodded and then he made the observation.

It would have been interesting to study the face of Charley Huyck during the next few moments. At first he was merely receptive, his face placid but with the studious intentness of one who has come to the moment: and as he began to find what he was after—an eagerness of satisfaction. Then a queer blankness; the slight movement of his body stopped, and the tapping of his feet ceased entirely.

For a full five minutes an absolute intentness. During that time he was out among the stars beholding what not even he had dreamed of. It was more than a secret: and what it was, only Charley Huyck of all the millions of men could have recognized. Yet it was more than even he had expected. When he at last drew away his face was chalk-like; great drops of sweat stood on his forehead: and the terrible truth in his eyes made him look ten years older.

"My God!"

For a moment indecision and strange impotence. The truth he had beheld numbed action; from his lips the mumbled words:

"This world; my world; our great and splendid mankind!"

A sentence that was despair and a benediction.

Then mechanically he turned back to confirm his observation. This time, knowing what he would see, he was not so horrified: his mind was cleared by the plain fact of what he was beholding. When at last he drew away his face was settled.

He was a man who thought quickly—thank the stars for that—and, once he thought, quick to spring to action. There was a peril poising over the earth. If it were to be voided there was not a second to lose in weighing up the possibilities.

He had been dreaming all his life. He had never thought that the climax was to be the very opposite of what he hoped for. In his under mind he prayed for Dr. Robold—dead and gone forever. Were he only here to help him!

He seized a piece of paper. Over its white face he ran a mass of computations. He worked like lightning; his fingers plying and his mind keyed to the pin-point of genius. Not one thing did he overlook in his calculation. If the earth had a chance he would find it.

There are always possibilities. He was working out the odds of the greatest race since creation. While the whole world slept, while the uncounted millions lay down in fond security, Charley Huyck there in the lonely room on the desert drew out their figured odds to the point of infinity.

"Just one chance in a million."

He was going to take it. The words were not out of his mouth before his long legs were leaping down the stairway. In the flash of seconds his mind was rushing into clear action. He had had years of dreaming; all his years of study and tutelage under Robold gave him just the training for such a disaster.

But he needed time. Time! Time! Why was it so precious? He must get to his own mountain. In six jumps he was in the office.

It was empty. The professor had not returned. He thought rather grimly and fleetingly of their conversation a few minutes before; what would Williams think now of science and consciousness? He picked up the telephone receiver. While he waited he saw out of the corner of his eye the car in the driveway. It was—

"Hello. The professor? What? Gone down to town? No! Well, say, this is Charley"—he was watching the car in front of the building. "Say, hello —tell him I have gone home, home! H-o-m-e to Colorado—to Colorado, yes—to the mountain—the m-o-u-n-t-a-i-n. Oh, never mind—I'll leave a note."

He clamped down the receiver. On the desk he scrawled on a piece of paper:

"Ed:

"Look these up. I'm bound for the mountain. No time to explain. There's a car outside. Stay with the lens. Don't leave it. If the earth goes up you will know that I have not reached the mountain."

Beside the note he placed one of the maps that he had in his pocket— with his pencil drew a black cross just above the center. Under the map were a number of computations.

It is interesting to note that in the stress of the great critical moment he forgot the professor's title. It was a good thing. When Williams read it he recognized the significance. All through their life in crucial moments he had been "Ed" to Charley.

But the note was all he was destined to find. A brisk wind was blowing. By a strange balance of fate the same movement that let Huyck out of the building ushered in the wind and upset calculation.

It was a little thing, but it was enough to keep all the world in ignorance and despair. The eddy whisking in through the door picked up the precious map, poised it like a tiny plane, and dropped it neatly behind a bookcase.

Huyck was working in a straight line. Almost before his last words on the phone were spoken he had requisitioned that automobile outside; whether money or talk, faith or force, he was going to have it. The hum of the motor sounded in his ears as he ran down the steps. He was hatless and in his shirt-sleeves. The driver was just putting some tools in the car. With one jump Charley had him by the collar.

"Five thousand dollars if you can get me to Robold Mountain in twenty hours."

The very suddenness of the rush caught the man by surprise and lurched him against the car, turning him half around. Charley found himself gazing into dull brown eyes and sardonic laughter: a long, thin nose and lips drooped at the corners, then as suddenly tipping up—a queer creature, half devil, half laughter, and all fun.

"Easy, Charley, easy! How much did you say? Whisper it."

It was Bob Winters. Bob Winters and his car. And waiting. Surely no twist of fortune could have been greater. He was a college chum of Huyck's and of the professor's. If there was one man that could make the run in the time allotted, Bob was he. But Huyck was impersonal. With the burden on his mind he thought of naught but his destination.

"Ten thousand!" he shouted.

The man held back his head. Huyck was far too serious to appreciate mischief. But not the man.

"Charley Huyck, of all men. Did young Lochinvar come out of the West? How much did you say? This desert air and the dust, 'tis hard on the hearing. She must be a young, fair maiden. Ten thousand."

"Twenty thousand. Thirty thousand. Damnation, man, you can have the mountain. Into the car."

By sheer subjective strength he forced the other into the machine. It was not until they were shooting out of the grounds on two wheels that he realized that the man was Bob Winters. Still the workings of fate.

The madcap and wild Bob of the races! Surely Destiny was on the job. The challenge of speed and the premium. At the opportune moment before disaster the two men were brought together Minutes weighed up with centuries and hours out-balanced millenniums. The whole world slept; little did it dream that its very life was riding north with these two men into the midnight.

Into the midnight! The great car, the pride of Winter's heart, leaped between the pillars. At the very outset, madcap that he was, he sent her into seventy miles an hour; they fairly jumped off the hill into the village. At a full seventy-five he took the curve; she skidded, sheared half around and swept on.

For an instant Charley held his breath. But the master hand held her; she steadied, straightened, and shot out into the desert. Above the whir of the motor, flying dust and blurring what-not, Charley got the tones of his companion's voice. He had heard the words somewhere in history.

"Keep your seat, Mr. Greely. Keep your seat!"

The moon was now far up over the mountain, the whole desert was bathed in a mellow twilight; in the distance the mountains brooded like an uncertain slumbering cloud bank. They were headed straight to the northward; though there was a better road round about, Winters had chosen the hard, rocky bee-line to the mountain.

He knew Huyck and his reputation; when Charley offered thirty thousand for a twenty-hour drive it was not mere byplay. He had happened in at the observatory to drop in on Williams on his way to the coast. They had been classmates; likewise he and Charley.

When the excited man out of the observatory had seized him by the collar, Winters merely had laughed. He was the speed king. The three boys who had gone to school were now playing with the destiny of the earth. But only Huyck knew it.

Winters wondered. Through miles and miles of fleeting sagebrush, cacti and sand and desolation, he rolled over the problem. Steady as a rock, slightly stooped, grim and as certain as steel he held to the north. Charley Huyck by his side, hatless, coatless, his hair dancing to the wind, all impatience. Why was it? Surely a man even for death would have time to get his hat.

The whole thing spelled speed to Bob Winters; perhaps it was the infusion of spirit or the intensity of his companion; but the thrill ran into his vitals. Thirty thousand dollars—for a stake like that—what was the balance? He had been called Wild Bob for his daring; some had called him insane; on this night his insanity was enchantment.

It was wild; the lee of the giant roadster a whirring shower of gravel: into the darkness, into the night the car fought over the distance. The terrific momentum and the friction of the air fought in their faces; Huyck's face was unprotected: in no time his lips were cracked, and long before they had crossed the level his whole face was bleeding.

But he heeded it not. He only knew that they were moving; that slowly, minute by minute, they were cutting down the odds that bore disaster. In his mind a maze of figures; the terrible sight he had seen in the telescope and the thing impending. Why had he kept his secret?

Over and again he impeached himself and Dr. Robold. It had come to this. The whole world sleeping and only himself to save it. Oh, for a few minutes, for one short moment! Would he get it?

At last they reached the mountains. A rough, rocky road, and but little traveled. Happily Winters had made it once before, and knew it. He took it with every bit of speed they could stand, but even at that it was diminished to a minimum.

For hours they fought over grades and gulches, dry washouts and boulders. It was dawn, and the sky was growing pink when they rode down again upon the level. It was here that they ran across their first trouble; and it was here that Winters began to realize vaguely what a race they might be running.

The particular level which they had entered was an elbow of the desert projecting into the mountains just below a massive, newly constructed dam. The reservoir had but lately been filled, and all was being put in readiness for the dedication.

An immense sheet of water extending far back into the mountains—it was intended before long to transform the desert into a garden. Below, in the valley, was a town, already the center of a prosperous irrigation settlement; but soon, with the added area, to become a flourishing city. The elbow, where they struck it, was perhaps twenty miles across. Their northward path would take them just outside the top where the foothills of the opposite mountain chain melted into the desert. Without ado Winters put on all speed and plunged across the sands. And then:

It was much like winking; but for all that something far more impressive. To Winters, on the left hand of the car and with the east on the right hand, it was much as if the sun had suddenly leaped up and as suddenly plumped down behind the horizon—a vast vividness of scintillating opalescence: an azure, flaming diamond shot by a million fire points.

Instantaneous and beautiful. In the pale dawn of the desert air its wonder and color were beyond all beauty. Winters caught it out of the corner of his eye; it was so instantaneous and so illusive that he was not certain. Instinctively he looked to his companion.

But Charley, too, had seen it. His attitude of waiting and hoping was vigorized into vivid action. He knew just what it was. With one hand he clutched Winters and fairly shouted:

"On, on, Bob! On, as you value your life. Put into her every bit of speed you have got."

At the same instant, at the same breath came a roar that was not to be forgotten; crunching, rolling, terrible—like the mountain moving.

Bob knew it. It was the dam. Something had broken it. To the east the great wall of waterfall—out of the mountains! A beautiful sight and terrible; a relentless glassy roller fringed along its base by a lace of racing foam. The upper part was as smooth as crystal; the stored-up waters of the mountain moving out compactly. The man thought of the little town below and its peril. But Huyck thought also. He shouted in Winters' ear:

"Never mind the town. Keep straight north. Over yonder to the point of the water. The town will have to drown."

It was inexorable; there was no pity; the very strength and purpose of the command drove into the other's understanding. Dimly now he realized that they were really running a race against time. Winters was a daredevil; the very catastrophe sent a thrill of exultation through him. It was the climax, the great moment of his life, to be driving at a hundred miles an hour under that wall of water.

The roar was terrible. Before they were half across it seemed to the two men that the very sound would drown them. There was nothing in the world but pandemonium. The strange flash was forgotten in the terror of the living wall that was reaching out to engulf them. Like insects they whizzed in the open face of the deluge. When they had reached the tip they were so close that the out-running fringe of the surf was at their wheels.

Around the point with the wide open plain before them. With the flood behind them it was nothing to outrun it. The waters with a wider stretch spread out. In a few moments they had left all behind them.

But Winters wondered; what was the strange flash of evanescent beauty? He knew this dam and its construction; to outlast the centuries. It had been whiffed in a second. It was not lightning. He had heard no sound other than the rush of the waters. He looked to his companion.

Huyck nodded.

"That's the thing we are racing. We have only a few hours. Can we make it?"

Bob had thought that he was getting all the speed possible out of his motor. What it yielded from that moment on was a revelation.

It is not safe and hardly possible to be driving at such speed on the desert. Only the best car and a firm roadway can stand it. A sudden rut, squirrel hole, or pocket of sand is as good as destruction. They rushed on till noon.

Not even Winters, with all his alertness, could avoid it. Perhaps he was weary. The tedious hours, the racking speed had worn him to exhaustion. They had ceased to individualize, their way a blur, a nightmare of speed and distance.

It came suddenly, a blind barranca—one of those sunken, useless channels that are death to the unwary. No warning.

It was over just that quickly. A mere flash of consciousness plus a sensation of flying. Two men broken on the sands and the great, beautiful roadster a twisted ruin.

But back to the world. No one knew about Charley Huyck nor what was occurring on the desert. Even if we had, it would have been impossible to construe connection.

After the news out of Oakland, and the destruction of Mt. Heckla, we were far too appalled. The whole thing was beyond us. Not even the scientists with all their data could find one thing to work on. The wires of the world buzzed with wonder and with panic. We were civilized. It is really strange how quickly, in spite of our boasted powers, we revert to the primitive.

Superstition cannot die. Where was no explanation must be miracle. The thing had been repeated. When would it strike again. And where?

There was not long to wait. But this time the stroke was of far more consequence and of far more terror. The sheer might of the thing shook the earth. Not a man or government that would not resign in the face of such destruction.

It was omnipotent. A whole continent had been riven. It would be impossible to give a description of such catastrophe; no pen can tell it any more than it could describe the Creation. We can only follow in its path.

On the morning after the first catastrophe, at eight o'clock, just south of the little city of Santa Cruz, on the north shore of the Bay of Monterey, the same light and the same, though not quite the same, instantaneousness. Those who beheld it report a vast ball of azure glow and opalescent fire and motion; a strange sensation of vitalized vibration; of personified living force. In shape like a marble, as round as a full moon in its glory, but of infinitely more beauty.

It came from nowhere; neither from above the earth nor below it. Seeming to leap out of nothing, it glided or rather vanished to the eastward. Still the effect of winking, though this time, perhaps from a distanced focus, more vivid. A dot or marble, like a full moon, burning, opal, soaring to the eastward.

And instantaneous. Gone as soon as it was come; noiseless and of phantom beauty; like a finger of the Omnipotent tracing across the world, and as terrible. The human mind had never conceived a thing so vast.

Beginning at the sands of the ocean the whole country had vanished; a chasm twelve miles wide and of unknown depth running straight to the eastward. Where had been farms and homes was nothing; the mountains had been seared like butter. Straight as an arrow.

Then the roar of the deluge. The waters of the Pacific breaking through its sands and rolling into the Gulf of Mexico. That there was no heat was evidenced by the fact that there was no steam. The thing could not be internal. Yet what was it?

One can only conceive in figures. From the shores of Santa Cruz to the Atlantic—a few seconds; then out into the eastern ocean straight out into the Sea of Sargasso. A great gulf riven straight across the face of North America.

The path seemed to follow the sun; it bore to the eastward with a slight southern deviation. The mountains it cut like cheese. Passing just north of Fresno it seared through the gigantic Sierras halfway between the Yosemite and Mt. Whitney, through the great desert to southern Nevada, thence across northern Arizona, New Mexico, Texas, Arkansas, Mississippi, Alabama, and Georgia, entering the Atlantic at a point half-way between Brunswick and Jacksonville. A great canal twelve miles in width linking the oceans. A cataclysmic blessing. Today, with thousands of ships bearing freight over its water, we can bless that part of the disaster.

But there was more to come. So far the miracle had been sporadic. Whatever had been its force it had been fatal only on point and occasion. In a way it had been local. The deadly atmospheric combination of its aftermath was invariable in its recession. There was no suffering. The death that it dealt was the death of obliteration. But now it entered on another stage.

The world is one vast ball, and though large, still a very small place to live in. There are few of us, perhaps, who look upon it, or even stop to think of it, as a living being. Yet it is just that. It has its currents, life, pulse, and its fevers; it is coordinate; a million things such as the great streams of the ocean, the swirls of the atmosphere, make it a place to live in. And we are conscious only, or mostly, through disaster.

A strange thing happened.

The great opal like a mountain of fire had riven across the continent. From the beginning and with each succession the thing was magnified. But it was not until it had struck the waters of the Atlantic that we became aware of its full potency and its fatality.

The earth quivered at the shock, and man stood on his toes in terror. In twenty-four hours our civilization was literally falling to pieces. We were powerful with the forces that we understood; but against this that had been literally ripped from the unknown we were insignificant. The whole world was frozen. Let us see.

Into the Atlantic! The transition. Hitherto silence. But now the roar of ten thousand million Niagaras, the waters of the ocean rolling, catapulting, roaring into the gulf that had been seared in its bosom. The Gulf Stream cut in two, the currents that tempered our civilization sheared in a second. Straight into the Sargasso Sea. The great opal, liquid fire, luminescent, a ball like the setting sun, lay poised upon the ocean. It was the end of the earth!

What was this thing? The whole world knew of it in a second. And not a one could tell. In less than forty hours after its first appearance in Oakland it had consumed a mountain, riven a continent, and was drinking up an ocean. The tangled Sea of the Sargasso, dead calm for ages, was a cataract; a swirling torrent of maddened waters rushed to the opal—and disappeared.

It was hellish and out of madness; as beautiful as it was uncanny. The opal high as the Himalayas brooding upon the water; its myriad colors blending, winking in a phantasm of iridescence. The beauty of its light could be seen a thousand miles. A thing out of mystery and out of forces. We had discovered many things and knew much; but had guessed no such thing as this. It was vampirish, and it was literally drinking up the earth.

Consequences were immediate. The point of contact was fifty miles across, the waters of the Atlantic with one accord turned to the magnet. The Gulf Stream veered straight from its course and out across the Atlantic. The icy currents from the poles freed from the warmer barrier descended along the coasts and thence out into the Sargasso Sea. The temperature of the temperate zone dipped below the point of a blizzard.

The first word came out of London. Freezing! And in July! The fruit and entire harvest of northern Europe destroyed. Olympic Games at Copenhagen postponed by a foot of snow. The river Seine frozen. Snow falling in New York. Crops nipped with frost as far south as Cape Hatteras.

A fleet of airplanes was despatched from the United States and another from the west coast of Africa. Not half of them returned. Those that did reported even more disaster. The reports that were handed in were appalling. They had sailed straight on. It was like flying into the sun; the vividness of the opalescence was blinding, rising for miles above them alluring, drawing and unholy, and of a beauty that was terror.

Only the tardy had escaped. It even drew their motors, it was like gravity suddenly become vitalized and conscious. Thousands of machines vaulted into the opalescence. From those ahead hopelessly drawn and powerless came back the warning. But hundreds could not escape.

"Back," came the wireless. "Do not come too close. The thing is a magnet. Turn back before too late. Against this man is insignificant."

Then like gnats flitting into fire they vanished into the opalescence.

The others turned back. The whole world, freezing, shuddered in horror. A great vampire was brooding over the earth. The greatness that man had attained to was nothing. Civilization was tottering in a day. We were hopeless.

Then came the last revelation; the truth and verity of the disaster and the threatened climax. The water level of all the coast had gone down. Vast ebb tides had gone out not to return. Stretches of sand where had been surf extended far out into the sea. Then the truth. The thing, whatever it was, was drinking up the ocean.

It was tragic; grim, terrible, cosmic. Out of nowhere had come this thing that was eating up the earth. Not a thing out of all our science had there been to warn us; not a word from all our wise men. We who had built up our civilization, piece by piece, were after all but insects.

We were going out in a maze of beauty into the infinity whence we came. Hour by hour the great orb of opalescence grew in splendor; the effect and the beauty of its lure spread about the earth; thrilling, vibrant like suppressed music. The old earth helpless. Was it possible that out of her bosom she could not pluck one intelligence to save her? Was there not one law—one answer?

Out on the desert with his face to the sun lay the answer. Though almost hopeless there was still some time and enough of near-miracle to save us. A limping fate in the shape of two Indians and a battered runabout at the last moment.

Little did the two red men know the value of the two men found that day on the desert. To them the débris of the mighty car and the prone bodies told enough of the story. They were Samaritans; but there are many ages to bless them.

As it was there were many hours lost. Without this loss there would have been thousands spared and an almost immeasurable amount of disaster. But we have still to be thankful. Charley Huyck was still living.

He had been stunned—battered, bruised, and unconscious; but he had not been injured vitally. There was still enough left of him to drag himself to the old runabout and call for Winters. His companion, as it happened, was in even better shape than himself, and waiting. We do not know how they talked the red men out of their relic—whether by coaxing, by threat, or by force.

Straight north. Two men battered, worn, bruised, but steadfast, bearing in that limping old motor-car the destiny of the earth. Fate was still on the job, but badly crippled.

They had lost many precious hours. Winters had forfeited his right to the thirty thousand. He did not care. He understood vaguely that there was a stake over and above all money. Huyck said nothing; he was too maimed and too much below will-power to think of speaking. What had occurred during the many hours of their unconsciousness was unknown to them. It was not until they came sheer upon the gulf that had been riven straight across the continent that the awful truth dawned on them.

To Winters it was terrible. The mere glimpse of that blackened chasm was terror. It was bottomless; so deep that its depths were cloudy; the misty haze of its uncertain shadows was akin to chaos. He understood vaguely that it was related to that terrible thing they had beheld in the morning. It was not the power of man. Some force had been loosened which was ripping the earth to its vitals. Across the terror of the chasm he made out the dim outlines of the opposite wall. A full twelve miles across.

For a moment the sight overcame even Huyck himself. Full well he knew; but knowing, as he did, the full fact of the miracle was even more than he expected. His long years under Robold, his scientific imagination had given him comprehension. Not puny steam, nor weird electricity, but force, kinetics—out of the universe.

He knew. But knowing as he did, he was overcome by the horror. Such a thing turned loose upon the earth! He had lost many hours; he had but a few hours remaining. The thought gave him sudden energy. He seized Winters by the arm.

"To the first town, Bob. To the first town—an aerodrome."

There was speed in that motor for all its decades. Winters turned about and shot out in a lateral course parallel to the great chasm. But for all his speed he could not keep back his question.

"In the name of Heaven, Charley, what did it? What is it?"

Came the answer; and it drove the lust of all speed through Winters.

"Bob," said Charley, "it is the end of the world—if we don't make it. But a few hours left. We must have an airplane. I must make the mountain."

It was enough for Wild Bob. He settled down. It was only an old runabout; but he could get speed out of a wheelbarrow. He had never driven a race like this. Just once did he speak. The words were characteristic.

"A world's record, Charley. And we're going to win. Just watch us."

And they did.

There was no time lost in the change. The mere fact of Huyck's name, his appearance and the manner of his arrival was enough. For the last hours messages had been pouring in at every post in the Rocky Mountains for Charley Huyck. After the failure of all others many thousands had thought of him.

Even the government, unappreciative before, had awakened to a belated and almost frantic eagerness. Orders were out that everything, no matter what, was to be at his disposal. He had been regarded as visionary; but in the face of what had occurred, visions were now the most practical things for mankind. Besides, Professor Williams had sent out to the world the strange portent of Huyck's note. For years there had been mystery on that mountain.

Unfortunately we cannot give it the description we would like to give. Few men outside of the regular employees have ever been to the Mountain of Robold. From the very first, owing perhaps to the great forces stored, and the danger of carelessness, strangers and visitors had been barred. Then, too, the secrecy of Dr. Robold—and the respect of his successor. But we do know that the burning glass had grown into the mountain.

Bob Winters and the aviator are the only ones to tell us; the employees, one and all, chose to remain. The cataclysm that followed destroyed the work of Huyck and Robold—but not until it had served the greatest deed that ever came out of the minds of men. And had it not been for Huyck's insistence we would not have even the account that we are giving.

It was he who insisted, nay, begged, that his companions return while there was yet a chance. Full well he knew. Out of the universe, out of space he had coaxed the forces that would burn up the earth. The great ball of luminous opalescence, and the diminishing ocean!

There was but one answer. Through the imaginative genius of Robold and Huyck, fate had worked up to the moment. The lad and the burning glass had grown to Archimedes.

What happened?

The plane neared the Mountain of Robold. The great bald summit and the four enormous globes of crystal. At least we so assume. We have Winters' word and that of the aviator that they were of the appearance of glass. Perhaps they were not; but we can assume it for description. So enormous, that were they set upon a plain they would have overtopped the highest building ever constructed; though on the height of the mountain, and in its contrast, they were not much more than golf balls.

It was not their size but their effect that was startling. They were alive. At least that is what we have from Winters. Living, luminous, burning, twisting within with a thousand blending, iridescent beautiful colors. Not like electricity but something infinitely more powerful. Great, mysterious magnets that Huyck had charged out of chaos. Glowing with the softest light; the whole mountain brightened as in a dream, and the town of Robold at its base lit up with a beauty that was past beholding.

It was new to Winters. The great buildings and the enormous machinery. Engines of strangest pattern, driven by forces that the rest of the world had not thought of. Not a sound; the whole works a complicated mass covering a hundred acres, driving with a silence that was magic. Not a whir nor friction. Like a living composite body pulsing and breathing the strange and mysterious force that had been evolved from Huyck's theory of kinetics. The four great steel conduits running from the globes down the side of the mountain. In the center, at a point midway between the globes, a massive steel needle hung on a pivot and pointed directly at the sun.

Winters and the aviator noted it and wondered. From the lower end of the needle was pouring a luminous stream of pale-blue opalescence, a stream much like a liquid, and of an unholy radiance. But it was not a liquid, nor fire, nor anything seen by man before.

It was force. We have no better description than the apt phrase of Winters. Charley Huyck was milking the sun, as it dropped from the end of the four living streams to the four globes that took it into storage. The four great, wonderful living globes; the four batteries; the very sight of their imprisoned beauty and power was magnetic.

The genius of Huyck and Robold! Nobody but the wildest dreamers would have conceived it. The life of the sun. And captive to man; at his will and volition. And in the next few minutes we were to lose it all! But in losing it we were to save ourselves. It was fate and nothing else.

There was but one thing more upon the mountain—the observatory and another needle apparently idle; but with a point much like a gigantic phonograph needle. It rose square out of the observatory, and to Winters it gave an impression of a strange gun, or some implement for sighting.

That was all. Coming with the speed that they were making, the airmen had no time for further investigation. But even this is comprehensive. Minus the force. If we only knew more about that or even its theory we might perhaps reconstruct the work of Charley Huyck and Dr. Robold.

They made the landing. Winters, with his nature, would be in at the finish; but Charley would not have it.

"It is death, Bob," he said. "You have a wife and babies. Go back to the world. Go back with all the speed you can get out of your motors. Get as far away as you can before the end comes."

With that he bade them a sad farewell. It was the last spoken word that the outside world had from Charley Huyck.

The last seen of him he was running up the steps of his office. As they soared away and looked back they could see men, the employees, scurrying about in frantic haste to their respective posts and stations. What was it all about? Little did the two aviators know. Little did they dream that it was the deciding stroke.

Still the great ball of Opalescence brooding over the Sargasso. Europe now was frozen, and though it was midsummer had gone into winter quarters. The Straits of Dover were no more. The waters had receded and one could walk, if careful, dry-shod from the shores of France to the chalk cliffs of England. The Straits of Gibraltar had dried up. The Mediterranean completely land-locked, was cut off forever from the tides of the mother ocean.

The whole world going dry; not in ethics, but in reality. The great Vampire, luminous, beautiful beyond all ken and thinking, drinking up our life-blood. The Atlantic a vast whirlpool.

A strange frenzy had fallen over mankind: men fought in the streets and died in madness. It was fear of the Great Unknown, and hysteria. At such a moment the veil of civilization was torn to tatters. Man was reverting to the primeval.

Then came the word from Charley Huyck; flashing and repeating to every clime and nation. In its assurance it was almost as miraculous as the Vampire itself. For man had surrendered.

To the People of the World:

The strange and terrible Opalescence which, for the past seventy hours, has been playing havoc with the world, is not miracle, nor of the supernatural, but a mere manifestation and result of the application of celestial kinetics. Such a thing always was and always will be possible where there is intelligence to control and harness the forces that lie about us. Space is not space exactly, but an infinite cistern of unknown laws and forces. We may control certain laws on earth, but until we reach out farther we are but playthings.

Man is the intelligence of the earth. The time will come when he must be the intelligence of a great deal of space as well. At the present time you are merely fortunate and a victim of a kind fate. That I am the instrument of the earth's salvation is merely chance. The real man is Dr. Robold. When he picked me up on the streets I had no idea that the sequence of time would drift to this moment. He took me into his work and taught me.

Because he was sensitive and was laughed at, we worked in secret. And since his death, and out of respect to his memory, I have continued in the same manner. But I have written down everything, all the laws, computations, formulas—everything; and I am now willing it to mankind.

Robold had a theory on kinetics. It was strange at first and a thing to laugh at; but he reduced it to laws as potent and as inexorable as the laws of gravitation.

The luminous Opalescence that has almost destroyed us is but one of its minor manifestations. It is a message of sinister intelligence; for back of it all is an Intelligence. Yet it is not all sinister. It is self-preservation. The time is coming when eons of ages from now our own man will be forced to employ just such a weapon for his own preservation. Either that or we shall die of thirst and agony.

Let me ask you to remember now, that whatever you have suffered, you have saved a world. I shall now save you and the earth.

In the vaults you will find everything. All the knowledge and discoveries of the great Dr. Robold, plus a few minor findings by myself.

And now I bid you farewell. You shall soon be free.

CHARLEY HUYCK.

A strange message. Spoken over the wireless and flashed to every clime, it roused and revived the hope of mankind. Who was this Charley Huyck? Uncounted millions of men had never heard his name; there were but few, very few who had.

A message out of nowhere and of very dubious and doubtful explanation. Celestial kinetics! Undoubtedly. But the words explained nothing. However, man was ready to accept anything, so long as it saved him.

For a more lucid explanation we must go back to the Arizona observatory and Professor Ed. Williams. And a strange one it was truly; a certain proof that consciousness is more potent, far more so than mere material; also that many laws of our astronomers are very apt to be overturned in spite of their mathematics.

Charley Huyck was right. You cannot measure intelligence with a yardstick. Mathematics do not lie; but when applied to consciousness they are very likely to kick backward. That is precisely what had happened.

The suddenness of Huyck's departure had puzzled Professor Williams; that, and the note which he found upon the table. It was not like Charley to go off so in the stress of a moment. He had not even taken the time to get his hat and coat. Surely something was amiss.

He read the note carefully, and with a deal of wonder.

"Look these up. . . . Stay with the lens. . . . If the earth goes up you will know that I have not reached the mountain."

What did he mean? Besides, there was no data for him to work on. He did not know that an errant breeze had plumped the information behind the bookcase. Nevertheless he went into the observatory, and for the balance of the night stuck by the lens.

Now there are uncounted millions of stars in the sky. Williams had nothing to go by. A needle in the hay-stack were an easy task compared with the one that he was allotted. The flaming mystery, whatever it was that

Huyck had seen, was not caught by the professor. Still, he wondered. "If the earth goes up you will know that I have not reached the mountain." What was the meaning?

But he was not worried. The professor loved Huyck as a visionary and smiled not a little at his delightful fancies. Doubtless this was one of them. It was not until the news came flashing out of Oakland that he began to take it seriously. Then followed the disappearance of Mount Heckla. "If the earth goes up"—it began to look as if the words had meaning.

There was a frantic professor during the next few days. When he was not with the lens he was flashing out messages to the world for Charley Huyck. He did not know that Huyck was lying unconscious and almost dead upon the desert. That the world was coming to catastrophe he knew full well; but where was the man to save it? And most of all, what had his friend meant by the words, "Look these up"?

Surely there must be some further information. Through the long, long hours he stayed with the lens and waited. And he found nothing.

It was three days. Who will ever forget them? Surely not Professor Williams. He was sweating blood. The whole world was going to pieces without the trace of an explanation. All the mathematics, all the accumulations of the ages had availed for nothing. Charley Huyck held the secret. It was in the stars, and not an astronomer could find it.

But with the seventieth hour came the turn of fortune. The professor was passing through the office. The door was open, and the same fitful wind which had played the original prank was now just as fitfully performing restitution. Williams noticed a piece of paper protruding from the back of the bookcase and fluttering in the breeze. He picked it up. The first words that he saw were in the handwriting of Charley Huyck. He read:

"In the last extremity—in the last phase when there is no longer any water on the earth; when even the oxygen of the atmospheric envelope has been reduced to a minimum—man, or whatever form of intelligence is then upon the earth, must go back to the laws which governed his forebears. Necessity must ever be the law of evolution. There will be no water upon the earth, but there will be an unlimited quantity elsewhere.

"By that time, for instance, the great planet, Jupiter, will be in just a convenient state for exploitation. Gaseous now, it will be, by that time, in just about the stage when the steam and water are condensing into ocean. Eons of millions of years away in the days of dire necessity. By that time the intelligence and consciousness of the earth will have grown equal to the task.

"It is a thing to laugh at (perhaps) just at present. But when we consider the ratio of man's advance in the last hundred years, what will it be in a billion? Not all the laws of the universe have been discovered, by any means. At present we know nothing. Who can tell?

"Aye, who can tell? Perhaps we ourselves have in store the fate we would mete out to another. We have a very dangerous neighbor close beside us. Mars is in dire straits for water. And we know there is life on Mars and intelligence! The very fact on its face proclaims it. The oceans have dried up; the only way they have of holding life is by bringing their water from the polar snow-caps. Their canals pronounce an advanced state of cooperative intelligence; there is life upon Mars and in an advanced stage of evolution.

"But how far advanced? It is a small planet, and consequently eons of ages in advance of the earth's evolution. In the nature of things Mars cooled off quickly, and life was possible there while the earth was yet a gaseous mass. She has gone to her maturity and into her retrogression; she is approaching her end. She has had less time to produce intelligence than intelligence will have—in the end—upon the earth.

"How far has this intelligence progressed? That is the question. Nature is a slow worker. It took eons of ages to put life upon the earth; it took eons of more ages to make this life conscious. How far will it go? How far has it gone on Mars?"

That was as far as the comments went. The professor dropped his eyes to the rest of the paper. It was a map of the face of Mars, and across its center was a black cross scratched by the dull point of a soft pencil.

He knew the face of Mars. It was the Ascræus Lucus. The oasis at the juncture of a series of canals running much like the spokes of a wheel. The great Uranian and Alander Canals coming in at about right angles.

In two jumps the professor was in the observatory with the great lens swung to focus. It was the great moment out of his lifetime, and the strangest and most eager moment, perhaps, ever lived by any astronomer. His fingers fairly twitched with tension. There before his view was the full face of our Martian neighbor!

But was it? He gasped out a breath of startled exclamation. Was it Mars that he gazed at; the whole face, the whole thing had been changed before him.

Mars has ever been red. Viewed through the telescope it has had the most beautiful tinge imaginable, red ochre, the weird tinge of the desert in sunset. The color of enchantment and of hell!

For it is so. We know that for ages and ages the planet has been burning up; that life was possible only in the dry sea-bottoms and under irrigation. The rest, where the continents once were, was blazing desert. The redness, the beauty, the enchantment that we so admired was burning hell.

All this had changed.

Instead of this was a beautiful shade of iridescent green. The red was gone forever. The great planet standing in the heavens had grown into infinite glory. Like the great Dog Star transplanted.

The professor sought out the Ascræus Lucus. It was hard to find. The whole face had been transfigured; where had been canals was now the beautiful sheen of green and verdure. He realized what he was beholding and what he had never dreamed of seeing; the seas of Mars filled up.

With the stolen oceans our grim neighbor had come back to youth. But how had it been done? It was horror for our world. The great luminescent ball of Opalescence! Europe frozen and New York a mass of ice. It was the earth's destruction. How long could the thing keep up; and whence did it come? What was it?

He sought for the Ascræus Lucus. And he beheld a strange sight. At the very spot where should have been the juncture of the canals he caught what at first looked like a pin-point flame, a strange twinkling light with flitting glow of Opalescence. He watched it, and he wondered. It seemed to the professor to grow; and he noticed that the green about it was of different color. It was winking, like a great force, and much as if alive; baneful.

It was what Charley Huyck had seen. The professor thought of Charley. He had hurried to the mountain. What could Huyck, a mere man, do against a thing like this? There was naught to do but sit and watch it drink of our life-blood. And then—

It was the message, the strange assurance that Huyck was flashing over the world. There was no lack of confidence in the words he was speaking. "Celestial Kinetics." So that was the answer! Certainly it must be so with the truth before him. Williams was a doubter no longer. And Charley Huyck could save them. The man he had humored. Eagerly he waited and stuck by the lens. The whole world waited.

It was perhaps the most terrific moment since Creation. To describe it would be like describing doomsday. We all of us went through it, and we all of us thought the end had come; that the earth was torn to atoms and to chaos.

The State of Colorado was lurid with a red light of terror; for a thousand miles the flame shot above the earth and into space. If ever spirit went out in glory that spirit was Charley Huyck! He had come to the moment and to Archimedes. The whole world rocked to the recoil. Compared to it the mightiest earthquake was but a tender shiver. The consciousness of the earth had spoken!

The professor was knocked upon the floor. He knew not what had happened. Out of the windows and to the north the flame of Colorado, like the whole world going up. It was the last moment. But he was a scientist to the end. He had sprained his ankle and his face was bleeding; but for all that he struggled, fought his way to the telescope. And he saw:

The great planet with its sinister, baleful, wicked light in the center, and another light vastly larger covering up half of Mars. What was it? It was moving. The truth set him almost to shouting.

It was the answer of Charley Huyck and of the world. The light grew smaller, smaller, and almost to a pin-point on its way to Mars.

The real climax was in silence. And of all the world only Professor Williams beheld it. The two lights coalesced and spread out; what it was on Mars, of course, we do not know.

But in a few moments all was gone. Only the green of the Martian Sea winked in the sunlight. The luminous opal was gone from the Sargasso. The ocean lay in peace.

It was a terrible three days. Had it not been for the work of Robold and Huyck, life would have been destroyed. The pity of it is that all of their discoveries have gone with them. Not even Charley realized how terrific the force he was about to loosen.

He had carefully locked everything in vaults for a safe delivery to man. He had expected death, but not the cataclysm. The whole of Mount Robold was shorn away; in its place we have a lake fifty miles in diameter.

So much for celestial kinetics.

And we look to a green and beautiful Mars. We hold no enmity. It was but the law of self-preservation. Let us hope they have enough water; and that their seas will hold. We don't blame them, and we don't blame ourselves either, for that matter. We need what we have, and we hope to keep it.

CHARLES W. DIFFIN

SPAWN OF
THE STARS

WHEN Cyrus R. Thurston bought himself a single-motored Stoughton job he was looking for new thrills. Flying around the east coast had lost its zest: he wanted to join that jaunty group who spoke so easily of hopping off for Los Angeles.

And what Cyrus Thurston wanted he usually obtained. But if that young millionaire-sportsman had been told that on his first flight this blocky, bulletlike ship was to pitch him headlong into the exact center of the wildest, strangest war this earth had ever seen—well, it is still probable that the Stoughton company would not have lost the sale.

They were roaring through the starlit, calm night, three thousand feet above a sage-sprinkled desert, when the trip ended. Slim Riley had the stick when the first blast of hot oil ripped slashingly across the pilot's window. "There goes your old trip!" he yelled. "Why don't they try putting engines in these ships?"

He jammed over the throttle and, with motor idling, swept down toward the endless miles of moonlit waste. Wind? They had been boring into it. Through the opened window he spotted a likely stretch of ground. Setting down the ship on a nice piece of Arizona desert was a mere detail for Slim.

"Let off a flare," he ordered, "when I give the word."

The white glare of it faded the stars as he sideslipped, then straightened out on his hand-picked field. The plane rolled down a clear space and stopped. The bright glare persisted while he stared curiously from the quiet cabin. Cutting the motor he opened both windows, then grabbed Thurston by the shoulder.

" 'Tis a curious thing, that," he said unsteadily. His hand pointed straight ahead. The flare died, but the bright stars of the desert country still shone on a glistening, shining bulb.

It was some two hundred feet away. The lower part was lost in shadow, but its upper surfaces shone rounded and silvery like a giant bubble. It towered in the air, scores of feet above the chaparral beside it. There was a round spot of black on its side, which looked absurdly like a door. . . .

"I saw something moving," said Thurston slowly. "On the ground I saw. . . . Oh, good Lord, Slim, it isn't real!"

Slim Riley made no reply. His eyes were riveted to an undulating, ghastly something that oozed and crawled in the pale light not far from the bulb. His hand was reaching, reaching. . . . It found what he sought; he leaned toward the window. In his hand was the Very pistol for discharging the flares. He aimed forward and up.

The second flare hung close before it settled on the sandy floor. Its blinding whiteness made the more loathsome the sickening yellow of the flabby flowing thing that writhed frantically in the glare. It was formless, shapeless, a heaving mound of nauseous matter. Yet even in its agonized writhing distortions they sensed the beating pulsations that marked it a living thing.

There were unending ripplings crossing and recrossing through the convolutions. To Thurston there was suddenly a sickening likeness: the thing was a brain from a gigantic skull—it was naked—was suffering. . . .

The thing poured itself across the sand. Before the staring gaze of the speechless men an excrescence appeared—a thick bulb on the mass—that protruded itself into a tentacle. At the end there grew instantly a hooked hand. It reached for the black opening in the great shell, found it, and the whole loathsome shapelessness poured itself up and through the hole.

Only at the last was it still. In the dark opening the last slippery mass held quiet for endless seconds. It formed, as they watched, to a head— frightful—menacing. Eyes appeared in the head; eyes flat and round and black save for a cross slit in each; eyes that stared horribly and unchangingly into theirs. Below them a gaping mouth opened and closed. . . . The head melted—was gone. . . .

And with its going came a rushing roar of sound.

From under the metallic mass shrieked a vaporous cloud. It drove at them, a swirling blast of snow and sand. Some buried memory of gas attacks woke Riley from his stupor. He slammed shut the windows an instant before the cloud struck, but not before they had seen, in the moonlight, a gleaming, gigantic, elongated bulb rise swiftly—screamingly—into the upper air.

The blast tore at their plane. And the cold in their tight compartment was like the cold of outer space. The men stared, speechless, panting. Their breath froze in that frigid room into steam clouds.

"It—it—" Thurston gasped—and slumped helpless upon the floor.

It was an hour before they dared open the door of their cabin. An hour of biting, numbing cold. Zero—on a warm summer night on the desert! Snow in the hurricane that had struck them!

" 'Twas the blast from the thing," guessed the pilot; "though never did

I see an engine with an exhaust like that." He was pounding himself with his arms to force up the chilled circulation.

"But the beast—the—the *thing!*" exclaimed Thurston. "It's monstrous; indecent! It thought—no question of that—but no body! Horrible! Just a raw, naked, thinking protoplasm!"

It was here that he flung open the door. They sniffed cautiously of the air. It was warm again—clean—save for a hint of some nauseous odor. They walked forward; Riley carried a flash.

The odor grew to a stench as they came where the great mass had lain. On the ground was a fleshy mound. There were bones showing, and horns on a skull. Riley held the light close to show the body of a steer. A body of raw bleeding meat. Half of it had been absorbed. . . .

"The damned thing," said Riley, and paused vainly for adequate words. "The damned thing was eating. . . . Like a jelly-fish, it was!"

"Exactly," Thurston agreed. He pointed about. There were other heaps scattered among the low sage.

"Smothered," guessed Thurston, "with that frozen exhaust. Then the filthy thing landed and came out to eat."

"Hold the light for me," the pilot commanded. "I'm goin' to fix that busted oil line. And I'm goin' to do it right now. Maybe the creature's still hungry."

They sat in their room. About them was the luxury of a modern hotel. Cyrus Thurston stared vacantly at the breakfast he was forgetting to eat. He wiped his hands mechanically on a snowy napkin. He looked from the window. There were palm trees in the park, and autos in a ceaseless stream. And people! Sane, sober people, living in a sane world. Newsboys were shouting; the life of the city was flowing.

"Riley!" Thurston turned to the man across the table. His voice was curiously toneless, and his face haggard. "Riley, I haven't slept for three nights. Neither have you. We've got to get this thing straight. We didn't both become absolute maniacs at the same instant, but—it was *not* there, it was *never* there—not *that.* . . ." He was lost in unpleasant recollections. "There are other records of hallucinations."

"Hallucinations—hell!" said Slim Riley. He was looking at a Los Angeles newspaper. He passed one hand wearily across his eyes, but his face was happier than it had been in days.

"We didn't imagine it, we aren't crazy—it's real! Would you read that now!" He passed the paper across to Thurston. The headlines were startling.

"Pilot Killed by Mysterious Airship. Silvery Bubble Hangs Over New York. Downs Army Plane in Burst of Flame. Vanishes at Terrific Speed."

"It's our little friend," said Thurston. And on his face, too, the lines were vanishing; to find this horror a reality was positive relief. "Here's the same cloud of vapor—drifted slowly across the city, the account says, blowing this stuff like steam from underneath. Airplanes investigated—an army plane drove into the vapor—terrific explosion—plane down in flames —others wrecked. The machine ascended with meteor speed, trailing blue flame. Come on, boy, where's that old bus? Thought I never wanted to fly a plane again. Now I don't want to do anything but."

"Where to?" Slim inquired.

"Headquarters," Thurston told him. "Washington—let's go!"

From Los Angeles to Washington is not far, as the plane flies. There was a stop or two for gasoline, but it was only a day later that they were seated in the War Office. Thurston's card had gained immediate admittance. "Got the low-down," he had written on the back of his card, "on the mystery airship."

"What you have told me is incredible," the Secretary was saying, "or would be if General Lozier here had not reported personally on the occurrence at New York. But the monster, the thing you have described. . . . Cy, if I didn't know you as I do I would have you locked up."

"It's true," said Thurston, simply. "It's damnable, but it's true. Now what does it mean?"

"Heaven knows," was the response. "That's where it came from—out of the heavens."

"Not what we saw," Slim Riley broke in. "That thing came straight out of Hell." And in his voice was no suggestion of levity.

"You left Los Angeles early yesterday; have you seen the papers?"

Thurston shook his head.

"They are back," said the Secretary. "Reported over London—Paris— the West Coast. Even China has seen them. Shanghai cabled an hour ago."

"Them? How many are there?"

"Nobody knows. There were five seen at one time. There are more— unless the same ones go around the world in a matter of minutes."

Thurston remembered that whirlwind of vapor and a vanishing speck in the Arizona sky. "They could," he asserted. "They're faster than anything on earth. Though what drives them . . . that gas—steam—whatever it is. . . ."

"Hydrogen," stated General Lozier. "I saw the New York show when poor Davis got his. He flew into the exhaust; it went off like a million bombs. Characteristic hydrogen flame trailed the damn thing up out of sight—a tail of blue fire."

"And cold," stated Thurston.

"Hot as a Bunsen burner," the General contradicted. "Davis' plane almost melted."

"Before it ignited," said the other. He told of the cold in their plane.

"Ha!" The General spoke explosively. "That's expansion. That's a tip on their motive power. Expansion of gas. That accounts for the cold and the vapor. Suddenly expanded it would be intensely cold. The moisture of the air would condense, freeze. But how could they carry it? Or"—he frowned for a moment, brows drawn over deep-set gray eyes—"or generate it? But that's crazy—that's impossible!"

"So is the whole matter," the Secretary reminded him. "With the information Mr. Thurston and Mr. Riley have given us, the whole affair is beyond any gauge our past experience might supply. We start from the impossible, and we go—where? What is to be done?"

"With your permission, sir, a number of things shall be done. It would be interesting to see what a squadron of planes might accomplish, diving on them from above. Or anti-aircraft fire."

"No," said the Secretary of War, "not yet. They have looked us over, but they have not attacked. For the present we do not know what they are. All of us have our suspicions—thoughts of interplanetary travel—thoughts too wild for serious utterance—but we know nothing.

"Say nothing to the papers of what you have told me," he directed Thurston. "Lord knows their surmises are wild enough now. And for you, General, in the event of any hostile move, you will resist."

"Your order was anticipated, sir." The General permitted himself a slight smile. "The air force is ready."

"Of course," the Secretary of War nodded. "Meet me here to-night— nine o'clock." He included Thurston and Riley in the command. "We need to think . . . to think . . . and perhaps their mission is friendly."

"Friendly!" The two flyers exchanged glances as they went to the door. And each knew what the other was seeing—a viscous ocherous mass that formed into a head where eyes devilish in their hate stared coldly into theirs. . . .

"Think. We need to think," repeated Thurston later. "A creature that is just one big hideous brain, that can think an arm into existence—think a head where it wishes! What does a thing like that think of? What beastly thoughts could that—that *thing* conceive?"

"If I got the sights of a Lewis gun on it," said Riley vindictively, "I'd make it think."

"And my guess is that is all you would accomplish," Thurston told him. "I am forming a few theories about our visitors. One is that it would be quite impossible to find a vital spot in that big homogeneous mass."

The pilot dispensed with theories: his was a more literal mind. "Where on earth did they come from, do you suppose, Mr. Thurston?"

They were walking to their hotel. Thurston raised his eyes to the summer heavens. Faint stars were beginning to twinkle; there was one that glowed steadily.

"Nowhere on earth," Thurston stated softly, "nowhere on earth."

"Maybe so," said the pilot, "maybe so. We've thought about it and talked about it . . . and they've gone ahead and done it." He called to a newsboy; they took the latest editions to their room.

The papers were ablaze with speculation. There were dispatches from all corners of the earth, interviews with scientists and near scientists. The machines were a Soviet invention—they were beyond anything human—they were harmless—they would wipe out civilization—poison gas—blasts of fire like that which had enveloped the army flyer. . . .

And through it all Thurston read an ill-concealed fear, a reflection of panic that was gripping the nation—the whole world. These great machines were sinister. Wherever they appeared came the sense of being watched, of a menace being calmly withheld. And at thought of the obscene monsters inside those spheres, Thurston's lips were compressed and his eyes hardened. He threw the papers aside.

"They are here," he said, "and that's all that we know. I hope the Secretary of War gets some good men together. And I hope someone is inspired with an answer."

"An answer, is it?" said Riley. "I'm thinkin' that the answer will come, but not from these swivel-chair fighters. 'Tis the boys in the cockpits with one hand on the stick and one on the guns that will have the answer."

But Thurston shook his head. "Their speed," he said, "and the gas! Remember that cold. How much of it can they lay over a city?"

The question was unanswered, unless the quick ringing of the phone was a reply.

"War Department," said a voice. "Hold the wire." The voice of the Secretary of War came on immediately.

"Thurston?" he asked. "Come over at once on the jump, old man. Hell's popping."

The windows of the War Department Building were all alight as they approached. Cars were coming and going; men in uniform, as the Secretary had said, "on the jump." Soldiers with bayonets stopped them, then passed Thurston and his companion on. Bells were ringing from all sides. But in the Secretary's office was perfect quiet.

General Lozier was there, Thurston saw, and an imposing array of gold-braided men with a sprinkling of those in civilian clothes. One he recognized: MacGregor from the Bureau of Standards. The Secretary handed Thurston some papers.

"Radio," he explained. "They are over the Pacific coast. Hit near Vancouver; Associated Press says city destroyed. They are working down the coast. Same story—blast of hydrogen from their funnel-shaped base. Colder than Greenland below them; snow fell in Seattle. No real attack since Vancouver and little damage done—" A message was laid before him.

"Portland," he said. "Five mystery ships over city. Dart repeatedly toward earth, deliver blast of gas and then retreat. Doing no damage. Apparently inviting attack. All commercial planes ordered grounded. Awaiting instructions.

"Gentlemen," said the Secretary, "I believe I speak for all present when I say that, in the absence of firsthand information, we are utterly unable to arrive at any definite conclusion or make a definite plan. There is a menace in this, undeniably. Mr. Thurston and Mr. Riley have been good enough to report to me. They have seen one machine at close range. It was occupied by a monster so incredible that the report would receive no attention from me did I not know Mr. Thurston personally.

"Where have they come from? What does it mean—what is their mission? Only God knows.

"Gentlemen, I feel that I must see them. I want General Lozier to accompany me, also Dr. MacGregor, to advise me from the scientific angle. I am going to the Pacific Coast. They may not wait—that is true—but they appear to be going slowly south. I will leave tonight for San Diego. I hope to intercept them. We have strong air forces there; the Navy Department is cooperating."

He waited for no comment. "General," he ordered, "will you kindly arrange for a plane? Take an escort or not as you think best.

"Mr. Thurston and Mr. Riley will also accompany us. We want all the authoritative data we can get. This on my return will be placed before you, gentlemen, for your consideration." He rose from his chair. "I hope they wait for us," he said.

Time was when a commander called loudly for a horse, but in this day a Secretary of War is not kept waiting for transportation. Sirening motorcycles preceded them from the city. Within an hour, motors roaring wide open, propellers ripping into the summer night, lights slipping eastward three thousand feet below, the Secretary of War for the United States was on his way. And on either side from their plane stretched the arms of a V. Like a flight of gigantic wild geese, fast fighting planes of the Army air service bored steadily into the night, guarantors of safe convoy.

"The Air Service is ready," General Lozier had said. And Thurston and his pilot knew that from East coast to West, swift scout planes, whose idling engines could roar into action at a moment's notice, stood waiting; battle planes hidden in hangars would roll forth at the word—the Navy was cooperating—and at San Diego there were strong naval units, Army units, and Marine Corps.

"They don't know what we can do, what we have up our sleeve; they are feeling us out," said the Secretary. They had stopped more than once for gas and for wireless reports. He held a sheaf of typewritten briefs.

"Going slowly south. They have taken their time. Hours over San Francisco and the bay district. Repeating same tactics; fall with terrific speed to cushion against their blast of gas. Trying to draw us out, provoke an attack, make us show our strength. Well, we shall beat them to San Diego at this rate. We'll be there in a few hours."

The afternoon sun was dropping ahead of them when they sighted the water. "Eckener Pass," the pilot told them, "where the Graf Zeppelin came through. Wonder what these birds would think of a Zepp!"

"There's the ocean," he added after a time. San Diego glistened against the bare hills. "There's North Island—the Army field." He stared intently ahead, then shouted: "And there they are! Look there!"

Over the city a cluster of meteors was falling. Dark underneath, their tops shone like pure silver in the sun's slanting glare. They fell toward the city, then buried themselves in a dense cloud of steam, rebounding at once to the upper air, vapor trailing behind them.

The cloud billowed slowly. It struck the hills of the city, then lifted and vanished.

"Land at once," requested the Secretary. A flash of silver countermanded the order.

It hung there before them, a great gleaming globe, keeping always its distance ahead. It was elongated at the base, Thurston observed. From that base shot the familiar blast that turned steamy a hundred feet below as it chilled the warm air. There were round orifices, like ports, ranged around the top, where an occasional jet of vapor showed this to be a method of control. Other spots shone dark and glassy. Were they windows? He hardly realized their peril, so interested was he in the strange machine ahead.

Then: "Dodge that vapor," ordered General Lozier. The plane wavered in signal to the others and swung sharply to the left. Each man knew the flaming death that was theirs if the fire of their exhaust touched that explosive mixture of hydrogen and air. The great bubble turned with them and paralleled their course.

"He's watching us," said Riley, "giving us the once-over, the slimy devil. Ain't there a gun on this ship?"

The General addressed his superior. Even above the roar of the motors his voice seemed quiet, assured. "We must not land now," he said. "We can't land at North Island. It would focus their attention upon our defenses. That thing—whatever it is—is looking for a vulnerable spot. We must. . . . Hold on—there he goes!"

The big bulb shot upward. It slanted above them, and hovered there.

"I think he is about to attack," said the General quietly. And, to the commander of their squadron: "It's in your hands now, Captain. It's your fight."

The Captain nodded and squinted above. "He's got to throw heavier stuff than that," he remarked. A small object was falling from the cloud. It passed close to their ship.

"Half-pint size," said Cyrus Thurston, and laughed in derision. There was something ludicrous in the futility of the attack. He stuck his head from a window into the gale they created. He sheltered his eyes to try to follow the missile in its fall.

They were over the city. The criss-cross of streets made a grillwork of lines; tall buildings were dwarfed from this three-thousand-foot altitude. The sun slanted across a projecting promontory to make golden ripples on a blue sea and the city sparkled back in the clear air. Tiny white faces were massed in the streets, huddled in clusters where the futile black missile had vanished.

And then—then the city was gone. . . .

A white cloud-bank billowed and mushroomed. Slowly, it seemed to the watcher—so slowly.

It was done in the fraction of a second. Yet in that brief time his eyes registered the chaotic sweep in advance of the cloud. There came a crashing of buildings in some monster whirlwind, a white cloud engulfing it all. . . . It was rising—was on them.

"God," thought Thurston, "why can't I move!" The plane lifted and lurched. A thunder of sound crashed against them, an intolerable force. They were crushed to the floor as the plane was hurled over and upward.

Out of the mad whirling tangle of flying bodies, Thurston glimpsed one clear picture. The face of the pilot hung battered and blood-covered before him, and over the limp body the hand of Slim Riley clutched at the switch.

"Bully boy," he said dazedly, "he's cutting the motors. . . ." The thought ended in blackness.

There was no sound of engines or beating propellers when he came to his senses. Something lay heavy upon him. He pushed it to one side. It was the body of General Lozier.

He drew himself to his knees to look slowly about, rubbed stupidly at his eyes to quiet the whirl, then stared at the blood on his hand. It was so quiet—the motors—what was it that happened? Slim had reached for the switch. . . .

The whirling subsided. Before him he saw Slim Riley at the controls. He got to his feet and went unsteadily forward. It was a battered face that was lifted to him.

"She was spinning," the puffed lips were muttering slowly. "I brought her out . . . there's the field. . . ." His voice was thick; he formed the words slowly, painfully. "Got to land . . . can you take it? I'm—I'm—" He slumped limply in his seat.

Thurston's arms were uninjured. He dragged the pilot to the floor and got back of the wheel. The field was below them. There were planes taxiing out; he heard the roar of their motors. He tried the controls. The plane answered stiffly, but he managed to level off as the brown field approached.

Thurston never remembered that landing. He was trying to drag Riley from the battered plane when the first man got to him.

"Secretary of War?" he gasped. "In there. . . . Take Riley; I can walk."

"We'll get them," an officer assured him. "Knew you were coming. They sure gave you hell! But look at the city!"

Arms carried him stumbling from the field. Above the low hangars he saw smoke clouds over the bay. These and red rolling flames marked what had been an American city. Far in the heavens moved five glinting specks.

His head reeled with the thunder of engines. There were planes standing in lines and more erupting from hangars, where khaki-clad men, faces tense under leather helmets, rushed swiftly about.

"General Lozier is dead," said a voice. Thurston turned to the man. They were bringing the others. "The rest are smashed up some," the officer told him, "but I think they'll pull through."

The Secretary of War for the United States lay beside him. Men with red on their sleeves were slitting his coat. Through one good eye he squinted at Thurston. He even managed a smile.

"Well, I wanted to see them up close," he said. "They say you saved us, old man."

Thurston waved that aside. "Thank Riley——" he began, but the words ended in the roar of an exhaust. A plane darted swiftly away to shoot vertically a hundred feet in the air. Another followed and another. In a cloud of brown dust they streamed endlessly out, zooming up like angry hornets, eager to get into the fight.

"Fast little devils!" the ambulance man observed. "Here come the big boys."

A leviathan went deafeningly past. And again others came on in quick succession. Farther up the field, silvery gray planes with rudders flaunting their red, white and blue rose circling to the heights.

"That's the Navy," was the explanation. The surgeon straightened the Secretary's arm. "See them come off the big airplane carriers!"

If his remarks were part of his professional training in removing a patient's thoughts from his pain, they were effective. The Secretary stared out to sea, where two great flat-decked craft were shooting planes with the regularity of a rapid-fire gun. They stood out sharply against a bank of gray fog. Cyrus Thurston forgot his bruised body, forgot his own peril— even the inferno that raged back across the bay: he was lost in the sheer thrill of the spectacle.

Above them the sky was alive with winged ships. And from all the disorder there was order appearing. Squadron after squadron swept to battle formation. Like flights of wild ducks the true sharp-pointed V's soared off into the sky. Far above and beyond, rows of dots marked the race of swift scouts for the upper levels. And high in the clear air shone the glittering menace trailing their five plumes of gas.

A deeper detonation was merging into the uproar. It came from the ships, Thurston knew, where anti-aircraft guns poured a rain of shells into the sky. About the invaders they bloomed into clusters of smoke balls. The globes shot a thousand feet into the air. Again the shells found them, and again they retreated.

"Look!" said Thurston. "They got one!"

He groaned as a long curving arc of speed showed that the big bulb was under control. Over the ships it paused, to balance and swing, then shot to the zenith as one of the great boats exploded in a cloud of vapor.

The following blast swept the airdrome. Planes yet on the ground went like dry autumn leaves. The hangars were flattened.

Thurston cowered in awe. They were sheltered, he saw, by a slope of the ground. No ridicule now for the bombs!

A second blast marked when the gas cloud ignited. The billowing flames were blue. They writhed in tortured convulsions through the air. Endless explosions merged into one rumbling roar.

MacGregor had roused from his stupor; he rose to a sitting position. "Hydrogen," he stated positively, and pointed where great volumes of flame were sent whirling aloft. "It burns as it mixes with air." The scientist was studying intently the mammoth reaction. "But the volume," he marveled, "the volume! From that small container! Impossible!"

"Impossible," the Secretary agreed, "but . . ." He pointed with his one good arm toward the Pacific. Two great ships of steel, blackened and battered in that fiery breath, tossed helplessly upon the pitching, heaving sea. They furnished to the scientist's exclamation the only adequate reply.

Each man stared aghast into the pallid faces of his companions. "I think we have underestimated the opposition," said the Secretary of War quietly. "Look—the fog is coming in, but it's too late to save them."

The big ships were vanishing in the oncoming fog. Whirls of vapor were eddying toward them in the flame-blasted air. Above them the watchers saw dimly the five gleaming bulbs. There were airplanes attacking: the tapping of machine-gun fire came to them faintly.

Fast planes circled and swooped toward the enemy. An armada of big planes drove in from beyond. Formations were blocking space above. . . . Every branch of the service was there, Thurston exulted: the Army, Marine Corps, the Navy. He gripped hard at the dry ground in a paralysis of taut nerves. The battle was on, and in the balance hung the fate of the world.

The fog drove in fast. Through straining eyes he tried in vain to glimpse the drama spread above. The world grew dark and gray. He buried his face in his hands.

And again came the thunder. The men on the ground forced their gaze to the clouds, though they knew some fresh horror awaited.

The fog clouds reflected the blue terror above. They were riven and torn. And through them black objects were falling. Some blazed as they fell. They slipped into unthought maneuvers—they darted to earth trailing yellow and black of gasoline fires. The air was filled with the dread rain of death that was spewed from the gray clouds. Gone was the roaring of motors. The air force of the San Diego area swept in silence to the earth, whose impact alone could give kindly concealment to their flame-stricken burden.

Thurston's last control snapped. He flung himself flat to bury his face in the sheltering earth.

Only the driving necessity of work to be done saved the sanity of the survivors. The commercial broadcasting stations were demolished, a part of the fuel for the terrible furnace across the bay. But the Naval radio station was beyond on an outlying hill. The Secretary of War was in charge. An hour's work and this was again in commission to flash to the world the story of disaster. It told the world also of what lay ahead. The writing was plain. No prophet was needed to forecast the doom and destruction that awaited the earth.

Civilization was helpless. What of armies and cannon, of navies, of aircraft, when from some unreachable height these monsters within their bulbous machines could drop coldly—methodically—their diminutive bombs. And when each bomb meant shattering destruction; each explosion blasting all within a radius of miles; each followed by the blue blast of fire that melted the twisted framework of buildings and powdered the stones to make of a proud city a desolation of wreckage, black and silent beneath the cold stars. There was no crumb of comfort for the world in the terror the radio told.

Slim Riley was lying on an improvised cot when Thurston and the representative of the Bureau of Standards joined him. Four walls of a room still gave shelter in a half-wrecked building. There were candles burning: the dark was unbearable.

"Sit down," said MacGregor quietly; "we must think. . . ."

"Think!" Thurston's voice had a hysterical note. "I can't think! I mustn't think! I'll go raving crazy. . . ."

"Yes, think," said the scientist. "Has it occurred to you that that is our only weapon left?

"We must think, we must analyze. Have these devils a vulnerable spot? Is there any known means of attack? We do not know. We must learn. Here in this room we have all the direct information the world possesses of this menace. I have seen their machines in operation. You have seen more—you have looked at the monsters themselves. At one of them, anyway."

The man's voice was quiet, methodical. Mr. MacGregor was attacking a problem. Problems called for concentration; not hysterics. He could have poured the contents from a beaker without spilling a drop. His poise was needed: they were soon to make a laboratory experiment.

The door burst open to admit a wild-eyed figure that snatched up their candles and dashed them to the floor.

"Lights out!" he screamed at them. "There's one of 'em coming back." He was gone from the room.

The men sprang for the door, then turned to where Riley was clumsily crawling from his couch. An arm under each of his, and the three men stumbled from the room.

They looked about them in the night. The fog banks were high, drift-ing in from the ocean. Beneath them the air was clear; from somewhere above a hidden moon forced a pale light through the clouds. And over the ocean, close to the water, drifted a familiar shape. Familiar in its huge sleek roundness, in its funnel-shaped base where a soft roar made vaporous clouds upon the water. Familiar, too, in the wild dread it inspired.

The watchers were spellbound. To Thurston there came a fury of im-potent frenzy. It was so near! His hands trembled to tear at that door, to rip at that foul mass he knew was within. . . . The great bulb drifted past. It was nearing the shore. But its action! Its motion!

Gone was the swift certainty of control. The thing settled and sank, to rise weakly with a fresh blast of gas from its exhaust. It settled again, and passed waveringly on in the night.

Thurston was throbbingly alive with hope that was certainty. "It's been hit," he exulted; "it's been hit. Quick! After it, follow it!" He dashed for a car. There were some that had been salvaged from the less ruined buildings. He swung it quickly around where the others were waiting.

"Get a gun," he commanded. "Hey, you"—to an officer who appeared —"your pistol, man, quick! We're going after it!" He caught the tossed gun and hurried the others into the car.

"Wait," MacGregor commanded. "Would you hunt elephants with a popgun? Or these things?"

"Yes," the other told him, "or my bare hands! Are you coming, or aren't you?"

The physicist was unmoved. "The creature you saw—you said that it writhed in a bright light—you said it seemed almost in agony. There's an idea there! Yes, I'm going with you, but keep your shirt on, and think."

He turned again to the officer. "We need lights," he explained, "bright lights. What is there? Magnesium? Lights of any kind?"

"Wait." The man rushed off into the dark.

He was back in a moment to thrust a pistol into the car. "Flares," he explained. "Here's a flashlight, if you need it." The car tore at the ground as Thurston opened it wide. He drove recklessly toward the highway that followed the shore.

The high fog had thinned to a mist. A full moon was breaking through to touch with silver the white breakers hissing on the sand. It spread its full glory on dunes and sea: one more of the countless soft nights where peace and calm beauty told of an ageless existence that made naught of the red havoc of men or of monsters. It shone on the ceaseless surf that had beaten these shores before there were men, that would thunder there still when men were no more. But to the tense crouching men in the car it shone only ahead on a distant, glittering speck. A wavering reflection marked the uncertain flight of the stricken enemy.

Thurston drove like a maniac; the road carried them straight toward their quarry. What could he do when he overtook it? He neither knew nor cared. There was only the blind fury forcing him on within reach of the thing. He cursed as the lights of the car showed a bend in the road. It was leaving the shore.

He slackened their speed to drive cautiously into the sand. It dragged at the car, but he fought through to the beach, where he hoped for firm footing. The tide was out. They tore madly along the smooth sand, breakers clutching at the flying wheels.

The strange aircraft was nearer; it was plainly over the shore, they saw. Thurston groaned as it shot high in the air in an effort to clear the cliffs ahead. But the heights were no longer a refuge. Again it settled. It struck on the cliff to rebound in a last futile leap. The great pear shape tilted, then shot end over end to crash hard on the firm sand. The lights of the car struck the wreck, and they saw the shell roll over once. A ragged break was opening—the spherical top fell slowly to one side. It was still rocking as they brought the car to a stop. Filling the lower shell, they saw dimly, was a mucouslike mass that seethed and struggled in the brilliance of their lights.

MacGregor was persisting in his theory. "Keep the lights on it!" he shouted. "It can't stand the light."

While they watched, the hideous, bubbling beast oozed over the side of the broken shell to shelter itself in the shadow beneath. And again Thurston sensed the pulse and throb of life in the monstrous mass.

He saw again in his rage the streaming rain of black airplanes; saw, too, the bodies, blackened and charred as they saw them when first they tried rescue from the crashed ships; the smoke clouds and flames from the blasted city, where people—his people, men and women and little children —had met terrible death. He sprang from the car. Yet he faltered with a revulsion that was almost a nausea. His gun was gripped in his hand as he ran toward the monster.

"Come back!" shouted MacGregor. "Come back! Have you gone mad?" He was jerking at the door of the car.

Beyond the white funnel of their lights a yellow thing was moving. It twisted and flowed with incredible speed a hundred feet back to the base of the cliff. It drew itself together in a quivering heap.

An out-thrusting rock threw a sheltering shadow; the moon was low in the west. In the blackness a phosphorescence was apparent. It rippled and rose in the dark with the pulsing beat of the jellylike mass. And through it were showing two discs. Gray at first, they formed to black staring eyes.

Thurston had followed. His gun was raised as he neared it. Then out of the mass shot a serpentine arm. It whipped about him, soft, sticky, viscid—utterly loathsome. He screamed once when it clung to his face, then tore savagely and in silence at the encircling folds.

The gun! He ripped a blinding mass from his face and emptied the automatic in a stream of shots straight toward the eyes. And he knew as he fired that the effort was useless; to have shot at the milky surf would have been as vain.

The thing was pulling him irresistibly; he sank to his knees; it dragged him over the sand. He clutched at a rock. A vision was before him: the carcass of a steer, half absorbed and still bleeding on the sand of an Arizona desert. . . .

To be drawn into the smothering embrace of that glutinous mass . . . for that monstrous appetite. . . . He tore afresh at the unyielding folds, then knew MacGregor was beside him.

In the man's hand was a flashlight. The scientist risked his life on a guess. He thrust the powerful light into the clinging serpent. It was like the touch of hot iron to human flesh. The arm struggled and flailed in a paroxysm of pain.

Thurston was free. He lay gasping on the sand. But MacGregor! . . . He looked up to see him vanish in the clinging ooze. Another thick tentacle had been projected from the main mass to sweep like a whip about the man. It hissed as it whirled about him in the still air.

The flashlight was gone; Thurston's hand touched it in the sand. He sprang to his feet and pressed the switch. No light responded; the flashlight was out—broken.

A thick arm slashed and wrapped about him. . . . It beat him to the ground. The sand was moving beneath him; he was being dragged swiftly, helplessly, toward what waited in the shadow. He was smothering. . . . A blinding glare filled his eyes. . . .

The flares were still burning when he dared look about. MacGregor was pulling frantically at his arm. "Quick—quick!" he was shouting. Thurston scrambled to his feet.

One glimpse he caught of a heaving yellow mass in the white light; it twisted in horrible convulsions. They ran stumblingly—drunkenly—toward the car.

Riley was half out of the machine. He had tried to drag himself to their assistance. "I couldn't make it," he said; "then I thought of the flares."

"Thank Heaven," said MacGregor with emphasis, "it was your legs that were paralyzed, Riley, not your brain."

Thurston found his voice. "Let me have that Very pistol. If light hurts that damn thing, I am going to put a blaze of magnesium into the middle of it if I die for it."

"They're all gone," said Riley.

"Then let's get out of here. I've had enough. We can come back later on."

He got back of the wheel and slammed the door of the sedan. The moonlight was gone. The darkness was velvet just tinged with the gray that precedes the dawn. Back in the deeper blackness at the cliff base a phosphorescent something wavered and glowed. The light rippled and flowed in all directions over the mass. Thurston felt, vaguely, its mystery— the bulk was a vast, naked brain; its quiverings were like visible thought waves. . . .

The phosphorescence grew brighter. The thing was approaching. Thurston let in his clutch, but the scientist checked him.

"Wait," he implored, "wait! I wouldn't miss this for the world." He waved toward the east, where far-distant ranges were etched in palest rose.

"We know less than nothing of these creatures, in what part of the universe they are spawned, how they live, where they live—Saturn!— Mars!—the Moon! But—we shall soon know how one dies!"

The thing was coming from the cliff. In the dim grayness it seemed less yellow, less fluid. A membrane enclosed it. It was close to the car. Was it hunger that drove it, or cold rage for these puny opponents? The hollow eyes were glaring; a thick arm formed quickly to dart out toward the car. A cloud, high above, caught the color of approaching day. . . .

Before their eyes the vile mass pulsed visibly; it quivered and beat. Then, sensing its danger, it darted like some headless serpent for its machine.

It massed itself about the shattered top to heave convulsively. The top was lifted, carried toward the rest of the great metal egg. The sun's first rays made golden arrows through the distant peaks.

The struggling mass released its burden to stretch its vile length toward the dark caves under the cliffs. The last sheltering fog veil parted. The thing was halfway to the high bank when the first bright shaft of direct sunlight shot through.

Incredible in the concealment of night, the vast protoplasmic pod was doubly so in the glare of day. But it was there before them, not a hundred feet distant. And it boiled in vast tortured convulsions. The clean sunshine struck it, and the mass heaved itself into the air in a nauseous eruption, then fell limply to the earth.

The yellow membrane turned paler. Once more the staring black eyes formed to turn hopelessly toward the sheltering globe. Then the bulk flattened out on the sand. It was a jellylike mound, through which trembled endless quivering palpitations.

The sun struck hot, and before the eyes of the watching, speechless men was a sickening, horrible sight—a festering mass of corruption.

The sickening yellow was liquid. It seethed and bubbled with liberated gases; it decomposed to purplish fluid streams. A breath of wind blew in their direction. The stench from the hideous pool was overpowering, unbearable. Their heads swam in the evil breath. . . . Thurston ripped the gears into reverse, nor stopped until they were far away on the clean sand.

The tide was coming in when they returned. Gone was the vile putrescence. The waves were lapping at the base of the gleaming machine.

"We'll have to work fast," said MacGregor. "I must know, I must learn." He drew himself up and into the shattered shell.

It was of metal, some forty feet across, its framework a maze of latticed struts. The central part was clear. Here in a wide, shallow pan the monster had rested. Below this was tubing, intricate coils, massive, heavy and strong. MacGregor lowered himself upon it, Thurston was beside him. They went down into the dim bowels of the deadly instrument.

"Hydrogen," the physicist was stating. "Hydrogen—there's our starting point. A generator, obviously, forming the gas—from what? They couldn't compress it! They couldn't carry it or make it, not the volume that they evolved. But they did it, they did it!"

Close to the coils a dim light was glowing. It was a pin-point of radiance in the half-darkness about them. The two men bent closer.

"See," directed MacGregor, "it strikes on this mirror—bright metal and parabolic. It disperses the light, doesn't concentrate it! Ah! Here is another, and another. This one is bent—broken. They are adjustable. Hm! Micrometer accuracy for reducing the light. The last one could reflect through this slot. It's light that does it, Thurston; it's light that does it!"

"Does what?" Thurston had followed the other's analysis of the diffusion process. "The light that would finally reach that slot would be hardly perceptible."

"It's the agent," said MacGregor, "the activator—the catalyst! What does it strike upon? I must know—I must!"

The waves were splashing outside the shell. Thurston turned in a feverish search of the unexplored depths. There was a surprising simplicity, an absence of complicated mechanism. The generator, with its tremendous braces to carry its thrust to the framework itself, filled most of the space. Some of the ribs were thicker, he noticed. Solid metal, as if they might carry great weights. Resting upon them were ranged numbers of objects. They were like eggs, slender, and inches in length. On some were propellers. They worked through the shells on long slender rods. Each was threaded finely—an adjustable arm engaged the thread. Thurston called excitedly to the other.

"Here they are," he said. "Look! Here are the shells. Here's what blew us up!"

He pointed to the slim shafts with their little propellerlike fans. "Adjustable, see? Unwind in their fall . . . set 'em for any length of travel . . . fires the charge in the air. That's how they wiped out our air fleet."

There were others without the propellers; they had fins to hold them nose downward. On each nose was a small rounded cap.

"Detonators of some sort," said MacGregor. "We've got to have one. We must get it out quick; the tide's coming in." He laid his hands upon one of the slim, egg-shaped things. He lifted, then strained mightily. But the object did not rise; it only rolled sluggishly.

The scientist stared at it amazed. "Specific gravity," he exclaimed, "beyond anything known! There's nothing on earth . . . there is no such substance . . . no form of matter. . . ." His eyes were incredulous.

"Lots to learn," Thurston answered grimly. "We've yet to learn how to fight off the other four."

The other nodded. "Here's the secret," he said. "These shells liberate the same gas that drives the machine. Solve one and we solve both—then we learn how to combat it. But how to remove it—that is the problem. You and I can never lift this out of here."

His glance darted about. There was a small door in the metal beam. The groove in which the shells were placed led to it; it was a port for launching the projectiles. He moved it, opened it. A dash of spray struck him in the face. He glanced inquiringly at his companion.

"Dare we do it?" he asked. "Slide one of them out?"

Each man looked long into the eyes of the other. Was this, then, the end of their terrible night? One shell to be dropped—then a bursting volcano to blast them to eternity. . . .

"The boys in the planes risked it," said Thurston quietly. "They got theirs." He stopped for a broken fragment of steel. "Try one with a fan on; it hasn't a detonator."

The men pried at the slim thing. It slid slowly toward the open port. One heave and it balanced on the edge, then vanished abruptly. The spray was cold on their faces. They breathed heavily with the realization that they still lived.

There were days of horror that followed, horror tempered by a numbing paralysis of all emotions. There were bodies by thousands to be heaped in the pit where San Diego had stood, to be buried beneath countless tons of debris and dirt. Trains brought an army of helpers; airplanes came with doctors and nurses and the beginning of a mountain of supplies. The need was there; it must be met. Yet the whole world was waiting while it helped, waiting for the next blow to fall.

Telegraph service was improvised, and radio receivers rushed in. The news of the world was theirs once more. And it told of a terrified, waiting world. There would be no temporizing now on the part of the invaders. They had seen the airplanes swarming from the ground—they would know an airdrome next time from the air. Thurston had noted the windows in the great shell, windows of dull-colored glass which would protect the darkness of the interior, essential to life for the horrible occupant, but through which it could see. It could watch all directions at once.

The great shell had vanished from the shore. Pounding waves and the shifting sands of high tide had obliterated all trace. More than once had Thurston uttered devout thanks for the chance shell from an anti-aircraft gun that had entered the funnel beneath the machine, had bent and twisted the arrangement of mirrors that he and MacGregor had seen, and, exploding, had cracked and broken the domed roof of the bulb. They had learned little, but MacGregor was up north within reach of Los Angeles laboratories. And he had with him the slim cylinder of death. He was studying, thinking.

Telephone service had been established for official business. The whole nation-wide system, for that matter, was under military control. The Secretary of War had flown back to Washington. The whole world was on a war basis. War! And none knew where they should defend themselves, nor how.

An orderly rushed Thurston to the telephone. "You are wanted at once; Los Angeles calling."

The voice of MacGregor was cool and unhurried as Thurston listened. "Grab a plane, old man," he was saying, "and come up here on the jump."

The phrase brought a grim smile to Thurston's tired lips. "Hell's popping!" the Secretary of War had added on that evening those long ages before. Did MacGregor have something? Was a different kind of hell preparing to pop? The thoughts flashed through the listener's mind.

"I need a good deputy," MacGregor said. "You may be the whole works—may have to carry on—but I'll tell you it all later. Meet me at the Biltmore."

"In less than two hours," Thurston assured him.

A plane was at his disposal. Riley's legs were functioning again, after a fashion. They kept the appointment with minutes to spare.

"Come on," said MacGregor, "I'll talk to you in the car." The automobile whirled them out of the city to race off upon a winding highway that climbed into far hills. There was twenty miles of this; MacGregor had time for his talk.

"They've struck," he told the two men. "They were over Germany yesterday. The news was kept quiet; I got the last report a half-hour ago. They pretty well wiped out Berlin. No air force there. France and England sent a swarm of planes, from the reports. Poor devils! No need to tell you what they got. We've seen it firsthand. They headed west over the Atlantic, the four machines. Gave England a burst or two from high up, paused over New York, then went on. But they're here somewhere, we think. Now listen:

"How long was it from the time when you saw the first monster until we heard from them again?"

Thurston forced his mind back to those days that seemed so far in the past. He tried to remember.

"Four days," broke in Riley. "It was the fourth day after we found the devil feeding."

"Feeding!" interrupted the scientist. "That's the point I am making. Four days. Remember that!

"And we knew they were down in the Argentine five days ago—that's another item kept from a hysterical public. They slaughtered some thousands of cattle; there were scores of them found where the devils—I'll borrow Riley's word—where the devils had fed. Nothing left but hide and bones.

"And—mark this—that was four days before they appeared over Berlin.

"Why? Don't ask me. Do they have to lie quiet for that period miles up there in space? God knows. Perhaps! These things seem outside the knowledge of a deity. But enough of that! Remember: four days! Let us assume that there is this four-day waiting period. It will help us to time them. I'll come back to that later.

"Here is what I have been doing. We know that light is a means of attack. I believe that the detonators we saw on those bombs merely opened a seal in the shell and forced in a flash of some sort. I believe that radiant energy is what fires the blast.

"What is it that explodes? Nobody knows. We have opened the shell, working in the absolute blackness of a room a hundred feet underground. We found in it a powder—two powders, to be exact.

"They are mixed. One is finely divided, the other rather granular. Their specific gravity is enormous, beyond anything known to physical science unless it would be the hypothetical neutron masses we think are in certain stars. But this is not matter as we know matter; it is something new.

"Our theory is this: the hydrogen atom has been split, resolved into components, not of electrons and the proton centers, but held at some halfway point of decomposition. Matter composed only of neutrons would be heavy beyond belief. This fits the theory in that respect. But the point is this: When these solids are formed—they are dense—they represent in a cubic centimeter possibly a cubic mile of hydrogen gas under normal pressure. That's a guess, but it will give you the idea.

"Not compressed, you understand, but all the elements present in other than elemental form for the reconstruction of the atom . . . for a million billions of atoms.

"Then the light strikes it. These dense solids become instantly a gas—miles of it held in that small space.

"There you have it: the gas, the explosion, the entire absence of heat—which is to say, its terrific cold—when it expands."

Slim Riley was looking bewildered but game. "Sure, I saw it snow," he affirmed, "so I guess the rest must be O. K. But what are we going to do about it? You say light kills 'em and fires their bombs. But how can we let light into those big steel shells, or the little ones either?"

"Not through those thick walls," said MacGregor. "Not light. One of our anti-aircraft shells made a direct hit. That might not happen again in a million shots. But there are other forms of radiant energy that do penetrate steel. . . ."

The car had stopped beside a grove of eucalyptus. A barren, sun-baked hillside stretched beyond. MacGregor motioned them to alight.

Riley was afire with optimism. "And do you believe it?" he asked eagerly. "Do you believe that we've got 'em licked?"

Thurston, too, looked into MacGregor's face: Riley was not the only one who needed encouragement. But the gray eyes were suddenly tired and hopeless.

"You ask what I believe," said the scientist slowly. "I believe we are witnessing the end of the world, our world of humans, their struggles, their grave hopes and happiness and aspirations. . . ."

He was not looking at them. His gaze was far off in space.

"Men will struggle and fight with their puny weapons, but these monsters will win, and they will have their way with us. Then more of them will come. The world, I believe, is doomed. . . ."

He straightened his shoulders. "But we can die fighting," he added, and pointed over the hill.

"Over there," he said, "in the valley beyond, is a charge of their explosive and a little apparatus of mine. I intend to fire the charge from a distance of three hundred yards. I expect to be safe, perfectly safe. But accidents happen.

"In Washington a plane is being prepared. I have given instructions through hours of phoning. They are working night and day. It will contain a huge generator for producing my ray. Nothing new! Just the product of our knowledge of radiant energy up to date. But the man who flies that plane will die—horribly. No time to experiment with protection. The rays will destroy him, though he may live a month.

"I am asking you," he told Cyrus Thurston, "to handle that plane. You may be of service to the world—you may find you are utterly powerless. You surely will die. But you know the machines and the monsters; your knowledge may be of value in an attack." He waited. The silence lasted for only a moment.

"Why, sure," said Cyrus Thurston.

He looked at the eucalyptus grove with earnest appraisal. The sun made lovely shadows among their stripped trunks: the world was a beautiful place. A lingering death, MacGregor had intimated—and horrible. . . . "Why, sure," he repeated steadily.

Slim Riley shoved him firmly aside to stand facing MacGregor.

"Sure, hell!" he said. "I'm your man, Mr. MacGregor.

"What do you know about flying?" he asked Cyrus Thurston. "You're good—for a beginner. But men like you two have got brains, and I'm thinkin' the world will be needin' them. Now me, all I'm good for is holdin' a shtick"—his brogue had returned to his speech, and was evidence of his earnestness.

"And, besides"—the smile faded from his lips, and his voice was suddenly soft—"them boys we saw take their last flip was just pilots to you, just a bunch of good fighters. Well, they're buddies of mine. I fought beside some of them in France. . . . I belong!"

He grinned happily at Thurston. "Besides," he said, "what do you know about dog-fights?"

MacGregor gripped him by the hand. "You win," he said. "Report to Washington. The Secretary of War has all the dope."

He turned to Thurston. "Now for you! Get this! The enemy machines almost attacked New York. One of them came low, then went back, and the four flashed out of sight toward the west. It is my belief that New York is next, but the devils are hungry. The beast that attacked us was ravenous, remember. They need food and lots of it. You will hear of their feeding, and you can count on four days. Keep Riley informed— that's your job.

"Now I'm going over the hill. If this experiment works, there's a chance we can repeat it on a larger scale. No certainty, but a chance! I'll be back. Full instructions at the hotel in case. . . ." He vanished into the scrub growth.

"Not exactly encouraging," Thurston pondered, "but he's a good man, Mac, a good egg! Not as big a brain as the one we saw, but perhaps it's a better one—cleaner—and it's working!"

They were sheltered under the brow of the hill, but the blast from the valley beyond rocked them like an earthquake. They rushed to the top of the knoll. MacGregor was standing in the valley; he waved them a greeting and shouted something unintelligible.

The gas had mushroomed into a cloud of steamy vapor. From above came snowflakes to whirl in the churning mass, then fall to the ground. A wind came howling about them to beat upon the cloud. It swirled slowly back and down the valley. The figure of MacGregor vanished in its smothering embrace.

"Exit MacGregor!" said Cyrus Thurston softly. He held tight to the struggling figure of Slim Riley.

"He couldn't live a minute in that atmosphere of hydrogen," he explained. "They can—the devils!—but not a good egg like Mac. It's our job now—yours and mine."

Slowly the gas retreated, lifted to permit their passage down the slope.

MacGregor was a good prophet. Thurston admitted that when, four days later, he stood on the roof of the Equitable Building in lower New York.

The monsters had fed as predicted. Out in Wyoming a desolate area marked the place of their meal, where a great herd of cattle lay smothered and frozen. There were ranch houses, too, in the circle of destruction, their occupants frozen stiff as the carcasses that dotted the plains. The country had stood tense for the following blow. Only Thurston had lived in certainty of a few days' reprieve. And now had come the fourth day.

In Washington was Riley. Thurston had been in touch with him frequently.

"Sure, it's a crazy machine," the pilot had told him, "and 'tis not much
I think of it at all. Neither bullets nor guns, just this big glass contraption
and speed. She's fast, man, she's fast . . . but it's little hope I have."
And Thurston, remembering the scientist's words, was heartsore and sick
with dreadful certainty.

There were aircraft ready near New York; it was generally felt that
here was the next objective. The enemy had looked it over carefully. And
Washington, too, was guarded. The nation's capital must receive what
little help the aircraft could afford.

There were other cities waiting for destruction. If not this time—later!
The horror hung over them all.

The fourth day! And Thurston was suddenly certain of the fate of
New York. He hurried to a telephone. Of the Secretary of War he implored
assistance.

"Send your planes," he begged. "Here's where we will get it next. Send
Riley. Let's make a last stand—win or lose."

"I'll give you a squadron," was the concession. "What difference
whether they die there or here?" The voice was that of a weary man,
weary and sleepless and hopeless.

"Good-by, Cy, old man!" The click of the receiver sounded in Thurston's ear. He returned to the roof for his vigil.

To wait, to stride nervously back and forth in impotent expectancy. He
could leave, go out into open country, but what were a few days or
months—or a year—with this horror upon them? It was the end. Mac-
Gregor was right. "Good old Mac!"

There were airplanes roaring overhead. It meant . . . Thurston abruptly was cold; a chill gripped at his heart.

The paroxysm passed. He was doubled with laughter—or was it he
who was laughing? He was suddenly buoyantly carefree. Who was he that
it mattered? Cyrus Thurston—an ant! And their ant-hill was about to be
snuffed out. . . .

He walked over to a waiting group and clapped one man on the shoulder. "Well, how does it feel to be an ant?" he inquired and laughed loudly
at the jest. "You and your millions of dollars, your acres of factories, your
steamships, railroads!"

The man looked at him strangely and edged cautiously away. His eyes,
like those of the others, had a dazed, stricken look. A woman was sobbing
softly as she clung to her husband. From the streets far below came a
quavering shrillness of sound.

The planes gathered in climbing circles. Far on the horizon were four
tiny glinting specks. . . .

Thurston stared until his eyes were stinging. He was walking in a
waking sleep as he made his way to the stone coping beyond which was

the street far below. He was dead—dead!—right this minute. What were a few minutes more or less? He could climb over the coping; none of the huddled, fear-gripped group would stop him. He could step out into space and fool them, the devils. They could never kill him. . . .

What was it MacGregor had said? Good egg, MacGregor! "But we can die fighting. . . ." Yes, that was it—die fighting. But he couldn't fight; he could only wait. Well, what were the others doing, down there in the streets —in their homes? He could wait with them, die with them. . . .

He straightened slowly and drew one long breath. He looked steadily and unafraid at the advancing specks. They were larger now. He could see their round forms. The planes were less noisy: they were far up in the heights—climbing—climbing.

The bulbs came slantingly down. They were separating. Thurston wondered vaguely.

What had they done in Berlin? Yes, he remembered. Placed themselves at the four corners of a great square and wiped out the whole city in one explosion. Four bombs dropped at the same instant while they shot up to safety in the thin air. How did they communicate? Thought transference, most likely. Telepathy between those great brains, one to another. A plane was falling. It curved and swooped in a trail of flame, then fell straight toward the earth. They were fighting. . . .

Thurston stared above. There were clusters of planes diving down from on high. Machine-guns stuttered faintly. "Machine-guns—toys! Brave, that was it! 'We can die fighting.' " His thoughts were far off; it was like listening to another's mind.

The air was filled with swelling clouds. He saw them before the blast struck where he stood. The great building shuddered at the impact. There were things falling from the clouds, wrecks of planes, blazing and shattered. Still came others; he saw them faintly through the clouds. They came in from the West; they had gone far to gain altitude. They drove down from the heights—the enemy had drifted—they were over the bay.

More clouds, and another blast thundering at the city. There were specks, Thurston saw, falling into the water.

Again the invaders came down from the heights where they had escaped their own shattering attack. There was the faint roar of motors behind, from the south. The squadron from Washington passed overhead.

They surely had seen the fate that awaited. And they drove on to the attack, to strike at an enemy that shot instantly into the sky, leaving crashing destruction about the torn dead.

"Now!" said Cyrus Thurston aloud.

The big bulbs were back. They floated easily in the air, a plume of vapor billowing beneath. They were ranging to the four corners of a great square.

One plane only was left, coming in from the south, a lone straggler, late for the fray. One plane! Thurston's shoulders sagged heavily. All they had left! It went swiftly overhead. . . . It was fast—fast. Thurston suddenly knew. It was Riley in that plane.

"Go back, you fool!"—he was screaming at the top of his voice—"Back—back—you poor, damned, decent Irishman!"

Tears were streaming down his face. "His buddies," Riley had said. And this was Riley, driving swiftly in, alone, to avenge them. . . .

He saw dimly as the swift plane sped over the first bulb, on and over the second. The soft roar of gas from the machines drowned the sound of his engine. The plane passed them in silence to bank sharply toward the third corner of the forming square.

He was looking them over, Thurston thought. And the damn beasts disregarded so contemptible an opponent. He could still leave. "For God's sake, Riley, beat it—escape!"

Thurston's mind was solely on the fate of the lone voyager—until the impossible was borne in upon him.

The square was disrupted. Three great bulbs were now drifting. The wind was carrying them out toward the bay. They were coming down in a long, smooth descent. The plane shot like a winged rocket at the fourth great, shining ball. To the watcher, aghast with sudden hope, it seemed barely to crawl.

"The ray! The ray. . . ." Thurston saw as if straining eyes had pierced through the distance to see the invisible. He saw from below the swift plane the streaming, intangible ray. That was why Riley had flown closely past and above them—the ray poured from below. His throat was choking him, strangling. . . .

The last enemy took alarm. Had it seen the slow sinking of its companions, failed to hear them in reply to his mental call? The shining pear shape shot violently upward; the attacking plane rolled to a vertical bank as it missed the threatening clouds of exhaust. "What do you know about dog-fights?" And Riley had grinned . . . Riley belonged!

The bulb swelled before Thurston's eyes in its swift descent. It canted to one side to head off the struggling plane that could never escape, did not try to escape. The steady wings held true upon their straight course. From above came the silver meteor; it seemed striking at the very plane itself. It was almost upon it before it belched forth the cushioning blast of gas.

Through the forming clouds a plane bored in swiftly. It rolled slowly, was flying upside down. It was under the enemy! Its ray. . . . Thurston was thrown a score of feet away to crash helpless into the stone coping by the thunderous crash of the explosion.

There were fragments falling from a dense cloud—fragments of curved and silvery metal . . . the wing of a plane danced and fluttered in the air. . . .

"He fired its bombs," whispered Thurston in a shaking voice. "He killed the other devils where they lay—he destroyed this with its own explosive. He flew upside down to shoot up with the ray, to set off its shells. . . ."

His mind was fumbling with the miracle of it. "Clever pilot, Riley, in a dog-fight. . . ." And then he realized.

Cyrus Thurston, millionaire sportsman, sank slowly, numbly to the roof of the Equitable Building that still stood. And New York was still there . . . and the whole world. . . .

He sobbed weakly, brokenly. Through his dazed brain flashed a sudden, mind-saving thought. He laughed foolishly through his sobs.

"And you said he'd die horribly, Mac, a horrible death." His head dropped upon his arms, unconscious—and safe—with the rest of humanity.

FRANK BELKNAP LONG, Jr.

THE FLAME MIDGET

ALTHOUGH the sun was warm and shining brightly, I experienced a sense of dismal foreboding when I drew near to Richard Ashley's little South Carolinian retreat. Live oaks and palmettos screened the small laboratory building and the high yellow fence beyond. Huge, brown mushrooms, which looked like the conical dwellings of gnomes and other demons of fable with a lineage rooted deep in earth, studded the grass about me.

As I advanced over the narrow pathway which led to the laboratory door, I told myself with some bitterness that no other bacteriologist of Ashley's standing would have conducted his researches so far from the citadels of organized science. Ashley had once labored in a great white laboratory by the sea, and this little inland retreat seemed peculiarly noisome by contrast.

I don't like profuse and suggestive vegetation. I don't like little buildings nestling in the midst of clustering shadows, with dank earth odors all about them. But Ashley was a strange chap.

There is a sect of Eastern fanatics which insists that human beings are but thinly disguised counterparts of certain animals. Some men exhibit characteristics which link them with the birds of the air, others with tigers, pigs, and hyenas, and still others with the invertebrate phyla. I have often thought that the imaginative gentlemen who adhere to this cult would have classified Ashley as a mole or an earthworm. I am not being facetious when I say that Ashley was a deep one.

He resented and fled from all warm, human, personal contacts. I don't believe there was ever a woman in his life. Even friendship was impossible to him. But occasionally he'd get into an intellectual jam, or run head-on into a stone wall; and then he'd send for me. I was his good man Friday.

As a human being I didn't admire Ashley at all. But as a scientist—and I think scientists are the salt of the earth—I respected and revered him.

I was halfway down the path when the laboratory door opened suddenly and Ashley came out. He came out blinking into the warm, bright sunlight, and stood for an instant with his hand on the doorknob, peering intently through thick-lensed spectacles at the hatless and perspiring young man who was approaching him over the lawn.

He resembled a corpse. His features, especially the skin on his cheekbones, had the sickly pallor which usually accompanies a stoppage of circulation. There were black half moons under both his eyes, and the veins on his forehead stood out horribly. His expression was a peculiar one, difficult to describe. Though torment and apprehension looked out of his eyes, he seemed somehow still master of himself and even a little defiant.

"You took your time getting here, didn't you?" he said, petulantly, as though he were addressing a child.

I had come three hundred miles by bus, in response to his urgent telegram, but it was no good being angry with him. He was tormented and in trouble. A wave of compassion swept over me when I saw how his hands were shaking. When he tried to hold the door open for me he sagged against the jamb. For an instant I thought he was going to fall.

As we passed from the palmetto-shadowed lawn into the interior of the laboratory I watched him out of the corner of my eye, striving to repress his hysteria. I continued to shoot sidewise glances at him until we reached the large, sunlighted room where he worked over his slides and cultures.

His composure seemed to return a little when he shut the door of that room. He seized my hand and pressed it gratefully.

"Glad you came, John," he said. "Really glad. It was decent of you."

I looked at him. A trace of color had crept back into his cheeks. He was standing with his back to the window, gazing in a kind of trance at the long row of microscopes which had claimed his attention for five absorbing months, and the pale-blue jars full of polluted water which contained an astonishing assortment of microscopic organisms—diatoms and wheel animalcules and prototropic bacteria, all tremendously important to him in his patient labors.

The laboratory was bathed in limpid shafts of warm and slowly reddening sunlight, and I remember how the optical tubes of the microscopes glittered as I stared at them. Their brilliant sheen seemed to exert an almost hypnotic influence on my companion. But suddenly he tore his gaze away and his lean fingers fastened on my arm in a grip that made me wince.

"It's under the third microscope from the end of the table," he said, with twitching lips. "It put itself on the slide deliberately. I thought, of course, that it was a microörganism at first. But when he stared steadily up at me I found myself thinking its thoughts and obscurely sharing its incredible emotions. You see, it would have been invisible to the naked eye. With devilish cunning it put itself where I would be sure to see it."

He nodded grimly toward the long, zinc-topped table which ran the length of the laboratory. "You may look at it if you wish. The third microscope."

I turned and stared at him intently for an instant. His eyes seemed abnormally bright, but the pupils were not dilated. I am rather proficient at detecting the stigmata of drugs, hysteria, incipient insanity. Without a word I moved to the end of the table, bent over and glued my eye to the instrument of science.

For a moment I stared down at tiny, moving blobs of matter on an immersion liquid which was tinted a beautiful rose-pink. Shapes grotesque and aberrant, grotesque and revolting, weaved in and out and devoured one another on a mucid area no larger than my thumb. Hundreds of shapes with enormous, greedy "mouths" and repulsively writhing bodies darted in and out between slothful tiger animalcules, and flat, segmented horrors which bore a nauseating resemblance to the proglottids of fish tapeworms and other intestinal Cestoda.

Suddenly, as I stared, an organism shaped like an inverted bell swam toward the center of the slide and remained there with curious oscillatory movements of its tapering body. It was utterly unlike the hundreds of other loathsome, squirming little animals about it.

It was quite large, for one thing, and extremely complex in structure, consisting of an outer translucent shell or chrysalis, and a cone-shaped inner shell, also transparent and curiously iridescent in texture. As I peered more intently I perceived that the inner shell enveloped a little form, serving as a sort of matrix for the actual inhabitant of the bell.

The little form was shockingly anthropomorphic in contour. There is something horribly disturbing about the human form when it is simulated by creatures of nonsimian origin. Vaguely man-shaped fishes, reptiles and insects—and there are a few such in nature—invariably repel me. The debased but distinctly manlike face of a skate or ray fills me with detestation. I shiver when I see a frog with its legs extended. Perhaps this fear reaction is caused by man's primitive, instinct dread of being *supplanted*.

Ordinarily the revulsion is fleeting and quickly forgotten. But as I gazed down at the little shape within the bell, the horror which I experienced was pervasive, unsettling. It wasn't just a shivery premonition. I had a feeling I was gazing on something alien to normal experience, something that transcended all the grotesque parallelisms in Nature's book.

The little shape was in all respects a perfectly formed little man, dark-skinned, with pointed ears and pointed chin. Purely by accident it resembled a whimsical creation of man's fancy. Purely by accident it was goblinlike, gnomelike. But it was not whimsical. It was horrible.

A human shape, starkly nude and so small it was invisible to the naked eye tenuously suspended within a bell-shaped receptacle. It rested on its back, with its little arms tightly folded across its chest. Its abdomen, arms and legs were covered with fine, reddish hair. Suddenly, as I studied it, sick with revulsion and horror, it opened its little slitted eyes and stared steadily up at me.

Something seemed to speak to me then. Words rippled across my mind in slow, sluggish waves.

"You are his friend. I will not harm you. Do not fear me."

I spun the microscope, gasping out in unbelief and horror. Ashley laid his hand on my arm and drew me swiftly away from the table.

"You saw it?" he asked. "It spoke to you?"

I nodded. I stared at him in furious unbelief. I clenched my hands in blind terror. I said: "What is it, Richard?"

I was trembling like a leaf. My face was twitching; I could feel the blood tingling in my cheeks as it drained away.

"It has traveled for hundreds of light years through interstellar space," he said. "Its home is on a tiny planet encircling a sun of inconceivable density in a star cluster more remote than Earth's nearest stellar neighbors, but an immeasurable distance from the rim of the galaxy. It came in a little space vessel which is hidden somewhere in the laboratory. It refuses to tell me where the vessel is concealed. Through some undreamed-of development of the power of telepathy it can transmit a whole sequence of thought images in a flash."

I nodded grimly. "I know," I said. "It spoke to me. At least, words formed in my mind."

Ashley grasped at that admission as though it were a life line which I had flung him suddenly in sheer compassion and at grave risk to myself.

"Then you do believe, John. I'm glad. Skepticism would be dangerous now. It can sense all opposition to me."

He fell silent an instant. He was staring with fixed intentness at the tube of the microscope which contained the little horror.

"I know that it is difficult to accept a reality in startling opposition to the whole trend of modern scientific thought," he said. "Since the age of Kepler the thinking portion of mankind has inordinately glorified bigness, vastness, extension in space and time. Scientifically minded men have thrown their thoughts occasionally outward toward remote constellations and mysteriously receding nebulæ, and dreamed vain dreams in which mere size has figured as a stepping stone to the eternal.

"But why should size be of any particular importance to the mysterious architect of the mysterious universe?"

"One associates size with force, power," I replied, my eyes on his white face.

"But size and power are not coincidental throughout the universe," exclaimed Ashley. "The radiant force fields at the core of many midget suns would shatter the stellar giants into glowing fragments. Van Maanen's star is no larger than our Earth, but its density exceeds that of the solar disk. If this little star came within a few million miles of Pluto s orbit, it would disrupt the Sun and turn it into a nova. A tiny fragment of its inconceivably concentrated substance no larger than a bolide would pull mighty Jupiter from its orbit. A few spoonfuls of radiant matter from its core colliding with the Earth's crust would cause a more cataclysmic upheaval than the eruption of a major volcano.

"In size it is simply negligible in the cosmic scheme. Compared to the Sun it is a gadfly speck, but it would be capable of blasting a heavenly body millions of times larger than itself.

"The little figure which you have seen was spawned on an unimaginably energized planet no larger than a large meteor, encircling a sun heavier than Van Maanen's star, but smaller in circumference than little Venus. A pygmy sun containing within its tiny bulk a concentration of matter so intense that its atoms may actually have become negative in mass.

"The thin, transparent sheaths in which the little figure appears to float are nonconductive energy sheaths. When the figure extends its arms the sheaths divide laterally, and a searing emanation streams out."

Ashley's voice rose in pitch. He appeared to be approaching a crisis in his recital.

"That radiation surpasses high-frequency electric waves in its destructive power.

"You are, of course, familiar with the theories of the noted research biologist Dr. George Crile as to the nature and origin of life. Crile believes all life is electromagnetic in nature and directly activated by the solar disk. He affirms that the Sun shines with unabated radiance in the protoplasm of animals.

"According to Crile every cell of an animal body contains tiny centers of radiation called radiogens, which have a temperature of six thousand degrees centigrade. These minute hot points are invisible even under the most powerful microscopes. Tiny, incandescent suns, hotter than the solar photosphere and more mysterious than the atom, they generate fields of force within us, producing in all the cells of our bodies the phenomenon of life. But these force fields do not flow outward from our bodies in searing emanations. They are so inconceivably tiny and infrequently spaced that their excess heat is dissipated by the water in our tissues.

"The little figure which you have seen is more lethally endowed. The product of a hotter and more concentrated sun, its radiant energies are not damped by what Crile has defined as interradiogen spaces within itself. Its entire body is a mass of radiogens. When the protective sheaths are withdrawn this terrific energy flows outward in channeled waves, searing everything in its path.

"Two days ago, in my presence, it withdrew the sheaths. One channeled wave streamed eastward across the Atlantic Ocean and was dissipated before it reached the shores of Europe. But the one that streamed westward killed twenty-four human beings.

"One death occurred right in this vicinity. A tenant farmer named Jake

Saunders was sitting quietly in the living room of his home with his wife and children when the ray pierced him. He threw up his arms, cried out and slumped jerkily to the floor. His flesh turned black. Although the Sun was shining in a cloudless sky, the local papers blindly assumed that a bolt of lightning had blasted the poor devil. In a New York paper which arrived yesterday all of the other deaths are casually ascribed to freak electrical storms throughout the country. One would think that such tragedies were of everyday occurrence."

"But if the wave crossed the continent thousands should have perished," I gasped. "How do you account for the fact that only a few were fatally affected?"

"The unimaginable thinness of the radiant beam," he said. "It is a single lethal filament, nonspreading until it contacts an animal substance. Then it spreads in all directions, blasting and searing the body in its path. Before it leaves the body it becomes a narrow thread of force again. Extend a thin wire from New York to San Francisco, and the number of men and animals directly in its path would be small indeed."

I was too horrified to comment. I glanced at the microscope, in silent dread and revulsion. Somehow I could not doubt one word of Ashley's recital. I had seen the little shape with my own eyes. It had stared up at me and communicated with me. Only its assurances of amity awakened my skepticism, causing my mood to grow darker as I mused on the implications of Ashley's words.

"I have been in constant communication with it for three days," said Ashley. "It was drawn to me because it believes I am superior to most men in intellectual acumen. The quality of my mind exerted a profound influence upon it, attracting it like a lodestone.

"The world from which it comes would be incomprehensible to us. Its inhabitants are motivated by passions and desires which are alien to humanity. The little shape is a sort of emissary, sent across space by its myriad brethren to study conditions on the remote terrestrial globe at first hand. Although they possess instruments of observation infinitely more complex and powerful than our telescopes, and have studied Earth from afar, they have never before attempted to communicate with us. When the little baroque returns its brethren will come in vast numbers.

"When they come they will probably exterminate the entire human race. The little shape does not admire us, and when it returns its observations will reflect no credit on mankind. It thinks us needlessly irrational and cruel. Our custom of settling disputes by a process of wholesale extermination it regards as akin to the savagery of animals. It thinks that our mechanical achievements are less remarkable than the social life of the ants and bees. It regards us as unnecessary excrescences on the face of a comparatively pleasant little globe in space which should afford limitless opportunities for colonization.

"As an isolated individual it respects and even admires me. There is nothing paradoxical in this. Mankind as a whole shuns and fears the dangerous animals which individual men frequently cherish as pets. It regards me as a kind of superior pet—possessing certain likable characteristics, but sharing a heritage, and following conduct patterns which are repellent to it."

I glanced at the microscope in apprehension. His candor disturbed, frightened me.

"Isn't it reading your thoughts now?" I asked.

"No. One must be within two or three feet of it. Its telepathic equipment breaks down beyond a certain radius. It cannot overhear us. It does not even know that I intend to destroy it."

I stared at him, startled.

"If it does not return," he said, "they will not raid Earth immediately. They will send another emissary to search for it. Although they can travel with the velocity of light, the star cluster from which they come is so remote that another emissary would not arrive before the twenty-second century. Another two hundred and fifty years would elapse before that emissary could return and make his report. The first raiders would not arrive before 2700.

"In eight hundred years mankind may succeed in developing some means of defense sufficiently powerful to repel and destroy them. Atomic armaments, perhaps."

He ceased speaking abruptly. I noticed that the muscles of his face were twitching spasmodically. He was obviously laboring under an almost unbearable emotional strain. Suddenly his hands went into one of the spacious pockets of his laboratory frock, and emerged with a flat, metallic object no larger than a cigarette case.

"This is used for purposes of demonstration in the metal industries," he said, as he extended it toward me on the palm of his hand. "It is a midget induction furnace. It will melt virtually all known metals in three or four seconds—even molybdenum, which has a melting point of nearly five thousand degrees Fahrenheit."

I stared at the object, fascinated. Superficially it resembled a little crystal radio set. It consisted merely of a small, spool-like object about a half inch in height, resting in the center of a flat surface of highly burnished copper. Two curving prongs with insulated stems branched from both sides of the little spool and projected a full inch beyond the gleaming baseboard.

"High-frequency waves set up a searing, blasting heat within the metal a few seconds after the furnace is turned on," he said. "I telegraphed to Charleston for the apparatus yesterday, but it did not arrive until an hour ago."

I had a pretty good idea then why he had sent for me. Richard Ashley was about to endanger his life. If the little horror survived the terrific heat generated by the blast furnace, it would certainly turn upon Ashley and destroy him. It would destroy both Ashley and myself. And since its protective sheaths could resist an *internal* incandescence of thousands of degrees centigrade, Ashley would be taking a long, grim chance.

My friend seemed to sense what was passing through my mind. "Perhaps you'd better not stay, John," he said. "I've no right to ask you to risk your neck."

"You want me to stay, don't you?" I asked.

"Yes, but—"

"Then I will. When do we—burn it?"

He looked at me steadily for an instant. I had a shaky feeling he was weighing the chances against us.

"No sense in putting it off," he said.

Unwaveringly, I met and held his gaze. "Right, Richard," I murmured.

"It will be difficult," he said. "Difficult and—dangerous. It will start reading my mind as soon as I approach the microscope, and if it becomes suspicious it will remove itself before the slide begins to melt."

He smiled with an effort. His hand shot out. "I'll try to make my thoughts behave," he said. "Wish me luck."

"I know you'll succeed, Richard," I murmured, as I returned the pressure of his fingers. He had laid the little induction furnace on the edge of the laboratory table. With a grim nod he picked it up and advanced with rapid steps toward the long row of sun-dappled microscopes. His broad back concealed the gleaming instruments from view as he approached the far end of the laboratory.

I watched him with indrawn breath. When he reached the extremity of the table he swung about and stooped a little. I saw his elbow jerk back. There was a faint, sputtering sound. It was followed by a blinding flash of polychromatic light. For an instant he remained bending above the table. Then he straightened and came slowly back to where I was standing. His face was gray.

"There isn't much left of the microscope," he said. "The slide is liquid, molten. Take a look at it."

Curiosity drew me swiftly toward the end of the table. The little induction furnace had indeed flamed destructively. The microscope was a twisted, blackened wreck. The optical tube lay prone in a gleaming mass of metallic ooze on the zinc table top.

Ashley had moved to the opposite side of the laboratory and was stripping off his soiled and faded frock.

"I'm going for a walk," he exclaimed. "I've got to get out in the open, away from all this. I'll crack if I don't."

I nodded sympathetically. "I'll go with you," I said.

A few minutes later we were walking side by side along a narrow dirt road under the open sky. Crickets shrilled in dust barrows under our feet, and warblers, wrens and chickadees chirped from the low branches of shortleaf palms and tulip trees. On both sides of us gently rolling hills stretched away to glimmering, haze-obscured horizons.

I glanced at my companion in deep concern. He moved like a man entranced, his body swaying a little as he advanced over the sun-baked soil of the deeply rutted and winding roadway. My concern increased when I perceived that he was silently muttering to himself.

With a shudder I tore my gaze from his white face and stared straight before me. For a long time I continued to keep pace with him in silence, my mind occupied with plans for getting him away from the little laboratory and into an environment where the memories of his grim, three-day ordeal would cease to play on his tormented nerves.

Suddenly he lurched against me. I heard him gasp in horror. A chill premonition swept over me as I swung about, staring. His features were contorted with fright and he was trembling all over.

"*It's still alive*," he choked. "It just spoke to me again. It has taken refuge *inside my body*."

"Richard," I exclaimed, "have you gone mad?"

"No," he choked. "It is really in my body. It says that when it came to Earth it berthed the space ship in my right kidney."

"Impossible!" I gasped. "How could it—"

"The space ship is microscopic, too. It can pass freely through all the organs and tissues of a human body. For three days the tiny vessel has been suspended in the pelvis of my right kidney by radiant microscopic mooring lines."

His voice rose hysterically. "It suspected that I intended to destroy it. It left the slide and listened while we were discussing it. When I blasted the slide it had already returned to the space ship."

His eyes suddenly took on a glaze of terror. "John—it has decided to kill me. It says that it will *take off* from my body, and carry me with it high above the Earth. It is mocking me, taunting me. It says that I will perish in splendor, will shine as a star. When the ship takes off the energy blast will turn my body into a field of radiant force. I will become a—"

Suddenly his speech congealed. He threw out his arms and staggered violently backward. For four or five seconds he continued to move away from me, his tottering steps swiftly increasing the distance between us. He moved with an incredible acceleration, his limbs trembling and jerking and his torso twisting about as though invisible forces were tugging at every atom of his receding body, pulling him in divergent directions and threatening to tear his fleshly tenement asunder.

There was an instant of utter silence while the air about me seemed visibly to quiver; to quiver and shake and buckle into folds like a film of violently agitated water. The gently sloping hills, the clustering pines and tulip trees and the winding road ahead all quivered in ominous instability. Then, suddenly, the whole of this wavering, fearfully silent world exploded in a blast of sound.

For a moment there was only sound. Then Richard Ashley rose from the Earth. In a burst of salmon-colored flame he shot high into the air, his body rotating like a revolving pinwheel.

He rose with tremendous velocity. As he soared toward the clouds long tongues of sanguineous fire shot from his body, ensheathing his limbs in a radiance so dazzling that even the sunlight failed to obscure it. He became a vessel of lucent flame, a day star throbbingly aglow. For an instant he flamed more redly than red Aldebaran high in the pale heavens. Then, like a comet receding from its zenith, the radiant force fields which streamed luminously outward in all directions from his skyward-soaring body dimmed and dwindled and were lost to view in the wide firmament.

Richard Ashley's body was never found. The local police conducted a thorough search for it, and even attempted to wrest a confession from me by cruel and illegal means. I had made up an absurd little story which they did not believe, but were unable to disprove or discredit. Eventually they were compelled to release me.

But though I am once more free to come and go as I please, I have made the tragic discovery that anxiety can take on many and terrible forms. Night and day I am haunted by a memory which I cannot erase from my mind; a fear which has assumed the compulsive character of a phobia. I know that some day it and its kind will return across wide gulfs of space and wage relentless war on all of humankind. In a peculiar, but very real, sense I have become Richard Ashley's heir. When he vanished into the sky he left behind him a legacy of horror which will darken my days until I am one again with the blind flux of the mysterious universe.

ANTHONY BOUCHER

EXPEDITION

THE following is a transcript of the recorded two-way messages between Mars and the field expedition to the satellite of the third planet.

First Interplanetary Exploratory Expedition to Central Receiving Station:
What has the Great One achieved?

Murvin, Central Receiving Station, to First Interplanetary Exploratory Expedition:
All right, boys. I'll play games. What *has* the Great One achieved? And when are we going to get a report on it?

Falzik, First Interplanetary Exploratory Expedition, to Murvin, Central Receiving Station:
Haven't you any sense of historical moments? That was the first interplanetary message ever sent. It had to be worthy of the occasion. Trubz spent a long time working on the psychology of it while I prepared the report. Those words are going to live down through the ages of our planet.

Murvin to Falzik:
All right. Swell. You'll be just as extinct while they live on. Now how's about that report?

Report of First Interplanetary Exploratory Expedition, presented by Falzik, specialist in reporting:
The First Interplanetary Exploratory Expedition has landed successfully upon the satellite of the third planet. The personnel of this expedition consists of Karnim, specialist in astrogation; Halov, specialist in life sci-

ences; Trubz, specialist in psychology; Lilil, specialist- in the art; and Falzik, specialist in reporting.

The trip itself proved unimportant for general reporting. Special aspects of difficulties encountered and overcome will appear in the detailed individual report of Karnim after the return of the expedition. The others, in particular Trubz and Lilil, were largely unaware of these difficulties. To anyone save the specialist in astrogation, the trip seemed nowise different, except in length, from a vacation excursion to one of our own satellites.

The majority theory is apparently vindicated here on this satellite of the third planet. It does not sustain life. According to Halov, specialist in life sciences, it is not a question of can not; since life of some strange sort might conceivably exist under any conditions save those of a perfect vacuum. But so far as can be ascertained there is no life of any remotely recognizable form upon this satellite.

This globe is dead. It is so dead that one may say the word without fear. The euphemism *extinct* would be too mild for the absolute and utter deadness here. It is so dead that the thought of death is not terrifying.

Trubz is now working on the psychology of that.

Observation checks the previous calculations that one face of this satellite is always turned towards its world and one always from it, the period of rotation coinciding exactly with the orbital period. There seems to be no difference in nature between the two sides; but obviously the far side is the proper site for the erection of our temporary dome. If the hypothetical inhabitants of the third planet have progressed to the use of astronomical instruments, we do not wish to give them warning of our approach by establishing ourselves in the full sight of those instruments.

The absence of life on this satellite naturally proved a serious disappointment to Halov, but even more so to Lilil, who felt inspired to improvise a particularly ingenious specimen of his art. Fortunately the stores of the ship had provided for such an emergency and the resultant improvisation was one of the greatest triumphs of Lilil's great career. We are now about to take our first rest after the trip, and our minds are aglow with the charm and beauty of his exquisite work.

Murvin to Falzik:

All right. Report received and very welcome. But can't you give us more color? Physical description of the satellite—minerals present—exploitation possibilities—anything like that? Some of us are more interested in those than in Trubz's psychology or even Lilil's practice of the art.

Falzik to Murvin:

What are you asking for? You know as well as I do the purpose of this expedition: to discover other intelligent forms of life. And you know the double purpose behind that purpose: to verify by comparison the psychological explanation of our race-dominant fear of death (if this were a formal dispatch I'd censor that to "extinction"), and to open up new avenues of creation in the art.

That's why the personnel of this expedition, save for the astrogator, was chosen for its usefulness *if* we discover life. Until we do, our talents as specialists are wasted. We don't know about minerals and topography. Wait for the next expedition's report on them.

If you want color, our next report should have it. It will come from the third planet itself. We've established our temporary base here easily, and are blasting off very soon for what our scientists have always maintained is the most probable source of life in this system.

Murvin to Falzik:

All right. And if you find life, I owe you a sarbel dinner at Noku's.

Falzik to Murvin:

Sarbel for two, please! Though what we've found, the Great One only— but go on to the report.

Report of First Interplanetary Exploratory Expedition, presented by Falzik, specialist in reporting:

The site of the Expedition's landing on the third planet was chosen more or less at random. It is situated on the third in size of the five continents, not far from the shore of the largest ocean. It is approximately indicated by the coordinates —— and ——[1] in Kubril's chart of the planet.

In the relatively slow final period of our approach, we were able to observe that the oceans of the third planet are indeed true liquids and not merely beds of molten metal, as has been conjectured by some of our scientists. We were more elated to observe definite signs of intelligent life. We glimpsed many structures which only the most unimaginative materialist could attribute to natural accident, and the fact that these structures tend to cluster together in great numbers indicates an organized and communal civilization.

That at least was our first uplifting emotional reaction, as yet not completely verified. The place of our landing is free from such structures, and from almost everything else. It is as purely arid a desert as the region about Krinavizhd, which in some respects it strongly resembles.

At first we saw no signs of life whatsoever, which is as we could have wished it. An exploratory expedition does not want a welcoming committee, complete with spoken speeches and seven-string sridars. There was a sparse amount of vegetation, apparently in an untended state of nature, but nothing to indicate the presence of animal life until we saw the road.

It was an exceedingly primitive and clumsy road, consisting of little more than a ribbon of space from which the vegetation had been cleared; but it was a sign, and we followed it, to be rewarded shortly by our first

[1] The mathematical signs indicating these coordinates are, unfortunately, typographically impossible to reproduce.—*Editor.*

glimpse of moving life. This was some form of apodal being, approximately one-fifth of the length of one of us, which glided across the road and disappeared before we could make any attempt at communication.

We continued along the road for some time, suffering severely from the unaccustomed gravity and the heavy atmosphere, but spurred on by the joyous hope of fulfilling the aim of the expedition. Lilil in particular evinced an inspired elation at the hope of finding new subjects for his great compositions.

The sun, markedly closer and hotter here on the third planet, was setting when at last we made our first contact with third-planet life. This being was small, about the length of the first joint of one's foreleg, covered with fur of pure white, save for the brown dust of the desert, and quadrupedal. It was frisking in a patch of shade, seeming to rejoice in the setting of the sun and the lowering of the temperature. With its forelegs it performed some elaborate and to us incomprehensible ritual with a red ball.

Halov approached it and attracted its attention by a creaking of his wing-rudiments. It evinced no fear, but instantly rolled the red ball in his direction. Halov deftly avoided this possible weapon. (We later examined it and found it to be harmless, at least to any form of life known to us; its purpose remains a mystery. Trubz is working on the psychology of it.) He then—optimistically, but to my mind foolishly—began the fifth approach, the one developed for beings of a civilization roughly parallel to our own.

It was a complete failure. The white thing understood nothing of what Halov scratched in the ground, but persisted in trying to wrench from his digits the stick with which he scratched. Halov reluctantly retreated through the approaches down to approach one (designed for beings of the approximate mental level of the Narbian aborigines) but the creature paid no heed to them and insisted upon performing with the moving stick some ritual similar to that which it had practiced with the ball.

By this time we were all weary of these fruitless efforts, so that it came as a marked relief when Lilil announced that he had been inspired to improvise. The exquisite perfection of his art refreshed us and we continued our search with renewed vitality, though not before Halov had examined the corpse of the white creature and determined that it was indubitably similar to the mammals, though many times larger than any form of mammalian life has ever become on our planet.

Some of us thought whimsically of that favorite fantasy of the science-fiction composers—the outsize mammals who will attack and destroy our race. But we had not yet seen anything.

Murvin to Falzik:

That's a fine way to end a dispatch. You've got me all agog. Has the Monster Mammal King got you in his clutches?

Falzik to Murvin:

Sorry. I didn't intend to be sensational. It is simply that we've been learning so much here through—well, yes, you can call him the Monster Mammal King, though the fictionists would be disappointed in him—that it's hard to find time enough for reports. But here is more.

Report of First Interplanetary Exploratory Expedition, presented by Falzik, specialist in reporting:

The sun was almost down when we saw the first intelligent being ever beheld by one of our race outside of our planet. He (for we learned afterwards that he was male, and it would be unjust to refer to an intelligent being as *it*) was lying on the ground in the shade of a structure—a far smaller structure than those we had glimpsed in passing, and apparently in a sad state of dilapidation.

In this posture the fact was not markedly noticeable, but he is a biped. Used as we are on our own planet to many forms of life—octopods (though the Great One be thanked that those terrors are nearly wiped out) ourselves hexapods, and the pesky little mammalian tetrapods—a biped still seems to us something strange and mythical. A logical possibility, but not a likelihood. The length of body of this one is approximately that of a small member of our own race.

He held a container apparently of glass in one foreleg (there must be some other term to use of bipeds, since the front limbs are not used as legs) and was drinking from it when he spied us. He choked on his drink, looked away, then returned his gaze to us and stared for a long time. At last he blinked his eyes, groaned aloud, and hurled the glass container far away.

Halov now advanced toward him. He backed away, reached one forelimb inside the structure, and brought it out clasping a long metal rod, with a handle of some vegetable material. This he pointed at Halov, and a loud noise ensued. At the time some of us thought this was the being's speech, but now we know it came from the rod, which apparently propelled some form of metal missile against Halov.

The missile, of course, bounced harmlessly off Halov's armor (he prides himself on keeping in condition) and our specialist in life sciences continued to advance toward the biped, who dropped the rod and leaned back against the structure. For the first time we heard his voice, which is extraordinarily low in pitch. We have not yet fully deciphered his language, but I have, as instructed, been keeping full phonetic transcriptions of his every remark. Trubz has calculated psychologically that the meaning of this remark must be:

"Ministers of the Great One, be gracious to me!"

The phonetic transcription is as follows: [1]

---

[1] For the convenience of the reader, these transcriptions have been retranscribed into the conventional biped spelling.—*Editor.*

AND THEY TALK ABOUT PINK ELEPHANTS!

He watched awestruck as Halov, undaunted by his former experience, again went directly into the fifth approach. The stick in Halov's digits traced a circle in the dirt with rays coming out of it, then pointed up at the setting sun.

The biped moved his head forward and back and spoke again. Trubz's conjecture here is:

"The great sun, the giver of life."

Phonetic transcription:

BUGS THAT DRAW PRETTY PICTURES YET!

Then Halov drew a series of concentric ellipses of dotted lines about the figure of the sun. He drew tiny circles on these orbits to indicate the first and second planets, then larger ones to indicate the third and our own. The biped was by now following the drawing with intense absorption.

Halov now pointed to the drawing of the third planet, then to the biped, and back again. The biped once more moved his head forward, apparently as a gesture of agreement. Finally Halov in like manner pointed to the fourth planet, to himself, and back again, and likewise in turn for each of us.

The biped's face was blank for a moment. Then he himself took a stick and pointed from the fourth planet to Halov, saying, according to Trubz:

"This is really true?"

Transcription:

YOU MEAN YOU'RE MARTIANS?

Halov imitated the head movement of agreement. The biped dropped his stick and gasped out sounds which Trubz is sure were the invocation of the name of a potent deity. Transcription:

ORSON WELLES!

We had all meanwhile been groping with the biped's thought patterns, though no success had attended our efforts. In the first place, his projection was almost nil; his race is apparently quite unaccustomed to telepathic communication. In the second place, of course, it is next to impossible to read alien thought patterns without some fixed point of reference.

Just as we could never have deciphered the ancient writings of the Khrugs without the discovery of the Burdarno Stone which gave the same inscription in their language and in an antique form of our own, so we could not attempt to decode this biped's thought patterns until we knew what they were like on a given known subject.

We now began to perceive some of his patterns of the Solar System and for our respective worlds. Halov went on to the second stage of the fifth approach. He took a group of small rocks, isolated one, held up one digit, and drew the figure one in the dirt. The biped seemed puzzled. Then Halov added another rock to the first, held up two digits, and drew the figure two, and so on for three and four. Now the biped seemed enlightened and made his agreement gesture. He also held up one digit and drew a figure beside Halov's.

His *one* is the same as ours—a not too surprising fact. Trubz has been working on the psychology of it and has decided that the figure one is probably a simple straight line in almost any numerical system. His other figures differed markedly from ours, but his intention was clear and we could to some extent follow his patterns.

Using both forelegs, Halov went on to five, six, and seven with the biped writing down his number likewise. Then Halov held up all his digits and wrote a one followed by the dot which represents zero and is the essence of any mathematical intelligence. This was the crucial moment— did these bipeds know how to calculate or was their numerical system purely primitive?

The biped held up eight digits and wrote a new figure, a conjoined pair of circles. Halov, looking worried, added another rock to his group and wrote down two ones. The biped wrote a circle with a tail to it. Halov added another rock and wrote a one followed by a two. The biped wrote a one followed by a circle.

Then Halov understood. We have always used an octonary system, but our mathematicians have long realized the possibility of others: a system of two, for instance, in which 11 would mean three, a system of four (the folk speech even contains survivals of such a system) in which 11 would mean five. For 11 means simply the first power of the number which is your base, plus one. This system of the bipeds obviously employs a decimal base.

(Trubz has been working on the psychology of this. He explains it by the fact that the bipeds have five digits on each forelimb, or a total of ten, whereas we have four each, a total of eight.)

Halov now beckoned to Karnim, who as astrogator is the best mathematician among us, and asked him to take over. He studied for a moment the biped's numbers, adjusted his mind rapidly to the (for the layman) hopeless confusion of a decimal system, and went ahead with simple mathematical operations. The biped followed him not unskillfully, while the rest of us concentrated on his thought patterns and began to gather their shape and nature.

The growing darkness bothered the biped before it incommoded Karnim. He rose from his squatting position over the numerals and went into the structure, the interior of which was soon alight. He came back to the doorway and beckoned us to enter. As we did so, he spoke words which Trubz conjectures to mean:

"Enter my abode and stay in peace, O emissaries from the fourth planet."

Phonetic transcription:

YOU'LL BE GONE IN THE MORNING AND WILL I HAVE A HEAD!

Murvin to Falzik:

What a yarn! A planet of intelligent beings! What a future for the art! Maybe I never was sold on this expedition, but I am now. Keep the reports coming. And include as much phonetic transcription as you can— the specialists are working on what you've sent and are inclined to doubt some of Trubz' interpretations. Also tell Trubz to get to work as soon as possible on the psychological problem of extinction. If this being's a mammal, he should help.

[Several reports are omitted here, dealing chiefly with the gradually acquired skill of the expedition in reading a portion of the biped's thought patterns and in speaking a few words of his language.]

Report of First Interplanetary Exploratory Expedition, presented by Falzik, specialist in reporting:

Halov and Trubz agree that we should stay with this *man* (for such we have by now learned is the name of his race) until we have learned as much from him as we can. He has accepted us now and is almost at ease with us, though the morning after our arrival, for some peculiar reason, he seemed even more surprised to see us than when we first appeared.

We can learn much more from him, now that he is used to us, than we could from the dwellers in the large massed structures, and after we are well-versed in his civilization we stand much more chance of being accepted peaceably.

We have been here now for three of the days of this planet, absorbed in our new learning. (All save Lilil, who is fretful because he has not practiced his art for so long. I have occasionally seen him eying the *man* speculatively.) By using a mixture of telepathy, sign language, and speech, we can by now discuss many things, though speech comes with difficulty to one who has used it only on formal and fixed occasions.

For instance we have learned why this *man* lives alone far from his fellows. His specialty is the making of pictures with what he calls a *camera*, a contrivance which records the effect of different intensities of light upon a salt of silver—a far more complex method than our means of making pictures with photosensitized elduron, but one producing much the same results. He has taken pictures of us, though he seems doubtful that any other *man* will ever believe the record of his *camera*.

At present he is engaged in a series of pictures of aspects of the desert, an undertaking which he seems to regard not as a useful function but as an art of some strange sort. Trubz is working on the psychology of it and says that a reproductive and imitative art is conceivable, but Lilil is scornful of the notion.

Today he showed us many pictures of other *mans* and of their cities and structures. *Man* is a thin-skinned and almost hairless animal. This *man* of ours goes almost naked, but that is apparently because of the desert heat. Normally a *man* makes up for his absence of hair by wearing a sort of artificial fur of varying shapes known as *clothes*. To judge from the pictures shown us by the *man*, this is true only of the male of the species. The female never covers her bare skin in any way.

Examination of these pictures of females shown us by our *man* fully confirms our theory that the animal *man* is a mammal.

The display of pictures ended with an episode still not quite clear to us. Ever since our arrival, the *man* has been worrying and talking about something apparently lost—something called a *kitten*. The thought pattern was not familiar enough to gather its nature, until he showed us a picture of the small white beast which we had first met and we recognized in his mind this *kitten*-pattern. He seemed proud of the picture, which showed the beast in its ritual with the ball, but still worried, and asked us, according to Trubz, if we knew anything of its whereabouts. Transcription:

YOU WOULDN'T ANY OF YOU BIG BUGS KNOW WHAT THE DEVIL'S BECOME OF THAT KITTEN, WOULD YOU?

Thereupon Lilil arose in his full creative pride and led the *man* to the place where we had met the *kitten*. The corpse was by now withered in the desert sun, and I admit that it was difficult to gather from such a spectacle the greatness of Lilil's art, but we were not prepared for the *man's* reaction.

His face grew exceedingly red and a fluid formed in his eyes. He clenched his digits and made curious gestures with them. His words were uttered brokenly and exceedingly difficult to transcribe. Trubz has not yet conjectured their meaning, but the transcription reads:

YOU DID THAT? TO A POOR HARMLESS LITTLE KITTEN? WHY, YOU—[1]

His attitude has not been the same toward us since. Trubz is working on the psychology of it.

Murvin to Falzik:

Tell Trubz to work on the major psychological problem. Your backers are getting impatient.

Falzik to Murvin:

I think that last report was an aspect of it. But I'm still puzzled. See what you can make of this one.

Report of First Interplanetary Exploratory Expedition, presented by Falzik, specialist in reporting:

Tonight Halov and Trubz attempted to present the great psychological problem to the *man*. To present such a problem in our confusion of thoughts, language and gesture is not easy, but I think that to some extent they succeeded.

[1] The remainder of this transcription has been suppressed for this audience.—*Editor.*

They stated it in its simplest form: Our race is obsessed by a terrible fear of extinction. We will each of us do anything to avoid his persona! extinction. No such obsession has ever been observed among the minute mammalian pests of our planet.

Now, is our terror a part of our intelligence? Does intelligence necessarily imply and bring with it a frantic clinging to the life that supports us? Or does this terror stem from our being what we are, rather than mammals? A mammal brings forth its young directly; the young are a direct continuation of the life of the old. But with us a half dozen specialized individuals bring forth all the young. The rest of us have no part in it; our lives are dead ends, and we dread the approach of that blank wall.

Our psychologists have battled over this question for generations. Would another—say, a mammalian—form of intelligent life have such an obsession? Here we had an intelligent mammal. Could he answer us?

I give the transcription of his answer, as yet not fully deciphered:

I THINK I GET WHAT YOU MEAN. AND I THINK THE ANSWER IS A LITTLE OF BOTH. O.K., SO WE'RE INTELLIGENT MAMMALS. WE HAVE MORE FEAR OF DEATH THAN THE UNINTELLIGENT, LIKE THE POOR LITTLE KITTEN YOU BUTCHERED; BUT CERTAINLY NOT SUCH A DOMINANT OBSESSION AS I GATHER YOUR RACE HAS.

Trubz thinks that this was an ambiguous answer, which will not satisfy either party among our specialists in psychology.

We then proposed, as a sub-question, the matter of the art. Is it this same psychological manifestation that has led us to develop such an art? That magnificent and highest of arts which consists in the extinction with the greatest esthetic subtlety of all other forms of life?

Here the *man's* reactions were as confusing as they had been beside the corpse of the *kitten*. He said:

SO THAT'S WHAT HAPPENED TO SNOWPUSS? ART . . . ! ART, YOU CALL IT YET! AND YOU'VE COME HERE TO PRACTICE THAT ART ON THIS WORLD? I'LL SEE YOU FRIED CRISP ON BOTH SIDES ON HADES' HOTTEST GRIDDLE FIRST!

Trubz believes that the extremely violent emotion expressed was shock at realization of the vast new reaches of esthetic experience which lay before him.

Later, when he thought he was alone, I overheard him talking to himself. There was something so emphatically inimical in his thought-patterns that I transcribed his words though I have not yet had a chance to secure Trubz's opinion on them. He beat the clenched digits of one forelimb against the other and said:

SO THAT'S WHAT YOU'RE UP TO! WE'LL SEE ABOUT THAT. BUT HOW? HOW . . . ? GOT IT! THOSE PICTURES I TOOK FOR THE PUBLIC HEALTH CAMPAIGN . . .

I am worried. If this attitude indicated by his thought-patterns persists, we may have to bring about his extinction and proceed at once by ourselves. At least it will give Lilil a chance to compose one of his masterpieces.

Final report of the First Interplanetary Exploratory Expedition, presented by Falzik, specialist in reporting:

How I could so completely have misinterpreted the *man's* thought-patterns I do not understand. Trubz is working on the psychology of it. Far from any hatred or enmity, the *man* was even then resolving to save our lives. The First Interplanetary Exploratory Expedition owes him a debt which it can never repay

It was after sun-up the next day that he approached us with his noble change of heart. As I describe this scene I cannot unfortunately give his direct words; I was too carried away by my own emotions to remember to transcribe. Such phrases as I attribute to him here are reconstructed from the complex of our intercourse, and were largely a matter of signs and pictures.

What he did first was to show us one of his pictures. We stared at it, and drew back horrified. For it represented a being closely allied to us, almost to be taken for one of us, meeting extinction beneath a titanic weapon wielded by what was obviously the characteristic five-digited forelimb of a *man*. And that forelimb was many, many times the size of the being resembling us.

"I've been keeping this from you," he informed us. "I'll admit I've been trying to trap you. But the truth is: I'm a dwarf *man*. The real ones are as much bigger than me as you are bigger than the *kitten*. More, even. And their favorite pastime—only they call it a sport, not art—is killing bugs like you."

We realized now what should have struck us before—the minute size of his structure compared with those which we had seen before. Obviously he spoke the truth—he was a dwarf specimen of his race.

Then he produced more pictures—horrible, terrifying, monstrous pictures, all showing something perturbingly like us meeting cruel extinction at the whim of a *man*.

"I've just been keeping you here," he said, "until some real members of my race could come and play with you. They'd like it. But I haven't got the heart to do it. I like you, and what you told me about your art convinces me that you don't deserve extinction like that. So I'm giving you your chance: Clear out of here and stay away from this planet. It's the most unsafe place in the universe for your kind. If you dread extinction, stay away from the third planet!"

His resolve to spare our lives had made him happy. His face kept twisting into the grimace we had learned to recognize as a sign of *man's* pleasure. But we hardly watched him or even listened to him. Our eyes kept returning with awful fascination to those morbidly terrifying pictures. Then our thoughts fused into one, and with hardly a word of farewell to our savior we sped back to the ship.

This is our last report. We are now on the temporary base established on the satellite and will return as soon as we have recovered from the shock of our narrow escape. Lilil has achieved a new composition with a captive pergut from the ship which has somewhat solaced us.

Murvin to First Interplanetary Exploratory Expedition:

You dopes! You low mammalian idiots! It's what comes of sending nothing but specialists on an expedition. I tried to convince them you needed a good general worker like me, but no. And look at you!

It's obvious what happened. On our planet, mammals are minute pests and the large intelligent beings are arthropodal hexapods. All right. On the third planet things have worked out the other way round. *Bugs,* as the *man* calls our kin, are tiny insignificant things. You saw those pictures and thought the *mans* were enormous; actually they meant only that the *bugs* were minute!

That *man* tricked you unpardonably, and I like him for it. Specialists . . . ! You deserve extinction for this, and you know it. But Vardanek has another idea. Stay where you are. Develop the temporary base in any way you can. We'll send others to help you. We'll build up a major encampment on that side of the satellite, and in our own sweet time we can invade the third planet with enough sensible ones to counteract the boners of individual specialists.

We can do it too. We've got all the time we need to build up our base, even if that *man* has warned his kind—who probably wouldn't believe him anyway. Because remember this always, and feel secure: *No being on the third planet ever knows what is happening on the other side of its satellite.*

LESLIE F. STONE

THE CONQUEST
OF GOLA

HOLA, my daughters (sighed the Matriarch), it is true indeed, I am the only living one upon Gola who remembers the invasion from Detaxal. I alone of all my generation survive to recall vividly the sights and scenes of that past era. And well it is that you come to me to hear by free com- munication of mind to mind, face to face with each other.

Ah, well I remember the surprise of that hour when through the mists that enshroud our lovely world, there swam the first of the great smooth cylinders of the Detaxalans, fifty *tas* * in length, as glistening and silvery as the soil of our land, propelled by the man-things that on Detaxal are supreme even as we women are supreme on Gola.

In those bygone days, as now, Gola was enwrapped by her cloud mists that keep from us the terrific glare of the great star that glows like a malignant spirit out there in the darkness of the void. Only occasionally when a particularly great storm parts the mist of heaven do we see the wonders of the vast universe, but that does not prevent us, with our marvel- ous telescopes handed down to us from thousands of generations before us, from learning what lies across the dark seas of the outside.

Therefore we knew of the nine planets that encircle the great star and are subject to its rule. And so are we familiar enough with the surfaces of these planets to know why Gola should appear as a haven to their inhabi- tants who see in our cloud-enclosed mantle a sweet release from the blasting heat and blinding glare of the great sun.

So it was not strange at all to us to find that the people of Detaxal, the third planet of the sun, had arrived on our globe with a wish in their hearts

---

* Since there is no means of translating the Golan measurements of either length or time we can but guess at these things. However, since the Detaxalan ships each carried a thousand men it can be seen that the ships were between five hundred and a thousand feet in length.

to migrate here, and end their days out of reach of the blistering warmth that had come to be their lot on their own world.

Long ago we, too, might have gone on exploring expeditions to other worlds, other universes, but for what? Are we not happy here? We who have attained the greatest of civilizations within the confines of our own silvery world. Powerfully strong with our mighty force rays, we could subjugate all the universe, but why?

Are we not content with life as it is, with our lovely cities, our homes, our daughters, our gentle consorts? Why spend physical energy in combative strife for something we do not wish, when our mental processes carry us further and beyond the conquest of mere terrestrial exploitation?

On Detaxal it is different, for there the peoples, the ignoble male creatures, breed for physical prowess, leaving the development of their sciences, their philosophies, and the contemplation of the abstract to a chosen few. The greater part of the race fares forth to conquer, to lay waste, to struggle and fight as the animals do over a morsel of worthless territory. Of course we can see why they desired Gola with all its treasures, but we can thank Providence and ourselves that they did not succeed in "commercializing" us as they have the remainder of the universe with their ignoble Federation.

Ah yes, well I recall the hour when first they came, pushing cautiously through the cloud mists, seeking that which lay beneath. We of Gola were unwarned until the two cylinders hung directly above Tola, the greatest city of that time, which still lies in its ruins since that memorable day. But they have paid for it—paid for it well in thousands and tens of thousands of their men.

We were first apprised of their coming when the alarm from Tola was sent from the great beam station there, advising all to stand in readiness for an emergency. Geble, my mother, was then Queen of all Gola, and I was by her side in Morka, that pleasant seaside resort, where I shall soon travel to partake of its rejuvenating waters.

With us were four of Geble's consorts, sweet gentle males, that gave Geble much pleasure in those free hours away from the worries of state. But when the word of the strangers' descent over our home city, Tola, came to us, all else was forgotten. With me at her side, Geble hastened to the beam station and there in the matter transmitter we dispatched our physical beings to the palace at Tola, and the next moment were staring upward at the two strange shapes etched against the clouds.

What the Detaxalan ships were waiting for we did not know then, but later we learned. Not grasping the meaning of our beam stations, the commanders of the ships considered the city below them entirely lacking in means of defense, and were conferring on the method of taking it without bloodshed on either side.

It was not long after our arrival in Tola that the first of the ships began to descend toward the great square before the palace. Geble watched without a word, her great mind already scanning the brains of those whom she found within the great machine. She transferred to my mind but a single thought as I stood there at her side and that with a sneer "Barbarians!"

Now the ship was settling in the square and after a few moments of hesitation, a circular doorway appeared at the side and four of the Detaxalans came through the opening. The square was empty but for themselves and their flyer, and we saw them looking about surveying the beautiful buildings on all sides. They seemed to recognize the palace for what it was and in one accord moved in our direction.

Then Geble left the window at which we stood and strode to the doorway opening upon the balcony that faced the square. The Detaxalans halted in their tracks when they saw her slender graceful form appear and removing the strange coverings they wore on their heads they each made a bow.

Again Geble sneered, for only the male-things of our world bow their heads, and so she recognized these visitors for what they were, nothing more than the despicable males of the species! And what creatures they were!

Imagine a short almost flat body set high upon two slender legs, the body tapering in the middle, several times as broad across as it is through the center, with two arms almost as long as the legs attached to the upper part of the torso. A small column-like neck of only a few inches divides the head of oval shape from the body, and in this head only are set the organs of sight, hearing, and scent. Their bodies were like a patchwork of a misguided nature.

Yes, strange as it is, my daughters, practically all of the creature's faculties had their base in the small ungainly head, and each organ was perforce pressed into serving for several functions. For instance, the breathing nostrils also served for scenting out odors, nor was this organ able to exclude any disagreeable odors that might come its way, but had to dispense to the brain both pleasant and unpleasant odors at the same time.

Then there was the mouth, set directly beneath the nose, and here again we had an example of one organ doing the work of two, for the creature not only used the mouth with which to take in the food for its body, but it also used the mouth to enunciate the excruciatingly ugly sounds of its language forthwith.

Never before have I seen such a poorly organized body, so unlike our own highly developed organisms. How much nicer it is to be able to call forth any organ at will, and dispense with it when its usefulness is over! Instead these poor Detaxalans had to carry theirs about in physical being all the time so that always was the surface of their bodies entirely marred.

Yet that was not the only part of their ugliness, and proof of the lowliness of their origin, for whereas our fine bodies support themselves by muscular development, these poor creatures were dependent entirely upon a strange structure to keep them in their proper shape.

Imagine if you can a bony skeleton somewhat like the foundations upon which we build our edifices, laying stone and cement over the steel framework. But this skeleton instead is inside a body which the flesh, muscle and skin overlay. Everywhere in their bodies are these cartilaginous structures—hard, heavy, bony structures developed by the chemicals of the being for its use. Even the hands, feet and head of the creatures were underlaid with these bones—ugh, it was terrible when we dissected one of the fellows for study. I shudder to think of it.

Yet again there was still another feature of the Detaxalans that was equally as horrifying as the rest, namely their outer covering. As we viewed them for the first time out there in the square we discovered that parts of the body, that is the part of the head which they called the face, and the bony hands were entirely naked without any sort of covering, neither fur nor feathers, just the raw, pinkish-brown skin looking as if it had been recently plucked.

Later we found a few specimens that had a type of fur on the lower part of the face, but these were rare. And when they doffed the head coverings which we had first taken for some sort of natural covering, we saw that the top of the head was overlaid with a very fine fuzz of fur several inches long.

We did not know in the beginning that the strange covering on the bodies of the four men, green in color, was not a natural growth, but later discovered that such was the truth, and not only the face and hands were bare of fur, but the entire body, except for a fine sprinkling of hair that was scarcely visible except on the chest, was also bare. No wonder the poor things covered themselves with their awkward clothing. We arrived at the conclusion that their lack of fur had been brought about by the fact that always they had been exposed to the bright rays of the sun so that without the dampness of our own planet the fur had dried up and fallen away from the flesh!

Now thinking it over I suppose that we of Gola presented strange forms to the people of Detaxal with our fine circular bodies, rounded at the top, our short beautiful lower limbs with the circular foot pads, and our short round arms and hand pads, flexible and muscular like rubber.

But how envious they must have been of our beautiful golden coats, our movable eyes, our power to scent, hear and touch with any part of the body, to absorb food and drink through any part of the body most convenient to us at any time. Oh yes, laugh though you may, without a doubt we were also freaks to those freakish Detaxalans. But no matter, let us return to the tale.

On recognizing our visitors for what they were, simple-minded males, Geble was chagrined at them for taking up her time, but they were strangers to our world and we Golans are always courteous. Geble began of course to try to communicate by thought transference, but strangely enough the fellows below did not catch a single thought. Instead, entirely unaware of Geble's overture to friendship, the leader commenced to speak to her in most outlandish manner, contorting the red lips of his mouth into various uncouth shapes and making sounds that fell upon our hearing so unpleasantly that we immediatey closed our senses to them. And without a word Geble turned her back upon them, calling for Tanka, her personal secretary.

Tanka was instructed to welcome the Detaxalans while she herself turned to her own chambers to summon a half dozen of her council. When the council arrived she began to discuss with them the problem of extracting more of the precious tenix from the waters of the great inland lake of Notauch. Nothing whatever was said of the advent of the Detaxalans, for Geble had dismissed them from her mind as creatures not worthy of her thought.

In the meantime Tanka had gone forth to meet the four who of course could not converse with her. In accordance with the Queen's orders she led them indoors to the most informal receiving chamber and there had them served with food and drink which by the looks of the remains in the dishes they did not relish at all.

Leading them through the rooms of the lower floor of the palace she made a pretense of showing them everything which they duly surveyed. But they appeared to chafe at the manner in which they were being entertained.

The creatures even made an attempt through the primitive method of conversing by their arms to learn something of what they had seen, but Tanka was as supercilious as her mistress. When she thought they had had enough, she led them to the square and back to the door of their flyer, giving them their dismissal.

But the men were not ready to accept it. Instead they tried to express to Tanka their desire to meet the ruling head of Gola. Although their hand motions were perfectly inane and incomprehensible, Tanka could read what passed through their brains, and understood more fully than they what lay in their minds. She shook her head and motioned that they were to embark in their flyer and be on their way back to their planet.

Again and again the Detaxalans tried to explain what they wished, thinking Tanka did not understand. At last she impressed upon their savage minds that there was nothing for them but to depart, and disgruntled by her treatment they reentered their machine, closed its ponderous door and raised their ship to the level of its sister flyer. Several minutes passed and then, with thanksgiving, we saw them pass over the city.

Told of this, Geble laughed. "To think of mere man-things daring to attempt to force themselves upon us. What is the universe coming to? What were their women back home considering when they sent them to us? Have they developed too many males and think that we can find use for them?" she wanted to know.

"It is strange indeed," observed Yabo, one of the council members.

"What did you find in the minds of these ignoble creatures, O August One?"

"Nothing of particular interest, a very low grade of intelligence, to be sure. There was no need of looking below the surface."

"It must have taken intelligence to build those ships."

"None aboard them did that. I don't question it but that their mothers built the ships for them as playthings, even as we give toys to our 'little ones,' you know. I recall that the ancients of our world perfected several types of space-flyers many ages ago!"

"Maybe those males do not have 'mothers' but instead they build the ships themselves. Maybe they are the stronger sex on their world!" This last was said by Suiki, the fifth consort of Geble, a pretty little male, rather young in years. No one had noticed his coming into the chamber, but now everyone showed surprise at his words.

"Impossible!" ejaculated Yabo.

Geble, however, laughed at the little chap's expression. "Suiki is a profound thinker," she observed, still laughing, and she drew him to her gently hugging him.

And with that the subject of the men from Detaxal was closed. It was reopened, however, several hours later when it was learned that instead of leaving Gola altogether the ships were seen one after another by the various cities of the planet as they circumnavigated it.

It was rather annoying, for everywhere the cities' routines were broken up as the people dropped their work and studies to gaze at the cylinders. Too, it was upsetting the morale of the males, for on learning that the two ships contained only creatures of their own sex they were becoming envious, wishing for the same type of playthings for themselves.

Shut in, as they are, unable to grasp the profundities of our science and thought, the gentle, fun-loving males were always glad for a new diversion, and this new method developed by the Detaxalans had intrigued them.

It was then that Geble decided it was high time to take matters into her own hands. Not knowing where the two ships were at the moment it was not difficult with the object-finder beam to discover their whereabouts, and then with the attractor to draw them to Tola magnetically. An *ous* later we had the pleasure of seeing the two ships rushing toward our city. When they arrived above it, power brought them down to the square again.

Again Tanka was sent out, and directed the commanders of the two ships to follow her in to the Queen. Knowing the futility of attempting to converse with them without mechanical aid, Geble caused to be brought her three of the ancient mechanical thought transformers that are only museum pieces to us but still workable. The two men were directed to place them on their heads while she donned the third. When this was done she ordered the creatures to depart immediately from Gola, telling them that she was tired of their play.

Watching the faces of the two I saw them frowning and shaking their heads. Of course I could read their thoughts as well as Geble without need of the transformers, since it was only for their benefit that these were used, so I heard the whole conversation, though I need only to give you the gist of it.

"We have no wish to leave your world as yet," the two had argued.

"You are disrupting the routine of our lives here," Geble told them, "and now that you've seen all that you can there is no need for you to stay longer. I insist that you leave immediately."

I saw one of the men smile, and thereupon he was the one who did all the talking (I say "talking," for this he was actually doing, mouthing each one of his words although we understood his thoughts as they formed in his queer brain, so different from ours).

"Listen here," he laughed, "I don't get the hang of you people at all. We came to Gola (he used some outlandish name of his own, but I use our name of course) with the express purpose of exploration and exploitation. We come as friends. Already we are in alliance with Damin (again the name for the fourth planet of our system was different, but I give the correct appellation), established commerce and trade, and now we are ready to offer you the chance to join our federation peaceably.

"What we have seen of this world is very favorable; there are good prospects for business here. There is no reason why you people as those of Damin and Detaxal can not enter into a nice business arrangement congenially. You have far more here to offer tourists, more than Damin. Why, except for your clouds this would be an ideal paradise for every man, woman and child on Detaxal and Damin to visit, and of course with our new cloud dispensers we could clear your atmosphere for you in short order and keep it that way. Why, you'll make millions in the first year of your trade.

"Come now, allow us to discuss this with your ruler—king or whatever you call him. Women are all right in their place, but it takes the men to see the profit of a thing like this—er—you are a woman, aren't you?"

The first of his long speech, of course, was so much gibberish to us, with his prate of business arrangements, commerce and trade, tourists, profits, cloud dispensers and what not, but it was the last part of what he said that took my breath away, and you can imagine how it affected Geble. I could see straightway that she was intensely angered, and good reason too. By the looks of the silly fellow's face I could guess that he was getting the full purport of her thoughts. He began to shuffle his funny feet and a foolish grin pervaded his face.

"Sorry," he said, "if I insulted you—I didn't intend that, but I believed that man holds the same place here as he does on Detaxal and Damin, but I suppose it is just as possible for woman to be the ruling factor of a world as man is elsewhere."

That speech naturally made Geble more irate, and tearing off her thought transformer she left the room without another word. In a moment, however, Yabo appeared wearing the transformer in her place. Yabo had none of the beauty of my mother, for whereas Geble was slender and as straight as a rod, Yabo was obese, and her fat body overflowed until she looked like a large dumpy bundle of *yat* held together in her furry skin. She had very little dignity as she waddled toward the Detaxalans, but there was determination in her whole manner, and without preliminaries she began to scold the two as though they were her own consorts.

"There has been enough of this, my fine young men," she shot at them. "You've had your fun, and now it is time for you to return to your mothers and consorts. Shame on you for making up such miserable tales about yourselves. I have a good mind to take you home with me for a couple of days, and I'd put you in your places quick enough. The idea of men acting like you are!"

For a moment I thought the Detaxalans were going to cry by the faces they made, but instead they broke into laughter, such heathenish sounds as had never before been heard on Gola, and I listened in wonder instead of excluding it from my hearing, but the fellows sobered quickly enough at that, and the spokesman addressed the shocked Yabo.

"I see," said he, "it's impossible for your people and mine to arrive at an understanding peaceably. I'm sorry that you take us for children out on a spree, that you are accustomed to such a low type of men as is evidently your lot here.

"I have given you your chance to accept our terms without force, but since you refuse, under the orders of the Federation I will have to take you forcibly, for we are determined that Gola become one of us, if you like it or not. Then you will learn that we are not the children you believe us to be.

"You may go to your supercilious Queen now and advise her that we give you exactly ten hours in which to evacuate this city, for precisely on the hour we will lay this city in ruins. And if that does not suffice you, we will do the same with every other city on the planet! Remember, ten hours!"

And with that he took the mechanical thought transformer from his head and tossed it on the table. His companion did the same and the two of them strode out of the room and to their flyers which arose several thousand feet above Tola and remained there.

Hurrying in to Geble, Yabo told her what the Detaxalan had said. Geble was reclining on her couch and did not bother to raise herself.

"Childish prattle," she conceded and withdrew her red eyes on their movable stems into their pockets, paying no more heed to the threats of the men from Detaxal.

I, however, could not be as calm as my mother, and I was fearful that it was not childish prattle after all. Not knowing how long ten hours might be I did not wait, but crept up to the palace's beam station and set its dials so that the entire building and as much of the surrounding territory as it could cover were protected in the force zone.

Alas, that the same beam was not greater. But it had not been put there for defense, only for matter transference and whatever other peacetime methods we used. It was the means of proving just the same that it was also a very good defensive instrument, for just two *ous* later the hovering ships above let loose their powers of destruction, heavy explosives that entirely demolished all of Tola and its millions of people and only the palace royal of all that beauty was left standing!

Awakened from her nap by the terrific detonation, Geble came hurriedly to a window to view the ruin, and she was wild with grief at what she saw. Geble, however, saw that there was urgent need for action. She knew without my telling her what I had done to protect the palace. And though she showed no sign of appreciation, I knew that I had won a greater place in her regard than any other of her many daughters and would henceforth be her favorite as well as her successor, as the case turned out.

Now, with me behind her, she hurried to the beam station and in a twinkling we were both in Tubia, the second greatest city of that time. Nor were we to be caught napping again, for Geble ordered all beam stations to throw out their zone forces while she herself manipulated one of Tubia's greatest power beams, attuning it to the emanations of the two Detaxalan flyers. In less than an *ous* the two ships were seen through the mists heading for Tubia. For a moment I grew fearful, but on realizing that they were after all in our grip, and the attractors held every living thing powerless against movement, I grew calm and watched them come over the city and the beam pull them to the ground.

With the beam still upon them, they lay supine on the ground without motion. Descending to the square Geble called for Ray C, and when the machine arrived she herself directed the cutting of the hole in the side of the flyer and was the first to enter it with me immediately behind, as usual.

We were both astounded by what we saw of the great array of machinery within. But a glance told Geble all she wanted to know of their principles. She interested herself only in the men standing rigidly in whatever position our beam had caught them. Only the eyes of the creatures expressed their fright, poor things, unable to move so much as a hair while we moved among them untouched by the power of the beam because of the strength of our own minds.

They could have fought against it if they had known how, but their simple minds were too weak for such exercise.

Now glancing about among the stiff forms around us, of which there were one thousand, Geble picked out those of the males she desired for observation, choosing those she judged to be their finest specimens, those with much hair on their faces and having more girth than the others. These she ordered removed by several workers who followed us, and then we emerged again to the outdoors.

Using hand beam torches the picked specimens were kept immobile after they were out of reach of the greater beam and were borne into the laboratory of the building Geble had converted into her new palace. Geble and I followed, and she gave the order for the complete annihilation of the two powerless ships.

Thus ended the first foray of the people of Detaxal. And for the next two *tels* there was peace upon our globe again. In the laboratory the thirty who had been rescued from their ships were given thorough examinations both physically and mentally and we learned all there was to know about them. Hearing of the destruction of their ships, most of the creatures had become frightened and were quite docile in our hands. Those that were unruly were used in the dissecting room for the advancement of Golan knowledge.

After a complete study of them, which yielded little, we lost interest in them scientifically. Geble, however, found some pleasure in having the poor creatures around her and kept three of them in her own chambers so she could delve into their brains as she pleased. The others she doled out to her favorites as she saw fit.

One she gave to me to act as a slave or in what capacity I desired him, but my interest in him soon waned, especially since I had now come of age and was allowed to have two consorts of my own, and go about the business of bringing my daughters into the world.

My slave I called Jon and gave him complete freedom of my house. If only we had foreseen what was coming we would have annihilated every one of them immediately! It did please me later to find that Jon was learning our language and finding a place in my household, making friends with my two shut-in consorts. But as I have said I paid little attention to him.

So life went on smoothly with scarcely a change after the destruction of the ships of Detaxal. But that did not mean we were unprepared for more. Geble reasoned that there would be more ships forthcoming when the Detaxalans found that their first two did not return. So, although it was sometimes inconvenient, the zones of force were kept upon our cities.

And Geble was right, for the day came when dozens of flyers descended upon Gola from Detaxal. But this time the zones of force did not hold them since the zones were not in operation!

And we were unwarned, for when they descended upon us, our world was sleeping, confident that our zones were our protection. The first indication that I had of trouble brewing was when, awakening, I found the ugly form of Jon bending over me. Surprised, for it was not his habit to arouse me, I started up only to find his arms about me, embracing me. And how strong he was! For the moment a new emotion swept me, for the first time I knew the pleasure to be had in the arms of a strong man, but that emotion was short lived, for I saw in the blue eyes of my slave that he had recognized the look in my eyes for what it was, and for the moment he was tender.

Later I was to grow angry when I thought of that expression of his, for his eyes filled with pity, pity for me! But pity did not stay, instead he grinned and the next instant he was binding me down to my couch with strong rope. Geble, I learned later, had been treated as I, as were the members of the council and every other woman in Gola!

That was what came of allowing our men to meet on common ground with the creatures from Detaxal, for a weak mind is open to seeds of rebellion and the Detaxalans had sown it well, promising dominance to the lesser creatures of Gola.

That, however, was only part of the plot on the part of the Detaxalans. They were determined not only to revenge those we had murdered, but also to gain mastery of our planet. Unnoticed by us they had constructed a machine which transmits sound as we transmit thought and by its means had communicated with their own world, advising them of the very hour to strike when all of Gola was slumbering. It was a masterful stroke, only they did not know the power of the mind of Gola—so much more ancient than theirs.

Lying there bound on my couch I was able to see out the window and, trembling with terror, I watched a half dozen Detaxalan flyers descend into Tubia, guessing that the same was happening in our other cities. I was truly frightened, for I did not have the brain of a Geble. I was young yet, and in fear I watched the hordes march out of their machines, saw the thousands of our men join them.

Free from restraint, the shut-ins were having their holiday and how they cavorted out in the open, most of the time getting in the way of the freakish Detaxalans who were certainly taking over our city.

A half *ous* passed while I lay there watching, waiting in fear at what the Detaxalans planned to do with us. I remembered the pleasant, happy life we had led up to the present and trembled over what the future might be when the Detaxalans had infested us with commerce and trade, business propositions, tourists and all of their evil practices. It was then that I received the message from Geble, clear and definite, just as all the women of the globe received it, and hope returned to my heart.

There began that titanic struggle, the fight for supremacy, the fight that won us victory over the simple-minded weaklings below who had presumptuously dared to conquer us. The first indication that the power of our combined mental concentration at Geble's orders was taking effect was when we saw the first of our males halt in their wild dance of freedom. They tried to shake us off, but we knew we could bring them back to us.

At first the Detaxalans paid them no heed. They knew not what was happening until there came the wholesale retreat of the Golan men back to the buildings, back to the chambers from which they had escaped. Then grasping something of what was happening the already defeated invaders sought to retain their hold on our little people. Our erstwhile captives sought to hold them with oratorical gestures, but of course we won. We saw our creatures return to us and unbind us.

Only the Detaxalans did not guess the significance of that, did not realize that inasmuch as we had conquered our own men, we could conquer them also. As they went about their work of making our city their own, establishing already their autocratic bureaus wherever they pleased, we began to concentrate upon them, hypnotizing them to the flyers that had disgorged them.

And soon they began to feel of our power, the weakest ones first, feeling the mental bewilderment creeping upon them. Their leaders, stronger in mind, knew nothing of this at first, but soon our terrible combined mental power was forced upon them also and they realized that their men were deserting them, crawling back to their ships! The leaders began to exhort them into new action, driving them physically. But our power gained on them and now we began to concentrate upon the leaders themselves. They were strong of will and they defied us, fought us, mind against mind, but of course it was useless. Their minds were not suited to the test they put themselves to, and after almost three *ous* of struggle, we of Gola were able to see victory ahead.

At last the leaders succumbed. Not a single Detaxalan was abroad in the avenues. They were within their flyers, held there by our combined wills, unable to act for themselves. It was then as easy for us to switch the zones of force upon them, subjugate them more securely and with the annihilator beam to disintegrate completely every ship and man into noth- ingness! Thousands upon thousands died that day and Gola was indeed revenged.

Thus, my daughters, ended the second invasion of Gola.

Oh yes, more came from their planet to discover what had happened to their ships and their men, but we of Gola no longer hesitated, and they no sooner appeared beneath the mists than they too were annihilated until at last Detaxal gave up the thought of conquering our cloud-laden world. Perhaps in the future they will attempt it again, but we are always in readiness for them now, and our men—well, they are still the same ineffectual weaklings, my daughters . . .

ROSS ROCKLYNNE

JACKDAW

WHEN BELGARTH arrived back on the home planet, Emonso, with his crew and galactic-roaming ship, he felt that he had a first-order intellectual riddle to discuss with his sectional recreation governor. If the problem were indeed next to being unsolvable, he was aware that not only would he add considerably to the recreational facilities of his race, but would also put himself up for prompt promotion.

Belgarth did not trouble to act in his capacity as captain when the ship hove in sight of the home port, but delegated the automatic job of landing to his subordinate officer, and immediately took wing for his commander's offices.

"Took wing" does not convey the method of his departure and eventual arrival. To be truthful, he selected a sixth-dimensional route which, as far as he was concerned, turned his giant ship inside out, scrambled it unrecognizably, but left him most indubitably on the outside, looking down on a similarly twisted caricature of a city.

Looked at from such a convolution of space, the city was a riddle, even to Belgarth. Which is a good commentary on the mental processes of Belgarth and of the Emonso, that wise race of the universe, other than which there is none older, other than which none shall exist longer.

Belgarth proceeded to figure it out, his many eyes winking in series of five, seven, and nine, as he turned off certain mental operations whose supplied data were immaterial to the problem at hand. The small cube which stood on one corner at the southwest end of the city must, naturally, be Main Street—in a sixth-dimensional matrix. Since Governor Orth's bubble palace was at Main and Omono, Belgarth need but follow a path indicated by the topology of a five-dimensional cube two dimensionally imposed on practically any three-dimensional geometric figure.

Which he did with a great deal of ease, wishing meanwhile, and with some disappointment in the facility of the solution, that he had taken the time out to set his synapses into a pattern which would have permitted the somewhat more complex eight-dimensional path.

Governor Orth—thoroughly three-dimensional—untwined the several sinewy sections of his body from the chair behind his desk, and focussed several of his eyes on Belgarth as he materialized.

"Oh, you, Belgarth," he said in slightly annoyed tones. "Always bothering a person, and without the least excuse. Have a good time? Never mind —that problem you posed on your return from your last expedition was a sheer washout as far as the Research Corps was concerned. They figured it out in nothing flat. If you must bring in problems which solve themselves, have the care to add your own elaborations—at least we can have some fun proving the elaborations are such. What's on your mind this time?"

"Plenty," said Belgarth. He settled himself comfortably around a chair, selected half a dozen cigars from Orth's humidor, and fitted them into his several mouths. He began to blow concentric smoke rings, his main eyes thoughtful. He began to talk. "I've had my ups and downs, governor. You know that. Through a lucky break I came out of the Upper Level Research Corps to command of a Recreation ship. I happened to hit on the solution of a problem our whole race had been working on for some million years, and you personally, off and on, for over ten thousand years. My luck with a command netted a few puzzles—the peculiar relationships of gravitons to chronons for one, which, of course, was cracked, but only after a thousand years of concerted effort from the entire Third Level Corps. Good enough. And, of course, I brought back a few flops—the one you mentioned just now, warped time, which I understand wasn't a problem at all.

"But, like all Recreation ship commanders, I've rather been looking forward to finding something that would give the whole Emonso some recreation that would endure for an indefinite length of time. *That* would be a contribution!" he added feelingly, and paused.

Orth frowned uncertainly at him. "You've found it?" he said cautiously.

"I think I have."

Orth said slowly, "I see." He pressed a button which actuated a sixth-order field that would retain the conversation from this point on. He settled a little more completely around his chair. "We can discuss it now, Belgarth —you have the data, with suspense, emotion and factual material well correlated?"

Belgarth was surprised. "You don't prefer a semantic account?"

"Not at all." Orth's reply was definite, if bitter. "Facts and figures are killing me, Belgarth, *killing* me! My ship commanders seem to have forgotten entirely the unformularized psychological aspects of certain situations and events—the least they could do would be to include them as errata, for later correction and elimination—it would give *life* to a problem.

But go on, go on, Belgarth, and draw it out as long as you wish—my next thousand years are yours, if you make it good."

Belgarth nodded in sympathetic understanding and immediately plunged into his tale, from which the major quotes have been mercifully eliminated:

On the fourth day of the one hundred third year of our tenth cruise we found a solar system. We were all exultant, and as speed was braked, I ordered a celebration. After all, when for year after endless year, for star after star, for light-year after light-year, you don't run across something which is likely to result in a problem, it gets pretty monotonous. You know and I know that there are a thousand and more different ways in which a solar system can evolve—all of us suspected that this system, with nine planets instead of the usual fifteen, would present a different solution.

After the celebration, I got my computers busy taking readings. We did find some interesting things, which will be noted only in my written report; however, the secret of the system's formation was no secret at all. Six of its planets had been swept away following the original nebula-star-nebula mix-up—swept away by a double star some four and a half light-years distant. So, save for a rather unusual disfiguration of the add-four law, this system was like any other of its class.

Choe, my main computer, swore. I agreed with him, but of course was powerless to relieve the disappointment of my crew save by agreeing upon a landing on one of the planets. All of the planets, save one that was ringed, and another beyond it, were more or less habitable, so I gave my crew their choice. They took a vote on it, and surprisingly enough were unanimous in that they picked out the third planet from the central sun. I noted at that time, by the way, governor, that this planet as seen from space was blue—or, rather, azure. Sometime I intend to find out exactly what emotional effect that color has on the Emonso—it certainly has one— Give it to one of the Minor Corps, sometime, if I don't get around to it.

So we did land, after making one slow revolution around the planet at a distance of several hundred feet. We brought the ship down on the shore of a salt ocean. A ruined city—that is, its main sections, rose some ten miles away. We were on the outskirts, deeming that best, since, if there were inhabitants in the city, we did not wish to frighten them too much.

We were all a little more excited than is usual in landing on a planet. For one thing, life in this universe which the Emonso alone have troubled to explore, is rare. We had, in our slow circuit of the planet, discovered cities, roads and cultivated lands—sure indications of life. For another thing, we were all of us certain, down to a man, that the life which had built those cities was on the wane, if not completely gone. What had caused it? A blight, or a natural death such as might come with what we of the Emonso still recall as "old age"?

A great, complete silence brooded over this planet.

Still, we did not wish to believe that that silence *was* complete. We wanted to observe. We allowed our opinions to remain theoretical. I ordered out half a dozen scouting ships, with the stern injunction to touch nothing, no matter what happened.

As it happened, my own command was more applicable to me than to the others. Choe and I took one of the scout ships, Choe at the controls. We sped directly east, away from the ocean, maintaining a discreet height above the planet's surface.

It was an interesting planet. This particular section, a thousand miles of it, was rather mixed up physically. There was the strangest combination of mountains and snow and lakes and deserts and vast forests, with cities now and then, ruined, churned cities, but cities nevertheless.

As we progressed east, cities and roads became more complex, better constructed, and more numerous. But the cities were more thoroughly demolished. We saw no moving vehicles, no signs of intelligent life at all. Now and then, however, we saw herds or packs of animals who were, respectively, the hunted and the hunters.

We came to another ocean. After some three thousand miles, we sighted a continent with some islands hugging its outskirts. The islands had been inhabited, but the evidences of civilization were completely leveled. On the continent proper, cities and farmlands were crowded together unsymmetrically. We could not see them in detail, since we were too close to them and moving too swiftly. Yet, we did note that destruction had been applied here, also. These cities were debris, the debris of a holocaust whose nature we seemed emotionally unfitted to conjecture about.

"There!"

Choe's ejaculation burst out at the very moment we had fixed our minds into a pattern which expected lifelessness. We jerked ourselves from that state of mind quickly. In the next few minutes, we made up our minds that life, intelligent, tool-building life, was present.

The creature who operated the craft must have seen us from the distance, for he came flitting up from the heart of a city ahead of us, and had matched our altitude by the time Choe saw him. He was coming straight toward us, the Sun burning with a hot brilliance against the wings of his strange vehicle.

I say "strange" advisedly. Not because I did not understand its method of locomotion immediately, but because we of the Emonso are and have been so used to such simpler means—dimensional transit, operated mentally over comparatively short distances, or the light-beam heterodyning and rocket principle combined. This craft swam in the air by means of solid propellers, and buoyed itself up with plane surfaces projecting from the main body of the ship. Nonetheless, it was fully capable of matching our present rather slow velocity—which it did not have to do, since it was in our direct line of flight.

As we approached closer, we noted an unusual exhibition on the part of the alien craft. Rings of fire were spouting in intermittent blasts from its nose. Above the rumble of our ship's jets, we heard a chattering—a sort of *rat-tatting* sound. And as the ship neared us, its motors thundering, we definitely heard the sound of small metal pellets striking against our transparent foreplates. I shivered a little, thankful that those foreplates were capable of deflecting spatial flotsam driven with full meteoric velocity.

Choe was tense, uncertain. "I'd better change course, Belgarth! We'll crash into each other."

"Maintain course," I snapped back. "The inhabitant of the airplane will certainly have the courtesy to veer off, since he must realize that we are the visitors, not he."

It happened in the manner I predicted. The plane was almost on us, the peculiar chattering still emanating from it, when its motors crescendoed, and it swept directly over us with inches to spare. We did not change course, but naturally I had actuated a sixth-order field which gave us a still-life picture of the being. Both Choe and I were somewhat puzzled over the unusual behavior of the creature, and thought it best to study him, his structure and general appearance, so that we could correlate the data later on, and thus acquire the correct visitor's approach.

Choe had touched the electron lock, and the picture was draining off onto the screen, when we were aware that our visitor was not yet done greeting us. His plane buzzed around our craft, dipping, diving, chattering; we heard the spang of hard-driven pellets striking against the impervious bulkheads. Finally Choe and I decided that until we grasped the psychology of the inhabitants, it would be wise to let a friendly meeting go until another day. Our ship put on a burst of speed which, rather uncivilly of course, left the other ship far in the distance, soon to disappear.

Then we turned back to the life-size picture of the creature.

He was strange, naturally; but then we would doubtless have been strange to him. First of all, his external appendages and organs went mostly in twos. Two eyes, two ears, two arms, two legs—but only one mouth; which, if you can twist your mind around, governor, is not absurd at all—in fact, our *eight* mouths are, in a way, the real absurdities. However, this being had hair on his head, part of which fell over its forehead. It was dressed in stiff khaki garments, on the coat of which gleamed several pieces of designed metal which I conclude must have been for ornamental purposes. The shoulders, which were in reality rather narrow and sloping in proportion to the broader hips, were given an artificial squareness by padding in the upper garment, the general effect being aided by little brushes of gold string projecting from the shoulders.

So much for a general description. The being used artificial means to enhance its personal appearance, and therefore was probably vain. We now studied the facial expression. Certainly, neither Choe nor I, though we leaned backward in an effort to give the creature its due, could find any trace of pleasantness. The muscles of the ovular face, we decided, when relaxed would give the skin a fairly smooth appearance. However, these muscles were not relaxed. The mouth, for one, was contorted, and the eyes were slits. The general effect of this was an unnatural formation of tight little hollows beneath the cheekbones, and unattractive shadows in the corners of the lips, in addition to an unsymmetrical bulge of muscles along both sides of the face.

We drew the picture into its field, and stored it away for future reference.

"What do you make of it, Choe?" I demanded.

"The creature was ill," Choe said positively.

Such was my opinion, governor; at least it was a good enough opinion to hold until we met more of the beings.

We arrived back at the ship in a state of excitement. In the remainder of our four-day trip, we met no more inhabitants. Indeed, it was hard to believe that people could live in the rumpled terrain, the ruined cities which we saw from the air. However, we were sure that at least one of the other scouts had seen indications of human life.

On the contrary. Instead of gathering data of that nature we were the only ones able to give it. We had to tell our story over and over, for none could make head or tail of the creature's actions. We searched backward in our experience for something corresponding to the rain of pellets which had smashed against our bulkheads. Certainly, we reasoned, the creature must have known that the pellets would not penetrate to the interior of our craft, since that would have damaged our bodies. Therefore, he must have been saluting us, or perhaps starting up some system of communication which, according to his psychology, we should have understood easily. We all regretted profoundly that we were unable to see inside the creature's mind. We felt that we would have made some unusual observations, and perhaps been able to render some much-needed assistance.

In the following days, we made additional scouting trips, taking slightly different routes. Only one of the scouts reported anything out of the ordinary. He was met, somewhere in the eastern hemisphere in north temperate latitudes, by a great fleet of planes. It was quite an exhibition. The scouting ship was thrown about a bit by some spectacular explosions which occurred in the air about. The planes were evidently dropping tokens of some sort which were timed to explode either on the ship or around it. Some of the planes, their pilots seemingly in the grip of some overwhelming emotion, lost control of their ships, smashing themselves against the scout ship. It was a rather dangerous display, and the scout ship outdistanced the welcoming horde, not even taking the time to secure pictures.

We all decided that the peculiar behavior of the inhabitants would be a hard nut to crack. We had landed in a civilization which was definitely and without question entirely foreign to anything we had ever seen or heard of before. Feeling that we might unintentionally be violating some law of courtesy by not returning the enthusiasm with which we were met in like manner, I no longer sent out scouting ships, but confined operations to a fifty-mile isosceles triangle of which our ship was the apex.

The city we explored in that general area evidently had been an important one. It was built around a bay, from the waters of which projected the hulks of sunken ships. Destruction was widespread. The buildings, unlike those of the eastern cities, were not high. Nonetheless, since that city belonged to the same civilization, we thought its contents should be a satisfactory index to the contents of other cities.

Some of the buildings, by the variety of implements in them, we identified as living quarters. We found immense quantities of food incased in metal and glass containers. The people evidently found the preparation of their own meals a more efficient method than distribution from a central kitchen. Furniture and rugs and other appurtenances to living were luxurious in quality. We did not err in believing that this was a wealthy civilization. Why the greater part of it had been destroyed we could not begin to conjecture. There were no people, but if there had been, a group of a considerable number could have lived indefinitely on the foods and in the homes and buildings whose interiors were still intact.

We followed streets which were heaped with the debris of wrecked vehicles.

We found airports—and these seemed to have been visited with greater destruction than the cities themselves. There were airplanes, but they had been twisted and torn apart until they were almost unrecognizable.

At the end of our third day of exploration we grew depressed.

As Choe said, despondently, "So many great things—so many valuable things—but utterly useless without someone to use them. Useless."

We pursued a quick four-dimensional route back to the ship, arriving in the interior to find the crew in a state of wide-eyed excitement.

"Ships! Thousands of them!"

The general cry was true in its statement, as I soon noted. From the west, the very sky was darkened with the numberless planes which were sweeping toward us. And truth to tell, I was relieved. At last some of the puzzles with which we were faced would be solved. A delegation from the remnants of the people had come to welcome us. This time they would land. This time they would seek a more basic method of communication, forgiving us whatever transgressions we had made on courtesy.

Of course, I was wrong. Very wrong.

The explosions began to occur. The planes swooped, motors roaring. Missiles began to strike against the ship. I at once ordered those few in my command who were outside the ship inside. They came quickly, for geysers of rock and earth had commenced to rise near them.

It was awesome. Ship after ship, in solid, unswerving lines, roaring down from the blue vault of the sky, loosing their explosive tokens. The very ground around us became pitted, corroded, churned. The ship shuddered under the concussions, but, of course, nothing was damaged. However, craters were opening around us, rendering the foundation on which the ship stood unstable. I caused the ship to be lifted slightly, intending to place it in another spot, until the enthusiasm of our visitors wore itself out.

It was hard to land. No sooner were we in the air than we were literally enveloped by hundreds of flying ships. We were afraid of damaging them, they were so numerous. However, our upward motion seemed to make them more intense. The ships began to crash in unending streams against our bulkheads, deliberately throwing themselves against us, absolutely and completely destroying themselves as they exploded into flame. We hastily landed—and so the strange exhibition continued, all through the long day.

My story, governor, is so far unbelievable. What I have yet to tell flatly contradicts common sense. Briefly, after each ship had rid itself entirely of its explosive tokens, it climbed to a dizzying height, poised, and then came roaring down. At the full top downward speed of which it was capable, and with an accuracy of aim which was commendable, each plane would hurtle directly, and without hesitation, at our ship. The scream of its flight would be cut abruptly. A staggering crash, the ship shudders a little—and that was the end of that plane.

The sun was almost obscured by the horizon formed by the great salt ocean, when the final note in the senseless drama sounded. All this time, we had had our radio receptors on to the all-wave length. Nothing had sounded. Now a voice began to speak. Of course, we could not understand. But we all breathed with relief. Proper communications were starting. We all preferred to overlook the holocaust that was still being enacted outside the ship. For of all those thousands of ships, the last ten were at that moment in full downward flight toward us. In another ten seconds, they had demolished themselves. And far up in the sky, limned darkly against the blue, the dark shape of one lone airplane circled.

From that ship, the voice was coming.

We listened eagerly, hoping to understand some inflection of tone—hoping to gather some clue which would inform us of the correct method of procedure we were requested to follow. Unfortunately, the voice was not understandable in any of its phases. It was *not* a melodious voice. It grated on our nerves. The words were spoken at what must have been the full power of the being's lungs. Sometimes it dropped to a roar, jerked itself upward to a high-pitched scream, dropped downward to a tearful sob and then swept upward to so shrill and bestial a sound that all of us automatically closed our auditory centers.

Still, there was *something* hypnotic about that voice!

We were fascinated. The voice was, to our senses, of course, a poison with which we were enthralled. The sensation, remembered now, makes me shudder. The longer we listened, the more we disliked the horrible, insidious rhythm. At last, I ordered the receptor shut off.

Our nerves relaxed. It was good to hear the quiet. But then the sound of the airplane above us again became audible. We glanced up through the hull, which I had caused to become transparent.

One of my lieutenants said slowly, "I fear the worst, Belgarth."

So did we all. And the worst happened. The plane was a three-motored affair, by far the largest of all the horde which had destroyed itself so senselessly. It began to descend, and when still an appreciable height above us began to loose its tokens. The reverberations seemed to shake the world. Spouts of earth geysered upward, and our ship shook from stem to stern. On that one downward dive, the pilot of the ship must have entirely emptied his ship of explosives, for he zoomed away—and the next time came at us with but one intention in mind.

To hurl the ship against our impervious flanks, exactly as the other thousands had done.

He came dropping from the sky. We heard the shrilling scream of his passage. Another second and— We all gasped.

In contradistinction to the actions of the other ships, this one swerved, made what seemed a desperate attempt to avert disaster. It did escape direct collision, but its wheels scraped us. The craft turned head over heels, struck the ground at a low slant, tumbled over the gouged surface for half a hundred yards, and slumped to a stop.

When we got there, we pulled the pilot from the plane, which burst into flame, but a moment later he was dead. A metal lever, which we judged afterward must have steered the ship, had plunged clear through his body.

Choe and I cast each other one astounded glance.

This creature was the same we had seen on our first scouting trip!

Furthermore, he was—had been—the only intelligent living creature on the planet at the time of our arrival.

Belgarth fell quiet for the first time since he had started his story, puffing abstractedly on the butt of his last cigar, using the mouth he had been talking with. As abstractedly, he noticed that the shiny, curved walls of Governor Orth's office were shrinking and expanding. "What's that?"

"That's the children," said Orth impatiently. "Never mind them. They're blowing a new room—the pressure of their bubble is affecting this one. Go on with the story— Say, are you sure you aren't elaborating?"

"I assure you I am not."

"The denial may be an elaboration in itself. Never mind—only I didn't want you to take me too literally. This story can stand by itself."

"It can," said Belgarth in satisfaction. "However, governor, there isn't much more to tell. We searched the scene of the holocaust which had taken place around us. Hundreds of the planes were merely shattered. We searched inside them and found *nobody*. With which data we rightly concluded that none of the planes had been personally piloted. They were robot planes. They had been operated by our dead being. He had kept his plane well out of the exhibition, by means of a complex instrument board directing the other planes in their spectacular show.

"And wasn't it reasonable to suppose that, since the one intelligent being we had seen had also turned up directing that horde of ships, he was also the only intelligent being alive on the planet? Such was my conclusion, and that of my lieutenants. Nonetheless, we did not rely on reason and intuition alone, governor, but organized ourselves in such a manner that we could completely comb that planet, from north to south poles, from eastern to western hemispheres—comb it *thoroughly*.

"Which we did. It took us one full year to do it, using every man and every device at hand for the job. When we were finished, we were satisfied, beyond a shadow of a doubt, that the planet was completely devoid of intelligent life; that but one creature, who now lay frozen in the refrigeration chambers of our ship, had inhabited it at the time of our arrival.

"We pulled up stakes and came back to Emonso, satisfied that we had found a real problem for the Emonso to play with. Briefly! What is the intellectual shortcoming, *in us*, which prevents our being able to comprehend the mental processes which motivated that single intelligent being's actions?"

The problem had already occurred to Governor Orth, in the specific form in which it was stated. He absently detached from the stalk which projected below his fourth eye a gleaming, spheroidal jewel—faceted minutely, if one were to look closely—and began to rub it back and forth on his velvety skin. Belgarth, watching him, knew that he was thinking, and thinking most profoundly. He repressed a multiple smile. Sagely, he was aware of Orth's next question before it was uttered.

"You collected no more data?"

"None. I suspected that you would prefer to be among the first to participate in a possible solution. You wish to eat now?"

"Now," and the machines which dutifully translated their two telepathic commands—machines which reposed at the core of the planet Emonso—spread Orth's desk with a repast on which the two creatures at once fell.

Then, "Take me to see this being," commanded Orth, and Belgarth led the way along a simple three-dimensional route, for he knew that Orth needed much time to think. They found a small ship on the street where an Emonso had left it, climbed in. Belgarth took over the controls. They rose over the shimmering city, the bubble-houses contracting and expanding with each minute change in atmospheric pressure. Then they were slanting down toward the landing field where reposed the giant cylinder which Belgarth had brought back from a section of the universe that was far away beyond the visible stars.

Orth stood looking down at the frozen being. "A strange creature," he commented. "How did he compare with others of his kind—that is, surely you found sample skeletons?"

Belgarth was vaguely surprised, and also impressed. That Orth should have directly impinged on a subject, research into which had netted Belgarth a singular fact, was a favorable commentary on Orth's acumen. Yes, Belgarth admitted, he had found sample skeletons—his crew had collected a few hundred which had immediately been classified into child, male and female groups. All, he went on, were pitted and corroded in a most unusual manner, so irregularly in individual cases that one could guess at the agency of either diseases or corrosive forces. Belgarth expressed his opinion that this peculiar skeletal characteristic was a marker which might point the way toward a solution of the manner of death of the beings.

"But the average dimensions," exclaimed Orth impatiently.

Belgarth looked at the still, frozen white face. He felt slightly uneasy. He had come to Orth with a problem which he truly felt to be beyond solution. He expected a rise in rank from his work in presenting the various ramifications to the Emonso, whose sole purpose in existing was the exercise of the intellectual centers of their large brains, which was in one word, recreation. Yet Orth had directly put his finger on a peculiarity of the situation which Belgarth had come across purely by accident. Therefore, Orth must be working from a preconceived, and therefore precedented plan. But where, in all the universes which stretched endlessly through the cosmos, had there been a precedent for the thoroughly confounding incidents which had occurred on Sol Three? He reluctantly told Orth that the male being at which they looked was distinctly slighter in build, both longitudinally and laterally, than the average adult male.

He added apprehensively, "You have discovered a fundamental on which to build factual, eliminatory, correctional and suppositional data?"

"Naturally," snapped Orth, thoughtfully placing his spheroidal jewel back on the stalk from which it had come. "It is fundamentally necessary to find the relationship of the nucleus of the problem to its environment. The environment, in a large sense, is the universe. In a restricted sense, it becomes that environment which is in direct contact, or the most direct contact, with the nucleus. This being is the nucleus of the problem. We must discover his relationship to others of his kind, both physically and psychologically."

Belgarth was relieved. "That fundamental applies to any problem."

Orth went on. "Psychologically, we are completely in the dark. Our minds move—or moved—in different orbits. However, the different exterior physical relationship is so pronounced that I believe we have discovered what may well be one of the most important—if not the most important—indicators toward a solution. How far we shall progress with it remains to be seen.

"Our information so far is almost completely negligible in quality. Briefly, we are certain *what* the creature was. He was an intelligent being who was the sole inhabitant of a world on which once lived other intelligent beings. It is a logical certainty that he lived at least part of his life rubbing shoulders with others of his kind, since it is an absurdity that he was the product of spontaneous conception. Therefore, he was present when the civilization of which he was a part met its doom. How he was affected by that, what part he played in it, come under the heading of *who* he was. If that information comes adequately into our grasp, we may understand his actions when you and your crew and ship were added to his environment.

"Belgarth," he concluded, abruptly turning away from the frozen enigma, "you will outfit a ship. In addition to the regular crew, you will include half a dozen Upper Level Research Corps philologists who are superior in basic thought pictorialization. You will set the ship's control for an automatic landing in your previous landing spot on Sol Three. During the voyage, we will use the Sleep."

Orth went in one direction, to arrange affairs for his departure. Belgarth went in the other, toward the ship port, faintly annoyed with Orth for plunging so avidly into a problem which Belgarth would have sworn did not have even a foothold for a solution.

The planet Earth swings heavily in its lonesome orbit. It has been millions of years—perhaps a billion—since Belgarth landed his ship there. The cities, the roads, the cultivated lands—all are gone. There is no iota of evidence which could prove that once a race of beings had its inception there. There is no iota of evidence which could prove that once the Emonso landed there. For the Emonso have long since forgotten Earth, even as the record of their own history has entirely been destroyed by the corrosive action of time. They have forgotten the problem which was alone Orth's reason for going there. They have even forgotten that the problem was not solved.

No, not solved; for which the Emonso are entirely blameless. They were an old race, and there were none that were wiser. They were so old that they had forgotten their own beginnings. They were so wise and they looked so high that the millions of years had atrophied something in their minds. The atrophy, of course, was a good thing—but it did not help them to understand.

On that day which again saw Belgarth on Earth, with Orth as his companion, it was spring, and the rains were descending in abundance. The great salt ocean was shrouded in mists, as was the great city which had long ago been built on its shore. Eucalyptus and pepper trees gratefully accepted the offering of the heavy, unemotional downpour.

The great ship landed in the precise spot from which Belgarth's ship had taken off more than two hundred years before. Belgarth and Orth were seated around chairs in the lounge, studying through portable view-plates the land exterior to the ship. There was not much to be seen, and Orth's brow was clouded. Where was the remainder of the senseless exhibition which had taken place? Where were those robot ships which had smashed downward to their doom?

Belgarth was in the grip of a depression. It might have been the after-effects of the hundred-year Sleep from which he, as well as Orth and the rest of the inhabitants of the great ship, had just awakened. Or it might have been the almost tangible forlornness which swept across the tangled, ruined face of Sol Three. Belgarth was sure it was the latter.

He indicated the gouged, eroded terrain which swept away from the ship. Here and there, like ancient tombs, mounds of earth rose.

"Time has been at work in the two hundred years since I was here last," he muttered heavily. "The very surface of the ground has changed. Those mounds—beneath them lie the ships which hurled themselves against the flanks of the ship. I wonder . . . I wonder what two hundred years has done to the rest of the planet?"

"Probably ruined everything that might have aided us in solving the problem," Orth said grumpily. He played with his minutely faceted jewel, his face thoughtful. "I am thinking mainly of the word-records of this planet. What if their books are of the old-style, electric-sensitive, type-filament wire? Climate may have rusted them, or magnetic storms ruined them. Worse still, what if they recorded happenings on an organic material, to be translated optically rather than auditorially? Before you left this planet, Belgarth, you certainly should have gathered books and other exhibits which would not have been ruined by the two hundred years that you knew would pass before we could get back. That was a blunder."

Belgarth was aggrieved. "A blunder! Yet you yourself advocate the complication of a problem whenever possible."

"An oral complication or elaboration, yes. But a complication which physically distorts or destroys the data on which the problem is built is rather like cheating, Belgarth, and is an indicator of childishness—for then one does not discover problems, one conceives them. As you say, this problem is a hard nut to crack—there's no sense in artificially strengthening the hull, is there? One had as well deliberately ignore fundamental factors in the problem in order to prolong a solution."

Belgarth said woundedly, "What will be our method of operation?"

"The philologists, of course, are our only hope of a direct and final answer. They know their business, so we'll let them take their own course, which will first of all be a hasty survey as to whether there is more than one language. Having determined that, they will seek out that language which was most widely used, and proceed to break the various periodicals of current history into basic thought patterns."

"What if," Belgarth interrupted a trifle sarcastically, "those basic thought patterns are not the ones which our minds accept? Remember, we may be the wisest and oldest race in the universe, but even minds may be relative. For instance: We are so old that our own beginnings are unknown. We do not know by what methods we evolved. Were our primitive ancestors actually concerned only and completely with happiness and recreation? Were all peoples on all inhabited planets driven upward along the path of evolution by a desire to enjoy? We don't know. In all our millions of years of universe exploration, we have never found a really primitive race of intelligent beings. I would venture to say, in fact, that this civilization is as young as any we have ever discovered."

"I don't know what you're getting at." Orth's eyes blinked in progression as he ran his mind over the exact phrasing of Belgarth's speech, striving to extract the kernel of information he was trying to impart. "And what do you mean, this civilization is young? They have complex cities, and appear to have advanced greatly in science—or were you elaborating on that point? And didn't you say the furnishings of the residences were luxurious? That points to a desire to enjoy— Oh, your conclusion, whatever it is, must be ridiculous. Remind me to discuss it with you later. Isn't that downpour incredible?"

Belgarth fastened his attention on the rain. "It's lessening a little."

Orth untwined his complicated structure from his chair. He lighted a cigar and began to move up and down the length of the room. Finally he stopped and pointed his cigar at Belgarth. "Get the philologists moving. Tell them to take their time, but to report back here to the ship whenever they run across a datum which seems to them an important one. They can send their reports telepathically, to be recorded on a sixth-order field, or personally if the datum is unusually applicable.

"Furthermore: Start the crew combing through the city. They are to look for skeletons exclusively, and are to record exact measurements. I want thousands of measurements, the final requisite being to find without question of doubt the exact average dimensions of the adult male. Your mere hundreds of measurements, Belgarth, were pitifully inadequate. To find an unquestionable figure, we really should look over millions of skeletons. That can be done later, if necessary. Too," he said thoughtfully, "we should examine the skeletons of those beings with whom our being lived his life. Come to think of it, maybe we'll find the birthplace of the creature right now, ourselves."

Belgarth paused before he left the room. He looked back curiously. "You seem to attach an unusual amount of importance to the being's stature. Why?"

Orth spoke with a strange, quizzical expression, as if he were aware that the thought which he uttered was at variance with common sense. "If the being were slighter physically than the average males of his age, he may have desired greatly to be as large as they."

Belgarth stared. He burst into a short laugh. "You mean that the reason he killed himself was because he wanted to increase his dimensions to that of the average person? Even if it could be accomplished, that would certainly be the wrong way to go about it. And besides, why would anybody want to have different dimensions than the ones he has?"

"That might have been a prime motivating factor in the life of these beings."

"Aha!" Belgarth burst out triumphantly. "Now you're coming around to the 'ridiculous' theory I suggested!"

Orth was annoyed. "No such thing."

"No such thing," mimicked Belgarth angrily. "I guess you arrived at your theoretical conclusion by following an entirely independent line of thought. Well, governor, I think that conclusion is about as ridiculous a thought as any I ever heard in all my five thousand years of adulthood."

He left the room. By the time he came back, he and Orth had entirely forgotten the incident, for of such stuff were the Emonso made.

"What do we do now?" he demanded. "The philologists are taking scout ships out now, and the crew are on their way to the city. That leaves us inactive."

Orth was watching the rain outside through the view-plate. He gestured. "The rain is stopping. I suggest we take a walk around the ship for exercise."

There was only a slow patter coming down as they walked slowly. Orth was thinking. He said finally:

"It will be important if we find the birthplace of the creature. As I see it, being the only inhabitant of the planet, it is likely that the first time you ran across him he was 'at home.' At least, that conclusion is temporarily acceptable."

He stopped in midstep as a raucous sound burst through the air. Both creatures stared upward instinctively. What happened, happened so fast that neither was able to prevent it. A tattered, wet bundle of ebon feathers came streaking down out of the sky. It swept past Orth, fluttering momentarily in front of him, and then went streaking away.

Both Emonsos stared after it in astonishment as it alighted on the topmost branch of a eucalyptus. It was a winged creature with small bright eyes, and in its beak it held the jewel which Orth had been wearing on the stalk under his fourth eye.

Belgarth laughed. "A peculiar creature," he said. "I'll go get it back."

Orth took his attention away from the bird and made a disclaiming gesture. "Not now. We've got something more important to do. Get out one of the scout ships."

Scarcely half an hour later, the little scout ship came down into the atmosphere again, and Belgarth landed his ship atop a building whose roof was the exact spot of the take-off of the plane which had given him his first glimpse of the enigmatic creature who now reposed in a refrigeration museum on far Emonso.

This building was intact, though the city around it, in most part, was inconceivably demolished. Here and there rose other buildings which seemed to have escaped the holocaust through some miracle.

Brow knitted, Orth led the way to the roof entrance after studying the lonesome miles which stretched away into the quiet, encircling horizon. The dust of two centuries puffed upward under the tread of their multiple feet. They passed through dark, musty corridors which creaked and sagged threateningly. They entered room after room, descended level after level. Each room on the upper levels had been used, and used, apparently, for but one day. They identified beds for what they were. Covers and blankets were rumpled, rotten dust, and the centuries had gotten in their work. Windows were open or shut. The glass had fallen from all. Weather had crept inward and woodwork was rotting.

They identified stoves. Food receptacles stood about. Tin containers, which had been opened with a sharp instrument, were scattered about as if whoever had opened them did not care where they fell.

There was evidence that only one being had used these living quarters. There was evidence that he used them once, and then moved on to another room or suite of rooms; for on the third level from the bottom, they found suites which were untouched save by the years.

They moved through the city. They entered other fairly intact buildings, which had been used until there were no more ready-made beds available.

They walked through the streets, caught up in the brooding desolation of a vanished glory.

They came to a statue.

Belgarth stared upward at it, noting the progress the weather had made toward disfiguration. He was academically interested in the fact that the green patina of age was the only indication of ruination. Evidently, the statue was constructed of an extremely durable material. His glance roved over a face which had a noble breadth of forehead, a strong though sensitive mouth. In Belgarth's mind pulsed a faint dawning of recognition.

It was not until Orth had made an impatient motion and had gone on ahead of him that Belgarth realized exactly what it was he recognized. He experienced one of the few emotional shocks of his life.

Orth came moving back at his shout, his face puzzled.

Belgarth said, in a voice he forced to casualness, "There he is, governor —one and the same!"

He indicated the colossal statue, which reared upward a full hundred feet from the middle of a square in the heart of the city. Neither of them had ever seen anything like it before. Orth had simply accepted it as a peculiarity to be glanced at, to be wondered at, and to be forgotten. He perceived the powerful, symmetrical lines of the colossus, digested Belgarth's mite of information, and came to Belgarth's more strongly supported conclusion. It was the same man.

"And yet not the same," said Orth, his voice hushed unconsciously. "The figure you showed me, Belgarth, was scarcely that handsome. Nor was there that much nobility in the face."

Belgarth glanced sidewise at him, amused. "He has achieved dimensions greater than those of the average male—by about fifteen times!"

Orth was thunderstruck. "So he has!" he exclaimed. "Why . . . why, Belgarth, that was a shot in the dark, but damned if it isn't truth." His voice was drowned out in a deluge of his own thoughts, and the thoughts, to him, an Emonso, were uncommonly chaotic. His eight mouths opened and closed, and finally he burst out violently:

"Now . . . *now* the problem becomes worse! Why did he have his image set up here where his fellow beings could see it? Why did he increase his dimensions by proxy? And why did he give himself the soft, kindly expression which certainly was not his? I can see the purpose in erecting a life-size statue of a person after that person dies, but I can see no purpose in erecting a statue which is a lie. Do you think that we have inadvertently run across the very crux of the problem in this ridiculously malformed statue, Belgarth?" Orth was panting, angry, irritated, hopeless at the same time. He added vehemently, "Yes, I am convinced of it. If we knew for what reason he erected this statue while he was alive, we should entirely understand why he eventually destroyed himself."

"He was vain to the point of absurdity, remember," Belgarth offered. "The decorations on his chest proved that he desired to improve himself artificially. The statue may have been, in its way, another decoration. Although," he added, perplexed himself, "I fail to see in what way it improved him."

Orth said, in a burst of inspiration, "It may have been intended as a representation of him which, when looked at by the populace, psychologically impressed them as being the real thing."

Belgarth burst into a chiding, multiple laugh. "You're off the track. Such a characteristic might be an attribute of barbaric minds, but certainly not of civilized ones. Look around you. This is a scientific, fairly highly developed civilization. You know the rule. Where there is a scientific culture there is also a semantic mentality."

Orth deflated. "That may apply solely to the Emonso," he said sulkily. He sighed, and grinned wryly. "All right, Belgarth. We'll stick to the rules. Well—let's go back."

The two creatures turned from the enigmatic colossus, and a certain curtain of glumness fell about them. The statue was voiceless. It would never speak, because it was inanimate. The inanimateness of the world about them, the lonely, destroyed world, would never allow them to know the true answer, because a dead world, too, cannot speak. For the first time, they had run up against an intangible barrier which their mentalities seemed incapable of penetrating, and it was depressing. Their scout ship lifted.

They went back to the ship. They listened to the telepathically inscribed reports of the philologists, learning the further depressing news that books and periodicals of current history were composed exclusively of an organic material. But the philologists assured Orth that, although such printed material was almost entirely destroyed through the vicissitudes of climate and organic decay, still they would be able to collect a plethora of material with which to work.

Governor Orth was not much impressed when they reported having accidentally found printed photographs of the being who lay on far Emonso. Such photographs, or drawings, in some cases, seemed to occur with some frequency in most of the current periodicals.

Orth said glumly, "Another 'decoration.'"

Belgarth smiled to himself. Although, as an Emonso, that wisest of all races in the known universe, he would have wished for a quick solution and would have done nothing to prevent it, still he felt a certain pride in having uncovered what would doubtless prove a real source of pleasure to his race that would last thousands or perhaps millions of years. As for his promotion, that was already a certainty.

At the end of a month, the crew, which had been at work uncovering skeletons, turned in an imposing list of figures. Belgarth ran the figures through his mind, which immediately returned to him an average figure.

He informed Orth, "The being was four inches shorter than the adult male of this climate."

"Send the crew to the place of the creature's birth," said Orth morosely. "Just a routine. I am already quite sure of his physical relationship to others of his kind."

The philologists had, in the meantime, reported themselves to be having a difficult time. They had found a language which had been in almost universal use. They were now breaking that language down into basic thoughts. So far, they had found whole paragraphs and pages which did not respond to the process. Such material resolved itself into incomprehensible gibberish, said the philologists. However, they would continue to try, at least.

After another two weeks, the chief of the group himself reported directly to Governor Orth.

"It's this way, governor." He groped for words. "Languages which are not rooted in our own tongue cannot be translated from the basis of word-meanings alone. Another root-connection must be found. Obviously, that connection can be found only in thought-patterns which are common to our minds and the minds of the others.

"So what do we do, governor? It's this way. We arbitrarily select a a basic thought-pattern upon which we consider the thoughts of all intelligent creatures are built. For instance: The ultimate and even the direct purpose of all intelligent creatures is to solve puzzles. We use that as an absolute axiom, which proves its own truth. Then we proceed to work our way down from that, adding other less basic thought-patterns, and applying them to the language data at hand, until we have a mass of interlocked thoughts which correspond."

"I understand the process," said Orth impatiently.

"Of course. Well, say that that doesn't work."

Belgarth interposed. He said frowningly, "Has there ever been a situation in which it did not work?"

"You mean with that particular arbitrary axiom? Not that I know of." He added grimly, "I am almost certain that it always *should* work. It didn't in this case—positively."

Belgarth and Orth exchanged glances. Both were running over their sensations at the time of seeing the statue. Each knew that the other was experiencing sensations similar, and probably identical—a mental barrier, impenetrable, almost other-dimensional.

Orth said grimly, "Go on."

The philologist went on. "So that doesn't work. We then select another arbitrary axiom. Namely: All intelligent creatures seek intelligently that relaxation of mind and body which is known as recreation or happiness."

"And *that* didn't work," said Orth.

"No. Nothing translated itself further than two or three basic thoughts. What do we do then? Why, we play our trump card!"

"And that is?"

The philologist grinned triumphantly. He was evidently exhausted from his task, and various parts of his body were stained with chemical reagents used in restoring the organic materials upon which the enigmatic language was printed. But he was proud of himself for knowing his business, even those parts of it which the Emonso had formulated millions of years ago, but had never found necessary to use.

"This one," he said softly, "has to work—you know. It's a kind of rewording of the second axiom: All intelligent creatures—we are defining intelligent creatures as those with semantic mentalities, remember—seek happiness by devoting themselves to the happiness of others entirely, forgetting themselves. Isn't that beautiful? Of course, as an axiom, it's a bit extreme to apply literally and exactly even to the Emonso, but it might conceivably apply to an utterly alien race. Well, we're going to work on it . . . but I thought you'd like to know that if this fails . . . but, of course, it can't . . . that if this fails . . . well—" He paused awkwardly.

Orth involuntarily raised his hand to the stalk under his fourth eye, but not finding the jewel which he commonly wore there, dropped it.

He said, his voice bitter, "All right, I get it. Report your progress as you go along— No, come to think of it, I'll take it in one dose. Let me know when you're—finished."

Three days later, the crew, working with excavated skeletons in the probable land of birth of the being who was the nucleus of the problem, came back with their figures, which Belgarth boiled down for Governor Orth's information.

"He was four inches shorter than his countrymen. His chest had an expansion of two inches less. His shoulders were one and a half inches narrower than his hips, an absurdly high ratio compared to that of the average adult male. His bones were far under the average in thickness and strength, and probably did not support strong muscles. Is that enough?" Belgarth was sarcastic. "It seems to me that you have arrived at a conclusion identical to mine, with far more expenditure of energy. Briefly, he would have had to go some to increase his dimension to that of the average."

Orth sighed and said nothing.

Three days later, the chief of philologists called Orth by television from his place of operations. Orth, before he faced the man's image, got hold of Belgarth.

"Why doesn't he come with a personal report?" said Belgarth, puzzled.

Orth laughed shortly. "Ha! Why doesn't he! He's embarrassed, and he feels that he's in the wrong, and he's not got the moral stamina to tell me about his failure in the flesh. Failure. That's right. You see if I didn't call it right. Not that I blame him."

In the lounge, after one look at the tragic, shocked face of the philologist, Belgarth realized that Orth's prediction had been fatally precise.

"No success," said Orth coldly.

"None," the philologist said hollowly. He made a bitter gesture. "Oh, we had more success this time than with the other two tries. But—would you like to hear what our third arbitrary axiom gave us? For a while, we actually thought we were on the right track, and we were hammering away, and things were clicking into place, and we thought the problem was nearing solution. It was funny how neatly everything was turning out." He fell into a brooding silence. He said in a slow monotone:

"We thought we had found out who the being was. His full title would probably have been Captain of Games—you see? This planet was divided into sectors, with artificial boundaries. Each sector—and there were hundreds of them—was presided over by a Captain of Games. Every once in a while, some captain would pick a sector to wage a game with. The whole population of the sector would be geared to turn out materials for the game, and millions of the population would participate in the game. It was not for their own enjoyment, but in order to give diversion and relaxation to other populations. Sometimes one sector would take on several other sectors. Distant sectors would enter into the spirit by joyfully turning out materials for both sides. Sometimes the whole world would be thus engaged, playing the game against the first sector, gaining a great deal of happiness from finally winning the game. In this case, the populace of the losing sector would be made unhappy, but they wouldn't care, because they had sacrificed their own happiness for others.

"So much for the general picture. We discovered that our particular Captain of Games started the biggest game in all history. It was wonderful, governor, the way things were working out—until suddenly we struck a blank wall, and the words wouldn't translate."

"Wouldn't translate," said Orth hollowly.

"That meant that your third arbitrary axiom wasn't applicable, either," said Belgarth, just as hollowly.

"That's what it meant. It also meant that our translations up to that point were the sheerest hogwash. The being who concerns us was in a position of great importance. But he was not a Captain of Games—I doubt if there ever was such a title. No, the third arbitrary axiom must have led us so far astray that it verged on the ridiculous. So"—the philologist was plainly frightened at his own thoughts—"these people just think differently. They think—thought, rather—so differently that I tell you right now, positively, with absolute certainty, that you'll never *never*, even if you put the whole Emonso to work on it, ever solve your problem. That's my answer. It's final. I'm bringing my men back to the ship."

His face faded, and Orth and Belgarth sat there quietly, thinking their own thoughts.

The ship of the Emonso stayed on Sol Three for another two weeks. Orth, doggedly following a routine, had the entire crew busy loading the ship with exhibits of a dead civilization. The philologists were sent out again, with instructions to return with all the reading matter they could find, books and periodicals, in addition to photographs. The crew brought back bricks, chairs, mirrors, the rusted motor of an airplane, anything and everything they could find which might later prove useful in an ultimate solution.

Orth had an unquenchable desire to visit the ruined city that lay to the north. He and Belgarth pursued a quick four-dimensional route which set them down in the middle of a crumbled street.

"Whatever he was," said Belgarth slowly, "I personally think that somehow he caused this. The same explosive tokens which fell around our ship two hundred years ago must at one time have fallen in this city, and other cities like it. But why?" He shook his head, and his voice echoed back to him.

Orth said, "The statue would tell the story—if it could speak. Mark my word, Belgarth, if the problem is ever solved, it will all go back to that. To the being's smallness relative to his fellowmen. He didn't want to be just as big as the average adult male. He wanted to be bigger. He wanted to be fifteen times bigger. That's why he built the statue."

They picked their way along slowly.

Orth added heavily, "You go on from there."

But Belgarth did not speak. What Orth had said seemed a logician's triumph. Being such, it was remarkable in that it did not explain anything. It did not explain any phase of the being's actions.

They took one last look at the quiet city, and went back to the ship, landing outside the air lock. No sooner had they touched solid ground, than the attention of both was attracted to a harsh cry emerging from a nearby tree.

Just visible on a topmost limb, a black bird with bright, shoe-button eyes was apparently cursing them with the full power of its lungs.

"Well!" said Orth, and he broke into a laugh. "Vociferous little devil, isn't he? Wonder if he's the one that took the jewel I was wearing."

"We could take a look and see," offered Belgarth. "Four-dimensional." Orth nodded his agreement, and both creatures set their synapses into a certain pattern, and were forthwith looking at the world from an accustomed convolution of space. They identified the top of the tree as a series of transparent, concentric spheres hanging without support in the air. In another second they were solidly entrenched on top branches, leaves in their faces, an astonished bird, bested in its own element, fluttering upward with a frightened squawk.

In the crook of two branches, there was a nest. It was literally overflowing with pieces of colored, shining glass, with bits of colored string, with jagged, shiny metal fragments, with any liftable object which might have stood out against a drab background.

Orth took the jewel and placed it where it belonged. The bird recovered. It beat its wings in Belgarth's and Orth's faces until Belgarth, almost losing his hold, angrily brushed it away.

Belgarth frowned at the collection in the nest. He mused, "Peculiar. What do you suppose it wants with all that useless stuff?"

"Nothing peculiar about it," Orth shrugged. His thoughts were still wandering futilely through the blind alleys of what he considered a more pertinent mystery. "The brains of most creatures of this type are all thalamus—all emotion. This one apparently likes to collect pretty things, even if it can't find any possible use for them." He glanced down at the ship, and made a gesture. "Ship's ready, Belgarth. Let's go."

Belgarth agreed. The jackdaw cawed its threats at the moment the two wise creatures from Emonso disappeared into a four-dimensional matrix. Having scared its enemies away, it came back to peck jealously through the trivia in its nest.